Shadow of the King

Also by Helen Hollick

The Kingmaking
Pendragon's Banner

Shadow of the King

being the third part of a trilogy

HELEN HOLLICK

ST. MARTIN'S PRESS ❧ NEW YORK

Library of Congress Cataloging-in-Publication Data

Hollick, Helen.
    Shadow of the king / Helen Hollick.
      p.   cm.—(Pendragon's banner ; bk. 3)
    ISBN 0-312-17000-9
    1. Arthur, King—Fiction.   2. Great Britain—History—
To 1066—Fiction.   3. Britons—Kings and rulers—Fiction.
4. Arthurian romances—Adaptations. I. Title. II. Series:
Hollick, Helen. Pendragon's banner ; bk. 3.
PR6058.04464S48   1997
823'.914—dc21   97-18589
                                                     CIP

First published in Great Britain by William Heinemann

First U.S. Edition: September 1997

10 9 8 7 6 5 4 3 2 1

For Hazel and Derek.

Who have shared
memories, laughter and tears.
And who are more to me than just friends.

Acknowledgements

My first thank you must go to Lynne Drew, my Editor at Heinemann. She has been so patient, so encouraging, particularly with this, the third book of my trilogy – by far the hardest work I have ever been faced with. Lynne has the gift of being able to guide and suggest, without being intrusive.

I have so many friends to thank. Friends who have given me their support and encouragement through all the years when writing was nothing more than an ambition and a dream. Mal Phillips – I value his sensible opinions and judgement; Mic Cheetham, my agent, is always there with her cheerful advice and encouragement; Joan Allan, willing to have a chat when I need one. I have spent many an hour standing in a windswept stable yard, happily discussing horses and history – my two great passions – with Joan Bryant. And Sharon Penman's wonderful letters have boosted my confidence on dull days when I have not a word in my head – she is a very dear friend, and one who so well knows the ups and downs of an author's career.

Sue and Geoff Williams have a special place on my list for their laughter and friendship, and thank you – the words are quite inadequate – to Sue for the ponies. 'Briallen' (Welsh for Primrose) appears in this story especially for her.

Researching the background details of my books takes time. I am so grateful to those who were kind enough to give their expert help and advice: Dorset County Museum for their advice on the post-Roman name of that county; the staff of my local library, Higham Hill, Walthamstow; Steve Walker MRCVS, for taking the time to tell me about the equine illness, strangles; Graham Scobie, Publications Officer at Winchester Museum for his useful correspondence.

My family deserves a special thank you. Iris, my mum; my sister Margaret and the useful discussions we had about Wookey Hole; and for his eagerness, my nephew Tom.

Very much love goes to Ron, my husband, and to Kathy, my daughter. They never (well, rarely!) complain at the monopoly over my life that Arthur and Gwenhwyfar have taken these past, many, years. I think the rewards are, at last, beginning to show.

Two of my dearest friends undertook the organization and navigation of a memorable time during the summer of 1995 touring northern France and Brittany. For me, it was a working holiday, researching the background details of Arthur's campaign there. I would not have undertaken the trip without their help. I am sure they will recognize some well remembered moments! To say thank you, *Shadow of the King* is dedicated to these two dear friends: Hazel and Derek Cope.

Places

BRITAIN

Alclud *Dumbarton*
Ambrosdun Prima *Ambersbury Banks, Epping, Essex*
Ambrosdun Secunda *Loughton Camp, Essex*
Ambrosium *Amesbury, Wiltshire*
Anderida *Pevensey*
Badon *Liddington (Castle)*
Caer Cadan *Cadbury (Castle), Somerset*
Caer Gloui *Gloucester*
Caer Lueil *Carlisle*
Caer Rhuthun *Rhuthun (Rhuthin), North Wales*
Castellum Prima *Barbury (Castle)*
Cerdicesford / Camlann *Charford, on the River Avon*
Cerdicesora *Christchurch Harbour*
Chalk Hills *Chilterns*
Cille Ham *Chillham, Kent*
Corinium *Cirencester*
Cornovii *Cornwall*
Cwm Dolydd *Lea Valley*
Deva *Chester*
Din Dergel *Tintagel*
Durotrigia *Dorset*
Durnovaria *Dorchester*
Durovernum *Canterbury*
Fortress of 3rd Ambrosiani *Higham Hill, Walthamstow*
Great Wood *New Forest*
Guoloph *Over Wallop, Hampshire*
Hibernia *Ireland*
Iceni Way *Icknield Way*
Lindinis *Ilchester*
Llan Illtud Fawr *Llantwit Major*
Llongborth / Portus Adurni *Portchester*
Londinium *London*
Môn *Anglesey*

Muchinga *Mucking, Essex*
Noviomagus *Chichester*
Radingas *Reading*
Rutupiae *Richborough*
Tanatus *Thanet*
Vectis *Isle of Wight*
Venta Bulgarium *Winchester*
Vercovicium *Housesteads (Hadrian's Wall)*
Vicus *Wickham*
White Hills *Mendips (The Caves – Wookey Hole)*
Wooded Ridge *Epping Forest*
Yns Witrin *Glastonbury Tor*

GAUL

Antessiodurum *Auxerre*
Avaricum *Bourges*
Augustonemtum *Clermont Ferrand*
Bononia *Boulogne*
Caesarodunum *Tours*
Condivicnum *Nantes*
Dariorigum *Vannes*
Juliomagus *Angers*
Lutetia *Paris*
Place of the Lady *Vézelay*
Place of Stones *Carnac*
Vicus Dolensis *Dèols*

RIVERS

Cuneito *Kennet*
Dolydd *Lea*
Hafren *Severn*
Liger *Loire*
Meduway *Medway*
Rhenus *Rhine*
Tamesis *Thames*
Terste *Test, Hampshire*

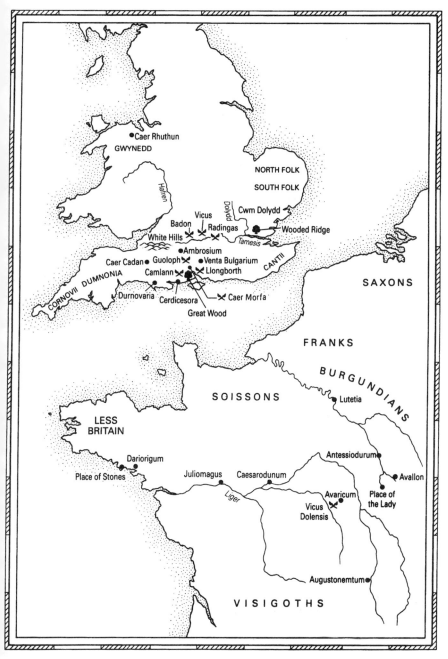

Britain and Gaul circa 500

FAMILY TREE

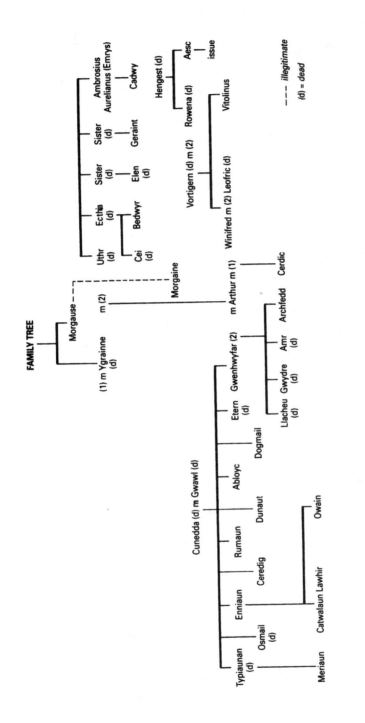

Circa AD 468

--- *illegitimate*

(d) = *dead*

Shadow of the King

PART ONE

The Ragged Edge

May 468

§ I

Above the great height of Caer Cadan, the sky swept blue and almost cloudless. The bright, sparkling blue of an exuberant spring that was rushing headlong into the promised warmth of summer.

The flowers along the already dry and dusty lane that ran around the base of the stronghold, were massed in a profusion of splendid colour. Gwenhwyfar was gathering healing plants – bugle for bruising, poor robin, a renowned cure-all – and flowers for their colour and scent to brighten her chamber: campion; the meadow goldfinch, that some called broom; wild parsley; cuckoo pint . . . She darted forward to snatch her fifteen month daughter's hand from clutching a butterfly. The child's wail of protest heaved like a cast war-spear up to the soaring sky, hurtling past the defensive earthworks of high banks and deep ditches.

The guard on watch, slowly pacing the wooden rampart walkway, heard and looked down, concerned. Grinned to himself, as he watched Gwenhwyfar hug the child and soothe her. It was a glorious day, and all seemed well with Arthur Pendragon's kingdom of Britain.

Archfedd, a fat-as-butter child, was much like her mother: copper-bright, unruly hair, green eyes flecked with tawny sparks of gold, set, determined expression. She reached again for the butterfly, the sobs coming louder as it fluttered out of harm's way. Gwenhwyfar chided her. 'Hush child! They are not for catching, you will tear the wings.' And she had the temper and mule-stubborn pride of her father, Arthur, the Supreme King. Gwenhwyfar neatly deflected the rising anger by giving the child a handful of flowers to hold. The girl's squawks subsided into a few half-hearted, tearful breaths as she absorbed herself with the new occupation of systematically shredding the petals. Gwenhwyfar left her to it. Better petals than wings.

Horses! The thud of hooves, jingle of harness.

The lane twisted away from Gwenhwyfar's line of sight, slipping between earth banks topped with wattle fencing made from entwined hawthorn and hazel. In the pasture beyond, mares grazing content on the new spring grass, lifted their heads and began to prance, snorting, into a bouncing, high-stepping, exaggerated trot. Their foals, those that had them, ran at heel, long-legged and gangling, with bushed, fluffy tails twirling in a frenzy from this sudden excitement. A stallion answered the mares' showing-off with a trumpeting call, and the sound of horses approaching came closer, nearer. They would be around the bend, in view, soon.

Gwenhwyfar lifted her daughter, settled her comfortably on her hip, legs around her waist, stood looking along the hoof-rutted, narrow lane; waiting, expectant and hopeful, her heart thumping. The banner she saw first, bobbing above the fenced, man-built banks; the bright white of the linen and the proud, bold, red dragon with its gold-embroidered eye and claws. Arthur. Her husband was home!

Running a few steps with initial pleasure, Gwenhwyfar halted, suddenly undecided, a great clasp of insecurity and fear gripping her. She stood, again waiting, apprehensive, chewing her lower lip. What had he decided after this week of discussion with his uncle? Had Ambrosius Aurelianus persuaded him? Ah, but then, the Pendragon would not need much convincing. Wherever there was the prospect of a fight, Arthur would find some excuse to be there.

The lead horses came into sight, the King's escort, the riders wearing the uniform of the Artoriani, white padded tunics, red cloaks. Then the Pendragon's banner and the turma's own emblem – and Arthur himself, riding easy in the saddle, his face lighting with pleasure as he saw Gwenhwyfar and his daughter waiting for him. The happiness faded as he drew rein, looked directly into his wife's eyes. He waved the men on, watched impassive as they jog-trotted past and began to make way up the cobbled track that sprinted steeply to the gateway into the King's stronghold.

Shifting Archfedd to her other hip, Gwenhwyfar returned Arthur's stare. He ran his hand down his stallion's chestnut neck, almost an uneasy gesture.

'You are going then?' she said, more as a statement than question.

He nodded, a single, brief, movement. 'I have to, Cymraes.'

As he knew she would, Gwenhwyfar flared a retort. 'Who says you have to? Your men? Me? No Arthur, you do not have to answer this asking for help. Gaul must look to its own defence – as we have had to all these years.'

The Pendragon dismounted, throwing his leg over the two fore-pommel horns of the saddle, and slid to the ground. With the coming of summer, he would be thirty and three years of age – but he wore the ragged eye-lines of a man ten years older. It had been a long and often bitter struggle to place the royal torque around his neck and keep it there. Arthur had been King for eleven years. And he intended to stay King for, at the very least, twice as many more.

4

'I am not answering Gaul. I need to give aid to Less Britain, for Armorica is also of my kingdom. I personally own an estate three times the size of Aquae Sulis there – do I turn my back on British people because their land happens to lie across the sea?' He stepped forward but made no attempt to touch his wife, knowing she would shrug aside his hand. 'The Roman Emperor himself is pleading for my help – personally asking for my Artoriani to join with his loyal allies against the barbarians who seem intent on destroying what remains of Roman Gaul.'

Archfedd was too young to understand the distress in her mother's eyes, the determination in her father's. She was wriggling against Gwenhwyfar's hold, her chubby arms stretching for her father to take her. Arthur reached for her, tossing her high as he took her up, catching her in his strong hands, her dimpled smile rippling into giggles of delight. All the while he held Gwenhwyfar's eyes. 'If Gaul falls to the plundering of Euric's Goths, Less Britain may be next. I cannot allow that threat to happen.'

'And Britain?' She retorted. 'Who will see us kept safe while you are gone?'

Archfedd, her father's attention no longer on her, was demanding to be put down. Arthur set her beside a clump of bright-coloured flowers, showed her how to pick the stems, gather a posy. He straightened, turned and took up the reins of his stallion, hauling the chestnut away from cropping the rich grass. It was difficult for him to spit the answer out, for he knew Gwenhwyfar's response. His own heart held the same uneasy misgivings. He mounted, said the one name.

'Ambrosius.'

§ II

Stroking the stone in his hand one last time along the length of his sword's blade, Arthur tested the sharpness of the edge with his thumb. It could slice the wind, this sword. He had taken it for his own from a Saxon in battle and used its beauty to persuade the British men of the army to proclaim him as King – by telling them a fanciful tale of its forging. One side of his mouth twitched into a smile as he remembered that moment of blood-pulsing, glorying triumph. *The man destined to carry this sword will be the greatest of all kings.* That is what he had told them, those men who now formed the élite permanent, disciplined ranks of his cavalry, his Artoriani. And with them had come the militia men and the young warriors of Britain, men who fought when and where needed for their King as the brotherhood of the Cymry. *The Supreme, the Bringer of Peace*. Huh! He ran his thumb down the shimmering strength of that craftsman-forged blade; snorted self-contempt. Peace to Britain, but not his wife. He could not use a sword to cut the ice wall that had formed solid between them these past few days.

Arthur raised his head. A horse was being pulled up from a canter beyond the open doorway. An exchange of cheerful greeting mingled with the outside sounds of voices, children playing, wood-chopping; hammering, the sounds of a king's Caer. A young, confident-faced man strode into the Hall, paused to adjust from the daylight brightness to the shadow-muffled interior, head up, eye seeking the King among the many. Bedwyr. He saw Arthur, threaded his way towards him. Stripping off his helmet and loosening his cloak, his footsteps thudded on the timber boards as he happily nodded greetings to others in the Hall, kissing a serving girl who laughed a welcome. He stopped before his older cousin with a smart salute. Arthur, the sword still across his lap, accepted the acknowledgement of formal homage.

'We go then?' Bedwyr's enthusiasm showed white teeth against the darkness of his beard-hidden grin.

At least someone was delighted at the prospect.

Sliding the thirty-six inches of potential death into the protection of its sheepskin-lined scabbard, Arthur nodded assent. 'You have heard then? Word spreads faster than a diving hawk. Ships will be sent within the month to fetch us.'

Bedwyr rubbed his hands together in anticipation. 'Time to get drunk beforehand then?' Added, 'Durnovaria is buzzing with the news – talk in the taverns along the road home is of nothing else.' With a laugh, finished with, 'It seems people are pleased at the prospect to be rid of you!'

Arthur laughed with his cousin as he pushed himself upwards to his feet, slapped his hand on the young man's back. 'I like to keep my people happy! And aye, we'll have a hosting for all those wanting to come on this mad-fool escapade. Barley-brewed ale and the best Gaulish wine!' He began to fasten the jewel-studded, bronze buckle of the leather scabbard strap around his waist, glanced up to see Gwenhwyfar enter the Hall from the far door, coming in from her small patch of garden. She wore pale green, the colour of new-budded leaves, with ribbons of a darker shade braided through the copper-gold of her hair. His stomach tightened, as it often did whenever he saw her, especially as now, with shafts of dancing sunlight shimmering around her. He felt the sudden stomach-twisting lurch of desire as she came across the Hall to welcome Bedwyr.

'What is this?' She laughed, pointing at the whiskers around the young man's chin. 'Three weeks away and you sprout a bush!' She hugged her husband's cousin, her own good friend. 'How is Geraint? Looking after my Enid, I trust?'

Bedwyr embraced her in return, batting playfully at the fingers tugging at his beard. 'Geraint's Enid is settling well into married life – you must no longer look upon her as your handmaiden, she is a freeman's daughter, married now to a prince!'

Gwenhwyfar retorted with matched seriousness, knowing he teased. 'How am I to find a new nurse for Archfedd? Enid was so good with my children – which is of course why Geraint took her, needing to find a replacement for his motherless brood.' She relented, 'I expect no man of Geraint's young age to stay a widower. Enid went to her marriage bed with my full blessing.'

'Which is more than I have for going to Gaul,' Arthur sniped.

She ignored him, kissed Bedwyr's cheek a second time and turned to go into the private chamber built along the rear of the Hall.

Arthur had not slept there these past nights, lying instead among the unmarried men who used the warmth of the King's Hall for their sleeping place. He had tried, that first night of his home-coming from Ambrosius to enter his own rooms, but the atmosphere had been as chill as the longest winter's night. He was not welcome; he stayed away.

Sensing the animosity, Bedwyr fashioned a sympathetic expression. 'It seems not everyone is enthusiastic about the prospect of Gaul then?'

'Na, not everyone.' Arthur turned the subject. 'Does Geraint accompany you? I need to have word with him.'

Nodding, Bedwyr confirmed, 'Aye, he rides with Enid, they will be here within the hour. I came ahead.' His grin was returning. 'He is eager to come with us, though I suspect my Lady Gwenhwyfar may find an ally with his wife.' A thing to be expected; the couple had been married but two months.

Arthur sighed, steered Bedwyr into the corner where the flagons of ale and wine were stored. Gwenhwyfar was angry with him because she was afraid. Afraid because she might lose him.

This escalating trouble in Gaul was not their fight, but the barbarian invaders were increasingly demanding too much land for their own. Land that was once Roman. Some of it had been given legally, as reward for services to the Empire, but men like Euric of the Visigoths wanted a kingdom and cared not how much blood need be spilt to get it. He was not a man to stop until the whole of Aquitainia was his – and from there it would be Soissons and the land given in friendship to the Burgundians – or Arthur's Less Britain. Gwenhwyfar was afraid because she knew he had to go; was afraid because the ache in her bones was screaming that he

7

might not come back. Anger was an easier emotion to let loose, to face than fear.

The Pendragon too, was afraid, for all those same reasons and more. This was a risk he was taking, agreeing to go into Gaul and help in the fight that would soon be coming there. It was not the fighting – any battle anywhere was a risk. You came out of it dead or wounded or alive. But to leave your kingdom to fend for itself for a whole season? A risk that sent the shudders of fear coursing through his belly. Especially when that kingdom itself was poked, prodded and battered on all sides by its own share of troubles. And when the majority of men on the Council supported the King's uncle, not the King. Men who would like nothing more than to have Ambrosius as supreme. Not Arthur.

He motioned for a slave to pour them each a tankard of ale, said in answer to Bedwyr's last comment, 'Enid has no need to fear, I cannot take Geraint with us.'

Bedwyr took a deep draught of the ale, enjoying the rich, barley-bitter taste, raised his eyebrows at his cousin, half-questioning, then nodded, understanding as he wiped residue from his beard. 'Ambrosius?' he queried. Needed no answer.

Ambrosius Aurelianus, youngest brother to Arthur's father. Ambrosius who styled himself the last of the Romans in Britain, titled himself Comes Britanniarum because he did not agree with the barbarian title of *rex*, King. Oh, on the surface these last few years, he had patched his differences with the Pendragon, but the suspicions were still there, on both sides. Stronger for Arthur, who was certain his uncle was waiting his chance. His God-given chance.

Ambrosius had backed Arthur into this corner from where there was no escape except agreement. Ambrosius, guiding the Council, insisted that Arthur give aid to Roman Gaul, out of duty, out of loyalty, out of necessity. For all those reasons, Arthur had no choice. He had to agree, had to go. Giving the ideal opportunity for the uncle to be rid of the annoying nephew.

Half-listening to Bedwyr's excited chatter about his recent visit with Geraint, Arthur's eyes watched the closed door to the chamber at the rear. His chamber; his wife's. He had to settle this thing with Gwenhwyfar soon, before this wound festered and turned putrid.

Easier to command the sun to cease its shining!

§ III

The evening gather was more than the serving of the day's main meal – a time for laughter and conversation, of sharing brave deeds and excited dreams, to air complaint or suggest change, a time when all were welcomed to the King's Hall.

Bedwyr this evening was entertaining those within listening distance at his end of the trestle-table with stories of his visit to Durnovaria, while Geraint, seated next to him, and amid much laughter, exposed the younger man's more gross exaggerations.

Late evening; the sky had already slid into the dusky purple of day's end, and night, with the accompanying scent of damp earth, woodsmoke and the heady, overpowering perfume of may blossom, was wrapping herself, protective, around the world. The door opened slightly, Arthur's gatekeeper slipped in, making his way between the crowded tables rowed along the length of the Hall, exchanging word here and there as he passed. He came to Arthur, talked quietly into the King's ear. The Pendragon frowned, chewed thoughtfully at the chicken wing in his hand. Those nearby eased their chatter, aware something was happening; discreetly, curious eyes were glancing at the King, watchers, with ears pricked, listening for a snippet of conversation.

'It seems,' Arthur declared, setting down the bones and sucking grease from his fingers, 'that my ex-wife seeks an audience.' He barked a single stab of amusement, caught Gwenhwyfar's eye as he added, 'She begs my immediate attention.'

Gwenhwyfar frowned. 'Winifred asking polite permission to enter our Hall?' She lifted her goblet in a mocking toast, 'I drink to a first-time event!'

Laughing with her, Arthur added, 'Aye, usually she barges in like a Roman warship under full sail, demanding my attention. I often have the impression that it is I being summoned to her!' Amusement spread through the Hall. They all knew Winifred, Arthur's first wife, his much disliked ex-wife.

Despite the fact that they were legally divorced thirteen years past, and that she was now widowed from a second husband, Winifred perversely thought herself the official, and only, Lady Pendragon, Arthur's legitimate wife, and mother of his only known surviving son.

Gwenhwyfar muttered a few profanities. The evening that had been tolerably enjoyable had of a sudden turned most disagreeable.

'Send word, Arthur, that she is to take lodging at the tavern, our gates are closed to visitors.'

A wry smile twitched Arthur's wind-browned face, crinkling the lines around his dark eyes deeper. Gwenhwyfar was talking to him again. 'I wonder what the bitch wants this time?' He spoke his thoughts aloud, pouring more wine for himself and his wife.

'To stir trouble. What does she ever want?' Gwenhwyfar laid her hand on his arm. 'Send her away, I have no stomach for her this night.'

Closing his fingers around her hand, Arthur shook his head. 'Na, best listen to the Saex-bred sow. On occasion her information – for all her intention of dung-spreading – has proved of use to me.' He nodded to his gatekeeper, 'Go fetch her up, but keep your distance – her venom is more potent than that of a disturbed adder!' Those in the Hall, Arthur's men and their wives, the people of the Caer, Arthur's people, laughed, sharing his humour. Aye, they all knew Winifred's reputation!

Winifred. An infected thorn in Arthur's backside. He ought never have taken her as wife, but at the time it had been a decision beyond choice. He had not been a king then, only a raw youth, and Gwenhwyfar had been betrothed to another. Admitted, against her will, and the betrothal had been torn aside through the brutal murder of her youngest brother, but all that had happened too quickly to stop his marriage to the Princess Winifred, only daughter of a Saex-born bitch and the tyrant who had then ruled as king. Vortigern.

Talk resumed, muted, eyes and heads turning frequently to the door to look for the lady's coming, though it would take a while for Glewlwyd to walk the distance back to the main gate, for her to ride through and up the track, to dismount . . . The door opened, thrown wide, admitted a woman alone, although the shadows of her escort were beyond in the new-lit flickering torchlight. She stepped through, walked with calm dignity along the central aisle, walked straight to where the King sat. She wore no jewels against the plain black of her Christian woman's garb, her sun-gold hair tucked firmly away beneath the gleaming white linen of her veil. Only a gold-and-silver crucifix dangled from a chain at her waist, its glint catching the flaming light of torches and candles as she walked.

She stopped a few paces before the King's table and sank to her knees. From the Hall came a few gasps. Never had Winifred submitted herself in homage before – even Gwenhwyfar caught her breath. Arthur alone, unimpressed, kept his expression masked. Too many times had Winifred tossed her tricks of humble innocence at him.

The gasps grew stronger, more audible, as the black-clad woman prostrated herself, laying flat as if she were doing penance before God.

Gwenhwyfar's fingers tightened in Arthur's hand, her eyes flicking him a puzzled question. *What was Winifred about?*

Impatient, slightly embarrassed, Arthur admonished, 'Get up, woman. You are impressing my guests but irritating me. Oh for Mithras' sake, get up!' He stood himself, strode around the table and hauled his ex-wife to her feet. And then he did feel surprise, for Winifred's eyes held real, distressed tears, nothing fake, nothing planned. Tears that had been falling, for her eyes were puffed and red, her cheeks sore. He had never felt compassion for Winifred. Too often had she brought him pain and anger, but this once, just this once, and only passing briefly, did he feel the great weal of sadness that was pouring from her. A dozen thoughts of tragedy swirled through his mind. What had happened? The foremost conclusion that her estate on the south coast had been raided – pirates obeyed their own law of kill or be killed and gave no respect for peaceful agreement reached between Saex and British. The sea wolves would as easily raid their own kind, the English, if the lure of gain was enough to entice their greed, and Winifred's steading south of Venta Bulgarium was as enticing as a bee's nest crammed with sweet honey.

Arthur took her arm, motioned for a slave to bring a stool for her to sit upon, said, concerned, in the softest tone that he had ever used with her, 'What is it? What is wrong?'

§ IV

The Pendragon hunkered down to his heels beside the distressed woman, casting a quick glance above his shoulder at Gwenhwyfar, sitting at the table. She shook her head, a slight gesture, indicating her own concern. Gwenhwyfar thought like Arthur, a warrior woman, his Cymraes, his British woman. She understood the dangers, the threats, the possibilities, as much as he. Returning that glance, she lifted her hand, palm uppermost. *Ask*, she was saying, *what is wrong.*

A few others had gathered around, Enid among them, Geraint's new wife, the woman who had for so long cared for Gwenhwyfar's sons. She offered Winifred a fine-woven linen square to dry her tears; someone else, more wine. Winifred took both, smiled a wan thank you. Took also a breath, said with quavering voice, her eyes holding her ex-husband's, 'I need your help, my lord.' She looked up, stared, only slightly defiant, at Gwenhwyfar before returning her gaze to Arthur. 'You know the agony of losing a son.'

Gods, Arthur thought with a sudden lurch to his heart-beat, *is Cerdic dead!* The strangest thing, he did not feel the gloat of pleasure that he would have expected. Neither was there sadness or pain – for that would not be there for Cerdic – merely a flickering of sorrow for another's grieving, a bitter memory of his own losses, that was all. It might have been that she was telling him of a valued dog's passing, not the death of his son by her.

Cerdic, conceived in the last months before Arthur had found legal cause to set the Saex-bred princess aside in divorce. Winifred's persistence in claiming the child was Arthur's only legitimate-born heir had been as annoying as flies constantly buzzing on a hot day. Beyond that irritation, and then only as an indistinct shadow for the future, Arthur rarely considered the boy. But then, he had once had other sons; sons born to Gwenhwyfar, the woman he had always loved, would always love.

Amr, Gwydre, Llacheu.

Amr, drowned when he was but two years old. Gwydre killed by the bloodied tusks of a boar at his first hunt, at eight years old. And Llacheu, Llacheu the eldest, Arthur's firstborn, conceived while Winifred was still his legal wife, started while Arthur loved with his Gwenhwyfar. Llacheu, killed by the spear of traitorous rebels. Rebels who had since paid the bloodied price for that killing of Arthur's most loved son, Llacheu, who had been on the verge of young manhood. First born, last dead.

And then Cerdic, a pestilence that Arthur had, on more than one occasion, threatened with the punishment of death. A boy Arthur detested, but had eventually acknowledged, to silence the malicious threats of the mother. The enforced acknowledging of one son serving to conceal another. A child born in shadow, illegitimate, to a girl he had barely known, but could, in another time, another world, have loved.

Winifred knew of this child, the boy, Medraut. Gwenhwyfar did not.

Such thoughts, rapid come-and-gone thoughts, skimmed through Arthur's mind, and more . . . where was Medraut now? He would be two, three years of age – and where was his mother, Morgaine? The lady who had once dwelt by the lake of Yns Witrin. Morgaine? Another thought of sudden-roused alarm: Winifred was an accomplished actress, knew how to turn the sympathy of the crowd. Was this something to do with that secret-born son? Arthur thrust the disquiet aside. Surely it could be nothing along Medraut's path, for this distress was genuine. Winifred would not weep over a bastard brat of the Pendragon's. Na, this was for Cerdic, her own-born.

And so he answered, calm, with inner assurance, 'We have seen the new-born with life that could not take hold, and have watched our other sons learn to talk and walk and run, only to see the light go out from the laughter of their young eyes.' He paused, the hurt returning as he remembered. 'Aye, we know the pain of a son's death.'

'Then help me!' she said urgently, taking his hand between her own, clinging tight as if he were her last link to life. 'Find our son! He has gone, to I know not where! More than two weeks since he took a horse and left me with no word of where or why he was going! I do not know what to do.' Her rush of words slowed; with awkwardness, added, 'In my desperation, I came to you.'

Arthur was staggered, angered. He stood, stepped back a pace, a roar of outrage building in his chest. Tragedy? Killing? Death? He had thought there was some enormity of wrongdoing, some powerful darkness or dread that would need facing – and all it involved was this? Her damned, insolent brat running off!

'By the Bull's Blood,' he bellowed, 'you try my patience!' He stormed back around his table, reaching for a wine goblet as he passed; drank, in an effort to control his temper. The strategy failed. 'Your son,' he sneered, 'I dislike intensely. Nothing would please me more than to know he has been tidily dispatched into Hades. You were careless enough to lose him. You find him!'

Winifred's anger was rising, to equal his. The Hall was in uproar, voices mingling in mixed reaction, most agreeing with the King, others, women, a few mothers, calling for the boy to be found.

Linking her arm through Arthur's, Gwenhwyfar grasped a chance to snipe at the other woman. Once, long ago it seemed now, Gwenhwyfar had pledged to see an end to Winifred for the murder of a dear and much-loved cousin. One day she would find the opportunity to see her revenge. Not yet, not now. It would come, the right time in the right place.

To Arthur she said, 'The boy has developed sense at last! He has discarded his mother's cloying skirts and gone in search of more pleasant pastures.' To Winifred, with a sweet, sickly smile, 'He is nigh on three and ten, have you tried the local whorehouse?' Triumph! Winifred's face had suffused red, her eyes had narrowed. Gwenhwyfar's idly tossed spear had thrust home at first casting!

Ignoring the woman at Arthur's side, Winifred taunted her former husband with bitter words. 'Call yourself King? Protector? Lord? By Christ, you cannot even give compassion to your own wife and child!'

'Ex-wife,' the Pendragon corrected tartly. 'And I care not a . . .' But Gwenhwyfar interrupted his anger, silencing him with her upraised hand.

'It is not a matter of compassion, Winifred. My lord Arthur cannot search for your son, he leaves within the month for Gaul. A king cannot turn his back on public necessity to pursue personal need. His people are his family, they must come first.' She smiled, at Winifred, at Arthur, the one returning a glare of hatred, the other a stare of pleased astonishment. It seemed Gwenhwyfar had given her blessing to Gaul.

He spread his hands, helpless, palms uppermost. 'As much as I would like to help you, Winifred, I cannot, yet.' He rubbed his chin, thoughtful, with his fingers. 'If he has not run home to you with his tail tucked atween his legs by the time I get back, I'll see what I can do. We all know what mischief boys get up to.' Men in the Hall chuckled, joined by their womenfolk. Aye, they all knew the whims of boys! Bedwyr, sitting at Gwenhwyfar's left hand laughed loudest. 'Have no fear Madam,' he called, 'I ran away. Admitted, I was older and circumstances were different, but I was gone some time, travelling to Rome and further. Look at me now!' He patted his spreading stomach, full of Arthur's good food. The Hall laughed louder.

Cold, her face stone, Winifred turned on her heal and strode for the doors. Why had she come? Why had she sought Arthur? She should have known he would show no concern, no fears. Cerdic could lay dead for all he cared – no, no she would not consider that. Cerdic must become King after Arthur. He must. She paused before going out, hurled at him, 'If you will not help, then I will seek the aid of my mother's brother. Unlike you, Aesc is faithful to his kindred. He sees the importance of the spear side of the family – it is he who is nurturing Vitolinus, my brother. He will find Cerdic and have him at his hearth as well. Two to destroy you, Pendragon, two of my blood to bring about your end!' She left, sweeping out into the night, calling for the horses to be brought up.

The mixture of chatter swelled higher, incredulous, excited, indignant.

Arthur seated himself, motioned for the Hall to sit also, to resume their meal. Gwenhwyfar selected a portion of duck, lifted her goblet for a slave to pour more wine.

'You go to Gaul, but know this, I do not like it.'

'Na,' Arthur spoke through a mouthful of best beef.

'It is a foolish quest.'

'Aye.'

'You are beginning to annoy me, Arthur.'

He looked at her. Grinned. 'Only beginning to?'

'Fool.'

The meal continued, the food finished. Dishes were cleared, wine and ale served and served again. The King's harper tuned his fine instrument in readiness to entertain.

'Her spies, it seems,' Arthur said to Gwenhwyfar, as if he were talking merely of the vagaries of the weather, 'are not as efficient as mine.' He took Gwenhwyfar's hand in his own, their arms twining together, thighs close, beneath the table. They would seal the declaration of pax tonight, in the privacy of their chamber. Loving, a good way to end the storms of disagreement.

'You know something Winifred does not?' she asked.

He retrieved his hand to join in the applause for the harper, taking his place of honour by the hearth. Along with a chorus of demanding and cajoling voices, the Pendragon called his own suggestions for a song.

'I have heard talk of where Cerdic is.' He smiled impishly at his wife, relieved that they were friends again. 'And if what I have heard is the truth, he can stay where he is, as far as I am concerned, until the four winds forget to blow.'

§ V

Cerdic knew his mother would be angry with him, but cared not a cracked pot for it. Her screeching, those last few days before he plucked the courage to leave, had been like a fox-chased, panicked hen. That, added to her incessant scolding – by Woden, anyone would think he had murdered the bishop, not merely lain with a whore!

God's breath, but he would soon be ten and three years of age – was it not time he became experienced in the matter of intimacies? He had started with the youngest daughter of his mother's falconer. A year older, as ignorant in these things as he – but those first few embarrassed fumblings were soon behind him, and by the third time in the cow-byre with her, he had mastered the way of it. Well enough to mount his pony and ride with confidence into Venta Bulgarium – Winifred's Castra they sometimes called it – to visit the whores' place on the east side of the town's walls.

Unfortunate that on coming out he had run slap into one of the priests, who had marched him straight to the bishop, who in turn, had vigorously informed Winifred. The subsequent whipping might have been less harsh had Cerdic not insisted on demanding to know why the priest had been intending to enter the place also.

The punishment he could have tolerated, regarding it as justified for being caught – he would not make that mistake a second time – but the constant recriminations, the tight, straight lips, the fuss! He was not a child!

His mother irritated him. She was thirty and one years, and as soured as last week's milk. She had aged, these past two years since taking the Saxon Leofric as a second husband. Cerdic had liked him, wanted him as his father, preferring him over the man who already officially held that title. Cerdic hated Arthur, wanted to kill him. Knew that one day that wanting would come about. One day, when he was a man full grown.

Leofric was not to have become a father though, for the marriage was short, over before it had began. It was the shellfish, they said around the settlement, over-eating of tainted shellfish that had brought on a bloody flux that had emptied his bowels and his life, one short, sharp night but two weeks after the marriage. A few, a very few, and only people from a distance beyond his mother's place, had whispered of poison.

In those two short weeks, Leofric had been a man of his word. He had taken Cerdic as his adopted son, insisting that a boy needed to know the ways of a man, promising to teach him properly how to use a sword and shield. Promising that they would sail together to his lands along the Elbe River, he had talked about sailing further, up to the North Way and even, if the Gods saw fit, beyond. Cerdic loved the thrill of the sea – though he had never stepped foot aboard a boat. It was in his blood, his spirit; the deck moving beneath his feet, the smell and feel of salt-spray . . . Ah, Cerdic had loved Leofric!

But Leofric had died and Winifred was again a woman alone. Within a week of the burial, she had resumed her first married title. Lady Pendragon, she claimed, carried more weight than that of wife to a Saxon. Her father's name was still spat upon; that of her mother and grandfather, the great Hengest, even more so. It was an empty title of course, Lady Pendragon, for it was no longer hers, belonging rightly to that other woman of Arthur's; but then, Winifred had never been a woman to care what was right or wrong, unless the rules should happen to suit her own need.

Those few rumours of poison had been softly whispered, soon hushed, but Cerdic believed them. For no other reason than it was obvious his mother's second marriage had been a mistake. She would be angry, he knew, for his leaving without word of asking. And angered too, at the brief, final message he had sent her. From spite, from revenge for all those years of her domination? For proof of freedom?

I have gone, he wrote on a wooden tablet, purchased and sent from Llongborth, *to use my manhood as I wish. Not as you order.* He had laughed as he had boarded a Saex ship, paying his way with a generous bribe. Laughed aloud, not caring about his mother's anger, enjoying it. The message he had sent deliberately to provoke.

Let her weep or wail, shout and scream. He was gone to the River Elbe. Gone to claim as his own all that had once been his legal stepfather's; the ships, the land, the wealth and the trade; claim it as Leofric had requested. As the father Cerdic had so wanted had written, signed and

16

had witnessed in his will. It was all to be Cerdic's now. There was some of the wealth to be divided with a niece, a woman who had disappeared in Gaul during the time of the Saxon killings – but she was dead, no doubt, and would not be coming again to her birth-home. A niece? She could be forgotten, or dealt with.

Ja, his mother would be angry. And Cerdic, who had taken a woman and was now, he considered, ready to become a man, cared naught.

June 468

§ VI

The sea had a mild swell, with a few ponderous waves and an over-enthusiastic following wind that billowed and buffeted the square, blue-grey sail. There was no need for the oars, if this strength continued; the crossing down to the mouth of the Liger river would be fast. There was a way to go, however, and already rain clouds were gathering in a squall to the west – wind and sea could so abruptly change for the worse.

Arthur was leaning on the stern gunwale, peering at the white-foamed wake scudding behind the craft. The land was now only a thin, grey smudge on the horizon. Greater Britain, the last he would see of it for a month or two. He snorted private amusement; the weather might be more hospitable on the other side of the sea. Grey days and drizzling rain had persisted across the south coast of Britain for three weeks. The Liger Valley was normally more clement, kinder to weary bones and a marching army.

Another man joined him, walking unsteadily across the deck. He grabbed the gunwale, rested his hands on the curve of the smooth wood, stood as Arthur did, leaning forward, staring at the swirl of water below. Only, his fingers gripped tighter as his stomach rose and fell with the motion. His skin had tinged pale and his mouth curved distinctly downward. Bedwyr, for all his experience of adventurous travelling, was not one for the open sea.

'The horses settled?' Arthur asked, peering over his shoulder at the horse-line, ranged along the centre of the flat-decked craft. A few had ears back, heads high and eyes rolling, but they had the men with them to stroke their necks, talk soft, keep them calm. They had all – save four – loaded well into this craft and the others of the flotilla. Those four they had left behind, it was not worth the risk or effort to force them up the narrow ramps onto the flat decks of the transporters.

Without speaking, Bedwyr nodded. At this moment he did not give a damn about horses, boats or anything, save blessed, firm, dry land.

'The swell will be somewhat stronger on the voyage back,' Arthur proclaimed, unsympathetically, 'for we will be returning nearing winter, November happen, the seas can be rough that time of year.'

'Are you so certain we will be away such a short while? I do not know this man Syagrius, King of Soissons and the Northern Gauls. Can he be trusted? We cannot hold off the Goths on our own.'

Those same thoughts had nagged occasionally at Arthur's mind also, but it was too late to question now. They were committed to this thing, had to see it through. 'I knew Syagrius when he was a young lad, preening his new-acquired feathers of manhood,' Arthur said. 'I would not rate him high on my list of commanders to be well respected; but Rome has commissioned him in this fool adventure along with us. He has supplied us with these ships. I imagine he would not unnecessarily spend his treasury without expecting to make good use of the end result. We will know soon enough, if he does not meet with us at Juliomagus.' Arthur casually shrugged his shoulders. 'Well, then, we leave Gaul to sort its own affairs; we secure Less Britain; then turn around and come home.'

It all sounded so simple, with the excitement of the sea rushing past the ship's keel and the wind crying through the sail's rigging. With everything ahead planned and hopeful.

'More important,' Arthur continued, 'can we trust those fat-arsed bureaucrats in Rome? Too many of them are interested in only their own gain – offer a bribe of the right weight in gold and anything can happen.'

A stronger gust of wind bounded from the west, pitched the boat deeper into the swell. Bedwyr groaned, leaned further over the side and vomited. Arthur slapped his cousin hard between the shoulders. 'Aye,' he chuckled, 'talk of Rome often has that effect on me also!'

Bedwyr glowered at him. 'Jesu Christ Arthur, why did you agree to this damn-fool idea?'

'You were keen enough these last few days – feasted and drank as well as the rest of us last night.'

At the unwanted reminder of the indulgence of food and wine, Bedwyr again spewed what was left in his guts over the side. 'To my regret.'

Seasickness was a curse not visited on the Pendragon, nor his father before him, nor Gwenhwyfar. Arthur folded his arms along the rail, his body swaying easily with the lift and rise of the craft. Last night. The traditional farewell feast, something the Artoriani had initiated years past. Gwenhwyfar had been there with them at Llongborth, where the ships were moored ready for loading, waiting for this day's tide. She had sat beside him, laughing, joining with the rowdy singing; dancing with him, swirling around and around to the lively reels. Her forced smile had hidden her fears, her bright eyes the sorrow of parting. *'Not for long,'* Arthur had assured her during those few, brief hours of privacy that they had shared in their tent. *'I will be returning soon enough.'*

Bedwyr wiped the back of his hand over the sour taste left on his lips. 'I might be eager for a campaign in Less Britain, and happen across the borders into Gaul, but God's love, I had forgotten the misery of these damn, wallowing boats!'

Arthur said nothing. He was looking again at where that distant land merged between sea and sky. His thoughts were there, with Gwenhwyfar and his child daughter. The land was almost gone. Was it land or cloud he could see? He had sounded so confident last night, so assured, as he had held her close, loved with her.

Why then, did that confidence feel as heavy as lead now?

Because he knew in his heart that he ought not be here on this ship? Ought not be so blind, trusting of an unreliable young pup of a king, nor of reassurances made by an empire that, through its entire history, had broken more promises than it had kept.

§ VII

It took much courage, and a certain amount of bravado, for Winifred to enter her maternal uncle's settlement – were it not necessary for her son's future, no enticement or threat would have brought her to within a day's ride of the place. Aesc was much like his father, the big and brash Hengest, famed for his strength of muscle and mind, a bull of a man, set in his ways and proud of his inheritance. Hengest had been a soldiering seeker of fortune. The youngest brother of a vast brood, with little prospect of laying claim to anything of value before the seizing of the great opportunity of Britain. Vortigern, Winifred's father, had been the key; a man as greedy and ambitious as Hengest, and a man with an eye for a woman. Little encouragement had been needed on Hengest's part; he was a mercenary ready for the fight, and had a daughter ready for marriage. Vortigern, the Supreme King had willingly accepted both offers, and Hengest waited quiet in the wings for the land and gold he had been promised in exchange. Except, beyond a small, wind-swept, surf-washed island, and an occasional bag of coin, neither had material-ised. It came as no surprise to Vortigern's opponents that Hengest, tired of waiting for the pledged reward, decided to take what he wanted by force. Only he had reckoned on Vortigern's successors being as weak as that king. Had reckoned without the Pendragon.

Aesc, perhaps, was reaping better reward than his father. The Pendragon was no limp-minded King, to him went the strength of victories and the generosity of grants that went with peace. Aesc was allowed the title rex, though as a subject-king beneath Arthur, with all the dignities accompanying such a title. Aesc ruled as he willed, conditioned upon annual homage and sufficient tithing to the Pendragon – and the continuation of peace. *Fight me and you lose all.* Arthur's words; words meant. Aesc held prime land in a prime position for the flourishing of trade. To him, the longships called first on their voyages from across the sea; to him fell the first pickings of wealth. Aesc was content with the treaty of peace that he held with Arthur, for it allowed him the ability to collect what he wanted most. Wealth.

Winifred had never much liked her mother's brother. She saw him as the barbarian son of a Jute war-lord, with the manners and stench to match a rutting boar. The feelings were mutually exchanged. Aesc saw his niece as a spoilt, arrogant woman who had turned her back on the tribal laws and beliefs of her kindred. Both were content to use each other for personal benefit when it suited a need.

As now. Winifred needed Aesc to persuade her son home. Rebellious, he was steadfastly ignoring his mother. She had no one else to ask for help, Arthur would prefer the boy dead, and Ambrosius Aurelianus had no place for him among his plans to restore Britain into Rome's fold.

She rode through the open gate into the settlement, expecting to see the common *graubenhauser* buildings, dwellings of little more status than midden huts in her opinion; was surprised to find a grandly built, timbered Mead Hall, surrounded by a cluster of solid wattle-walled houses and barns. The place thrived, was bustling and busy, the people bright-clad, healthy skinned. Wealth and prosperity oozed from beneath every reed-thatched roof, abounded in the surrounding hidage of fields, orchards and grazing land. Her uncle was doing all right for himself it seemed!

Aesc came open-armed to greet her, his smile and boom of accompanying laughter full of welcome. He lifted his niece from her mare, embraced her as valued kindred, Winifred responding with a smile that successfully masked her inner feelings of contempt.

From the Hall also, accompanied by her attendants and brood of sons, stepped Aesc's woman. Anhild, fifth-born daughter to Childeric of the Franks. Her dress and jewels were lavish, her manner superior – she was a king's daughter and a king's wife. Her dowry had brought the basis of her husband's present wealth and the accompanying extensive exchange of trade with northern Gaul. She greeted Winifred coolly, aware her guest was a divorced wife and daughter to a deposed, disgraced king, conveniently forgetting that her own father had been in the same position for a while. But then, Childeric held more friends than had Vortigern, and his exiled dethronement had been a temporary setback only. He was allied now with Syagrius of Soissons. While it suited him.

Childeric could change his allegiances as often as the wind swung around.

The two women embraced, their cheeks touching in token of friendship; both felt the cold of the other, both broke apart with barely disguised dislike.

'The Pendragon is making much of a nuisance of himself in Gaul, so I hear,' remarked Anhild. 'My father reports that the Gaulish landowners complain more of his Artoriani's looting and whoring than they do against the Franks, Goths and Saxons combined.'

Winifred retained her pleasant smile – loathsome woman, as fat as a toad and as ugly – 'The Pendragon is of no concern to me, Anhild, only his title and kingdom. The sooner he loses both, the better. It is his son who occupies my thoughts. It is for Cerdic that I have come to seek my uncle's aid.'

'Ah yes,' Anhild replied, her Frankish accent distorting some of the Jute words, 'your independent son.' Her condescending smile broadened as she motioned three of her boys forward, smaller images of herself, though they bore the red hair of their father. 'My childer would never run away from their mother. We are too devoted to each other.'

Your childer, Winifred thought, *would never have enough brain to find their way out of this settlement without someone holding their fat-fleshed hands.*

Aesc invited Winifred inside his Mead Hall, called for wine and food, served his kinswoman himself. Congenial, outwardly friendly and welcoming. All smiles and laughter, an eagerness to please. It was a waste of time, this coming here, Winifred knew it the moment Aesc had lifted her from her mare. Her Jute kin would not give aid in attempting to persuade – or force – Cerdic back to Winifred's Castra; it had only been a vague hope that they would, a last resort.

She sipped her wine, ate the food, though the drink tasted bitter and the meal stuck in her throat. Aesc would not help. Her uncle was over-fat and over-full of his own laziness. He had his kingdom, his wealth and his pleasures. Why should he stir himself for a mere boy?

A young man entered the Hall, swaggering with self-importance, another reason for Aesc being unwilling to help her. Ten and five years of age and with all the arrogance of his untried, incautious age group, the newcomer paused within the shadow of the Hall, his hand resting on the pommel of his Saxon short-bladed sword, the Saex. Winifred caught her breath as the youth came through that open doorway. She saw the very image of her father. Her brother Vitolinus was another Vortigern, the same chiselled chin, long, thin face and nose, small darting eyes. There was even a scar to the side of his face. Involuntarily, Winifred's hand went to her heart, its beating fast and startled. Only the hair was different, his being thick and fair. Rowena, their mother's, hair.

He strode up to Winifred, acknowledging his uncle with a curt nod to his head; stood, legs apart, fists on hips, before her, eyeing her, weighing her. 'Well, I never thought I would see the day! My sister, deigning to visit the poor relations of the family. Come to spy on us, have you?' Vitolinus thrust his pointed face forward, reminding Winifred of a weasel. 'Whatever it is you want, sister dear, forget it. You'll have nothing from us.'

Her composure returned, Winifred spread her nostrils as if some foul stench was before her. 'I want nothing from you, little brother, I come for adult council with my uncle.' They were talking Latin, a language neither Aesc nor Anhild understood. She added tartly, 'Go away, boy. My business does not concern a whinging brat.'

Vitolinus's smile was more of a sneer. 'No? I would have sworn you were here to talk of Cerdic!' He turned away, whistling, nodded again to Aesc, tossing, in English, 'My men and I have brought home a fine buck from our day's hunting. I'll go help the butchering.' He sneered again in Winifred's direction. 'The stench of offal is more appealing than the company of your guest.'

One interesting facet. Winifred noticed Anhild's expression of contempt, and Aesc's own narrowed eyes. Ah! Did they dislike her brother as much as she?

Aesc offered more wine, said, as he gestured for a slave to pour, 'I sympathize with the worry of a mother for her son, my niece, but Cerdic is better off where he is.' He sat back in his comfortable wicker-woven chair, folded his hands across his ample lap. 'I am content with the ruling of my Kent lands, but that one there,' he pointed briefly to the door through which Vitolinus had just departed, 'that one wants a kingdom of his own. He intends to gain back his father's.' Aesc shrugged, accepting an inevitable outcome. 'While your son remains on his acquired stepfather's land, Vitolinus will forget him. If, when your son becomes a man, he should have the notion of trying for what the Pendragon now holds . . .' He spread his hands, shook his head. 'Vitolinus has higher entitlement to that land than Cerdic. I gave a home to my nephew when he sought my protection from your' – his insincere smile showed blackening, broken teeth – 'shall we say, intended incarceration.'

Winifred too sat back, folding her hands. Murder would be a more appropriate term. Unfortunately her plans for Vitolinus's demise several years past had failed when the wretched boy had escaped her custody. Her frown deepened. He had disappeared the day Arthur had beaten her injured son, the day after that fire at her farm-steading. Aesc had been there, to pay homage to the Pendragon and agree renewed treaties, and the boy Vitolinus had run to his uncle and his Jute kin, spreading tales and lies about his sister and his future. Well, perhaps not so far-fetched tales. Winifred had held every intention of being rid of the boy, her brother. But Vitolinus threaten Cerdic?

Could a worm threaten a wolf?

September 468

§ VIII

'Bull's blood!'

Arthur savagely threw the parchment scroll he had been reading across the tent. It hit the leather wall, bounced a few inches, then lay, curled up on itself on the rush-woven matting. He was pacing the tent, arms waving, animating his deep, frustrated anger, his expression dark thunder. Bedwyr, his cousin and second in command, and Meriaun, Gwenhwyfar's eldest nephew, were seated on the only two stools. Wisely, they considered it prudent to remain silent. The officer of the Roman Imperial Guard, who had brought the letter, stood at rigid attention near the door flap, his indignation growing redder on his face, his helmet, with the splendid red-dyed horsehair plume and gold and silver plating, clamped tighter between the curl of his arm. Proud, rich dressed, his armour – and ego – was old but immaculate, both a reminder that Gaul was still very much a subservient province of Rome, governed by and answerable to, the Emperor. He disliked this pretentious British King, was affronted at being treated as if he were an imbecile.

'Have I this aright?' Arthur asked, scathingly. 'The sender of this letter, the present Prefect of Rome who is, in this instance, acting in his capacity as Ambassador of Gaul, bids me welcome. He greets me with flowered words as a guest here, entreats that I make my men as comfortable as may be . . . as if I am here on some informal courtesy visit?' Arthur stooped to retrieve the offensive letter, rolled it tight, then, changing his mind, shook the scroll loose, batting irritably at the perfectly neat script with the back of his other hand. He continued his pacing, the eyes of Bedwyr and Meriaun anxiously following his movements. 'This Roman aristocrat,' Arthur glanced at the signature, 'this Sidonius Apollinaris, then proceeds to inform me that a friend of his has been arrested for writing a treasonous letter against the Emperor, and he begs that I am to make no matter of it.' Arthur's nostrils flared. The couched implications were plain enough. A sour taste spilled into his mouth. 'By the gods,' he roared, 'were I to lay my hands on such a treasonous turd, I would have his balls first, then his blood!' *Gods*, he thought, *all this way, all these weeks and miles, all this damned wasted time! Is Rome playing me so easily for the fool?*

25

The Roman officer coughed, unable to retain his pent silence any longer.

'Arvandus, that said traitor, is arrested and on his way to Rome in chains, for trial.' Coldly, he added, 'In Rome, we deal with misdemeanours by the means of civilized methods.'

Bedwyr caught Arthur's eye, stemmed an explosive retort by saying hastily, 'It could be a mistake.' He spread his hands wide, searching for a more appropriate word. 'A misunderstanding?'

Again the Roman spoke, his tone haughty, condescending. 'Rome will sort the matter. Punish those who are guilty.'

Arthur stepped a pace nearer to him. 'We sail, Mithras alone knows how many hundreds of miles, in answer to a plea from your Emperor. He begs us to unite with those loyal to Rome against the barbarian Euric who is seeking for himself a kingdom. We then sit here for bloody weeks, doing sod-all except scratch our arses – and I am calmly told, by a man appointed by Rome to govern Gaul, that a friend of his has written to Euric of the Goths, suggesting that he does not sign the offered treaty of peace with Rome but destroys the British instead!' He threw the parchment a second time, kicked it at the Roman as it rebounded off the tent wall, strode after it and caught hold of the officer by the throat; shook him, like a dog with a rat, the reason for his anger bursting from him like cooked meat in over-stuffed pastry. 'What bloody treaty of peace? I do not give a dog's turd for this traitor, or for Rome's bloody laws – what treaty? If those stool-sitting arseholes in Rome have been suing for peace with Euric, why have I not been consulted of it? And if a peace treaty was the intention all along, why was I damned well brought here?'

The officer was spluttering and choking, his face suffusing red; he had dropped his helmet, his fingers were grappling with Arthur's hands, attempting to loosen that tight grip around his throat – and Arthur let him go, let him drop like a stone to the floor, discarding him, leaving him to heave and choke for breath. The other two men, Bedwyr and Meriaun, ignored his discomfort.

'Rome is not likely to want a fight if it can be avoided,' Meriaun pointed out to Arthur. 'After all, you have used the same tactics back home often enough to secure peace.'

'We would not be here if it were not for treaties,' Bedwyr added, trying to smooth Arthur's ruffled temper. 'Britain is free, at least for a while, of any uprising because of various such signed scrolls of parchment.' He rose from his stool, strolled to a table, questioned with his eyes whether anyone wanted wine. Arthur accepted, Meriaun shook his head. Bedwyr ignored the Roman, a man who had never seen a day's fighting in his life, despite the fancy uniform; would probably not know which end of a spear to hold. The mental insult was unjustified, but such men were not soldiers, they were couriers, the Emperor's lap-dogs; trained to fetch and carry, to look smart, salute. Say aye or na to command.

Reluctant, the Pendragon had to acknowledge the truth of his younger cousin's point. Calming his racing breath, he took the offered goblet of wine, drank; said, refusing to concede entirely, 'Aye, but we proved ourselves first. The Saex settled along our eastern rivers and coast know me for my strength, know they cannot defeat my Artoriani. They agree peace because the alternative is slaughter. This,' – he crossed to the offensive letter, picked it up, looked at it with disgusted loathing and lobbed it out the open doorway – 'this is admitting defeat before even a blade has been unsheathed!' He turned again to the Roman who stood warily shaken, his fingers massaging a bruised throat. Arthur asked again, 'Why was I not informed that a treaty had been offered to Euric?'

About to answer with his first-come thought – that Rome's business was none of this British king's – the man shrugged his shoulder instead. 'We have always made friends with the barbarians. This new king of the Goth's dead brother, Theodoric, was a follower of Rome, he led his men for us. We have many such treaties with these new, petty kingdoms. They live in peace under our laws and rule. It is so with the Burgundians, the Franks,' – he smiled derisively – 'the British.'

Arthur smiled back at him, seeming pleasant enough. Bedwyr, pouring more wine for himself groaned.

'I,' Arthur said, patiently, 'have signed no such treaty with your poxed masters in Rome.' He held up one finger to stem the protest hovering on the imperial officer's lip. 'Nor is any treaty proffered by the dignitaries of Less Britain valid. I am King of Britanniarum, Less and Greater. The island across the sea is mine, and so is Armorica, as you still call it. I personally own an estate a few miles from Condivicnum. I rule in my own right, with my laws, my word. I, Arthur Riothamus the Pendragon, not you.' He poked the man's chest with one finger, sending him wobbling backwards a step. 'Not this traitor Arvandus, nor Rome's Governor, Sidonius Apollinaris, who is so proud of his fawning, overrated letter-writing; not Anthemius your Emperor – nor his puppet-master Ricimer, the man who pulls the strings of all Rome's snivelling governors. I, Arthur, have the title Pendragon in Greater Britain; and in Less Britain, that of Riothamus. I am Supreme King.' Each word had been punctuated by a prod that increased in intensity. The officer was backing away, found the open tent flap behind him.

Arthur moved suddenly, alarmingly fast, had the man's arm up behind his back and was trundling him from the tent, marching him across the flattened grass that officiated as a parade ground towards the horse lines.

'Get on your mount and go back to the imbecile who sent you! I will hear nothing of treaties, letters, or peace. I have been asked here to fight and fight I will. As soon as Syagrius of Soissons joins with me.'

The officer was unhurt, but affronted and humiliated. He had come as ordered from Rome to officially, and politely, inform this arrogant bastard of a king that a traitor had been arrested before rumour permeated the wrong impression – and had been treated in response as less than a midden boy! These British had less manners and fouler language than Euric and his barbarian Goth whoresons!

He scrambled onto his horse, gathered up the reins and began trotting for the open gate, set between the wooden-fenced palisade. He had to say something, something to avenge his dignity.

'Syagrius?' He shouted, looking back over his shoulder at the gathering, laughing men; at Arthur, the British King. 'Syagrius has no intention of joining you. It was he who suggested offering a treaty with Euric, not Rome!' He dug his heels into the horse's flanks and galloped off. Remembering, too late, that his ornate parade helmet lay on the floor of Arthur's tent.

§ IX

Arthur stood beyond his tent watching the splendours of the sunset fade into the purple of approaching night. Evening was different here in Less Britain, quicker, more vibrant. Back home, the coming of night seemed to settle with a gentle, softening sigh. Here, it shouted at you.

He wondered if the day had been as hot in Britain. Or was it raining there? Almost he could smell the pleasing, fresh, dampness of the Summer Land, the scent of damp earth and water, the approach of a low-lying mist. Here, everything was dry, brown, beneath the arid scent of sun-baked heat. Another sigh. In the name of all the gods, he should not have come!

He heard Gwenhwyfar's voice – seeming so close that he almost felt that were he to turn around she would be there, behind him, her copper hair tossing, her green, tawny-flecked eyes flashing. *'Why must you go?'*

The men were preparing for night, shaking out their blankets, finishing supper, heading for the latrine ditch.

'I need to aid Less Britain, it is as much a part of my kingdom as the lands of Geraint's Dumnonia or your brother's Gwynedd. I am the Supreme Lord, I swore to protect, to keep peace.'

Had she been angry with him because she had seen the whole thing was a slaughterhouse mess of disguised half-truths, deceptions and hollow fabrications?

He looked again around the sprawling camp, the rows of tents, across at the picketed horses, the smith's bothy, the grain tent; the paraphernalia that accompanied a king's army. Looked at his men, his Artoriani, trained, disciplined, professional men. Almost four hundred had accompanied him, twelve turmae of his best. Volunteers. He had not demanded of any of them, although they had all wanted to come. He had answered this urgent – huh, where was the urgency now? – plea for help from the Emperor with the proviso that he would bring no more than half of his Artoriani. He could not bleed Britain dry, not – for all the agreed treaties of peace – with so many of the Saex settled along the coasts and rivers. Not when Ambrosius Aurelianus, his uncle and a pro-Roman, was so much more popular with Council than himself. And not with an ex-wife determined to see her son wearing the Pendragon's royal torque around his own neck one day.

Not that the last mattered with Cerdic gone, out of her reach. There needed to be some secure, loyal force left behind, some stabilizing deterrent. Someone to keep care of Gwenhwyfar and their daughter if something happened to him.

I have to add British weight to the counter-defensive. His argument had sounded reasonable enough, back at Caer Cadan, even knowing that Ambrosius just might get enough of a taste for ruling to not want to give it up if he came back after this campaign.

Arthur swore silently to himself, started walking towards the horse lines. He would see the animals were settled before seeking his bed. *If he came back* ... what in the Bull's name was wrong with him this night?

The men seemed cheerful enough as he strode past the tents, some of them calling out in good humour, sharing lewd remarks about the local womenfolk, exchanging jests and comments with him. They all seemed happy enough to be here. But they had come expecting a fight. That was what they were trained for – what they lived for. They were brothers, comrades, men who lived and fought and died as one family. His family. And he had told them that Less Britain and Gaul was in danger from Euric and his rabble; that his people, their people, were threatened, as once, not so very long ago, the people of Britain had been threatened. The men had answered that they were willing to join with those allied to Rome against these Goths. To fight.

Some of the horses were already dozing, their heads drooping, ears flopped, hind legs resting. One or two, recognizing him, whickered softly as he approached, ran his hand along a neck, gently pulling at an ear; touching a muzzle. You knew where you were with horses. They did not lie or cheat. They served, proud but without arrogance, with strength bound within gentleness. A horse gave you all it could without question. As did the Artoriani, his men.

Arthur groaned, laid his face against the mane of the next horse in line, a broad-headed grey. Rome had no need of his fine, brave men. Bringing them over, all this expense and time and effort had been a knee-jerk panic reaction, a show of bravado, a threat. *Live in peace with us, Euric, as did the brother you murdered, or face the consequences* . . . only the consequences had turned out to be as threatening as a broken spear. He had not seen that possibility back in Britain – or had he not wanted to see it? Had he, like his men, been so enthusiastic for a fight that he had turned his eye, and sense to the reality? He patted the horse. Too late to realize the suspected truth now. One nagging question persisted; had he only listened to what he had wanted to hear or to what he had been meant to?

He moved to another horse, Bedwyr's chestnut. His own favourite stallion, Onager, he had left in Britain. A damn good horse in battle, but a bad tempered brute with a will of his own. He would have been unsafe in the confines of those flat-bottomed transport ships.

By seeking a treaty of peace, Rome was only doing what he had done as King, except on a larger, grander scale. Why fight if the need to spill blood could be averted by other means? He had settled peace in such a way back home – but by the Bull, he had not wasted all this time and energy in moving men and horses about unnecessarily! Ah, he countered his own thoughts, but then, he supposed it had been necessary. To bring his trained men and horses all this way had taken a deal of effort and organization. The loading and unloading of ships, the sea crossing, the march up from the estuary along the course of the river here to Juliomagus, their base camp for now. Manoeuvres that had taken weeks, not days to complete. If Euric had decided on taking an immediate defensive, all this land would be blackened ruins by now.

The town of Juliomagus, one mile or so distant, had been engulfed by the night, only a few scattered watch-tower lights glimmered in the darkness. The stars were different here too. Bolder, more sharp, a few down on the horizon he remembered seeing as a boy at his father's estate down-river near Condivicnum. Only he had not known the great Uthr Pendragon to be his father then, for his identity had been hidden until it was safe to announce him for the son he was.

Juliomagus had survived one bloody attack already, a few years past. The Saxons had been raiding along the river, building their homestead-ings on the numerous islands, and, growing bolder, had tried for something more than holding a few scattered villages. The fighting had been bitter, but in the end Odovacer, their leader, had been driven out, sent running.

The whole of Gaul was a simmering cauldron. If watched it would bubble away without harm, but if left to its own there was every possibility that the heat would grow too high and the thing would boil and spurt over like a volcano blowing its top.

Arthur wandered back to his tent. It was that which niggled him.

He did not much like being a pot-watcher.

October 468

§ X

The remnants of an autumn dawn lay over the levels of the Summer Land. The Tor, eleven miles distant as the raven would fly, sat like a faery island, rising solid amid the white, shape-shifting mist, and as the sun rose, deep, black shadows lengthened away from the ramparts and ditches of the King's stronghold of Caer Cadan. The heart-place of Arthur, the Pendragon. Finger shadows, stretching out across the moving mist, shadows cast from tree and bush and scattered copses of alder, ash and willow, the tumble of uneven ground. Another morning, another day.

Gwenhwyfar shivered, drew her cloak nearer around her shoulders. It was chill this morning, summer had faded into the sharp tang of autumn; already the colours had altered from pleasant green to the fire-bright bursts of red and yellow and orange. With the lifting sun, the mist too was turning gold. How this great welt of loneliness and despair gripped her, clutched at her, like the unrelenting chill of a frozen winter! Arthur was gone, ridden away with the laughter and hopeful excitement of his men. Gone to chase the lure of a promised fight. Gone, not knowing when – if – he would be back. As he had been gone so many, many times before.

Why then, this portent of dread within her stomach? Because he had taken ship across the sea? Because, already, he had been gone longer than he had intended? Because the crows circled the Caer each night before going to their roost, the wind blew from the east, the old apple tree had not borne fruit . . . so many nonsense reasons to explain the questions that held no answers.

The mist lifted, evaporating with the new-risen burst of sun-warmed day, leaving the Tor once again stranded in the mortal world of the Christian God. Gwenhwyfar, seeing the magic of the whiteness disappear, had the thought that it was not so easy to chase away the fears that lunged through her night-dreams, that muttered so persistently at the back of her waking mind.

Nail-studded boots scraped on the wooden stairway, emerged out onto the rampart walkway. She recognized the step, the heavy tread, turned with a smile to greet Ider, the Captain of her personal guard.

'My lady?' His voice showed concern, a question, aware of her sadness and fears. No sign though, in his words or eyes, of the unutterable devotion that he felt for her. He had a wife of his own, and a family, but still he loved his queen. As did nigh on every man of Arthur's élite cavalry of nine hundred men, the Artoriani.

'I have come for this day's orders,' he said. Routine went on, King present, King absent, the daily routine of a stronghold.

She managed a wide smile, brighter, appearing content, knowing she did not fool Ider.

He stood as strong and tall as an ancient oak tree, his heart and kindness as gentle as the willow. He crossed to the palisade fencing, stood next to his lady, rested his arms along the top of the wooden fencing, stood gazing outward, as Gwenhwyfar had. He breathed in the dew-wet smells of this new day. A rich aroma of earth and marsh, of water, and autumn withered grass, a distant tang of the sea. Arthur's summer land.

'It is in my heart,' he said at length, the northern burr of his accent pronounced even after all these years in service to the Artoriani, 'to be with my comrades, my brothers, across the sea in Gaul, following the Dragon Banner. A soldier needs the pull of a battle to keep an edge to his sword. But then,' he turned with a barrel-wide grin and an exaggerated inhalation of wafting smells, 'then I catch the aroma of the remains of last night's supper of ham cooking for breakfast down there, and change my mind!' He nodded to the scatter of wattle-built dwelling places and huts that made the Caer into its life-place, chuckled.

Gwenhwyfar laughed with him, laid her hand for a moment on his chest, against the leather of his tunic. 'Glad I am that you did not go with my husband, you have always had the wicked ability to make my heart smile.'

Ider stepped back a pace, his expression displaying hurt. 'And I thought you valued me for my good looks, strength and skill with a sword!'

Amused, the heaviness of heart, for a while at least, lifted, Gwenhwyfar teased back, 'Those come without question, my lad!' She made her way to the steps, began to descend, the sun striking the brilliant copper-gold of her braided hair. For all the affection he held for his wife, Ider felt a knot tighten in his stomach. She was an attractive woman, Gwenhwyfar, her figure slim, despite the bearing of children, her skin fresh, unmarked, teeth white, all her own. Her thirty years leant nothing but maturity and poised wisdom to her being.

If Ider were her husband, he would not have been so eager to leave, to go to fight for a foreign cause. But then, Ider was not a king. The role of husband, he supposed had to come second, behind that of being the Pendragon. Even with a wife as lovely as Gwenhwyfar.

December 468

§ XI

Sorrowfully, Ambrosius surveyed the ragged, incomplete building before him; the half-height walls, the tumble of stone, a scatter of timber, the rutted wheel and foot-churned ground. Half-built, abandoned for the other work, the other construction up on the hill, where, it was said, the great Vespasian once made a stronghold, back in those times when Britain was being harnessed to Rome's superiority. There was to be a fortress again there. Ambrosius's fortress, his place of command, his stronghold from where he would refasten those loosened straps and chains. The men were up there, labouring to dig the defensive ditches, toss up the huge ramparts, build the stone and timber palisade. Inside would come the dwelling places for the men and their families; the principia, the administration offices. He was determined to have a Roman-built praetorium for his own house, not the British-built timbered Hall.

He sighed, long and loud. He would have preferred this half-complete building finished rather than have a fortress saddled on him. Council wanted a stronghold, wanted preparations ready, in hand. He did not, but Council would have their way. He turned away, resigned, and saw his son hobbling with his cumbersome crutch and dragging, lame leg. Another thing that must be accepted, but stuck like a fish-bone in the throat. His only son was limp-legged and useless.

Cadwy tried a cheery expression, aware that he was a constant disappointment to his father. He pointed with his crutch to the building works up on the hill. 'It goes well, father! Soon it will be finished.'

Ambrosius returned a forced smile that did not reach the eyes. Aye, soon it would be finished and then Council would be pressing for him to use it, to take over the permanent leading of this God-forgotten damn country. He did not want that either, but who else was there to do it? Who else could herd this lost and weary province back into Rome's protective pastures? He gestured at the abandoned building behind him, said, the sadness all too obvious in his voice, 'I would rather it had been my school for teaching God's word that was nearing completion, not this place of war.'

'War?' Cadwy stayed determinedly cheerful. 'Surely father, the fortress is a precaution only, a standby in case Arthur . . .'

'. . . Does not come back?' Ambrosius finished for him. Added, in a loud, slow voice, as if he were talking to a child, not a man of ten and eight, 'Arthur will not be back. Council will not allow him back.'

Abandoning the pretence of a smile, Cadwy shook his head, pleading with his eyes for his father to accept that although the leg was twisted and wasted, there was nothing wrong with his head and mind. 'Can Council stop him?' he asked cautiously, 'Arthur has many men, he is a war-lord unparalleled in battle.' Difficult for Cadwy, for he liked the Pendragon, admired and respected him, but the loyalty had to go to his own father. A father who gave all to his Christian God and spared no love for his son.

Ambrosius twitched his hand, dismissive. He was a man who believed firmly in the ways of Rome, the old ways of law and order and justice. It was Council, the British equivalent of the Senate, who should have the voice of power, not kings or princes. Command should be by an appointed governor. If Council decreed that he ought be that governor, then who was he to go against the will of the Council? His nephew frequently did exactly that, but then his nephew – aye and his nephew's dead father, Uthr Pendragon – were in Rome's eyes almost barbarian. Ambrosius took a patient breath. What had become of Rome, to allow such men the respect of recognition?

'Arthur's men are across the sea and he fights with horses. His cavalry is what makes him good. Take away the horses and you are left with nothing.' He began walking up the sloping ground, in the direction of the rising fortress, pacing with deliberate long strides, making it hard for Cadwy to keep up. He knew what he had just said was not true, but he could not admit that, not even to himself. He had to believe what Council said and decreed was the right of it, the only way of it. Had to. 'Arthur's men,' he stated, 'may find a way to return, but he will not be able to transport the horses.' He added no more, for this part of it – huh, if he were truthful, all of it, but this part in particular – left a sour taste in his mouth, left behind a putrid smell of poison and treachery. Council were already seeing to it that the ships would not be available to bring back Arthur's valuable war-horses. Horses that cost much in time and gold and experience to breed and train.

Resentful, for Cadwy could smell that stench of naked treason, the young man almost snapped a sharp retort, but dutifully swallowed the thought that his father sounded pleased. It was no secret that these two, the Pendragon and Ambrosius, nephew and uncle, had little liking for each other. Opposites in nature and mind. Instead, Cadwy steered a safer course, asked, 'You would not use horse then?'

'Not like Arthur does, no.'

More disappointment, although he had already known the answer. Cadwy could ride a horse; could, if he were shown how, even fight from a horse. It had been the one thing that had pulled him through the burning, paining illness that had crippled him at the age of seven years; the hope that when he was grown he could ride a horse and join with the Pendragon's cavalry. Arthur had become King that month, as Cadwy began to surface from the horrors of those long months of agony and near-death. A great battle there had been, over on the east coast, against the mighty Saxon war-lord, Hengest. Arthur had won his sword in that battle, taken it from an ox-built Saex and slaughtered the sea wolves with its shining strength. Cadwy's nurse had told him the tale of that battle – as many, many others had been retelling the same thing throughout the land of Britain. He had so wanted to be a part of that glory, the hope and excitement. He could be still, if his father would only let him ride a horse suited to war. No use regretting. It would not happen, he was a lame-leg, a nothing. And his father intended to take the Pendragon's place.

He hurried his awkward steps to stay apace of Ambrosius, the thought flashing like a stabbed spear into his mind, that he did not want to fight Arthur. He slowed, unable to keep up, turned back down the slope. He would need to take the easier track that led up the east side, not this steep, grass way.

His father was near the top, pausing to say something to the men stone-facing the highest rampart. Another bitter thought, best kept secure to himself. When the fight eventually came between Arthur and his father, Cadwy so hoped it would be the Pendragon to win.

§ XII

The Mass of the Nativity, for all its meaning of birth and celebration was, for two particular people in the congregation, a solemn, reflective occasion. For them, the service was poignant, a reminder of their own born sons. The joy of the birth of the Christ child being over-shadowed by disillusionment and regret.

The splendid holy building at Venta Bulgarium. Winifred and Ambrosius Aurelianus sat, each in shadowed isolation upon their privileged seating of high-backed, cushioned and ornately carved chairs. The Bishop was intoning his sermon. Several of the nobility arrayed on the front rows of hard, wooden benches had their chins tucked well into their chests, though only one had the indecency to snore.

Venta was one of the few towns that could still boast a bishop. Aquae Sulis had old Justinian, a frail man who had to be carried everywhere by litter and often stank of the bowl flux; Gwynedd had Bishop Cynan, firmly installed as shepherd of men at the wondrous recently built chapel of Valle Crucis – Winifred intended to travel there one day, to see if it really was more splendid than this, her church. Eboracum was a deserted town now, save for the Saex who seemed not to mind the annual flooding. Durovernum was partially destroyed, its crumbling stone walls protecting the establishment of Aesc's Jute settlement, Canta Byrig, his capital town.

Deva, Caer Gloui and Caer Lueil, the minor towns that had once seen the wealth of Rome, had never quite recovered from various tragedies of flood or assault, or abandonment. Only Venta Bulgarium flourished, because Winifred sank much of her wealth into it, and Ambrosius, Governor of Britain, patronized its church.

Compared to the simple standards of the period, the building was a superb place. Twice the size of any other known British church and built in the style of an equal-sided cross. A single narrow, green and blue glass window was set in the eastern wall – solid-built of stone. Above, a slate roof, not straw or reed-thatched, topped the vaulted, carving-encrusted rafters. Standing on the linen altar cloth were a golden crucifix the height of a man's forearm, two chalices and a silver salver.

Winifred had financed much of the construction and decoration, bringing in the best Roman architects, the best masons and carpenters. It was intended to be grander and superior to the wattle-built shacks that normally served as church or chapel, a place where pilgrims would come to worship the Christian God. A place to generate wealth for the Church – and Winifred. Travellers needed somewhere to sleep and eat. Farmers came to sell goats and cattle in the wide-spaced forum, traders brought their pottery, jewellery, cloth. The Church – the bishop – or Winifred, owned between them the taverns and open-fronted shops, collected rent for the stalls. Were doing very nicely out of her investment.

Winifred fingered the crucifix that dangled from her corded waist-belt, feeling its shape, its smoothness, trying to feel its meaning and comfort, finding instead only the cold of emptiness. Arthur had mocked her devotion to the Christian faith, accusing her of using religion to further her own gain. To a point, happen she had, but she did believe, that was not faked. Believed, but found no comfort. God had deserted her, had allowed her son to turn his back on her. She knew she ought regard this as some sign of testing her faith, of her true love of God; but she could not find the strength, the willingness. God and the Christ she loved, but not above her son Cerdic.

And Ambrosius, sitting opposite her on the spear side of the aisle, chased similar thoughts in a crazy whirl around his mind. He ought be listening to the bishop's words, ought focus his attention on God, not Cadwy, his misshapen, useless son. The doubts and bitterness had been encroaching stronger of late. The questions, the asking why. Why, if God favoured him to become the sole lord of Britain, had He not blessed him with a strong, capable son? A son able to command an army, able to ensure the taking of what had been Arthur's? To follow, as his heir.

Cerdic had turned his back on his mother and her oppressive Christianity, had returned, with determination of will, to the people and pagan beliefs of his stepfather. Cadwy felt no love for this Christian God that was supposed to offer love and comfort. Where was the comfort in knowing your earthly father despised you?

The nativity, an adaptation of the pagan celebration of life and rebirth. Winifred, as the bishop finished his monotonous diatribe at last, felt a tear slide down her cheek. All she had fought for, lied, cheated and even killed for. All she had built and sown and harvested. All had been for Cerdic. He had to become king after Arthur, for without him as supreme, what was left for herself? Nothing, save the loneliness of an unwanted, set-aside ex-wife.

Ambrosius mouthed the words of the chant, reciting by rote of habit. What was there for him after he had taken what was offered, now that Arthur was away, unlikely to come back? If there was no one to pass his gain to, no one to ensure the continuation of all he had worked and struggled to achieve, what was the point of gaining it?

The bishop offered the Blessing, took up his mitre and crosier and, with his retinue pacing in solemn splendour, proceeded down the central aisle, his soft doeskin boots scuffing on the bright colouring of the intricate, patterned mosaic flooring. He had his own thoughts, his own ambitions.

The position of archbishop had never been refilled after the tragic massacre of so many of the Church a few years past at Eboracum. Both Ambrosius Aurelianus and the Lady Winifred were sure to have been impressed by that splendid sermon of his today. He smiled benignly at the poorer people of his flock huddled towards the rear of the grand church. Archbishop, the title sat well in his ambitious thoughts.

February 469

§ XIII

It was raining. Not the soft drizzle of a British springtime shower, but a harsh, wind-blustering swathe of winter, stinging needles that pulsed in from the wave-tossed river. Juliomagus was sodden. Water cascaded from low-hung eaves and cracked, broken gutters; the street drains, unrepaired for years, were blocked beyond use; consequently, the mud seethed with sewage, fetid and stinking. The heavy wheels of ox-carts became stuck; people were truculent and irritable as they hurried about their business, heads dipped, shoulders hunched. At the Forum, where the market traders had set their stalls, requirements were bartered for quickly, no one caring to browse or chat.

Arthur, however, was in no hurry. Several citizens, scuttling, bent against the rain, knocked into him, cursed, as he strolled along the Via Apollo. He was talking, hands animated, to Bedwyr, expressing personal preference for the town's selection of wines. In turn, Bedwyr was challenging his cousin's choice, both men heedless of the discomfort of rain.

'The Red Bull,' Bedwyr insisted, 'serves the best Greek. Your nomination of the Grape cannot hold a candle to it!'

'Nonsense, the Grape's wine is stored the better, their amphorae are kept in cool cellars, the Bull's stores are nigh on in full sun!'

Bedwyr was having none of it. He pointed at the sky. 'Sun? Do they get sun in this dull place?' The disagreement colourfully continued as they strolled the length of the next street and around the corner. They had reached the eastern corner of the Forum.

Normally crowded, the wide, square market-place was woefully empty. Traders' stalls dripped sorrowfully, displayed wares looking soggy and unexciting. Foodstuffs, cloths and the like were ruined, although the sellers would undoubtedly find some way of making a financial gain.

'The Grape has one unquestionable advantage though, cousin!'

'Which is?' Bedwyr queried.

'The dark-eyed Diana!'

Bedwyr laughed. Aye, he had to concede that point. Diana was indeed a most enticing serving lass.

The Pendragon's eyes were skimming across the expanse of the mud-puddled market-place, roving to the opposite side, in the direction of a huddled group of slaves squatting miserably beside the inadequate shelter of a tavern wall. They sat, dismally hunched against the wet as best they could, movement restricted by the ropes that tethered them to wooden slave-posts. Always a depressing corner of any Forum, the slave market. Arthur usually avoided them. He had his own slaves, what man did not? But those on sale in decaying towns such as this were frequently a sad lot. Today's offerings were probably no exception; the usual selection of old men, women past their prime, skinny, scabby children. Saxon most of them, the occasional Frank or Burgundian.

He was supposed to be making his way to a designated meeting with Sidonius Apollinaris, one-time Ambassador of Gaul and Prefect of Rome, a man now somewhat discredited by his friend's treasonable letter, an incitement against peace. There was no hurry; let the intrusive little man wait. Arthur and his men had been kept waiting these long months, all damn summer and winter. One promise and assurance after another delayed or set aside. Sidonius had requested this meeting to explain the latest set of excuses for keeping the Britons encamped with nothing to do, nowhere to go, no one to fight with or against – and aye, there was a degree of explaining to do! Having a few bones of his own to pick over, Arthur had agreed to meet – aside, there was little else to do in this town, especially on such a miserable, wet morning.

'Now, Diana might be alluring, but what of that fair-skinned beauty?' Making his way obliquely across the Forum, Arthur pointed at a girl, her hands bound and tethered from a neck ring to the slave-posts by a rope. She was standing, dressed well for a slave, arguing fiercely with the slave-master, her head tossing, foot stamping. A second man, fat-bellied and porcine in appearance, was joining in, a goatskin was dropped in the mud at his feet, in one hand he held out a leather pouch which jingled a few coins, the other hand making grabs for the girl, who darted nimbly aside while pouring more complaint at her master. Intrigued, Arthur, with Bedwyr at heel, wandered closer.

'I am not worth that piddling amount!' she was declaring heatedly. 'A few bronze coins and a stinking goatskin? Woden's breath, I am a noblewoman's daughter, you cannot sell me for the price of a' – she spat at the man attempting to purchase her – 'for the price of a piss pot!'

Arthur folded his arms, grinning. A slave negotiating her own payment? He had never seen or heard such a thing!

'Take my offer or go without, Tadius!' the fat man protested. 'It is a good offer; you'll not sell such a shrew for better in this town!'

Tadius obviously agreed, for he took the leather pouch. The girl shrieked her rage. 'My mother was the sister of a thegn – of Leofric of the

Elbe! She was wife to one of Odovacer's trusted generals! I am of relation to royal birth, damn it!' Tadius was ignoring her, unfastening her tether. 'By the Hammer!' she cursed, 'I am related by marriage to the King of Britain, Riothamus himself – I ought be valued as a royal concubine, nothing less!' She fell forward to her knees as the slave-master jerked her rope, breath knocking from her.

'You're a tongue-shrilling damn nuisance!' The man countered. 'No wonder I was offered you so cheap – Odovacer, the Saxon war-lord, probably sold you into slavery himself to be rid of you from his encampment!'

'I was abducted by the stinking Gauls, as you well know, you turd!'

Standing with his familiar expression of one eyebrow raised, the other eye half-shut, Arthur's interest had heightened. Leofric of the Elbe? Winifred's deceased husband? Surely there would not be two of the same name and title?

The fat man had hold of the rope, was jerking it to encourage the girl to stand, succeeding only in dragging her forward. Panic was behind her eyes, although she was masking her fear well.

'There are some men who enjoy a bit of spirit in their bed,' the Pendragon said, to no one in particular. ''Tis easy enough to stop a tongue from clacking.'

The fat man hauled the rope harder, causing the girl to gasp as the other end choked at her neck. He was grinning, jowls flapping, an ugly, insidious man. 'Why think you I buy her? To converse with over dinner?'

Arthur grimaced. He was no moralist, had no prudish censorship, but this thing brought a sour taste to his mouth. The girl could be no more than nine or eight and ten, Fat Man was in his sixth decade at least.

Arthur jiggled his fingers at the money pouch secured at his waist. He had not much coin – bronze and silver was becoming rare, nothing had been minted in Britain since Vortigern had died. Idly, casual, he took a ring from his finger, tossed it in the air, caught it, saw the slave-master's greedy eyes follow its movement. Fat Man had stopped tugging at the rope, the girl ceased her shrieking.

Bedwyr tapped at his cousin's arm. 'Leave it, what want you with her?'

Arthur waved him silent. His eye had never left the slave-master. 'As she says, a noble-born, even a king, might be interested in her.'

The man laughed, derisive. 'As much as such a profit would be pleasing, no man of that rank would be seeking a bed-mate in this midden heap of a place!'

Raising one eyebrow higher, Arthur considered the situation. He had obviously not been recognized. On the two occasions that he had visited this Forum, he had not lingered, the tavern he frequented was on the far side of the town, and the citizens of Juliomagus most certainly did not venture into his own army encampment down-river. There was no reason, save for the quality of his appearance, that he would be recognized. His cloak was fastened close, hiding his sword and the royal torque around his neck. Save for the dragon ring on his left hand, there was nothing to show who he was. 'I may be interested in her, assuming she does not carry the cock-pox.'

Sensing a better deal, Tadius answered quickly. 'She's clean, a maiden pure.'

The latter Arthur very much doubted. The girl was looking at him, kneeling in the mire, her expression pleading – anything, anyone rather than the fat man. A maiden? Arthur studied her. Na, she had the look of the world-wise about her, no naive innocence lingered behind those blue eyes.

Fat Man snorted his contempt, tightened his grip around the rope. He had no intention of losing his bargain. 'You are a bloody soldier, one of those cursed British, as bad as any Saex or Goth! We did not invite you here – we want you gone, want rid of you. You plunder us for food and whores and wine; you brawl, make a nuisance of yourselves. Your poxed, bastard king promises to pay, to settle all debts with us, the honest traders and merchant men – huh! Aye, that he will, on the day pigs fly in the sky!'

Arthur stood very quiet, very still. Bedwyr, a step behind, knowing his cousin so very well, had his hand resting lightly on his sword pommel.

Tossing the ring once more, Arthur flipped it in the slave-master's direction. 'That is good gold, the gem is small but a quality garnet, for all its lack of size.' He indicated the purse of coins. 'I doubt that will match my offer.'

The slave-master examined the ring. He doubted the garnet was real, glass probably, and the gold would be poor quality, but for all that it was of a higher value than the other offer. He nodded acceptance, put the ring in his pouch and reached for the girl's rope, tossing the coin pouch back to its owner, who ignored it, let it fall.

With surprising speed, a dagger came into Fat Man's hand. 'You agreed the deal Tadius. She is mine!'

Arthur's hand had, even faster, clenched around the man's pudgy neck – and he was sailing forward, not far or high, but far enough for Arthur to laugh, 'I'll be damned, a pig flying!' Then he had his sword out, the blade slicing through the slave rope. He picked up the severed end, his blade hovering above Fat Man's groin. 'I get the girl, or your balls? Your choice.' A heartbeat pause, no answer. Arthur grinned. 'It seems I get the girl.' He grasped her hand, brought her to her feet. 'You'd better be woman-clean, girl. Riothamus, despite popular opinion, may be a bastard, but he's not, yet, a poxed bastard.' Casually he shrugged back the folds of his cloak, let the glimmer of his torque show, a coil of twisted gold shaped like a dragon. Only one man wore such a thing.

'Come, Bedwyr, we are late for that meeting.' Holding the slave rope as casually as if it were a dog's lead, Arthur walked away, heading for the northern exit from the Forum, the girl trotting obedient, wide-eyed and silent at his heel.

Tadius re-examined the garnet ring, ignoring the fat man, who breathless was struggling to his feet. 'God's Fortune!' Tadius whistled aloud, 'That was the Pendragon, this is the real thing!'

Fat Man, at his shoulder, peered at the ring, unimpressed. 'If he can squander such things on a whore, happen it's about time he paid some of us honest townsfolk.'

Tadius laughed, put the ring safe away. 'Honest folk? God's balls! Honest? Here? There be no such person!'

§ XIV

Sidonius Apollinaris welcomed the Pendragon – or Riothamus, as he was titled in Less Britain and Gaul – with wide arms and a wider smile. If he was annoyed at the late arrival of his guest, he made no mention of it. Instead, he ushered Arthur and Bedwyr into the luxury of a private room at the rear of the tavern, raising his eyebrow only slightly at the British King's request to have the bedraggled girl accompanying him sent to the kitchens for food and a chance to dry her clothes and hair. Sidonius was a man who took the unexpected in his stride – storing such glimmers of tantalizing information away in his brain for later, private reflection.

There was another man in the room, seated, sipping wine. He rose as Arthur entered, bowed formally. A young man, bright-eyed, clear-skinned, tall and clean-shaven. He bounded forward, offered his hand to Arthur, not caring to wait for formal introduction. 'My Lord, I am Ecdicius; my elder sister being Sidonius's good lady wife. I have heard much of you, am honoured to meet you.' His hand was pumping Arthur's arm, his grin broad and genuine. Sidonius, Arthur noted, seemed slightly embarrassed at this reckless enthusiasm.

'My brother-by-law,' with a light laugh Sidonius explained, indicating that his guests be seated and offering them wine, 'is an incurable romantic. He has a notion of riding with you to sweep the Goths from Gaul forever, in one deft charge.' He shook his head at the naivety of such an impossible idea, seated himself on a cushioned chair, arranging his body straight, small feet neatly placed together. 'He has an unfortunate disability not to be able to recognize the realities of life.' His accompanying smile was sated with indulgent affection.

Sipping his wine – it was good stuff, the best he had tasted here in this town – Arthur answered, 'Given the men, horses and financial backing that I was promised, more than a year since, I could do just that.' His false smile did little to hide his annoyance. Sidonius, ordering the slaves to bring in food and more wine, either did not hear, or chose to ignore the comment.

Bedwyr, sitting beside Arthur, asked eagerly, 'Are you the Ecdicius who after that disastrous harvest a few years past, fed all your estate tenants from your own granaries through the entire winter?'

Ecdicius nodded assent. 'Not just my tenants, the folk of the settlements and their families also. About four thousand in all.' His beam of pride was extravagant. Incredulous, Bedwyr encouraged him to tell more.

'I sent horses and carts to bring all those poor people onto my estate. I saved them from starving.' Ecdicius flapped one hand dismissively. 'It was no large thing, a simple matter of helping one's neighbour.'

Sidonius snorted. 'Damn fool nigh on beggared himself! Used all his grain surplus and a good deal of gold to buy in more to feed classless peasant farmers and their whores and brats! Let them find their own way or go without I say. There's always someone else to take over an empty farm.'

Ecdicius kept his smile, but his retort was barbed, for all his outward pleasantness. 'Aye, there is many a Goth who would like to get his hands on good farm land.' He had been baited with this same line of contempt for his generosity many times. 'Is it not a lord's duty to care for those less well off in the time of need? By following my duty, I am assured of loyalty from my tenants and servants.' There was mischief in his eyes as he added, looking direct at Sidonius, 'I do not constantly need to watch the shadows growing larger behind my back.'

Sensing something more than family disagreement over the treatment of servants and tenant farmers, Arthur searched for plausible reasons. Why would a man need such a large, loyal following? He tried a blind stab at one. 'Have you, then, an ambition to become Emperor like your father Avitus?'

Ecdicius laughed, head back, large hands slapping his thighs. He had a bold, full-of-humour bellow. 'What? And have a dagger plunged into my back a few months later? No thank you my lord Riothamus! My father was foolish enough to want to wear the purple, he held that dubious pleasure for less than a year.' He sat at ease, spread his arms along the back of the couch. 'I am content with what I have. A wealthy estate, a loving wife and an articulate brother-by-law who is soon to become Bishop of Augustonemetum'

This was news to Arthur.

Sidonius shrugged his hands modestly, though the flicker of annoyance and bitterness was not lost to the Pendragon's keen, watching eye. 'It is an honour that has been offered to me.' The modesty was false. 'I have humbly decided to accept the position.'

Polite, hiding his amusement – and satisfaction – Arthur offered congratulations, while rapidly digesting the information. So, Sidonius was thought to have been involved with that treasonous letter sent by Arvandus to Euric of the Goths! Because of it, he had fallen from his high place of favour in Rome. That Arthur knew already, though the reason had not been made clear. Nothing had been openly said or declared, there was probably no evidence to support the suspicions. But this sealed the lid to the coffin, did it not? To be forced into accepting a bishopric! Hah! Happen there was justice in this world after all.

'I hear,' Arthur decided to stir a few muddied puddles, 'that Arvandus was saved from execution by a sentence of exile instead. The man was your friend, Sidonius, was he not?'

Quickly, too quickly, too hotly, Sidonius denied it. 'He was a colleague, nothing more. The man was foolish in not understanding the intricacies of Roman law, that was all, was unfortunate enough to fall foul of others with more evil intent than ever he could dream of.'

'So, plotting with Euric to destroy us British and then to overthrow all traces of Roman rule in Gaul is not evil intent?' Bedwyr responded, not bothering to hide the disgust in his voice.

'That episode was all a misunderstanding, I assure you.' Sidonius had to say that, had to believe it, for he too had very nearly been lured into the plotting, had only escaped by reason of his own eloquence and wit. Arvandus had been his friend, they shared the same views, the same beliefs, knew that the only hope to rekindle prosperity and peace in Gaul was to let Euric become the legal, and only, lord. Sidonius had attempted – discreetly – to give defence for the arrested traitor – not expecting the idiot to trumpet his guilt all over Rome. Nothing had been proved to involve Sidonius, beyond a wrong-made friendship, but in consequence he had lost his exalted position as Prefect of Rome and his lands had been confiscated. Offered instead the binding chains of a bishopric! An offer only a fool would refuse.

A slave was refilling Arthur's goblet. He smiled at her, a pretty young thing. That reminded him of the girl he had bought. What in the Bull's name was he do with her? He grinned to himself. Happen he could think of some use. He sat back, relaxed, all the anger and frustrations of these long, slow passing weeks suddenly evaporating.

What do you do with a dignatory against whom you cannot prove corruption and treason? You bind his hands and silence his tongue, you bury him alive. You make him a bishop.

Raising his goblet, Arthur saluted his host. 'A good choice of career, my friend, I am sure you will make an admirable bishop.'

Ecdicius echoed Arthur's toast. 'Oh he will, my lord, my brother-by-law has a taste for telling others what to do, as long as it causes no discomfort for himself.'

Sidonius scowled, deeply regretting allowing his brother-by-law to accompany him here to Juliomagus, and bitterly regretting the suggestion of this meeting. It would be an idea to get to the business side and be gone. He cleared his throat.

'I have been asked to suggest that you move your men on, my lord Arthur. You would be more effective as a deterrent near Avaricum.'

'Effective? With the few men I have? My men, Sidonius, my Artoriani! Where are the men I was promised by your Emperor? Men we British were supposed to be joined with in this fight against Euric and his Goths? Where are the horses I need? When will Syagrius be joining us? He was supposed to have brought several thousand infantry to me last summer!' Arthur's anger was rising. Too many damned questions and never a satisfactory answer! 'I have been here a year around waiting to see this business done with, yet have done nothing but scratch for lice and fleas!'

Sidonius retained a pleasant smile. He had been warned of this British King's foul temper. Euric a barbarian? Huh! It was in Sidonius's experience that the Goths were generous, mild mannered and welcoming. Not Euric personally, but his brother certainly had been. He had much liked that brother, a firm, large man, given to much laughter and a pleasant outlook on life. He had treated Sidonius like a visiting king. A pity that Euric was so different, had murdered him; but it was Riothamus, Sidonius was thinking, who needed to be made an end of.

A ridiculous notion to bring him here in the first place. Nothing could hold back Euric from obtaining his ambition, nothing and no one. Rome realized that, these months on, there would not be the funding or the will to hold back the encroaching tide of inevitability. Syagrius, King of Soissons, knew it too. The funding had dried up; there was little left in Rome's vaults, little save dust and empty coffers. Not even enough to send the British home.

Sidonius held his fixed, amiable expression. Arthur must never learn of that. Must not learn that bringing him here had been an appalling mistake. God's truth, the anger that would be unleashed, the uproar . . . the cost of compensation! No, Arthur must be assured that reinforcements were on their way, that later in the summer the ships would be waiting to take him and his men home again. In the meanwhile, Arthur must be made to leave Juliomagus. The presence of his rabble of men could no longer be tolerated.

And with Fortuna's blessing, the problem would soon be solved. Euric would have a hand in that, when eventually he decided to make his move. Either the British would be wholly slaughtered, or at the least, there would be fewer of them to need bother with.

§ XV

Mathild stretched languidly, relishing the feel of a comfortable mattress beneath her body; the absence of fleas and bedbugs and the warmth of fine-woven, soft blankets. She lay, arms and legs limp, relaxed, her eyes closed, for fear this might all be a dream. If she opened them, she would find herself back in that bug-hopping, faeces-stinking slave pen. Then the man beside her moved, turning in his sleep, and she realized she was awake, this was real, she *had* passed the night in the King of Britain's bed. She had pleased him, she knew – was this day not *Frigedæg*, the Lady's own day? A self-satisfied smile crept over her face. Frig, wife to Woden, the Lady who blessed the union of man and woman, who was most surely giving blessing to her daughter this day.

'That expression on your face can only be described as smug.'

With a snap, Mathild opened her eyes. Arthur was awake, watching her. She blushed, feared that he had read her erotic thoughts.

Happen he had, for his hand brushed over her breasts, her body responding eagerly. Arthur chuckled. 'You are no stranger to a man's touch, my Saex whore. Who taught you the art of pleasuring?'

About to say 'my husband', Mathild choked back the truth. He was dead. Slaughtered with the others, men, women and children, by the Gauls when they came to destroy the English who had lived peaceably, for many years, on their island settlements along the Liger. And then they wondered why Odovacer had called the men together! Wondered why they had marched to take their revenge at that wicked day of burning, killing, and slave-taking! No, she would not talk of the husband she had loved. Instead, she answered in her own tongue of the English, 'I am a noble-born, a daughter of the goddess Frig. Her gentle hand guides my *Wyrding*.'

To her great surprise, Arthur understood. 'So, your fate is decreed by the Lady.' His hand was stroking lower, more intimate. 'Not so, my expensive whore. From now, I command your future.' He spoke also in English, was amused at her wonderment. Returning to Latin, he explained, 'I find it most useful to understand what my enemies have to say about me.' He laughed. 'Or what my whore may whisper in my ear.'

She was as eager as he for the sharing of pleasure. Her husband she had missed with great sorrowing. To be used as nothing more than a receptacle for need by the men who had taken her as slave had been hard to endure these past two years. Mathild had pride for herself and her people, had accepted what fate, the *Wyrding*, that her goddess, the Lady, had sent. But oh! How much more pleasant, how much more worthwhile, to become the bed-mate of the British King, Arthur Riothamus, the Pendragon! She would make an effort to please him, would serve him well. Her task all the easier, from the intimate delight that she was receiving from him.

Later, she announced into the night-dark tent, 'I have many whispers that I can tell to you.'

Arthur lay still. His heartbeat, after the exertion of love-making, was easing. He was tired, wanted to sleep. Outside, beyond the leather walls of his command tent, he heard the voices of the night watch changing. Day would be here soon, not much chance for more sleep. 'And what whispers would they be?' He asked through a casual yawn.

'That Syagrius of the Romano-Gauls, and his allied Franks, have no intention of coming to join you. That Rome will continue to play games with you before Euric of the Goths chooses his own time to slaughter your British in a bathing of blood.' She paused, then added, her voice hard, the anger as bitter as sour fruit. 'That Cerdic, your son, has become Lord of the Elbe, and is gathering warriors to his hearth.'

Arthur attempted to sound disinterested, as if all this was old, long-known news. 'You hear many whispers, my Saex whore. From where do they come?'

Mathild smiled, the indifference did not fool her, for his body had stiffened, his breathing had quickened. Ah! Mathild knew many things! She was a woman of learning, could read and write both the Latin and Greek styles as well as her own English runic lettering. She knew too, how to read a person's thoughts from the movement of eye or muscle or limb. She had seen the splendours of Rome and the wonders of the dancing lights that shimmered in the sky up in the clear coldness of the North Way, for she had travelled those many miles as a child and young woman with her mother's brother, Leofric of the Elbe. How she had loved the thrill of his fast, splendid longships that sped like swans over the seas! She had even set foot in Arthur's land, once, had seen the crowds and bustle of the city of Londinium, as it had been then, when she was younger. It had gone now, she had heard, that town, fallen into disuse and disrepair, save for the few peasant-folk who had built their poorly made bothies among the crumbling houses and falling walls. She had seen Arthur there, when he had been serving as an officer under the then King of the British, Vortigern. She had been a child, but had seen and recognized the gleam of ambition in that young Pendragon's eyes. She had seen Winifred, his wife, also. Seen and disliked her. As she now disliked her arrogant, power-grasping son, Cerdic.

And so, in answer to his question she said, 'I hear many things on the wind. A slave is considered to be mute and deaf, with no sense between the ears.' She shrugged. 'It is a pose worth adopting.' Then she paused, followed in a rush, 'I have never met Cerdic, yet I dislike him. He has that which should not be his! My uncle was tricked into leaving his land to Winifred's brat, he was murdered for his wealth and title. Leofric was a respected man. What was his should, by all rights of inheritance be mine.' Mathild lay rigid. It was not for a whore, a slave, to speak so forthright, so bitterly. She had no rights to anything, not freedom of thought or life, no right to go where she pleased, to own any possession, not even the clothes she wore. She had a slave ring around her neck; belonged to the man who had paid a garnet ring for her.

But no man could take her mind, her past; no matter how ill she was used or beaten or starved. Both her mother and father were children of noble-born men. Her own husband had been a thegn, one of Odovacer's bodyguard. And no man, not even the Supreme King of Britain, Arthur the Pendragon, could take away her determination to one day, one day, reclaim all that was rightfully hers.

In the darkness she did not see the slow, calculating smile that accompanied the fast-forming thoughts that were rapidly scheming in Arthur's mind. He had intended to make use of her only this one night – for all the love he had for Gwenhwyfar, aye and all the assurances he had given her, he was a man who needed the comforts of intimacies. A few short months away from his wife he could endure, but within the turn of a few weeks it would be nearly the year around since he had left Britain – and the pleasures he gave and received with Gwenhwyfar were becoming desperate to be sated.

Mathild would serve a passing purpose in that area, for she was pleasing enough – but for certain, Fate, Wyrd or the Roman Fortuna, some benevolent goddess by whatever guise she wore, had surely set this woman Mathild on his path.

When this thing was sorted, here in Gaul, when Rome finally shifted its arse and decided either to let him and his Artoriani fight or find suitable shipping home, he might just undertake another voyage after seeing to matters in Britain. Take a few of his men, two, three turmae ought be sufficient, and escort Mathild back to her dead uncle's land along the Elbe river, aid her in claiming her inheritance.

Arthur wriggled deeper beneath the bed covering, brought Mathild closer for her voluptuous warmth. He would need write to Gwenhwyfar soon. Ought he tell her of the whore he had bought for the price of a garnet ring? She would be angry at that. Rather he would word it, I have purchased a lawful way of removing Cerdic. That would please her, and happen, would set her understanding better over this need for another woman while he was so long away.

March 469

§ XVI

'Hit it man!' Bedwyr bellowed, 'It's a bloody sword you're using, not a pitch fork!' Exasperated, he turned, swivelling at the waist, to face Arthur who stood a yard or two behind. He spread his arms. 'Jesu's love, cousin, these mud-wallowers are hopeless!'

Thrusting his fingers through his leather baldric strap, the Pendragon, masking his own frustration, merely shook his head. 'They are all we have, Bedwyr, we must make fighting men out of them.' Added ruefully, and slightly under his breath, 'Somehow'.

Another rider made a pathetic attempt to cut at the straw-filled man with his sword. He pushed his horse into a canter, going too fast too soon. The horse, realizing the uselessness of the man on its back, stopped abruptly to crop grass three feet before the target. The rider, leaning forward, urging the horse on with frantic kicking legs and flapping arms, tumbled in a haphazard heap over the horse's shoulder.

'Oh Christ's patience!' Bedwyr roared, striding forward to pick him up by the neckband of his tunic. Shaking the poor man as if he were a rat, Bedwyr scolded with his tongue. 'Call yourselves riders? Horsemen? God's blood, you're nothing but a bunch of plough-pushers!'

The faces of the ninety or so trainees fell longer, more disillusioned. They had come to join the Artoriani, filled with the hopes and dreams of glory – fight with Arthur, make a name for yourself! Half of this group were from Juliomagus itself, others from Caesarodunum or Condivicnum, coming from the towns, settlements or farm-steadings, drawn to Arthur's cavalry like ants to spilt honey. All young men who were sick of Rome's apathetic attitude towards the threat of the Goths. Arthur had accepted them, enrolling them as Cymry – only the best, the élite, became Artoriani, but Cymry, comrade, brother, was enough. To fight under Arthur's Dragon Banner was enough.

Bedwyr took a long, slow, deep breath. He and Arthur's officers had to make soldiers out of these lumps. If Syagrius were to come, as promised, there would be no need to recruit these imbeciles, no need to count on the inane. But it seemed Syagrius was delayed, yet again, would not be coming now until next month.

Arthur, last night, talking with his officers, had raised again the issue

52

of going home, but even for that they had to rely on Syagrius, for it was he who had provided the ships, the horse-transporters, the seamen to bring them here.

'What these men need,' Arthur said, with that familiar thoughtful expression of one eye half-closed, the other eyebrow raised, 'is some incentive.' He stood a moment, considering; the next, he was running, pushing through the line of men. The horse that the rider had fallen from, a fine bay, though its head was common, was still eating grass. Arthur vaulted into the saddle from a run, taking up the reins as he landed, and urging the animal into a gallop all in one movement. Startled, the horse tossed its head, snorted and leapt forward. Arthur galloped it across the training field, wheeled at the far end and, without slowing, galloped back. The bay was going fast, eager, excited – and then Arthur performed several of the movements that were everyday exercises to the Artoriani: dismount at the gallop run a few paces, vault across the horse's back to land on the far side, vault again; turn around in the saddle through a full 360 degrees. He had crossed the field, was swinging the animal to come again . . . Bedwyr ran forward, laid a javelin on the grass . . . Arthur saw, rode to take the thing up. Would he miss, so fast he was going? He leant down from the saddle, plucked the shaft up, rode on, the horse not breaking pace once, the javelin held high above the rider's head. Arthur halted, bringing the horse to a stand in one flowing movement. And then he circled, turning the horse this way and that, round and around, and as he manoeuvred, he threw the javelin, tossing it high, up above his head, catching it with each change of direction . . . and was off again, galloping straight at the straw-man target – and was past, the javelin quivering as it thudded neatly into where the heart would be.

At the far end, Arthur slowed, eased the horse to walk, caressed its neck, praising and patting, walked on a relaxed, loose rein back to the group of impressed men.

'That,' he said simply, 'is what it is to be Artoriani.' He dismounted, gave the reins of the sweating animal to its deposited rider and, with a final slap to its rump, Arthur sauntered away, as if the display of horsemanship was an everyday occurrence.

At the edge of the field, near to where the ordered lines of tents began, a man waited, his arm looped through the reins of his horse. As Arthur approached, he began to applaud, genuinely impressed.

'That was a fine display, my lord! Do all your men ride as competently?'

Acknowledging the praise, Arthur answered truthfully, 'Many are more proficient than I. That was nothing compared to some.' He held his hand forward for the man to clasp in greeting. 'What brings you to my camp, Ecdicius?' Indicated the way to his command tent. 'May I offer you wine?'

Agreeing with enthusiasm, Ecdicius fell into step beside the Pendragon, who motioned for a cavalryman to take his guest's horse.

'I come for one reason only, Lord Riothamus.' Ecdicius paused, seeking how to put his thoughts, though he had rehearsed his speech over and over. He stopped abruptly, stepped in front of the Pendragon, his expression earnest, entreating. 'Take me as one of your Artoriani, teach me to fight as your men fight.' His features crumpled into a crease of desperation. 'You will not be staying in Gaul, you have your own land, your own kingdom to defend – someone must have at least a partial awareness of how to keep these barbarians at bay. I want to learn, want to know how my beloved country can survive when you are gone!'

Arthur placed his hand on the man's shoulders, steered him forward into his tent. Ecdicius was ten years Arthur's senior at least. He was well meaning, his compassion and sincerity whole-hearted, but to learn all Arthur knew in a matter of weeks? Ecdicius interpreted Arthur's frown as a negative reply, for his fists bunched, his face contorted. 'Teach me anything, even the rudiments of a cavalry charge, show me the basic needs. Give me something so I can drill the men who would fight behind me, as men fight behind you, as a cavalry team, as comrades, as one brotherhood.' Eager again, determined, 'I can do it, I will. I mean to form myself an efficient cavalry.'

'Your wine.' They were inside the tent, Arthur's personal quarters, cluttered as usual with papers, wooden writing-tablets, strewn clothing. The bed, a portable leather-strung cot, was rumpled in one corner, unmade. Women's undergarments were clustered with the blankets.

Arthur seated himself on one of the two stools, indicated to his guest to seat himself also. 'How many men have you?'

Eager Ecdicius responded with, 'Twenty. They have their own mounts, good quality stock, some with the Desert breeding in them, as do yours.' He sat, leaning forward, the wine goblet, untasted, clasped tight between his hands.

'The horses I have brought are not my best. I would not bring the cream of my stock across the seas.' Remembering his trained war stallions and the breeding herds, Arthur fell silent. How many of the mares had foaled well this year? They needed good colts, sure-footed but fast, courageous but easy-tempered. The foundation stock had come from Gwenhwyfar's father, Cunedda – his stallions from his father and grandfather. Fine, proud horses that were, so legend said, bred from the wind by the gods; horses that could do well on poor feed if necessary; horses that could carry a man all night and fight with courage and stamina the day after. They came from the desert lands, those original horses, given as gifts by the Romans to Cunedda's family. The horses now, Arthur's horses, were sturdier, broader, with shorter, thicker legs; but they retained the intelligence, deep chest, bold eye and distinctive concave face. The desert breed, adapted through cross-breeding with the smaller native-bred ponies for the changeable climate and rougher terrain of Britain.

He ought to be at home, helping train the two- and three-year-old colts, helping put the mares to this year's selected stallions. Gwenhwyfar was overseeing all that, she was capable, more so than he, but he liked to be with the horses . . . Gwenhwyfar, he ought to be with Gwenhwyfar.

Ecdicius was prattling something about these men he had, his ideas for a training programme; Arthur only half heard, he was looking at Mathild's garments strewn over the bed.

'What will you do about a woman?' Gwenhwyfar had asked.

'It's a part of soldiering to take a whore occasionally,' he had answered, truthfully, adding, 'but we will be gone only the few months, I expect I can make do with the memory of you.' A few months? Hah!

He had written to Gwenhwyfar yesterday, telling her that the army would soon be moving on again, that only the gods and Rome had the knowing of when they could turn around and march for home. Had said nothing of Mathild. Happen he ought have done. Ought have told his wife that it was she he loved, not a slave-woman acquired merely for the comfort of his needs. It was Gwenhwyfar he wanted with him, his Cymraes, not for all her pretty smile, intelligent conversation, and aye, soft skin, not Mathild.

His thoughts were broken by Ecdicius repeating a question.

'Do you read Vegetius? A wonderful man, wonderful strategy.'

'Oh, er, aye,' Arthur rallied his mind back to the present, 'Vegetius is useful. Arrian's *Tactica* if you can get a copy is informative, or there is Xenophon of course.'

Ecdicius was delighted with the advice. 'My brother-by-law has a vast library, he must have copies. He is to soon publish a collection of his poems, I shall arrange for you to be sent a copy.' He thumped the palms of his hands on his thighs with a resounding slap, announced, 'But I must be on my way! It is agreed then, my men shall join with you as a separate turma. Aquilla Turma, I think, our standard shall be the Eagle, after the honour of Rome!'

Arthur stood as his guest came to his feet with that last declaration. What? How did . . . he remembered making no such agreement for Mithras' sake!

'Until the morrow, then.' And Ecdicius saluted and ducked from the tent. Arthur stood, dumbfounded, then laughed. If a civilian landlord could outmanoeuvre the Pendragon so smartly, then aye, happen he did have the makings of a reasonably good cavalry officer!

§ XVII

'No! My answer is no!' Aesc, lord of the Kent Saxons, angrily banged the flat of his palm down onto the table, causing the pewter tankards and plates to bounce. A chicken leg, balanced on a heaped bowl of cooked fowl, wavered and tumbled, rolled to the floor where a hound, snarling at his companions, greedily snapped it up. Several men seated at lower tables ranked along the Mead Hall glanced up at their leader's bull-roar, saw Aesc was only reprimanding Vitolinus, returned unconcerned to their food and drink. Vitolinus was always in one sort of trouble or another; he seemed to have a gift for rubbing people up the wrong way.

'But why?' Vitolinus protested vehemently. 'I could take thirty or forty men this very night and . . .'

Aesc thrust himself with such force from the table that his chair toppled backwards with a crash that boomed and echoed through the length and height of the building. His hand snatched out to catch hold of his nephew's neckband, dragging the young man also to his feet. Aesc shook him, bellowing, 'I said no! I have agreed peace with the Pendragon. If I ever decide to break that peace I will do the cattle-raiding or the settlement-burning.' He shook Vitolinus again, 'I would lead my warriors. I, Aesc of the Kent Jutes, not a mere whelp who still drinks milk and has a handful of straw-piddling pups as hearth-mates!' He tossed the lad aside, sending him skidding across the timbers of the floor on his backside. Several men laughed, Vitolinus was not much liked, tolerated only because he was Aesc's kindred, the son of their lord's dead and buried sister.

Righting his chair, and with a contemptuous snort, Aesc reseated himself, stretched forward for a third helping of roasted fowl.

Vitolinus clambered to his feet. His arm was bruised, his pride hurting worse. His expression was always that of a scowl, enhanced by the scar that ran from ear to chin down the side of his long, thin face. Behind Aesc's back, his hand formed an obscene gesture; he turned and stalked, furious, from the Hall. Many a man breathed a sigh of relief at his going. Where Vitolinus sat, there would always be a storm blowing. Few of the older men in that Hall would grieve at a permanent ending to Vitolinus.

Aelfred was younger, and like many of those of his age group, admired

Vitolinus. He slipped from his own place at table and joined his friend, catching up with him a few yards from the Hall door. The sky was almost dark, a few stars stealing from behind wispy cloud cover. No moon this night. Vitolinus acknowledged his companion with a grunt, indicated he was heading for the kennels. His favourite bitch had whelped, he would need to check the pups before seeking his bed.

They stood a while, watching the proud mother suckle her litter of eight. Aelfred pointed out a large, fat pup. 'That one'll be a fine dog when he grows! See how he shoves the others aside to get at her teats!'

'Ja, a hound who knows his own mind.' Vitolinus made no effort to hide the anger that burnt inside him. 'As do I.'

Aelfred was silent a moment, leant his weight on his arms, straddling the closed gate of the hound pen, said, 'So you want to lead a raiding party against the British?'

Vitolinus only grunted as a reply.

Vaguely, Aelfred observed, 'Aesc is our lord, he must know what is best.'

'It is in my mind that old men prefer the warmth of a hearth fire to the cold of battle.'

Aelfred was not shocked by Vitolinus's rebellious words. Aesc's nephew was known for his provocative opinions. And aside, he agreed.

'It is also in my mind,' Vitolinus continued, knowing his companion's thoughts well enough, 'that those same old men need reminding occasionally of who we are, where we come from. Are we the Pendragon's slaves? Or are we warriors, proud men who take what we want, when we want?'

The air moved as the outer door opened, another young man entered, joined them at the hound pen.

'Thought I would find you in here,' Cuthbert grinned. 'A fine litter – I would like one of the bitches when they are weaned.'

'You've nothing to barter for such a hound!' Aelfred teased, 'Vitolinus has enough blunt spears and worn, holed cloaks already!'

Playfully, Cuthbert batted at his friend's shoulder, laughed, 'Mayhap not, but he needs sharpened spears and willing hearts to form the basis of an army!' He spoke to Aelfred, looked at Vitolinus.

Aesc's nephew, resting his elbow on the gate, nestled his chin on his cupped hand, pointing with the other, offered, 'You can have that black and tan, she's small but seems game enough.' He straightened, threaded his fingers through the baldric slung diagonally across his chest. 'I need no payment, only an oath of loyalty.'

There was no hesitant thought, no decision-making, Cuthbert was instantly on his knees before his young lord. 'Need you offer reward for such a thing?' he asked, 'You have my loyalty without condition.'

Aelfred too, knelt, 'And mine.' His features were earnest, sincere. 'And many another, were you to ask!'

Touching their heads with his fingertips, Vitolinus nodded grimly. He was heartsick of this unquestioned obedience to the Pendragon, heartsick of being treated as a child, a useless nothing. He was ten and six, old enough to lead men, the son of Vortigern, grandson of Hengest, old enough to try for a kingdom of his own. His father's kingdom; the kingdom Arthur had stolen.

As if reading his thoughts, Cuthbert stated, 'If Aesc will not help you gain what, by birthright, is yours, then there are plenty of us who will. We are warrior-born, the sons of warriors, we wish to use the spear and sword, not the plough and pitchfork.'

Vitolinus smiled, a scheming, unkind smile that sat well on his weasel-like face. He knew those sentiments ran in the blood of the young men, knew and fostered them! He would be King of Britain! To take everything from Arthur and with the same sword-thrust, keep the prize from the greed of his sister Winifred! That was his double ambition. And ambition had to be tickled at the right moments. If Arthur's hold was to be defeated, it had to be done now. Now, while he was over the sea, while the God-mumbling Ambrosius Aurelianus was fumbling his way around in the dark.

His smile widened, the glint in his blue eyes triumphant, gloating. 'Then I see no reason to plod behind dull-minded oxen any longer!' He raised his companions to their feet, cuffing each of them affectionately around the ears. 'Pass word to all who would give me their pledge. I will be going from here at the rising of the new moon, five days hence, to prepare to take my kingdom. I will wait at Cille Ham, while the moon swells three nights for any who wish to join me.'

Stroking the shadowed beard-growth around his chin, Aelfred considered Vitolinus's proposal. 'It will not be easy to send out word without the older folk knowing but it can be done.'

Cuthbert asked, hesitant, for he had no wish to offend, 'Cille is old, is he trustworthy? 'Tis the older men who side with Aesc's decisions.'

Vitolinus sauntered across to the door, patting his friend's shoulder in a fatherly manner as he passed. 'Cille, in most circumstances, I would not trust even if my life depended on it! But, he fought when he was our age with the great Hengest against Arthur, at that time when the British took final victory. I know for certain that he has an old itch that he yearns to scratch.' He had reached the door, had it open. 'He will support us.'

April 469

§ XVIII

Never before had Cadwy defied his father. Never before had he found the courage to do so. But this? This was unacceptable, horrible.

He stood before Ambrosius, uncomfortable from the press of the crutch beneath his armpit, despite the leather and straw padding along the crossbar. Stood as straight as his deformity allowed. 'No,' he declared, raising his chin with as much pride as he could muster. 'No, I will not offer myself to God, I will not take holy orders.'

Ambrosius was clearly shocked, for he seated himself, took an over-large gulp of wine. No? No! What was this from his son, what was this defiance? Calm, swallowing anger, Ambrosius said, 'There is nothing else suited for you. A bishopric would sit well. The duties are demanding I grant, but mentally, not,' – he paused, licked his lips, tried so hard not to look at his son's deformed leg – 'not physically.'

Wanting to sit down himself, to take the weight from the pain that ushered from his hip to knee, Cadwy forced himself not to look for a stool. His father was a good man, had a weight of problems as heavy as the drag of his own lame leg, had only the best of intentions at heart, but always, always, where Cadwy was concerned, the wrong intentions. He did not understand, could not see beyond this wooden crutch and dragging leg that Cadwy was in all other respects a normal man with the desires and ambitions of any young male of ten and nine years.

Slowly, measuring his words, Cadwy tried to explain, tried to show his view of this thing without hurting or wounding his father's pride. 'It is an honour to be recommended as taking the new-vacant position of Bishop of Aquae Sulis, father, and I thank you for your concern in putting my name forward, but' – his eyes sought his father's, failed to locate, hold them, instead, he took a clumsy step forward – 'but I cannot give myself to a life as a priest. I want a wife, children.' His expression was pleading, begging, 'A grandson for you.'

The hurt came deeper, more wounding, when his father bitterly laughed, stood, and turned away from him.

Fighting tears, tears that would not become a lad of his age, Cadwy said, through a choking throat, 'As a priest, even as an exalted bishop, I could never find a way to prove to you, father, that despite my lameness, I am, inside, as much a man as any other.'

He half-held his hand, pleading. Ambrosius did not turn back. Cadwy made for the door, his crutch loud-tapping on the flagstone floor, his left boot dragging. As he reached the door, Ambrosius spoke, his voice taught, rasping, emotion raw. 'Along but one path could I have found pride in you, along a path to God. Reject that route and you reject me.'

No choices, no regrets.

'Allow me to live my life as I choose, father, or equally, reject me.'

There came no answer, no movement, only a solid-turned back. Cadwy opened the door, shuffled through, closed it silently behind, not seeing his father's disappointed misery.

Ambrosius sank to his knees, clasped his hands in prayer. Why, he questioned, why does naught come easy for me? I try, I give my heart and soul into doing what I believe is right, yet each time, along every path, around every corner, I meet failure. Bitterly, he moaned, bowed his head. Why could he not be strong, successful, obeyed and respected like his elder brother Uthr had been? Why could he not achieve, as the son, his nephew Arthur, seemed always to achieve?

Why, for Emrys, as his British given name had been, did everything always take a wrong turn?

§ XIX

It was raining when Cadwy rode up the steep, cobbled lane into Caer Cadan. His twisted leg was aching horribly, his teeth were clenched to ignore the torturing stabs that seemed to lance his entire body.

The past days had dragged through the sullen anger of an interminable week of glowering half-politenesses and barely veiled displeasure. The decision to come here to Caer Cadan had formed yestereve, an hour or so after the messenger had ridden in. Gwenhwyfar was taken seriously ill, he had told Ambrosius, was dying. I will go, Cadwy had offered, see how she fares. His father had responded with a sharp, instant forbidding of no, and there had come another bitter quarrel.

Was he to be kept prisoner then? Cadwy had demanded, shuttered away, snared, because he would not do as his father bid? In anger, Cadwy had saddled his horse and left his father's household with no word of farewell. He would see the queen for himself, could not believe that her life was so desperately near its end. Gwenhwyfar and Arthur had always shown him kindness and respect, had never patronized or shown pity. He would go to her, if for nothing else, to show his respect for the sadness of death.

The gatekeeper acknowledged him with a nod of recognition, directed him to the King's Hall where Lord Geraint would be, and in answer to his question said, with a slow shake of his head, 'My lady be no better, my lord. The medics say there's nothing more to be done for her, save pray.' And that they had all been doing these past three days without the need of asking.

With his good leg, Cadwy kicked his mount forward, a fresh burst of pain jolting from the movement. It was a dismal day, for all the fresh growth of a new spring and this great Caer echoed the flat, dull, greyness. The place seemed empty, where was the familiar bustle and pride? The air of power and authority? Those few people about their daily tasks passed barely a nod at him as he rode; no one smiled, there was no idle chatter, no laughter or merriment. The women were mostly inside their dwelling places; the men, those that had not ridden with Arthur to Gaul, must, Cadwy concluded as he approached the Hall, be away drilling or training or something.

There were few children about – one or two only, hurrying on whatever errand they had been sent. Even the geese and chickens were quiet. This great place was hushed, its breath held, shuttered. Waiting. A darkness stalked beside the cobbled track. Lurked, unwelcome, uninvited, beside every building, behind every fence; in every corner, every hollow. The darkness of death waiting to claim Arthur's Queen.

He dismounted, stiffly, grateful to a young lad who ran from the Hall to take his horse; as grateful to enter through the doorway into the dry. He had expected more people to be in here, the people of the Caer, a settlement in itself. There were always men in a Hall, mending leather, fashioning a hunting spear, putting an edge to a blade ... the women would be cooking, sewing or weaving, but this place, the spacious interior of this vast King's Hall was all but empty, apart from a few small groups huddled in the shadows to each side. They were looking up at him, their faces ashen, sleep-lacking and lost. It was like a tomb, this Hall that ought to have been vibrant with life. A dank, inhospitable tomb.

Someone was coming from the far end, his hand stretched out in welcome. Cadwy limped forward to meet him, grateful to be greeted by someone he knew – Geraint of Durnovaria. He walked quicker, the drag of his leg more pronounced, took Geraint's hand firm in his own. Asked straight away, 'How is she?' Nothing seeming so important as this asking. Nothing more urgent to know.

A sudden, grasping thought hit him with the strength of an axe blade. Had this been the reason for his father's forbidding him to come here?

61

The cause behind the enmity that had been steadily growing between them? Had Ambrosius realised that which Cadwy had, until this moment, not? That the son would rather sit at the Pendragon's hearth, than at his own father's. Cadwy thrust the uneasy thoughts aside. He would need to examine them later, in his own time, when there were less important things to ask ... He gasped at his own dawning truth. Important? Aye, Arthur's Queen was more important to him than was Ambrosius.

Geraint too, had the dark rings of sleepless nights under his eyes; he too had that same pale skin, taut, drawn cheeks, as others of this grieving place. The dreadful hush, the sense of foreboding and waiting, pressing in from the timber walls, down from the height of the vaulted, dust and cobweb-strewn rafters. Even the spirit faces carved along their length sat quiet, anxious.

Geraint himself helped remove Cadwy's cloak, escorted him nearer the central hearth fire, a blaze of brightness and warmth in this dismal place.

He had not initially answered, reluctantly blurted, 'She is dying, we think. The fever has raged for several days. Beyond prayer, there is nothing more we can do for her.' Geraint served two bowls of hot venison broth, indicated they should sit at a nearby trestle bench. Cadwy complied, spooned the steaming food, the warmth chasing the ache and chill from his body. Geraint swallowed only a few mouthfuls, did not taste the goodness of the meat. No one felt much like eating, no one felt much like doing anything while Gwenhwyfar lay in her bed so ill, courting death.

A door at the far end opened, a woman came through. Everyone in that Hall looked up at her, their eyes enquiring, several of the men and women half-rose to their feet. The woman motioned them to be seated, with a slight shake of her head. No change, nothing of any difference. She came, with quick, firm steps across the timbered flooring, her smile wide and welcoming. Cadwy recognized her as Enid, Geraint's wife, one-time nurse to Gwenhwyfar's sons.

Pushing himself to his feet, Cadwy mastered the urge to wince as his leg violently protested. Wearily, Enid waved him down, sat herself, taking a place next to her husband on the bench. 'Her breathing comes a little easier,' she said, as she took the bowl of uneaten broth from her husband, ate a few spoonfuls. With a slight shrug to her shoulder added, 'But it may only be my fancy that it seems so.'

Cadwy thought she was going to weep, but they did not come, the tears, for Enid was a strong woman, and the time for tears was not, yet, here.

'My father knows of a doctor who resides in Venta Bulgarium,' Cadwy offered. 'Happen he . . .'

Enid touched his hand, her smile soft and grateful, her eyes so very tired and saddened. 'There is nothing more that can be done.' She left her spoon in the bowl, sat with her chin in her cupped hands, weary. 'No one can do the fighting for her now.' And then she added, so very softly that Cadwy barely heard, 'Save Arthur.'

The young man came to his feet, the pain ignored. 'I could fetch him! A fast horse, the wind behind a good ship . . .' It was something he could do, some useful, welcome thing!

Geraint patted the air with his hands, gently bid the lad to be reseated. 'Na, na, 'tis well meant and we thank you. Do you think we have not already considered it? The journey would take weeks, we have no sure idea of where Arthur is. We have only a few more hours, at most a day or two.'

Reluctant, Cadwy sat.

In an attempt at consolation, Enid said, 'It is good of you to come. Your father would . . .'

Cadwy looked up sharply, his eyes flashing. 'Would not come.' He finished bluntly for her. 'My father has, for all his life, nursed a grudge of jealousy against his elder brother.' He shook his head, offered unexpectedly, 'It must come hard upon him to also live beneath Arthur's shadow.' He shrugged, was amazed to see, as he stretched his hand to pick up his goblet of wine, that his fingers shook. 'Even harder to accept that the Pendragon left him with the responsibility of Britain on his shoulders and that he has not the strength to keep it as Arthur left it.'

How often had Cadwy talked of one day learning to fight from a horse, one day joining the Artoriani, being with Arthur? Arthur, always Arthur. Never had he expressed a wish to fight alongside Ambrosius. He had assumed his father did not want him, was disappointed because he would not be able to fulfil those dreams of being a normal man. The truth hit him as hard as a hammer blow. Did Ambrosius resent his son, not because of the lameness, this twisted disability, but because he was jealous of Cadwy's regard for Arthur?

He groaned, swallowed the wine down. And this day he had compounded that jealousy by riding away. All he had wanted was for his father to be proud of him. It was too late now, he was here, he could not reweave the threads he had so wantonly unravelled.

'Can I see her?' he asked tentatively, expecting to be denied. For all the realization of his father's feelings, Gwenhwyfar meant much to Cadwy, for he had few friends, few people he could trust enough not to mock him behind his back, remark on his disability or sneer at him for being weak and unable. He wanted a wife, a child, but was enough of a realist to fear he would never have either. Most women seeking a husband respected only the strength of a man, not the awkwardness of a crutch and a stumbling gait.

Enid rose, her head nodding in agreement, led Cadwy along the length of the Hall, past the few dejected, sorrowing occupants whose eyes followed as they passed. While hands worked, minds were turned to that private chamber where Gwenhwyfar lay, covered by the shadow of the next life. All hearts tore and ached for her safe keeping in this.

Through that private door, Cadwy stopped, gasped, his hand covering his nose and mouth against the stench of sickness and clutching death that assaulted him, all thoughts of his father clean forgotten. Gwenhwyfar lay, small, withered, against the expanse of the bed, beads of sweat proud on paper-thin skin that stretched over gaunt cheeks; her eyes closed in deep, dark-ringed sockets, while her fingers plucked, restless, at the bed covers. The room was hot, airless; a fire burned in the hearth, the hiss of steam rising from a cauldron of boiling water.

Distressed, Cadwy shuffled across the room, plucked a stool from beside a table, sat by the bed. Was it any wonder Caer Cadan shouldered such heaviness of heart? He took up her hand, held it firm in his own, willing her to know he was here, willing her to live.

§ XX

Cadwy sat with Gwenhwyfar through the night, listening to the spatter of rain dribbling outside, hearing the hiss and crack of wood on the hearth-fire and her harsh, laboured breathing. He wiped the sweat from her face and hands with a damp linen cloth, dripped the potion that Enid had left, between her dry, cracked lips. Held her hand, holding her, keeping her, in this world.

The night seemed long, endless. His thoughts came crowding, insistent, whispering and fluttering in his mind. Fleeting thoughts that flickered from one subject to another like a leaping hearth-fire, dancing around and around in a never-tiring, engulfing circle. His lameness, unvoiced hopes and dreams; his disappointed father; the future. Arthur. Gwenhwyfar . . . His lameness . . . Around and around.

Even in his drifting sleep they came, those thoughts, entering disguised as dreams; dreams where he was trying to run to save Gwenhwyfar, to run and run but he was caught by cloying mud or the grip of an incoming tide, bound by tightening ropes, held by clutching hands. He could not run, could not save her. Dreams where his father stood, condemning, disappointed. Dreams where Gwenhwyfar's life was fading, ebbing into that final darkness.

He awoke with a jerk, startled, not having intended to have slept. It was that sleep-filled hour when it was not quite night, nor yet morning. Something had roused him, some noise. He looked at the fire. It had burnt low, but the dried dung and wood were still glowing red, friendly, there were no logs that could have fallen or cracked. The rain had stopped, only the occasional drip, drip, from outside. An owl called, mournful, somewhere not too near.

Something was different, something important. Something, some sound, was missing. That harsh, clutching-at-life sound. Almost as if he could not bear to look, he leant nearer Gwenhwyfar. Her hand felt cold in his, limp and lifeless. Breath held, fearful, anxious, he bent closer. Was this it? The end? And her eyes fluttered open! Vague, distant eyes, but eyes of tawny green flecked with sparks of gold; eyes that were blurred, and tired, but eyes that attempted a smile. Alive, breathing. Here. Alive!

'Arthur?' she murmured, her lips dry, barely moving.

Cadwy's insides twisted, lurched. *No! Not Arthur! Me, Cadwy! Cadwy!* 'I am here.'

Her fingers moved in his clutching hand. 'I have dreamed such frightening things.'

'They have all gone now.' Cadwy stroked the damp hair from her hot – hot but not feverish – forehead. 'Rest now. Sleep.'

'Have I been ill?' Her voice was a whisper, hoarse. Hard to hear clearly.

'Aye.' His was choking, full of relief and despair and rage. Relief that she was alive, despair that he might never experience the deep love shared by a man and a woman, and rage against Arthur. Arthur, her husband, who ought be here with his sick wife, not off fighting some barbarian foreign king in a barbarian foreign land.

A slight, very slight smile touched her lips, a barely perceptible squeeze to his hand. 'Stay with me,' she asked.

'I will stay.'

Her eyes closed, the lashes fluttering down. A light sigh floated from her lips, and her body relaxed. She slept. A peaceful, unfevered sleep.

Bowing his head, Cadwy prayed – to which god he knew not – to the one Christian god? To the pagan deities? He cared not which one among them listened to his murmured, relieved, words of thanks.

May 469

§ XXI

One of Winifred's greatest delights was the stirring of a still pond into muddied waters. The feasting had been a congenial affair, extravagant, but satisfying. The selection of shellfish in particular, an extravaganza of mussels, oysters, whelks, periwinkles and scallops. The tender roasted, stuffed hare also of exceptional, succulent taste. Winifred sat, relaxed, at ease with her guest; sipped her wine – best Greek, her last amphora. When – if – she would be able to import more of the same fine quality was anybody's guess. The Saxon Leofric had been a mistake as a husband, but he had been able to secure the best goods for her. Most of these were used to furnish this private apartment within the holy abbey of Venta Bulgarium; fine carved tables and chairs, intricate tapestries. Bronze candelabra, expensive Roman glass and the rare red Samian pottery. The best wine and food, served to the few honoured guests that Winifred received here.

'More wine, my lord Ambrosius?' The polite, smiling hostess. Concealing her relief when he declined. 'I hear,' she said, with that well-practised lightness of innocence, 'that your son is now residing at Caer Cadan with Lady Gwenhwyfar.'

Ambrosius's answer was a mere clearing of his throat, a lowering of his eyebrows. Winifred felt a warming glow of delight. They were true then, these rumours! All of them? Oh, she must know! She affected a little laugh. 'People are talking, my lord.' Again, a light-hearted chuckle. 'They say he sleeps within her private chamber.' *They say*, she thought, smugly, *that he sleeps* with *her!*

'And who, madam,' Ambrosius retorted, setting his half-empty goblet of wine down sharply on the table beside his couch, 'are "they"? Tongue-waggers? Inane peasants? Illicit traders? What do they know of circumstances?' His anger gave away his embarrassment, his hurt.

Displaying feigned righteousness, Winifred laid her hand flat across her breast. 'Tale-tellers indeed, my lord. Wicked people who would impart any lie to gain a bellyful of food and a night's comfort.' The sort of people she entertained at her steading a few miles from here. People who kept her well informed of news and tattle. Forcing aside the regret at using the last of the wine, she motioned for the slave to top up her guest's drink –

for she must loosen his tight-held tongue somehow. 'Nevertheless, my lord,' she said with a loud sigh, 'there is talk.'

And what talk! Whirling down the wind like a winter storm! Cadwy, the lame-leg, only child of Ambrosius Aurelianus, wooing and bedding the Pendragon's Queen! Did Arthur know of the rumours, she wondered? But was it true? Could a lame-hobble lay with a woman who, so rumour also said, had been held in death's arms not a month or so back? A second thought. Would Gwenhwyfar be unfaithful to her husband? Would she be so openly foolish? Winifred thought not, but then, Arthur had a whore in his bed over there in Gaul – a flaxen-haired slave-girl. Through her planted spies, Winifred knew of her. As, surely, must Gwenhwyfar.

She motioned for the slave to serve Ambrosius with honey and apple cakes. A Saxon recipe, but she doubted Ambrosius would bother himself with such minor culinary thought. Common knowledge, of course, that Ambrosius was disappointed in his son – how much more so, now that this scandal had occurred? As well known that the Governor of all Britain had never held a liking or approval of Gwenhwyfar. Feelings fostered and honed over the years by Winifred's subtle interference.

Biting into one of the cakes – a little sweet for his taste – Ambrosius nursed his varied annoyances. Annoyance that this meddling woman, whose nose always seemed to be poking into the business of other people, was prying into areas that were not her concern. Annoyance that his son was behaving in this way – combined with the older, deeper awkwardness over Cadwy's lameness. He had intended his son to be destined for high office within the church, a bishopric certainly, but now? What could there be for Cadwy with this outrageous scandal dangling over them? Could Cadwy ever raise his head in public again? Huh, if Arthur came home, would Cadwy be left with a head? It must be stopped, this whole, intolerable, wickedness, must be put to an end. But how? Already Ambrosius had written to his son demanding his return home. Short of sending his men to drag the lad away, there was little Ambrosius could do to enforce the order. In the meanwhile, he had to endure the knowing glances, the sidelong nudges. Outright comments. Dirt and dregs. The things that meddlers like Winifred thrived upon.

Curtly, he deflected the probing. 'These tales are lies, there is nothing save malicious gossip behind them. Aside, my son is a man grown, his life is his own.'

The smile left Winifred's face, replaced by an expression of crumpled sorrow. She said, with such sadness that Ambrosius's head came up, 'Sons. What aching heartbreak can be inflicted on us by our sons.'

A long silence. Embarrassed, Ambrosius thought that the normally

hard woman sitting opposite him was about to weep. He finished the too-
sweet cake, refused the offer of another. Searched for something
appropriate to say, alarmed at this unusual revelation into Winifred's
personal vulnerability. Noisily, he cleared his throat, electing to alter the
conversation. 'You invited me here, madam, I am sure, with intentions of
discussing matters other than the wilful disobedience of our respective
offspring.' Fervently he hoped so. Cerdic, Winifred's son, was not a lad he
was inclined to think over-much upon.

Her poise had returned, that fleeting glimpse of despair thrust aside.
She was shocked at herself for allowing that flicker of grief so openly to
manifest itself. See what the strain of Cerdic's foolishness was doing to
her! She folded her hands neatly in her lap, tilted her head, drew breath
to tackle the subject she had invited Ambrosius here to discuss.

Her guest relaxed. Ah, that was the Winifred he knew! There, against
the ice blue of her eyes was the familiar glower of hatred, the incessant
quest for meddling or vengeance, at both of which she excelled.

'My brother,' she demanded, 'What are you intending to do about
him?'

For a wicked moment, Ambrosius was tempted to laugh. He might
have guessed this was the reason behind such an appetizing dinner! The
half-saxon whelp Vitolinus. A whoreson irritation.

Tentatively he asked, 'What would you have me do, madam?'

Several vapid suggestions rummaged through her mind, but Winifred
kept the more unpleasant ones to herself, answered simply, 'Stop him.'

'Ah.' Ambrosius leant his arm against the padding of the couch arm.
His own furniture was impoverished, shabby, by the standard of items in
this luxurious room. 'That would not be prudent.'

'Prudent?' She spluttered contemptuously. 'In God's good name! My
brother is running rampage along the borders of the Cantii territory and
you judge putting an end to him would not be prudent!'

'Dealing with a hot-headed, cocksure boy is one matter. Fighting a full-
blown war another entirely.' Ambrosius attempted to phrase his answer
politely, but there was a hint of terseness in his reply. He was Governor
of Britain; the Lady Winifred, for all her bloated self-importance, was
not. He continued speaking, cutting off her retaliatory response.
'Vitolinus is but an itching sore, no more than a minor irritant.' He held
his hand up, palm outward, again silencing an interruption. 'Would you
have me start a war over a mere boy?' A war which he had every
intention of starting when he was ready. A war that he had no desire to
let Winifred know about. Yet.

'Vitolinus has burnt two or three peasants' farm-steadings, stolen a few
head of cattle, nothing more serious.' Ambrosius waved his hand,

dismissive. 'I have sent protest to your uncle, Aesc. He assures me that the boy shall be dealt with.'

Incredulous, Winifred gaped at him. 'Arthur,' she sniped, 'would have hoisted Vitolinus's head on a spear ere now, aye, and for less reason!'

'I,' Ambrosius retaliated coldly, 'am not Arthur.'

No, Ambrosius was not. They were opposite ends of the spear, these two men of one kindred. Arthur, a battle-hardened war-lord, a realist, willing to make peace and uneasy friendship with the English, understanding that the might of Rome would never raise to power again; a pagan. Ambrosius a man of God and learning, who believed passionately in the way things once were, and would, he was determined, be again.

Claiming a more mellow tone, Winifred asked, 'Is it that you do not have the men or finance to put an end to my brother's raiding?' Refrained from adding, *or is it that you do not have the balls?*

He must have read the unspoken thought though, for Ambrosius retorted abruptly. 'When I judge it the right time to fight, I assure you I will have all I need.'

Soon, within weeks, a few months at most, she would see the fruition of his words. When the harvests were safe in, when Aesc least expected a counter offensive, when Vitolinus overstepped the mark too far, gave Ambrosius the full excuse he needed to take the Cantii lands back into Rome's possession. He was not about to impart all that to Winifred however. Aesc was her uncle, and for all she wanted her brother dealt with, there was no certainty that those same malicious feelings stretched to the rest of her Saex kin.

An uneasy silence. A minute dragged by, two. Unexpected, Winifred announced, 'He should take a wife.'

Puzzled, uncertain of this sudden turn of conversation, Ambrosius frowned. Who? Who should? Vitolinus?

'Cadwy,' Winifred opined, fluttering her hand. 'Find him a wife. That will put an end to this nonsense with the Pendragon's whore.' Poor Gwenhwyfar, to lose her boy lover to a wife!

Ambrosius sat quite still. Was this woman totally mad?

'I am quite serious,' she stated, correctly interpreting that open-mouthed look of horror on her guest's face.

'My son, madam, is a cripple.'

Winifred curled her fingers around the stem of her fragile and expensive glass goblet, sat back into her wicker chair, her smile indulgent. Said as if explaining some obvious matter to a child. 'It is his leg that is crooked, not his cock.' She sipped the wine. 'There are women who would not decline such a husband if the right compensations were agreed.'

'Compensations,' Ambrosius spoke slowly. The abhorrent idea had never occurred to him. Added tentatively, curious, 'You know of such a woman?'

Winifred sat straight, the image of calm reassurance. 'Of course.' She looked Ambrosius square in the face, holding his eye. Announced, 'Myself.'

Spluttering through a mouthful of wine, Ambrosius half rose to his feet, incredulous. 'You? Wed my son? Indeed, you are mad!' If he realized how rude his words sounded, he made no notice of it. Emphatically, he shook his head, his mouth open, shocked, speechless. Horrified.

Similar thoughts occurred to Winifred. Whatever had made her say this thing? Her last marriage to Leofric had been a disastrous mistake, a mistake she had needed to rectify almost immediately. She did not want to repeat the experience . . . yet had this idea been entirely impulsive? Opportunities offered themselves at unexpected moments, and had to be grappled immediately, lest they escape usage. Ambrosius was not telling her all his thoughts, was hiding something. War with Aesc, a strong probability. He was also intent on taking Arthur's place – whether he returned from Gaul or not, that much was obvious. When he became King – assuming Aesc did not butcher the man ten minutes into the first fighting – someone would have to be appointed as his heir. Cadwy with his deformity could not, by law, or in all practicality, become King. And Winifred, despite the present estrangement with her son, was still determined to see Cerdic King of Britain; would follow any path to gain him that royal torque. Any path.

She indicated that Ambrosius ought reseat himself. 'I am somewhat older than your son, I grant you,' she pronounced candidly, set, now that she had spoken, with the preposterous idea. 'He is but nine and ten to my two and thirty, but there is no reason why I cannot still bear a child. A grandson,' she promised, 'could become all that your son might have been.'

Winifred drained her wine, a flutter of doubt drying her throat. What in the good God's name was possessing her? Cadwy, that limping crutch-hobbler as husband? She swallowed. Wife to the son of the Governor of Britain, another foot wedged firm in an opening door, that possessed her. The fault for not conceiving another child would, naturally, be laid to Cadwy. She relaxed. It would work, this union between herself and Ambrosius. It could – just – work.

She signalled for her glass to be refilled, lifted the goblet in a salute. 'As wife to your son, my lord Governor, I would bring you a generous dowry. Enough men and their payment, to bring down not only my brother, but my uncle Aesc also.' 'And' – her expression clearly signalled, although no word passed her lips – 'and Arthur.' Her smile was self-pleased, smug. She doubted Ambrosius would ever agree to such a suggestion, but the paleness of his skin, the way his tongue flicked over dry lips showed all she needed to know. He was tempted. She savoured the wine, the last goblet of fine Greek. A pity if he would not accept her. It would be so very pleasing to steal Gwenhwyfar's lover from her bed!

§ XXII

While Winifred dined with Ambrosius to encourage an ending of her brother, Vitolinus was watching as flames engulfed the house-place of a British farm-steading. The screams from inside had ceased, his men were sauntering away, the amusement over, were beginning the slaughter of the livestock. They would only take the meat that could be carried to their boat. The rest would be left to rot.

Cille stepped behind Vitolinus, stood, much as the boy, legs spread, arms folded. Watched as the final roof beam groaned and collapsed inward, sending a fresh eruption of flames into the night sky. Soon, there would be nothing left to burn; come morning, only the charred timbers would remain heaped behind the stone pillars of the door-way. Among it all, the bodies, probably huddled in one place, the burnt flesh and bones fused and gnarled into a grotesque remainder. Cille said, 'It is a pity about the women, they would have provided extra entertainment for your young men.' Not for himself. He was becoming too old for this, for fighting, for war. Even for women. A warm hearth-fire and a belly-full of ale suited his needs better now. He sighed. This was the work for younger men, not for the likes of himself. He had been flattered that the lad had sought his advice and guidance. But was this, this shabby burning and killing, truly the work for a warrior such as he had once been? Na, he would be away soon, back to his own hearth.

Vitolinus had merely grunted. He had no urge for the forced taking of poxed British women. It was death he wanted. An ending to the British, to all that had once been Arthur's.

'The old man here was a fool,' Cille added, 'to hide his family inside.' He shrugged, but then to his mind all born of the British blood were fools. Had this been his steading, he would have taken the lives of his womenfolk quickly, with his own knife, and then sought an honourable warrior's death for himself, not cowered behind burning walls. He shook his head. Ja, a pity about the women, the men needed something to crow over, something more than the rise of flames and slaughtered meat. He rubbed the back of his hand across his mouth and chin. It did not matter. There would, no doubt, be other women.

'So, do you return to our boat, go back up the Meduway? Or do you try for some more sport?' Although he was an older man against the ten and six of Vitolinus, he tactfully looked to the younger lad for the decision-making. Vitolinus was the son, grandson and nephew of kings, to him fell the position of liege lord; this was his war. The sky would fall on the lad's head when the Pendragon returned home, not on mere followers. Aside, Vitolinus was intelligent enough to look for guidance when it was needed. As he did now, for the lad was turning, with a distorted grin, his eyes reflecting the glare of orange, smoke-wreathed light, the scar running along his cheek giving him a look of hideousness.

'The night is but young, my old friend, and as you say, 'tis a pity about the women.' He sprung full around, with a bark of laughter, slapped his companion and adviser on the back as he sauntered past, heading for the shadowed woodland rising to the west of the steading. To the men he called, 'Hoist the choice of carcasses into the trees for safe keeping, we will collect them on the return journey.' And with an expression that was more sneer than grin, exclaimed, 'I have a taste to roast more than one whoreson's family in their beds this night!'

Cheering, raising their voices in battle song, the young men gathered up their weapons and swaggered away from the flames of what had, an hour before, been the farm of an elderly couple and their grandchildren.

Reluctant, resigned, Cille followed behind Vitolinus. Ja, soon he would go home. But not yet.

§ XXIII

The sun filtered, dappled, through the overhead canopy of leaves and branches. It was shaded, cool beneath the trees, but insufferably hot for so early in the year in the open. If this continued, the wider, shallower, rivers would soon be running low; grass, even that in these woodlands, was already dry and brown. Arthur only hoped that Euric and his Goths, somewhere away to the south, were as uncomfortable and irritable in this heat as he and his men.

He rode, as always, at the head of the Vanguard, setting a steady pace in the wake of his competent scouts. The line of march was ordered much as the Roman legions would once have tramped across enemy territory. First, the pioneers, whose job it was to make a way for the army coming immediate behind – this current stretch of woodland was easier than the past few days, the trees and undergrowth not so dense, so tangled. Sharpened axes and brute strength had been needed over-often on this campaign. Even the women, the whores and their rag-tag scrabble of children, marching within the safety of the baggage, had been required occasionally to help clear the overgrown, neglected Roman roadways running for mile upon mile through these seemingly never-ending woodlands.

No one rode, except the cavalry. If you could not keep up, you were left behind. It was the way of things for an army on the march.

With the pack-mules and ponies trundled the blacksmiths, the medics, armourers, leather workers. The boys trudged here, boys who, in later times, would be called squires. Gweir, Arthur's servant, was luckier than most, for he had acquired a pony, rode it proudly, for all the animal's poor conformation and age. Here too, escorted by a select, experienced guard, travelled the army papers, the paraphernalia of war. Maps, details of logistics, a clutter of letters, half-read or half-written by the Pendragon.

Then, the Artoriani, the élite, Arthur's cavalry, riding with the standards and emblems of each turmae, a second forest of fluttering, rustling colour. Beyond the riders, the infantry, the mercenary forces, men, whom, had they been fighting in Britain, would have called themselves Cymry. These were an ill assortment, a straggle of volunteers who had, since those first days after landing along the coast of Less Britain, come in small groups or singularly to join with Arthur. Young men and old, freemen and slaves. All seeking a part in the great fight that lay ahead. Beyond necessary question, Arthur never asked from where they came. If a son defied his father, or a husband a wife, a slave his master, what cared the Pendragon? He needed the men, their hearts and their loyalty. For that, he asked nothing more than a given name and next of kin if known.

The rearguard was formed partly of Artoriani, experienced, battle-hardened men, intermingled with Gauls, those yet to learn. Ecdicius and his small retinue rode proudly here, alongside Arthur's men. He was proving useful, this adventurous nobleman. Quick to learn, slow to comment. The sort of man Arthur welcomed as an officer and friend.

Easing his backside in the saddle, Arthur stretched cramped, sore muscles. It had been a long, hot day. A longer, hotter week. Evening would be upon them in an hour or so, and the air would cool, thank the gods! Another half-hour on the march and they would make camp. Their last. The morrow would see them at Avaricum, and there the march ended. Arthur had made his mind, quite when, he was uncertain, but the decision had come – happen unconsciously, during a dream. They were going no further. Either the Goths came to him before the ending of the August month, or he would go home.

He had nigh on two thousand men following, eager, behind his red-blazoned Dragon Banner. The men of Riothamus they privately called themselves, those who were not Artoriani, marching with hearts as high as the sky and grins as wide as the Liger River. And at last, word had come that Syagrius was to join them. The King of Soissons was about to move south with his army, would meet the Pendragon at Avaricum.

Arthur twisted in the saddle, surveyed the column that was his army, listening to the familiar, comforting sounds. The tramp of feet; shouts, chatter, laughter. The occasional oath, a cadence of sound against the background of soft-treaded hoof-beats, the creak of leather, neighing, braying. He glanced upward, at the swathe of bluest sky, hanging bright, unclouded, above the trees. A magpie screeched somewhere to his left, answered by another, further ahead. Three days past the word had come from Syagrius, the King of Soissons, that Euric was again on the move, and that he, Syagrius, would be coming with all haste to meet with Arthur. Together, they could put an end to this barbarian scourge.

A scout was riding in, coming at a trot, sweat glistening on his forehead beneath his war-cap, wet, dark, patches on his mount's coat. At Avaricum? Hah! Had Syagrius not said the same for Condivicnum, Juliomagus, Caesarodunum? Arthur was reluctant to admit, even to himself, that he would only believe his one-time friend intended to take part in this thing when he stood there, before him. Even then, Arthur harboured a suspicion that Syagrius had no intention of soiling his own hands with blood.

The Pendragon returned the scout's salute, questioned for a report with his expression and eyes.

'Trees are down, sir, quarter of a mile ahead.'

'No way round?'

'No sir.'

Arthur's reply was a colourful oath. Did no one travel in this damned country? Did no one consider that it might have been prudent to ensure the roadways were kept clear? God's breath, did not one of these damned Gauls have a brain to think with? Time and again the column had needed to halt while obstacles were cleared from the road. Great trees, fallen, half-rotten, submerged by years of undergrowth. Gape-holed bridges, unsafe, unkempt. Arthur was beginning to believe that the whole of Gaul was like this derelict north-western corner. And men like Ambrosius back home thought Britain was in disrepair? Bull's blood, Britain was a thriving phoenix compared with this!

'There is another river ahead also, sir.' A slight hesitancy in the scout's voice brought a frown to his King's features.

'Go on, surprise me. The bridge is down,' Arthur drawled.

The scout grinned, raised one hand in surrender. 'Took the words right out of my mouth, sir.'

Arthur halted the column. God's holy truth! Why in all Hades had he agreed to come to this bloody country?

§ XXIV

Ragnall was used to keeping herself to the background, away from the forefront. Hers was the world of shadows and half-light, of walking with her head bowed, veil or hood held close, sight cast down. She was ten and six years, and had never smiled into a man's eyes. Never expected to. A girl who was to face the rest of her life as a woman of Christ had no reason to be smiling at mortal men.

Her father's voice, beyond the closed doorway, was rising, angry, but then her father, Amlawdd, had always been prone to sudden-flared tempers regarding his daughter. It was the disappointment, she supposed. Other fathers could be proud of their daughters, would expect the prospect of a good marriage, a useful alliance, an honoured son-by-law. Such as those would not come for Ragnall. Who would ever want her as wife?

She sighed, lifted the rolled parchment from her lap, tried again to read the delicate print of the Gospel. Her sight was not so good, the words faint and small, and the voices beyond the abbess's closed door too distracting.

They did not want her here, the holy women. She was an embarrassment. Neither did her father want her. For the same reason, although he also had the guilt and memories to contend with. She rose from the stool, carefully re-rolling the parchment scroll, placed it on the table, walked aimlessly around the room.

It was functional, but austere and cold, much like the abbess to whom it belonged. This was the outer, public chamber, before her private rooms. No one was allowed in there without invitation, although those few who had been privileged enough reported that it was no more comfortable. Her fingers fiddled with the one ring that she wore, twiddling it absently around and around. Nor did she want to be here, cloistered as a nun, with only a duty towards the Christian God to fill these endless days. Ragnall wanted the sun on her face, the wind in her hair.

She looked at the ring. It had been her mother's, the only thing of hers that she possessed, the only thing of importance that she had brought with her from her father's Hall, six years past, when she had been a child of ten. Most of the jewels and fine woven clothing that had once been her mother's had gone, over the years, to his succession of whores and bed-mates. Aye, and even before her mother's death had such things been given. They said she had died of an illness. Ragnall could not remember much of her, except her smile, sun-blonde hair and her golden laughter. It had not been illness that killed her, though, of that she was certain. Her mother had died of despair, for Ragnall was like her mother. They both needed the sweet freedom of the sky and the sun, not the shuttered darkness of binding chains.

Amlawdd had not loved her mother, no more than he loved her, his daughter. But then, Amlawdd had no love for anyone save himself and the woman he boasted that he would have as his, one day. His was a love for greed, lust and gluttony. He loved the Lady Pendragon, he said, but few of his stronghold believed his declaration. He wanted her, but wanting was not the same as loving.

Ragnall paused in her walking before the shut door, studied the iron nail-studs, ring handle and hinges, the oak wood of the panels. This had been alive once, had stood as a great tree in a forest, its branches spread to the sun . . . Ragnall let her head fall back, her arms spread, imagining the warmth of such a freedom . . . and the door opened. Ragnall squeaked, leapt back a pace. The abbess stalked through, her mouth a thin line of disapproval, her double chin firm, set.

'You see,' she said, brandishing her arm at Ragnall. 'The child is possessed. Her mind is not in this earthly world, nor is it in God's. I cannot tolerate her here any longer.'

Amlawdd trotted, red-faced, blustering, behind, still arguing. 'I pay you enough, damn it, for her keep! You've been happy to take my gold!'

The Lady Branwen turned imperiously to face him. 'Even were you to double the sum, I would not keep her. Her disruptiveness is harming the peaceful nature of my convent. She must go.'

'And to where must I send her? To a brothel perhaps?' If Amlawdd intended to shock the abbess, it did not work. Lady Branwen merely scowled, turned to Ragnall and grasped her chin, tilting the girl's head painfully up, back, her eyes scrutinizing the scarred and puckered skin, the one undamaged eye. 'Even the basest of whores need something beyond their sex to draw a man.'

Branwen had seen much ugliness and unpleasantness during her life.

At least here, secluded as Abbess of the Convent of Mary the Mother at Yns Witrin, she was spared many of the horrors of the outside world. The girl Ragnall was too much a reminder of the devil's work. She had tried, God knows, Branwen had tried to tolerate her rebelliousness, had tried to ignore the ugliness of those dreadful scars . . . but no more, no more!

In her own turn, Ragnall had no wish to stay in the gloom of this place, but there was nowhere else to go. She begged, 'Have I not been of use to you all these years?' She held out her hands, one with long, slender fingers, the other as twisted and gnarled as an ancient oak tree's roots. Pleaded, 'Half my body was disfigured by the flames of the fire I fell into, but half is untouched, capable. I can read and I can sew. I have tended the gardens, sown and reaped the corn. My voice joins well with the songs of God . . .'

Branwen held up her hand for silence. 'You manage to do all these things, I agree. But you have never willingly and obediently done them. Your disfigured body, child, completes these tasks while your mind is far from prayers and God.' Lady Branwen folded her hands inside the sleeves of her black robe. The matter was ended.

'Your daughter will leave here, my Lord Amlawdd, when you do, at the ending of this called Council.' She swept to the door, opened it wide. Angry, Amlawdd strode through, disappeared across the courtyard beyond, his oaths trailing in his wake.

Ragnall dipped a reverence to the abbess, walked through the door, which shut, with an unalterable finality, the moment she was through.

There would be many more people arriving on the morrow – indeed, already the little town was swelling with important visitors. Ambrosius Aurelianus, the Governor of all Britain, had called for his Council to meet here, on the Glass Isle. Happen one of them would take pity on a girl with nowhere to go.

Ragnall sighed, walked across the courtyard with her head bowed, her hood pulled well forward. Happen, but she doubted it.

§ XXV

Cadwy stood watching as the man dismounted, exchanged polite greeting with the abbot awaiting him in the crowded courtyard. Ambrosius turned, their eyes met, Cadwy betraying in that first, unguarded instant the pleading to be accepted, loved, for what he was, not condemned for what he was not. His father's eye mirrored, just briefly, that same echo from the heart. Quickly veiled, shuttered, behind the stern exterior.

Clearing his throat, Ambrosius began to walk towards the group awaiting him on the steps of the new, wooden-built, basilica building. The difficulties of formality, the intricacies. He was here at Yns Witrin, neutral ground, to meet with the Council of all Britain, ostensibly to persuade the chieftains and landowners to supply the men he needed to join against the growing menace from the Cantii Saxons. Primarily, he was here to assert his authority. Made all the more difficult by the woman standing central among the men and the disconcerting, unexpected presence of his son beside her. Mastering a calmness that he did not feel, Ambrosius approached Gwenhwyfar. She had always been a slender woman, but now, after being so ill, her body was thin, the skin paper over bones, cheeks hollow, eyes sunken. At another time he might have shown concern, but not here, not before these people. Inclining his head to her as he mounted the steps, he did nothing more to acknowledge her, the rightful queen, stepped instead, one pace to the right to greet Amlawdd, lord of the coastal lands to the north west of this, the Glass Isle.

As Ambrosius intended, Amlawdd's pleasure at being singled in this way was obvious. He had always been a proud, if somewhat slow-witted man, but he had ambition. A fact which Ambrosius fully intended to trade upon. Pleased, Amlawdd knelt in public homage, an act reserved normally for a liege lord, for the King. Furious, Gwenhwyfar, made to step forward, to protest. Cadwy took her arm, shook his head, mouthed a warning. Instead, it was he who moved, thrusting his weight onto his sound leg to counterbalance the lameness, he who said, loud, so all might hear, 'My lord Aurelianus, the queen asks me to speak for her, to offer her welcome to this, her Council.'

Amlawdd jumped up, his face reddening. Glancing apprehensively at Gwenhwyfar, he wiped his sweating palms down the front of his fine-woven woollen tunic. He had been at the wrong end of her sword blade once before. Once was enough! A hush fell over the gathered men, the elders, chieftains, high-born traders and merchantmen, the freeborn who served, by election or birth, on the Great Council. In the courtyard too, a silence fell among the men and women who had come to Yns Witrin to seek God and be witness to the deliberations of Council, though not necessarily in that order of preference. The abbot, the highest ranking official of this cluster of buildings that was firmly establishing itself as a holy-community settlement, bustled forward to protest, was stilled by a hand-motion from Ambrosius.

Passive, he half-turned, again inclined his head in Gwenhwyfar's direction. To her, ignoring Cadwy, he said, 'You will, naturally, forgive my forwardness in the calling of this Council without representation to you. A woman who has been as ill, as I believe you to have been, would not, I assumed, have had the physical strength to attend, let alone lead a battle campaign.'

Tawny sparks flashed against the green of Gwenhwyfar's eyes, a sharp retort hovered on her lips, but she bit the anger down. He was right, curse him, she had not much strength, and would never be able to lead men against Vitolinus. She was damned if he was going to usurp her position before all these important men! She held his eyes a heartbeat longer, then, smiling, addressed Amlawdd.

'It is good, my lord, that you are so eager to lend your sword in the defence of my husband's kingdom.' Her smile so encouraging, so intensely false. To Ambrosius, to them all, 'I will be sure to inform the Pendragon of your loyalty when he returns.'

A few nervous coughs, shuffling of feet, no one daring to meet her eye as she cast around the embarrassed faces.

'Has there been further news on that matter then, my lady?' Ambrosius queried. 'Is the Pendragon to abandon this foolish quest and resume his rightful duties here, in his own lands?'

Several gasped, including Gwenhwyfar and Cadwy.

So easy, so subtle. Ambrosius smiled, as easily and as falsely as Gwenhwyfar. He climbed the last two steps, walking through the parting men, entered through the doorway of the building that had been constructed solely, upon his orders, for the purpose of this meeting. Men filed after him, skirting their way around Gwenhwyfar, averting their eyes from her, looking at their feet, their neighbour, the way ahead, any direction save at her. The wife of the Pendragon, the King who had just, with those few words, lost his kingdom.

§ XXVI

Evening was settling, the remnant of the afternoon's rain-clouds scudding over the bruise-purple sky. The wind was rising, Cadwy could hear its voice growing more insistent among the clusters of tossing trees. The small holy settlement snuggled at the foot of the great Tor was already preparing for night; the last meal taken, doors closing firm against the coming darkness.

Cadwy knew Gwenhwyfar had gone up the Tor. He had seen her setting out, going up the rain-puddled lane, her cloak wrapped tight about her shoulders, wisps of copper-gold hair escaping her hood. She was so frail, so thin. He had watched her as she had stepped onto the miz-maze path that made its ancient pattern up and around the place of the goddess. Was she still up there? He could not see up onto the summit, for his sight was not as sharp as it ought to be. Distances were a blur, a fuzzed-edged picture. There was a tall standing stone up there, black against the fading colour of the sky. He knew it was there, for he had heard of it, but see it he could not.

Would she come down before night descended? Ought he attempt to find her? Did she want to be found? She had been weeping as she walked, that also he knew, by instinct more than sight. She had gone up there, to seek solitude and healing. Would not want him hobbling after her. Cadwy sighed, began the weary trudge back along the muddied lane. She would not want his poor attempts at comfort.

Below this incline, nestled in the sheltered hollows beneath the Tor, huddled the Christian settlement, the dwelling-places, shops and taverns that had sprung up around the enclosing walls of the abbey with its attendant cloisters, and the smaller, wattle-built chapel dedicated to Mary the Mother.

The lane ahead scuttled under a tangle of droop-branched, overgrown trees, their foliage, black against the greying sky, casting wary shadows beneath. Cadwy jerked to a halt, head up, nostrils flaring, scenting the wind. Something had moved, something other than the wind-swaying shadows. A darker shape rose from a huddled clump. Cadwy peered into the gloom beneath those suddenly unfriendly trees. This was a pagan place, the Tor of Yns Witrin, a place of magic and fear and superstition – aye, despite the resident community who insisted it now belonged to the Christian God. The Old Ones, Cadwy secretly thought, were not to be so easily dislodged.

'Who walks there?' he called, his voice commanding, impatient. A feint to mask his fear. 'Who watches me?'

'Only God, and myself. You have nothing to fear from either of us.' A young woman's voice. Sweet, soft, a hint of rare-used laughter.

Cadwy's heartbeat doubled. A lady? *The Lady?*

The priestesses of the Mother Goddess had once had their sanctuary here, at the base of the Tor, near where the lake lay, dark and silent, even in the driest of summers. This too, had been the place of the Underworld god Avallach. There were doorways, it was said, that led from within the Tor down into his dark kingdom. Cadwy took a steadying breath. There was no Avallach, only the one, Christian God. And the last Lady had gone, years past, drowned, they insisted, in the pagan waters of her Goddess. Summoning courage, he stepped forward, one single, lame pace. 'Show yourself. Why need you hide in the shadows if you mean no harm?'

She sounded young, a girl just passed into womanhood. Her voice reminded him of summer, warm evenings scented by honeysuckle and roses. 'I do not hide, I was merely waiting for you.' It was a half-truth for she had not intended to show herself, was waiting for him to pass. Something involuntary had made her move though, some urging inside her that had ran away with her sense.

He could see her now, her cloaked body blending with the shadows, her face hidden by a hood pulled well forward. He pointed at her with his crutch, a crude gesture of defence. Surely this was some night-creature, some pagan deity come back with the fall of night to do mischief?

'It is a late hour for a woman to be out alone,' he said stiffly.

She ignored his censure, said, 'Your father has men looking for you. He wishes to speak with you.'

'And you came looking for me? Up here?'

There was a smile in her voice as she answered. 'No, but since we have unexpectedly met, there is no reason why I ought not give you the message.'

The explanation was simple. Earthbound. Cadwy's fear dissipated, he felt a little foolish. Pagan spirit? She was nothing more than a novitiate from the Convent of Our Lady Mary! He lowered his crutch, his pathetic weapon, settled it beneath his arm. So they were searching for him? Let them look! He had no wish to speak with his father. This night, or ever.

'Anger can be a two-edged sword, my lord. Its bite difficult to heal unless tended straight'way.'

Cadwy started. How did she know of his inner anger? How could she perceive that his stomach was a tight, clutching knot of rage and shame? The superstitious fear began niggling again.

'We, all of us,' she added matter-of-factly, 'feel the pain that our fathers unwittingly inflict. But do we not, in our own lifetime, give as many wounds as we receive?'

The clouds, ragged-edged, shape-shifting, were running before the blustering wind, sailing faster across a background sea of dark, night-blue sky. Suddenly the moon came up, her full roundness opening from behind the blackness of the Tor, her light blossoming against the backdrop of night, her pale silver-brightness sparkling. Shadows leapt, like a mettlesome horse suddenly allowed its head, their shapes changing, then settling, quivering beneath the gentle caress of soft light. The moon, the chariot of the goddess.

Cadwy made to walk on, but the path was mud-bound, slippery, his lame-legged foot went from beneath him and he toppled forward onto one knee, cursing beneath his breath.

Ragnall darted forward to help him, her hand going to his arm. 'Take care, my lord,' she said, concerned, 'this path is notorious for its bad footing after rain. 'Tis impassable in some weathers, most especially when the ice comes after the snow.'

He was grateful to her tact. They both knew it was his clumsiness that had made him fall. Bless her, most others would laugh or mock his unsteadiness.

Voices, male, coming nearer, breath panting as they came up the incline. The light of their torches, needed beneath the trees, bouncing and spluttering, swallowed the softness of the fragile moon-shadows, frightening away that suspended moment of magic. Three men in the uniform of Ambrosius came busily around the bend of the lane.

Cadwy glanced briefly at them, then back with curiosity at the girl, whose face also was looking to the newcomers. He gasped, his hand coming, unbidden, to his mouth. The flickering torchlight had struck full upon her features, the crevices of skin, the tight scars, twisted mouth and puckered, sightless eye. Bile rose to Cadwy's throat as in that single fleeting second he saw the hideousness of Ragnall's distorted face.

To his shame, he fled, hobble-running past the men, pushing them aside, slithering in the mud-ruts, breath sobbing in his throat. Certain that she had, after all, been a creature of the Old Ones.

It was only later, much later, in the quiet stillness before dawn, that he saw, in his sleep-troubled mind, the tears that had welled from her other eye. Pale, moon-silvered tears that had splashed from the side of her face that had been left untouched by whatever damage had caused so much suffering. An eye so wide and so lovely.

§ XXVII

The Tor was a safe place for Ragnall; its solitude and peace surrounded her with the comfort of love that she so desperately needed. For all their conviction that the Glass Isle was now a place of the Christian God, the spirits of its older name, Yns Witrin, still lingered up on the height of the Tor. You could hear them, the echoes of their whispering, if you knew where and how to listen. It was the place of the female, the Tor, a woman's place, where the Goddess listened to the tears or laughter of her daughters.

The path was steep, slippery from the recent rain, but Ragnall climbed with the confidence of familiarity. Nor did she mind the night. She was happier in the dark, for none could see her ugliness where there was no light. Up here, where the wind sang and the stars were only a fingertip's touch away, Ragnall could feel beautiful. The Goddess did not judge a woman for her sins, only for what she was, a daughter of life.

The abbess, Branwen, would have had the girl whipped raw, or worse, had she known of her coming here, but Ragnall took care that none should discover it – easily done for few paid much heed to her. The Christian God and His followers, Ragnall felt, professed love to all save the pagan and the deformed.

She stopped as she neared the crest of the path, took time to slow her breathing. The wind would be strong once she crossed from this sheltered side to the open summit. She would need her breath out there.

A few years back, she had been shown these paths, introduced to the freedoms that the Tor gave, by the one who had then lived here. Morgaine her name had been, the Lady of the Lake, last priestess to the Goddess. She had been Ragnall's only friend – they were mutual friends, both outcasts, both feared for their difference. When she had gone, with the boy-child that she had borne three years past, Ragnall had felt desolate, had almost taken that most precious thing, her own life, but the Goddess had comforted her with her songs that whispered in the wind, and Ragnall had faced her loneliness, sure that one day, one day, she would be able to dance in the sunlight. She missed Morgaine, but understood why she had found the need to go. Ragnall alone knew where she had gone. Not even the child's father had the knowing of that. Aye, and Morgaine had confided that detail also. Who the father of her son was.

Ragnall stepped out from the shelter of the hill, her cloak and hair billowing as the wind screamed past her. She laughed, exhilarated by the force, the passion of its passing. Laughed, because they would all be so shocked were she ever to tell them of that knowledge. What a nest of ants it would stir! She would never tell though, never betray her only friend, Morgaine, and the trust of the Goddess.

She had to lean forward against the buffeting wind, head bowed, to make her way along the ridge to where the single Stone lunged up towards the cloud-ragged sky; did not see the other woman there, leaning against its timeless solidity. Both saw each other almost at the same moment, both gasped in instinctive alarm. The woman by the Stone dropped her hand to her side, drew a sword blade that, although shorter and lighter than a man's weapon, looked none the less deadly. The Goddess must have been watching, for she tossed her protection, sent a tendril of wind scurrying through this woman's cloak, hurling it around her arm, trapping the bright blade among its folds, giving Ragnall that small moment to catch her wits.

'You startled me,' she confessed. 'It is rare to meet another up here.'

'The Christian kind do not venture this far,' Gwenhwyfar replied, uncertain, wary, attempting to distinguish, unsuccessfully, who this woman could be. Decided on forthright attack. 'I am Gwenhwyfar, wife to the Pendragon. Who might you be, and what do you here?' She had untangled her sword, held it downward, the blade glinting softly under the scudding moonlight.

'I live within the shelter of the Holy Sisters' place but I am here for the same reason as you.' Ragnall lifted her head higher, uncaring whether the scars showed on her face up here, where nothing of the real world mattered. 'I come to face my grief, to let it run loose, unfettered, where none will judge or condemn.'

For a long moment Gwenhwyfar regarded the girl, seeing, in the fleeting cloud-shadows, a hint of the damage to her face. Her thoughts this past hour had taken the twists and turns of the lonely and frightened, skimming through doubts of the future, regrets of the past. Touching on laughter, lingering on tears. The smiles of her sons, the grief that befell them. And the fear, that thundering fear, that hammered for her husband. She had been thinking, standing with her back against the cold of the granite Stone, of the last time she had stood up here on the Tor. Llacheu, her first-born, had been growing in her womb then. She had been staying with the Holy Sisters too, but had sought the presence of the Goddess to heal her fragility, the damage that had been done to her. How the circle turned!

Gwenhwyfar smiled, slid her sword back into the safe keeping of the scabbard slung at her waist, held her palms wide in peace and friendship. 'There are not many of us,' she said, 'who remember that it is the Mother who is the first to comfort our tears, not the Father.'

The Tor was a lonely place, by night or day. It squatted, rising high above the levels that were water-bound by winter, marsh and grazing land by summer. Floating like an island among the swirls of white, morning mist, or lazily drowsing beneath the cricket-chirruping heat of a summer sun. It sat, brooding the cluster of lesser hills about her skirts, benignly watching, like an indulgent mother, the blunderings of Man scuttling beneath her gaze. A lonely place, but a place where, if you cared to listen with your heart, not look with your eyes, you could find love and contentment, given without condition.

Two women seeking the sanctuary of its healing calm. Gwenhwyfar, weary and heartsore and frightened of the future for her husband and daughter, sat companionably and silent beside Ragnall who shared the same fears for herself. Together, they watched the stars wheel across the sky, shared the first, beautiful colours of the new day, their backs leaning against the Stone that had stood, almost since time began, on the summit of this hill where surely once the gods, whoever they were, had walked and shed in their footsteps the patterns of peace.

§ XXVIII

Cadwy found his father in the chapel of Mary the Mother. The hour was early, the sun barely a hint in the rain-whisping sky. Cadwy waited at the rear of the small, square-built place. If his father, kneeling at the altar a few yards away, knew his son to be there, he made no sign. Ambrosius expressed no surprise, however, as, his prayer finished, he rose and turned, suppressing a wince of pain from joints that protested at the kneeling and bending. Of course he would have known the man entering the chapel to be Cadwy. He would have heard the shuffle of a lame foot, the tap of a wooden crutch.

'I sent to speak with you last night.' For all the moderation in his father's tone, Cadwy still heard admonishment, criticism.

'I was about other matters, last night,' he retorted.

Ambrosius shot his son a speculative look as he walked past, heading for the doorway. What would his son be doing, where had he gone? He had not been in either of the two taverns, nor anywhere within the small town. Could he have been at the brothel a mile outside? Mentally Ambrosius dismissed the thought as nonsense, opened the door but did not pass through.

'I think it time, Cadwy' – again, Ambrosius tried to ensure that his voice was mild, friendly – 'for you to leave Caer Cadan. To come home, with me.'

'Why?' A single, short-made answer. Full of rebellion.

Ambrosius sighed, shut the door again. He walked to the first line of wooden benches, moving slowly, for his knees were sorely aching this morning. 'Because I ask it. Is that not enough?'

Cadwy remained silent, glowering.

Seating himself, Ambrosius ignored the obstinacy. 'People are talking.'

'I see. 'Tis the tongue-wagging that annoys you.'

Shaking his head slowly, taking deep breaths to remain calm, Ambrosius rubbed his hands along his thighs. The palms were sticky, sweating. His head was beginning to thump too. He did not want to argue with his son, did not . . . Very patient: 'Aye, talk bothers me, for it is malicious talk, lies, most of it, I trust.'

Cadwy's head came up, his arms were folded defiantly across his chest. What did he mean by that? That Cadwy had shamed him, shamed himself? 'I have done nothing to offend you – save fall prey to an illness that left me twisted and useless in your sight.' His eyes bore into his father's face, directly offering a challenge to deny it. 'At Caer Cadan I am valued.'

Ambrosius could not help it. He laughed.

Coldly, Cadwy asked, 'What do you want from me, Father? To take what I have found away from me? Why? I have been happier this short while at Caer Cadan than ever I have.'

For the first time in many years, Ambrosius looked at his son and saw him for what he was, a young man of ten and nine years, tall, like all of this line, with a slightly over-long nose set against high, firm cheek-bones. Dark eyes, dark hair. Cadwy looked much like his mother, yet he had the similarities of the Pendragon blood too. He supposed those male characteristics marked him to be alike himself, Ambrosius – Cadwy's father, Uthr's brother – Arthur's uncle. The passion in his son's words hit home. Ambrosius paled, his skin crawling, chalk-white, though sweat trickled down his back, pricked his forehead, upper lip. Christ's good soul! Was it true, then? All of it? Swallowing bile, he stammered what he had intended to say to the son of his flesh.

'I need support. I need loyal men beside me, behind me.' Again he swallowed. 'I need the respect granted to a war-lord.' This was not easy, begging for his son to come back to him. 'I need you with me, Cadwy. It looks bad that you are with the Queen not with me.'

'So, you resent my happiness.'

'I did not say that.'

'You implied it.'

'I imply nothing save what is spoken or thought by others.'

'Of course, you would take leave to listen to them rather than myself.'

This was getting out of hand, becoming nonsense. 'I want you – ' Ambrosius spoke slowly, trying to keep the quiver of anger from his asking, 'I want you to be sensible, responsible. When I leave to put the Saxon Vitolinus back into his place, I need to have someone I can trust to speak for me. Someone of my flesh, my blood.' He tossed a challenging glance. 'I have no choice, I have only you. I cannot trust you, however, while you bed in Gwenhwyfar's Hall. You must leave Caer Cadan. 'Tis fortunate that communication is travelling slow and with great difficulty, for if the Pendragon should hear of these rumours . . .'

Then Cadwy laughed, head tossing back, clenched fists resting on his hips. 'Oh I see, I understand it all now!' He propped his crutch beneath his arm, leant his weight on it. 'If Arthur hears the rumour that I am tumbling his wife, he just might be incensed enough to abandon Gaul and come racing back to relieve me of my balls! You'd not be happy with that would you?' He laughed again, genuinely amused. 'The matter of me keeping my manhood intact is naught, for you are convinced that my lameness makes me a gelding anyway. Ah no, it is this other thing you fear. You have not yet secured enough power to ensure that Arthur cannot fight his way back into Britain. And Vitolinus will sorely drain your resources.' He made for the doorway, cast it wide open, limped through, his father following a few paces behind. 'I am almost tempted to lie, to say that I am indeed bedding the Queen, only I would never so dishonour my Lady Gwenhwyfar.'

Ahead of his father, Cadwy missed the relief that passed across Ambrosius's face. The rumours were not true then, thank God!

'I need your support, son,' he implored. There were more than a mere few who were saying that Ambrosius could not keep his own house in order, let alone an army, a country.

Cadwy turned, intending to sneer some caustic retort, checked his hurtful words. His father was ageing, though he was barely forty and two years. Grey was flecking his hair, his skin was drawn, tense. He looked ill. Sympathy lurched into the son. He made to step forward, to offer his hand to his father. The crutch tapped on the stone floor, and the man, Ambrosius, involuntarily recoiled. That brief moment of reconciliation was lost, tossed away.

Some half-heard rumour that would hurt his father turned from thought to words and Cadwy snarled, 'I would almost think this was a planned scheme of Lady Winifred's, were I only to see her purpose.' His father's face had drained paler, he plunged on, determined to ram the knife deeper. 'She needs to be rid of her brother Vitolinus, needs also to ensure Arthur never returns, the both to make way for her son. And she has always used you for her purpose. Is that how it is this time also, father? Save she would not want me back with you, would want to continue the further soiling of Lady Gwenhwyfar's name.'

Cadwy froze when his father said, with a tone of ice hatred, 'On the contrary. The Lady Winifred wants you as far as possible from the Queen's bed. In her own, in fact. I am considering agreeing to her suggestion of alliance. Of marriage with you.'

Stunned, speechless. Cadwy stared at his father; then the anger came, the outrage. 'I'll not be ordered into such a marriage. You shame me, sir, shame me!' The path was narrow, on a steep incline, and wet from the rain. Cadwy could not, leaning on his crutch so, walk fast away, but he made an effort at it.

'It would be a way of showing you were with me, boy, not the Pendragon,' Ambrosius called.

Cadwy stabbed his free hand into the air, an obscene gesture.

'You will obey me, boy!'

Cadwy halted, spun around, his crutch skidding, flying out. 'I am no boy. I am a man grown, and I choose my own life. My own wife.'

Ambrosius strode up to him, pushed past, sneered into his face, 'You prove you can be a man, then happen I will treat you as one.' He stalked away, angry that he had lost his temper, angry that he mentioned this idiocy about Winifred. Damn the woman, this was her doing, putting that fool idea into his head. Never would he want her as a daughter-by-law. Yet, yet, it would mark Cadwy in his place to enforce such a thing. He marched on, his body screaming from the pains shooting up and down his legs and back. Marched on, angry. Try as he might, he could not find love for his son.

§ XXIX

Unfortunate that it need be this night that the Lady Branwen, haughty abbess of the Glass Isle, discovered to where Ragnall so often disappeared.

Chance brought events colliding together on a course set for harsh words and angered exchange. Lady Branwen arose from her bed shortly before dawn, with a headache thumping as if all the horses of hell were pounding across her forehead. These past days had been full of distress for her – the Isle in turmoil with the influx of so many come for this Council; and in consequence a few too many of her women turning attention to the lure of the outside world rather than God's pure Word. And her own memories, long forgotten, had resurged, unbidden, unwelcome. Heavy with lack of sleep, she splashed cold water on her face, dressed, elected to walk a while. The freshness of a new day might chase the weariness from her. She would welcome time alone, to think.

Without making disturbance, she let herself out of her private chamber, slipped past the little building that housed the sleeping nuns. Her boots scuffed the dew-wet grass, leaving silvered tracks. To her left, among the thicket of ash and alder, a few birds were tuning their morning song. Ahead, the Tor rose devil-black against the paling grey of early dawn. You could never escape the presence of the Tor, for it glowered there, a constant reminder of the Heathen, God's cursed. She walked up the rain-muddied lane, setting a good pace despite the soft footing.

It was Gwenhwyfar who had aroused these memories, she who had brought these troubles flooding back into mind. Always, in the past, it had been Gwenhwyfar who vexed Branwen so. She breathed deep as she walked, filling her lungs with the crisp air. She had known Gwenhwyfar from childhood, for she, Branwen, had been wife to one of her brothers, the second eldest-born of Cunedda's large brood. Ah, so many of them dead now. Cunedda himself, her lord husband, Osmail; their second-born son. Why had Gwenhwyfar come here to haunt her with the past? Stirring those things that ought to have been buried deep.

Branwen halted, tossed her face up to the swift-lightening sky. Eyes closed, head back, arms spread wide, she pleaded in her mind for God to give her comfort, to ease the ache in her heart. It had been His will that her man had been taken, that she should remain here, in this mist-bound place. His decree that she ought raise His word above the old beliefs that so obstinately would not die. But why, why did these wretched memories have to return?

She opened her tired eyes, looked straight at the ancient miz-maze path that descended from the Tor, and her head cleared, her brows furrowed, lips thinned. Hussy! Heathen-spawned whore! An anger more bitter than any poisoned berry poured through Branwen, a choking, all-grasping, all-consuming rage.

Ragnall, making her way carefully down the dew-wet steepness of the slope saw the abbess, stopped, fear gripping her. There was nowhere to hide, to run. She searched frantically back up the path behind her, up to the summit where the Stone was showing clearer, blacker, against the sky. Had Gwenhwyfar gone, descended on the other side? Alone, she had to face the wrath of Lady Branwen.

The girl had known that one day she would be discovered, knew the consequences. Until this morning, she had taken such great care never to be seen, never to walk on these slopes unless the safety of darkness cloaked her, for the Tor was forbidden to the Holy Sisters. It was a place of evil, and it had many times been made clear that harsh punishment would be meted to any who flaunted a preference for the darkness of the devil. Only one, to Ragnall's knowledge had broken that rule. A girl, much of her own age, three years past . . . Ragnall shuddered, tried so hard to blot out the fearful memory of what had happened to that girl.

The abbess hurried up to her, her face contorted with the indignation of one defied and disobeyed, her breath hot, eyes wide, blazing disgust and anger. Her fingers clamped around Ragnall's wrist, dragged her without pity or care away from the place of the Goddess.

The girl wanted to scream, wanted to plead for forgiveness, to defend herself, but no words would come as she slithered and fell, dragged behind the enraged woman. A scream, so terrified, so engulfing, was lodged in her throat. If she opened her mouth it would be let out, never to stop, for too clearly, far too clearly, could she see that other girl's death.

As a child, Ragnall had fallen into the flames of the hearth-fire of her father's Hall. The terrible scars on her body were nothing to those that remained in her mind, nothing to the screams that still choked her in the dark hours of night when her hand and face and body throbbed from the remembered pain of that terrible day. Ragnall knew the pain of fire and could see before her eyes, as the Abbess Branwen took her back to the holy place of the Mother Mary, that other girl's tortured death by burning.

§ XXX

Gwenhwyfar elected to stay a while longer, savouring the unique, comforting solitude that the Tor offered. She was in no hurry to make her way back down to the Christian settlement – was in no hurry to be further humiliated and angered by the arrogance and ambition of men who were plotting to destroy her husband.

Although many came to the Glass Isle for the benefit of their soul, earthly curiosity still sat with a greater need on their shoulders. This calling of Council had attracted an unusual amount of visitors to the holy place, some of whom, it had to be admitted, were more interested in the ramifications of politics than the peace and blessings of the Christian God. The settlement was a small, clustered town of taverns, dwellings and trading stalls, set cheek by jowl against the timber-built abbey with its attendant chapels and buildings. They slept where they could find, crowding the taverns or guest places within the monastery; word had spread with great speed that this Council met with an intention to overthrow the Pendragon. They gathered with a morbid interest in the verbal murder of their King.

Gwenhwyfar sat looking eastward, her back comfortable against the granite of the Stone, watching as the sky paled, the light spreading like an army on the march across the Summer Land. Darker clouds were gathering in the distance. It would rain again soon. Once she thought she heard a girl's scream, but the wind was powerful up here, it could as easily have been some small animal taken by an owl. She felt weary, with no energy or spirit. Was it her recent illness that caused such languor? Or an inner failing? Arthur was losing his kingdom and there was nothing – nothing – she could do to stop it save wait and watch. And hope he would come home again, soon.

The sun was rising, a red-golden, warming orb. A rain-laden mist rose, coming from nowhere, covering the sunken lands that nestled lower than the high-tide level away over at the coast. It was a mist that swelled with the onrush of day, breathing over the willow and alder-pocked grassland that even in the hottest days of summer held soggy, bog-bound areas of waterlogged marsh.

The birds were busy at this first coming of the day: the cries of the lapwing, the piping of plovers mixing with the harsh calls of rooks and the shrill chattering of starlings . . . Gwenhwyfar closed her eyes. Rested her head on the Stone. She was so tired, so bone-weary, heartachingly tired.

The mist had gone when she next looked; she must have slept. Day had begun in earnest, and she was of a sudden hungry. Raking a hand through her tousled hair, she came to her feet, took one last, long gaze around the panorama of land that belonged to her husband. This was Arthur's own held dominion, these marshes of the Severn Rivers. And over there, where the hills were smudged against the skyline, lay Dumnonia, also his, and beyond that, Cornovii – and the Land's End, a few, wave-tossed islands . . . and the sea. The sea over which he had gone. Gwenhwyfar fancied she could hear it, hear the swoosh and rush of waves darting on a shingle shore, smell its salt tang. Maybe it was only the sound of the gulls that brought the fancy, those birds that, even in these finer days, preferred to ramble for food among the dykes and marshes.

Slowly, she picked her way down from the Tor, ambled along the lane, idling here and there to admire a plant, watch a bird. This day would need be faced, and the next. And the next. It was how she was surviving this vast, empty loneliness, staggering from one day through to the next.

'My Lady! Lady Gwenhwyfar!'

She stopped, startled, as she lifted the latch that would open the door into the tavern where she lodged. Turned her head at the urgent calling of her name, saw Cadwy running, as best he might, up the narrow street that sneaked between the outer wall and this row of higgle-piggle traders' shops and dwellings.

She stood, waiting for him, took his arm to steady him as he came up to her, panting, red-faced, distressed. He gasped a few incoherent words, none, save the name of the girl Ragnall, making sense. Firm, a little irritable, she commanded him to regain breath, start where things made sense.

He shook his head, waved his hand, urgent. There was no time! No time!

'Ragnall,' he gasped again. 'Caught coming from Tor.' He had his hand on his chest, trying to ease the pounding of his heart and the burning of his lungs. 'You were up there. You told me you were going there. Did you meet her? Ragnall? You must do something!' His frantic eyes sought Gwenhwyfar's, willing her to understand the urgency, the importance. He swallowed, tried again. 'I have been looking for you. You must stop this!'

Something was terribly wrong with the girl Ragnall, that much she realized. 'Stop what?' she asked, calmly.

'They intend to burn her. They accuse her of being a devil child!'

Irritation flashed into Gwenhwyfar's mind and expression. She was tired, drained of energy. 'We shared each other's company through the night. She seems a pleasant girl. We laughed together over many things.' Aye, Gwenhwyfar thought, and comforted a few tears. What nonsense was this Cadwy saying? 'Who accuses her of such an absurdity?'

'Lady Branwen, the abbess.'

Gwenhwyfar almost laughed. Almost, but not quite. The gravity of Cadwy's frantic expression, the knowing of the Lady Branwen's capabilities stopped her. Oh aye, Gwenhwyfar knew the cruel side that lay behind the Lady Branwen's pious bigotry! She had been victim of it herself, once, back in the days of childhood.

Cadwy had his breath easier. He grasped Gwenhwyfar's arm, began to urge her along the street. 'Hurry!'

She brushed his clasped arm aside, 'Wait, wait! What can I do about it?' She was at a loss, confused. Tired, a little disorientated.

Blank, Cadwy regarded her slow-witted dullness. 'You are the Queen. The Pendragon's wife. You can speak for her.' She seemed not to understand. 'The abbess has called for an immediate trial. They are gathered in the Council basilica, my father presides in judgement.' Again, Cadwy pulled at her arm. 'There will soon be a decision made!' Tears were welling in his desperate eyes. If they did not hurry, it might be too late!

Trial indeed! What folly was this? It was no crime to walk on the height of the Tor – why, if it was then . . . Gwenhwyfar smiled to herself. Aye, she had a glimmering of an idea. Deftly, she spun Cadwy around, pushed him from her. 'Go, delay things, I come as soon as I may.'

His face brightened. 'You will hurry?'

She nodded, thrust open the door to her lodging-place. 'Go!'

§ XXXI

The anger welling inside Gwenhwyfar was aroused by more than the injustice that seemed to be thrown at an innocent young girl. She swept through the doors into the crowded Council chamber, pushing aside the two sentry guards who stood as a matter of formality on such an occasion to either side. Taken by surprise, they hurriedly crossed their ceremonial spears, barring entrance, but she sliced them apart with her drawn sword, strode into the building, creating a stir from inside as the crowd turned their heads, tutting and frowning at the disturbence.

Here were the nobles and eldermen, high-born merchantmen and free-born traders. Bishops and the clergy. The abbot of the Glass Isle and, seated opposite him, the abbess, Lady Branwen. At the head of the room, beyond the crowd, swollen by those of the settlement who had managed to push their way in, Ambrosius Aurelianus, dressed formally in a purple-edged toga, was seated on a chair of state. Sprawled at his feet, visibly shaking from cold and fear, Ragnall. They had stripped her of outer garments, displaying her disfigured body. Proof of her devilry, they said; proof that God had punished her for her sins.

Although hurried, Gwenhwyfar had attired herself carefully. It would not be wise to appear dishevelled and slovenly before such austere and august company. She had chosen a robe of green silk, the colour of new-budded spring, and a cloak of finest woven wool that draped to her ankles, in a contrasting, darker shade. It billowed behind her, like a green cloud of rustling leaves and wind as she strode through the parting crowd, seeming like a visiting Goddess herself.

Her copper-gold hair was braided and decorated with the glittering sparkle of emeralds and garnets. At her throat, her gold-twined torque, shaped as a dragon. And in her hand, blade down, now that she was through the doors, her unsheathed sword.

She stalked forward, head proud, green eyes flickering tawny sparks of outrage. It occurred to her, in a moment of fleeting sorrow, that it ought be Arthur where Ambrosius sat, presiding over this gathering. But had Arthur been here, there would be no need for her anger. Had this court of judgement been called with Arthur as King . . . No use pursuing that brief thought. Arthur was not here. She need deal with Ambrosius. And Branwen.

Politely, if somewhat restrained, Ambrosius acknowledged her entrance, waved aside the two guards hurrying after her. The Council and gathered onlookers – mostly men – pressed behind her, heads craning, standing on toe-tip, not wishing to miss a single moment of this excitement.

She had reached Ambrosius, halted before the first step of the raised dais and, watched by all present, offered her sword to him, hilt first. Hesitant, puzzled, sensing some trick, Ambrosius came to his feet, took it.

And Gwenhwyfar sank into a deep reverence of obedience. Save to her own husband, she had never before offered such humility.

Murmurs of astonishment; mutters of incredulity. All in that Council knew Gwenhwyfar too well, reckoned her to hold as much force, self-will and impudence as Arthur himself.

Gwenhwyfar had decided how to fight this thing as she hastily dressed. Ah, there was more than one way to fight a battle! Straight out, with brute strength – or by stealth and cunning. She had no hope of winning by force, there were not enough men present to back her. Oh, there were a few who would remain loyal to Arthur, but not many. Ambrosius had seen to that. Arthur's men had either gone with him or had not been invited here . . . Gwynedd was not summoned to Council at Yns Witrin, nor were Dyfed, Rheged, Caledonia . . . only representatives of the south were here, the wealthy south, who ran spear against shield with Ambrosius.

She offered her sword and tipped her face up to her husband's uncle, the man who was proclaiming himself as Supreme Governor of all Britain. Her voice did not quaver as she spoke, her words winging, clear and regal. 'We have our differences, my Lord Aurelianus, angers that will never be quenched. In absolute loyalty to my Lord Pendragon, I cannot, nor will not, acknowledge you as Supreme Lord.'

'But I am, undeniably, in command of this Council of judgement this day,' Ambrosius countered. Murmurings from the watching crowd, a few hands applauding, nods of agreement.

Briefly, Gwenhwyfar inclined her head. 'You are, undeniably, about to command the murder of an innocent – and that of the rightful Queen, wife to Arthur the Pendragon.'

The murmurs rose in volume, excited chatter, speculation. Ambrosius was about to deny such an outrageous charge, but Gwenhwyfar did not give him opportunity.

'But then,' she continued, 'that would suit your ambition, would it not? To be rid of me so easily.' Her smile, directed solely at him, was taunting. There were many things she disliked about Ambrosius Aurelianus, many a reason that she could find in her heart to justify his end – but, she knew that, for all that dislike, he was a fair man, no murderer of women.

His answer was honest. 'I have no wish to be rid of you, madam, only your husband.'

Hers was as direct. 'I am Arthur's wife. You need be rid of me.'

Declining to argue the point, Ambrosius flapped his hand. 'Neither have I a taste for murder.' A doubt flickered in his mind. Was that the truth? He would gladly have Gwenhwyfar sent somewhere in safe-keeping, somewhere a long distance off, but na, he would not have her murdered. He held his hand out, intending to raise her up.

She ignored the gesture. 'If you order the brutal killing of this young woman, Ambrosius, then you must burn me beside her, for we are equal in guilt, if guilt it be, to walk in innocence on the Tor of Yns Witrin.'

'What nonsense is this?' Lady Branwen, impatient at this play-acting, annoyed at the interference, came to her feet. Ordered, 'You interrupt a court of law, madam. Be gone!'

With slow dignity, Gwenhwyfar stood. Her height was taller than the abbess, her poise and dignity the more acute. A willow against Branwen's elm. Once, Gwenhwyfar had feared her, when she was a child at home in Gwynedd. No longer. She felt only pity, now, for Branwen.

Ragnall's trembling had eased at Gwenhwyfar's entering, relief filling her. She knew not how this woman could save her, only that through the night they had sat together companionably, listening to the distant, comforting, heartbeat of the ancient goddess, sharing their secrets and pain. As the abbess spoke, however, the fear began its insistent quivering again. She dared not glance up, dared not lift her head. Instead, she curled smaller, foetal, the tears brimming from her undamaged eye.

Gwenhwyfar asked, 'What charge is brought?'

Branwen answered tersely, although it had been Ambrosius Gwenhwyfar had addressed. 'The charge of consorting with the devil.'

Gwenhwyfar raised an eyebrow at the woman. 'Your evidence?'

Without hesitation, using spite-ridden words, Branwen retorted, 'She was caught walking on forbidden heathen ground.'

Gwenhwyfar laughed, her head back, hands going to her hips. 'Then aye, you must burn me also! I was with Ragnall for all the night. It was I who took her up onto the summit of Yns Witrin.' She glanced around the crowded Council chamber, her stare lingering across one or two known faces. 'I would warrant in the days when the Lady resided here, many a man in this audience found his way across the lake onto the Tor.' A few men laughed, echoing her amusement. 'My Lord Ambrosius, if such be the charge against this young woman, then there will, I think, be quite an array of us condemned to this fire of yours.'

More laughter. The tension had eased. This whole thing exposed so easily for the ludicrous sham that it was.

Affronted, irate that the sway of opinion had shifted, Branwen begged Ambrosius to intervene, to command silence. Persisted with her intent. 'This girl bears the marks of God's cursing.' Roughly, she dragged Ragnall to her feet to again publicly show those hideous scars.

Gwenhwyfar bit down a repulsive shudder. Ragnall had told her, out there in the hiding darkness, of her injuries and of how she had come by them, but she had not seen for herself, under the cloak of darkness. She managed to mask her reaction, thrust a moment of panic aside. God's truth, how could she proceed with this next thing? The girl was indeed hideous ... yet her nature was gentle, her voice sweet, her laughter infectious. She must go on, for she was too far along the road to turn back! It might not be winning for Arthur, but even some small, insignificant victory over Ambrosius would mean much.

She turned, slowly, deliberately sought out Cadwy, who had so hopefully followed her through the crowd, was standing at the forefront, anxious, concerned, angry at his father's part in this. Why, though, was he so fearful for a girl he had met but the once? A girl from whom he had recoiled because of her deformity. Because of guilt and a heavy conscience? He had behaved shamefully to her, reacted exactly as others often did to himself.

Gwenhwyfar directed her words to the crowd. Her eyes to Ambrosius. 'Do we then, burn all who bear the scars of misfortune?'

The Lord Aurelianus caught his breath, saw this other trap neatly set, with no way to escape.

'Commit Ragnall to burn, Ambrosius, for these prejudices, and you so commit your son.'

Uproar. Branwen calling for a right to issue punishment for offences against God. Those of Council and interested spectators shouting her down.

Beneath the tumult, Gwenhwyfar spoke quiet words to Ambrosius. He listened, nodded once. Aye, it was as she said, it was the law. Although for Ragnall, he could see it doing naught but making a bad situation worse.

Gwenhwyfar stepped aside, her part done, her mouth dry. Now it was for others to do and say.

'Hear me! Hear me!' Ambrosius called for order, called again, and a third time. Quiet was slow to descend, but gradually it fell.

'Hear me!' Gruff, reluctant, they listened. 'There is but one way to settle this. By law, no maiden can stand condemned if a man be willing to take her into his protection.' Ambrosius paused, let his gaze slide over the men present. 'Will any here take Ragnall as wife?'

Gasps, shouts of incredulity – some of horror and outrage. Ragnall herself looked up, her mouth open, shocked. Then laughter came, and derision, fingers pointing, men mocking. Shamed, Ragnall dipped her head, fought back new tears of humiliation. It was her own father who laughed the loudest, he who called, 'Have her as wife? That hideous creature?' His amusement rang to the rafters. 'No man would be so much the fool.'

'I would.'

The silence fell as rapidly as a thunderbolt. All eyes turned to Cadwy. He came forward, stood before the girl, took her unscarred hand in his own, tipped her head and, balancing his crutch, gently wiped aside her tears. 'I would have her as wife.'

Gwenhwyfar closed her eyes, silently concluding a prayer. If Cadwy had not responded as she had bargained ... Ah well, was life not one long sigh of – 'if'?

June 469

§ XXXII

Arthur stifled a yawn. He had slept badly again and now had to sit listening to this imbecile whinging about lost slaves. Several times he found his mind wandering, the despair and aching loss hammering persistent in his brain and heart.

'And, so, my lord,' the little man stammered, anxiously twisting his woollen cap around and around in his fingers, 'if you could, in your royal benevolence, but see your way to ...' He trailed off, fiddled more earnestly with his head-gear. Exactly how did a mere farmer command a king to return his slaves?

Rubbing tired eyes with the fingers of one hand, Arthur reread the letter held in his other, trying to concentrate, to blot out the memory of those words spoken two weeks past. He groaned. Why could the Bishop Sidonius Apollinaris never write plainly? All this flowery, meandering language and exaggerated flattery! '*I am a direct witness of the conscientiousness which weighs on you so heavily, and which has always been of such delicacy as to make you blush for the wrongdoing of others.*' What a piled heap of bullshit!

'Your benefactor is mistaken,' Arthur stated blandly. 'I have no interest whatsoever in the laws and justice of this country, beyond that which affects my men.' The little man coloured, said nothing. 'I also have been informed, on many occasions, that I have no conscience or morals. A strong king cannot afford the first, and I have never been overimpressed by the latter.' Arthur read on, scanning the second paragraph, let the parchment roll up on itself, took up the leather-bound book, an accompanying gift from Sidonius, from the table beside him. It was a small volume, its rough-cut parchment pages well stitched, bound between a stiffened leather cover, the text carefully copied in lines of neat, small, handwriting. The *Carmina*, a publication of the bishop's prolific poetry. Arthur frowned at the thing. Was he expected to read it? He had no use for such egotistic prattlings. As if it were some everyday wax-tablet communication, Arthur tossed the book across the width of his tent to Bedwyr, who sat cross-legged, consuming a second bowl of breakfast on Arthur's rumpled bed. The book fell short, fell to the floor; a page, loosened by the discourteous handling, fluttering out. 'You have time to read, cousin, you have the thing,' Arthur declared.

The farmer had followed the book's trajectory with his sorrowful eyes, his mouth curving deeper into a drooping expression of despair as it fell. Books were expensive items, he had never even seen one until this day. All he wanted was his slaves back and to return forthwith to his farm. It was only a small, unassuming place, situated fifty miles south of Avaricum, but it was pleasant enough, bordering the banks of the river Allia. And it prospered. For several years running, the harvest had been good, yielding a high crop of grain and grape. At least, it had prospered until this British man came here with his army.

These past months, as Arthur had marched along the course of the Liger, young men in their hundreds had deserted the land to flock to join with Riothamus. All well and good for the free-born, but when the slaves ran off, who was there left to do the work? In desperation, the smaller landowners had put their enjoined case before the newly consecrated Bishop of Augustonematum. Sidonius had been most sympathetic, but not exactly helpful. In this little man's private opinion, written letters never achieved as much as the spoken word. Now, if only the eloquent bishop were standing here in the King of Britain's command tent . . . No doubt the good bishop thought himself correct to urge that Riothamus was a fair-minded man, that a case of wrongdoing, if put before him, would be judiciously and impartially judged. But the farmer wondered, shuffling uncomfortably from foot to foot, whether the bishop truly understood the reality of situations. He was not an educated man, he was a farmer, he could not read or write, nor was he assertive or vocal. He farmed his land, raised his sons, kept himself to himself, but even he could see that he was going to get nowhere, because this British King was not the amiable, courteous, gallant that Sidonius had expressed him to be.

As each minute passed, he began to wish fervently that he had never allowed himself to be persuaded by the bishop to come here, to plead in person to this King. Never had he seen so many men encamped in one place. More than two thousand, he had been told. Why, even when the local folk gathered back home, their small number of twenty and four seemed a huge crowd! But all this, the noise, the bustle – the stench! And they all seemed such large, boisterous men. Several times he had been buffeted – they assured him, accidentally – as he came through the throng of tents and men. He was only a humble man, was finding the enormity of everything quite beyond him. Nor did it help matters that this man Arthur was known to have been fostering foul, black moods these last weeks. Word had been passed around, even as far as his humble farm-steading, of the British King's loss, of the message from Britain, telling of his wife's illness. It was sad to lose a wife – he himself had lost three – but death was a part of life and had to be accepted. To the farmer's modest opinion, it was not fitting for a king to grieve so long for a mere woman. A day or two of public mourning was quite sufficient, a Mass spoken, some gift in her name made to the Holy Church. But this excessive reaction? Unfitting, unnecessary. There were, after all, plenty of women to fill an empty bed-place.

'There are no run-way slaves within my army, I assure you,' Arthur stated. 'If you were careless enough to allow them to escape, well,' – he spread his hands, expressive, his meaning unspoken – 'they will be long gone by now. Saxons, were they?' He did not wait for answer. 'Scuttled back to their homeland, I would warrant.' He was lying, but then the Pendragon was a proficient liar.

'I beg your pardon,' the farmer blurted, becoming desperate, 'I know they came to you.' The British King said nothing in response. Emboldened, he continued with his contradiction. 'A few of your officers rode by way of my farm. Some many weeks past. They were recruiting, they said.' He nodded his head sharply, as if to emphasize *so what do you think of that?* 'Within a day, my slaves had gone! Vanished! Stole out in the night.' Gloomily, he added, 'They took some bags of grain and baked bread with them too.' For good measure, finished, 'And some of my best wine.'

Mithras' blood, Arthur thought, *save me from such imbeciles!* 'Do you think, then, that some of these men who intend to fight with me, to save *your* lands and *your* farms, have been lenient with the truth about where they came from?'

The farmer missed the sarcasm, mistakenly took the statement as compliant acquiescence. Eagerly he nodded; then cast a slow, conspiratory glance over his shoulder, took one, bold step forward. He licked his lips.

Anticipating a shared secret, Arthur leant forward from his stool. 'I think,' the farmer opined in a loud whisper, again glancing over his shoulder to ensure no one else, aside the King and his cousin were listening, though the tent was empty save for the three of them, 'I think your officers deliberately enticed away my slaves!'

Feigning incredulity, Arthur sat back, a shocked expression to his face. 'Surely not?'

The farmer nodded, once. Triumphant.

'Would you know these officers again? Recognize them?' Arthur questioned, again leaning forward.

'Oh aye, I clearly recall all four. I even saw two of them as I made way through your encampment!' Emboldened, the farmer straddled his legs, folded his arms. 'Most distinctive they all were. One had a scar running from here to here.' The farmer brought his finger down his cheek, from eye to chin, 'And another was dressed in a wolf-skin, an older man, craggy-faced. Too old for effective fighting, I would wager.' The farmer shook his head. What hope had the citizens of this fair province when they were protected by a rabble such as this? Enticers of slaves, old men, a king reported to blub like a child every night because of the loss of a wife . . . He sighed. They needed real soldiers, legions, the Eagles. Euric this barbarian would not have dared linger so long had the soldiers of Rome been here in Gaul. Ah, real, proper soldiers they had been!

Arthur looked to Bedwyr, commanded he find these two officers, bring them without delay to his presence. His lazy smile was reassuring. The farmer relaxed. Had he misjudged this British King? Was he about to give justice after all?

It was some ten minutes before two men ducked through the tent opening and saluted their King, followed at heel by Bedwyr, who again seated himself comfortably on Arthur's bed. His face, like the King's, was impassive, but the laughter was there, bubbling almost beyond control, beneath the surface, sparkling in his eyes.

One of the officers was indeed rugged of face and as tough-looking as old leather. He wore a shabby, but much loved, wolf-skin. He was Mabon, a trusted, long-serving, loyal man, who had also served the other Pendragon, Uthr, Arthur's father. The other officer was younger, but as loyal. Mabon spoke first, his face thrusting forward, eyes scowling, expression as fierce as the wolf-head that served as his cloak hood. 'The others are hunting my lord King, for this night's supper.'

Arthur nodded curtly, wasted no further time with formalities. He addressed the farmer, pointing his hand at the two officers. 'Are these the two?'

'Aye lord, I would recognize them anywhere!' Proud of his personal achievement, the farmer stood, arms folded, chin jutting. 'I saw them speak to my slaves – enticing them away!'

The Pendragon's voice came harsh, a bark of contempt and wrath. Frightened, the farmer scrabbled backward a pace or two. 'Then I trust you are no more than a fool, not a deliberate mischief-maker intent on wasting my time!' Arthur bounced to his feet, came menacingly close. The man backed away further, mouth opening and closing, speechless, eyes bulging. Arthur's anger was in full spate. Gods! They had begged him, these people of Gaul, to come here, pleaded for his help! All these months he had trailed in the wake of the ineptitude of this country's damned government, had been promised, and promised again, the reinforcements he so needed to get this thing finished and done with – promised support, financing ... all of it empty words spouting from empty breaths. Those few who saw sense, who recognized the reality of Euric's cold shadow blotting the sun, had willingly enough joined him – aye, and those few who were not free to choose their own destinies, but what cared Arthur for that? He needed men, men willing to fight. Slave or free-born, he cared little. It was their strength he needed, not their background. He lashed out at this unfortunate who epitomized all the crass stupidity typical of his kind.

'These two men are among the most trusted of my officers, they are too valued to employ their time on mere recruitment!' Arthur flapped his hand, effectively dismissing his men, trusting they would not show open grins this side of the entrance. Another lie, of course. His valued, experienced men obtained the numbers he needed to fight, for they knew Euric's numbers now. Numbers far greater than Arthur had under his command.

He nodded to Bedwyr, who rose, gestured with finality that the farmer was to leave, the matter settled. Bewildered, wondering where he had been mistaken, the little man bowed, made to leave, his hopes shattered. How would he run his farm with no one save himself and five young sons to work it?

'There will be a great battle in these parts soon enough,' Arthur stated, making the man pause, turn reluctantly around. 'If I do not have sufficient men to fight it with me, then you'll not need workers for your farm.'

Arthur was turning away, reaching for other letters on his table, said, his back to the tent entrance, 'Euric, if I cannot stop him when he comes, will take more than your slaves.'

Bedwyr, peering through the open flap, one arm resting on the tent pole, watched the man go tottering down through the lines, head ducked, face red against the trail of laughter that cantered after him. He only hoped those Saxon slaves had the sense to keep their skinny carcasses hidden for a while.

'That was neatly done,' he chuckled, turning back into the tent and sauntering over to stand behind his cousin. 'Of course, he knew you lied.'

'He had no means to prove it though.' Arthur sighed, handed his second-in-command the parchment he had been scanning. 'It came this morning.'

Quickly Bedwyr read, his expression altering from brief amusement to disbelief, dismay. 'They are as near as that?'

Resigned, Arthur nodded. Euric and his Goth army were less than sixty miles distant.

'And Syagrius?' Bedwyr queried. 'Where is his promised army? The men we were expected to join with, the men who are supposedly to meet us here, to be at the forefront of this fight?'

The Pendragon laughed, a harsh, mocking sound. 'Still encamped at Lutetia. Apparently they like the climate better there. It is not so,' – he laughed again, wilder, desperate – 'not so potentially deadly.'

§ XXXIII

Mathild signed with her hand to the small group of Saxons hunkered to the south side of her personal tent. The six men acknowledged the 'all clear' with appreciative grins and trotted off, chattering amiably, returning about their business. It had been a close-run thing. If they had been spotted by their former master . . . Mathild smiled to herself as she watched them go, good men, good Saxon men. No Saxon deserved the fate of being taken as slave. She was certain that Arthur would not have turned them over to that greasy-looking Gaulish peasant. He needed them too much for himself. But had they been seen, well, it would have created a nasty incident. Sensible to lay low a while.

She considered returning to the Pendragon's tent, decided against. He was in no mood for women, for her, these past two weeks. Not since that messenger had come from Britain, from the man Ambrosius, telling him that Gwenhwyfar was dying. Arthur grieved for her, his conviction that he ought not have come here to Gaul, stayed so long, magnified that grief. He needed no reminder that he had also betrayed his love by taking a whore to his bed. Could she as easily cease her needing for him?

Mathild did not share Bedwyr's optimism that the queen might yet live. The messenger had spoken of an illness, of the expectation that the queen would not survive – had said that further news would follow. But nothing had come, no word, nothing. Did she secretly feel gladdened at that? If Arthur no longer had a wife, he would have need of another, one day.

She shook her head, lengthened her stride more purposefully towards the women's corner, the whores' tents. She had found friends there and a chance to share women's gossip. A chance to ascend to her true-born status also, for the army whores treated her for who she was by birth, and what she was, the daughter of a noble-born and the mistress of a king. His mistress ja, but his wife? As much as she loved Arthur, that she did not truly want, not in her heart. She wanted to go home, to her own kindred along the Elbe River, to claim her rights of land and wealth. As wife to the Pendragon she could have more success in claiming it, but Arthur would never help her. Not now. Never again would he leave his own Britain. If ever he was able to return to it.

She was greeted with smiles of welcome by the women. Sharing a few passing comments, a brief exchange of idle chatter, she was invited within Marared's tent, where a whirlwind of young children were tumbling and playing. A vivacious, pretty girl, Marared was among the favourites of the whore camp, her tent always a beacon to those who were looking for a warm bed. The children were a gaggle of varying-coloured hair, different-shaped faces, skin tones. All hers, none with the same father. The eldest, ten years old, shook his brothers and sisters from him, emerged from the heaving pile with a red, laughing, face. The mock-fight had been fast and furious, with all seven of them against himself. 'There are times,' he declared, 'when I discover how it must be to fight many times your own number in battle!'

'Ja,' Mathild agreed, helping him out of the mêlée, 'these ruffians need the discipline of a Decurion's drilling!' She patted the nearest on his backside as he swarmed past with the others. 'Get you gone so I can talk with your mother and be able to hear my own voice!' Squawking and shrieking, they ran out to join other children. They would find employment around the camp, carrying, cleaning, chopping wood, mending clothes. The whores' army, they were called, the brats who marched with their mothers behind the men. Often never knowing which man had sired them, not caring. One father was as good as another.

The eldest, last to leave, tossed a query at Mathild as he passed. 'Be there news?' he asked. 'Are we to fight soon?'

'What? Am I one of Arthur's officers to have the knowing of such?'

'Na,' the boy jested, 'but you be his whore and that makes you know all that goes on!'

Indignant, Mathild swiped at his ear. He ducked, ran, giggling, to join his siblings.

'That lad'll be the end of me!' His mother laughed, proudly. 'Come you in, m'dear and we'll share this jug of wine I've acquired. 'Tis good stuff.' Her eyes twinkling, added, 'Comes from an officer, pleased with his night's sport!'

Mathild sat, accepted the wine. It was indeed good quality. They talked of women's things, of the youngest babe, the next that was on the way, of Mathild's new gown, fashioned from fine-woven wool, a present from the King some weeks before. Shared amusement over the morning's trickery, their laughter growing the louder as Mathild impersonated the farmer, mocking his predicament.

They fell silent, laying back on the ragged bedding that served for eight children. The wine was too strong.

'Will he let you go, think you? When the fighting comes?'

Mathild did not answer immediately. Would he grant her freedom? 'I think,' she confided, 'that he would let me go now, were I to ask, but' – she lifted one hand, emphasizing her uncertainty – 'I think also, that I would not ask. He is so lost, so empty. He will soon once again need the comfort only a woman can offer. I would be here for him when that need comes.' Remembering her own past pain, she added, 'It is hard to accept the loss of the one you love, and Arthur loved Gwenhwyfar, for certain.' She lay a moment, staring up at the stained, ragged ceiling of the patched, worn tent. He loved his wife as much as Mathild had come to love him. 'I think,' she whispered, saying her floating thoughts aloud, 'that, should he want me again, I will not wear my amulet or use the secret things that stop a child from forming.' She turned her head, 'What think you?' But the other woman had her eyes closed, her mouth open. A gentle snore emanated into the room.

Mathild regarded the ceiling again, watched it swirl and blur. Ja, that wine was good. Too good.

§ XXXIV

Arthur was standing, his fingers hooked through the leather baldric that carried his sword, watching the distant, glittering light of the first stars. It was a calm, quiet evening, the coolness most welcome after the heat of the day. He was thinking of nothing in particular, a myriad of thoughts, come and gone as sudden as that bat flickering in and out of the trees and between the tents. He had never known a time when he had felt so miserable, so utterly despondent and alone. As a boy, when he had learnt of Uthr's death, his grief had felt like a weight crushing him. He had not even known Uthr to be his father, then, but he had loved him, and the losing of that man had come hard. And then, once, he thought he had lost Gwenhwyfar, thought she had been taken, butchered by the Saxons, by Hengest and his rabble when they had turned rebellious against Vortigern. His feelings then had been those of horror and distress – but he had had the comfort, however slight, of hope. And it had proved right, for he had found her, alive and well, carrying their first child. Llacheu, his first-born son, the son who had been killed . . . Arthur tore his mind from those cruel thoughts. What point this aimless dwelling on the dead? Gwenhwyfar was gone. Dead. Finished. Ah, love of the gods, how could he exist without her?

Movement behind, the gentle swish of a woman's robes and aroma of subtle perfume, the tent flap lifting, a wedge of light flooding out into the darkness. Mathild. He was grateful to her, for she was one of those rare women who knew when a man needed the solitude of silence or the companionship of talk.

She came to stand beside him. With sincere fondness, slid her arm around his waist, stood, looking as he did, up at the stars pricking the darkening sky, sharing his reverie. Absently, he laid his hand over hers, his fingers twining with her own. She would never love him as deeply as she had once loved her husband, but Arthur, despite his sudden tempers, was capable of being a kind and loving man. You had to know him, know the man, the reality that lay hidden beneath the hard exterior.

'What will you do?' she asked, knowing he would understand to what she referred.

'Stop him from coming further north.' He sighed, squeezed her fingers again. 'That is all I can do. There is no choice in the matter.'

'Is there much hope of being successful?' She did not add any more. They all knew the answer. Without Syagrius, without his substantial, promised reinforcements, knew the answer too clearly.

'Hope?' Arthur said, with a sardonic laugh. 'Hope took a swift horse an hour or so since, and is heeling hard for home.' He turned to her. 'You are a good woman, Mathild, you will make someone a good wife. Choose your next husband wisely.'

She smiled back at him, her feelings for him plain in the unwitting shine of her eyes. 'I will find it hard to meet with another man like you.'

He smiled. 'I hope so! There are, fortunately in some eyes, few like me!'

The camp was settling for the night, to sleep or to gather in comrades' tents for dice or board games. For the sharing of ale and wine, or the exchange of tales of bravado and boasted prowess. A congenial, high-hearted camp, even with the knowing that soon, they were to meet with Euric.

'Come with me.' Arthur led her back inside the tent, stood her in the centre, strode to the table where he rummaged through the scattered pile of letters, wax tablets and documents. Lists, petitions, correspondence. Took up two scrolls, rolled and sealed, one larger than the other. He crossed back to Mathild, handed her both. 'Open the smaller one.' He pointed to it, took a step backward, stood watching as, curious, she glanced from him to the things in her hand. Encouraging, he nodded his head.

106

Puzzlement increasing, she wandered to the bed, sat, put the larger scroll down, began breaking the seal of the smaller, read. When she looked up, tears glistened on her cheeks. Her voice was tight, the words coming in a quivering whisper. 'It is my freedom.'

Arthur shrugged, as if this were but some light, inconsequential matter. 'Have you ever felt anything but free? You are too independent a woman.'

She bit her lip to stem the great flood of emotion. Looked up at him, more tears coming. 'I can go home?'

He nodded.

'Now?'

He shrugged again with one shoulder. 'If you wish.'

She reread her manumission, signed with Arthur's flourished signature, *Arthur Pendragon, Riothamus*. Sat, feeling limp, awash with such a mixture of feelings, not knowing what to say, do.

Casually, aware of her consternation, Arthur crossed to the wine, poured for himself and her. 'I would like it were you to stay this one last night, but that would be for you to choose, not me to demand.'

A third time she looked up at him, her face and heart glowing with a happiness so great she thought she might burst open, like a seed head that was overfull of pollen.

Embarrassed, Arthur indicated the second scroll. 'Why not open that one also?'

Almost reluctant – for what further happiness could he give her? – she did so. She read quickly, abandoned her restraint of tears, let them fall freely as she hurried across the tent to hold him, to bury her head in his shoulder as she cried. The second contained legal freedom for all the Saxon slaves currently enlisted in Arthur's force of the Cymry.

Feeling a little awkward, Arthur slid his arm around her. 'Well,' he mocked, 'had I known it would upset you so much, I'd not have written the document!'

She pulled away, wiped at her tears with her fingers, laughing aloud. 'I am not upset. I am,' she fumbled for words, admitted, 'I know not what I am.'

Drinking his wine in gulps that betrayed his own mixed feelings, Arthur half-turned away from her, said, 'They too, the men, may leave when they wish.'

Incredulous, her laughter faded. 'But you are already too short of men.'

He gestured acceptance of the inevitable. 'A dozen or so less will not make much difference.' He drank again, finished the goblet. It would, but he was beyond caring.

Mathild crossed to him, threaded her arm through his, sought his eyes

107

so that he might see her earnestness. 'Most of the men here are from my own people, kindred of those who have their homes along the Elbe. Most are loyal to me, for I am the daughter of a nobleman, a warrior lord. They will do as I do, say as I say.'

Arthur patted her hand. 'I had counted on that. They will see you safe home.'

She dipped her head in agreement. 'But so too will they serve me here. Free men fight the better for knowing that they do so out of choice, not desperation.'

Aye, that was true enough!

She had to stand on toe-tip to reach up and kiss him, for Arthur was tall and she slight. 'I will stay, these next few days, see this through. After, whichever way it may go, after, I will return to my home.'

They lay quiet as the stars trod their ancient path across the arch of black sky. Together, warm, she nestled between his arms, her head pillowed on his chest, hair fanned in a tumble of golden spray. Arthur was awake, staring at the darkness inside the tent. Awake and thinking again of all those unwanted, unbearably sad memories. An owl called somewhere, mournful, desolate and haunting. An owl, the spirit bird. Did Gwenhwyfar come, riding astride its back? Or Llacheu? Gwydre, Amr? Or was it his own spirit, come to make ready to take him to the beyond?

Mathild stirred in her sleep, mumbling some unintelligible word. In his sorrow he needed comfort, could not have borne it had she gone from him also.

§ XXXV

Someone else lay awake twenty or so miles from the Pendragon's encampment. She lay with her three-year-old son huddled close, deep asleep. They were curled beneath her cloak, for the nights were chill, after the warmth of the day. The stars had blazed so bright, and crisp, a thousand silver fires burning in the vault of the sky. She had watched the constellations in their slow wheel, watched a star fall with the blaze of brief but magnificent glory, seen a planet rise, and wander its path.

Morgaine had come with her son, she knew not why. Some inner urging or instinct? Come to see him again, the father of this boy, the man she loved. But having come, her courage had left her. He would have no wish to see her, have no wish to see for himself the child spawned from his seed.

Medraut was much like his father, brown, slight curled hair, though lighter in shade, intense eyes that seemed as if they could see right through to your soul. The same nose, long, straight. As she had set out from the place that had become her home, Morgaine had told the boy of Arthur, the Pendragon, the one they called Riothamus. Told him of his strength and courage, his wisdom and laughter, speaking aloud all the memories that lay so vivid in her mind.

They were so close now, two, three more days would bring them to the place where the army camped, waiting for Euric the Goth to come further north; but the closeness was bringing its own terror, feelings that drowned her expectant hopes. Only the once had they lain together, her and Arthur, although he had come to her place at Yns Witrin more times than that. Only the once had she known him intimately, yet she had loved him, loved him with an intensity as bright as the brightest star, from as far distant as girlhood. Five years of age she had been when first she had seen him. The only man – only other being – to be kind to her, to have smiled on her. For that, if nothing else, her love had been seeded.

Why had she come? She ought not have come. Those days, that time, when she had been the last priestess of the Goddess, the Lady by the Lake, that was different then. She had held an aura around her then, a shielding cloak of mystery and pagan sanctity. For that reason, he had come to her. Why would he be wanting her now? Now, when she was nothing more than the mother of a bastard child.

She lay, looking up at the stars. 'If another one falls before I count to the number of one hundred,' she whispered to herself, 'I will turn around on the morrow, and go home.'

A star fell. It had been a pointless promise. Morgaine knew that she could not go without seeing him, seeing his face, hearing his voice, just one more, one more, last time.

July 469

§ XXXVI

Gwenhwyfar was enjoying the wedding celebrations. Her strength was improving daily, the vitality returning, like the welcome spread of spring sunshine, through her limbs and body. Her face was filling out again, the skin a glowing colour of pink health, not the sallow yellow of illness, and her eyes had that familiar sparkle returning, the glint of tempered fire and vivacious laughter. Caer Cadan was the natural choice for the marriage of Cadwy and Ragnall, for neither of their respective fathers had inclination to offer hospitality. The King's stronghold held adequate room to house many guests, warranted the prestige and facilities for a splendid feasting – and would be an opportunity to remind those who were on the verge of forgetting that they still had an acclaimed King. Aye indeed, Gwenhwyfar was enjoying herself.

The Christian ceremony over, with its solemn pledging of vows and the bishop's intoned blessing, the guests were demanding feasting and revelry. Both of which Gwenhwyfar, in the name of her lord, Arthur the Pendragon, was intending to give in grand and unforgettable style. Wild boar, venison, roasted fowl and hare; basted pork and tender young mutton; the best imported wines, ale in plenty and the sweet, heady apple-mead so well brewed in these Summer Lands. Musicians played, acrobats, dancers, conjurors with their sleight-of-hand tricks and astounding illusions provided a wondrous variety of entertainment. It seemed the whole world had trooped to Caer Cadan!

The Hall was crammed with the higher nobility, petty kings and lords; from Dyfed, Powys, Rheged, Dumnonia – respected men from Arthur's subject lands. Among them, Gwenhwyfar's brothers, come from Gwynedd. How could she not delight in such, most welcome, company? In addition, filling those sought-after spaces at table or ale-barrel, elders, merchant-men, traders. A clamour indeed of talk and laughter! Open invitation had been sent by swift messengers to the four winds – and they had responded with an alacrity that put those pressing for Arthur's demise to shame. Outside, too, beyond the light and noise of the King's Hall, were lesser revellers, over many to count, with such a whirl of dancing, feasting and drinking! Clustered groups seated around the well stacked fires, knots of men and women gathered in discussion, sharing

110

laughter and good-natured debate. And all with their wives and children and servants ... Everywhere, there came a bustling exuberance of laughter and merriment, gay contrast to the dour proceedings at Ambrosius's called Council, at Yns Witrin.

At that Council, Ambrosius's men, his declared supporters and sympathizers, had publicly declared for him – but with what practicality? They were, compared to the multitude gathered here, a minority, if outspoken, voice. Ambrosius had his embryonic army of the Ambrosiani, but they were not the élite, proud force of Arthur's followers, men who had made free choice to fight beneath the King's banner.

No one in this Hall would, this day, dare go openly against their King, and the loyalty would last a while, at least long enough. For Arthur surely – surely – was to be home soon. Aye, this wedding had been well timed, for all its unplanned spontaneity!

Only Ambrosius and those few of the Church hierarchy to attend were sitting stone-faced, aware they had been successfully outmanoeuvred for a while. Ambrosius sat at the high table, talking occasionally, observing the merriment with drawn brows and unsmiling expression, his eye going repeatedly to his son and new-taken wife. That this marriage was nothing short of disaster was, to him, an obvious fact; yet the girl was smiling, and Cadwy seemed more animated and at ease than ever his father had seen him before. Could this union prove worthwhile? Was there some small hope? A grandson would be too much to pray for, too presumptive a gift to ask of God. Yet were it possible? . . . Ambrosius dismissed the thought. How could it be so? He observed also Gwenhwyfar and her obvious determination to prove that she was no longer ailing, that death had been successfully cheated. He was ignorant of the Pendragon's deep misery. The messenger, he had sent in all good faith, wishing to inform a king of his wife's illness, to warn of her last days. Ambrosius was a proud man, but he was not vindictive or callous. He could not know that his sent word had been received incorrectly, that Arthur thought Gwenhwyfar dead – nor that all subsequent communication, both written and verbal had been delayed or misdirected. Had not been delivered.

So, in as much innocence and ignorance as Gwenhwyfar, he watched the queen as she danced and talked, laughed and sang, appearing as if she had never been ill. Watched, unaware that on the morrow her body would ache and the tiredness would return. That was Gwenhwyfar's knowledge alone, a lingering weakness that at all costs must be shielded from public view. For, leaderless, the lords would drift to Ambrosius's hearth. Discomfort was for the next day, this was the now, a now where she had to show these men – and Ambrosius Aurelianus – that were an army to be brought against the rightful King, the queen would be strong enough to draw her sword and lead one even greater in his name.

For Ragnall and Cadwy, the day had begun as an ordeal. Neither of them particularly easy in company, both timid and shy of strangers, they had found themselves unwillingly cast as principal players in this whirlpool of joyful celebration. Ragnall, still frightened of the threat of death hanging over her – though Gwenhwyfar and many others had repeatedly assured her of the invalidity of that punishment – attempted to smile, to show happiness. But other fears were crowding her, fears real and imaginary. Together, they had shuffled a few brief, stumbling steps, as custom decreed, to begin the dancing. Holding Cadwy's hand awkwardly, Ragnall had wondered at his motive for taking her as bride. She had no beauty, only ugliness, no grace or elegance. He knew not enough of her to be aware of the laughter that longed to escape from deep inside her, nor did he know of her sweet singing voice or her love of tale-telling. He did not know her at all, for until this day they had been apart since the ordeal of shame and fear at Yns Witrin. Nor did she know him, but this did not matter. He had given her the gift of freedom – albeit that freedom might be short-lived, for no woman could be certain how a husband would treat her in marriage – his features were strong, his countenance gentle and compassionate. He did not seem a man who would tend to violence towards his lady. Ragnall did not mind his limping, his awkward gait, for she saw only her own ungainliness. Wished so much that she would find some way of pleasing him as wife.

Cadwy, for his part, was as mindful of his own disability. How must she think of him as he shuffled and lurched those few, embarrassingly public steps? Acutely, was he aware of the glances and smothered sniggers. For all the joyfulness, the comments directed at the couple who had caused the celebrations were overloud and over-rude. Cadwy reddened at the cruel jesting, his fist clenching, schooling his expression to remain plain, untroubled, but Ragnall saw, read the thoughts behind his narrowing eyes, took his discomfort as shame of her.

Her fear increased as the afternoon drifted into evening. With the dark would come that other part of the ceremony, the final, complete taking of a wife. Could she endure it, the snide comments, the cruel thoughts? How could a man take her into his bed? What enjoyment or pleasure could her gross deformity give? Ah no, there was little happiness in Ragnall's heart, for she knew that once in the privacy of their bridal chamber, Cadwy would drop his mask of restraint and show his abhorrence of her.

Winifred, among the guests, was all smiles, enjoying herself immensely. The invitation to attend this day's merriment had been a general one –

one Winifred had determined not to miss. Mischief was so much the easier discharged among a large and prestigious gathering! Smug, as she always was, she observed with amusement Ambrosius's obvious discomfort. Her first words to him, upon her immediate arrival, were to the effect that she regarded his approval of this marriage as a slight against her. '*At least I could have bred you a grandson with four limbs and an intelligent brain. One wonders what her spawn will resemble!*' That her barb had struck home was clearly evident. Ambrosius's grim reaction told, all too plain, that his thoughts were dwelling along those same lines. He could not, of course, know that Winifred was delighted by this preposterous marriage, for the ending of Ambrosius's line: all the better for her purposes of Cerdic's inheritance, and for the annulment of her own, highly rash, suggestion that had been instantly regretted. Not that she would have, for a moment, expected Ambrosius to agree to the idea. Still, she really ought not make such ill-judged offers again! And a third reason to enjoy the occasion. A rare chance to stir the political waters and annoy Gwenhwyfar with the one muddied stick!

A pity that the wretched woman had recovered from that illness. Ambrosius, in Winifred's considered opinion, had missed his chance there. Had *she* been consulted, Arthur's wife would not have survived. Easily enough achieved, with the result uncontested. Making her way slowly around the edge of the uproar of lively, drink-heightened dancing, Winifred paused to gossip here and there, tossing in her little comments, poking here, digging there. Ambrosius was a fool. Poison was the answer to so many riddles.

A rustle of movement spread through the Hall like a wafting breeze. Winifred's eyebrows rose, anticipating more interest, more fuel to heat the next few months with gathered tattle. It was time for the couple to depart for the bedchamber. Winifred closed her eyes briefly, sent a swift, silent prayer of reprieve. Woden's breath! This could have been herself, needing to face the ordeal of bedding with a youth who was only half a man! She rose from her seat, joined with the general throng of guests pushing their way towards the upper end of the Hall. Winifred quirked a smile that tilted half her mouth, her mind anticipating the scene of these two unfortunates attempting to create some mild spark of passion in their bed. She had forgotten her own comments to Ambrosius, that it was not Cadwy's manhood that needed the crutch.

Ragnall stood, her hand placed lightly within Cadwy's before the open door of Gwenhwyfar's own personal chamber that was for this night to be theirs. She ensured her head was tucked well down; her veil she had replaced as soon as possible during the evening, had pulled it well forward. They were all laughing at her, she knew, sniggering and

113

exchanging lewd, vulgar whispers. It always happened on occasions like this, so she was informed, part of the ceremony. She would not know, personally, for never before had she attended a marriage celebration. She had not been old enough at her father's stronghold, and weddings were not the thing of a nunnery.

Cadwy, too, was nervous, although he took the humour with courage. He knew his own capabilities, even if they did not. But what of her? How was this intimacy to be concluded for Ragnall?

Gwenhwyfar stepped forward, raised her hand for silence, parried a few hecklers, a few tossed jests with quick, amiable wit. 'My lords and honoured guests,' she said when quiet had eventually settled enough for her to be heard. 'The night grows late, already the moon is high and full. I fear that come the morrow I will be left with a surfeit of roasted meats and fine wines.' More calls, shouts of disagreement. 'No, I agree with you sir, I hope indeed all the wine will be consumed, but I fear it will not be so!' Gwenhwyfar indicated the great oak doors that were swinging inward, the guests turned, shuffling feet, murmuring, questioning. Four men were rolling in a great cask, trundled it to the centre of the Hall, where they manoeuvred it upright, began the task of prising away the sealing wax from the lid.

'My guests, there has been a grave oversight,' Gwenhwyfar apologized. 'This casket of fine barley-wine was overlooked. I considered it right that it ought be brought in to you straight'way, for I believe it to be of the finest brewing. Please, go, sample its taste!'

They surged forward almost as one, pushing and jostling for their tankards, glasses and goblets to be filled. It was cleverly done, for in that first moment when all attention was focused on the issuing of the most prized of all wines, Gwenhwyfar swivelled around and hastily ushered Cadwy and Ragnall through the door into her chamber. 'You will have privacy,' she said. 'Bolt the door, none shall dare attempt to open it beyond perhaps hurling a brief flurry of jests.' She smiled at Ragnall, a reassuring warmth of comfort, dipped her head at Cadwy. 'I bid you both a good night.' And she withdrew, shut the door, waited a moment until she heard the two bolts slide deftly into place.

There was a token exclamation of disapproval, a few half-hearted disappointed comments, but the barley-wine was, as Gwenhwyfar had promised, an exceptional brew, and most gathered in that Hall had been dreading the traditional ceremony as much as the bridal couple. After all, just how did you put two disfigured cripples together into a marriage bed? Both men and women found the thought abhorrent, neither sex willing to admit outright that the ideal of a marriage partner was for beauty and strength, virility and passion. Hardly qualities of those two!

Na, the wine held better interest. There could be no embarrassment in emptying the contents of such fine, strong-brewed stuff!

§ XXXVII

The sounds of enjoyment beyond the bolted door, were loud, but indistinct, muffled, although the occasional roar of laughter came clearer, more startling.

Cadwy sat on a stool, close to the fire, nursing a goblet and leaning forward, his arms resting heavily on his thighs. He had made no attempt to prepare for bed, just sat, staring into the flames, occasionally sipping at the wine. The confusion, the conflict of emotions were whirling in him with all the force of a snow-melt mountain stream. Gushing and tumbling, going this way then that.

For a while, Ragnall had stood close to the door. He had politely offered her wine also, but she had, as politely, declined. He had attempted to persuade her to sit, but adamantly she had remained standing. For perhaps half of one hour they stayed in their chosen positions, with no sound passing, save the crackle of the fire and the revelry beyond that shut door.

It was Ragnall who moved first. Although she was nervous, frightened of the future, of what tomorrow would bring, she had to put an end to this unbearable silence.

Cadwy looked up to see her kneeling before him, her head bent, veil tipping forward to hide all her face. He wanted to reach out, touch her, show her that she had no need to be feared of him, but he could not. He did not have the courage or the boldness. Did not know where, or how to begin.

'Am I so displeasing to you?' she quivered. 'If,' her voice was little more than a tremulous whisper, 'if we were to extinguish the lamps, my disfigurement would be hidden from you.'

Ashamed of himself, inwardly cursing his rudeness and lack of thought by ignoring her for so long, Cadwy tipped her face up to him, his fingers gentle under her chin. With his other hand, he slid the restricting silk veil from her head. Her disfigured side was away from the fire, blurred in shadow, and the side of her face that was lit showed her to be a young woman who could easily, were it not for misfortune, have been handsome.

'Na,' he said, 'I like you as you are; the flicker of lamp and fire light strikes pleasing colours in your hair.' He surprised himself, it was no idle

115

comment, for it was true. She had black, raven hair, which shimmered like the polished jet beads of a woman's ear-rings or necklace. He toyed for a while with a strand, sliding its softness between his fingers, then ran them down the smooth skin of her cheek, soft and supple beneath his touch. 'You are not displeasing,' he said, with truth on his lips. He sighed, 'Yet, I must be a disappointment to you.' Forcing a self-mocking laugh, he indicated his twisted leg. Her response was immediate, defensive.

'Not so, my lord!' She blushed, lowered her eyes from his. 'I find you most,' she hesitated, risked a quick glance at him, 'most pleasing.'

A surge of hope coursed through Cadwy, hope and pleasure, the despondency and doubts beginning to waver. Something Gwenhwyfar had said at Yns Witrin, that day when they were baying for Ragnall to die, came suddenly back to his mind. So deep wallowed was he in his present despair, that he had forgotten it until now. 'You are both most suited,' she had said.

Aye, they were! They were indeed! He snorted laughter, took Ragnall's hands in his, leant forward and attempted a tentative kiss. She responded, eager, with no fear or sign of revulsion. His second kiss lingered, and he found his hands to be going tighter around her, wandering, more intimate.

Breathless, flushed, they broke apart as a bellow of laughter sounded from beyond the door, as someone heavy of build crashed against it. Their faces turned together, alarmed, embarrassed, but there came nothing more, save loud voices, jesting with each other. The new-married couple, it seemed, had become forgotten.

'What a pair we are!' Cadwy smiled. 'Each of us uncertain of our appearance to the other. We both know full well,' he tossed his head over his shoulder, jerking a look at the door, 'what they think of us. Need we question ourselves also? Even if we are fools about all else, we at least know how painful those sneering glances and barely whispered comments are.'

Ragnall's answer was spoken with the tears thick in her voice. 'If it would please you,' she offered, 'I can wear my veil full over my face while in public. I will not shame you.'

Incredulous, Cadwy rose to his feet, pulling her up with him. How could she think so ill of him? 'I am not ashamed of you!' he protested hotly. 'Indeed, I have a pride in you, pride for your courage and determination! Your voice has such a sweet sound, your goodness is as obvious as winter berries on the holly tree. I would not hide you from the world! Why, your . . .'

But Ragnall, blushing at this sudden outpouring, put her fingers to his lips, stopping him from talking. No one, save for Gwenhwyfar, had cared

116

to speak so kindly to her. 'I am not used to such compliments,' she declared. 'More of this and my head will be turned!' Confused, and more than a little embarrassed, she moved away from him, steadying her quick breathing, taking time for her hot face to cool. For want of something to do with her hands, she took up the jug of wine, refilled his goblet.

She tried again to sort some form of sense from this whirl of inexplicable madness. 'If it is my voice that pleases you so much, I can wear my veil when I am alone with you, so that my disfigurement shall not spoil your pleasure.'

'There is no need . . .' Cadwy began, and she crumped to her knees, sinking down to the rushes, where she squatted, hunched, miserable and shaking, weeping. His run was hobbled, but urgent. He hunkered next to her, took her, cradling her into his arms, again and again asking with desperation what was wrong. What had he said to so upset her?

At last she managed to control herself, to ease the sobbing, to gulp a few words. 'Do I try to hide this ugliness from your dear eyes, or from the discomfort of others who sneer and talk behind your back? I know not what to do! Know not which way to please you.'

He was confused. Why this anxiety, this distress? Please him? She already pleased him. 'Be beautiful for me then.'

She bit her lip, astonished, a little hurt. 'Then others will sneer and talk. They will say, "Look at the hag Cadwy has taken as wife!" '

Cadwy countered, 'Then wear your veil in public.'

Her expression of horror deepened, she caught her breath, exclaimed, 'You, then, cannot bear for them to see me thus? I knew it!' And she rushed to her feet, scuttled to where her veil had fallen, retrieved it and fastened it, with trembling hands, to hide her face as well it could.

As quickly, for all his lameness, Cadwy was at her side, removing it again. 'Truly, I am not concerned over your looks. What you are is within you, not shaped outwardly on the parts that we all see.' He smoothed her ruffled hair, smiled warmly at her. 'Wear your veil as you see fit, when and where it pleases *you*. Where it helps you feel comfortable, at ease, with me or in the public eye. I care not, for I care only for you, Ragnall, for you.'

He kissed her again, and took her, before she could protest, to the bed that was Gwenhwyfar's and Arthur's. Claimed her for his wife, to prove to her, that, truly, it was not her appearance that mattered, not to him. That it was what you did together, as man and wife, that counted. She was so trusting, so truly innocent – and blithely unaware of his possible inability as a husband. Other women may have sneered or mocked, but not she.

It was Ragnall who needed the confidence, the kindness and

understanding of a man for a woman, and incredibly, to his immense joy, Cadwy discovered for himself that a lame leg made no difference to the ability of his manhood.

For Ragnall, the night brought a swathe of emotion and pleasures that never would she have dreamt of experiencing. And greater was the sheer, utter delight, for the first time in her life, of being informed that she could have choice. She was free to choose for herself what she did, when and how.

For any woman, but especially for Ragnall who had been ordered by the whims of others, the greatest desire, the keenest pleasure was to have her own mind.

§ XXXVIII

At the rustle of silk and waft of expensive perfume, Gwenhwyfar turned her head to see Winifred seating herself. She made no gesture of welcome, but equally no protest at the uninvited intrusion. For a while they sat in silence, surveying the dancing, that whirl of activity circling and cavorting along the centre of the Hall. Each electrically aware of, and steadfastly ignoring, the other.

'That was neatly done, the diversion from the unpleasant necessity of bedding the marriage couple.'

Gwenhwyfar inclined her head in acknowledgement. Made no answer however.

'You are full recovered to health now then, my dear?' Winifred enquired, her voice light, pleasant, seemingly genuinely interested.

'Quite recovered, I thank you.' Gwenhwyfar's retort was shorter-breathed, sharper. She had no wish for conversation with this woman.

Winifred persisted. 'Your daughter? She is well also?' Craning her neck to search around the crowded Hall, added, 'I see her not here.'

'Most well.' Archfedd was outside with the children of her own age, being too young to mingle with such honourable company. As Winifred well knew.

'There are fine numbers here, some many notable people.'

There seemed no point in answering. Gwenhwyfar kept her counsel, forced down a scathing retort.

'Though I see there are as many missing. Geraint of Dumnonia for one.'

Blood of the Bull, but this woman could be insufferable! Those not attending were Arthur's most vehement opposers, and for each of those, twice as many supporters were here. Geraint, the exception. 'A first child is about to be born to his wife,' Gwenhwyfar retorted, although she saw no need for explanation.

Another long, silent pause. The noise of excitement was rising, the drinking taking precedence over most other entertainments.

'You have not heard when Arthur plans to return?'

'Soon,' was the terse answer.

Winifred chuckled, dipped her head meaningfully in Ambrosius's direction. 'Ah, but is *soon* not already too late?' She patted her gown straight, smoothing a few creases. In public she wore the plain black of a Christian woman, but even this was of fine-spun, softest wool, worn with a gossamer-soft silk veil to cover her sun-gold hair. 'Will he be happy to leave his whore behind, do you think? Or will he bring her back with him, secrete her away somewhere?' Winifred had the ability to offend while wearing such a pleasant, friendly smile.

'If you are hoping to goad me into anger, Winifred, you had best try a different tactic. I know of Mathild. From Arthur himself.' Aye, Gwenhwyfar was jealous of the fact, but she was practical. No man such as the Pendragon could be expected to pass this length of time without the company of a woman.

'And do you know that Euric was, according to my last received communication, moving northward? That, very likely, the two armies have, by now, met?' She could see, by Gwenhwyfar's quick, indrawn breath and sudden paling skin, that this was, indeed, unknown news.

Mastering her composure, Gwenhwyfar countered the woman's smug gloat, her words coming in a rush of protest. 'There has been no exchange of communication these past many weeks. I understand the sea-crossing is made fierce by strong winds.' *Nor do we know for certain where my husband encamps, I have no knowledge that my latest letters have reached him.* But that she had no intention of admitting or confiding.

Satisfied at achieving the reward of reaction, Winifred began the thrust of her second blow. She folded her hands onto her lap, deliberately took time before expanding her information. 'The Saex pirates, as they are still insultingly termed, have little fear of these high, summer winds at sea. Their longships handle well under any condition. For the right price.' She applauded an acrobat who had performed some incredible contortion routine within a small space at the side of the Hall, her praising hands clapping politely, joining other, more exuberant delight. 'I, my dear, have always made it policy to pay more than what is right.' Turning her head towards Gwenhwyfar, her condescending smile was as rancid as stale cheese. 'The reward far outdistances the commitment.'

Tartly, Gwenhwyfar sniped, 'I have no fear for Arthur. He is a capable war-lord, has the best men with him.'

Indulgent, Winifred nodded agreement, infuriatingly patted Gwenhwyfar's hand. 'I agree with what you say, but even the best will not be sufficient against five, happen six times his number.'

Sharply removing her hand, Gwenhwyfar made to rise, thought better of the action, remained seated. Her response was curt. 'My Lord Pendragon does not fight alone. Syagrius is to . . .'

Winifred interrupted with an amused laugh. She came, gracious and with dignity to her feet. 'Syagrius? Oh my dear, you ought use Saxon messengers. Have you not heard that news either?'

Blankly, Gwenhwyfar stared at the odious woman. The question was rhetorical, for Winifred, starting already to walk away, tossed the answer over her shoulder. 'Syagrius marched only as far as Letetia.' She halted, turned her head to regard the Pendragon's second-taken wife, to observe how pale her cheeks had turned, how wide her eyes, how fast her breathing. 'He dismissed his army. Went home.' She feigned shock, her hand going to her chest. 'My dear, were you not aware that the Pendragon is to fight alone?' She walked away, but her words trailed after her, through the noise and laughter of celebration. 'I happen to know that Euric of the Visigoths follows my policy of paying high to ensure his success. I could tell you how much he has paid Syagrius if you were enough interested.' She beckoned to a slave. 'Take wine to Lady Gwenhwyfar. I believe she is a little unwell.'

§ XXXIX

Restless night, the long darkness before a battle. It always seemed so very long, as if the stars hung there in the sky, paused, breath held, their timeless dance suspended, quiet, and unmoving. The waiting, the reluctance – the anticipation – of what would come on the morrow, at this place called Vicus Dolensis.

The horses grazed or dozed, fidgeting, their ears flicking, legs shifting, sensing the underlying tension of the men, few of whom slept. Gathered around the hearth fires, men squatted, checking war-gear for loose stitching, blunt edging, cracks, breaks. Others lay huddled, curled beneath their cloaks, dozing from one anxious dream to another. Many sat, putting an extra edge to the blade of sword or dagger or axe, exchanging tales of past battles and brave heroes; of women loved and women lost. Some kept their council, caressing the treasured memories of the past, regretting a future unfulfilled.

. Always Arthur walked through the encampment on the night before battle. It pleased the men, gave heart to those in doubt or wrestling against fears, cheered the old campaigners, gave chance to exchange shared laughter or give comfort or courage. But who was there this night to prop the sagging weight of his own heavy heart? Who was there to talk to him, to give an encouraging smile, a friendly slap to the shoulder or a hand-clasp of faith? Who was there to hold close, to caress, to touch, to give and receive love? That especial love that could only leap between a man and his wife. The wife he mourned.

Arthur stood to the edge of the camp, aware the watch-guard was uneasy at his presence so near to the danger of the unprotected dark. The trees here, covering the higher ground that sloped down to the vast stretch of flat land below, were tall, straight, and thick-shadowed beneath the moon. He could so easily take two, three paces and be lost within their sheltering darkness. He could slip away, now, be many miles gone by dawn. No doubt that there were already a few – huh, on an uneasy night such as this, more like many – who had already done so. Had slid quiet away, to hide, to wait, watch, for a few hours, then disappear, go home.

If he, Arthur, were to go, would there then be a fight on the morrow? Or would the men talk between themselves, lay down their weapons and ride away? Would Euric the Goth accept that inglorious way of winning?

Before, there had always been some point, some reason, for the fighting. Honour; to control the land; to retain or gain what was his by rights. To fight for revenge or power, or glory, or gain . . . whatever, there was always a reason. What reason was there for this? Gaul was not his country, most of these men sitting anxious around their fires waiting for a dawn that they did not want to arrive, were not his men. This was not his fight, his problem. Why in all the gods' names had he not turned around months past and simply gone home?

Pulling a thin branch off the nearest tree, Arthur absent-mindedly shredded it of its leaves between his fingers. Why? Gods! How those damn questions trundled around and around in his brain!

Why had he come? Why had he stayed? Why did Gwenhwyfar have to die!

His throat was dry and taut, his chest hurt from the tight, choked breathing that clutched like a clenched fist at his lungs. Arthur bit his lip, threw the mangled branch from his hand. He wanted to shout, scream, roar his anger, let loose his great grief. Started as a dead branch cracked, loud in the stillness, not four paces from him.

'Mithras, Bedwyr,' he laughed, shaken, 'you nigh on set me leaping like a frightened deer!'

Bedwyr stepped forward, his white teeth glistening behind his wide smile. 'Thought I might find you out here.' He stood next to his cousin, looked out into the darkness of the trees a moment. He had been searching for Arthur this past hour – had understood the need for solitude once he realized where Arthur had gone. 'I know I have said this before, Arthur, but I must say it again – she may not be dead. That messenger only said . . .'

The Pendragon swung irritably away. 'I bloody know what that messenger said! She was ill, was not expected to last the night through. Damn it, man!' He faced Bedwyr again, fists bunched, body rigid, so wanting to hit out, to punch someone, something. Release the anger of loosing her, of not being with her. Of being here instead. 'If she had survived, do you not think I would have heard?'

Lifting his hands in protest, Bedwyr was about to express a contradiction, sighed, let them drop again to his side. They had travelled this path before, what use to say again that aye, Arthur might be right, but equally they had heard no further message confirming the first. Had heard nothing of Britain since that grey-faced youth had brought them such immeasurable sadness.

'I came to say that our officers await you for final orders. Do we move down onto the plains, come dawn, meet Euric as we planned?'

Arthur nodded, realized Bedwyr would not see his slight movement in the dark. 'Aye. We will make this a fight to be remembered. One way or the other.'

There was a reason behind the fighting that was sure to be bitter and bloody, come sunrise. It would be good to release all that stored anger and frustration. Good for all of them, not just for Arthur alone.

And then, after this thing was finished, those who could would go home without any shadow of shame or regret clinging to their shoulders. Those who wanted to go home.

Those who had something – someone – worth going home to.

§ XL

Vicus Dolensis. This was marsh; stretching as far as the horizon, a flatness, oozing runnels of bog-bound, shallow river and sluggish, stream-laced, marsh. Unsuited to cavalry, ground that Arthur would have avoided if given choice. The decision had not been his to make. Three hours past, the site of this battle had been in Arthur's hands; three hours past, his cavalry had been drawn up almost two miles northward, where the ground was firm, suited for horse.

The two armies had met, fought. The Goths, thousands of men, skirmishing half-heartedly, their slow, backward pacing unnoticed at first, unforeseen. For all his experience and gift for fighting, Arthur could not oversee a whole battlefield, not when the enemy had so many men dispersed. Steadily, the Goths had drawn Arthur's cavalry forward. No choice, once the strategy was realized, but to follow, to go with them, trying, struggling, to break that slow step, back pace. Knowing that the marshes, the vastness of this water-bellied wilderness, lay behind Euric's men. Marshland, where infantry could fight well on foot, where horses would be next to useless.

Arthur had never, save once, fought within marsh without it being him to choose the ground, him to call the tune. That once had been his first fight, long, long past, when he was a raw youth in service to King Vortigern. He had learnt since then. Learnt never to trust the treachery of marsh and bog, unless it suited his tactics. And this day, this long, sun-scorching day, it did not suit him at all. It fitted well for Euric, and it was he, it seemed, who paid the harper this day.

And the Pendragon seemed almost not to care, but pressed forward, recklessly trying to outmanoeuvre the enemy. The alternative was to turn and run like whipped dogs – and that, Arthur could not, would not do. The Artoriani had never retreated, save as planned strategy. To fall back now would be their certain end, for already their numbers were dwindling, the horses tiring. To retreat would be the end of them all. Huh! Was it not the end anyway? But it was one thing to finish with honour, quite another with the defeat of shame.

Not half of one mile to the east, the waders and waterfowl went unconcerned about their business of feeding. The geese, honking and clamouring their annoyance, had taken flight in great skeins when one wing of Arthur's cavalry, led by Ecdicius the Gaul, had swung about in a brave attempt to cut any further backward movement of Euric's damned hoard. They had circled, the geese, screaming protest, only to land further off, to begin again their preoccupied flat-footed dabbling among the wind-teased, whispering reeds and water grasses.

The sun was high, a bright, glaring ball against the vivid, heated blue of a cloudless sky that swept as endless as the marshes into the distance. Since sunrise had the battle flurried, swaying back and forth, like the relentless sweep of the tide. Two armies intent on savagery. Kill or be killed. With nothing, no compromise, in between. So many already dead. Among the first, Meriaun, Gwenhwyfar's nephew.

Arthur's horse floundered. He was a good stallion, a dark, polished-elm bay, with bold eye and deep chest. A good horse, yet the Pendragon would rather have had Onager beneath him; that bad-tempered, unpredictable bugger of a chestnut. Onager, who could fight with teeth and heel as bravely and efficiently as any soldier. A second time, the bay's legs went from beneath him, and this time he went down, his hooves skidding in the churned ooze of mud. Arthur grabbed for the mane, saw, too late, an axe scything down, rolled desperately, felt the whish of air as it thudded past, taking the bay's head from its neck in the one, savage, blow.

On one knee, the gush of horse-blood spouting, the mud thick and squelching, Arthur raised his shield, deflected a second blow, though the pain from a sword-slash that had lain open his arm from shoulder to wrist was ramming like a ballista bolt. He knew, knew, that this was the end. And he did not care. He thought he would have minded when the end came. Minded losing, dying.

Already he was bleeding from too many wounds to count, from shoulder, arm and thigh. One more blow from that axe to his shield and surely his arm would shatter as thoroughly as the wood. One more blow from that axe . . .

The axe did not come for a sword was swinging from behind, the bloodied, dulled, blade forcing through the air . . .

The end. Arthur never knew the end of that battle, for it came from behind. Unseen, unfelt. A great exploding end, of sudden pain across his shoulder, down his back, a stunned nothingness that turned, slowly, slowly, from red to black. Empty.

PART TWO

The Empty Loom

§ I

'Oh Christ! Christ Jesu!' Over and over, with struggling, tortured breath, Bedwyr repeated the oath, with every stumbling, exhausted step; he fell, staggered again to his feet, pushed on, willing his trembling, aching, legs to move; dragging his precious burden. 'Christ, Jesu Christ!'

The trees were no more than fifty yards distant now, only fifty yards, and the ground was beginning to rise sharply. They were clearing the feet-cloying, mud-sucking pull of the marsh – yet it could have been one hundred and fifty, one thousand and fifty. Fifty yards, fifty yards too far!

Like a child ineffectually swiping with a wooden toy, Bedwyr menacingly waved his sword at a Goth approaching too near, his accompanying snarl producing some little effect, although it was Mabon, striking out using the King's own great sword, that drove him back.

Illtud came forward, stumbling, as tired and bloodied as the others. He could barely walk himself, yet he bent, took hold of the Pendragon, helped Bedwyr carry the muddied and bloodied body. It had been Illtud who had seen the King fall, Illtud who had screamed for help, had, in a flood of anguish and fear grabbed at the King's own sword and thrust it into the guts of the man who had felled the Pendragon. Illtud who had then pulled his King's body clear of the fighting with the aid of these last few standing men; Illtud who had thought, in that last moment, to clutch up the ragged, stained, Dragon Banner. He wore it, tied ignobly around his waist, where it draped like a battered beggar's cloak. The sword he had passed to Mabon. For all his greater age, he was the better swordsman.

Fifty yards. Fifty yards of firmer ground, but it was the solid ground of an incline, an incline that would be as nothing to fresh, alert men, but this small group trying their best to take their King from the field of battle was nearing the limit of endurance. They had been more, for they had rallied to Illtud's cry for help, but steadily their numbers had been cut down, falling to the axe or sword or exhaustion. If you fell, it was unlikely that you would get up again . . . Fifty yards. Their one hope that the Goths too were spent, as weary, as bloodied and drained. Doggedly they pursued, but few were coming nearer now, only the occasional one who found some small reserve of strength, and the British were proving a match with their cussed perseverance. For the British were determined that Euric would not have the body of the Pendragon.

Bedwyr, gasping for some extra, unfound strength, forced himself up the hill of rough, tussocked grass. He caught Illtud's grim expression, a young officer who had served well these past three years within the Artoriani. Sweat beaded through the spatter of blood and marsh-mud; mouth open, a face masked with pain and distress. His own, Bedwyr knew, must mirror the same grim image. He looked down, closed his eyes, not wanting to see the awfulness of what had been Arthur, his beloved cousin, his lord and King. The matted hair, grey skin, bruised and bloodied. The last thing they could do for him, the last loyal thing. Give him a peaceful burial. Christ Jesu alone knew what Euric would do to a defeated king's body ... and he might not be dead. There was some small, desperate hope that Arthur was yet alive, though the pallor and stillness shrieked otherwise, and if those terrible wounds had not slain him, then surely this inglorious hauling and dragging to a place of safety would finish what the Goths had initiated. 'Christ Jesu,' Bedwyr prayed again, 'let him still live, let this not be all in vain!'

'Amen,' gasped Illtud, staring stoically ahead. Bedwyr had been unaware that he had spoken aloud. Happen he had not, happen Illtud had been mouthing the same despairing prayer.

Swallowing vomit that threatened to rise, Bedwyr turned his thoughts to concentrating on tackling this incline. One step, another, and another. Once they reached the protective safety of those trees, and night came ... another step. One foot, the other foot.

Behind, littered across this northern end of the stretching marshes, lay the dead and dying, men and horses. The horses. The Artoriani's fine horses, all gone, dead, butchered by the Goths. The only way that infantry might succeed over cavalry: be rid of the horses.

Forty yards. Small groups still fought, desperate and exhausted, their blows slow and clumsy, unable to let go, to end this thing, the madness too strong, too powerful to release them into sanity, save through the ultimate finality. Darkness would bring an ending, but few British would crawl from the mess of that battlefield, the place of slaughter. Up on that slight incline, the small group moved closer, each supporting the other, Bedwyr, Illtud, old Mabon. Two Decurions, several unranked Artoriani. Save for those few who might live long enough to be protected by the hand of darkness, all that was left of the Artoriani.

Thirty yards.

Bedwyr glanced ahead, caught his wheezing breath with a groan of disbelief, of wretched despair. Saxons, well-armed, tall, fair-haired Saxons, ten and five of them, running, war-cry screaming, axes swinging above their heads, coming from the shadow of the trees, from where it was thought to be safe. Despairing, the British closed ranks, Mabon coming to the fore, his legs planted, sword raised. They would all die, here, now, rather than let the enemy take their King. But it was the Goths who fled, who faltered, dropped their weapons and ran with cries of alarm, scuttling for the marsh and the comforting shield of their comrades.

Euric had lied to his men yester-eve, as he talked to them of this fight. Their superior numbers, he had told them, would bring an easy victory. By the mid of the day, he had boasted, they would be roasting meat and drinking fine wine in celebration. He had said nothing of the British discipline, the British strength and courage. Said nothing of the terror of those horses. If they had not managed to reach the advantageous ground of the marshes in dignified retreat, if they had not felt so acutely the cowardliness of turning and running ... Ah, but Arthur would never know that Euric had not planned that as strategy, that it was pure chance – and fear – that had taken his men backwards towards those treacherous marshes. Euric was not a man who studied strategy or cunning. He was no great warrior, no great leader. But he had the luck of the devil, and he had more, many more, men.

Incredibly, the Saxons divided, raced past the braced, upright huddle of British, swept down the incline, like hounds chasing a scatter of rats, and two women were coming, running, kirtles hitched to the knees. One Bedwyr recognized, knew. He closed his eyes, willed the strength to stay in his knees, but they buckled, he fell forward. Illtud too, he saw, was kneeling, and a few of the others.

Mathild, tears streaming her face, put her hand under his arm, urged him to his feet. 'We must go, my lord, my small guard will not hold them for long.' She kept her eyes from the one laying on the ground, from the man who had lain and loved with her. The other woman, though, had gone to him, her tears also falling, her black hair tumbling forward to hide the paleness of her skin. Bedwyr had never seen her before, knew not who she was, but obviously she knew Arthur, for she spoke his name, took the coldness of his hand into hers. Wept for him.

The Saxons were coming back, trotting up the hill. The Saxons whom Arthur had freed, the men who had been taken into slavery by the Gauls, given back their dignity and courage by the British King, given weapons and armour in return for their sworn oath to protect Mathild of the Elbe, and return her to her own kind. For at least a while they would not be harried.

'Come,' Mathild ordered, 'They may yet be after us again. Let us be gone.' She was capable, firm-minded, not one of the men thought to do aught else but obey. Two of her Saxons lifted the Pendragon and those last few yards, that distance that had seemed so great before, was covered in a matter of moments.

It was over. The killing was over. Now the result was about to begin.

§ II

They marched for two hours, the British exhausted, passing through the threshold of pain, following without question where the Saxons led. It was dark beneath the canopy of trees, but they had reached a wide, slow-flowing, shallow river and turned along the path that ran parallel with its course. The Indre, Mathild told them, it would take them to safer territory. They did not question her, for they cared little for anything beyond the immediate necessity to place one foot before the other.

The other woman walked beside the two Saxons who carried between them the Pendragon. She had spoken three words only, 'I am Morgaine', but this meant nothing to Bedwyr or his companions. Only Mabon thought he had once heard the name, but with mind fogged and so utterly tired, he had no strength to pursue the thought of questioning further. She walked in silence, in her arms a boy, of little more than three years of age, his thumb stuffed in his mouth, his wide, frightened eyes staring and staring at the man they said was dead. Arthur would have known her, for her son was his son, she it was who had once had the title of Lady, who had lived serving the Goddess by the Lake of Yns Witrin. But that was a while and a while ago. She was only Morgaine now. Morgaine the Healer. And Arthur was dead.

Mathild spoke briefly to Bedwyr, though his body was too tired and his mind too dazed to listen with care. 'I came back to watch,' she explained, 'though Arthur's orders were that I was to go, put as many miles of safety as possible between us.' She glanced ahead, at the Saxons carrying, as reverently as if they were carrying a god, her beloved lord. 'I could not go without seeing this thing finished. Not after the sharing of so much, with one so – ' Her words faltered, choked. 'So kind to me.' She mastered the tears, for Bedwyr's sake as well as her own. Were one to break, they would all crumble. This forced pace, the matter-of-fact passing of information was nothing but a shield, a wall to shelter behind. Keep the anguish and despair caged, tight-reined. Once out, it would run like wildfire fanned before a summer wind. 'I wish now,' she said candidly, 'that I had not come back, yet if I had not . . .' She did not finish. No point in saying that which Bedwyr would know for himself.

'She was there, among the trees. We met by chance.' Mathild indicated Morgaine, but said no more. They had shared but few words, the two women, while watching with growing horror the killing below that incline, spread before them out along the edge of the marsh. But those few words were enough, enough to convey that they watched for the same man, enough to cling together for support and comfort when they saw the Dragon Banner cut down, knew one of those men dying nearby to be the man they both loved.

Neither of them, Mathild knew, would ever forget this day.

'We will stop soon,' she announced, 'when my men think it safe to do so.' She trusted these men, men who, before they were taken into the indignity of slavery, had been acclaimed warriors, skilled soldiers, who had fought beneath the command of the Saxon leader, Odovacer – for two of them, beneath her own husband. Arthur had been no fool when he accepted such slaves into his army. Had been no fool when he had given them their freedom, weapons and armour, demanding nothing in return save their sworn oath of loyalty to Mathild, Lady of the Elbe. An oath not truly required, for they were her people, her blood.

'Get her home,' he had ordered that last evening, 'whatever the gods bring for me against Euric, get the lady home to her land along the Elbe.'

'Soon,' she said again, 'we will halt. And do what has to be done.'

§ III

They walked until it was too dark to see where they put their feet. The farm-steading was a lowly place, a barn, a few dung-stinking cattle pens, a round, wattle-built dwelling. The man of the steading had come out at their arrival, looking them over suspiciously, nose wrinkled, axe solid in his hand. Reluctantly, he agreed to allow them to build a fire, rest a while. He would not let them inside his house-place, a snarl and his back turning as he stumped away from them, his decided answer on Mathild's polite asking.

'Please,' she begged, running after him, 'at least grant shelter for our wounded.'

'You be nothing to do with me or my kin, neither you nor them soldiers. Your fight t'ain't naught to do wi' me. Use my field to rest in, but be you gone by mornin'.'

The door to the house-place had been open, and as he shambled through into the dim-lit interior, Mathild had an impression of children watching, and a woman gathering them inside as her man entered. The door was shut firm, the poor, ragged family on one side, the last remnants of Arthur's once-proud Artoriani on the other.

The fire they had built was small, but enough to heat a few, rough-made oatcakes. Barely enough for tired men, but better than an empty belly. The flames gave only dim light. Morgaine saw as best she could to

Arthur, cleaning away some of the grime and blood, tending him with the love that she had felt for him since the days of early childhood, when he had been the first, the only other being to smile with warmth at her. Her boy was curled asleep, with a cloak wrapped snug around him, his back firm against the solidity of a tree.

Only Mathild heard the other woman's low intake of breath, followed by a quick, flurried movement. Alerted, she observed Morgaine a moment, saw her hands lay still over the place where the heart should beat, saw her fingers move to where the rhythm of blood should pulse within the neck. Watched as Morgaine put her cheek to Arthur's blue-tinged lips.

Unhurried, Mathild licked oat crumbs from her fingers, stood, wandered towards Morgaine, as if to offer assistance. No one followed her, not even with their eyes. The British were too tired, heads drooping, most already sleeping where they sat. The Saxons, the few that were not sent to scout behind for signs of being followed, too busy with the sharing of the only wine skin.

Mathild squatted opposite Morgaine, boldly put her own fingers to the naked skin of Arthur's chest, felt nothing. Searched for the beat in his neck and put her cheek to his lips, as Morgaine had. Sat back on her heels, each woman looking direct, challenging, into the eyes of the other.

Morgaine looked away first, her eyes flicking, briefly, to Arthur's sunken face, before going back again to Mathild. 'He lives,' she said, 'but it will not be for long, for in this darkness I know not what damage has been done. I cannot heal what I cannot see.'

'A few hours, and it will be light.'

Morgaine shrugged, said nothing. A few hours? It might be too late in a few hours. Yet he had clung, somehow, and if only by the most slender, fragile of threads to life thus far.

Running, boots scuffling fast. The Saxons around the fire were on their feet, weapons drawn, and for all their tiredness, the British were not far behind them.

The women stood, Morgaine moving swiftly to her sleeping boy. The relief showing clear when their own kind came into the small clearing, the Saxons sent behind as scouts. The relief lingering momentarily only, for the news was bad.

'We are being followed. Thirty, mayhap forty men.'

A few flurried questions. Were they sure? Was that possible, in the dark? How far behind were they? Immaterial questions, for already Mabon was kicking earth and turf over the fire, already they were gathering cloaks tighter, collecting possessions and weapons, preparing to move out.

With a despair that Bedwyr thought could become no deeper, he looked at the body of Arthur. Morgaine had lain him out, had half-covered him with the banner, his Dragon Banner. 'Have we time', he enquired, 'to bury him?'

The Saxons looked from one to another. They had not, but they could not leave the Pendragon, nor could they make much speed with taking him.

'I will see to him,' Morgaine said. 'I will hide with him and my son in the darkness until they have gone by, then I will see to his grave.'

Bedwyr, the Decurions and Illtud were all for protesting, but Mabon silenced them with a rough growl. ''Tis sense. We can do no more for him. 'Tis our duty now to head our eyes for Britain, take word of this bad day home.' He shook his head. An unwelcome but necessary task.

Still they were for protesting, but it was useless argument. They each, in turn, bid their farewells to their King, Illtud taking the bloodied and torn banner. The Dragon Banner, Arthur's. Mabon had given Bedwyr the sword, the great sword that Arthur had taken in battle from a Saxon, and as he stood by the man he had once called lord, Bedwyr held that sword before him. 'I will take this,' he said, 'but I would with all my heart that there was one worthy to use it as you have used it.' He swung away, trudged after the others, already beyond the clearing.

Mathild kept her counsel. She saw no reason to tell them that Arthur was not, yet, quite dead. For if she did, they would insist on staying, or carrying him again. And either option, she guessed, would bring his end. And theirs.

She hoped only the one thing. That, should the gods grant him their favour, and if by some great miracle he should survive, she hoped that some day, if it were not possible for him to do so himself, that the woman Morgaine would send word of it.

October 469

§ IV

Gwenhwyfar was playing with Archfedd. She was a happy child, full of giggles and smiles; enjoyed, as much as her mother, this shared, especial moment before she was taken to her bed. Beyond the solid walls of the chamber, the wind howled around the height of Caer Cadan. Occasionally, the hearth-fire and braziers would flicker as a tendril of the outside rage found its way through a gap or crack, then the colourful tapestries that graced the walls would lift also, flap weakly. Neither mother nor child noticed. They were safe and warm, cocooned in this, their place, their home.

The door opened, not unexpected, allowing in a rush of cold air, a gust of power that ruffled everything within. Gwenhwyfar did not look up or round, for her back was to the door, but Archfedd pulled her favourite wooden doll closer, her eyes widening, mouth shaping into a silent 'oh'.

The door was shut, thudding closed, shutting out the anger of the night. Feet shuffled, the damp smell of rain on woollen cloaks, hair and skin. A cough. The unmistakable presence of men.

Gwenhwyfar swivelled around, Archfedd's other doll in her hand, not worrying to rise, expecting the newcomer to be Ider, or another officer. Her face paled, eyebrows furrowed. Slowly, she stood up, the doll falling, forgotten, to lay face down among the scattered floor rushes. Her eyes told her what she saw, but her mind was numb, silent and dark. No one spoke, there came only the sound of the wind and the vivid crackle of logs burning in the fire.

There were three men. Three men, wind-tousled and rain-wet, two of whom Gwenhwyfar would never have expected to enter her private chamber unannounced. Her eyes roved from one to the other – questions poised, stuck like a bone in her throat – rested on the third man, tall, square-chinned, dark-haired and eyed. Dark, sad, tired, red-rimmed eyes.

'Bedwyr?' she whispered, almost afeard to utter the name aloud. 'Bedwyr? Why come you here? And with Ambrosius?' Her gaze flickered to the third man, knew him as an officer, Illtud. Found the same haggard, twisted look about his expression.

The door was behind them. Was it to open soon, was another man, a man so cherished, so loved, to come banging through at any moment? But it remained shut. No one else entered. And no one spoke or moved.

The three-year-old girl could sense something was wrong, this quietness was frightening. The three men, standing so still before the door, intimidating. She clutched her doll tighter to her chest, toddled to her mother's side, slid her pudgy hand between Gwenhwyfar's cold fingers, snuggled her small body against the comfort of her mother's leg. Gwenhwyfar was not even aware that she was there, for her eyes, her mind, was directed upon Bedwyr, upon the sword that he was holding in his hand.

Only one man had the honour of owning such a sword. It was unique, forged, so story told, by the gods and given to the world of mortals by the hand of the Goddess. Arthur's sword. Still her thoughts were unmoving, frozen, unable to bear to think upon the meaning of all this. Arthur's sword. Arthur.

She swallowed, her throat tight, constricted, the scream that was swelling in her stomach churning higher.

It was her eyes that asked the question. Bedwyr's brief, downward nod that answered.

She put the back of her hand to her mouth, did not notice the pain from her teeth, stuffing that scream away, back down. She shook her head, one slow, unaccepting movement, the one word coming, denying. 'No.'

'You have my deepest sorrow, madam. This news is not palatable to either of us.' Ambrosius felt awkward, knowing she would not believe him, but it was the truth. He had not expected it to be so – indeed had looked forward with anticipation to Arthur's death. The realities were always different to the thoughts of ambition and imaginings, though. Reality was so final. Held so much pain. You never remembered that in your thoughts and schemes for what might one day be.

Now that the silence had been broken, the men moved, came further inside. Bedwyr crossed the room to pour wine, Illtud going to the inner door, clutching up the little girl as he passed, lifting her with a high swing into his arms. She laughed. She recognized this man, from where or when she did not know, remembered only that he had played with her in the sun, swirling her around and around, like her father had used to do before he went away. Recollected, on that same thought, that they had gone away together. Happen they were returned together also?

'Will my Da be home soon?'

Illtud ruffled her hair, tucked her closer in his arms, made for the inner door that passed into the King's Hall. 'Na, lass. Na, he'll not be home.' What else could he say?

Illtud closed the door behind him, took her to find her nurse, to speak quietly to those in the Hall who pressed close to hear with ashen faces and tear-brimmed grief what he had to tell.

Gwenhwyfar acted with automation, taking the wine flagon from Bedwyr, offering the two remaining men fruit and nuts from the side table. She sat in her chair, her fingers fiddle-fiddling with her pewter tankard. Her eyes gazing at the sword, laying where Bedwyr had placed it, across the bed-furs. On the side where Arthur would have lain.

They sat a long while in silence. One of the dogs, Blaidd, who had been her eldest son's favourite hound, came from the warmth of the fire to nuzzle at her with his wet nose. Absently she fondled his silken ears, running her hand over his body. He had pined for the boy a long while after that killing, refusing to eat or settle, until one night when Gwenhwyfar had taken him out with her for a walk beneath the quiet of the stars. They had been up in the north then, where the rivers ran deeper and wider, had sat together, woman and dog, her arms clasped around the roughness of his neck, her head buried against his coat while the dawn rose. And they had come away with the grief lain to rest. But not buried, not forgotten.

'I would know what happened,' she said, breaking the stretching silence.

Bedwyr cleared his throat, spoke, telling all as it was, as if giving report. Telling all, knowing she would not want half-truth or delicate covering of the facts.

When he finished, she asked a question.

'And so you know not where he is buried.'

Bedwyr shook his head. No. 'It matters not. He is gone.'

Silence again. Bedwyr added wood to the fire. Poured more wine for himself. Gwenhwyfar had not tasted hers.

Then another question.

'It puzzles me. Happen I am tired, or confused.' Gwenhwyfar searched Bedwyr's strained, dark-lined face for a clue to her worry. Found none. Had to ask. 'Why did you go direct to Ambrosius? Not come here, to me, at Caer Cadan?'

Bedwyr hung his head, wiped his trembling hand around the stubble of his mouth and chin, trying to find the courage to answer her.

Ambrosius spoke for him. 'Bedwyr thought you to be dead. He knew of no one else to take the news to.'

She thought on this a moment. 'Dead?' she enquired, 'How so?'

'I sent a messenger to the Pendragon when you were ill, to inform him that we expected you not to recover.' Ambrosius felt the need to justify himself. 'You were so very ill. We none of us expected you to survive.'

Again she mulled this answer in her mind. 'But you sent again? Informing him of your mistake? And I sent letters to my husband, several, after I recovered.' She added with strained sadness, 'Though I received none in return'.

'Gwenhwyfar, we had none of these. No messenger, no letter, came. We knew nothing. Arthur was – ' Bedwyr hung his head, feeling awkward, stunned, heart-stricken with his own grief. His voice choked. 'Arthur was desolate.'

Gwenhwyfar rose, placed her untouched wine on a table, walked across the room, the dogs' and mens' eyes following her, expecting something, some outburst. Tears, anger, something other than this stiff, rigid silence.

Her cloak was draped over a stool, she took it up, walked for the door, clicked her fingers at the two dogs, who rose and padded beside her.

'I would walk a while,' she said. 'Sort my mind.'

She let herself out into the harsh weather. Neither of the men made attempt to stop her.

§ V

The unthinkable had happened. The Pendragon was gone, dead, with none to follow him. Ahead stretched a void of uncertainty and anxious fear for Britain.

Subdued, going about its business cloaked by a mantle of dark grief, Caer Cadan survived through the passing of the night and day; its women keening husbands or sons who would never return; the men, the Artoriani who had remained behind, nursing the loss of comrades, friends and brothers. They were numbed, desolate.

The wind had dropped, but the sky hung low and petulant over the autumn landscape of the Summer Land. Trees with leaves fluttering from their limp branches; dull, browned and faded grass; the winter waters already returning, over all, the cold swirl of grey. More rain was in the sky, threatening with the banks of cloud that rushed from the west, building behind the Tor that lunged from the Lake, that at this time of year had spilled and swelled over much of the flatness.

Only the messengers were busy, sent on the fastest horses to all who should know, by Ambrosius. Council was summoned for the next new moon, at his own stronghold of Ambrosium. It had to be. Someone must lead, someone must attempt to keep a steady course over the confusion and disquiet. And someone had to lay a hand on the rein that kept control over the Saex.

137

Ambrosius stood beyond the Hall, looking at, although not seeing, the height of the rampart walls. He had visited Caer Cadan on but a few occasions only. Each time had been impressed – though reluctant to admit it – by the unity of Arthur's men. Caer Cadan was a thriving community, the heart, the soul, the very being of Arthur's Britain, while he had been King. Yet now, suddenly, overnight, it too had died. Ambrosius could feel it, feel the limp emptiness that was the nothingness of a shell, a dying body. A month or two, some day after the winter solstice, there might well be nothing here save the abandoned buildings of what once had been.

Gwenhwyfar stood on the ramparts with her back to the Caer, gazing over the solitude of the Summer Land, her husband's land, hers now. Ambrosius would not take it from her, though he could allow her to keep only that which had belonged to Arthur as personal possession. The Summer Land, Dumnonia. The rest, Britain, was his.

If he could keep it.

A step behind, shuffling. He recognized the tap of a crutch, knew his son approached. Did not turn around.

'She has stood up there since dawn,' Ambrosius observed aloud, pointing with his finger to Gwenhwyfar. 'I hear she passed but a few hours within her chamber during the night. I doubt she slept.'

Cadwy made no answer.

'How fares the child? Does she understand much of what is happening?'

Shaking his head, Cadwy acknowledged that Archfedd did not. 'A child comprehends little at her age. I doubt she remembers much of her father.' He steadied his own breathing, added, 'It is for us, the adults, to come to terms with our disappointments and griefs.'

His father nodded. Aye, it was so. Suddenly, unexpectedly, he confided, 'I know not how I am to contain the Saex. Word will soon spread among them.' He opened his hands, palms uppermost, let them fall. 'Bad word always does, like mould in a barrel of badly stored fruit.' Aesc of the Cantii. Vitolinus. Until now, uncle and son had argued and fought as much between themselves as the younger had irritated and annoyed the British. That would change. There was reason to unite now. Now that Arthur was gone.

Then there was Aelle of the South Saxons and his three sons. Three years they had been settled along the coast near Noviomagus after that first fighting. Three years while they settled themselves firmer. Entrenched with the British while Arthur had been away moving further backward, further into the shadows of the Great Wood.

There was little that Cadwy could answer, for there was only the truth.

'The Saex will rise when they hear Arthur is dead. We can but hope that they are not as ready as we may fear. It may be a year, happen two, before we need fight them all at once.'

Astonished, Ambrosius regarded his son through narrowed eyes. 'All at once? You think the tribes of the Saex will unite together? Against us?'

Sadly, Cadwy shook his head, began to limp away in the direction of the small dwelling-place that was home for himself and Ragnall. 'Against Arthur's British? No, father, they would not. Against you? Aye, they would.' He trudged away, glancing once, as he walked, up at the ramparts where his father had been watching, up at Gwenhwyfar, standing bereft, alone. The Saex would unite against Ambrosius. Arthur they would never have beaten, for he had been a war-lord, the Pendragon. Ambrosius Aurelianus was of the same family, but he was no soldier, no fighter. Never would the honour of the title Pendragon be bestowed on him.

And that the Saex knew all too well.

§ VI

Bedwyr's boots scuffed on the wooden flooring as he ambled along the walkway. He frowned. Gwenhwyfar was alone, staring out into the emptiness of the landscape. He strolled to stand beside her, near enough to be a companion, not so close as to intrude. He folded his arms along the top rail; stood, much as she, gazing out into the world.

'We will have frosts early this year,' he said amiably.

'It will be a long winter.'

He rested his chin on his hands. 'I recall the first time I looked across and saw Yns Witrin under snow. A sparkling bright day it was. Great blue-black shadows stretched across the whiteness. Everything shimmered. You could see the shape of the Tor clearer, more bold against the snow.'

Gwenhwyfar made no answer this time, kept staring, staring out at nothing. He stole a glance at her. Saw a single tear slither, unchecked, down her cheek.

'The pain,' he said, 'never goes. But it does ease.'

'No,' she said after a while. 'It just becomes buried under a mountain of other pains.'

There was no comfort, no words, that he could offer. He needed them all for himself, although he had grown used to this thing. No, you could never become used to losing someone you loved. Bedwyr had loved

Arthur more than he had his own brother. When Cei had died, he had mourned, aye, and grieved, but for a while only. The forgetting had come easily there. But it would not be so for Arthur.

'As a boy, I worshipped Arthur,' he admitted. 'He was my god.' He bit his lip. Gods were supposed to be immortal. Gods did not die. His own tears were coming, trickling faster. 'At least, though, I have the one comfort.' He turned to her, instinctively opened his arms, 'At least I no longer mourn your loss also.' And she went to him, moving swiftly into his embrace, her face going into his shoulder, his hold tight, protective around her.

They stood together, the guard on patrol altering his routine walk, turning earlier, to step in measured pace back again along the walkway. His own few tears streaking his firm, wind-weathered face.

Bedwyr held her, as if she were sister, lover, queen and wife. She meant much to him, for as a boy he had laughed with her, and loved her. She had been his first love, the first to stir a lad's thoughts to the novelty of women. Whether she ever knew it, he was unsure. Probably she suspected, for he had followed her around like a faithful whelp all those months when she had lived with them in Less Britain. He snorted a single note of self-contempt, said to the sky, his chin resting on her head, 'I was so jealous when I discovered that it was my cousin, Arthur, who you loved, not me.'

She made no answer, but her hands, clasped around his strong body, squeezed harder. 'I was a lad, naive. I had no idea why you and he were always disappearing together. When, much later, I found out, I was so angry with him – but of course it was too late for me by then, you were already his wife.' He moved slightly, held her away from him to see into her eyes. Smiled at her. 'Mind, you'd not have had me in his stead. I was only ten and one years at the time!'

As he hoped, she returned the smile. She put her hand on his heart. 'You are a good man, Bedwyr. Happen, had you been older, I might have chosen you.'

'Really!'

Her smile widened slightly as she confessed, 'There are many who are dear to me, you are among the dearest. But' – she dropped her hand, turned away – 'but no one, no one ever will fill this cold, empty space left within me.'

'I do not think,' Bedwyr replied slowly, 'that anyone will ever be fool enough to try.'

Turning her head, she saw Ambrosius striding across the expanse of the parade ground that stretched before the main doors of the Hall, his purple cloak fluttering as he moved, preparing to leave. There was one man who would not grieve for Arthur for long. She ought go down, bid him farewell. Ought do many things, not stand up here, idling time by.

She watched Ambrosius mount his horse, move off. He looked up at her, saluted. She ought at least acknowledge him. Did not. Could not.

From up here, she could see the spread of the Caer, with its clutter of rectangular dwelling-places, stables, geese-, goat- and pigpens. The blacksmith's place, the tanner and the leatherworker, the small but efficient hospital, the chapel, kennels and the two enormous granary barns. An army settlement which extended beyond the defence walls, down the cobbled lane to the civilian buildings that had sprung up on the level ground below the great height of the stronghold. Down there were two taverns, a bakery, a potter, a jewel-smith, apothecary and a fuller.

What would happen to them now? Now that there were to be no more Artoriani?

'I suppose they will all eventually follow Ambrosius,' she said with sadness. 'There is nothing for them here, now.'

Bedwyr frowned, uncertain to what she alluded, but did not question her.

'And I?' she asked, 'Where shall I go?'

Spreading his hands, he indicated that he was not following her conversation. 'Caer Cadan is your home.'

'No.' She turned to smile at him, patient, half-indulgent. There was no sparkle in the expression. 'No, this was Arthur's place. There is too much of him here for me to stay.'

'All the more reason not to go. At Samhain, the night of the spirits, it is to here that he will come.'

She walked a few paces, heading for the stairway. Stopped. Said, 'He will never come back here. He has no reason to.' She choked on a sobbed breath, gathered her cloak tight between her white fingers. 'Do you not see? He searches for me in the other world. He does not know that I am not there in that world, that I am here, alive in this.'

§ VII

Mathild's plans had materialized with more ease than she could have envisioned. The Goddess of Fortune had most certainly smiled on her!

A succession of events had aided her intentions, as if everything were, indeed, meant to be. Wyrd, the Saxons called it. Fate.

First, as the touch of dawn was tingeing the eastern sky, they had found a small boat – flat-keeled, oared, suited to these wide, shallow and sluggish rivers. They, the Saxons and the British, had marched at an exhausting pace, covering a handspan of miles before full light, only once looking back, when the sky behind had reflected the sudden, bright, glow of fire. The farm-steading, poor hovel that it was, had not deserved such a finality of destruction. The group, weary, heart and footsore, although exchanging no word, thought as one. Hoped that the family, for all their inhospitality, had got away from the ferocity of the pursuing Goths. Morgaine and her son also. And that she had first succeeded with the safe burying of the body.

The boat, no doubt, belonged to some similar poor steading, lying hidden by the trees from the river. They did not delay to find out, but took the craft for themselves, Bedwyr insisting on leaving a pouch containing two gold coins, his last minted money, beside the mooring-post. The Saxons thought him moon-mad; for them, stealing craft was as common as a land-man raiding cattle, but they said naught. It was well known that the British were a crazed race.

Rowing was no less tiring than walking, but by taking the oars in turns, at least there was occasion to rest, to sleep. Not to remember. That was still, then, too raw to face. Thus, to the town of Caesarodunum they travelled; found there many questions and rising alarm. Euric and his rampaging Goths, the citizens cried, would be upon them by the next dawn! The gates were to be closed, the militia stood to arms. A fuss and panic, with the wealthy taking to their horses or river barges. The poorer, wailing and crying for salvation in the narrow, crowded streets.

None of the small, tired party of British or Saxons stayed longer than the one night, the excuse of their need to take word further afield readily accepted. They purchased sturdy, though malnourished, ponies; rode as fast as practical north, the nights and days becoming a blur of exhaustion and despondency. Heading, on that weary trudge through thick forest or floundering marshland, for the nearest port with sea-going vessels. Where the second touch of the Wyrd laid help at Mathild's feet.

For most the summer the seas between this northern coast and that of Britain had been high, with a rough, wallowing swell. Trade and fishing, seriously disrupted, had consequently suffered. Boats, those that had dared put to sea, had become damaged or had failed to return. There would be no crossing, Bedwyr was curtly informed, until conditions eased. When would that be? His polite question met with a shrug of shoulders and a blank expression. Only the Saex, the pirate traders who plied their adventurous living up and down the Gaulish coast were foolhardy enough to risk such doubtful seas. Eagerly they agreed to take Mathild north along the coast, past the Roman lighthouse at Bononia and on as far as the Elbe and her homeland.

The British? They would need make their own passage.

Mathild thought of them occasionally on that first day apart with regret. Bedwyr had been a friend, uncensorious of her relationship with Arthur; the men, she had known these past, long months as they camped or marched as Artoriani. But for all that, they were British, not Saxon, and she had a task before her to face. To claim her right to title, wealth and land.

That Arthur had given her these Saxons as her own guard was no mere gesture of affection. He had known well enough her intention, once free, to follow her own path. Delighted in it. Aye, and with the granting of these men and her manumission, encouraged it. She had not told him the full truth, however, for he had assumed Mathild was to confront the boy who had so presumptuously taken her uncle's place and be rid of him. It had been one comfort for Arthur, that last night, to believe Mathild would ensure Cerdic stayed not long in the world after his father's passing. Her one doubt, one tinge of guilt. She had not corrected, at any time, that assumption.

For all their fondness of the man Leofric, for all their loyalty to his surviving kindred, many a Saxon thegn would not support a woman, returned from exile and widowed, against one who might, with the strength of Thor's hammer, lay claim to land far richer than the wind-whispering marshes of the snake-pathed Elbe. They would not rally to her, not if it came to outright fighting. They might, however, if she put before them a tempting alliance. One that would secure no tarnish of blood feud, and if she had a son.

Arthur would have been horrified to learn of her plan – indeed, she was herself when, truly, she examined her intention. But the Wyrd thrust her a third sign of what was meant to be, for as the month turned to August she reached the first bustling harbour that nestled beside the sea estuary, and met with Cerdic, disembarking from his own vessel. And all her schemes, her plans, her manoeuvrings, thought up through these long months during the quiet hours of darkness, were not needed.

He was flush-faced, excited. His crew, who cared naught for difficult sea conditions, had tossed caution to the wind. Pirating, it seemed, suited Cerdic well. As did the pretty-faced woman, whose eyes caught his, and whose enigmatic smile aroused his interest and rapacious need.

Within the week, Mathild's charms and expertise in the art of loving had him chained to her as fast as a caught thief to the whipping post. Her easy success heightened by the secret knowledge that what pleasured the son had been taught her by his own father. As the night of the dead passed, and there came no haunting spirit from the Pendragon to chide her conquest, Mathild subtly suggested they keep their shared bed warm with a more lasting arrangement.

It suited Cerdic well; for all his youthful age he had a shrewd mind, was well aware that not all Leofric's people willingly accepted him. Mathild was true kindred to the dead man, he was not. The solution to change that position was attractive, as attractive as the woman who would make him a most pleasing wife, though he was but one month short of the age of manhood. His would be a double celebration, his four and tenth birthing day would also be his marriage day.

When that day came, and Mathild shared the marriage bed with her new, young lord, he had a third reason to salute Woden. For she was already swelling with child, his child.

Or so she told him.

July 470

§ VIII

Ambrosius Aurelianus was finding it difficult to control his temper. He sat presiding over Council where once his nephew had sat, in the padded, armed chair on the raised dais. They were bickering, the Councillors seated opposite each other along the narrow, gloomy chamber. Disagreeing, arguing. Like spoilt children squabbling over the last lick of honey in the pot. And Ambrosius had condemned Arthur for losing patience on occasions such as these! Hah, this would try the patience of God himself!

He listened, brows furrowed, fingers clenched, for half of one minute more, then came abruptly to his feet. 'Enough!' he roared as he strode down the two steps, along the central aisle. 'What is this foolishness? This inane argument?' He glowered left and right, at the bishops, the elders, noble-born, merchant-men, the wealthy traders, petty kings and lords. 'There is no case for disagreement here. I summoned you to discuss the basis of strategy, how we move and when, not if! Not *should* we!' He had reached the end of the long, narrow room, turned on his heel, strode back again, amused, even through his anger, that Arthur too, had paced in this self-same manner.

He stopped at the head of the right-hand row of stools, gathered his breath a moment before turning to face his Council; a softer, calmer expression forced onto his countenance.

'Gentlemen,' he began patiently. 'Last year, the nuisance of Vitolinus was just that, a nuisance. He raided a few settlements, butchered a few cattle. He was an irritant, a flea, a buzzing fly. Nothing more. Last year, he was as much a nuisance – and an embarrassment – to his uncle, Aesc of the Cantii. Things have very much changed this side of the winter snows. Great things. Most notably, you have a new Governor of Britain. For many of us,' he smiled here, received the response he intended, 'this is a God-sent blessing!'

Most were listening to him, a few still mumbled between themselves. Stern, he boomed, 'But that blessing is as advantageous for the Saex as it is for us!'

The mumblings and mutterings were becoming fewer. 'Aesc will not recognize my authority. We could have war on our hands before harvest!'

Ah! He had their full attention now.

Striding back to his seat, Ambrosius had a last chance to think – as if he had been doing anything else this last eight and forty hours!

Emissaries had been sent with the snow-melt – the last winter had come hard throughout Britain, heavy drifting snow falling over settled, packed snow. The people and farm-stock, cattle, sheep, swine froze and starved. Only the healthy or wealthy had come through this winter past – and if the harvest proved as bad as some predicted . . . Ambrosius shut that thought firmly aside. Enough to worry on for the time being. One by one Ambrosius's messengers had returned. Few carried pleasing news – even from the British! Too many petty kings had sent scorn flying back – aye, Council had said that move by Arthur, to allow such men their independence was a bad one. Had Britain continued under one government, one lord, had he not allowed so much freedom of self-rule . . . But what was the point of ifs and buts? The now had to be faced.

These rebellious British in the north would be content if left alone. Could be dealt with later. The Saex? The Saxons were waiting to see what happened with the British, and between themselves. Waiting to see who made the first move. Who would prove to be the stronger.

Every leader's nightmare, that the enemy would agree to settle their differences and unite.

For a while, Ambrosius was safe there. The Anglians considered themselves too aloof from Aesc's Jutes of the Cantii territory to join in a chosen fight with them. Aesc's father, Hengest, had been a mercenary soldier, homeless, landless; the various independent lords of Anglia and the North Humbrenses were noble-born, princes, kings from their own birthright, they scorned the line of Hengest with as much distaste as they did the British. For the others, the South Saxons were too new-settled, with not enough strength to brave a foray beyond their insignificant lands; likewise, the Saxons along the Tamesis; the East and Middle Saxons and those settled along the South Ridge were no threat. At least, not yet.

Aesc had little to lose if he decided to run against the British, and much to gain. He was wealthy enough to be able to buy himself into some other place, should he come out of a fight the worse off. He held lands, through his wife, in Northern Gaul. As easy for a Saxon to live under Childeric's law as under Ambrosius's. He could lose his life and respect, but to a Saxon neither were of consequence when weighted against the kudos of possible victory. It was regarded as honourable for a Saex to be killed in battle; respect was given to the war-lord, the leader, the Bretwalda . . . Ah, there was the danger! It needed only one man, one arrogant Saex who thought he had more strength than others of the English kind. One Saxon to award himself the title Bretwalda and become the Supreme, Woden-blessed, King. Aesc seemed to be courting that title. Little to lose. Much to gain. King of all Britain. King, at least, over the English.

Ambrosius had reached his seat, settled himself comfortable. Could Aesc aspire to such a height? Or was that privilege waiting some other for the next year, or the next? For the Lord Winta of the Humbrenses? For the Anglian Icel; or Aelle of the South Saxons?

'My lords and gentlemen,' Ambrosius began. It was no good, he would have to be honest, could not conceal the situation with half-lies, half-truths. As Arthur would have done. 'My emissary was returned from Aesc two days past, the last of those I sent out.'

A few in the Council sat forward, interested.

Ambrosius studied all their faces, their expressions. Some eager, glowing with the prospect of a fight – the tribal lords mainly, the petty kings, those who had agreed to remain under the supremacy of Ambrosius, men such as Amlawdd who expected much from the new supreme leader. Too much? Others seemed dour or irate. The bishops, the clergy. They could ill-afford a war. A few even seemed bored. One man, elderly, admitted, and known to be hard of hearing, was asleep. Ambrosius sighed. Arthur would have had his sword out to such an insult. Christ's good name, why was he forever thinking what Arthur would have been doing?

So, it was the whole truth, not hiding anything. 'My entrusted man, who, in peace, had taken word that Aesc was to submit in homage to me as overlord, came back with his ears sliced from his head, his fingers severed and his tongue cut out!'

Shouts of rage, men stamping to their feet, hands and fists waving. The elderly lord, as deaf as stone, slept on. Cries for action to be taken against all the heathen Saex.

'Aesc has declared war!' Ambrosius called, raising his voice, attempting not to reach an undignified shout. 'He has joined with Vitolinus! We need fight the Jutes of Cantii.'

'Can we?' someone called, thinking practically. They were crowding forward, huddled together before Ambrosius. Anxious, alarmed, their given opinions and suggestions mingling.

'Strike the impudent bastards now!'

'Burn them in their hovels!'

'Drive them back to the sea!'

'Aye, we ought have done so years ago!'

'Have we the men?'

'Of course we have!'

Patting the air with his spread hands, Ambrosius appealed for calm.

'That is the point,' he emphasized. 'We have not!' He stood to regain attention. Could see now why Arthur had spent so much of his time on his feet at these meetings. 'Arthur had not as many men in his army as I – but his men, the Artoriani, were professionals, drilled and drilled again. I have but a few hundred with as much dedication and spirit as they, and half of them are what remains of that Artoriani! The rest, the bulk of our fighting men, come from militias and tithed quotas. Arthur relied on such as padding, extras for garrison duty and reserves. He could fight where and when and how he chose, not relying on any save his own bound, brotherhood of men!'

'Then he had no right to take them from Britain!' Someone shouted it out, the Bishop of Venta Bulgarium, Ambrosius thought. The cry was taken up, variations on the same theme.

Angry, Cadwy pushed forward, making way by striking out with his crutch, earning himself black stares, curses; but, determined, he thrust his way to the forefront.

Ambrosius had been embarrassed to discover his son here, but it was an emotion that he had been forced to swallow. The lad was here by right of being the appointed lord of a stronghold. Badon was his, the fortified Caer that dominated the Great Ridge Way. One of Arthur's places – Gwenhwyfar's. She had given it to him. Why, Ambrosius could not understand. A cripple with a hag for a wife, to hold and, God forbid, soon, too soon, need to defend it. There were others more suited to the granting of such a prestigious holding, but Cadwy had it, and there was nothing Ambrosius could do against it.

'My lord, I wish to speak.' Formal, Cadwy addressed his father. Few in this council followed correct procedure. Ambrosius nodded permission.

'I have the floor, my lords! I will speak!' Cadwy found he had need to repeat his claim for attention several times. He rapped the foot of his crutch on the stone floor, gained reluctant ears and eyes.

'May I remind you all,' he said candidly, 'that it was Council who voted that Arthur Pendragon must take half of his men away into Gaul? He had no wish to go beyond the boundaries of Less Britain. You forced his decision. Must I also remind Council that it was you yourselves,' and he lifted his crutch, swung it in an arc, pointing it at each and every man, 'at Yns Witrin, who unanimously voted that Arthur, our King, was not to be encouraged home!'

Disagreement, cries of 'no', 'lies' and 'shame'. Cadwy countered swiftly. He fumbled beneath his toga – Council insisted on dressing in the traditional style – brought out a parchment, waved it at the dissidents. 'This is a copy of the reached agreements, as written by the clerk of that

Council.' He flourished it higher. 'Your voting is recorded by black ink on a scrolled parchment!'

Bolder than his fellows, recently appointed, the Bishop of Aquae Sulis spoke out. 'We have no need of Arthur. We will call out the militia and assemble our own men – and we will send for Rome to help us!'

The suggestion was well received, was taken up. 'Send to Rome!'

'Aye, Rome will help rid us of these Saxon parasites!'

Men were bustling to their seats, someone called for the vote, hands were raised, aye had it. Cheering, patting each other on the back, men began to leave the chamber, assuming business for the day to be concluded.

Ambrosius fumbled for his own chair, slumped, head in hands. For not even one year around had he ruled in Arthur's stead, and already his hopes and dreams were proving to be nothing but ash and dust. He groaned.

Why had he not seen that Arthur, for all his arrogance and temper and faults, had been right?

§ IX

'I am thinking,' Cadwy said into the echoing emptiness of the Council chamber, 'that it is no easy matter, to be a king.'

His father lifted his head from his hands, though his fingers remained spread across his cheeks. They had all gone, save for Cadwy and the clerk, a scrawny novitiate, who was gathering together his scribe's equipment.

'I am no king,' Ambrosius answered, but without the strident conviction that this retort usually conveyed.

Cadwy shrugged. 'Title is unimportant, it is the doing that counts.' He walked a few paces nearer his father, his crutch tapping, leg dragging. 'And what will you do? Nothing? Or follow Council's blindness and make appeal to ears that will no longer hear?' His words were a direct challenge, he expected rebuke.

Ambrosius sighed, eased the tiredness from his eyes and face by rubbing his fingers across the tight skin. 'Do? What can I do?' He stood, spread his hands. 'God's truth, Cadwy, I do not know for certain what to do.' He snorted self-derision. 'I am, unfortunately, not an Arthur.'

Quirking a half-smile, Cadwy cocked his head to one side, uncertain whether he could tease his father. 'There is no reason why you could not be. You only have to rid yourself of a few prejudices, learn how to lie and fight, and become a total bastard.'

Eyes narrowing, Ambrosius regarded his son carefully. There was something different about him. The style of hair and the dress unchanged; he still favoured his weight onto the undamaged leg, giving his body an imbalance. His eyes were brighter, more alive, but it was not that.

To his son's surprise, the father also smiled. 'I thought you already regarded me as a bastard.'

Cadwy laughed outright. 'Oh aye, I do, but that is a personal viewpoint, others think of you as a saint. Hardly a description that can be applied to Arthur's memory!'

'His men thought him even higher! A god.'

'Alas, gods are immortal. Arthur was not.'

It occurred to Ambrosius that this was, perhaps, the first amicable conversation he had held with his son. 'Your wife,' he asked, after clearing his throat several times, 'she is well?'

Cadwy's expression brightened, glowed with pleasure and pride. 'Most well. The child is due within the next month.'

Clearing his throat again, for he found himself feeling unexpectedly awkward and ill at ease, Ambrosius added, 'I wish her safe delivered.' More unexpected, he truly meant it. A grandson. A grandson! He chuckled, invited his son to walk with him from the chamber. 'This would displease Arthur. Something Winifred said once to me has proven to be so.'

'Really?' Cadwy was tempted to ask further of the matter, thought better than to pry over-close, but his father, opening the door for them both to pass through, volunteered the information himself.

'She implied that a grandson could make up the ground lost between us.'

Slightly hesitant, 'If you wish it to be so.'

'Of course, it may be a girl-child.'

'It may.' Cadwy met his father's eye, defiant, bold, announcing either would be welcomed, as equally loved by the child's parents.

They walked together, Ambrosius matching his pace to his son's. Evening was settling, the swifts were busy, swirling and swooping, noisily darting after their supper, the sky a warm red, promising another day of sun on the morrow.

'If Ragnall bears a girl-child,' – again that defiant tone had come into Cadwy's speech – 'she will be named after my mother.' He expected some reaction, an indrawn breath, a rebuke. Nothing. They walked on, along the narrow cobbled streets of Aquae Sulis, easing past an ox-pulled cart, a

150

woman carrying a basket of soiled linen destined for the fuller's place, some drunkards singing loudly, out of tune, before a crowded tavern.

Abruptly, Ambrosius announced, 'Your mother was no beauty, she would often remark that her features were plain, that her eyes were too small, her mouth too large. Yet to me,' and his voice choked with the memory of the wife he had loved so dearly, 'to me, she was more beautiful than ever a Venus could be.'

She had been murdered, when Cadwy was a child in arms. Murdered by the brutality of Saex pirates who came raiding one autumn afternoon. Raped and murdered, their child daughter with her. The boy had been spared, for a slave had hidden him. A cruel jest, that, having been spared, the boy had later fallen so ill, become so lame.

Hah! Ambrosius checked himself. He was in danger of becoming sentimental, and that he could not allow.

They had reached his apartments, a grand building, suited for the High Governor of All Britain. Ambrosius offered dinner, but the younger man refused, declaring he had arranged to meet with friends.

'So what will you do now?' Cadwy asked.

Deliberate, Ambrosius misunderstood. 'Dine alone, I imagine, with but the servants for company.' He produced a smile, was glad to receive a laugh in return.

'I will enter with you then, after all, I thank you.' Cadwy offered his hand, in friendship, as pax. 'My companions will not miss me, and your kitchen will, no doubt, have better fare than a backstreet tavern.'

It was confidence and pride that had changed Cadwy, Ambrosius could see that now, confidence in himself. Arthur had held confidence. In what he was, what he was doing. Was that why Ambrosius had so despised him? Because he had nothing for himself save self-doubt and indecision? Arthur's father had been the shining star and, after him, Arthur had blazed as brightly – brighter. For Ambrosius, there had always been the shadow. Always following, two paces behind. Now he was the one ahead, but still he stood in the half-light of their presence. He had to take up the torch, blaze his own trail. Had to!

'Are you to heed Council?' Cadwy questioned during the meal that was simple but well cooked. They had talked around this issue, exchanging light conversation, ambling on solid territory, mindful of putting a foot wrong, of damaging this new-found, emerging acquaintance.

The oysters were good. Ambrosius took another, levered open the shell with his eating knife. 'My Councillors have fat arses and narrow brains.'

His son's hand paused over the selecting of a leg of roasted chicken or a wing of duck. 'You are not going to endorse application to Rome then?'

'Christ's good name, no! Help us? A remote, poxed island? If Rome would not aid Gaul, what chance do we have?'

'But Council . . .'

'Council is turd-scared of the need to spend our insubstantial treasury. To send for help, and sit and wait, would be more economical in the short term than funding an army, than fighting a war. Sit and wait, in the hope that trouble may never materialize, will go away.'

'But such a choice,' Cadwy remarked with all seriousness, 'would invite trouble, entice the Seax.'

Lifting his goblet in salute, Ambrosius drank to the observation. 'Which is why I must raise myself an army as strong and as dedicated as Arthur once had. I have a fancy to lead an army into victory, to kick the arse of this impudent boy, Vitolinus.' He lifted his hand, sucked his cheek. 'My only problem, I do not know how in hell to do it!'

'And what of Rome?' Cadwy could not resist asking the question, for too many times had he heard his father defending what had once been.

'Rome,' Ambrosius opined, 'is not the power she once was.'

Cadwy's eyebrows rose. Was this his father talking? Had he partaken of overmuch wine, perhaps? 'You have changed your views somewhat,' he tried, tactfully.

Another oyster, another goblet of wine. 'It galls for me to admit Arthur was right about Rome, that the old ways are gone, can never be again. But he is not here to belch derision. A man may be allowed to change?'

'Certainly.' With a wicked grin, 'Happen you will be taking the title King, next?'

Ambrosius tossed a laugh. 'Ah no, there is a limit! To totter delicately out from the shade is one thing, but to prance naked in the sun? I think not.'

For there they were of like mind, Arthur and Ambrosius. Stubborn, on matters of principal. A genetic trait of the Pendragons. To be as stubborn as bloody-minded mules.

September 470

§ X

The sea crossing had been appalling. The voyage up-river, although short, tedious. And the welcome? As cold as the easterly wind. But then, Winifred had expected nothing else from her son.

Cerdic was taller by the height of almost two handspans, and his features were maturing, bearing the first stubbling of beard-growth along his chin and upper lip; very much the confident young man, far from the image of the dependent boy that the mother remembered, though his scowl had remained as aggressive and his manner as offensive. Winifred found herself to be quite amused at his childish hostility towards her. He had yet to perfect the ability to impart scathing insult without rousing his own anger. A trick he would, no doubt, soon learn. His father had used it to perfection.

Winifred did not consider her uninvited, unannounced and unwanted arrival as discourteous or inconsiderate. She was Cerdic's mother, and to her respect was due without comment or question. Her son thought otherwise, and made those thoughts perfectly clear. He had no love for her, did not want her on his land or in his settlement – much less, living as guest beneath his own roof. Where he could, he ignored her or answered in monosyllabic grunts. By the third day of her coming he was tempted to board one of the Saxon long ships and disappear with the crew on a trading expedition, except there were things that needed tending within his settlement, and he was damned if his wretched mother would drive him away from his own home. The occasional day of hunting would provide some legitimate respite from her uncompromising, critical tongue.

The settlement over which Cerdic's Hall presided – Leofric's Hall as it had once been – seethed out in a raggle-taggle bustle from behind the rummage of slave and cattle-pens, boat-sheds and warehouses erected along the river bank, where the natural tidal current drifted into a sheltering bend. Boats and ships of all kinds were moored alongside the wharves, between slipways, or in dry dock for repair. The river itself was crammed with fishing vessels, barges, trading ships and the impressive, sixty-foot, single-masted, thirty-oared long ships. Magnificent craft, built for speed and durability, craft that could cross the open sea, or slide,

153

silent, up-river – the English warships. Pirate craft. Winifred had counted eight of these huge sea-beasts when her own barge had ponderously moored. She was impressed. Cerdic was obviously doing well for himself. How much better could he do, then, with the aid of her wise advice and judgement!

This was a riverside settlement where life revolved around the swing of the tides; where fishermen returned from the open sea with their catch, merchants and traders met to buy and sell or exchange their cargoes of lead, iron, silver and gold. Where they came with expensive silks, brocades, wines, fruits and spices. The luxuries of ivories and exotic animals from the Africas, and for the everyday trading of grain, wool, leathers, pottery; hunting-dogs and slaves, the fair-haired or the dark-skinned, as black as ebony. Along the banks, stacks of timber, crates, amphorae. New ships being built. Old ones awaiting dismantling.

Despite her misgivings, her anger and hurt at the way he had so viciously and callously left her, Winifred had privately to admit that she was proud of her son's acquisition. That pride did not extend to his choice of wife, the reason for Winifred's coming. Mathild, Winifred disliked. From the day she had heard – from a trader's lips – of her son's marriage, that decision was made. Reasons, had she needed them, were plentiful. Cerdic was too young, she was too old, being all of ten years his senior. Her past was suspect and she had been wife to another. Cerdic needed pure blood for a wife, for his future queen of Britain, for the mother of his sons, Winifred's grandchilder.

Meeting Mathild confirmed the contempt. Her faults, in Winifred's eyes, included pride, lack of respect and the ability to lie with an ease that came too glibly. Lies accompanied by an offhand manner that suggested a quick wit and too many hidden secrets. Ah no, Winifred would not tolerate a daughter-by-law who breathed enough spirit to become a possible rival. It was rare for Winifred to meet her match and Mathild showed, from the first introduction, that she held no fear or awe of her husband's sharp-tongued mother, a fact which delighted Cerdic and intensely annoyed Winifred. Only one other person had treated her with such disdain. Arthur.

Mathild reminded Winifred of that man, for both held a single-minded obstinacy and a wilfulness deliberately to misunderstand or misinterpret. The child too, the son Mathild had borne Cerdic, brought Arthur to mind. Something about the eyes, the shape of the nose? But then, the Pendragon was his grandsire, a strong resemblance was to be expected. Or so Winifred judged, those first few days, until her gold, placed in the right hands, and tattle gleaned from the right lips, began to sow other suspicions.

Mathild was feeding the boy herself, giving her own milk, employment frowned upon by her mother-by-law, a cause for more sparring. The day had been wet with drizzle, although it had not stopped the men from setting off through the marshes with their dogs and spears in search of game to hunt. The women had remained within-doors, Winifred reading, comfortably settled beside the hearth-place of Cerdic's own private chamber, Mathild standing at her loom in the corner, or occasionally going into the main Hall to supervise some task necessitating her head-woman's presence.

Late afternoon. The men would return soon, with wet cloaks and tired hounds, muddied boots, cold hands, empty bellies. The child had awoken, cried for his own feeding, hushed into gurgles of contentment when offered his mother's breast.

Winifred frowned, could not resist a barbed comment. 'You will lose your figure by suckling a child. A woman your age ought be more mindful of these things.'

'My son is of more importance than the shape of my breasts.'

'Your husband will not agree with you.' Winifred's immediate response was accompanied by a snort of derision. 'His eye already roves to younger, firmer, girls.'

Mathild chuckled – she had quickly discovered how to defend against the more hurtful remarks. Winifred could not tolerate being mocked, or outmanoeuvred. 'Cerdic may bed with as many fillies as he pleases. It is of no consequence.' She regarded Winifred candidly. 'My son is of more importance to me than is *yours*.' Added, 'Did Cerdic not mean more to you than did your husband?'

Ruffled, Winifred snapped, 'My husband was a bastard.'

The smile was there in the voice, though not on the face, as Mathild quipped, 'Cerdic, then, is much like his father.'

She shifted the boy to her other breast, fondly watched his eager guzzling. He had brown hair with a slight curl, large eyes, a placid, contented temper. Features like his father, but spirit and character? No. Cynric would be different there.

Setting aside the scroll she was reading, Winifred stood, strode over to Mathild, her shadow slanting across the child's face. She was a tall woman, Winifred, austere in her Christian, holy woman's robing, her face pinched, without humour or sparkle of contentment. She achieved happiness by causing the pain of others.

'I have been asking questions about you, madam.'

I wager you have! Mathild thought.

'You were taken as slave after your husband was killed.'

'I have made no secret of that.'

'A woman is used for only one thing by a slave-master.'

The babe, full-bellied, was drifting into sleep. Mathild laid him across her shoulder, adjusted her clothing. 'Nor is that secret.' She looked up at the woman standing so ominously over her. 'It seems you have been asking the wrong questions, or have received the wrong answers.'

'I think not.'

Unexpectedly, Winifred reached forward and took the child. Anxious, Mathild checked an impulse to retrieve him, but Winifred was holding him with care, cradling him, rocking him into deeper sleep, soft-crooning to him. 'He will be a fine boy, Cynric, Arthur's grandson.' A pause. Winifred spoke her next words slyly. 'Or is he?'

Even Winifred, used to countering with implacable lies, was impressed by Mathild's instant answer.

'I know not, madam. Only you know the truth of Cerdic's siring.'

'You fight without rules, Mathild,' Winifred answered with a sneer, 'like a man would, like Arthur would.' She ambled to the cradle, lay the child tenderly in his bed, covered him. It had come as some surprise to herself, on first seeing the boy, that she held these maternal feelings. But then, why not? She was his grandmother. He was the child of her child – or was he? She turned to Mathild, challenged her outright. 'You were, for some time, with Arthur. I have suspicion that he sired the child, not Cerdic.'

The incredulous laugh was, at least, plausible. 'And how do you decide on that?'

Winifred seated herself, casual, picked up her scroll, but did not unroll it.

Mathild stated blandly, 'Arthur was killed in battle in July. Cynric's birthing was in March, a full month before his time. The months do not tally.'

Winifred's retort was as instant. 'Early July, and Cynric was, so I understand, full-formed. Early-born childer often have no hair and no nails. They are puckered little things.' She tapped the scroll in her hand. 'Oh, the months can be made to tally, my dear, with Fortune's blessing, a little manipulation and the helping of many lies.'

Mathild said nothing.

'You do not deny being the Pendragon's mistress, I note.'

Mathild chose fruit from the bowl, small, sweet apples. 'It is not a thing that I am shamed of. Arthur, to me, was a kind, good man.'

Winifred's turn to laugh. 'We are talking of the Pendragon, girl. Such description is not for him.'

'From you, no, but then, he loved you not.'

'Ho!' the other woman sniped. 'Did he, then, love you?'

That one hurt, a lie, could not come to Mathild's lips. Had he loved her? She knew well that he had not. Instead, she answered with the truth. It was, after all, good enough, for it was more than he had given to Winifred. 'He was fond of me. Arthur had love only for one. For Gwenhwyfar, his wife.'

'My son obviously does not know that his father bedded you.' Winifred sniped. 'Indeed, he hates the man enough to slit such a woman open from belly to throat.'

Tossing the apple core into the fire, Mathild issued her own challenge. 'He does not. Nor is he likely to know. None would be fool enough to so inform him.'

Raising her eyebrows, Winifred chuckled. 'Do you intend to intimidate me by threatening me with some veiled, dark foreboding?' Her laugh increased. 'You do not frighten me.'

For a moment, Mathild stared into the flicker of hearth-fire flames, watched the flesh of the apple core shrivel, brown, then blacken. When she looked up, her expression was serene, confident. 'Nor do you intimidate me, madam. I am not prepared to justify myself to you. I know when my son was conceived, and to whom. I will not deny that he could, just, be Arthur's, nor will I listen to suggestions that his is any other than Cerdic's seed. Cynric is his father's child. With that you must be content.'

'I dislike you, Mathild, you are not suitable as wife to my son. I intend to have him be rid of you.'

'Equally, I may decide to rid myself of you and him.' Mathild was smiling again, a composed, self-assured smile that held nothing of amusement or humour. These lands along the Elbe were, by family right, hers, and she had a son now. 'It would not be difficult,' she said, 'to persuade the men that it would be wiser to follow my son, not Cerdic. We are a tribe with deep loyalties. Cerdic is not of the blood. I am, as is Cynric.'

Eyes narrowed, nose pinched, Winifred came abruptly to her feet, swept in three short strides to stand before Mathild, her fingers clenching, wanting to go around this impudent girl's white throat. Anger quickened her breath. 'Do you dare threaten my son's leadership?'

Calm, Mathild rose also, stood, her head tipped slight to one side. 'That I would not. I would suggest, however, that you ensure no mention of this day's fanciful conversation reaches his ears.' She walked away, towards the door that led out into the Hall. It was a dangerous proclamation, but Mathild had sound motive for her determination, the loyalty of her men.

157

Winifred, of course, crowed derision. 'An arranged death is no difficult undertaking.'

With no flicker of fear or doubt, Mathild regarded the older woman. 'Another murder, lady, might just be questioned.' She depressed the door latch, tossed parting words. 'Already have I arranged my security against you Winifred. Were I to die under any but the most natural circumstances, there are those loyal enough to me to ensure I do not enter the next world alone.'

Winifred took her meaning wrong. She snorted contempt, mocked, 'So you threaten my murder!' She seated herself, laughed at the absurdity.

'Oh no, madam,' Mathild said, 'not yours. I will enter Valhalla with my husband.'

§ XI

Skirmishes up and down the border-land, a British farm-stead burnt, a Saxon family butchered. Ambrosius's men were gathering strength, gaining courage, but then, so were Vitolinus's followers. Petty cattle-raiding by the Saxons had already escalated into the mindless, bloody murder of farming families; Ambrosius retaliating by thrusting across the border of the Cantii land on punitive raids. It was not enough. Winifred's brother had a grievance, justified in his mind, and a young, hot-headed man with an ambitious cause to follow was not to be easily pushed aside.

With the Pendragon gone, Vitolinus rapidly grew in confidence. The arrogance of his father and the dominance of his sister were swelling within himself also. Before, there was always the knowing that Arthur could come back, would not give up his kingship to the challenge of a spot-faced youth. Others of the Saxon kind, the various tribes, petty kings, Ealdormen and warrior-class thegns, were indifferent to the lad's claims while Arthur still lived; agreements were honour-bound, until necessity dictated otherwise. The Pendragon had ensured treaties made with the English were adhered to, from both sides of the boundary. His death in Gaul laid all that void, but most were reluctant, even then, to deliberately upset the apple-barrel. They had their land, their settlements and farm-steadings. Trade was increasing. The Saxon kind were not, below surface need, a warrior race. They were farmers, settlers, family-raisers. Seeking peace and prosperity. Why muddy calm waters?

Nor, to the Saxons, was Vitolinus wholly English. He was untried and mistrusted, too many remembered those half-truths and forgotten promises made by his father, the British King, Vortigern. '*Come fight with me,*' he had encouraged, '*and I will pay you in gold and land.*' Now here was the son who looked so like the father, even down to the jagged scar raking across his cheek, claiming those same offers. Fight with me, make me King and all Britain will be yours. The same empty promises? Not even his own uncle, Aesc of the Cantii, had believed or backed him. Until Arthur was dead.

Mistrust and suspicion was a double-edged blade, cutting to either side. While Arthur remained King, peace, however uneasy, however delicately balanced, between English and British remained intact. Borders had been established, limits of settlement, of respect, and what was, or was not acceptable agreed. With the placing of Ambrosius as Supreme Governor of Britain, those same boundaries were challengeable. All of the English knew that peace to be vulnerable. Ambrosius Aurelianus was a man of the old kind, the old, prejudiced, blind-eyed order of the Romans, who looked upon the Saxons as invaders, barbarian, savage, unlearned and unworthy. It was a matter of time before the British reassembled, regained their strength and determination. A matter of time, only, before the English had to once again put an edge to their weapons and fight for what had become theirs.

Arthur had promised not to fight as long as there was peace. Ambrosius professed to determine for the opposite. To drive the Saex back to the sea, to cleanse Britain of all savagery and heathenism.

'I need more men,' Vitolinus coaxed, sitting cross-legged before the hearth-place of his uncle. Already he had emptied a chestful of plundered silver and gold before the gathering, had marched the rows of chained and grimed slaves before them, giving the best of the women to the more influential among Aesc's guests. 'With more men, I can crush Ambrosius before he has chance to come into his full strength.' Vitolinus spoke, eloquent, confident. 'The British run around in circles, like chickens with their heads cut off. Ambrosius is no leader, he has not the balls for an outright, bloody fight. His head is full of his Christian God and the ideals, the misguided notions, of the past.' He was toying with his dagger, running the blade across his thumb, fondling the fine carving of the handle, fixed his eye on his uncle Aesc who sat, leaning a little forward, on his king's stool of honour. 'My father,' Vitolinus said, 'became king because the people of Britain, the ordinary folk, the tribesmen, their warrior kind, wanted no more of the Roman law, harsh taxation and injustice.' His lazy smile became a broad grin, the scar on his face creasing menacingly. 'My father had a greed for wealth and power, yet he was no soldier. He left the fighting to others, the English. Your father, uncle, my grandsire, the great warrior Hengest, gained for Vortigern a royal torque and a kingdom. Without the blades of the Saxons, Vortigern would have been nothing. Yet, like fools, we believed him when he promised to do well by us.'

Vitolinus pushed himself to his feet, sheathed his dagger, drew instead his sword, the short-bladed Saex. 'Well, we took the kingdom of Britain once, in the name of Vortigern. Let us take it again, in the name of the English!'

He was anticipating a roar of agreement, a storming to their feet of all the men listening, a drawing of weapons, unleashed enthusiasm. Instead, a few murmurs, one or two mildly nodding heads.

It was Aelle, from the south coast, Aelle, chieftain of the settlers of the South Saxons, who spoke, coming regally to his feet, the faces of his three sons quietly watching him. 'And do you, then, Vitolinus a half-Wealas, expect us to follow where you lead? In *your* name?' It was a mild question, betraying nothing beyond its simple asking.

'I do.' Vitolinus had also inherited those unfavourable traits from his father that he shared with his elder sister; self-opinionated arrogance and conceit, an ill-judged vanity for control and dominance. Among those of his own age and inclination, objectives that were somewhat admired and encouraged; but for those such as Aelle, a man of superior years, breeding and worth, added to nothing save insolence and disdainful presumption.

Aelle gestured for his sons to rise, enclosed his cloak firmer around his shoulders, and made polite respect to Aesc, host to this assembled gathering. 'Then you are as much the fool that your father was, and as ill-bred as the bitch-sow who is your sister.' And he was gone, his sons walking close at heel, gone with him the thirty or so men who had accompanied them, rising from the gathering and disappearing into the night. Others slid as quiet away, the great circle rapidly diminishing, men who had come as representatives from the Eastern Saxons and the settlers of two, three generations who had established steadings along the Tamesis river and its tributaries.

A long silence drifted with the woodsmoke rising from the stacked hearth-fire.

'It seems,' Aesc observed, himself rising from his stool, 'that you must fight Ambrosius alone, my nephew.' He began to stride away, back to the light and warmth of his Hall that beckoned beyond the spread of this, the gathering ground. 'Prove yourself able to succeed in more than the slaying of women and children, and mayhap they' – he nodded his head into the night – 'will think again.'

Vitolinus remained where he stood, fists clenched, grit-jawed. Angry. 'Ja,' he vowed, his nostrils flaring, eyes narrowed, to those, his friends, the young men, young warrior-kind, who had stayed. 'They will think again, when I force them to kneel before me, and honour me with the title

Bretwalda, high lord.' He rammed his sword back into the sheath at his hip, spat contemptuously into the blaze of flames. 'They will indeed think again when I have taken Ambrosius' head.'

April 471

§ XII

In the land of the Cantii and at the insignificant steading of the old warrior Cille, spring leapt into life a week or so behind the milder climate enjoyed by the southern areas of Gaul. When it came, bursting forth with a rejoicing of new-leaf budding and enthusiastic bird-song, the blood of the young Saxons stirred with it. Tales around the winter hearth-place had been plentiful and vigorous, stories of war and glory, of new beginnings and future expectation. With the dazzling yellow of the spring sun, the time came for the young men to tie the coloured war ribbons to their spears, and meticulously sharpen their sword-blades, axe-heads and daggers. To spread the heating of a warriors' blood-lust, Vitolinus, at the old man Cille's suggestion, had paid the travelling harpers well. When, as April shifted nearer the bloom of May, he called for others to join his small band of followers, the young, untried youths, keen to blood their blades, answered him. They sought adventure, manhood and a chance to swagger their achievement before the maids. Glory would not be found behind the ox and plough.

Initially, it was planned well. Vitolinus had realized, perhaps belated, and on Cille's advice, that he had to work with others of his kind to gain what he wanted. His uncle, Aesc, would not take part in the foolery of young men – yet neither would he condemn nor put firm end to it. A youth's blood ran with the urge to prove his bravehearted strength by the spilling of blood on the field of battle. So it was with the male of whatever species. Who were the older and the wiser to interfere?

Fortunate for Vitolinus, another Saxon had the cry of the battle-blood in his heart. The South Saxon, Aelle was waiting his chance to extend his borders, waiting patiently to claw for himself more than those few, small, scattered settlements that he held along the south-eastern coast. And Vitolinus wanted to strike at Ambrosius. An easy matter for the two secretly to negotiate their plan through the long winter. The one with his battle-scars and experience and with bold, firm-muscled sons; the other eager, sharp.

The Shore Fort of Anderida, slightly eastward of the island of Vectis, was a bastion of dogged Romanized perseverance. An irritating itch that lay beyond the stretch of Aelle's finger reach. It would fall to him one

162

day, but that day seemed too distant along the horizon. He wanted it destroyed, needed it gone. With no Anderida to heckle his warriors, to burn his steadings, slaughter his cattle, he could concentrate on dominating this stretch of the southern coast, could build on his strength and achieve his aim, his hope. Gain power, credence and wealth. None could be his while British Anderida stood, defiant, at the corner of the land Aelle intended to make solely his.

When more ships came, he could do it; when many more men carried arms beneath his banner, he could rid himself of the pestilence that fortress entailed. Vitolinus was a boy, a piddling whelp, but he was easy to manipulate. A few crooned suggestions, some flattering praise, the occasional, idly slipped-in, propositions, and he was trapped like an eel! However uneasy, such a temporary alliance could form a mutual benefit for two ambitious men. Aelle had no concern whether Vitolinus succeeded against Ambrosius. The Governor of Britain would last well enough for another day. Once the coast was secured as the Saxon's own, then Aelle – or his sons – could see to him. If Vitolinus was, by some unexpected hand of help from the gods, successful . . . ja, it could prove useful to Aelle to be united, for a while, with the half-bred whelp, Vitolinus.

The plan was simple enough. Using two of his uncle's long ships, Vitolinus sailed into the harbour at Anderida two days before the spring month ended, fire-arrowing the craft moored there, and attacking the sea-ward wall. Simultaneously, Aelle and his men marched on the western side of the fortress, battered at the gateway beneath the spanning arch of the main entrance, and scaled the massive stone walls that soared high beyond the twenty feet. The Pendragon had seen well to his coastal and border forts, but neglect and rot had set in rapidly once his demand of discipline and authority had wavered. Undermanned, underequipped, attacked on both sides together, the place fell – the fight valiant but brief. Within the passing of two hours, the might of what once had been a proud Roman fortress was ended, its defenders dragged, some wounded, still alive, to burn in the victory fires piled high with gathered timber and dead bracken. An inglorious end to such a noble place.

Aelle was well satisfied. He had won his eastern boundary. And Vitolinus, cheering and laughing with the South Saxons, had for himself a foothold in the south, from where he could march, undetected, unexpected, into firm-held British territory.

He would move north, taking Ambrosius's defence from the south. A few settlements burnt along the way, but the march must move swiftly, no time to delay, to tarry. Later, they could return and leisurely settle accrued accounts. For another reason, then, had Vitolinus so wanted to approach the British territories from the south. After settling with Ambrosius, he would march on Venta Bulgarium.

Would visit his murder-minded sister, Winifred.

§ XIII

Unlike Arthur, Ambrosius had few cavalry. He fought in his own style, with ranked, disciplined infantry. He had ensured Vitolinus had been watched through most the winter – the shabby steading of the warrior Cille was no difficult place to observe, with its tumbled dwelling-place, poorly tended fences and encroaching woodland. But Ambrosius's spies were paid men, not loyal comrades of the Artoriani. Paid men worked only as well as the gold clinked in their waist pouch, and when rain fell heavy or a cold wind blew, they were inclined to prefer huddling around the warmth of a camp-fire rather than stand in the shadows watching the closed door of a small, rough-made, Saxon dwelling-place.

Cille was an ageing man. There would be no more fighting for him this side of the Otherworld, but though his joints were stiff and cramped, his mind was active, his senses alert. He knew well enough that Ambrosius's poor excuse for spies were watching him and the lad. Knew well enough when to set Vitolinus out, secret, under cover of darkness and rain-scudding clouds.

When word came that Vitolinus was gathering the young warriors to Cille's hearth, Ambrosius made ready. There would be a fight, that was certain – and he greeted the prospect with enthusiasm, now that it was upon him. One victory, one good, well-fought victory, and he would gain the respect, the kudos that he needed to put the memory of Arthur aside.

Inadequately informed, he had not calculated the unexpected. Unable to move as swiftly and precise as once the Artoriani had, the British found little time to move into a suitable position, so unexpected and unpredicted was Vitolinus's coming at them from the southward. A few, a very few of Arthur's men had survived the massacre in Gaul and had struggled homeward. Four complete turmae of cavalry, one hundred and twenty men of the old Artoriani, were encompassed now into an effective cavalry wing of the Ambrosiani. Experienced, battle-hardened men, who knew what it was to face a rampaging enemy, who knew how to deal with a mewling cub which had not yet learnt what it was to face the spilling of blood in battle.

There were a few who whispered, of course, that Ambrosius had never taken the responsibility to lead men into battle. He had fought himself, once, with Arthur in the north, but he was a man of book-learning, not raw experience. He knew the theory of how a battle ought be deployed, knew well enough the tactics and logistics of war, and below his authority he had those experienced officers, men like Bedwyr and old Mabon who had fought beneath Arthur's command. Experience counted for much, but so too did a cool head and a determination to prove capability. Ambrosius would show that he was as good as ever his elder brother or younger nephew had been! Vitolinus, the son of Vortigern and that Saxon whore-witch Rowena, was a stabbing thorn that needed plucking. Chance to achieve both aims may not come again for Ambrosius.

It was a shabby, shambling affair, the fight, when it began. A young man no more than a boy, with an arrogance the width of the Tamesis estuary, leading an ill-prepared rabble – the young Saxon Cantii warriors, for all their numbers of several hundred and their surprise appearance from the south, could never boast the title, army. And these, arrayed against a man who followed the rules of war as written by the book. A man who had taken no account of the bloody mess that was the reality of battle.

It was not a battle, this ill-thought, ill-timed yearning for a fight, that happened at the place called Guoloph, along the Roman road north-west of Venta Bulgarium. It was not how the scribes had written the glories of battle to be. This was a bloodied scramble, a muddle of snarled oaths and wounding blades, of hand-to-hand mauling and killing. Feet kicking, teeth biting, fists punching. When the rain, threatening for most the morning, finally dropped from grey, hard-packed clouds, and the ground beneath their feet turned treacherous from churned mud and spilt blood, the two sides fell apart, breathing hard, growling and cursing, teeth bared, hackles high. Dogs squabbling over the same bone.

Only later, did men give it the grand title of battle. Later, when, in retrospect, British harpers told of Ambrosius's first-led fight, and English story-tellers recounted the inglorious ending of Vitolinus.

§ XIV

Winifred had not dared admit, even to herself, the extent of her fear when first she heard that her brother was marching up through the forests of the south, up from the coast, swinging out along the Roman road, heading for a battle with Ambrosius. He had come too close to her wealthy steading outside Venta Bulgarium – and the fear ran high through all those who dwelt on her land. Many knew well enough that there was no love between brother and sister, as many could too readily make guess at the prospect should Vitolinus take the victory over the British.

Winifred's fear had rapidly turned to anger when word came, back along that same Roman road, that the fighting was over. The British – Ambrosius – had won. The anger welled, now that she was safe; her brother, that toad-faced, poxed, weed-stunted, shrub should dare, *dare*, to threaten her . . . indirectly maybe, but she knew well her danger had the outcome at Guoloph proved different.

The anger became scathing derision when, through the storm of rain and thunder that had persisted across the night and into the next day, a few tattered, blood-smeared Saxons came stumbling into her steading. Breath-panting, sweat-pocked, they huddled behind a young man, face bruised, arm torn and bleeding. The man they had, but yesterdawn, hailed as a son of Woden.

The torn and battered young man fell to his knees before the steps of Winifred's grand Mead Hall, and with tear-empassioned voice, begged for her aid. Vitolinus knelt before his elder sister, hands clenched, begging her protection.

'My army is scattered, or slaughtered,' he sobbed. 'They were untried and untested boys, yet the British hacked them to pieces. Where was the mercy your Christian kind so often extol?' Pleading, he looked into his sister's blank, hardened face. 'Ambrosius will be hard at my heel,' he stammered, 'He will string me up by my balls for this . . .' He choked, the full rein of cowardness after failure unleashed. 'Talk with him, Winifred! He will listen to you. Offer anything. Save me, for the love of our lady mother, I beg you!'

Winifred stood on the top step of her Hall, her cloak held tight around her throat against the damp, chill of the evening. A pathetic creature, her brother. Her father too, beneath his mask of greed for power, had been naught but a bullying coward. At least, for all his faults, Arthur had never been one to plead or beg.

'For our mother?' she sneered, answering him. 'My mother once pushed me back into the flood-waters of Caer Gloui, would have let me drown – unless the Pendragon had caught me, and then I would have hanged. Why did she do this, to her only daughter?' She narrowed her eyes, looked with loathing at the thing that ought be a man, grovelling before her in the mud. 'Why? So that she could save you, a snivelling, cheating heap of mouldering cow-dung.'

She descended the steps regally, her cloak swishing behind her. She was not alone, for those of the Hall were gathered in the door-place, watching; others from the steading grouped at a discreet distance behind the shabby bunch of defeated young men.

Winifred reached the last step. Whimpering, Vitolinus crawled to her, fastened his hands to her ankles.

'Come, brother,' she said, her voice less harsh, less judging. 'Things be not that bad. As you rightly say, I have influence with my Lord Ambrosius.'

A hesitant smile flickered over Vitolinus's face. He began to rise, tentative, embraced his sister for her generous forgiveness. The dagger went into his stomach easily, but she twisted the blade, pushing it in deeper, her arm holding him around the neck, choking off his breath and voice.

Killed in such a manner, it took Vitolinus a while to die.

One death Winifred would openly own to. No regrets for the way it was done – though there were some who later said that it was unChristian. More praised her courage, her thinking. The best way to put an end to scum, with the feel of a cold blade.

Na, Winifred had no regrets at the sorry ending of her brother. She would have killed him as easily, had she found chance, on the day of his birthing.

May 471

§ XV

The British saw the battle at Guoloph as a resounding victory. Given that Vitolinus, the perpetrator of the unrest was dead, it could not, reasonably, be taken in any other vein. Conveniently, it was immediately forgotten that his ending was by murder. None saw him as British – despite his father having been once their King. He had incited war and death, no matter how it had come about, was fitting retribution. To the English, Vitolinus's failure was regrettable, but few did more than shrug their shoulders or shake their heads. He had been a hot-headed young man – good for him for trying – but the crops needed planting, the weeds hoeing. The son of a foreigner, a half-bred Wealas boy, would not be over-missed, on either side.

Ambrosius was delighted with the victory. Deaths had been few, though many had suffered terrible wounds; his Council was pleased that the matter had been dealt with quickly and efficiently – no need for expensive campaigns or costly negotiation of terms. The Cantii Saex were firm under Ambrosius's boot, he had proved himself a capable leader both politically and now militarily. He was praised as a heroic leader, and before the month was half-completed, men began to forget the Pendragon, for he was no longer needed. Whereas once the young men came to join the famed Artoriani, now they would come to seek a place within Ambrosius's army. With not so much eagerness and hope, it had to be admitted, but it was early days. Soon, when he had the economy on firmer feet and his army was at full strength, he would begin the task of pushing the Saex back.

'*Send them into the sea from whence they came!*' With the flush of first victory, the rally cry spread swift throughout southern Britain, especially where the borders ran against the English-held lands. Victory ran proud through those chieftains and petty kings who had thought it prudent to fight alongside Ambrosius, but Arthur had freely granted land and status to those who readily supported him and Ambrosius was, as yet, an unknown quantity. Their loyalty was not to be disappointed. Success, they found, brought all the trappings of generosity.

Ambrosius's victory banquet was lavish, by his standard of modesty. All those of importance were invited to join him at Aquae Sulis. Praise for those who had taken a stand against the Saex was bountiful, as was the promised reward: land, title, cattle, jewels and weaponry ... Ambrosius was not a fool. Loyalty must be earned, and the winning of one small skirmish did not buy unquestionable faithfulness. Not when so many were so fickle, and so prone to bouts of absent-mindedness. Arthur had earned loyalty by achievement and ability. Ambrosius had much ground to cover in sparse time. He needed to give, and give generously, to those who would follow – and remain – with him.

The banqueting hall within the public buildings of the Basilica at Aquae Sulis was moderate, but sufficient. Only the most important, the especial invited, were to join Ambrosius at his High Table. Lower down, there would be no official seating, for too many were of high and equal rank, so as was common at these larger gatherings it was made a free-for-all, come, sit-as-you-please.

To his delight, Amlawdd was to be one of those invited to be seated with the Supreme Governor. He had his own wanting for reward. Patient, he had waited for Gwenhwyfar's grieving to take its natural course; patient again, had retained his thoughts and ambition until the right moment came to unleash them. He knew for what he would ask, it was his understanding that the thing had been promised him while Arthur was still King, now was the time to claim it. Unusual to ask for reward – it was for the giver to offer, not the receiver to seek – but in this instance, Amlawdd took his chance, knowing Ambrosius was desperate for firm alliance. All he need do was wait, speak when opportunity presented itself.

He was greeted well by Ambrosius, who embraced him and gave loud praise, overheard by those many already seated in the banqueting room.

'Amlawdd!' he exclaimed. 'Another of my loyal men at the battle of Guoloph come to share in this victory feast!' Ambrosius indicated that he should sit, to Amlawdd's great pleasure, at the Governor's right hand.

'Did I tell you how splendidly Amlawdd fought for our cause?' Ambrosius smiled wide; heads were turning to listen, those at the High Table, others seated nearby along the rapidly filling seats of the lines of trestle tables. Soon the food would be brought in, the serious eating and drinking started.

Putting his hand on Amlawdd's shoulder, Ambrosius gave further praise, 'My friend Amlawdd personally slew more than a dozen of the Saex scum!' Ambrosius encouraged polite applause. 'Aye,' he laughed, 'was your sword not almost as bloodied as mine own?'

Chuckling happily, Amlawdd settled himself comfortably among the noble guests, accepted wine as the girls began to pour the offered drink, took a few olives from the dish before him. The slaves began to bring in the courses, great dishes of pork, beef, fowl, swan and hare, and fish of all kinds, piled vegetables, pastries, many needing to be carried by two men; all greeted with applause and delight.

Ambrosius spoke gross exaggeration and disfigured fact. He had slain two men, wounded three or four others, had all but soiled himself when a Saex axe-head missed scything away his left ear by but a hair's breath and, to his sure knowledge, Ambrosius's blade had been as clean and bright then, as it was now. To be fair, that was not the Supreme Lord's fault, for his personal guard had been so thick about him and the enemy so weak, that he had not found chance to do more than shout orders and avid encouragement. Soon the tables were littered with spent dishes, half-eaten carcasses, discarded bones; frothing with spilt ale, stained with slopped wine.

'So!' Ambrosius waved his hand for the slaves to come forward with the sweeter courses. The noise was tremendous after an hour or more of feasting, so many guests eating, talking and laughing together. 'What can I offer you, my lord Amlawdd as token of my appreciation?' Ambrosius had to raise his voice so that he could be heard. 'You hold good land already. Do you require cattle perhaps? Slaves or furs?'

Amlawdd grinned, enjoying this show of amicable companionship. Arthur had never offered such friendship outside his own ring of trusted officers. Bold, he answered, 'My lord, I seek but one thing.'

Ambrosius raised his eyebrows, gestured for the man to continue.

'You may have once heard that a certain lady promised to be my wife if ever her husband had no further need of her?'

Ambrosius stroked his clean-shaven chin. Aye, so he had heard.

'I ask, then, lord, that you grant me permission to take Lady Gwenhwyfar as wife.' Amlawdd held Ambrosius's eyes, daring him to refuse.

Pursing his lips, Ambrosius considered. It was indeed as Amlawdd had said; Gwenhwyfar had once made such a bargain to secure Amlawdd's loyalty to Arthur who had been in desperate need of fighting men. It had been a trick, of course. Never had she intended to offer herself as his wife . . . and yet. Yet the Pendragon had now been dead a few months short of two years round. Was it not time that the woman buried her grieving and gave herself to another? Add to that, Gwenhwyfar was somewhat of an embarrassment. She was, to some, a figurehead; technically, to those who opposed Ambrosius – and there were more than a few – she remained queen. To those of the northern and western tribes, she had the right to rule, not himself. Aye, she ought be put somewhere safe, where she could come to no mischief.

Shrewdly, Ambrosius observed Amlawdd's expectant anticipation, weighed what he intended to gain from such a match. Merely a woman to occupy his bed? Or did he see this as a chance of seizing power? To be consort of a queen was no small achievement. Had Amlawdd the wit for that? Or would such a granting be sufficient to ensure loyalty? Amlawdd could call on many men were Ambrosius to need them. Making decision, he nodded. 'It is agreed, if the lady will consent to have you.'

Amlawdd beamed his pleasure, this had passed better than he could dared have hoped! 'Were my lord to give specific request, could she refuse?'

Hah! Neatly said! Had Amlawdd more cunning than he was given grant for? Well was it known that Gwenhwyfar was becoming a problem for Ambrosius, he could not lock her away, nor ignore her, for there was no legal cause, yet he must be rid of her. She had not interfered with his running of the country, beyond a few disparaging comments, had not openly opposed him, but surely it was only a matter of time for both, and more, to happen. For her to go directly against his wish – order – in this: could that amount to treason? Possibly. Probably, given the right lawyers, the right circumstances. And to grant Amlawdd such obvious pleasure . . .

Ambrosius smiled, said, 'We shall ensure she agrees. How can I do less for a man I am honoured to call friend?'

Amlawdd inclined his head, acknowledged the extreme compliment paid him.

'You will, of course,' Ambrosius continued, 'require her eldest brother's consent.' He selected a wedge of ewe's milk cheese. 'He is legally responsible for her.'

Nodding vigorous agreement Amlawdd answered, 'I intend to ride to Gwynedd within the week. Lord Enniaun is a man of good sense, he will see that it is wise for his sister's child to have a new father.' His grin of triumph was shaped broader than a new moon.

Ambrosius knew what he was doing, even if Amlawdd was fool enough not to realize it. All he wanted was to possess Gwenhwyfar, that much was clear, but how soon would the other things come to ride high in his mind? Gwenhwyfar held, as estate from her husband, much land. She was the wealthiest woman – aside the Lady Winifred – in perhaps all Britain. If enough men remained loyal to the memory of her husband, she could, with the ease of snapping her fingers, try to resume her right to be Queen. Ambrosius knew all that well enough. The wager, was Amlawdd enough of an ass to think no further ahead than the pleasures of his bed?

June 471

§ XVI

Winifred was perhaps the only woman to be openly unimpressed by Ambrosius's self-claimed achievement in battle. In fact, she was furious. Vitolinus *she* had dealt with, not the Supreme Governor. Where was *her* accolade, *her* triumph? And what of those who had so blatantly aided her traitorous brother? Her uncle, Aesc, was he to go unreprimanded? And the Saxon Aelle with his three bragging sons, was there to be no punishment there? How foolish it was, she raged aloud, to leave the Saex be. What if they rose a second time? What if Aelle or Aesc managed one day to take Britain for themselves? And her private thoughts: what if they take what is by right mine, through Cerdic?

By letter, she petitioned Ambrosius to take action, received no satisfactory reply. She journeyed to confront him personally, only to be brushed aside with patronizing remarks addressed to her womanhood and lack of understanding regarding politics. Ambrosius, it seemed, had come full into his rank of pompous, superior male arrogance. He was supreme and would take advice from no one. Hah! Should she be surprised? Was he not of the Pendragon family?

Seeing that potential danger – for herself and Cerdic, if not for Britain – Winifred's temper stewed, setting the servants scuttling, slaves cowering. Her tempers were well known, this latest one matching anything that had ever been initiated in the past by aggressive disagreement with Arthur. Even now, after all these past weeks, Winifred shuddered when she considered what would have been her own fate had Vitolinus and his English rabble fared better at Guoloph ...

Well, if Ambrosius would not listen to her, would not ensure that such a rebellion would not occur again ... there was another who would! Commissioning a fast craft, Winifred took sail to the Elbe.

Cerdic must be made to see sense, all this fool talk of not wanting Britain for his own must cease. Britain was ripe for the picking and it was the time to set about the harvest. She would never be Queen, but King's mother held its own, particular power. It would need suffice as the next best thing.

*

'No.'

Winifred sat, back straight, hands folded in her lap, ankles crossed. A fine lady dressed in the softest spun wool, purest linen veil. 'That is your final word?'

'It is.'

'Then I call you coward. You are no son of mine.' There was no spite in her voice, no rise of inflection or anger, but the menaced poison behind those spoken words were thick and threatening.

Cerdic had never been as self-controlled as his mother and would never be as adept at schooling his features or temper to suit his need. At her insult, he lurched to his feet, bottom lip quivering, face reddening and fists clenched. The result she had intended, for a loss of self control made him vulnerable and weak. 'I am no coward!' he bellowed at her. 'And I tell you,' – he was waving his fist at her, nostrils flaring, face contorted – 'the day you are dead and out of my life will be a day of festival and rejoicing!'

Mathild moved to her husband's side, threaded her arm through his, attempting to calm him by offering her support. Arguing with Winifred, shouting at her, being abusive was not the way to handle this bitch. Mustering her dignity, in contrast to her husband's outburst, she declared, 'We are not interested in Britain, Lady Winifred. We have enough for our needs here.'

'Pah!' Winifred also stood, her height appearing even greater for her proud, upright deportment, her high-held chin and her confident air of command and authority. Cerdic would seem the more imposing had he not been inclined to be overweight and did not hunch his thick-set neck so deep into his sullen shoulders. She had told him so often enough, but huh! Did he listen to her, his mother?

Scornful, she mocked them both, her hand flicking a dismissive gesture. 'You are, then, fools! This sluggish river enough? When you could have Britain at your feet?' Her head came back, mouth opened in a hollow grunt of derisive laughter, a sound like the careless snarl of a wild beast. 'For how long will it last, this idyllic settlement of yours?' She paced around them, prowling. 'The Franks are slavering over claiming more territory, and since Arthur so carelessly failed to stop them, the Goths are driving the Gauls higher northward.' She ceased her walking as she came face to face with Cerdic again, stared callously at him and her daughter-by-law. 'You have, I would judge, but a handful of years before your precious river falls to the dominance of another nation. Assuming the floods do not bring about your eviction first.'

Cerdic rasped a bitter answer. 'Leofric had wealth enough here, aye and his father before him.'

'Leofric was as much the fool as you are,' came the swift response, although a twisted smile formed with it. 'Though he had some small prick of sense in his brain. He wanted me to give him a part of Britain.'

'Pig's swill!'

'Is it, Cerdic?' Winifred rasped. She sauntered back to her chair, seated herself, almost regally. 'You must, of course, make up your own mind.' She settled herself more comfortable, preening her veil, spreading her skirt. 'But you will never make much more of yourself than what you already are while you remain here.'

'I am a thegn, and already I have the honour of the title Ealdorman.'

'King would be so much finer.' Leaning forward, Winifred altered her tone to that of enticement. 'Take opportunity while you can, son! Land, wealth. The authority to do as you please. You have a chance to be a king, Cerdic, a king!'

Cerdic thrust Mathild's hand from his arm, took one menacing step nearer his mother. 'And if I were king, what would there be for you?' His laughter sounded hollow, with almost a madness thrusting through the hard sound of it. 'You failed to become a king's wife, a king's mother is your next hope.' He had stepped closer to her, stood over her, his breath foul on her face. 'It is not for me that you urge this thing, but for your own glory. The mother of a king can wield great power, should she so wish.' His lips drew back in a sneer, 'And if the son would let her.' Slowly, he shook his head. 'I do not want Britain. I will not take it, not for your benefit.'

Eye for eye, Winifred returned her son's stare. Her answer came, domineering, as from a woman used to be obeyed. 'And I say, Cerdic, that you will.'

He swung away, hurled his fist against the wattle wall, a small puff of plaster trickling to the floor. The fine tapestries quivered.

Mathild felt compelled to challenge the other woman, to salvage some of her own authority as mistress of this Hall, this settlement. 'I too am a mother. I think of my son, Lady Winifred, as you do yours. His birthing-place is as mine, this river, the Elbe, not Britain, not some foreign country where the Wealas-breed live. He shall inherit wealth and power enough from his father when he is grown to manhood, without the need to spill his blood for it on some distant, hostile shore.' She indicated the child's cradle to the far side of the room, where the boy lay curled tight in sleep. 'It is for Cynric's future that I and my husband must think. Not for our own.'

Her hand shaking with derision, Winifred pointed at the child. 'You think of the child before your husband, madam. Why is that, I wonder? Because you think also of his shameful siring?'

174

Mathild caught her breath, her fist going to clasp the material of her gown at her throat. Cerdic's head had snapped from watching his mother to scowl at his wife, then back to Winifred as she spoke again.

'She has deceived you, Cerdic. From the very first, she has tricked and used you for her own gain.' Winifred leant back in the chair, her shoulders pressing against the wickerwork, her fingers loose, relaxed, along the carved armrests. 'A mother's power behind her son can be great indeed, depending on the status of that child's father. Mathild has never had love for you, Cerdic. Her loyalty lays elsewhere, with what her son may get her when you are gone. For he has as much claim to Britain as have you, has he not, Mathild?' Winifred's gaze burnt into Mathild, rousing a rage that burnt putrid in the younger woman's stomach, but she allowed no time for answer. 'Her loyalty has rested all this while with the man who planted the seed of that boy, laying asleep over there, in her belly.' Abrupt, she stood. 'You fool, Cerdic! Do you believe *you* sired that child? Arthur had the doing of it. Your own father bedded this whore before you took her to your bed.' She held open her hand, emphasizing the obvious. 'You have not the manhood in you to sire a child, nor the balls to take what by right ought be yours! Arthur was always so much the better than you!'

Like thunder erupting from a black sky, Cerdic hurled the table next to him over, smashing the pots and tankards that stood upon it, scattering fruit and wine. The dogs leapt to their feet, barking; he hurled over a stool, a chest, roaring his hurt pride and rage.

Mathild, stifling a scream, tried to run for the child, frightened that harm might befall him; Cerdic lunged in her path, grasped her shoulder, spun her around, struck his knuckles across her mouth, sending her staggering backward against the wall, blood welling from her nose and a split lip. She fell to her knees, tears coming with the blood, pain, and sudden fear.

'You bitch!' she stabbed at Winifred, who stood superfluous, watching, mildly amused. 'You lying bitch!' she hurled again, holding fingers to the blood, her other hand stretched towards Cerdic, pleading. He stood, panting, trembling, eyes widened and breathing hot with fury. Mathild clambered, unsteady, upright. 'She lies, husband! Cynric is your son. Your child. Do not listen to her. She has, since first you wed me, tried to prise us apart, to dirty my name and my honour for she knows that I would dissuade you to leave this place, our territory, our home.'

Haughtily, Winifred protested. 'I act only in your interest, son.'

Cerdic caught his mother's smug expression, turned on her. 'For me?' he snarled, 'My interest? When have you ever acted for me, Mother? For anyone other than yourself?' He stalked through the debris scattered over the rushes, kicked aside one of the dogs ferreting for food among the spillage. 'All you have ever done is to make my life a misery.' Cerdic drew back his hand with the intention of striking her also, but Mathild was behind him, seized his wrist.

'She is not worth your anger, my lord! Send her from here, be rid of her. We have no need of her spite and her barbed, dung-stirring tongue.'

Twisting from her grasp, Cerdic swung around, viciously pushed her from him. 'You disgust me, woman! Think you I have not heard before this, of how you lay with the bastard who was my father? Think you I have not heard the tongue whispering that Cynric may not be of my seed?' His foot sent another stool hurtling across the chamber. 'I have ears to hear with, eyes to see and a brain to reckon the months with!'

Mathild's anger was rising as high, she realized the need to fight, for herself and for her son. To belittle Winifred. 'Ja, I laid with Arthur. I was his bought slave, what choice had I? I was ill-used by him, as he ill-used all women.' Her lip was sore, already swelling, her head swam, fuzzy, dizzy, she fought the swaying faintness. 'Cynric is your child. The rumours are lies, lies spread after she had last come here.' Mathild thrust her pointing finger at Winifred. 'She has stained the innocence of truth with her black heart and evil mind. Set rumour running for her own gain.' Unsteady, Mathild stood before her husband. 'Who would you believe in this? Ugly, rattling tongues, wagging after the drink has slurred the senses? Her? Your bitch mother who has no worth save her own arrogance? Or I, your loving wife?' Mathild spat saliva onto the floor at Winifred's feet. 'Have I lied to you as she has? Have I ordered or demanded of you, as she does?'

Cerdic nursed the flesh of his hand where he had struck out, the knuckles were bruised and grazed. His breathing was fast, his eyes darting. Truth? Lies? He had never known the difference between the two, for his mother held no value for either. He would not recognize truth, even if it were sworn on any oath named. He wanted to believe Mathild, so wanted to, but how could he judge? How could he know the truth from a lie?

Attempting to regain calm, Mathild brushed rushes and straw from her woollen gown, pushed a fallen pin back into her hair.

Momentarily, Winifred had been alarmed, fearing that Cerdic would strike her also, but the moment had passed. She was again in control. 'I swear, on your father's grave,' she said to him, 'that on this, I do not lie.'

Mathild swung around, her eyes flashing rash, unchecked triumph. 'Then your oath is false, my lady! To my certain knowledge, Arthur the Pendragon has not, yet, need of a grave.'

§ XVII

Winifred's skin drained white. Cerdic stared at his wife, his mouth open.

Mathild swallowed. Gods! What had she said? She nodded once, slowly, her split lip twitching into a slight, mocking smile. 'The truth? I will tell you both the truth. When last I saw Arthur, he was clinging to life. By a narrow thread, I grant, but he was not, as the others believed, dead. I know that he is alive.'

Winifred's hand had come to cover her mouth, her breathing had almost stopped. She mastered the panic, the uprush of disquiet, forced herself to move, slowly, back to the chair, to sit. This could not be true – yet she knew it was, knew this to be no fool jest. It was the sort of bloody-minded thing that Arthur would do to her, cheat her of his death.

'My father is alive?' Cerdic said, through a long, snarled breath. 'You have known, all this while, that he is not dead?'

That brief triumph faded from Mathild. This was not knowledge that ought have been made public. Not to these two.

'Have I then, been bedding his whore while he still lived?'

'What difference does that make?' Mathild quavered, with false bravery. 'Whether he be in this world or the next, what I once was to him . . .' But she never finished. In senseless jealousy, unreasonable rage, Cerdic smashed his fist into her face. She fell, but his fists, his feet, kept battering at her, kept pounding into the body that had been touched, soiled by the man he hated above all else.

His mother pulled at him, desperate, tugging at his arm, her voice crying in her throat. 'Leave her, Cerdic! We must know where he is! Do you not see? She must tell us, we must know!'

The child had woken, was laying in the cradle, wailing, frightened and confused at the noise, the shouting.

Hammering at the closed door, shouting. It burst inward, men coming in, swords drawn, anxious, alarmed. Mathild's men, Saxons. A maid-servant in the open doorway, hand to her mouth at the blood and the mess, began to scream.

Cerdic swung towards them. 'Get out!' he bellowed. 'Get out of here!' He pushed at them, lunged with his fist, booted with his foot, driving them from his private chamber, slammed the door shut, stood, breathing hard. Shaking.

She was dead, Mathild, he knew that. No woman could survive such brutal treatment.

'You fool!' Winifred snarled. 'Will they follow you now without question? Without glancing at you with thoughts of murder in their minds? She was their kindred by blood.' With difficulty, she was attempting to control her own shaking body, swallow down the rise of vomit that had come into her throat. She fetched a cloak, threw it over the body, hiding it from sight, then wine from the far side of the chamber; with trembling hands, poured, drank a few, quick gulps, poured for Cerdic, handed him the tankard.

'You have one chance to survive beyond this night, Cerdic, to live into the next dawn and the dawn after that.' Her hand went to his arm, gripped it tight, urgent. 'You must say that some madness took possession of her, that she had tried to murder your son – I will be witness to it – that to protect him, you acted as only you could.' Her other hand took hold of his chin, her fingers biting into his jowled cheeks, forcing his head to turn, to look at her. 'They will follow the boy! Without question, they will follow him.' She slowed her breathing, becoming calmer, now she knew how to deal with this day's madness. 'You must be his father. And I must discover, and ensure somehow that yours is truly dead.'

Cerdic pushed her grasping hand from his face. Bitter, he laughed. 'And what of Britain? Do you still command me to take Britain?'

She moved away from him, turning her eye from the heap on the floor that had once been his wife. 'If I do not manage to finish those men who have loyalty for Mathild above you – or her son – then Britain may be the only safe place for you.'

Her smile allowed a small sliver of triumph to settle into it. She knew who most of those men were, she had made it her business to know. They were the ones who had come north with Mathild from Gaul. The ones who had fought with Arthur. Easy enough to pay the right people with the right gold. Winifred laughed, low, to herself. Ah no, Mathild would not be going into the Otherworld alone. She would have her men with her for company. And by chance one of them might talk of Arthur, before he died.

§ XVIII

Another spring come and gone, with the days rapidly sprinting towards the full heat of summer.

The man stood beside the palisade wall, looking down into the valley that ran, almost as a second defensive barrier, around this side of the decaying Roman town. Avallon had once been a busy, important place, bustling with the trade that had come from the road that trundled north-west through Gaul, passing below its high citadel walls. No more. Few used that Roman road now that Rome's influence was waning. There was no safety in travel, no profit in trading along an obsolete route. Avallon too, was dying. Once a proud town, its buildings were beginning to crumble, becoming shabby; where the many taverns had swelled with laughter, only the one sold wine now. Where the young had set their market stalls, opened shops, sold pottery, skins and cloth, now only broken shutters swung aimlessly in the wind and few cared to visit Avallon.

He, this man, was one of the few. Of dishevelled appearance, hair in need of cleaning and combing, simply dressed in rough-spun, woollen tunic and plaid bracae. He was watching a woman and child make their way along the track. They seemed small from up here, overshadowed by the tumble of trees that cluttered the far hill, dwarfed by the steepness of Avallon's own imposing height.

He could hear their voices floating up to him on the clear, still air, she chiding the boy for idling. He ought to call out, show them he was watching, but he did not.

Unchecked, a single, despairing tear wavered down his beard-stubbled cheek. He closed his eyes, seeing in his mind not the woman walking down that narrow, steep-sided valley with her son, but another lady, one who had green eyes and unruly copper-coloured hair, not Morgaine's dyed, red hair.

He could see her, that other woman, her shape, her size, that hair tossing and cascading around her shoulders. But he could not image her face, or recall her voice. It was there, on the edge of memory, hanging like a half-awake dream, always just beyond his reach, never near enough to see clearly, to touch.

He ought be grateful to Morgaine, for she had so patiently healed him of his terrible wounds, brought him back from the edge of the Otherworld. Her nursing, skill and love through those long, long months when he had lain so ill, so weak and so helpless, ought be appreciated, rewarded. She loved him, he knew that, but for her he felt nothing.

After the passing of all these seasons, the hardship of winter, the glory of spring, surely he ought feel some stirring, some lift of caring feeling? But Arthur felt nothing. Nothing save the gaping emptiness that surrounded and swallowed him. His Gwenhwyfar was gone, gone ahead to the Otherworld without him, and he had lost everything that had once been his, in this. His men, his kingdom. His courage and his hope.

Morgaine happened to glance up, saw him standing up there behind the timber palisade wall, waved, encouraged her son to wave also, but

179

Arthur did not return the acknowledgement. She could heal deep inflicted wounds from spear, sword or axe, could ease away the ravings of a fever, nourish the weakness and return strength to a body that had been so sorely punished. Nothing could she do for the inner hurts, the bruising and lacerations to the heart and soul. Arthur was her life, her being, her meaning, yet she was daily, almost by the hour, aware that he had no feeling for her.

Arthur stood, his mind not registering the blueness of the sky, the gold of the sun or the fresh green of the trees. When the others had gone, believing him dead, Morgaine had stayed with him. Cared for him in the hovel of a deserted goatherd's hut that she had found tumbled beside the river. Fought, for many weeks, against the spirit of death that had so determinedly courted him. She had cooled his fever, warmed him when he lay shivering and cold. When those immediate dangers were passed, struggled with his weak and feeble body to bring him here into the safe territory of the Burgundians, to the place where she lived, a few miles outside the town of Avallon, within the dedicated, discreet community of pagan women who served the Mother Goddess.

All this she had done for him out of love. He ought feel something of gratitude to her, not this damning darkness of resentment. He could not fight it though. Had not the strength or inclination.

Better it would have been, for Morgaine, for himself, to have died there in that stinking goatherd's hut.

For, without reason to live, it was all, all of it, so pointless.

§ XIX

Although Ambrosius Aurelianus wore the impressive title Supreme Governor of All Britain, it was a hollow decoration, or at least, the element 'All Britain' was exaggeration. By the factor of his strength and popularity among the north and western tribes, Arthur had been the only man, since the extinction of Roman influence, to rule as unquestionably supreme. Save, perhaps, in the extreme north, above the line of the old Antonine Wall where not even Rome had survived for more than a handful of years. To the Pendragon, the British tribes had acknowledged their homage, claiming lesser titles of king or prince beneath his seniority. To Arthur, the English had also knelt, either willingly, or forced through defeat. By right of inheritance, he had been lord over his own Dumnonia and the Summer Land. Aye, Arthur had been a war-lord who commanded much power and respect.

Only the territory of Ambrosius had not bowed to him. Centred around the wealthy and well-to-do towns of Aquae Sulis, Venta Bulgarium, Caer Gloui and Corinium – Londinium having been shamefully lost to the Saxons through the tyrant Vortigern's incompetence – the populace preferred one of their own kind to lead them, someone who valued Rome and the Empire, someone who would restore that same stability of law and order. Who would reintroduce the hierarchy's necessary status and wealth and lower unreasonable taxation.

Arthur had veered towards the old, pre-Roman way, to the independence and tradition of the British tribesman. Ambrosius Aurelianus advocated the opposite, the rights and privileges of the citizen. Naturally, with its deep rooted sense of pomp and grandiosity, southern Britain came down heavily weighted in the latter's favour. As naturally, the wilder lands of Britain would have nothing to do with him.

With Arthur's going, that gradually splitting rift had fragmented even further. Britain was no longer a single island state. With no steady hand firm on the steer-board, the tribespeople were returning to how it had been before the Roman Eagles had marched up from Rutupiae way back in Claudius's time, in Anno Domini Forty-three. Gwynedd, Powys, Rheged and their sister lands; the wild hills above the Wall – all were now independent, forming themselves into rough-hewn embryonic kingdoms, answerable to none save their own lord. The ending of Arthur had escalated the ending of Britain as a united province. Only the one enclave, Ambrosius's held lands, remained steadfastly Roman.

And then, of course, there were the English.

There was little Ambrosius could do about the British tribes, as unruly, snarling a bunch as ever had been. Nor was there much inclination among the Council to consider them. The tribes, never truly Roman, would, it was widely accepted, revert to type. Let them! But the English? Ambrosius had pledged to finish them, send them scuttling for their boats and the sea. For the Saex, he promised his loyal followers, Britain would become as uncomfortable as squatting on an ants' nest.

The problem with rash-made pledges. Easy to make, difficult to accomplish.

Inexperience of soldiering did not deter Ambrosius, for he was a man of faith and he had good men beneath him, battle-hardened, war-scarred men, who for all their previous questionable loyalty, would serve him well. At least until someone else lured their interest. As there was no one now that Vitolinus was despatched – and even were he not, it was doubtful British men would follow a half-Saex cur – Ambrosius was safe at least for long enough to achieve his aim to firmly entrench the level of respect that Arthur had once acclaimed.

His first move was to occupy English-held territory, to dominate and suppress. He ordered a formidable line of fortresses and strongholds to be built at strategic points. He placed patrols and militia guards along the key trade routes. Arthur had never advocated such methods, preferring to be able to move his men fast and effectively when needed, where needed. To tie men to one area went against the use of his efficient cavalry, but Ambrosius was ever an infantryman. He would do things the Roman way. What was left of the proud Artoriani, Arthur's élite cavalry, Ambrosius sent to man the new fortresses that set watch over the English settlements. They were no longer Arthur's men, for they were his to command now.

August 471

§ XX

Amlawdd, for all his impatient character, was astute enough to realize he must wait, pick a right moment to approach Gwenhwyfar. Apprehension was behind his reasoning. Gwenhwyfar was no ordinary, demure woman. One false step and he could lose more than pride! The lady was too well practised with sword and dagger for any man's safe comfort – as he well knew from past experience. Even the hope of amassing all the Pendragon's wealth and land kept his hand steady on the reins. Whatever was Gwenhwyfar's would, as her husband, become his. The prospect of making attempt for the supreme kingship, though, for all his dreams of ambition, was low on his list. Even Amlawdd, with his imprudent and ill-thought ideas, recognized his limitations. No, to be lord over such prestigious land was enough. With both the Summer Land and Dumnonia marching alongside his present, modest, coastal holding, he would be master of the entire south-east . . . a fine enough ambition.

It was not, then, until August was into full gallop that Amlawdd rode, intent upon his quest and with an escort of but four men, to Caer Cadan. He had chosen a fine, warm, day; a pleasant ride beneath a sapphire blue sky that was skittered with mare's tail and distant mackerel clouds.

The marshes were already drained for dry weather had come early, the Summer Land lay as a worked tapestry of flowers of many colours and the varying greens of grass and tree. No breeze stirred the alder or willow; running streams gurgled laughter, lazy rivers trundled their meandering course. The Tor, the whale-hump island that rose above these miles of flat, marsh levels, seemed to be sleeping, drowsing under the heat. Ahead, the Caer lay camouflaged against a background of blue-hazed, grassed hills, with only a few thin, spiralling wisps of cooking-fire smoke to give notice of its being there.

No banner flew above its ramparts. Gwenhwyfar had refused her own and she would not fly her husband's Dragon. There seemed to be no guard patrolling the walkway. A solitary gatekeeper snarled his growled challenge as Amlawdd drew rein at the summit of the cobbled lane's incline. The visitor dismounted; handed, with jovial cordiality, a small wooden box to the man who came stumping from his guardhouse beside the open-thrown gates, bid him, with polite courtesy, take it immediate to Lady Gwenhwyfar. 'With my good wishes and compliments.'

He could have ridden straight in, made his way direct to the Hall that he could see built on the highest ground, bold against the skyline. Could have marched in and demanded his right to hospitality. Did not. Ah no, Amlawdd intended to follow correctness to the letter. In case the lady should not be in a mild temper this day.

He waved his men to dismount, settled himself on the grass bank below the palisade fencing, lay back to enjoy the calm pleasure of early afternoon sun on his face. He had bathed first thing, been shaved, had his hair trimmed. Had even chewed on a fresh hazel stick to clean his teeth. His clothes, best doehide boots, leather tunic settled over linen shirt, and fine-woven woollen bracae, were recent made. His cloak, a favourite, a deep blue and red plaid, the slaves had cleaned and hung above a smoking fire for several days. There ought not be any remaining fleas or lice sharing it, not after such strenuous treatment.

He must have dozed, for the clouds seemed thicker bunched as he opened his eyes on hearing the tread of a shuffling, approaching step. Congenially, wearing an open, pleasant smile, Amlawdd bounced to his feet. The gatekeeper had returned without the box. A good sign. Promising!

He was a gruff man, the gatekeeper, elderly, his left leg swinging in a stiff limp. Undoubtedly an old soldier. He tossed his head over his shoulder, muttered through toothless gums, 'My lady'll see you. You're to go up.'

Polite, Amlawdd thanked the man, mounted, proceeded through the gate at a walk, did not see old Glewlwyd spit and make a contemptuous, horned sign as he rode past. If matters had been left to this trusted old man, scum such as Amlawdd would be sent, no questions asked, bouncing and rolling direct over the ramparts.

Were he to have known the nature and intention of the visit, Glewlwyd might have been sorely tempted to do so anyway.

§ XXI

The concentration on the little girl's face would almost have looked comical had her intent not been so serious. Brows slightly furrowed, lips parted, she stared ahead, eyes directly focused between the pony's neat, pricked, black-tipped ears. Archfedd would soon be five years old; it was well time that she learnt to ride, and Briallen, named for the spring primroses that had bloomed so profusely in the year that the mare was born, was to be as much her tutor as her mother, Gwenhwyfar.

'A little kick-kick with your heels to make her walk on . . . aye, that's it!' Gwenhwyfar clapped her hands as her daughter again successfully moved the pony into a walk. Her legs were too short for such a fat pony's round belly, but Briallen had known enough children, knew her job. A patient, steady mare, alarmed at nothing save the thought of missing out on her next feed. Sure-footed, pretty, intelligent, the colour of sun-dried hay, with a dark mane and tail that tumbled down like the wild waterfalls of her native mountain home of Gwynedd. All the Artoriani children of Caer Cadan had learnt to ride on Briallen, including Gwenhwyfar's sons, Llacheu and Gwydre. Now her daughter, Archfedd.

'Good,' Gwenhwyfar encouraged, 'keep her going, now turn her – well done!'

Horses were approaching the area running beside the Hall that served for courtyard and stable-yard alike. Gwenhwyfar frowned, ignored the men coming to a halt, dismounting. Her back was to them as she watched her daughter ride, but the pony was going forward, she would need to turn with her . . . and Amlawdd was striding across the yard, both arms outstretched, smiling hugely. Politeness could dictate no other response, Gwenhwyfar would need welcome him. She nodded a cursory acknowledgement to him, called for her daughter to halt. 'Gently on the reins, cariad, do not pull at her, the bit will hurt her mouth badly if you do.'

'A fine young lady,' Amlawdd observed, 'every inch her mother!'

Ignoring the flattery, Gwenhwyfar instructed her daughter to dismount, watched with approval as the girl moved her legs from the saddle horns and dropped neatly to the ground.

'Shall I take her to a stall and brush her, mam?' Archfedd asked, taking the reins over the pony's head and patting her neck.

Na! Gwenhwyfar thought, desperately, *do not leave me with this imbecile!* But what help could a child be, save as a distraction? She nodded, 'Of course, find her a handful of chaff as reward for her hard work.'

Grinning, Archfedd produced a chunk of stale, fluff-covered, bread from the leather pouch at her waist, showed it proudly. 'I have this for her!' Scenting it, the mare pushed her nose, eager to eat the titbit immediately, but the girl authoritatively shoved her aside. 'You wait, greedy pony!'

Joining the conversation, Amlawdd attempted friendliness. 'You will spoil her, make her fatter than she is!'

His effort failed, for Archfedd only scowled at him. Briallen was as round as a barrel of ale, but it was not for strangers to say so!

Indicating a side doorway into the Hall, flung open for the light and air, Gwenhwyfar gestured for Amlawdd to walk with her, ordered that his escort be comfortably attended. She served him herself, pouring wine, offering food, anything to delay the need to sit, converse with him; thanked him politely for the gift, the expensive myrrh from the eastern trade routes. A luxury few in Britain could afford to buy from the traders who sailed from those distant lands.

Genially he patted the bench with his hand, gesturing for her to be seated beside him, chatted pleasantly of his journey, the weather, the prospect of an excellent harvest. She answered him well enough, able to talk of minor things, but her breath caught, inaudibly, as he slightly shifted position, took her fingers up in his hand.

Gwenhwyfar did not dislike Amlawdd. Indeed he was a man so innocuous that it was impossible to like or dislike him. It was his kindred, one brother in particular, long dead, that she hated. Amlawdd had so much of his appearance, though without the rank stench of stale wine and dried sweat, she could never look at him without the tremor of memory returning. That brother had beaten and mistreated her husband, raped her, murdered her own beloved brother. She gazed, eyes tear-misted, across the Hall, at the bustle of the women preparing the evening meal around the hearth-place. That was all so long, long ago, but the memories lingered. Memories would always linger.

Amlawdd had been talking. Gathering her wits, Gwenhwyfar apologized, asked him to repeat what he had said. Her mind was so easily distracted these days. There was no inclination to do anything, to go anywhere. She would sit for hours, staring at nothing, her mind blank. She had once been so active and alert, but since ... since he had gone ...

'I said that I have been into Gwynedd recently.' Amlawdd was stroking the skin along the back of her hand. Idly, Gwenhwyfar watched his fingers moving there, wondered at why she did not withdraw from the touch.

'Gwynedd?' she asked, vague.

'Aye,' Amlawdd cantered on with his rehearsed speech. 'Your brother Enniaun was most welcoming. We passed several weeks together in mutual pleasure, hunting through those deer-filled forests of his. There are still some small patches of snow on the tops of the highest mountains, you know!' He had been amazed at that, indeed, as a man born and bred along the coastal marshes of the Summer Land had been amazed at all the beauty and awe that the mountains of Gwynedd offered. 'I feel it a privilege to be honoured by your brother's calling me as friend. He is a most generous and wise man, will make a most pleasing kinsman.'

186

Dumbly, Gwenhwyfar stared at him. Why was he telling her all this?

For Amlawdd, the conversation seemed not to be going as well as he had hoped. Deliberately he had talked of her childhood home – an opening move to put her at ease. She ought have responded with enthusiasm, with exchanged pleasure. Momentarily he fumbled for what to say next, decided to come straight out with his reason for being here. 'As you know, I have no wife. I asked permission of your eldest brother for me to consider the taking of another.'

Frowning, the thought trundled through Gwenhwyfar's sluggish brain. *Why ask Enniaun?*

Beads of sweat began to prickle Amlawdd's forehead. 'My dear, you are a woman alone, unprotected. Your daughter has no father.' He lifted her hand to his lips, turned it over, kissed the palm, his eyes on her face. Relieved that she did not snatch away from him. 'I offer you my sword and shield, lady. I offer you myself as husband. I truly want you as wife.'

Blankly, Gwenhwyfar stared at him. The silence became embarrassingly long.

Gamely, Amlawdd stumbled on. 'Your brother believes it to be an excellent match and already the Supreme Governor has given us his blessing. Our union can take place,' Amlawdd vacantly waved his free hand, 'well, almost immediately.'

'No!' Gwenhwyfar shot to her feet, snatching her hand from his grasp, her startled cry echoing and bouncing between the timber, tapestry-covered walls. The heads of servants and Caer-folk lifted alarmed, one or two men came a step closer, hands on their dagger-hilts.

Hurriedly, confused, Gwenhwyfar waved their startled concern down. She was not in danger, needed no help. For all that, her faithful Ider, standing just within the shadows of the open doorway, checked that his blade was loose in its sheath. He did not trust this Amlawdd of the Mount of Frogs. Never had. Amlawdd had once ordered him killed, only his men had bungled the doing. Ider had conveniently set aside the fact that he had gone to Amlawdd's fortress for the same purpose, to kill him.

Gwenhwyfar recovered herself, managed to smile at her visitor. 'Sir, forgive me, your words have flustered me.' She kept the smile, though her heart was lurching. Enniaun, her own brother, had agreed to this? How could he? Then the thought, how dare he! And Ambrosius had been consulted in this obnoxious thing – God's breath, had everyone, save herself, been involved in decision-making about her future? She must find a way out of this without giving offence, gain time to think straight. Aye. Gain time. Her smile widened, reaching to her eyes. 'This is so unexpected, so generous. I,' she faltered, took breath, plunged on, 'I would ask time to make a reply. My husband, you understand, meant much to me. It is a serious matter to take a successor, I will need to consider, and seek advice.'

Her answer seemed plausible enough for, coming to his feet, Amlawdd beamed pleasure. For a moment, he had thought she was going to reject him. 'Naturally, my dear, I understand. But this you must understand also, you need to take a husband.' He lowered his voice, glanced surreptitiously around to ensure none stood too close, could overhear. 'Ambrosius needs to have you placed somewhere that gives him security. You are, however unintentionally, a threat to him. It would be wise to take a husband, to retain your freedom.'

The false smile vanished from Gwenhwyfar's face, that muddled panic disappearing with it, a flare of anger interceding. She had not missed the subtle threat. 'Freedom? What mean you?'

A second time, Amlawdd glanced around. 'Ambrosius confided in me,' he shrugged his shoulder, flapped a hand, 'oh, some while past, that he could not leave you to stir possible trouble. It is a steadying husband, loyal to the Governor, for you, my lady, or the safe confine of a nunnery.' He was lying, but Gwenhwyfar had no knowing of that. Were she to refuse him, the last was a suggestion he would most assuredly put to Ambrosius.

Wild, dizzying, angry thoughts chased across Gwenhwyfar's mind. Breathing steadily, trying to mask her alarm, she controlled herself. By the blood of the Bull she must get herself out of this! She replaced the smile, her senses coming rapidly alert.

'I thank you for your confidence. A husband would be more acceptable than the piety of a convent!' She signalled for a servant to approach, gave orders for Amlawdd and his men to be found comfortable quarters.

'I trust you will enjoy your stay at Caer Cadan,' she said. 'I will inform you of my decision as soon as it be made.'

Again, a dazzling smile set Amlawdd at his ease and, aware that he had been dismissed, he had no choice but to withdraw from the Hall with the waiting servant. He bowed, smiled and left, encouraged that Gwenhwyfar had amicably returned his reverence. He would see her at the evening Gather, speak again with her, nudge her decision in the right direction.

Only Gwenhwyfar was not at the Gather. A mild chill, he was told.

Amlawdd did not know enough of Caer Cadan to know who was attendant and who was gone. Had he been aware that Ider, captain of Gwenhwyfar's guard – all her guard – were missing, and that horses had left the Caer through the western gate, their going muffled by the natural noise of the evening, he might have showed alarm. As it was, the food and the wine at Caer Cadan was, as always it had been, most plentiful and good.

§ XXII

They rode the best horses, not necessarily the fastest or most sensible, but the most valuable. Onager, the bad-tempered chestnut who had once been Arthur's war stallion, Gwenhwyfar rode herself. He was difficult to handle, being strong of muscle and temper, with snapping teeth and perpetually flat-back ears and likely to kick any who came too close behind, but she was a competent rider, and perversely, was fond of him. As Arthur had been. She rode him often, for he was a link with the past, something alive that had been Arthur's.

They had packed hurriedly but efficiently, Ider agreeing with Gwenhwyfar, in hasty conference, that it seemed likely they would not be returning to Caer Cadan for some while.

'I am not safe here,' she had confessed, pressing her hand on Ider's arm, as he dutifully protested that she would always be safe within his protection.

A few clothes, items of value: jewels, rings, necklaces. Arthur's great sword, wrapped in the tattered, blood-stained Dragon Banner, Gwenhwyfar carried rolled within her own saddle-bundle. It was never far from her, that sword. As with Onager, it had been a part of Arthur, an extension of his soul, his being, the last thing he had touched. Had been in his hand as he died . . . it lay in her bed at night, that sword, held close on those many occasions when the drowning loneliness swamped too deep.

Ider carried Archfedd, drowsing after a full hour's ride, beneath the wrap of a cloak, though she had been awake at first, eager and excited at the prospect of a night adventure. Her only protest, which threatened wailed tears, that they should not leave her pony behind. So Briallen had come also, making herself useful by carrying one of the packs.

Twelve of them left Caer Cadan, heading almost due south for the coast, and Durnovaria. Gwenhwyfar and Archfedd, Ider and her personal guard. Among those men another as loyal and devoted as Ider, Gweir. He was ten and nine now, a young man, although it could be one year more or one year less, for he was not certain of his birthing year. Arthur had found him, a ragged, scrawny boy of ten summers, while campaigning up beyond the Wall. He had been furious at first, the boy, at the thought of being taken as slave, but with no family, no home and no hope, he had soon seen sense. The sense turning to awe and within a short time, love, when he discovered the identity of his new master. Gweir lived for the Pendragon, even after being awarded his freedom. Would have died for him too, at that last, awful battle, had he been given chance, but the lad had been out of things almost from the first, when a club had knocked him senseless. He had awoken to find that the sway of battle had drifted from where he had fallen, and that it was nearly all over. Gweir was one of the few to have returned, to have struggled, weary and heart-sore, home to Britain, to Caer Cadan. At least the hurt of Arthur's passing had been eased by the joy of finding his lady alive, that the report of her death had been false. Most of those who came back elected to continue soldiering, it was their life, their being. They joined with Ambrosius for the sake of Britain, but Gweir stayed with Gwenhwyfar, promoted as one of her trusted guard.

'Will Lord Geraint give us the protection we need?' Gweir had pushed his horse forward, rode beside his Queen, giving respectful distance to Onager's quick heels. She nodded confidently at him. 'Aside the men who ride here with me this night, the lords Bedwyr and Geraint are the most trusted among all those I know.'

Although there was no moon, they rode easily, for the road was maintained even here, as it crossed the ridge of hills running as a border between the Summer Land and Geraint's Durotrigia. Gwenhwyfar lifted her head confidently, spoke again to Gweir. Although he would not be able to see her movement in the darkness, he would hear the sincerity in her voice. 'I can trust all those men who loved my husband.'

Gweir bowed his head, beneath his breath muttered, 'Amen to that.' Gwenhwyfar regarded him curiously a moment. For how long had he been a follower of Christ? She said nothing. A man's religion was his own business.

The distance between the two strongholds was not far in miles – not many over twenty – an easy ride, even in the dark, but in the measurement of safety Geraint's land was immense. Protected on the west and north by the strength of Arthur's – Gwenhwyfar's – land; southward by the sea and high, rugged cliffs; and east by a firm-fortified ditch and rampart earthwork. Unless overwhelmed by an army the size of a legion, Durotrigia was safe enough.

Geraint was proud of his heritage. Green, rolling hills, gentle breeze-whispered woodland, fish-filled rivers and streams, all nursed by a subtle, warm climate. The father of his fathers had settled this south-western corner and thrived ... until the General Vespasian had come with his Roman Eagles and massacred men, women and children in the name of the Emperor. Geraint's kindred, the Lord of the Durotriges had been slaughtered defending his vast and impressive stronghold of Maiden-Hill. One daughter, a babe in arms, lived, carried away by a woman as her own; one of the few, on that sad, bitter day, to survive. From her, and the few of her kind, the memories lingered through the telling of tales of the time before Rome. Geraint was lord now, as that distant, shadowed lord had once been, but the Maiden-Hill would never be a lord's place again. Too many spirits wept upon its high, rampart walls.

On the surface, Gwenhwyfar had no idea why she was riding through the night like a cutpurse thief. She only understood the heart-thump of panic and clamour of danger screaming a warning. She had not imagined it, for Ider had seen and felt it with her, he had not hesitated when she had summoned him, urgent, into her chamber, told him quickly, succinctly, of her need to leave and its reason.

Ider's only objection, which he sensibly kept to himself, was that it might have been better to have finished Amlawdd and had done with it. But then, happen that was what Ambrosius hoped for. The murder of Amlawdd would give him excuse to destroy Caer Cadan. Aye, better to leave, gain time to think this thing through. One thing Ider – all the men, although none need voice opinion – held for certain. With their last breath, they would fight to prevent their lady marrying against her will. Aye, they rode eagerly into the land of the Durotriges. Geraint's tribal people held dear to their hearts the way it had once been, the way it ought to be. Arthur, as Geraint's lord, had been their cherished King. Under their protection, Gwenhwyfar would be safe.

None dared consider the consequences for Caer Cadan and the Pendragon's lands. That bridge would need be crossed when the track led to it.

§ XXIII

They arrived after everyone had settled for the night, with all but the lamps of the watch-guard extinguished, hearth-fires smoored and the lord of the stronghold gone already to his bed. The gatekeeper eyed them suspiciously, holding his burning torch high to examine their faces. Gruffly acknowledging recognition of the lady, he sent a lad to waken his lord, directed the party to ride inside, slamming the gates shut again, almost on the last horse's swishing tail.

The place was a rambling, hotchpotch of wattle and timber dwellings and shops, erected haphazardly among and against the remaining Roman buildings. Durnovaria. The main road that ran north–south, was empty, except for a dog chained before a closed tavern and a one-eared tom cat that hissed disrespectfully at them from the top of a crumbling back-garden wall. The hooves echoed and clattered on the dew-wet cobbles, but no light shone from behind shuttered windows, no door creaked open. For all that, there was a feeling of being watched; aye, some disturbed from their sleep peeped out to see who rode by at so early an hour.

The Hall was situated where once the basilica had dominated the forum-place, and was partly built with the stonework of that once opulent building. Smaller than the Hall at Caer Cadan, though no less impressive, it stood, by far the largest building, dominating the town with its solid air of indestructibility and security. Geraint was there, on the steps, to welcome them, cloak thrown over old bracae and tunic, the first garments to hand, with hair tousled, eyes sleep-bleared. He came forward to meet them.

If he was surprised to see the Pendragon's lady, he made no sign out here in this public place, though there were only a few of the watch and a handful of the curious to see. Enid came bustling down the steps, a wool cloak tossed over her night-garment. She hugged Gwenhwyfar, took Archfedd from Ider, the child waking briefly. She would be settled with Enid's own children, wriggling into the warmth of their bed like a hound-pup pushing into the comfort of her litter-mates.

With her men allotted quarters, the horses taken off to stabling, Gwenhwyfar asked Ider to enter Geraint's private chamber with her and their host. For as captain of her guard he would need be involved with plans or decision-making.

It was near dark inside, with only one night-lamp burning, Enid lit more while Geraint poured wine for them all. Ider squatted before the hearth-fire to stir life into its embers, and offered a smile of encouragement to Gwenhwyfar, who seated herself wearily on a stool before the reviving flames. She looked so tired, her eyes black-bruised, skin taut over her thinned cheeks. He wished he could do more to help her, but what could he, a mere captain, do for a queen?

Enid resisted a longing glance towards her rumpled bed. Geraint sipped his wine while Gwenhwyfar gave reason for their being here. She asked a few questions, digested the answers.

'Amlawdd will not be much amused when he learns of your departure,' Enid observed with her usual practicality. 'May he not even be offended?'

Her husband snorted. 'Hah! Let him, he's naught but a troublemaking, frog-footed marsh-wallower.'

'He is close to Ambrosius,' Enid retorted as a reminder.

'I could not stay,' Gwenhwyfar stated, agitated. 'I have no explanation. I just – ' She broke off, lifted her hands, let them fall into her lap. 'I just could not.'

'May I speak?' Ider said, tentative, eyeing his host for permission, addressing Gwenhwyfar. 'We did the right thing in coming where Amlawdd will not dare follow. He may well be angry, but we have gained the time we need to think, to plan.'

'To plan for what?' Geraint asked. 'A war with Amlawdd? That is a high possibility given his aptitude for stupidity!'

Sighing, Gwenhwyfar studied her hands, the ring on her marriage finger. The ring Arthur had given her. A ruby, the colour of blood. His blood. She choked back tears. 'I need to make decision on my future.' She looked up, anguished. 'But it is so hard, facing tomorrow and tomorrow, when all I want is yesterday.'

'It will ease,' Geraint said, leaning forward to touch her hand. 'The grief does ease.'

She nodded, attempted a smile. How could she disagree? They thought they were right. She knew they were wrong. If only he had been brought home to a grave. If only she had been given chance to say her goodbye, send him safe, into the Otherworld . . .

'I think we ought send word to Amlawdd, explain your coming here.' That was Enid. 'If we can make him think that there is a possibility of you accepting his proposal, he may be diverted from any anger.'

Geraint agreed. Gwenhwyfar, with a show of venom, did not.

'I will never marry that toad!'

'Mayhap not,' Enid interjected. 'But it will do no harm to allow him to think otherwise. At least until – ' She paused, searching for a way to put her thoughts tactfully. 'At least until you have settled yourself.'

Her husband was not so delicate with his wording. 'It needs to be faced, Gwen. You must remarry – no, do not jump up in some rage. Look at the sense of it, woman!'

Sense! Gwenhwyfar's face had flamed red, her anger taut. *Never*, she wanted to scream, *never*!

Ider would have offered himself as husband were he of higher rank. Ah, but dreams and wishful thinking were of no help.

Geraint spoke again, practical and insistent. 'Gwen, you are too vulnerable, too useful. You need a husband – if for nothing else, to keep ambitious wolves from your door.'

'Geraint, I . . .'

'No, you must listen! Amlawdd will not take no for answer. Only the taking of a husband can block him, and others. For if not Amlawdd, there will be others. You are too wealthy, too alone, for there not to be.'

She knew Geraint to be right, knew he spoke sense and truth. But to have another man touching her, laying with her? She had only ever known and loved Arthur, save for that one abuse by another.

Enid had picked up her sewing, was darning a hole in her son's bracae.

There was always mending or weaving, or spinning to be done. Her thoughts were cantering with the pace of her quick-fingered needling. 'What of my Lord Bedwyr?' she commented.

Geraint rubbed at the stubble of his chin. It would be dawn soon, no chance of returning to his bed. He would go straight to the bathhouse when this was all settled. 'Think you it necessary I send a messenger for him? Ought he know of this?'

Indulgent, Enid smiled at him. 'I did not mean that,' she laughed. To Gwenhwyfar, coaxed, 'Is there not something more than kindred and friendship between you both?' The daughter of a high-born family, Enid had come to Gwenhwyfar as nurse to her sons, had become, through the passing of years, through the sharing of laughter and tears, much valued as a friend. She was well qualified, and astute enough, to make intimate comment.

Bedwyr? Aye, Bedwyr was a good friend, more than a friend. Gwenhwyfar had some love for him, but not the sort of love you gave to a husband. Bedwyr, as husband?

Hating himself, Ider offered, 'You could not do better than to take him, my lady. None would dare challenge him.' Except myself! He bit the feeling of jealousy down, swallowed it. He had a wife of his own, and a brood of sons and daughters. He ought not think of his Queen in so intimate a way, for all that his thoughts were kept secret to himself.

Toying with the ruby ring on her finger, twiddling it around and around – it was looser than once it had been – Gwenhwyfar tried to sort her swirling mind. What to do? Oh, what to do?

The hole darned, Enid set her mending aside, tucking the needle safe into its holder. She stood, her expression and air efficient, authoritative. 'It is not wise to come to decision now, my lady. You are tired and distraught, you need calm and peace. Stay with us a while. Send word to Amlawdd – and my Lord Bedwyr – that you are here, that you will make a decision before the winter snows fall. God has his guiding hand on the shuttle of life, give Him time to weave a pattern for you.' Enid was a firm believer in leaving the uncertainties of the future to God and the tapestry of fate.

§ XXIV

Bedwyr arrived at Durnovaria with a flurry of joviality and a saddle-bag bulging with presents. His coming was like a summer whirlwind, swirling everything in its path and setting it down again blown, flustered and

194

breathless. He had that effect, particularly on the women, both unmarried and those with husbands. He was a good-looking young man, tall, muscular but not heavily built, with unruly brown hair and a constant twinkle in his eye, and grin to his lips. Every maid lost her heart to him.

Stretching his long legs from his offered stool to soak the warmth of the central hearth-fire in Geraint's Hall, he happily accepted the exuberant fuss that flurried around his evening arrival. The day had been grey, with a light drizzle and a chill sea wind hustling from the south. Even as he had entered the town he had acquired a crowd, those who knew him tossing generous greetings, others admiring the new horse he rode. A spirited chestnut, a present, he shouted to those who asked, from Ambrosius himself! A bribe, more like, but why question a good gift over-closely?

Gwenhwyfar was the only one to greet him quietly. Standing with Geraint and Enid to give welcome, her smile was simple, her embrace equally so. For his part, he had slid his arm around her waist, placed a light kiss on her forehead and given her a boyish wink. There was no need for more between the two. An exchanged greeting between friends who needed no opulent gesture, a plain acknowledgement that he was here, for her, for no other reason. They would talk later, alone.

Already she felt better. Bedwyr's presence could light a dark room with sun and gaiety, his easy chatter and endless, absurd stories lifting the dullest of moods. Several times he glanced at her, watching as she sat, quiet, hands folded in her lap, legs crossed at the ankles, to one shadowed side of the Hall. She was troubled, he could see that. He knew part of the reason from the letter Geraint had sent, urging him to come down to Durnovaria as soon as he could arrange leave from his command. Bedwyr enjoyed soldiering, enjoyed the position of authority and high command, but Gwenhwyfar was more important.

One thing Bedwyr would never understand. How Arthur could have placed his country's needs before his wife's. Had she been some hag-bound old harpy, then aye, it would be explainable, but to leave Gwenhwyfar? For so long? Bedwyr commanded because he had rank and title, but he had no ambition, no aspiration for power. All he wanted was a woman in his bed, a warm fire to sit beside, a bellyful of good food and a goblet brimming with best wine. Soldiering was a way to pass the time until he found a woman willing to share these modest wants.

He had been greeted at Durnovaria with wide smiles and friendly laughter. As with any stronghold, Geraint's no exception, visitors with news were highly welcomed – and Bedwyr had much news to tell!

The land above the Tamesis river, settled by the Saxons and Anglians, had surrendered to Ambrosius without blood being shed. The fortresses that he had ordered built were full-fledged garrisons, establishing regular patrols, with the British presence beginning to dominate the English settlements. Trouble would come, Bedwyr said. It was only a matter of the right time and the right opportunity. All agreed with Bedwyr on that.

Well into the evening Bedwyr talked, relating stories, news and gossip, not all of it true, but again and again he returned to Ambrosius. 'These fortresses of his, they are built to keep peace with the English.' Bedwyr's tone implied that, were you to believe that, you would believe the earth circled around the sun. 'Their very presence is stirring the Saex to thoughts of war. It might cleanse a wound to rub salt into the bleeding, but, ah, we all know the pain of the treatment.'

To Gwenhwyfar, he talked of marginal things. Later, when most had sought their sleeping places, he had the chance to exchange a brief, quiet word with her, to hear from her own lips Amlawdd's proposal, her rejection of it.

Though Amlawdd had angrily retreated to his own stronghold with a grievance as furious as a winter tempest, Bedwyr agreed wholehearted with Gwenhwyfar's tactics. Amlawdd was no great threat, they could well enough ride his storms. Before they parted for their own beds, Bedwyr jested to her, 'If you are in desperate need of a husband, I would consider obliging you.'

Gwenhwyfar added her laughter to his, lightly kissed his cheek with affectionate fondness. It was only later, laying awake watching the dim-lit shadows moving across the walls of her allotted chamber, that she wondered just how much Bedwyr was jesting. And how much he was serious.

As with most nights, sleep came for her only after the tears of despair had dried on her cheeks. She missed Arthur, his smile, his tempers and irritating habits. His embrace, his loving. Their relationship had often been tempestuous, but their passion as strong. Gwenhwyfar was a woman who needed the intimacy of love, and for that, she needed Arthur. Or a husband to take his place. It would be good to have someone to cling to in the loneliness of the dark. To be held and comforted by a man's touch. By Bedwyr? If she could never again have Arthur's love, would Bedwyr, with his bright eyes and sun-shimmering laughter, do instead?

§ XXV

With so many living within a busy stronghold, privacy was a luxury awarded to the very few. An honoured guest such as Gwenhwyfar might be offered accommodation within a small dwelling-place, but Bedwyr slept among the unmarried men of Geraint's house-guard in the Hall, comfortable on hay-filled pallets, covered by animal furs or thick-woven woollen cloaks. By day, there were always people around, free-born, servant or slave. Enid with her brood of children, Geraint himself. This huge, extended family arrangement was ideal for someone who wanted to avoid, for whatever reason, the embarrassment of being alone with someone. Unless the chance was deliberately sought, there could rarely be opportunity for lengthy private conversation.

And that Gwenhwyfar was avoiding Bedwyr was as plain to Enid as it was to the man himself.

So it was, on the third day, that Enid suggested her guests ride to the ancient stronghold where once Geraint's ancestors had held court. The day was pleasant enough, Bedwyr was enthusiastic. Gwenhwyfar had no choice to disagree without seeming churlish.

They took six men as escort. Geraint's domain was safe territory, but Gwenhwyfar was still the anointed queen; she rode nowhere without Ider and her guard. Many years ago, when she had assumed herself out of danger while in similar safety, her small guard had been attacked, herself injured by Amlawdd's son. Arthur had been so furious at the careless lack of precaution. Never again had any of his Artoriani allowed their lady to be placed in danger. Whenever, wherever, a guard escorted her.

They left the men and horses, under Ider's watchful eye, at what would have been Maiden-Hill's eastern gate and walked together up what would have been a busy trackway passing through the banks and ditches that reared one behind the other. A few young, green-shooted saplings were trying for a foothold along the lush grass of the first ditch, but wandering sheep and deer would not give much chance for them to survive. Congenially, through panting breath, Gwenhwyfar and Bedwyr debated theories of how the impressive pattern of gates would have been structured, the size and number of buildings that would have been inside the enclosure that was ahead. At the third bank, Bedwyr called a halt; stood, hands on his hips, catching his breath.

'This is some climb!' he panted. 'No wonder Geraint's ancestors thought themselves safe, tucked away up there.' He ducked his head behind him, indicating the rest of the steep incline.

Gwenhwyfar had her hand on her chest, taking lungfuls of air. As fit as they were, the climb had winded them. 'The Romans were too new here, then, for their threat to be understood.' Her breathing easing, she studied the ground below and above. 'They could not have defeated this stronghold without the sophistication of their fighting machinery.'

Holding out his hand to haul her upward, Bedwyr answered, 'Family tradition, Geraint told me, relates that his ancestor was killed outright by a ballista bolt between the eyes.' He winced. 'Messy.' He received a nod from Gwenhwyfar by way of response, this last haul was too steep for talking.

The wind from the coast caught them square on the face as they stepped out from the shelter of the track. Before them lay acres of sheep-cropped grass, securely enclosed by the top rampart bank. Gone was the palisade fencing, the wooden guard-towers, the round houses, granaries, cattlepens, storage pits and sheds. Gone, the Hall, the heart of the community. Nothing, save the wind and the grass, and the remains of one square, stone-built building. They ignored it, for it was a tawdry Roman temple.

Leaping up the incline to the top of the last rampart, Gwenhwyfar shaded her eyes from the buffeting wind, her hair whipping away from loose hairpins, her cloak swirling around her legs. The stronghold was impressive. 'This is magnificent!' She marvelled as her eyes roamed over the expanse of enclosed land and then outward. Was that the sea there in the distance? Clouds were gathering. Rain.

They walked around this top rampart, following where once the fencing and walkway would have strode, pointing out intricacies of the next gateway, a faded shadow where once a track had lain. Gwenhwyfar exclaimed at a hare, set running almost from beneath their feet. Bedwyr cursed, he had no spear with him.

'Na,' Gwenhwyfar chided, 'let the goddess keep her fleet-footed messenger. There has been enough killing in this place.'

It took an hour or more to walk the entire circuit, by which time their cloaks were drawn tight against the wind, and their hair was as ragged as a wind-teased seed-head. The clouds had surged nearer, heaping higher and wilder. A few dithering spots of rain fell.

'Would there be shelter beneath the banks?' Gwenhwyfar queried, peering at the lowering sky. Already she was cold, had not much inclination to become wet also in this late-summer storm.

'The temple would be better.' Bedwyr was already running, her hand clasped firmly in his, his head ducked against the sudden cloud burst. Boots slipping on the sudden-wet grass, they ducked through the doorless entrance, stood breathless, laughing together as they shook the rain from cloaks and hair.

It was not much of a building, half a roof, one wall cracked and bowed. One puff of wind from the right direction and surely it would be down. Roof tiles scattered on the floor among an accumulation of debris, leaves, grass, sheep droppings. The remains of a fire. Someone else had sheltered here, then. Bedwyr squatted down, began poking at the cold ashes, peered around for dry timber. 'There may be enough for a fire if you are cold,' he offered, raising his eyes questioningly at Gwenhwyfar. She was standing by the door, her arms clutched around herself, watching the sheet of dark rain blanketing the expanse of desolate fortress that had once, so long, long ago, been active with the bustle of life.

She shook her head. 'No,' she smiled, a sad half-complete expression. 'No,' she repeated, 'I am not cold, now we are out of the wind.'

Bedwyr came to his feet, crossed the small space and stood before her; after a moment, put his fingers out to tuck away a loose strand of hair behind her ear. 'I love you,' he said. There was no laughter, no jesting. 'I always have, ever since I was a boy.'

She dipped her head, not knowing how to answer him.

'I would never let anyone else take you as their own,' he added.

Gwenhwyfar nodded her head, a small, slight movement. Aye, she knew that.

As if she were a fragile, terracotta-made doll, Bedwyr slid his arms around her, drew her to him, nestled her head into the dip of his shoulder, cradled her softness against his strength. His fingers stroked her copper-coloured hair, and his lips brushed her forehead. She made no response, but then, neither did she move away.

There was no intention for anything more, but they were a man and woman, alone, sheltering from the rain. Both with their own, separate, need. It was nothing frenzied or passionate, their love-making, not the sweating, breathless coupling of the desperate; rather this was a shared giving and taking, the need to be loved, the wanting to give comfort and protection. Something gentle and immensely tender.

§ XXVI

Bedwyr must have drifted into sleep, for he awoke with a start, some abruptness in a dream grunting him alert; found the rain had stopped and Gwenhwyfar gone, though her perfume, the vague scent of summer meadow flowers, lingered. Damp and chilled, he collected his cloak that they had lain upon, shook away the dead grass, twigs and earth, and fastened it around his shoulder; stepped outside.

Everything was fresh and gleaming, the grass sparkling as if some faery-creature had wide-scattered handfuls of tiny diamonds. The sky, where the rain had passed, was a cloud-skeined cobalt blue. A flight of wild geese threaded past in their pondering formation, their cries and beating wings eerie and mournful in the silence of this ghost-murmuring place. Gwenhwyfar stood on the top rampart, her back to him, facing the sea, the wind blustering at her loose-tossed hair and folds of her cloak. She stood, straight and still. Arms wrapped around herself, staring into the heavy weight of the past.

Beyond these deep ditches and high ramparts lay the rolling hills. Beyond them, the sea. Wind-whipped, white-tipped, sea-crested horses, prancing their wild dance with the tide. The Britannic ocean, over which he had sailed with his men. Over which he would never return.

'I miss him,' Gwenhwyfar spoke to the buffeting wind, her voice carrying to the spirits who must surely be watching, listening, aware. To his spirit? Did he hear? Was he there, trying to be near her? If he was, why could she not feel him, feel something of him – a whisper on the wind, a half-seen shadow? He had believed her dead, but surely he knew now . . . surely? But why did she never feel that, if only she could turn around quick enough, she would see him standing there, with that familiar smile. Why did she never see his face in her dreams or hear his voice? Imagine his touch? Why was there this nothingness for her, beyond the empty darkness of this desolate ache?

Did he miss her? Were his tears as many, was his pain as searing? 'I miss you!' she shouted again to the wind. 'Miss you so much, but I am so, so very angry with you!' She let her head drop back, her breath clamped tight in her chest, tears wet on her face. 'So angry that you went, that you'll not be coming back to me. So angry that you loved me, angry because I ought to hate you for hurting me like this!' She lifted her arms, her fists clenched. 'Why did you go?' She cried, 'Why? Tell me, why?' Her fingers went to her hair, combing through its loose thickness. 'How could you do this to me, Arthur?'

Watching, the pain tore at Bedwyr's heart as if a sword were twisting there. She might lie with him, marry him, but he would never possess Gwenhwyfar. Not until Arthur's spirit was laid. And how did you fight a ghost?

Nothing, only the sigh of the wind as it toyed with her hair, the geese in the distance. No snarl of thunder, no great burst of light. No roar, no cry, no sound. There was nothing, no feeling of him nearby, no memory

200

of his voice. He was not here, not with her. Gwenhwyfar was quite, quite alone. She let her arms drop, head and shoulders sag.

Uncertain whether to leave her to herself, or go to her with some offer of comfort, Bedwyr walked slowly, hesitant, across the wide expanse of sheep-nibbled grass. His toe caught against something, the light nudging its rain-wet shine into a sparked gleam. He bent, picked up the object. It had once been bronze, gleaming, worn proudly.

Gwenhwyfar had turned, seen him, was wiping at her falling tears, attempting a smile.

'Is all well?' he called, almost carelessly, as if nothing of serious importance had occurred.

She nodded, sniffed loudly, that smile winning through. 'Aye,' she said lifting her chin. And suddenly, she realized that she was, almost. 'Aye,' a slight laugh. 'I think I am. What's that?' She came down the bank, her impulsion and the steepness making her run, girlish, lovely. She took the thing from Bedwyr's outstretched hand – a buckle, a bronze baldric buckle, green and old, a few moss-bound garnets still decorated its hinge. She studied it a moment, solemnly handed it back.

While Bedwyr examined it, she looked across to where she had stood, up to the rain-washed, fresh-cleaned sky, then across to the ruined temple where not long ago she had willingly given herself to the touch of a man who was not Arthur.

'Everything has a start and a finish,' she said, with a soft, resigned sigh, 'but there is always something lurking unexpected to remind us of how it once was.' She placed her hand on Bedwyr's arm. 'I am searching for the thing that will help me forget, that is all.'

Her smile deepened as she stood on toe-tip to kiss his cheek. 'I am well. He has gone, I must accept that. I must look to the future, not the past, for that is a path of sad darkness. I must try to face into the sun again.' She patted his shoulder, a light, loving touch, walked away, heading for the gateway and the descent.

'Do I let it be known that you are to be mine?' Bedwyr called to her departing back.

She kept walking, her heart churning, breath thrashing. She needed to take a husband, if only to protect herself against those who wanted her as wife. But did she want to love again? Could she face being so hurt again? Her voice, for all her jangling thoughts, came calm. 'After Samhain,' she said. 'After the night of the dead, then aye, you can let it be known. Give me until then.' *Your last chance, Arthur*, she thought. *Your last chance to come back to me.*

He watched her walk down the steep track before following, glanced back over his shoulder at the temple. She might agree to be his, or somebody's, wife, but inside, she would always be Arthur's.

Bedwyr knew that, for as he had loved with her it was another name that she had murmured on the shadow of her breath.

Arthur.

§ XXVII

'Arthur!'

He heard his name being called, half-checked, his head lifting fractionally, fingers pausing, then bent back to his work. The figure he was carving was of a woman. He would tell Morgaine that it was of the Goddess. The wood was birch, smooth to the touch, pale, silvery, feminine. It was half-finished. The gown he had managed, the folds appearing easily beneath the blade of his knife, the feet and hands, perhaps, could have been a little more delicate. The face he would leave until last. Today he was shaping the head, working patiently, carving each separate curl down the long mass of loose hair. Later, he would find something that he could use to darken it a little, make it redder. Morgaine would know it was an image of Gwenhwyfar, but she would not make comment, would take it, delightfully thank him, make much of setting it in place of honour on their dwelling-place shrine. She was always polite, accepting, smilingly quiet even when he shouted at her.

She called again, her voice coming nearer. Arthur shifted uncomfortably, he was quite well hidden here beneath the trees unless she came up the path alongside the river. She did.

'There you are!' She beamed, fastidiously skipping across a scatter of rocks that served well as stepping stones, her hem held high above her knees to avoid the spray. The river ran fast here, making ready to descend in a series of waterfalls a little lower down. 'Did you not hear me call?'

Arthur had not looked up. She cast herself down beside him, in a flurry of bright-coloured swirled skirt and jangling bracelets. Still he did not look at her.

'Is it not a glorious day?' She sighed, lay back, stretching out, sharing the shade of his tree. Arthur, his back against the trunk, grunted a non-committed answer.

'Look at those clouds,' she persisted cheerfully, tucking her hands behind her head. 'The gods riding their white chariots across the sky. I wonder what they think of us?'

'What a useless pile of dung we are, I expect.' He meant to be sarcastic, but she giggled, thinking the comment amusing.

'I have left Medraut playing with his friends,' she said. 'They are planning a running contest. I told him he has no chance of winning.'

Arthur only grunted again, concentrated on his carving.

'What's that?' she asked, mildly curious.

'Nothing that concerns you.'

'You have a gift for carving. That bowl you made me was lovely.'

'Anyone with an ounce of sense in his brain can turn a lump of wood into something worthwhile.'

'Well, I cannot.'

He made no answer.

Morgaine toyed with the curled shavings, heaping them, fingering their soft, silkiness, wondered whether to collect them up for Medraut to play with later. Arthur was so hard to talk to, she could never entice him into conversation, tease him into even a smile, let alone laughter. With the boy he was as distant – though he took interest in his upbringing and education, teaching him his letters and numbers, telling him the histories of Greece and Rome. He never showed feeling, though, seemed so aloof, remote. Not once had she seen Arthur embrace the lad, yet he cared for him, she knew. The time last year when Medraut had fallen from that tree . . . it was Arthur who had run to him, Arthur who had carefully set the broken leg in splints, carried him to the house-place. Arthur who had watched over him during those first few fevered nights of the lad's discomfort and pain. Through eyes half-closed against the hot glare of the sun, Morgaine studied the man sitting cross-legged beneath the shade of the trees, patiently carving the figure of a slender woman. She wished she could understand him. Wished she could do more to help him.

Wished she had the strength to let him go back into his own world.

She pushed herself to her feet, dusted down her skirt, her bangles jangling and clanging. 'I called for I am about to set supper cooking. Will you be long?'

'Might be.'

'It will be ready for you when you come in.'

No, she would not wish for that last. She would rather they, all three of them, were dead rather than be without him.

September 471

§ XXVIII

Ecdicius of Gaul was too tired to dismount. He knew that if he tried to drop to the ground his legs would buckle, he would crumple into an undignified, quivering heap. His body ached. Beneath his leather and iron-linked armour he stank and itched from runnels of sweat, his face was dirtied and bloodied, bruises and welts would appear on his legs, arms and torso by the morrow. But by all the love of the good God, how wonderfully, exhilaratingly happy he felt! The grin beneath the loosened strap of his battered helmet was as wide as the Ligre river in full flood, and not all the shaking of his body was from exhaustion. Some of it was sheer excitement and incredulous disbelief.

They had done it, by God, he and a handful of men had defeated Euric's rabble of Goths, had sent them running, tails tucked tight between their legs! They had done it! The siege of Augustonemetum was lifted – by no more than a mere eight and ten mounted men. Less number than he would invite to dine at his table!

Bodies, Goths only, for not one of his own men had lost a life, lay fallen, sprawled in a grotesque trail across the plain. They had been brave men, those of the Goths who had tried to make a stand of it to the rearward of their fleeing army, but God's hand had most surely been cupped around Ecdicius and his cavalry this day! That first, unexpected, madly heroic charge had been responsible. From the cover of the hills, Ecdicius had led his men at the gallop, straight across the plain, straight through the milling crowds of the Goths busy with their besieging, ferocious assault on the town.

From above the battered and blood-marked walls, the citizens had watched, open-mouthed, heart-held, as the horses thundered through, leaving bloodied chaos and panic in their churned wake, their riders not giving a single backward glance. Hooves, teeth, lances, swords. It must have seemed as though all the hounds of hell were let loose to those confused, panicked Goths!

They fled to the sanctuary of the hills, unaware of how few their attackers were in number compared to their own. What chance had a poorly armed, common foot-soldier against the crushing, terrible deadliness of a cavalryman?

Ecdicius had swept through on that first charge with the ease of a hot knife through goose fat. He had wheeled, pursued the fleeing numbers, leaving behind the dead and the screams of the dying. A few, the more experienced, the harder-armed warriors, had tried to cover the rear, tried to salvage some dignity from the blind panic, but there had been no attempt to rally, or re-form. Shattered, defeated, stunned and appalled, the Goths had kept going, up into the hills and away.

They would be back, of course, on another day, at another town probably, before long, back to Augustonemetum for another try at taking it as their own. But for today and tomorrow at least, the citizens were safe. They opened the gates and poured out in a great spill of joyful cheering and shouting. Ecdicius grinned at his men, ordered their banner to be held high, and rode leisurely towards the procession that came flowing out to meet them.

A multitude of hands reached to take the bridles that were thick with foam and blood, clasped manes, tails, saddle straps; others reached to kiss away the dirt and grime from the faces of the eighteen men. Proud, they were led back into the crowded streets of the town. At the Forum they dismounted, eager helpers unfastening armour straps, helmets and grieves. The few wounds were marvelled over, reverently touched. Jostled and cheered, hugged, embraced, the eighteen Gauls found themselves carried high on shoulders, eighteen exultant men, grinning and laughing, enduring the high enthusiasm with good grace, though their bodies ached and their tiredness was immense.

At the steps of what the bishop proudly called his cathedral, Ecdicius was deposited on his own feet. Slowly, as if he were faced with climbing the steepness of a mountain, for his aches were many and his limbs heavy, he ascended to meet with the man waiting there at the top. The bishop himself, his brother-by-law, Sidonius Apollinaris. The most important man – save for Ecdicius!

Eager, Sidonius swept half-way down to greet his kinsmen, clasped hands, stood back for a few heartbeats, then took the town's hero tight in close embrace, tears streaming his face, words for once lost to this eloquent bishop's voice. They cried together a moment, laughed at their absurd emotion; then, with arms about each other, led the way inside the grand, stone-built church that stood as tall as three storeys and could seat along its benches the prominent citizens of all the town.

Ecdicius sank to his knees before the central altar, his men forming behind, their banner furled in homage to their God, heads bare and bent in submission and thanks. His mind only half listening to the bishop's inspired prayer, for he was idling, mulling over his own wonder and praise. His plan had been ambitious, formed of desperation, but it had worked, against all the sensible, wise odds. It had worked! He closed his eyes, let his heart and mind drift. Among his thoughts, the realization that today, this day, was his birthing day.

'May our God be praised for this glory . . .' The bishop's words were booming and resounding around the echoing building.

Sidonius had balked at this position of bishop, had been forced to take it, or face ruin and exile, but since this was now his vocation he plied all his mobile strength and character into doing the job to the very best of his ability. He was judged a fair-minded man, who cared much for the ill and poor; a revered man, loved by the people. He was wise and educated; some even believed him to possess powers, for did he not, at that time when the prayer books went unaccountably missing, recite the entire Mass from memory? Did Sidonius Apollinaris not have the wondrous ability to read from the scrolls without the need to move his lips? Today's prayer of thanksgiving was one of the bishop's best delivered, and would be remembered for many a year to come, but Ecdicius heard little of it, for he was making his own prayer, his own thanks. And he was thinking of one other, one who had not held the fortune that was blessed for them this day. Of Arthur, the Pendragon.

The bishop was ending, giving the blessing, and they were being shepherded outside, into the bright sunlight and great tumult of cheering. Tonight and for the next few nights to come, there would be feasting and dancing – such celebration as the town had never witnessed before, and would not see again.

Ecdicius turned to grin at his brother-by-law and at his sister, Sidonius's wife, who had come to greet her beloved brother. 'Is it not fortunate,' Ecdicius shouted above the din and clamour, 'that the Pendragon taught me how to drill cavalry, how to lead and fight a charge?'

Sidonius half-heard, catching only the words Pendragon and cavalry, but he returned the grin, nodded vigorously. Refrained from saying that if the Pendragon had fought the harder, the better, Gaul would not have need to fear the Goths now. Best left unsaid. Ecdicius had always held these silly notions that were put into his head by the dead and defeated British King.

December 471

§ XXIX

Saturnalia, the time of winter feasting and merry-making, had become for the Christians a celebration of the birth of Jesu Christ. A pagan feast that they had blatantly adopted for their own, its symbolism nearly fitting their beliefs. The evergreen for eternity, the blood-red berries for the shedding of the mother's birthing-blood and for Christ's own; the giving of gifts as the Magi had given Christ; a season of peace, goodwill. The symbolism of renewal, the passing of the old and the coming of the new. An opportunity for Gwenhwyfar to cast aside the past and look ahead to the future. A new life. New husband.

Geraint's Hall was crowded and jovial. Garlands of holly and ivies were draped along the rafters and placed behind the warriors' shields hung along the walls between the coloured, exquisitely woven, tapestries. A great log burned in the central hearth-fire; lamps, candles, torches, brought much light and warmth. At one end, the children played, Archfedd with Enid's own, and others of Geraint's officers and companions, their childish laughter shrieking with excitement, hands and faces sticky from honey-sweetened nuts and fruits.

Gwenhwyfar had dressed elegantly, wearing her favourite emerald-green gown, her amber necklace and earrings. Green ribbons were twined and plaited into the complicated braiding of her rich, copper hair, her green eyes sparkled in the dance of fire and lamplight. She smiled widely, amused, at Bedwyr who, rather drunk, was making a good-natured ass of himself in trying to imitate the three professional acrobats. He fell heavily from his fourth attempt at walking on his hands, lay on his back, spread-eagled, puffing like a stranded fish, while his audience cheered, clapped and guffawed. Geraint suggested he try balancing on someone's shoulders, Enid protested, alarmed that Bedwyr might take the jesting encouragement seriously.

'Great God, husband, he'll break his neck!'

Geraint chuckled happily, he too had partaken of too much wine. But why not? It was midwinter, the rain and cold was as hostile as a barbarian army outside, while in here, inside his Hall, it was warm and dry and pleasant. They had plenty of good food, good company. Good wine. Aye indeed, if a man could not enjoy his drink at Saturnalia, what was the point of celebrating? 'As long as he does not break his manhood, does it matter?' he jested, nudging Gwenhwyfar who sat beside him.

She also had consumed a glass or two too much of Geraint's fine, imported wine. She giggled, made a ribald answer. 'I suppose a crutch would not be suitable for all parts of the anatomy. Could a sling be fitted, I wonder?'

Geraint roared delight. 'Have we material wide enough to fit Bedwyr's adventurous piece?'

His wife tutted, shook her head, though she was laughing as much.

The subject of their amusement had scrabbled to his feet, was boldly fiddling inside his woollen bracae. 'Na,' he announced, 'everything appears functional!' Earned for himself more laughter and cheers.

Beaming, his face red from drink and exertion, Bedwyr settled himself on Gwenhwyfar's left, took his wine-glass up from the table and saluted her with extravagant gesture. 'I would do nothing that might jeopardize our partnership.'

'You had best take yourself off to your bed then, stay there in safety,' Gwenhwyfar teased.

Rolling his eyes, lips sporting a leer of approval, he answered rapidly, 'A fine idea! Come with me! Let us ensure all my equipment is kept practised!'

'Fool!' Chuckling, she batted at him with her free hand, her other had been taken by him as soon as he had seated himself. Bedwyr was proud to claim Gwenhwyfar publicly as his own, made much of ensuring all knew that he had won her, not caring to take regard of the disparaging comments that had drifted southward. The stirring was done by Amlawdd, of course, sour jealousy being behind the wide spread of malicious gossip. As personal friend to Ambrosius, Amlawdd saw himself as a figure of high importance, felt slighted by Gwenhwyfar's refusal, and therefore justified to make loud and continuing protest against Bedwyr. He was all hot air in pumped bellows, all words and mouth. Amlawdd would never find the courage – or stupidity – openly to make a challenge for Gwenhwyfar' hand. Did the imbecile not realize that the lady would never have him? Bedwyr let the fool spit his venom and slander, allowed him to save face before others of Ambrosius's court. Time enough to deal with anything more serious, should it arise, after the winter snows had fallen and melted again. Come spring, Bedwyr would be a month or two blessed as Gwenhwyfar's lawful husband, she could even be carrying his child. What could Amlawdd do about losing her to the better man then? It was said that empty amphorae made hollow noise. Hah! Amlawdd was as empty as a dry, fire-baked, new pot!

Sliding his arm around Gwenhwyfar's waist, Bedwyr brought her nearer, enjoying the supple feel of her slender body against his, relishing the joy of knowing what lay beneath her garments. Silk-smooth skin, long legs, and even though she had borne children, firm breasts and a flat stomach. The anticipation of sharing her passion, her immodest need, was already rousing him, the excess of drink doing little to dampen his eagerness. The Hall would be rising soon, drink-filled men and women seeking their dwelling-places within the settlement or, for the unmarried and the servants, beds within the protection of this Hall.

Gwenhwyfar, for all Amlawdd's protest and blustering, had emphasized that she was committed as Bedwyr's lady, though they had not yet been blessed by the priest and were not joined in legal marriage. They shared a need, and a companionship, the warmth of a bed; the formal details could come later, after Saturnalia. Gwenhwyfar had promised him that after Saturnalia they would exchange vows, make the thing legal. They were already bound together in companionship, she said, was that not enough for a while? In turn, Bedwyr had a concern that she was not going to consent to the formalities for they were supposed to have been wed two months past, on All Hallows Day, the day after Samhain. She had balked, suggested Saturnalia instead. He was impatient to slip the security of a marriage band on her finger, but, ah, surely he could wait until she was ready? She was his woman, no one else's – only that memory of Arthur formed a rival. And he had no fear of the dead.

The professional acrobats were performing some fabulous, breath-taking contortion, earning themselves splendid applause. Slaves were distributing wine as if the amphorae could never be emptied. Merrymaking, happiness. It was Saturnalia, a season for enjoyment and pleasure. Gwenhwyfar twined her fingers tighter into Bedwyr's clasp, joined the enthusiasm. Pushed back the voice whispering a name, a memory.

She *would* forget Arthur. She would! She had to.

But that damned, persistent voice would not let her.

§ XXX

The night lay quiet, except for the normal sounds – the bark of a dog fox, the call of an owl. No wind. With the temperature dropping, there would come a frost. Bedwyr slept on his back, hair tousled, arm outstretched, facial muscles twitching as his sleeping mind chased some dream. Beside him, Gwenhwyfar lay awake, listening to the darkness outside their small, private, dwelling-place, her eyes watching the pale hearth-fire shadows creep across the far wall. Archfedd was asleep in the other bed, curled

209

safe and warm against her nurse, a young lass of not more than ten and four, given to care for the child by Enid. Beside the last warmth of the hearth, the dogs were piled, Bedwyr's three brindle hounds and Gwenhwyfar's two, Blaidd and Cadarn. Both presents from Arthur: Cadarn for herself, Blaidd for her son, Llacheu. She remembered Arthur's face as he had held the two squirming pups, both from the same litter, his smile wide as he had dumped one in the boy's lap, the other in hers. The touch of his lips against her forehead as he had followed the giving with a light, almost casual-given kiss. Llacheu, playing with them when they reached that gangling, legs-longer-than-the-body stage . . . his wild shout of laughter as Blaidd had stolen a boot, the resulting game around their room as he had attempted to claim it back . . . Arthur's extensive cursing one wet night, when the dogs had come in from outside and shook their coats vigorously. Memories.

Bedwyr was more good-natured than Arthur, would shrug insults and nuisances aside with an indifference that could so easily be taken as uncaring. He believed more in the law, in the judicial intervention of right. Arthur would never have trusted to such unreliable uncertainty. If something angered or offended him, he would see to its sorting himself. Never would Arthur have allowed Amlawdd's tongue to have shouted the insults that had reached their ears these last few weeks. If Arthur had heard those vile things that Amlawdd had called her, the man would have been dangling by his balls from his own stronghold walls by now. Bedwyr had taken the man as a jest, had laughed, slid his arm around her and loudly proclaimed that they had nothing to fear from the jealous defeat of a toad-spawned, mannerless boor.

Nothing to fear? Happen not, but the words had stung. No woman liked to be called harlot, whore and slut. No woman cared to have her children cursed, her honour tainted.

Bedwyr would be returning to his garrison soon, within the week – before the snows came, he had said, as they were preparing for bed. His leave had finished, three weeks taken, he could not reasonably extend the time away from duty.

'Oh,' was all she had answered.

'Are you to come with me this time?' he had asked, as he had blown out the last lamp, scuttled beneath the fur-coverings. His place of command was a wooden-palisaded fortress set above the marsh-spread valley of the Dolydd river. Nothing grand, he had said, a plain fortress, and command of two further outposts set at stages up the valley. *'We keep a weather eye on the coming and going of the Saex as they bring their boats up the river to their little hovels.'* He had told her that when first he was posted there, oh, back into the new-end of summer. An out-of-the-way place, where Ambrosius had hoped to keep him apart from the likes of Geraint and Gwenhwyfar . . .

'I will come.'

She sighed, closed her eyes to try again for sleep that would not visit. *I will go with you*, she thought, said soft, aloud, into the darkness, 'but I will not wed with you. Not yet.'

Amlawdd had called her a whore, and worse, for deceiving him. Amlawdd had said that she had promised herself to him, aye, promised, even before the Pendragon was fool enough to get himself bloodily slaughtered. He was right, she had, but as a trick, as a means to gain time for Arthur.

Bedwyr mumbled something in his sleep, shifted, lumbering his body over onto his belly, taking most of the fur coverings with him as he turned. Gwenhwyfar lay a moment, her feet and body growing cold. No use trying to retrieve them, Bedwyr seemed to weigh as much as two oxen when he slept, was as possessive of his bed-coverings as a cat was of a captured mouse. It was being a soldier, she supposed. Arthur had been the same. He would roll himself into the bed-furs, leaving little for her. The difference, Arthur had been easy to wake. One prod, one mild kick. One kiss . . .

She sighed again, deeper, more drawn, left the bed to fumble in the dark for her cloak, hunkered down beside the fire with the dogs who flapped their tails with a welcome, happily allowed her to wriggle into their heaped warmth.

To gain time. Why was she stalling the deadline of marriage? Why would she not consent to make this new-begun thing binding between them? She ate with Bedwyr, laughed with him, slept with him. Had agreed this very night to go with him as a commander's lady. Why would she not go as his wife?

It was warm among the bundle of dogs, and comforting. She had her arms around Blaidd, Cadarn was resting his old, grey-grizzled muzzle across her feet. Warm and soothing.

She slept.

A stranger trudged wearily up the lane that trundled steeply up the incline between the ditches and ramparts. It was an hour after sun-up but still the gates at the top were closed; beyond, only a few thin wisps of hearth-place smoke spiralled into the frost-blue air.

He hammered on the iron-studded oak-built timbers, shouted for entrance. He had come a long way, on foot. A long, weary trek, his heart as heavy as his tired, blistered feet.

A face, grizzle-bearded, sleep-riddled, peered over the top rampart of Caer Cadan, demanded who made so much noise so early in the day.

'I have come to speak with the Queen. I have word for her, important word.'

'She ain't here. No one's here save us few. Gwenhwyfar's gone.'

The man, a Saxon, though he had taken care to dress himself British-fashion so as not to draw over-much attention, ran his fingers through his dank hair.

'To where has she gone?'

'Durnovaria. South of here.'

The Saxon almost wept. He had just come north, from the South Saxon Coast. He sat, desolate, tired, head in hands. For weeks now, he had been living like a beggar, walking the roads, sleeping in ditches and sheep-folds, constantly looking over his shoulder in case she had found his trail.

He had masked it as well he could, travelling through the great dark forests of Gaul, first, working his way to the River Rhenus, to put her off the scent, before finding a ship to bring him across the sea to Britain. A waking nightmare! He was the last alive, for she had dealt with the others, torturing them, his companions, his friends, before ending their lives. Dealt with them as she had dealt with their mistress.

Oh ja, it was known that it had been her, Winifred, that half-British witch who had been behind the murder of Lady Mathild. He did not believe the lies that they had said about that good woman. Not as most of them had! That she had tried to kill her own son.

At least the boy was safe. Cerdic had proclaimed that, as the funeral pyre had burnt high, taking Mathild's spirit on her last journey to the gods. 'Cynric is my son,' he had said, 'my son and hers. In him, her spirit shall live on!' Ja, it had better or Cerdic would answer for it! There were those along the Elbe who had never trusted Cerdic. He was not one of them by blood, for all his adoption by the Lord Leofric. Adoption was not blood-tied, not blood-bound kindred. Cynric was of her blood. And his. Arthur's, not Cerdic's. Though that was their private view, those men who had come with Mathild from Arthur's camp, after he had set them all lawfully free from the misery of slavery.

They had served Arthur with loyalty, repaying his asking of no questions of whence and from whom they had come. Had served Mathild, as one of their own kind, with loyalty even deeper. And now he was the only one left alive, the only one who knew two things of importance. That Cynric might not be Cerdic's son. Oh, the dates, the calculations might be wrong, that was all women's matters and women's words, but he knew this for certain: Mathild had been as sick as a poisoned dog each morning on that journey from Gaul to the settlement along the Elbe. It could have been the fear, the grief; the poor food, the fast-set pace. Or it could have been for a woman's reason.

And that the Pendragon might be alive, not dead as they were all meant to believe. A secret Mathild had kept to herself, sharing it only with them, her few trusted, loyal, personal guard. '*Tell Gwenhwyfar*,' she had commanded of them. '*If ever something should happen to me, tell Gwenhwyfar that I believe Arthur to be with the ladies of the Goddess in Gaul.*'

He looked up at the bright sunlight, heaved himself to his feet. Durnovaria. More than twenty miles. Ah, at least it was not raining.

January 472

§ XXXI

It had snowed overnight, although it only amounted to a light fall of a few inches. The air was dry, but the wind came direct from the east, bitter, with a bite as raw and mean as a boar's temper. The skin on Gwenhwyfar's cheeks felt as though it were being ripped apart by dozens of small knives. She had ceased to feel her fingers, curled around the leather reins, after five minutes of riding. It did not help, trekking along this part of the valley that was open to the full exposure of the wind, but the other track threading through the density of trees, Bedwyr assured her, was an inadvisable route. 'Impassable at times!' he had explained heartily, his usual boyish grin decorating his face. 'The earth around here is mostly heavy clay – the Green Track is well named, bright green grass in every hollow – God knows how many poor souls lie at the bottom of those bogs!'

The bogs would be frozen, the ground hard and firm. On the dexter side, happen he was right. The Wooded Ridge looked to be a wild place, straddled by gnarled oaks and sturdy limes that marched up each side of the escarpment, dense and alarmingly inhospitable.

They turned from the flat meander of the valley, rode up a rising track. A short but steep climb, up through those shouldering oaks, to come out abruptly onto the crest of a hill that gave view to a panoramic spread, as breathtaking as the scramble upward. Bedwyr called a halt. The signal tower built here was manned by five men, all eager to conduct their commander up to the top height to inspect the brazier, kept ready at all times to send urgent signal southward if ever there were need.

To compensate for the cold, the valley spread below was at least worth looking at. The wide marsh, snow-covered, blue-gleaming beneath the winter sun with the frozen river under its ice-covering making its ambling way through the middle to join, a few miles further down, the Father river, the Tamesis. A herd of deer milled along one section of the snow-bound bank, searching for water. The Dolydd broadened out further down, below the Command Fortress of the Third Ambrosiani, but its width and depth was unpredictable, variable. The flat valley formed a natural flood plain for the high tide waters of the Tamesis, regularly engulfed the marshy ground. Wisps of smoke, grey-trailing against the

214

background of white snow, gave evidence of small settlements and scattered farm-steadings. Not all Saxon, as many were farmed by British landholders. There were two Roman Villas even, though neither were able to boast the same grand status as they had once enjoyed. British and Saxon, living and farming amicably, side along side, sharing grazing land, felling trees, ploughing fields, harvesting their crops. One farm using a neighbour's prime bull, another a best ram. A valley community, accepting each other, intermarrying, becoming one people.

Beyond the ooze of marsh lay good farming land for crops, vegetables especially, mulched by the regular floods. Livestock grew fat and sleek on the verdant grass. Alder and willow dotted here and there in clumps and copses, swathes of hazel and birch, hornbeam; on the edges, a few elms. The woods that tramped this eastern ridge and gave reluctant way at the northern end into the wild, thicket wood were home to boar, deer and badger; though the bears, Bedwyr had assured her, were long gone. Gwenhwyfar was relieved. She had once been badly frightened by a bear.

They were riding to visit the two outposts under Bedwyr's command. Ambrosdun Prima and Secunda. 'As commanding officer,' Bedwyr had laughed, 'I have to put in an appearance every so often, in case the men forget I exist!'

For two days, they had been at the main fortress, the command post of the Third Ambrosiani – a grand title for what was in reality little more than two Cohorts, one hundred and forty men, including the non-combatants – medical orderlies, blacksmiths, armourers, clerks and so forth. One third of this number manned the two outposts.

Neither the Saxons nor the British for that matter particularly liked the chain of fortresses that Ambrosius had ordered built at such strategic sites. Unwelcome, unwanted, their occupants found themselves faced with hostility and surliness. Bedwyr's Command Fort of the Third Ambrosiani, named, as with all the constructions, after its Supreme Commander, and the legion manning it, sat on the first spur of high ground to dominate the valley, surveying a commanding view from the east bank up and down river. Striding to the north, the eastern ridge began to rise ponderously up to its maximum height of around three hundred feet. The fortress was, compared to what had once been built by Rome, nothing outstanding. Ditch and rampart with stone-built walls, albeit badly morticed and lain. Within, a tumble of timber buildings; barracks, a small hospital, stabling, commander's house, headquarters building. The house was built to Roman style, but without the comforts. No hypocaust heating, no private bath house. Gwenhwyfar did not mind their exclusion, for she had been without the luxury of either for many years at .Caer Cadan. A bath house was something Arthur had always been planning to have built . . .

The men whole-heartedly welcomed her, for many were ex-Artoriani. Bedwyr had managed to persuade Ambrosius to keep them together, to retain them as cavalry; how, no one was certain, although he had an acknowledged glib tongue. These were the men who had not gone with Arthur into Gaul, who felt bruised and heart-sore at being left behind. The remainder of their comrades were settled into other such patrolling fortresses to the north and south of Bedwyr's command. For those who would have chance to serve Gwenhwyfar again, a light came back into their lives. She was their Queen, their beloved King's wife.

If anyone was to replace the Pendragon as her husband, then Bedwyr was an acceptable candidate. None resented her decision to re-marry.

For her coming, they had ensured the house-place to be clean and tidied, a vase filled with evergreens had been lovingly placed upon the table in the entrance hall, a bowl of nuts and dried fruits set for her in the bedchamber. The braziers were lit. Effort made, trying to make the place home for her. Each man aware that it could never offer the same comfort and atmosphere of Caer Cadan. Gwenhwyfar appreciated their under-standing, pledged that she would try to make the place her home, for their sake.

Archfedd Gwenhwyfar had left for now with Geraint, for the girl enjoyed being with others of her own age, and Enid was a capable woman. The child would join with them soon, come spring, when the weather was more suited for children to travel. One insistence however. She had brought her own guard. Ider, Gweir, and the others. How their faces had lit with delight as they rode through the open gates into the fortress that first late afternoon! So many old friends, old comrades. The Artoriani together, almost. Aye, more than a few heads were heavy and sore next morning! Wine and ale and memories had flown fast and free that first night!

From this high ground, Gwenhwyfar asked, 'What is that place?' She pointed to a hazed smudge to the south-west. An officer stepped up beside her, she recognized him as one who had been a good soldier under Arthur.

'Londinium, lady.'

She arched her eyebrows, shielded her eyes from the brightness of the low winter sun. 'Surely not?'

'Aye, 'tis not as clear today. On occasion you can see as far as the low hill of the Cantii land, and the sun-glimmer shining off the Tamesis itself.' She looked where he had indicated, then across to the lower ridge opposite and the wide spread of land below this hill-height, all covered

216

by a white-woven blanket, blue-shadowed by the roll of hills and white-capped pockets of woodland.

'I had heard that there were still those who made their homes in Londinium.' Gwenhwyfar spoke her thoughts aloud.

'Those too poor to move home have little choice. They scratch a living among the ruins, manage well enough. A few traders call at the decaying wharves, but the Saex seem to leave the place be.' The officer was shading his eyes, looking towards the distant smudge that was the town. 'They seem not much to like our once-splendid buildings,' he mused.

Gwenhwyfar laughed, turned away. She could hear Bedwyr and the men clambering back down the four flights of wooden stairs within the tower. 'Very sensible of them,' she stated. 'From what I recall of Londinium, there was little worth the effort of liking.' Her opinion was clouded, mind. Her time in Londinium, those many years ago, had been shadowed by tragedy and horror.

The entourage rode on, down the far side of the hill, across cattle-grazed common land, crossing brooks, skirting a willow- and alder-guarded lake, looking faery-tinted in its lace-decorated whiteness. Laughed heartily at the wild-fowl skidding and sliding, bemused, on the frozen ice.

The first outpost, Ambrosdun Secunda, was the smaller of the two. Built as a stronghold with its sister a few miles further north, long before Rome was anything more than a few shepherd's huts clustered among the Seven Hills. Hanging to the top end of a valley, it dominated the north-western approach and the undulating, bog-bound trackway that Bedwyr had mentioned. Ambrosius had ordered the ditch and ramparts refortified, a palisade fence built, the trees that had encroached in the interim few hundred years to be cut back. Once again, the place looked impressive, imposing.

They spent the night there, sharing a feast of venison and roast fowl, exchanging laughter and gossip with the men. Then went on again in the morning, for the short ride to the larger fortress where they were to spend several days.

Ambrosdun Prima. Squatting on the open ridge that commanded a view that led the eye southward to where the Tamesis ran, and beyond, north-west to the hazy escarpment of the chalk hills where the ancient track of the Iceni Way strode. East, the valley that ran to that side of the Wood Ridge. Left to its own, the wild wood would gradually return, reclaim what man had cleared. Oak, beech, hazel, lime, elm and birch. Those trees that had encroached during the years that the fortress was kept only as a useful stockade for penning roaming cattle, were now the timber of the palisade fence, the double gateway with its watch-tower and the usual array of inner buildings.

Again, the welcome was eager, men pleased to be serving Gwenhwyfar again. Men who had been so proud to be Arthur's men, Arthur's cavalry. More than a few shook their heads in sadness and regret for what had once been and would never be again.

Bedwyr was busy most the day, inspecting the fortress inside and out, hearing cases of military matters, minor squabbles, major needs. Gwenhwyfar settled herself into the commander's dwelling, a small but adequate house. The evening meal was formal but pleasant. It was snowing again as the first watch of the night came on duty, settling as Bedwyr darted into his bed, wriggling for warmth against Gwenhwyfar, already burrowed into the bed-furs.

A man managed to struggle to the gates of the Third Ambrosiani a moment before the guard slammed them shut for the night. He was ushered, cold in his feet, hands and bones, weary and stubble-faced, into the guard room. He insisted the watch officer be summoned. Eventually the guard gave ground, sent word for him to come, though they knew he would be annoyed at having to turn out with the snow falling heavier and colder at the summons of a mere, ragged, Saxon.

The Saxon sat before the single brazier, head in hands. He could not believe this. Could not believe the gods were being so cruel. His first question, first demand, as he limped into the fortress, 'Where be the Lady Gwenhwyfar?'

Was this some great jest that Woden was playing upon him? She had gone to the outpost. Again, he had missed her.

§ XXXII

'If you agree to wed me come the spring, will you change your mind to that also?'

Gwenhwyfar made no reply to Bedwyr's impatient question, stirred her oat-porridge with her spoon. Breakfast was growing cold, she ought eat it, was not hungry.

A knock at the door. Bedwyr growled for whoever it was to enter. The officer of the watch, come with a flurried blast of cold air and the duty roster, hastily rearranged to accommodate the piled snow carpeting the fortress and blocking the gates. Bedwyr checked the list, nodded agreement. The officer saluted, left. He knew Gwenhwyfar, had served with her dead husband since the days when Arthur was a lad, wet behind the ears and taking orders from Vortigern. Most of the men had been delighted when Arthur had set his first wife, Winifred, aside and taken Gwenhwyfar instead – aye, even the devout Christian men who were not so certain of the ethics behind divorce. God said you should have but one wife, one husband. He shut the door behind him, chewing his lip, thoughtful, decided he would have a word with young Ider when chance offered. Something was wrong with the lady, that look of unhappiness went deeper than lingering grief.

Gwenhwyfar had to make some reply to Bedwyr. What? How could she answer? She set down the spoon, raised her eyes to him. 'I am sorry.' Looked away, focusing on a careful drawn map of Britain siting the Roman Forts of the Saxon Shore. Incongruously, she wondered how many still survived. Portus Adurni certainly, for it was safe at the edge of Geraint's territory. Llongborth, they called it now, the place where Rome had built and docked her great warships, where Syagrius had sent the transport ships for Arthur . . . She closed her eyes. Everything, everything always came back to Arthur! She drew a deep breath, returned her gaze to Bedwyr who sat, both hands clasped around his own, empty, porridge bowl. She could only reply with honesty. 'I am, have always been most fond of you, Bedwyr. I receive pleasure in your bed, but . . .'

He interrupted, finished, with a sour taste in his mouth, 'But you do not love me.'

'No!' Gwenhwyfar risked a tentative smile. 'No, I mean –' She shook her head, spread her hands, 'I do love you, in some certain way.' Brought her hands together, toyed with her fingers, her rings. 'I would marry you now, this day, if it were not for –' She pulled her ruby ring off her finger, replaced it. And in a rush said what had been scuffling in her mind these long weeks past. 'If it were not for the fact that I cannot accept that Arthur is dead.'

Vigorously pushing himself from his stool, Bedwyr snorted a single bark of derision. He turned away from the table, from her, ran his fingers through his thick, dark hair. 'Christ, Gwenhwyfar!' He turned back to face her. 'I was there, remember? I saw him. Blood-covered, ash-faced, limp. Dead.' He rubbed his fingers, for his hands were suddenly very cold. Said, quieter, 'I helped drag his body from that bloody place.' Then he lashed out with his foot, sending the stool tumbling and bumping across the room. A leg broke, the seat cracked as it slammed into the wall. Angry, resentful and bitter. 'Sod it, Gwenhwyfar. I saw him! I was *there!*'

She bowed her head, laid her hands in her lap. She could not help or stop the tear falling. 'But I was not. I can only think of him as alive. I still expect him to come blustering, angry at some imbecile's stupidity, through the door.' She looked up. 'When I lay with you Bedwyr, I will myself to remember that I am no longer his wife.' She remained looking at him, though she wanted to glance away. 'I feel as though I am cheating him, that I am unfaithful . . .' She raised her hand to stop the words that were about to leave his lips. 'Stupid, I know. Stupid I am.'

Shaking, her legs seeming as if they could not support her, she rose from the table, steadying her balance by placing her hands flat on its surface. 'Until I can accept he is gone, then no, I will not wed.' And again, she said, meaning her words, 'but I will, soon, when I am ready. I have promised you. I will not go back on my word, but please, do not force me into more than I can yet give.' She walked to an inner door, let herself quietly out into the privacy of what had been their shared bedchamber.

Bedwyr stood, looking, feeling blank. He ought to go after her, argue, tell her she was wrong, that she must take for herself a husband. Why was she being so damned stubborn?

Instead, he slammed out the door that led to the parade-ground, took up a shovel and furiously helped with the digging to clear the main gate.

Eight days the snow lay, a rising wind drifting each fresh fall into the cleared gaps. Two roofs fell in under the weight, one a barrack's block, the other a small bothy where the geese were night-housed. All eight birds perished. Ambrosdun Prima ate well that night, at least.

Gwenhwyfar was restless. She needed to be alone, needed to think. Damn this snow penning her in, and damn Bedwyr for being so hurt. She would become his wife, soon. After she had had time to think! The few personal belongings brought with her, clothing, jewellery, unguents and oils, combs, pins, the paraphernalia every woman carried, were packed, waiting and ready for her to leave. Each morning Ider tramped through the gateway as soon as the men had it cleared, walked a few yards from the fortress. Each morning, reported back to his lady that the track was impassable. Gwenhwyfar waited, snared in an awkward situation, regretting the need to go, yet not regretting a friendship that had flourished into something more intimate. Would yet blossom into something permanent.

Bedwyr had not set aside hope. All she needed was time. Time to heal, time to accept what was done, face what was to be. He could wait – but not without her with him!

'Where are you intending to go?' he had asked her.

She had shrugged, uncertain herself.

'To Gwynedd? To your brothers?'

Shaking her head, she replied no. 'Enniaun, my eldest brother was never a dreamer, his feet are firm set in this world. He would never see the sense of my delaying an offer of marriage.' She had laughed at herself, her absurd predicament. Half in jest, added, 'I may decide on entering a convent for a while. One founded by Winifred happen?' He had not responded with any shared amusement. Both knew a holy house was her only option if the likes of Amlawdd were to be kept at bay.

The snow cleared as if some magician had swept his hand over the land, commanding the whiteness to be gone. The wind had turned, bringing for a few consecutive days a milder clemency. It would freeze again within the week, turning the tracks into rock, thick-icing the rivers and streams, numbing fingers and toes to the bone, and daubing trees and bushes with garlands of hoar-frost. But allowing enough time for Gwenhwyfar and her guard to saddle the horses and start south.

Bedwyr would have left with them, but he opted to stay one more day, preferring to say his farewell here, where there were fewer men to witness his sorrow at her going. If only he knew when she would be back, would be his without doubt! When? A month? Two? More?

There was some commotion at the gate. Ider grunted at his men to close firmer around their lady as they rode out through the tunnel beneath the watch-tower. They caught a glimpse of a man struggling to free himself from the harsh grip of pinning arms. He tried to shout something as Gwenhwyfar rode by, but a soldier's fist caught him square in the mouth, splitting his lip, knocking out two teeth.

Struggling, the man begged to be released, pleading his need to speak with the lady. The watch officer saw Gwenhwyfar and her guard set safe on the track. Aye, the weather would hold for a day or two. He turned to the Saxon, kicked him in the groin. 'Why would the Lady Pendragon have wish to speak with scum like you?' For good measure, kicked him again, ordered, 'Take him to the punishment cell. See what mischief he had in mind.'

Not until evening, after the trumpets for the setting of the first watch had sounded, did anyone think to inform Bedwyr that a Saxon lay battered and beaten in the stinking, stone-built hovel that served for a place of punishment.

The commander was in no mood to bother with the problems of local settlers – already, even before the serving of the evening meal, he was deep into his drink. 'Throw him out. Let him tell his sorrows to the wolves.'

Fortunate that the night was milder than any other recent night. Fortunate too that several of the boys from the settlements in the valley had chosen this full-mooned night to creep up through the woods and out onto the cleared, cattle-grazed land to see what the British were up to

221

in their wooden-built soldiers' fort. It was a game for them, seeing who had the nerve to wriggle the nearest. The watch knew they were there, knew them to be youngsters about their innocent games, occasionally would shout they had been seen, usually ignored them, providing there were but only a few of them and they stayed well out from the first ditch.

This night, the watch guard spat over the palisade fence, mouthed an obscenity. The boys had found the Saxon, one of their own kind, were carrying, dragging, him back to his own world. The guard had little care whether the whoreson survived. One less Saex in the world would be of no consequence.

March 472

§ XXXIII

'I intend to extend my territory.'

Aesc's hand, pouring his guest a tankard of the new-fermented, strongest brew of ale, never faltered. 'Anderida be not enough for you, then?' he queried with a mild chuckle, after settling himself in his own chair, with his own, filled tankard.

Aelle, chieftain of the South Saxons narrowed his eyes, lifted his chin slightly and formed a half-smile. 'Would the Isle of Tanatus have been enough for Hengest, your father?'

Conceding the point by saluting with his tankard, Aesc of Kent pondered the implications of this news. Asked detail. When? How? Receiving for answer a mere, mild shrug.

They were in Aesc's private chamber, cleared, for the necessity of male talk, of children and wife. She had gone with her nose pointed in the air, sniffing disdain, they had scurried off happily enough. Aelle was a broad man, gruff-voiced, stern-faced, children were not at ease in his powerful presence. Indeed, were it to be admitted, few men, save his own three sons, relaxed comfortably in the same room.

He took time to answer more fully, enjoying the strong drink, helping himself to dried meat and hunks of fresh-baked barley-bread. He intended to pursue his plans, whatever the outcome of this visit to the Cantii lands. He would go further north from here, seek out the Saxon leaders of the eastern settlers; on his return, those along the South Ridge. If necessary, he would go for what he wanted alone, but how much better it would be, how much more effective, more permanent, if they were to unite and be one. 'I have made no plans as yet.' He flapped his hand, idly. 'Mere ideas, an eagerness, if you like, to set thoughts on a more advanced step.'

'Ambrosius,' Aesc mused, stretching his feet to the warmth of his hearth-fire, 'is determined on his security. His string of bristling fortresses seem reasonably strong.'

Aelle formed his fingers into a derisive gesture. 'Anything can seem strong in the drowse of a summer heat. It is when the winds come that the firmness of walls and the solidity of a roof matter most.' He shook his head, slow, meaningful, emphasizing his figurative point. 'Na, my friend, I assure you Ambrosius Aurelianus's playthings are about as secure as castles made in the sand.'

The Kent, Aesc, grinned. 'We but have to wait for the tide to turn.'

'Ah no, my friend,' Aelle corrected, taking a deep, satisfying draught of his ale. 'The tide has turned already. We but wait for it to come in.'

April 472

§ XXXIV

Ambrosius Aurelianus had, as so often occurred during the colder months of winter, been unwell. The bowel flux had eased, and the stomach pains, but intermittent fever and weakness had lingered for many weeks. His skin was a mixed tincture of ash-grey and liverish-yellow, clinging gaunt over hollow cheeks and sunken eyes. Although he was only forty and five years, his hair was turning a premature grey, and was receding from the crown of his head in a monk-like tonsure. He was constantly cold.

Cadwy, his son, was ambling around, picking at a bowl of fruit, touching a gold crucifix, admiring a tapestry. He had flung off his cloak, loosened the fastenings of his tunic, for the room was hot and smoke-stuffed with so many braziers kept constantly stoked. His father wore two cloaks, yet still he chafed at his fingers to bring some warmth into them. A slave brought in a tankard, solemnly handed it to Ambrosius who reached for it, took a reluctant mouthful. Cadwy watched his father drink, wipe residue from his mouth.

'Without this foul stuff, the stomach cramps return and I will be spending the night shivering in that ice-hole of a latrine.' Ambrosius grimaced, took a breath and gulped the rest down, with the slave scurrying forward to take the empty tankard. Sliding deeper into his chair, Ambrosius laid his head against its high back a moment, closed his eyes. For all the disguising of spices and sweet honey, the drug tasted bitter. 'What I would give,' he sighed, 'for a glass of fine wine.' He drew in his breath as if savouring the aroma of a luxury imported wine, opened his eyes, sat up straight. 'However, my physician would never allow me to drink it – even if I could get hold of some. What brings you here, boy? Stop fiddling with my things and spit it out!'

Nervously clearing his throat, Cadwy limped to a stool, seated himself, laying his crutch on the floor behind. 'Ought you not be abed, father? You look tired.'

'I am perfectly all right!' Ambrosius snapped, 'I have enough fussing from my physician without your unwanted additions.' He was damned if he would spend all day and night pandering to the weaknesses of his body. He shuffled himself into a more upright position. So much to do! Orders to send, letters to read, to write. Judgements to be made, petitions to scrutinize. Three senior officers needed appointing and one of the recent-built fortresses had burnt down – an accident, with the fire started in the blacksmith's bothy, so he understood. Did he rebuild or abandon? Then Amlawdd sent at least five letters a month demanding the rebuffal of marriage by Gwenhwyfar be settled in court. Ambrosius had glanced through the latest, sent just before Cadwy had entered, had tossed it aside. When was the fool man going to understand that he had been rejected and there was nothing illegal about Gwenhwyfar's decision? He ought to send word that Amlawdd was to sort which of them had the lady with Bedwyr privately, in whatever fashion he thought fit. That one of them would probably end up dead was suddenly of no consequence. God's truth, was he surrounded by fools? Abed! The good Christ, when would he have chance to linger abed!

Gruff, Ambrosius asked, 'What is it you want?'

A drink! Cadwy thought. *Something very strong and very fortifying.* Said, 'I have come because I have grave concerns.'

'Personal or public?'

'Public. I would not bring personal matters to you!' Damn the man, did he think it was easy sitting here, having to be polite, having to breathe shallow to staunch the threatening rise of nausea? Gods, his father stank! A combination of sitting so long in this warm fug, the cling of administered drugs and the putrid aroma of illness. 'I come about Amlawdd.'

Ambrosius's eyes narrowed, he successfully concealed a groan. What had the imbecile done now? It had seemed a good idea at the time, to promote the man as a personal friend, given his wealth and number of men. 'What about him?'

Why did he feel this insecurity, this nervousness? Again and again, Cadwy repeated to himself, *I am a man grown, I have a wife, a child.* He ought not fear this man sitting hunched, so obviously ill. Ought not. So why in all hell's name did the sweat trickle down his back? Why were his palms sticky, his voice in need of constant clearing? Love of God! Could a son never shake off a father's disapproval?

Leaning forward, palms flat on his thighs, Cadwy lunged into his reason for coming. He doubted Ambrosius would listen, but he had to try. Ragnall had asked it of him, and for her he would do anything. Even face his father in his lair.

'Amlawdd collects the taxes.'

Ambrosius shrugged. Someone had to do it, and Amlawdd was good at the evil job, being too thick of heart to bend before bleating sorrows and hard-luck cases. Few refused Amlawdd's blank-eyed stubbornness and determination, Ambrosius chuckled to himself, save of course for the

226

Lady Gwenhwyfar! This brought on a coughing fit, a slave rushed forward with a draught of water, held it to his master's lips. Cadwy had to wait for his father to collect his breath again.

'He is causing misery and destitution.'

'An unfortunate necessity.'

'No! 'Tis not a necessity, not at this time of year!' Cadwy smacked his fist onto his knee, angry. 'The last winter was harsh for so many. Nor was the harvest as good as expected last year, people are near to starving, father. Amlawdd has not the slightest feeling of concern or justice. He rides in, takes what is demanded and leaves.'

Ambrosius was rubbing his hands, he was so cold, so damned cold. Was he listening?

'The poorer people are desperate, father – Amlawdd takes what little they have left – even their children if they cannot pay! Twice now have I heard that! He takes the children to sell into slavery!'

Ambrosius merely shrugged. 'Then they ought have set aside the legal requirement. Any free-born British man has the right to attend the Justice Courts to contest his taxable dues.'

Cadwy shot to his feet, hammered the air with his fist. 'British-born, but not Saex! You have taken away what few legal rights they had. You are beating them into submission by pushing them into the ranks of the poor and slaves!'

Coming to his feet also, matching his son's anger, Ambrosius bellowed, 'The Saex? If they do not like the way things are, then they can pack their possessions and go back to where they were born!'

'Most along the South Ridge were born there, father!' Cadwy retaliated, his nerve rising with the anger. 'My stronghold oversees many a Saex farm-steading. Most of them are second- or third-generation-born settlers! The farmland around my holding is all they have ever known!'

Turning away, clutching his cloak tighter around his shoulders, Ambrosius mumbled some callous remark. Cadwy heard. He stumbled forward, forgetting the need for his crutch in his great rise of rage.

'Gwenhwyfar granted me Lord Pendragon's stronghold at Badon because she trusted my judgement! I am no Saex-lover. Call me that if you are so wrongly bigoted. I regard myself as a just and fair lord. Condoning the burning and destruction of innocent people's steadings because they happen to be of Saex descent is not just! Arthur would never have done it!'

'Arthur? Arthur had no initiative when it came to raising taxes, that is why his economy was always so poorly managed! He taxed the wealthy to provide for their protection. Well, I say be rid of the reason for the protection!'

'So you will not admonish Amlawdd for his excessive zeal?'

'Not where the Saex are concerned. No.'

Retrieving his crutch and placing it beneath his arm, Cadwy made his way to the door. 'There is unrest coming, sir, even in my own land, where I give care for my tenants.' He looked direct at the man before him, at the sunken face, the thin body. 'The Saex will not go back to their boats, father. They cannot, for there is nowhere for them to go. Arthur made peace with them because he knew we could never fight all of them, not if they united their strength.' He turned, had the door open. 'I trust you will not be giving them a reason to join hands on the same spear.'

§ XXXV

Eadric lay quietly on his straw pallet that was placed in the corner shadows, watching the hearth-smoke curl up to the roof-hole, and the family cluster around their father, helping to remove his cloak and boots, offering him ale and hot broth. The three boys were particularly noisy, asking questions, dancing around, getting under foot, excited by their father's return. Gundrada brought the broth, placed the bowl in her father's hands; it would warm them more thoroughly than anything else. Shyly, she smiled at Eadric as she noticed him watching her, silently poured a second bowl, brought to him. He laughed to himself as he thanked her, saw her face redden. She was a shy little thing, as timid as a young doe. As pretty.

The boys were demanding to know all of their father's visit. Gundrada wished to know also, but knew better than to ask. He would tell them, in his own time, when he was warm and settled.

The eldest of the three lads persisted, 'Did you speak with Aelle of the South Saxons?'

His father laughed, ruffled the boy's thick crop of fair hair. 'That I did not.' The disappointment this announcement brought was as heavy as an iron pot. 'I did see him though and hear him!' The excitement increased, rose in volume. Gundrada's mother had to speak sharply to her brood, sent them scuttling to bring in more wood for the fire and to bring the evening milk from the goats. Cuthwin winked at Eadric, settled himself, legs stretched to its heat, before the fire.

'And how are your hurts? Almost healed?'

Eadric nodded assent, said gallantly, 'With your daughter's fair hands doing the healing, who could expect aught else?'

Cuthwin mopped the last of the broth with a chunk of bread, handed the empty bowl to the girl, who was again blushing. 'A good girl, my daughter, she will make some man a fine wife.'

Making no answer, Eadric shuffled to make himself more comfortable, for that he had already decided upon. Had he not found plenty of time to think upon it, these past few weeks? He shuffled again, easing the ache of his broken ankle, the throb of cracked ribs. They had done a thorough job, those soldiers up at the fortress.

Other matters seemed to take precedence for a while; settling the stock animals outside, penning the geese and chickens, feeding the sow and the cattle. The preparing and serving of the evening meal – despite his broth, Cuthwin ate like a starved horse – the lighting of the lamps, and Eadric's bandages to be ended. He had only the two now, covering the torn, inflamed area of his arm and the ones binding the splint to his leg.

'So,' Cuthwin made a beginning when his boys were seated by his feet. His wife was, as always were she not cooking or cleaning or scolding, at her loom. Gundrada sat near Eadric, where she could watch him discreetly through her lashes while she spun wool. 'Aelle is intending to raise a great host. To unite all of us English under the one banner against the British.'

Eadric released a low whistle. 'That is some proud ambition!' he murmured.

'Will you go with him, Father? Will you fight the bastard Ambrosius?'

'Hush child!' the lad's mother admonished sharply. 'Such language is for grown-up folk, not childer!'

Cuthwin folded his hands across the broadness of his belly, regarded the curl of hearth-smoke wreathing upward. He had thought much of this question on his walk home from this called Council. This was to be a thing for every free-born man to decide for himself, whether to accept Aelle as Bretwalda, overlord, whether to fight when the call came, or not.

Cuthwin stretched. It had been a long walk. The menfolk had not all dared take the easy route down-river by boat – like as not, the British commander had already guessed that some matter was in hand, but still, it was best not to draw obvious attention. Cuthwin had drawn the short straw. Had been one of those to walk from the meeting-place at Muchinga aside the Tamesis river. Plenty of time to think.

He was not an old man, but he had done his share of fighting. Four elder sons lost fighting in Vortigern's wars, two daughters, buried beside his first wife. Cuthwin had welcomed the settled life of a farmer, his held land was his own, he owned the best breeding sow this side of the Lea, lived comfortably, ate well. Did he want to put an edge to his Saex sword again? Fit a new shaft to his war spear?

He shifted his gaze, watched his wife speed the shuttle through the warp threads. This farm-steading was, by right of law, hers, for it had passed to her from her father. A farm was no place for a woman with no menfolk; she had accepted Cuthwin as a good man, despite his being a Saxon. She was British, his wife, as so many of the wives were. Ah no, he had done his share of the fighting.

Opening the leather pouch at his waist, Cuthwin withdrew a small brooch, his sons crowding closer to see the better. 'Na, boys, this is not for you, you are not yet old enough to tie the ribbons of war onto a spear. We must give this to Eadric.'

Solemnly, the brooch was handed across. This was some item of importance, some especial thing, no mere decoration. Eadric settled it into the palm of his hand. Bronze, slightly shorter than the length of his thumb, the edges raised, forming a dish shape. In its centre, a mask. Human. Eyes, nose, mouth. Eadric flicked a glance at the older man, questioning with his expression.

'It is from Aelle,' Cuthwin said, his voice lowered, as if the walls might hear and spread this secret word. 'All who decide to fight with him must wear it when the summons to battle comes.'

'And when might that be? I cannot yet stand on my own feet.'

Grunting, Cuthwin made a vague gesture with his hands. Who knew when a lord king made his final decision? 'It will not be for a while. We have not enough swords, not enough spears. And the Masks of Aelle have yet to be spread.' He jingled his waist pouch, he had several to give to those who wanted them, as did other men of the valley. 'It is my mind,' Cuthwin added, speaking slowly, thinking as he talked, 'that it would be good to have an elder son again, a husband for my daughter.' Avoiding his wife's eye, continued, 'It is also in my mind that we may need to fight the British again before too many more winters pass.' He sighed. 'Under the Pendragon, there was no fear of another war. It was good to know that crops planted would be crops harvested. This Ambrosius Aurelianus, I think, does not cherish peace as much as his nephew did.'

'He is a Roman, seeking the way things once were. Arthur was British, he accepted what was.'

Cuthwin frowned across the dim-lit smoky room at his guest. If his lads had not found him, Eadric would have perished that night from the cold or the beating. Both. He knew little of the Saxon stranger, for Eadric had kept his own council, save that he had no family and had made the journey across the sea for a reason. But then, had not they all at some time done that?

'You speak,' Cuthwin observed, 'as if you had known the Pendragon.'

Eadric did not answer. Instead, he tossed the little brooch, caught it again, and slid it into his own waist-pouch. 'I am thinking,' he said, 'that it would be good to have a home and a wife. To raise childer and crops.' Gundrada smiled secretly at him, quietly accepting his offer. 'I will wear Aelle's badge when the call comes, I will fight against Ambrosius, although never will I take arms against the Pendragon's lady.'

Cuthwin's brows rose. Ah, he had known Arthur then!

'And before I put an edge to my war-blades, and before I take your daughter to the marriage bed, I have a task to complete. I need to talk with the Lady Gwenhwyfar.'

The older Saxon whistled, was eager to ask on what matter, and through what circumstances, but held his council. It was not for him to pry into another's business. 'Be that why you were up at the British fortress?'

Eadric nodded. Cuthwin shook his head, bewildered. 'Yet they treated you as they did?'

'What they did to me was dishonourable, but it was not of the lady's doing. What I intend to do is also a matter of honour.' He held his hand out for Gundrada to shyly take. 'When I have discharged my promise, I will return, and we will be wed and raise our children. And hope that perhaps this badge of Aelle's will stay untouched, un-needed, in my pouch.'

May 472

§ XXXVI

Bedwyr hated tax-collecting. Arthur had too, he remembered, when it came to taking tribute from the poor. A necessary evil he had called it. Mind, obtaining due tithe from the wealthy had often compensated! All that blustering and protestation could be a joy to handle. The majority of settlers and farmers in his jurisdiction of command, up and around Cwm Dolydd, though, were not wealthy. The harvest last year here, as elsewhere, had been frugal and the winter exceedingly wet. Not as many as in some years had died from the cold, but enough had neared starvation. Aye, Bedwyr always hated the spring collection of taxes. How did you take a farmer's last surviving sow? His only sack of grain?

He rode at the head of his turma of men. They all rode with swords loosened and spears ready. The ox-cart was filling rapidly with payment already collected, grain, barrels of ale, furs, leathers. Christ God, what was he going to do with the girl-child? Selling a child into slavery was commonplace, but Bedwyr had no stomach for it, even if in all probability the child had more chance of surviving under a master than with her malnourished parents. She could not be more than five years of age.

For the fourth time, the men had to dismount, manhandle the cart through the mud. The two oxen were militant beasts who saw no reason to work any harder than they needed. Bedwyr cracked a slight smile; one of the men, he noticed, was playing with the lass, tickling her under the chin, making her grubby little face shine with laughter, instead of putting his shoulder to the cart. Bedwyr turned away. If the others did not mind this shirking, why should he notice?

Another muddy lane led up through thick, hazel hedging to another steading-place, slightly larger this one. The freeholder had been a favoured mercenary soldier, given high reward. He had a British wife, one daughter of marriageable age, three under-age sons; held four hides of land, which in the Roman was about sixty acres, one fish-pool, ten sow pigs, one boar, four oxen, twenty geese, four beehives and ten goats. Bedwyr knew all this from his official scroll. He was surprised, therefore, when rounding the last bend in the lane, to see a young man leaning on his spade, watching the soldiers from the fortress ride in, taking a rest

232

from digging what was obviously a vegetable garden. The man nodded, he was a Saxon, unmistakable from the colour of his hair, manner of dress. The daughter was wed then, the scroll would need be altered.

Cuthwin, the landholder, came from around the back of the dwelling-place. Bedwyr caught a glimpse of three impish lads peering curiously after their father, heads hastily ducking back as the British commander winked at them.

'It's waiting for you, the tax be by the gate. Grain and furs. The pig's in the pen over yonder.' Cuthwin spoke gruffly, barely moving his lips, his Latin clipped and uneasy.

'I thank you,' Bedwyr said, gesturing an accompaniment with his hand, and talking in the Saxon language. Cuthwin was an honest farmer, for all his curt manners and abrupt ways. Given the situation, who could expect anything less?

'No need to give thanks for starvin' us,' the Saxon bowled back, craggily. 'You'll not get a thank you in return.'

Bedwyr surveyed the farm, neat kept, well stocked, even this side of winter. 'You do all right for yourself, old sir.' He indicated the younger man, still leaning on his spade, still intently watching the British commander. 'With another hand to guide the oxen, you will plough well later this year.'

Cuthwin sniffed loudly, rubbed his bushed beard and regarded Eadric, who without haste set his tool against the low, stone wall and sauntered over to stand beside Bedwyr's horse. He ran his hand down its neck, appreciating the smooth coat, fine muscle of the crest. 'A good horse. One from the Pendragon's desert bred stock, I'd wager.' He spoke British well, with an accent deeper than most the Saxons in this area.

Shrewdly, Bedwyr surveyed him, taking note of his stance, his confidence, hearing the marked difference in speech. 'Do I not know you from somewhere?'

Eadric gave the horse a final pat, pulled one of his bay ears through his fingers, and let the animal lick at the salt taste on the palm of his hand. 'Mayhap you do. I know you.' He returned Bedwyr's stare, said lightly, almost offhand. 'I helped you drag the Pendragon from that bloodied field of battle.'

Bedwyr gasped, swung down from the saddle, stood looking eye to eye. Slowly he nodded, accepting the statement for fact. 'One of Mathild's men.' Bedwyr loosed his held breath, added, 'You are a long way from the Elbe; could you not find a wife nearer home?'

Lifting a slight smile to one corner of his mouth, Eadric shook his head. 'I am here at Cuthwin's farm because of your men, though Gundrada, his daughter, is good enough reason to stay.'

Frowning, Bedwyr queried the answer. 'My men?'

'Aye, my lord. Your men beat me so bad I have not been long from the bed-place.' Eadric indicated his leg, that was bent, slightly misshapen, touched a vivid scar to his temple.

Still, Bedwyr did not understand. 'You enjoy riddles, my friend. I cannot fathom this one.'

'No riddle, my lord. I came up to the fortress just as the winter snows cleared. I needed to speak with the Lady Gwenhwyfar. I was beaten for my trouble.'

At that Bedwyr formed a wry smile, not quite enough to laugh. 'Why would a Saxon from Mathild's Elbe river wish to speak with my lady?'

The answer came back swiftly, Eadric's head high, eyes piercing, sincere. Proud. 'That be for me to tell the lady.' Then he relaxed his expression, a weariness entering his spirit, gazed at Bedwyr's men, sitting on their horses a few yards away, came to a decision. 'I will tell you though, my lord, for I believe it will be the only sure way that my lady will hear what I have to repeat.' He glanced, pointedly, at the other men, included Cuthwin in his flickering eye. ''Tis for your ears alone, sir.'

Now Bedwyr was growing curious. He passed the reins to one of the men, put his hand on Eadric's arm, guided him to the house-place. Inside, Gundrada squeaked with alarm, though her mother barely glanced up from her cooking-pot at the two men. Her nose did wrinkle at the thick mud cloying on their boots as they stamped in over the doorsill, but she made no comment, as she would shrilly have done, had either Cuthwin or Eadric entered so, alone.

'Get you gone,' Bedwyr ordered, tipping his head to the outside. 'I need speak with this man.'

Gundrada hurried away, risking only one quick, frightened glance at Eadric, who smiled encouragement at her. Her mother grumbled. 'My stew be nigh on cooked.'

'We'll see to your stew,' Bedwyr assured her, holding the door wide, ushering her through with an encouraging gesture of his hand.

'You mind you do! If it burns, it'll be the waste of a fine hare.' She stalked outside, nose tipped high, muttering protest. Bedwyr slammed the door shut, stood with his back leaning against it, arms folded. Tell me, his expression said.

The dwelling-place was larger than most farm-steadings, Cuthwin being of higher status financially. An aisled timber-built structure, with at one end the family place, lower down, the cattle stalls, all empty this time of day and year. Pegs for hanging harness. Three fattened chickens scratched, content, at the straw-scattered, beaten-earth floor.

The living space seemed comfortable, though sparsely furnished with a

234

wooden box-bed to one end and loft space above, where the boys slept. Another bed, smaller, lay to one side. An old oaken chest, a sturdy table. Several stools, baskets, pots, flagons, barrels. In one corner, the inevitable loom. Hunkering down on his heels before the hearth-place, Eadric poked more kindling onto the fire, blazing the flames higher.

Bedwyr waited. This was obviously something of importance, there could be no hurrying for great matters.

Finally, Eadric lifted his head. He was nervous, for his tongue licked at his lips, hand rubbed hand. 'Since June's month have I been hiding my tracks, looking over my shoulder.' Bedwyr made no interruption, let the Saxon speak. June? All but the year around. A long time. 'Those first months I was running from the Lady Winifred, ensuring she could not know where I had gone.' He spat into the fire, sending a hiss of steam flaring out. Bedwyr's eyebrows rose. Winifred had long claws if her malice was stretching as far as the Elbe! But then it was her son's place now that Leofric the Saxon was gone. Was she making it her own also? 'Why?' he asked simply.

Eadric took a deep breath, poured the next out. 'Because I am certain that she was responsible for my Lady Mathild's death. Because she could not let those of us who served that good lady live to tell others what she knew.'

Pushing himself away from the door, Bedwyr approached the opposite side of the hearth-place, hunkered on his heels as Eadric did. 'And that is?'

'Mathild told us, I and several of my comrades – they are cruelly dead now, that bitch's doing. How my lady knew this thing, I know not, but there was no reason to doubt her.' Squarely, the Saxon regarded the British commander. Bedwyr, an Artoriani officer. Cousin to Arthur, the Pendragon and, so word on the wind chattered, a man who would soon be husband of that same lord's widowed wife. 'Mathild gave us secret command, if death came to her. We were to bring word to my Lady Gwenhwyfar. Word of the Pendragon.'

Bedwyr raised one eyebrow higher, his breath, though he realized it not, was tight held. Everything seemed paused, stilled and waiting, waiting for this thing that, with a prickling itch to his scalp, he had feeling was going to be so difficult to hear.

'The Pendragon was not buried. She believed he did not die. He lives.' Eadric shrugged. 'At least, he did last year, when Mathild was murdered for the knowing of this.'

For a long, long while, Bedwyr sat very still, very quiet. The flames of the hearth-fire crackled, the stew bubbled, began to burn. A hen, from the far end of the dwelling-place announced her intention to lay. He drew his fingers down his nose, across his clean-shaven chin. Bit at the rough skin around one nail.

'If this be some evil jest . . .'

''Tis no jest my lord. I carry out a promise to my lady. She wished your lady, Gwenhwyfar, to know the truth.'

'Jesu.' Bedwyr breathed. 'Jesu Christ.'

§ XXXVII

Utter stillness. Gwenhwyfar sat, unmoving, her ankles crossed, hands folded on her lap. Still, except for the steady rise and fall of her breathing, the occasional blink of her eyelids.

A cuckoo was calling outside, from somewhere in the small copse behind the chapel. A bell began to ring, calling the women to prayer. Someone walking quickly, her feet scrunching on the gravel path, her shadow flickering briefly beneath the closed door as she strode past.

Eadric, his woollen cap held tightly between nervous fingers, shifted uncomfortably from one foot to the other. He was looking at the floor, scrutinizing the dried rushes. He dared not look up, look at her white, pale, face.

Clearing his throat, Bedwyr moved forward, poured a goblet of wine, offered it to her. Gwenhwyfar took it, held it between her hands. Eadric could see the white there also, stark, against her clenched, tense knuckles.

The abbess, a good, kindly woman, bent over Gwenhwyfar, encouraged her to drink. 'Take something, my dear, it will help.'

Shaking her head, Gwenhwyfar offered the cup to her. 'No, no I want nothing. Thank you.' She tried a smile. It would not come.

'You are certain,' the abbess asked, addressing Bedwyr, 'that this information is the truth?'

He could only shrug. 'I have no reason to doubt it. What this Saxon has told me fits with what I remember.'

Gwenhwyfar stood, smoothing down her gown, her hands travelling over the plainness of her simple-styled dress. She had found quiet here at the abbey, quiet, but not peace. The sisters were kind and caring, doted on young Archfedd, respected Gwenhwyfar's wish for solitude, fussed her without being obtrusive. In the gentle abbess, a woman who had a natural gift for understanding the needs of others, she had found a lasting friend.

She could have returned to Durnovaria, stayed, lived within Geraint's household, but the small community of sisters with their gentle way of life suited her the better, and the abbey to which they were attached was a short distance only from the bustle of that busy town. And the companionship of Enid, should she want it.

Gwenhwyfar tipped her head back slightly, closed her eyes. She felt tired, drained of energy and life. A husk beaten of its kernel, an empty shell. Her body felt heavy, weary. She could feel the pulse-places throbbing, every muscle crying out, for want of rest and sleep. She steadied herself, aware of her fragility, opened her eyes, regarded the Saxon, Eadric.

'I do not doubt that which you have told me to be the truth. For what good reason would your lady lie?' She managed a weak smile. 'And I could never quite believe that Arthur was gone.' She wanted to scream, rage, curl into herself and weep. Wanted to be alone, to think. So much to think on! This had turned her world, her life, again on its heels. All this long, long while trying to accept that Arthur was dead – finally on the edge of believing it – and now to learn from this Saxon that he might not be! To know that when last the Lady Mathild had been with him, his body had carried a faint heartbeat of life. That to her later secret-acquired knowledge, he had survived.

Bedwyr was watching Gwenhwyfar intently, understanding the thoughts that must be gathering and tumbling in her mind. Understanding how her heart must be leaping and juddering. Had he not thought and felt the same? The glorious knowing that what they had assumed to be the truth was not so – and the immediate following of seemingly a thousand racing questions. All beginning with why. And following close behind, the dismay that now she would not be his.

And how would the Supreme Governor react when he heard this news of Arthur? If he heard. Ought he be told? Ought anyone?

Glancing at those in the room, Bedwyr pondered on that. The abbess would say nothing. Eadric had already proven his worth by holding his tongue until now. No one else knew, save Mathild who was dead. Lady Winifred and Cerdic, who had for their own reasons, whatever they were, held silence, and the people with whom Arthur sheltered. He was standing, chewing a torn nail, worrying on other, crowding questions. What to do now? How to react? Who to tell? Who not to. How to let Gwenhwyfar go from him?

Gwenhwyfar must have read his frown. 'I have my own mind to set straight before deciding how many others to bowl over with this news.' She moved to his side, placed her hands within his, said, 'Even if this is true, and Arthur is alive, there can be no recrimination upon what happened between us. We acted in honour and faith.'

237

He attempted a grin, did not manage one.

Gwenhwyfar kissed him lightly on his cheek. How hard he must be taking this! How hard were they all? Christ in his mercy, it was as difficult to swallow down this medicine as had been the hearing of Arthur's death!

'What will you do, lady?' Eadric summoned courage to ask. He felt nothing but relief now that his part was ended. He could return to Cuthwin's farm, wed with Gundrada, raise a family. Aye, and happen one day tell his grandchilder the story of how it was he who had told of King Arthur's return from the dead.

'Do?' she said, her fingers twisting, as so often they had these past months, her wedding band. 'Do?' She laughed, high, a hint of crazy uncontrolled quivering behind the sound. 'I have no idea.'

§ XXXVIII

The baby, a girl-child, had finished suckling, was drowsing, her mouth a perfect rosebud shape, eyes closed, content, against her mother's breast. Ragnall did not want to disturb her, this perfect, beautiful little girl, the product of her own womb. The boy, Aurelius Caninus, was playing before the hearth-fire with a set of wooden animal figures carved for him by his father, humming to himself some childish, monotonous tune. Caninus was almost two years old, a sturdy boy with the mischief and spirit of a prized hunting dog. They had called him that, 'little whelp', for his grit determination. His father was so proud of the lad. As was his grandsire. Of course Ragnall loved her son, but her daughter completed the circle, brought her the fulfilment of all possible joys. Her beautiful, golden haired, blue-eyed angel.

Reluctant, Ragnall lifted the babe, settled her in the cradle, over her shoulder warned Caninus that soon it would be time for his own bed. The boy ignored her, continued setting his animals in line. The baby's arm jerked in a muscle reaction, slept on. Her mother stroked the fluff of pale hair, covered her carefully, steeled herself to tackle the boy. Always there was a fuss at bedtime. Tears, screams, shouts and flying fists. 'Just a few more moments,' she warned, knowing the moments would stretch on too long. Easier to give in, let him have his way, though she knew it was spoiling the child. He would be better as he grew, more manageable.

Eventually, it took over an hour to settle him, by which time Ragnall felt exhausted. She considered going to her own bed, but Cadwy had promised he would return this day. It was already dark.

She sat with her sewing, quiet before the crackle of the fire, listening to the gentle sounds of sleep from her children. Slept. A log shifted, startling her awake. Her sewing had dropped to the floor and for a moment she was disorientated, uncertain. Other sounds? What had wakened her?

Sounds beyond the closed door, horses, men's voices. Ragnall hurried to her feet, ran to the doorway, flung it wide as Cadwy was about to do the same from the far side. They laughed, embraced, each glad to see the other. Five days Cadwy had been gone.

Ordering a slave to fetch fresh wine and hot broth, Ragnall fussed her husband, took his rain-damp cloak, removed his boots, sat him before the fire, added more fuel.

She did not ask what cause had been behind his urgent summoning by Geraint of Durnovaria. Cadwy would tell her, in his own good time.

He discussed it much later, after the lamps were growing low, as they lay together in their bed, having celebrated his homecoming as husband and wife should. Ragnall listened, intrigued, astonished. Incredulous. Her first question had been the same as theirs, those men whom Geraint had called together to talk with himself, Bedwyr and Gwenhwyfar. Cadwy, Mabon and Ider.

'But if Arthur is alive,' she said, 'why has he not come home?'

'There can be but two reasons.' Cadwy answered, pulling the delight of her naked body closer to his own. 'Either he cannot, or he does not wish to.'

'I would go for the first of the two,' Ragnall responded with surety, settling her head comfortable against his chest. 'Arthur was a King, he would not abandon us.'

'A defeated King.'

'Huh! One lost battle against all those he had won? Na. I tell you, for some reason he cannot get home. Bad wounded – happen he has lost a limb, a leg or arm. His pride would not let him be seen as a maimed man.'

Cadwy nodded dubious agreement, smoothed his wife's black hair. She could be right, probably was, but why had Arthur never sent word? He began to drift into sleep, murmured some half-answer to a question Ragnall had put to him, jerked awake as she prodded him with her elbow. 'I said, is there no clue as to where he might have gone?'

Cadwy yawned. It had been a long day, a long ride. He wanted to sleep. Closing his eyes, he began to relax, enjoying the sensation of warmth that was creeping through his body. 'He was left, assumed dead, with the woman and her child. He may be with the Ladies, with the one called Morgaine.'

Ragnall jerked upright, her hair falling to hide her breasts and the scars on the skin. 'Morgaine!' She echoed, 'Did you say Morgaine?'

Cadwy's eyes snapped open. 'Aye. A woman with a boy-child.'

'Named Medraut?'

'How should I know?' Irritable, that comfort of drowsing sleep vanishing, Cadwy gathered the bed-furs closer against the cold that her sudden movement had caused. 'I doubt they knew the lad's name. Why? Do you know of her?'

Excited, Ragnall grasped his shoulder. 'Aye,' she said, quick, breathless. 'If it be the same Morgaine, then aye, I do. So did Arthur!'

Interested, catching her headiness, Cadwy pushed himself up onto one elbow. 'Bedwyr said that he thought, from her manner and her grief, that the woman knew the Pendragon. She was a healer, he said. So who is this Morgaine?'

Ragnall sat with her fingers pressed against her cheeks and nose. 'My God,' she breathed, slowly releasing her held breath, 'it must be she!' She laced her fingers, rested her lips against them, thinking, rapidly trying to remember. 'Morgaine was the Lady, the priestess of the Lake at Yns Witrin. I talked with her often.' She flashed an apologetic glance of guilt. It had been forbidden to speak with the pagan priestess, forbidden to enter the realms of the heathen. 'She was kind to me.' Even now, even after Cadwy was mending her confidence in herself, Ragnall felt the need to place some defence for actions of the past. Cadwy waved her, impatient, on. He had no care for the petty, blinkered rules of a hag-riddled abbess. 'Go on!'

'Morgaine had a son. She bore him at the abbey. A few of the sisters guessed who she was. They kept that knowing well from Abbess Branwen, of course!' Ragnall searched her memory, fought herself back to that time. It was difficult to remember accurately the good things that had happened, so few were they between the many harsh sadnesses. 'Morgaine left when the child was but a few days old. She had let me hold the babe.' Ragnall smiled broadly at that pleasing memory. 'He was a fine, healthy boy. Morgaine told me that his father would have been proud of him.'

Cadwy snorted. 'A bastard brat, aye, I guessed as much.'

Ragnall pursed her lips, stern censure crowding her expression. 'Aye, a bastard born. With the King as his father, what else would he be?'

Cadwy had only half-listened. 'These whores who bed for pleasure, never caring about the consequence of a . . . Jesu, what was that you said?' He sat up, kneeling, grasped Ragnall's arms, almost shook her. 'The King, his father? Arthur?'

Ragnall nodded.

'You are certain?'

Again, a nod. 'She told me so herself.'

'Arthur has a living son?' Cadwy's voice betrayed doubt.

Patient, Ragnall nodded a third time. Her husband was taking an annoying while to comprehend all this!

'If Morgaine was his mistress, this boy is his son . . . Jesu and all the Angels in Heaven!' Cadwy's face grew vigorously animated. 'Arthur is more than likely to be with her!' He released Ragnall from his grip, swung his legs from the bed, began hurriedly fumbling for his clothes. 'We are closer to finding him – should we decide to search! I must inform my lady!'

'Hold, husband.'

'Bedwyr need know of this also, and Geraint. We had elected to do nothing as yet – put out a few spies, ask a few discreet questions in Gaul. Geraint was all for writing to that pedantic old letter-scribbler, Apollinaris or his brother-by-law, the one who had ridden with Arthur, but we reckoned that if they had any knowing of Arthur being alive they would already have informed us.' He spoke hurriedly, talking fast, all on the one, excited breath.

'Husband!' Ragnall's stern admonishment pulled him short, his leg half-way into his bracae. 'Has it occurred to you that this might be the reason for the Pendragon not returning?'

Cadwy stared at her, her face deep-shadowed in the low light. He did not see the disfigurement there any more, not even in the full light of day or bright-lit lamps. No need to see the outer shell when the inner core was enough to give contentment and love. 'You mean, he may have elected to live with this whore of his?' He shrugged. 'Even if that is so, my Lady Gwenhwyfar ought know of it.' He continued dressing. Ragnall sighed.

'You have just returned from Durnovaria. Need you leave again so immediate? 'Tis the middle of the night.' Coquettishly added, 'And it is raining out there.'

Hesitating, Cadwy dutifully repeated he must leave straight away. The pitter-pattering of the rain was loud, rattling heavier on the roof. His bed beckoned, tempting. Ragnall moved, the dim light shape-shifting over her unscarred naked shoulder giving a glimpse of her breast. 'Damn it!' he cursed, removing the one boot, his bracae and tunic. 'I'll ride at first light.'

Content, Ragnall pressed against him as he wormed beneath the furs.

Tomorrow, she had every intention of riding south with him.

Except that as the sun warmed the morning, rain-leaden sky into a more promising shade of mist-wreathed grey, two riders and their clattering retinue of attendants reined in before the doors of Cadwy's modest Hall.

Ambrosius Aurelianus and Lord Amlawdd. Both rain-damp, chilled, and with a dull aura of bad tidings swirling about their glum, slumped shoulders.

§ XXXIX

Ambrosius assumed his son's agitation was due to this unexpected arrival. He seated himself wearily, suppressing the insistent nag of a headache that had been with him since yesterday. God's truth! What hope was there for the two of them to form a relationship if every visit resulted in this flustered embarrassment? And what hope had Cadwy of commanding this stronghold in an emergency? If the arrival of his own father set him into such a twittering, red-faced whirl, what would a horde of spear-waving Saxons beyond his ramparts do?

In contrast, Amlawdd sprawled, legs spread, before the hearth-fire. His was the ease of arrogance. Not for him the detecting of subtle nuances or the noticing of the uneasy glances exchanged between husband and wife.

Both men accepted warmed wine from Ragnall and the offer of food, Amlawdd saying nothing, merely taking and drinking; Ambrosius polite and asking after the health of his grandchildren. Ragnall's face lit immediately with the animated radiance peculiar to a mother's pride.

'Your granddaughter is a content, lay-abed babe. She wakes and gurgles for her feed then snuggles again into her cradle like a hedge-pig seeking his winter sleep. Your grandson, mind,' – her smile was wide with pride – 'has more energy than a colt turned out onto his first spring grass!'

'I have a small gift for him in my saddlebag,' Ambrosius admitted, his face tinged with red, for fear he would be construed as spoiling the boy. 'Nothing of consequence, a carved animal for his collection.'

Ragnall was delighted. 'I will send for his nurse to bring him when you have eaten.'

'The last time I saw the boy, he was overexcited and exceedingly rude to me. He needs discipline, not child's toys.' Amlawdd spoke gruffly. He had found the indifference he felt for his daughter continued with her children. Amlawdd's priority was for himself, his own needs and ambition. There was not enough room in his head or heart for the details of others.

Seeing his wife's lips compress, her eyes narrow, Cadwy intervened by

242

cordially asking how long his father intended to stay, was relieved to hear the answer of only an hour or so, to take refreshment, change horses.

'Amlawdd and I need ride on.' Ambrosius sounded tired, but there was anger behind his weary voice also. 'We seek Bedwyr, who is, as I understand, again at Durnovaria.'

Ragnall could not stem the gasp escaping her mouth. Ambrosius did not miss it, but said nothing.

Her father was not so tactful. 'What ails you, girl? What is that woman-stealing bastard to you?'

Frantically searching for some unobtrusive answer, Ragnall appealed with her eyes to her husband for help. Cadwy had seated himself with his guests. He realized his father guessed there was something amiss here at Caer Badon, for Ambrosius, for all his annoyances, was astute and observant. He must have seen the baggage ready for loading on the ponies, would undoubtedly discover the intended destination. He could think of no rapid lie, decided on the truth. Or near enough to suffice. Calmly he took a sip of the warmed, red wine, said, 'By concidence, I returned but yesterday from Geraint's Hall.' At his father's questioning frown, he tossed an indulgent smile at his wife. 'My Lady Enid admonished me stoutly for not taking my wife and new daughter. For the sake of peace I decided to return, fetch them. We were preparing to depart as you arrived.'

Amlawdd scoffed, announced disparagingly. 'Women are timewasters. A double ride – and of such distance – merely to show off a puking brat? Wanton foolishness!'

Cadwy spread his arms, lifted his eyebrows, helpless, to the roof. 'Aye, my Lord, I agree, but even you must acknowledge there is no arguing with a lady who has set her mind.' To his surprise, his father chuckled.

'If you would indulge a father's whim and delay an hour, we could ride together. It will make a merrier party, having the children with us.' Ambrosius asked this of Ragnall, who generously agreed. What else could she do?

'Caninus thinks much of you, his grandsire. He will enjoy your company.'

'Pah! What nonsense is this, Ambrosius?' Amlawdd swung irritably to his feet. 'We go to arrest Bedwyr on suspicion of treason – and you advocate taking a woman and babes with us?' He stalked around the hearth-place, stood, fists bunched on his hips before his Supreme Lord, angry. 'God's justice man, is your head going as soft as your belly?'

Ragnall gasped, her hand going to her mouth at her father's gross indiscretion. Cadwy had leapt to his feet, his hand touching his dagger hilt. 'How dare you, sir!' he hissed. 'How dare you insult my father at my hearth?' With a snarl, Amlawdd had his dagger out, instant, into his hand.

Careless, almost offhand, Ambrosius waved the hostility down, ordered both men to sit, put up their weapons. 'Leave it be, Cadwy, Amlawdd meant not his words in the way you heard.' To Amlawdd, said, 'We do not go to arrest Lord Bedwyr, merely to ascertain why, yet again, he is not at the fortress I gave him to command.'

Amlawdd grunted, sat, reached for more wine. 'We know why. He either goes to bed the lady who ought be my wife, or plots to raise a rebellion against us.' Added with a growl, 'Or both.'

Cadwy openly laughed, earning himself a dark, thundercloud look. 'I assure you, unless there should come another, greater, leader, Bedwyr remains loyal.' Cadwy spread his hands, emphasizing the absurdity of Amlawdd's claim. 'He does, I admit, often ride south to see the Lady Gwenhwyfar.' He cast a challenging glance at Amlawdd. 'She did, after all, openly refuse you, is betrothed to him.'

Amlawdd spat into the fire, sending up a hiss of steam.

'Aye,' Ambrosius said, bringing his cloak tighter around his body. He was cold, close to shivering, and his stomach was paining him again. 'Bedwyr rides to see the lady. But I have heard a whisper on the wind that is, as yet, a rustling on a light summer breeze.'

Puzzled, Cadwy swivelled slightly on his stool to look the keener at his father's tired, drawn face. Ambrosius nodded, just the once. Saw in his son's eye that Cadwy had heard similar whisper. 'Aye, it seems the Artoriani might not, as we thought, be ended.'

§ XL

For a long, heart-thumping moment, Cadwy stared at his father, at his calm, almost indifferent expression and, although he was tired, his almost careless poise. How could he have heard of Arthur being alive? Had rumour spread further than the Saxon Eadric had thought? Careful, Cadwy said, 'You take this news with some amount of ease.'

Ambrosius shrugged. 'I have always suspected, been prepared. For all that some might have it, I am no fool. Son, I am aware that not all those in authority are eager to be my followers. Arthur had as many friends as he had enemies.' He lifted his shoulder a second time, a resignation to the acceptance of the inevitable. 'It takes only one spark to set dry kindling crackling.' He gestured his hand at Cadwy. 'You have obviously heard these wild whisperings also.'

244

Amlawdd was not as calm as his Supreme Commander. Came rapidly to stand before Cadwy, his hand tight-clasped on his sword pommel. 'Aye, your son has heard! Is he to support the bitch who so cleverly gave him this stronghold?' Spittle dripped from Amlawdd's mouth, so vehement was his accusation. He left no chance for Cadwy to respond, to defend himself from this verbal attack. 'Why do you ride again to Durnovaria – do you take your wife to safe quarter? Hah!' He stepped even nearer, his breath smelling of stale wine and bad teeth. 'Are you not in the thicket of it all, Cadwy? You plan to join in this thing and oust your own father!' His voice was rising, nostrils flaring. Amlawdd was a large-built man, bull-headed, bull-minded. Although shaken, even alarmed, Cadwy controlled his fear against this threatened intimidation, remained sitting, forced his own hand to stay away from his dagger hilt.

This was false accusation – although he was not entirely certain of what he was being accused. Tactfully, he responded on one issue. 'I have been charged to defend Badon against attack. That is my duty, my honour will ensure that duty is complied with. I will fight against any who may attack here. If you were to take hostile action, father,' – he glanced away from Amlawdd's sneering expression, to Ambrosius – 'then, aye, I would fight you.'

Ambrosius, waving Amlawdd to stand down, choked back a raw grimace. Even as little as one year past he would have bellowed outright laughter at the suggestion of his son fighting. Now he was not so sure. Cadwy had changed since taking Ragnall as wife. No, that was not accurate. Cadwy had changed since being closer in friendship to Gwenhwyfar. And was Gwenhwyfar plotting against Britain's Supreme Governor? The evidence – however shallow – seemed to suggest so. 'I have no intention of marching against Badon. The Saex, though, may do otherwise now they are united. And who knows where Bedwyr may decide to lead his comrades.'

Cadwy frowned. Now he had entirely lost the drift of conversation. 'Excuse me,' he questioned, eyebrows deepening, his fingers rubbing at his temple, confused. 'The Saex? Bedwyr? I do not understand this.'

Impatient, seating himself straddle-legged across a stool Amlawdd snapped. 'You said you have heard the rumour! Well, that rumour has come to be true knowledge.'

Cadwy caught his breath, as did Ragnall, who came to stand behind her husband, her hands resting taught, on his shoulders.

'Aelle of the South Saxons is elected Bretwalda. Supreme over the united Saxons.' For so great and threatening a thing, Ambrosius Aurelianus spoke mild, as if he were issuing a statement of the weather prospect for the afternoon.

Puffing his cheeks, raising his eyebrows, Cadwy placed one hand over Ragnall's. Thank all the gods that might be listening! It was not of Arthur that they spoke!

'I have heard such rumour,' he said. Refrained from adding that it was not long since he had warned his father that this might happen, that the Saex had had enough, were on the brink of rising. To avoid an unnecessary clash of bitter words, he kept his eyes from Amlawdd, whose harsh methods had been one of the direct causes for this joint need to unite.

Sneering, Amlawdd, aware that Cadwy refused to catch his eye, assumed it to be for a different reason. He leant forward, elbow on knee. 'And have you also heard of Bedwyr's treason?'

'Bedwyr?' Cadwy stilled his fingers from rubbing against Ragnall's hand.

'Do you also collaborate with that bitch-woman and Geraint? Do you plan, with them, to reunite the Artoriani, to rise against us?' The venom was deadly, the glare in Amlawdd's eye and poison on his tongue black with hatred.

Ambrosius cocked one eyebrow. He would prefer Amlawdd to direct his accusations with more tact. Too often he assumed above his authority; acted, spoke, as if he were on some equal level with Ambrosius. Ah, well, that is what came of giving patronage to an imbecile.

Puzzled, not rising to Amlawdd's attempt at angering him, Cadwy stated, again to his father, again ignoring Amlawdd, 'I know nothing of Bedwyr plotting against you, Lady Gwenhwyfar also is innocent in this charge.'

The sneer of contempt was triumphant on Amlawdd's face. He slapped his thigh with his hand, threw back his head. 'Why, then, has Bedwyr so often been absent from his command so often with that bitch-breed Gwenhwyfar?'

Cadwy irritatingly smiled. 'I would suggest that he has a personal interest in the lady that is not to your liking.'

His lip curling, Amlawdd thrust, 'You deny involvement with this conspiracy then?'

Vehemently came the answer. 'I do!'

Clearly, Amlawdd did not believe it.

'I would suggest, father,' Ragnall declared, giving a reassuring squeeze to her husband's shoulder, 'that you concentrate on the reality of the Saxon danger, and not look for treason where there is none.' Added with a courage that Amlawdd had never, before now, noticed, 'My Lord Bedwyr has no time for rebellion. He is preoccupied with convincing Lady Gwenhwyfar that her place is legally in his bed.' She dipped a reverence at Ambrosius. 'I will give instruction that we are to journey together.'

Ambrosius pushed himself to his feet. He was chuckling. 'Talk your way around that one, Amlawdd!' He slapped his hand on his shoulder. 'Your daughter seems to have more wit than either of us have given her credit for.' He was laughing. Did not believe a word of it, for the rumours that Bedwyr and Gwenhwyfar were involved in something of greater significance than the matter of marriage were too strong.

And if they were not plotting his demise, what else of importance could be so determinedly occupying their attention?

§ XLI

The argument that erupted less than an hour after arriving at Durnovaria was more explosive than even the fabled eruption of Vesuvius. Amlawdd was ready to pick a fight, Bedwyr in a mood determined to oblige him. Naturally, Bedwyr hotly denied the accusation of treasonable intent. As naturally, Amlawdd loudly proclaimed that he lied.

Ambrosius and Geraint between them managed with some difficulty to keep the two men from each other's throats. The urgent matter of the Saxons uniting under one leader kept the quarrel reasonably at bay, though the growling and snarling exchanged between the two, from their opposite sides of the table, was more vehement than any Saxon war-cry.

'I will be needing commanders whom I can rely on without question,' Ambrosius said pointedly to Bedwyr. 'Can I rely on you to be where you are meant to be when the Saex rise against us?'

Angry at the reiteration of the accusation, Bedwyr leapt to his feet, his stool scraping on the timber floor of this, Geraint's Hall. They were gathered at the top end, where the lord's table was permanently sited, before the largest hearth-fire. Below, in the Hall proper, the tasks of daily life were dutifully attended, with more than one surreptitious glance cast at the rise and fall of voices. Several heads turned at Bedwyr's abrupt movement, glances exchanged. Word had spread quickly that a fight was imminent – more tasks than usual seemed to need urgent tending in the Hall this day.

'I tell you again, Lord Aurelianus, I am no traitor! If you seriously think I am, then, damn it!' Bedwyr slammed the table with his fist. 'Have my head now!'

Amlawdd growled something beneath his breath, the words not quite discernible, the meaning plain.

Patient, Ambrosius repeated what he had already said. 'I am satisfied that you have no intent against me, yet I must argue that you leave your place of command over often.' That was due to the lax way Arthur had run things. Letting his higher officers follow their own pursuits. Ambrosius would have none of it. 'Desertion, Bedwyr, I could well call it desertion!'

'Ask the men to stone me. See how many would agree to do it!'

'Christ God, you push your luck, boy!' Amlawdd was on his feet also, hands spread flat on the table top. Geraint and several of the other gathered officers groaned. 'Back you, would they?' Amlawdd jeered. 'And you say you do not gather an army to your side!'

It was enough to push Bedwyr over the edge of patient reason. His dagger was out as he leapt across the table, scattering papers and maps, his free hand going for Amlawdd's throat. The men met, tumbled to the floor, rolling over, scuffling, breath rasping from exertion and anger. A confusion of dogs jumped up, barking, prancing around, two starting their own fight.

It lasted but moments, hands reaching instantly to clamp on both Bedwyr's and Amlawdd's tunics, hauling them apart, to stand bent, breathless, glowering, ready to start again if chance allowed.

From their private quarters the women had come, enticed by the sudden clamour of noise, Ragnall with the babe still at her breast, Enid, several of their maids. And Gwenhwyfar, storming into the Hall, her cloak flying behind like the unfurled wings of some swooping bird. She grasped Bedwyr's dagger, taking it from him, flung it aside. 'Is this what we are brought to?' she rebuked. Turning to Amlawdd, she removed his weapon in the same manner. 'Grown men behaving with no more dignity than dogs! Mithras! What makes that of me? A bitch on heat?' Her eyes flashed between the two of them, the green sparking with the gold flecks of her anger. Beneath, they were grey-bruised, the rims red. She had been weeping. Weeping, it seemed, these past few years with never-ending tears.

What had happened to them all? To her? Why was everything spiralling into this whirl of chaos?

She did not need these two men snarling their endless squabble over who should have her. She needed . . . What? What did she need? Needed to know, in her own mind, in her own heart, whether Arthur would be coming home.

Amlawdd wanted to preen over her as his wife, Bedwyr wanted her as a woman. Standing, her fists clenched, she made her decision. To do what she wanted. To find Arthur, discover for herself why he had not returned.

Face it outright. If he preferred to stay with this other woman, then . . ..
She would face the *then* when it came.

Decision.

'Neither of you will have further cause to bicker and squabble like infants mewling over a broken toy.' She eased the taut breath, solemnly regarded each man there in turn. Ambrosius Aurelianus, who had so wanted to return Britain to the protective fold of Rome. A few years back, he might have succeeded, but not now. It was too late, they were too far along the rock-strewn path of independence and the Saex were too firm-entrenched. Geraint, a princeling who wanted only to rule his own quiet corner in peace and prosperity but who was, by the very nature of his position, drawn into a wider circle of events. Amlawdd who wanted to satisfy his greed for being the best, who could never admit to falling so far short of his ambition. Cadwy, who was perhaps of them all the only man there who thought with a clear head, who put his duty to country and kindred above the scheming of personal worth.

She looked across at Ider and the lad, Gweir, who had come into the Hall as she had, with the onset of disturbance. Two men who would willingly follow her into the Otherworld if she asked it of them. At Enid. At Ragnall. Ragnall, who had an hour past told her of the woman Morgaine and Arthur's son, Medraut.

'I am going to Less Britain.'

Several eyes widened at her announcement. A spark of hope, of relief from Bedwyr, Ider and Geraint. They knew that what she then said was veiled truth, a feint to put the opponent off-guard. 'Across the sea, I may find the peace that I am looking for.'

Her glance met again with Ragnall, with that woman's disfigured, misshapen face. And their smiles met. 'If I can find that,' Gwenhwyfar said. 'Then, by chance, I can see an end to all this fighting.'

June 472

§ XLII

The forest was dense, quiet and enfolding, giving the impression that she, Gwenhwyfar, was the last person left alive on this earth, aside from the old hermit striding ahead of her. She even had her doubts about him. He was thin – lanky – and tall, far taller than any other man she had known, even Ider who stood several fingers above six feet. His sun-browned bare arms and legs protruding from beneath the faded grey of his robe were like sticks, bone stretched beneath a taut cover of aged and worn skin; his hair streaked white like a badger's pelt, gnarled hand clasping a staff, almost as tall as himself. His stride was long, Gwenhwyfar found she had to trot to keep up with him as he threaded a way along the twisting, narrow, but well-trodden path.

Ider had wanted to come with her, but the old man had not allowed it. 'No,' he had said, the one word only, a man of little conversation, making one or two simple sounds do for lengthy explanations. He stepped over a fallen trunk with no effort, no scramble or difficulty. Gwenhwyfar had to hitch her gown, scrabble over best she could, and quickly, for he was striding on, not waiting for her. If he turned a twisting corner, she feared he would be gone, disappear into the darkness beneath these trees. Less Britain was a large, formidable land, these woods greater than the whole of the Summer Land of home. She had no inclination to become lost within the silence of these crowding trees.

'I seek those who are of the Goddess, the women who call themselves the Ladies,' she had said earlier, when they had come to this place, to this old, Christian man, living alone in his solitary hermitage. 'I have heard that such women live here, in these woods, though they may not be the Ladies I seek.'

Sitting cross-legged, straight-backed outside his door, the Gospel resting open on his lap, he had silently watched her men make camp, observed the cooking of their meal, said nothing, made no acknowledgement. Did not move until the sun began to slide downward into the purple-blue of evening.

Startled, Gwenhwyfar had looked up to see him at the entrance of her tent. 'It is to the heresy of the pagan you ask to go, but come, I will show you,' he had said, and she had followed.

250

The sea-crossing had been uneventful, tedious. They had sailed from Llongborth and had ran before a fresh wind across the Channel Straits, then down, around the toe of Less Britain, encountering few other ships, no Saxons, no pirates. Disembarked at the sheltered harbour town of Dariorigum, sought information, were directed back along the coast to here, the old hermit who lived near the Stones. Even the horses had travelled well, aye and Onager! Gwenhwyfar had deliberated over the bringing of him, such a bad-tempered, unpredictable animal, on a long sea-crossing. Arthur had left him behind for that reason, but then, Arthur had transported several hundred horse, they had only their six riding animals and three pack-ponies. Bad-tempered he might be, but he was a bold, strong horse, could go for miles on little feed; his heart rode as high as his temper. And aye, she had brought him for another reason. He was Arthur's.

'How far do we go?' she called, lengthening her stride to keep up with the hermit. For an old man, he was quick-paced. She expected no answer, received none.

Ahead, the trees were thinning. Through the tree shadow filtered the rich gold of a sunset. The hermit gestured that she should step out ahead of him into what seemed to be the lower end of a clearing. She went forward, stopped, incredulous.

Stones. Row upon row of grey, lichen-mottled Stones. Upright, or toppled over, varying in shape, wide or narrow, some squat, some taller than a man, others small, like a child – rows of them, a hundred, hundred Stones lined in ranks stretching away up and along the clearing bordered so densely by the sentinel guard of dark forest. A marching army, frozen into these timeless ranks of stone.

These were nothing like the ancient sacred circles and avenues that Gwenhwyfar was familiar with – not even the Great Henge could rouse the breath-held awe that this place generated. Tentative, reverent, she walked forward, her fingers going out to touch the nearest time-weathered monument, but she drew back, reluctant to make contact with its cold surface.

For the constructions in Britain – smaller, much smaller than this great wonder – no one remembered who had erected them or why. Old beyond ancient, holy, mystical, magical places. Nothing else. No reason, no use. They *were*, that was all, just *were*. The forgotten. The ended, stretching away into the distance of the past, back to the dawn when time itself was on the verge of being. But they were places of peace, of welcome also. To wander around those circles back home, touching each standing stone with a warm caress of greeting, brought the overwhelming inner feeling of calm.

But these Stones Gwenhwyfar could not touch. She felt no fear or dread; there was no leering shadow of evil or malicious intent, she just could not reach out, touch the surface of the nearest Stone. She walked forward a pace, imagined that the Stones were parting before her, making a path, stepping aside, not wanting to be a part of this, her time, her existence. It all seemed very polite, so tolerant and indifferent, as if those spirits that lay here, remembered only by the marking of these Stones, had dutifully accepted her presence, offered her polite courtesy, yet would be relieved were she to go. She was not wanted, but would not be turned away. They were waiting, she was certain, for someone, or something, to come, were prepared to wait until the other end of existence. Until the very ending of time.

As Arthur was waiting. She knew that, she could feel it, so strong was it here amongst the Stones. Waiting . . . for what? For her? To be freed? To decide? Ah, that she could not yet know.

Impulsive, she curtseyed low and deep to one Stone that seemed larger than some of those others nearby. A trick of light, the fading glow of sunset, the coming of dark . . . Did it seem that the Stone answered her with some slight, shifting movement? She turned. The hermit was waiting at the edge of the trees, not stepping out from their night-darkening protection. He, a Christian man, would not come into the domain of the pagan.

'The Ladies,' he said, in a voice that was as clear and fresh as spring water, 'are beyond these lines of Stones. Follow their march, on the morrow.' He lifted his head a little higher, his blue eyes glittering a Christian challenge. 'If you are not afeared.'

Gwenhwyfar walked back to him, her smile indulgent. 'The Stones do not mind those who come to do them no harm.'

He snorted light contempt, indicated that they were to return along the same path. 'May I ask why you seek the heathen, when it is the words of Christ that ought be in your heart?' he said, after they had walked in silence for some many yards.

Again, Gwenhwyfar was behind him, having to trot occasionally to keep pace with his long stride. 'It is the heathen who can answer the questions I must ask,' she replied.

He walked on, head high, his staff stabbing into the ground with every pace, saying no other word until they neared the camp. She could smell the smoke of her mens' hearth-fire, hear the faint murmur of their voices. Ider would be waiting, anxious, at the edge of the trees, not settling until she returned.

'You have the look of a woman who has lost something that must be found,' the Hermit announced. 'I will pray that Jesu may help you find it.'

They stepped out into the clearing, where a shallow river ran down to where the hard earth slipped into sand, and the sand into the sea. Ider, as she expected, grunted, nodded at her, turned to join his men. The hermit went direct to his bothy, slipped inside.

At dawn, Gwenhwyfar made her way, with only Ider for company, along that same twisting path and out among the mist-wreathed columns of Stones. She walked the few miles with her heart light, her steps making no sound on the dew-wet grass. Where the Stones ended, she found the place where the Ladies dwelled. They were of the Goddess, but were not the Ladies she sought. There had once, and not so long ago, been many such scattered groups throughout all of Less Britain and Gaul, but their following was dwindling now, here as in Britain, with the young girls going to serve Mary the Mother of God, rather than the Goddess, Mother of Earth. None of the five knew of one called Morgaine who had a boy-child named Medraut, but then Gwenhwyfar had not expected them to. For a journey to end it must have, somewhere, a beginning, and no journey could end too soon after its starting.

By mid-morning, she and her men were again on their way. At least now, from the telling of the Ladies by the Place of Stones, they had some vague idea of where they need ride, where they need look.

July 472

§ XLIII

Bedwyr, riding through the gateway into the outer settlement of Ambrosius's stronghold was surprised, and not pleasantly. The place was busy, full with people occupied with the various needs of daily routine, but they were civilians, a good portion of the men clad in the garments of Christianity. Where were the soldiers, armed men, trained professionals? He halted his horse by a trough, let it extend his head to drink. July had been hot and humid, a long, uncomfortable month of sticky, itching skin and irritable, flaring tempers. In a few months time, when the bite of winter was nipping sharp at fingers and feet, they would look back and long for this heat – as a fall of snow would be most welcome now! Christ God, this was supposed to be a fortress! A bell began to toll, striking one, solemn note. Bedwyr's eyes followed a group of monks as they made their way through a stone archway into a shaded courtyard from where the summons came. A gaggle of five young boys ran from a narrow side-street, dodged around his horse and scampered after the monks, one pausing to grin a quick apology.

Bedwyr dismounted, led his horse after them, but stopped this side of what was an obvious boundary. Through the arch, in contrast to the business of the streets, order, neatness and an air of calm solitude. The monks, and the boys – more of them now, at least four and twenty – were entering a low, single-storey chapel, stone-built in the traditional equal cruciform shape. So Ambrosius had his abbey built, and his school for boys. His fists clenched, Bedwyr turned away, clicked his tongue for the horse to walk on, headed for the lane that ascended steeply upward to where another gate stood open. The fortress proper. Well, he hoped that Ambrosius knew what he was doing, that those simple-clad, sandalled monks knew how to wield a staff and club as easily as they did gospel and crucifix. He shook his head as he began the climb up the cobbled track. If not, that fine, recent-built place would soon enough be blackened and lying as a smoking ruin.

He had to wait for the most part of an hour. He was offered wine, fresh baked bread, sheep and goat's cheese. He drank the wine, nibbled the cheese, paced the floor, barely noticing its splendid mosaic pattern depicting the ascension of Christ. There were soldiers up here within the

254

fort, guards at the perimeter wall. A half-century, about forty men, drilling on the parade-ground before the principia building. Others loitered around the barrack blocks, some grumbling between themselves, as soldiers always did, at the unfairness of the fatigues rota. A few men looked up as Bedwyr passed by, saluted a superior officer smart enough, but with a reluctance, no snap of enthusiasm or interest. Someone had come to take his horse and he was escorted here, into this ante-chamber of this Roman-style house-place. And asked to wait.

'My business is important,' Bedwyr had said, twice now, received in response the same answer: please wait, Lord Ambrosius will not be long.

More wine, more cheese. A door opened and closed somewhere among the rooms that ran behind this one. Footsteps, but no one came. Another quarter of one hour. Another door, more steps, and Ambrosius entered, his hand extended in greeting. 'You ought have joined me at Mass, Bedwyr,' he chided, 'we have a new-appointed abbot, his words are most uplifting.'

The thought that there were more important matters that needed attention beyond the listening to a new abbot's monotonous liturgy crossed Bedwyr's mind, but he held his tongue, answered with a polite mumble. 'Another time?'

'Indeed! Please, sit. May I offer wine, something to eat?'

'Thank you. No.' Bedwyr remained standing, ignoring the offer of a couch. Pointedly, he looked at the two servants who had entered with their master. Ambrosius dismissed them. From his waist pouch Bedwyr brought out a small, bronze Saxon brooch, handed it to Ambrosius, who took it, frowned, passed it back.

'They have reached your part of the woods, then?' Ambrosius seated himself on a couch, patted a cushion into place behind his back, his good humour evaporating.

Bedwyr put away the saucer-shaped brooch that carried the mask of a human face, fastened the leather thongs of the pouch. 'It is in my mind that they have been worn for some months, hidden beneath folds of a cloak or kept safe within a pouch.' He patted his own. 'That they are now beginning to be worn openly is, I think, significant.'

'Yet there is no whisper on the wind of a hosting. No mumbling of a meeting point.'

Pursing his lips, Bedwyr agreed to this, but added, 'There are war spears, I have seen them, though I was told they were for hunting.' He lifted one hand, fingers curled as if cradling a sword pommel. 'There is a sharp edge being put to the sword and axe. Nothing tangible, nothing obvious, more a pricking at the nape of the neck.' He let his hand fall; he wanted to shout, to get angry, to say all the things that were in his head and heart to the man before him. To tell him of this inadequacy and inefficiency. To say that Britain desperately needed Arthur back . . . but he was sworn to secrecy, could not betray his King, nor Gwenhwyfar. Could not betray the confidence of men such as Geraint, Cadwy, the trust of Lady Ragnall. 'The Saxons are about to rise,' he said, pushing thoughts of Arthur from his mind. It might all be wrong, Arthur might be dead. 'And you are not making ready.' It came out, not as an admonishment or judgement, but with a hurt cry of saddened pain.

'Aelle will not call for a hosting this year.' Ambrosius placed his palms, fingers spread, on his knees, spoke with a conviction of certainty. 'But if he does, I shall be ready.'

Scornful, Bedwyr challenged the assurance. 'Ready? How? Do you plan to pray for a victory?' He swung away from Ambrosius, faced the wall, leant one hand upon its smooth, dark-red, painted plaster. 'When Aelle comes—' He turned around, managed to keep the anger from his voice. 'He will be coming with an army at his back!'

'And if he does not come?'

It was not an answer Bedwyr had expected. He stood, mouth open, the words that he had intended to say trapped as irrelevant. He frowned. 'Of course he will come.' He heard the question in his voice. Did Ambrosius know, then, something he did not? He had to, for he was sitting too calm, too self-assured.

'His eldest son will not be able to fight. Aelle will not act without Cymen.'

Bedwyr had gasped, his face coming alight with a glimmer of hope, happen God had not deserted them after all! 'Is he ill? Mortally so?'

Ambrosius shook his head. 'Not ill. Few die from a break to the leg, but he will not be from his bed until the leaves change, too late for battle by then. The Saex will not fight during winter.'

The answering comment was a curse, one of Arthur's favourite colourfully embellished oaths. The anger was rising. 'Are you so certain they will not? Or next spring, what of then? Do we still sit here, on our backsides, running our thumbs along our blades, waiting?'

Refusing to rise to the bait, Ambrosius leant deeper into the comfort of his couch. His back was aching, his shoulders stiff. He had lain awkward during the night, would take a hot bath, have his slave massage the tense muscles. 'I have placed my resources where I think them to be effective, Bedwyr. If Aelle cannot form a hosting there will be no battle. When the time comes, you will have your orders. I expect you, and others who hold like command, to contain the Saex in their own territories. Your east Saxons will not meet with Aelle of the South.' Ambrosius pushed his cushion a little higher up his spine, confident in his judgement.

256

The anger was seething, bubbling below the surface. 'Are you mad? Contain the Saex? Is that what you want us to do?' Incredulous, Bedwyr stood before Ambrosius, too stunned by the utter stupidity to release that checked anger. 'My few men against God alone knows how many? We'll be slaughtered – if we ever even manage to fight our way out of our fortress.' He strode across the few paces between them, thrust his face close into Ambrosius's. 'Aelle understands the rule. You obviously do not. United we win. Detached, we die.'

'No, Bedwyr, I say again, the Saex will not fight. You and your men will ensure they have no heart to fight with. No men, no weapons to fight with. You misunderstand me, Bedwyr.' Ambrosius stood, folded his arms, threading his hands into the loose sleeves of his robe. 'I am not intending to wait for them to attack us. We attack them. Through the winter, we burn and destroy. Come spring, there will be no Saex left to fight. Not even the women or children.'

For many long seconds Bedwyr stood there, staring at the man dressed in the style of a monk. 'My God,' he said, appalled, 'you are to commit us to a war that will be bloodier than any slaughter ever made.'

'No,' Ambrosius stated, blandly. 'I am to do what I set out to do. I intend to destroy the Saex.'

§ XLIV

So they had taken a barge up the River Liger, had stayed a few days at Juliomagus, then continued on to Caesarodunum. From where the letter Winifred held in her hand had come. She tapped the scrolled parchment against her lips, thinking.

That Gwenhwyfar had gone in search of Arthur was obvious. How she had discovered him to be alive was inconclusive, but not difficult to realize. Winifred had known that she could not ensure the silence of all Mathild's men – mind, it came as some personal satisfaction to know she had almost achieved it. Precautions against failure had, naturally, been taken, had reaped reward, although Gwenhwyfar had led the spies a merry, winding dance these last months! Agreeing to wed Bedwyr, changing her mind, living a while at the Holy House of Durnovaria . . . Oh, a time Winifred's paid spies had, trailing and observing. The cost was mounting, ah, but worth every spent piece!

For although Winifred knew Arthur might live, she had no clue, no hint of gossip or whispered speculation of where to look for him. Torturing Mathild's men had gained her nothing. Her smile was smug, cat-like in her gloating self-satisfaction, for Gwenhwyfar, it seemed, was inadvertently to solve the riddle.

She folded her arms, watched her grandson toddle across the courtyard outside, miss his footing and fall onto his knees. His nurse ran to him, all hugs and consolation, but the boy stubbornly pushed her aside, scrabbled to his feet and tried again. Winifred quietly applauded, her expression as proud as any doting grandmother's should be. Cynric was a determined whelp, for the three months that he had been here at Winifred's steading, a few miles from Venta Bulgarium, she had not heard him cry or wail once. A boy a handful of months into his second year, Cynric had the resilience of a warrior. Stubborn, with a mind made to succeed at all cost. Like his father.

Huh! Was there any doubting that Cynric was Arthur's child?

Winifred shed her breath with a loud, partially impatient sigh. It was a pity that Cerdic was the mismatch of the family. Pig-headed, aye, but to all the wrong leanings. Determined, but only in the area of a determination to do all in his power to oppose his mother.

It was a marvel that she had been allowed this short while to have the boy with her, happen even Cerdic had a small grain of sense in his granite-bound brain! Winifred placed her palms together, the fingers pressing under her chin. There had been fighting again along the Elbe, the peoples moving up from the south and from the east, causing confrontation with those already settled along that busy, important waterway. Cerdic was safe enough – for at least a while, a few years or so; happen, if he were fortunate, more than that, but three times now his waterside buildings had been burned to the ground, his fortified settlement attacked. Added to that, so many of those who were supposed to be loyal to him had left, taken a craft or walked away, preferring to offer allegiance to some other man of status. Too many remembered the killing of Mathild to remain loyal to Cerdic. Those first few months after her death had been difficult, disquieting, for he had found need to prove himself worthy over again. There were not so many supporting Cerdic now. Those few who stayed remained for the boy, the child of Mathild's body, but there were not enough of them to secure the boy's safety, that was now certain, or else Cerdic would never have sent him here, away from the sporadic raiding, safe with his grandmother.

Winifred chuckled, mayhap the turning of events would force her son to consider the taking of Britain as his own. There would soon be precious little for him along the Elbe.

As she watched the boy that wandering thought came again to mind. Whose child was he? Cerdic's? Arthur's? She would never know for certain, but this she did know, Cerdic enjoyed his women, he had lost his boyhood at the age of three and ten. Yet no woman, outside of Mathild's bed, had borne him a child.

Cynric noticed his grandmother watching him, laughed happily up at her. He adored the woman, for she allowed him anything he wanted, unashamedly indulged his every whim. Winifred blew him a kiss from her fingers. She, in return, idolized the boy. He, she hoped, would not turn out to be the bitter disappointment that his father – whichever one of them was the father – had proved to be.

August 472

§ XLV

Antessiodurum was a town teetering on the brink of Christian fame. Narrow, steep-rising streets, buildings huddled shoulder to shoulder – a town that was doing well for itself. The abbey with its complex of buildings was already impressive, nestling as it did beside the river and below the domineering height of the town. A congenial place to be, Antessiodurum, if you had the time to wander and admire. Along both banks of the wide, slow-moving river idled clusters of trees, cool with green shade, while in the water fish lazed beneath the span of the only bridge. Fields of fertile soil supported recently-harvested crops of corn, and strong, healthy vines. Drowsing heat and murmured pleasantries; trade agreed over a goblet of local wine, a crowded town where no one cared to hurry, where there was time to sit all day in the sun.

Gwenhwyfar hated the place.

Accommodation had been the first difficulty. The world with all his children, it seemed, had decided to visit Antessiodurum this same week, drawn by a festival, a celebration to the glory of some local, minor, Christian deity. Eventually they found a tavern that was little more than a flea-ridden hovel, where the food was mildly edible if not wholly appetizing. Ider had long since taken it upon himself to sleep across his lady's door-place, not trusting even his own men to see to her safety. The horses had, through the same necessity, been stabled in shoddy stabling where the hay was musty and feed smelt of mildew.

No one knew, or admitted to know, of the pagan Ladies. Ask a question, receive a shrug, uplifted arms, slow-shaken head, blank or askance expression. 'Ladies? No, not here, this is a Christian place.'

Gwenhwyfar began to despair, even to doubt the wisdom of this fool idea. Would she not do better to turn around, find some obsolete place in Less Britain and settle there in quiet oblivion for the rest of her days? As many in Britain would prefer.

She sat at a table outside a street taverna, Ider standing behind, leaning one shoulder against the wall, his expression gruff, as always when on duty, his eyes narrowed, watching all who passed with a glower of suspicion. Once or twice his hand tightened around his sword pommel. Ider, too, had little liking for this place. Antessiodurum reminded him of an old villa he had once visited as a child with his father. Grand on the outside, giving the appearance of ordered wealth. Inside, comfortable enough, with servants and wine and good food, but Ider had noticed the threads of spreading cracks on the plaster walls, the patched tunics of the serving girls and the small portions offered only the once, no chance of a second mouthful.

Gwenhwyfar sipped her wine, had not touched the greasy stew in the bowl before her. The barge journey up the Liger river had been frustrating for its slowness, for the river was low, the exceptional summer heat rapidly drying its many tributaries. Many times, the craft had laboriously to follow the shrinking navigable channels, and with the river more than a mile wide in places, each manoeuvre to change direction became an unbearable delay. The horses drooped beneath the heat, listless and bored, the monotony of the scenery lulling the passengers into a hypnotic daze. The relief was enormous when they disembarked a few miles after the river had swung to the south. To ride again, to be in command of their own pace!

Leaning her elbow on the table, Gwenhwyfar rested her cheek on her fist. With passing interest, watched two young women walk by, catching a glimmer of their conversation. She smiled to herself. Either that erotic description had been exaggerated boasting or the dark-haired girl had a stallion for a bed-mate. She chewed at some dead skin by her fingernail. Na, that would be impossible to do . . . Christ and all the gods, she was sitting here, speculating on some wretched whore's sexual exploits!

She signalled to Ider, made to move away, heard her name called. The street to their left was steep, narrow and busy, but Gweir called again, waving his hand frantically to draw attention. He thrust his way through a group of women waiting to buy bread, danced around a man carrying two bolts of cloth, pounded on up the incline, stood, panting for breath, before his lady, his grin broad.

'I have found them!' he declared, 'At least, I think I have.' His face was alight, animated, the pleasure of success running not far behind the promise of leaving this seething town.

Excited, Gwenhwyfar grabbed his arms, bent slightly towards him. 'Where?' she demanded. 'Tell me!'

'To the south. The Place of the Lady!' His grin broadened at Ider, his arms folded, countenance scowling. 'A great hill, rising high, high.' Gweir raised his hand over his head, 'Above the valley. We follow the river south, there will be a track before the water swings west.' He laughed, danced a few delighted steps. 'The woman who told me—' He flushed, suddenly embarrassed at the pleasurable memory of these past few hours: he had learnt more than a destination from that delightful creature. He floundered, forgetting what he was about to say, blushed at Ider's snort of amusement. 'The place is known, but few go there, especially men.'

Gwenhwyfar kissed his cheek. 'I am not a man.'

Oh the relief! They could be gone from this wretched town within the hour. That passing idea of returning to Less Britain was quite, quite, forgotten.

§ XLVI

The track, zig-zagging up the side of the hill, seemed to take forever to climb, the riders sweating as profusely as the horses before they were even half of the way up. Gwenhwyfar brushed hair from her eyes, wiping perspiration with the same action. She blew out her cheeks, kicked Onager forward again. He was a bold strong animal but even he was labouring.

The day was hotter than yesterday and the day before, a more insistent, oppressive heat that drained energy, made for bad tempers and irritability. The blue, unblemished sky had hazed over after the sun had passed through the midday zenith, with dark cloud building ominously from the south. Rain would be welcome, but not if it came with a crushing storm. Several women working at the vines unbent to stand, one hand to an aching back, the other shielding eyes at Gwenhwyfar and her men, their bodies turning, curious, as the party rode by. No one spoke; it was too hot for words. At first sight of them, Gwenhwyfar knew they were in the wrong place. Morgaine would not be known here, not among these Christian women.

'Different than Antessiodurum,' Gweir remarked with false amusement. 'There, everyone would rather talk than work. Here . . .' And he swept his hand behind, across the spread of the vines clinging like limpets to the steep, sunward slope. 'Do we turn back?' he asked, disappointment catching at the tiredness in his throat.

'At Antessiodurum,' Gwenhwyfar answered, 'it was only the men who lazed and talked. I saw enough women with their backs bent double and their hands gnarled from hard labour. Na, we have come this far, we may as well go on. There may be someone who can be of help to us.'

One of the men, turning to look behind, remarked, 'There are more travellers on the road. Two, three riders?'

The view from up here was tremendous, overlooking the spread of the parched valley, dark trees dotted against sun-burned, brown grasses and

262

withered crops. One single track wound through the centre of the valley, bald, bleached white against the baked earth, the horses too far away to see clearly or make out detail, a dark smudge against the stark emptiness.

Ahead, higher up the slope, another woman had ceased her work, had straightened. Her face was brown-tanned, the skin cracked and wrinkled from exposure to sun and wind. She looked to be over the age of half a century, was probably no more than thrice ten years. Gwenhwyfar reined Onager in, allowed him chance to rest. 'A storm comes,' she said, attempting pleasant conversation. 'You tie the vines to minimize damage?'

The woman nodded. 'They are robust enough if regularly tended, as any child would be.'

'You wear the black habit of a holy woman,' Gwenhwyfar observed. 'I had been told that this was the Place of the Lady.'

The woman studied Gwenhwyfar, her ageing, crinkled eyes taking in the dark blue of her robe, the purple of her linen cloak, the sword with jewelled scabbard hanging from a leather, bronze-studded baldric slung oblique across her chest. Seeing also the men, strong, armed, wearing white, padded tunics beneath crimson-red cloaks. The horses, tired but well fed, well kept, well bred.

'We serve the Lady Mary, though once, long ago, this was a sanctuary of the other Lady. You wear the garb of a royal woman.' She added her own question, 'Yet your guard is few and you carry no banner?'

'I need no guard nor proclamation of who I am when I come in peace to visit friends.'

The woman sucked her lips against partially toothless gums. 'Equally, 'tis best to travel quietly among possible enemies.'

Gwenhwyfar made no immediate response. Apart from those distant riders and the women working among these vines, the world appeared as if it could be silent and empty. Conflict, death and battle had no hold in this serene valley. 'My enemy is also your enemy. I fear Euric the Goth as much as you. It was my husband, the Pendragon, who attempted to rid you of him.'

The woman raised her eyebrows, impressed. 'He was a brave man to try, but also he was the fool.' She expected Gwenhwyfar to respond with some form of animosity or hostility, was surprised to receive instead an amused smile.

'Aye,' Gwenhwyfar agreed, 'as I also told him, on more than one occasion.'

The woman laughed, she had a pleasant, young laugh. 'Men give so little credit for our feminine sense!' She indicated the top of the hill, hanging high above, and the cluster of white-painted buildings, clinging to its eastern edge. 'You will find no men up there, beyond the wayfarers' tavern outside the gate.'

'I am not looking for a man.' It was a lie, but justified as it was a partial one only. 'I seek a woman. Morgaine.'

'Not a name to be found among our Christian kind.' A flutter of wind lifted the white of her veil. The smell of rain came strong, insistent, with the breeze. The woman bent back to tying the vines. 'Continue up,' she said. 'There will be shelter for you inside the abbey, for your men and horses, at the tavern.'

Thanking her, Gwenhwyfar signalled to move, halted again, turning slightly in her saddle. 'Do you know of Morgaine?'

The woman stood, her posture straight, shoulders held proud. Her head had turned up the valley, to where the track, having passed this citadel, lifted again to the hills. She was not seeing the rising ground, nor the dark welt of trees covering the slopes. 'I have not always served this lady,' she said, her voice and thoughts distant, set in the past. Her eyes met with Gwenhwyfar's, held. 'Aye, I know of the one they call Morgaine.'

Thunder rumbled, some many miles to the south.

§ XLVII

The men had not been allowed beyond the gateway. Ider had loudly protested, announcing that where his Lady went, he went also. The gatekeeper, a woman with steel-blue eyes, firm jaw and almost half his height, sidestepped his insistence by allowing Gwenhwyfar to pass through the iron-worked gate, and shut it promptly behind her, marooning Ider on the outside. He rattled at it a few times, demanding to be let through, drew his sword, a helpless gesture. He stepped back, searched the high wall for a place to climb. Useless! The sanctuary within was as well fortified as the most formidable stronghold. The wall, sturdy, mortice-filled stone, stood above twelve feet, the drop this side being deeper than the other, given the steepness and shape of this sharp-rising ground. By stepping back a handful of paces, he could clearly see many of the buildings within, stacked, it seemed, roof upon roof as they climbed up to the higher summit. Timber-built, most of them, small dwelling-places, perhaps a few workshops. He stamped again to the gate, rattled irritably at its lock. Within, he could see a tannery, women working on the drying skins and a larger building behind – there must be somewhere for a wine press, storage for the amphorae and barrels of fermenting fruit. Women? Women only beyond that gate? He found that hard to believe.

A chapel stood at the summit, wood-built and reed-thatched, with a crucifix, gold inlaid and taller than two men, erected with reverence high above the door lintel. The single cobbled track led straight and steep, bending sharply to the dexter side at a well where several women were gathered. He called out to Gwenhwyfar, 'My lady!'

She did not seem to hear, for she did not turn around or acknowledge his shout of concern. Instead, the gatekeeper came again, peered through the iron railings. 'She will be quite safe young man,' she admonished with a firm finality. 'None shall harm her here.'

Ider muttered something beneath his breath, which could have been a profanity; the woman did not choose to hear. She shuffled away, her keys jangling from the chain at her waist. Gwenhwyfar he could no longer see, for she had turned the bend in the track. He faced the opposite direction, his back to the gate, watching down the hill.

The men were seeing the horses fed and settled; the lodging at the tavern appeared adequate enough, simple food but clean accommodation. Beside it, a forge and a tumble of shabby dwelling-places, the beginnings of a small settlement that would increase, no doubt, with the passing of time. The first spots of rain were falling, the sky blackening, thunder becoming more persistent, louder. To one side of the gate, there was a small shrine built into the wall. Flowers had been placed there, though they were already drooping for it was too humid for wild things to survive for long. Ider hitched the hood of his cloak over his head, hunkered into the partially protecting overhang of the alcove, his sword laying across his thighs.

He would not move from here until Gwenhwyfar returned through that gate.

Gwenhwyfar knew Ider would not go far, hoped he would have the sense to make himself comfortable within the tavern, guessed he would remain close to the gate. Ider's was a loyalty of devotion, never would he let anything happen to her. It was good to have such friends.

The climb up the cobbled track left her breathless; she found her legs and back aching long before she and the woman accompanying her reached the chapel at the top. The abbess, a woman of advanced years, but with eyes as bright as a blackbird's, came from a building at the side of the chapel to meet her, hands outstretched in welcome and with a warm smile, as if she were greeting an old and cherished friend.

'Welcome, my dear! Welcome! We are delighted to offer our hospitality to such an honoured guest!'

Taken aback, Gwenhwyfar questioned, 'You know who I am?' She had never met this woman before, nor did she see how advanced warning of her coming could have reached here.

The woman laughed, gestured for her to follow along a path into the comfort of her private quarters. 'My dear, I have no idea who you are; nor, if you do not wish to tell of it, do I need to know. It is enough to know that you visit us.'

Liking this abbess for her honesty, Gwenhwyfar replied with as much frankness. 'I do not know how long I intend to stay . . .'

The woman laughed, ushered her into the comfort of a small but pleasant room as thunder crashed overhead, releasing those few drops of rain into a downpour. 'I think,' she said, with a knowing nod to her head and bright sparkle in her eye, 'that you will stay at least an hour or so, while this storm passes.'

Gwenhwyfar accepted the wine offered, agreed to that, but added, 'I would be honoured to stay at least the one night.'

'I will see that a room is made ready. Stay as long as you need, my child.'

§ XLVIII

The stone wall to the east of the convent was low, the hillside, dropping as it did, almost vertically downward on the other side, creating seclusion and protection. The storm had grumbled through most of the night before taking itself off northward, but had done little to dispel the uncomfortable heat. Two days later, the air still hung as heavy as lead, a persistent haze muffling the expanse of sky. Gwenhwyfar sat on the wall, watching a lizard scurry from one hiding-place to another, pausing, hesitant, between its chosen places of safety. Archfedd would have been delighted in the creature, its yellow-green skin, darting swiftness and reptilian beauty. A stab of longing for home and her daughter shot through Gwenhwyfar. Perhaps it was the height, the permeating contentment of the convent, that reminded her so of Caer Cadan, the looking down the hillside and out across the valley and up the winding track that straddled the steep, rising ground. Archfedd was safe with Geraint and Enid, happy running as one of the pack with the children of Durnovaria's stronghold. She had no worries for the child, though occasionally, when thoughts wandered homeward as on this day, she missed her dreadfully.

Reaching forward, Gwenhwyfar picked a cluster of leaves and fruit that would, before long, ripen and reveal the hardened shell of a walnut. The slope was dense with the trees, the nuts self-seeding over the years, creating a massed forest that tumbled downward, forming an impenetrable natural barrier. Absently, she pulled the leaves off one by one, tossed the fruit away, watched as it tumbled and rolled down the hillside, became lost among the tangle of grass, fallen dead leaves and young, tangled, saplings. She stood, wandered along the path, her fingers idling across the cracks and splits on the wall, brushing the softness of mosses and the intricate patterns of lichens. Beyond the wall, the unmanaged trees became clearer as the slope gave way to less hostile ground. Vines were planted here, southward-facing to catch the full benefit of the sun. Below, way below, the valley floor was cultivated with scattered fields and pasture for grazing, the meandering river an oasis of fresh green against sun-baked brown. Further away, as the land began again to rise, the cultivation gave way again to trees, those dense forests that dominated so much of Gaul. The track, winding upward cutting like a white scar through the dark foliage. That was the track she would need follow, tomorrow or another tomorrow. To ride up, between the sentinel trees, upward to the crest of those hills, to find on the other side ... Gwenhwyfar closed her eyes. All this way, these weeks and miles of journeying. One last track to follow. A few more miles, a morning's ride ... She wanted to go home, to turn round and ride away. Courage had failed, the need to know dispelled by the desperate desire to not find out.

Horsemen, riding along the valley, crossing the river, turned to take the track that led up to this high place. She recognized the four riders as her men by their red cloaks and white tunics, distinguishing Gweir's dun stallion at the forefront. They led a pack-pony, a deer straddling his withers. They had been hunting then, successfully, it seemed. She hoped they would have the courtesy of presenting the Abbess with some of the meat, knew they would, for her men were not a selfish breed.

She rubbed her hands. The wind was chill up here, at this great height. She would soon have to find the strength to discover what lay on the other side of those wood-covered hills. If not for herself, for the men who had faithfully followed her here. And for all those that waited their return.

She could no longer see Gweir, for the shoulder of the hill hid the upward track. Two days they had rested here, although she knew her men had not been idle. She had not seen things with her own eyes, but she knew Ider well enough, and Gweir and the others. They were not men to sit in the sun when something needed tending.

How far had they ridden, she wondered. Had they already been over that hill? Already talked about what – who – might be there on the other side? Morgaine, certainly, with a boy-child. Sister Brigid, the woman tending the vines out on the hillside, had told her that much, had elaborated a little while the storm had raged outside that first evening.

'A while past,' she had said, 'I turned away from the pagan blackness and into the light of the Christ.' She never related what had swayed her decision and Gwenhwyfar never asked. Enough to know that before, she had been among the Ladies of the Goddess, and had lived in their secluded community on the far side of those hills that were, this afternoon, shadowed in the mist of a shimmering heat-haze. Enough to know that the one called Morgaine had been away on some journey, private to herself, and had returned with a man, wounded and close to death. The sister had known no more, whether he had survived, whether he was still there. That was for Gwenhwyfar to discover. When – if – she was ready to.

Gwenhwyfar wrapped her arms about herself, closed her eyes against the tears. Was it not better to have that slight, however improbable, edge of hope? Tomorrow, or the day after, she would need to find the courage to face what might well be, the final breaking of a heart that was already so bruised and battered, but from where that courage would come, she knew not.

§ XLIX

Gweir found his commanding officer sitting, as expected, at the table set outside the tavern. At least the man had been persuaded to move from that gateway. Further than that Ider refused to go. At night, once dark had fallen, he rolled himself in his cloak and slept across the threshold of the shuttered gate. Obsessive, some lesser men would call it. Others, Gweir included, would use the word devoted.

Gweir straddled a chair, mindful not to block the larger man's view of the convent gateway, helped himself, with an upraised eyebrow of asking, to wine.

'Good hunting?' Ider asked.

Gweir nodded. 'Shall I send a haunch of venison up to the Ladies?'

Ider returned the nod, watched a group of chattering sisters walk by, acknowledged their greeting. 'And last night?' An innocently asked question. Received as innocent a reply.

'Interesting.'

Stool balanced and with his shoulders propped against the wall behind him, Ider's feet had been set upon the corner of the wooden table. He dropped them to the floor, sat forward, resting his stubbled chin on the knuckles of his linked hands. 'How interesting?'

Refilling his tankard, Gweir drank again, not so thirstily this second time, answered casually. 'Last night I scouted up through those woods to the north of the road.'

Ider remained silent. This he knew, this they had discussed before Gweir had set silently out on foot as dusk had settled.

'I found them.'

'They see you?'

Gweir laughed cynically, finished his wine, did not bother to answer the question.

Ider had realized at Antessiodurum that they were being followed. Whoever the two horsemen were, they were not good at their job, not discreet enough, not careful enough. Unless that was their intention. Occasionally to show themselves, to keep Gwenhwyfar's guard guessing?

Rubbing his fingers across his nose, under his eyes, Ider asked, 'Same horse?' Confirming what he already knew.

Gweir dipped his head. 'Same horse. The roan. Why stable it alongside ours back at Antessiodurum? Why deliberately show themselves?' He folded his arms, resting them on the table. 'And you were right, it is ill.'

Ider sucked his cheek, considering. 'Get close enough to find out for definite?'

Gweir nodded. 'Discharge from the nostrils, swelling under the jaw.'

Ider swore.

Flicking his head backward in the direction of the convent, Gweir asked, 'Do we tell her?'

'That we have an unwelcome shadow who seems to enjoy playing games, or we've been stabling with the strangling disease?' Ider stood up, stretched. He was an impressive man to look at, strong built, strong minded, dependable and unfalteringly loyal. Slowly he unsheathed the sword from the scabbard hanging at his side, tested its oiled, gleaming, blade with his thumb.

'No matter, for both tis the same answer.' He looked to the wall, behind which he knew Gwenhwyfar to be safe. 'She already has over much to think on. This is our concern.'

He put the sword away, strode in the direction of the stabling. Those two following could be dealt with anytime, when they became too much of a nuisance. For now, they were a minor irritant, nothing more. Disease among the horses, however, was always a worry for a cavalryman.

§ L

There was only the one road. From a high vantage point, the two men watched its snaking path as it dropped downward to the valley, taking turns to doze in the morning warmth. By noon it would be unbearable again and they would need seek the shelter of shade, but while the sun rode low it was fairly pleasant. The one awake nudged his companion with his foot, startling him alert. He pointed, grunted. The second man sat upright, narrowed his eyes to study better the lone rider. The dun horse again. The second time that he had ridden up this winding road alone.

'Where does he go?' the first man mused, speaking thoughts aloud. His tongue was Saxon, with a Gaulish accent, though his dress and appearance, as with the other man, was clean-shaven, respectable Romano-Gaulish.

'Does it matter?' The second man shrugged apathetically, and rolled again to his back, set his hands behind his head. 'Our orders are to wait and watch where the woman goes. I can be content with that.' He closed his eyes. Sought the sleep that had been interrupted.

Irritated, the other man got to his feet. 'You're a lazy bastard. It'll be your fault if we've been discovered here.'

The response was a lewd gesture, accompanied by, 'So what if we have? We're travellers, journeying in the same direction, nothing wrong with that. It is the others they must not know of.' Without opening his eyes, he swung his arm up, flapped a hand somewhere behind his head, vaguely indicating the haze-shrouded hills at the far end of the valley. He smirked laughter. 'But how would they know? We are the decoys. If we find out anything interesting, one of us goes back.' He wriggled his buttocks more comfortably into a hollow. 'Meanwhile, I am enjoying the easy life. Let the woman stay where she is for as long as she likes, I say.'

The other man began collecting up his belongings, kicked his toe among the flattened grass where he had sat to encourage it to spring up again. 'I'm going after him.'

'And what if he sees you?'

'He won't.'

The second man heaved himself upright, fumbled in one of his saddlebags. He tossed a leather pouch of gold coins at his companion. 'I'd rather you did something useful. Ride into Avallon. Get me another horse.'

Catching the small bag, the first man weighed it in his hand, then let it fall. He picked up his saddle, walked away into the covering shelter of the trees. 'Get your own bloody horse. You should have taken more care of the last one.'

Gweir rode relaxed but alert, feeling more than knowing that he was being watched. He let the dun pick his own pace. The road ran steep in places as it bent and twisted its path upward through these woods. He looked back once, appreciated, not for the first time, the impressive domination of that lone, high hill, upon which sat the Place of the Lady. It would take a determined army to assault that citadel. The sun, gaining strength in the east, reflected on the whitened walls of the chapel, built on the very crest of the highest ground, caught on the gold of the crucifix erected above the door-place. *The hand of God*, Gweir thought, before he set the dun at the next, even steeper bend, *marking his blessed territory.*

The horse pricked his ears, turned his head to the north and whickered. At Gweir's urging, continued forward. Another horse answered, from a distance, well back into the trees, possibly from near where that rise of high ground gave a good view down the valley. So that was where they had moved to. Ah well, that would save him the bother of coming out again tonight, to look for himself.

It was the bay that had called. The roan lay dead, partially buried beneath leaves and bracken. Gweir had found it last night. They had cut its throat with no time or reason to tend a sick horse.

He looked ahead, up the climbing road, his ears and senses alert for movement, for sound to either side among the darkness of the crowding trees. If there was to be an ambush, it would come here, where the going was slow, a long haul. Not that he expected one. Not yet.

'They are waiting to find out what we're up to, why we are here.' That was Ider's opinion, spoken last evening in a soft growl as he discussed tactics quietly with the men around their corner table in the tavern.

'Who else knows why we are making this journey?' one of them had said. 'Beyond our friends?'

'More to the point,' another had added, 'what is their intention?'

Ider had grunted his opinion. 'Probably, the same as us. To find whether the Pendragon is still alive.'

Loosening the sword at his side, Gweir tested that it would come quickly free should he need it in a hurry. His lips formed a half-grin. 'If that be the case,' he had answered Ider, 'they are more worthless than we thought.' The daylight had been fading, but the lamp set on the table, flickering in the evening breeze, had illuminated his features. 'For the answer to that riddle, we already know.'

Gweir touched, as if it were a talisman, the roll of linen tied behind his saddle. Yesterday, he had seen him, admittedly at a distance, too far to see clearly or to hail, but it was enough. Gweir had known him.

Quietly, calmly, he had informed Gwenhwyfar, this morning, as the first, faint caress of light had began to dim the stars' dance. She had met him a while later, in the stables behind the tavern, and had given him this thing.

'Take it to him,' she had said. 'Tell him that I am here.'

'Ought not you to go, my lady?' Gweir had said to her.

She had shaken her head, pushed a strand of loose hair from her eye. 'Na,' she had answered him. 'I cannot go.'

This morning, he had not understood. All this way, all this long journey – ought she not have been eager to see Lord Arthur for herself?

But riding up the steepness of this lonely road, Gweir had realized the truth of it, for he felt that first unease that she too must have felt. What, if after all this distance, all this effort, Arthur did not want to return to Britain, to his men, his kingdom? His wife?

§ LI

With livestock to keep safe, there was always fencing to be mended or tended. Goats especially, stupid animals, had an obsession with pushing through, finding weak timber, loosened posts. Arthur hit twice more with the mallet, tested the corner post for firmness, grunted, satisfied when it did not move, looked up as a horse came into the yard, picking its way across the sun-hardened mud ruts. A dun, well bred.

Few turned onto the uninviting track that meandered down the valley to this clustered settlement where the women of the Goddess dwelt. Those few, men, who did come, rode here for one reason only. For the pleasures a woman gave. And for the most part, the women welcomed them. Not here though, not at Morgaine's isolated dwelling. Men did not come to this place. How word spread that there was already a man here, Arthur had never cared to ask, but spread it did.

His hand went automatically to the dagger sheathed at his waist band. He took a few paces forward, his eyes squinting against the bright glare of the sun. Stopped.

Something familiar, alarming. Arthur's heart quickened, the unexpected rearing up to meet him, square on. Gweir? By all the gods, Gweir! He licked his lips, wiped his hand down the outside of his thigh, the sweat on his palm sticky, annoying. Had he known, all this time, that someone, some foolish whelp, might just come looking for Morgaine, might come asking after where she had buried the body, what she had done with the man who had once been strong enough to be King?

For his part, Gweir was as afeard as Arthur. All this while, all these miles. All the tears. What did he say, now that he was here, face to face with his lord? How did he begin?

'We thought you were killed on that dreadful day.' It was as good an opening as any.

Arthur shrugged his shoulders. 'As you see, I survived. You also escaped the clutch of the Otherworld.'

Gweir lifted his hand in a slight gesture of unimportant dismissal. 'I missed most the fighting, was left for dead early in the day.' Gweir threw his leg over his horse's withers, slid to the ground. 'I made my way back home. Back to Caer Cadan.' He did not say it, but it was there, deep in his voice, hurting, screaming. *Why did you not also come home?*

Again Arthur shrugged, how could he answer? How could he say aloud that there had been nothing for him to go back to? That he had not the courage to face what once had been, with the blood of defeat stinking so strong on his hands? In the end, all he could say was, 'I walked with death for a long time, and when I was recovered, there was nothing left in my spirit to guide me back.'

Standing beside his horse, one hand to the reins, Gweir felt a surge of sudden, uprushed anger. All those tears, all those damned, wasted, tears! 'Not even for us?' he said bitterly. 'Not for all those men who would die a hundred deaths for you?' Then softer, perplexed, added, 'You turned your back on so much, so many.'

'They say,' Arthur replied, a tightness catching in his throat, 'that when learning to ride a horse, if you fall you must get on again straightway, else your nerve shatters.' He spread his hands, the mallet dangling, 'I fell, and there was no horse for me to mount.'

Gweir stepped forward, leading his dun, held the reins out to Arthur. His eyes, imploring, said, 'Here is mine. Take him. Come home.'

Arthur's smile was sad. ''Tis not as simple as that, lad, I would that it were.'

'Where is the difficulty?' Gweir protested. 'If ever you loved your men and your country, if ever you loved your wife,' – Arthur winced – 'then mount this horse. Now.'

For a moment, Arthur held the lad's hurting eyes, recognized the pain there – did he not feel that same pain biting into his own, twisting soul? He shook his head, turned away.

His head hanging, Gweir shut his eyes against the well of tears. He had not intended to say all that, had not expected to be so angry. What had possessed him? Hastily, he untied the roll of linen from behind his saddle, ran the few steps that separated him and his lord, held the bundle to him.

'She said to give you this. Said, this would tell you all you need to know.' Gweir put the thing into Arthur's hand, stepped back as the Pendragon looked for a moment at it, unwrapped the covering. A leather scabbard, functional, nothing exceptional. Inside, a sword. He knew that pommel, knew the firm feel of power and strength that flowed from it into the skin of your hand; knew its wonder. Knew all that without need to draw the blade.

If his heart was pounding before, it now leapt faster. He licked dry lips, looked from the sword to Gweir, back to the sword. His sword. The sword he had taken in battle from a Saxon, the sword he had last seen at . . . He looked up at Gweir, asked simply, 'She?'

Boldly, Gweir spoke out. It was the best way, best to fight with the edge of your blade, not the flat. 'Bedwyr took the sword back to Britain, he thought it a thing he ought do. Found, as you would have found had you returned, that further word never reached you, that you had been mistakenly told false. Bedwyr gave the sword to her, and now she has brought it here, returned it to you. For you to do with as you will.'

Dumb, with no word in his mind or mouth, Arthur stared blankly at Gweir, his lips slight parted, brow dipped in a questioning furrow.

'You were told wrong, my King, thank the Lord,' Gweir responded in a rush of words. 'She lives. Like me, like you, Gwenhwyfar lives. She is at the convent at the Place of the Lady, not a handful of miles from here, waiting for you.'

§ LII

Arthur leant his forehead down into the goat's warm flank, his fingers working automatically, stripping the milk from her full udder, sending it hissing into the wooden bucket. She was a good animal, this one, content to stand quietly, rarely kicking or fidgeting. Not like her eldest daughter, a demon to milk. Arthur frequently threatened to butcher her. If it was not for her consistent yield, he probably would have done so by now.

His busy fingers slowed, stopped. The goat lifted her head, thoughtfully chewing, enjoying the feed placed in the bucket before her. Arthur shut his eyes, pressed back threatening tears.

A child's feet, running. They were returned, Medraut and his mother. She called something to the boy, then he was at the byre door, his fingers fumbling with the stiff latch. Arthur scrubbed the back of his hand across his cheek, continued with the milking. Medraut, breathless, his face flushed from the exhilaration of running in the heat of the afternoon, was at his side.

'Mam says, can she have the milk as soon as you have finished?'

Arthur grunted agreement.

'There were a lot of people in Avallon today, and we saw soldiers marching along the Roman road.' Receiving no reply, the boy gaily chattered on. His father was often silent, quiet, often answered with only aye or no, or a grunt. 'They were Burgundians, Mam said, hundreds of them, all singing and laughing as they marched! I wonder where they were going?' He was darting about, full of a child's exuberant energy as he talked, swinging his arm as if it held a sword, parrying and thrusting, fighting an imaginary opponent. 'The leaders wore chain armour and bright coloured cloaks, and their helmets had horse-tails on the top.'

'Many weapons?'

'Oh aye, spears and swords and great axes!' Medraut changed his imaginary weapon to an axe, which he swung haphazardly from side to side. Arthur had finished the milking, was moving the bucket to where it could not be knocked or kicked over. You only did that once, when milking; leave a full bucket where it was vulnerable. 'You use an axe like that in battle, boy, you'll be dead within the first few minutes.'

Medraut's lips pouted.

Moving to the stacked woodpile to one side of the cluttered byre, Arthur casually lifted the chopping axe from where it hung on a roof-support post. He set a log end on, on the earthen floor and, gripping the shaft with both hands, brought the axe down, clean through the centre, the wood falling in two equal halves. 'You can split a skull as effectively.' Arthur set the two billets of wood to the top of the pile.

'Have you ever killed a man with an axe?' Medraut was impressed, his question asked with awe. He was a lad of six years, an age when warrior heroes and super-strength gods filled his mind and dominated the breathless stories he asked for.

'You use anything you have in battle, boy, including fists and teeth, knees and feet.' Arthur held the axe in his hand. It was heavy, not well made, an axe adequate for wood chopping, not sturdy, lightweight, reliable enough for battle. 'The axe is a weapon for the ranks. Mine was the sword.'

'Have you been in many battles then, Da? Before you came to stay here with us?' Medraut knew little of his father's past. That he had come from somewhere else, injured and unwell, he knew. He vaguely remembered a long walk with his mother, once, dimly remembered a lot of men fighting, but his mother had never talked of it, and neither had Arthur. It could all have been a dream. He often dreamt of battle and soldiers, marching and fighting, dreamt of being a hero, brave and strong.

Arthur snorted through his nose. 'A few,' he answered. He sighed, placed the axe back where it belonged. 'A few.' He turned his back on the woodpile, bent to lift the bucket of creamy, warm milk. It was there, hidden between the logs of wood, his sword, the sword that had once made him a King.

Opening the door for his father, Medraut was still chattering about the men he had seen, asking questions, reciting his observations, not noticing that Arthur's answers were grunts or monosyllabic. 'Some of them had their hair tied in a tail on top of their head, they looked like horses. Who was that man we saw riding away from here? What did he want?'

Abruptly, Arthur stopped, the milk slopping over the brim of the bucket. 'What man?'

'The one riding a dun horse. We were coming down the hill, we saw him riding away.'

'Oh. He was seeking directions, had taken the wrong track.'

Medraut was only a child. Morgaine, his mother, would have caught the rise of inflection in Arthur's voice, would have heard the catch in his throat and seen the quick rise of breath on his chest. Being a boy, Medraut had no reason to doubt his father's answer.

§ LIII

The horse held his head out stiffly, easing the discomfort of the swollen, misshapen glands beneath his jaw. Onager was ill. He was off his feed, his body slumped; eyes dull and disinterested. The nasal discharge had altered from a clear trickle to the thick, opaque flux common to the strangling disease, an illness that spread from horse to horse with rapacious speed – the young were the most vulnerable, together with the unfit and the old. Onager was a good horse, in his prime, well-fed, well-groomed, but as a colt he had not contracted a dose of this wretched illness, was paying for that earlier escape now.

The jaw abscess was hardening, was ready to burst, the danger being that it would burst internally, would drain inward. Gwenhwyfar stroked her hand sympathetically along his neck, his coat harsh and rough beneath her finger-touch; her misery compounded by a combination of lack of sleep, profound disappointment and anxiety. She was regretting that impulsive decision to bring Onager. Was regretting coming at all. What a fool she had been!

To know that he was alive. Is that what she had told herself all these weeks, these months? Just to know that he was alive? Was she a fool, born under the madness of a red moon? She wanted him back – had assumed he would come back to her, with her. Fool! Her soothing fingers had wandered to the hard lump beneath Onager's jaw. It would need lancing, to ensure the pus drained away correctly, a task she detested. A foul, messy job. Do it now, or leave it another day?

Two days past Gweir had ridden out of the valley, had said little on his return.

'*Did you see him?*' Gwenhwyfar had asked, flushed, breathless.

'*I saw him.*'

'*And?*'

'*And I left his sword with him, as you asked.*'

That first night had passed slowly, hot and airless, with Gwenhwyfar unable to sleep. She had prowled her room, lain down, got up. Told herself the agitation was for Onager, ill in the stables. Knew that for the excuse it was. Tomorrow Arthur would come, they would wait for Onager to recover and then go home. Oh, would tomorrow never come?

The day came, but Arthur did not. Another dawn. Sun-up, midday. Evening, a haze of dark clouds, gathering into another grumbling storm.

'*You told him I was here?*' She had asked Gweir, several times.

He had bitten his lip, tried to avoid meeting her eyes. He had nodded. '*I told him.*' But how could he tell her Arthur's last words? '*I have for myself another life, another home.*'

The stables were lit by only two lamps for the night. More were unnecessary. The men had gone to their beds, although Ider would not be far away, probably having a last drink with the tavern-keeper. The gates to the convent would have been locked more than two hours past. She would sleep near Onager this night. Rain pattered lightly on the stable roof. Again, Gwenhwyfar fingered that ripening swelling.

Footsteps beyond the door. Ider had said he would come to see all was well, before he slept. The lamps flickered briefly as it opened and closed, chivying a draught. 'We must make decision on this tomorrow,' Gwenhwyfar said, her head tilted, peering closely at the abscess. 'We cannot afford to leave its lancing over-late.'

The aisle between the stalls was long and narrow, much of it in darkness. The man's boots clattered on the cobbling, a smell of a rain-wet cloak. He lifted the lighted lamp as he came abreast of it, carrying it high, stretched forward, felt the hard lump, ran his hand affectionately down the horse's neck. The animal lifted his head, ears pricking, attempted a soft whicker of greeting. 'Ah, my handsome lad, I can see you are not well, but we will get you better.'

Gwenhwyfar stood very still, her fingers remaining on Onager's crest, her heart pounding, mouth dry, lost for the right words to say.

Arthur set the lamp safe into a niche high in the wall, placed his fingers lightly over hers. His hand was cold, the skin sun-browned. He was thinner than she remembered, his cheeks hollowed, eyes tired. His hair needed cleaning and combing, a shave too, for the stubble was thick on his face. An uneasy, embarrassed silence. 'You would have been thinking that I was not going to come,' he said, his voice so familiar.

'I was starting to think that.'

For want of something more to say, he touched Onager again. 'This needs lancing. Tonight.'

'It will go another day.'

'No, it will not!' he said it wildly, with more aggression than he had intended. His mind was a muddled jumble. His stomach knotted into an ache of disbelief and elation and fear, mixing and tumbling with uncertainties and doubts. Churning with a need that was so great that its shout was deafening his senses. He had thought her dead, gone! But here she was, standing before him, green eyes, copper hair, lovely. His Gwenhwyfar.

She span around, fury blazing on her face. 'What do you know of it? What do you care?' She too was sun-browned, and her face thin. She knocked his hand away from the horse, snarled, 'What right have you to tell me what to do?'

'I have every right, he is my horse.'

'You forfeited that right when you elected to stay with your whore!'

'Morgaine is not my whore.'

Gwenhwyfar laughed contempt. 'Do you expect me to believe that?'

'I do not know what I expected!' Arthur drew in his breath, fought to swallow this stupid rise of anger that was sparking between them. He lowered his gaze from her flashing eyes, his fingers fiddling with a buckle on his belt, nervously raised his eyes again half-smiled. 'I did not expect us to fight.'

She snorted, made to push past him, to move away, to put a distance between them, her heart was hammering, her breathing rapid. He grasped her arm. With great effort, he said, as calmly as he could, 'I thought you to be dead. Until Gweir came, I had no way of knowing different.'

'And you never cared to make sure? Forgot your daughter, your country, your kingdom – and for what? For the by-blown daughter of the woman who caused your son's murder!' Nostrils flaring, she removed his clasping fingers from her arm. 'You disgust me!' With quick steps, she stalked away, going into the darkness so that he might not see how her hands, her body, shook.

'How could I go back?' Arthur shouted. 'For months I lay close enough to death to remember nothing of it.' He spoke to her retreating shadow, made no attempt to follow. Cried. 'Would Britain have taken me back? After I had been directly responsible for all those dead? I had lost everything. My men, my pride!' He spread his hands, let them fall. Said very quietly, 'so I thought, you.'

She had stopped.

'I could not go back, Cymraes.' He lifted one shoulder in a shrug that told more of the grief, of the defeat that had tormented him these last three years than any words could express. Arthur had always held the reputation of never quite telling the truth. It was an image he had specifically nurtured, along with the implacable, ruthless exterior. Only Gwenhwyfar had known him for what he was, a man with so many doubts and fears. 'I could not, Cymraes,' he said again. 'Without you there to help me, I had not the courage.'

Gwenhwyfar closed her eyes, her fists at her sides clenched, her shoulders taut. 'The tears I have cried for you. The loneliness!' Her own grief was there, her pain. 'All those tears,' she said, as she slowly turned around to look at him, 'And you were with another woman.'

He shook his head, hesitantly stepped to her. 'No, there is nothing between me and Morgaine. In another life, happen there might have been, but not in this. I lay with her once. I did not know then, what—' he took a deep, steadying breath, confided, 'what I later realized. There can not be anything between us.'

'You ask me to believe that you have no love for her?'

'I love you. And I thought you were dead.'

The trembling reached her voice. 'You also. I believed you dead, also.'

They stood a pace or two apart, eyes not meeting, not daring to look one upon the other.

Arthur nodded, so Gweir had told him, in the sun-shadowed stillness of the byre. All morning he had waited, he had told Arthur, patient, beneath the shade of the woods, waiting for a time when the woman and the child might not notice him. They had left, together, walking up the incline, had disappeared over the brow of the hill, and Gweir had ridden down from his hiding place.

'You and I have both suffered,' Arthur attempted. 'Unnecessarily, it seems.'

Gwenhwyfar was weakening, the anger caused by alarm and the flutter of unease going out of her. 'You ought to have come home.'

'Aye.' He stretched out his hand, his smile widening. 'I was wrong.' He took those last few steps, took her hand. 'But I am not wrong about my horse.'

Gwenhwyfar's answering smile was shy, guilty. 'I know you are not.'

He touched her cheek, caressing her lightly with his fingers and thumb. He would have kissed her, but Onager moved, restless, in his stall. The animal was in discomfort, needed tending.

Businesslike, feeling his feet on safe ground for the first time in many months, Arthur's dagger came into his hand. Unnecessarily, he tested the blade, although he knew it to be honed to keen sharpness. The kiss could come later. Perhaps more than a kiss.

§ LIV

The rain was easing, the clouds breaking up into ragged streamers, blown by a freshening wind. Soon, the new day would steal in. Beneath the mantle of darkness, the world lay at peace, asleep. Gwenhwyfar, curled on a bed of dried bracken in an empty stall, mumbled incoherently in her sleep.

Arthur had been outside, to sluice a bucket of its foul contents – the wound beneath Onager's jaw still seeped yellow pus, but the draining stuff had eased. He stopped at the doorway to the stall where Gwenhwyfar slept; stood, one hand resting on the shoulder-high post. He had thought that he would never see her again, never hear her voice, feel her touch. In one sense he *had* died, for he had been nothing but an empty, dead husk these past years. A part of him could not believe, accept, that he was standing here, looking at her, watching her breathe, live. This was all some cruel dream. He would wake soon, would wake to face, over again, the misery of knowing she was gone from him, for ever. He stepped further into the stall, his hand – it was shaking – stretching out to touch the delicate skin along the inside of her arm. Leapt back, snatching away with a muted gasp. She was cold! Ice-cold, death-cold! Teeth biting into a forefinger, Arthur steadied his uneven breathing. Fool! Of course she would be cold. Was it not cold in here? Stalls for twenty horses, with only eight filled and a draught whistling like an ice-dragon's breath flurrying through every conceivable gap? He unfastened his cloak, laid it across her body, tucking it beneath her exposed arm. Gwenhwyfar. His Gwenhwyfar.

Leaning his head against the partitioning wall, he closed his eyes, sank down to his heels and bowed his face into cupped hands. She was alive, and he had not known of it! She had come for him, still cared for him, expected him to go back with her to Britain. To do what? To lead men, to be King again? How could he? How could he command men to fight, when he had not even the courage to wear his own sword? He had stayed here, hidden away, rather than make that long journey back to Britain, stayed here because it was easier to let them believe him dead rather than let them see him for the weak, cowering failure of a man that he had become.

He dozed where he sat, hunkered on his heels. The outer door opening with a crash as a gust of the rising wind caught it, woke him and Gwenhwyfar together.

Startled, they both jolted awake, Arthur hurriedly scrabbling to his feet, his dagger coming automatically into his hand, Gwenhwyfar slower, sleep-tangled beneath his covering cloak.

It was Ider coming in, unshaven and sleep-tousled, coming, as Arthur had ordered, to wake him. Behind him, the faint light of first dawn seeped through the open door-place. Ider lifted his hands, palms outermost to show he held no weapon. 'Whoa!' he soothed, ''tis only I. How is the horse this morning?'

Arthur tucked his dagger safe into its sheath, grinned to hide that sudden-come jolt of alarm as he stepped forward hand outstretched, to greet his old friend. It had been dark last night, raining, with little light to see clearly by, outside the tavern. Only briefly had they spoken then, Arthur asking where he would find Gwenhwyfar, Ider awkwardly expressing his joy at seeing again his Lord King alive and well. 'Mithras, Ider,' he teased, seeing the man in better light, 'if you put much more bulk around that belly of yours, you will break your horse's back!'

'Bulk!' Ider chortled, his broad hands patting the ample bulge around his midriff, 'This is solid muscle!'

'Solid flab!'

Gwenhwyfar, bedding caught in her hair, the cloak folded over her arm, came to Arthur's side. Her eyes were bright, gold flecks dancing against the green. She prodded Ider's prolific weight with her finger. 'This,' she said, 'is an ale pot. It has wondrous powers, for it renders its wearer senseless at night and has the ability to fill faster than it empties.'

The two men roared their laughter, Ider's face flushing a modest red, Arthur's arm going around Gwenhwyfar's shoulders, to stand as often they had stood, close, companionably, together. She did not move away, turned her head to look at him, green eyes meeting brown. The laughter left his face as he returned that solemn gaze. He had kissed her, after they had dressed the lanced wound with a pad soaked in oil and vinegar, after they were sure Onager was safe enough for the remainder of the night. One kiss, his lips lightly on hers, but it had been almost a chaste, tentative thing, like two people who did not yet know each other well enough for intimacy, fumbling around politely in a darkness of uncertainty.

Ider cleared his throat, squeezed past, intent on inspecting Onager. The horse's ears were cold, though Arthur had covered him with a blanket. He busied himself with changing the dressing, tried not to let his eyes or ears stray to the two people who stood a few yards away. They were all in turmoil! Lives turned topside-out.

Gwenhwyfar brought her fingers up, touched them lightly to Arthur's chin, slid her palm across his cheek, held his face in her hand, her eyes taking in his features, looking for all those half-forgotten familiarities. The flop of hair that tumbled over his forehead, his nose, long and straight. Firm, determined jaw. Those dark eyes that so well kept all thoughts, secrets and fears tucked behind. Of what was he thinking now? Of her, of them? Of the past, the future?

'It is you,' she said. 'I dreamt that you were only a memory. I called you, but you did not come.'

He placed his hand over hers, pressing the palm firmer to his skin. 'If I did not come, it was because I could not.' And then he said, 'And if I do not return with you, it is because I cannot.'

Her eyes widened, then darted, flashed, realizing what he had said, meant. 'You are staying with her? Choosing her over me? Christ and all the gods in heaven!' She hurled away from him, tossing his cloak from her, 'And I believed you! Last night, Mithras help me, I damned well believed you!'

He answered with the first, stupid thought that came into his head. 'I only came to see Onager.'

'You bastard!' She spat. 'You toad-spawned, whoring bastard!' Gwenhwyfar could move quickly, for she had always been lithe and quick on her feet. Before he could defend himself, take a step back or raise his hands, her palm flashed out, struck him across his cheek, reeling his head backward, leaving a red streak across the flesh.

'Take your bloody horse!' she screamed, 'Take him and go! I hope you both rot!' She whirled, a flurry of brown skirt and copper hair, was gone, running from the stables, up the hill through the gate into the sanctity of the woman's place, the Place of the Lady.

Ider stroked his broad hand down the softness of Onager's nose, stood blindly torn between his devotion to Gwenhwyfar and his love for his King, the Pendragon. Arthur was aware that he was there, unsure and uncertain. As confused as he was himself.

'What do I do, Ider? How do you tell such a woman that the man she once knew is no longer living?' He turned his eyes to seek some form of guidance from the big man standing by the chestnut horse. 'I am Arthur, but I am no more the Pendragon. I forfeited the right to that title when I left the remainder of my men to die, without me. Left those already dead for the crows.'

Ider disagreed, but how was it his place to say so?

A fool thing to do, for the horse was ill, needed rest and quiet to recover, but Arthur took his halter rope. 'Sometimes,' he tried, explained, as he went towards the open door, leading the horse, 'Sometimes, there can be no going back.'

He would have his horse, at least, to remind him of what he had once loved. And lost, a second time over.

§ LV

When Arthur did not return, Morgaine was not unduly worried, it would not be the first time that he had stayed drinking himself into a stupor at the Wild Boar tavern in Avallon. He would find his way home eventually, come staggering through the door, with boots muddied and clothes rain-sodden, wearing a sore head and a poor temper.

She had company, for old Livia had arrived, seemed set to stay a while – a well-intentioned woman, but a nuisance on occasion, for she was not one to notice subtle hints.

'Arthur not here?' she had queried, in her high, old-age creaking tone, stumping through the always-open door, setting herself firmly in the only chair. 'Part of my roof is off. That storm did much damage the other night.' Impossible to say no to Livia, she asked as a command, but then, no one would say no to an old woman who had no man or son of her own.

'I will send him over tomorrow.' Morgaine knew Arthur would be annoyed at the offer to help, but Livia could hardly be expected to repair such damage herself, and they were her nearest neighbours. The two women drifted into other, varying conversations, Morgaine taking up her distaff and spindle, Livia, enjoying the companionship of idle gossip. Medraut busied himself with his third attempt at carving a pony. Da made shaping the wood appear so simple, but the blade never seemed to obey his fingers as neatly. It was an odd-looking pony, with stumped, uneven legs and too square a head, but Medraut was pleased with his efforts. Morgaine chided him for the mess of shavings on the floor. Medraut ignored her.

Night had set, Livia was content to stay, for she had no reason to return through the dark to an empty and lonely dwelling place. She enjoyed company, and Morgaine always made her welcome, at least whenever Arthur was not around to grumble his objections. They had been talking of the latest child born in the village, a sickly girl, expected not to live long. Livia, as was her right as an elder, had attended the birth. There was not much that the old woman did not know, few things that she missed; her opinions, and more important, her blessings, were regularly sought throughout the community – aye, and beyond, for her knowledge of healing and use of potions were unrivalled. 'Business, has he?' she asked suddenly, almost in mid-conversation. 'Arthur? Over in that Christian Valley?' She spat her contempt for those Ladies who she called putrid love-lacks.

Morgaine could not hide her startled surprise, covered it as well she could with some vague, excusing answer, her mind simultaneously hurling a roar of complex questions. Why would he choose to go there? Why had he not told her? Was this connected with Arthur's silence and distracted mood of these past two days? He had been more reticent than was usual, abrupt, and even coarse when he had to speak. After that stranger had come. Arthur had said he had taken a wrong track, lost his way, but Morgaine had not believed it for one moment. No one could mistakenly follow that narrow, half-hidden path that began between two straggly bushes from the road. Ah no! The rider of that dun horse had come for a purpose. A purpose that had set Arthur into quiet brooding.

He was not content here, had no caring for her company, no need for her as a woman, save for her ability to sew and cook. He had never made attempt to share her bed, sleeping always where old Livia would sleep this night, wrapped in a fur before the hearth. He had not made this place his home, not looked upon it as his. This was Morgaine's dwelling, and though Medraut called him Da, he did not acknowledge her as a wife, or as his woman, the mother of his child. Not that Morgaine would be prepared to let him go. He did not sleep with her, on occasion did not speak to her for days on end, but he was here, he was hers. And to accept him as he was was better than not to have him at all.

'He is usually at the tavern,' Morgaine said, flippant, attempting to deflect the matter by offering her guest a second, large, helping of stew. It had been intended for Arthur, but as he was not here ... 'Arthur keeps his own mind, his own company. He will return home when hungry, I have no doubt.'

'Aye. No doubt.' Livia chewed the meat on toothless gums. Morgaine was a talented woman with a stew-pot, and Arthur kept her well supplied with good, fresh, game. Ah, if she were but a few years younger ... what she would have done with such a man! Wasted on Morgaine. Fool child. She let him have too much of his own thinking, did not use enough of her bed to keep him in the house-place. Keep a man content and occupied during the night and the days would look after themselves. 'You ought to be breeding him more children, lass, then he would have no cause to go a wanderin' after other women!'

Morgaine flushed. Livia noticed, guessed at the wrong conclusion. 'You have a seed growing?'

'No.' The accompanying sigh was revealing. 'No, there is no chance of a child.'

Livia snorted her derision. 'Babes do not get made by chance, girl! They get put there. If he will not willingly come to your bed, ought you not make your way into his?'

Morgaine pressed her lips together. She had tried that once, some while after Arthur was healed of his wounds, was well enough to begin work around the shabby place that was her home, mending fences, building a byre for the goats, a pen for the geese. She had held him, touched him, made it known that she was his, if he wanted her. Never would she repeat the shame of that night! The shame, and the hurt as he had turned his back, told her to go whoring with someone else.

She would not tell Livia of that; would not admit, even to herself, that the jealousy had started to seep its insidious roots into her from that night. He went somewhere else for his needs, probably to that little slut who served at the tavern . . .

'Why didn't Da take that big sword with him?' Medraut's question broke her thoughts. He had only partially listened to the conversation, most of it women's stuff, falling meaningless on his ears. Morgaine attempted to make light of the boy's words, although her heart started lurching like a wild, Beltaine drumbeat. 'What sword? Your Da does not have a sword.' Sword? Why would he need a sword? From where would he obtain a sword?

'Yes he does. He has it hidden in the woodpile. That man gave it to him. I saw him, when you sent me back to fetch your cloak. I saw them talking, saw him give it to Da.' With self-pride, the boy added, 'They did not see me, of course!'

Livia busied herself scooping the last of the stew from the cooking pot, but she had noticed Morgaine's sun-darkened skin turn almost white. 'A man came here, did he?' The old woman asked. 'Would that be one of the men keeping watch on the riders staying at the Place of the Lady?' she said, sucking gravy from a hunk of bread. 'Or one of the riders themselves? The British woman's escort?'

§ LVI

Through the night, Morgaine worked up her own storm, until, by morning, her anger was as furious as any wild wind. Anger fuelled by fear, stirred by jealousy. By asking subtle, seemingly innocuous questions, she had gleaned valuable information, for Livia was readily eager to pass on her accumulated gossip and speculation – information that fermented during those quiet, dark hours into a potent, black brew.

That Arthur had gone to see this British woman, she had no doubt. Who she was, why she was here, she could only speculate. And guessing could so easily make for wrong answers. Come dawn, she had narrowed her mind to two choices. Follow him to the Place of the Lady, see for herself who this woman was and make an end of her, or seek out the two Saxons camped, as they appeared to believe, secretly in the woods. There were no secrets in the Avallon Valley! Too many knew too much of another's business. As Arthur ought to well know.

How dare he assume to steal away without consultation, without informing her! That he might not be coming back never occurred to Morgaine, perhaps because she did not want to consider such a thought. Admitted, Arthur had been with her, living with her as nothing more than a kinsman, but rarely had he talked or shown a longing of going back to Britain, of picking up the dropped and shredded threads of his old life. Those days, she was sure, had gone for him, were as dead and left for the crows to pick over as the men he had left to rot on that battlefield.

But as, by noon of that day, she made her way up through the steep hang of dark woodland, she began to question her own assurance. Was the past dead? Arthur did not talk beyond a basic necessity of conversation. He never talked of himself, his hopes his fears, his plans, his daughter. He shared some of himself with the boy, encouraging and teaching him, but was that from mere duty? Was there any love for the lad, his own son? Certainly there was no love for the mother. Polite courtesy, obligation, nothing more than that.

And from where had this sword come? From this British woman – why was she here? Why now, after all this time had passed? 'She could be his wife.' Livia had been convinced of her opinion. 'He had a wife, did he not? Two, I believe.' There was no deliberate intention to be malicious, but Livia had an unequivocal habit of hitting where it hurt. 'Or a mistress. He had several of those.'

Morgaine was not listening to the ramblings of the old woman. No, it would not be Gwenhwyfar, she was dead. Morgaine stumbled over a gnarled root, tumbled to her knees, scraping the skin. She knelt there, among the dead leaves and new grass, watching the blood ooze without seeing or feeling its sting. But was she? There had been something said, months past, something she had heard muttered on a wind from Britain, something about Lady Gwenhwyfar's grief? She licked her finger, brushed the spittle against the grazed skin, walked on, ducking beneath the sweep of branches, more watchful of where she put her feet. Britain thought Arthur to be dead. But someone must have heard that he was not, someone had come all this journey to make sure. What had Livia been saying about these men in the woods, the Saxons? Why were they here? Who had sent them?

She found the two men easily, guided by the lazy smoke of their fire. A slovenly pair, taking few precautions, for they thought themselves safe up here in these uninhabited woods. Concealing herself, she watched them a while, bickering and snapping at each other like two spoilt children. One lost the argument, hauled himself, grumbling and complaining to his feet, lifted up his hunting spear and disappeared into the trees in search of evening supper. The other man lolled, bored, half-dozing in the shade, supposedly keeping eye on the road that snaked downward below their hidden vantage point. He did not hear or sense Morgaine approach, felt only the cold death-touch of her dagger against his throat. She smelt the trickle of his urine, the dark stain on his bracae spreading, obvious. A coward as well as a fool.

'Why are you here?' she hissed, her voice an insistant snarl in his ear.

'We watch the travellers.'

She knew that. 'Why?'

'Because the one who hired us believes they will lead us to a man who ought be dead.' He answered open enough. But then, the blade was biting harder, a trickle of blood meandering down his throat.

Morgaine thrust more questions, her knee digging hard, uncomfortable, into the small of his back. 'What man might this be?'

'The Pendragon.'

So it was the lure of Arthur that had brought them here. She narrowed her eyes, pushed her dagger deeper, determined, her disgust erupting against this puke-smelling worm. 'And the name of the one who hired you?'

The man hesitated, fearing future consequences more than the immediate threat. Morgaine persuaded him to think otherwise.

'Winifred!' he blurted, as the dagger prodded in a more intimate area. 'Lady Winifred paid us!'

Winifred! Not a mistress then. Morgaine knew of Winifred, knew the open hatred she had for Arthur. Once – aye, and not so long past – had never understood it. How could a woman love and yet hate with such equal ferocity? Now she knew. The hate came with the threat of loss. While it – he – was yours, you could love, but that hatred came in so easily, stepping hand in hand with jealousy.

'And is it Lady Winifred who rests at the Place of the Lady?' Doubtful, but she asked anyway. The name that came brought a cold, heavy dread to her stomach.

'No, not Lady Winifred. Gwenhwyfar, it is Gwenhwyfar.'

Almost, she was tempted to kill him. Tempted to slide her blade in between his ribs and end his miserable excuse for an existence. Almost. Something held her hand. Something sinister worming its blackened way into her red-enraged thoughts. She let the dagger dangle loose in her hand, sat hunkered to her heels, thinking, planning, barely noticing that he scuttled a few yards away, putting safe distance between them. He could have bolted, but he saw her now as a slip of a woman, was ashamed of his fear, sensed that perhaps his life was not in any danger from her.

She sat quiet a long while, sliding the blade through her fingers, through and through again. 'And what if Gwenhwyfar finds him, the Pendragon, who ought be dead?' Morgaine knew that answer also, knew enough of Lady Winifred.

The Saxon shrugged. 'As you say. He ought be dead.'

Morgaine rose to her feet, threaded the dagger through her waist-girdle, her smile a malicious, scheming smile, one that, had she known it, would have set as easily on the face of her mother, Morgause, the woman Arthur had called witch, the woman who had brought fear and hatred to him as boy and king.

'Are you two alone to murder one such as the Pendragon?' she scoffed. She could not see this pair of fools mastering the ability to butcher even a suckling pig!

At least he had the decency to flush. 'Others of us are concealed a day's ride behind. There is many an armed band roaming Gaul; beyond a cursory glance, we have passed unnoticed.' He met her cold, marble-faced stare head-on, confessed, 'If the Pendragon should be found, one of us is to fetch them forward.' The rest he left unfinished.

Morgaine unfastened a leather pouch that hung from her waist girdle, tossed it at him. He caught it neatly, one-handed. 'The woman will not leave this valley.' The Saxon had no reason to contradict her; the hair was rising on the nape of his neck. This was no threat, no boast. A statement. A curse.

That narrow-eyed, evil smile again. 'You will ensure that it is so.'

'What of the Pendragon?' the man queried as, greedily, he pulled open the leather thongs, tipped several rings into the palm of his hand. All were of good gold, one, the one shaped as a dragon, with an impressively expensive ruby for its eye.

It had been Arthur's ring, a symbol of his supremacy. Morgaine had removed it from his bloodied and broken hand when he lay mortally close to death, kept it safe, secreted, intending for him to have it one day, should he ever ask its whereabouts. But he had never asked, never questioned what had happened to his ring, or his banner, or his sword. Never had he talked of his kingdom, or of Gwenhwyfar. That he thought of her, Morgaine knew, but of the other things? Who knew of what Arthur thought?

There came no answer to the Saxon's question. When he looked up again, his eyes as wide as his gloating smile, the woman was gone. No trace of her, no sound of her going. No bush moved, no branch or leaf stirred. It was as if she had never been. He shivered. There were tales about these woods and the women who lived near here. Priestesses of the old Goddess. Witches, some called them.

He had no doubt that he had just met one.

§ LVII

When Medraut shouted, gleefully, that Da was come home, a great tide of relief surged through Morgaine, sending her stomach churning, her head spinning. He had returned! Had chosen her, Morgaine, over Gwenhwyfar! She ran from the house place, her hands flour-covered from the baking, her delight almost childish. Then she saw the horse. A war-horse and, irrationally, all the jealousies and petty imbalances welled into her. She waited, feet planted wide, arms folded, barring access onto the dusty track that led through the gateway into the open, hard-baked yard that dallied between house place, byre and a variety of outbuildings.

'Where did he come from?' she asked, pointing, with an expression of repugnance, at Onager. She had never challenged Arthur's authority before, nor queried his action, questioned his doing, always accepted that his word, his way, was law. He was here and she would do anything – anything – to keep him here, but the horse, like that sword, was a threat. A reminder of the past, too close a link with an alternative future that did not, would not, involve her.

Arthur's anger and pain was knotted so tight within him that, superficially, he failed to notice the unusual aggression. His anger was directed at himself, leaving no room for analysing the reaction and feeling of others. At the Place of the Lady he had said and done all the wrong things – acted the opposite of what he had intended. But then, what *had* been the intention behind going there? To establish whether Gweir had told him the truth? Why would the lad have lied over such a thing in the first place? Had he gone merely to have seen Gwenhwyfar, to have talked with her? Why? What would either have achieved? Gone to explain what had happened to him? Or had he intended to leave here, go back with Gwenhwyfar? As she had wanted. As he wanted – in the name of all the gods, that ever were or ever would be, as he wanted!

But he could not. He had not the courage to confront his own weakness, his fear. Both had reared up at him like some pain-angered monster. And he had turned and fled. Not even Gwenhwyfar had been able to keep that raw fear of what had been at bay.

He answered Morgaine curtly. 'He is mine.'

'We have no room for a horse.'

'I will make room.'

It was late afternoon and it had taken Arthur many hours to coax Onager slowly up that steep, winding road. Stopping often, resting, encouraging. Occasionally forcing. They were both tired, bone-weary, mind numbed, dead tired. Arthur had realized the idiocy of taking the horse fifty yards from the tavern stables. Pride, irrational anger, frustration, all those things made it too late to turn back. To admit he was wrong – huh, to admit it for one thing, meant facing again all those other things.

Morgaine persisted. She did not want Arthur to have a horse. He could so easily ride away from her on a horse. 'From where did he come? What do you want him for?'

As he pushed past, elbowing the woman out of his way, pushing her against the low, wattle-built wall of the sow's pen, Arthur regarded Morgaine with a look that could almost have been interpreted as contempt, except he barely saw her. He headed direct for the byre, settled the horse in an empty stall where in winter the one or two cattle they kept would be sheltered. He busied himself fetching bedding, water, feed. Everyday things to keep the mind occupied, thoughts shut aside.

Medraut, hovering at the doorway, was uncertain what to do. His Da was in a strange mood, and his mother was angry – why, he did not understand. He had never known her to be openly angry at his Da before. It had something, he thought, to do with that sword, or perhaps, was it the horse? His mother disliked horses, he knew that, for she had told him so. He could not see why, for although it was obviously ill, this horse was a beautiful one. He stepped a pace into the byre, stood sucking the tip of his thumb. 'Have you brought him here for Mam to heal?'

Arthur, scattering bedding, regarded the boy. He was small, Medraut, thin, with mouse-brown hair and wide, dark eyes that always, for some unexplained reason, held a little more than their fare share of fear in them. Had he been born a pig or a sheep he would have been despatched as a worthless runt. Six years old, painfully shy, with seemingly no confidence or courage. Arthur tried to remember what it had been like to be six years of age. All he could recall of his childhood was the stench of fear and the presence of evil. And the unbearable longing to have known his father.

'No,' he said. 'I have brought him here for us to heal, you and I, lad.'

The boy's face lit with a sunburst of pride and pleasure. Arthur would never have had such an expression at that age. His early life had been one of constant blows and taunts. There was no obvious cruelty in Morgaine, he had never seen her strike or rebuke the lad with unnecessary harshness, and yet she was not close to him, not as Gwenhwyfar had been to her sons. He had never seen Morgaine fuss the boy, be it at bedtime or when he had fallen, hurt himself. That occasion when he was so ill? Morgaine tended him, administering potions, draughts and cordials, but it had been Arthur who had held the boy close, who had stroked the wet hair from his forehead. Given him the comforting reassurance of love and protection.

Gwenhwyfar had always shown love. In contrast, Morgaine was remote, kept her feelings close guarded. She never questioned, never queried. Some days, Arthur forgot she was there.

'*From where did he come? What do you want him for?*' Arthur shook the last armful of bedding, frowned. Morgaine, questioning? He shrugged the thought aside, beckoned the boy forward.

He ran, delighted, but Arthur clasped at his shoulder, stopped him short. 'Never run up to a horse, lad, they startle easily – especially this one. When he is well he'll use his teeth and feet and not need an excuse for it. I have fought battles on this horse.'

Medraut's jaw dropped as wide as his eyes, his esteem for this splendid creature doubling. Onager stood almost six and ten hands measured at the withers, bigger than the few scruffy, ill-bred ponies from the valley. A rich, dark chestnut horse, with a short back, deep chest and fine head. His eyes were bold, set to either side of a wide forehead that sat above a dished, slender face. This was a horse that would surely gallop for hours and never tire, a horse that could race the very wind! Medraut loved him, he was superb!

Gathering the boy into his arms, Arthur took him closer, let him reach out to touch that high, proud crest, stroke down the neck, pat the shoulder. Patient, Arthur explained what was wrong, what need be done to make him well. Emphasized that Medraut was not to go near him unless he, Arthur, was here also. Solemnly, the thumb going back into his mouth, Medraut promised.

The door creaking open attracted their attention, Arthur swung around, the boy in his arms. Morgaine stood, silhouetted against the low, late afternoon sun. They could not see her face for it was in deep shadow, only her voice told that she was displeased.

'I do not want the boy near the horse.' Arthur made no answer. 'Horses are not to be trusted.'

Setting the boy to his feet, Arthur nudged him in the direction of his mother, and the outside. 'Run along lad – do you not have chores to attend?' The boy gone, he said, 'What I do, where I go, is of my business, not yours. You are not my keeper, Morgaine.'

Tartly, her fists on her hips, head upright, she responded with the only weapon she had. 'Mayhap not, but I am the mother of your son.'

Arthur returned to tending the horse. Taking up a handful of straw, he twisted it into a plait, began grooming Onager's dulled, poor coat. When the light brightened, he assumed Morgaine to be gone, leaving the door wide. He guided the plait of straw across the horse's shoulders, using firm, even strokes along his back and rump, down his quarters. Aye, Morgaine was that, the mother of his son.

She was also his sister. Uthr, the first Pendragon, had the siring of them both.

Arthur had not known it, then, when he had lain with her at a time when a great fear had clouded all sense, all reason. He had gone to the Lady by the Lake for her healing, his eldest son was ill and it was all he could think of to save him, to go to the pagan woman who lived, then, at Yns Witrin. Would he have lain with her if she had not asked? If she had not given the impression that it was a thing demanded by the Mother, the Goddess of all life? If he had not thought that the union might bring some benefit of healing to his most precious boy? Possibly. Probably – but alternatively, he might have discovered her siring first. And then, Morgaine would not have held this weight of shame and guilt over him. Not that she knew. No one else knew, only he realized the father of Morgause's daughter.

Arthur dropped the straw wisp, laced his fingers into Onager's long mane, leant his cheek against the warmth of the animal's coat.

It was growing dark outside. Night. Morgaine would be putting the boy to bed, preparing supper.

He ought tell her the reason why he stayed here. Tell her that he stayed because there was nowhere else to go. That here there was no one to sneer that he was a failure, a lost man with not the guts to pick up his sword again. No one to lay blame for the massacre of his men.

Morgaine settled Medraut into his bed, an arrangement of furs and blankets set on a wooden platform above one end of the dwelling. Medraut liked his 'room', this private, upstairs place. When he was older, he intended to ask if the wooden ladder could be hoisted up at night. That would make it even more secretive.

Eagerly enthusiastic about the horse in the byre, Medraut had been chattering happily about the animal, unaware of his mother's tight-lipped silence. Tucking a blanket around him, her patience finally snapped.

'No more of this! You are to stay away from that creature,' she commanded.

Wildly alarmed, the boy protested. 'But I am to help Da make him better! I promised I would!'

Morgaine snatched hold of the boy's shoulder, her fingernails pinching cruelly into the delicate skin. 'If I catch you near that beast, I will whip you!' And added, her face pressing vindictively close to the boy's, 'And I shall whip the horse too!'

Medraut dug his teeth into his lip, held his tears until she had gone with the lamp, leaving him alone up here, under the roof beams in the darkness. He could hear her moving about down below, preparing supper for herself and his Da. One solitary tear trickled from beneath his lashes, then another.

He turned his face into the bracken-filled pallet so that not even the night spirits would see him weep.

§ LVIII

Arthur was disappointed that the boy did not come to help with Onager. He had seemed so eager at the outset, but that was children for you. Full of boundless enthusiasm the one moment, off with their friends, fishing or swimming, the next. He supposed he had been inclined the same as a boy, except, as a bastard child he had had few friends, and always, had chosen the company of the Pendragon above other things. Although he had not known Uthr to be his father then.

Medraut was down by the lake, over to where a large cluster of dwellings huddled beneath the shaded slope of trees. The morning had been overcast and the wind chill, but by early afternoon the temperature was picking up. Naturally the pack of boys had headed for the lure of the water. Arthur could hear their shouted, excited voices floating on the wind, could imagine them romping and splashing at the lake edge. He might walk Onager down there later, lead him along the shore, let him graze the succulent grass that abounded there. He forked a pile of dung from the horse's bed, rested his shoulders and back against the partition wall. Closed his eyes. He was so tired. Had no energy, no enthusiasm for anything.

Morgaine had nursed a temper that first day, although not one that could ever have matched her mother's. Morgaine was not as clever as her, nor as subtle or vindictive. Why she should be so upset about the horse, Arthur could not imagine, nor did he care enough to enquire.

Yesterday, she had changed tactics, had brought him a breakfast out to the byre where he was sleeping, fresh-baked wheat bread smeared liberally with honey, a tankard of barley ale. Had she guessed to where he had gone? On several occasions yesterday he had almost told her. *'I went to see my wife and she was more beautiful than ever I remembered.'*

She would have gone now, Gwenhwyfar, saddled the horses and be heading home. Disappointed, angry? He had no way of knowing.

Arthur wiped his hand over his face. The palm was sweaty, the fingers shaking, blurring before his vision. He sighed. So tired.

The goats would need milking again soon, and the sow's pen cleaning. He placed an affectionate smack on Onager's rump, the horse's ears flicking backwards with the sound. At least the animal was improving, he had eaten a feed mixed with a generous handful of healing, dried nettles, was chewing at hay stacked in the manger. The pus had stopped oozing. Onager had been lucky, a mild dose of the illness it seemed. A few good feeds, a few days of grazing in the summer sun and he would soon recover. What in all the gods' names was Arthur going to do with a war-horse? Onager would never pull a plough or wagon, Mithras's love, what had made Arthur bring him here?

He could hear Morgaine singing as she worked at her loom, some song that he did not recognize. He put the wooden fork with the stable tools that leant against the stack of the woodpile, cursed as it fell, his fingers fumbling to stand it upright. Why were his hands so clumsy? Damn it, why was Morgaine so happy? He could feel this black mood of despair engulfing him, cramping its tentacles around him, feel the darkness oozing deeper and thicker. A great pit opening before him, going down and down into the darkness. All he had to do was look up, reach out for the light, summon the courage, go after Gwenhwyfar, say he was sorry, beg her forgiveness, but he was too tired. So much easier to step into that hole and drift downwards. He wanted to sleep, fought against it, for the darkness would surely come, swallow him for ever if he drowsed into sleep.

He had dreamt last night. Dreamt of home, of Caer Cadan and, strangely, of Yns Witrin, the Tor that rose proud above the flat levels of the Summer Land. His Summer Land, the land of the seven rivers, summer-sluggish, that swelled and flooded in spring from the run-off from the surrounding rounded hills. Flat pasture, willow-bordered, spongy beneath your feet even in the hottest, driest summer. In winter, a constant movement of birds, for the levels swarmed with lapwings, golden plover, redwing, snipe, rook and gull. Hawk and kestrel.

In his dream, a light, golden evening was settling after what must have been a brilliant day. Late summer, for the grass was sun-browned, the lake not as high as it would be in the dazzling green of early spring. A boat, coming across the lake from the Tor, one person paddling, a woman, brown-cloaked, hood pulled forward. Two other women waited on the shore, both with their backs to him, waiting for the boat. He knew who they were, the one dressed as a Christian woman, with her dark gown and white veil, her gold crucifix glinting in the evening sunlight, and the other woman, with her plaid, a rich red cloak. Her tumble of copper hair.

He had tried to call, attract their attention, but they were intent on watching the boat. And then Gwenhwyfar had turned, but she had not seen him, was unaware that he was there. His sword was in her hand – and then she and Winifred and the boat that carried Morgaine were gone. Only the sword remained, the blade quivering in the grass as the wind, that danced down from the height of the Tor, whispered past.

Arthur gasped, found he was on his knees, his head bent forward, his vision reeling and spinning, an ache hammering against the side of his skull. Sweat slithered down his spine, from beneath his armpits. He saw the shadow move at the doorway, heard the rush of movement, the dagger scything downward, and he rolled, head ducked, back curved, rolled over and up onto his feet, crouching low, hands spread, his movements slow, clumsy.

There were two of them, two men, Saxons, blonde-haired, drooping moustaches, blue, cold eyes. One man with blurred senses against two intent killers.

Arthur's fingers fumbled at his waist for his dagger, dropped it. He leapt backward as one man came again with his short sword, the Saex, the blade whistling as it sliced the air, missing Arthur's midriff by the width of a hair. Arthur stumbled, sending the stable tools, a bucket and several other items tumbling and rolling, part of the woodpile crashing as his hand grappled for a hold to steady himself.

He needed a weapon! His hand closed around the stable fork, he jabbed the prongs at the nearest man, swung forward to drive the second backward, but that first man's sword had an edge like a midwinter's night. The blade sliced through the wooden shaft, leaving Arthur holding a next to useless stump of stick. He used it haphazardly, as a defence, waving it before him to keep the attackers away while he manoeuvred around, closer to the woodpile. He slid the stick into his left hand, felt frantically with his right among the stacked logs. The two men stood, side by side, their grins widening, one shifting his blade, menacing, from hand to hand as they closed in, their breaths strong and foul from an excess of stale wine and strong cheese. Desperate, Arthur side-stepped a pace, his fingers still scrabbling between the crevices of the stacked logs – blood of Mithras, where in all hell was it? Where was his sword?

He heard a woman screaming, a man laughing, ducked and twisted as both men lunged forward, head-butting one, his fist pounding into the chin of the other. The first doubled over, winded, his arms going around his stomach, sword falling to the earthen floor. The second reeled, but lurched forward, mouth drawn into a snarl that showed a row of blackened, decayed teeth. Arthur again rolled, coming up with the dropped short sword in his hand, driving it upward within the same moment as the man raised his own weapon, and drove it in, through the abdomen.

No time to take breath, to gloat at the one's death, for the first man was again on his feet, a log of wood firm in his hand, coming hard at Arthur, enraged at the death of his companion. Arthur had his back to Onager, the horse shifting nervously in his stall, ears back, eyes rolling. Simple to manoeuvre around, reverse the positions. As easy to lunge forward, drive the Saxon back a step. Onager's hind foot lashed out, crumping against the Saxon's thigh. The sound of the bone shattering, and the scream, ricocheted around the byre.

Shaking his head to clear the muzziness and blurred vision, Arthur ran outside. Three men were coming through the gateway, swords drawn. Another had been searching inside the grain-barn. Saxons, everywhere. Why? What were Saex doing this far into Gaul? No time to think, to reason, the man from the granary was entering the house place, the eyes of the others swivelling in that direction also, as Morgaine's screams were rising against the excited roar of male laughter. Saex-sword raised, Arthur hurtled across the small, square yard. He would rather have had the secure feel of his own cavalry sword in his grasp, with its greater length and stronger bite, but all Arthur had was this bloodied one. He ran, foot-kicked the door wide, sending one man sprawling face forward as it back-slammed, killing another almost within the same instant with a side-thrust of the blade, ripping it, double-handed, through his ribs and lungs.

Morgaine was on the floor, her skirt pushed up over her head, a heavy-built Saxon grunting on top of her, another hauling at his shoulder, urging him to hurry, make way. Arthur's sword slammed between the waiting man's shoulders, driving in to the hilt. Blood spewed from the dying man's mouth, choking off the startled death-cry. Two-handed, Arthur attempted to pull the short-bladed sword out, had to leave it, turn, bending low, as a man flew at him from behind. Arms grabbed him, a fist thudded into his abdomen, under his jaw.

Morgaine was still screaming. He toppled forward, dizzying into semi-consciousness.

§ LIX

Gwenhwyfar did not look back, not once, not even when they passed by the track that trailed southward, following down into the Avallon valley and to the lake where the community of pagan women squatted between the shoulder of the hills and the shore. There was a dwelling-place there which housed a woman and her son, and a man who had once been so splendid a King. She shut them from her mind. Angry, so disappointed.

She rode ahead, her horse picking its way, sure-footed, across roots and tangled overgrowth. They would meet the main Via Agrippa some time soon, ride onward through the night, for a full moon and clear skies were expected to light the way.

They ought to have left that same day as he had . . . No, she refused to think of that, think of him. They ought to have left, but had not, the excuse being that Gweir had not yet returned, but by this mid-morning she had decided not to wait longer, ordered the men to saddle the horses. They rode slowly, in no great hurry, following the valley up that steep winding track that Gweir had ridden to find . . .

Gwenhwyfar closed her eyes, let the horse pick his own way along this narrow, faint-marked trail.

'The two Saxons have moved,' Gweir reported, that afternoon after Arthur had come, and gone. 'They have split, one waits among the lower trees, the other has ridden hard in the direction of Antessiodurum. There is mischief in mind, I am sure.'

Mischief indeed if Gweir were not to return! He would catch up, knew the direction they headed, the quicker way home, straight up the Roman Road to the coast and a ship that would take them back to . . . to what? She had promised herself that she would not cry. No more weeping, no more tears.

Gwenhwyfar rode ahead of her men so that they would not witness that broken promise.

§ LX

The wind had eased a little to the east, was becoming chill again, as it had in the morning. Medraut shivered, decided it was time to return home. He called farewell to the other boys and, scrabbling into his clothes, trotted along the upward-winding track.

He thought it was his friends that he could still hear, playing down by the lake, but when he looked back, they too had gone. Then he heard the screaming clearer, and ran, head down, arms pumping, the voice unmistakably his mother's.

Slowing, out of breath, legs aching, he rested a hand on the rear wall of the small granary. The screaming had stopped but he could hear laughter and unfamiliar, guttural voices, men. And another sound. He dropped to his belly and squirmed beneath the raised building, wriggling between the stone pillars that supported the wooden floor, an effective means of keeping vermin from the grain. His eyes saw another form of vermin, more vicious than the rats that came creeping stealthily by night, more frightening than the great eagles that he occasionally saw sailing on the winds high above the hills. Five men in the yard, big men, loud and brash. One was holding his Da, the others, one with a bloodied nose, were hitting him, beating him. Medraut could see his Da's blood spattering from above his eye, could hear him gasping as fists and feet thudded into his body. What could a boy do? A boy of six years against five grown men? He could run for help, but they lived apart, their dwelling well to the outside of the lake community. And beside, it was mostly women down there. A few had husbands, but they were old men, farmers, and they all lived too far away.

If he had a sword he could . . . a sword! His Da's sword! He knew where his mother had hidden it, for he had peeped over the edge of his sleeping platform, watched as she had put it there, beneath the mattress of her own bed. He knew how to get inside the house-place too, without being seen. The gnarled old walnut tree behind reached past the window opening that gave more ventilation than light. It was small, but then, so was he. It was a route he used often if he needed to sneak out something without his mother knowing; food usually, a chunk of bread or wedge of cheese.

It was dark inside, with the door partially shut and no lamps lit, but

Medraut knew his way around, and his eyes became quickly adjusted to the dim light.

Morgaine lay huddled, curled, on the floor, arms wrapped around herself, sobbing.

'Get up, Mam, Da needs help!' Medraut shook her, pulling frantically at her arm, her shoulder, but she shook him off, curling deeper into herself, her sobs jerking louder. 'Mam! Please!'

Desperate, Medraut ran to her bed, tugged aside the mattress and dragged out the scabbard. It was heavier than he had anticipated, he needed both hands to pull the blade from its sheath, both hands to carry it back to the window and irreverently shove it through.

They were still hitting his father, those horrid men. What could he do? He could barely lift the weapon, could never use it – and then he thought of Onager.

The boy had ridden occasionally on the backs of ponies, once on a bigger horse that was used occasionally to pull a wagon into Avallon. It was not the same as riding a war-horse – but how different could it be? He managed to get the horse's bridle on, by balancing on a stool and coaxing the animal's head down. The saddle he abandoned, for he was unsure how all the straps went; it would take too much time to think it all out. He found some rope, wound it around the hilt of the sword and looped it around his shoulder, climbed atop a barrel and with held breath, clambered onto Onager's back. He had done well, the horse had only nipped him twice!

The byre doors stood open, beyond, he could hear the men jeering, hear their shouted words, though they spoke in a language he did not understand. He knew how to make horses move. He took up the reins in one hand, steadied the dangling sword with the other and brought both his heels back in a mighty kick.

Onager plunged, head down, back arched, squealing. Medraut let go both reins and sword, clutched frantically at the horses's mane, managed to stay aboard through several of those enormous bucks. Onager careered forward, they were well beyond the door now, near the pile of muck and dung that was rotting for use on the fields, another buck and . . . but at least it was soft. The Saxons had scattered, convinced this was some fire-breathing creature of the gods. Dizzy, Arthur managed to dodge the animal's crazed path, ran, breath gasping in his throat for Medraut who sat in the muck, holding the naked sword as high as he could manage. Arthur took it, swung around as, gathering their senses, two of the men came at him.

It had been a long time since he had held this sword in the grip of his hand. A long time since he had swung it, used its strength and beauty to destroy and maim, but the time fell away as simply as dew beneath the scorching sun, it was as if it had never been from his grasp, never been from his side.

And there was another man, with another sword, coming from the gateway, yelling and hacking at the Saxons. A few moments only, and the five men lay dead, and Gweir stood leaning upon his sword, grinning at Arthur.

'It is good,' he said, 'to fight again with my Lord Pendragon.'

§ LXI

The man in the byre talked easily, helped along by subtle persuasion of Gweir's boot coming into contact, none too gently, with his shattered thigh. He was, he then willingly told them, one of a group of men who had followed the Lady Gwenhwyfar across Gaul, men who had been paid to ensure that the Pendragon was undeniably dead, paid to retrieve his head.

'Do we finish him?' Gweir asked, when nothing more of interest was forthcoming.

Arthur was seated on a pile of old mildewing sacking and straw. His brain reeled and his vision seemed as if he were walking through a heavy, moorland mist. What in ever the gods' names was wrong with him? It was not the beating, for this dizziness and disorientation had been bothering him before then, since yesterday. Two vivid bruises were welling on his cheek and beneath his eye, more would be on his body. He would tend them later, no hurry now. He stood, feeling the room sway, held his hand out to the boy who stood wide-eyed, open-mouthed, inside the doorway. Growled at Gweir, 'Aye, do it.' To the boy, in a kinder tone he teased. 'Come with me, lad. Since you let him loose, you can help me catch Onager. Unless he's found a patch of sweet grass, he's likely to be half-way to Rome by now.'

The boy's face dropped, and the thumb went back to his mouth. Arthur ruffled his hair, swung him up into his arms. 'You did well, lad, I'm proud of you.' Amazing, the sudden difference of expression, from dismay of doing wrong, to elation.

A brief, high-pitched gurgle came within the byre. Medraut attempted to turn his head to look, but Arthur distracted him, carried him away with long strides. Gweir emerged, bent to wipe the blade of his dagger on grass tufting beside the sow's pen.

Morgaine was standing in the yard, her face blotched and puffed by tears, the skin beneath ash-white. She had one hand stuffed into her mouth, fear raged in her eyes, hair straggled across her face. It needed redying, for the brilliant red that it had been these past weeks was fading, the paleness of her own natural colour streaking through the artificial pretence. How many colours had Morgaine used? Red, black. A rich, dark brown? Never fair, as she had been as a child, never spun gold like her mother. The thick, black kohl that she used to line and darken her eyes had run in streaks down her cheeks making her appear haggard, and twice her two and twenty years. As Arthur and the boy emerged into the evening light, she pointed, with trembling fingers, at the men sprawled in various postures of death. 'He is not here,' she quavered. 'The one I spoke with, he, is not here.'

Arthur dipped his head over his shoulder. 'There is another, in there.' He did not understand, but did not question. Added, not without a tint of cruelty, 'His throat is cut.'

Onager had not moved from beside the muck heap, as Arthur had known. He would not move without a rider while the reins hung loose, every war-horse of the Artoriani was trained so, such entrenched discipline could save an unhorsed rider's life in battle. Arthur tossed the boy onto the horse's back, picked up the reins. 'Hold his mane – and keep your heels still!' Smiling at the boy's delight, Arthur returned the animal to the safe confine of his stall.

Inside, he said dispassionately, addressing Morgaine, 'That your man?' She stood beside the bloodied, twisted body, chewing her thumb-nail as her son would have done, too numbed to answer.

Slipping the bridle from Onager's head, and lifting the boy down, Arthur glanced at her, caught from the corner of his eye a spark of red on the dead man's left hand. A ring. Curious, he handed the bridle to the boy, walked forward, hunkered beside the body, his narrowing eyes never leaving that ring. Gweir had come up behind Arthur as he lifted his head to ask of Morgaine, in a quiet, dark voice, 'How did this Saex bastard come by my ring?'

Morgaine was too dull-writted not to answer. Nothing like her mother! Morgause would have been laughing, or sneering at the incompetent failure of the dead. Rape would be a meaningless thing for the woman who had entertained more men in her bed, for her own gain, than any tavern whore. Morgause would have held her tongue. Even through the pain of torture would not have answered Arthur – answered any man. Morgaine though, had fear on her face, and guilt. Emotions unknown to her mother. 'He was not supposed to kill you, only her. I thought he understood that.'

Arthur squatted, very still, very quiet. His eyes had dropped again to that ring, his ring, his dragon ring. The last time he had worn it was on the morning of that last battle. And again, in his tortured mind, he saw that day. Saw his men, his brothers, his friends, hacked down and dying. Saw and felt the deep, raw, pain of his failure.

Gweir stepped across the body, removed the ring, held it on the open palm of his hand. The Pendragon's ring. Reverently, he handed it to Arthur, who took it, slid it onto his left hand, where it nestled comfortable, familiar, as if it had never been removed.

'Ambrosius,' Gweir began in desperation. He faltered. Would the Pendragon heed him? He had turned away from his lady wife, why would a King listen to a man who was once a slave boy? In a rush of speech, he ploughed on. 'Ambrosius is making the biggest balls-up that Britain has been saddled with in many a year. War's brewing – if it hasn't already boiled over.' He bit his lip, swallowed, lifted his eyes to Arthur and pleaded, 'We need you, my lord. Britain needs you.'

The Pendragon was staring at Morgaine, his expression hard, jaw clamped, eyes narrowed. If he heard, or listened to Gweir, he made no sign, save that he irritably gestured for him to leave the byre. 'Take the boy with you,' he snapped.

Head bowed, disappointed, Gweir obeyed.

'You gave my ring to this Saxon?' His gaze had not left Morgaine. His brain was sluggish, reluctant to function, comprehend, but a few things were beginning to make sense. At the beginning how many times had he almost gone from here? Two or Three? And on how many occasions had something happened to stop him? The sow farrowed over-early and that house-place fire, both during those months when he was first recovered, when he had talked of going home. Coincidence? And those stomach cramps and the dysentery that had seized him . . . His head was muzzy. It all meant something. He was trying to think. He shook his head, it was as if he had drunk too much barley-brewed wine and was drugged from its numbing effect . . . and he saw it all.

'You bitch!' The dark hatred that came into the shadow of his eyes was intense. Not like her mother? What a simple fool he had been! Na, she was not as confident or competent as Morgause, but Morgaine had her own talent, her own art. Was she not a healer? Did she not know the properties of herbs and roots and plants? Aye, she knew them well enough to be able to cure a sickness as well as plan an illness. The bread, so thickly smeared with sweet honey. The stew, so strong with flavourings? Drugged!

'God's breath!' Arthur snarled, his disgust reeling. 'Even your own son? He was ill, so very ill. You poisoned your own son, so that I might stay?'

His hand came over his mouth, fingers pinching the nostrils to stem the rise of repugnance and nausea. Stunned, he repeated, 'You bitch.'

Morgaine flinched at that stark loathing, but held her head high, defiant. 'I wanted to keep you here. I knew of no other way.' She clasped her hands, twisting the fingers through and through each other. 'You do not love me enough to stay for me alone.'

Abruptly, Arthur was on his feet. 'Love you?' he bellowed. 'How could I love you? You are as corrupt and tainted as ever your witch mother was. You disgust me!' The outrage was swelling with the full force of realizing who she was and what she had done. 'Was it her idea,' he sneered, 'for you to get with child by me? Was that her way of destroying the memory of our father?'

Morgaine had stuffed her fingers in her mouth, her eyes stared wide in horror. Her breath was quickening, sickness rising to her throat. 'I do not know my father!'

With loathing thick on his voice, Arthur answered, 'You are Uthr's daughter, as I am his son. Did she not tell you that?' He took the bridle down from its peg, buckled it again onto the horse, fetched the saddle, led Onager from the byre.

Gweir was dragging one of the bodies by the legs, taking it to the fields for burial, Medraut sat hunkered before the house-place door, alarm and confusion plain on his young, anxious face. 'Bring my cloak from the house, boy, and your own,' Arthur commanded him. Obedient, Medraut scrabbled to his feet, ducked inside the dwelling.

Morgaine had followed Arthur outside, weeping silent tears.

'The boy comes with me.' Arthur said. 'I will not leave him to the mercy of your evil. Gweir, leave that scum for the ravens to clear.' The young man nodded, dropped the dead man's legs.

Morgaine did not know what to do, what to say. All she had wanted was to keep Arthur with her. She was not like her mother, oh she was not! She had not understood everything that had happened, for it was all tumbling too quickly, too much, too fast. The Saxons, this British man – who was he? – Arthur . . . Uthr. *Uthr was my father?* Arthur was going out the gate, leading Onager. Was leaving . . .

She grasped the one thing that made sense to her, shoved all else aside, to the back of her mind where she need not, yet, think upon them, those cruel things that Arthur had said. Thought only of the thing she had planned. 'It is pointless going after her. She will be dead,' Morgaine announced boldly. 'These Saxons would have attacked her first, realized you were not with her and come to find you. Finish you.' She tipped her head, daring Arthur to contradict her.

Arthur glanced at Gweir, who was shaking his head, spreading his hands. 'I followed the dead one in the byre from the woods, stayed with him as he met with his companions, then trailed them here.' He caught his breath, gasped fearfully. 'Jesu!' he yelped. 'They split into two groups – I naturally followed those coming here . . . Jesu!' he repeated, 'My Lady Gwenhwyfar!'

But Arthur was already a step before him, he dropped Onager's reins, was running from the yard, through the open gateway, yelling, 'Where is your horse, Gweir?'

'Just around the bend of the track . . .'

'What road was my wife to follow?'

Gweir answered as they ran, explained the trail Ider had expected to take. The horse was as Gweir had left him, the dun, a native pony of Britain crossed with the blood of the desert breed. Not as tall as Onager but as brave-hearted, almost as fast.

'Bring Onager and the boy,' Arthur ordered. 'Follow as fast as the horse can manage!' He was in the saddle, heeling into a gallop.

Morgaine was left alone with the pain riding high, billowing outward, engulfing her. He was gone. Arthur was gone! How was she to bear it? And Uthr was her father. Her mother had demanded that she lay with her own brother?

Gweir too had gone, he had put the boy up into Onager's saddle and, leading the horse, set out to walk where Arthur was going. Morgaine was alone, with only the dead for company. The dead, those who had come to murder Arthur. And she had brought them here. A Saex sword, short-bladed, stained with blood, lay on the mud of the small, rutted yard, its blade glinting in the late afternoon sunlight. She went to it, picked it up.

Old Livia, coming up to discover the cause of the noise that had drifted down the quiet valley, found her, new blood draining from her open wrists. As well that Livia was also a healer, and one with more skill than Morgaine.

§ LXII

The going along the first, upward-winding, rutted track was slow, Arthur having to keep the dun to a frustrating trot in many places. At the road he could push faster. Already Arthur's back was aching, his thighs sore. It had been a long while since he had ridden such a horse!

There were few travelling the road, especially at this late part of the day. With the overrule of Rome gone and the ever-present threat of thieves and barbarian raiders, traffic had dwindled. Once, the Legions would have marched up this road, led by the Caesars themselves. Couriers, with their urgent-carried messages; trundling ox-drawn wagons laden with army supplies or weighted with goods of trade, cloth, wine, pottery. Civilian carriages, the lighter, two-wheeled type and the heavy, family four-wheelers. The fast, extravagant chariots. Arthur put the dun into a canter, knowing he was corn-fed and fit, capable of keeping the pace for several miles.

Evening was approaching, enveloping dark spreading rapidly from the east, eating the last of daylight. They, she, could be anywhere! Had she joined this road yet. Could some delay have kept her behind? Would she still be in those woods? Would the Saxons, following, be hurrying or dallying somewhere, waiting for their companions? All these thoughts, fears and worries bursting through Arthur's mind as he rode. Gweir was certain they would not have delayed longer than this morning. Even riding at a sedate pace, she would have come up, out of the woodland, have reached this road . . .

More dark than light. Ahead, a glimmer of yellow, voices, laughter. A tavern, a stopping place! Arthur slowed, the dun was dripping sweat, breathing hard, but keen to go on, loath to walk when a more exciting pace was offered. He danced through the gateway, head snaking, nostrils blowing. Several men were about, tending horses, unloading a heavy ox-wagon. Their heads came up together at the clatter of Arthur's sudden, wild appearance, the innkeeper himself coming down the steps, wiping his hands on his apron.

'Hail friend! You travel with some urgency!'

The dun was fidgeting, refusing to stand still, pawing the cobbles, swinging round.

'Does a woman, a British woman and her escort stay here the night?'

Fool question, she would not stop this early onto the road.

The keeper shook his head, and then offered the finest words Arthur had heard in many a while. 'No my lord, but she rode by, happen an hour past.'

'And Saxons? Have any fair-haired Saex passed this way?'

The man stroked his beardless chin, shook his head, 'We see a few Franks and Burgundians. Saex, you say? Na, no Saex.' He spat a globule of spittle to the ground. 'Don't think I'd be inclined to serve Saex.'

He gestured with his hand, indicating north. 'The lady now, she was a handsome woman.' The man shook his head, a pity she and her party had not stopped. They seemed of the wealthy type, he could do with such trade. Here was a second chance. Although this man's dress seemed not so affluent, it belied his accent and way of command. 'Will you dismount,

305

lord? Rest your horse, take wine and some stew, my wife has prepared a
. . .' He scratched at an itch behind his ear, sighed.

Arthur was gone.

§ LXIII

'My lady?' Ider's voice was soft, so that it did not carry further than it
ought. He brought his horse beside Gwenhwyfar's. 'There is a horse
coming behind. Fast.'

Gwenhwyfar could not see her captain's face in the darkness, the
moon had not yet risen and although the silvered starlight was enough to
follow the straight road, it was not sufficient to illuminate detail. For all
that, she knew he was concerned. Ider did not fuss unnecessarily.

'An urgent messenger?' she offered. 'A lover late for his assignation?'
She laughed, irony in the sound, 'Or the outraged husband?'

Ider's guffaw was low. 'Any of those, my lady. Equally it could be
Saxon.'

'Or Gweir.'

He nodded agreement, but his voice was not convincing. 'Aye, or
Gweir.' Why would Gweir be pushing his horse so fast, in the dark? 'I
suggest we pull off the road, let him, whoever he is, pass.'

Gwenhwyfar agreed, she was in no hurry. They had walked the horses
all this distance, ambled, almost. Really, she had no care what happened.

They got off the road and into the concealment of the trees barely in
time, for although the tattoo rhythm of the hoofbeats had sounded
distant, the rider was soon upon them. Ider grimaced at the man next to
him, who jabbed his thumb downward. It was Gweir's horse, but the rider
was not Gweir. Llwch already had an arrow knocked onto his bow, barely
waited for Ider's brief, but sharp, command.

Arthur heard the sound, so familiar, the whistle of an arrow in flight.
He yanked at the dun's mouth, hauling him to the left, cursed as the barb
found target in the same instant as the horse lost balance. Horse and man
tumbled downward, the animal skidding along the road surface a few
yards, Arthur crumping into a heap. 'Mithras bloody God!' he yelled as
he scrambled upright, sword already to hand. *Saxons*, he thought, *Saxon
ambush.*

Ider's men exchanged glances, emerged, leading their horses, but
Gwenhwyfar was ahead of them, leaping across the ditch that drained the
road, up the embankment, running, legs, cloak and hair flying, screaming

Arthur's name. She slithered to a halt, breathless and fearful. 'Jesu and all the gods! Are you hurt?' Her hands were already fumbling at the arrow shaft in his upper arm, her eyes searching frantically for any other hurts, found none. 'What in all hell do you think you are doing, scaring us so?' The reprimand came sharp. 'Bloody fool,' she added. The men had come forward, were sheepishly gathering at a discreet distance.

'Who shot this arrow?' Arthur demanded as he shooed Gwenhwyfar's fussing hands aside and broke off the shaft as close the flesh as he could.

'I did, lord,' Llwch confessed, twisting his horses's reins in his fingers, thankful that the dark hid the deep, embarrassed blush to his skin. 'We thought Gweir's horse was stolen.'

'Llwch. I might have guessed. You always did have a bloody bad aim.' The Pendragon was laughing, relieved to have found them – her – unhurt, unharmed. The men laughed with him. Llwch was superb with a bow, he claimed he could hit a bat's wing blindfold.

A while to bind Arthur's arm and tend the cuts scored on the dun's legs, more would need be done come first light, this would do for now. Arthur talked as they worked, telling in brief, concise words of the Saxon attack, his suspicion that more were following. 'They'll catch up, watch for a few days, take us at night, while we're camped somewhere.'

Ider grinned. The moon was rising large and lovely, hanging above the trees that marched twenty paces back from each side of the road. He signalled for two of the men to find a suitable camping-place, hidden, yet from where they could watch. Hitched his sword belt more comfortable. 'They're in for a surprise then.'

Gwenhwyfar put her hand to Arthur's chest. 'Us? We?' she queried. 'You are staying?'

Arthur placed his hand over hers, took her fingers, brushed her lips with his own. 'If you'll consent to have back a fool?'

Her answer was a returned kiss, more lingering, more urgent. As they broke apart, he said drily, 'I have to stay. Someone must show Llwch how to shoot straight!'

October 472

§ LXIV

Bedwyr sat on his horse, the reins loose between his fingers, one arm resting across his thigh, his men, ten of them, sitting, perhaps not so seemingly relaxed, behind him. Eadric the Saxon stood on the track before them, his axe casual across his right shoulder. The women and the boys he had sent into the house place. As well Cuthwin was no longer here to witness this day's bad work, as well that the fever had taken him to a better place three months back. He shifted the weight of the heavy axe, his eyes still not losing their hold, locked into those of Bedwyr's.

'You will need fell me first,' he stated, 'before you take my harvest and burn my farm, as others of your kind have been doing to the south of here.'

Bedwyr eased his behind deeper into the saddle, his fingers pulled at the strap of his war-cap. 'I have no wish for killing,' he replied. Eadric the Saxon spat on the ground. 'Nor,' Bedwyr added, 'have I much of a wish to disobey orders.'

Eadric spat a second time. 'And whose orders would they be? Those of the Roman fool Ambrosius?' He let the axe-head down, let its weight swing to the ground between his feet, his hands holding the shaft, ready to move, use it, if he must. 'It is the shame that your King was not found. The Pendragon would never have permitted the spilling of so much innocent blood.'

'No blood has been shed,' Bedwyr countered.

Blood, no, but to the south and along the Tamesis valley those past months, farm-steadings had been burnt to the ground, livestock herded away, harvests taken. The Saxon families were not killed, but with no shelter, no food left them for the winter, how long would they survive? 'There are other ways to die,' Eadric said sadly. He took one step forward. 'Without this farm, I cannot support my wife nor the bairn growing large in her belly. Without this farm there will be nothing for her brothers when they are grown into manhood. Without this farm—' He lifted the axe so that the gleaming head lay in the open palm of his broad, strong hand. 'I, as with the others of my kind, will have no choice, but to fight you, and your kind.'

Bedwyr looked about him. This was a pleasant valley, it had seen little

308

killing, save for the hunt and the stalking of nature's own endings. He had no heart to start shedding blood now. He sighed, long and slow. Had his mind already been made before he came here, before they had saddled up and rode from the fortress? Made two weeks since, when the first written orders had arrived? He took up the reins, turned his horse. 'When the Pendragon left,' he said, 'Britain had a prospect of peace and trade. Ambrosius's southern lands are still prospering, but only because he is taking from the Anglian, the Jute and the Saxon. He has taxed and taxed again, is bleeding these peaceful, settled lands systematically dry. He is trying to rid us of the Saex, he says, but he will not. If bees nest in the hollow tree at the far end of the orchard, you leave them there, harvest their honey for your own use. You do not poke them with a stick, make them swarm in anger. I will not serve a man who deliberately sets women and children on the track to starvation, even if they are Saex. I am a soldier, I am no cold murderer.' He heeled his horse into a walk. 'Peace be with you, Eadric the Saxon, I'll not be the one to destroy you.' One by one, the men followed, aware of what Bedwyr, their lord commander was doing.

One asked. 'To where shall we go, sir?' They could not stay at the fortress, for now they were no longer Ambrosius's men.

'I will ride to Geraint, take service with him,' Bedwyr shrugged, truly he had no plan, he was doing things as he went along. 'Mayhap we will consider resurrecting the Artoriani, place a challenge to the one who is destroying all that the Pendragon once fought for.'

Nods and murmurs of agreement at that, it was a good suggestion. They were once, most of them, Arthur's men. Would willingly be so again, even if they need follow his kindred, not the man himself.

Feet, running from behind, the youngest of Cuthwin's sons. Bedwyr halted his horse, the lad proffered something in his hand. A brooch, another of those round saucer-shaped brooches with a mask pattern. 'Eadric says, to honour you and the King you once both served, he will have no use for this.'

Bedwyr took it, thanked the boy, put it safe in his waist pouch. If only all the threats of war were so easily settled!

December 472

§ LXV

'If they march,' Amlawdd warned in his irritating nasal whine, 'we will be knocked aside like year-old saplings before a charging boar!'

Ambrosius Aurelianus barely bothered to flick a long-suffering glance at the man. He had been belly-aching about more or less the same thing for the past half of an hour – had been ignored at the start of this Council, was being ignored now. There was no point in repeating the obvious, for it served no purpose and solved nothing. If the Saxon force, assembled at the place they called Radingas, decided to move within the next eight and forty hours, Britain would be lost. Would become the land of the Saxons, of the English. General opinion, though, was agreed that this was to be their wintering place. There would be no fighting this side of the winter snows.

The east was already fallen, out of any direct British control, all treaties, agreements and enforcements systematically and irrevocably destroyed, as was the line of fortresses that Ambrosius had so ambitiously planned. At least no British men were slaughtered, but, as most had ridden south under Bedwyr's banner of the double-headed dragon, effectively abandoning the entire East Saxon region north of the Tamesis, it was a fact of little consequence. They were classified as deserters; faced, under the stricture of law, the sentence of death by stoning.

A few had refused to ride with the traitor Bedwyr, had returned to Ambrosius. Joined by the loyal fortresses of the Cantii border and those in the valley of the Tamesis, the Governor of All Britain at least had an army to his name. But they were not enough. Even with calling out the entire levy due to serve, the Saxons held the advantage of three to one.

'Is there no word from Lord Geraint?' someone asked from the rear of the crowded Council chamber at Ambrosium. 'Surely he will bring men to reinforce us?'

Someone else took up the cry. 'Aye, he will not let Britain fall to the barbarian heathen!'

Amlawdd was standing, legs straddled, beside Ambrosius's chair of state. He answered with endemic scathing. 'Geraint? Pah! He shelters the traitor Bedwyr and his scum followers! Geraint keeps his own land for his own kin, cares nought for anyone or anything north of his borders. We are on our own and I say we ought take up our arms and hit the Saex first! Hit them while they sleep, burn their camp, halt them afore they make decision to march onto the Ridge and become unstoppable!'

A few ears were beginning to cock in his direction, a few murmurs of reluctant agreement, silenced as Ambrosius raised a hand so that he might speak.

'Geraint has not yet answered my urgent-sent plea. For all my friend Amlawdd may think of him, he is a man of honour. Admitted, Bedwyr resides with him, but Geraint gives shelter to kindred, as he is duty bound to. He has not publicly declared for rebellion. Geraint may yet come to our aid.' Did he speak with too much of a hesitancy in his voice? With too much fervent hope? 'Aside those here at this meeting, a handful of lords to north and west have pledged to send men.' He shrugged dismally. 'It may be enough.' He knew it would not be. The voices of Council rose louder, one clearly heard.

'We ought never have let ourselves become so isolated! Arthur retained petty kingdoms under his sovereignty for this one especial reason. When he needed men, he had them.'

Someone else shouted, 'Arthur deliberately kept the Saex contained and contented. Under his rule, this bloody mess would never have raised its head higher than his balls would have let it!'

'If only he were to come again! We would have chance of victory under a leader such as Arthur.'

The number of voices increased, a few, Ambrosius noted, decrying that last statement. Amlawdd one of them, of course. He had not hidden his open pleasure at Lord Bedwyr's fall from grace, was personally seeing to it that these latest, gossip-mongering rumours of Arthur were firmly quashed and ridiculed. Arthur would come again in time of need? Fool nonsense! Childish prattle to bolster unsteady nerves. No one spoke of Arthur when the gold chinked in their pouches, when the grain was stored high in their barns. No one spoke of Arthur when they had sent the Saxons running at Guoloph!

Ambrosius would not speak of him. The Pendragon was dead, gone, buried and mouldering. The maggots and worms had already heaved and twisted through the bloated, decaying corpse, the stinking, rotting flesh moving as if in life beneath the darkness of the earth. Arthur was gone! That last speaker had been his own son, Cadwy.

Slowly, drained from tiredness and an ominous hint of returning illness, Ambrosius stood. The faces blurred, the walls moved, he closed his eyes, all but briefly. He must not be ill. Must not! Spoke, mustering

311

calm and confidence. 'We have, then, the one option. We initiate the fight.'

Delighted, Amlawdd punched the air with his fist, men were on their feet, beginning to herd forward, excitement overruling any former reluctance, the roll of adrenalin pumping. Others, generals, petty chieftains, were gathering the drape of their togas over their arms and hurrying for the outside. The one cry loud on their lips, passing from ear to mouth, a babble of expectant anticipation, spreading through the fortress and beyond its secure walls to the scatter of encampments. Within the hour, men were putting a sharper edge to their spears, swords and daggers, were checking straps to harness, helmet and armour. Women were seeking their loved ones, or those who needed a woman. One word hovering and dancing, leaping and cavorting.

War!

January 473

§ LXVI

The Ridge Way. The Tamesis River flowed from the west a while, before turning abruptly south, its flood-plain fed by hungry, running tributaries dashing down from the high ground that was topped by this ancient and majestic track. The Tamesis, a geographical and cultural boundary. Below, to the south, British land, lifting to the heights of the soft-coloured, bright-aired Downs, above its flow, the outriders of the forests that ran up dark and foreboding to the fledgling Saex Kingdoms of the East and Middle Saxons. An undisputed frontier, a great protective curved boundary that effectively separated English from British.

Except the English had gathered to the British side and were massed near a place of early, peaceful settlement, called in their English tongue Radingas. The settlers, the farmers and landholders, there and along this part of the gentle Tamesis valley, were of a third and fourth generation, their land given as reward by Rome itself. More British now than Saxon, some even converted to Christianity, they found themselves inextricably caught between the cultures of the two. Ostracized by one, treated with contempt by the other. Old men, young boys, unsure on which side to carry their spears. No farmer cared to fight, not when the land needed ploughing, sewing or harvesting. No farmer cared to leave his cattle ready to calve, his sheep ready to lamb. But then, no farmer cared to pay taxes to a greedy and scornful over-lord – and it was not yet spring, not yet the time of nature's urgent need for those who farmed the land. There was little choice. The long-established settlers of the Tamesis Valley tied the war ribbons to their spears, and made their way across their winter-sleeping fields to the fortified encampment beside the great Ridge, swelling the numbers of discontented English. If Arthur had been King, they would have stayed at home, mending their ploughs, watching the skies for the first signs of winter snow, sifting the bad sowing-grain from the good. But he was not. Ambrosius was Supreme. Ambrosius Aurelianus, a man who answered only to his Christian God, and acclaimed the ways that were Roman ways. The English cared nothing for Rome and what little was left of it. Cared even less for the Christ God.

On the eve of midwinter, the British had come, crying their Christian-

God war-shouts and hefting their war-spears along the Ridge, driving the English outposts before them, sending the Saex scuttling for shelter behind the high, solid-built timber palisade walls of the English encampment. The fighting had been bloody and short. One gateway had given way, several British had pushed through, raising an expected victory cry, but the English were many within, and the broken defences were soon rebuilt by a barricade of the dead and dying. The night attack failed. The dawn of the new day saw the bodies of the British dead piled before barely charred, sentinel-like oak timbers.

A loud-sung victory for the English. The British had come and were beaten back. Those few of the Saxons who had wavered at the prospect of battle, took up their weapons and made with all speed for Radingas. There was now hope, and Aelle, the acclaimed Bretwalda, High King of All Saxons, was to lead them to a victory even greater. One that would resound in song from mead-hall to mead-hall, from father to son; to son, to son.

The rain came in cold, vicious squalls lashing from the north-east, and the English saw no reason to leave the safety of their camp, the warmth of their tents and the comfort of their women. It was a time of feasting. They drank their mead and ate their fill of ox and deer, boar and fowl, toasted their gods, and told their tales of heroes past and adventures achieved. When the winds eased and swung to a more benign south, they would be ready, with cleared heads and high hearts. Aelle of the South Saxons would call to his brothers, and they would march. When the feasting was done, when the mead had run dry and the tales were all told.

Despite the failure to dislodge any of the Saex whoresons from their encampment, the British were of good morale, eager to fight – and to fight well. They had not expected to achieve much in that previous attack, had attempted the idea more as a challenge, a warming-up, a flexing of muscles. Did not look upon the incident as defeat or loss, seeing it merely as an exercise, a chance to explore the Saex strength and seek out weaknesses. After all, few fortified places could be taken with ease.

Sunrise, the third day of the Roman month of Janus. An appropriate month, Ambrosius thought, if you disregarded the pagan element. Two-faced Janus, the pre-Christian god who looked ahead and behind. Behind, the failure. Ahead, the victory. It was time for battle.

After the Nativity and midwinter feasting, more men had arrived, not many, but every extra man was welcomed and valued. Powys had sent fifty, Rheged another thirty or so, the Mid-Land tribes over two hundred between them. The mild weather helped, and the eagerness for a fight. After that short bout of cold wind, the sun had shown through spindle-thrift clouds for most days, persuading the birds to sing for their mating territories over-early. Even the buds of the elderberry and hazel were bursting into too early spring-worn green.

Briton and Saxon spent that night straddling the Ridge Way, camped no more than two miles apart. Dawn saw the Saxons dividing into two forces, Aelle of the South Saxons commanding one, Aesc of the Cantii Jutes the other, holding the advantage of deploying on slightly higher ground. The British saw no reason to make private complaint, drew a similar stand. Ambrosius and his own men, the infantry of Britannia Secunda taking the northward division, Amlawdd with the militias and tithe-bound men the southern. Battle-lines drawn, division facing division astride the ancient track that led south to north. A pause, waiting for the last few stragglers to make their way into the rear, a chance for individuals to make a last peace with their own god.

Ambrosius bent his knee to pray, head bowed, lips silently moving the intoned words. Coinciding with his Amen, the sun rose, filtering a pale, subdued glow onto the winter-bare ground – and the Saxon lines rippled and shifted, their spear tips and swords gleaming faintly in the weak burst of new light. Ambrosius called his horse forward, mounted, settled himself into the saddle, and raised his arm, commanded his column to advance at the run. There came a great shout, and the British rushed forward to meet the slow-advancing Saex. The crash and clash of weaponry, the yelling and shouting and cursing reverberating across the lower lands that fell away to each side of the high ridge, sending winter birds into wild, raucous flight. As wild, the furious mêlée of men.

Although they held the higher, advantageous ground, the uprush of the British, so determined, so intent, allowed the Saxons not one pace forward from their first-drawn lines. With Amlawdd and the tribes' warriors beating and hacking at Aesc's Jutes, and Ambrosius himself leading against the Bretwalda, Aelle, it became an even match as more and more of the Saex, peasant men many of them, poorly clothed, ill-armed, fell dead or dying. Twice more. The sun rose to the zenith, slid westward, the gather of winter-dark clouds bringing dusk early. The Saxons broke, began to fall back, steadily, pace by pace, fighting still, but drawing back. Night enveloped the Ridge, with a sudden-come bluster of wind-driven rain, and the Saxons turned and ran for the sheltered safety of their fortified place at Radingas.

Dismounting his horse, weary, blood-grimed, battered and aching, Ambrosius, again that day, bowed his head in prayer. They had seen off the Saex, it was a victory, but such a small one. Such a very small, temporary, one.

§ LXVII

Gwenhwyfar tugged her fingers, sensuous, through Arthur's thick, dark, hair; on down over the naked, rapidly cooling skin of his back, running across the haphazard pattern of scars. More than she remembered, her touch lingering over the newer, unfamiliar disfigurements. Many of them, too vicious. 'If ever, at any time, I grow tired of you, remind me of this. Remind me of what we have just shared,' she murmured.

He quirked a light smile, one that tilted the side of his lips; nuzzled his face deeper into the softness of her body. They had made love several times on the long, slow, journey home, kindling each other's needs, rediscovering each other's body, but those few uncertain explorations had been bound by an unspoken hesitation that harboured flickering doubts and wary apprehensions. Wounds heal, but the pain can take a while to cease its blistering throbbing, and the scars remain, red and evil before paling, puckering white against a dark, healthy, skin.

Now they were home, or near enough. They had rested a while at the first town – Antessiodurum, Gwenhwyfar's least favourite place, giving Onager time to gain strength and recover, giving themselves time to be certain of their decisions. But Arthur had never looked back over his shoulder, and the boy, Medraut, made no murmur of returning to his mother. Hard, those first few days, for Gwenhwyfar to accept the child, another woman's born son; harder still to sit quiet and calm as Arthur had told her everything of Morgaine, of her birthing, of her father. His. Unexpected, she had shown no anger or recoiling horror, Gwenhwyfar had accepted the fact. Arthur had sired a son on his own half-sister. What was done was done, threads in the multi-coloured tapestry of life were too close-woven to be unravelled. The dark knotted too tight to unravel within the gold.

'I remember her,' Gwenhwyfar had said. 'A ragged, poorly child with scalds and hand-marked weals on her skin.' Morgause had not cared for the girl, had abandoned her, left her, for the other elderly priesthood women to see to her upbringing. 'While I was waiting for you, that time at Yns Witrin, to come to me, Morgause was there with the child.' Gwenhwyfar remembered the sadness of the girl, the pity she had felt for her.

Watching the boy, sleeping curled as a babe, thumb stuffed between his teeth, she had remembered her own sons. They had seen troubles and sadnesses, even witnessed fear and the dark shadow of death. But never had they known the loneliness of the uncherished, the unloved.

'*I could not leave him,*' Arthur had said, that first night together. '*I could not abandon him to an echo of my own childhood.*'

And Gwenhwyfar, the mother in her, had understood that. Understood more. She could perhaps birth Arthur more sons, but they would be too late, too young. Cerdic was grown, a man with a son of his own. Cerdic would most certainly come if he knew he could claim his father's land with the ease of taking a choice bone from a new-whelped pup. Medraut was not hers, but then nor was he Winifred's. That was the importance, the difference.

After leaving Antessiodurum they had ridden north along the road that became more travelled the further they journeyed. Stayed a while at Lutetia, on the island town of the Parisii, Arthur in no great haste to follow the last few miles to the coast and a ship home. Gwenhwyfar in no great urgency to hasten him.

He had been sleeping badly. Restless dreams tossing with perspiration and sharp, fearful cries. The enveloping blackness of memories, galloping with the hard-forced pace of those unbidden night-riders, hostile on their red-eyed, black-coated mares. The sound of battle, the clash of sword on sword, the scream of men killed and dying. The red of blood, the black of death! Horror and fear revisiting, returning. Gwenhwyfar, warm and safe and strong. Her arms around him, comforting, reassuring, hand soothing the stark sweat of fear, closeness easing the ragged breath of drowning, suffocating, beneath that returned stench of the past.

It had to be faced, had to be done, they had to return to Britain. But it was so hard, so dreadfully hard!

On to the coast; the craft they had found had battled her way steadily through the strong winds. It was the wrong time of year for the sea, but she was a game little ship. Again, she raised her prow with the uplift of the heavy sea-swell the surging wind from behind, shadowing like a swooping king eagle, flecks of salt-spray keening into the breathless-passing air. Arthur stood on the foredeck, legs spread, hands gripping as if there was no tomorrow to the gunwale. Ahead, a grey-misted hint of something that was not sea nor sky, rising higher, clearing, coming nearer as the ship kicked her way forward.

Britain. Home. Almost home.

Gwenhwyfar had come behind him, her tread muffled by the shout of waves and wind, her cloak and hair billowing as excitedly agitated as the single, square, bleached-blue sail. He had jerked as her arm slid around his waist, his hand flying, instinctive, to the pommel of his sword. Covered his disquiet with a laugh.

Gwenhwyfar rested her head on his shoulder, warming into his returned embrace; stood, silent a while, watching the shape-changing grey mist congeal into the more solid shape of land. He was afraid, she knew that. Every muscle was tense, every nerve-end screaming, jagged. Afraid of going home, returning. Afraid of the fighting that surely would be waiting.

She linked her fingers through his. 'You will be at ease,' she comforted, 'once you are back.'

He answered, betraying himself with a shaking huskiness to his voice. 'What if they no longer want me?'

Her answer was succinct. 'For those who once followed you, it will be as if you had never been away. For those who did not,' she chuckled, kissed him, light, reassuring, on the cheek, 'well, they did not want you in the first place. It did not bother you then. Ought it bother you now?'

He supposed not, but for all her flippancy, this was not going to be easy. For too long had he been gone. Ambrosius was the Supreme now. Hard enough to have fought for, and won, a kingdom once. To retrieve it after so blindly letting it go? He closed his eyes, let his weight sink against Gwenhwyfar's solidity. To fight again, knowing he had once failed, knowing he had irresponsibly killed so many men . . .

§ LXVIII

'I'll not fight for that incompetent imbecile!' Bedwyr slammed his clenched fist onto the table, his expression as conscientiously fierce as the action. 'Ambrosius has brought this mess upon himself, must get himself out of it, or die.'

Patient, Geraint choked down the temptation to match Bedwyr's blazed anger. 'Ambrosius is a good man, has done only as he thought best. You can not censure a man for pursuing his beliefs.'

'Pah!' Bedwyr thumped onto a stool, sat opposite Geraint, leaning his arms onto the table, his eyes glowering, mouth pouting. 'You censure me? I believe in the Artoriani. Want to ride with them, take back what is ours!'

Disciplining his hands to relax along the carved arms of his oak-wood chair, Geraint inhaled three deep and slow breaths. 'No, you want to become king. That I cannot condone, not yet. Not while the Saex have risen under one leader. There are times when, for all our hatreds and disappointments, we cannot afford to fight among ourselves. That—' He leant significantly forward, one finger raised. 'That was always the Pendragon's belief. It ought be yours also.'

Bedwyr eased forward, the weight of his upper body taken by his tight-folded arms. 'I fight in the Pendragon's name, for Arthur, for when he returns.'

The man opposite did not intend it to be audible, but the sigh was stronger than he realized. Geraint rested his head against the high back of his chair, closed his eyes. For how many days now had they been sparring with this self-same argument? These same words, round and around and around? In the name of the good God, was it not blindingly obvious that Arthur was not coming back? Was not going to return?

Two months since, a rider had galloped up to Geraint's Hall of Durnovaria, his horse lathered, ridden hard the distance from the port of Llongborth, the man come from across the sea, one of those who had accompanied Lady Gwenhwyfar. '*The Pendragon is found! He is alive!*'

How that joyful, and so expectant, news had then travelled! Despite the hushed warning that it was to be kept tongue-locked within their own knowing.

Two months past. And still the Pendragon had not come.

'It is my belief that it was false news, Bedwyr.' Geraint pushed himself wearily to his feet. 'We must face the fact of our own eyes, our own sense. Something – some tragedy, illness, treachery, I do not know what, something, has befallen them. Him. Whatever it was that had prevented the Pendragon's return three years past is still as prevalent now. If Arthur could have returned, he would have done so. If not . . .' He eased a second sigh. 'We must accept, Bedwyr. We are, for all our hopes, our ambitions and dreams. We are, God help us, on our own.'

Bedwyr remained at the table, leaning on his arms, his lips as tight folded. 'The men are here, Geraint, waiting to fight. To fight against the Saex. To fight for Arthur and Britain.' He lifted his eyes and face, his chin, lightly stubbled with beard-growth, jutting determined. 'They strain at the leash, anxious to fight this Saxon army, but they will not do so, not under Ambrosius's banner. They will not follow a man who ordered the murder of old men, of women and children. Of those who farm, are settled and live at peace with Britain.' He unfolded his arms, lay his palms flat on the rough surface of the wooden trestle table, pushed himself up, as wearily as Geraint had done. Taking up his cloak from where it lay over a bench, he swung it around his shoulders, fastened the ornate pin. 'This garment,' he said, settling the folds of the cloak comfortably around him, 'is the red of the Artoriani. Beneath, I wear the white tunic. We—' He idled his hand in a general direction of the outside. 'Those of us who knew Arthur, who rode with and loved the Pendragon, have faith that if he can return to lead us into victory – and restore the peace that victory brings – if he can return, he will.' He ambled to the door, lifted its latch. 'If we must ride against the Saex, then we ride under someone who will preserve all that Arthur stood for. We'll ride as Artoriani, Geraint.' He half-turned, his eyes pleading to be understood, pleading for some unknown god to be listening and take pity. 'We'll ride under Arthur, when he returns to lead us.'

He left the room, the door closing with a quiet thud.

Geraint stood before the brazier, warming himself. His bottom lip was tucked between his teeth, and his head shook, slowly, from side to side.

Dreams and hopes were one thing. The realities, another entirely.

§ LXIX

Deep into the mead, Aesc, self-styled king of the Cantii Saxons, was morose. This whole venture went against the grain of all sense. Why face degradation, blood and pain for the sake of obtaining land when he already had sufficient lordship over land enough? Talked into this fool thing by a honey-tongued ambition chaser! Ach, Aelle of the South Saxons had much to gain, little to loose, but he, Aesc? . . . Curse the idle god who had allowed him to slip, unsuspecting, into this damn situation! He drained his tankard, slopped more mead into it, drank again. What, in all the power of Woden's thunder, had possessed him? He had lost men, good fighting men – could lose so much more! His wife his sons, his land, his wealth . . . mead dribbled from his mouth, he rested his forehead against the rim of the drinking vessel, groaned. He ought have stayed at Canta Byrig, stayed in his own land, remained lord of his own future!

A hand, thick-wristed, muscle-armed, slapped onto his shoulder, a chortling laugh sounding behind. 'My friend! More mead? This is excellent stuff, is it not? Something else we do better than the poxed British, ferment a fine brew!' As he spoke, Aelle's other hand gripped firm around the mead-jar, poured a generous measure for the seated Cantii king, set the jug down again. Aelle placed himself next to his fellow Saxon, his tactfully appointed joint commander. 'Have you thought on what I asked of you? Do you join us when we march on the morrow?' The joviality was, perhaps, a little false, a little too extreme, too hearty. Aesc, if he realized it, made no move or comment against that grand, extravagant, show of friendship. The South Saxons needed the Cantii in this thing as much as the other way around. Without either side backing the other, the whole uprising would crumble into scattered pockets of weak minded, weak armed rebellion. Soon crushed, soon ended. Together, they almost stood a chance of succeeding.

'You could have more than that insubstantial corner of Britain.' Aelle's arm was gripping firmer around Aesc's shoulders, his lips close to the Cantii's ear. 'Much more. All yours, and mine, for the sake of one more effort, one last fight!'

The mead tankard thudded to the table, slopping the rich, dark drink over the side. Aesc half-turned, his surly, drink-sodden features growling behind the cragged, grimed skin, puckering beneath the unkempt, mead-stained beard and moustache. Why in Woden's name was he still here at Radingas? Why in all the gods' names had he not gathered together his men and arms and returned home? There was nothing here, save defeat and shame. And a sore head to face come morning.

'Fight?' He sneered. 'Fight? As we fought ten days past, do you mean? Do we, then, chase a second opportunity to piss our breeches and run?'

The control to retain the good humour came with well-schooled patience. That was why Aelle had attained the position of Bretwalda – overlord, Supreme King – among the Saxon peoples. Aelle, not any other king or princeling. He was a large-built, sturdy man, strong-muscled in arm and thigh and brain. A man who could think as efficiently as he could fight. 'Ah,' he said, batting the air derisively, 'that was a mere skirmish, a battle of no significance, save to test our strength against theirs. Let us be magnanimous about it, allow the British to make merry and crow loud about their poxed little victory. His fingers returned to grip, claw-like into Aesc's flesh, the bite hard, even through the padding of cloak and tunic. 'Let them win a small battle. We, my comrade, shall win the war!'

Almost insolent, Aesc picked at the clasping fingers, setting them loose, pushed the hand aside. 'War? Why did I get myself embroiled in your farting war? This is your need, not mine!'

Assessing the hostility, Aelle moved himself a fraction along the bench. He must take care, for as mule-minded as Aesc could be, he was an essential ally. They must fight together! Together, they had strength and determination; together, the British could be defeated. 'Agreed, it is I who require the more land, to enlarge that which I have already laid claim to, but it is we, my friend, we who can drive the British into the hills, we who can send them scurrying across the sea to their God-mumbling sanctuaries in Less Britain. It may take us a while, may take the spilling of much of our blood. The losing of many battles.' He leant slightly more forward, more intimidating, more sincere. 'But I say again, you and I with our unity can win!'

Aesc growled something inaudible and Aelle knew he had him, had his alliance again. Quickly, he moved on. 'I have learnt that the British remain at the place they call Badon. 'Tis a fortress guarding the Ridge Way – ja, as you rightly say, you know this –' Aesc had grunted his indignation at being told what even a babe in arms ought know. Protested, 'I know more of the British defences than do you South Saxons! My father, Hengest rode with a British king, remember? My sister married him. My niece, Winifred, married another!'

Calming, talking easily, low-voiced, unhurried, Aelle skirted the rebuke, continued. He must make certain that Aesc would march with them come the morrow! He must! 'Forgive me, I do not tell you what you know, merely sort my own thoughts aloud so that we may compare our strategies.' Tactfully, neatly done! 'Badon is a fortress formidable on the north side, easier to take from the more gentle sloping south. We need to swing around, secure the British, then attack.' Added, almost as an after-thought, 'Ambrosius is again ill, I hear.' His excitement and enthusiasm increased as if urging an already running horse into a flat gallop. 'We could take them so easily, Aesc! From the south, we could take them as if they were poisoned rats sealed in a nest-hole!'

The Canti conceded. What Aelle said was the truth. 'Do we have the time to lay siege?'

'Ja! We do!'

'What of Prince Geraint? What if he comes riding hard from the south?'

'Is that now likely? All this while and he has not made a move. 'Tis more likely he has sided with Bedwyr. They are waiting for us to finish Ambrosius, then . . .'

Impatient, curt, Aesc interrupted. 'Then we will need start a new fight! I knew singing the praises of a short sharp war was a mead-soaked exaggeration!'

The other man chuckled a gust of amusement. 'Since when, friend, did a warrior not exaggerate the course of battle!'

The sour retort. 'Since he discovered his hair was becoming thinned and grizzled, his back and bum ached from laying on damp, hard ground, and that the delights of a wife's teats, the warmth of her bed and the knowing that he could savour the same enjoyment the next night uninterrupted, began appealing to him more than the possibility of having his balls hacked off by some raw British recruit!'

Aelle roared amusement. 'You are right! Of course, you are so right!'

Shoving the empty mead-jug from him, Aesc swivelled to full face his Bretwalda. Asked one, earnest, sober, question.

'So, Ambrosius is ill. Geraint, it seems will not aid him. What, then, my Overlord, do we do if the other rumour proves to be truth?' He belched, wiped the back of his hand across his mouth. 'What if Arthur truly is returned?'

322

§ LXX

Arthur gripped the top lip of the palisade fencing, the knuckles of both hands whitening under the tension of that anxious grasp. Below, slaves were lighting the torches and braziers. The cobbled courtyard of Geraint's inner, private sanctuary of royal dwellings leapt with the dance of illuminated shadow, the uneasy proximity of a winter's evening recoiling, while beyond the wooden palisade, the darkening sky pressed closer, leaning its cold breath up against the outer walls of Durnovaria. There were no stars. No moon. January had been a dull-weathered month, encased in louring grey cloud that refused to scud or billow into anything more than an omnipresent weight. If snow or frost touched a more northerly part of Britain, it had not dared to ride here, to this milder, more southerly, climate.

Durnovaria, the town beyond the royal enclosure, rustled into the casual stroll of a typical evening routine. Shops and bothies were closing, taverns filling with those seeking warmth, food and drink after a day's laborious toil; streets emptying of daytime traffic, mothers calling their young children in from play, husbands returning home. Doors and window shutters bolted, the chill of night closed firmly out. The day ended so soon after it had begun this time of year.

A wind was stirring, becoming attentive to the banner flying from the roof of the northern guard tower and scuffing at Arthur's cloak. It smelt different. Here in Britain, the wind carried a heady scent of damp soil and mouldering autumn leaves, mixing with the saline tang of sea and sheep-grazed upland grasses. Always, the tantalizing promise of distant summer and optimistic hope.

Three days had he been back. Three long, never-ending days of heart-racing, unnerved panic. He had come up here, onto the rampart walkway, to escape the loud press of people in Geraint's Hall, their swell of excited talk and heated debate. They had been feasting, the men, Geraint's loyal, warrior-class followers, and his own Artoriani. A handful more than three hundred men, where once he could have boasted three times that number. They were men who had remained loyal to his memory, his name, men who had ridden with Bedwyr rather than go against all they had previously fought for. Men who, whatever way you cared to look at it, had deserted Ambrosius and their country, leaving both to God's mercy and their fate. By Arthur's law, and the law of soldiering laid down by Rome, and even before that, by the law of tribal honour, one in every ten of those men ought be stoned or clubbed to death. Desertion was the greatest sin for any fighting man, from the humblest shield-bearer to King himself. Arthur's fingers gripped tighter. Aye, to King himself. Desertion. A deliberate leaving, a conscious thought not to return. One man in ten? Happen, he ought be the first.

They were celebrating down in the Hall, unaware of his torment, this torrent of crazed, mixed emotions. They rejoiced at his homecoming, their saving, as they saw it. They were swilling beer, draining wine and devouring pork, venison, beef and fowl as if the morrow was to bring a judgement from the gods and the world would end for all time. As well it might, considering the news brought in not one hour since.

Arthur closed his eyes, lifted his hot face to the cold caress of the night wind. Too many were in that Hall. The stench of human bodies, male sweat, wine-sopped breath and passed wind mingling with the pleasanter aromas of roasting meats, hearth-smoke, honey-sweetened mead, the apple perfume of cider, and the odour of fresh-fermented beer. He had never felt comfortable in confined spaces, never settled at ease within the enclosure of walls. God's truth! They wanted him to fight, to lead them! He swallowed, forcing down that hard lump of gathering fear.

What had he expected for Mithras's sake? To come home unnoticed? To ride up to Caer Cadan, pull off his boots and sit quietly before his hearth for the rest of his days? He had hoped, perhaps, for a few cheerfully called greetings, a few slaps on the shoulder. One or two might have expressed a notion that he would take up where he had left off, a suggestion he would quickly have parried. A few, a foolish handful, may even have wanted to fight with him again. He had not expected so many to be so eagerly waiting for him. And more would come, Bedwyr had informed him, when they knew he was once again their King; more, many more would come.

King! How could he dare take up that privilege again? Had he not abandoned that right when he remained in Gaul? And why would men want to fight beneath him now? Now that he had so irresponsibly slaughtered his own, had so horribly shown that he could fail?

Horses were coming up through the town from the outer gates, passing through the gateway below and to Arthur's left. Too dark to see the riders muffled in thick winter cloaks, Arthur too deep in his own fear-bounding thoughts to attempt an identification. Probably more fool men come to give thanks for his return, men who had heard the news that was spreading as rapidly and widely as ripples on a calm pond.

Give thanks! Did the imbeciles not see? Did they not understand? Even if the Saxon army was marching for the Ridge Way fortresses, what could he do about it? Lead the British? He was no longer a leader, did not have the credibility to expect men to follow him. Fight with them? Hah! He was too damned scared ever to fight again.

Sounds in the town had been subtly altering, daytime folk giving way to prowling night-users – young, adventurous men seeking the taverns or a whore. Both. Cutpurses and thieves seeking the bleary-eyed and wine-sodden. Arthur was cold, the chill in the strengthening wind biting at his hands, face and body, but he stood looking out into the darkness, hands clutching that rampart palisade.

The new-arrived horses had been led away, he had heard the distinctive clatter of their shod hooves going in the direction of the stables. From the Hall, the talk and laughter had faltered, then risen again as the newcomers, whoever they were, obtained momentary attention. He ought go down, see who they were, greet them. Why? Who would they be? Misguided men hoping to follow the Dragon Banner? More men blindly not seeing that to follow Arthur meant to meet a certain end? As those others had met death at the marshes near Vicus Dolensis.

One quarter of an hour passed, creeping to the half. Foot-treads on the wooden stairway, two voices, female, met by the barked challenge of the night-watch. Gwenhwyfar's polite, identifying answer followed by belligerent anger as she spoke to the one accompanying her. A woman's retort, stubborn and haughty. Arthur's breath quickened. He did not turn around.

'So!' The second woman was behind him, standing close, he could smell her perfume, her natural female odour heightened by artificial elegance. 'So,' she announced again, 'it is you. You are not worm-meat as we all believed.'

'As they believed. I understand you knew different some while since, Winifred.' He turned, slowly and with deliberate indifference. Gwenhwyfar casually manoeuvred herself to be beside him, should he need her support. In whatever form. She alone understood the disquiet that was rocking his self-belief. She had always understood Arthur, not needing to hear the words or discuss the cause. Her own belief had been shaken, almost destroyed when he had not returned to her, but that was behind her, set aside, for she now understood why. Without someone to stretch a hand into the darkness, the pit of despair was a fearful place. And he had been there alone, with no one, nothing, to comfort him or offer hope.

Winifred feigned amusement at his caustic accusation. 'I? How could I know that you were not dead? The discovery of it came as a great shock, I can assure you.'

'I wager it did!' Arthur offered his arm to his wife, Gwenhwyfar thread her own through it. Her perfume was more subtle than Winifred's, more natural. 'How,' Arthur added cynically, 'I have no idea, but someone with your name attempted to ensure that belief remained.'

Winifred laid her palm on his upper arm, leant forward, ignoring Gwenhwyfar's strident glower, placed a light, mildly affectionate, kiss to his cheek. 'Nonsense! I am pleased, na, relieved, to have you so wonderfully alive!'

Arthur laughed outright at that, some of his old confidence and trust in his own judgement returning, like the welcome embrace of a good friend.

'You paid handsome to have us killed.' Gwenhwyfar did not echo her husband's lighthearted acceptance of attempted murder. 'Put your gold to better use another time, Winifred,' she suggested.

Prepared and waiting for them, Ider and her guard had made short work of those hired scum in Gaul; a swift skirmish, puddles of blood on the road three miles from Antessiodurum and, left behind, a shallow, unmarked grave. Killers dealt with dispassionately, brutally. Hired mercenaries who would murder no more.

At least Winifred had the grace to appear genuinely affronted by the accusation. She did not make enough protest for proof of it, however, as any innocent would have instantly demanded. Instead, indignant, she quivered, 'I have ridden with all speed to give you greeting, Arthur.' Huffily, she folded her hands regally into the drape of her cloak. 'And this is the welcome I receive!' She tossed her head, Arthur noting how her hair was as sleekly golden as he remembered. He smiled, scornful, to himself. Morgaine had coloured her hair so often with roots and powders; it had never before occurred to him that so many women pandered so brutally to their appearance. He glanced at Gwenhwyfar, at her copper-gold torrent of mane, bound relatively disciplined into two braids. The light was poor here, the only glow emanating from the stairwell, but even with so little to see by, he noticed the lighter streaks, the subtle, shadowed differences, the silvered-grey strands nestling comfortable among that tumble of curls. He was glad she had no care of showing her increased age, that Gwenhwyfar had no concern for concealing the truth. Suddenly, he loved her so much. Felt a deep longing, an overwhelming need, to have her always with him. Gwenhwyfar thought of more important things than the necessity to colour her hair, to paint her eyes and lips or to lighten her skin with chalk and ground lead, to fool others into believing she was something that she was not.

He moved his arm around her waist. 'It grows cold up here, we ought return into Geraint's hospitality.'

Winifred blocked his path. 'There is much uncertain talk down there in that Hall. It is not right that you spend time up here, musing, while

Ambrosius is in urgent need. When do you ride to his aid? Soon, the morrow, I trust?'

Arthur stared at her. Breath of all the gods! Not her also! His heart was racing again, his throat running dry, hoofbeats pounding in his brain. 'My uncle has done well enough for himself so far,' he heard himself say. Even Gwenhwyfar looked up, startled, at that. 'I have been home but three days.'

'Aye!' Winifred actually stamped her foot, a child's tempered reaction, 'Three wasted days! My uncle is apparently swarming up the Cuneito Valley.' Tartly she glared at Gwenhwyfar. 'Are you not concerned that it may be your fortress, Badon, to fall in their path first? Do you not care that Cadwy and Ragnall and their childer would most certainly have perished?' She paused for effect, enjoying the satisfaction of bluntness.

For Arthur, the ground seemed to rise and fall, the torchlight dim and blur. A rush of blood swooping through his brain; his vision, senses, darkening and screaming. The word *no!* was swelling in his throat, pushing and heaving to break out. Sweat glistened on his face, trickled, uncomfortable, down his back. If his legs had not felt so heavy, had not been weighted by lead, he would have run, would have bolted down those stairs, raced for the safety of the private chamber allotted him, slammed and barred the door. He could not lead those men, Mithras help him, he could not! He met Winifred's intense gaze, his answer coming, surely, from some other man's mouth. 'I ride on the morrow, as soon as may be, with any who should care to join me.' He was shaking, his hands and legs almost uncontrollable.

'Thank you,' Winifred said, with direct sincerity. 'It is a relief to hear you say it.'

Gwenhwyfar snorted. What nonsense was this! What obscene game was Winifred pursuing now?

Arthur patted her hand, the shaking was easing, the control returning. He indicated for Winifred to go ahead of them, said to Gwenhwyfar, loud enough for his first wife to plainly hear, 'She speaks truth, Cymraes, she is genuinely relieved that I am returned to become King again, for she almost made a mistake.' He was openly grinning again, as Winifred spun around to glower at his deliberate sarcasm.

Gwenhwyfar's query as to what he meant was made with her eyes, her expression. His answering squeeze was reassuring. He explained as he walked her past Winifred, began descending the stairs down to the bright friendliness of the torchlit courtyard. 'She miscalculated, did not reckon on those Saxons already here laying plans for the taking of land that she has marked for Cerdic.'

Gathering her skirts, Winifred swept past them both, head carried high, feet quick-tapping as she walked, proud, offended, for the sanctuary of hospitality within Geraint's noisy Hall.

'Cerdic,' Arthur continued, raising his voice so that she might hear, 'ought have challenged Ambrosius, but for his own cowardly reasons, did not. He may well decide to try again when next time I am believed dead.' He chuckled, louder, 'Unfortunately, unless I stop his mother's uncle and Aelle of the South Saxons now, there will be nothing for him to try *for* when I am gone. Will there, Winifred? With me dead, all hope for Cerdic would be lost.' His laugh echoed around the square of the courtyard, several guards and men seeking the latrine turning to look speculatively at him.

Winifred, entering the Hall, repeated Arthur's announcement. Men were coming to their feet, anxious, excited, begging to collect weapons, leaving to see to their horses. Bedwyr was standing alongside Geraint, grinning. Earlier, someone had brought in the Dragon Banner, had lain it across the table before the lord of this Hall. He lifted it, as Arthur entered yodelled the war cry of the Artoriani. 'Pendragon!' he roared, 'Pendragon!'

The men wanted to ride, wanted Arthur to be their King again. They took up the shout, lifting it to the rafters and beyond, through the smoke hole, through the thatch. The shout, 'Pendragon, Pendragon!' raced upward to the grey cloud, pierced its cold blanket and thrust on, outward. Even mighty Jupiter and congenial Saturn must have heard the acclaim that night in Geraint's Hall!

Arthur ambled into their midst, enduring the slaps to his shoulders, the grasping and shaking of his hand, the great, vigorous burst of cheers and jubilation. *Blood of the White Bull*, he thought, *I am committed to fight because I could not admit to the bitch who was once my wife that with this fear I could piss myself with enough water to put out a fire the size of Nero's burning Rome.* He reached the raised dais, Geraint's table, took the white banner decorated with the leaping red dragon from Bedwyr. His banner, the Dragon that Gwenhwyfar had made for him and his Artoriani. *Must I preserve my kingdom from Saxons, so that my own whelped Saex-breed may one day take it from me?*

Geraint knelt before him, unsheathed sword in his hand, given in offering of hommage. *'To you, lord, I give my sword and shield, my heart and soul. To you, lord, I give my life, to command as you will.'*

None could possibly hear those words, through the exultant roar of voices. The combined voice of the Artoriani.

§ LXXI

Winifred, Lady Pendragon, as she obstinately referred to herself, had not finished with her one-time husband. Once decision was taken that he and his Artoriani would be riding from Durnovaria at first light, she found it next to impossible to seek him out for private audience, but she had always been persistent, finally caught up with him as the hour approached midnight. It had been his custom, in the past, to walk through his men's encampment on the eve of marching or battle; they appreciated his presence. This night, his tour was even more important. He needed to re-establish his authority and his friendship, needed to greet each and every one of the two hundred and seventy-four men who would ride with him on the morrow. Arthur had the gift of making every man special, every man important. Duach, who carried a stiffness to his shoulder from one of their first battle's together; Drwst, who had a fist and a punch as hard as iron; Glewlwyd, who had the strength in his grasp to hold a sword all day in battle and not once let go that grip – he too had been with Arthur from the first, aye, and with his father, before him, with Uthr Pendragon. Anwas, who they called The Winged because of his fleetness of foot; Hael, The Generous; Halwyn The Unsmiling; Gwrhyr, who could speak any language within a day of hearing it . . . many men, many old and so very dear friends. Peredur, as ever, had a jest to share that was as bawdy as a whorehouse. He was called Long Spear for his well-endowed manhood, a good man, Peredur. Chuckling at the jest, reminding himself to repeat it to Gwenhwyfar, Arthur barely noticed the shadow emerging from behind the next tent, felt his heart lurch and race as it materialized into a cloak-flapping shape. 'Mithras, woman!' he raged, 'What in the name of all the bloody gods are you doing here?'

Winifred stepped into the feeble light cast by the few campfires, tossed back her hood and laid her hand on Arthur's arm.

'You never used to startle so easily. What, are you growing old and tired?'

Irritated, he walked on, thumbs thrusting through his sword belt. Why did he let this damn woman annoy him so? If the gods were ever good enough to allow him to live his life over, he would certainly ensure that this item of baggage was not loaded onto his wagon!

To annoy him further, she threaded her arm through his, ignored his attempt to shake her off. 'Has it occurred to you, Arthur, that it is not I who lie? Why would I have wanted you dead? There is another who may have desired that convenient ending.'

Arthur managed to brush her intimate hold aside. 'Ambrosius?' He snapped, tetchily, 'I do not see him behind murder.'

'Ambrosius?' Winifred scoffed, 'God praise him, he is too pious for such a sin.' Determined she again threaded her arm, walked to match his striding pace, 'I do not talk of him.'

He knew she was stirring mischief, knew he ought give her a few choice words and send her away, under armed escort if need be. Damn her, the question came out! 'Who then?'

Winifred had two voices, one strident and harsh, used more often than anything to get her own way; the other wheedling, drowning in caring innocence, bordering on the sickly sweet. Also used to obtain her way. It was the second she used. 'Are you aware Gwenhwyfar was to marry?'

Arthur had slowed, decided it best to ignore the informal way that she was walking with him. His lips compressed, his left, free hand, going to the pommel of his sword for self reassurance. Walked on. There was much to do before daylight, weapons to have an edge put to them, horses examined for lameness, harness and armour checked for loose stitching, cracked leather, loose joints and buckles. 'Aye, I understand that Amlawdd sniffed around. I would not expect aught else of that web-footed toad.'

She had to lengthen her stride to keep up with him. 'Not Amlawdd, dear-heart, he is but a predictable fool kept deliberately sweet-fed by Ambrosius. 'Tis better to keep a rogue under close eye.' She cocked a knowing eye at her ex-husband. 'As I believe you often did?'

Absently he nodded agreement. Which is why he tolerated her nearness. Better to keep her in clear sight than hidden away. What did she want? Trouble, he was certain. Trouble by stirring clear water into black mud. Winifred excelled at that.

'It is not my place to tattle idle gossip,' she oozed. Arthur snorted, almost laughed outright at her hypocrisy. 'But it is well rumoured that Bedwyr and your wife are not innocent of each other.'

'Gods, you're a bitch!' Arthur halted abruptly, fiercely shook her arm away, faced her, angry.

They were at the end of the row of pitched tents, Winifred had not halted with him, but walked on. She swung left, heading away from the muted darkness of the encampment, returning to the bustle and light of the royal place. Over her shoulder, she tossed, 'That I am. How else would I have survived being the wife of such a bastard?'

§ LXXII

They could, perhaps, withstand a siege for a few days, food was not a problem – they could always eat the horses, although even among the most cynical, this would be considered unlucky, a legacy surviving from pre-Roman paganism. Horses had been valued by those early British tribes, valued and prized, worth as much as gold or any splendid jewel. The concept of not eating horse-flesh had never faltered, standing during four hundred years of Roman belief, and unwavering through the doctrine of Christian values. There was nothing to show that the Christian faith honoured the horse, but British men would not eat one. Unless a great need meant they had to.

Water was the problem. The Ridge Way fortresses were built as intimidating watch-places, designed to mark the ancient track striding from south-west to north-east, not intended to withstand siege. The old tribes, those who had built them, would have had each of the four main strategic forts along this stretch of the Way occupied against inter-tribal raids, not against the massed, amalgamated force of the Saxons. Until Rome came, sieges would have been superfluous, the British warrior would have come out to fight, not remained trapped and cowering behind walls put there for the safe-keeping of women, children, cattle and ponies. Warfare had changed so much since Rome had decided on the taking of might and power by force.

Like the other three, Badon was above the water line. Taking the horses down for daily watering was no difficult task; collection and carrying by leather bucket similarly no more than a part of a day's expected toil. The constructed dew ponds provided enough water for need, but not for an army seeking shelter from Saxons that had swept, so unexpectedly, up the Cuneito Valley, shrouded so cleverly by the heavy woodland, short hours of daylight and murky, low cloud. The forts were there to glower down upon the Way as it marched past the soaring, impressive ramparts. The southern side was vulnerable, and Aelle chose to exploit it.

A second, inconvenient problem. Ambrosius was again unwell. He had fought the returning sickness and diarrhoea off before that first fight, that victory, had swallowed powders and mixtures one end, inserted other such things at the other, to no avail. Even prayer had failed him. When he needed his strength, when he needed to be seen, to enforce courage and endurance, to instil the protection of the Good Lord, all he could do was lay on a bed and wretch into a bowl. When he was not squatting over a chamber pot. Ragnall, may God bless her, was his strength, constant at his bedside, spooning unpleasant-tasting medicines, emptying the results. Ambrosius marvelled that any had ever doubted her sweet nature, her uncomplaining goodness. Like his son, he no longer noticed the puckered scarring, the clumsy limp or twisted fingers. Mind, he was too ill and too preoccupied to notice anything beyond the clamour of derisive shouts and abuse that hurtled from beyond the rampart walls, and the pain in his belly.

The second day. Two, three days more, they could survive, not beyond that. What hope of the messenger getting through to Geraint? Huh! Even if he did, help would not arrive in time. Their only hope was that word had reached Durnovaria of the Saxon advance. That Geraint had realized the implications. And acted.

Cadwy had helped his father – all but carried him from the Hall and up the steps to the walkway. Ambrosius leaned heavily on the boy, sweating profusely, his breathing coming in pained gasps. His belly and bowels were empty, had nothing else to eject, but the feel, the belief, that he must soon visit that stinking latrine persisted. The day was duller than yesterday, the cloud billowing lower. It might rain later. Beyond the palisade and high, grass-topped, chalk-cut ramparts and ditches, the ground sloped down into the crowded swell of woodland that strode too close to the the lower slopes of Badon. 'Why were they not cut back, those trees?' he asked, his accent critical.

His son's answer was brusque. 'Because I have not the manpower to fell so many, nor has there been a need.' Cadwy resented the question. He had tried to keep the creeping scrub tamed, had cleared to one half mile all around the ramparts. Always intending to do more, go further, when he had time.

The Saxons appeared in no hurry to flush them out, were unconcerned at the grey coldness of the day. The current work parties were piling branches, leaves, turf, into the outer ditch, steadily filling it in, a few British spears and arrows found their targets, but the men were mostly under orders to preserve their weaponry. Those arrows that went wide would be gathered, sent back with the next Saxon uprush. The last had endured for most the morning. Not enough of the enemy had fallen, too many of the British lay awaiting burial, when someone found time or thought to order it.

The woods, deeper, denser between the undulating hollows of the hills, were full of Saxon men, some scurrying, busy about given orders, others taking their ease, tending wounds, adding an edge to their weapons, relaxing, playing dice, drinking or eating a meagre meal. Aelle was down there. His spread-winged Raven had been sighted on several occasions during that last assault. No doubt he was discussing the next move, the next tactic. As Ambrosius ought be doing.

But what in the Lord's name was he to do? Several of his officers were shuffling a few yards away, their helmet-straps hanging loose, blood staining here and there, awaiting him. He wished – he snorted at the irony – that Amlawdd was here. For all the man's irritations, he had a sense of bravado and gut feeling for these situations. It had been Amlawdd who had pressed home the victory at Radingas, but it was no good dwelling on what was not. Amlawdd was commanding at Castellum Prima, had precise orders to remain there, whatever happened here at Badon. The small force he held there could do nothing against the hundreds of Saex crowding these slopes, would be needed to hold that fortress when they had finished here . . . Ambrosius groaned aloud.

Cadwy, too, had been dwelling on the fancies of wishing. 'If only those rumours of Arthur had proven true.' Stoically he watched the Saxons finish the filling-in of a few more yards of ditch. They would be across soon. Were it summer-dry, not winter-sodden, the British could have sent fire-arrows down, burned the wood and grass.

His father made no answer, he dared not, for those officers were within hearing, along with too many of the men. But aye, as reluctant as he was to admit it, even to his own thoughts, he would have embraced that rumour were it true.

Ambrosius Aurelianus closed his tired eyes in prayer. He had so wanted to succeed, to lead with pious and clear-sighted wisdom. So wanted things to be like they were in the days of his father and grandfather. Now, would give anything to see the Dragon Banner, and Arthur, come riding out of that valley.

§ LXXIII

They camped overnight beyond Sarum, the Artoriani. The few families farming below its brooding walls welcomed them as if already a battle, a war, had been won. Sarum, the ancient defended place, with its battered ramparts and broken gateways, was proving its use yet again. For the Saex, it seemed, were no more than five and twenty miles north. Cattle, goats and swine were being herded into its protective enclosure, the air reeked of fear and panic. The relief, the immense joy that swept through that small community! 'The Pendragon?' They asked, doubtful, disbelieving, when first the cavalcade of horse and men made stop for the night, 'but is he not gone from us? Is he not dead?' To Arthur, their elation when seeing the truth with their own sight, caused personal embarrassment. So loud were the praises, the cheering, the offerings of food, gifts, wine – best wine – nothing spared, nothing hidden. One landholder, of old Roman stock, offering two of his slave women should the men of the Artoriani need them. Arthur declined the generous-meant offer, with thanks and gratitude. 'You are returned!' they all cried. 'Returned to help us, save us, in this dark hour of approaching death!' The cry taken up, repeated, shouted and gloried.

A thousand, thousand Saex, the chief man had declared in fast, agitated breath, were gathered up towards the Way, laying siege to Ambrosius, trapped, these past two days at Badon.

This was news! News that explained the intense panic! How, Arthur cursed, did Ambrosius manage to get himself besieged? Mithras's blood, the damn fool! The numbers he dismissed as exaggeration. Hoped that he was right to do so. If not, it promised to be one hell of a fight. For all the love of all the gods, he hoped, prayed, he was right!

They slept on the open ground, wrapped beneath their thick-woven, as good as waterproof, cloaks. The tents they had not brought with them, nor pack-ponies. No accoutrements save what was necessary for battle. What could not be carried in a saddle-pack or across the shoulders, was left behind. Each man carried his own weapons, own equipment and enough corn to feed each horse for three days. Arthur needed to move quickly, and at the far end of the journey, quietly. The only exception the young lads, not yet old to enough to join the ranks of fighting men, boys who would in the years ahead be honoured with the title squire. They had their uses, aside from duties of serving, for they rode the spare horses. Wagons, baggage and army whores could follow on at the slower pace with Geraint and the infantry. They had no place with the three hundred Artoriani. An exact figure. Ten turmae, twenty and six to each, with four officers. Being pedantic, three hundred and two. Arthur and Gwenhwyfar.

She slept curled against him, both of them doubly warm beneath shared cloaks. Slept without murmur, as they all did. The march had been an endurance, almost forty miles to Sarum. With as much again to cover on the morrow, now that they had this further information. New plans, new route. They would leave before dawn, swing out along the road heading north for the Dyke that Arthur had built as a tormenting boundary between his land and that claimed by Ambrosius. God's breath! How long ago that seemed! Follow it, then strike up the valley of the Cuneito, marching eastward, to swing around and behind the Saex. Further to ride, longer for Ambrosius to hold out. A risk worth taking, for surely Aelle would be expecting reinforcements from Geraint to come the most direct route, from the south.

Dawn limped in, dark and dismal, replaced by a reluctant, dull, sulking day. At least, everyone said to himself, as they rode up past Ambrosium, it was not raining.

One question Arthur had to ask, before they met with the Saex, before the fighting began. His stomach churned each occasion he thought of it, looming nearer with every mile set behind them. He had to know. They were walking the horses down the Cuneito valley, leading alongside the south bank of the river, resting them. The woodland was thick, quite dense, the surrounding area quiet and unnerving. Arthur had dropped back, was beside Bedwyr; there was no room here for more than two abreast. Gwenhwyfar walked ahead, leading her bay. The men talked in low tones, suppressed by knowing that the Saex might just be wise enough to post scouts this low down, and inhibited by the grey, low cloud; spirited chatter, jesting or singing seemed inappropriate. Gweir's voice was the closest, telling his companion of Gaul. Exaggerating, as all young men do, with such a wondrous story to tell.

'Do you love her?' Arthur managed to keep his voice neutral, as if he were merely asking some minor, military matter.

Bedwyr had no need to ask of whom Arthur spoke. Only a matter of time before the questions were asked. And the answers had to be made. Just as good now as later. He spoke as casually, successfully masking the gallop of his heart-beat. 'I always have. My boyhood fancy never grew from me.' He checked his horse from snatching at a mouthful of grass.

'How much?'

'Enough to know she does not love me in the same way as she loves her husband.'

There was no answer that Arthur could make to that.

They had not argued about her coming, Arthur and Gwenhwyfar, as once, perhaps they would have done. She had sorted her saddle-pack, had the armourer put an edge to her sword and ridden out beside her husband. No glance, no challenge. Arthur accepted the gesture as it was meant. Was grateful for it. Nothing would have induced him to beg her to come; equally, nothing would have prompted him to order her to stay. Leaving the children had been hard – Archfedd had grown so! No longer a babe, but a girl, with fiery eyes and tossing head – ah, so like her Mam must have been at that age! Medraut too, he missed, for he had grown used to the boy's wide-eyed, awed company. They were safe with Enid; given a while to settle, would establish a friendship. Or was that another hope? Archfedd was quite the ferocious bully. Her idea of acquiring a friend, according to one tale Enid had laughingly told, was to hit another child over the head with some implement – a toy doll, a stick, whatever – and make demand that he or she *would* be a friend! It seemed the girl had a thing or two yet to learn about the subtle gaining of allies. Medraut, timid as he was, stood little chance of beating her tyranny.

One of the scouts was returning, the column ahead shuffling aside to let him canter past. He reached the Pendragon, dismounted, fell into step beside Arthur as Bedwyr gave ground to him, gave his report, brief but concise. The column halted. Arthur passed the order to mount up.

Ahead, several people gathered beside the old road, incredulous when they recognized the Dragon. The villa, rambling behind overgrown trees, seemed shabby, its once white-painted walls peeling and mouldering; the gardens were once maintained to the highest standard. Arthur had stayed there for a few days when he had served under Vortigern – when Winifred was his wife, he remembered grimly. Old Phillipi, the owner, had been alive then, a gentle, wise old man. The villa had seen better days then, but with the old master's passing, and a son who preferred to spend what little gold there was on wine and women rather than roses and maintenance, was its sad demise so surprising?

Arthur acknowledged the acclaimed greetings from the small crowd, promised, 'We go fight the Saex! Keep yourselves safe until I ride this way again!'

They were jog-trotting now, to make up time, for already the day was sliding rapidly nearer dusk and darkness. They would press on, as long as they could. Arthur rode beside Gwenhwyfar again. She wore male apparel, bracae, padded under-tunic with a leather, bronze-studded over-tunic. Her hair, bound into a single braid, thick as her wrist, bobbed and bounced against her back as they trotted, hands light on the reins, riding easy, natural.

'I have been told of you and Bedwyr.'

Her eyes remained ahead, looking through the gap between her horse's ears. What to answer? Petty? Spiteful? *As I discovered Morgaine for myself. And Mathild, and . . . how many others?*

The way it was. The only way, the fact of it. 'I was told you were dead. I mourned, I grieved, but I could not remain alone and at the mercy of filth such as Amlawdd.' She turned her head, regarded him, her green, tawny-flecked eyes honest, hiding nothing from him. The meaning was there, plain, in her expression, in those eyes. *Where was my choice?* 'A woman cannot remain alone and unprotected.'

They rode on a while in silence, Arthur mulling over her answer, wanting to ask more intimate questions. How often did you sleep with him? Did you enjoy being with him? Is he better than I am? At last he said. 'Do you regret losing him?'

She softened, the smile touching her cheeks, eyes, her whole face. She stretched out her hand for his. 'If that was so, would I have ridden to Gaul? Would I have spent that long while searching for you?'

Arthur withdrew his hand, curled the fingers around the reins. Feeling the pressure, Onager laid back his ears, raised his head, his tail swished twice. Arthur had to say it. Had to know if what Winifred implied had substance. 'Your intention may have been to ensure my end.'

A lucky guess, intuition, a knowing of how Winifred wove lies and deceptions, made Gwenhwyfar say, 'Na, if *I* had wanted you dead, I would have succeeded.' She held his gaze. Added, after a significant pause, 'I am not Winifred.'

He took her hand again, reprimanded Onager's sullen temper. Arthur's heel clamped into his side, daring the animal to kick.

Behind, Bedwyr had observed the exchange, although the conversation he could not hear. He sighed. It had been so difficult. Losing her, so close to gaining her, so close! His heart, pulled in two equal directions, one for the love he had for Gwenhwyfar, the other for his cousin, Arthur the King. Ah, but Bedwyr had always been philosophical. Gwenhwyfar would never choose the lesser of the two, the boy if she could have the man. She had not wanted him, not for who or what he was, anyway. He had been a means, a useful tool, someone to buffer her against bastards such as Amlawdd, someone to be there in her misery and darkness. He could accept that.

He would never admit that Gwenhwyfar had been, always would be, his only deep, especial love. But then, who needed that when there was sure to be a succulent, fair-haired whore waiting for him, somewhere, sometime. Soon he hoped, for he knew he lied to himself.

§ LXXIV

Over-confidence! Arthur was grinning like a moon-mad boy, jubilation spreading through the men as word passed along the column. Gweir, returned from scouting ahead, sat his horse with a matched expression. He could not have brought better news to his weary and apprehensive companions.

'So,' Arthur declared, 'Vicus is straddled with the drunk and the whoring, is it? Hah!' His bark of delight rippled through the overhanging canopy of winter-bare trees as he twisted in the saddle to speak direct to his men, their pleasure at this unexpected turn of events as evident as his. 'A fine rearguard that bastard pair Aelle and Aesc have left us to deal with! Mithras, I was hoping for a real fight!' They took up his laughter, heeled their horses forward as he signalled to ride on, Gweir bringing his dun alongside Onager – at a respectful distance.

He was a good scout, Gweir. He claimed the ability to move fast and undetected came from his deprived years of childhood. Too often, he would laugh, he had to fend for himself out in those wild lands up beyond the Wall. Keeping your head down from grey wolves or Saex wolves – the one was much like the other. Clinging to the camouflaging trees that encroached beside the old road, Gweir, to his surprise but relief, had found no Saxon outposts, no set watch or guard. Could not believe his fortune when, crawling on knees and belly through the untended, uncut tangle of low shrub and grasses, he reached the small town of Vicus. He had heard the singing, the occasional woman's scream, much laughter and merrymaking. Needed only to see the huddle of guards at the gate swilling wine from a passed-around wineskin to be sure. He had waited, all the same, watching from his safe place of hiding, seen them slump, drunk, fall sodden to the world, against the outer wall, leaving the gate way open, unguarded. No one had come to reprimand them, to replace them, haul them away. Easy to conclude there was no one sober enough.

Would that be maintained, Arthur wondered, mulling over the lad's report. A chance worth the taking. Some things needed quick decisions, others detailed planning. Arthur – and several of the men with him – knew Vicus well, knew its street layout and gateways. The defendable places, the insecure. A half-hour's ride, less, if they pushed the horses on at a pace faster than the jog-trot so far employed. They were warm, the animals, neck and flanks perhaps showing more sweat than he would have liked, but then, this was winter. Even Onager, and those like him with the Arabian breeding, had thicker, denser coats. Their breathing was easy, however, energy unsapped.

Arthur's stomach was churning at the anticipation of a fight, mixed emotions of plunging fear and the rising excitement. He glanced at Gwenhwyfar, who lifted her head, gestured her thought by touching the sword at her hip.

'Cut off the rear, and it will be an easy gallop up to Badon.' She almost purred at the prospect.

As her husband, Arthur ought soon suggest that she fall back, seek safety with the boys and spare horses. He *ought* to have insisted that she never left Durnovaria. But then, Arthur never had been a man for doing as others thought he ought do. He nodded at her. Aye, his thoughts exactly. 'You will fight with us?' Only a slight hesitancy, a slight doubting as he asked it.

'Would you prefer,' she answered, cat-eyed, blank expression, 'that I had stayed to keep Winifred company at Durnovaria. Joined with her in her fast?'

He replied with a matching, teasing, solemnity. 'If I could ensure an end to the Saxon uprising by letting nothing but sips of water past my lips for the next few days, I would have stayed with her myself!'

Gwenhwyfar laughed merrily. 'What? You? Fast?' The gurgle increased. 'Has that shield you carry gone to your head?'

Grimacing, Arthur swivelled his eyes over his shoulder, tipped the oval shield to an angle, wrinkling his nostrils in disgust at the design painted on its toughened leather skin. The Chi Rho. All shields were painted so, Ambrosius's first task on learning that the Pendragon was no more, to replace the Red Dragon with the symbol of God. Arthur had no other shield, had accepted this one with no time to have it altered.

'With the Dragon on my banner and this Christian symbol on my shield, I assume I am covered from both directions.' He raised his hand, gave the signal to move out.

§ LXXV

That feeling of being alive but facing death, the sensation of the heart pumping, sweat glistening. The pull of aching muscles, the bite of a blade into thigh or arm. God's love, but it was wonderful!

It was over all too soon and, on reflection, when Arthur, breathing hard, squatted his backside onto the winter-damp steps of Vicus's shabby, timber-built Basilica, nothing more than a slaughter of the unsuspecting and drunk by the experienced. Most of them, the Saxons, had been old men, the unfit, the wounded, those left behind to keep the road open for a safe retreat, should – Woden prevent it – Aelle need to withdraw. The inactive waiting, poor command and that element of over-confidence contributing to this, a minor, easily accomplished victory. Aelle had obviously not expected the British to come this far eastward. Most certainly did not expect the Pendragon.

Arthur marvelled that he had so easily forgotten the exhilaration of the enjoined fight. That surge of elated power created by a war-horse in full gallop, mane flying, ears back. The sheer pleasure of feeling so alive while death danced so close. Na, he had not forgotten; perhaps had thrust it away to the furthest depth of his mind because he had not wanted to remember. Some things were best forgot, and even though his men were jubilant, excited, proud of this success, he still asked whether he was suited to lead them. He had failed once, he could fail again. The next battle he led those good, proud, unquestioning men into could so well be their last.

Gwenhwyfar sauntered along the main Via Prima, wiping her sword with a torn shred of a Saxon's cloak. Her face was grimed with sweat and dirt, spotted with blood specks. She positioned herself next to her husband, finished wiping blood off the blade. Flushed, eyes bright-sparkling, her hair, never controlled at the best of times, bursting in exuberant wisps from its restricting braid. 'That was good,' she said, as if she were speaking of nothing more simpler than an afternoon stroll.

'Mm,' Arthur answered.

She sheathed the sword, propped her elbows on her knees, rested her chin on the knuckles. 'Only "mm"?' she queried, slipping a sidelong glance.

The men were clearing up, helping their wounded, reverently lifting their few dead – three only, incredibly only three! Occasionally, one would glance up, see Arthur watching and raise an arm or hand in victorious salute. Ah! It was so good to be riding under the banner of the Dragon again! Riding with Arthur, the Pendragon! The Saxons they were tossing into a pile beyond the gateway, no time or want to bury them. Arthur had given orders for their burning, come dark when the smoke would not be seen climbing into the sky. The Saex wounded were finished quickly and dispassionately by a knife to the throat. Men of the Artoriani disliked torture where it was not necessary, had not the resource of enough men to leave guard over any suitable for slavery.

'The gods alone know how I managed to ride through that gate,' Arthur confessed to his wife, staring ahead, embarrassed to say aloud the truth, though he knew she understood it. 'Once into that charge, there was no choice, but—' He cast a swift, guilty squint at her expression, which remained impassive. 'But by the bull, before that I was trembling like a rain-sodden cur in a thunderstorm!'

The tactics had been to ride quietly, as near as possible to Vicus, under the sheltering cover of dense trees; then spring into a gallop, burst through those still-unclosed, unguarded, gates and create havoc. The plan worked as if it had been no more than a predictable child's game using toy pieces. And only three British dead!

Arthur held his fingers of his right hand out before him. Steady, controlled. 'I almost dropped my sword twice, and Mithras alone knows where the first spear I cast ended up. Certainly not in its target!' He was beginning to relax, the tightness in his body easing, leaving him. A hint of laughter was gathering behind the recounting, not yet ready to come out, but there, hovering, waiting its moment.

Sensing it, Gwenhwyfar uttered a swift, silent, thank you. She, perhaps alone above anyone, had realized and understood the great fear that had clawed mercilessly at Arthur's gut. To fight, to face battle, took courage and endurance. Arthur had plenty and more of both, but he had also seen the horror of defeat and failure – as on occasion they all had, but he had gone away after it, taken by a woman who wanted nothing of death and fighting. He had not even had his sword to touch or to cherish, to remind him of other, better endings. It was best not to allow that tick of doubt to rise, to grow, like yeast in bread. For a nerve broken was a nerve difficult – occasionally impossible – to mend.

They all had fear, any man, be he British, Saxon or Roman, felt the spectre of trepidation while waiting for battle to begin; all knew the dread that sank into the stomach like a weighted stone. Knew how it would vanish like mist under a rising sun when the bloodlust began to flow, when the battle-cry was bayed and taken up; when the thing was entered. Arthur's fear would be harder to conquer, and this small skirmish was nothing to prove that it had been exorcized. To rebuild self-pride and confidence took more than the slaying of a few unwary drunkards, more than just remounting a horse and sitting there while it stood, cropping grass. The hurdle need be faced and jumped again. And again. The dawn of his coming through was there, though, the darkness not quite as black, as cloying and smothering.

'So what now?' she asked. She had not talked with him about the fear. It was something for him alone to face and to conquer. Instead, she was here, beside him, with him. Her horse had galloped next to Onager, her sword slashing beside his as, dismounted once inside that gate, they had advanced through the mud-slurried, dejected streets of Vicus. She covering his left, he, her right. Aye, the rest of the Artoriani had been there also, but what mattered was that she was there, her presence, with her loyalty and love, there.

'Now?' he repeated, pushing himself to his feet. Gods, but he ached! 'Now we feed the horses and ourselves and, come dusk, we ride like souls fleeing hell along the road to Badon.' He took Gwenhwyfar's hand, hauled her to her feet, caught a brief flickered flare of her nostrils, a grimace. Instant concerned, alarmed, he raked his eyes over her, searching for a wound, an injury.

'I'm well,' she reassured, patting her palm onto his chest. 'You, however!' She leaned back from him, appraising as he had, 'You are filthy and you stink!'

The light came into Arthur's face as brilliantly as the summer sun casts its magnificence into the new-born day. His head tossed back, the barked guffaw drawing attention from several of his men. He clamped his hands to Gwenhwyfar's shoulders, and smacked a resounding, firm, loving, kiss to her lips.

'So, my dear Cymraes, do you!'

§ LXXVI

Three or so hours it took them to ride from Vicus along the Via Ermin to Badon. A ride completed in near silence and beneath the shrouding mantle of midnight darkness. No moon would rise, no soft glow of star could penetrate the thick mass of rain-building cloud that pressed close over the earth, like a lid above a box. They rode the fifteen miles at the walk, any metal item that could clatter or jangle muffled: weapons, buckles, harness. Hooves were bound with rags, leather slips secured around the muzzles of war-dogs and horses to ensure no bark or whinny could betray their presence. The wind came from the west, blew in their faces, scudding their cloaks behind them like wings spread from some soaring bird. The eagle king, come to claim his land.

Of course, one of the Saex could have made it away, one among the English might have not been so inebriated as the others. Or it was always possible that a messenger had been sent back from Aelle and the army ahead, laying arrogant siege to the British fortress. Anything could have alerted the Saex of the Artoriani. Even instinct, that gut feeling that a good leader has; the knack of knowing. As Arthur *knew* that Aelle was ignorant of his coming.

Leaving the easier route of the road, they dismounted, led the horses, cut across country, boots squelching in the many pocketed muddied hollows, cursing silently as they thrust a way through tangled thorn and unyielding scrub, slowing the pace more, and taking care. So much care. They could have taken the smaller, narrower, and easier to travel road that would run, straight as an arrow, up to the fortress. But that way was easily watched, and they would be vulnerable on foot; easily seen, mounted.

They began to climb, the flickering, smoke-shifting, pale glow of many camp-fires leading them on; the Saxons, half of one mile ahead, strung out in scattered copses of tents clustered around tended hearth-fires. Some would be sleeping, others nursing weapons, talking quietly to ward away the tedium of a long, quiet, night-watch. Ha! Well, things would not be so quiet or monotonous soon enough!

So Gweir and the two others sent ahead with him, had reported. They had watched since dusk, secreted against the browns and greens of earth and grass, observed the Saxons, taunting the British entombed behind

342

the high rampart walls, held their breath as a foray to try again at the secured gates was beaten down. But at even their safe distance, Gweir could see the British were suffering, their defence edged with a lack of resilience that was rapidly crumbling towards the inevitable. Would Ambrosius be tempted to surrender soon? It depended on how many men he had already lost, how many could continue. And on Arthur bringing up the Artoriani without sign or sound.

Gweir sent a boy back, riding on one of the swift Arabian breeds that ate the ground beneath the hooves as hungrily as a starving beggar devoured fresh-baked bread. The English were unaware that they had been observed, were unaware of the Pendragon's closeness. One group, set to keep eye to where the steep slope fell into the flat spread of land, were unknowing that Gweir and his companions were close enough to hear their muttered conversation, smell their wine-tainted breath, even. They, the three Englishmen, watched the sky now, their blank eyes staring up at the blackness, waiting for a sunrise that they would never see.

One hour before dawn, when men drowsed at their most languid and when senses drifted with the slow turn of the night, the litter of hearth-fires with their bundled accompanying sleepers had died to glowing embers, the muttered conversations, muted laughter shrinking as more men rolled into their cloaks or sought the shelter of rough-pitched hide tents. One hour before dawn.

Ambrosius stood, awake, unwell, unable to find the comfort of sleep, staring into the blackness of that night. The land curved darker beneath a lighter sky. It fell away steeply on this side from the well-protected watch-tower, while on the other side of the fortress the dips and undulations rolled from the high ground, vulnerable, down to meet the spread of woods and pastures. He knew how many Saex were dreaming of battle-glory around the red glows of so many fires. Knew where Aelle and Aesc had erected their swaggering tents among the encircling army. They even had whores down there, those heathen Englishwomen among the men, so sure were they of their position, of the outcome. Ambrosius turned his head to the south. Bedwyr would not have come, not even to Badon. But Geraint, why had he not come? Again, as he had done so often these past many hours, Ambrosius asked his God why help had not arrived.

'Am I to end here then, Lord, so despicably? Is this to be my punishment for the sin of pride?' He bowed his head, had to accept the Lord's will but, Christ in his mercy, that acceptance was so hard to achieve!

A light, chill rain began to drizzle, not enough to bring the water they so needed; would even a good rainfall be enough? . . . No, not now, it was too late. Everything was too late. All he ought have done, those he ought have listened to, heeded!

The sounds came as if the wind were rising, swaying through the trees, a nondescript, shush of sound, gathering momentum, swelling, growing as the daylight drifts unnoticed at first from darkness into pale dawn. Movement, a soft uprush of shadows darting, light flickering, voices, low and unnoticed. Ambrosius watched, gazing intently at the camp spread in a pocked mêlée against the night-dark land. He frowned, concentrated his sight into one area. What was that? What . . .? Lord God in all His greatness!

Ambrosius leapt down the stairway, running, his heaving belly quite forgotten. The watch-guard, weary, several wounded, turned, puzzled, to watch him, whispering between themselves. He was shouting, raising the fortress, calling for the officers. Men came running, many half-dressed, scrabbling into boots and tunics, buckling on armour and helmets, carrying spears, swords, bleary-eyed from sleep. Were they under attack? From what quarter? Where?

Excited, speech gabbling from his panting breath, Ambrosius could only point, indicate, beyond the walls. Cadwy was there, limp-hobbling, shoving his way through the confused crowd.

'Father, what is it? What is happening?' He set his hands to the older man's shoulders, almost shook him in his urgency to know what was wrong, anxiously surveyed the men already running into positions of defence along the rampart walkways. There came no sound from beyond, none of the usual baying and howling of attack, no torrent of abuse, hurl of flame-lit arrow or wind-swishing spear. If they were under attack, where was the noise, the bestial clamour for blood? He made out one or two words from his wheezing, coughing father, heard them but did not understand. 'Attack?' he repeated. 'The Saex are under attack?' He sounded as if he were addressing his young son, querying some infant's imaginative story. 'Attack?' he said again. Ambrosius, wiping at the spittle on his chin, nodded vigorously, waved his son to go see for himself.

Cadwy needed no second urging. Ragnall had come from their chamber, her hair loose, unbound, a thick cloak tossed around her night apparel, the darkness shrouding the disfigurement of her face that so few people, save for strangers, noticed now. She called for a cloak to cover Ambrosius, placed her arm around him, led him to the warmth of within-doors. The man was shivering, his teeth chattering, eyes bright with what could well be a new fever setting in. Delirium? She glanced at her husband, but he was already away, his crutch moving wildly as he thrust his way to the stairway and the ramparts, officers and men crowding with him.

The cheer boomed through even the thick, oak-solid walls of the Hall. An exultant ululation of rejoicing, of freedom, of new-given life. Ambrosius smiled, swallowed another of the spoonfuls of warm broth Ragnall was offering him. 'The Saex,' he said, eyes twinkling, finger raised, 'are all in panic. Someone scatters them with blade and fire.'

'Who?' Ragnall asked, as the cheering of Badon's small population, gathering to see what was happening below in the darkness, swelled in voice and joy. 'Who comes?'

'Geraint?' Ambrosius ventured. 'It could be Geraint.'

Ragnall was squatting on her heels before him, the bowl in her hand, the spoon forgotten, tipping, dripping broth. She met her father-by-law's excited eyes, matched them with her own eagerness. 'Or Arthur,' she ventured, in almost a whisper, as if to say the name aloud would chase this avenging spirit away. 'Could it be Arthur?'

Ambrosius touched her hand with one finger. 'I hope so, my child, in the name of our God, I do hope so!'

The horses came in at the gallop, bringing the corpses of the watch, some still kicking the last of their life-thread as they were dragged like meat skewered on the spit. Some riders wielded sword or club, others carried fat-spitting torches that were tossed inside the openings of tents. The hearth-fires, and the sleepers curled beside them, were deliberately trampled. Difficult for a war-horse, trained not to tread on a body laying on the ground, but obey they did, for Arthur's horses had always been as disciplined as the men when it came to battle. Fire, too, held no fear for these brave-hearted creatures, nothing could stop one of the Artoriani war-horses, save for its rider's hand on the rein or a spear clear through the heart or jugular.

The screams, the panic flared and grew along with that rising blaze of fire. Unprepared, swilled with wine and mead, satiated from the comfort of a warm whore and the belief that the fortress would be theirs come the morrow, the English barely fought back. Those camped nearer the rampart walls stood greater chance, for the alert had given them time to arm themselves, to form rank, to fight back. Aelle stood within his shield ring of thegns, bellowing orders, calling to his sons who fought their way to join him. What had happened to Aesc of the Cantii he knew not, nor had he time to ponder long on the matter; he was fighting for his very life, or already gone to join the gods. Either way, there was little, at this moment, that Aelle, Bretwalda, Lord of all the Saxon kind, could do about it.

Dawn brewed, reluctant to face the dull, persistent drizzle, the bleaching light casting over what had been not two hours before, a besieging camp-place. The coming of light showed tents ripped or fallen, many smouldering, with bodies scattered around. Men huddled, weeping, dying. Blood, dismembered limbs. The horror of carnage.

It was not over. The cavalry, the riders, were beating the Saxons back, but the English had made formation now, a solid wedge, impregnable, determined to survive. It was the Pendragon, the British could see that now, from the vantage-point of the high ramparts, they could see the Dragon Banner as it dipped and swayed. Several times, men would point and shout, 'There! There he is, on that brute of a chestnut!'

'Arthur. Arthur has returned to save us!'

When he was certain with his own eyes that it was indeed the Pendragon, Cadwy had the gates ready to be thrown open and formed the men, those still able to fight – and God's praise, there were many of them, some bandaged, some limping, one with his face half-torn and hacked from an unlucky stopped arrow, another without a hand, one without an eye – serious, hard-borne woundings, but still they came to form up into line, still they wanted to be a part of this glorious thing that was happening. It was, surely, to be a battle that would be sung about to the children of their children's children, and they did not want their sons telling that the father lay doing nothing save nursing a bloodied wound in the Hall of Badon while the Pendragon rode to victory outside.

The gates swung open and the men marched out, clamouring the battle-cry to add their weight to Arthur's men, Arthur's three hundred men, who had, in that one, astounding, triumphant charge, slaughtered more than nine hundred of the English.

§ LXXVII

Aelle and four, five hundred of his men stood firm, their wedge formation as solid as the trunk of a mature oak, back-pacing steadily, foot by foot, giving ground to the Artoriani, but not giving men or lives. Then there a came a disturbance from the rear, men were pouring from the fortress, cheering, spears and swords raised, come to join their comrades – but met by Aesc of the Cantii instead!

Somehow, later, he said by the protection of Woden himself, Aesc had fought his way clear of the British, managed to scramble around, attempted to link with Aelle. They saw the fortress gates open, unprotected, and changed direction and tactic as easily as a hawk pulls from a dive. Aesc drove hard for the fortress, fought like a man crazed to win his way in, and almost managed it.

The fighting at the gates was furious, bloody, and soon over; but Arthur had to call some of his men away, ride hard to intercept and deal with it, and once his own formation was distorted, it gave chance for Aelle to break and run.

The Saxons headed for the easy path of the road, intending to head to the Via Ermin, then swing east for the relative safety of Vicus, that they called Wickham, the Roman settlement.

Arthur cursed as he felled a fair-haired brute coming at him open-mouthed, screaming abuse and baying for blood. A bay horse was beside him, rearing, blood gushed from the man's crushed skull as he came down, Gwenhwyfar's sword finishing what the hooves had not completed. She had kept close to Arthur throughout, her horse Onager's shadow, fighting alongside him, blow for blow; his Cymraes as he affectionately called her, a tribeswoman of the British. Her father had taught her how to fight, how to use sword and shield or spear, her father and her brothers, some of whom were now dead and passed to the Otherworld, the kingdom of God's heaven.

That slow ride through the darkness, and then the waiting for all the muffles and rags to be removed – how Arthur's heart had pounded, how his stomach had churned with the vomit of fear! This was to be a battle. No skirmish, no pandering bickering. Close on two thousand Saxons were laying siege to the fortress of Badon. He had a few less than the three hundred, given the dead and wounded and those left behind to patrol Vicus.

Gwenhwyfar must have known his thoughts, must have held some sharing of his apprehension, for she had spoken, her voice no more than a whisper in the concealing darkness. 'They may be many more than us, but we have the night and surprise as our allies. And we have the horses.' Aye, the horses. Unless they made firm, rock-steady formation, few infantry could survive against well-ridden, well-managed horse.

Almost, just as he had been about to give the arm signal to move forward, Arthur had nearly turned, nearly rode away. The fear had risen up within him, choking his breathing, clutching his throat, screwing his belly into a heated knot of twisting pain. He had pulled the rein, urged with his heel, had swung Onager's head, but he had turned in Gwenhwyfar's direction and she had saluted him, touching the hilt of her sword against her forehead. She could not be seen clearly in the darkness, but he had known how she looked.

Her cloak was green plaid, the different greens of the natural world woven together in the traditional patterns: light, spring green against the

347

darker, mature colour of summer, the mellow of autumn and the sleeping green of winter. Green to heighten her eyes, show the copper-gold of her hair. At her throat, she wore the golden torque of her royal rank, and on her left hand, his ring, the ring he had given her as a marriage gift. Nothing else adorned her leather tunic, save for the gleaming bronze of buckles and the silvered pommel of her sword. Her reassuring smile and her apparent calm had stopped him from fleeing, had rekindled the courage that had began to warm in him at Vicus. He had raised his arm, and they had moved forward. From walk into jog-trot, pushing immediate into a canter – and the release into gallop.

Aesc, they did not kill. They did not treat him kindly, but he was spared death. At least for now, until the Pendragon could decide what punishment to mete him.

Aelle, the Bretwalda, was running, although he would not go far. The road to Vicus was closed to him, he could only head into the woods, where the dogs would sniff him out, or along the Way, where the horses would ride over him.

It was to last throughout the day before it was ended, a day of harrying and following, of moving in, encircling, attempting to thrust into the wedge that Aelle's men formed so hastily whenever the horses came too close, a day from before dawn to after sunset of determination, sweat and exhausting energy. A day that had followed two of fast riding and another fight a few miles down, along the road.

There was another skirmish beneath the place where the white horse galloped in her endless race against the wind. Fatigued, despairing, unable to go much further, Aelle ordered his men to make a stand. They would fight, kill as many of these British as they could before meeting Woden themselves. It would be a brave death, an honourable death for his fine men.

Many died at that place, more of the English than the mounted, elated British, but it was a fight of honour, and the men were buried with their weapons in one grave to mark the respect that each side felt for the other.

When Arthur and his queen returned to Badon, with Aelle led like a dog by a chain around his neck, stripped naked, with leather thongs twisting tight into his wrists, Ambrosius greeted them beyond the gates that had been cleared of the dead, the dying and the wounded. Nothing could be done to clear or hide the ground that was churned and scraped. The blood still puddled in the ruts, spattered against the stonework of the arch, the solid wood of the gate. The smell lingered too, the smell of blood and death and grieving.

Ambrosius stood, head erect, proud. Arthur rode Onager forward, dismounted, went to greet his uncle, unsure what to expect, uncertain what to say. Ambrosius talked for him.

'It is with regret that I cannot return your kingdom to you as it was when you left it, but I can at least let my heart rest that it is indeed returned to you, and not delivered up to a Saxon.'

'I thank you, uncle, for taking care of my people and my land while I have been gone.' Arthur reached forward his hand in offering of peace. Grateful, with relief, Ambrosius took it. He had expected a sword to bring his justified end, a torrent of curses and reprimands; had not expected this, Arthur's forgiveness.

As they shook hands in greeting, Arthur noticed something glint at his feet. He frowned, bent, picked up a brooch, saucer-shaped with a mask of eyes and mouth indented on it. The Saxon brooch of rebellion.

He looked at it a moment then leant forward and pinned it to Ambrosius's shoulder. 'Wear it,' he said, 'to remind you always of this day, and' – Arthur quietly indicated the graves being dug on the slope below the ramparts – 'of who was lost.' He sighed. He was tired, every muscle in his body ached, every nerve-ending was screeching to be eased or scratched or bathed. He itched, he stank, his belly needed filling, his bladder emptying.

Gwenhwyfar came up beside him. Ambrosius caught his breath at sight of her, as begrimed, as bloodied as her husband. He stammered a greeting, added, speaking of Arthur, 'You found him then?'

Gwenhwyfar nodded.

Ambrosius allowed a small, weary smile. 'I am glad. Perhaps now I can see to the running of my monastery and my school. My work is with the kingdom of God, I think, not the kingdom of man.' With his eye he sought dismissal. Arthur gave it. 'Go in peace, nephew,' Ambrosius said, making the sign of the cross. 'Go in the peace of God.'

'Peace?' Arthur echoed. 'How long will peace last? There is another Saxon yet we may need to face.'

Ambrosius's eyebrows lifted.

'Cerdic,' Arthur answered. 'My son Cerdic.'

'Ah,' Ambrosius mused. 'Cerdic.'

The burying was begun. The Saxons they took to the byre that would burn and send souls to Woden, the British they lay in Christian graves, clustered beneath the ramparts of Badon. In one of them lay Cadwy, who had tried to fight so valiantly to keep the Saxons from entering his fortress, the fortress he held in the name of Gwenhwyfar, wife to the Pendragon.

PART THREE

The Remnant

March 476

The ship's prow nosed into the reeds, carried forward by the heavy roll of the incoming tide, the flurry of movement rippling through the stems, whispering, as if unseen fingers were stroking a harp's finely tuned strings. A moorhen paddled away from the wooden keel that loomed dark and high, her scolding at this sudden intrusion vociferous in the empty stillness of the early morning.

Cerdic was the first to leap ashore. Leaping the gunwale, he plunged into the knee-high water, thrust his way to the firmness of land, head back, arms wide, exultant, triumphant. He had brought his ships across the sea to this isolated British inlet that was his mother's held land, would soon be his own. Four other keels jostled their formidable way into the reeds, disgorging men who hauled at the mooring ropes, their voices loud against the quiet of the murmuring breeze and the flurry of anxious bird-calls. The women and their children came after them, hesitant and uncertain in this unknown place that was, from now forward, to be their home.

Drawing his Saex, the short sword of the Saxons, from its sheath, Cerdic held the weapon before him, its blade glinting in the bright sun of this, the first day of the Roman month of Mars. The month dedicated to their god of war. More significant to Cerdic and those first few men wading up out of the reed-lapping, incoming tide, this was their own special day of the calendar week. Woden's day. Cerdic held the weapon by the polished wood of the rounded pommel, held it high above his head, and called upon his god, his creator, his ancestor, to grant his blessing and favour.

'Woden!' he cried. 'Hear me, hear your son, Cerdic!' The men and women, jostling their children before them or holding the younger ones in their arms, straddling their hips, gathered behind their lord, almost two hundred people in all. Some of the men also drew their swords, others held high their spears or shields. The boy was brought forward, to stand beside his father. He would see his sixth birthing-day this year, too young to be at the forefront, assisting with the business of the gods, but this was to be their land now, and one day Cynric would be their leader.

He must be here for this, their coming, the names of father and son linked together in the tales that would be woven around this day.

'Be with us,' Cerdic called to the sky, aware that they all watched, attentive and expectant. 'Woden! Give us courage and endurance to make what we will of this land. Grant us aid to build our homes and plant our crops, let our women bear us sons, give us daughters who will bring us the union of husbands and allies!'

A cheer soared behind him as the men and women proclaimed their approval and echoed his prayer. They had elected to come with Cerdic, these few, abandoning what remained of their old home along the Elbe, to start again. A new life, a new beginning.

Cynric was proud of his father, excited at this great adventure. The sea-crossing he had not liked, for his stomach had heaved as much as the roll of the waves, but now that they were ashore and the motion of the craft was leaving his legs, he was again starting to enjoy himself. Although he understood little of what was happening. Someone had fetched the white kid from one of the ships, set it down before Cerdic. Cynric watched, interested. His father had taught him the importance of sacrifice.

'Woden!' Cerdic cried again, 'And Thunor! As this blood spills on this ground before me, then so shall the blood of any who dare oppose me spill!' He lowered the sword and drew its sharpness quickly through the bleating kid's throat. The red blood streamed, puddling in the dew-sparkling grass, the animal's legs kicked, its eyes rolled into the blankness of death. He slit the belly open, lifted out the guts and entrails, the steam and stench rising together into the sea-tanged air, the gulls, whirling overhead, crying and swooping, already sensing an unexpected meal. No twisted growths or black evilness there! Cerdic turned to the men, those behind the first row craning and peering to inspect the offal. 'The portents are good!' he cried, letting the mess slide through his fingers to lay beside the blood-soaked carcass. Cynric wrinkled his nose, took a half-step backwards from the foul-smelling, slimy stuff.

'Woden!' His father raised his voice, tipped his face up to the spring-blue morning sky, 'Woden, be with us!' They cheered, and raised their voices to the skies, setting the waders and shorebirds wheeling and calling in alarm.

Then they set about bringing one of the ships up from riding the shallows, left it beached, forlorn and desolate, lying on the tall reed-grass, a ship so graceful and beautiful when on the sea, clumsy and inelegant on land. They stripped it of all that would be of use; the oars and sail fashioned into makeshift tents to provide shelter, the wooden benches, the water barrels, ropes; all they left was the hull and the single mast.

354

Cerdicesora, they agreed to call the place, this lonely stretch of coastal marshland along the southern coast of Britain. Some, a few, went off to hunt duck and to catch fish, the children sent to gather fuel for the fires. Most of the men set to felling the trees, for the strong barrier of a palisade fence would need be erected before nightfall. If the British came to drive them away, then they would fight, but the women and children, the goats, sheep, cattle and pigs that they had brought across the sea would need protection. If the British let them alone, then so be it. They had come in peace to their new home. At least a peace that would last a while and a while. A handful of men, some young, some old, could not yet take on the might of the Pendragon.

As evening fell, the mead jars were passed around, and Cynric sat beside his father, sharing the pleasure and euphoria. Ja, it had been a good day! Dusk descended with the delicate, twilight shading of a clear-skied spring evening. The stars beginning to murmur their presence, subduing the day into what would be a frosted night.

It was then that they burnt the ship, the one they had heaved up onto the land. An offering to the gods. Tomorrow, they would clear more trees, begin the permanent building of their settlement, but this day, their first, was the most important, this day of their coming, and it needed something special, something ultimate to mark its ending. They stood in silence as they watched it burn, watched the flames wander at first, then run and twist into leaping, engulfing spasms that roared and cracked and shouted. The screaming and pleading of the four women slaves, brought from their old home for this purpose, had ceased with the uprush of fire and dark smoke. With pleasure and pride, Cerdic's people gave the craft to their gods.

Never again would they see what was left of the trading settlement on the Elbe river. Many had wandered away soon after Mathild's passing, those who had resented Cerdic's coming, disliked his taking of authority; then, for three years in succession the floods had destroyed their homes, washed away the new-sown seeds or sprouting corn. Men had drowned with their families; cattle, goats and sheep were lost to the rapid spew of water that had engulfed the banks and swamped the low-lying land. The water-bloated bodies and the stink of mud! And then last year, after the floods had receded, the Franks had come raiding for what little was left.

They could fight, but for what? For sodden timbers? Drowned pastures, shattered keels, and abandoned hopes? Na, better to try for something worth the taking. And Cerdic could offer that. There was land that ought be his, land that boasted fertile fields and hoarded riches of gold and precious jewels. Let the Franks overrun the mudflats of the Elbe! Cerdic could offer a better place to the Saxons. Britain.

They stood in silence and watched as their craft was taken by the gods. With the guidance of Woden's hand, they would build for themselves new homes, farm new pastures, establish new trade.

Or die fighting for it, and have for themselves a grave of British earth.

§ II

Winifred was roused from deep sleep by her anxious maidservant, leaning over the bed, shaking at her arm. She carried a lamp which flickered, highlighting the pale fear on her features, was dressed in undershift, her hair loose and night-tangled.

'My lady!' Her voice came trembling, quick. 'We are all to die!'

Impatient, irritated, Winifred shrugged the girl's arm from her, rose from the bed, flung a cloak across her shoulders. 'What is it? What ails you?' She glanced beyond the partially open door. 'Jesu's love, it is still night-dark outside!'

The girl stammered a few words, not making sense, something about men, pirates, inside the gates. A second time Winifred glanced out the door. Her private quarters gave direct view onto a little courtyard beside the abbey of Venta Bulgarium, a building that had taken much gold to construct, much effort to plan and enhance. Worth it all, for Winifred's Holy Place of Venta was known as the most magnificent in Britain; three storeys high, built of stone and roofed with tiles – this was no wood-and-thatch hut, but a building of substance, of worth and value.

'Nonsense, child!' Winifred was about to turn back for her bed, had her hands to the cloak to remove it. The door crashed open, bringing a chill of night air and a blaze of light as two men marched through, carrying flaring torches which they set into the wall brackets. Broad-chested, fair-haired, leather-armoured Saxon men. And behind them, a third.

'Hello, Mother.' Cerdic walked in, arrogantly selected the only chair, seated himself. The girl attempted to duck past, to run from the room, but one of the Saxons caught her, held her to him, impervious to her wriggling and kicking, attempted to fasten his mouth over hers.

'Cerdic!' Winifred's breathing had quickened with her surprise and a flutter of alarm. Her hand was on the cloak, gathering it tighter. Cerdic? Here? The questions coming into mind with an immediate third. Why?

He was one and twenty years, not as tall as his father, but wider-built, more deep-chested. Arthur had never carried bulk or any hint of running to fat. Cerdic already had the makings of what would become a flabby, belly paunch in later years. He wore his hair – much darker than his companions – in the Saxon way, loose, its slight curl touching the padded tunic that covered the broadness of his shoulders. Above his lip, a moustache descended into a full-bushed beard, the skin behind, wind-weathered, the eyes narrow, crinkled. His clothing was expensive. The tunic, set beneath lavish, iron-ringed, leather armour, was of a rich, verdant green, edged with three rows of gold embroidery. Softened leather bracae, fine-made laced boots. The clasp of his darker green, woollen cloak, fur-trimmed, winked the merit of its own decoration of rubies and emeralds. A sword dangled from a baldric fastened with a buckle of jewel-crusted gold, and a fine-made warrior's axe, rested through his belt.

Winifred's heartbeat was racing, her throat had dried, constricted. God's breath, Cerdic, come here! Why? For what reason? She mastered the pounding fear, a technique she had learned so early on in her life. Fear made others despise you, fear was a weakness. Fear was not a permissible emotion, must, at all cost, be controlled. Dear God, Cerdic!

Dignified, she seated herself on a stool. 'There is a story Jesu told about a prodigal son. Have you returned to me, then, or are you come to finish your father?' There, control. Be the first to call the challenge.

Lazily, Cerdic stretched his legs before him, motioned for the second man to fetch him wine. The oaf, for that was the only description Winifred could find for this Saxon, ambled to a side table, poured wine from the flagon for Cerdic and himself. Ignored the other man, whose hands and attention were full with the handmaid. The delicate blue-glass goblet was absurdly incongruous in his paw-sized hand. Nothing was offered to Winifred.

'I have come,' Cerdic answered, drawled, sipping at the wine, 'to accept the land that you intend to give me.' He smiled, a malicious, gloating expression. He had the satisfaction of seeing his mother's stiff tension, that flicker of anxious uncertainty.

'What land? I have no land to give you. It is your father's land that you must take for yourself if you wish to become King.' Rising from the stool and walking to the table, she fetched herself wine. Easier to retain impassiveness when your hands were busy. To the Saxon, in an acid tone as she passed, 'Let my handmaid alone! Paw at one of your own breed!'

His hand over the girl's breast, he leered back at Winifred, showing yellow, gapped teeth, a stink of stale breath wafting from him. The terrified girl was sobbing, her eyes pleading at Winifred to help her as he ripped away the torn remains of her nightshift. Naked, desperate, she tried to struggle free, to cover herself with her hands.

357

'Cerdic!' Winifred rebuked. 'Do you have no command over your filth?'

Cerdic pushed an embroidered cushion more comfortably into the small of his back, sipped his wine, held the glass up against the light of the flickering torch, examining the workmanship. He would have some of these fine things for his own. Said, his eye on the goblet, 'Oslac. If you need to rut so desperately, I suggest you take the whore outside.'

Oslac grinned, nodded. Clasped a handful of the girl's hair, began to haul her from the chamber, her screams rising.

'Cerdic! I demand you stop this insult!'

The goblet emptied, Cerdic held it out for a refill. 'Sigebert, when you have finished scratching at your crotch, I would appreciate more wine.' Added, 'You may have your turn at her when Oslac is finished.' He turned his eye to his mother. Small, skin-crinkled eyes, reminiscent of an ill-tempered boar, narrow and calculating, hideously dangerous. 'Unless,' he said, 'as she protests so loudly at the use of the little bitch, my mother would offer to take her place?'

Back straight, ankles crossed, hands folded in her lap, Winifred settled herself on a stool, closed her ears to the girl's shrilling out beyond the door. He was not jesting, Cerdic. And both of them knew it.

'Your father,' Winifred said disdainfully, 'never held a liking for you. I now see why.'

'Feelings run mutual regarding father and son, Mother.' Cerdic rolled another mouthful of wine around in his mouth, swallowed it slowly, thoughtfully licked his lips, savouring the strong, red, taste. The other man, Oslac, returned, adjusting the lacing on his bracae, his grin leeringly expressive as Sigebert hurried outside for his turn at the girl.

Winifred concentrated on steadying her breathing, willed her facial muscles to relax, her fingers to remain still. She knew enough of hatred to recognize its stench when it squatted, odious, before her. She could not allow her son to see that she was afraid – not of him, but of what he might, irrationally, do – there was a difference, subtle, but all the same, a difference. Cerdic was spoilt, conceited and pretentious. As a boy she had endured his rages, his wilful tempers – privately even admired them. He would need anger, determination, guts, to face Arthur, to take Britain for himself. But it was one thing to smile secretly at a little boy's ragged tantrum, quite another to face one tossed maliciously, intentionally, by a grown man. And she had seen that adult temper. Seen it unleashed, vehemently, at Mathild. Winifred's breath quickened. Why was he here? It was not at her that he ought be setting loose this energy of will, but at Arthur, at the kingdom. Cerdic's rightful kingdom . . . hers.

'You have, then,' she was mocking him, 'found your senses, have come to destroy your father. It is time you showed your manhood!'

Cerdic rose to his feet, walked around the room. As he passed Oslac, he motioned his head at the door in a quick gesture, said something that Winifred did not quite hear. Something about the men of her guard. Oslac – did that loathsome grin never leave his smirking face? – ambled from the chamber.

'Na,' Cerdic said, 'I do not want anything from my Father. It is your lands that I have come for.'

'My lands?' she echoed, incredulous, 'Never!' For how many years had she schemed and lied – aye, and murdered – to obtain all that was now hers? Her established settlements, these rich buildings at Venta Bulgarium, her founded churches and holy places? Land given her as divorce settlement by Arthur, land entitled to her by will from her father and her grandsire. Her land, her wealth. Hers!

She breathed deep, her nostrils flaring for air, steadied her rise of vehement anger. 'You could take all of Britain from your father, you could become King – I can help you . . .'

Cerdic interrupted her. 'I have come to Britain with barely one hundred men, with us are women and children.'

She hastily stood, crossed the room and took his arm, her nails gripping the padded tunic. 'I can get you more men! An army! I have gold to pay them, jewels . . .'

'I know you have,' he answered with a leer of greed. 'It is that which I have come for.'

Angry, stepping away from him, she spat, 'You would steal from me? Is your head, then, as empty as your balls!'

His axe, a lord's bright-bladed, light-weighted weapon, came somehow into his hands. He brought his arms back, and with his full weight behind the blow, brought the blade crashing through the fine-made table, splintering the wood, shattering the delicate glass goblets, a pitcher of wine, a fruit bowl that stood upon it.

Her hand and arm shielding her face, Winifred cowered into the wall, stifling her scream, fearful of flying debris, lowered the protection as Cerdic turned away, turned his back to her. She darted past him, pulled open the door, shouted for her guards. Her son came behind her, caught her arm, pulled her back into the room, callous laughter twisting his face.

'There are no guards. We cut their throats as we came in. They dared bar my entrance.' He stepped away from her, returned to the chair, sat. The axe he laid across his lap, one hand resting lightly on its wooden shaft.

'They were English,' she said. 'You have butchered your own kind?'

'As I will butcher anyone who stands in my path.' His eyes flickered to hers, held them. 'Anyone,' he repeated.

From somewhere, Winifred found the courage to laugh. There was a stool beside her; though she was trembling, she made herself sit, seem relaxed.

'Even your father?'

Cerdic's eyes held nothing of amusement, ignored her taunting. 'You hold land along the south coast, running against the Vectis Water.' Seated in Winifred's comfortable wicker-backed chair, he propped his boots on a low footstool. 'I have already made it my first settlement.'

Winifred was furious, she would not be treated as if she were some pox-riddled gutter girl. How dare this whelp, this churlish pup, do this to her! 'After all that I have done for you,' she sneered. 'You ungrateful dog turd!'

'Hah!' Cerdic sprang to his feet, stood over her. 'For me? What have you ever done for me?' He thrust his face forward, she could smell his breath, feel his spittle on her face. 'You did nothing for me, Mother. You wanted it all for yourself, everything. For me? Ja, you want me to take my father's place as King. Why? Because you intend to be the influence behind me, to dangle me on your chain. Do this, Cerdic, do that, Cerdic. Do it my way, Cerdic!' He kicked out at her stool, toppling it, sending her sprawling to the floor. 'Your way, always your way! Well, no more. I made that decision when I left you. And now I have made other decisions, and my first is to take what is yours to be mine!'

Shaken, her body quivering with rage, Winifred scrambled to her feet. 'While I live, you will not have my land.'

Cerdic dropped his gaze to the smooth wood of his axe shaft. It fitted into the palm of his hand so neatly. Snug and comfortable. He looked up, slowly, his heavy-lidded eyes opening wider, and as slowly. He said nothing, merely looked at her, lazily blinked, once.

Abruptly, Winifred closed her mouth, bit back the torrent of abusive words that had been hovering. For a long, silent pause, she regarded him. Cerdic, the son she had borne, tutored, nurtured, loved. Loved? Had she ever loved him – had she ever loved anyone? It was not a word familiar to Winifred, love. Yet she had, in her own, peculiar way, loved Arthur. Even if that love was one honed out of jealousy and envy. Arthur was strong and powerful, he feared nothing and no one – or so he cleverly gave the impression. Between the two, father or son, who would she support if it ever came to a fight? Arthur or Cerdic? If she would be Arthur's queen, then it would be the Pendragon without doubt. With her son? As his adviser, mentor, guide . . . Ah, it was the power she wanted, that which she loved.

360

A rap at the door, Oslac entered without waiting for permission, two heads held by the hair in his hand, blood dripping from the severed necks. Two of Winifred's guard, meant to intimidate her, no doubt.

'Do you think I will give way to such paltry threats?' she retorted curtly, barely glancing at the bloodied trophies. 'What are a few dead to me?' Did Cerdic think her so feeble-minded? So soft-bellied? She, Winifred, who had murdered for her own gain; Winifred, who had from childhood, schemed and bartered and fought to achieve her wealth, her position. Wealth and position that she fully intended to keep. Threaten her? Had she, then, bred a fool?

Cerdic stood, the axe in his hand. 'Your land is to be legally, undisputedly mine. On that land, my people can settle and thrive without threat or intimidation. More will then come to join us, with the swing of the seasons, they will come. And then I will found my own kingdom. Mine, Mother, not yours, not my father's, mine. I will become Bretwalda of the English, the founder of a dynasty, the . . .'

The absurdity! Winifred laughed, head back, hands on hips, mouth open, laughed. 'You? Do all that for yourself? You could not even sire your own son – your father had to do it for you!'

Cerdic's lip lifted into a snarl. The axe was in his hand, he lifted it, swung, brought it down, his breath bellowing from between his enraged, clenched teeth, with the exhalation of effort. Blood, bone, sinew spattered among the shards of green glass and splintered wood.

She had not screamed or moved, so quickly had he killed her.

Oslac scratched, unconcerned, under his armpit, the drip of blood from the two heads adding to the mess on the floor as he raised his arm. He had understood not a word of what had been said, for they had spoken in Latin, and he knew only the English tongue. He sniffed. 'Bury her, do we?' he asked, 'With the others, to stop their spirits walking?'

Cerdic wiped his hand beneath his nose, licked his lips. He was shaking. *Gods*, he thought, *what have I done?* 'Aye, put them with their severed heads between their legs, to bind them to the darkness of the earth.' He left the room, went to where it was dark and private, and brought up the contents of his stomach, his belly heaving and twisting. Then sat, his back against a wall, letting the cold of the night dry the sweat that was on his skin, the quiet calm his shaking. After a while, the thought came that he had wanted his mother's land, and now, by right of inheritance, it would be his.

In control of his guts and his thinking, Cerdic rejoined his men who, if they had noticed anything, said not a word. There was one last thing to do, now that he had obtained what he had come for. Cerdic had recognized him when they had battered down the wooden gates of this place. The priest had been one of the first to run forward, protesting, demanding that the Saxons leave. Cerdic had recognized him.

He rapped orders, watched as they butchered that man, that unfortunate priest. They would toss the bloodied bits into a shallow pit, not like the others, no burial grave for this one. This one, who would never again be entering a whorehouse, or running to tell tales to a mother about a boy eager to sample his first taste of offered delights. Ah, vengeance had its own reward, and Cerdic found it to be a good way to settle a heaving stomach and a shrieking conscience.

Their business done, Cerdic and his small band of Saxons left, weighted with treasures and trinkets, carousing their success. Three words, remembered from those tedious days of childhood tutoring thrumming in Cerdic's mind as they marched home, southward. *Veni, vidi, vici.* I came, saw, conquered.

The guilt had already passed, replaced with the smell of undominated freedom.

April 476

§ III

With men working together as a unit, a team, Cerdic's Hall took shape. It was the first permanent building to be erected, for the Mead Hall was more than a prestigious place of residence for the head man. It was a meeting hall for Council, where judgements of law would be made or collective decisions discussed and argued over, be it for planning the next harvest or the next war; a workplace, where women would cook, weave and sew, where men mended harness, sharpened weapons, fashioned a new spear. A feasting hall, a sleeping place . . . the Mead Hall, the heart, the centre, of a community. Although as yet this embryonic settlement of the West Saxons was not a community. They were fledgelings, grubbing an existence under tents, foraging for food, living hand-to-mouth, day to day, but not for much longer. Cerdic's people were here to stay, and the raising of the Hall was a statement of their intransigent intention.

The oval palisade fence had been the first essential construction. Defence and confinement, to keep domestic animals in, the undesirable – human or animal – out. Built of oak, a wood that smouldered rather than blazed, rising higher than two men standing one atop the other, and with the width of two, spread handspans, it encompassed an enclosure of several acres that would, eventually, be a permanent home to the founders of Cerdic's kingdom.

With that completed, the men felled yet more timber for the Hall. Oak again, for the upright supports, door-frames, roof rafters, wall-plating and the crafting of the great, curved pairs of timber crucks needed to support the weight of the roof. The plank floor was to be suspended, the height of a man above ground level; the space underneath to take the foundations for the weight-bearing uprights, and to keep the living quarters warm and dry. The dark cellar would eventually be used for storage, reached by a low entrance set modestly beside the steps leading upward to an imposing, intricately carved, doorway. Cerdic's Mead Hall was to be a magnificent building. Roofed with timber shingles, not thatch, half as wide and long again as the one he had inherited from Leofric – oh, his was to be a chieftain's Hall, worthy of mention in song!

And others would come with the passing of the seasons, see it, admire its crafting, its significance of power. Men would come, bring their wives and children, offer their shields and spears into Cerdic's service in exchange for the right to build their own dwelling within the protective hand of Cerdic's authority.

The foundations were well laid, the massive uprights in position. The door-frames fitted, skeletal openings. Today, the first of the roof-beams were to be hoisted, slotted into the half-lap joints. The weather had been kind, dry, but not hot. If it lasted until the shingles had been laid ... Ah, would the gods be that generous?

Cerdic stood, fists resting on his broad waist, legs spread, head back, eyes squinting into the light, as the first of the heavy beams was pulled upward, the ropes creaking from the suspended weight, men's muscles straining. The beam was swung around, manhandled, eased forward, slotted with deceptive ease neatly into the waiting joint; at the far end, another beam, with another team of men. They were working high off the ground, the height of five tall men. The crossed ends of the exposed upright supports to the fore and aft of the apexed roof would be carved and decorated, painted with the grotesque faces of house-place spirits to ward away the forces of mischief and evil. Glad Cerdic was, that he need not clamber about up there! Once, he had groped his way up the mast of one of his ships. He had been younger then, no more than ten and six years, but still the dizzying height had spun his brains, churned his stomach. He had left the sorting of the square sails to the experienced sailors after that. And the building of his Hall roof to the carpenters.

Someone approached from behind, his shadow passing across Cerdic's feet, stood beside his lord. Belched, wiped his mouth with his tunic sleeve, pork grease dribbling down his chin, the hunk of meat, well-chewed, between his black-nailed fingers.

'Going well,' Oslac observed, indicating the busy industry. 'Be settled in soon, eh?'

Cerdic made no answer. Oslac was a good soldier, reliable, strong armed, sure-aimed, though his manners left much to be desired. He also stank of rancid wine, stale sweat and piddled urine – but then, most of them did.

'How long do you reckon then? Before we move on?' Oslac spoke through a mouthful of pork, mouth open, teeth masticating, oblivious of Cerdic's responding frown.

'Move on?' Cerdic asked, his tone severe. 'I do not intend to move on.'

Oslac swallowed the chewed meat, picked at a shred stuck behind his gum. 'We're not going to stay here forever, are we? Stuck on the edge of these marshes, with all that land out there ripe for the taking.' He threw the bone away, northward, to where, beyond the palisade fence, the sea-marshes gave way to the outskirts of woodland – laying further back now that so many trees had been felled, the new-cut stumps stark against the foot-trampled undergrowth.

'Until I am ready to expand. We stay here, on my own-held, undisputed ground.'

'But I thought we were here to fight!' Oslac's voice could whine, petulant, like an irritating child. 'That's what I came for. To kill British.'

'And that is what we shall do,' Cerdic's acerbic tone was lost on Oslac, who failed to notice the lift to his nostrils, the narrowing of eyes, warning signs. 'When we are secure here, when we have ploughed, sown and harvested our fields, stored our barns to the roof-beams with grain, have fattened cattle, milk-yielding goats. When the traders' ships come first to our harbour, not others along the coast. When the women have borne us the next generation of warriors. Then, when we have the power of permanence behind us, then we will fight.' Stability meant survival. Attack now, and the Pendragon would have all the excuse he needed to sweep in from the west and wipe them out, while they were vulnerable and exposed.

Winifred's death had been a mistake, Cerdic had realized that on the swaggering march back from Venta. He had done it in a rage of temper, it had not been intentional, not been planned – but she had pushed him once too often, the bitch. And it had been so easy to lift that axe and . . .

For now, he must keep his head down, remain quiet, then he would be forgotten, ignored as of no consequence. Only a few of the British were blustering their protest at Winifred's death, but Cerdic had taken steps to repair the damage done in that fit of temper – and he had more or less succeeded. His bile had risen at having to write so placatingly to his father, to petition his innocence, pleading that Winifred had forced his hand . . . and the bribing of so many of the British Council had cost him dear, but then, the ploy had worked, for his father seemed content to let things ride.

Although you never knew with Arthur quite what he was thinking, what he was planning.

'There's enough of us,' Oslac said, piqued. 'We could make a fight of things whenever we wanted. And why has the Pendragon not come to us? Challenged us?' He spat pork-stained saliva to the grass. 'They say, so I've heard, that he hasn't the stomach for battle any more.'

'They are fart-arsed fools, then,' Cerdic retorted as he walked away, only the white of his clenched knuckles betraying the rage burning inside him. The idleness of gossip! Arthur was afraid of nothing, so Winifred had maintained. Hah! Boasted, bragged! How often had she flagrantly compared him with Arthur? Your father is not afraid of the dark, of thunder, of the pain of a tooth that needed pulling. But he would learn to be afraid! When he was ready, Cerdic would show him that there was something to be feared – the destruction that his son would unleash. The death that he would bring.

'He's lost his balls,' Oslac muttered, persistent. 'He'd have come otherwise, after you murdered your own mother.' Possibly it was not meant to be heard, but it came out louder than intended.

Cerdic's fists clenched, his teeth clamped together. He would have slain Oslac then, at that moment, except it would have tainted the building of his Hall, the cold spilling of blood as the beams were raised.

No one crossed Cerdic. No one doubted his word, contradicted his planning, told him what to do and when or how. Mathild had discovered that, and his mother. No one openly mentioned murder. He took several deep breaths, calmed himself. They would need make sacrifice to ensure luck and fortune. Blood must be sprinkled over the lintel, hearth and threshold of the Hall, in the name of Woden.

Easy enough to arrange the chosen one to be Oslac.

May 476

§ IV

The ride north. Tiring, rain-sodden, aggravatingly slow. The mud thick and cloying, the horses bad-tempered and unwilling in the face of continuous, needle-tipped, rain-squalled wind. And all for nothing!

Ambrosius Aurelianus sat hunched, cold and aching before the feeble heat of a sulky brazier, nursing a bowl of venison broth between his chapped, stiff hands. He dipped the wooden spoon into the bowl, brought out a chunk of meat. At least this was hot! It tasted good, too, the meat tender, root vegetables not soft or mushy, subtly flavoured with herbs. He ate hungrily, enjoying the meal.

The Hall was busy with many people indoors on such a foul afternoon, yet the building was quiet. Not silent, for the bustle of everyday movement created sound – footsteps coming and going across the timber flooring, the clatter of cooking pots and utensils, the growl and snarl of squabbling dogs, the slap of leather as one man cut and shaped the straps he would need to fashion a new bridle. A hen sat brooding, crooning to herself, unmolested, in a dark, straw-piled corner – though the dogs would find any eggs soon enough. The women talked as they worked at the two looms, their voices muted, dulled into a respectful murmur, but they had all, everyone in that Hall, stopped, fallen silent, looked up from whatever busied their hands, as Ambrosius had entered, wet and chilled. And he had known, as he walked into that dismal silence, an hour past, that he was too late. Caw, a man devoted to his God, who had once been a king in the north, his friend and kinsman, Caw was dead. The illness had taken him to the Holy Kingdom before his request, uttered on dry, cracked, pain tensioned lips could be fulfilled. '*Bring Ambrosius to me. I would make confession to Ambrosius.*'

'Why me?' Ambrosius had asked himself on that journey north, to the Gwynedd stronghold that Lord Caw had made his own, for himself and his great, many-numbered family. *Why me?* Because they had known one another in the innocent time of childhood? Because Ambrosius's wife had been Caw's favourite sister? Because and because . . . Who could unravel the many possible answers to an obscure riddle? Caw had asked, Ambrosius had come. Too late. Caw had died two days previous.

A girl, dark-haired, dark-eyed – as many of them from north beyond the Wall were – came a second time before him, offering to top his bowl with fresh broth, the harsh, red bruising of tears still swelling her eyes. She was Cywyllog, Caw's youngest surviving daughter. Ten and seven years of age, quiet-voiced, neat, precise movements that gave an air of calm, rooted, efficiency. She was dressed plain in dark colours, muted browns and greens, her black hair bound in a single braid. No jewellery or decoration to ears, neck or arms. A few of her elder sisters carried, from their mother's pagan influence, the blue tattooing of the north, the needle-pricked patterned markings on cheeks, forehead and arms, but not Cywyllog, for the girls born to the second and third wives were raised in their father's Christian faith. They were married to northern men, those older girls, several had grandchildren born. Cywyllog barely remembered them, for she had come south to the sanctuary of Gwynedd with her father and mother – his second woman – in the late spring of 464. Had lived here, within the seclusion of Caer Rhuthun's palisaded walls, mostly in peace, since. Save for that one short time, when the eldest of her brothers had come seeking sanctuary . . .

Caw had produced a large family. Daughters, a sprinkling of sons; some were married and settled, many, after coming south, had entered into the service of the Church; as many were dead. The first-born had been male, as was the last. Cywyllog had nurtured a deep, personal, affection for them both – though the one was dead, murdered, she insisted, ten years past, and the other was merely three years of age.

Ambrosius accepted the second helping of broth with gratitude, invited her to sit a while, to talk. She shook her head. There was much to do, much to arrange. Lord Enniaun was soon expected, she explained, they must make ready to receive their honoured benefactor. With a smile that brought no light or sunshine to her face, she whisked away. Ambrosius felt cheered. It would be good to meet with Enniaun, Lord of Gwynedd. Happen the journey north was not wasted, then, after all.

As he spooned the broth, he glanced around. Caw's Hall was small, frugally furnished, parsimonious in comparison to a lord's usual necessary splendour. But then, Caw had been a dispossessed king. His land, his title, wealth – some had even whispered among themselves, his manhood – had been forcibly taken from him by the stronger eldest son, Hueil. That last had proven malicious gossip of course, but for the rest . . .

There were not many younger people within the Hall; most, the majority, a tired, older generation. A few children had trotted, shoulders hunched against the discomfort of drizzling rain, beside the horses when Ambrosius and his escort had made way through the open gates, up through the mud-slush into the stronghold. It was not a place of the young, this, for the younger men had not ridden southward with their ousted lord, opting for the better excitement of the prospect of war against Arthur with Hueil. Caw had made the same mistake as Ambrosius. It was all very well putting your faith firm and solid into the goodness of God – but a devout monk could not be a successful king.

Hueil. Ambrosius set his empty bowl topside-down on the floor – tradition, to show he had finished, enjoyed his meal, and practical, to dissuade the wretched dogs from scrambling for it. Hueil.

A young man of such potential promise. Where – when – had it all gone awry? Ah, with the evil of pagan mischief and the lure of a woman! He would have been ten and four when his mother had died, the woman who had followed the heathen ways of the Priestess. With her pagan influence banished, Caw had turned his mild interest into whole-hearted Christian faith. For a while the boy followed, eager to imitate his earthly lord and father. But Caw's devotion was perhaps too rigid, too blind to the path of greed, and Hueil was a young man who had the strength and passion of the warrior in him.

At twenty years of age, he had left Alclud in the North and ridden south and south, to join with Arthur the Pendragon, to fight with, and under, him.

But Caw would not fight for his own land, had trusted too deeply that God would triumph over the sea-raiders who came in more numbers every spring to steal his land, his cattle, his women. And Hueil, turning against Arthur, had been lured by the witch-woman Morgause to the taking of his father's kingdom by force. Ambrosius leant forward, his elbows resting on his knees, chin propped on his clasped hands. The war that followed had been bloody and bitter. Many men had died, men from the north beyond the Wall and from the south. Arthur's son, Llacheu, among them. He sighed, long and slow.

'That is a sound of deep regret, my friend! What troubles you so?'

Ambrosius looked up sharply, saw a tall, tall man, red hair grizzled and streaked with grey eyes merry, lips firm. For that brief, quick-glimpsed moment, he thought he was seeing Cunedda, the Lion Lord of Gwynedd, but he was dead, gone these many long years . . .

'Enniaun! My dear Lord Enniaun, I did not hear you enter!' Ambrosius was on his feet, pleasure lighting his solemn expression, hand out-stretched, greeting Cunedda's eldest surviving son, aware that the Hall was filling with newcomers, men, cloaks drenched, dripping puddles on the floor, their accompanying dogs trading aggression with those of the Hall.

'Your reverie was certainly deep!' Enniaun laughed, straddling himself before the brazier. 'Guilt of conscience or musing for the future?' His laughter resonated through the Hall, raising smiles from those within hearing. For a moment the gloom of the place lifted, colour returned, life seeped through the walls, drifted among the roof-beams.

'My uncle knows no guilt, he is a man of God.'

Ambrosius swung around, startled at the sarcastic remark, a faint gasp issuing from his lips. Arthur! Arthur, here? In this place? 'I was thinking of Hueil'. The words sprang from his mouth unchecked, unbidden.

Arthur swung his heavy, rain-sodden cloak from his shoulders, handed it to his body-servant, moved to the poor, insufficient warmth of the brazier.

'It would be difficult not to, I suppose,' he said after a short while. 'It was to here that he forced his father to flee; it was to here that he later came, seeking safety for himself.' Arthur was the only man to have entered who retained his weapons. He was the Supreme King, he would not shed sword or dagger, leave them on the threshold. As he spoke, he rested his hand on the hilt of his sword, aware of the silence, the rabid course of mixed feelings; on some faces, barely veiled hostility.

A woman was threading her way through the crowd of newcomers, copper-haired – though that too was bearing streaks of silver – her features, eyes, nose, similar to those of the Lord Enniaun. Her green eyes were sparking, forcing down the huddled press of animosity.

'Hueil,' she said, loud so all heard, 'was rightly executed by the King for the traitor and murderer that he was.' Gwenhwyfar stood beside Arthur, the gold of the torque at her throat gleaming as vivid, as royal, as her eyes. 'We have come to pay our respects to his father, the man Hueil would have also murdered, had he not taken the wisdom to flee into the safe protection of my brother, Lord Enniaun.'

Low murmurings as the rise of aggression faded, the Hall went back about its business, welcoming those new-arrived. None could dispute the truth of what Gwenhwyfar said.

Only one kept the steady clench of hatred in her jaw. Cywyllog was chivying the younger children out from their corner. Her father's Hall was small, of no size to accommodate so many comfortably. Those who had no reason to remain must leave, find for themselves some other place out of the rain. She steered her brother before her, taking him through a side door, directing him to the dwelling of Christen, his nurse. He was reluctant to go, for he wanted to see the splendid men and the King, Arthur.

'You ought have no wish to see him! He murdered our brother, there, over there on that rock, he threw Hueil against it and struck off his head!' The boy swivelled his eyes from the shelter of the door-way to the grey slab of limestone, watched the rain heave and bounce against it, pictured his brother's blood streaming down its sides instead of the shiny wet of the rain. 'I know what happened,' Cywyllog hissed in his ear, 'for I was here, I saw. It is Arthur who is the murderer, not our brother Hueil. Now be off with you, I have much to do.'

The boy wrenched his gaze from the rock – he would go nowhere near it by night, skirted it by day, for it scared him. It had been used as a savage execution block and he feared he might see the blood, hear the scream. His sister had told him of it all often enough, of how one day she would take revenge on Arthur for the death of their brother. 'Will you kill him?' The boy asked her. 'Will you do as you have said you will one day do? Take a dagger and cut out his heart, or blacken his belly with poison or . . .'

Cywyllog slapped her hand around her three year old brother's mouth. 'Hush, child! Do you want him to hack your head off also? He will do if he hears such unguarded talk!'

Fearful, Gildas glanced through the open door into the crowded room, caught a glimpse of the Pendragon, tall, powerful, austere. He ran, hurtling through the rain to the safety of his nurse's warm lap.

§ V

'Does it not make you feel' – Ambrosius searched for a tactful word – 'uncomfortable? Being here at Caer Rhuthun?' They were walking back from Caw's burial in the family plot a mile beyond the stronghold's walls, were lingering, politely, to the rear of the family. It had been a reasonable ceremony, efficient, correct, with a suitable number of mourners. Ambrosius had made a fine eulogy, Enniaun had spoken a few words. Arthur had assumed it wise to be silent, remained on the edge, faded into the background. Thankfully the rain had stopped, although the day was dark and sombre, and with the mountains swathed in low, dull wreaths of cloud, the prospect of it staying dry was not promising.

'No. Should it?' The Pendragon would not have, ordinarily, come here – at this time or any other, but he and Gwenhwyfar had been visiting Lord Enniaun, essentially to redraft old treaties of alliance, additionally to great old friends, family faces. When Enniaun decided to pay his respects to Caw's grieving family, Arthur opted to travel with him. It would have been churlish, even taken as a slight against the family had he not, and for practicality, it was the same road home. Company was always welcome to ease the tedium of travelling.

Clearing his throat at Arthur's unembarrassed, matter-of-fact reply,

Ambrosius regretted asking the question, but felt he need add something relevant. 'It was a nasty business, the family took it hard.'

They had reached steeper ground, the path beginning to rise, churned, wet and muddied, walking made difficult by the slush. Ambrosius's boot slithered. He lost balance, almost toppled, but Arthur was a man used to quick reaction, urgent movement. He seized his uncle's arm, steadied him, said, as bluntly as before, 'Aye, it was a nasty business. The consequence of war always is.' Arthur dropped the hold on the arm, continued walking. 'I took it hard. Hueil was responsible for more than starting a civil war. He caused the murder of my son. Remember?'

Oh, Ambrosius remembered! He had been there, fighting that war with Arthur. They had been almost friends then, for that short while when they shared a common ground – the sorting of Hueil of the north and his wanting more than just a ragged cluster of settlements and a decaying stronghold. Few doubted the ultimate necessity of ending Hueil's life, taken for that of the boy's. It had been the manner of the doing: an execution without trial while Hueil had sought the forgiveness of God.

Arthur had pulled ahead, striding out to catch up with his wife and her brother Enniaun. Ambrosius remained behind, walking slower, mindful of the precarious ground and the grumbling discomfort of his stomach. A nasty business? Aye indeed. All of it.

Linking arms with Gwenhwyfar, Arthur grinned at her eldest brother. 'Somewhat poor condition this stronghold of yours, Enniaun!' he teased. 'Ever heard of cobbles?'

'Not my stronghold, Pendragon! I freely gave it to Caw, it was his to do with as he pleased.' Enniaun grunted as his boot sunk ankle deep in a mud rut. 'Cobbles cost coin to buy, labour to lay. Not wishing to speak ill of the dead, but my Lord Caw was a – how shall I put it? – a frugal man.'

Tight-arsed bastard, Arthur thought the words, prudently kept them to himself.

Enniaun, glancing at him, guessed the thought. He laughed. 'Oh I agree!'

'Who will hold Rhuthun now then, brother?' Gwenhwyfar asked, her other arm linked through his, so that they walked three-abreast, herself secure from slipping between the solidity of two men. 'Or are you to take it back?'

'Various surviving sons' – Enniaun nodded at the backs of those of the family walking ahead – 'are already squabbling over it, with a few daughters adding their shuttleworth.' He tossed a gruff laugh at Arthur. 'I ought give it to you Pendragon, that would set things hopping! Jesu, it would start another war!'

'Gods, no! I have enough trouble brewing down south, without facing additional storms up here among your ball-freezing mountains!'

They had reached the gate, a narrow, dark and gloomy construction; were forced to stop, wait their turn to pass through, respect necessitating that the grieving family go first. Their public show of grief, loud and evident with raised, wailing voices, doubled into reverberating echoes as they filed through the low, dank, tunnelway.

Low, confidential in Arthur's ear, Enniaun whispered, 'Were you not pleased at one event down your way?'

'Winifred, you mean? Aye, in some aspects it is a relief to be rid of her.' Shifting a skimming, sideways glance at Gwenhwyfar, Arthur added with what seemed a careless shrug, 'But even Winifred did not deserve to die in that way.'

Gwenhwyfar, who had been inspecting the amount of mud plastered around the hem of her robe, snorted in a manner that conveyed distinct disagreement. From which Enniaun, knowing his sister well enough, deduced there had passed angry words between husband and wife.

'She ought to have been hacked to pieces long before this!'

'She was once my wife.'

'She murdered. She lied, she cheated . . .'

'I agree, but she was also, once, my wife.'

Arthur had not understood the unexpected, disturbing feelings that had seeped into him after hearing of Winifred's murder. He should have rejoiced, as Gwenhwyfar had, exclaimed his delight that he was, at last, rid of her meddling interferences. Yet he had gone off quietly by himself, riding out onto the lake-shimmering Summer Land levels, felt the raw exposure of an inexplicable sadness. Guilt, he assumed, for never loving – liking – her, for treating her so badly. Ah, guilt. The repercussions that emotion could rouse after the dead had departed!

Predictably, Gwenhwyfar had greeted the news with favour. For so long had she loathed Winifred, an odious woman who had set herself so determinedly as a rival. Her only regret that she was not the one to be responsible for her ending. In retrospect, the satisfaction was as rewarding, but at that first hearing of the news she had felt cheated. The bitch was done with, that was what mattered. For all Arthur's inexplicable disquiet over her passing, she was, finally, firmly, thankfully, done with.

'And the son?' Enniaun asked, as he motioned for Arthur and Gwenhwyfar to proceed before him under the archway. They had touched on the matter of Cerdic only briefly during the few days together, never quite pursuing the subject in its entirety, for Arthur had steered away from it. For that, too, was laying on his mind, heavy and

373

weighted. He was responsible for many things, had, by necessity made unpleasant, harsh – often cruel – decisions. For himself, personally, for his life outside that of being the Supreme, the King, he had not always made the right choice. Inadvertently, occasionally deliberately, he had hurt people, even those he loved. On his orders, men lived or died, faced the bloodlust of war or the benevolence of forgiving mercy. But that was part of living, the choice-making, the decision-taking. Cerdic was a force let loose into the world, started by Arthur's seed. Started unintentionally, yet was that not the ultimate reason for laying with a wife, to procure children?

'My son' – Arthur's answer was poignant – 'took an axe and used it to hack his own mother's skull into two pieces. He made petition to me that he was defending himself, had killed her for her inciting of war between Saxon and British. We know that is all bullshit, but legally I cannot act against him.' He paused, added, 'He is a murderer, and I sired him – what does that make me?'

Where once the apparition of death, for all its ugliness, would not have clung to Arthur, its dark foreboding now worried him, lingering like a malignant presence gnawing at his stomach. Gaul had changed him. He had met fear, and fear, once encountered became a shadow that followed like a starving stray dog. Kick it, shout at it, but it was always there, sniffing at heel. One day he would die. There was never the cheating of the inevitable, but it was the manner of it that clutched black and unforgiving at him. To be killed by an axe-blade in the security of your own chamber, and by one of your own blood, your own creation . . . The thought filled him with dread.

They were walking under the long and narrow arch of the stone-built gateway, their conversation reverberating, the words *took an axe, took an axe* seeming to echo louder than the others, obscene and ominous.

'For all the declaration of his innocence, you ought to have had an end to him, I say!' Gwenhwyfar announced with finality, as they emerged through the tunnelway.

Ambrosius had almost caught them up, had heard her declaration.

'As I have so urged,' he said vehemently. The group, Arthur, Enniaun and Gwenhwyfar turned to look at him, waited for him breathlessly to come up to them.

'What of the murdered priest? And the rape of the girl, Lady Winifred's handmaid? It was a disgraceful business, and it has been overlooked, set aside!'

'English, too, were butchered, uncle, do not forget them,' Arthur added, knowing Ambrosius would dismiss their killing as nothing of consequence.

Ambrosius waved his hand fastidiously. 'What the Saex do between themselves is their business, not mine.'

Arthur sighed. He had already argued through this conversation with Ambrosius at Council. 'I will not commit my men to a war in order to bring about the murder of my own son. If he meets me in battle, then that is his doing, not mine.'

Cerdic had been clever – had more wisdom than Arthur would have given him credit for. By sending immediate petition of his innocence, and declaring that his mother had acted treasonably against the Supreme King, there was little, legally, that Arthur could do. The sending of the heads of three of Cerdic's own Saxons had, of course, helped to sway Council's mind in Cerdic's favour, a decision bustled along by an eloquent representative attending Council in Cerdic's stead – a merchant-man, paid well, no doubt, to lie as efficiently as he had. The men responsible for those other, shameful killings executed; Winifred's affluent steading a few miles outside Venta to be given by Cerdic to the bishop of that same town; other possessions of his mother's promised with flourished generosity to notable men of influence who sat on the Council. Oh aye, Council had voted for Cerdic! Had agreed that what was his mother's ought by right pass to him, to do with as he pleased; that her death had been unfortunate but unavoidable.

They had all known Winifred for what she had been, and here Arthur could not disagree with them, had cast his vote with those who proclaimed aye – silencing Ambrosius's protests. He knew Cerdic to be lying, but there was that small element of doubt. For how often had Winifred boasted, threatened, that it would be she who made Cerdic into King in Arthur's stead?

Ahead was the timber-built Hall, low, rectangular, the reed-thatch of its roof sodden from the rain, the courtyard squelching with mud and rain-ruts. The mourners were making their way across, through the open doors, into the welcome of dry warmth. To the left, the Stone, brooding, leering its stark reminder of the past.

It had once functioned as a foundation for a taller, phallic, man-height shaped stone, the Stone, the ritual symbol of the warrior, the sacred Stone on which oaths were sworn, allegiances made. Caw had ordered its removal, despising its heathen connection, but the base had proven beyond him, a rock, part of the structure of the stronghold, it seemed, impossible to remove or destroy.

A small boy was standing a few yards inside the gate, momentarily alone, dejected, the streak of shed tears marking his cheeks. He watched the King emerge from the darkness of the tunnelway, saw, hanging at his side, the scabbard, the sword pommel ... the sword. That sword, the

Pendragon's sword. A sheathed blade that had been drawn, glinting, in the afternoon sunlight, here, in this very courtyard . . . the boy screamed, ran, slithered in the mud, fell, tumbled back to his feet, ran on.

He was barely noticed; Gwenhwyfar was discussing Cerdic with her brother, the nonsense, in her opinion, of Council's decision to allow him to settle in peace along the south coast. 'There will be war,' she said. 'My husband has been the fool in this.'

Arthur saw the boy. Heard his strangled, fear-ridden cry. Wondered.

I hate you! I hate you! Did hatred run so deeply putrid through the line of kindred then? Eldest born to youngest. Father to son?

Cerdic. His son, grown to manhood, grown up with so much stark, twisted hatred. What was he to do about Cerdic? He did not chastize Gwenhwyfar for her scolding tongue, how could he, she had the right of it. There would come war between father and son, and there was always this other question, hanging, insidious, in Arthur's mind. *What did Cerdic intend to do about his father?*

The boy had gone. Gildas, they had said his name was. Ambrosius was to take him back to Ambrosium, to the school that was flourishing there. Arthur's other son, Medraut, wanted to be a student there also. Medraut, who seemed more suited to book-learning than the wielding of sword and shield. A safer occupation, book-learning. Safer for whom? For the son or for the father?

The boy Gildas would be better off there, where he could forget about the darkness of execution, of blood and war. Forget about the past, and the necessary, cruel ending of elder brothers.

A pity that Cerdic could not be so easily dealt with.

September 476

§ VI

'What's that?' Gwenhwyfar knelt on the bed, her arms going, automatically, around Arthur's waist, her chin resting on his shoulder as she peered over his shoulder at the document he was reading. 'Anything interesting?'

'Mm?' Engrossed, he had not heard her enter their chamber. Beyond the open door someone was chopping wood, and a hunting party had returned with all the clatter and shouting that usually accompanied a successful expedition. It was good to have Caer Cadan busy and prospering again. He caressed her cheek as a greeting. 'A letter arrived from Gaul.' He chuckled wickedly. 'Sidonius Apollinaris. Will the old goat never cease his writing?'

Gwenhwyfar settled herself more amiable, snuggling beside her husband as he shifted to make room for her. It was more comfortable to sit on the bed than to endure the hard seat of a chair or stool. His thigh had been throbbing these past few days, the rain and the damp disagreed so abominably with the ache of old wounds. He was one year over forty, and on some days, when the broken bones and wounding scars of the past loudly reminded him of their existence, felt twice that.

'Apparently,' Arthur said with a chortle of amusement, 'our intrepid cousin, Bedwyr, has been making himself useful during his travels abroad. He persuaded Euric to let Sidonius out of imprisonment. Hah!' He laughed outright. 'I imagine shutting the old man away for over a year was the only thing Euric could think of to stop so many of these damned letters!'

They laughed together, Arthur drawing her nearer with his arm affectionately around her. She was eight and thirty, a few silver streaks were becoming pronounced in her hair, crow's-foot lines appearing around her eyes. But to him, she would always be beautiful, even when she was old, toothless and stooping, she would be Venus.

'Does he include news of Bedwyr?' She peered again at the letter, scanning the neat, accurate writing for information, took it to read closer. Arthur watched her, noted the anxious dip of her eyebrows, the way her tooth chewed at her lip as she quickly read. She had wept quiet tears for several days when Bedwyr had left, almost two years ago now. He went, he had said, because he found it difficult to sit still in one place, saying that he wished to travel along the great rivers, to reach, eventually, the centre of the Eastern Empire, Constantinople. Arthur wondered whether it had been an excuse. He knew that Bedwyr had almost married with Gwenhwyfar – guessed there had been more than platonic formality between them, but had never pursued the detail. Had she slept with him? Often, he almost asked her, let the rise of courage slip away. The truth did not always need knowing.

'There's nothing beyond passing mention of gratitude to him, and to say that Bedwyr then moved on towards Rome.' The disappointment that clouded her expression was obvious.

'Do you miss him?' Arthur asked quietly, the lurch of his heartbeat booming in his chest. He wanted to leap up, shake her, make her say no or make her confess that she had loved Bedwyr, lain with him, wanted him . . . and what would he do then? Hate her? Punish her? She had thought herself a widow. It was not adultery to be with another man when your husband was dead. And if there was punishment, ought it not be levelled at himself?

Gwenhwyfar's restless shrug however, was indifferent. 'I suppose so. Bedwyr was—' She paused. What was he? A good companion, a good friend? Reliable? Sexually exciting? 'Bedwyr was here when I needed someone.'

Arthur drew his finger lightly down the sun-tanned gold of her arm. *Here, when I was not.* Jealousy, he thought, was an irrational, uncontrollable emotion. The silence hung uneasy for a moment. Gwenhwyfar had not responded to his touch, had even moved slightly away from him, her attention deliberately secured on the letter.

She sat upright, reading intently, Bedwyr set aside for other, intriguing news. 'Odovacer has overthrown Orestes after demanding a right to land, has taken Rome!'

'It would have been wiser to have granted the army's request,' Arthur answered laconically. Added, matter-of-factly, 'When an elected leader asks for something, it usually means there is an intention of taking it, one way or another.'

As Cerdic would one day, sooner or later, try to take more land. The thought struck them both, but it passed without verbal referral.

Instead, Gwenhwyfar asked, 'And the boy? What has happened to him? Does Sidonius say? He is so young.' It was always the innocents who were hurt in a rebellion. The children. The sons.

The man Orestes had, for some time, been in supreme command of the army of Rome – what was left of it – and strategically, had placed his young son on the throne as Emperor of the West. Ten months past, that was. Emperors lived such short, interrupted lives.

Not this one, he had Fortuna guarding him, it seemed. 'Na,' Arthur reassured her. 'Read on. He is in exile, enjoying the hot sun and blue sea of the Bay of Neapolis. I doubt there will be any support to reinstate him, and he will be no threat to a man like Odovacer, his replacement.'

'Orestes dead then?' Gwenhwyfar read quickly, ran her finger under the passage describing his lurid murder, grimaced at the excessive detail, hoped this was another of Sidonius's many colourfully exaggerated flourishes. The previous paragraph describing the destruction, burning and killing brought about by the rebellion made her doubt it. 'Did you ever meet him?' she asked, lifting her head from the writing, and letting the scroll roll up on itself. 'Odovacer?'

Arthur took the letter from her, dropped it to the floor, lay back, taking Gwenhwyfar with him, tucking her between his embracing arms. Her hair smelt new-washed, deliciously of herbs. 'I never had the fortune of that pleasure.' He spoke wryly, but his hold had tightened around her. The memories of Gaul remained, grim even after this while. He rested his cheek against her head, closed his eyes. Gaul. Pictures sauntered into his mind; dark, never-ending woods, sun-dappled roads, wide, shallow and lazy rivers. That battle. That final, destructive, haunting battle.

Mathild. She had known Odovacer. He frowned, could not remember the exact knowing. He had not thought of Mathild for some while. A year, two? Longer than that? Was it Sidonius's letter that brought back this unexpected recollection? She had been with him many times while he sat reading just such a communication. Sat next to him on the creaking bed in his tent, combing her hair or easing the tense ache in his shoulders with her deft fingers.

The detail surfaced. 'Mathild's mother was wife to one of Odovacer's generals. Her family were butchered when their Saxon village was raided.' She had been taken into slavery and Odovacer disappeared to serve under a variety of rising generals. Had worked his way since then, steadily, to the top of the pile.

'Any woman who had known this man, Odovacer, must have had her wits about her. He sounds dangerous,' Gwenhwyfar observed.

Arthur took her face between his hands, his thumb brushing the softness of her cheek. 'She was as fiery as you, Mathild. You would have liked her.'

Gwenhwyfar doubted it. 'Not while she was sharing your bed. I would have sooner cut her throat.'

A teasing smile lifted Arthur's lips, his eyes sparkling. As he would have cut Bedwyr's had anything persisted between him and Gwenhwyfar.

She delicately touched her lips against his own, silencing any further word, reminding him of the unspoken pax that rested between them.

Mathild. Arthur had told her, on that long, slow, journey home from Gaul, of Mathild. The jealousy, the rise of heart-burning ill-will had compressed her lips then, but sense and practically had eased away the hostility through the passing of months. Arthur was a man who enjoyed his women. Mathild, at least, had seemed to be a woman of worth, not some lice-bitten, pox-ridden, gutter-slut. And who was Gwenhwyfar to chide? Had she not also betrayed their exchanged marriage vows? Occasionally, especially when Arthur was gone on some visit to a distant stronghold, or meeting of Council, she lay at night remembering Bedwyr's hot caress, the different touch of his exploring hand, the feel of his breath, his mouth on hers. Remembering, but not wanting. It was Arthur she wanted, Arthur she loved. The rest had no more significance than the fantasy arousal of a passing dream.

'It would seem to me,' she said after a while, 'that we all have a darkness shut into our souls, one that we will need explain when we stand in the sunlight of the next world.' She moved slightly, kissed his mouth again, more possessive, decisive.

Arthur ran his hand along her back, down across her buttocks, pulling her, insistent, nearer. Teasing, he announced, 'I think events have arisen that make me need someone in my bed. Shall I make do with you, or send out for the tavern whore?'

The look Gwenhwyfar gave him was supercilious. She disentangled herself from his hold, rose gracefully from the bed and ambled to the doorway. Lingered, watching the men lifting the deer carcasses from the pack-ponies.

'Will he last long, do you think, Odovacer? The first man without Roman blood to wear the purple of an Emperor since Augustus Octavian. Surely he will be dead before the year is out?' She spoke with her back to Arthur.

'He is a man to be reckoned with, uses his head as well as his balls. But I agree, there'll be Romans ruling again in Rome before the winter.'

With deliberation, Gwenhwyfar closed the door, slid the bolt home with a firm thrust, turned, leant against the wood, her eyes narrowed, seductive. 'You would not rather have Mathild, or someone like her, here?'

Stretching out, folding his hands behind his head, crossing his boots at the ankles Arthur pursed his lips, considering. *Would you rather have Bedwyr?* He thrust the irrational jealous thought aside, knowing it to be the mischief of mind-tricks. 'Na,' he said. 'Her hips were too boney for my liking. If I must purchase my meat, I expect something substantial to chew on.'

Ponderously, Gwenhwyfar unpinned her hair. Unrestricted, the copper silver-streaked mane tumbled free, cascaded over her shoulders, across her breasts, down past her waist and hips. Slowly, unhurried, she walked back to the bed, her fingers releasing the lacing of her gown, let it slide to the floor about her feet; unfastened the under-tunic, her breastband. Stood naked, sensuous, one step away from Arthur.

She was as slim as she had been in her youth, the faint marks against her belly and thighs the only signs of her childbearing. The skin of her arms, neck and face was golden, tanned from the hours out in wind, air and sun; her legs long, slender.

'If you found me in a slave market,' she enquired, 'would you purchase me for the price of a ring?'

His stomach knotting with wanting, Arthur held his hand out to her. She took it. 'If anyone ever owned you,' he answered, his voice husky, 'he would be a fool to sell you.'

'Oh.' She knelt on the bed, leant over him, her natural perfume, her body, her nearness, rousing him to that last, full attention. 'You intend to keep me, then?'

Arthur drew her down, brought her body close, moulding together with his. 'I am not a fool.'

§ VII

Something thudded against the outer door with a loud, penetrating thump, followed by what sounded like the hounds of Hades let loose after a wild she-cat. Within the chamber the dogs leapt wildly at the inside of the closed door, barking furiously.

'What in the name of the Bull is going on?' Arthur sprang from the bed, found his bracae in the hastily discarded heap of clothing tumbled on the floor. Pulling them on, hopped to the door, flung it wide.

Two children fell through, locked together, snarling, hurling abuse, tangling with the excited dogs. Fists punching, feet kicking. Arthur leapt back as a sandalled foot caught him on the shin. He cursed loudly, shouted at the dogs to lay down, be quiet, bent in attempt to grab hold of the two twisting children, cursed again as human teeth sunk into his hand. 'Mithras's blood!' he yelled, yanking furiously at the tunic in his other hand. 'Stop this! Break it up, I say! Now!'

Breathing hard, snarling, eyes enraged, the two children came apart.

The boy Medraut, and Archfedd, blood trickling from her left nostril. Both of them would sport bruises to face and body by next morning.

Enticed by the noise, several people were gathering around the door, a few of the Artoriani, women, some more children, curious onlookers. Ider was pushing his way sternly through, clearing a path none too gently, the commotion at the private entrance to his King's chamber alarming him. He reached the threshold, stood, arms folded, grim-faced, watched Arthur shaking the two children as if they were pups caught raiding the meat-store, relieved that it was false alarm, not some brutal murder attempt.

'What in all the gods' names is going on?' Arthur was bellowing. 'How dare you brawl in the vicinity of my chamber!' With each angry word he shook both of them; realized something wet was staining his left hand, he pulled away. 'Bull's blood, Medraut, you have ink all down you!' He released Archfedd, intending to inspect the state of the boy more closely. The girl flew past him and began laying into the lad again with her feet and fists, beating at his chest, kicking at his legs. Medraut cried out, tried to dodge behind Arthur.

The roar of rage from both the Pendragon and Ider, who lurched forward to help separate them, could have been loud enough to raise a war-standard. Ider took hold the boy, dragged him away, Arthur grasped the girl, his daughter, trundled her like a beer barrel a few paces into the room. She struggled, arms whirling, hair flying. Gods! For a ten-year-old, she possessed the strength of a grown man! Her fist accidentally caught Arthur's chin, knocking his head upward, sending his brain reeling. 'Enough!' he roared, furious, pinning her arms to her side. Lifting her forcibly off the floor he strode across the room, flung her onto the bed. 'Calm yourself this instant, or I'll take my belt to you here and now!'

Gwenhwyfar had risen and tugged a shift over her body, her hair falling loose and tousled, her eyes soft with contentment. They had slept, Arthur and she, curled together for more than an hour. Shameless! Love-making during an afternoon – as well they were married, else tongues would be wagging! This outrageous interruption had spoiled their tranquillity, destroyed the lazy pleasure.

Roughly, she took hold her daughter, steered her to a stool, sternly pointed for her to sit, and sit still. Archfedd's eyes were glowering, hot coals, her jaws clamped into anger. Her hair was red, like her mother's although darker, perhaps not as curled. Most of it had escaped its braiding, for it tumbled, untidy, dishevelled; her tunic was torn at the shoulder. She sat, reluctant, crunched into her ball of tight fury.

Arthur dealt with the boy. 'So?' he demanded curtly. 'What is this about?'

Medraut was shaking, his fists clenched as rigid as Archfedd's, his jaw as set, though tears were rapidly welling in his eyes. Ider had him clamped firmly with vice-like hands grasping his shoulders, and his voice trembled as he tried to answer his father, a mixture of outrage, fright and agitation. 'She tore it,' he stammered, 'my parchment. She ripped it into pieces.' He was breathing hard, clearly upset. 'I was almost finished!'

Ider released the lad, but stood ready to clutch hold should renewed fighting between the two whelps seem imminent. Arthur hunkered to his heels. At ten, he had been a tall lad. Medraut was still short, skinny, somehow managed to convey the image of a poor-kept peasant's boy, though he was well fed, well clothed. Educated. Arthur rubbed his stubbled chin with his hand. Would these two offspring of his not even try to become friends? Or at the very least, agree to differ! Five times in two weeks; bickering, squabbling. A blackened eye, a scraped shin.

'Parchment is expensive stuff. From where did you get it?'

'He stole it from Father Cethrwm's chamber!'

Arthur scowled at Archfedd, 'I am speaking to the lad, not to you. Keep silent.'

'Stealing is a grave accusation, Archfedd!' Gwenhwyfar rapped at the same instant. 'You must have proof before you claim such things.'

'I have proof!' Archfedd bounced to her feet, her face tipped up to her mother's, her passion intense. 'I saw him take it!' She flung her arm at the boy, pointing, accusing. She did not think of him as her brother, for she despised him. Thought him a coward, a liar; a mewling little runt. It was a mistake, on her father's part, to have brought him home from Gaul. He was not of Pendragon blood, she was certain. Some guiling whore had wrongly convinced her father that he was. 'I was in the chapel and . . .'

'Be silent, girl!' Arthur commanded. Biting her lip, Archfedd sat, her hands clasped in her lap. Would no one ever listen to her?

'Boy? Did you steal it?'

Medraut stared direct at his father. All he had wanted to do was write out a psalm that he had learnt last week, to keep it for himself, to be able to re-read it whenever he fancied. He liked the psalms; he liked writing; but he never had the courage to tell his father that. Was never able to say that he hated weapon-training, sword practice, the daily drill of javelin-throwing. He could never hit a target; always ended on the floor or with multiple bruises. Oh, Archfedd was good with weapons – the little show-off! But could she read as well as he? Could she form her letters as beautifully? All right, so she could ride a frisky horse without falling off – so what? He preferred being in the quiet sanctuary of Father Cethrwm's chapel, reading the expensive books kept there. Reading the Bible. That pleased the Father. He had said only last week that he, Medraut, would have made a fine scholar, had he not been born as a king's son. Well, he did not want to be a king's son! He wanted to go to Ambrosius's School of Learning. He wanted to become a priest!

'Father Cethrwm would not mind me having it. He says my writing is better than hers.' Medraut sneered over Arthur's shoulder at Archfedd, realized, too late, that he had made an error. His father's expression had darkened, his eyes narrowed. Medraut was wary of his father, he knew his anger, his strength, had seen it used against others, had felt the lash of Arthur's belt across his back. So had Archfedd, but Medraut conveniently forgot that.

Unable to take a step backwards, Medraut pushed his body harder against Ider, standing behind him.

'Answer the question, boy!' Arthur's admonishment snapped out, as fierce as a wolf's bite.

Defiant, attempting to hide the fact that his heart was pounding and that he desperately needed to visit the latrine, Medraut lifted his chin. 'I borrowed it.'

'You stole it.'

For a long moment Medraut said nothing, staring eye to eye with Arthur. He could never please his father for he was useless with sword and spear, was afraid of the horses, especially the stallions; was clumsy, inept. He dropped his gaze, hung his head. Could not even brave this out, as Archfedd would have done. 'Aye,' he whispered, meekly. 'I stole it.'

Arthur stood, turned his attention to his daughter. Her chin was up, defiant, she had done wrong and she knew it, but unlike Medraut she would not hide from punishment. She would grow to be a lioness, Archfedd, like her mother. 'And you started a fight because of this?' Arthur asked her. What had he told her, warned her, about fighting, two days past? Two days, for Mithras's sake! 'I am most displeased with you, daughter.'

'He started fighting, not me!' she countered, hotly, bounding to her feet. 'I told him he had no right to use that parchment and he said I was a spoilt brat!'

'Only because she called me a pagan whore's bastard!' Furious at her twisting of the truth, Medraut rushed forward, fists swinging. Arthur made a grab for him at the same moment as Ider, Gwenhwyfar restrained Archfedd as the girl prepared to lash out with her feet again.

'Gods' blood!' Arthur cursed. 'Have I sired a pair of demons?' He waved his hand, dismissive, at Ider. 'Take him to Cethrwm. It was his property, he can deal with it. And as for you,' he swung to Archfedd, 'you are confined to the Hall for one week.'

384

'But Mam was taking me to Lindinis on the morrow!' The answering wail of protest was fraught with disappointment.

'Mam,' Gwenhwyfar promptly retorted, 'will be taking you nowhere.'

'He was in the wrong! He ought be punished, not me!' Archfedd, spun around, ran for the inner door, pausing as she fumbled at the latch to cry, 'I hate you, hate you both!'

Arthur stood, looking blandly at Gwenhwyfar, who opened her arms, spread her hands. There was a twinkle of laughter in her eyes as she exclaimed, 'And she is barely is ten. I dread to think what she will be like in another three years, when her body begins to change!'

Arthur ambled to the outer door, shooed the last of the curious onlookers away, kicked it shut with his foot. 'Oh, I know just what she will be like.' He turned around, grinned at his wife. 'Just like you.'

Gwenhwyfar grinned back. 'Oh dear,' she laughed. 'We are heading for a rough sea then!'

November 476

§ VIII

The onset of another winter. Chill, hostile winds; trees bare and dejected against a drained, colourless landscape that lay ill-willed and sullen beneath a bored, frowning sky.

Morgaine sat hunched, her arms clasped around her drawn-up knees, her back pressing against the hard discomfort of the granary wall. She did not feel the bite of the cold that ate into her numbed fingers and feet, did not care that her dress was drab, torn and faded. The building behind her was empty, save for cobwebs, a scattering of mouldered ears of corn, and a few half-starved rats. The steading was broken and shabby; fences, buildings, neglected and untended. One goat, the last, thin and lice-scabbed, grazed for some small sustenance at the remaining autumn straggle of weeds. The cattle, the hens, the sow had gone long ago. The fields that had once harvested the smile of golden corn and reaped sweet, rich hay had returned to wildness. Even the house-place was half-tumbled, its roof rotten, fallen in at one end, with the door leaning on sagging hinges.

Morgaine had slept poorly, tossing and quivering as the vivid dreams rode rough through her troubled night. They were coming more frequently, the previously occasional visitation haunting her almost nightly this past week. Mayhap the dreary onset of winter had sent them hustling around her hearth-fire. Or was it the past resurging spiteful and insistent?

Her mother came in all the dreams. Morgause. The lurid vehemence of a red sun always behind her, shadowing the sharp features of her face. But Morgaine knew it was her. That arrogant, supercilious stance, that cruel, derisive laugh. And Arthur was there also, behind, a little to the left, standing, sometimes with his hands empty, hanging by his side, occasionally with a sword, jagged and broken. And always, always, blood. Running, savage. Gaping, raw. From head, from hands. Flowing, oozing. Always, the blood.

Morgaine's forehead rested forward, touching her knees. She had her eyes open, for she dared not see again the pictures that lay behind them, dare not reconjure those images that had woken her, two hours past. She lifted her head, stared without seeing, at the leaden sky. Her fault, her mistake, her negligence. *Mea culpa. Mea culpa.* Who had she been to think she knew better? What wisdom did she possess, what science, what knowing? None! She knew nothing, had nothing! Her mother, while she lived in this existence, had almost become the Goddess on Earth. Morgause had known everything that needed to be known. And she was dead. Slaughtered, murdered. That darkened, unseen face, haloed by the corn-gold of hair, blood soiled. Morgause would live, would be queen, the all-powerful, the all-seeing, the all-knowing, had Morgaine, her wretched daughter, not disobeyed her.

That was why the dreams came. Sent from Morgause, from the red darkness of the otherworld, sent to set right a wrong. Sent to show Morgaine the path that she must follow to undo the wickedness that she, by disobeying her mother, had set so terribly in motion.

Twice – twice! – she had allowed him life, when death should have brought about his ending. Ah, she had been beguiled by the whisperings of those who worked against the wisdom of the Goddess. Uncaring, she had listened to their mischief, their malice, rather than the words, the command, of her mother. Listened to the silliness of her heart, of the betraying image of love. Love? Hah! What was love? Pain, rejection, contempt, that was love! She had given love, she had given life. And had received nothing save pain and contempt in return.

She stood, her bones and muscles stiff, her mind and body exhausted, for she had sat a long while listening for what she must do. Inside the house-place she collected her cloak, put several items in a coarse-woven drawstring bag, her personal things. A whale-bone comb, a handful of ivory and silver hairpins, a bronze mirror. The most useful of her dried and ground herbs. And a wooden box. She could not face the trauma of sleep without the contents of that box, a gift left to her by her friend, old Livia, who had taken the final journey to the otherworld as the last winter had rolled into spring. A precious gift. The warm, safe, comfort of the Poppy.

She took nothing else. It was not the time of year for travelling, but what use staying here, where the demons of the Dream could so easily find her? Better to move on, go back.

Set things, if she could, as they ought have been, as she had been commanded. Eleven years past.

October 477

§ IX

'Thrust! It's a spear you are using, not a damned swine-prod!' Gwenhwyfar bellowed her reprimand across the practice ground, her hands cupped around her mouth to carry the shouted words further. 'Dear gods,' she muttered, as the cast spear arced too flat, fell, bouncing and slithering, along the dew-wet grass several yards ahead of the target. 'Useless.' She yanked her own spear from the ground before her, strode, long-legged, impatient, the width of the field, glaring at the boy who stood, head down, embarrassed, fingers fiddling with a leather pouch at his waist.

'Like this. You throw like this!' Gwenhwyfar came alongside him, weighed the spear in her hand and, taking aim with her eye, brought her arm back, launched the weapon with strength from her legs, buttocks and shoulders. The spear sailed in its low trajectory – not too high, for the wind was wilful this morning, and struck, with a satisfactory thud, just off-centre of the red circle painted in the heart-place of the straw man dangling from an upright post. The shaft quivered, jutted from its target. The one time Medraut had managed to hit the man, his spear had glanced off the sacking, fallen to the grass.

'The first volley of spears, after the archers have released their arrows,' Gwenhwyfar lectured, curtly beckoning Medraut to walk with her as she strode to retrieve the weapon, 'must make their mark. Not that many kill, but enough wound and disable. Enough are rammed into shields to render them useless. The second volley follows quickly, inflicting more of the same. By then, the horses are in full gallop.' She twisted the shaft, tugged the spear loose, pleased that it had sunk in deep. Were he real, the man would be dead.

Medraut had fetched his own spear, was holding it limply. Why did the bloody thing never fly as straight for him? It did not help that he could not see the target clearly from the distance across the practice ground. Closer, he was better – and his sword-fighting was improving. At least, so he thought.

They returned to the throwing point. And he did try, but his foot twisted as he brought his weight forward. The grass, damp from warm days and cold nights, was slippery. It would have been a good throw, almost, for he had put his strength behind the casting, but the aim was off, yards wide. The blade dug into the grass.

'Well,' Gwenhwyfar announced, with an audible sigh, 'let us assume your opponent also has a spear. He would have thrown by now. You,' she added rather pointedly, 'would now be dead, unless you had brought your shield up quick enough.' She placed her fists on to each hip, stood, legs slightly apart, her blue cloak hanging loosely from her shoulders, lifting gently in the wind. 'However,' she added scathingly, 'seeing as you made a balls-mess of shield practice yesterday, I am assuming you would have failed that simple defensive move also. It would be kinder to slit your throat now, have a quick end to it. You are never going to make a soldier.' She did not add the rest, the other words that automatically ought to follow. *You may be a King's son, but you will never make a King.*

It was disappointment that made Gwenhwyfar exasperated, disappointment harnessed with regret. Her eldest-born son would have been two and twenty. Would have fathered sons of his own by now . . . if Llacheu had lived, the menace of Cerdic's omnipresent shadow would have been nothing more than the annoyance of harvest-flies on a hot summer's day. If Llacheu had lived. Or Gwydre. Or Amr. Arthur would have had a son to follow him, a son to be proud of. Instead, he had Medraut.

She had accepted the boy, taken him into her household with barely a murmur, though his presence was daily a reminder of her own loss. And of Arthur's infidelity. Why had *she* borne him a son who lived, who thrived? Why her, why not Gwenhwyfar? She tried not to be harsh on him, not to let the dismay taint her voice too openly. 'Never mind.' She put her hand briefly to his shoulder before walking away. 'With more practice, who knows?' They both knew it would take more than practice. Medraut could not see straight, aim straight. He was clumsy, finger-fumbling, slow with his reaction in evasion and attack. He was, as she had said, useless.

Medraut took the spear to the armoury, stacked it with the others of its kind. It was a square, stone-built room, situated to the rear of the blacksmith's bothy. Spears of all lengths, some heavy, bold-bladed, others more lightweight, the javelins; swords, daggers, a few shields. Leather-lined war caps stacked to one corner; in another, the linked chain of mail tunics. He would have liked, one day, to have worn some of that mailed armour. It seemed unlikely. If he could not throw a spear straight, what hope had he of one day becoming one of the Artoriani? Medraut was not hurt by Gwenhwyfar's annoyance. How could he be? She was right. Dismally he left the armoury, trailed along a narrow and rutted side-path that skirted behind this cluster of work-place buildings, found himself at the chapel.

Again a small construction, erected as with all Christian places, in the form of an equal-sided cross; its wattle walls white-plastered, the reed-thatch of the roof new-repaired in places, golden-patched against weather-darkened brown. As always, save on the coldest days when the wind blew direct inside, the door stood propped open. Medraut entered, breathed deeply of the sweet scent of beeswax candles, fresh-spread herbs and the subtle air of peaceful contentment. A posy of flowers stood in a pottery flagon on the stone altar, their bright colours joyful and pleasing. He sat on the rearmost bench, studying the pictures decorating the inside of the walls. They were probably not as marvellous as the beautiful paintings that Arthur's cousin Bedwyr would no doubt be seeing in Rome and Constantinople, but to Medraut they were wondrous. Each section depicted a story about Christ's time on earth – the feeding of the five thousand, the healing of the sick, the crucifixion, and his favourite, Jesu calming the storm on the sea of Galilee. Medraut sat facing that scene now. His stomach was churning, the choke of tears burning his throat. His whole body felt battered, bruised and aching, as if he was out in the temper of that storm, buffeted by that wicked wind, threatened by the oppressive mass of thunder clouds and frightened of the great sweep of angry waves that tossed and plundered the tiny, valiant boat. Steadfastly, he stared at the white-clad figure to the left of the scene. The man standing so calmly at the edge of the water, arms outspread, radiating his love and compassion.

The tears that had threatened to flood down Medraut's cheeks dried, the heart-thump eased and the pain sauntered away, left his body, left the chapel. Calm. Acceptance. What was to be, had to be.

Father Cethrwm had painted the pictures, taking many months to complete them to his satisfaction, and Medraut had helped. He had mixed the bright tinctures, carefully filled in the areas of colour that Cethrwm had indicated. Part of his soul had entered these scenes, and to come here to look at them, the deep reds, the vivid blues, the golden yellows, rekindled hope and quiet belief in Medraut. There was something for him out there in the future. Something.

'What are you doing, skulking in here? I hope Father Cethrwm has his things locked away.'

Archfedd.

'I have as much right to be here as you. Go away.'

'No.' Archfedd flounced to the nearest bench, intending to be deliberately annoying. Medraut ignored her, even though she sat jangling her bracelets and drumming her heels in a rhythmless beat against the bench leg.

'You will never be King, you know.'

She was in her eleventh year, her body already maturing to womanhood, a capable child who knew her own mind. A smaller version of her mother, so Arthur often said. Most things that Archfedd attempted, she excelled at. Riding, sword-practice, running. She was not so good with people, not tactful like her mother, not able to keep thoughts to herself, set safe away in her mind. She was a girl loyal to her friends, intent against her enemies. She repeated what she had said, with more animosity. 'I said that you will never be King.'

Aye, he knew he would not. 'If you have come to gloat, forget it. I know I'm bastard-born and not much good with weapons. But—' And a sudden courage came to him. Could it have come from the still peace of the chapel, or through the bitterness of self-disappointment? He only wanted to please, to show his father and Lady Gwenhwyfar that he could, given the chance, be of value, be a son worthy of the great Arthur Pendragon. He would please them one day. One day they would be proud of him. He stood, regarded his half-sister, addressed her with conviction. 'But remember this, Archfedd. I will not always be a boy of eleven years old!'

He stalked out the door, pretended that he did not hear her answer.

'And I'll not always be a girl. One day I will be grown also, Medraut the bastard-born.' She had come to the doorway, stood, one arm raised above her head, learning on the timber frame, watching him saunter away. Said the one thing that she knew would hurt him as surely as a plunged dagger blade. 'I'm legitimate-born. I will be Queen when my father is gone.'

§ X

The hut was still there, rough, wattle-built, crudely circular, set beside the Yns Witrin road where the track crossed the log-laid causeway. It was low country here, oozing with rivulets of water that overnight could raise the quiet extent of willow-pocked marshes to a desolate landscape of floodwater.

A poor quarter of the country, an equally as poor hovel but, for what it was, it had been kept well enough. The roof adequately thatched, the walls recently replastered with daub made from animal blood and dung mixed with mud. Herbs and medicinal plants grew strong and healthy in a walled garden to one side of the stream, a tethered goat grazed a little beyond that. Clothing, that had been washed that day stretched, almost dried, over a few scraggy shrubs of hawthorn. It ought be fetched in soon, for the autumn warmth of the day was giving ground to the chill of evening. There would be a frost this night.

Morgaine was not hurrying. Through the months she had wandered across Gaul, taking her own path, her own time, spending a few nights in a peasant's bothy, several weeks in towns along the way. Earning her keep, never wanting for anything. She had a gift of healing, her remedies and potions eagerly welcomed anywhere and everywhere. And she had herself to offer, should there be the chance of higher payment. Morgaine paused before stepping onto the raised pathway of logs, ran her hand through her hair, pushing it back from her forehead. She was travel-grimed, weary; hoped for a dry bed and a warm supper. She would get it here, at this hut, if the occupier was not busy.

She was not. She came to the doorway, bucket in hand, intending to bring the goat into the night-shelter of the lean-to bothy at the back of the dwelling, to milk it. Stood instead, head cocked slight to one side, waiting for the woman to approach nearer. 'Good greeting to you,' she called, 'you travel late on the road, 'tis nearing evening.'

Morgaine crossed the log way, seated herself on a wooden bench set before the hut, enjoying a chance to rest in the last of the day's sunshine. 'Not so late,' she contradicted. ''Tis not yet darkening.'

The girl – for she could not have been more than ten and five years – licked her lips nervously. She welcomed visitors, indeed counted on them, but it was usually men who came to her hut by the causeway, not women. And this woman, with hair dyed as black as a raven's wing, and penetrating deep-blue eyes that seemed darker than they ought be, alarmed her for some unexplained reason.

'I will be preparing supper soon,' she offered tentatively. 'You are welcome to share with me, although,' – she slid in a small, flustered giggle – 'I may have custom to attend.'

Morgaine raised her hand, dismissive. 'You need not concern yourself overmuch. I ask only a bowl of broth and a bed for the night.'

The girl, her milking bucket wedged under one arm against her hip, chewed a finger-nail. She had only the one bed, a blanket-covered pile of dried bracken, and that, if any men paid call, she would be needing. Disconcerted, she wondered what to do. The law of hospitality bid her make any traveller welcome, yet no woman had ever wanted to stay at her wayside whore-place.

Could this woman read her mind? It seemed that she could, for Morgaine smiled, reassuring, said, as she rose, walked to the open doorway, 'Mayhap this night you will not have custom.'

Inside, the hut was dark, musty, as most small dwellings of that kind were. A hearth-place situated centrally with the smoke-hole above it in

392

the roof. A stool, the bracken bed to one side, a stone-weighted loom. Cooking pots, pottery amphorae; from one timber support hung two glass-bead necklaces, intertwined with a bunch of drying herbs. It was humble but tidy. It would suit Morgaine. This hut had once belonged to another whore, Brigid, who had been the messenger-woman of Morgause, Morgaine's mother. Brigid, who had also worked for the Pendragon, feeding him suitable information. Oh, he had found out, eventually, that Brigid had two paymasters, that she was a traitor to his kingdom. Morgaine had been misguided then, had thought Arthur to have the right of it, had thought that love was the most important thing. Not the commands of her mother, given through Brigid's tongue.

Aye, this whore-hut would suit Morgaine well. Easy enough, in the early light of the next dawn, when a cattle-drover called by to ease the itch in his groin, to inform him that this was her place now. He never questioned further, one whore was much the same as another. He had no reason to notice the patch of garden – even if he had, would have assumed the fresh-dug earth was for the planting of new herbs. Why would he suspect that it made an ideal grave for the girl who had been whore here the evening before?

February 478

§ XI

They located a small herd of five deer after about an hour's easy riding. The woods that spanned the undulating ground to the south of Caer Cadan were winter-quiet, the trees dormant, lifeless in their naked state of bare branches. The day had been dull, although the snow clouds that had trudged across the skies these last few weeks had at last retreated. Pockets of snow remained, huddling between tree roots in the lee of bramble and hawthorn bushes, lining the shadowed places of ice-fringed streams. It was cold, the breath vapour from rider and horse steaming, the light beneath the thickly crowded trees, for all their lack of a leafed canopy, poor.

Arthur pointed with his bow, indicating the does feeding, some few hundred yards distant, as yet unaware of the newcomers in the woods. He grinned at Gwenhwyfar riding a few yards to his left. She smiled back, the prospect of an easy kill cheering them both. The quicker they could bring down this night's supper, the sooner they could return home to the warmth of a hearth-fire and a tankard of wine. One of the dogs whined, chastized immediate by Gweir, who had already dismounted, secured his horse. They were well downwind; the deer grazed, unconcerned. Arthur, too, dismounted, signalled for the boy, Medraut, to climb down from his pony, tether him alongside the others. The dogs were similarly secured, the handler left to crouch with them, ready to slip the leashes when needed. Hunting was a synchronized effort, each rider and bowman working as a team, needing, necessarily, to work in silence without command or communication, but needing to act implicitly.

He was nervous, the boy, the last hunt, a month past, had been disastrous, not his fault, they all said, it was a thing easily happened, yet had he not stepped on that dead branch, had the snap of its breaking not ricocheted around that clearing . . . it had taken three hours to find their quarry again. Archfedd had not let him forget it. She was not with them this day though, laid up as she was with a swollen and bruised knee after that fall yesterday. He ought not smile, ought not feel this gloat of pleasure; the girl was in pain, could have been severely injured. At least the pony was unharmed, though the fall had been a crashing one. Gwenhwyfar had told Archfedd not to jump Briallen over the ditches,

394

not in icy conditions. But she had ignored the advice, as ever, jumped the mare anyway. There had been a terrible row after, Gwenhwyfar determined to thrash Archfedd for putting a good mount in unnecessary danger, Arthur countering the anger by saying the injured knee and the forgoing of a hunting trip was better punishment. Medraut agreed with his father on that. Archfedd took a whipping as stoically as a warrior faced a battle wound. Not coming today though . . . hah! That had hurt her indeed!

He attempted a smile at his father, put one finger against his lips to indicate his awareness for the need of stealth and quiet. Arthur nodded, tested his bowstring, indicating Medraut was to do likewise. Arthur, Gweir and a third bowman took position beside Gwenhwyfar and the two other mounted men, Medraut staying close to his father, as he had been instructed. Ready, arrows knocked to the bowstrings, the horses moved off slowly, almost ambling. Deer were not so mistrustful of four-legged creatures and, downwind, the scent of human was masked. The bowmen, on foot, walked to the far side of the horses, Arthur beside Gwenhwyfar, his hand upon her thigh. She playfully tapped his fingers as they stealthily worked erotically higher, mouthing at him to wait until later. He grinned up at her, boyishly, winked. He was still handsome in his rough, rugged way. Grizzled hairs were starting to show more pronounced against the dark above his temple, but it was as thick as if he were still young, no sign of receding from the forehead or balding on the crown. The skin around his eyes, chin and jowls, was wrinkling, perhaps developing a slight sag where once it lay firm, but the eyes themselves shone bright, mischievous. *Later?* that wink implied, *I'll hold you to that.*

Gweir stopped at the first position, stepping from beside the horse, shrinking against the solid width of an old oak. The horses moved on. Arthur tapped Medraut on the shoulder, their turn to drop aside. He had skilfully chosen two trees close together, Medraut to stand a little to one side of and behind his father. The third man positioned himself, the three experienced men and the boy forming a V-shape ahead of the grazing deer. There they must wait, immobile, poised and ready, while the horses unhurriedly continued to circle upwind, to manoeuvre behind the quarry. Walking in fits and starts, the horses grazed a few mouthfuls of grass here and there. Unhurried, unsuspicious, unalerting.

Upwind, Gwenhwyfar and, spaced a few yards apart, the other two horsemen began to tighten the noose, edging closer to the group of does, starting the drive forward. The occasional click of the tongue, a light slap of a rein against the leather saddle. Innocent noises, almost natural, but a doe lifted her head, some half-doubt alerting her. The horses gave no threat, but there was a slight, uneasy scent to the air. Chewing the mouthful of grass, she walked a few yards downwind, head high, eyes alert, ears listening, nostrils scenting for that vague, half-caught smell of human. The other four followed gradually, browsing, unconcerned, as they went with her, nudged forward by the three innocuous horses those few, distant yards behind.

Medraut held his breath. His arm was quivering, for the bows needed to be held in the firing position. They, he and the three men, blended well with the trees and bustle of hawthorn and hazel bushes, dressed as they were in natural colours, browns and dark greens, their hoods pulled over their heads. He kept his half-slit eye on one deer, as his father had told him. *'Pick your prey, a deer nearest you, one that looks likely to come to your side of the ambush.'* He had laughed, Arthur, when telling this, ruffled the lad's hair. *'Works as well when ambushing men, only they have a better power of reasoning than beasts.'* Medraut had grinned at the advice . . . Ah, he so wanted to do well on this hunt!

It was a delicate task, herding the prey forward. Too slow and they could simply trot away, melting into the shadows of the trees, too fast and they could panic, running to one side, or flee too soon. If they simply disappeared, it was not too much of a matter, for the dogs would scent them out again, but it would all be time, and daylight, wasted.

Gwenhwyfar, riding to the right, clicked her fingers. Another deer pricked her ears, listened, attentive, watchful. A flurry of wind taking scent to wary nostrils . . . and they were running!

The best shot was to aim for the centre of the chest as the deer came head-on, from as close range as possible. If the animal ran to the right, a good aim would be difficult, the bowman had to turn. To the left was desirable, for an arrow could be loosed into the side. *'For Mithras's sake though, boy,'* Arthur's words flickered through Medraut's mind as the deer came nearer, his fingers tightening around the drawn bowstring, *'do not shoot straight to your left or right – you could easily hit another man and anyway, the quarry would be moving too fast in relation to the arrow flight.'*

Medraut gathered his breath, forced himself to wait, one eye shut, the other squinting, intent on the doe with a pale muzzle. He had been practising with the bow. It was easier to handle than a spear, for he could take better aim, aligning his eye with target and arrow head . . . Just one more yard, one more . . . Medraut released the strain on the taut bowstring, let the arrow loose, heard the whine of its brief flight, fancied he heard the thud of its finding the mark. The doe faltered, staggered, scrabbled a few more paces, her legs working, chest heaving, fell forward. Dead. Medraut cheered. His exultation sweeping away caution, he leapt in the air, hoisting his bow, yelling his delight, 'I did it! I did it!'

Simultaneously, the second deer staggered, picked herself up, ran on.

The third was also hit, but the lodged arrow barely broke her stride. The other two leapt away, unharmed. Arthur had reached for a second arrow, knocked it quickly into place, but they were gone, too far to shoot accurately between the trees and undergrowth. He was pleased, stepped forward, slapped his son on the shoulder, took him to the fallen deer. 'Well done, lad!'

Medraut grinned up at him, satisfied, pleased. Two arrows protruded from the carcass, one, Arthur's, clean through the chest, the other, Medraut's attempt, penetrating the neck. It was so much cleaner when the quarry fell easily. Gwenhwyfar rode up, slid from her horse. 'Well done,' she said to the boy.

'What about me?' Arthur chided, feigning petulance.

'What about you?' she teased.

Gweir trotted up, his face glowing. The third man was sounding his hunting horn, the notes spiriting through the woodland, the baying of the dogs answering almost immediately, aware of the oncoming excitement, the tracking of injured deer. The two trails were found with ease. One was of clear, bright blood, a long chase probably, for it would be a minor wound; the other dark, thick and sticky. They followed for one quarter of a mile, found the deer collapsed, already dead, the arrow buried deep in its belly. For the other, they took to the horses again, letting the hounds run free to follow the scent unhampered by leash or handler.

The dogs brought the animal to bay after half an hour's searching. Arthur was tempted to let Medraut finish the doe, but it was senseless to prolong death unnecessarily. He motioned for Gweir to do it. One arrow, at close range. The three carcasses would provide well for supper that night in the King's Hall.

Riding homeward, while the adults exchanged teasing jests and bellowed raucous hunting songs, Medraut dared ask his father a thing that had been on his mind for several months.

'Da?'

'Aye, lad?'

'Can I go to Ambrosius's school?'

Gwenhwyfar had been laughing with Gweir and the other men, she had not heard. Arthur checked his mare from snatching at an appetizing clump of grass, rode in silence a while. Medraut bit his lip, hung back slightly from the merry group. He had been stupid to ask. His father was not a Christian. Arthur referred to Mithras, the soldier's god – though in all reality, he was not a dedicated follower. And he was needed at Caer Cadan, to be trained as a warrior, to fight, to lead, but oh, by all that was dear to him, he wanted to go to Ambrosius's school! To read the scriptures, to learn how to perfect the technique of using styli and ink. To hear the histories, the great works of poetry and oratory! He wanted to learn, to become a scholar, not a soldier.

'Is that what you truly want? To leave Caer Cadan, go to Ambrosium?'

Medraut rode, looking intently at his hands, gripping around the reins. He did, oh he did! But to say so, to tell his father that he would rather be with the monks of Ambrosius Aurelianus's religious school . . . It would sound so ungrateful, so hurtful. He said nothing. It was only a hoped-for dream after all, a boyish wanting.

'I wanted to be the greatest leader, when I was a boy,' Arthur said. 'Even before I knew who my father was. Not King, I did not know that I had the birthing to be King, I just wanted to be a good leader, good enough to have men eager to fight with me.' He had eased his mare slower than the others, had pulled back so that he rode beside Medraut. 'Wanting something so badly can hurt, more than a wound sometimes.'

Still Medraut made no reply.

'Are you that unhappy living with me at Caer Cadan?'

Medraut's head shot up, protest quick on his lips. 'Na, father, I am not unhappy, it is just that . . .' He broke off. He did not want to leave, he was happy, but equally, he wanted to be at Ambrosius's school.

'You helped me kill that deer well today. Happen you have a better talent with a bow than you appear to possess with spear or shield?'

Medraut's smile was tentative. 'I will keep practising until I am as good as you.'

'Aye, lad.' Arthur released a slow, resigned, sigh. 'I'll ask Ambrosius to ensure that you do.'

June 478

§ XII

Had he been a more cynical man, Ambrosius could have been forgiven for believing that Amlawdd arrived at the time he did to be deliberately annoying. Always a man for routine, Ambrosius insisted on following a rigid day: prayer at dawn, a light breakfast of goat's milk and cheese, the morning devoted to correspondence and judicial matters, midday hours delegated to his school of learning, attention directed during the afternoon to overseeing the stronghold's farming estate and expanding settlement. With the third hour firmly set aside for a strict continuation of Roman order and civilization. Ambrosius spent an hour relaxing in the steam and hot-waters of his bathhouse. Such a typically Roman thing – and with so many estates forgoing the costly upkeep and maintenance of a private bathhouse, Ambrosius's modest little building had become something of a personal symbol for his immovable sense of loyalty to Rome. This single, self-indulgent luxury, a daily ritual of private solitude with only the presence of a necessary body-slave had become an opportunity to relax, to quietly peruse mental ideas of worldly plans and Godly thoughts.

The law of hospitality decreed that a guest be welcomed, offered shelter, sustenance and the sharing of comfort. In Roman terms, this included use of the bathhouse. Ambrosius was preparing to wander down the hill to his small complex of buildings as Amlawdd and his eight-strong bodyguard entered the outer courtyard at Ambrosium. Initial formalities concluded, he was obliged to extend the courtesy of asking Amlawdd to accompany him. Naturally, Amlawdd accepted. Masking his annoyance, Ambrosius disrobed in the modest changing-room, his nostrils wrinkling against the putrid stench that wafted from Amlawdd's travel-grimed body.

'Damned uncomfortable journey,' Amlawdd complained. 'Saddle needs seeing to, my backside's been chafed raw. See?' He thrust his buttocks outward for inspection, rubbing at the fatted folds of skin with his hand. Ambrosius murmured some appropriate comment of sympathy, declining to look at the overlarge rump.

'Nothing that a whore's touch can't cure though, eh?' Amlawdd belched and passed wind simultaneously, loosing a worse stench into the confined space. Surreptitiously dabbing at his nose, Ambrosius gestured for Amlawdd to proceed before him, to enter the hot pool.

Waves heaved as Amlawdd leapt into the gently steaming water splashing against the tiled edge, slopping over the top to puddle the hypocaust-heated mosaic flooring. Sedately, Ambrosius descended the three shallow steps, waded to the edge of the pool and, gripping with his hands, allowed his legs to float before him. He laid his head back into the relaxing warmth, closed his eyes; tried to close his ears against Amlawdd's prattle. For most of it he succeeded, not hearing the repetitive detail of that tedious journey . . . *'lazy brute of a horse wouldn't go faster than a trot, only slightly lame, damned thing's fit only for sausagemeat'*; complaints against the poor state of the roads . . . *'Mud wallows, Arthur ought make repairs an urgent priority'*; the coldness of the wind . . . *'Gets right round your balls, when it blows from the east'*; the inhospitality of a passed inn . . . *'The whore there smelt of pig's muck!'*

Ambrosius said nothing. From Amlawdd's similar stench, he assumed he had rutted with her anyway.

'This school of yours has expanded since last I was here, Ambrosius . . . must be making a gold piece or two from fees, eh?' He idled a few more lumbering swimming strokes, trod water. 'Think I might start something similar, get a few of those eunuch monks of yours to teach the lads.' He scratched at his private parts. 'Better still, have a few young girls, eh? I see you've got some around the place.'

Ambrosius averted his eyes from the obvious pleasure that this erotic statement evoked in Amlawdd, did not condescend to clarify the inaccuracies. That men who offered their celibacy to God were not geldings; that the girls attending his school were novitiates of the women's holy house and were the educated daughters of noblemen, not whores. Useless explaining to a dolt like Amlawdd who had interest only for the perverse and the crude.

'You ought spend more of your profit on personal comfort, Ambrosius. Look at these tiles, man, they are a disgrace!' Amlawdd had swum to the poolside. It would be the one part most in need of repair. He picked at the loose edging, pulling a cracked tile away, tossed it out to the floor where it shattered, unrepairable. Ambrosius's body-slave immediately trotted forward to gather up the pieces. 'This water's not as hot as it ought be either. I would supervise your slaves more carefully if I were you. Here, you!' Amlawdd beckoned to the slave, a thin-faced man in his late second decade. 'Feel this, it's damned cold!' Guffawing, Amlawdd splashed water over the slave, drenching him. 'He'll make sure it's warmer next time, eh?'

So he went on, passing comment, making criticism, rankling Ambrosius with references to the quality bathhouse that he intended to build. Ambrosius took several calming, deep breaths, blotting out the rambling monotony. Amlawdd . . . a bathhouse? How many times had Ambrosius endured this same boasted conversation?

The water was becoming chill. The stoke-hole had not functioned as efficiently since it had partially collapsed a year past. The rebuilding had been unsuccessful, the quality of bricks poor, the mortar too soft. Shivering slightly, Ambrosius left the pool, settled himself on the couch for the slave to begin work with the wooden strigils, scraping away the sweat and grime, followed by massaging oil into his skin. The experienced kneading of taut, tired muscles brought a pleasurable, clean glow, marred by the raucous, indecent song that Amlawdd bellowed while floating on his back in the pool, his rotund belly bobbing, visible, like a white, bloated corpse.

'You have not enough flesh on you to keep a bed-flea occupied,' Amlawdd observed between choruses. 'You're thinner than my black-haired bitch from Gaul – and that's saying something! A hay-fork has more meat on it than she has. *Oh, for a feast, I stuffed the hare and stuffed the pig, and stuffed the girl who served it!*' Fortunately for Ambrosius's bruised ears, the lewd song had only a further three verses and, his massage finished, he had the excuse to retire to the sanctuary of the changing-room.

'Arthur has taken most of my best horses, you know,' Amlawdd called after him, climbing from the pool, adding a comment that a massage would be the more satisfactory from a female body-slave.

Ambrosius ignored him, was tempted to ignore the previous comment also, but felt obliged to answer. 'It is the Pendragon's policy to purchase good stock. You have the misfortune to have stallions that relate to the old breeding lines of Gwynedd.'

'Purchase!' Amlawdd sat up, jerkily thrusting the slave aside, bellowed again. 'Purchase? I think not, sir! He took them, stole them, two weeks back! Eight of my best-bred colts and five mares. Said it was for tax tribute, pah! The bastard's no more than a common thief.'

Draping the final fold of his toga, Ambrosius called up a vague semblance of polite sympathy. 'Taxation has always been a cause for contention.' His glint of amusement went unnoticed by Amlawdd, who was wriggling himself into a more comfortable position on the couch. 'Harsh measures can even lead to uprisings, I believe,' he added, but again the sarcasm was lost. It had been Amlawdd's suggestion to tax the Saxon settlers heavily which had led to the beginning of Ambrosius's downfall. That Arthur would make the same mistake was highly doubtful. The

Pendragon was lenient in those areas where trouble could arise, took only from those who could afford to pay – and, damn the man, took within the bounds of reason, never too much, never more than necessary. Ah, but why should he worry over the failings of the past? Ambrosius had no wish to rekindle thoughts of leadership. There were a few, a mere handful of like-minded men, who would willingly donate a fortune to re-alight the flame of Rome, to return Britain to sanity and discipline. But to what point? Even Ambrosius had to admit, now, that what was gone had gone. A clay pot that was broken could not be mended.

At least here in the calm confines of his stronghold, within the walls of his religious school, he was his own master. A little piece of what was once the Roman way flourished here. Ambrosius realized that his mind had been wandering, that Amlawdd was still making complaint against Arthur. Huh, was he ever not?

'We ought be looking ahead, I say, to securing our future. What do we do when he has gone, that's what we ought be asking!'

It was a question they all mulled over, aye, even Arthur, quietly, to himself. Who would follow the Pendragon, when death eventually came to claim his corpse?

'There is Medraut, the bastard-born . . .' Ambrosius suggested.

Amlawdd heaved himself from the couch, gesturing a crude sign of dismissal, stalked into the changing-room, began to dress. 'We have two choices. We look to the daughter or to Cerdic.'

Were the second option not so absurd, Ambrosius would have laughed outright.

'She will not be far from reaching the age for breeding. Find her a suitable husband, get her with child,' Amlawdd said.

'And you, I have no doubt, would be willing to offer yourself for such a role?' It was pointless adding that edge of mockery.

At least Amlawdd had the decency to laugh. 'Of course! I could not secure the mother, why not have a go at the daughter?'

'The daughter,' Ambrosius replied, 'has the promise of an even sharper temper, so I hear.'

'My blade could cut her down to size!' Robed, clean, Amlawdd headed for the doorway, his stomach audibly growling for food and drink. 'How was your last brewing of ale?' he asked. 'Mine was poor, but I know you stock other stuff of a superior quality!'

Ambrosius suppressed a groan. Amlawdd knew, full well, that there was always sufficient wine.

'Breed with the daughter, aye, but it would also be wise to nurture Cerdic.' Later, Amlawdd continued the conversation as if there had been

402

no substantial interlude. They sat in Ambrosius's private chamber, already one flask of wine had been emptied, refilled.

'Cerdic has reneged to the Saxons.' Ambrosius's pinched tone indicated that the subject ought be ended, Amlawdd ignored the reprimand.

'Cerdic is half-British. He wants a Kingdom, would as easily return to being British if he knew he could have what he wanted. Have it handed him on a platter.'

'Nonsense!'

'Nonsense, is it?' Amlawdd crammed the last of his meat pasty into his mouth, spoke while he chewed. 'I have it from Cerdic himself.'

§ XIII

Ambrosius was uncertain whether his sense of outrage was that more intense because the man, obese from a cumulation of years of over-indulgence, crude-mannered and sprawling slovenly on the best couch, was either an outright fool or a serious threat. Had he heard right? Had he truly understood what Amlawdd implied – that Cerdic could be, was willing to be, bought?

'Cerdic has only one want. To rule as his grandsire ruled.' Amlawdd sublimely picked meat from between his teeth.

Spluttering protest, Ambrosius rose indignant and angry to his feet. 'Vortigern?' he bellowed. 'Christ and all the holy saints! You would return us to that era of heretical darkness? For all Arthur's faults, for all his petty annoyances and irritations, he has taken better care of this land than ever that poxed tyrant Vortigern did!' He took a breath, blustered on, 'We have peace. Prosperity and trade are again rising, there is law and order in our towns . . .'

'I merely meant,' Amlawdd brusquely interrupted the tirade, 'that Cerdic wishes to be King by right of inheritance. Bear in mind that he could secure us a much stronger peace for he can dominate the English as no other British-born could.' Added with a sneer, 'Not even Arthur.'

'And you know all this?' Ambrosius barked. 'How? Have you spoken with Cerdic? By Christ, if Arthur hears of this . . .!'

Lifting his buttocks to ease the discomfort of flatulence, Amlawdd passed wind, making the action sufficient answer to the threat. 'Things will travel along one road or the other,' he said. 'One day, Cerdic will have sufficient men to fight Arthur. The Pendragon is three and forty, Cerdic a much younger man, he will undoubtedly win. I see it as prudent

403

to show favour to the fortunate now, rather than later. When it may be,' Amlawdd's black toothed smile was obscene, 'too late.'

The horror of what he was suggesting made the blood run cold through Ambrosius's body. As he reseated himself, he felt chill, his stomach, his guts, turning uncomfortably. Amlawdd was suggesting a treaty of alliance with the Saxons! By God's grace and truth, was proposing that good, honest, sensible men declare for Cerdic! He swallowed vomit, felt the pain of the flux twisting in his bowels.

Amlawdd belched, stood, stretched arrogantly, drawing attention to the muscles in his arms, his strength. 'Well, it was a tiring day, I'll be away to my bed, my men ought have found a whore of some sort to be warming it for me by now. Think about it Ambrosius. We put Cerdic as supreme over Britain, and end all possibility of hostility. Or we look to having a bastard whelp, born of the father's own sister.' He had strolled to the door, was buckling his sword and baldric into place. Ambrosius's complexion had paled.

'The boy Medraut is here in your school, is he not?' Amlawdd said. 'Arthur bedded his own half-sister to get him. Did you not know? Ah, I see you did not.'

Sitting, arms flopped, head tipped forward, mouth slight open, unbelieving, incredulous, Ambrosius attempted to digest what he was hearing. What evilness was being spoken in the tranquillity of his private quarters? What foul, devil-spawn had been set loose in Ambrosium? In Britain?

'It is true. The mother told me herself.' Amlawdd opened the door, admitting the subdued night noises that drifted from the settlement beyond the outer walls of Ambrosius's private compound. Men, the worse for drink, dogs barking, a young woman's suggestive laugh, reminding him of Morgaine, a delicious woman! Regrettable that she had moved on, away from her hut by the causeway, so closely convenient to Amlawdd's stronghold. But then, she was not so far away, was more suitably placed for contact with traders – Saxon traders. Her whoring set so usefully near the busy, winding road to the lead mines. He might well take that route home.

The bell hung beside the monastery chapel on the far side of the compound tolled its calling to Compline.

'There's your God wanting you, Ambrosius. I'll be away to the more enticing settlement. Of course, incest would not worry Arthur, he is a heathen, so is she for that matter. Neither of them care who, or what, they rut with. The brat could cause a problem though, do you not think? Do we really want such a creature as our King?' Amlawdd tapped his finger against the side of his nose. 'Think on it. I am going with Cerdic, at least he was born from between a good Christian woman's legs, not spawned on the lust of a devil's ride. I would rather not risk having my place in God's kingdom tainted.' Amlawdd lifted his eyebrows, emphasizing his point, left the room.

Ambrosius could hear the mocking, the scornful ridicule that crept and slithered, black and soiled, beneath the surface of the laugh that was not quite audible on Amlawdd's tongue. Amlawdd. Confessed as a traitor! How many, like him, were tempted to turn to Cerdic? Cerdic, who ran like a rogue wolf with the Saex. Cerdic who had hacked his mother, that good Christian woman, to pieces with an axe. Cerdic, son of Arthur – and Medraut, the other son. Oh God in His wisdom, how many knew of this, this sickening thing about the boy?

Ambrosius fell forward to his knees, his lips mumbling in fervent, desperate prayer. What to do! What to do? He vomited, the muck spewing onto the mosaic flooring, the mess staining the benign face of God, peering upward from the pattern of the tiled picture.

§ XIV

There was another boy who could be a valid contender for the royal torque when Arthur was gone. From the same family as Arthur, claiming right of succession from a past Emperor of Rome. Aurelius Caninus. Ambrosius's grandson. How useful that he too, was a pupil of Ambrosium. Useful for Amlawdd's purpose of setting his eggs in different baskets.

For the immediate, it was Medraut who had to be dealt with. Medraut, for all his incestuous begetting, could become a problem in future years. Only the devout, the fanatical followers of this Christian God, would trouble themselves about the pedantics of kindred between a man and a woman's intimate relationship. Of course it was not encouraged, inbreeding was not a way to produce healthy sons, but then, it did ensure a purity of blood line. There was many a petty king or chieftain who had secured a line of inheritance through coupling with his own sister or daughter – men who would not oppose Medraut inheriting from his father for this reason alone. Ambrosius was such a dour perfectionist. You would always find flaws in man, especially where women were concerned. Did Ambrosius think old Caw to have been such a pure Christian? Hah! Not all those sons and daughters were born to legitimate wives or taken whores. Amlawdd knew of at least four children born to Caw's own

405

daughters. Cywyllog, that pinched-faced girl he had seen on arriving yesterafternoon being one of them.

Caninus? If Medraut were out the way, Caninus could become King once Arthur was dead. But who would back him? He might be properly born out of a coupling between legally vowed husband and wife – but who would trust the issue of a misshapen hag and a lame-legged father? There would be too many whispering speculation as to where the unseen twisting and warping would fall in the son. In the sanity? Or the spreading of his seed? Few would readily follow Caninus without someone to urge his acceptability, someone to guide him, advise him. Amlawdd would never be accepted as King, but the title Regent sat well enough in his mind.

It was not by chance that he found the boy that next morning. Ambrosius was ill, confined to his bed. It was natural that Amlawdd would seek out the lad, express his concern for the grandsire's health.

In his eighth year, Caninus was a tall, lithe boy. Brown-haired, hawk-eyed, carrying the trait of the Pendragon kin, the long, slightly overlarge nose. Easy enough to draw the boy aside, engage in conversation. And the main thrust behind its purpose falling like meat served onto a platter. Medraut came from the scriptorium, head down, a scroll clutched between his hands as he trotted in the direction of the latrines.

But this was too simple! Amlawdd easily recognized the wrinkle of Caninus's nose, the glint of sneered malice. 'The Pendragon's son,' Amlawdd vaguely indicated the lad as he turned a corner, disappeared. 'I hear he is a most promising pupil.'

'He is a bastard whelp, with the balls of an ox.'

'You do not much cared for him then?'

Caninus guffawed. 'About as much as a pig cares for the slaughterer's knife.'

For a while, Amlawdd altered the line of conversation, directing talk to hunting, fighting, things that would be of interest to a boy. Said, so casually, 'You seem the better lad, the more capable; it is the shame that Medraut has precedence over you. Were he not to survive into manhood, of course, it would be you to become the next King.'

So easy done! Light came into the widening of the boy's eyes, Amlawdd could almost see the thoughts whirling in his brain. King! Power. Respect.

Amlawdd lightly patted the boy on the shoulder. 'When you grow a little older, I would think about clearing the dead wood from your path, lad, were I you.'

§ XV

The new dwelling place that Amlawdd had suggested she move to suited Morgaine well. This bothy was larger and more comfortable than the damp hovel that had stood beside the marshland causeway. For a bed, she had piled dried bracken and mosses, scattered with sweet smelling herbs and covered by a thick, soft-woven blanket. There was a stool, a wooden chest for her few clothes, cooking pots and utensils, a selection of wooden bowls and two fine-made plates of Roman Samian ware. Both had chipped rims, but were serviceable enough. The wattle-built bothy was her public place, where she would sit and watch or dream when alone, and where her visitors came. They were frequent, the men who came to her, men who travelled the road to and from the lead mines. And the complex of caves that tunnelled deep into the White Hills behind were ideal for her private needs. At first, she had avoided the leer of that cave opening, going only to draw water from the river that rushed from the dark, gaping mouth, but eventually she had plucked courage to take up a lamp and duck into the darkness, using the rush of the river that first time as her pathway guide. Several times she had gone into the darkness since then, using her tallow candles, thrilled yet scared by the crowding of the weight of rock above her, the mystery and magic of this deep, dark world. It was surprisingly warm and dry further in, once past the first cave with its mosses and lichens. She found things on the dry floor: pots, tools, animal bones. People had lived in here. For how long, and when, she did not know. And then she had found the underground lake, dark and mysterious, lapping against a small beach. She swam there regularly, delighting in its deepness and the cold bite that set her skin crackling and glowing as she rubbed herself dry after. It amused her that once again, even if only in secret, she was the Lady by the Lake.

These inner sanctuaries provided her privacy, the pockets of eerie shadow gave her mystery, and concealment to those who came visiting. There were the formations of rock that stabbed down from the ceiling or roared up from the limestone floor – places to silently hide behind and between, should she not wish to entertain a guest; places of darkness, from where she could listen or watch, unnoticed, unknown.

The men would come to the opening, peer into the darkness, call out, wait a while, then shrug and go. It was good to have their attention or not, as she chose. Those she did lay with were generous with their gifts of payment of grain or meat or fowl. Eggs, cheeses, bread, fish. A woollen cloak, an ivory comb. Morgaine and her reputation, once she had settled herself as Lady of the White Hills, rapidly spread along the road from the lead mines to the coast. She became the enchantress, the woman who could pleasure a man and cure all ills, the faery woman who came up from the Underworld into the land of mortals.

Once, soon after she had come to the caves, a man had not turned directly down the track after he had enjoyed her services, but had hidden, deciding to watch her a while. She had come out the bothy and gone into the caves. Curiosity had overcome his fear. Scuttling into her dwelling, he had found for himself a lamp and some candles, had run after her, heart beating that happen she had already vanished, but he could see the distant pool of light from the flaring torch she carried, and followed her, not knowing that Morgaine was full aware of his noisy-footed, clumsy presence. He had then seen her, this courageous, or foolish, man, had seen the goddess herself walk naked into the water of the Underworld, had seen her black, raven hair streaming like rippling weeds against the darkness of the lake, her skin white and smooth – and he had watched as she sank below the surface, did not appear again.

Yet she was there, out in the sunlight, the next day. That same woman, with the black hair, pale skin. There for him when he came to pay for her again. He could not have known that she had found, quite by accident, that by taking a lungful of air and swimming fast beneath the surface, she would come up into another cave, another black, empty space, that she could only feel, not see. Only a sense of vast emptiness told her that she stood at the edge of another cavern. She dared not move from out the water here, for fear she would be swallowed up into the hollow of nothingness. Only occasionally did she go there, to prove that she was more powerful than the god of the dark. For when she went, she would always come back; he could never hold her, take her for his own into his Underworld realm.

She never allowed anyone else to follow her into her private world – but that one man had proven useful, for he had spread word among the many who used the Lead Road. Word of a Goddess from the Lake of the Underworld.

Most days, more than one man would come. Occasionally, they came in small groups, twos or threes. Usually, she would oblige them with what they wanted; always, if they were not of British blood.

For the Saex came along the Lead Road. Saxon traders, to buy the lead, cart it on lumbering ox-wagons back to the coast and their waiting ships. British lead, to use or to trade for high profit. The difficulty of the journey made all that much more rewarding by a visit to the Lady. Who had more than her body to sell.

In secret, Amlawdd sent weapons to Morgaine's caves. Swords, shields, daggers and spears. Quietly they were pushed in among the pigs of lead, hidden, transported, safe. And the Saxons paid well for this extra, illegal trade.

Especially Cerdic.

It was Morgaine's greatest thrill when he came himself, dressed moderately as an overseer, or a rich buyer. To entertain Cerdic in the way she knew best! To tell him all Amlawdd deliberately, and others unintentionally, passed to her listening ears. To tell him of Arthur. To know that she was undoing the mistake of the past, that she was stirring the potion that would one day put an end, as her mother had wished, to the Pendragon.

And doing it by using his own son.

July 478

§ XVI

Gildas was five years old, a quiet, serious little boy. He loved listening to the stories of Jesu and adored the man Ambrosius Aurelianus who had brought him to this wonderful place of Ambrosium. His other home, that stronghold of Caer Rhuthun, he had hated for its dark gloom and stench of drenching blood that covered everything that could be seen or touched. His sister, Cywyllog, was happier here also; she would often sing to him, take him for walks along by the river or through the cool shading of the woods. Never had she done that in Gwynedd. There had always been a clutching of fear and danger there, never much happiness or laughter. Gildas was too young to understand why. Caw, his father, had been a man with strong discipline for obedience to his will. No one had said no to Caw, save for his eldest son Hueil, and the Pendragon. A man who had put his own purpose before the need of others, who sought his own pleasure, protected by the belief that he followed the will of God.

It had been easy enough for Hueil to take Alclud from him, to make himself lord in his father's place. As easy to rally the north to his voice, not so easy to defeat Arthur. Gildas did not understand any of that family history either. All he knew was that Arthur had killed his brother. Through the law of family rights of blood-tie, the Pendragon and all his kindred were to be mistrusted and regarded as an enemy.

That was the difficulty. Ambrosius Aurelianus was kin to the Pendragon, but he was a good and holy man, to be loved and respected. Medraut was Arthur's son. Gildas liked him too. Medraut was in his twelfth year, almost man-grown, yet he had time for the younger boys, enjoyed playing with them, reading the scriptures to them, telling stories, patching up scraped knees and cut elbows with soothing salves and honey words.

Cywyllog said that Arthur had murdered Hueil. It was true, Gildas knew that, for the blood was still there, metaphorically, on the stone in the courtyard at Rhuthun. Medraut, though, had told him another version of that same story.

'*After the battle, which was terrible and bloody, and where many men from both armies died terrible deaths,*' Medraut had said, using the sing-song voice

410

of the story-teller, 'Hueil fled, riding his horse without mercy, for Arthur's son, his last remaining son, had been killed.'

'But you are his son,' Gildas had queried.

'This was another son. I was not born then, and my mother is not Queen Gwenhwyfar. Hueil rode to Rhuthun where lived his father, a Christian man, who would surely forgive him and take him, as the eldest son, into the sanctuary of protection.'

'My father loved all his sons.'

'Stop interrupting! He took Hueil into his stronghold, but only until a court of law could be arranged to try him, legally, against the accusation of treason. That was the Roman way, the established way of law and justice.'

'Ambrosius's way?'

'But not the Pendragon's. Arthur, my father, followed hard on Hueil's heels and demanded that he be given over for execution as a traitor and murderer. Caw and Ambrosius and others argued for things to be done in the correct way, and in the end, Arthur agreed. What men were there – and there were many, for Arthur had chieftains and nobles in his army – formed a court. Hueil was summoned to state his case before them. He came out from where he had taken shelter in your father's chapel. As King and the highest of judges, save for Christ Jesu and God the Father, Arthur stood by the sacred stone, one hand, his left, placed upon it. Hueil came up to him, giving the impression of humble repentance. He made to kneel before Arthur, but instead, leapt forward, a dagger in his hand! He plunged it at the Pendragon, striking for the throat! Arthur was a soldier, a man swift with weapons and fighting. He struggled, his fingers found the hilt of his sword, he broke free, knocked Hueil aside. Hueil stumbled, fell across the stone. Arthur raised his sword – and struck Hueil's head from his neck. The blood ran thick across that sacred stone, and all agreed, save for Caw and the kindred of Hueil who mourned his passing, that justice had been done.'

Gildas had asked Ambrosius whether this telling was more true than the one his sister told. It was, Ambrosius had said. Medraut's version was the more accurate.

It was a puzzling thing for a boy of five years to fathom. Why had his sister lied to him?

He was wandering through the complex of alleyways that snaked between various essential buildings of the monastery, the rear of Ambrosius's bathhouse, the stables, cow-byre, pig-pens and kennels where the hunting hounds were kept. Ambrosius would not allow them in his living quarters for his house, he said, was for God's servants not flea-ridden creatures.

The door to the kennels was shut. Unusual for midday, but one of the bitches had whelped yesterday, happen that was why. A yelp, anguished, pitiful, and laughter, malicious, wicked. Then a scream. Gildas recognized it, the tone, the pitch. His sister!

He pulled at the heavy door, panting hard as it refused to give. Ran along the narrow walkway around the back, where he knew there to be a window. Climbed to a barrel, peered through, sobbing as the sounds inside increased. A group of boys, six of them, the eldest two almost four and ten years of age, with the youngest, Maelgwyn, his own age, and Caninus, eight. Now there was a boy to hate! They were all throwing stones, had a basket full of them, aiming at the bitch and her new pups – and at Cywyllog who was cowering over the litter, trying desperately to protect them with her own body.

Gildas gasped, shrieked. There was a pause inside, then a stone whistled through the window opening, caught Gildas on the forehead. He tumbled backward, fell, scrambled up, his arm hurting, his head aching. He must get help!

It was the hottest hour of the day, the heat had been unbearable this past week. Everyone was inside, resting until the midday sun eased. He ran, calling for help, rounded a corner, was in the main courtyard – and there was Medraut, squatting in the shadows of Ambrosius's carefully tended line of ornamental trees, reading.

Medraut looked up at the boy's frightened shout, leapt to his feet, the scroll falling, abandoned; ran, concerned, for blood trickled from a cut to the lad's head. 'You are hurt! What has happened?'

Gildas explained, his words tumbling almost nonsensically, but Medraut understood. It needed only three words. *Caninus. Stones. Pups.* 'Fetch others, an adult,' he ordered. 'Brother Illtud is in the scriptorium.'

Medraut ran. He never knew what made him take up the broken hunting spear that had been carelessly left laying against the kennel wall. He saw it, took it up. Taller, stronger than Gildas, he had the kennel door open, was inside, his eyes for a moment blinded by the darkness contrasting with the bright sun outside.

The bitch was bleeding. Two of her pups lay dead, their small, delicate heads smashed. Cywyllog was sobbing, blood soaking her tunic, her arm hanging limp. And Medraut was so angry. So very, very, angry.

Everything that he had been taught came to him. He heard Gwenhwyfar's voice in his head. '*Calm and controlled when you face an enemy. Keep your feet light, your body balanced. Go for disabling if you cannot kill.*'

The spear's blade was loose, but he had no need of it, used the shaft instead as a staff, lunging forward to strike at the nearest boy's legs, catching three of them, one after the other, not expecting his intention. He continued with the momentum, brought his weapon up, laid it hard

412

to the left, across the shoulders of another, swung it immediately right, catching Caninus across the jaw. The boy screamed, fell back, blood pouring from his mouth. The others fled.

A few moments only, a mere handful of heartbeats. Medraut was breathing hard, was shaking. His first battle, his first fight.

Men were crowding in, Brother Illtud, Brother Paulus. Their anger as great as Medraut's, at the senseless, wicked cruelty.

Gildas's head throbbed through most that night, his puzzlement over family loyalty even more compounded. 'Medraut,' his sister said from her bed in the infirmary, when Gildas went to see her before supper, 'may be the son of the Pendragon, but he has courage in his blood.'

Did that mean it was all right for Gildas to like him now? Or were his sister's injuries affecting her reasoning? One thing for certain, Gildas would never speak a good word for Caninus and those other boys as long as he lived!

And with his jaw broken, it was doubtful that Caninus would, through future years, think with any fondness of Medraut.

§ XVII

Arthur was appalled at Ambrosius's condition. Regretted not coming earlier. He had not always agreed with his uncle – more often than not, outright opposed him. Most of the time they did not even like each other, although there had been the odd occasion when mutual need had brought them together to ride the one path. And he had been ill on and off for so long, they had all become accustomed to his need occasionally to take to his bed and to the thin, sallow face, the tired eyes, the discreet, painful cough. But not this! Ambrosius was nothing more than a living skeleton. Sitting rigid, self-conscious on a stool beside the bed, Arthur could count every bone in his uncle's limp, gnarled hand. He was not old, Ambrosius – Mithras, not much older than he himself! A handful of years older – eight, nine? Death in battle was one thing, but this, this wasting away, this slow, painful death-in-life ... Arthur put his hand over his eyes, brought the fingers down over his nose, mouth, chin. Christ God, would it not be kinder to finish the man, swiftly, with a blade across the throat?

'I have not long, it will soon be ended.'

Arthur physically jumped, his facial skin blushing red. Bull's blood, how had Ambrosius read his thoughts! He searched for something to say. 'You have suffered a long while, uncle.'

'As Christ suffered. I cannot ask to be less than my Lord.'

There was nothing that Arthur could answer. He did not believe, did not have enough knowing of the right words even to pretend.

Ambrosius coughed, a dribble of blood-tainted spittle trickled from his mouth, a slave bent forward to wipe it away tenderly, tears in his eyes. 'Marcus has been a good body-slave,' Ambrosius said, his voice rasping. 'I have written his manumission release on my death.' Marcus turned away, not caring to show his grief. Ambrosius summoned energy. It was so tiring to talk, but talk he must. He must tell this to Arthur.

'I asked for you to come. You must arrange for Medraut. He is condemned to the fires of hell if you do not.'

'Medraut? What has he done? I understood that he is in everyone's favour since the episode with the pups.'

That had been two weeks since, but word of it was still buzzing around Ambrosium, monastery and settlement, it was one of the first things told to Arthur on his arrival early this morning. To his credit, Medraut found the matter highly embarrassing and had, on his father's questioning, shrugged the incident aside as nothing of much importance. For all that, Arthur had ruffled the lad's hair, muttered something about being proud of him.

'Not that, that is of no consequence.' Ambrosius closed his eyes, had to take several painful breaths. Arthur knew full well what he was referring to, damn it! 'Though, my grandson's part in it was not to my liking.'

'What do you intend to do with Caninus?'

Ambrosius's eyes snapped open, his withered fingers sought Arthur's hand. 'You take him. His mother, God rest her departed soul, spoiled him over much. Take him to Caer Cadan. Whip some discipline into him, he is not for the peaceful life of a monastic order. He will be better placed as a soldier.'

Arthur laughed wryly. 'Exchange your lad for mine, eh?'

Urgently, Ambrosius's fingers picked at the bed linen, had an intensity about his eyes. 'Aye! 'Tis the only way to save him!'

Assuming he spoke of Caninus, Arthur agreed to the request. 'I'll not have him at Caer Cadan, though. He can go to Geraint, he has a better talent than I with boys. He will knock some sort of shape into him.'

Agitated, Ambrosius attempted to sit up, his hand reaching for Arthur. 'Ensure Medraut makes his vows to God. Keep him under God's hand, 'tis the only way to salvation for him!'

Recoiling from the touch, Arthur retrieved his hand, wiped away the clammy feel of death on his tunic. Bluntly, he answered, 'I need Medraut. He is my son, he must follow me as King.'

'He is God-cursed!'

414

Then the Pendragon understood what this was all about. Medraut's birthing. He sighed. 'Your God, Ambrosius, not mine.'

The retort snapped back, clear, forceful. 'His! Medraut is of the Christian faith!'

'*Not if your God has rejected him for something that is not his fault.*' The thought remained in Arthur's mind, he could not taunt a dying man with deliberate irreverence. Said instead, 'It is for Medraut to choose, not for me to order.'

Curling his hand into a clumsy fist, Ambrosius thumped the bed-covering. 'He does not know of the sin that covers him! How can he make choice?'

'Then, if he does not know, how can he suffer? To sin, you must be aware of the offence.' Arthur could not quite believe this. Here he was, sitting beside a dying man, discussing the Christian religion!

'Promise me that you will tell him, that you will let him make his choice!' The appeal in Ambrosius's eyes was brutal in its demanding. Arthur chewed his lip, his fingers toying with the buckle of his belt. It was hot in this room, with the shutters closed, hot and stifling. He would need to go soon, he had always disliked being enclosed within walls . . . he nodded. 'I can do that.'

'Promise me, Arthur! Avow it!'

Arthur shrugged, grunted.

'On your life, and his, Pendragon! Swear it!'

Arthur spread his hands, stood, scraping the stool backward as he came to his feet. 'When the right time presents itself, I will tell him.' It was a lie, but lies never bothered Arthur.

Closing his eyes, Ambrosius nodded, content. There was something else that he meant to tell his nephew. Something important? Later. He was so tired, so dreadfully tired. He would tell him later, when next he woke. What was it about? Ah, yes. Later then.

Before the day ended, Ambrosius Aurelianus died. He had not woken again, had not told Arthur of Amlawdd and Cerdic.

May 482

§ XVIII

Cerdic stood at the edge of the wharf, legs apart, fists on hips, his smile generous and welcoming. The two ships eased alongside, both with sails furled, splendid, in full regalia of shields hung at prow and stern, along the gunwales, each one exhibiting bright-painted motifs of eagles, boars, coloured patterns or magnificent creatures. Men stood behind, oars uplifted, like line-planted wooden forests, their grins wider than the depth of a ship's keel. As the leading ship bumped alongside, a great impressive roar left the lips of the two crews. Ropes were tossed, fastened in a flurry of activity, the second ship manoeuvred, moored behind her sister. One man, standing much as Cerdic had, fists nestled on hips, balancing with the sway of the boat, leapt from the deck of the first onto the wharf, his arms outstretched, pleasure immense. Cerdic strode to meet him. They embraced, clapped each other on the shoulder. From the second craft came two more men, all three with similar features, same-coloured hair, but these two were younger, sons of the first. Cerdic embraced them also, the pleasure at their coming genuine. Port, with his sons Maegla and Bieda, come from the Saxon lands to join with his kinsman-by-marriage.

'Cerdic! Husband to the daughter of my mother's sister!'

'Port! Noble warrior, cousin!' More embracing, more enthusiastic back-slapping.

Bieda, the younger son by one year, noticed the boy hanging shyly behind Cerdic. Guessed him to be Cynric. 'A fine lad!' he announced, gestured with an exaggerated sweep of the hand for him to step forward. 'Come boy, show yourself.'

Self-conscious at being singled out, Cynric stepped up beside his father, who put his hand, protective and proud, to his shoulder. Cynric straightened his back, lifted his chin, stared this man, Bieda, straight in the eye, as seemed natural to do. They were here to help begin the fight for a Saxon kingdom, father had said, and must be honoured with all respect and greeting. Port, he had explained, was an important man.

'As important as you, Papa?'

'Almost.' Would Cerdic have answered the truth? That Port was, possibly, more so than himself? For, unlike Cerdic, these were men experienced in battle, hardened men, warriors, who could boast the scars of wounds received, aye, and tell a tale of the many that had been given! Port had twenty and one hundred warriors to his name, each and every one of them experienced, tough, frightening men, men who knew the exhilaration of the victory, the anguished pain of losing. Cerdic had an advantage however, for Cerdic had the higher wealth, an edge of status, and the claim of a right to territory. Port had nothing. Save for his men, two ships, and a ravaged homeland.

The Saxon lands were disintegrating, worthless, becoming ragged around the edges, for the Franks, with Clovis as their new-chosen king, were becoming too much of a nuisance. Securing for themselves a wider and vaster territory, Clovis was pushing the tribespeople from their settlements. Port had fought against the Franks, had realized the impracticality of a few hundred needing to face, again and again, the many thousand.

With good chance, the Franks would soon turn south again, leave the Saxon wetlands alone; instead, harass Soissons, the Alamani and, if the men of Clovis proved as strong and determined as all indication gave, even press the Goths and Burgundians. But it was the Saxons who were being pressed at this moment. Cerdic had sent invitation to any who cared come, to any who cared join with his intention of taking a portion of Britain for his own. To Port, and many a chieftain of lesser rank, the prospect was alluring. An only choice. Try for something better rather than stay and drown as an unstoppable tide rolled in with the force of a moon-heightened spring flood.

They answered. They came. Many as crew members on board trading ships, working their passage across the sea channel; a few, in their own small craft. Port was the only man of rank to equal Cerdic, to own two such superb long ships. Warriors' craft these, not the heavier-built, shorter, and by far not as beautiful, trading vessels.

'He has the look of his mother about him,' Port observed, referring to the boy. He had been fond of his cousin Mathild, a girl with laughing eyes, a wise smile. A pity that she was dead, but these accidents happen. His own wife had died in much the same way; a fall, a tragic blow to the head. Like Mathild, she had never opened her eyes again.

'Has the look of the Pendragon also!' The older son, Maegla, scuffed the boy's dark, slightly curling hair with his calloused-palmed hand, before lightly tapping the tip of the boy's long, straight nose.

Cerdic's jaw stiffened. Port noticed the pinched anger. He chuckled. ''Tis all the proof we need, to show that we come to fight for the man who has the right to wear the royal torque of Britain!'

That slight tension eased, the shoulder slapping resumed, the laughter.

The crews were coming ashore, with shouts and hilarity, leaping from the deck, striding across the two gang-planks, eager to receive the welcome of the men, the shy kisses of the women. Eager for the feasting that would come at dusk and, with that, the giving of gifts.

Battle was all-important. It warmed the blood, kept a man's heart and desire alive. But the preliminaries, the making of new allegiances, the crafting of new friendships? Ah, that was as good!

Mead, ale, beer, wine. Roasted, fattened bullocks, pork, lamb. Duck, hen, wildfowl. Fish and cheeses of all kinds. Fine-ground wheat and barley loaves, spiced or scattered with the seeds of poppy, caraway and fennel. Fresh-made butter.

The feasting would be grand and special for these next three days, when the men that Cerdic had asked to come to him and join as one under his banner, would unite together in his Hall, in his stronghold of Cerdicesora. Partake of his hospitality and declare for him, for Cerdic.

And then, when the time was right, together they would fight.

June 482

§ XIX

Like most of the men, Arthur did not care to make his way through the dark to the stinking latrine, away to the northern corner of the stronghold. As they all did, he used the wattle fence of the pig-pen behind the rear door of Geraint's Hall. Geraint himself stood beside him, their urine puddling the mud at their feet.

The late-night sea-damp air was chill, casting their breath in clouds of vapour. Both of them were the wrong side of sober – Geraint was noted for his selection of fine wines and strong beers – but who would stay clear-headed for a parting feast? The ride tomorrow would be long and hard, with the day after facing . . . ah, no man would think too far ahead when there was feasting in the lord's Hall. The time for dwelling on battle was during that half-dark hour of dawn, when the wind stung your face, the shout of the enemy and the crash of spear on shield reached your ears. That was when death leered over your shoulder, not now, when the wine flowed and enjoyment was to be chased.

Arthur adjusted himself, waited for his friend and cousin to finish. From beyond the fencing a snuffling, sucking sound of feet in mud, and a huge snout lumbered over the top of the fence, wet, hairy, scenting the wind. The sow, ready for farrowing any day, was investigating the smell, the sounds. Startled, Geraint jumped backward, his urine splashing over his boot. He swore. Arthur doubled in laughter.

'Damn the bloody thing!' Geraint cursed, 'I'll have her for my supper when I return! Sod it!' He wiped at the wetness spreading over his bracae, shook his foot.

'Frightened of a pig's snout! Pissed yourself, eh, Geraint?'

Geraint growled something non-complimentary, earned for himself more laughter. Arthur fell into step beside him as Geraint paced back to the light and noise emanating from the Hall, slapped his arm around his cousin's shoulder.

'Pay no mind, our boots will all be squelching come a few days. The marshes around Llongborth are wetter than a babe's night napkin, so I hear.'

'You talk for yourself,' Geraint jibed back. 'I have no intention of removing my backside from my horse. If you want to paddle around up to

419

your arse in sea-water and bog, that is up to you.' They ducked through the low door, the rear entrance, stood a moment inside, mutually surveying the scene of wild celebration.

The eating had finished, with the trestle tables cleared away, the dancing and entertainment begun. Mixing with Geraint's men, the Artoriani, the élite cavalry – though it had taken this while to rebuild the numbers, find the horses, train them, drill in the rules of discipline. Were they as good as before? So many had died in Gaul.

'We British? Fight on foot, as the Saex do?' Arthur retorted, scornful. 'What, when we have chance to keep our feet dry?'

Geraint chuckled. 'Unless another bloody sow should scare the piss out of us?' The two men laughed at the shared jest, made their way, companionably together through the crowd, heading for their place of honour beside the warmth of the hearth.

A girl swung by, head back, hair tossing, her mouth open with enjoyment, saw Arthur. She stepped aside from the group, slid her arm through his. 'Come! Dance with me?' she carolled, guiding him into the whirl.

'What? These old bones get giddy. I'd not last a heartbeat!' But for all the protest, Arthur swept his arm around her waist, took hold of a hand in the line, joined in the reel.

She was lovely, her hair gleaming as bright as her eyes, her figure lithe as it bent and twirled with the exotic pace and step of the dance. She was dressed in a loose tunic of spring green, a thin gold and silver torque at her throat, silver ear-rings, gold bangles on her bare arms, sandals of narrow gold thread. More than one young man – and aye, those not so young – watched her, Arthur noticed.

'You will have my wife reprimand me for dancing with so beautiful a girl, you know,' he chided as a couple twirled down between the formed parallel lines of fellow dancers who clapped the beat.

'Would she much mind?' the girl answered, as they joined hands to swing each other around.

'She can be a jealous woman.'

'I could always dance with someone else.'

'Then I would be jealous. And as I am the King, you dare not offend me.' They were at the head of the dance, their turn to go down the line, two hands together, swirling around and around.

Breathless, hand on chest, panting and dripping sweat, the dance ended, Arthur drew the girl aside. She placed a kiss, light, on his cheek; he touched her hair with his hand. The enjoyment of celebration left her eyes, she put her fingers over his hand.

'How do we, the women left behind, bear it when you all go off to war?

How do we not dwell on the knowing that you might not be coming back?'

Arthur quirked the side of his lips into a slight smile. 'So many questions!' He took her fingers, squeezed them. 'I would ask your mother, for I have no answer for you.'

Archfedd withdrew her hand, a temperamental pout forming on her mouth. It was no good asking her. 'She rides with you.'

Nodding once, Arthur affirmed that she did. 'Gwenhwyfar comes with us on the morrow, aye. It is her wish, and mine.'

About to blurt some harsh word of disgust, Arthur stopped her answering by placing a finger to her lips. 'Do not say it, Archfedd. Do not form what is in your mind into voiced word. Your mother comes with me because I need her.' He held the finger up, reinforcing her silence. 'And no, you cannot come. Not because you are woman-born, but because you are my daughter.' *Because, unlike your mother, you have no experience of war; because you are six and ten years of age, at the dawn of your life; because if Cerdic wins, you will only be safe here, within Geraint's stronghold.* He kept all that to himself, especially the last, which even he recoiled from thinking about. If Cerdic was somehow to take the victory when they met, what would he do to Archfedd? Arthur swallowed a rise of foul-tasting bile. No, of that he could not, would not, think.

'A man asked that he would marry with you, a long while past now,' Arthur said, casually.

'Oh?' Archfedd attempted not to look interested, but the flattery was obvious. Her mother had promised that she would have say in the choice of husband, and as yet there was no acceptable contender. 'Who?' she asked, several faces flitting through her mind. Handsome and courageous men, all.

'Amlawdd.'

'What! That ill-mannered, lecherous, toad-foot?' Archfedd's wrinkled nose and expression of disgust replaced any need for further word.

'I had a feeling that would be your answer.' There was laughter in her father's voice.

'You are teasing me!' Archfedd complained, flouncing slightly away from him.

'About Amlawdd's asking? Na, I am not.' Arthur relented as the alarm spread over her face, put a finger under her chin. 'Do not fret, my answer was similar to yours, only the language was somewhat coarser.'

Her relief was extensive.

'When I return,' Arthur altered direction, 'we must consider finding you someone suitable.' She would not be safe from scum such as

421

Amlawdd until she had a husband of her own. Not now that she was of an age ready for marriage. And grandsons could be as useful as sons.

Archfedd tossed her head, her contempt acute. 'No old goats or unwhelped pups. If I agree to marry, I'll not wed any but the strongest warrior!'

Her father gathered her to him, held her possessively close, protective, urgent. Love of Mithras, she was so much like her mother!

A sudden come thought, unexpected, from the past. *'If I marry, I will only wed with the strongest leader, a man who will unite Britain and drive out our enemies.'* He had been a lad when Gwenhwyfar had boasted that. A bastard-born lad who had not known his father, had not known that the great Uthr Pendragon was his sire. Later, when he had known, after Uthr's death, when Cunedda had told him the truth of it, she had again said that she would not wed with any but the best. *'Would you consider a Pendragon the best?'* he had asked.

Obviously Gwenhwyfar had, though how she came to that conclusion Arthur had often, since, wondered. Him, the best? Aye, the best liar, the best whore-layer, the best . . . ah, the list rolled on.

At that moment Arthur glanced up, across a cleared space where three jugglers were amusing onlookers with their skilled craft. She was there, enthralled, admiring; the rich, warm light from the torches burnishing her hair into the colour of beaten copper, the gold tips of hairpins glinting as she moved to applaud their talent enthusiastically. Whatever happened between them, whatever Arthur did, whatever flurried argument sprang up, there was always this thing, their shared love, to draw that tying thread tight again. He loved her, his Gwenhwyfar.

She lifted her head, saw Arthur cradling Archfedd to him. Watching her daughter, Gwenhwyfar smiled. She would know, almost, what he was thinking, for she knew her husband, knew his thoughts, his hopes. His fears.

Knew as well as he what Cerdic would do to Archfedd if ever he managed the unthinkable. To beat his father in battle.

§ XX

Llongborth, the ship port where once the galleons of the Roman sea legions, the navy, put into harbour. The élite of shipping, the triremes, the quinqueremes, with their multi-banks of oars, their ability to manoeuvre with breathtaking skill; to turn within their own length, disabling the enemy by ramming or by smashing through the oars. Magnificent craft that could set fear scudding in the heart.

They were gone, those awesome ships with their skilled oarsmen and superb ability. The harbour had succumbed to the sole use of traders, even before Vortigern's time, with Saex pirates on the prowl from along the coast, even that use had dwindled. The wharves were no longer kept in good repair, the lighthouse not maintained. Llongborth was the eastward boundary of Geraint's territory; to here, the ships that had carried Arthur and his men to Gaul had come, for the especially designed quays – even in poor repair – were better suited to load horses and cargo efficiently, without excess fuss.

The inlets and marsh-land creeks that dominated this stretch of the southern coast were impossible to patrol. With Saxon settlements established to the east, and Cerdic entrenching himself on the west, this pocket of land with its puzzle of waterways to the north of Vectis was a last stronghold of British command. Cerdic had the temerity to offer part of it to his new allies, Port and his two sons.

Scattered, isolated settlements that sprung up along the empty, windswept and desolate stretches of the coast could be overlooked. Natural, uninhabited inlets that were being transformed into Saxon harbours could be tolerated.

The giving of what was not yours to give, could not.

Llongborth, with its past status, its potential for rebuilding, regrowth. Llongborth, with its position for trade, for the building of new craft and the safe sheltering of old, made it a prize worth the having. Both Geraint and Arthur had known that it was only a matter of time before the Saxons tried for Llongborth. The only surprise was that it had taken Cerdic so long.

Marsh. The emptiness of rippling water, wind-brushed reeds and the mournful cry of the curlew. The ceaseless, steady pulse of the tide, the smell of mud, seaweed and the sea. A mist-hazed blue morning. The sun climbing, golden, to the east, trailing fingers of shadow over the emptiness. Two miles distant, the human encroachment, the wharves and half-derelict buildings of Llongborth itself. Just ahead, the mast of a single ship, her broken keel aslant on a sandbar, abandoned to the tide, the wind and the barnacles. Left to rot. As, at the end of this day, would be the bones of the dead.

The shield-wall of Saxons, ranked, bright-coloured and solid. Spear tips, helmets, swords, catching the first cast light of the sun. The banners and standards lifting lazily as an offshore wind sauntered past.

The British horses, grey, bay, chestnut and dun. Harness jingling as heads tossed, feet stamped. The snort of excitement through distended nostrils, a shrill whinny, an impatient kick. Grass-stained foam flecking from the bit. Restless shifting. Ears flicking. Muscles firm and strong, beneath coats that rippled with the gloss of fine condition. Horses with stamina and strength. Corn-fed, bold-eyed, strong-hearted.

Between the two armies a careless silence. The sigh of the wind, a cry of a bird. Nothing more.

The Saxon line, a blur of indistinguishable colour and shape. The horses walked, pranced, side-stepped; reins curbing the tension, the will to go. Forward. Legs swishing through the marram grass. Ahead, the archers, bows strung, the first arrow knocked ready.

The Saxons. Standing. Shield linked against shield. Immobile, immovable.

Individual thought of fear, expectation, and elation. A quickened heartbeat, a muttered prayer. Incongruous thoughts. The remembered taste of a good wine, a potent beer. The smile on a child's face, the loving caress of a woman. The cry of the wolf on a winter wind, or the joyful, soaring song of a lapwing on a summer's day.

The archers. In line. Halted. Bows raised. Eyes to the side, to their lord, sitting on his horse, a chestnut, as red as a setting sun. Geraint.

The horses. Their paced, measured walk, a few yards behind. Arthur's arm fell. Geraint raised his spear – and the sky was black with the skimming, fearful hiss of death. One arrow, two, three. Archers, men who knew their craft. The arrows waiting, tips pinned into the soft mud, easily lifted, fitted, shot. Again and again and again.

The horses came on, side-stepping around the archers, walking, still walking. Waiting for that moment when the terrible rain of death would end. The sound, as it shushed above the horse's ears, tossing their heads, shortening their pent, tight-held stride. They knew what was coming. Man and beast knew what lay ahead.

Eyes to the left, to Arthur now. To the Dragon Banner, fluttering white, red. The glint of spur, the flash of a sword. Quiet beneath the arrows, horses' hooves moving through the grass, the jingle of harness, the creak of leather. Then the arrows ceased and Arthur lifted his sword, raised it high. The signalmen took up the order.

Trotting, steady jogging. Riders firm, deep in the saddle; one hand on the reins, held behind the shield. Spears raised, the lightweight javelins. Thrown. The second spear coming easily into hand, heavier, more destructive. The horses. Held in, reins tight, checked. Necks bent, heads in, jaws taut, wanting to go; manes tossing, eyes white, nostrils red, flaring, snorting; mouths open, pulling against the hold of the bit, cutting, curbing. Blood-flecked foam.

Arrows in shield, in flesh. Spears crippling, disabling. Death. Wounding. Pain. The shield wall, standing firm. Holding. Where one fell, another stepped forward.

Cantering. Strides lengthened and stretching. Hooves galloping, the ground vibrating, thundering, drumming. Breath hot. The men, mouths open, voices, indistinct in the single, shouted war-cry.

From both sides, from British, from Saxon released that terrible howl, defying death.

The last few strides. Faces near enough to be seen. Clear beneath the protection of helmets. Eyes, blue, brown. Bright, excited, fearing. Breath gasping, quickened. Fingers gripping, palms sweating. Bodies taut. Legs, feet, braced, balanced. The reins slackened, let loose. Horses' necks low, stretched, hooves pounding. Legs, manes, tails, blurred by speed and wind. The shield-wall standing firm. Met. Hooves, teeth. Plunging, screaming. Sword, dagger, axe. Crashing through, destroying. Man against man. Blood and terror. Men who did not flinch, slay or be slain. Bloody heads, limbs maimed, amputated, mutilated. Kill or be killed.

The shriek of pain. The agony of bloody destruction.

Battle.

Dusk and the ending of a day that was long, sorrowful and bloody in its passing. Only the few were unwounded, with so many dead, British and Saxon. For neither side the victory; for both, the grieving of death. The horror of such terrible killing.

The Saxons would write, later, in their chronicles: *Port came with his two sons, Maegla and Bieda, in two ships, and killed a Briton of high rank.*

Geraint.

The British, for him, they wrote, *After the war cry. Bitter the grave.*

June 476

§ XXI

'I admit I know the Pendragon not well, but he seems quiet, withdrawn. As if some great trouble lay heavy on his heart?' Owain spoke carefully, for he had no wish to offend his father's sister, his aunt Gwenhwyfar.

She was a wonder to him, twenty years his senior, at eight and forty she was a woman who had retained her strident looks. Was it her laugh that kept the youthfulness dancing around her? Or her wit, her understanding? She was slim, agile. He had seen her, only this morning, practising with his own three sons, parrying with a blunted sword, casting a spear. God's truth, even he, at eight and twenty, found an ache in his back and shoulders after strenuous exercise!

And if Gwenhwyfar carried her age, what of the Pendragon? One and fifty, a man of wise age! To younger men, was not any age approaching twoscore seen as elderly? Arthur was young in years, however, when compared to two men of the past for whom Owain had much interest – he enjoyed the histories, especially those early years of the Empire. In particular, the careers, both political and military, of Augustus Octavian and Vespasian. Grand, impressive men, who had died at the ages of six and seventy and nine and sixty. Old? Hah! Arthur had a way to travel yet!

They were walking, he and his aunt, along the firm, wet sand of the bay below Caer Arfon. The tide was ebbing, a sharp wind blowing across the strait from the island of Môn. Behind, to the horizon, rose the mountains; snow-topped Yr Wyddfa, caressing the summer blue of a cloud-scudding sky. Gulls wheeled overhead, and away down the shore the waders were scurrying for the exposing mussel beds.

Gwenhwyfar bent, lifted a stick washed in by the tide, tossed it for the dogs to chase. The two of them raced off, paws scattering wet sand, tongues lolling, ears flapping, barking joyously. Arthur was ahead, walking alone, head down, hands thrust deep through the leather of his baldric, his long stride taking him further away from the slower pace of his wife and her nephew.

How could she answer Owain's question? Four years it had been. Four years since that dreadful, bloody day at Llongborth, when so many, so many had died. So many, yet nothing had come of it for either side. No one the victor, a stalemate, an equal withdrawal. Save that Llongborth was lost them, now. That had come about later, more than one year and two seasons after that day, after the terrible deaths of that battle. None of the British kind cared return there for any reason and the place had become abandoned, left to the crows and the waterfowl, and the Saex. For the British, too many ghosts walked with too much pain at Llongborth.

So many gone, that day. Of them all, the most painful, the most missed, Geraint.

How long had he been friend to Arthur? He had been there, fighting beside the Pendragon at the beginning, when Vortigern ruled, when Hengest's shadow had darkened the land. Been there, seeming always, at Arthur's shoulder. Without Geraint, what was left? More, without Geraint, who would be there with Arthur?

'It was on this day that we fought at Llongborth.' Need she say that? Ought he not know? But then, why would they remember a battle fought so long ago, so far away? Why ought they remember, here, in Gwynedd, for they had their own many deaths to remember. Cunedda, her own father, killed so long, long ago, by Hibernian sea-raiders. Catwalaun, Owain's eldest brother, slain last year by the kindred of those same men, but killed over there, on Môn. Môn, the Gwynedd island, where once the powerful druids, the Myrddin, the wise men, had lived and worshipped – and died under the brutal hand of Rome. After Cunedda's passing, Môn had become Hibernian. Again and again, Gwynedd had attempted to send those unwanted and unwelcome settlers back across the sea or to their pagan gods. Enniaun, Cunedda's son, Gwenhwyfar's brother, had tried. Failed. But not his son, Catwalaun, Owain's brother had the doing of it – but they, both of them, lay cold, buried beside the Lion Lord, Cunedda.

Aye, Gwynedd had her own dead to remember.

Now there was Owain, the second son of Enniaun, left to rule. It ought be Maelgwyn, for he was Catwalaun's son, but Maelgwyn was a boy of three and ten, too young to keep the sand-shore of Gwynedd empty of pirates. Too unsuitable. Maelgwyn would never make a good king for Gwynedd, they all knew that, save for Maelgwyn. Illtud was trying to teach the boy sense and morality, trying to thrash into him that greed and lust and cruelty were not traits that brought respect and pride. His was a good school, Llan Illtud Fawr. The pity that many students were not as good.

And Arthur? Was it any wonder that these last months he had seemed morose and ill-humoured?

'We have trailed through a bad winter – did the snows come early here in Gwynedd?' Gwenhwyfar looked, as she spoke, to the crown of Yr Wyddfa, the Snow Mountain. Even in early summer there was a thin shawl of white around its height.

'The Strait between here and Môn froze. For the one night, when the tide was at lowest ebb, but all the same, I have never known a winter so cold as this last.'

Gwenhwyfar nodded. Nor she.

The dogs were back, growling and barking over the delight of the stick. Gwyn and Mêl – one named for the white in his coat, the other for the honey-gold of her eyes – descended from Blaidd, the dog of Gwenhwyfar's son, Llacheu. They were good dogs, though young and foolish. Mêl especially seemed to have little sense in her brain. She was Archfedd's, but Archfedd had gone hawking with Owain's wife and sons. Mêl was not a dog to take hunting, fool animal would try to catch the hawk, like as not.

Arthur was half a mile or so ahead, too far to call out to him, attempt to catch up. Gwenhwyfar threaded her arm through her nephew's, swung him around to return to the Caer. 'Had there been a noted victory – for either side – at Llongborth, I think we would rest the easier. A battle with no outcome leaves a wound that is open and raw, one that weeps pus and stinks of rotting flesh.'

There would be more fighting, that was known anyway, but when it came, it would be all the more bitter, all the more necessary, for fighting without settlement made each side the more determined to prove their worth. And Cerdic was not a man to shrug and let a thing pass. He had Llongborth, but had it by default. It was said – and aye, not by the British alone, there were Saxons who whispered around the hearth also – that Cerdic was not a man of worth and valour. He had been carried, bleeding and whimpering, from the field at Llongborth. Wounded, but not deeply, he had left his men, commanded to be taken to a place of safety.

Had he stayed, then happen the outcome at Llongborth might have ended different. For until Cerdic quit the field, the Saex were making the better of the day.

That, Arthur dwelt on, these long months as time wheeled through the slow passing of the seasons. Cerdic, when he had replaced the dead and wounded, would come again.

That and the other thing. That many of the weapons hastily collected with the wounded after that day had been of British crafting.

No unusual thing, for naturally the Artoriani and the men of Geraint would use their own-made arms.

But not the Saex. Geraint had been slain by a Saxon using a British spear.

428

Arthur had it, kept it in place of honour above his King's chair at Caer Cadan. Kept it as a reminder to all who saw it, a reminder that one day he would discover who it was who sold the Saex superior British weaponry.

And whoever it was would pay dearly for the death of Geraint.

§ XXII

The lake was calm, as if it were embroidered on a tapestry. The only movement the ripples that spread from a busy pair of grebe. In those places where the mountains cast their shadow, the water lay deep and black, almost menacing. In contrast, the rest of the lake sparkled bright and blue. White puffs of cumulus wandered somnolent across the greens and browns reflected from Yr Wyddfa's lower slopes. It was a breathtaking view; the lake, and the mountain horseshoe; sun-bright colour, shadowed darkness.

Gwenhwyfar lay on her back, her arm behind her head, watching the cloud shapes lazily change, imagining faces, animals. A dog, a tree, a wine amphora. As a young girl, this had been one of her most special places. Always, she and her youngest brother had looked forward to coming to the stronghold down along the valley. Dinas Emrys they called it now, although they had known it in childhood as Dinas Mynydd. Vortigern, the tyrant king, of all people, had ordered it built. He had been a young man then, the royal torque still new, and chafing at his neck. That had been at the time when he had ordered Cunedda into Gwynedd from the north, from beyond the Wall, expecting him and his people to sink into the morass of oblivion. Hah! Vortigern had not known Cunedda! It was Enniaun who had, later, given it, with its land and prestigious citing, to Emrys – in the days before he had adopted his Roman name, Ambrosius. Strange how the stories about the place had grown out of virtually nothing regarding the two names, Vortigern and Emrys, the one reviled for his evil and alliance with Hengest the Saxon, the other revered for his goodness and service to God. But that was the way of stories, one small thing exaggerated into a mountain of untruths.

The horses, hobbled, grazed nearby, the chink of harness and the steady tear and chomp of their eating accentuating the drowsing heat of the day. The dog, Gwyn, lay stretched out, panting, legs twitching as he dreamed of chasing hares. Mêl was away with Archfedd, the girl too young and full of energy to waste a sun-hot day by lazing, sleeping, on the warm grass.

'That is a good sign,' Gwenhwyfar said. 'Look, a dragon-cloud in the sky.' Dragons! They were the foundation of the story that surrounded Dinas Emrys. The red dragon, the white. The British, the Saex. Good, evil. God, the heathen.

Arthur lay on his stomach sprawled next to her, one arm flung carelessly across her, his hand cupping her breast. He had been drifting into sleep.

'White or red?' He mumbled.

'White, of course.'

Stretching, shifting his cramped leg, Arthur twisted around, sensuously caressing her as he moved. 'Saxon then. Bad omen.'

'Oh nonsense! It's a cloud!'

Carried on the silence, amplified by the wide stretch of water, came young laughter. Gwenhwyfar craned her neck. She could see the horses, grazing as hers and Arthur's were, taking advantage of the lush grass on the far side of the lake. Of Archfedd and the lad, no sign. She was wearing kingfisher blue, ought be easily seen, unless they were up among those trees.

'If she is laughing, then she is not in trouble,' Arthur stated unconcerned, snuggling his face into the deliciousness of his wife's hair. 'When she screams, I'll pursue her.' His hand had wandered to Gwenhwyfar's tunic hem, was inching higher, beneath, enjoying the smooth feel of skin along the inside of her thigh.

'He seems a reasonable lad, Natanlius?'

Arthur noted the question in her voice. 'Reasonable as in suitable escort for the day, or reasonable as in future son-by-law?'

She batted at his hand. 'Stop it. They will see.'

'Who will see? My daughter and that young, rutting stag of hers?' To provoke her, Arthur rolled on top of her, pinned her arms with his hands. 'I would wager my sword they will be too occupied doing what we are about to do.'

'They had better not!' Gwenhwyfar thrust with her hip, toppling him off, sending him rolling slightly down the hill. She lunged to her feet, hand shielding her eyes from the brightness to scan the woods anxiously. Nothing, only Mêl's joyous barking.

Arthur sat, legs crossed, chin cupped in his palm, elbow on his knee, watching Gwenhwyfar, mystified. When she went to the horses, bent to start untying the hobbles from her mare, said, 'You allow a pair of ripe fruit to wander off together, without muttering a word of protest, yet expect neither to have a nibble at the sweetness?' He shifted his chin to the other palm. 'It is no wonder that women puzzle men.'

'It does not concern you that this lad may be tumbling our daughter?'
Gwenhwyfar's outrage was forthright.

'She is twenty years of age. About time someone tumbled and wed
her.' He held up one finger, stemming the torrent of indignation that he
knew was about to follow, 'But aye, it concerns me.' Casual, he stood,
scratched at an itch on his buttock, strolled towards her and, grabbing
her around the waist, pulled her to the grass. 'It concerns me,' he
quipped, 'that on a beautiful day such as this, a lad more than half my age
may be doing what I ought be doing.'

Gwenhwyfar made only a token show of protest. As Arthur slipped her
unlaced tunic over her head, she surrendered to the pleasure of lying
naked with him on the sun-warmed, sweet grass. His love-making,
serenaded by the sound of droning bees and bird song, was lingering and
intense. Her response, passionate.

§ XXIII

Natanlius was fun to be with, Archfedd liked him, her pleasure with his
company made all the more acceptable by the knowing that her father
and mother, too, approved of him. The last-born son of six brothers, he
had joined with the Artoriani a moon-month after he stepped across the
threshold from boy to manhood, for there was only himself and his next-
eldest brother in his family. The others had been killed at Llongborth.
His father too, had died soon after that dreadful day. To join the
Pendragon and his Artoriani was a certain way to seek vengeance, for
they all knew, all of Britain, that one day Arthur would again fight with
Cerdic. And on that day, Natanlius intended to be there, with the
fighting, to help in the attempt to kill that Saxon whoreson, as his
beloved father and brothers had been killed.

Thoughts of battle and killing were far from both their minds this day,
though, as the two young people abandoned Arthur and Gwenhwyfar to
their own company, and rode their horses through the shallows of the
lake to the lush grass on the far side, left them grazing there to explore
the coolness of the river that tumbled down through the shaded trees.

They climbed upward, Natanlius occasionally taking Archfedd's hand
to help her up some steeper part, or to steady her as she clambered over
the occasional fallen tree. She did not need his help, but it was nice to
feel her hand in his, to see that bright smile on his fine young face
beaming at her.

He was twenty years of age, with laughing hazel eyes set in a merry expression. A sure aim with a bow and spear, quick and nimble on his feet, he could ride even the most unmanageable of horses. It had not taken Natanlius long to be promoted to a higher officer's rank within the Artoriani, even less time to gain the King's trust and liking.

Archfedd had noticed him before; there were many young and handsome men among the Artoriani, all of whom smiled at her, exchanged laughter and pleasantries, but for the journey to Gwynedd Arthur had selected this one to be among the personal guard to his daughter.

The path had risen quickly, steeply, the river cutting a deep gully to their left side. Below, the tumble of water pushed and buffeted its way over rocks and boulders, leaping and running on its mad, downhill rush. In places, the path was easy to walk, at others, it narrowed precariously.

'Take care, it is slippery here,' Natanlius advised, reaching out his hand. But too late, Archfedd's foot slid on a tree root. He lunged for her, fastened his firm grasp around her arm, caught her before she tripped. Breathless, she held onto him, not daring to look down that drop to the waterway below, as he walked her a few paces to a safer, wider part of the path. Had she fallen . . . she had her fingers twined in his, their bodies close, could smell the exciting aroma of male sweat, the leather of his tunic, a faint odour of wine and strong cheese on his breath.

It might have been wrong, but surely the King had known what might happen when he allowed a young officer to take his daughter into the seclusion of leaf-shading trees? The first kiss was brief, his lips light on hers, but she answered him, her arms going about his neck, drawing him nearer, to kiss her again, firmer, more insistent.

Happen it was a good thing that her dog, Mêl, came bursting out from the undergrowth where the path divided, her tail wagging, tongue lolling, her insistent barking urging them to hurry, for there was the promise of better scent-trails ahead. Laughing, still breathless, but not now from the danger of falling, Archfedd clutched the hem of her skirt into her hands and ran on up the right-hand path after the dog. Natanlius pounded after them.

The river had fallen behind, only trees and outcrops of rock surrounded them as the path lurched into a steeper incline. Natanlius pulled the girl up, did not let go her hand as they emerged from the shade into a level, grassed clearing. They had found the river again, only here, it ran slower, widening into a tranquil shallow pool, before dropping abruptly over a rocky edge into the white foam of a forty-foot or so waterfall.

Archfedd went to see it closer, taking Natanlius with her, clinging to his strength as she peeped cautiously over, down into that cascading torrent. Immediately below, another pool, hissing and boiling with the spray, rock-edged, no doubt deep.

'Come away,' Natanlius urged her. ''Tis dangerous so close to a fall.'

Archfedd needed no second asking.

Mêl had disappeared again, they could hear her barking joyfully somewhere ahead, was chasing squirrels or birds, no doubt. Fool dog would not know what to do with one were she to catch it! Archfedd called to her, knowing she would not come until her own interest brought her back.

The climb up, although enjoyable, had been hard work and Archfedd felt the uncomfortable trickle of sweat down her back; a hot enough day without the effort of exercise. The pool appeared to be only a few feet deep, the stones and rocks shining beneath the dance of surface sunlight, the clear water so cool and inviting. In a moment, she had her boots off, her skirt hitched high about her thighs, was stepping in, enjoying the delicious coldness that stung her legs, tickled her toes. 'Come in!' she teased Natanlius. 'Strip your bracae and tunic and come in!'

Natanlius was tempted. But to kiss a pretty girl beneath the shade of the trees was one thing, to strip naked and romp in the water with her . . . Ah no, not when that girl happened to be the King's only daughter! Instead, he removed only his sword belt, and sprawled on the grass to watch her. Plucking a blade, he chewed at its sweetness, trying not to look over-closely at those long, inviting legs.

The mountain rivers were cold, too fast-flowing for the sun to warm their passing, too cold to stand paddling for overlong. Archfedd scrambled from the water, flung herself full-length beside Natanlius, lay with her eyes closed, enjoying the heat of the sun falling full on her face. A shadow dropped across her, and then the touch of his mouth against hers, the feel of his hands on her body, her breasts.

'Do you think,' Natanlius whispered, 'that the sixth son of a noble lord would stand chance of asking a King's daughter to become his wife?'

'That would depend on what manner of a man that sixth son was,' Archfedd answered with a shy giggle as she guided his hand up under her skirt, along the length of her damp legs, 'and on whether the King's daughter liked him enough.' She pulled him nearer, closer, her senses pulsing as she became aware of his want for her.

The dog Mêl had trotted into the clearing, plunged into the water to drink and found a stick bobbing there. She enjoyed the game of chasing sticks. Dripping water from her coat and mouth, took it to her mistress, and with an enthusiastic bark, dropped it onto the man who lay atop of her.

Suppressing an oath, Natanlius rolled from Archfedd. Twice now the dog had stopped him from taking his manhood over far! He did not know whether to praise the dog or curse it. Archfedd, however, was irritated. The presence of this man had aroused her; she had never known the close intimacy of a man. Oh, the occasional light kiss, aye, the feel of a man's hand around her waist, beneath her breast, but not this closer, more exciting, urgent thing. She liked Natanlius, wanted him to be her first man, her man, her husband. As her father had, no doubt, intended.

Annoyed at the bitch, she took hold the stick and tossed it away, forgetting that the bitch would chase it. Mêl went after it, racing over the short, sun-browned grass to where it had disappeared among the greenery of bushes . . . only they were not bushes, but the tops of trees, trees that had their roots forty feet below, where the river had gouged a ravine from its race over that waterfall.

Archfedd screamed, thrust Natanlius from her, ran to where a moment before her dog had been.

The man did not think, acted only with instinct; he plunged over the edge where the dog had fallen, almost falling himself, grasping branches to steady his descent, grabbing at slender trunks, bracing himself with his feet that tangled in bracken and bramble, jarred against rock. Slithered, slid and tumbled. He was down, a little bruised, but in one piece.

Archfedd had run to where the trees gave way to bare rock, to where she had first looked down onto the cascade of water, knelt there, watching for Natanlius, eye searching for her dog. Natanlius appeared from the tangle of trees and bracken, she cupped her hands around her mouth, called desperately. 'Can you see her! Is she there?'

He did not hear, the noise of the water was deafening. He made his way carefully over the wet, slippery rocks, knelt at the edge of the foaming, white-bubbling pool. Damn silly dog could be anywhere, engulfed under the hurl of the water, submerged in the pool, swept downstream . . . he saw something dark bobbing among the turmoil of water – a lump of bark. Then something else! There she was, trying to swim against the current, trying to keep her head above the frantic swirl of water! He called her, urging her to him. The dog heard, for she struck out towards him, but the strength of the plunging river swept her aside. Again and again, she tried to come to him. Natanlius looked around for a branch, something to reach out to hook her with. He dared not go into that water himself. Who knew how deep it was? He could be swept away, carried, tossed and bludgeoned down to the lake . . . He lay down, stretched out as far as he could above the foaming noise, reached out his hand – and a surge of water lifted the dog forward. He had her ear! He hauled, grasped her ruff with his other hand, dragged and pulled her –

434

rolled on his back, lay gasping and panting. The dog crouched beside him, shivering, cold and frightened. Vomited water over his arm.

Opening his eyes, Natanlius surveyed where he had plunged down, his passing marked by torn branches, battered ferns, a few dislodged rocks. How in all Hades was he to get up again? Grasping the dog by her collar, he set her at the sheer wall, pushing her rump before him, encouraging her to scrabble for a foot-hold, found a hand-hold for himself, a low branch, and heaved. Clutching hold of anything firm that held his weight, breathing hard, he worked his way upward, thrusting the dog before him – and hands clasped at her, took her, came again to grasp his hand, pull him up that last yard, and he lay panting, winded, more than a few scratches on his face and hands.

Archfedd was crying. She rubbed at his hands, his back, not knowing what to do for him, how to thank him. Feebly, he pointed at the dog. 'I'm in one piece, see to the dog,' he gasped.

I wonder sometimes, he thought, *whether women are worth all the trouble they cause.*

Then Archfedd was beside him again, her arms going around him, her head burrowing into his shoulder. He put his hand on her hair, held her close, until her trembling eased. *Aye*, he answered his own thought, *happen they are.*

August 486

§ XXIV

Caer Cadan, the King's stronghold, subdued without the presence of Arthur and the others – even Archfedd, Medraut missed. At least her criticisms were offset by laughter and a love of life. Cywyllog's continuous censuring was melancholic, her character dismal. Even during the celebration of their wedding, she had barely smiled.

Why in the name of God had he wed her? What had possessed him? What foolish idiocy had driven him to want her for his own? Na, that was not wholly true. He had not pursued her ... It had just happened, last winter it had been, during the time of the Nativity Festival. As often before, Lord Geraint's widow and her family had come as guests – with her, Aurelius Caninus.

Caninus, grandson to Ambrosius Aurelianus, inheritor of all that noble man's estate, and kin to Arthur; below Medraut and the whoreson Cerdic, his heir. He had none of the honour of his father, Cadwy, or the gentleness of his mother, Ragnall. That good woman who had, with her infant daughter, passed into God's Kingdom from the ravages of fever barely three months after Badon. Caninus was a lad new into manhood, and overproud of it, he had an arrogant charm that drew the maids like dull-painted moths to the brilliance of the flame. Young smiles did not see behind the handsome mask of confident, carefree boastfulness. A girl could be so easily flattered at exaggerated compliment and expansive attention. He danced, he talked. Performed, Medraut thought, like a dressed actor playing a well-rehearsed part of the bachelor lover. A vain coxcomb, with, as Medraut knew, a vile streak of cruelty. Watching him prance and exhibit before the ladies, even Arthur became exasperated by his swaggering. To the maids, however, he brought a merriment of honeyed words and blatant adulation. More than one was lured into the tumble of the stored hay while Caninus resided at Caer Cadan.

One declining. Cywyllog.

When Ambrosius died, there had been difficulty over deciding where the students of his school ought go. Many opted to remain within the monastery of Ambrosium, but the younger ones, it was thought, would be better to go to Brother Illtud at his new-founded school of Llan Fawr Illtud. The boys Gildas and Maelgwyn went there, along with Davydd and Sampson. Caninus went into Geraint's household and Medraut returned with his father to Caer Cadan – along with several of the noble-born young women who would take position as handmaids to the Queen.

Cywyllog was too sensible to listen to Caninus's ridiculous flattery, too practical to be taken in by his boasted prowess. And beside, she too knew of his malicious streak – she wore the scar still, pale above her left temple, where a stone meant for a litter of pups had cut deep.

Was Medraut impressed by this? Was it her stoic contempt that first drew him to, as he thought, admire her? It must have been, for by the first budding of early spring he had sought permission from his father to wed her. Arthur had queried his choice, suggesting, although not outright, that the girl was dour. And now, these few months later? There was no passion, no warmth, and as for love . . . Why had Cywyllog accepted him? The answer to that had come plain enough on the night of their wedding. Vengeance. She could not stab at Arthur, hurt him or his pride and manhood, but she could his son. Oh there was enough to legitimize the marriage. Medraut could not complain that she did not fulfil her duties, neglect him for any need that he might have, be it for a full belly of food or cleaned boots; a new-woven cloak, or the intimacies demanded by marriage. She was clever, Cywyllog. Too late, Medraut had discovered that.

He would have liked to have ridden north to Gwynedd with his father, but someone had to stay, someone need oversee the daily training of the war horses, listen to the complaints of the common people, make judgements, punish the wrongdoers, take on the temporary responsibilities of a king. Medraut was not the King, but he was his son, and deliberately Arthur had placed the burden on his shoulders. In private, the Pendragon doubted the lad would have the stamina or stomach to see the duty through. For that reason, he left others, trusted, wiser men, to keep unobtrusive eye on him, and the daily workings of Caer Cadan, but like it or not, Medraut was his heir – unless he chose Caninus . . . na, that was not an option Arthur would be tempted to consider.

Unexpected to them both, father and son, Medraut managed well, for he had a good ear for listening, a knack for making sensible decision – save the fool decision to wed with Cywyllog. Happen he had not inherited a talent for the intricacies of battle and war, but the gift of the ability of organization and administration did not go unnoticed by all within the Caer, nor by his father, who was impressed by the sending of regular written, accurate reports and accounts.

Two events happened on the same day at Caer Cadan. News reached them that Archfedd had wed with Natanlius, and Lord Bedwyr, Arthur's cousin, arrived home from his years of journeying abroad. Both filled the

Caer with an air of celebration and joy – and Medraut ordered a feast be prepared for that evening's Gather.

He had barely met Bedwyr, and then only as a child when first he had come to Britain. He remembered the tall, deep-voiced man only vaguely, for he had disappeared soon after the victory of Badon. Medraut had been too young then to wonder why, but he had heard enough in the intervening years to understand the reason. Hard it must be for a man who had loved a woman, expected to take her as wife, then to see her happy with another. Aye, even if that other was her husband.

He found Bedwyr an easy man to befriend, was disappointed to learn that he intended to ride on, north, to join with the Pendragon.

'I have been too long absent,' Bedwyr explained, sharing a congenial flagon of wine with Medraut in the privacy of what was Arthur's own chamber – Medraut's, while his father was away. 'I doubt the ladies – nor the King – will forgive me, were I to languish here, waiting for their return.'

Talk of the women reminded Medraut of his half-sister's marriage. Bedwyr was pleased at the news – though he expressed astonishment at how the years had passed him by. 'She was a child when I left!' he declared. He asked after Natanlius, probing as to his background, his family; seemed eager to meet with him.

The marriage delighted Medraut. A husband might quieten that quick temper of hers! Too much to hope that Arthur would grant them a stronghold somewhere far distant from Caer Cadan ... Ah, to be free of Archfedd's barbed sarcasm ... raising his goblet of wine, he proposed long health and happiness to the couple, enthusiastically echoed by Bedwyr.

Was it then Medraut had his idea? Or later, when they prized open the sealing wax from a third flagon of Arthur's best wine?

'I can take a few days to be gone from here – the Caer will run smooth enough without me. Why do I not ride part the way with you? I have a fancy to purchase some especial bridal gift for my sister – what do you suggest?'

And so they had talked, and decided. Medraut would leave with Bedwyr in two days. They would ride north-west into the White Hills, Bedwyr going on, northward to Gwynedd, Medraut to the place where the silver was extracted from the mined lead and cast into bowls and plates, spoons and goblets. He would purchase his half-sister something beautiful and expensive for her new life as wife to Natanlius.

Happen it would impress her enough to ease the taint of mistrust that had been between them both throughout all these years.

438

§ XXV

With an escort of four men, Medraut and Bedwyr rode from the Caer soon after dawn, when the clouds were gathering to the west, boasting rain. It would be welcome, for the sun had blazed too hot, too long.

A steady jogged pace, the two men easy in their conversation, talking as if they had known each other many years, not but a few days. Crickets chirruped among the heat-dried grass of the Summer Land; a lark sang; further on, another. The steady rhythm of the horses' hooves, the creak of leather, jingle of harness. He ought not think such thoughts, but oh, how joyous it was to be riding away from his wife for three, happen four days!

Yns Witrin to their left, the dark cone of the Tor rising to meet the louring sky. His mother had come from there, so his father had told him. Where was the place of his own birthing, Medraut wondered? Beside the lake that even in the hottest summer lay at the foot of that pagan, mystical hill – or away up there on the summit, where the eye of the Goddess could have watched over his mother's labour? Had his mother sat, gasping through the birth pains, with her back pressed against the Stone, the sacred symbol of oath and eternity. He could see it clearly, bright, illuminated, as the early sunlight struck against its granite surface. He asked Bedwyr if he knew how tall it was. The older man confessed that he had never climbed the Tor to find out.

'Ask your father,' he suggested. 'He has been up there.'

Medraut had heard that it was the height of a man, difficult to judge from this distance. One day, he must go up there. He had never liked to, though, for Ambrosius and the monks at Ambrosium had instilled into the boys the evilness of the old ways, the pagan places and heathen gods. That was all an anomaly to Medraut, though. If the non-Christian way was so bad, why was Arthur a good King? Why did people follow him, love him? The Pendragon was no Christian . . . but then, there were not over-many within the Church who held a fondness for him. His mother must have. The questions came marching in again. Easy to think, to puzzle as you rode, to let the mind wander and sieve through the many possible answers.

Where was she, his mother? Alive, dead? Did he care? Not really. He barely remembered her. Gwenhwyfar had been more of a mother than his natural one – even though she had an inclination towards indifference. Gwenhwyfar had no love for him, why should she? But at least she had, from the first, shown him kindness, had seen he wore warm clothes, had a full belly. Nursed him through illnesses. Did he remember Morgaine for that? He could not even recall her face.

The road was a good one, well maintained – that was something they could no longer lay at Arthur's feet – the main roadways were all repaired. Holes filled, drainage ditches redug – and not just here, in the King's own land, elsewhere also. Roads constructed with the strength of Rome, that ran to north, south and west. East, ah, that was Saex territory. Let them see to their own arrangements, Arthur said.

He parted amicably from Bedwyr, who turned to join the road that would meet eventually with the eastern bank of the Hafren river, and the north. The White Hills loomed grey and cloud-covered, an undulating cluster of hills, cut by the rift of the Great Gorge and pocked by natural caves and man-dug mines. A lure for Rome when first she made decision to claim Britain for herself. Corn, fine hunting dogs. Tin and lead, all these plentiful in Britain. From these mines came the lead that lined the great bath at Aquae Sulis, that brought water along the aqueducts to many a town and fortress. Lead that gave its precious extraction, silver. Lead for making pewter, coffins.

The mines within the White Hills were still operable, though not so busy and economical as they were during the height of Rome. Nearby, a cluster of settlements where the craftsmen gathered, and it was to here that Medraut was headed, where he passed two contented days, selecting the stuff he wanted to purchase, and watching, fascinated, as the silversmith created his beautiful ware. For himself, he purchased a silver ring, detailed with the figure of a running stag. He wore it on the second finger of his right hand. On the smallest finger, sat a battered gold ring that had once been his father's.

He was almost tempted to stay, build himself a hut, learn how to take the raw ingots of silver and turn them into such wondrous items . . . what a thing to do with your hands and mind! A King's son become a silversmith? Na, he had duties and responsibilities at Caer Cadan. Well enough to take his ease for a few days, his father would not begrudge him that, but more . . .

The journey homeward was not so buoyant, no Lord Bedwyr as company, and only a sullen wife to greet him. He had waited until late morning before giving the order to mount up, hoping the grey skies that had persisted these few days, would clear, but the drizzle fell heavier, with a distant rumble of thunder. No choice but to leave in the rain.

The road was crowded by standards of normal travel, traffic slowed by the ponderous lumbering of ox-carts making their slow way through the mud, to or from the mines. There was much cursing and grumbling, sour faces and hunched shoulders. Many of the slaves hauling at stuck wheels and recalcitrant beasts, Medraut noticed, were either northern-born or Saex. Twice he passed rich-dressed merchants coming from the direction of the coast, again, Saxons. He supposed it was economically wise to sell the pigs of lead to foreigners. To the Saex? But then, trade was trade.

He decided to leave the road, divert to follow the river, for no reason, save for a whim. His escort passed muttered grumbling between themselves, soon silenced by a stern look. Then his horse went lame, a stone, a jagged rock, whatever, had sliced into the underside of his foot. It would be a long walk for one of the men – obliged to exchange mounts – unless it was rested a while. Eagerly, Medraut seized the excuse to delay. They would make camp by the river, allow the horse to stand in the coldness of the water. By morning the rain might have stopped, the cut healed well enough.

One of the escort mentioned the caves. 'Up through the woods, my lord,' he said, indicating the faint path. 'There is a woman up there knows all about healing and such.'

One of the men laughed.

At the time, Medraut wondered why.

§ XXVI

How foolish! Medraut felt awkward, ill at ease and ridiculously immature. He stood, embarrassed, one step inside the open doorway, fiddling with his wet, woollen cap, dripping rain on the earth floor of the bothy. She sat before her fire, her skirt, that was wet-stained at the hem, pulled up over her knees, her bare toes almost in the embers. Her legs were sun-browned, scraped smooth of hair, as were her arms. Dark hair, damp. She had recently been out in the rain then. Her eyes and lips were coloured with the ochres and paints that some women wore. His wife Cywyllog did not, for painting the face, she said, was a blasphemy against God. Medraut could not see how. It made this woman attractive and alluring. Interesting.

'Well,' she said, having scrutinized him up and down, twice over, 'I see a man before me, yet he has the shyness of the boy about him.' Her heart was hammering. Mother! She had never expected him to come here. Mother be protective, not here! But then, what had she expected? Never to see him, never to meet accidentally, never to have their paths cross? By remaining in Gaul she could have ensured that. Not by coming here, so close to where he was. She retained the seductive smile, for she was experienced at that. You could not be a woman who pleasured men without that ability to smile, to laugh, to give the illusion of enjoyment. While inside you were screaming.

'My horse is lame,' Medraut stammered, looking at the floor, the bothy wall, anywhere but at her, and those slim, enticing legs. 'I hoped you might have a suitable salve. I have payment.' He unhooked a small wineskin from his shoulder, hung its strap on a hook directly to his left on the wall, atop a cloak, wet also from the rain.

The woman inclined her head in acceptance, leant backward, resting her weight on one elbow. If he could come, what of Arthur? The smile at the corner of her lips twitched, gloating, triumphant. If only he would, how much easier it would be! She did not turn to look, for she knew the jar well enough. It was there, on the left-hand shelf, beside the casket of jewellery. A small pottery vase, well stoppered with wax, its contents a dark, bitter liquid. Intended, one day, for him.

'I have a salve to heal all needs,' she said. *And potions to end them*, she thought.

Medraut knew his answering smile gave him the appearance of a full-moon fool, knew also how red his face was burning. What had he expected to find here, in the name of God? A hag, a curled old woman, muttering toothless over her foul-stinking remedies? Now he understood the men's laughter. '*A woman up there, knows all about healing and such*' ... Aye, and such! His blush deepened. Why had he come here ...? Why did he not go, walk away?

Because she would mock him, laugh at him? He could see it happening, see himself hurrying back down the hill, slipping and sliding on the rain-wet grass; her standing in this doorway, hands on hips, head back, laughing. Cywyllog mocked him, though not with laughter. Hers was the censuring of long silences or harsh, narrow-eyed glances, and the bite of unnecessary sarcasm.

He stood there in the doorway, uncertain what to do or say. Chewed his lip. Damn the woman, she was not making this easy for him!

'Are you to come inside?' she asked, kicking her eyes briefly in the direction of a blanket-covered bed to one corner. Inviting, luring. Cywyllog's, was a box-bed, hard and unyielding. Like her.

'I just want the salve,' he managed, through dry mouth and uneasy breath.

Shrugging her shoulder, Morgaine unfolded herself, came to her feet, her bracelets chiming, the blue-painted patterns tattooed along her arms rippling, giving the illusion that the twined shapes of snakes and vine leaves were slithering up the skin. Her skirt tumbled to fall as it should, the bright colour attractive, but hiding those long, lovely legs. The

442

thought raced across Medraut's mind that he would have liked to have seen higher – a thought hastily thrust aside. His eyes, however, were focused on those painted patterns. Where had he seen such before?

'A lame horse? What form of lameness?' Twice she needed to ask the questions.

'His hoof, a cut.'

She nodded, gestured with her hand that he must step aside from the doorway as she needed to pass through. 'My salves I keep in a room to the back of this.'

Embarrassment re-emerging, he hastily stepped a pace to the side. A chance to glance around while she was gone.

The bothy was wattle-built, reed-thatched, windowless. A central hearth-place with tripod and cooking pot suspended over it, the normal fug of smoke gathered beneath the roof, writhing its way through the narrow smoke-hole. The bed, a stool; shelves crammed with pots and jars, a wooden chest, for her garments, no doubt. Cooking utensils. A table, small, ornate, out of place here in this hovel. It was a wealthy person's piece of furniture, exquisitely made, inlaid with ebony and some bright, shining, coloured stuff such as you would see inside an opened oyster shell. It was not that which drew his attention, but the things laid out upon it. A whalebone comb, an array of ivory and silver hairpins and a bronze mirror. The handle was twisted around itself, decorated to resemble a tree, the branches and leaves spreading upward to form the back of the polished metal mirror. He wandered over to it, his hand going out, almost as if it had motion all its own, to lift the object up. He knew he would find a doe carved, half-hidden, timid, behind one of those stemmed branches . . .

He almost dropped the thing as he heard her returning to the door, his skin prickling, drained white, his hand, his body, trembling. He took the pot from her hand, ran from the place. He steadied himself, forced himself to walk, dignified, calm. Ignored her call.

'Come again, Medraut. You will always be welcome.'

September 486

§ XXVII

Bedwyr found Arthur relaxing within the contented security of Gwenhwyfar's family domain. Gwynedd, the land of sky-tipped mountain and
soaring eagle; of the proud, red deer, the bristled ugliness of the boar, and
the slink of the grey wolf.

For several months, they had resided among the splendour of the
mountains, Arthur himself disappearing for a few weeks to ride north, to
Caer Lueil and beyond, to the High Lands rolling, seemingly forever,
beyond the Roman Wall. That monument to a distant era that stretched
from sea to sea, that was now obsolete and rapidly becoming neglected
and ruinous. In the north, Arthur was Supreme King in name only. They
outwardly honoured him, paid a minor annual tribute, fawned and smiled
while he resided overnight in Hall or settlement. Forgot him as soon as
his banner dipped out of sight into the next valley. It was enough for
Arthur. If the peace held, if none cared or dared to challenge his ultimate
authority, then so be it, leave it as it was. It would remain so until his
ending, and then . . . who knew?

Arthur had returned to Caer Arfon three days earlier, was assisting in
the breaking-in of a young colt, a fiery bay with a will of his own.

Teaching a horse to respond to a rider's wish was no quick, single-
morning task. To train an animal for the requisites of war – as Arthur
needed – took skill and time and patience, took the knowing of a horse's
mind. It was all about trust and respect. Beat a horse, hurt or frighten it,
the horse would serve, but unwillingly, with fear and wariness. Gentle
him, and the animal would do anything, go anywhere. The colt had
passed through its third summer, had been handled from a yearling,
taught to lead quietly, stand, turn. To wear saddle and bridle. The next
stage, to carry a rider.

Already comfortable with the saddle and used to having a man lean
over his back, the colt stood quiet for his handler while Arthur made a
fuss of him, patting, stroking, talking softly, fondling his ears and muzzle,
giving a small handful of corn. Gently, taking his time, Arthur moved
along the colt's neck, patting and stroking, talking, almost crooning,
nonsense words.

'There's a lad, handsome boy. Your sire would be proud of you, your

444

mother elated! There, my son of the wind. Stand, my beauty, stand.' Arthur leant his weight over the saddle, his feet firm on the ground. The colt's ears flicked backwards, but unconcerned, listening more to the soothing voice rather than being attentive to what was happening. Arthur eased his whole weight over, feet dangling, and then, judging the right moment, sat astride, calm, immobile, hands resting loose on his thighs, legs dangling. The colt was more interested in that second handful of corn that Arthur's helper was offering him, a lad who had the trust of many of the young horses. Relaxed, in no hurry, Arthur took up the reins. He nodded, clicked his tongue as the handler, leading the horse simultaneously, gave the order to walk on.

Within half of an hour, Arthur was directing the colt alone, following the fence of the circular gyrus, the horse training ground, he tapped the horse's sides with his heels, used his voice and tongue, and the colt broke into a rhythmic trot.

Arthur was pleased, a fine animal, a good horse for the Artoriani.

'A Roman once said of the Syrians,' a voice called laconically from inside the gateway, 'that the only mares they could ride with any efficiency were the whores of the local brothels, and even then, they could not maintain a distance. It pleases me to see that we have higher standards here in Britain!'

Looking across the sanded ground of the gyrus, wearing a deep frown of annoyance at having his concentration interrupted, Arthur burst into a wide, gladdened, grin. 'Bedwyr!' he exclaimed, 'By all that is good! Bedwyr!' He halted the colt, beckoned for the handler to come forward, take him, slid down from the animal, giving him the last of the corn from his waist pouch and a rewarding pat. Strode across to the gateway, arms outstretched, delighted. 'You are home? Ah, it is good to see you!'

The men embraced, looked each other over for signs of age, illness or harm, found none, embraced enthusiastically again.

'Jesu, but you have led me a merry dance!' Bedwyr complained, as arms about each other's shoulders, they left the training ground. 'First, I ride to Caer Cadan, then to Dinas Emrys, then here. You are more difficult to pin with a spear than a wounded boar!'

'Had you arrived a few days since, then I would have been up above the Wall – but Gwenhwyfar is here, with Archfedd and her new-taken husband.'

'Aye, so I have heard.' Bedwyr slapped Arthur's back half in congratulations, half in jest. 'What manner of an untried whelp have you taken as son-by-law, then?'

'One who has delusions of young love and romance.'

'Hah! That will soon be rubbed from him.'

They laughed loud, delighted with the company of each other, euphoric at the reunion, strode down the hill towards the imposing ramparts of the stronghold of Caer Arfon. The pleasure repeated with Gwenhwyfar, and her daughter. Then the questions came, the whys, wheres and hows. The demand for tales of his long journeying, to hear of where he had been, what he had seen. A louder demand to know what gifts he had brought home, especially from Archfedd who had leapt to engulf her father's cousin in an embrace of fierce possession.

'Gifts?' Bedwyr jested. 'Is my return not gift enough?' Relenting, he accounted the truth. 'I have left them at Caer Cadan, safe waiting your return. Silks as fine and delicate as any maid could wish, perfumes and unguents, jewels that sparkle brighter than the summer sun reflected on a mountain pool, fleeces thicker than three skins of the bear, leather, ivory, skins . . .' Gwenhwyfar begged him to say no more, Archfedd pleaded to return south on the morrow!

They dined, Gwenhwyfar's nephew, Owain, commanding a feast of especially fine quality be prepared, and the best wine amphorae be opened. Late into the night, Bedwyr entertained with his stories of distant, exotic countries that baked under a sun hotter than the hottest summer's day, of rivers wider than the space between the walls of the Caer; of strange beasts and dark-skinned people. A wondrous variety of language and foods. Inevitably, the delights of the whores.

'They ride well? None of them Syrian then, I assume?' Arthur quipped, his expression straight and serious as he sipped his wine. For a moment Bedwyr was puzzled at the reference, remembered his jest from earlier in the day, laughed outright.

More wine, more talk, more laughter. Archfedd had fallen asleep, her head pillowed on her husband's shoulder, Natanlius, his arm proudly around her, attempting to keep his eyes from closing. Gwenhwyfar lay stretched along a couch, a goose-down cushion clutched between her arms as a pillow, a deep smile on her sleeping face. Owain had retired for the night. Arthur and Bedwyr alone sat awake pouring yet another glass of fine wine.

'You heard of Syagrius?' Bedwyr asked.

For a while, Arthur was silent, savouring the sweet taste of his wine. Then slowly and with no tinge of regret, said, 'I heard. Clovis of the Franks took Soissons, had him executed.' Another mouthful of wine, thoughtfully swallowed. 'He was once, a long time past, a friend of mine. After Gaul, I will never again trust any man who dares call himself friend.' The words were poignant, tinged with those bitter memories.

Bedwyr too sat silent, swilling his wine around in his glass. He would not argue with that. 'He ought have come to our aid. Ought not have abandoned us as he did.' Bedwyr drained his glass in a quick, tossed motion. 'He tried seeking sanctuary with Alaric, the new king of the Goths. Even our past enemies, it seems, did not trust his honey words. He was returned to Clovis.'

'Alaric.' Arthur ran his finger around the rim of his empty glass. 'The successor to Euric. I ought have been delighted to hear of that bastard's death, but somehow, as each year passes, the word death grows more menacing. It stalks too close to my heels to be mocked, I think.' He snorted a puff of self-derision. 'I even found myself dismayed to hear Sidonius Apollinaris had died of a fever. No more of his damned embellished letters, I ought have felt some small pleasure at that.'

They sat a while, silent, each brooding his own thought. Bedwyr was about to speak, realized Arthur had drifted into sleep. He looked so much older. More hair greying at temple and forehead, skin more puckered and wrinkled. Contemplated Archfedd with the fresh dew of youth radiating about her; her husband Natanlius, eager in his pride, shining with his new-found love. And Gwenhwyfar.

Ah, Gwenhwyfar would always be the beauty, even when she was old and shrivelling. For all the excitement and adventure that he had experienced these past few years, he had missed Gwenhwyfar.

May 487

§ XXVIII

Coed Morfa: the marsh beside the woodland. The wind swept up the channel, blustering aggressively, bending the reeds beneath the hiss of spray tossing the gulls and sea-birds as if they were of no consequence. Billowing behind the sail of the Saxon long ship, which was cruising parallel with the far bank, the blue-grey chequering of its weave undulating with each freshening gust.

Natanlius was not a tall man, though stocky-built, deep-voiced; he held Archfedd before him, his hand firm around her broadening waist, his expression grim. Oh, the Saex ships came frequently enough to their established south settlement, over there on the far side of the water, but rarely further up, never before, this far – at least, not as openly. Archfedd gripped her husband's forearm, sharing his anger, hiding the flutter of fear within her belly, telling herself that it was only the child moving. It was not so much the ship that caused their anger, but the emblem streaming from the mast. The White Dragon. Cerdic.

The bitch, Mêl, sensed the stir of unease. She nosed the wind, scenting for danger, met only with the familiar smell of the tide and the salt tang of the marsh. Pressed herself closer against her mistress's legs, growled softly. Absently, Archfedd ruffled her head, soothing, behind those flattened ears.

'Can he see us?' she asked. 'Will he attempt to make a landing?'

'I doubt it, to both questions.' Natanlius had no need to sound optimistically confident, common sense told that he was right. They stood, not out in the open, but against a cluster of wind-twisted trees that marked these patchy, irregular coastal woodlands. Their cloaks, though fluttering in the wind, were the earth colours of dark green and brown and the horses were secured on the far side of the copse. It was no good hunting for wild duck dressed in bright colours. They had a brace already, had been stalking a fat mallard when the ship had appeared. As for her landing, the wind was too strong to bring such an immense craft – for all her sleekness and manoeuvrability – to this side of the channel, and soon, the tide would be turning. 'Na,' he said again, 'we are safe enough.' *For now. But for how much longer?* He kept the thought to himself.

The oars were out, they could see them dip and lift, see the wild cream of foam as they swept downward into and out of the water, the power of that craft immense, magnificent. Formidable. The ship shuddered, came to a halt as the oars, in unison, backswept through the tossing, white-crested waves. For a moment it stood, poised, waiting. Deciding?

Archfedd was certain she could see someone standing at the prow, a well-built figure . . . Imaginative fancy, the distance was too great to make out such detail, but did she need to see? Cerdic would be standing there, surveying this empty stretch of coastland. His narrowed eyes would be sweeping the ripple of wind-dancing reeds for sign of settlement and stronghold. To look for the rise of hearth-smoke, the movement of riders, the shadowed smudge of wattle-built walls. He would be disappointed, there was nothing to be seen. As with all marsh country, settlements and farm-steads were wide-spaced, isolated dwellings hugging the islands of higher ground, or squatting beside the shelter of the trees that began their solid march a few miles inland. Nor would he see anyone among the reeds, or softly paddling a coracle along the tide-filled channels. If Cerdic could see, then so would the wild fowl, the occasional deer or boar, and if they could see, then that man's family would go hungry that day.

And if there was nothing to see, except the dull pewter of a wind-lashed sky and the sweep of marsh below, why did he watch?

Her husband must have been pursuing the same line of thought, for he spat saliva from his mouth, intending offence. Coed Morfa and its stronghold two miles inland, had been the domain of his father and of his father, and of how many more fathers before? From the time before the legions had taken up their belongings and boarded their ships to return to Rome, had one of his line been here. Natanlius proudly placed his hand over the swelling of the child. Unless this one was a son, he would be the last of that long, distinguished line. His brothers, the four of them, had fallen at the bloodshed that was Llongborth. Their father had never recovered from the wounds that were terrible about his body. He had gone to join his sons and Lord Geraint one month exactly to the day after that wicked battle. The fifth brother had followed their path into the next world six months past, taken there by fever. Leaving Natanlius as Lord of Coed Morfa.

His hand around his wife, Natanlius stiffened, his grip tightening. Cerdic would not have it from him! Would not take what was his! Not while he had breath in his body to keep any poxed Saex shadow from falling here!

The ship rose and fell with the swell; with the sail furled, the oars kept her steady. What was Cerdic watching? This, the British shore? Or could he be surveying that other side, the Saxon land?

'He has quarrelled with Port and his bastard sons,' Archfedd declared, attempting to find some acceptable explanation, 'and is contemplating a way to land an army with the intention of marching, unexpected, to the rear of his settlement.'

Natanlius guffawed. 'If only!' A tempting idea, but doubtful.

Two gulls were noisily shrilling over possession of a fish. The waves were flattening, rolling, as the tide came to its height, that short period of confrontation between ebb and flow.

'Will you be sending word to my father?'

Natanlius nodded. 'I may go myself.'

Grabbing at his hand, Archfedd spun around, eyes wide, anxious, her heart bounding with sudden fear. 'Leave me here alone?' She flickered a glance over her shoulder at that White Dragon ship. 'What if he comes while you are gone?'

Amused at her absurdity – as if he would leave her unprotected – Natanlius caught her chin between his fingers, tipped her face so he may kiss her, lingering over the pleasure of her eager response. 'I have no doubt you would be more than capable of putting a boot into his arse, were he to be so foolish.'

She batted at his nose with her finger. It was not true, she could not fight as formidably as her mother. All the same she pursed her mouth for a second kiss.

When they looked again, the ship had swung about, had loosed the sail and was making heavy way, back down the channel into her own territory.

Natanlius hid the sigh of relief. Unlike Archfedd, for she did not yet know, he had heard that Cerdic was growing stronger, that soon there would not be just the one ship making her way up the Coed Morfa water, but many. Only a matter of time before Cerdic marched to join his acclaimed land to the south of here with Port's, over there, on the far bank.

Coed Morfa, British territory that lay in between the Saex lands, vulnerable and exposed. Why had Cerdic come in his splendid ship?

Why else, but to gaze upon what he wanted. Would soon fight for. Coed Morfa.

August 487

§ XXIX

So annoying that he need be called away these few days after his daughter had arrived at Caer Cadan, but that was the unfortunate thing of being King, the final responsibility of authority rested with him. Even were he to have Bedwyr here – he had gone into the East Anglian territory on some other, minor, business for Arthur – he would need sort this thing himself. Irritably, Arthur curbed Onager's eager stride, glowered at the rain-dark sky. If she birthed the child while he was sorting this latest in a long line of disruptions at the lead mines . . . that was nonsense, she had more than the six weeks to go until her time. A grandsire. Him, the Pendragon! The thought filled him with elation. The babe could be female, of course, but equally as much chance that it could be a grandson. A boy. A future Pendragon. That he already had a grandson was immaterial. Cynric was a Saxon. Meant nothing. *He* would trace his lineage back to Woden, not to the pride that was the title Pendragon.

They had left the flat of the Summer Land behind, were climbing into the higher country of the first of the White Hills range. Slightly more sheltered here, where the trees grew higher and thicker. The rain had fallen almost incessantly these past three days, with no promise of it easing, judging by the dark hang of the sky and the distant rumble of thunder. Spring this year had ventured late, tottering pathetically after a dismal winter, bringing with it cold winds and squalls of rain. June had fared somewhat better, with pale, half-hearted sunshine, but those winds had persisted. Much of the Summer Land remained underwater, isolated lakes and swollen, overflowing rivers and streams. Arthur was not alone in being sick of damp clothes and wet boots.

The grumblings at the lead mines – involving the legality and authentication of the various official stamps used in marking the pigs of lead – had rumbled on through the months, with one useless procurator replaced by another, and a series of officials sent to attempt to sort the muddle of bureaucracy, resulting in the ultimate need for Arthur himself finally to intervene. Too much lead – and more important, extracted silver – was going amiss, only the King's authority, it seemed, would get to the bottom of the problem.

The road that ran beside the rise of hills had fallen quieter as late afternoon dwindled into an early-arrived evening. Wagons and travellers with any sense would have already been seeking shelter for the night. Those last few on the road were hurrying to a final destination, not eager to make another, unnecessary stop.

Ahead, by five miles or more, lay the Great Gorge, limestone cliffs that towered several hundred feet above a winding pass that cut, like a vicious sword wound, into the side of the Hills. Arthur hated the place. The precarious track that ran, slippery and muddied, beside the gurgling run of the river. The small slit of sky so high and distant above, cliffs to either side rising sheer, dominating, brooding. Trapping. He would rather not ride up that gorge, but his business lay with this latest appointed procurator who resided at the largest mine, at the head of it. He could go the other route, up and over the top, the longer, exposed road. In this rain? Adding almost a whole day to the journey? Na, he would brave the gorge.

Ahead, an ox-wagon had turned to make the ascent of a narrow side-track, the Saxon drover whipping the beasts to pull against the cloy of mud, shouting abuse as a wheel lodged in a rut. The stone roads were bad enough for wagon haulage. Idiots to travel the lesser roads, Arthur thought absently, giving only a passing glance at the cart as he rode past the junction. A man, mounted, flanked by two body-guards respectfully, if somewhat slowly, moved aside from the road, their heads dipped in acknowledgment of rank. Well-dressed, a man of some wealth. A merchant-man. Saxon.

Arthur ignored him.

Behind, the Pendragon guard sniggered muted laughter. 'What is the jest?' he asked Gweir, riding beside him.

'That fat Saxon has taken the track after the ox-cart.'

They would stop soon, make camp. Arthur edged Onager into a jog-trot, pushing the pace slightly faster. They would camp this side of the gorge, ride through at first light. 'And what is comical about that?' he had to ask, having decided on no rational explanation for himself. The Saxons were certainly fools to travel a rough track so close to nightfall, but no merchant cared about the welfare of man or beast. Trade and payment their sole concern. Where was the jest then?

'The whore lives up there.'

The whore. What whore? Whores spread their wares along any track that a man might travel. These roads around the mines would provide ample trade.

The hills were deep misted with the rain, trees dripping, the dampness seeping upward. It was cold, the light fading, so depressing, hills, in the rain. At Caer Cadan they would be huddled around the hearth-fires, filling their bellies with hot food and warming wine.

Gweir rode his beloved dun. Arthur regarded him, one eye half-closed, other eyebrow raised, his expression questioning.

'*The* whore. The Lady of the White Hills,' Gweir explained. 'You must, surely, have heard of her?'

Arthur had, but had not realized it was to this side of the hills that she dwelt, thinking her further to the north.

Gweir then added, 'She was the one Medraut visited.'

Ah, he could see reason for the laughter now. 'When was that?'

Gweir shrugged, wiped at rain trickling uncomfortable down his neck. When? How did he know when? He pulled his dun to a walk, set in beside one of the men, questioned him, kicked into a trot to catch up with the Pendragon.

'Last year, while you were in Gwynedd. Antonius was one of the escort.'

Again, ah.

'The tale is well known among the men,' Gweir continued. 'Lord Medraut came running down from that hill as if the hounds of Hades were after him. The men reckon either her price was too high for the lad, or her legs too long for him to reach into the important parts!' Gweir chuckled. Poor Medraut, with the misery of such a sullen wife, the ideal butt of many a jest.

It was wrong to make mockery of the King's bastard son, of course, but with him away these last two months, visiting at Llan Illtud, the old stories had naturally resurfaced, safe in the knowing that he would not hear.

'You seen her, this whore?' Arthur asked, casually.

'Me? When I need a woman, I go for one a little nearer home!'

'That,' Arthur answered with a broad grin, 'is because you have no need to hide your habits from a wife!'

Ahead, a suitable sheltered place to make camp. Arthur ordered a halt. He had a prickly, uncomfortable feeling rising along the nape of his neck. It had been there since that ox-wagon had lumbered into view. More precise, the merchant travelling with it. What was the familiarity about him? There was many a Saxon trader Arthur had met in passing or spoken with along this route, why this unease?

It hit him, with the force of an axe blade, while the world, save for the night creatures and the watch guard, slept beneath the canopy of darkness. Had it come to him in a dream, or was it merely that thoughts came clearer when there was not the distraction of daylight? Whatever, he had been sound sleeping, curled beneath the thickness of his cloak,

453

oblivious to the patter of rain. He sat up, arrow straight, eyes wide, lips slightly parted.

That man, that Saxon, turning off onto the whore's track. There were easier paths to the nearest mine. Why would he take the wagon with him to pay visit to a whore?

And more important, why had he been so intent to hide his face?

§ XXX

With the horses secured, Arthur and Gweir walked the last mile. Away from the track, the going was easier. They walked carefully, aware of the need to make as little noise as possible, but the rain drizzling from the canopy of the trees, and the soft ground, absorbed small, unavoidably made sounds. At the edge of the trees, they hunkered to their heels, observing the bothy that squatred before the dark opening of a cave. With the rain falling, dawn would come late, the sky lightening with reluctance from darkness to slate-grey. No glory of a welcome, golden sunburst this morning!

Arthur was wet and in sour mood. The ride yesterday had been dispiriting, his sleep non-existent. And that black, predatory hole of a cave entrance exaggerated his bad temper. Gweir had assured him the whore lived in the bothy, but what if they had to go in there, into the caves? The sweat on Arthur's forehead and upper lip was not from the exertion of walking. Gweir would have to go in. He most certainly would not.

Three horses, unsaddled, were tethered to the lee side of the bothy, each standing with a hind leg resting, head drooping. Two men dozed beneath the makeshift protection of the ox-cart, the ox himself grazing unconcerned at the weather, over to the left. The drover, presumably, was the bundle beneath a sodden cloak, huddled beside what had been a pathetic attempt at lighting a fire.

The Saxon merchant-man? Assuming the two beneath the wagon were his bodyguard, he, could only be inside with the woman.

The decision. Whether to disarm these three outside or kill them. There was no cause, outside Arthur's suspicions, that they were about any wrongdoing. Even Saxons were permitted to rut with a whore! He glanced at Gweir, who mimed binding hands together, nodded his agreement. To kill them would be murder. Aside, their tongues may be useful.

They went for the two under the wagon first, assuming they would be the better armed, the more dangerous. Drovers were often slaves and simple-minded: you had to be to keep sane – oxen were such stupid creatures. Within a few short moments, the two were secured and gagged several yards down the track: one unconscious, the other too dazed to make a sound, with more than a few bruises and aching bones between them. Gweir dragged the third man from his sleeping place, his frightened whimpering silenced by a crack to the temple from Arthur's boot.

When the daylight finally came, miserable and slovenly, Arthur indicated that he was going into the bothy. Gweir nodded, grinned, whispered, 'If she's any good, let me have a turn at her before we leave?'

'You are welcome to all of her. No damn whore is worth all this effort!' Arthur drew his sword from its sheath, instinctively running the pad of his thumb along its sharpness. He stepped out from the cover of the trees, shoulders hunched, head bent low – was about to run the twenty or so yards to the closed doorway – froze, tumbled back into the shelter of the trees, heart pumping, cursing colourfully beneath his breath.

Gweir, with his own sword drawn, had heard it also. A horse, coming up the track. As stealthily as if he were approaching a nervous buck, he made his way to Arthur, exchanged a curious glance. They watched. The horse was a bay, four white feet, white face. He was muddied, tired, had been ridden through most the night by the look of him. His rider, cloak hood pulled well forward against the rain, dismounted, circled the ox-wagon, walked to the tethered horses, inspected them, examining their quality, looking for any brand or distinguishing mark. Stood a moment, considering the implication of their presence. Decision made, he marched for the closed door, his left hand stretching forward to thrust it open. His hood falling back, exposing his face.

Gweir reacted as swiftly as Arthur grasped his arm, gripped hard, for the Pendragon had risen with a startled, angry gasp, was about to step from the trees. Gweir pulled his lord downward. 'No!' he hissed. 'If you had a wife like his, would you not be secretly visiting places like it?'

Annoyed, Arthur shook the restraining hand off, but he hunkered down again, his sword lying exposed across his thighs. With a wife like Gwenhwyfar, he had already visited such places – but never while a wealthy Saxon was taking his pleasure.

They watched Medraut enter, waited for the shout and the flurry of activity that was bound to follow. It was normal, if a whore was busy, either to wait your turn or find yourself alternative arrangements. One minute passed. Two, three. No sound from that bothy. Nothing, no disturbance, no clatter or indication of fighting. No woman's scream, no reopening of the door with an embarrassed or grieved customer scuttling through. No man who valued his balls would deliberately walk in and disrupt another's purchased entertainment. Not unless the thing was arranged.

Arthur's eyes narrowed, his knuckles whitening against the grip on the sword pommel. Arranged. Organized. Deliberate. He spoke low, the control over his fury menacing. 'That bloody whoreson is not here for the woman, he is meeting with the Saex.'

'We do not know that . . .' but Gweir's protest fell on closed ears. Arthur was already running for the bothy. Gweir had no option. He followed.

Slamming into the door, kicking it open with his boot, Arthur was through, rolling with the impact, instantly up on his feet, nostrils flaring, sword ready to strike if necessary. Gweir silhouetted against the daylight in the doorway. Froze, both stood quite still, stunned. This, neither had expected. The implications began to slither into Arthur's brain. The answers to so many uneasy, puzzling, questions.

Medraut's expression was a mixture of horror and embarrassment. He stood, pressing his back against the far wall. Morgaine Arthur recognized immediately. She was hunched at the end of the tumbled bed, a fur loosely covering her nakedness, her hair unbound, uncombed. Her head had jolted up as Arthur had roughly entered, her eyes widening in fear, a gasp escaping her lips. She made no other sound, but the trembling was visible.

Arthur shifted the grip of his weapon, stepped forward across the four paces of the room, brought the sword-point, with deliberate leisure, into the hollow of the Saxon's throat. Except for the flicker of fear in the eyes and the slow, uncomfortable swallow, the man did not move. He was sitting on the edge of the bed, birth-naked. Wickedly, Arthur brought the sword lower, to point at the private parts, a sneered smile coming to his mouth at the Saxon's hastily stifled, indrawn breath.

'Father, I . . .' Medraut had to say something, had to explain.

'Do not beg, boy. Not of me.'

Medraut hesitated, the viciousness in that retort was acid sharp. He knew his father's potential for anger – had witnessed it often enough, but could not place why he was so enraged over this. Was it so unreasonable for him to be here? Aye, he had a wife – but then, so did his father. Could that be it? Arthur did not want others to know he was visiting a . . . Medraut could not bring himself to think of that word about his mother. No, no that could not be it. Why bring Gweir if that was so? Unless . . . was the anger for the same reason as his own?

That last time when Medraut had come here, unsuspecting, tricked by the men . . . What if his father had stumbled on the knowing about

Morgaine just this moment, as unsuspecting? What if his father had not known the woman here to be Morgaine? Expected to find a healing woman, as he, Medraut, had? To come in innocence to find her, Morgaine, was here, was a . . . Could his father be shocked and enraged for that reason?

'I – father –' he blurted, trying to ease the pain that he was certain was also coursing through his father. 'It, this, is not what you think!'

Arthur did not take his slit eyes from the Saxon, said to his son, 'I would like to believe that the pair of you had lured this turd here for my benefit, but knowing this bitch as I do, I doubt it.'

'Medraut,' the Saxon said, hiding his fear by pretending arrogance, 'could not lure a starving hawk to the bait. He is too incompetent even to clean his own arse.'

'Well, you would know all about that, wouldn't you, Cerdic?'

Medraut gasped, lurched forward, skin draining pale. Bile was rising in his throat. Cerdic? Had his father said the name Cerdic?

Arthur flicked his gaze, briefly, to Morgaine. Her head had dropped forward, tears were splashing, matting the fur. 'And you, madam? You thought this would never be discovered?'

'Took you many years,' Cerdic chuckled. 'I think we had a good enough sailing!'

Arthur jabbed with the sword, Cerdic winced, edged backward.

For how long then has my mother been here? Medraut was thinking, *For how long has she been a whore to this Saxon? This Saxon, my own half-brother?* He fell to his knees, vomited profusely. No one paid him heed.

'Who else is in this?' Arthur snarled. 'Someone must be bringing the trade in? Who supplies the weaponry? The arrows, the swords, the spears?' Bull's blood, they had been such blind fools! For all these years they had known of a Whore of the Hills – there was even a lewd song circulating about her – but no one had known her to be Morgaine, Medraut's mother, the Pendragon's . . . what? What had she been? What she was now? And why should they know? She did not use that name, Morgaine. None other, save himself and Gweir – ah, and Medraut – and Cerdic, it seemed, knew her for who she truly was. God's blood! Under the scent of their noses she had been the means of that dreadful trade, a whore's house, where none would suspect the visits of men, British or Saxon, where none would question a wagon waiting outside.

'Gweir,' Arthur ordered, 'search outside, if it is not already loaded, there will be weaponry somewhere.' Gweir nodded, made to leave, paused as his lord added, 'While you are out there, make an end of the scum secured to that tree.' To Cerdic, 'You ought choose a more competent guard. Yours were asleep.'

There was only the one scream. The drover. The other two at least had the honour to die silent.

'They made me do it.' Morgaine lifted her tear-swollen eyes at the sound. 'They forced me, I had no choice. I came to Britain because I wanted to see you, to see my son . . .' She shrieked as Arthur lurched forward, grabbed her by the hair and dragged her from the bed. 'Who?' he bellowed, 'Who forced you? Certainly not Cerdic, he might have visited you here, but he could not have set this little treachery into motion! Who?' She was on the floor, he was shaking her, kicking her. The memory of all those dead at Llongborth – all those British men slaughtered by weaponry provided by a traitor, a British traitor. Enraged, he had no mercy for her.

Medraut stumbled to his feet, lurched against his father, attempting to stop him. Cerdic seized the opportunity to run. Like he had always maintained, Arthur was a fool. Had the position been reversed, he would have not hesitated, Arthur would be dead, instantly run through. Kill first, then think about the situation. That was Cerdic's policy.

As Medraut frantically hauled at the Pendragon's arm, Cerdic edged for the door. One, two, three paces. Four . . . and he was outside, running for the sheer terror of survival. He saw the horse, Medraut's, scrabbled into the saddle, heeled it into a gallop . . . ducked as a thrown dagger whistled past his shoulder, yelled for the lazy brute of an animal to move faster. Gweir, running from behind the bothy, tried to launch himself forward, to grab at the bridle, but the horse swerved, was into the trees, away.

Swearing, Gweir turned to Arthur, who cursed more vehemently and more explicitly. 'Shall I run for the horses? Do we track him?'

'To what point? There will be a craft waiting for him somewhere down-river. He'll be away, out to sea.' With the first person he should meet, dead, either for his clothes or for sniggering at a naked man riding a horse. 'I hope your balls get chafed, you dog turd!' Arthur bellowed into the trees, to where the horse had disappeared. He swung around as a flurry of movement swept from the doorway. Morgaine! Mithras, he needed her, needed her to talk!

Hurtling after her, he shouted for Gweir to head her off, but Morgaine had always been slender, quick on her feet, and she had only the few yards to go. Desperately, she threw herself into the cave, ran into the darkness, splashing into the torrent of the river. It was high, running swollen from the rains, coming up almost to her thighs, the current strong. The first cave too, was wetter than usual, water running down the rock walls, dripping into puddles, small pools. Thrusting her body into half-swim, half-run, she followed the water course. She had no light, but needed to go further in, hide herself. She ducked under the water, again tried to swim, but had to claw her way to the surface, grasp at an overhang of rock to gasp for breath.

Sobbing, she realized that this day, this one time when she desperately needed it, her route of safety could not help her. The water was too high, too strong a current. Swallowing tears and river, bruised from a battering against rocks and boulders and fighting for breath, she hauled herself out. The ground was drier here, the air warmer. These inner caves were almost a constant temperature, warm for such heavy darkness. She felt along the walls, fumbled for a niche between the rock that she could press herself into. This was a cave she knew, but not so well as to be able to move freely about without light. She pressed her nakedness against the solidity of the rock, was surprised to feel it wet in places, trickling water, forced herself to be still. To hide. It would be the only way to remain alive, for Arthur if he found her, she knew without doubt, would have her killed.

§ XXXI

Arthur stood one pace inside the darkness, groaned. He could not go in there. Knew he would have to.

Gweir fetched light, two lamps and a bundle of tallow candles from the bothy. They took a lamp each, sheltered the flame with their hands and stepped out into the darkness. The feeble glow was a pathetic glimmer, overpowered by the immensity of the surrounding nothingness, the strident awe of complete blackness. Arthur raised his to head height, attempting to widen the pool, choked down fear as menacing shadows leapt and danced, exaggerated the cracks and crannies into ominous chasms. Where in Mithras's name was the ceiling? The walls trickled with moisture. Ferns and mosses grew on the rocks, on the walls the light sparked colour, seeming to make everything move as it swayed, making shadows flicker. Icicles of rock, thrusting from the floor, dangling from above. Did the floor heave?

'My lord?' Gweir had served the Pendragon long enough to know this fear of confined spaces. 'My lord, I will go in. You wait here.'

'Sod off.' Determined, Arthur strode ahead, holding the lamp as high as he dared against the drip of water. A maze of tunnels, gape-mouthed, or low, narrow and menacing. He followed the river, stepping cautiously over tumbles of rock, runnels of water, his boot crunching once on a scatter of bones. He dipped the lamp downward, closing his mind to the

459

sudden sway of rearing shadow and darkness, shuddered. There was nothing to show they were human, could well have been the remains of a wolf's or bear's dinner. But there again . . . he swallowed hard, ignored the heavy hammering of his heartbeat, tried to shove the fear from his mind. The walls were pressing inward, the ceiling squeezing downward. There must be a ceiling somewhere, just beyond the reach of light.

No sunlight came here, no sweet bird song or hiss of rain. The ferns and mosses that adorned the first entrance cave could not grow here, nothing here, only rock and blackness. No sound beyond the eerie, monotonous drip of water. No point in calling out. Morgaine would not answer. He did though, just to break that oppressive silence. Was rewarded by a battering of his own voice, hurling and bouncing from one wall to another, around and around, echoing, repeating. Mocking.

There were shelves and pockets lodged among the rock, darker spaces beyond . . . other caves, other paths. She could be anywhere.

They stayed with the run of the river, to guide them back, as much as to go forward, searched for what, in the stark confine of this darkness, seemed an hour or more, but was less than a score of minutes. Arthur was shaking and sweating, his breathing rasping.

'We would be better to set a guard outside, my lord.' Gweir suggested, anxious for his lord, becoming as uneasy in this underground world. 'We will not find her in here, and she must come out, eventually.' Practical, he added, 'She may have already ducked behind us.'

Gods! Arthur had not thought of that. 'Could she seal the entrance?' he gasped, the horror panting on his breath, 'Shut us in?' Never to see daylight again, to die in here confined, in the evil of blackness . . .

Gweir assured him not.

This was ridiculous! Arthur lifted his lamp high, swung it in a circle, illuminating the path, narrow here, wetter than other places, with water seeping along the walls, puddling at their feet, running into the flow of the river. Gweir was not afraid, so why was he? He forced several deep, calming breaths. He would have to conquer this thing, damn it! Would have to! He banged his hand, hard, against an overhang of rock, ran the palm against the surface, wrinkling his nose at the cold feel beneath his hot skin. Screamed as the solidity began to give way, to topple forward.

Gweir, without the cramped restriction of fear, acted faster than his lord. Dropping his lamp, he pitched forward, hauled at Arthur, hurling him away, downward, into the river. The wall ahead crumpled with an enraged roar, a sound louder than anything Gweir had ever heard. Louder than the clash of battle, louder than the howl of a winter-raged wind or the crash of overhead thunder. Rocks fell and rolled, hitting against his legs, his shoulders. Rocks that shouted and bellowed as they fell in their might of anger, water gushing into the holes and crannies left behind.

And then there was silence, a dreadful stillness, where only the water dripped, and the river drifted.

§ XXXII

Medraut had waited outside the cave, too distraught to follow his father, attempt to find his mother. It was unseemly for a man to weep. God's mercy, but how Cywyllog would lash him for this weakness that was upon him, were she to know! At this moment he cared not one grain for what she would think; he sat, knees bent beneath him on the rain-sodden grass, weeping like an abandoned child. He had ached for so long over the decision whether to come here again. Or did he forget the woman who had birthed him? Set behind him, the knowing that she lived as a whore to the traders of the lead mines. A whore to British and Saex, freeman and slave. His mother. Morgaine.

All these months had the anguish wrestled in his mind, his conscience. Why now? Why had he made his mind to come now? He could have come on the morrow, or the day before, but no, it had been this day. What cursed devil had brought him here, this day!

And *why* had he come? To talk? To see her? To confirm what she was, to hope that he had been wrong?

Jesu, what a naive fool he had been!

He dropped his head into his hands, unable to believe what he had witnessed, unable to accept the shrieking horror of it all. His mother, his own damned, God-cursed mother, a fornicating whore. He had walked into that bothy – light of the Cross, how could he have been such a fool – so sure that he had been wrong, that she would welcome him . . . He had just lifted the latch and walked in!

They had been coupling, she astride him, her head back in a leer of pleasure as the man beneath had grunted and heaved.

Medraut had stood there, inside the doorway, frozen, horrified, watching the ugly pleasure of it. And when they had noticed him? She had leant back, exposing her nakedness, and they had laughed. Mocking, shaming.

His stomach heaved, and again he was violently sick on the grass. Cerdic. The man had been Cerdic. The Saxon. Mother of God, his own half-brother! He groaned, shut his eyes, trying to stop the images slamming in his head. His mother and him . . .

. . . Plunged to his feet as he heard the grumble, then the great, monstrous roar of noise from within the cave, and with it a sound like the clash of a smith's hammer on metal, a frightening, eerie sound. Terrified, he stood, immobile, convinced some dreadful creature would emerge, teeth bared, slavering, dripping blood . . . Nothing. Cautious, he crept to the entrance, peeped in, soft voiced called. 'Father? Gweir? Are you there?' Gained courage, tried again, louder, ran inside a few yards, genuflecting for protection, realized he would be useless without light. Ran to the bothy, searched, sobbing again, when he realized Gweir had taken everything.

He returned to the cave, stood at the entrance shouting. No answering call, no muffled cry. No responding reassurance that they were unharmed, on their way out. Nothing, only his own voice coming back to him.

What could he do? Fetch help? From where?

The road! The miner's road! Fool, why had he not thought of that before now!

By chance, he found the tethered horses, recognized Onager, took Gweir's dun, not trusting that brute of a chestnut – he might be an old animal now, but he could still pack a kick like a mule. The dun was a good horse, sure-footed, agile. Medraut mounted, headed him for the track, pushing him as fast as he dared on the rutted, muddied, slippery ground. Smoke! A camp-fire!

His breath was sobbing in his chest as he came upon Arthur's men, the escort. Words tumbled in a confusion of anguish, he had to repeat himself, to make them listen, make them understand.

All day to search, to fetch up men from the mines, men experienced with the underground, used to the dank and the dark. All that day, most the night. Dark mattered not, inside those caves where the lord blackness ruled.

They brought Arthur out two hours before dawn. They had found him, sodden, cold, shivering and mumbling, his soul straying between the conscious world and the merciful haven of a release into another. He was injured and ill with a fever, but he was alive.

Medraut had spoken of a woman. Of her, they found no sign. But from that day, the Whore of the Hills was never again in her bothy by the cave.

Gweir, they left to lay where he was. A covering of rock and debris, as good as earth and mud.

The blackness of one lonely grave as good as another.

October 487

§ XXXIII

Cerdic knew they mocked him, the British – ja, and the English. No easy thing to hide, the embarrassment of riding for your very life, birth-clad through the woods, to meet, of all damned people, Amlawdd! That he had been going up to Morgaine for himself was obvious – almost, at that instantly suppressed snigger of amusement, Cerdic had been tempted not to warn him of who else was up there at the bothy by the caves. Then they had heard the noise, a boom, louder than ever any roar of thunder could be, followed by a sound that resembled the mighty clash of musicians' cymbals, a great whoosh of air from where the caves were. Amlawdd had stopped his laughter then, had offered Cerdic his own cloak, and together they had made their way through the woods, south, to where Cerdic's craft was moored.

Autumn was settling in now, firing the marshes into the reds and golds of her fine, warm colours. The days were shortening, the nights coming with a nip of frost that bit at your cheeks and fingers. If Cerdic had never unduly cared to take Britain for his own before, he did now. For his father to find him with that woman, to have seen the expression of contempt and loathing on Arthur's face, and to hear the laughter afterward. He could hear it now, the sniggering, the pointing fingers, the lewd comments.

He stood at the quayside at Cerdicesora, surveying the bob of trading boats and long ships, waiting for his men to ready his craft, a beautiful ship, one of the best. His wealth was steadily mounting, the trade coming into his harbour and his prestige was rising along with it – most had now forgotten the shambles that had been that battle at Llongborth – until that damned stupid episode with Morgaine had reminded them. Curse Amlawdd for not keeping his tongue from wagging, for spreading it to all who cared listen!

Those who had whispered against him after Llongborth were quick to revise the old tales, of the fool that Cerdic of the West Saxons was. '*He ran from Llongborth,*' they mocked, '*but at least there, he had his balls tucked in his bracae!*'

Cerdic stood, legs spread wide, hands clasped behind his back. Oh they would mock him on the other side of their faces, soon enough! One day, and one day not too far distant, he would have the strength to call his father to war. Damned annoying that it was still not yet the time! He had not the men behind him to call out an army, had not the superiority needed to face the Pendragon in battle.

The craft was ready, the men waiting at the oars, the sail ready to be hoisted. He stepped across the gang-plank, grunted order that they were to cast off. With allies he could do it, could fight Arthur and the British. There were the sons of Aelle further along the coast with their men of the South Saxons, and could he persuade the Cantii to join with him? They had been so sorely defeated at Badon – was it not time to rise again, to prove their worth?

But first, he needed the alliance of Port and his sons. It was worth the trying, again, to convince him to join with the West Saxons, before opportunity was lost. Arthur was inactive, confined to his bed with a broken leg, broken collar bone and cracked ribs. He would not be out again this season. Was it not a ripe time to raid into his territory, take what they could, stir a few fires into life?

He had suggested it a month past, when first he learnt of his father's injuries – unfortunate that it had been the other one to die, the one they called Gweir. Damn his father and his cursed luck! But Port would have none of it.

'Not yet,' he had said, 'not this side of the winter.'

'When?' Cerdic had asked, resentful of the need to have this other Saxon as so firm an ally. 'When can we raise a war-host against the Pendragon?' The answer, 'When we are ready', was no comfort, even though Cerdic had said the same thing often enough.

He would go to Port again, try to persuade him that action must be taken now, before the glow of autumn turned into the snows of winter. He knew it was foolish to contemplate rising against his father now – knew Port would again tell him so, tell him to go home, gather more wealth, more men – but Arthur was bound to his bed, damn it, in pain and discomfort. And he had been one of those to laugh loudest – to spread the story further abroad of how he had seen Cerdic fleeing naked, down through those woods, 'with a backside raw with fear, and cheeks at both ends red with shame!'

May he rot in the fires of the Underworld! May the bones of his leg fail to heal, twist and warp and cause him an eternity of pain!

Frustrated, Cerdic barked orders at his men to turn about, to put ashore, abandon the voyage. What was the point of going to see Port again? He was right, they could not fight yet – and knowing his bastard father's luck, he would be up, out of that bed within a few weeks, strutting around as if nothing had happened to him.

Ah, but one day. . . . one sweet beautiful day, things would be so different.

§ XXXIV

Arthur thought if he kept his eyes shut and lay very still, he would not wake, but remain asleep. He did not particularly want to wake up, not with the prospect of another tedious day drifting in front of him; not if Gwenhwyfar's black mood was as bad as it had been yesterday. And the day before that. He could hear her moving about the chamber, or could it be Archfedd? She had arrived last evening – without Natanlius, for he had need to stay at Caer Morfa. Something was dropped, a wooden bowl by the sound of it, followed by a subdued, but explicit, oath. Gwenhwyfar.

Yesterday she had spent most the afternoon at her loom over in the far corner. She was never one for enjoying weaving, always attempted it when her tempers were foul. He could not understand her logic – why pull the knot tighter if the rope was already tangled?

His shoulders hurt, his ribs ached, though he was healing; the bruises were turning a putrid yellow now, the vivid purple easing. His damned leg was itching beneath the splints and bandaging. He squeezed his eyes tighter closed . . . it was no good, he was awake.

'Did I disturb you?' Gwenhwyfar said. She was squatting on the floor, gathering the apples that had fallen with the bowl, inspecting each one to see if it had bruised. A good fruit harvest this year, for which they were all thankful.

'Na, I was already awake.'

Polite conversation, each of them treading warily around the other.

The bowl of apples in her hand, Gwenhwyfar stood, walked to the bed, set the apples on the table beside it. 'Do you want one of these, or shall I fetch you something else to break your fast?' Why did she feel so tight inside? So irritable? It was not her monthly course coming, they had ceased over a year since. She had a headache, but it was only mild, and she had awoken with it, fresh air would see it gone.

'They'll do,' Arthur answered her, easing himself into a sitting position, wincing at the ache and pull of battered bones and muscles. She looked tired, he thought, her eyes listless. He supposed it was not easy for her having him bed-bound, and he would be the first to admit that he was a poor patient, too restless to be confined within doors for so long.

465

'Why not ride into Lindinis today?' He suggested. 'A change may brighten you up.'

'I have too much to do here.'

'Nonsense, there is nothing urgent that needs tending.'

Awake less than five minutes and already they were quarrelling!

The door from the courtyard opened slowly. Archfedd peered around it, her face brightening into a smile as she saw her father awake and sitting up.

'Morning, Da, Mam,' she said cheerily as she breezed into the chamber, carrying two baskets, the larger crammed to its brim with gathered berries and a smaller one filled with fungi. 'For you,' she said, placing the fungi on the bed beside her father, and leaning forward to place a kiss on his cheek. 'The hedges are crammed with berries this year, a sign for a hard winter ahead, do you think?' She sat on the bed heavily, drawing her legs up beneath her, Arthur winced again. She put the second basket down beside her, atop the furs.

'It will not bother me if we are snowed in until next April,' he answered testily, rummaging with his finger through the fungi and selecting a handful of buff-coloured mushrooms. He sniffed at their fresh, pleasant aroma, that resembled the smell of new-sawn wood. 'I cannot get out anyway.'

'You will be full mended within a few weeks,' Gwenhwyfar snapped in response. 'Why must you be so damned petulant whenever you are ill? If you had not gone whoring in the first place . . .' Abruptly, she fell silent. Arthur looked up sharply from the basket of mushrooms. Archfedd half-turned, her breath caught.

For a long, awkward, moment, no one said a word, then Archfedd cleared her throat, picked up the basket of berries, stood. 'I had better take these to the store-room,' she said.

'Stay here!' her father snapped.

'Berries are best sorted when fresh-picked,' she countered, already heading for the door. She knew her parents' arguments, had no wish to stay for one that had all the indications of a full-blown tempest. A pity, she had so enjoyed herself this morning, strolling along the hedges that edged the horse paddocks. It had been a bright, sun-clear morning with a hint of frost in the air – the autumn scents were so different here than at home, at Caer Morfa. It was mostly marsh there, the dampness of the reeds and the saline tang of the sea permeated into everything. Oh the great woods a mile or so behind were pleasant, but she missed Caer Cadan, the wide openness, the hills to the horizon, and the beauty of the ever-changing colours of the Summer Land. She shut the door behind her, leant against it a while. She had so wanted to share her news with them this morning! Last night, she had been too tired, the ride here being so tedious. Her mother had been tetchy then, she remembered, had assumed it was because her father was confined to his bed, was being difficult.

Their voices were rising from inside. She was almost tempted to put her ear to the door and listen. Whatever had her mother meant? She knew her father had an eye for women – what man did not? – but she thought this woman, Morgaine, had been involved with her two half-brothers, not with her father. The excited talk of exactly why the accident had happened had been so muddled, and they were all so worried, aye, and frightened when first it had happened, her husband and herself included. Coed Morfa was openly vulnerable to Saxon attack; it was only her father's imposing strength that was keeping the floodwater of war at bay.

Fortunate that he had not been that dangerously hurt – oh aye, bones took a while to mend and would often ache for months after, but the breaks were clean, he had suffered and recovered from far worse, or so Mam had assured her, during that initial anxious week. How fast she and Natanlius had ridden here when word was sent! They near on broke the horses! But thinking back, she never had discovered the truth behind it all. They had returned home after a day or so, once they were certain her father was in no mortal danger. She chewed her lip in thought, eased her basket to a more comfortable position. Happen now would be a good time to find out something more precise. Who could she ask? None of the men would talk, not about their lord King to his own daughter. But Medraut would if she made him.

A half-smile crept onto her lips. She would take these berries to the store-rooms and then seek him out.

'And what exactly do you mean by that?' Arthur asked his wife, coldly.

'What I said. If you had not gone visiting your whore, this would never have happened.'

'Morgaine was not my whore.'

'No, of course not. It was by accident that she birthed you a whelp!'

'I laid with her once and once only.'

'Once each night, aye that I would believe!' She was being unreasonable, Gwenhwyfar knew, but now that those words that had been rumbling in her head were loosened, she could not stop. Almost, it was a relief to be arguing.

They had not quarrelled about Morgaine at all – because all those years past, in Gaul, beyond that first awkwardness and uncertainty of meeting again, when they had found each other to be so wonderfully alive and well, there had been no room for harsh words between them. And anyway, she was no longer a part of his life. You could not feel angry at someone who was no longer there to rub the hurt the wrong way. But that niggling worm of jealousy had began to bite into Gwenhwyfar again since the accident in the caves. The doubts, the suspicions. He had gone to the White Hills to sort the matter of the lead and ended up in a whore's bothy, a whore who happened to be Morgaine. She could not, just could not, accept it for coincidence.

When he had returned from Gaul, so splendidly with the momentous victory at Badon, so much had settled back, so quickly, to as it had been before, as if he had never been away. Yet, there had been differences, subtle, happen unseen to many, but she knew them to be there. He had held more fears, for one, did not harbour the great confidence that he had once boasted; was more restless and uneasy, especially during the long winters when confined within-doors, with little to do. He had never been one to sit idle. He was harder now, too, more bitter. The disappointments of Gaul had been many, most especially the entire pointlessness of it all. He and his men had been ill-used, and he had greatly resented it at first, but all that had eased as time passed. He rarely spoke of Gaul now, except perhaps when snippets of news reached them, and even then, it was with sarcasm or indifference.

The dreams began troubling him again though, after that accident in the cave. Dreams where he called out, shouting for the dead and dying. And occasionally, a name. Her name, Morgaine.

How long had she been there, Gwenhwyfar wondered, selling her body to the men of the Lead Road? And, more persistent, the nagging thoughts, when did Arthur learn of her, and how often had he seen her?

Unknown to either of them, someone was beyond the inner door, a door that was not quite latched, that allowed every word to filter out to him as he stood there, hand raised to tap on the door to seek entrance; stood, not wanting to listen, but unable to move.

'Was it because you found Cerdic bedding with her that angered you more that day, Arthur? Your son bedding your poxed whore – a second time over?' Oh no, she had not forgotten Mathild either!

'Damn you! I knew nothing of Morgaine, had no idea she was here in Britain. Why should I? She was nothing to me in Gaul, would be nothing to me now.' Arthur's frustration was mounting. Gwenhwyfar was pacing the room, her arms animated, head tossing – all he could do was sit in the bed, lean slightly more forward.

'After all these years together, and still you lie to me.'

Arthur slammed his fist onto the bed-furs, sending the basket of carefully gathered mushrooms bouncing and rolling to the floor. 'I do not lie!'

Gwenhwyfar's voice was rising, the hurt and anger running away, uncontrolled. 'You would have me believe that both your sons knew that Morgaine had become the most notorious whore in southern Britain – yet you did not!'

Arthur's anger too, had reached its height. He flung the bed-furs from him, made to get from the bed, but the door thrust open. Medraut burst through, his face white, nose pinched, mouth twisted, ugly, with his own anger.

'You call my mother a whore,' he roared, 'but what are you?' He stormed across the chamber in three swift strides, stood before Gwenhwyfar, his fists clenched, face thrust almost into hers. 'Have we not all heard of how you bedded with my father's own cousin – and aye, not just while you thought him dead! There are enough who say you continue to tumble together!'

Gwenhwyfar did not have time to think, or consider action. Her hand came back, slapped sharp across Medraut's face, her breath hissing. 'How dare you!'

Arthur was half from the bed, swinging the leg bandaged into its splints as best he could. If he was angry before, the rage in him now was blinding, although it had shifted ground, from Gwenhwyfar to Medraut. He got no further than one pace, toppled, crying out in agony as pain hurled through his body.

Gwenhwyfar shoved Medraut aside, ran to her husband, fearful, concerned. Medraut's hands, too, went to attempt to help his father up, but Gwenhwyfar barred his way. 'Get out of here,' she screamed. 'Get out!'

§ XXXV

'Shall I find you a rope?' Archfedd said to Medraut. 'You have as near hung yourself, you ought make a thorough job of it.'

Evening. The frost was sharper, already, as the first stars were beginning to prick the sky; the ground was glistening, whitening. She had tracked her half-brother down at the stables, found him grooming one of the horses, was leaning against the doorsill, watching, mocking, him.

It was all over the Caer, what he had done, what he had said. Were he not the King's son, like as not that rope would have been forcibly provided for him. Archfedd, though, had an advantage over those men whose anger was so roused by the insult shouted to their Queen. She was the daughter of the King – and that Queen. The curiosity that had intrigued her that morning had almost been sated. She had discovered more of what had happened in that whore's bothy near the Lead Road this day than in all the others put together.

'So-o you are the bastard son of a pagan whore-witch. 'Tis no wonder you never spoke of her, that word was kept so efficiently quiet.'

'Everyone knew that my mother's name was Morgaine. 'Twas no secret.'

'Na, but no one knew that she and the whore who served the Saex lead-traders were one and the same.' She sauntered further into the stables, running her hand over the rump of the nearest horse, holding her hand to another's muzzle for him to smell. 'Fortunate for you that Lord Bedwyr be away on my father's business. Your balls would be making fine decoration for the Caer walls by now, were he not.'

'I am not afeared of Bedwyr.' Medraut said it boldy, knew as well as she that it was a lie.

The contempt was thick in her voice. 'No wonder also, why it is that my father has never seriously considered you to be his heir!'

That hurt. Hurt even more than hearing his father and Gwenhwyfar talking so crudely of Morgaine. He had remembered so little of his mother. The few memories that he had cherished had been the happier ones – the sound of her laugh, the swirl of her hair in the sunlight. All those were gone now, after he had seen her doing what she had been doing. Hard enough to bear that, without hearing the only other two people in this whole world that he cared for talk of her as they had.

Medraut had never held a wish to be King after his father. He knew he could not be, he did not have the courage or the strength. Had no talent for weapons or fighting, but Archfedd's taunts had so often been stabbed at him, had so often thrust home into his belly and twisted there. He lifted his head, his eyes holding hers, said, 'He has no one else. I will have to be King after him.'

The horse had been licking at the salt on Archfedd's hand, she moved away from the animal, went to stand before Medraut, leant forward and insultingly wiped her sticky palm on his cloak. 'Oh, but there is someone and, with Fortune's blessing, mayhap two.' She smiled at him, haughty in her firm superiority. 'The Pendragon has a grandson already born. And I am again with child.'

Medraut pushed past her, thrust the grooming brush onto a ledge. 'Are you that much the fool, sister? Children will not hold off Cerdic when he comes. Nor for that matter, will they be able to better me.'

470

'You?' she called spitefully as he walked out through the open doorway. 'If it came to choice between you and Cerdic, all the people of Britain would choose him! He at least was legitimate-born to the daughter of a king, not a by-blown brat conceived of a poxed whore!'

For three days, Arthur lay tossing in a drenching sweat of pain. Through the day and most the night, Gwenhwyfar sat beside the bed, wiping the hot fever from him, and spooning strengthening buttermilk into his mouth.

When at last he lay quiet, she asked, 'You did not believe him, did you? It is not true, what he said.'

Arthur attempted a smile, held his hand for her to take. 'I'll not believe him, if you believe me.'

Gwenhwyfar's smile chased the lines of sadness and fear away from her eyes and mouth. She bent forward, kissed Arthur lightly on the lips.

It was a fair bargain.

March 488

§ XXXVI

Arthur removed his war cap, let the bite of the wind ruffle his hair. Clouds were massing, bringing in rain. This was wild coastland, these cliffs of Dyfed, almost as wild as the sea. There were three ships, small against the grey horizon, straining at their blue-grey sails like horses eager to be away, galloping. Spray would be billowing over the gunwales, for the waves were rough, the wind lively. It would not worry the crew, for the Hibernians, like the Saex, were brothers of the sea. A good sailor, it was said, was born within the sound of waves booming onto the shore, and the feel of the sea tossing in his belly.

Arthur had come here to see for himself how the sea-wolves were tormenting this rugged line of Britain's western coast. He did not much like what he had already seen. His horse stamped a hind hoof, impatient with standing at the edge of this wind-tousled cliff. There was grass beneath his feet and he wanted to run. Arthur absently patted his chestnut neck. The winter coat would be thinning soon, this rough, thick one giving way to the smooth shine of summer. Brenin – King – son of Onager, sharing the same chestnut colouring but with more white to his hind feet and a star on his forehead. As handsome and bold as his father, thankfully, with his dam's sweeter temper!

'Always a ship.' The man sitting his horse beside the Pendragon said. 'One, often two or three. They come in closer on days when the wind is favourable.' Vortipor of Dyfed, a man barely into his thirtieth year, already high in power. Dressed richly, blue cloak adorned by gold braiding and a brooch the size of a man's clenched fist. Rings on his finger, a gold hoop in his ear, at his throat, a torque as thick as his wrist. Vortipor, probably the second wealthiest man of all the British, beneath the Pendragon. His land stretched from coast to mountain, inherited from his father and secured by the benefit brought him by his recent-taken wife – the benefit of gold. He had been fortunate with betrothing her, the widow of a merchant, a man who had hoarded gold with the voracity of a squirrel collecting nuts. Her young daughter was a problem, for by law, the father's wealth would pass to her upon her mother's death, not to the husband, but she was just a child yet, the mother of no great

472

age. Why worry about the future, when the threats of now were more prevalent?

'They will be harassing my shores in greater number, now that spring has tumbled out of her bed.' Vortipor heeled his horse so that he could regard Arthur direct. 'I need the assurance of more fighting men to aid me. Good men. Your men. As you have seen for yourself, I have coasts to protect. Valleys to patrol.'

Only the one craft was visible now, rain threading from the darkening clouds was sweeping, curtain-like, over the restless toss of the sea.

'So far, they come only to plunder – taking slaves and women mostly, some cattle, but last year the Land-Trotters arrived, seeking to settle.' Vortipor briefly wondered if the Pendragon was listening, for his expression was so immobile and distant. Damn it, he needed help! Was entitled to help! 'We drove them off, burnt their huts, tortured the men, killed the few women they had brought with them. But I cannot continue to do so alone, not if more of them come. As this year, we expect.' More had been coming across the sea from Hibernia each year, seeking new places, now that Môn had been cleared of their rats' nests by the Gwynedd lord.

Arthur was listening, but his thoughts were wandering, idling. He welcomed being out here, in the open, beneath the wild touch of the wind and the first spattering of rain. To have the smell of sea air in your nostrils, the sounds of the rugged waves in your ears. Even darkness was unintimidating out here. The golden glimmer of the moon, the silver sheen of stars, the call of an owl or vixen. It was walls that shut all these things out. Walls that leant in on you, crowding, crushing. Arthur filled his lungs with the unfettered smell of the open. The winter had been long and long in passing. Fraught with the physical pain from his leg and shoulder and ribs, damaged by the mental anguish of knowing now that Medraut could never follow him as King. To be King, you need be either respected or feared. Medraut they would treat with contempt and suspicion.

The sea. Wide. Open. On the other side, another land on a distant shore. The sea, harbouring a different menace. He had Cerdic to worry about, Vortipor had the Hibernians.

'You have enough to pay men handsomely for the use of their swords,' Arthur said. 'You ought have a sufficient army loyal to you.'

'Not an army such as yours.'

Arthur replaced his war cap, fastened the strap. He turned Brenin, heeled him into a trot, heading away from the cliffs, dipping down into the hollow of the valley, out of the wind, away from the heavier rain that was starting to squall. 'Then train them, Vortipor, as I have had to do.'

Vortipor watched the King ride down to join his waiting escort. 'Four turmae. That is all the men I need!' he called.

'One,' Arthur shouted back, trotting onward.

'Three!'

'Two.'

'I accept.' Vortipor scratched at the beard growth around his chin. Two turmae of Artoriani. It would be enough, with his own men and those mercenaries he already paid. More than he had hoped. The Pendragon had spared only one turma for Gwynedd and Ceredigion together last year. None for Amlawdd.

Vortipor kicked his mount into a trot, going in the direction opposite to that which Arthur and his men had taken. The Pendragon was to head north, up to Powys and Gwynedd. He, Vortipor would ride for home, back to the voluptuous delight of his wife. Amlawdd. Hah! He had tried to take her for his own, had failed, it was Vortipor she had accepted as her mate.

A second time, then, that Vortipor had fared better than that contemptuous weasel!

He halted his stallion on a rise, turned, could just make out the Pendragon's banner disappearing into the shadowed cleft of the valley. For now, they all relied on Arthur to sustain their strength and defence. God's truth, it was fortunate they still had him! The Artoriani were the most efficient that gold could buy. Under Ambrosius's brief rule ... Vortipor closed his eyes against the fear that shuddered through him. Best not think of it!

He pushed his mount into a trot, shook his head sorrowfully. They needed Arthur, but the man was a fool where women were concerned. Eight days he had spent here in Dyfed, intended to pass as many in Powys and Gwynedd, add as many more for the journey here and travelling back ... almost the month he would be gone from Caer Cadan. A month around and he had left his wife alone with Bedwyr! God alone could guess what advantage they would take of it, were even half of the spread rumours true.

And then there was Amlawdd, invited by the Pendragon to remain as guest at the Caer while he was away on his King's business.

The rain was scalding hard now, coming straight in grey sheets of coldness. Vortipor urged his horse into a fast canter. He supposed the Pendragon knew what he was doing. Gods, he hoped so, for if Amlawdd was to take advantage of the King's absence ... 'Christ and all the Holy Saints,' Vortipor swore the oath aloud, 'I would rather follow that Saxon whoreson, Cerdic, than bow to that oiled bastard, Amlawdd and his protégé whelp, Aurelius Caninus!'

April 488

§ XXXVII

'If that bloody man does not leave here soon, I swear I shall slit his throat!' Gwenhwyfar flounced to the couch, flopped into it, began removing her boots, her fingers irritably unlacing the leather thongs.

'You must wait your turn then,' Bedwyr laughed, offering little sympathy. 'There is a queue from here to Rome for that privilege!' He was at Arthur's desk, sorting through the paraphernalia of letters and petitions; tossed the parchment in his hand onto a growing pile of correspondence that needed primary attention. 'What is his latest offence?'

'Amlawdd,' Gwenhwyfar spoke the name as if it were poison, 'has ordered the men to go out on overnight patrol on the morrow.' There came no response of indignation or anger. She lifted her head abruptly, frowned across her chamber at Bedwyr, suspiciously asked, 'Did you know about it?'

Bedwyr twirled a stylus between his fingers, had the decency to redden slightly. He cleared his throat. 'Um, aye.' Embarrassed, he poked at the inside of his cheek with his tongue. 'Did you, er, countermand it then?'

'And allow the men to believe that I am not in command while Arthur is away?' she retorted. Added sharply, 'Although it seems I am not.'

She kicked off the second boot, began searching for her house-shoes, peering beneath the couch, a table, her agitated manner indicating all too well her ruffled temper. 'If ever my husband invites Amlawdd as guest here again, while he is gone to visit the tribal lords, I'll—' She peered around the room, her hands flapping like wind-tossed flags, 'I'll slit his throat also!' She knelt on the floor, felt beneath the couch. 'I do not require him here for my protection. I have a Caer full of Artoriani for that – did have, until you stupidly agreed to have most of them sent off!'

'I'm here to protect you, not Amlawdd. And it was not stupid.'

Standing again, she did not hear him. '. . . I spent all that while alone while he was in Gaul.' Where in damn hell had she put those shoes? 'Ider stays closer to me than my own shadow.'

'As do I.'

'And Arthur calmly suggests to Amlawdd that I need protecting? From what? Who? Inane morons who send the Artoriani on unnecessary patrols mayhap?' She stalked to the hearth place, snatched her shoes from beside the log pile.

'I had reason, Gwen.'

'Damned insufferable, interfering bastard!'

'Who, me?'

Gwenhwyfar paused, the left shoe half on her foot. Relented, laughed. 'No, bonehead. Amlawdd.' She crossed to him, patted his shoulder affectionately. Thank the gods for Bedwyr! If it were not for his humour, she would probably have thrown herself in desperation from the watch-tower by now.

Lightly, with one hand, she ruffled Bedwyr's hair, idled her other through the letters on the desk. Oh, Arthur had told her why he intended to encourage Amlawdd and the boy, Caninus, to come to Caer Cadan. The whispering on the wind had grown louder in its rustling through the winter. There was no doubt it was Amlawdd who had supplied those traded weapons to Cerdic. No doubt either, that he was aiming to advance Caninus as Arthur's successor. Typical Amlawdd, to plant one foot in either camp. No doubts, but no proof. 'My lands are vulnerable while I am away,' Arthur had told her, 'I would feel easier with those two firm in view.'

He had not told her how he had intended to get them here, but whatever it had been, it worked, for Amlawdd was at the gates of Caer Cadan no less than two days after Arthur would have taken his leave from him. More than four weeks past, that had been. Arthur had already promised Vortipor the men he needed, and had visited Gwynedd. He was in Powys now, so his last letter, arrived four days since, had said.

It was a wise decision to entice Amlawdd here, yet the mood between Gwenhwyfar and Arthur had not been as warm and congenial as it ought when he had left, and yet again she wondered at part of the reason behind that invitation. For if she and Bedwyr were watching Amlawdd and his young ward, then equally, had they eyes on them?

She tossed the insidious thought aside. Arthur trusted her, he did not believe that she was bedding with Bedwyr. Did he? Those vile comments that Medraut had disgorged – for all that it was nonsense because he was angry with the pain of hurting inside – it had rekindled those flickering doubts that she knew had never entirely fled from Arthur's mind. Once before, long, long ago, he had fought with a man over just such a stirred lie. Who was it? Strange how your mind forgot such things.

She had wandered over to the couch, sat, was fiddling with her ear-ring – my God, she thought, of course! It was Hueil! Hueil who had accused her of adultery. They had fought, he and Arthur, and Hueil had

476

drawn a dagger, which had somehow wounded her eldest boy, Llacheu. She unthreaded the ear-ring from her lobe, held its delicate silvered beauty in the palm of her hand. How the wheel turns in its circle. That time, Llacheu had escaped, not badly hurt; but later, because of Hueil's treachery, her son was to be brutally slain.

If he had lived. Or had Amr not been drowned, Gwydre not gored by that boar. She sighed. There was no unpicking the pattern once it had been woven. She breathed deeply through her nose, rethreaded her ear-ring where it belonged. 'The Artoriani, tomorrow. Explanation please, Bedwyr. And make it good.'

Bedwyr set down the parchment in his hand, leant back in his chair, tipping it slightly. 'It is Amlawdd's Birthing Day – had you forgotten? He has organized a celebration feast for the Gathering and he suggested—' Bedwyr paused, idly waved a vague hand – ordered would have been more appropriate, but Bedwyr's own pride was as near to bursting as Gwenhwyfar's – 'that the Hall would become overfull with Artoriani and his own men. That could cause trouble, which would look ill for your hospitality.' And would augur bad fortune for Amlawdd during the coming year.

'What men?' Gwenhwyfar interrupted.

'Er, those arriving on the morrow.' Hastily, Bedwyr added, 'A few only, he assures me, guests, nobles, a few lords. Friends.'

'Friends? Amlawdd? Does he possess any?'

Seeing the rise of temper about to boil again, Bedwyr lurched on, 'I did not think it wise to insist our men pay honour to a man we have small patience with. For them to have deliberately kept away could cause embarrassment for you . . . so—'

'So you played into Amlawdd's hands and have allowed the Caer to fall into half-strength defence. My God, Bedwyr—' Abruptly she stood, strode across the room to face him across her husband's desk. 'Arthur will be furious with us for this!'

Patience wearing thin, Bedwyr slammed his chair forward, barked, 'Damn it! It was Arthur's bloody suggestion!'

Incredulous, Gwenhwyfar stood, her palms laid flat on the desk top, staring at the man before her.

'He suggested it when he was at Amlawdd's stronghold. It is all a part of his strategy.'

'What strategy?' Gwenhwyfar asked coldly. 'And why did he not tell me of it?'

Opening his mouth to yell some equally belligerent answer, Bedwyr paused, said instead, 'I do not know why, I think because he did not want us to give the wrong reactions. He is rather hoping that Amlawdd may do something rash on the morrow.'

Gwenhwyfar let her head drop forward, closed her eyes. She was tired, had been awake for most the night and through the morning.

'Arthur is taking a risk with this,' she said, looking up, her eyes holding a slight, questioning glance.

'To hunt, you need release your hawk,' Bedwyr answered. 'There is always the risk that she will fly free and not return to you.'

'And Arthur hopes that Amlawdd and the boy will try for freedom?' Bedwyr could only shrug, spread his hands.

'And us?' Gwenhwyfar asked. 'Has he thought that we too may fly free, were he to unleash our tether?'

§ XXXVIII

Medraut squatted before the hearth-place, one hand clasped around yet another goblet of wine, the other idly poking the dull glow of the fire into more cheering bursts of flame. An hour yet until the evening Gather, the feasting of Amlawdd's Birthing Day. He took two gulps of wine. Sighed. He was bored.

'You would do better to find useful employment rather than be under my feet,' Cywyllog admonished, threading a new colour of wool onto her shuttle.

Medraut made no answer. He had long since ceased responding to his wife. On his mind, a persistent question. Why did his father allow him to stay here at Caer Cadan? Because he was his heir? But he would never become King. He was too stupid, too afraid. It would have to be Archfedd's boy, Constantine, who followed the Pendragon. Natanlius was capable to rule as Regent until the lad came of age. So why else did Arthur tolerate his continuing presence here? He was of no use to anyone, did nothing save sleep and drink and avoid his wife.

There was only the one answer. No other had come, not in all these past weeks of thinking. He was here because his father did not trust him.

So many times had he wanted to explain about that awful day with his mother in that bothy; how he had come to be there, that he had not known about Cerdic – had not even known the man to be Cerdic. Gods! The thought of his mother and that . . . his stomach again turned, nauseated. That was why he had so badly abused Gwenhwyfar that day, of course. Because he was hurting at what his mother had so ashamedly become. Those words had hurt, had rubbed salt deep into the wound, and

478

he had lashed out, screaming from the pain of it. He jabbed the stick into the fire. How he hoped the bitch who had birthed him was roasting in the flames of Hell!

'If you had any sense, not that you have—' What was Cywyllog scolding now? 'You would be more civil to Lord Caninus. You would fare better under his service than wasting your days here. God's truth, why ever I wed with you I will never understand!' She hustled the shuttle through the warp threads. 'Does your father treat you with the respect you deserve? Na, he does not. Does he give you the authority that you ought have? Hah! He ignores his own son and gives responsibility of the Caer to that womanizer, Bedwyr! Why? Because you are a useless fit-for-nothing.'

Turning his head, Medraut regarded his wife. How could a woman be so consistently spiteful?

Impatient with him, she dropped the shuttle, swung away from the loom, her skirt brushing the hang of the stone weights, setting them swaying and bobbing, clicking against each other. 'Caninus will be the Pendragon's successor, not you. We all know that. As much I am saddled with a dumb ox for a husband, I have no wish for widowhood. Expect death when he takes the royal torque as his own, or make alliance with him now. Without it, he cannot let you live.'

Medraut stared at her, made no answer. Had she been pretty once? he wondered. Curiously, he could not remember. He did not even recall liking her when he was a child at Ambrosius's school. He tried to conjure images of the past. Gildas, her youngest brother, came easily to mind; that small, serious face, those incessant questions of his, concerning death and murder. That was linked to his brother Hueil, although Medraut did not realize it at the time. Cywyllog had deliberately poisoned the boy's mind. Was that where the rot had started festering in her? With Hueil's execution?

Years of scowling had puckered Cywyllog's mouth and nose, had narrowed her eyes. Her hair she swept back into a tight coil; at night she kept it braided; he had never seen it swing loose and lovely, like Gwenhwyfar's, or his mother's . . .

'Ask yourself why Amlawdd is here with the lad.'

The answer slipped from Medraut's mouth. 'Because he is a whoreson bastard who would delight in placing Caninus as King now, rather than politely wait for my father to die?' He had meant it as sarcasm, but Cywyllog darted forward, grasped his arm, her face thrusting near his own, pointed, shrew-like.

'Exactly! And if we are to survive the coming slaughter, then we must show our support for Caninus now!'

Shrugging off her clasping fingers, Medraut slowly rose to his feet. 'What slaughter?' he asked, suspicion meandering into his wine-dulled brain.

Aware she had let her tongue over-loose, Cywyllog covered her blunder. 'It is common speculation. Caninus will try for the kingdom one day. When he does, it would be better were you to ride with him. He may even parcel some of it out to you. That is more than you can expect from your father!'

Medraut drained the wine, ambled to the small table, refilled his goblet from the flagon.

'You could have a good point, wife,' he said.

Cywyllog closed her eyes, relaxed. Almost, she had said too much too soon. Yet she had to make this fool man agree with Caninus, and had to make him see sense before tonight!

Turning around, Medraut propped his backside against the table edge. 'You are forgetting two things, though, woman. One, I will never willingly betray my father, and two, Cerdic is unlikely to allow a whelp like Caninus to steal what he regards as his.'

§ XXXIX

The prospect of celebration and feasting would normally be greeted with enthusiasm and good cheer, but few within Caer Cadan held an eagerness to drink Amlawdd's good health. Reluctance heightened during the passing of the day, with the arrival of several dozen of Amlawdd's swaggering men, acting as generously donated escort to the few invited merchant-men and traders from the scattered settlements along the busy coast and Hafren estuary.

'There are too many men in this Hall that I do not know,' Gwenhwyfar whispered. Bedwyr agreed, but said nothing, his unease amplifying as each half-hour passed. The Hall was crowded with the followers and supporters of both Amlawdd and Caninus, men from the settlements held under Amlawdd's lordship, strong men, fighting men. Strategically picked for that escort duty.

There appeared nothing sinister about Amlawdd's attitude. He was eating, drinking and making merry with the rest of them; roaring for the harper to play a tune, laughing often with the eight and ten year old lad, Caninus, who sat beside him in the place of honour at the high table – Gwenhwyfar's graceful gesture. 'No, my lord, today is for your honour, not mine. Please, you and your chosen guests be seated at the high table.'

Her excuse not to need be seated near any of them. She and Bedwyr sat, content, at a lower, quieter table. Mind, she had ensured Arthur's carved, oak chair be removed from the public Hall. He might sit at Arthur's table, but most certainly Amlawdd would not have Arthur's chair!

His men were drinking with no immoderate care, voices growing louder with the rise of laughter and jesting banter. Those from the Caer were to drink with care. Mind and reaction were too easily muddled by the effect of a strong brew. *Keep a clear head this night, by order of the Queen.* Bedwyr had seen to it that word had spread. In Gwenhwyfar's name, it would be obeyed.

No objection had been raised by any of Amlawdd's men – not even by Caninus – to the search for secreted weapons as each guest had entered the Hall. It was customary for swords, daggers, to be left outside the main door when entering, only an eating knife was permissible and the King could carry his sword. Amlawdd himself had made an expressive show of leaving his sword with the door-keeper, of there being nothing hidden in his boot, under his tunic. 'We want no unpleasantness on this special day, do we?' His voice had boomed laughter right up into the smoke-wreathed roof-beams.

With the main feasting ended, the trestle tables were cleared, the benches pushed to the sides of the Hall, and the dancing and entertainment begun. Making polite withdrawal to Amlawdd, Gwenhwy-far left the Hall, as was the Queen's right if she so chose. Bedwyr sat alone at a table in one corner, nursing a goblet. Watching. Trouble was coming, he was certain. It was as recognizable as a thunderstorm gathering along the horizon. The difficulty here, to judge from which direction and in what form. And when.

The young men of Caninus's admiring group of friends had already singled out the prettier young girls of the Caer for themselves, their fumbling hands becoming more intimate with the progression of each whirling, breathless dance, and the consumption of more of the fine wine and ale. Amlawdd, also, had secured for himself a pretty redhead. To Cywyllog's annoyance. She had done all as he had asked, hidden the daggers in those empty barrels over near the latrines. None suspected, none would realize, that as each man went out weaponless, he returned with a hidden blade.

A while since, Amlawdd had gone to relieve himself. Cywyllog, serving ale to a group of loud-laughing men, saw him re-enter, the red-haired serving girl clinging to his arm. Both were rumpled, the girl's tunic partially unfastened. With quick steps, Cywyllog made her way through the press of the crowd, snatched a tankard up from a table as she passed.

'Ale, my lord?' she said, thrusting the tankard into his hand, as she neatly elbowed the red-hair aside.

'When?' she hissed into Amlawdd's ear. 'You leave things too late!'

'On the contrary.' He leered drunkenly into her face, spewing fumes of wine and beer, his speech slurred. He patted the girl on the buttocks, indicated she was to lose herself. She scowled, lingered a moment, for she had hoped for good payment. At Amlawdd's growl, she trotted off to find reward elsewhere. 'It will begin soon,' Amlawdd said to Cywyllog. 'Rest easy. My Lord Bedwyr seems sufficiently bored, happen we can liven the celebration up for him in a while, eh?' Amlawdd laughed, pressed his hand over her breast. 'You've fine teats, woman, hope your man appreciates them as much as he appreciates what you're doing for him!'

Cywyllog scraped his paw from her body, held on to his wrist. 'I do this for myself and my murdered brother,' she snapped. 'I have been long and patient in the waiting for it!' She jerked her hand away from his arm. 'Just make sure you and Caninus remember what I have done for you, when the time comes for remembering!' Tossing her head, she whirled away from him, slammed the ale flagon into the hands of a passing serving girl, and withdrew from the Hall, head pert, steps quick-tapping on the wooden floor.

Out in the fresh air, she leant against the wall, her eyes shut, savouring the coolness that fell on her face, swirled around her sweating body. She had been trembling as she had left that Hall, trembling because she had done it at last! Had taken her revenge on the Pendragon. By morning, his wife and companions would all be dead, and Caer Cadan would be in the hands of Amlawdd and Aurelius Caninus.

Suitable punishment for the Pendragon.

§ XL

Aiding Cerdic, Amlawdd had decided, was wasted effort. He could wait until the Day of Judgement before that one decided to make a move. But then, why worry? After all, he had a foot planted either side of the stream. His second intention was to supplant Arthur with Aurelius Caninus. When the Pendragon had vaguely suggested that he spend a while as guest at Caer Cadan, Amlawdd had leapt at the invitation like a cat catching a rat. Now was his chance to begin the Pendragon's downfall!

His plan: Caninus was to goad Lord Bedwyr into a brawl. Most the Artoriani were away on patrol, those left would eat and drink at the feast, and be unarmed. The fight would be brief and bloody, for his men would have their daggers. It would spill over beyond the Hall and Gwenhwyfar would be so tragically killed along with the bastard-born Medraut. In the confusion that would follow, Amlawdd would take command, in the name of Aurelius Caninus, and set the lad as King.

That was the plan, except Amlawdd was not talented as a leader, preferring his drink and his women rather than concentrating on important timing. A moment after Cywyllog had admonished Amlawdd for delaying, Bedwyr unexpectedly rose from table and retreated through the door into Gwenhwyfar's private chamber, before Caninus had managed to hurl even a single abusive remark.

She was already abed, reading through Arthur's last-sent letter. She greeted him with a smile, the dogs stretched before the hearth-fire doing no more than lift their heads and thump their tails in greeting. 'I complained of a headache. What is your excuse?' she laughed.

His hands in the air, palms flat, Bedwyr blew out his cheeks, shook his head. 'Preservation of sanity?' He quipped. 'My God, am I glad we do not have a surfeit of men out there – the excitement is so riveting, they would be slashing their own throats to provide entertainment.' He gestured with his hand and expression, asking whether he had permission to enter the chamber. She nodded.

He crossed to the table, poured himself wine, asked by raising the wine jug whether she wanted any. She did. 'I cannot stay long, I will need keep a watch on the Hall, have merely come to bid you a good night,' he said, his back to her as he poured, 'and to assure you that all will be well.'

There were times when Bedwyr wondered how he survived without having Gwenhwyfar as his own. Days when he remembered and remembered how they had talked and laughed together as a betrothed couple. Long nights when the intimacy they had shared made his manhood throb with wanting. His hand shook slightly as he poured her wine. She looked so lovely sitting there. He could not have her, she could not be his . . . Never would he betray Arthur, except in thought. Never at all would she.

She must have read something of those thoughts for as he turned, a goblet in each hand, she said, 'When my husband asks if I have been faithful to him, I will only answer him with the truth, Bedwyr.'

He stood, his head drooping, staring at the floor.

'I am fond of you, Bedwyr, we are friends. But this truth I must tell you, I have never loved you as I love Arthur. Nor shall I.'

Putting a brave face on his torment, Bedwyr settled a smile onto his mouth as he lifted his head. 'I am thinking I may travel again soon. I have a fancy to see the great pyramid tombs where the Egyptian kings lie buried. And Athens. There are many places I still have not seen.'

Holding out her hand for him to bring her the wine, Gwenhwyfar returned his smile. 'I will never stop you from following where your feet must lead, but do not waste your life running from what must be, Bedwyr.' As he began walking towards her, she added, the laughter shining in her eyes, 'You have loved with many a young girl, my friend. I would advocate that you find for yourself a wife – why not a dark-skinned Egyptian?'

Bedwyr's amusement echoed her own, he lengthened his stride, was distracted by a sudden rise of noise from the Hall. He turned his head, forgot the dog stretched in sleep between himself and the bed, tripped. Lurching forward, Gwenhwyfar's reaction was to try and steady him. One goblet fell from his grasp, the other, as he overbalanced, cascaded wine down the front of her undershift and over the bed furs, splashed down Bedwyr's tunic. Soaked, the red stain rapidly spreading, the fine-woven silk clung to her flesh, emphasizing the shape of her breasts. Throwing the emptied goblet aside, concerned, Bedwyr patted at the patch of wetness, knelt in a puddle of wine collected in a fold of the bed fur, tried to move away quickly, became entangled and tumbled forward, pinning Gwenhwyfar to the bed. She lay laughing helplessly, beneath him.

Medraut considered that he would probably be enjoying himself more, were he to be stuck, horseless, in the middle of open moorland, during the blackest part of the night, while a thunderstorm raged. Even the annual clearing of the midden heap would be preferable to hearing one more of Aurelius Caninus's grossly exaggerated tales of personal bravado. Because they had spent a while at the same school together, Caninus had assumed that Medraut would want to share in the entertainment and conversation of his friends. There was nothing further from Medraut's preference, but without offering insult, he had no choice but to accept the invitation to sit with the rowdy, half-drunken group. Mind, Medraut himself had as much wine in his belly – if not more.

'Not dancing?' Caninus, breathing heavily and sweating profusely from the exertion of the spirited reel just finished, flopped onto the bench. He reached over, took the wine from Medraut's hand and thirstily gulped the remainder of its contents, wiped residue from his moustache. 'I suppose with a wife as sour as yours, you would not have much inclination for dancing though, eh?' He nudged at Medraut's elbow, pointed at the redhead Amlawdd had been leering over for most of the evening. 'Now there's one worth a tumble in the hay! I would like to have more than just a look at those paps of hers!' He held the goblet for a slave to refill.

484

'You ought try for a whore, get your exercise on her if your wife's not accommodating you.' He guffawed, nudged Medraut's arm again. 'Even if she is, a little extra riding never did a man harm!' He turned to his friends, sharing the jest with them.

Although lank, Caninus was a young man with deceptive strength in his muscles; had very much the Pendragon look about him – brown hair, piercing eyes, long, straight nose. That was as far as the resemblance went, for his character and poor judgement were crude. Arrogant, churlishly abusive, and more often than not, drunk and in the company of whores. It was as well his kindred were no more. The two who had brought him into the world, such gentle, kind-hearted people, now long cold in their graves, and Ambrosius Aurelianus, his grandsire, a man of God. If ever there was a contender for a changeling babe, then Caninus was the one.

One of the men nudged Caninus's elbow, dipped his head across the Hall, pointed. 'Bedwyr.'

'Well, would you believe it!' Caninus chortled. 'We have found gold, my friends. Pure gold!' He eye-searched the crowded Hall, Arthur's men clustered in their groups to one side, Amlawdd's to the other. Amlawdd himself, talking to Medraut's scowling wife. 'Lord Bedwyr has played himself for a fool!' He stood, caught Amlawdd's eye, urgently waved at him to come across the Hall.

'What do you mean?' Medraut asked, suspicious, brows furrowed, part of his attention watching Cywyllog leave through the Hall's side door, part glancing around the Hall for his father's cousin. He had been sitting at that table over there a moment past . . .

Incredulous, Caninus regarded Medraut. Did he really not understand? Was the oaf either so drunk or so blind? Hah! Was it any wonder that he would never make King? 'Why think you we were sent here? Because Amlawdd is a great friend of Arthur's? Because I am his choice of heir? The Pendragon assumed Bedwyr would not dare bed the Queen while we were here to keep watch on the both of them. Obviously the Pendragon miscounted the lure of a whore's enticement!'

Amlawdd was striding over, his authority parting groups of men and women before him.

'We have him, Amlawdd!' Caninus crowed. 'Right into our hands, we have good reason for confrontation and not a word out of place said from our side.' He indicated Gwenhwyfar's chamber door, his grin broadening to match that glowing on Amlawdd's face.

Swinging around to face all those gathered in the Hall, Amlawdd raised his arms, roared in his mighty voice, 'Traitors! Damned, lying traitors!' Eyes, bodies, attention, swivelled to Amlawdd, conversation stopped, laughter ceased. In a few quick strides, Amlawdd was crossing the room, drawing a dagger from his boot. 'Bedwyr and the Queen, in there!' He pointed the dagger at the door ahead of him, 'Making mockery of the Pendragon!'

Daggers were coming into the hands of others, Amlawdd's men, their drunkenness sobering quickly. The few Artoriani looked to one another helplessly, bewildered. What was this? What was happening?

Medraut, too, was confused. Words reverberating in his wine-addled mind. 'If we are to survive the coming slaughter . . . show support for Caninus . . .' God's truth, what was this? He leapt to his feet, hauled at Caninus's arm, saw the dagger glinting there, in his hand.

'This is treason!' he cried, attempting to wrestle the dagger from the other young man's grip. 'You cannot displace my father!'

Grappling this unexpected opponent, Caninus attempted to shake Medraut off, tried to alter the grip on that dagger. It was no worry to him if Medraut died here, or later . . . His face was close to Medraut's as they struggled together, breath hot on each other's cheeks. 'Why defend him? What has your father done for you? Does he treat you with the respect deserved for a son? Does he listen to you, take note of what you say? Did you not warn him that his wife was bedding his cousin? Well, now we have proof!'

Breathing hard, Medraut knocked the dagger aside, it fell to the floor, skimmed away a few yards. There was confusion all around, men beginning to fight, Arthur's men, unarmed, attempting to defend the chamber doorway with weapons of stools, the jagged ends of a broken flagon. Amlawdd's men striking at them with sharpened blades.

'You cannot do this!' Medraut screamed, 'I will not allow you to depose my father!'

Caninus hit him, a punch to the jaw that sent him reeling, fastened his hand around Medraut's throat. 'Who are you to oppose me? You, the bastard spawn of a bitch who thought nothing of spreading her legs for her own brother!'

Medraut's hand had been trying to force that grip away from his windpipe. He let go, his skin draining white. Caninus released his grip, licked his dry lips, took a small step backward. That information had been told him in confidence by Amlawdd, it was to be used later, once supremacy had been secured for their own purpose, used to gain sympathy among the Christians, to discredit Arthur, to bring to themselves the advantage of righteous conquest. Once made public knowledge, Amlawdd could not use it to full advantage. It was to remain their final ambush, their secret weapon.

The words hammered in Medraut's ears. Mother's brother. Mother's brother. Arthur was his mother's brother? The sickness rose in his throat, caught at his guts, twisting and crushing. Was this true? Was this just another lie, another trick? Who would say with certainty that this spread of dung was lies? Arthur would know, but he was not here ... Gwenhwyfar?

With a snarl, Medraut shoved Caninus aside, pushed his way through the mêlée of men, across the Hall to the private door. Arthur's men let him through, he was the King's son. His fingers clicked the latch, thrust it downward, propelling the door open. In his rage and sodden distress, marched through with no announcement, no permission to enter.

Stood speechless, enraged, on the far side of the threshold.

§ XLI

The numbing agony had taken Medraut across the Hall and through that door, but he stood inside, the impetus gone, disbelief sweeping intention aside. My God! He thought, I was right. Caninus, Amlawdd ... we are right.

Before him, Bedwyr romping with Gwenhwyfar on the bed; laughing together, arms around each other ... Before his father, he had been disgraced; yet all the while he had spoken right, she was the whore he had said her to be. The surge of passionate rage set loose in a great roar. He had no weapon, needed none. He leapt the distance between door and bed, his hands going around Bedwyr's throat, feet kicking, teeth biting. Startled, Bedwyr attempted to push the assailant off, rolled from the bed, across the floor, in a flurry of desperate manoeuvres. Gwenhwyfar screamed, her reaction – that Amlawdd had sent men in to murder both her and Bedwyr – justified as men pushed in through the door, snarling and fighting each other, some with blades drawn. She fumbled for the dagger beneath her pillow, leapt for the one tumbling furiously with Bedwyr, was dragged from him to be flung across the room, her back slamming into the timber wall, her head crunching on the support beam.

Amlawdd truly believed at that moment that the gods were on his side and he had a chance of making Caninus King. He clawed his way deeper into the press of fighting, bellowing as he made passage with boot, knee, elbow and dagger. 'Traitor!' he roared, 'Whore!' and for good measure, added the cry, 'Murder!'

Women were screaming, clawing their way to the sides of the Hall, away from the danger. Blood was spilling onto the timbers of the floor, benches were turned over, a torch was knocked from its sconce, the flames exploring the edge of a torn tapestry.

Bedwyr was grappling with Medraut, was the one on top now. He had hold his hair, was thumping his head to the floor, felt the hot scythe of pain swarm across his shoulder, down his arm, saw the blood gush in a stream of red . . . *Jesu Christ*, he thought, desperately attempting to stem the flow with one hand, keep Medraut away from his throat with the other. *Jesu! Medraut is with them!*

§ XLII

Amlawdd struck out with his sword, laying it about him, left and right, his men cheering and shouting, the fight exhilarating. He heard Caninus squeal, glanced to his left to see him kneeling, clutching at blood soaking from his thigh. It ought be over soon, for his men were armed and defence of the Caer well under strength . . . and the surprise unguessed. He parried a sword, hissed as the blade came too close to his face. Ought be over . . . yet too many of Arthur's men also had daggers and swords. Five and ten minutes, slightly longer. Still the fighting, Amlawdd's men bunching together, grouping tighter, several back to back, the free use of weapons hampered by a neighbour's arm.

Gradually, with slow dawning, certain things began to register. The few burning tapestries had been torn from their hangings, the smell of damp smoke and wettened oak permeating over the stink of sweat and blood. The Hall was crowded with men. Arthur's men. The fighting was fading, one or two swords jabbing here and there, a grunt as a man lunged forward with foot or fist. Flaring nostrils, breath rasping. The glisten of sweat. Too many men. Artoriani.

Amlawdd lowered his sword, glowered as an officer of Arthur's élite force took the weapon from him. Someone was sobbing, gasping against the pain, curled on the floor. Contemptuous, Amlawdd spat at Caninus. One by one, his men were disarmed, herded together, surrounded by Artoriani.

'Did you think, Amlawdd, that we would trust you?' Bedwyr emerged from the chamber, holding a rough linen pad tight against his bleeding shoulder, his face grey, eyes blazing. Behind him, Gwenhwyfar, a cloak flung around her shoulders, a wine stain down the front panels of her undershift. At her side, Ider, breathing hard, blood on his sword. She leant heavily on his arm, her fingers pressed to the back of her head.

Thank God for Ider and his men who had burst into her room from the courtyard . . . and for the wisdom of Arthur's men.

Gathering her strength and dignity, she lightly pushed Ider's support aside, walked towards Amlawdd. Taking a dagger from one of the Artoriani, she held the blade to his throat.

'Did you think we would be such fools? That we would allow the Caer to fall to half strength?' She indicated the crowd of Artoriani in the Hall, all of them full-armed, full-dressed in war gear. 'That we were not close watching as each of your men picked a blade from out of a barrel? The Artoriani rode but the few miles, circled around, crept back through the gates while you swilled your wine and filled your belly with flatulence.' She pressed the dagger tip into his skin. 'Were my husband here,' she said, her voice level, menacing, 'he would have you executed, here and now. But he is not.'

'Na!' Amlawdd writhed in the grasp of the two men holding him. 'If he were, you would not be bedding with Bedwyr!'

She stared at him, long and cold and hard. 'I am Lady of Caer Cadan, while he is gone.' Added, 'Therefore I must do it.' Fast, she brought the blade round, slashed it through Amlawdd's throat, cutting through flesh and sinew. His eyes widened in disbelief, as he gasped for air. She has killed me, he thought, gods she has . . . No more thoughts, not in this world.

Caninus vomited.

Immediate, Gwenhwyfar turned to Medraut. Like Amlawdd, he was held between two men, his head hanging, body slumped. She stepped up to him, grasped his hair, lifted his head, the bloodied blade going to his throat also. 'Your father brought you here, raised you. He could have left you to the mercy of the whore who was your mother, but he did not. And this is how you repay him?'

Medraut could not meet her eyes. The shame that was in him felt as heavy as the lead mined from within the White Hills. Kill me, he thought. End it for me, end this misery. Knew she would not, for whatever else he was, he was also Arthur's son.

May 488

§ XLIII

Natanlius held the babe close, the child's tiny hand clamped around his own index finger. He was beautiful, perfect. Another son, a brother to Constantine, who was himself two months away from the year old. It was good for brothers to be born and grow together, as he had with his. He missed them, for they had been a close family; it was hard to be alone, the only brother to survive.

He smiled down at Archfedd, who looked exhausted. At least he had her with him now, and two sons. Together they countered the loss of brothers.

'Is he not a fine boy?' She asked.

Handing the child carefully back to her, Natanlius bent forward, kissed her forehead. 'Of course, but then he has a fine mother.'

The women were bustling about the room, clearing away the remains of the disruption that always seemed to accompany birthing. Bowls, linen, unguents and oils. The last of them bobbed a curtsey, left the room. Archfedd cradled her sleeping son. He was warm and content in this new-come world, his small face, tiny lips, closed eyes. That soft down of fair, curled hair.

'Father will be proud,' she said. 'Two grandsons to follow his name, to hold Britain when they are grown.'

'Let us hope there is a Britain to be held,' her husband replied gravely.

They had heard the news, a week past, that Amlawdd had attempted to overthrow the Pendragon, had failed. The poor fool, they all said, could he not see that he had walked into Arthur's baited trap?

To Archfedd's anger, of the three leading traitors only Amlawdd had paid for it with his life. That pathetic whimpering stoat, Caninus, her father had allowed go free – had even given him Amlawdd's stronghold! The Pendragon's rage had been as boiling as a winter-churned sea, they had heard. Amlawdd's men had waited, miserable and in fear, held in chains, given no food, little water, until the King had returned, riding home hard and fast from Powys. Most of them he had ordered hung. Their heads, so Archfedd was pleased to hear, adorned the gate towers of Caer Cadan, a stark reminder of what would befall those who went against their King. Of the third, Medraut, there was no word save that he had fled.

'Have you sent my father word of the child?' she asked, her green eyes glancing suddenly up at him. Natanlius seated himself on the side of the bed, tucked the shawl the tighter around his son's small, dimpled chin, took her hand.

'Of course. I sent a courier on my fastest horse.' Teasing, added, 'Expect your mother here by dawn!'

'Fool!' Archfedd answered, lifting her head so that he might kiss her again, knowing not even her mother, for whatever reason, could ride so far so fast.

She was much alike Gwenhwyfar, Archfedd. The same flashing eyes and unruly hair, though its copper shading had darkened as she grew older, was not so curled. Her face had shadows of her father in the features, though, in the shape of the chin, slant of the eyes, the higher cheek-bones. Her temper, too, was his. Nor was she the capable woman that her mother was. Oh, Archfedd knew how to use sword or spear or dagger as efficiently as any man – yet she did not possess the cunning that Gwenhwyfar had for a fight. Facing an opponent and coming away alive was more than being able to slash and parry with a blade. You needed to think quick, watch, wait, strike at the right moment, move fast. Move hard. Archfedd did not care for fighting; she was, perhaps, more the woman than Gwenhwyfar when it came to the things of the household. Sewing, weaving, the overseeing and preparing or preserving of foods; brewing ale, pressing wine. For Gwenhwyfar, her delight was a sword in her hand, or a horse beneath her, riding beside her lord husband. For Archfedd, her happiness lay in her sons and her home.

'If my father cannot visit us soon,' she said, 'we must take our sons to him, at Caer Cadan, so he may see for himself how handsome and strong they are.' The smile dropped from her face, a look of hardness taking its place. 'He must declare Constantine his heir,' she stated. 'You as regent, until he is grown.'

Indulgent, Natanlius patted her hand as he rose from the bed. She ought rest, restore her strength. Her labour had not been long for this, the second child, but birthing was always a difficult business. He tucked the bed-furs around her, told her to sleep, let himself from the room.

Outside, he elected to tour the rampart walkways. Saxon ships had been seen again recently, coming close to shore. One of his men swore there were signs that one might have moored.

He was a strong-hearted man, Natanlius, happen a little on the quiet, serious, side; the amusement of a jest chortling in his mind rather than coming out as a guffaw. His feet to be stretched towards a warm fire, a

491

bowl of venison stew between his hands – his idea of contentment. He enjoyed watching his wife at her loom, or playing with their first-born, took pride in her prettiness, her love. Would dread the day that he would ever need do anything to hurt her.

Took as much pride in his stronghold. And there he found the difficulty. Caer Morfa was his to protect and cherish so that he might pass it on to his sons, as his father had. He understood and accepted that Arthur, the Pendragon, might need one day soon to proclaim the eldest, Constantine as his heir, but liked it not. Too much sadness had already befallen the male seed of Arthur. He did not want its black shadow to reach out and touch the daughter or her sons also.

As it would. Neither of those two living sons, Archfedd's poisonous half-brothers, would allow children declared as heirs to grow into manhood.

Medraut, who had turned traitor and fled Caer Cadan, to who knew where. He was bastard-born, but had the right to become King.

And Cerdic. Ah, Cerdic would allow no one to stand in his way once he came full into his strength. Many believed, after all these years of peace, that there would not come a war between father and son. Cerdic wanted them to believe that, wanted them to pass year upon year looking to the horizon and seeing nothing save the smile of ripening corn and cattle, grazing fat. For when you looked long enough and saw the same thing again and again, eventually you stopped looking.

And failed to see the storm until it lashed, wicked, at your door.

October 488

§ XLIV

Twice, Medraut almost turned back. Only the presence of other travellers on the road kept him pressing onward. An old Roman road – the Saxons called them streets – running south, direct for the open mouth of the gates into Cerdicesora. A busy town by the outward look of the place, with a bustle of people coming and going, ox-wagons, donkey-carts, men and women on foot. Bales, bundles and barrels. A lively chatter of conversation, in a variety of tongues; an aroma of scents, pleasant and odious. Medraut's mule plodded patient at his side, the saddle-bags weighted with its cargo of silverware – not fine stuff, but good enough to sell. An inspired idea, it had seemed at the outset, this disguise as a silver-trader, for merchants were welcome anywhere, within Saxon or British habitation, and he had purchased a few finer pieces to make his plausibility the more creditable. It had cost him the last of his gold, those few pieces that Gwenhwyfar had given him, along with a warm cloak and a bundle of food. Three days he had sat, chained, in that cell, wretched in his deep misery. What a damned, idiot fool he had been! And then she had come, with Ider and two more of her guard, had him unchained and ordered him thrown from the Caer.

'I ought have you dead, as Amlawdd is dead,' she had said, her voice indifferent, with no care or feeling, as if she were addressing a stranger, not the boy she had raised from childhood. 'Your father would see you hanged when he returns.'

'Then why not have an end to me now?' Medraut had asked, not understanding this seeming benevolence.

And there was so much grief in her voice as she had answered, that Medraut had almost wept for shame. 'Because,' she had said, 'already your father has lost three sons to the darkness of death, another to the maliciousness of hatred and treachery. I would not have him be responsible for the loss of the fifth, and last, of his sons.'

He knew then, as he walked down the cobbled lane from the Caer, with no knowing of where he was to go, that he ought take his own life. Open his veins with his dagger, drown himself in the river, obtain poison; but he could not, he had not the courage even for that.

But was this exile the better choice? This living death? As he ambled through the busy streets of Cerdicesora, he again wondered, as he had so many times these past months.

Cerdicesora. A wealthy settlement if first impressions were aught to go by. The market stalls well laden, the children clothed, fed; the women bonny. The two taverns he passed were full, ale flowing plentiful from amphorae and jugs, the smell of hot pies and stews enticing. He would stop soon, fill his belly, quench his thirst, but first he need find Stefan, in the street of the silversmiths.

Stefan had been recommended him as a buyer and as a useful contact, for Stefan was silversmith to the ealdorman, Cerdic. Medraut asked directions, found him in the street of the silversmiths, over to the east of the town.

'These pieces look familiar crafted,' Stefan remarked, his myopic eyes squinting suspiciously at the wealas man, the foreigner, sitting opposite him on the far side of his smith's bench. 'They are, I think, not from your hands?'

'Oh I could not work as fine as that!' Medraut admitted with an amiable smile. 'I bought them off a man who cannot make the journey to Cerdicesora this season.'

The old silversmith nodded, again held the piece in his hand close for inspection. He allowed no expression onto his face, set the buckle down, picked up the next item, an exquisite silver ring, emblazoned with the device of a griffon. He scratched at the nape of his neck, rubbed his nose, sniffed a few times. Coughed. 'If you bought these pieces,' the old man said, 'you'd be wanting to make a profit.'

Medraut was leaning on his elbow, chin cupped between his fingers and thumb, waiting patient and quiet throughout. He removed his hand in a brief gesture of agreement.

The smith set the ring down, pushed the collection of pieces across the bench, shaking his head. 'I'll not pay more than they are worth. Sorry, lad.'

Slowly, Medraut straightened his back, laced his fingers, as if considering. He moved the pile back towards the smith. 'I ask for no higher payment. All I want for profit is something in kind.'

Stefan pursed his lips. There was some good silver amongst the things before him. The three plate dishes in particular would fetch a nice amount, mayhap from Lord Cerdic himself. 'And what kind of a something would that be then?' He asked.

For the third time that day, Medraut almost abandoned his plan. This was madness coming here, what in the name of God was he doing? Get up, go home! Hah, he had no home! He had nothing, save the clothes he stood in and the stained name of a traitor. His wife, that first dawn after the treachery of Caer Cadan, had taken her belongings – aye, and his – and fled north, back to the hills around Caer Rhuthun, had entombed herself in a women's holy house rather than be linked to the stench of the name Medraut. His father refused to think of him as son, and Archfedd, his half-sister, had refused to see him. He had gone to her to explain, to set his case, to try to tell someone that he had been so grievously mistaken, that he was a fool, and ashamed. But Archfedd had ordered him tossed beyond the gates of Caer Morfa as if he were a begging peasant. He had nothing and no one. The apology that he so wanted to give to his father and Gwenhwyfar must hang unuttered, unpenanced. There was only this one thing left him.

'I wish to be admitted into the Ealdorman's Hall. To speak personally with Lord Cerdic.'

The smith laughed, a wheezing, old man's chuckle, that crackled in his lungs. 'And you want me to see it so?' He shook his head, his eyes wrinkling with mirth. 'You wealas people are all fools! I have long known it!'

Close to losing his nerve, Medraut fought the instinct to bundle his wares and bolt for the door at the front of this dark little smith's bothy.

Stefan was sucking at a loose tooth. 'How do I know you are not harbouring plans to murder him?' He snapped, his amiability vanishing. 'I would not have blood on my hands because of you!'

Medraut stretched his right hand across the bench. Save for one ring, he wore no adornment, no ornate rings, no arm-bands, though there were the lighter marks against his skin where such things had rested. The one ring was a battered gold thing. 'This,' he said, 'was given to my mother by my father, from before the time of my birthing. It is all I now have of him.' He withdrew his hand, rubbed his left thumb affectionately over it. 'I have no honour of my own left to me, but on my father's honour.' He lifted his head, gazed earnestly at the smith, 'I do not come to murder Cerdic.'

He had thought of it. Oh, many nights he had lain, planning ways of putting an end to the whoreson. But what purpose would that serve? He would need kill the son also, Cynric, who was ten and eight, a man grown, and with a young wife already swelling with child. She, too, would need ending, to ensure the line was finished. Killing outside of battle was against God's law. If Cerdic was to die, then it must be done openly, where Arthur alone could take the victory from it. A knife wielded secret in the dark would not solve this thing.

'I have nothing,' Medraut admitted openly, 'only these few pieces of silver to sell. My father has cast me from him, my sister shuns me. My own people, the British, spit in my face. What have I left, but to find for myself a new home, a new people?' He shrugged, resigned to his fate. 'Cerdic seeks men to fight in his name. He gives them reward of gold and silver, spears and shields, food in their bellies, his Mead Hall to lay under and a woman to lay with. I have none of this from the British. I wish to speak with Cerdic, for I wish to join with him.'

April 489

§ XLV

Walking down the cobbled lane that ran steeply up through the heights of the ramparts, Gwenhwyfar could see Arthur on the far side of the nearest paddock. There were a few foals already, the early born, long-legged and gangling, dancing beside their fat-bellied dams. The sun was warm this day, the new-hatched midges bothersome; with the mares' tales constantly swishing. Arthur had stopped to talk to one of the foals, a handsome dark-coated colt – he would turn grey as he grew older, would make a fine height if the length of leg was anything to go by. Gwenhwyfar smiled as she watched Arthur offer the colt a crust of stale bread. He kept his waist pouch full of morsels this time of year for the foals, though he was all too often saying that it spoilt them to offer titbits. He was good with horses, more patient than with men. You could expect loyalty from a horse, and trust. Not so with men, sons.

Gwenhwyfar stood, shielding her eyes from the glare of the afternoon sun, watching as Arthur parted from the foal, walked to the small mound of earth in the far corner that was only just beginning to grass over. Had she done right to allow Medraut to run, to disappear into exile? At the time, she thought she had, was not so certain now.

Britain was at peace. A golden age of content, they were calling it. Aye, even the fusty, pedantic men of Council. The English lands, too, were settled and thriving. Intermarriages were common place, with the two cultures in certain areas, especially the East Anglian and North Humbrian lands, mutually blending together. English husband, British wife.

'They will grow stronger than the British one day,' Arthur had once confided to Gwenhwyfar. 'The English are a determined and rugged people.'

He had stopped beside the mound, stood with head bowed. If he mourned Medraut's loss, he had not outwardly shown it, though Gwenhwyfar knew the wounding had speared deep. For Onager, however, Arthur openly grieved.

She resumed walking, but had changed her mind about visiting Rhonwen at the tavern. Her fifth child was due within this week, with the pregnancy a difficult one, but she could always call on the woman later. Instead, she continued on down the hill, across the rutted lane, and let herself through the hazel-laced fencing of the foaling paddock. She, too, put out her hand to the grey foal, his soft, delicate nose whispering, curious, at her hand. No bread from her. It was Arthur who spoilt the foals.

Without speaking, she threaded her arm around her husband's waist, a squeeze of understanding comfort. He too, said nothing, enfolded her hand within his. Onager, a bastard of a horse at times, but how often had his courage and strength saved Arthur? No man among the Artoriani had thought it a weakness when Arthur had ordered the great horse to be buried here, in this spot where the sun settled for most the day. They all had special thought for their horses – for some of the men, more so than their wives. A horse, they would laugh, does not answer you back!

'Do you think it has truth behind it, this latest rumour?' Arthur asked.

What could she answer? Lie, and know that he knew she lied. Reply with the truth, and drive the spear further? 'It is never wise to trust rumour that cannot be substantiated, but aye, this one I believe.'

Where else would Medraut have gone? There were no other reports of him, and few loyal to Arthur would have cared to take him in. The ring of truth behind words whispered on the wind, was too sound to be ignored. Medraut had been caught into Amlawdd's net of intrigue, and Amlawdd had trudged dangerously close to Cerdic's heel.

Arthur sighed, linked Gwenhwyfar's arm through his own. Truth or malicious taunting, either way there was little he could do. They would know about Medraut one way or another, eventually, soon, when Cerdic made his mind to move the men he had been massing away from the thin line of his held land, and into Arthur's territory.

I ought have slit his throat when I had chance, Gwenhwyfar thought.

'Come,' Arthur said to her, 'I have more productive things to be doing above standing mewling over a horse's grave.'

§ XLVI

The Feast, an occasion that symbolized more than the consumption of food and drink. *Gegadorwiste*, the assembly for plenty, a gathering intended for celebration and social pleasure; for entertainment, the exchange of news, and to pledge homage. To eat and drink at the provider's table was to declare openly, for all to see, the agreement of support and a pledge to fight to the death. For the lord, the leader, to provide more than mere food and wine or mead, to give an image of plenty, an atmosphere of wealth and harmony, stability and coherence, in a world where conflict and uncertainty was the experience of the many. The English Feast.

Medraut hated them, and Cerdic held many. A great lord had the need to show his wealth and status; for Cerdic, the extra need to instil into his followers that he had every intention to become their King one day – and that the day of reckoning was fast approaching.

The summoning horn had blown three hours past – and what a gathering of fine-dressed, strong men, had made way to their benches! The usual shuffling for position of course, the best place: to be seated at the end of a bench, to be served first; the most prestigious of all, to be asked to the higher tables, where cushions made the seating more comfortable, and the choicest portions were served. Some of the usual scuffling by those who considered they ought be placed higher up the Hall, nearer the lord's dais; one or two exchanges of payment for the privilege to be seated at his table.

The Hall had looked splendid, draped with wall hangings threaded with gold and silver, and all the shields, spears and weapons hung there. The higher tables laden with gleaming silverware, brimming jugs of ale and wine, baskets of bread and fruit; servants waiting with silver bowls for the ritual washing of hands ... the ordered effect disintegrating as the hours wore on, as the Hall became hotter, the participants rowdier.

Medraut – although he was half-brother – did not warrant a seat at Cerdic's table among the honoured lords and thegns. He was seated lower down: not, for him, an honourable position, but Medraut did not complain – indeed, the further from his brother, the better.

The two hated each other with a distaste as strong as rancid cheese, yet Cerdic saw the wisdom of keeping eye on the one who could oppose him, and Medraut had no choice but to stay, although there were times when the temptation to walk out the stronghold gate and not return were often great.

He had settled well enough among the fighting men, learning to disregard their lewd humour and rough ways. He was not treated miskindly or made to look the fool. No man would openly insult the brother of their lord, even if that lord made such things regular habit. Cerdic made Medraut's life into misery whenever the two came into close contact – which was rarely, as Medraut saw to it that where his brother was, he was not. Until a Feast was called.

Feasting highlighted Medraut's harboured resentments. Cerdic had for himself a fine Hall, retainers, loyal men, and a pleasant woman to serve the wine, to share his bed. Cerdic had the courage to decide his own law, his own fate. What had Medraut to his name? A mother who had been a notorious whore, who had produced him through the sin of incest, and a father who now despised him.

They were bellowing laughter at the high table, the boom of merriment hitting the smoke-swirled rafters with the thunder of a thrown boulder. Cerdic, with Cynric his son sitting aside his right hand; Cerdic's woman, his wife, to his left. A small, demure lady, who rarely spoke, rarely lifted her eyes. There was no reason to believe that Cerdic treated her cruelly, yet there was no show of love between them either. She had borne him no children. Cynric himself had three daughters by different women – and one in the belly of his taken wife. They were sweet little girls, with dimpled smiles and flaxen hair, welcomed at Cerdicesora as all Saxon men welcomed their offspring, whether legitimate or no. Another bellow, more laughter. Cerdic's wife rose to bring the wine again to the men of the three highest tables. Medraut, sitting at the far end of a bench, was one of the last for her to serve.

'See,' Cerdic roared, wine dribbling from his lips, 'my wife pours wine for the whoreson bastard! The boy who poked his thumb at the great Pendragon, our father!' Cerdic was well into his drink, the gluttony of over-indulgence almost a prerequisite for the rules of enjoyment. He belched, pointed with unsteady hand at Medraut.

'On your feet, boy, let us all look at you so we might recognize a traitor when we see one!'

No use Medraut protesting, for that would only enrage his half-brother, and Cerdic in a temper was an ugly experience. Already Medraut bore scars on his shoulders from where Cerdic had ordered him a beating for defiance. On his feet, Medraut judiciously kept his head lowered, schooled the anger from his reddened face. The taunts would continue a while, until Cerdic found another unfortunate to condemn, or a loyal friend to praise.

'Before you,' Cerdic's voice boomed, 'stands a dog turd who slithered from the womb of a mare who could be ridden by any who fancied scratching at the itch on his piece. She had breasts like a cow's udder and a sex as open as the sky in summer. I know, for I rode her often – and I rode her at the gallop, no fancy trotting and prancing for me!'

Enduring the insults, Medraut could feel his heart beating faster, the pump of his veins thudding. He would insult Arthur next. As always. It came.

Cerdic had stumbled to his feet, was waving his tankard of wine around as if it were a banner. 'My father,' he sneered, 'has not the stamina I possess. He hides behind the woman who is his whore-wife – the bitch who takes his cousin to her bed. Why? Because, so I have heard, he prefers the company of his men!' They all jeered, the entire

500

Hall mocking and contemptuous, ridiculing the Pendragon. 'I have reason to believe,' Cerdic shouted, regaining attention, 'that I am the only true son born from him. My mother was a virtuous woman, a noble, wise lady.'

Aye, Medraut thought to himself, *was that why you so brutally killed her?*

'The others, they were not of his seed – and neither are you!'

Appalled at the sudden thrust of venom, Medraut dodged, as Cerdic threw the tankard at him. It caught his shoulder, tumbled to the floor. 'Are you then,' Cerdic screamed, 'an impostor? Eating at my table, begging warmth from my fire under the pretence of being a brother?'

'No, lord!' Medraut countered hurriedly, 'I come to fight with you against the man who treated me with as much wrong as he did you!'

'Fight? You, a snivelling boy, fight?' Cerdic put his fists to his waist, threw back his head and howled derision, the Hall echoing his mockery.

'I am three and twenty, my lord!' Medraut protested hotly, this insult one too many. 'Older than the boy who calls himself your son!'

The skin on Cerdic's face became blotched, patched red and white, the loose jowls beneath his chin quivering. 'How dare you!' He swung around from behind the table, striding the distance between himself and Medraut, took him up by the collar as if he were a recalcitrant pup and shook him. Almost, Medraut's teeth and bones rattled. As if he were something unpleasant, Cerdic abruptly dropped him, Medraut crumpled to the floor, winded, more than a little frightened. What had he said, for God's sake? He had only meant that he was of an age more fitting to fight than Cynric. To his relief, there came no blows or kicks. Instead, Cerdic hauled him upright, held him painfully by the throat, his fingers squeezing and bruising his windpipe. Medraut, choking, gasping for air, tried to pluck at Cerdic's grip.

'Do I want your poxed presence tainting the glory of my proud men?' Cerdic was shouting, his eyes pig small, cheeks puffed. 'How do I know the stench of a traitor does not cling to your foul breath? You? A snivelling whoreson against that bastard my father? Ah no, you will not fight with us come the next waning moon, you are not worthy to be among those who call themselves Cerdicingas!' Cerdic let go, pushing Medraut into the arms of a man standing close by. 'Get him from my sight!' Cerdic roared, his wrath suffused with contempt. 'Throw him to the sea, let the Mer people feed on his miserable guts!'

Medraut could not protest, make an attempted plea for forgiveness for his throat was aching, tight, as he tried to swallow, make a sound. The pain became almost unbearable – but anyway, did he want clemency?

Rough hands took him by the collar, the shoulder, the elbow, dragged him from the Hall, accompanied by ribald, drunken laughter, the finger of disdain and derision at his fall from grace, pointing firmly and unforgiving. Across the night-dark courtyard, lit with the flare of smoking braziers and torches, they took him. Loud voices hailing for the small water-gate to be opened. They marched him through, manhandled him along the echoing wooden walkway of the wharves, and tossed him over the edge, into the black coldness of the sea.

Cynric was the only one to remain seated at the high table. He watched his father's torrent of rage, knowing it to be unjustified, felt regret at Medraut's humiliation. Such was not the way to treat a man who had come to offer his sword. Even if the offering was riddled with suspicious patterning. Cynric would have won Medraut over, would have showered him with gifts and good feeling, made him one with the family. How much more that would have hurt the Pendragon – the knowing that another son had full and whole-hearted turned against you?

But too many men pledged loyalty to Cerdic through the colours of fear. Fear of his anger, fear of being left with nothing after the day of fighting finally came. His father was too demanding, too harsh. Regrettable, but many a man would not miss his going when the Reaper of Death came for him. For all that, all those in this Hall would be with him when the battle came, with him to the death. That was the way of the Saxon.

He would miss Medraut. They had held some good conversations together, discussing the differences of religion and culture between Briton and Englishman. Had talked of Arthur, the Pendragon. Cynric would have liked to have met him, his grandsire, under better circumstances: under conditions other than those of hostility, for although he would never dare breath word to his father, Cynric admired Arthur. A good leader, an excellent military strategist, and – even Medraut had admitted this – with exception of the one son, Cerdic, a good father.

With the exception of Cerdic? If he, Cynric, was to examine his heart for the truth, he would find the admission that he intensely disliked his own father. And if he could say that then why could not a father dislike a son?

May 489

§ XLVII

The coldness brought Medraut to his senses, though the pain that was in his throat caught alight with the rush of salt-water entering his mouth and nose. He could swim, but the weight of his boots dragged his legs, and the leather of his tunic hampered movement. The tide was on the ebb, with the current already strengthening. He would need grab hold some solid object soon, or be swept out into the eddies of the channel. He forced his arms into a few pathetic strokes, groping blindly. Everything was dark, the blackness of a moonless, heavily clouded night. Rain was falling, though only a soft drizzle.

As each wave lifted and tossed him, he could hear the voice of the wind and a soporific, swishing, rhythmic sound; dull, repeated, distant. It seemed a while that he had been in the water, was probably only a few minutes. Once, to his left, he saw the darker shapes of the wharves and moored ships; beyond those would be the Hall, people. The current pulled him further away, outward along the open desertion of the coast.

Something bumped against his shoulders, something hard, and unforgiving. He cried out. What now? Had they come to hit him? To finish him off? He thrust out with his arm, knocked against a cask, bobbing on the tide. His breath sobbing, Medraut pulled it to him, leant his arms and chest over it, the effort of heaving himself partially out of the water draining that last particle of strength. His vision swayed, the roar of the sea increased in his ears and a blackness that was darker than the night leered into his numbing mind and body. If it were not for that empty, floating cask, he would have drowned, would have sunk into the oblivion of the sea.

For what seemed a long while, he drifted there, aimless, carried by the disinterested tidal pull. Dark, so dark, with no light, no sound, save for the constant movement of the sea and that rhythmic pulse somewhere, way ahead. Had there been the bathing light of the moon he might have been able to see how far he had drifted, whether it was worth trying to swim, to save himself. But there was nothing, only darkness. And why would he care to live? What was there to live for? Better to close his eyes, let the sea have him.

No moon. When would the moon return? Soon. Full moon. His mind was slurring, tiring with the cold, numb ache of his limbs. There was something he had heard about the moon. Something Cerdic had said . . . and Medraut snapped his eyes open, alert, awake. To march at the waning moon. Cerdic intended to march into Arthur's lands, to fight within the month.

The next thought tumbled after the first. Did Arthur know? Was the Pendragon aware of the number of men Cerdic had beneath his banner now? Of the strength, the determination of those who called themselves Cerdicingas, the People of Cerdic?

And then, that sound registered. The familiarity of it jerked his senses, shouted at his shattered will to survive. He lifted his head, saw, not too far away, the shore resting darker than the pale gleam of the sea, the wide expanse of night sky. Recognized the sound of the sea caressing the reeds. For a moment, as he attempted to propel himself forward, he found himself in a new danger, for the energy of the tide swept him back, then hurled him forward, the waves strong, reluctant to release him from their snare. He had to make land, had to get himself from this current, else he would be swept out into nothingness. With one hand he paddled forward, determined, persistent. His feet touched on the muddied ooze of sand, scraped shingle. He had made it.

Arthur must already know of Cerdic's movements. But what if he did not?

§ XLVIII

Good intentions remain good while in the sublime regions of the mind. In practice, they seldom work out, as Medraut discovered. He sat in the lee of Caer Cadan's lowest rampart, huddled against the pre-dawn chill. Many days it had taken him to walk from the coast to the Summer Land; hard days, where on occasion he went without food or shelter. His feet were sore and bleeding, his chin in need of a shave, a bath would be welcome, dry clothes. The idea was to wait for the gates to open at dawn, enter the Caer and demand to be taken to Arthur. The Pendragon would be delighted at receiving the news Medraut brought, so much so, there would follow instant forgiveness, and embracing, smiles and a few tears. Ah, the stuff of harpers' tales! The problem was, tales were seldom true.

Waiting, with a ragged cloak gathered around his shivering body, he realized the joy of an errant son returning to a forgiving father would not occur. The cloak, he had removed from a Saxon fisherman's hut. It stank of fish. Now that he was actually here, he realized that, more probably,

504

Arthur would have him run through with a sword before exchange of a single word.

What he needed was to meet quietly with a friendly face, someone who would intervene between himself and his father. Someone like Gwenhwyfar.

The sky was paling over to the east, the darkness easing into grey and colourless pink. He could not wait by the ramparts, for he would be found, moved on or arrested. Would that be an idea? It would get him into the Caer – aye, and beaten, thrown into a cell. Na, he would wait for Gwenhwyfar, down by the tavern walls, where the beggars tended to collect, where she would occasionally come, as Lady of the Caer, to scatter bread or give discarded clothing. Hoped he would not need wait over long, for the swelling crescent of the new moon was drifting against the ocean that was the sky.

'. . . And that beggar has been seen again, hanging around the young horses he was, yestereve. Would you like him to be moved on?'

Examining a tooth in the hand-held bronze mirror, Arthur murmured a brief acknowledgement to the end of the officer's report. The usual stuff, the daily roster for drill and training, for duties. The lists of illness, injury, a recommendation for promotion. The tooth was becoming more painful, the gum sore, swelling. It would need come out, for there was obviously poison building beneath its rotten enamel. Not yet, the pain was bearable for a while longer. Arthur knew nothing worse than facing the tortures of the tooth-puller.

This beggar. He was becoming somewhat of a nuisance, hanging around the gates, scuttling into shadows when anyone approached, huddled and bent, his hood pulled over his face. Of course, the Caer had its share – more than that – of the poor who clung to the ragged muddle of wattle sheds behind the tavern at the base of the lane. Men and women – more than a few children – who came hoping to receive the benevolence of the King. Arthur did not ignore them, but neither did he encourage their presence. What was left from the meal at Gathering was sent down for them, along with the occasional ragged cloak or worn pair of boots. Hand-outs, charity. It was for the lord of a stronghold to take care of the infirm, the ill, the ragged and the unwanted. But to a degree only.

'What was he doing by the horses?' Arthur asked, irritated. He had more important things to tend this day, without the need to be bothered by a stinking peasant. Were Bedwyr here, he would pass the matter over to him, but he was still away from the Caer, over at Aquae Sulis, enjoying, it seemed from his infrequent letters, the hospitality of the local women rather than paying mind to matters of state.

'He was looking at them, sire, nothing more, ran off when my men approached.'

Arthur rubbed at the ache in his jaw. There were several petitions he should respond to this morning, and he would need seek advice about the increase of import tax. Always an unpopular decision. He should be at Aquae Sulis himself, discussing these issues, but he could not leave the strategic advantage of Caer Cadan and his men. Not while these rumours of Cerdic were running at a gallop. 'Have this beggar brought in for questioning. Ensure he gives answers.'

The officer saluted, withdrew from the chamber.

Gwenhwyfar glanced up from finishing her letter to Archfedd. She would like her daughter to move back to the Caer, for Natanlius's stronghold of Caer Morfa was too vulnerable, too close to Cerdic's land, but Archfedd was as strong-minded as her mother. Gwenhwyfar would never leave her husband or his men when the tide of danger began washing against the shield-wall; neither would Archfedd.

'I will check the yearlings this morning,' she said, rolling the parchment and dripping hot wax to seal it. 'That bay with the white legs may be promising, and the lame grey ought be brought up again for examination.'

Arthur absently nodded. Gwenhwyfar had taken full responsibility for the horses this season, for his thigh was aching more than it had in the past. Old wounds, old scars, the reminder of a long past and an increasing age. He was four and fifty, with hair more grey than brown, and all the aches and groans that went with someone of more than half a century of age. It was no small achievement, but when the east wind blew and the pain roared up from his leg, he wondered if the acclaim was worth it. With this damn tooth adding to his misery, he found himself asking that question more frequently. Had he a son to remove some of the burden from him . . . Llacheu, Amr, Gwydre . . . aye, or even Medraut. He had shown a talent for administration, a liking for the tedious, everyday bureaucracy that went hand in glove with kingship. Ah, no use regretting what was not to be, that was as senseless as trying to catch a rainbow.

The letter marked with the imprint of her ring, Gwenhwyfar ambled to the inner doorway, propped open at this busy hour of the morning, called for the courier, awaiting her order. Arthur had several similar parchments for Natanlius, already in the lad's leather bag. The man saluted smartly, jogged from the Hall to his horse, ready saddled. Arthur's couriers were the best; reliable, innovative men, who handled the responsibility of delivering the King's word with all the faith and expediency entrusted them. A light rain drizzled outside, though the grey skies were lifting; there would be sun by late afternoon. Gwenhwyfar tossed her thicker woollen cloak around her shoulders. She would be dry enough beneath its adequate protection. Her boots and bracae were old, comfortable friends; pointless dressing well when she intended traipsing around muddied fields, checking horses for signs of lameness, cuts and harm.

She crossed to Arthur, engrossed in the first of the pile of legal petitions, his hand cupping the pain of his jaw, placed a light kiss on the crown of his head. 'Get that seen to,' she advised. 'It will only become worse if you do not.'

'My tooth, my business. Go check your horses, woman!'

Gwenhwyfar smiled, kissed him a second time and walked with a light, jaunty step from the chamber. She would not ride down to the fields, for despite the rain it was pleasant enough. The air was fresh, heady with the smells of late spring, the may blossom in full spate, frothing white along the hedgerows that formed boundaries to the horse and cattlefields. From the height of the Caer, the land looked magnificent, even below the colourless grey of spring rain.

Lower down, she walked along the puddled, muddied lane, two head-collars and ropes draped over her shoulder. The hedges were alive with fledgelings, blackbird, thrush, sparrow, the peep-peeping of their demand for attention from tireless parents an orchestra of sound. Gwenhwyfar smiled at the sight of an ambitious young robin attempting to make a meal of a worm three times his own length. Men were working at the hedge a few yards further along, repairing a place where a mare had pushed through. They saluted, greeted her. She walked on, let herself through a gate, crossed diagonally over the expanse of spring-grown grass to the group of yearling colts gathered at the far side. Nine of them, brought into the smaller, easier-watched field for a variety of reasons. One lame, one with a deep cut to his knee, another not putting on the condition he ought. The others, fillies and colts, ran loose in the meadows further out, running free to develop muscle and sinew, strong bone, healthy coat, bold eye and sound wind.

She made soothing noises as she approached, eyeing the overall appearance of the nine – no, eight. Gwenhwyfar ceased walking, counted the fidgeting group again. Definitely eight. The dun with that bruising kick to his stifle was missing. Their field was not large, no more than five acres, well-hedged with hazel and hawthorn, the occasional taller tree dotted in between – the hole was in the next field, not this. To the eastern corner ran a drainage dyke, one of several that criss-crossed much of the farmed areas of the Summer Land. A copse of alder and willow had grown up in this moist corner, provided shade from the heat, shelter from wind and rain. He could be hidden beneath the trees, though he was a well-grown colt, already standing above thirteen hands.

Two of the colts had ventured near her, curious. She petted them, ran her hand along neck, shoulder and rump, inspecting their healing damage with touch and sight. One was almost mended, the other might need a week or two more. At least the cooler weather had not yet brought out the flies. The laying of eggs in open wounds caused such problems come the summer months.

She inspected a third colt, then made her way to the small copse, aware as she neared that no colt dawdled beneath the droop of spring-garlanded branches. She ducked beneath the nearest willow, parting the sweep of new-budded leaves, hurried forward, breath quickening as she found him, trapped, laying on his back, stuck in the ditch.

He must have floundered there a while, for the ground was churned and his coat muddied and drenched from his struggles to rise. Sweat lay dark along his neck and flank, his ears back, eyes rolling, frightened. 'Hush now, good lad, steady, my brave boy.' Gwenhwyfar dropped into the slop of the ditch beside him, the black mud deep beneath the channel of water slurping around her boots. She would need to push him over, roll him, so that he lay more on his side than his back. He might then be able to get his legs under, heave himself up. Shifting the weight of a horse was no easy matter. Getting behind him, she tried to push his quarters, but she had not the strength nor the solidity of a firm footing, for her feet were slipping. Twice she fell down on her knees. She would need help, need to run back to the lane, summon the men.

Gwenhwyfar gasped, startled, alarmed, as a man, ragged, in need of a wash, a shave, jumped into the ditch beside her. His hood had been pulled forward, but had flopped back as he leapt down, his features familiar . . .

'I'll push at his shoulder, you take your end . . . ready, one two, heave!' he instructed.

Three times they pushed, their whole weight and strength behind the need to get the colt onto his feet. The fourth time, it worked. The colt lurched, thrust at the right moment, and was suddenly, with much splashing of water and dripping of mud, up, heaving out the ditch, standing winded, head down, shivering. The man had leapt aside, Gwenhwyfar, her boot stuck in the ooze of mud, was not so fortunate. The colt caught her as he leapt, his hind leg thrashing for a foothold, slamming into her belly, knocking her aside, winded. She fell backward, her head slamming against an overhanging branch, lay there in the black mess of oozing water, dazed, semi-conscious.

She was aware of being lifted, carried. Aware of the sweep of trees

508

around her face as he took her further beneath the trees, carried her through another, small gateway, his pace a loping run, his head ducked low, bent over her.

She tried to talk to him, but the breath had been knocked from her. Tried to tell him that surely he knew he was running the wrong way, did he not remember the Caer was behind them? She could not have made sense, for he did not hear or did not understand. Vaguely, she remembered the officer this morning, making his report to Arthur. Something about a beggar hanging around the horses?

Was this him? Did they think him a beggar? And why was he carrying her so fast and so far from the Caer?

§ XLIX

'Then where in the Bull's name is she?' Arthur was bellowing at the officer of the evening watch. He realized it was unfair to reprimand the man, but life could be a whoreson sometimes and fairness rarely came into the reckoning. Aside, his jaw thundered with a pain that screeched louder than ever any battle-wound had. Without Gwenhwyfar here to sooth his temper, this man could take the brunt. The officer stared ahead, standing smart, at attention. With the gates of the Caer about to close for the night, and the Gathering in the Hall already delayed, the situation was beyond serious. Gwenhwyfar was not within the Caer; nor, it seemed, was she anywhere within close proximity.

Arthur had not been unduly worried in the beginning, when her handmaid had come to report she could not find the Queen. 'She is with the young horses,' he had said with a hint of irritation. Gods, was he expected to follow every move his wife made?

And later, Ider had come to him with the same concern, received the same answer. 'With your pardon, sire, she is not.' Ider had served long enough, and was loyal enough, to contradict his King. Aside, his guts told him something was wrong. Very wrong. He had informed the Pendragon of the muddied and fretful colt the men had found later in the morning. He had been in the ditch, they thought. But no sign of Gwenhwyfar. 'Have you searched the ditch?' Ider had. It was his first thought, that she might have fallen, injured herself.

Another mild search. Nothing. Arthur kicked out at the leg of his desk, swore. Where in hell had she gone? She ought have informed him, not just ridden off. Then a thought. Damn her, she had not taken it into her head to ride to Archfedd, had she? Mithras, if she were to go near that swarming nest of Cerdic's ... dangerous enough having Archfedd and her children remaining over close! 'What horse is missing?' he asked the officer, his words slurring slightly as his tooth grumbled. If she had taken her grey, she could be miles ahead by now, for he was fast, covered the ground well.

'None, lord.' Anticipating the next question, the officer added, 'Her grey is safe stabled.'

Again Arthur swore, more colourful. In his stomach, he knew that something was amiss. A thought. One that had, several times, already lurched into mind. He shoved it firmly back into the recess of impossibility, too abhorrent to contemplate. But it came again. Cerdic had her.

By full dark, the dogs were restless, Arthur had not eaten and, ignoring the hot throb along his jaw, had ordered his own stallion saddled, joined the men in searching the surrounding area, calling her name, holding burning torches and lanterns high, peering beneath hedgerows, along ditches, beside the rivers. A feeble gesture really, for it was too dark to search thoroughly. They would need resume at first light.

Few within the Caer slept that night. Ider paced the palisade walkway, staring out into the hollows of the sleeping Summer Land, starting at the crack of every unfamiliar sound; hoping, each time, that it would be her. Always disappointed.

Arthur made himself go to his bed. He removed his boots, bracae, tunic, drank three goblets of wine straight down. He lay beneath the bed-fur, the dogs stretched out beside him for warmth and comfort. He might have dozed, but he did not sleep. The medical orderly had given him something for the tooth, with the additional advice, unheeded, that it need be removed. All the things that could have happened to her paraded through his mind. He had never held much belief for a god, Christian or otherwise, there never seemed to be a free moment to think about a religion, or a deity. He blasphemed in the name of Mithras and the Bull, occasionally even used Jehovah as witness to his oaths. Soldiering was his religion; the truth, battle; the learning, military tactics. But he found himself praying this night. Quiet, in half-breathed words, softening on a whispered breath through half-parted lips. 'Oh God of all men, let her be not harmed.'

Dawn, sunrise. The hours of night passed slow and achingly hesitant. The Caer faced the new day hushed, dismal. Women standing around in bunched groups, their usual burbling chatter muted and subdued, their children held protective, the youngest resting on hips or clutched in their arms. The men tended their duties with an automation of familiarity. All combined with many solicitous glances towards Hall and King's chamber, alert for news.

Ider strode down from the Caer as dawn freshened into a mildly sunny day, determined to search for some clue, some showing of where she had been, what she had done. Where she had gone. Ider would die for Gwenhwyfar. The intense ache in his heart that she might be suffering was unbearable. She was in trouble, maybe lying injured, or worse, and he could not find her, was unable to help her . . . his worry heightened by the misery of remorse. Yesterday had been a rest day, a rare bonus. He had taken his wife to Lindinis, a treat for her also, to wander around the busy market, finger the cloth, inspect the pottery and pewter, smell the exotic wonder of spices and the intrigue of a multitude of herbs. The pleasurable enjoyment of the day had been shattered on returning home. It was his fault, he felt, though Arthur had attempted to persuade him otherwise. If he had been here, if he had watched over her! Nonsense, his wife had said, Gwenhwyfar had her own mind, would she have expected a bodyguard to go down into the field with her to inspect the yearlings? She knew she was comforting closed ears, for Ider had a separate love for his lady, one that a wife would never overcome. Ider was a good man, a kind father and a faithful husband in all other respects, from him, she had a fine home, well furnished, warm and dry. Two tapestries on the wall, three good cloaks and several gowns to wear. A set of silver spoons and two bowls made from the old red Roman ware – precious items, those bowls, for once such pottery graced every Roman table; now there was little of it left. She had given him, in return, a home and three boys, grown strong into manhood. They were Artoriani now, serving in Bronze Turma. With them, two beautiful daughters, wed also to Artoriani men. She was content. Her only regret that when a wild wind blew, Ider took so much of its weight on his own shoulders.

When he burst into Arthur's chamber an hour after sunrise, excited and agitated, hope had spurted through those who had seen him running. Ider had found important information, but the haggard, grey look on the Pendragon's face that was settled there from more than the raging of toothache, stopped the big man short, curbed his hurried enthusiasm.

'My Lord!' Ider ran to Arthur, dropped to kneel at his feet, his head bowed, tears sliding from beneath his closed eyes. 'Oh my lord, forgive me, I ought have been with her!'

Many – near all – the men held a love for Gwenhwyfar. For three of them, more than love. One, Arthur himself. His love went beyond the bounds of life. He had not remained faithful to her bed, had abandoned her during their numerous squabbles and differences, but throughout, she had been within him, as much a part of his being as was the blood that ran in his veins or the thoughts that jangled in his head. How old had she been when first they met? Twelve, nearing ten and three? One summer short of twoscore years past. A lifetime ago.

The second, Bedwyr. Bedwyr loved Gwenhwyfar, had loved her with an intimacy that ought not have been between a man and the wife of another. That was a happening the Pendragon had forced aside from memory, although it slithered into awareness occasionally. In the murk of a troubled, sleepless night, the faint hiss of its being taunted him. She had not always remained his, but better it had been for her to turn to Bedwyr, a friend rather than a stranger.

And then there was Ider. There was no reason to mistrust Ider, for his love was different. Ider's feelings ran far from the needs of a man. There was no lust, no longing. Gwenhwyfar was his Queen, his sun, moon, his waking and sleeping. That Arthur would trust her life to Ider's keeping was to trivialize a fact.

Arthur laid his hand on Ider's bent head; how to offer comfort when his own fear was lurching into the realm of the ridiculous? What thoughts had gone through his mind during the tormented length of night! Rape, murder, accident. Treachery. Worse, the wondering that she might have gone willingly, stolen away to be with someone else. Bedwyr?

Ider lifted his head, the pain of worry etched deep, raised slightly by new hope. 'Lord,' he said, 'I found this.' He gave Arthur a ragged tear of cloth, woven with shades of red wool. From a cloak? Like the one Gwenhwyfar wore on days when the drizzle spattered from low-pressed clouds. 'It was caught on the brambles beyond the copse of willows. There were footprints also, a man's boot, and scuff marks, as if he had staggered, fallen, while carrying something heavy.'

'Something. Or someone?' Arthur's question was sharp, harsh.

'He circled to the road, keeping to the shadow of the hedge. I found a place where he might have sat, waiting, for the grass was flattened, the flowers bent and broken. Two people, one laying, one sitting. And then, beside the road, laying beneath the mile-marker for Yns Witrin, this.' The second item that Ider handed to Arthur; brought the Pendragon's breath sharp, the nagging of his tooth instant forgotten.

A battered, old gold ring, looped on a plaited strand of Gwenhwyfar's copper hair.

Medraut.

§ L

The mule and cart had been easy to steal from the tavern stables. They were all into the business of drinking inside, the noise of talk and laughter muffling the rumbling of wheels on the cobbles. An anxious moment for Medraut when someone called out to him from the doorway, 'Keep me a tankard waiting – I'm to take a cask of ale up to the Caer!' He tossed back, 'Let the mule do the work, I say, I'm damned if I'm going to break my back!' The man guffawed, went inside. No one queried why the cart turned down the lane not up; few were out in the murk of a damp evening. The Caer gates would be shuttered soon, those of the settlement either warming themselves by their own hearth, or hailing the night with drink inside the tavern.

He needed the cart for Gwenhwyfar. He had carried her some way, but she was heavy, his own feet blistered and sore from ill-fitting boots. What it was to be a King's son in a King's Caer, with gold enough to pay for quality boots to be made to fit the size of his feet. Another anxious moment, later on, when he heard horses and men's voices. Of course she would be missed, they would be searching for her. He had to think quickly, act fast. A gate ahead, into the mares' field, urged the stubborn mule through, brought the cart up against the high hedge on the far side, closed the gate. No moon risen yet – God's truth, a few days only to fullness and then it would be waning. The horses came nearer, men were calling for Gwenhwyfar. Medraut prayed they would not have the dogs with them at night. Recognized his father's voice. Almost, he summoned the courage to run out, call at Arthur, urge him to listen, but they had passed by, the moment was lost. He would need wait a while, safe in the darkness. The searching, surely, could not last through the night, and Gwenhwyfar was comfortable where he had left her.

Come sunrise, the hill of Yns Witrin sat dark against the new-bright day. He had travelled through the night, had bullied the mule to trot, had searched around the edge of the lake, seeking a way onto the Tor. There were paths beneath the gently rippling surface, he had heard, but where they were, where they lay, only God and Morgaine, he assumed, knew. He found something on the far side, where the lane began to slope down into the Christian settlement, an upward path overgrown and shrouded by the profusion of spring. It would serve well enough, though he would need abandon the cart.

Gwenhwyfar lay motionless, her eyes closed, skin pale. He regretted the need to have tied her wrists and feet, using the halter ropes, regretted

513

this need to take her in such a shameful way, but he must speak with Arthur, had to come away from the Caer where there would be men to overpower him. The planning had come to him so quickly in those moments after the colt had struggled from the ditch. She had lain, breathing, but unmoving, not answering him, blood trickling from the back of her head. Unconscious. He had lifted her, intending to seek help, had crouched beneath the trees on seeing men in the distance of the next field. How would he prove that it had not been himself who had hurt her? Who would believe, at first sighting, that this was the result of accident, not his own action? From there, the plan had seeped into his brain. He could take her somewhere, shelter her until she awoke, then she could tell the truth of the thing. There was an old tumbledown goatherd's shed a mile or two to the north, he had passed several nights there already. It would suit his purpose.

When she did wake, as evening dipped into the first stars of the night, she was dazed and incoherent, drifting in and out of sleep. She would be missed by now, the alarm raised. Only the one solution, take her to safer ground and summon Arthur to fetch her, then talk with him, make him see that his son Medraut was no traitor. It seemed simple enough, especially once he had the cart and was making way along the road northward.

The cart he left beside the lane, turned the mule loose with hobbles so that it might not stray too far. He carried Gwenhwyfar again, pushing through the tangle of bush and high-grown bramble, disturbing the heady scent of the may blossom that burst in clouds of pollen around him, making him sneeze, his eyes water, nasal passages sting. Gwenhwyfar groaned as he lay her down beside the man-height Stone at the very top of the hill. Her skin was cold, a light tinge disfiguring her lips. He covered her with his own cloak, ragged though it was. The wind was strong up here, he would need move her a little down the slope.

The Tor of Yns Witrin, where God had not placed His footstep, nor caressed with His smile. Yns Witrin, silent, save for the song of the wind and the mournful cry of the kestrel. The Summer Land lay spread like a patched blanket beneath, the shadow of cloud skimming over the water-shining levels. Was this what it was like to soar in the sky like a bird? To feel the wind lift your hair, buffet around you? To be King over all in your sight! An immense thrill of power unfolded around Medraut, a strength that swelled behind and within him. The air was pure and light, the wind danced and twisted at his feet, scurrying through the grass, rippling it into waves of motion, before hurrying off up the valley, leaving behind a half-breathed sigh.

Up here, Medraut felt both invulnerable but humble, brave but scared.

514

Wise, while knowing nothing. There was a presence here, on the height of the Tor, a feeling that if you turned around quick enough you would see a movement, lost out the corner of your eye. The swirl of a cloak, the shining sun catching on a sword blade. Nothing tangible, but there all the same. The laugh of a woman, the footstep of a man. The perfume of the Goddess; or the hand of the god?

Yns Witrin, where he had come into being, where the Goddess, for whatever reason, had breathed the touch of life into the making of a child. A son. Medraut.

Unexpected, a powerful clutch of grief stabbed into his stomach. He crumpled to his knees, head bent into his hands, the sobs shuddering through his body. What a damned fool he had been, what a fool he still was! 'Oh God,' he cried, lifting his tear-streaked face to the cloud-mottled sky, 'I am a lost ship, drifting on an endless sea of despair. Is this my punishment then, for the wrong of my birthing? How do I right that wrong? Lord, hear me! Help me, show how I may prove to my father on earth that I have love for only him, that I would not betray him!'

Medraut leapt to his feet, his heart lurching in startled fear as a voice behind him, said, scathingly. 'I suggest you make a start by untethering me. I am not a goat.'

§ LI

The courier rode into the Caer a while after Arthur had ridden out, heading north. They gave him a fresh horse, sent him on at the gallop, his shouts reaching the ears of the King's guard at the same time as they heard the drumming of hooves. Arthur reined Brenin in, the young animal snorting contempt at the exciting pace being interrupted. Ider, riding beside the King, clenched his jaw. What now? Already they had been delayed by the blathering of the tavern-keeper, whining about the loss of his mule and cart. That the beggar had stolen it seemed evident, and the identity of him only a guessed conclusion, but one accepted by all within the Caer.

'My lord!' The courier brought his lathered horse to a slithering halt, the man as blown as the animal. Brenin tossed his head, side-stepped. 'Sir, message from Caer Morfa, from Lord Natanlius.'

Arthur heeled Brenin in a circle, cursed the animal's impatience.

'My lord believes the Saxons are making ready to march. He requests the Artoriani, immediately.'

The stream of profanities from the Pendragon made even Ider, who was no stranger to the crudities of language, raise an eyebrow. Arthur rode Brenin away from the men, dismounted, stood a few yards distant, staring ahead across the swift-shadowed levels of the Summer Land. The grass lay in its patched carpet of variegated greens, spring-grown, lush, spreading between the small copses and pockets of trees. Willow, ash, alder, the occasional elm. Hollows of water lay in pools and runnels, dazzle-glistening beneath the brilliance of the sun overhead, sailing the vastness of the wide, cloud-shuffling sky. The land of seven rivers; sluggish streams that carried away the winter flooding. In summer it smelt of silted marsh, drying grass and watermint. A kestrel hovered half a mile ahead.

The Tor brooded in shadow against the clouding sky. Yns Witrin, where Arthur had once started a life. And where, by all that was sacred and beloved of him, this day he would end that same living!

He mounted, hauled Brenin around, decision made. 'Ider, and you two men' – he pointed – 'will ride on with me. The rest of you, return to the Caer. You,' he ordered his Decurion forward, 'issue my command to the officer of the day. The Artoriani are to be ready to ride by noon.'

Four hours.

'Courier!'

'Aye, lord?'

'Ride on to Aquae Sulis. Give my orders that Bedwyr and his escort are to return immediately.'

'Aye, my lord.'

They rode in silence, Ider as before, beside the Pendragon, the two Artoriani behind, their swords loose in the scabbard, eyes watchful, ears listening. One crossed himself when a hare darted across the road, fled, ears laid along its back as it sped away. A symbol of superstition, the hare. It was the hare who carried the souls of the dead into the Underworld. The kestrel again, away to the left. When he plummeted downward there came the faint scream of his capture. Not the hare. The soldier was glad, for the death of a hare meant that another soul was left to wander, desolate and aimless, lost in the painful world of mortal men.

They found the cart and the mule, knew then that they had come to the right place. Arthur had never doubted it. The message Medraut had left him had been plain enough.

The Pendragon rode further along the base of the Tor, to where the lake lay, calm and peaceful, crinkled by a few, wind-brushed ripples, shadowed by the reflection of the hill. He dismounted, gave the reins to one of the men with the command that they were to wait. Ider he beckoned to follow.

'Let us hope the paths have not altered,' Arthur said grimly as he

516

stepped into the water, a gasp of protest leaving one of the men, waiting behind. Arthur glared at him, made another step forward, the water level covering no higher over his boot than his ankle. 'I advise you to step where I do, Ider, else you are likely to be up to your neck in it.'

Once, he made a wrong turn, floundered to his knee in water, Ider reaching to grab hold his arm, pull him to safety. Easy enough to follow, the firm path that meandered beneath the surface. Easy, if you knew where to look. The twist of reeds, a scrawny bush, the lighter colour of water against dark. The occasional glimpse of the silted path. Morgaine had shown him how, all those years past.

At the far side, within the cluster of trees, was the skeleton of a dwelling-place, one wall crumbled, the roof fallen in, no door, signs of where boar and other animals had pushed a way in, searching for shelter or food. To the left, a patch where once there might have been a garden.

Ider said nothing as they began to climb the height of the Tor. That the dwelling had been the place of the Lady needed no confirming. How Arthur had known his way across the mystery of the lake needed no asking.

The climb was steep and soon they were breathless, their bodies leaning forward, steps short, boots digging into the slope and deer-grazed grass.

The wind hit them with the force of a thrown battleaxe. Arthur had expected it, but not Ider, who staggered, slipped, his boot skidding, his leg pulling from under him. Arthur made no move to help him regain balance, for he had not seen. His eyes were ahead, narrowed and angry. The Stone, darkened from this angle, its shadow stretching like a pointing finger. Beside it, Medraut, sitting, knees bent, head bowed, arms cradling. And before him, Gwenhwyfar, standing, hair and cloak foaming about her. She lifted her head as Arthur appeared over the edge of the Tor, her eyes meeting with his. Her smile, as she saw him, so beautiful. His relief and hers washing with the force of a full spring-flood tide.

§ LII

For a moment, the discovery that Gwenhwyfar was well and unharmed was so intense that Arthur felt nothing beyond the gladness of thankful relief. He whispered a brief prayer to whatever god had protected her, and acknowledged the presence of the caring Goddess. And then Medraut moved. A small movement, he raised his head, but it was enough to shatter that benign feeling of goodwill. Arthur hurtled forward, roaring,

Ider coming a pace behind. Gwenhwyfar screamed for them to stop, Medraut scrambled to his feet, undecided whether to run or face the fury bearing down on him. He opted to run, but it was too late, Arthur was upon him.

The brawl was swift and furious, the blows mostly coming from Arthur, Medraut swung a few punches, but as his father was the stronger, better man, he resorted to ducking and protecting, as well he could, his head and face. Blood was already splashing from his nose. Gwenhwyfar attempted to wrestle Arthur away, clinging to his arm, hauling at him, shrieking for him to stop, but so great was his anger he barely heard, tossed her aside. With Ider she had more influence; the big man, about to hit out at Medraut, responded to her bawled command to leave it, to stand down. Expression a mask of taut passion, his fists clenching, limbs quivering. Difficult to obey but, breathing hard, he backed away.

Gwenhwyfar yanked his sword from its scabbard, laid it about Arthur using the flat of the blade, beating at his back, his legs. 'Stop it!' she screamed. 'For my sake, damn you, leave him!'

Arthur's fist connected with Medraut's jaw, sending him spinning. Dazed, the younger man fell, tumbled, rolled a few yards down the slope of the Tor, where he lay, sprawled like a squashed spider, winded and fearful, expecting the barrage of blows to continue. The Pendragon was leaping after him, found himself toppling, Ider's sword in Gwenhwyfar's capable hands tripping him. She thrust her body on top of his, as he rolled to his back and, dropping the sword, put all her weight into pressing his shoulders into the grass with her hands. 'Stop it Arthur!' she commanded. 'Do as I say!'

His nostrils were flaring, breath coming in great, unsteady gasps. Blood trickled from his mouth. Fury spurred, red hot, from his eyes.

'Aside a headache, I am unharmed. This has been all a mistake.' Gwenhwyfar dug her nails into Arthur's shoulder, denting the leather of his tunic. 'Arthur, listen to me!'

The Pendragon shut his eyes, filled his lungs with air, let the shuddering breath ease from his pounding body. With a groan he raised his arms, encircled Gwenhwyfar, bringing her close, holding her tight, so very tight, his face in her hair savouring her nearness, her scent, her life. As she returned that embrace of possessive relief, she felt his body judder, relax. The fighting was over. Now would come the accusation and the shouting, unless she intervened.

'I have come to no harm,' she said, again reassuring him. 'Medraut needed to speak with you. Things,' she pulled away, sat astride him, 'became out of control.' As she wiped at the blood on his chin with her fingers, she explained, briefly and in concise words, Medraut's muddled and desperate reasons for bringing her here. She opened Arthur's mouth to inspect from where the blood came. 'He wanted to warn you of Cerdic, but did not know how to go about approaching you. You have lost a tooth,' she smiled, added, 'It is a sad day when a son cannot speak with his father because the father has too much anger to listen. We are all too hasty to accept the first-made conclusions, no matter how wrong they are. Too slow to consider an alternative explanation.'

Raising his hand to investigate his gum, Arthur swore. He rolled Gwenhwyfar from him, tapped the tip of her nose with one finger, limped to his feet and strolled towards Medraut, who was tentatively scrambling upright, ready to bolt if need be.

'You boar's whelp,' Arthur growled, 'if you are damn well going to hit me, you could at least try to remove the right bloody tooth!'

Standing with head bent, hands bunched and gripping his tunic, blood dribbling from nose to chin, dripping onto the toe of his boot, Medraut knew not what to say or do. He had lurched from being the fool to a full-fledged imbecile. His father ought take up that sword laying naked on the wind-quivering grass and rip the blade through his throat. His death would be no loss to anyone. He raised his head, his eyes, face, expression, sodden with grief. 'I have been with my half-brother,' he stated, his voice cracking, dry. 'I went to him, deliberate. At first to hurt you, to make you realize that I was someone to be valued, to make you see that you needed me. And then I realized that you never would, because,' he swallowed down the pain of truth, spread his hands, pleading, asking for forgiveness. 'Because you do not.'

White, puffed clouds had been straggling across the sky, shading the spring colours of the Summer Land into muted greens and pale yellows. The lake, down beneath the Tor, lay dark, brooding, in its overpowering shadow; the insistent wind, up here on the height, petulant and chill. When the sun shuffled from behind the covering, a glow, a warm, mother's smile, embraced the world, the light catching against the Stone, casting shadows among the swirled, carved patterns.

'How could you live with the shame of knowing that I was born of your own sister?' The cry came, anguished, from Medraut's heart.

All his life Arthur had found the need to hide feelings behind a shielding armour of pretence. Pretence that beatings and sneering words did not hurt, pretence that he did not care if he were called bastard-born. Pretence that he was in control, in command. How could he pretend to his own son? How could he lie about Morgaine? He did not feel shame, because it did not matter to him. Relationships were only wrong to those who believed in Christian sin. Arthur was no Christian, but he could

519

not, for all his lack of belief and indifference, hurt Medraut any more than he already had.

'There are three methods of bringing discredit to a man, Medraut. One, by accusing him of adultery, the second by calling him bastard-born. The third, branding him as a coward. There have been plenty who have tossed the first two at me, but they have failed to bring me down because I am not the third. And then there is a fourth, for those who follow the Christian way of thinking. The accusation of incestuous birth. 'Tis only the priests of the Christian God who seem afeared of it. Happen they are right to, happen not.' Arthur drew breath. Gods, he had made a mess of both his living sons. He ought never have allowed Winifred to keep Cerdic. Morgaine ought never have birthed this one.

'On my life, and that of Gwenhwyfar's, I swear to you, son, that your mother had no knowing of her father. She was born after Uthr's death, those who say that we shared the same father have no proof of it, 'tis speculation – and stirring of trouble. There is only one who could say for certain, your grandmother, and she is long dead.'

'Then,' Medraut answered hesitantly, 'it may not be true?'

Arthur shrugged. 'That is for you to decide, what is truth, what are lies. Who would have reason to tell the one, or the other.'

Medraut turned away, stood looking out over the expanse that was the Summer Land. Had he been so much of the fool all this while? There was much to think on, much to decide and accept, much that he ought outface about himself. He swung around, turned back to his father.

'I have decided to go north,' he announced. He had not, but it seemed a reasonable enough thing to say. 'I came to tell that Cerdic is to march with the waning moon. He has many men. He intends to take Coed Morfa for his own.'

Arthur bent, took up Ider's sword, held the blade before him, watching as the ripple of the sun swarmed up and down its crafting. He tossed it, caught it again by the hilt, handed it to its owner. Ider threaded it back into the protection of its sheepskin-lined scabbard.

What more could the Pendragon say? He had never meant to hurt the boy, but Medraut had not been Llacheu, or Gwydre, or Amr. He was chance-born to a woman who had beguiled a man. Just over there, in the hollow of the Tor. With the Goddess sublimely watching and the Christian God frowning, no doubt, Arthur had lain with Morgaine, believing the act was as a gift to the Mother. Offer the beginning of one life to save another. How the gods must laugh at the simplistic trust of mortal men!

He looked away, much as Medraut had, out over the Summer Land, his land, to where the purple spread of hills hid the Caer that was his stronghold. It was open up here, uncluttered, unconfined. No walls, no darkness.

'I would have my body brought here,' he said, unexpectedly, 'to where my spirit can watch over that which means so much to me.' He loved this land, had fought so hard, so long, to make it good, to bring peace. Was all of it to be destroyed by his own son?

Cerdic, turned sour through the jealousy and ambition of his mother. Medraut, abandoned and ignored by the selfishness of his. And Arthur, the father, had stood by and rammed it all home with the toe of his boot. What more could he say to this one, who stood empty and battered before him?

'Lad, I cannot expect but to be what I am, who I am. No more can you, or Cerdic, or anyone. Our fates are there, before us, woven by the Three. All we can hope is that we can cling somehow with our bruised and torn fingers to the tangled threads that are life. And make some good out of the torn remnant that is left us.'

Arthur lightly placed his arm around Gwenhwyfar's waist, led her down the slope of the Tor, going the gentler way, following the path where Medraut had brought her up. Ider, a snarl on his mouth at Medraut as he passed, followed. To his mind, he would have cut the bastard's throat and had done with it.

'Father!' Medraut ran a few paces after them, stopped as Arthur turned, inquiring. 'What of Cerdic!'

Was the death blow any the better for being sharp and swift, or lunged from behind?

'Cerdic? I already know of Cerdic. The Artoriani will be ready to ride as soon as I return to Caer Cadan.' He half-saluted his son, hurried Gwenhwyfar away.

Medraut stood, blank, alone with only the sound and tug of the wind.

It was for nothing then, all this. His father had already known, and his stupidity had added delay.

He would go north. Why not? They must have fools in the north. One more may not be overmuch noticed.

§ LIII

Arthur pushed Brenin into a hand canter – it would be no use encouraging him faster. With eleven miles to cover and another ride at the end of it, the horses would be finished before the Caer came in sight. Especially while carrying extra weight.

Strange, after all these years with him, as friend, mistress, then wife, Gwenhwyfar had never ridden double behind Arthur. It was not an unpleasant experience. The only slight discomfort was the press of the saddle against her groin, but to counter that, Brenin had a smooth pace and a broad rump; she felt secure and, with her arms around Arthur's waist, wonderfully safe.

'You lied,' she said into his ear. 'To Medraut.'

Guiding the horse past a few ruts, Arthur made no immediate answer. Then, 'What did I say that was a lie? Morgaine was born after Uthr's death. None of us can be certain of her conceiving. There is a suspicion, that is all. I may not have told Medraut all the truth, but I did not, for once in my life, lie.' They cantered on another mile, then he asked. 'Would you have minded, if I had?'

Gwenhwyfar said nothing. Did she mind about Morgaine, about Medraut? Would it be the truth to say she did not?

'Are you well?' he called when she made no reply, his voice floating past her ear, carried by the wind.

Briefly she tightened her grip, smiled as his hand reassuringly touched hers. Aye, she was well, now.

'I have acquired yet another lump on my head, that is all,' she said, then laughed. 'I ought wear a war cap more often!'

'You ought take a guard with you!' Arthur growled back. Ahead, a bridge spanning a narrow, meandering river and an ox-cart laden with timber blocking it, one wheel shattered and buckled. Arthur drew Brenin to a jog-trot, assessing the situation as he approached. It would be cleared; ten, mayhap fifteen minutes. Too long. He heeled the horse from the road, across the parallel drainage ditch and pushing him into canter, set him to jump the river. Deeper than it was wide, a spread of only a few feet, it was an easy leap, for Brenin had the agility of a cat. Gwenhwyfar squealed as they landed on the far side, her balance toppling. Arthur put his arm behind to steady her, but she had already adjusted herself. She glanced behind, saw Ider's horse clear the ditch; behind him, the two Artoriani. Medraut had declined to ride with them, opting instead to bring the mule. 'You need your men,' he had explained to Arthur, 'more than you do me.' To that, Arthur had no disagreement. To need his men more than his son ... how deep could the truth hurt!

'Forgive me!' Medraut had called as he stood by the Stone at the height of the Tor, watching them ride away, small figures against a wide land. He would send payment as soon as he could for the mule and cart, but he would never go back. Not to Caer Cadan, not to his father. There was nothing to go back to, nothing to go back for.

Arthur had known it, had seen it there in his son's eyes – had known it before Medraut had realized it for himself. Would they meet again in this world? He ought have said something, embraced his son, given him blessing to travel safe along the road ahead, but he had remained silent, just walked away, down the path from the Tor, back to the horses. He had left the ring, though, that battered gold ring with Gwenhwyfar's hair still threaded through it, had fastened it to the mule cart. With it, a dagger, one that Arthur had carried for many years. Medraut would remember it from those days in Gaul. As a child he had often asked to see it, touch it, the brightness of its deadly blade, its jewelled hilt. *'Will I have a dagger like it one day?'* Oh, Arthur remembered him asking that! *'Aye, lad,'* he had answered, *'when you swear oath of homage, your chosen lord will, no doubt, give you such a weapon as your own. But if you do not remain loyal to him, you must either use it on yourself, or use it against the man you called lord.'*

§ LIV

The sweep of the rain-grey marsh and the permeating tang from the estuary were the Artoriani's companions. Caer Morfa and the inland run of the sea lay less than three miles to their left, with the Terste river and its tributary sisters behind. They had distinctly little room to manoeuvre here – Cerdic's intention by choosing this ground so close to the rise of the Great Wood.

Arthur could have waited, forced him to move, but this suited well enough. It could have been a better place for a battle, but he had fought in worse, and those tight-packed oaks and regal beeches would be of hindrance to both sides.

The woods had seemed so content at sunrise. The scent of leaf mould, dew-wet grass and wind-teased leaves; the gentle swirl of a light morning mist evaporating beneath the warming embrace of the sun. While they waited to move forward, Arthur had watched a tree-creeper jerking up a trunk, busy jabbing for spiders among the minute cracks of the bark. And then Cerdic's army had stepped forward from between the sentinel trees, locked their shields into the formation of the shield-wall, and cast their first introductory foray of arrows and spears. The nesting birds had flown, abandoning their young families, the tree-creeper had been brushed from her breakfast-hunting by the flank of a horse passing too close to the trunk. Her wing damaged, she had fluttered helpless beneath the surge of hooves. The first death.

Cerdic had chosen his ground well, Arthur had to acknowledge him that. The Saex fought on foot, men standing firm behind their shield-wall, the front rank the better armed, shield overlocking shield, spears ready for the horses, bowmen to left and right. He had the advantage of the high ground, with dense woodland behind.

Three hours after the first tentative steps into battle. The Pendragon would need send his men in again, to charge up that hill, set their tiring strength on that damned wall of men and shields a fourth time. Cerdic must have lost as many men as he, for the British bowmen were skilled at their craft, and the damage to that front line must be taking its toll of wounded. He must come around behind the Saex, break their courage and solidity.

Cerdic stood far enough to the rear of his shield-wall to be safe, but near enough to be seen by his men, to be a part of this ragged business. His hearth-guard were gathered close, their shields already prickled by British arrows, their Saxon short swords and heavy, sharp-bladed axes prominent, ready. Just in case, they told him, although they assured him with nodding heads and wide, confident grins, that the wall was strong, would not waver. 'Let the Pendragon set his horses at us, let them tire themselves coming and recoming up that hill if that is what they wish to do. We will be here to meet them, and send them away again!'

This battle was going well, better than that last disaster with his father. Cerdic closed his eyes briefly. Woden forgive him, but that battle at Portus Chester had been an experience he would not wish to face again! He had been unprepared then, minor skirmishes, raiding, the defence of one's own stronghold – ah, all that was different from this, the real, whole, bloody thing! He wiped sweat from his forehead; he was four and thirty years of age, already his hair was thinning on top – gods, but he hated all this! He resisted the impulse to step backward as a man, tumbling from the affray, fell, blood and spittle gurgling from an arrow through his throat. Vomit rose in Cerdic's throat, he swallowed, forced himself to ignore the man's open, staring eyes. So many of his Saxons were already dead or maimed, but, as they had said, the shield-wall was holding. He had good officers now, experienced men like Port and his sons, and the two newcomers, Stuf and Wihtgar, men who knew their job and did it well. The Saxons had every chance of victory, high reward had been promised to all those who survived the day. And for those who died in glory, an honoured welcome by the gods.

If the shield-wall held and if his ships were unopposed at the landing place along from Caer Morfa. Cerdic planted his feet wider, eased his sword from its scabbard. The three ships would bring his Saxons in, behind the Artoriani, cut off their rear, trap them between the two armies . . . Cerdic shouted encouragement to the men ahead of him as another charge by the Artoriani began to come up the hill towards them.

Arthur had judged it time to change tactics. It was obvious that the wall of men and shields up on top of that hill was not going to fall as things stood. To damage a solid structure, you needed to weaken its least strong point. He sent the horses in again, relying on the strict discipline of the Artoriani, and their superb ability as horsemen and soldiers. A fighting machine that could take into account every required nuance of strategy.

The horses jog-trotted, easing into a hand canter, facing the wall head-on. They would gallop, release into the energy of the charge within the last twenty or so yards only, for the high ground was taking its toll of energy and impetus. The bowmen would hold their flights of arrows above their heads until the last moment, until the horses sprang into their full, powerful pace. The Saxons were ready, braced, their spears bristling from between and beneath the line of shields, their structure immovable, again awaiting the impact.

The line shuddered, wavered, almost toppled – for the horses had changed direction in mid-gallop a few yards from the shields, a manoeuvre fantastic to watch, brilliantly completed. Within those few strides the Artoriani wheeled to left and right, their charging, strung-out line compacting into two groups, the pace barely pausing. The Saxons staggered as the assault hit hard at each wing, where the more vulnerable stood, where the line was thinnest, least protected, and the Artoriani hammered through, breaking the line of men as easily as if they were nothing but a stand of golden corn. Saxons ran to defend their flank, the centre stretching, less densely packed. And another wave of Artoriani came up the hill at the gallop, straight for that thinning centre, leaving no time for the Saxons to regroup, to rethink. A swift assault executed by a man who had spent more years at war than his son and his Saxon officers combined.

The hearth-guard clustered tighter around Cerdic, the fighting rapidly swelling to hand-to-hand, infantry against cavalry, sword clashing against sword, an axe blade, glinting in the sun before it swooped down, was raised again, bloodied, ragged with sinew.

'Do we withdraw?' Cerdic yelled, frantically signalling his guard closer.

'Na, my lord, we can fight them off!'

Woden protect me! Cerdic's mind shrilled, *How can we fight off this many!*

Arthur was ready to send in the reserves, the last two turmae of Artoriani and the bowmen, their weapons exchanged for the sword and spear. He had Brenin gathered on a tight rein, his hand lifting to signal the move forward. A galloper burst from the trees behind, causing Brenin to rear and plunge, Arthur brought him around, cursed. A courier, face bloodied, an arrow quivering deep within his horse's flank.

'My lord!' he shouted, anxious, near to tears, desperate. 'They are attacking Caer Morfa – three ships, many men. The stronghold is in danger of falling!'

§ LV

All timbers were of oak, the palisade, the Hall, dwellings, only the roofing, the reed thatching, burnt with a fury. They raked down what they could from the Hall and the more important buildings. Dwelling-places could be re-built, roofs re-thatched. Lives were the more important, and the need to secure the gateways. If the Saex broke through . . .

Gwenhwyfar smiled encouragingly at Archfedd. Both knew the smile and the encouragement were false. Gwenhwyfar had seen enough of battle to know this one was desperate, and that Caer Morfa was screaming its death chant. Her daughter had never seen fighting, not skirmish or raiding, close too. Aye, she had witnessed the aftermath, the pain of the wounded, the keening for the dead, but this, the desperation of having your home, your family, friends, your land, your life threatened by the attacking forces of savagery, this was new to her. New and terrifying.

They were in the Hall – roofless, for the thatch of the highest roof had been among the first to catch beneath the fire-arrows. As with any stronghold under siege, it was to the Hall that the women and children came, to the Hall that the men brought the wounded. 'Da will come, will he not?' Archfedd had asked, an hour or so past, as she had patched a minor arrow wound to Natanlius's shoulder. 'If he can, he will,' her husband assured her, placing a light kiss on her forehead before he went out again to join his men at the palisade. 'I have sent word, three of my best men, one will get through to the Pendragon, I am sure.' Comforting words of hope. For himself as much as her.

Archfedd had glanced at her mother for confirmation. She had resented Gwenhwyfar coming from Caer Cadan so hurriedly yesterday, saying tartly that she could look to herself and her family. Was so glad, now, that she had her mother's strength to shore up the sagging spirits of all those within the Caer. Including her own.

'If he can,' Gwenhwyfar had agreed. 'Aye, your father will come if he can.' Knowing he would not, because he fought with Cerdic those few miles away, up where the marshes washed against the rise of high ground, up where the open sky dipped to meet the wind-browsed trees of oak and ash and elm and beech. Up where he might himself be laying dead.

Gwenhwyfar finished bandaging a man's leg. The arrow had plunged deep, but fortune had been on his side, it was a wound that would heal. Movement behind her, she knew it would be Ider. She turned, brushing hair from her eyes with the back of her hand, leaving a bloody streak smeared along her forehead.

'I need more bandaging,' she said, starting to walk to where the children were rolling strips of linen. She indicated he was to walk with her. 'Well?' she asked.

Ider's hand was gripped tight on his sword pommel, his expression grim. He jerked his eyes towards another group of children, younger, sitting huddled with a few of the women. Among them, three boys, babes, the eldest a handful of weeks short of his second birthing day; for the second child, this was the day of his first full year in the world of men. They had planned a feasting for him, with honeyed cakes and pastries shaped into animals. The third, aye well, he was nought but three weeks into life, his only concern the milk that warmed his belly and the love of his mother's arms. Grim, Ider said, 'We ought consider them, my lady. Look to their safety.' Archfedd's sons. Arthur's future heirs.

Gwenhwyfar stacked a bundle of bandages in the crook of her arm, rubbed the cheek of the serious-faced little girl who had handed them to her. 'Be brave, sweetheart.' The girl smiled back at Gwenhwyfar, trusting her. She liked the pretty lady with the soft, calming voice, did not like the noises that penetrated into the Hall. Her Da was out there, Mam had said, fighting to keep them all from the knives of the Saxons. Gwenhwyfar made her way to the far end of the Hall, to where wounded men patiently awaited the attention of the medical orderlies, Ider at her side. She wanted no one to think she was in earnest discussion.

'Is it desperate?' she asked.

He nodded. 'It is. Half? One hour? If help does not come, the gates will not hold.'

She piled the bandages with others, asked where she might help next.

What to do? Wait or go? Was there any choice? Gwenhwyfar knelt beside a young lad. He could be no more then ten and three summers. He had burns to the side of his face, his arms; most of his body was charred and reddened, the skin blistered and peeling. He was in great pain, yet he smiled at her. 'The Pendragon will come soon, will he not? And when he does, I would like to see him beat the balls from their arses!'

'When he has finished with Cerdic, aye, he will come to our aid.' Gwenhwyfar took his left hand in hers, held it, a small part of him that was whole and clean. She sat there for a few, long minutes, easing his pain, by letting it flow into her. She was glad that he would not know that she had lied to him.

Ider tore a tapestry from the wall, its edges charred, its bright-coloured hunting scene smoke-blackened and spoilt. His teeth bit into his lip as he covered the dead boy with its once splendid glory. No lad in the spring of his life deserved to die in such a way.

Gwenhwyfar remained on her knees, looking nowhere in particular, looking everywhere around that Hall, at the wounded men and the frightened women and children. They would be safe enough, the Saxons were not generally known as mindless butchers. The able men, that would be a different matter, but a man knew his destiny when a fight began. For herself . . . She mattered not. She had lived her life, and when death marched nearer, you almost came to welcoming its shadowed presence. Archfedd and her three born sons, though, what would Cerdic have done to them? Gwenhwyfar closed her eyes, her hands clasped in brief murmur of prayer. What barbarism would be expected of a son who took an axe to his mother and to the woman who had borne him his son?

'Can we get them out?' she asked.

Ider held his hand to her, helped her rise. He nodded, once. 'Natanlius wishes it. As do I. We will open the gates and allow you to run.'

She wanted to scream no; she wanted to insist that her place was here, with these women and their precious families. Wanted to, but did not, for above being a woman and a mother, she was a queen, and her duties lay beyond the caring for one isolated stronghold. She need put the safety of the King's grandsons above all else.

'See to it,' she said. 'We will be beside the gates, as soon we can.'

'Not long,' Ider answered, laying his hand on her arm, his anguished eyes meeting hers. She knew then that the plan did not involve him coming with her. 'Do not leave it too long.'

She touched his face with her hand, a caress that would say so much more than any word. 'God keep you,' she said, and walked quickly away. There was too much to do, in too short a time. The grieving would have to come later.

§ LVI

They took the swiftest horses, Gwenhwyfar her grey, Archfedd a chestnut descended from her father's Onager. With them, a turma of men, thirty in all. It would deplete the numbers holding the Caer, but it would not hold much longer. Thirty more men for Arthur, assuming he was surviving the fight those few miles inland.

'No goodbyes,' Natanlius said to Archfedd. He reached up, ruffled his second son's hair. The lad sat before his mother, eyes wide and frightened, his arms tight around her waist, ropes securing him to her as added precaution. They would be riding fast when those gates opened, they could not guide horses to fight their way out and also hold onto the boys. Gwenhwyfar had the eldest, Constantine. A Decurion sheltered the baby.

The roar beyond the closed gates was increasing, the flames licking at the resistance of the oak timbers, billowing acrid smoke, spreading through the piles of brush and carcasses, both animal and man; the stink of burning covered everything.

'No goodbyes,' Natanlius said again. He squeezed Archfedd's knee, took a last look at her. They called her the Lioness, many of his people of Caer Morfa, as a term of respect. There were a few from further away who thought her too headstrong, too determined to stand firm for the things that her father advocated; mostly, those of the Church. Those few used the title as a curse, but she did not object. It added to the remembering that she was daughter to the Pendragon.

'No goodbyes,' she repeated back. She tried to smile, but the tears would not stop coming. They had been so happy together, this short while.

Natanlius would have swept her off that horse, called a halt to this whole, foolish idea. He turned, and went quickly to the head of the phalanx of men waiting this side of the gate, with swords drawn, spears ready. This way, she had a chance. The other, for her and his sons there would be nothing except slavery or a cruel death.

Ider took his place beside him. There would be fierce fighting when those gates opened, they would need the best men. He glanced around, only the once, at Gwenhwyfar. She had hurriedly dressed herself as they would expect a warrior Queen to be. Her red cloak, white padded under tunic, with the thicker, protective leather and bronze studded tunic above. Leather doe-hide bracae. Boots. She had her sword out, a dagger ready in her belt, a shield. Her hair, she wore tied at her neck, a thick single plait of grey-streaked copper. Around her neck, the royal torque.

She caught that glance of Ider's, raised her sword, with the blade touched to her forehead in salute.

And the gates were open, fast, hurling inward, the men leaping forward, screaming, yelling, to meet the Saxons who rocked backwards at the unexpected manoeuvre. They cut a swathe through, those brave British, scything a path through the formidable press of the Saex.

Virtually every man from inside that stronghold, formed a protective barrier, and, not understanding what was happening, the Saex reacted too late. The burst of horses thundered through and away. The Saex slammed their spears at them, tried to rush forward, cut them off, a few arrows were loosened. One or two horses were hit, brought down, their riders hacked, unmercifully, the horses butchered. But they got away, Gwenhwyfar and Archfedd. And two of Arhur's grandsons.

§ LVII

What did he do? Damn it, what could he do! The Artoriani had broken through that shield-wall. One more heavy thrust and they would have them all running, or dying. But he could not let Caer Morfa fall, not while ... Arthur thrust the protest from his mind. He was a soldier, a battle-hardened war-lord, could not let personal love come into this thing. Gwenhwyfar and Archfedd had insisted on staying. They knew the risk they took, knew what could lay before them. All the same ...

He had the reserves and two turmae to send in up that hill. Yellow Turma and his own, the King's Troop. A good leader needed the ability to think quickly, to change plan, alter direction with fast-made decisions, for the sway of battle could alter as swiftly as a peregrine's dive. He yelled for Yellow Turma's Decurion to come forward, told him briefly, concisely, that he was to ride to the stronghold, see what help he could, reasonably, give. 'Reasonably,' Arthur repeated, ensuring his trusted officer understood. The Decurion nodded. He did. If his small force would make no difference, if the stronghold had already fallen, the men were needed here, for it was Cerdic they must put an end to ...

Through the day, Arthur had been cursing that Bedwyr was not here with him. Bedwyr as second-in-command had been needed ... but was it not ironic that even if he were here, he could not have sent him to the Caer? Bedwyr would have fought and battled his way through to Gwenhwyfar, regardless of cost.

Arthur raised his arm, gave the command that his men were waiting for. To charge the remaining solidity of that shield-wall, finish it.

Bedwyr would have led his men into certain death for Gwenhwyfar.

'Whatever happens,' she had said to Arthur as they lay together last night – Mithras! Was it only last night? – 'Whatever happens, you must close your eyes and ears to what is around you, fight Cerdic, and only Cerdic. For until he is finished, this thing will not be ended.'

'There is the boy Cynric,' he had pointed out.

'Cynric,' she had answered obligingly, 'is Mathild's son. Not Cerdic's.'

Twenty yards from the shield-wall. Arthur released the tight hold on the reins, shifted his grip to his sword, used his heels on Brenin's flank and let the stallion plunge forward into a gallop.

He only hoped Gwenhwyfar was right, for it was Cynric who led the command down at the inland sea. Cynric who was besieging Caer Morfa.

§ LVIII

He stood before his father, enraged, his fists clenched, nostrils flared, jaw clamped. The passion of anger so overwhelming in Cynric that he could feel the desire rising up in him to take an axe and plunge it into his father's brain. The blood of war was still spattered on his clothing and skin, even his sword had not yet been cleaned.

'They were good men,' he stated through clenched teeth. 'And there was no need for that slaughter of women and children.'

'Are you, then,' – Cerdic spoke through one side of his mouth, the other being puffed and swollen, the eye black and disfigured – 'disagreeing with the action taken by two of my most supportive allies?' For a wound, a blow to the face by a club was nothing glamorous, but for Cerdic, the pain went deeper than anything marked on the surface. The broken bone of his nose would be permanently disfigured, and the blood that had gushed from him surely almost led to him bleeding to death. They had assured him that it was all superficial, but what did these medical people, those imbeciles, know of the needs of a man who had Woden for ancestor? A known fact that Kings had greater feeling than peasant folk.

'*I* was in command!' Cynric hurled back at him. 'Not your friends, Stuf and Wihtgar. I ordered the British men to be taken prisoner, the innocents to be treated with respect. Orders ignored by their men.'

'Innocents? Pah! They were poxed British. At least they met death swiftly. I would have let the men use the women and girls, first.'

'Ja, you would have done that.' Cynric began to turn away from his father, the disgust blatant on his face. 'But then, you are a bastard whoreson.'

Cerdic leapt to his feet, overturning the chair, knocking aside the table that had been placed at his right hand, scattering the bowl of fruit, the wine. He ran the few paces that separated them, caught hold Cynric's arm as he stepped away. 'How dare you, boy?' Cerdic roughly swung him

531

around, took a hurried backward pace, let go his spiteful grasp as he met with an expression that shouted contempt and hatred.

'How dare I, father? How dare I?' Cynric jabbed his father in the chest with his finger, pushing him back another pace, and another.

'I dare because I know that I will become King of the West Saxons when you are gone.' He jabbed again. Cerdic came up against his chair, tripped, sat down heavily, his son leaning over him, breath spewing the fury on his face. 'I dare, because it would not take very much for me to decide to take my kingdom for myself now. This day, this moment.'

Cerdic was quivering, struggling to contain his bladder. He never had much bravery, had not inherited his mother's quick thinking, nor her ability to disguise thought or fear. He could lie, but his untruths were plain seen.

'You promised your friends great reward for victory over the British, did you not? And for so thoroughly destroying the marsh stronghold, what do they get? The Roman isle of Vectis? Wihtgar is even now taking the first ship to claim his land, sailing to establish for himself a burgh. What do I get from all this, then, eh? What is there for me?' Cynric's hands tightened on the neckline of Cerdic's tunic, his father gurgled some half-heard response.

'Arthur, my grandsire, fought with you, fought an honourable battle. He set your troops running. How many did you lose father, six, seven, eight hundred men?'

His courage returning, Cerdic tried to prize the tight fingers away from his throat. Cynric would have drawn his dagger by now, had he truly intended murder. 'We slaughtered more than three hundred British this day at Caer Morfa!'

'Ja, Caer Morfa is become ours. It is peopled with the rotting carcasses and charred bodies of the British dead. Where is the victory in that? Where is the honour in the killing of so many women and children?'

'For every Briton dead, I gain another acre of land . . .'

'We have gained nothing today father. You ordered your men to retreat. You saw the Pendragon coming for you, saw your death in his sword, shit yourself and ran. As you did the last time, at Llongborth. The Great Wood may be ours, because Arthur will not be able to rebuild the stronghold that protects it, but we have penetrated no more than twenty miles, father. And we have the blood of innocents and heroes to carry with us to our graves.'

Cynric released his hold, almost tossed his father aside. 'If you had fought as you had boasted, we would, this first evening after battle, have for ourselves a kingdom.' He turned on his heel, walked the length of his father's Mead Hall, the eyes of those within, following him. No one else would say all that he had voiced, none of the hearth-guard, the thegns. Not elders or chieftains, not the ordinary man who fought in the shield-wall when Cerdic called him to battle, or felled trees, grazed sheep and planted corn when he did not. Only the eyes portrayed their thoughts. And every man in that Hall thought to himself, *Cynric will be the better King when he is called to lead us.*

Hunched on his chair behind the high table, Cerdic saw those thoughts, and the jealous doubts whiffled through the hollows of his own dark mind. *Cynric has more of his father in him than do I.*

'Boy!' He scrabbled to his feet, bellowed down the length of the Hall. 'Boy, do not turn your back on your King!'

Cynric halted. He was a tall young man, agile, long fingers, strong arms. A man with the nobility of the stag about him. Handsome with his dark eyes and mother's flaxen hair, his firm jaw, long nose and quick, humorous wit. He was much liked for his fair judgement, Cynric. He stood with his shoulders back, head high. Did not turn.

'Did you hear me boy?'

'I heard you.' Cynric slowly turned around, faced his father, regarded him a long, silent moment. 'You are not yet a King.'

The gateway at Caer Morfa. It had come so unexpected, startling, the opening of those gates. None of the Saxons swarming before it had remotely considered that they would be thrust open and the British would – so insanely – come out to fight. The scrabble of those first few moments had been little short of panic, the Saxons ready to flee for the safety of their ships, believing, in that mad whirl of yelling and shouting and sword-brought death that the Wild Hunt was escaped and coming for them. Indeed, had that not been the Huntsman himself out in the front? An oak of a man, as tall as that tree, as broad, as strong. Dressed in red cloak, white tunic, the uniform of the Artoriani – his roaring voice, his sword whirling pounding death on all who had the misfortune to be in his crazed path. When they gathered their wits and tried to cut him down, he fought on. Though they hacked and sawed at his blood-spewing body, still he stood there, defying death, fought on, refusing to let go of life and sword until the riders – the two women – had gone through, had reached the first line of trees, and were away to the road, to safety. Ider, someone said his name to be. Cynric would have had him buried with honour, but the Saxons, his father's friends, Stuf and Wihtgar, had ordered him dismembered and used in the burning of the Hall at Caer Morfa.

Cynric gazed down the length of the Mead Hall at the overweight figure of his father, and knew him for what he was, a man who had never known love, who had not experienced pity, and would never understand the word compassion.

All the British had fought well, sacrificing their lives for those two women and the children who had been with them. Cynric had caught a glimpse of one of the boys himself. He had pushed forward, grappling with one of the riders whose horse had fallen, a spear through its chest. The woman had been there, urging her grey horse on, her mouth open, the war-cry of the Artoriani shrieking from her lips. Cynric had finished the man, leapt up, trying to make a grab for the horse's reins – and he had seen the boy clinging to her beneath the fold of her cloak. He had hesitated. Gwenhwyfar. She could have been no one else, and that must have been one of Arthur's own grandchilder. Her sword was raised, Cynric had stood, transfixed, unable to move for that one, so very brief, moment when all else, the rage of fighting, the noise, the blood, the stink, had faded into the mists that swirled outside of time and life. She could have struck him, used that sword to end him, but she had not.

Their eyes had met, fleetingly gazed into each other's thought, into each other's soul. Why had she deflected that swordstroke? Mayhap Cynric would never know, not until he entered the next world and the gods saw fit to tell him. And he? He had stepped aside, brought the flat of his blade down on the grey's rump, urging it away faster. With what followed, he had been glad that he had. He would not have wanted that sorry ending for the Lady Gwenhwyfar and her kindred. His kindred.

'You bring dishonour to me, boy!' Cerdic rasped. 'I ought have you whipped for your insolence.'

Cynric was looking at his boots. They had blood on them, a spattering of the life of men. He was a Saxon lord, and he had honour and courage. He would fight for a land of his own, fight the British, whoever. But he would not fight with dishonour, with the blood of murder on his sword and shield.

It was they, his father's friends, who had butchered the lord of Caer Morfa. Not Cynric. Natanlius had not been as fortunate as the tall man. He had not been killed, but captured. Wihtgar had ordered him gelded and, while the man still lived, his intestines drawn from him. They used them as rope to fasten him to the broken door-timbers of his own Hall. Then they took the dismembered bodies of his officers and men, and piled them before that doorway, around him, adding bracken and hay and anything that would burn, poured oil over it all, and fired it, with the women, children and wounded huddled inside.

Natanlius had not cried out once during his slow death, but the tears had poured from his eyes. At his feet they had placed one body for him to see, to watch, as it burnt.

Cynric lifted his head. If his father ever had doubt as to how much his son despised him, he was made clear of it now. 'I have no need to bring you dishonour,' Cynric said. 'For you bring it to yourself. I asked for some reward from you, as is my due for fighting beneath your banner. I ask then, for the destroyed stronghold of Caer Morfa as my own.'

The hostility was thick, it could be severed with a dagger. Cerdic knew that his son was leaving him, taking a hearth-place for his own. The fear stabbed through him. If his son left, then others might follow, for Cynric was much liked, had much favour, most especially from the younger men. He could not let him go – least, not while this anger rested in his heart. Cerdic was not fool enough to miss that necessity, had learnt something from his mother.

'It is yours, as sign that our disagreement is passed and that we are again friends, as kindred such as we ought be.' It stuck in Cerdic's throat to be so pleasant, the smile that he forced onto his cheeks hard, without warmth. The atmosphere in the Hall, however, eased, the men visibly relaxed. A few hands dropped away from their daggers and sword hilts.

Cerdic's one fear, had passion overspilt between father and son, on what side would they have fought?

'I intend to bury the remains of the dead. To give the area a new name.'

Settling back into his chair, showing outward sign that he was content, relaxed, Cerdic gestured with his hand. So be it, he signalled.

'From this day, the day when so many brave men died, when so much honour was lost by the spilling of bloody murder, the British place of Caer Morfa will bear the title Natan Leag. The Forest of Natanlius.'

Cynric ignored the infusion of red that coloured his father's enraged face. He saluted, a mocking gesture of uncivil obedience, swivelled on his heel and left the hall. His last words echoed the dark length of that huge place. 'And if you were not my father, I would challenge you for the futile butchery you brought about this day. My grandsire may be British-born, not Saxon, but it seems to me, to be British is to fight and die with honour. Do not ask me to fight with you against Arthur again, Cerdic, for I will not.' Honour meant much to Cynric, and oath taken was oath kept. The shame that had been Caer Morfa ensured he kept his word.

It was a child they had lain there. Natanlius's own son. A babe, no more than a few weeks into life. It would not have been so sorrowful, that wicked burning, had the boy at least been dead.

PART FOUR

The Final Thread

May 500

§ I

A group of men stood, close together, talking low-voiced beside the blaze of the hearth-fire. Occasionally, one would cast a furtive glance at the woman who sat in the King's place.

Gwenhwyfar was aware of their hostile appraisal, guessed their thoughts as if they were being spoken aloud. What did they see when they watched her from beneath those half-closed, wary eyes? Confidence, an appearance of ease, that there was nothing wrong? Or did they see the copper hair that was now silvered grey, her wrinkled skin, her stiffened fingers that found it difficult to hold, let alone use, a sword? Did they realize, if she seemed so old, what age was her husband, their King?

It was they who had called this Council, the lords, the elders, men of the Church. Justly, she supposed, for Arthur was ill, and for a man nearing his five and sixtieth summer, their concern could be expected. Did they not think she shared their worries? They did not listen to the breath rattling in his throat, they did not watch the strength daily sapping from him in the sweat of his fever.

There were not as many lords as there ought be. How many had not come? Dyfed was not here, nor Powys, Rheged, Builth or Brycheniog. None from the north. Gwynedd? Hah, Gwynedd! Gwenhwyfar clenched her jaw against the vomit that rose. Thank all the gods that she was the last of Cunedda's children to have life. How her brothers, she closed her eyes, her dear father, would have wept to see Gwynedd as she now was! Would Council, Arthur, expect Gwynedd's loyalty? What, allow a murderer, a cheat and a liar to sit at the Council hearth? Maelgwyn, her own – God preserve her – her own kindred. Maelgwyn who had taken a sword to his own uncle, Owain, had murdered him for the prize of Gwynedd. Prince Maelgwyn? Scum, dog's dirt.

A side door into the Hall opened. Bedwyr stepped in, his expression and step jaunty, his hair tossed, wind-tousled. 'My,' he joked, 'the wind's stronger than an evening after onions for supper!'

A few men politely chuckled.

Bedwyr strode to Gwenhwyfar, saluted, made his obedience. She made a light gesture of implied question with her eyebrow. Imperceptibly,

Bedwyr shook his head. She had hoped that Archfedd would come, but she was new-wed to Llawfrodedd, Lord of Cornovii, a good man, but not wholly to Archfedd's liking. Between them, with Archfedd's land of Dumnonia, given her by her father for her eldest-born, Constantine, they had much to rule, much to see to. Though for all that she had gained in land and wealth, Archfedd still had to forgive them for advising her into this marriage. She did not want Llawfrodedd, for all that he seemed kind and generous, nor for all the alliance this marriage brought her father. Ten and five years her senior, and with a serious view of his responsibilities. His first wife, Archfedd declared unkindly to her parents, most probably died of boredom. *Natanlius is my husband,* she had added, on that wedding night, two months past. *The memory of his love will not fade merely because I must go to another's bed. He knows it is against my will.* Archfedd had always been stubborn. Too much like her mother, Arthur often complained.

Indicating that Bedwyr was to lead her to the hearth, Gwenhwyfar took his hand, rose from her chair. Would she have gone through with marriage to another, to Bedwyr? Who knew? Certainly not she. Happen, it was only the Three, the goddesses who wove the fate of men and women, who had seen the future rippling in the pattern of life. There was a difference though, between herself and Archfedd. She had not had two living sons to follow after Arthur. Archfedd did. And one of them might become Pendragon one day. For that, Archfedd needed the alliance of a husband who would fight for those sons. Archfedd knew that. It was the reason she had wed with Llawfrodedd. But, even for that reason, she could not forgive her father for making her do it.

Gwenhwyfar hid her disappointment. *Give nothing away in your expression, hold your planning close to your chest.* Arthur had instructed her what to do, say, at this Council, but she wished that it was he who was now making way to the hearth, calling the men to order. As she sat, making herself comfortable on the cushions spread for them, she allowed a slight smile to slip onto her lips. *And such an interesting, enjoyable chest ought have things held close. My body, preferably.* He might be ill, but he could still tease her.

Bedwyr sat beside her, at her right hand. To her disgust, Caninus seated himself, uninvited, to her left. Almost in his thirtieth year, a man with young sons of his own, but another man like Maelgwyn, out for his own gain, with blood on his hands and deceit in his mind. Oh, he had come to Council, for even after the treachery of the past he considered himself next after Arthur. Well, he would need to pursue another thought on that! Constantine of Dumnonia might yet be only ten and three years of age, but Arthur had been barely a year older when his father had been killed in battle . . . the grandson would be proclaimed the next Pendragon, not Caninus.

They sat, circular, as Arthur had introduced the tradition so many years past. Circular, so that each might see the others' expressions, read the others' thoughts. They began with the trivial things, the levies for the rate of taxation, the granting of rights for three settlements, a change to a minor law. The matter-of-fact, everyday items that Council was responsible for. All the while their minds on that door to the rear of the Hall, that closed door, where, behind, lay the King. Never before had Arthur missed a calling of Council through illness. Anger, belligerence, aye, then he had stayed away; but never would he have admitted the frailty of the body, the creeping hindrances of age, to so important a group of men. They were here, these lords, to gain what they could for themselves, to discover how ill Arthur was. How soon it would be before he died. She would need say something, show them that soon he would be well, on his feet, as strong as ever he had been . . .

The Bishop of Aquae Sulis cleared his throat. 'It grieves us that Lord Pendragon cannot be with us. How is the King's health?' He asked it politely, with a grave smile. 'We trust he will be not be incapacitated long.'

'It is a fever, nothing more. A few days to regain his strength,' Gwenhwyfar spread her hands. 'It was difficult for me to persuade him to rest, you know how the Pendragon loathes to lay abed when there are things to be done.'

They nodded, agreeing, sympathetic, offering their hopes for a fleeting return to health. Most of them lying, most, secretly delighted that he might soon be gone. Too many in this Council wanted the royal torque for their own decoration.

A man came quietly into the Hall, whispered to Gwenhwyfar. She gasped, half-rose to her feet. Bedwyr put his hand to her arm. 'What is it?' he hissed. Concern raced through the circle of Council, all sharing the same, unspoken thought . . . the King . . .? Only Bedwyr realizing that the gatekeeper would not be bringing word of Arthur.

'At the gate, asking permission to enter . . .' Gwenhwyfar put her hand to her mouth. *My god*, she thought, *surely he would not come here*!

Bedwyr stood, questioned the gatekeeper, sent him scurrying back to his post. He saluted Council, a hasty politeness, almost ran to the privacy of Arthur's chamber. His thoughts echoing Gwenhwyfar's. *My God!*

With the wind scurrying so playfully outside, only one of the two great oaken doors stood open. They would be shut at night, after the evening

Gathering had assembled. During the daylight hours, the Hall stood open to all, as was the custom of welcome, from King downward, to lord and landholder.

Sounds outside, disturbed, flurrying sounds, nothing definite, nothing particular, just a momentum of intense unease and anxious disquiet. Shadows fell at the door, stabbing across the timber flooring, the light blocked by the presence of men. They walked through, the one at their head dressed splendidly, jewels decorating his hands, arms, throat, a ruby dangling from his left earlobe. Gold and silver ornamenting buckles, cloak and tunic. He made much of carrying his naked sword before him, setting it, with opulent display, beside the threshold. That he probably bristled daggers within his boot and beneath his tunic, no one would dare challenge.

Cerdic came into the Hall, flanked by ten of his men, swaggered its length, halted before the hearth-fire. He ignored the British Councillors, all of whom had scrabbled, open-mouthed, to their feet. He regarded Gwenhwyfar, blinked at her several times.

'It has reached my ears that my father is dying.'

Gwenhwyfar rose, elegantly, not needing the steadying hand offered by a slave. For Council, she had robed herself as befitted a Queen – gown of silver-threaded silk, purple cloak, amethysts and diamonds sparking from ears, arms and fingers. Before her seated place, Arthur's sword, unsheathed. She lifted it as she stood, held it, blade downward, her hand light on the pommel, ready to swing it upward should need arise.

'Then your ears hear wrong. He has a mild fever. Nothing more.'

Cerdic shrugged. Men died of fever. Especially old men. He indicated that one of his hearth-guard was to clear a space for him in the Council circle. The Saxon stepped forward, shuffled two bishops and a lord aside. Cerdic sat, patting cushions comfortable, flapped his hand for the others to reseat themselves. 'Is this not Council?' he said. 'Do we not sit thus, we British?'

No one moved.

Cerdic sniffed loudly, cleared his throat. His men had arranged themselves, semicircular behind him, shielding his back from those who were pressing through the door, watching, twittering quietly, awaiting some order of what to do.

'I am the acknowledged son of Arthur, the Pendragon.' Cerdic pulled a small roll of parchment from his waist pouch. 'This,' he said, unrolling it and passing it for all to see, 'was signed by him and given my mother, stating that fact. As his acknowledged son, am I not entitled to sit in Council, is it not my right, as his only legal heir?'

§ II

The Caer at Din Dirgel was a place true to its name, a secretive stronghold that had for constant companion the restless buffeting of the sea. It was never silent here, for the waves beat with relentless force against the rocks, pounding, clamouring, roaring a right to be let in against the shore. The stronghold was built out among a promontory of the cliffs, with only a narrow way to its gatehouse. Archfedd's grandsire, Uthr Pendragon, had held it for his own, once, long ago. Her father had been conceived here, in that lofty, wind-riddled chamber, no doubt, that was now hers and her husband's. It was a place where the wind howled, or the mist curled; where waves battered and the sea moaned.

When the tide was low, she could make her way down the wind of steps cut into the rock walls, the descent perilous for it was seaweed-strewn, barnacled, wet and slippery. She went there rarely, for although she was no person to shy away from difficulty, she found the unsteady way down and the long haul back up again rather pointless. If she were to admit it, Archfedd was afeard of the angry fuss of this sea.

She had known the coast as a child, while she lived under Geraint's protection at Durnovaria, but there the sands had been below gentler cliffs, the sea not so high, or alarming – save for on stormy days, and then they had mostly stayed within the safety of the stronghold. Caer Morfa had rested close to the inland sea. She had known the tides there and the rush of wind and rain, but there was the calm flat expanse of sea-marsh, the ripple of rivers and tributaries, the wading birds, the bustle of fishing boats.

Her two boys enjoyed this wild sea, of course, but they were children. For most of her life, she had known naught but the openness of her father's Summer Land, the quiet of the vast skies, the lulling calls of the curlew and lapwing. Here, it was the harsh, squabbling shriek of the gull.

It was all steps and stone and seaweed here at Din Dirgel, no sweet grass, only the brittle sea grass, or that short-cropped by the constant tremor of a saline wind. No plants save those that could cling, short-rooted, to the cliffs and cracks, that could survive in the distinct salt-tang of the air. Even the people of the Caer seemed craggy and sea-dipped. The cliffs were exciting to walk along, but sometimes the wind became over boisterous, and once Constantine was almost blown over. Archfedd never allowed the boys near the edge after that, for he could have fallen, been picked up and tossed like an autumn leaf!

She was out along the cliffs this day alone, for the boys were with Llawfrodedd, inspecting the new-whelped pups. They had been promised one each, Archfedd too, but she did not want one. Mêl had been her dog. There would never be another to replace her. It had almost hurt as much to leave the bitch behind at Caer Morfa as it had to leave Natanlius . . . what had happened to her, Archfedd would not know. She had not wanted to. But then, she had not wanted to know how Natanlius and her son had died, either, yet she had heard. Gossip was never silent, even that of the well-meaning kind.

The sky was a sulky blue, one that could not quite decide between brightening or souring into the dull grey of threatened rain, and for once the wind was not so rough. A ship had thrashed her way through the tumbling waves a while past, blue-sailed, a brave little craft. Archfedd had wondered where she was going, where she was from. There was not much else for her to do here, in this small, lonely Caer. Llawfrodedd was a good man – as her father and mother had said – ten and five years her senior, deep-voiced and dark-eyed. He was kind and considerate to her, gave her all she wanted, except company and talk and, she sighed as she walked, something different to do with her days!

The stronghold was behind her. To her left, the sea. To the right, away a distance, the narrow road that led northward, up through the Cornovii land, through her own Dumnonia and joined, not far from Durnovaria, the greater road that had been started by the Romans, used throughout the dominance of the Empire, and had been repaired recently at the order of her father.

The letter had come two weeks past, sent to her and Llawfrodedd. It was not a summons, but invitation, a semi-formal yet hopeful letter, asking for them to come to Council, for her to come. Llawfrodedd had wanted to go, but she said no, it was too far to ride. He was not a man to press the matter, she knew best. They did not go. Now she was regretting it, now the other news had followed in its wake, that her father was ill. Only a fever, the trader had said. Would her mother send word if it were worse? Surely aye, she would, but what if she did not want to worry her – and what if Gwenhwyfar was still angry with her for that petulance over the wedding? Had it been her fault? She had not wanted to remarry, had not wanted to be brought here to this damned desolate, sea-trapped place.

Riders on the road. Two. Men on ponies, not well-bred horses, not messengers from Caer Cadan then. Traders? Men with another petty petition for Llawfrodedd to ponder over? Archfedd kicked at a rock, stubbed her toe, cursed, using one of her father's more colourfully explicit oaths. Llawfrodedd would have chastized her for that, with an upraising of his eyebrows, a slowly wagging head, had he heard. He meant well, was kind to her, offered all she needed or wanted. Save for a relief from tedium.

She considered walking nearer the road, decided against. What would be the point? Dull people bringing daily business to a dull stronghold. She walked to the edge of the cliff, stood, gazing down at the foaming surf. She was four and thirty years of age, a woman grown, nearing mid-age. She had known and loved a man, borne three sons, lost one to the violence of death. What more was there for her? What could there be for her here, for the future, save loneliness and despair in this empty, tide-washed, wind-tortured place?

'Archfedd?'

Her eyes snapped open, her body slammed rigid. She knew that voice, who was it . . .? She spun around, covered her mouth with her hands.

'You! You dare come here?'

'Can I not dare to visit my own half-sister?' Medraut dismounted from the pony, handed the reins to the other man, a servant, false bravado setting a smile to his face. Beneath his cloak he trembled. Would she hurl abuse at him, turn him away . . .?

'You have done well for yourself, I see,' Archfedd retorted with a proud toss of her head. 'Rings, to your fingers, a fine cloak, good boots. A servant. A pity the ponies are such poor, ragged things.'

Medraut's courage improved. She was berating him, a good sign. He had expected to be shunned or ignored, sent with a curse on his way. Talking too quickly, betraying his nervousness, he said, 'I have been a while in Less Britain, before that I travelled north, up beyond the Wall. And aye, I have done well enough for myself.'

The sky was healing darker, the wind whispering louder, shuddering in from the sea. Brewing a storm.

'I heard you were a while in Gwynedd.' Archfedd ignored the wind's pull at her cloak, the damp feel to the back of her neck. She was uncertain whether she ought be welcoming this man, talking to him, but, ah, Medraut, for all his faults, his unfortunate birthing, and for all she had disliked in him, was someone to talk with; someone who had known the people she had known, the places where she had been happy. And was, after all was said and done, her half-brother.

'For a while, a few years past, I was in Gwynedd, aye. I left after Maelgwyn murdered for his land, guessing there would come more fighting between kindred.' Medraut shook his head, the sadness and shame of that evil happening clinging to him, though he had not been part of it. His wife had, the witch! 'Maelgwyn's cousin had taken one of my wife's sisters, a daughter of Caw, in marriage, did you know that?'

545

Archfedd nodded. She knew that. It was old, dusty news . . .

'Did you know also that my wife is now Maelgwyn's mistress? She, who supposedly gave herself to God?'

Aye, she knew that also. Poor Medraut, things had never woven into the right patterns for him. 'Come,' she found herself saying, 'come into the stronghold, you must be in need of warmth and food, a dry bed. Though I warn you, 'tis a draughty, cold place. The wind finds its way in whatever the time of year.'

Medraut accepted with beamed pleasure. He had risked coming here, knowing the antagonism that had snapped so vehemently between them. Come with the hope that maturity and the loss of a husband had softened her. Glad that he had taken that chance, for it was good to see her again, to be with someone who would be willing to share the laughter of the past and reflect on the sadness of tears.

'Our father is ill. Had you heard?' They were crossing the narrow way between cliff and stronghold, Archfedd advising him to look straight ahead, not down. ''Tis a long drop and the swirl of the sea can make your head spin.'

'Ill? How ill?' Medraut stopped short, alarmed, his hand gripping tighter to the rope rail. All these years had he been gone, the hurting so deep that he had fled northward, seeking to lose himself among the obscurity of the high hills beyond the Wall. Then he had ventured into Gwynedd, by sea to Less Britain and a new life of his own, where no one knew him for what he was or what he had done.

He asked worried, frightened, 'Is he dying?'

'How do I know?' Archfedd tossed, churlish. 'I have heard nothing more, this stronghold lies beside an empty shore, and has a road that leads to nowhere else.'

'I cannot stay here, then, I must go to him!' Medraut began to retrace his steps, anxiously hurrying, waving and calling for his servant who was about to disappear into the narrow streets of the stronghold's ragged little settlement.

'Medraut, no!' Archfedd ran after him, caught the sleeve of his under tunic. 'You cannot go, you have just got here!' Her heart was bumping, her mind quivering. Her first visitor, the first person she could relate to, talk with – a friend – he must not go!

'I took ship to come back to Greater Britain. It was coming for tin from the trading harbours of these shores. I realized that I must make my peace with my kindred. I began with you, for you were the nearest, but it is with my father that I must mend old wounds. If he should die before I have chance to do that . . .'

Archfedd threw herself to her knees, clutching at the swirl of

Medraut's cloak. She bowed her head, let the tears sob from her. 'And I,' she cried, 'I must also make my peace with him!'

Strange, as they rode northward together, she felt a small, whispered note of regret at leaving the sea behind. So it was not Din Dirgel that had clutched, dark, at her then, losing her in a mist of despair. It was the knowing that she was not at peace with the ones she loved that caused her spirit to wander so restless and dissatisfied. 'You will come back?' Llawfrodedd had asked, holding her to him before they parted. His regret at her leaving had been genuine, for in his way he had much love for her.

As Archfedd and Medraut entered into Dumnonia, and followed the road which would meet with the Roman Way, she was glad that she had not needed to lie to him, that when she had answered, 'Aye, I will be home to you soon', she had meant it.

§ III

Arthur was aware of rising voices from beyond the door, that ought be firm closed but was not. He ached. His head, arms, legs, everything, everywhere ached. It would be better if he drifted back into the warmth of that sleep, easier, but one voice in particular was persistent, a voice he did not much like. Something was wrong. He tried to think what it might be. Could not. He groaned.

Someone came near the bed, a man. Arthur opened his eyes, closed them again. It was Bedwyr. 'Has Council ended so soon, then?' Arthur asked, his throat husky, his energy drained.

'Not yet.' Bedwyr had no idea what to say, or do. Cerdic was out there in Arthur's Hall, as bold as life, behaving as if he were some Augustus or a god. Jesu Christ, how many more Saxons had he waiting outside – how in all Hell had he come all this way unchallenged?

'What is it?' Arthur asked. He was not so ill as not to recognize trouble when he smelt it. And this, whatever it was, reeked of raw, sun-baked sewage.

Bedwyr took a breath, spread his hands. Told him.

'I assure you, the Pendragon is well,' Gwenhwyfar said again, feigning patience and calm – it would not do to show the fear that was coursing through her; bad enough that several of the Council had scattered to the corners of the Hall, were huddling behind the presence of the Artoriani – who waited Gwenhwyfar's signal. One nod from her and this impudent

547

turd would be run through. 'He had a mild fever, which has left him tired. He is a strong man, your father.'

Cerdic picked at a loose thread dangling from the hem of his cloak. A pity. His informer had been wrong then. That would be the last information *he* ever carried. He shifted his leg – damn fool idea this sitting on the floor. He gave orders from his gold-inlaid chair from where the people, his Saxon people, could see him and wonder at his wisdom and power. Of course he listened to his council, the Witan, but he did not always heed them.

They had strongly advised him not to come here, not to march as bold as mid-summer daylight into Caer Cadan, but he had disagreed with their advice. He needed to know for himself whether his father was dying, and this was the only way. He heard a noise behind, the unmistakable sound of a sword being drawn from its scabbard, and folded his arms, contempt lurid on his face.

'Is this, then, the hospitality and welcome given at the King's hearth to the King's son? I entered here under the green branch of peace and I brought two white doves to symbolize my awareness of your Christian preaching. Yet this is how you respond? By drawing a sword to plunge into my back?' He pinned Gwenhwyfar's gaze, realised that he had never seen her close to before. 'They say that you were once a beautiful woman,' he remarked.

'They say,' she retorted stiffly, 'that you are a deceitful bastard.'

'Ah no,' Cerdic sneered at her, 'that is my father they speak of.'

'Well, at least you have inherited something from me then.'

There came an in-drawing of breath, shuffled movement. Arthur entered the Hall from the privacy of his chamber, stood beside the door. He was pale beneath the spattering of beard stubble, although a few beads of sweat dabbed his forehead, and his skin was drawn thin over his cheeks. Perhaps there was too much brightness in his eyes? The fever had not wholly gone, but it was only there for those who knew to look. He wore his purple cloak, his white under-tunic, leather armour. Dignified, Gwenhwyfar rose from her seated place, walked to him, head high, proud, and made obedience to him, a deep submissive reverence. With the Queen so publicly – and unusually – acknowledging the presence of the King, all others in the Hall, by necessity, made from formal salute. All others, save Cerdic and his Saxons.

Arthur held his hand to her, made it seem as if it was he who led her to be seated before the hearth fire, though it was the other way around. His legs were shaking, his strength already sapping: he had not been from his bed for over two weeks.

'So the dog returns to his vomit,' Arthur said to Cerdic, after he had seated himself. 'I will not pretend to you. You are not welcome in my Hall, your presence is not recognized or required. Get you gone before I order my men to throw you to your death from my walls.'

'Do that,' Cerdic answered, 'and my people will ensure all Britain hears how you deal with those who come to you with offers to treat for peace.' Cerdic's narrow eyes glinted, he knew his father could not argue against that, knew he must be treated with respect and courtesy – at least as an outward sign.

Arthur had taken his sword from Gwenhwyfar, had placed it across his knees. His hand was touching it, lovingly. He could take it up, use it on the scum sitting opposite him. He had created that life, could take it away. Na, this blade was too worthy to have it blunted on the spilling of such poisoned blood.

'You came, hoping to hear that I was close to death. What if I had been? What then, Cerdic?' They were rhetorical questions, for Arthur allowed no answer, he plunged on, making this ordeal pass quickly, for he would not be able to hold himself so straight, keep the quivering from his dry voice, too long. 'As you see, I am not. Nor do I have any intention of discussing peace terms with you, for I know you to be a cheat and a liar, and aye,' – he held up one finger – 'I know this because that is what I also am.' Arthur beckoned his men forward. Gradually, more of the Artoriani had filtered into the Hall, more would be outside, ready, armed, eager to fight. 'Decurion.'

'Sir?'

'Escort these men from the Caer, and from my British land. Immediately.'

'Sir.'

Cerdic remained seated for a moment, his fingers locked together, an amused smile playing over his mouth. 'I have no need for escort,' he said, 'I will go, for I see you have not the wisdom to talk of a settlement between us. I will tell my people this, that the Pendragon has no time to listen to those who are not as great as he.'

Bedwyr, standing a few paces behind Arthur, almost vomited. He had seen more truth in the eyes of a wife caught lying about a lover! Arthur too, it seemed, for he made no answer. Cerdic made no salute, no form of reverence as he turned to leave. Arthur had not expected any.

'Cerdic,' Arthur called as the Saxons reached the open door. 'If you wish to see me dead, then I suggest it must be at the doing of your own hand.'

'Oh it will be so, Pendragon. I assure you. Soon, very soon, it will be so.'

Cerdic rode from Caer Cadan well satisfied. He had established for himself two things. One, his father was old and would not have the strength to fight as once he had. Second, he had proven to his son Cynric that Cerdic of the West Saxons was no coward, no scurry-away. And a third thing. It was time to fight his father again.

June 500

§ IV

They could not believe that they had missed their father by a day. Caer Cadan was deserted, but for women, children and a small guard. The Artoriani had gone, all of them, with Gwenhwyfar and their King, the Pendragon. Gone, to meet with Cerdic at the borders of Arthur's land and his own.

Archfedd sat her horse in the stable courtyard behind the King's chamber; she had never seen the place so empty. Eerie, not having the men of the Artoriani around, as if she had ridden into an abandoned settlement populated by the spirits of the past. There was the horse trough, there, the manure pile, the dung drying for use as fuel in the fires. Old Onager's stable – Brenin's now; the one for her mother's grey. Over there, the kennels where Mêl had been whelped and weaned. The hitching ring where, as a child, she had tied her pony Briallen, groomed her, pampered her. The door to the chamber – the family room, her home – was firm closed. Never had it been shut during the hours of daylight. Oh occasionally, aye, when the wind blew so strong that it whirled the hearth smoke into all the corners and into eyes and nose, or when the snow lay deep and drifting, a few times when her father and mother wanted the privacy due to husband and wife. But even if the door was shut-to, it was never *closed*, never loudly proclaiming 'There is no one here'. The courtyard was different too, clean, tidy, no piles of horse dung, no wisps of stable bedding, no buckets of corn waiting to be fed to horses banging, impatient for it, at stable doors. No wise-eyed heads looking out, ears pricked, inquisitive.

'It was not this quiet even when my father was away in Gaul with the men, when Mam thought him to be dead,' Archfedd said.

Medraut shifted uncomfortably in the saddle. When Arthur had been with him and Morgaine. Archfedd did not notice his discomfort, that was all a long time ago, she had been a child then, all she remembered was her Mam's unhappiness and her own enjoyment when she had been with the children of Geraint's stronghold. Distant days of childhood summer. She had swum in the sea, played on the sand and ridden in the undulating, sun-baked hills on Briallen. A child's order of priority. She had been well cared for and loved by Enid, Geraint's wife. Of course she missed Gwenhwyfar when she had gone over the sea for a while, but she would have missed that pony more!

They dismounted, put the horses in stables, dismissed the escort, Archfedd sending a slave to fetch water and feed for the animals. The few servants around – and the gatekeeper as they had entered – had nodded polite greeting to her, but it was not extended to Medraut. Archfedd assumed that they did not know him for who he was, took him as another of her escort. It was possible, for he was dressed soberly in plain riding gear, bearing no shield or elaborate sword, having no identifying badge. He had been away a long time. Twelve years. There would be those who did not recognize him

They shied away from the Hall, wandered instead through the low archway, along the side of the granary and into the maze of narrow alleyways between the huddle of dwelling-places; a village in itself, where the married Artoriani who chose to lived with wife and family. Here there were more people, women Archfedd knew.

The wife to one of the senior Decurions invited them into her house-place, a building eight man-strides by ten, reed-thatched, wattle-walled, one third two-storeyed, made as a slatted loft, hay scattered, several blankets. Here, the children would sleep. The central hearth-fire with the inevitable cooking pot, lazy smoke rising to linger between the roof-beams before meandering out through the smoke-hole. Simple furniture, a bed, stools, a wooden clothes-chest. In one corner, a loom. Cooking pots, wooden and pottery bowls. Herbs hanging from the beams, among the salted and smoked meats.

Bechan her name, with a brood of youngsters from babe to one almost man-grown. 'There are a few folk up at the Hall,' she explained to Archfedd, 'but with so many away it seems so large and empty. Come, sit, eat.' She ladled broth into wooden bowls, handed them to her unexpected guests. A few of the children were grouped, owl-eyed, squatting close for self-protection, at the far side of the hearth. Mostly girl-children, a few boys.

'Why so many gone, Bechan?' Archfedd asked, spooning the delicious venison broth. The ride had been long, she was hungry.

Medraut added, 'My father, to my knowledge, has never before drained so many Artoriani from the Caer. Always, he left a minimum of three turmae.' One hundred men, plus those who could not, for various reasons, report for duty. Caer Cadan was a place of great importance, the symbol of a King, its defence as strategic as any border. Only when Arthur had been thought dead had it fallen this silent, this unused.

'More broth?' Bechan asked Archfedd.

'I understand from the gatekeeper that the senior command here is placed with a man named Marcus Alexios.' Medraut persisted with his questioning, aware that she was reluctant to speak with him. 'I do not know him.'

'I believe I do,' Archfedd interjected. 'A big man, with hair as red as a fox's brush?'

'A competent man,' Bechan confirmed, offering her wine. 'Decurion of Blue Turma. He is out with a hunting party.'

Archfedd nodded. Aye, Marcus Alexios, as Bechan said, a competent man. But not one of her father's best, certainly not the one she would have expected her father to leave in command here. Bechan poured wine for Medraut, her lips pressed closed; busied herself with her youngest a while, seeing to soiled clothing, his feeding. Medraut exchanged a glance with his half-sister. There was something here that Bechan was not willing to speak of. It shouted at them with the clarion of the war horns.

'My father,' Medraut began, trying again, 'has been warring with Cerdic the Saxon since the day of his son's birthing.'

'You would know much of that matter, my lord.' It was not quite spoken with hostility, but there was a sharpness there, a distinct rebuffal.

'They have met in battle before.' He forced Bechan to meet his eyes, momentarily only, for the woman dipped her head, concentrated on suckling her babe. 'In the name of God, Bechan,' Medraut insisted, 'what is happening? What is different about this confrontation?'

'You need ask?' She responded with a quick hiss of anger. 'You, who served with Cerdic? Accepted shelter within his Hall.'

Annoyed, Medraut was about to snap an answer. Archfedd set her hand on his arm, a brief shake of her head.

'That was in the past, Bechan. We heard our father was ill. That is why we have come here. Surely—' She paused, regarded the woman with a look that showed all too plain whose daughter she was, her head dipped to one side, one eyebrow raised, the other eye slight closed. 'Surely,' she repeated, 'he is now well?'

Bechan had started to rock her child, backwards and forwards, the slow, rhythmical movement of a mother with her babe, a comfort from grief. She lifted the child to beneath her chin, held him, close, protective. She was silently weeping, her face buried in the bundle that was the child. Her eldest boy climbed to his feet, went behind her, placed his hands on her shoulders.

'Na,' she said, through her tears. 'Na, he is well enough but . . .' She lifted her head, wiped at her face, 'but would you expect a man of his years, who is still weakened by the fever to go into battle? That,' she said with sudden venom lashing at Medraut, 'ought be for a son to do!'

Medraut was shocked. Her hatred so virulent.

'My father says you are a traitor,' The lad sniped. 'He says, if you were a son worthy of his father you would not have turned against him, would not have taken up with the Saxons.'

Startled at the attack, Archfedd defended her brother, who sat stunned, mute. 'My brother is no traitor, else I would not be with him! What happened in the past has been misconstrued – and he was with Cerdic to spy for us, the British. His life was daily at risk.'

The boy spat saliva into the fire, sending sparks hissing, showing he did not believe her. The woman had not attempted to reprimand her son, to silence him.

'Is this how others think?' Archfedd snapped, jumping to her feet, her fists resting on her hips. 'Is this why we have been greeted by hostility and lack of manners? I remind you of who I am. Of who my brother is.'

Medraut dropped his head into the cup of his hands. Would the mistakes of the past never leave? Had they all, then, assumed the worst of him this while? The letters he had sent these years, to his father and Gwenhwyfar, the gifts. Had they not been recognized for what they were, a willingness to apologize, to ask forgiveness? Gwenhwyfar had answered him – once or twice only, he admitted – but surely with Arthur's approval? Now he was not so sure. Had he left it too long to come back? Twelve years too long.

'Aye,' Bechan said to Archfedd, her nose wrinkling as if there were some foul smell in the place. 'We know who your brother is. A Saex-loving cur who deserted his father. Who tore Lord Arthur's heart, and cared not that he had done so.' She said no more, but the words in her eyes were as plain as any spoken. Desertion, the worst crime a soldier could commit, worse even than murder or rape. Punishable by stoning to death.

Again, Archfedd hotly spoke up. 'My brother is no deserter. He is here – we are here – to join our father. We ride again within the hour.'

Medraut lifted his head from his hands, caught at her arm. 'You must stay here, I will go.'

'Aye,' Bechan sneered her contempt. 'You will go. To the Pendragon? Or are you to run to Cerdic, tell him what you now know? That no lord cared to answer your father's summons. That after Cerdic had threatened the King at his own hearth, the lords melted back to their own lands like mist on a summer's morn. Is that why you are here? To confirm to the Saex that the British lords are like you, cowards and unwhelped pups who will not fight with their King because they know he cannot win?'

'My father does not need the help of the lords,' Archfedd boasted. 'He has fought often enough with Artoriani alone. He does not make use of mercenary force unless it is necessary.' She spun on her heel, flounced for the open door, calling Medraut to follow.

Slowly, he stood. He brought a dagger into his hand, a slim-bladed, beautifully crafted thing. The battered, misshapen gold ring on his hand glinted. How, as a child, he had wanted that dagger as his own! How heavy it had been to carry since the day his father had given it.

He lifted his eyes, regarded the woman who was also standing, the babe, full-fed, draped over her shoulder, her son, arms folded in attitude of defiance, beside her. 'I am no traitor,' he said. 'I left my father because I knew how it pained him to see, daily, that I was, as you rightly say, a cowardly, unwhelped pup. I have never fought, I have never seen battle.' Medraut swallowed. 'In all my miserable life, I have never held the courage to harm another man.' He could hear Archfedd outside, making her way up towards the stables, bellowing orders to have fresh horses immediately saddled. He turned to go, but at the door-place retraced his steps, back again, to the hearth-fire.

'To take all the Artoriani with him, and leave so few here, I am thinking that it must be, this time then, necessary?'

The woman nodded. A single, jerked movement.

§ V

Cerdicesford, the English called it later, when the mess of battle was cleared away, when the ravens had glutted their bellies on the carnage, and the bones had began to bleach as the sun rode with blazing heat for most of that summer, across the sky.

Where the sloping hills came down to the marsh river, Cerdic waited for his father, and there took stand against the Artoriani. Ready, this time, with a thousand men behind his banner, ready to withstand the fear of the horses, ready to fight until an end should take one of them.

They rode, as ever, the Artoriani, wearing red cloaks and white tunics, their hearts high, large with courage. They rode with pride behind the Pendragon's Banner, the Dragon, knowing that they faced an opponent who this time would not run.

The officers, the Decurions. One of them husband to Bechan, a woman who had a brood of children to care for at Caer Cadan, who would be, within the first hour of fighting, a widow. The turmae, Red, Blue, Green, all the others, thirty men to each; bold, fearless men who loved their lord above all else. Even life itself.

Many, too many, almost all, put that love to the ultimate test that day at Cerdicesford.

Beside the Pendragon, his kindred, those he loved. To his left, his wife, Gwenhwyfar, her hair tied in a single braid for battle, in her hand her sword, the one he had given her, oh, so long, long, ago. Next to her, Archfedd. She had never fought before in battle, and Arthur had ordered her away, but she had too much of him and her mother bred within her. Too damned stubborn. Bedwyr would have preferred to have ridden with them, to have been beside Gwenhwyfar, for to die with her would be better than dying without her, but he had the left to command, his task it was to stop the Saex crossing the river, from coming behind. He failed. There were not enough of the British. Too many of the English.

To Arthur's right, his son, pale-faced and fearful. Not of the Saxons, even though there were so many. So many! Na, he was afraid that he might again fail his father.

'Take heart,' Arthur had said to him as they waited, the horses fretful, wanting to be released, to run, to charge that shield-wall of Saxons that prickled death, over there, beside the rush of the river. 'Dying is not so bad. It can only happen to you the once.'

He had smiled at his son. And Medraut knew, then, that whatever else might happen that day, he would do his best for his father, the Pendragon.

The stars. Uncountable, scattered, as if some great, godly hand had recklessly tossed them there against the beauty of that vast, unending expanse of darkness.

The land stretched quiet in sleep, with only the creatures of the night scuttling between the pockets of shadow. The air smelt deliciously warm and damp, a heady, pleasant, earthy scent of summer. The streams chattered as they rushed, the wider, slower rivers bumbling along, while the night-calm water of the Lake beneath Yns Witrin shimmered gracefully under the caress of a light, teasing, night breeze. A few waves lapped dreamily against the rushes. A frog plopped below the surface, a nesting waterbird rustled, agitated.

Gwenhwyfar, the protective height of the Tor at her back, knelt beside her lord, the fold of her bloodied and torn cloak draping over him. The night was mild, but he was cold, his hands, his face, without warmth. Her head was up, her green eyes gazing, unseeing, over the spread of the star-silvered Summer Land. An immense feeling of unbearable loneliness was tightening about her shoulders, heavy, weighted, like an ill-made cloak.

They had brought him here – she, Archfedd and Bedwyr – a difficult journey, knowing what they left behind, and what they faced. But it was best, to travel quickly and in secret, to seem no more than any landowner with a horse-drawn cart travelling north, away from the victory of the Saxons, and the revenge that would be Cerdic's. Though that word would not, yet, have spread. It would. Very soon, it would.

Archfedd was sleeping, curled beneath her cloak, the tears dried on her cheeks streaked against the spattering of blood. She would return to Llawfrodedd, raise her sons into manhood, but for Archfedd, for all the years that she was still to live, she would never laugh again, nor flinch at the cruelties that one man could inflict upon another. For Camlann, as the British named it – the battle that finally ended Roman Britain, and that made Cerdic into the first king of the dynasty of Wessex – Camlann would never be superseded by anything, anything at all.

Bedwyr was nearby, somewhere beside the lake, cleaning the wound to his arm, Gwenhwyfar thought. They would put Arthur's sword there soon, give it into the waters, so that none might find it and use it for their own. So that Cerdic would never, even by chance, have it.

At least Cynric had not been there, among the Saxons, at least he had not fought against his grandsire – his father? Once, Gwenhwyfar had heard that Cynric was said to have been Arthur's son. From that Saxon of Mathild's. It was nonsense of course . . . and yet . . . ah, it would have been well to know that Arthur's seed would one day rule the English with honour and respect.

A sigh, falling as quiet as an autumn-curled leaf, escaped Arthur's breath. Gwenhwyfar's head dropped to look at him, her fingers tightening, with such love, around his.

'I am for the Otherworld, Cymraes.' He announced it as a fact, a statement. Nothing hysterical or dramatic. It was so.

Gwenhwyfar squeezed his hand. His skin was slightly damp, she could feel his trembling. He was afraid. As was she.

'It seems,' he added, 'I have been long enough in this.'

Simply she answered, 'Aye, it would seem so.'

The stars. The souls of the dead. A thousand, thousand eyes watching, unblinking. Waiting. One fell, blazing a trail of a last triumph, burning brightly and briefly, before it faded, was gone. Gwenhwyfar followed it with her eyes. Was that one for Medraut, she wondered? He deserved a star to fall for him, to mark his passing. There would be no grave for him, no burials for the Artoriani who had died. For so few remained to dig graves, to tidy away the dead. He had died, as they all had, with courage in his heart. Had died knowing the Pendragon would not be far behind.

Again, she squeezed Arthur's hand as he said, 'From the humblest creature to the wondrous thing that is a star, everything must die when it comes to its time of ending.' She smiled down at him. With her other hand, touched the flop of hair across his forehead that had, since first she had ever known him, been so irritatingly untidy.

Not to him, but to the night darkness, to the stillness of the silent Tor and the starlit ripples on the Lake, Gwenhwyfar answered.

'As long as there is someone willing to tell the story and another eager to listen, a man such as you will be forever remembered. Though they may forget what you did and why, and they may mistake the minor parts played by others in the tale.'

The wind hushed across the Tor, dancing through the grass, teasing the reeds beside the lake, and whispered to itself as it twirled away up the valley towards the distant hills that marked the place that had been Caer Cadan.

'But none shall forget your name,' Gwenhwyfar said on a quiet, tear-caught breath. 'None shall forget the man who was the Pendragon. Arthur. My King.'

Author's Note

Few historians are prepared to accept the dates and events listed in sources such as the *Anglo-Saxon Chronicle*, Bede and Gildas as entirely accurate. Rather, these records represent a broad – and biased – sweep of events. It is so frustrating that there are so few undeniable *facts* for this muddled era of British history. We know what happened, occasionally where, but not precisely when. Even these early written records rarely agree with each other in the matter of dates. The timing of Easter, which was in disagreement for many years, stirred the whole confusion of dating into a further, fogged mess. The *Anglo-Saxon Chronicle*, for instance, lists some events – notably the 'history' of Wessex – twice, with a difference of nineteen years for the same event. So, if even in the tenth century, when it was written, they were not certain of the dates, what chance do *we* have one thousand years later? In the end, I gave up trying to make sense of it all and decided to leave the nit-picking to the professionals. I therefore freely admit that my dates are manipulated – within the realms of plausibility – to fit my tale; for after all, the three books of the *Pendragon's Banner* Trilogy are novels, loosely woven around the few definite things that happened. In this, the third book, I have, on the whole, used the earlier version of the nineteen-year discrepancy. For instance, Cerdic landed at Cerdicesora with his five ships in 476 or 495, and could have fought his battle at Cerdicesford in 500 or 519.

But of course, whether that battle was Arthur's Camlann, only Arthur, Cerdic, and those who lived and died at that time know for certain . . . We probably never will.

If dates cannot be agreed upon, the matter of Arthur himself is even more debatable! There is much passion and heated disagreement concerning the various theories of Arthur's how, when, and where. Indeed, it has not even been established whether he ever truly existed outside the realm of the imagination.

Cerdic is also an anomaly. He is named as a leader of Saxons – those men who were the founders of Wessex – but his name is British. It has been widely assumed that his father was British-born. I am not the only person to suggest that this father could have been Arthur.

Ambrosius Aurelianus existed. Gildas writes fondly of him as 'the last

559

of the Romans'. The fortresses that I have named after him in my story may, in fact, have nothing to do with him, but again, I am not the only one to have suggested it. I decided to use them because those in modern Epping Forest (Ambersbury Banks and Loughton Camp) are near to where I live – anyway, why not?

Gildas lived. Although again, my dates may not be accurate. We know he wrote some time during the early sixth century. His book complains about the moral decline of religion; it is not a history. He does mention the siege at Badon, although his dating is frustratingly ambiguous – and who was his 'filthy lioness'? He rebukes her son for murder in a holy place, but that is all we know of her. I have made her Archfedd, Arthur's daughter, but obviously I have no evidence whatsoever to back this! He probably knew Ambrosius, most certainly knew Maelgwyn of Gwynedd, Aurelius Caninus and Vortipor, for he soundly rebukes their crimes and sins. Why did he not mention Arthur? I believe because, by the time he was writing, Arthur was already dead and was irrelevant to his narrative. It might also have been because Gildas's loyalty could not lie with the Pendragon because of his eldest brother's death . . . the Stone exists at Rhuthun (Ruthin), the legend of Hueil's execution by Arthur along with it.

Geraint's death at the battle of Llongborth is fact. An early Welsh poem describing the event is highly dramatic and so sad. '*After the war-cry, bitter the grave*'. It was a battle that heavily featured cavalry, and is one of the first poems to mention Arthur's men. For the Saxons involved, Port is probably a fabricated name, but I have used it anyway. From the Saxon Wihtgar, the Isle of Wight apparently gets its name. Ambrosius did fight Vitolinus and gain a rather doubtful victory at Guoloph, and Aelle was the first Saxon Bretwalda, and did attack Anderida (Pevensey).

My version of the story of 'the Loathly Lady' – Ragnall – does not quite follow the known tale, for mine is more of an interpretation on a theme; and of course I have substituted Cadwy, Ambrosius Aurelianus's son, for the Sir Gawain of the more familiar medieval legend.

As for Medraut, the Mordred of later tales, he is usually portrayed as the traitor, the one who fought against his father – but an early poem does not support this. '*The battle of Camlann in which Arthur and Medraut fell* . . .' There is nothing here to suggest that they fought on opposing sides. For once, and to be different, I have made Medraut more of a 'good guy' – if a somewhat misguided one.

The contagious disease that we now call strangles is as much a worry to horse-owners of today as it was in the past. The illness is mentioned in Chapter V of Pelagonius's veterinary notes under the heading '*Cures and medicines for head ailments*'. The majority of cures appear only once in this section, but strangles is mentioned on *seven* occasions, indicating how prevalent this illness must have been during Roman times. Perhaps my one questionable fact would be that this disease mainly affects young horses and occasionally the old. However, given the lack of knowledge about contagion in the fifth century, I do not think it unreasonable to suppose that a horse like Onager could contract it.

As with many, totally unconnected legends, the Wookey Hole Witch came to be associated with the stories of Arthur. She was a reality, an old woman living in the caves whose skeleton was found with an alabaster ball. She actually dates from the early eleventh century and so could not possibly be Morgaine. Poetic licence can be allowed to stretch the imagination occasionally; and besides, people are known to have lived in the caves from about 2500 BC. It is not unreasonable to suggest that a lone woman could have been there in the fifth century.

Many of the British place and river names have been lost to us. On the whole, I have used what I have felt comfortable with, although these may not always be totally accurate. To the historian or professional, I apologize for any liberties; but again, I emphasize that this is a *story*, a novel. It is not meant as a scholarly, historical work.

Geoffrey Ashe's book *The Discovery of King Arthur* put the idea of a campaign in Gaul into my mind. Not everyone agrees with his theories, but I am grateful for the inspiration behind what – I hope – proves to be a good story! *Shadow of the King* follows his theory, in which he suggested that Arthur could have been Riothamus, a war leader who *did* exist. We have several references to prove *that* fact: in particular, a letter to him from Sidonius Apollinaris – a letter which I have used in my story. Riothamus *was* King of the Britons – but does this mean the British or the Bretons? Riothamus, like so many names of this period, was a title meaning something like 'King Most' or 'Supreme Leader'. Today, the title Prince of Wales refers to Prince Charles, but could equally mean George, the Prince Regent of the seventeenth century, or the Welsh Llewelyn ap Gryffydd, the only true *Welsh* Prince of Wales!

The battle at Dèols (Vicus Dolensis) *was* fought between 'the British' and the Goths. Syagrius's army did fail to arrive, and the British *were* slaughtered. Riothamus fled into Burgundy and was never heard of again.

Was he Arthur? Mr Ashe's theory has been hotly disputed, but I think it is as plausible as many alternative suggestions regarding Arthur. And there is no faultless evidence to prove that Riothamus was *not* Arthur! The one, major factor again is the dating. Sidonius was already Bishop of Clermont Ferrand when he wrote his letter to Riothamus. Was he inaugurated as Bishop before 469 or after the battle of Dèols? Or perhaps Riothamus was just a nuisance, a minor war-lord who plagued that area for several years. Perhaps he was Arthur. It is up to the individual to decide.

As for Ecdicius and the siege of Clermont Ferrand (Augustonematum), eighteen men against several thousand Goths? Surely not! Well, we have another letter from Sidonius Apollinaris praising his brother-in-law for just such a wondrous victory! The letter was written before 475 and there is no reason to disbelieve its contents. Well-armed cavalry can wreak havoc among poorly equipped, startled infantry.

But was Ecdicius trained by Arthur?

If Arthur truly lived, and if he *was* Riothamus . . . who knows?

January 1997

THE DIET TRAP

THE DIET TRAP

*Your seven-week
plan to lose
weight without
losing yourself*

PAMELA M. SMITH, R.D.

LifeLine
Press

WASHINGTON, DC

Library of Congress Cataloging-in-Publication Data

Smith, Pamela M.

    The diet trap : your seven-week plan to lose weight without losing yourself / Pamela Smith.

    p.cm.

    Includes index.

    ISBN 0-89526-259-2

1. Weight loss. I. Title.

RM222.2.S6228 2000

613.2'5—dc21   00-029895

Published in the United States by

LifeLine Press

An Eagle Publishing Company

One Massachusetts Avenue NW

Washington, DC 20001

Distributed to the trade by

National Book Network

4720-A Boston Way

Lanham, MD 20706

www.lifeline.com

Printed on acid-free paper

Manufactured in the United States of America

10 9 8 7 6 5 4 3 2 1

Books are available in quantity for promotional or premium use. Write to Director of Special Sales, Regnery Publishing, Inc., One Massachusetts Avenue, NW, Washington, DC 20001, for information on discounts and terms or call (202) 216-0600.

To my daughters, Danielle and Nicole
May the truth of who you are—beautiful masterpieces created
with purpose and promise—keep you forever free
of the diet trap and any snare of life.
Loving you is food to my soul.

CONTENTS

ACKNOWLEDGMENTS

I am forever grateful to so many people who have made The Diet Trap *a living reality.*

Special thanks to those at Regnery and LifeLine Press who helped fire my passion to help others "just say NO" to the diet teachings of our day—Jeff Carneal, Harry McCollough, Harry Crocker, and Al Regnery. And to Marji Ross, Jennifer Azar, Marja Walker, Nancy Bryan, Erica Rogers, and Tom Freiling for investing their incredible gifts into creating a worthy vessel to carry the message.

To Traci Mullins, my forever friend and visionary editor, who encourages me, gently guides me, resists redundancy, and makes writing fun and fulfilling. It has been a freedom walk for us both.

To my loving family—Larry, Danielle, and Nicole, my mom—and to the Martins, Phillips, Smiths, and Hensleys—for being my best cheerleaders and replenishers.

To all of my awesome clients whose life experiences, the hurdles and the victories, have shaped *The Smart Weigh* and laid the foundation for *The Diet Trap*. Thank you for your unwavering commitment to never diet again!

To Joe Lee, for believing that good food that's great for you can taste great too—and for entrusting your health to *The Smart Weigh* principles. You are an inspiration.

Information in this book is meant solely as a guide; it is not intended to replace a medically prescribed program. Before beginning any weight-loss and/or exercise plan, a licensed physician should be consulted.

PART ONE ■ DIETS MAKE YOU FAT

CHAPTER 1 ■ Diet Mania

Sometimes when we're stuck with a locked door in front of us there's a key hidden under the mat, or a window open on the side of the house.

—ANONYMOUS

For JoAnn, the moment of truth came when she couldn't button her favorite size-8 skirt. Ever since hitting her mid-thirties she had known that a little extra weight was creeping on. But that day, a "little" became depressingly close to "a lot." When she finally weighed herself, JoAnn, a thirty-nine-year-old mother of two, couldn't believe she had gained twenty-three pounds—as much, all told, as when she delivered her first baby.

Where did all those pounds come from? And when? Oh, JoAnn was aware that she'd been expanding—but she had blamed that on her lack of exercise, on not playing tennis because of a knee injury. She just needed to tone up. Or maybe she should go on a "serious" diet—at least half of her friends were doing that.

For Mike, weight had always been a major battle. He was a pudgy, stocky kid who never seemed to grow out of his baby fat. The family nickname for Mike was "Beefy King," a name that somehow followed him to school. Throughout his early teens, the extra weight was a nuisance that he hadn't really done much about, except to try to wish it away. That is, until he started playing football.

Then his bulk served him well. It helped "Beefy King" rise to be the starting linebacker for his high school team. It also landed him a scholarship to college. Mike played to great acclaim for three years, but then came the knee injury that took him out of the day's game, and ultimately, out of football. That's when his weight really ballooned—and that's when he first tried serious dieting.

That was fifteen years ago, and Mike has been on close to fifteen diets since. He's done Herbalife, protein shakes, Fit for Life, Butterbusters, Jenny Craig, even a hospital fasting program, to name just a few. And he's always been pretty successful—as long as he was "on it"—and especially if he was exercising hard to boot. But he can't stay "on it" forever. He gets the "misery factor" weight off, gets distracted or hurts his knee again, and then he's right back to eating and drinking whatever, whenever, and quits exercising. Worse, he always gains back more than he lost.

But as Mike sat before me, his diet history was only part of the story. The bigger issue was that he'd been hospitalized over the previous weekend with chest pains, and extensive testing had revealed a coronary artery that was 90 percent blocked. Blood tests measured his cholesterol at a dangerous 270, with a low level of protective HDLs.

Mike's moment of truth had come: He now *had* to lose weight, but in a different way from how he ever had before. Now he had to change his lifestyle permanently in order to lower his cholesterol, strengthen his body, and hopefully reverse the blockage without surgery.

Mike came to me because he just didn't know what to do. In the past, either diets he'd tried had failed him or he had failed at them. Deep down he knew they had all been unhealthy. But was it possible to lose weight, keep it off, and restore his health at the same time?

Susan had some of the same questions. Her fit-and-trim appearance was the envy of all her friends. They assumed it was easy for her; she must just be naturally thin. They never really saw her eating; but then, she was always a bit tired, but who wouldn't be with a schedule like hers?

What Susan's friends didn't know is that staying thin wasn't "natural" or easy for her, and never had been. They didn't know that she kept pictures of herself at a plump age of twelve on the refrigerator and bathroom mirror to remind her of what she never wanted to look like again. And she hadn't backtracked—but it had taken a lot of working out and a lot of dieting.

And I do mean diet. Susan sat with me and ticked off her dieting history. A bout of mono served as her first "diet" at age thirteen and gave her enough of a boost to show her she *could* be thin, and that she liked it—*a lot*. It also showed her that starving was her best bet for weight loss. But headaches stopped that several years ago. So she turned to her own version of every popular diet to come down the pike.

It started with protein shakes in college, then Fit for Life, then a vegetarian diet, then a no-fat diet.... Susan wouldn't just go "on" the various diets, she would adopt them as a way of life. What she ate depended on which diet she was on at the time.

It was the confusing array of new high-protein diets that brought her to me, seeking my direction on which one would be best for her, a vegetarian, to boost her immunes and keep her weight down. She ended her story with, "I'm so tired, and I get sick so easily, so I'm thinking the high-protein diet might be good for me, but is it what I need?" She was too weary to decide on her own anymore.

But it was the letter I received from Brenda that summed up the dilemma, confusion, and entrapment of a nation:

Pam,

*What am I doing wrong? I try to eat the right foods and I exercise,
but my weight is higher than it's ever been. At fifty-two, I weigh
forty pounds more than I did at thirty-two. Sure, I know it's been a
stressful number of years. There's been work to do, a family to tend to,
spiritual needs, emotional demands. It's hard to be "good" all the
time, but I've never been what I'd consider a big overeater. So why do
I seem to gain weight so easily?*

*Diets are not the answer for me—I've gone on enough of them
through the years, and I know better. I've probably lost a sum total
of 200 pounds, but I've gained back 210! Yet I have to admit,
going on a crash diet is so tempting to me right now. Especially one
of the high-protein/low- or no-carbohydrate ones that EVERYONE
seems to be on. I've read some of the stuff—and have seen shows from*
Oprah! *to* 20/20 *to* Larry King Live. *I'm so confused—maybe
eating carbohydrates is the problem. I know they're good for you and
will probably make you live longer—but will they make you live
longer* fatter?

*I watch my friends who are on the hot diets eating steak cooked in
butter and loading up on bacon and eggs, and I think, "How can people eat that way?" Yet, they are losing weight—no doubt about it.*

*Pam, I don't know what to do. Maybe we're supposed to weigh
more as we get older. Maybe our Baby Boomer struggle is to try to
hold tight to some image of our youth—and have it enshrined in
thinness. Or maybe that's a cop-out, and I'm just giving up. I'm so
confused. Can you help me make sense of all this?*

Brenda

Millions of Americans are crying out just like Brenda. They want a
thin and healthy body, but that body seems to be an impossible dream.

More than 120 million people each year report going on a weight loss diet. And, on any given day, about one-third of all adult women (30 million!) are desperately trying to lose weight, searching for the magic diet or workout that will catapult them to their ideal body.

They try everything to lose weight, no matter what the cost: high-protein diets, high-carbohydrate diets, food-combining diets, expensive weight-loss programs, drinks, potions, pills, herbs, spas, fasting, and feasting. And they do lose weight—some lose quite a lot. But the vast majority also gain it back, and with a vengeance—most with more than they lost, and most, with more fat than they started with. Many more simply fail to lose any weight at all.

The puzzle is this: How come one person can go on a diet, get rid of fat, and keep it off easily, while *nine* others get caught in a never-ending chain of disappointing diets that lead to despair and defeat? The odds are exactly that overwhelming—nine to one—that people who have lost weight on a diet will gain it back within a year. In fact, follow-up records of virtually every diet program indicate that one-third to one-half of dieters gain back even more weight than they lost.

THE AMERICAN WEIGH?

No doubt about it: Dieting is a national obsession—and problem. The United States is by far the fattest country in the world; the prevalence of overweight people has increased by 20 percent in twenty years. In 1962, 12.8 percent of Americans were obese; in 1980 it was 14 percent. Now, 22.5 percent are obese and more than 50 percent are overweight. On average, we eat 7 percent more calories than we did twenty years ago. Even the nation's children are pudgy; 25 percent—one quarter of them—are overweight. A 1998 Harris Poll found that 76 percent of adults were heavier than rec-

ommended for their height and body frame. In the late seventies, that figure was only 46 percent. The latest estimate is that 97 million Americans are overweight and most of them want to lose the excess poundage. Even more of them go on a diet each year, whether they need to or not.

How is all this weight gain possible in a country that spends billions each year on attempts to slim down? The U.S. Department of Agriculture surveyed American eating habits a few years ago and determined that only 12 percent of us have a healthy diet. And making a change—any change—is tough. Some have become so discouraged that they do nothing at all regarding their weight. A major poll in 1998 found that although 58 percent of Americans wanted to lose weight, only 46 percent were seriously trying. Why try again—only to fail?

This was where Sandy was when she came to see me for nutritional counseling. She started our meeting with "I'm forty-something and feel as if I've been fighting a war against my body for forty-something years. I think I've tried every diet created. I've swallowed pills, taken shots, and eaten carefully formulated foods and powders. I've fasted and drunk protein shakes. I've prayed and been prayed for. I've spent untold amounts of money on weight-loss programs guaranteed to work. And they do work. Actually I can lose weight quite easily—but not nearly as easily as I can gain it back!"

Sandy's most recent diet had resulted in a rapid loss of sixty-five pounds—down to the thinnest she'd ever been. She had been motivated by the invitation to her twenty-five–year high school reunion, and with dieting helping her to feel thin and beautiful, she had walked proudly through the door. Unfortunately, she broke the diet that night and continued to eat and overeat the rest of the weekend. As with any fad diet, Sandy gained back five pounds almost imme-

diately. Then came a vacation, followed closely by Christmas. She gained back the entire sixty-five pounds within five months.

That was a year ago. Sandy finally mustered up the gumption to try again—and started the Carbohydrate Addict's Diet after seeing the book's authors on a number of TV talk shows. She lost fourteen pounds in four weeks. But then Thanksgiving arrived, and she broke the diet—but just for that one day, of course. And now, three weeks later, Sandy was sitting across from me, having already gained back the full fourteen pounds. She was desperate.

Sandy's story could be the story of countless numbers of discouraged people just like her. A measure of our discouragement is how we suspend our good sense and do some pretty outrageous things, falling for some incredibly ludicrous schemes to lose weight. Americans spend $40 to $60 billion a year on the diet and weight-loss industry—and that dollar figure is increasing every year. The desperate search for *how to do it*—this time—usually ends with a headfirst fall into a new diet plan or scheme, or a revisit to an old (failed) one.

Yes, diet mania is alive and well today—even though statistics show again and again that diets never have and never will be effective on a long-term basis. Diet programs abound, complete with lots of advertising and many faithful followers armed with before-and-after pictures. There is a virtual weight-loss smorgasbord from which to choose our next diet: celebrity authors, diet doctors, model spokespersons, multilevel product plans in mall kiosks—even at churches. More than just a weight-loss game alone, there are diets to combat hypoglycemia, diets to prevent aging, diets to cure chronic fatigue and arthritis. There are high-protein/low-carbohydrate diets and low-protein/high-carbohydrate diets—sometimes written by the same author!

Diets and their teachings bounce us back and forth like pinballs between this and that. They get cycled and recycled. As soon as one generation forgets the worthless and dangerous diets of the past, out comes a "new-and-improved," "revolutionary" version with a new name. Many of these deceptive diets have been used and overused so much that they've even been accepted as good nutrition. We're bombarded with mixed messages. On the one hand, we hear the depressing statistics about diets being ineffective, unhealthy, about their even making us fatter. On the other, those before-and-after pictures in advertisements and infomercials seem too good to ignore.

This is the essence of the diet trap: We are sucked dry by life, fall headfirst into overeating and unhealthy choices, and are seduced into the newest diet that will show us how to regain control of our weight, our image, and our lives. But the diet ends up controlling us instead. Our hopes are misplaced, our road a dead end. For most of us, no amount of dieting or exercise will give us the physique of models and movie stars—it's an unattainable goal.

But exercise and better nutrition *are attainable.* Anyone can improve his or her health by exercising and eating well, even if that person doesn't become thin. Losing weight can be good for a person, but only if it's done in a healthy way. A lot of people, despite dieting, weigh more now than they ever have. Is it what they eat? Partly. Is it heredity? Yes, that's also important. But the secret to permanent weight loss lies elsewhere—it is being set free from the diet trap and embarking on a lifestyle of wellness. Until we are ready to go beyond dieting and look at the real issue—the way we live—then fatigue, unhealthy living, overeating, and being overweight will continue to have a powerful grip on our lives.

DESTINED FOR FAILURE

I've always proclaimed that the word "diet" is the original four-letter word. Think about it: The very word is spelled D-I-E-T, just a letter away from the word *die*. And that's how you feel when you're on a diet—as if you are going to die! This is one big reason why diets are bound to fail.

Diets are all about denial—focusing on what you can't eat. The temporary deprivation cries out for a nice reward. Going "on" a diet to go "off" the diet, being "good" to be "bad," eating "legal" foods only to "cheat"—all this leaves us exhausted, unhealthy, and usually unsuccessful. People feel guilty about eating unhealthy "bad" food. Yet their biggest nutritional mistake is not what they *do* eat; it's what they *don't* eat. They don't choose nourishing foods, and they don't eat the right foods in the right balance at the right time. Their eating is sporadic and erratic until, driven by hunger and low blood sugar, they choose the very foods they are struggling to avoid. Even when their diets are high in protein, if whole carbohydrates are lacking, the nutritional imbalance ultimately brings failure.

Physiologically and in some ways psychologically, dieters are no different from people who are starving. Like water and air, food is necessary for life. Obsessive behavior over weight and dieting creates all sorts of havoc that even health care professionals don't fully understand. For example, normal eaters will decrease their food intake after a high-calorie meal. Yet, in one study, when dieters were given just one high-calorie meal, they immediately felt the diet was over and began to overeat, even to gorge. The dieting had put them into a state of deprivation that triggered a physiological and emotional drive to eat, and overeat. Their metabolism, moreover, had moved into a "store" rather than "burn" path, so that what they ate was much more damaging. How many times has that happened to you?

It's happened to me a lot. Like many of you, I grew up with diet-ing as my second language—a bona fide member of the Dieting Generation. And with good reason: I inherited a tendency toward being overweight and had a family filled with compulsive overeaters and obesity. By the time I was eleven I had already gone on my first diet, an awful grapefruit and poached egg diet (it was called the Mayo Clinic diet, but did not originate there—nor has any stamp of approval from this respected medical and research institution ever been given). Was I overweight at the time? Not really. But I was growing and at the start of menses, and my body shape was chang-ing. My hips simply didn't conform to the popular "Twiggy" look of the day. Add to that an unhealthy dose of fear about my family's obe-sity problems, and I fell headlong into the diet trap.

I lost weight at first. But, sadly, I regained it—more than I had lost. It was the classic story: I lost five pounds only to gain that five and raise it three. The next year, on the next diet (five days of spinach and orange juice!), I lost ten pounds, and quite quickly gained fifteen. The pendulum was swinging higher and wider each year with each new diet. All the dieting was doing was leaving me a malnourished mess, yet weighing more and more. I spent half of my time discouraged and depressed—and the other half overeating to compensate.

In the last semester of my senior year at Florida State University, I got a wake-up call. I was anxious to graduate and take on the world of fashion design and marketing. I needed a class to fill a core requirement for my chosen field and stumbled on a class in nutri-tion. I was on one of my many diets at the time—lose-five-pounds-in-five-days-for-a-weekend-beach-party crash diet. It was straight out of the newest diet book on the block, *Dr. Atkins' Diet Revolution*, and it was working great! I had actually shown a loss of twelve

pounds in seven days! It was miraculous… and definitely the way I was going to eat for the rest of my life.

But then, sitting in this nutrition class in the early seventies, I was amazed to learn of the damage I was doing to my body by following this diet and all the others, by my naiveté and drive for thinness at any cost. And, like all crash dieters, I was paying a high price—poor health, mood swings, and a body that was yo-yoing between fat and lean. I was an "expert" dieter, but I didn't have a clue what I was doing. While taking the course, I began to understand that I knew precious little about health. I had not been taught—I had only been mentored by diet doctors and gurus who had become successful by selling quick ways to lose weight, not telling the truth about caring for the *whole* body.

After an emotional seesaw and much deliberation, I changed my major to nutrition. It was the first thing in my life that I really felt passionate about—I had to help others learn what I was learning and break free from the diet trap right along with me. That decision changed my life—and changed my dieting ways. I never went on a diet again.

WHOLE-BODY WELLNESS

As I learned more about nutrition and began to take care of my physical body, I was able to lose weight and, for the first time, gain health and energy. My nails became strong and long, my hair was shiny and full, my eyes were clear and sparkling. I no longer got headaches every day, nor did I sit on the cliff-line of depression. I could think clearly—even studying was less of a chore. I grew in understanding of why I did what I did, and why I didn't do the things I wanted to do when it came to self-care and healthy eating.

I have now been living this life of wellness and teaching it for twenty-two years. Throughout my years of nutritional and behavioral

counseling, people have come to me seeking a quality of life filled with energy and well-being. Many people have knocked on my door because they want to lose weight for good. Some need to manage stress better. Some want more energy. Others arrive very ill, in need of a nutritional plan to control serious disease—even to save their lives.

I started my nutrition practice as a Registered Dietitian for a progressive hospital's oncology unit—working with very brave patients and their families to fight their cancer with every means available. These challenging days led me into private practice working with people seeking wellness, helping them to get well and live well today, while focusing on preventing the diseases of tomorrow.

Early in my practice I sensed that, like my dieting college self, most of my clients needed simple nutritional education and guidance. They needed to be led beyond the cultural diet deceptions and myths to a true understanding of holistic health and nutrition. Rather than finding out what they *shouldn't* eat, they needed to learn what they *should* eat, when to eat, and how to balance their intake in a way that would benefit their bodies. My clients needed to learn how to break away from the typical American eating style while still living a normal lifestyle. And they needed to learn the vital part food plays in their well-being.

Different from the run-of-the-mill physicians and programs, I worked with my clients in a very focused, time-intensive manner. The foundation of their lifestyle changes was individual and practical. In 1985 I developed *The Smart Weigh*—a seven-week plan of practical education and lifestyle direction. Since then, over 12,000 people have followed the program—and hundreds of thousands more have adopted the principles found in my books: *Eat Well-Live Well, Food for Life,* and *The Energy Edge.*

The first step in *The Smart Weigh* plan was a lifestyle assessment

and blood work profile that helped me to learn about a client's health and weight history, eating and self-care patterns, and current nutritional status. From this information I could develop an educational and meal plan to fit within a person's lifestyle and preferences. Weekly sessions and consultations helped the person to adopt the newly learned principles and adapt them into habits.

As my clients put these principles into practice, most succeeded in achieving their goals: more energy, leaner bodies, weight loss and management, lower cholesterol, and stress resiliency—all direct benefits of the new way of eating and living. They began to learn how to maintain those goals for life. Their success was contagious, and the principles of *The Smart Weigh* overflowed to their friends and family.

And so, I offer you too a word of hope: *The Smart Weigh*—and its principles revealed in these pages—provides a plan for nourishing your body with the right foods at the right time, and for dealing with what's eating you. It will allow the healing and repair—the natural ability to lose weight that is scripted into every cell of your body—to flow through your being. It works because, quite simply, it's how we were created. Whatever our need of the moment—losing weight, gaining weight, controlling overeating, getting well— the goal is to learn how to get our body working for us and with us.

In this book, I have tried to break down a complex subject into seven simple principles. These principles are expressed in my *Smart Weigh* plan in Parts 3 and 4. They will equip you to plan your own proper balance of nutrients at each meal, according to the foods you like, and to develop a lifestyle that will propel you towards your goals.

If weight loss—even weight gain or just maintenance—is what you are seeking, I want to help you attain it. But I'm not interested just in weight management, or your hormones, or your heart, or your gut—I'm interested in your *whole* body and soul. Change in

one area shouldn't have to compromise the vibrancy of another. Just the opposite. That's why the information you will receive from this book is different from most. It's not a tunnel-vision view toward one goal at the expense of all others. Rather, it is designed to help you achieve whole-body wellness.

NO QUICK FIXES

The amount of personal pain among those striving to be something they cannot be is enormous. It impacts everything they do, everything they see. The effects of the stress and depression are impossible to evaluate.

Perhaps for you it's not so serious, it's just time to get in control of your waistline and back into last year's shorts. Sure you know that a healthy, lower-fat eating plan may be the right way to lose weight, but you don't really have a serious weight problem—you just need a quick fix! People that have a real problem with weight and overeating need to focus on long-term answers. But a slew of *New York Times* best-sellers are delivering quick results to people all around you. And, if they didn't work, they wouldn't be flying off the shelves, right?

Right. They *are* working; they *do* deliver quick results. But are they wise? A fast-acting diet is not your answer, whether you have eight pounds to lose or eighty. But you do need an answer, and that is why I've written this book.

Diets are confusing and robbing us of our health, wealth, and wellness. In a day when health care costs are immobilizing our country's economy, we see a huge segment of our population selling U.S. health to fad diets and diving headfirst into disease.

I say *ENOUGH!* It's simply time to clear the confusion—to cast a vote for new ways and a new weigh. It's time to get freed from the diet trap—for life.

CHAPTER 2 ■ The Top Seven Diet Myths

Don't think you are necessarily on the right track just because
it's a well-beaten path.

—ANONYMOUS

A friend swears that by cutting out all wheat from her diet she
dropped ten pounds almost instantly. Another woman over-
hears her, tells her friend, who tells her coworkers. One of them
sends it out to his Internet address book... and that's how diet
myths are born.

Unfortunately, buying into half-truths about weight loss is as
dangerous as jumping out of a plane with an unchecked parachute—
and no sky-diving lessons.

This is the boring, unchangeable truth about losing weight: *A
pound of fat equals approximately 3,500 calories. If you eat 500 fewer calories a day, at the end of a seven-day week, you can lose a pound. If you exercise away another 500 calories a day, together with cutting your calorie
intake, you could lose two pounds of fat by the end of the week.*

Anyone who tells you that you can lose more fat than this is misleading you—whether they intend to or not. Even if you could, it
would be dangerously unhealthy. Oh sure, the scale can go down a
lot quicker than one to two pounds a week on a fad diet—that's
what makes them so attractive. But the extra pounds being stripped

away are simply the fluid being temporarily purged from your cells and the muscle mass that follows. Not the fat. (I'll explain all this in detail in Chapter 3.)

The bottom line: A human baby produces a certain number of fat cells, depending on genetics and how he or she is fed. The baby never loses these cells, and the body can add more if overfed for an extended period of time. It appears that the more fat cells we have, the hungrier we feel; they are continually signaling the brain to feed them. If we drastically cut our food intake by going on an unbalanced fad or semistarvation diet, our bodies slip into famine mode. Our metabolism slows down, using fewer calories than usual for the same activities, putting our fat cells into the "store" mode. This is why there are plateaus in dieting (which occur in even healthy, sensible weight loss). The body is working hard to maintain weight for survival. It is also why weight is regained so quickly when the diet is over. The body reads that the time for feasting is here, and it had better "stock up" fat in the cells to prepare for the next famine.

WHO DO I BELIEVE?

One reason it may be so easy to accept diet myths is that health and diet advice is always changing. If you believe every sensational headline, it can seem that way.

Most of us simply don't like sound nutritional advice. In focus groups people complain that the advice makes them feel guilty, angry, and confused. They don't want to take the time to keep track of a diet and are confused over nutritional guidelines: a food that is praised today may be trashed tomorrow. That accusation is understandable. A nutritional message is sometimes difficult to decipher and to follow. For example, consumers tend to interpret "low fat" as meaning "no fat," an unachievable—and undesirable—standard.

Getting 25 to 30 percent of your calories from fat is considered a sensibly low-fat diet by mainstream nutritionists—but to many fat-phobic teens, it is a fat gorge.

What is unchangeable is how changeable medical science is. It's constantly evolving and growing, and so of course the medical advice is constantly being modified. Reliable advice must be based on good science, and good science means continuing research that utilizes ever more refined methods for arriving at the truth. Diet myths remain the same year after year because they are based on wishful thinking, not on solid research. So untruths can stick, year after year, and even become public health beliefs. We'll explore all these myths, truths, and half-truths thoroughly in the next chapter, but for now keep in mind these warning signs of a bad diet.

WARNING SIGNS OF A BAD DIET

1. FORBIDDEN FOODS. Any diet that restricts or cuts out whole food groups is guaranteed to cause problems. Not only will the deprivation lead to binges; it cuts out exposure to essential nutrients and nutraceuticals (pharmacological agents in food that are vital for vibrant living). Although choices need to be made wisely, all types of real food fit into a healthy diet.

2. VERY LOW CALORIES. A normally active woman trying to lose weight should consume no fewer than 1,500 calories per day. A normally active man trying to lose weight should consume no fewer than 1,800 calories per day.

3. SPEEDY RESULTS. For healthy, permanent weight loss, you should aim to lose no more than one to two pounds per week.

4. NO EXERCISE. A healthy weight loss plan should encourage at least thirty minutes of moderate-intensity exercise four to five days per week.

5. INFREQUENT MEALS. It's best to eat before you get intensely hungry. For most people, that's at least every three to four hours.

Here is a brief rundown on some dieting myths that have become mainstream beliefs about nutrition in our culture.

MYTH NO. 1:

High-protein diets help you drop pounds fast!

REALITY: If you're on a high-protein plan that limits carbohydrates, you may appear to lose weight more quickly because your body is dumping a lot of water weight. This happens for three reasons. First, you are cutting out sweets and refined starches. They are triple threats—loaded with fat, sugar, and calories (more on this later). Second, when total carbohydrate intake is low, the body must turn to the stored carbohydrate supply (known as glycogen) for energy. Since these molecules are bound with water, the water is released to provide fuel when the glycogen stockpiled in the muscles and liver is burned. And third, excess protein, unlike carbs, must pass through the kidneys, which need to draw additional water from tissues to flush out the protein waste products. So all that water you excrete shows up on the scale as lost pounds. But that loss is temporary, as you'll see the moment you return to your normal eating habits.

And of course, high-protein fare holds risks and dangers. Diets heavy in animal protein—meats, dairy, even poultry—are linked to higher incidences of colon cancer, kidney disease, and osteoporosis. A lot of evidence exists showing that the body has to work extra hard to process the protein that it doesn't need, and those waste products open the door to disease. That's a big concern when considering the current popularity of high-protein diets. An even bigger concern is robbing your body of precious whole carbohydrates that more than twenty years of research have proved to prevent disease and promote wellness and longevity.

Read more about these deceptive high-protein diets on page 30.

MYTH NO. 2:

Carbohydrates pack on the pounds.

REALITY: You can gain weight by eating carbohydrates *only if you overeat them.* Whole-food carbohydrates in the least processed form— harvested grains, fruits, or vegetables that have been prepared without destroying their nutritive value or fiber—are vital fuel for your body. These complex carbohydrates are broken down slowly during digestion, gradually and steadily releasing glucose into the system to be burned. But refined carbohydrates—complex carbohydrates that have been stripped of their fibers and most of their vitamins, minerals, and phytochemicals, such as white bread and pasta, crackers, and cookies can add to your weight by creating chemical gymnastics in your body that may increase your appetite and your craving for fuel. Refined carbohydrates break down quickly during digestion and are almost immediately released into the bloodstream to be metabolized—leaving your body's efficiency on a high/low roller coaster.

Whole-food carbohydrates can actually aid in weight loss because their fiber satisfies you longer—a sure way to curb cravings. In addition, fiber-filled foods are nutrient-rich, contributing to overall body wellness. But the simple truth is that when you exceed the amount of calories your body needs to maintain your weight, everything is fattening. The portion size is often your biggest enemy. It may be wise to measure what you eat against the recommended servings—and serving sizes.

Read more about low-carbohydrate diets on page 30.

MYTH NO. 3:

Eating certain combinations of food helps you lose weight.

REALITY: This concept does only one thing: it helps to sell diet books. The body has a very efficient digestive system, and no matter what

combination of foods you consume, it will disassemble them naturally and digest them equally. The digestive system is not a trash compactor! What goes in first doesn't have to be digested before what follows. In addition, proteins and carbohydrates are primarily digested in different spots anyway—they don't interfere with each other's breakdown. Eating them together does not cause weight gain or gas, unless you are eating large quantities of fat and refined starch. Avoiding one and eating the other at a meal just throws off the balance of nutrients, forces dehydration, and makes the scale artificially drop. If the diet eliminates even more foods with important nutrients, such as dairy products (which provide valuable calcium), the ensuing unbalanced eating can be even more hazardous to your health.

Read more about deceptive food-combining diets on page 44.

MYTH NO. 4:
To drop pounds, simply cut all fat from your diet.

REALITY: Not only is this statement untrue, following the advice can actually backfire on the would-be dieter. An insufficient intake of fat not only throws hormones out of whack, but also appears to slow metabolism (how many calories we burn per minute to fuel our essential bodily functions). Drastically low fat intakes also appear to turn on the appetite thermostat for fat by triggering the release of the fat-craving hormone, galanin. Taking in a moderate amount of fat is actually more effective in speeding weight loss than banishing fat altogether.

Low-fat diets became a big nineties fad when people started replacing fat with highly refined, high-sugar/fat-free products, and lots of them. The truth is, the road to health and weight management is not paved with fat-free brownies. "Eat anything as long as it's fat free" is no more healthy or smart than "eat anything as long as it doesn't contain carbohydrates."

Read more about the dangers of no-fat/high-carbohydrate diets on page 42.

MYTH NO. 5:

You don't have to exercise to lose weight.

REALITY: Actually, it is possible to lose weight by following a sensible diet and limiting calories without working out. But it's not a good idea. Records of dieters show that weight loss is maintained only when a routine of exercise continues after the calorie limitation has ended. In addition, exercise helps to preserve and build lean muscle mass during the weight loss, and more muscle leads to boosted metabolism, even when the body is at rest. What's more, exercise is simply good for you, head to toe.

MYTH NO. 6:

You can lose weight safely and effectively by using weight-loss drugs, herbal supplements, and "superfoods."

REALITY: You've seen advertisements promising that you can lose weight without changing what you eat one single bit. *You can even eat more!*—and do it all, even build muscle—with *no exercise!* Why, basically, you can lose pounds while you sleep. Of course, the question of the day is, Where does it go? Are your sheets greasy when you wake up in the morning?

The lose-it-while-you-sleep hype has become a $6 billion-a-year business. Herbal supplements and power drinks for weight loss and energy are readily available in health food stores and even some gyms. They are widely used by bodybuilders and athletes, and recommended by trainers, friends, and multilevel marketers alike. Metabolife, Thermadrene, Blue-green Algae, Chromium Picolinate, Fat Trapper, Exercise in a Bottle, and DHEA are just a few of the

popular products being hawked, and multilevel plans offer scads more. The products seem so natural, so safe, so *quick*, but most people aren't aware that some can have serious repercussions—and can even kill you.

It would be hard not to have heard about the Fen-Phen or Redux craze and fall for them. Those are just a couple of the many drugs still coming down the pike to help in the weight-loss battle. Many more medications will follow. But because they are drugs—with risks right along with potential benefits—they shouldn't be a first choice! Prescribed weight-loss drugs should be used only if you are likely to have eminent and serious health problems as a result of your weight—not just appearance problems. And they should only be used as part of an overall program that includes long-term changes in your eating and physical-activity habits.

MYTH NO. 7:
If a certain food tastes good, it's more than likely bad for you; and if it's good for you, it's going to taste like cardboard.
REALITY: Healthy eating is not a prison made of rice cakes! But if you feel this way, you have a lot of company. In a Gallup Poll commissioned by the American Dietetic Association, 56 percent of adults surveyed said they no longer found eating pleasurable because of their worries about fat, cholesterol, carbohydrates, and calories. Nearly half said they believe the foods they like are not good for them.

This may be why another public opinion survey in 1999 showed that although diet and nutrition is important to 85 percent of American adults and getting enough exercise is important to 84 percent of adults, only 41 percent feel they are doing all they can to achieve a healthy lifestyle. An unwillingness to forego favorite foods was the main reason cited for not doing more to achieve a balanced diet.

This myth is simply that—a myth. Eating well is not about giving up all the foods you love, it's about opening the door to a whole new world of fresh, flavorful, and fun foods that bring your body natural energy and healing.

THE BIGGEST MYTH OF ALL

The biggest myth of all is that fad diets work for the long term. Yet, convincing a disciple that his or her newest cure is doomed to failure is difficult at best. Body logic and nutritional science are no match for a good diet salesperson or convert especially after the first rush following the rapid water loss.

The truth is that all of these diets do work, for the short term. They show quick results on the scale. Believe me, you *will* lose weight on *any* diet that cuts your calories below what you burn. No matter how seductive the claim of the diet—NEW! MIRACLE! STRAIGHT FROM EUROPE! GROUND-BREAKING! REVOLUTIONARY!—add up the calories and you'll see that you are losing weight for one reason: you are consuming fewer calories than before. Although you may be "allowed" by your diet to eat "as much as you want" of certain high-calorie foods—eggs Benedict (without the muffin), fried steak and gravy—there is a limit to how much you can eat for long. The fat fills you up, and you cut calories without counting them. But after you stop the diet, watch out! Because of the imbalance your body is left in, you don't have to eat more than before to gain back the pounds.

Forgive me, but let me say it one more time (and several more times throughout this book!): When you lose weight quickly on any fad diet, it's only because the diet has manipulated your carbohydrate and protein intake to cause quick dehydration. And that's only for the first two weeks. If you continue to lose more than one to two

HOW TO CREATE YOUR OWN FAD DIET

(Excerpted from www.faddiet.com)

NOTE: This is especially effective if you have a doctorate degree in something obscure like genealogy. That way you can call it the "Dr. Scardsmayo Diet." Follow this up with a book, and you'll be rich.

Here are the basic ingredients you will need to create your own fad diet:

1. A book that lists the nutritional values of every food under the sun.

2. A good idea about what foods the grocery store carries (so that you can include those it doesn't).

3. A bag of chips (you'll need a snack while you work).

4. No nutritional knowledge whatsoever.

5. A picture of someone who was slim five years ago, but is now larger. The larger person has to own an outfit that is at least ten years old.

6. Pick a promised weight reduction. Most people don't think they can lose more than four pounds per day, so keep it a little less than that, but be positive. Also, put an official sounding disclaimer in there for good measure. Here are some examples:

   ■ Lose up to 12 pounds in 3 days! (Actual weight loss ranges from 8 to 12 pounds depending on the person, their metabolism, and the digestibility of the potassium manganate encountered.)

   ■ I lost 13 pounds between Monday and Thursday and you can, too! (My experience may not be yours; however, I am a very average person who has never excelled at anything.)

   ■ Follow Dr. Jingleheimerschmidt's program and get down the pounds! (Consult a doctor before starting Dr. Jingleheimerschmidt's program, especially if you ever experience shortness of breath when climbing more than eight flights of stairs.)

pounds per week, it's because the diet is turning for fuel to your muscle mass as well as fat. Although your body fat will be burned, you are losing a great deal of lean body tissue as well. This is because muscle is a more readily available fuel than fat, and when the body

is being starved of carbohydrate energy, it turns to the most efficient source—protein, not fat.

The truth is that the only desirable kind of weight to lose is fat, never muscle. And the best way to restrict calories and control appetite is not by being tricked into it, but by learning how to eat to meet the demands of your body with the proper supply. Losing weight should really be considered "releasing weight," because you sure don't want to *find* the weight that you've lost!

Losing weight is best accomplished through a "leaning down" process that comes from a balanced intake of nutrients. Smart weight *release* occurs only when you (1) burn more calories than you take in, (2) fan the flame of your metabolism by eating strategically and exercising, (3) crack the code of the fat storage mechanism to put your body into a "burn" rather than "store" mode, and (4) change your perspective about the way you eat and live. To be set free from the diet trap, you must throw out your old belief systems and learn to separate fact from fiction.

I compare going on a fad diet to using throat lozenges for a strep throat infection. The throat pain you are soothing and the redness you might be reducing are symptoms of the real problem: a dangerous infection. It will persist, even become life threatening, until treated properly with antibiotics. Similarly, weight issues need to be addressed with *real* answers, not with temporary, feel-good, look-great-on-the-scale measures.

A BETTER CHOICE

The best diet? One that focuses on real foods that you like and can live with, one that is generous in complex carbohydrates, moderate in lean proteins, and light on fat. Eat small, balanced meal portions often throughout the day, drink water, and exercise.

Unlike the diet designers you may have followed or been taught by in the past, I emphasize eating, not starving or manipulating the body. The emphasis is not just on what to eat, but on how and when to best stabilize body chemistries, boost the metabolic burn, handle stress, and release your full energy. *The Smart Weigh* is a week-by-week building plan that enables you to function close to your peak in seven weeks: thinner, more fit, and equipped to continue on that positive road to your goals—for life.

Remember this: *You don't need to learn how to diet; you need to learn how to eat in a healthy way.* The strategies in the pages that follow will cut through controversies and diet teachings; they will change your perspective about the place of food, exercise, and rest in your life; and they will greatly enhance your understanding of your body.

You can take charge, feel better, have abundant energy from morning till night, and look more radiant and healthy. Forget the "miracles." Save your money, your time, and maybe even your life— do it *The Smart Weigh.*

Let's start by taking a closer look at the popular diet schemes of today. Armed with a thorough understanding of why they are dangerous and ultimately ineffective, you'll be able to protect yourself from being seduced by their empty promises.

CHAPTER 3 ■ Six Weight-Loss Schemes to Avoid

There is no right way to do a wrong thing.

—ANONYMOUS

So what are the most popular destructive weight-loss schemes of our time? The variety is endless—all protein, or all carbs; all liquids, or all grapefruit; all eggs, or all cabbage soup. At times, it seems that the wackier the diet, the more the American public swallows the theory. It makes some people (the authors, diet businesses, or investors) very rich, while a lot of other people (those who follow them) get hurt. Any diet that focuses on one food group at the expense of others is unhealthy at best, downright dangerous at worst.

All quick weight loss diets boil down to being variations on six main themes (a.k.a. schemes) of deception: (1) the high-protein/low-carbohydrate diet; (2) the high-carbohydrate/low-fat diet; (3) the semistarvation diet; (4) the food combining diet; (5) the blood or body type diet; and (6) the "lose it while you sleep" diet. Many of these weight-loss schemes have come back from the seventies like bell-bottoms, just under a different name or new packaging. All work, *quickly*, by the same mechanism—throwing the body into a state of imbalance. This promotes sudden weight loss primarily from dehydration.

All fad diets are based on nutrients, not on foods. Specifically, fad diets are based on a manipulation of carbohydrates, protein, or fats. On any of these diet schemes, 10 percent of your body's fluid weight can be lost in just two weeks—which, depending on your weight, can fulfill the sensational promise—"Lose twenty-five pounds in twenty-five days!" If you weigh 210, it's not difficult to lose fifteen pounds in fourteen days. Even after the first two weeks, these diets will continue to make the scales go down (for the short term) by eating away at your valuable lean muscle tissue, which weighs more than fat. Over time, the waste products from your tissue breakdown will depress your appetite, so you'll continue to lose weight because you are eating less.

But the moment you "cheat" or stop the diet, the tide turns. Your body's survival mode turns your appetite on *high*, releasing galanin, a brain hormone that regulates your body's desire for fat. The higher your galanin level, the higher your craving for high-fat foods and the more fat you will store. You don't even have to gorge to regain weight; your sluggish metabolism will do that for you. Since you are burning calories at a slower, less efficient rate, a little overeating goes a long way. And sadly, the weight you gain back is water and fat, not muscle.

Years of this kind of dieting will leave you in terrible shape. With each loss/gain cycle, the percentage of lean muscle mass decreases and the percentage of fat increases. Eventually, you begin to deposit fat in new places, and finally diet yourself into a pumpkin shape! And your body will make it harder to lose weight each time you try, because your slower metabolism (due to the body's higher fat percentage) takes on a life of its own.

The reality is that your metabolism can be your greatest ally... or your worst enemy. If you've been an on-again, off-again dieter, the

dieting itself could now be making you fat. Why? Because for every pound of fat you gain, your body burns just two calories a day at rest compared to an average of fifty calories for each pound of muscle. So if you lose five pounds of muscle mass on the latest high-protein/low-carbohydrate diet only to regain it as fat, you're burning 240 fewer calories a day. That's bad news for your body and your weight. And that's without considering the hazards and side effects of the fad diets themselves.

And the hazards are many. On an unbalanced diet, you do lose—you lose your health, your energy, your time, and your money. What you gain back is your weight—in spades. While being fat is not automatically the big problem in health, especially if you are fit, major studies have found that "yo-yo dieting" is downright bad for you. In a study of 11,000 Harvard graduates, researchers found that weight cycling adversely affects longevity. Rapid weight loss from extreme dieting has been shown to result in everything from high levels of blood cholesterol, decreases in memory and mental performance, irritability, depression, and altered reaction time, including deficits in hand-eye coordination that led one study to conclude that "driving while dieting" is hazardous!

Sure, you can lose ten pounds in ten days, shocking your body into dehydration and muscle cannibalism. But at the same time you also put a deadly strain on every organ in your body: your heart, liver, gall bladder, kidneys, and pancreas included. You can shed pounds—and shave years off your life.

How many diets do we have to go through before we figure out we've been misled, and that we're missing the real issue? Diet promoters need a new gimmick with the start of each new diet season, and you've got to give them credit for the job they do. It's not easy to come up with a dieting "revolution" every year! It's not easy to

build a book around an old story, retold. But the real issue is not even touched, and it's the issue of our souls. For whatever reason, when life leaves us hungry and empty and looking for a quick fill, the bait is set for the diet trap. And then, when this doesn't fill the hole or slim the body, our wounded beings start looking for the next quick cure of body and soul.

THE SCHEMES UNMASKED
High-Protein/Low-Carbohydrate Diets

High-protein/low- to no-carbohydrate diets are like nuclear bombs—they really work, because they devastate everything. But they seem like such a dream—and a wonderful dream, at that. Eat bacon, steak, and butter to lose weight! After years of being steered toward a healthier intake of grains, fruits, and vegetables, finally a diet to cause meat-lovers to rejoice: cut out carbohydrates, eat high-fat protein (and a lot of it), and you'll lose weight. Voila!

Oh, there's a trade-off: none of those comfort foods like pasta, bread, or potatoes—and certainly no dessert. Oh, and there's one more trade-off: evidence that the odds of getting heart disease and cancer increase hasn't changed a bit. Such foods increase work for our kidneys, promote stones, and thin bones, increase gout, raise blood fats, and shorten life span. And because the lost weight comes back with a vengeance, these diets make us fat, fatter, and fatter still.

Today's protein-praising diets echo the popular regimens of the seventies. The big diet schemes then were six: *Dr. Atkins' Diet Revolution*, Dr. Stillman's *Quick Weight Loss Diet* (I lost my hair on this one!), Dr. Tarnower's *Scarsdale Diet*, the *I Love New York Diet*, the *Drinking Man's Diet* (I was grounded for a month on it), and Dr. Taller's *Calories Don't Count Diet*. Then along came protein powder diets: the *Cambridge Diet* and the *Last Chance Diet*. They are all mar-

keting spins, twists, and turns, and hugely successful—at least for the companies behind them.

Atkins came back (with a NEW program, of course!), and a lot of other voices have joined the high-protein/low-carb choir: Drs. Michael and Mary Ann Eades are promoting *Protein Power*; H. Leighton Steward and company are touting *Sugar Busters!*; Richard and Rachel Heller are championing *The Carbohydrate Addict's Diet.* These diet books are seducing the public with almost unlimited amounts of meat, cheese, eggs, cream, and butter, while strictly limiting portions of carbohydrates such as grains, legumes, even some healthy fruits and vegetables.

The arguments that fuel these weight-loss schemes are based in half-truths that sound very convincing to the average person who isn't educated in nutritional science. Basically, they claim that when we ingest carbohydrates, our body turns them into sugar, stimulating the pancreas to release the hormone insulin, which accelerates the conversion of calories into fat. When we restrict or eliminate carbs, advocates say, our body will burn stored fat for energy and we'll lose weight.

Reality

Calling the latest fad diets high-protein may be somewhat of a misnomer. The average low-carbohydrate/high-protein dieter gets a whopping 50 percent of his or her calories from *fat*, upping the ante for long-term disease risk. This type of diet—high-protein; high-fat—has been linked to higher incidences of colon cancer and kidney disease. Many researchers have accumulated a lot of evidence showing that the body has to work extra hard to process protein that it doesn't need, and the waste products produced open the door to disease. The more protein you eat, the greater the risks.

Questions have also arisen about the link between eating too much protein and developing the bone-weakening disease osteoporosis. This may be because calcium, essential for strong bones, is drawn from the body along with excess protein in the urine. As protein intake increases, the amount of calcium excreted in the urine increases as well. This can be a problem if your calcium intake is low.

And, of course, skewing your diet toward protein is apt to lead you away from other important sources of nutrients, particularly plant-based foods and all their myriad of vitamins, minerals, and phytochemicals. Again, it's not just what you *are* eating, it's what you *aren't* eating that's the problem. Don't necessarily think of protein as the bad guy in the fight to lose weight; it's critical for metabolic boosting power. And studies have shown that it's better at suppressing hunger than carbs or fat, so eating enough of it (15 to 20 percent of your total calories) will help you stick to a reduced calorie meal plan when the going gets tough. And taking in protein with carbohydrates helps to regulate blood sugars. But packing in proteins at the expense of carbs can ultimately result in sluggishness and walk you right through the door of disease.

Researchers at Brigham and Women's Hospital and Harvard Medical School in Boston report that women who consume two to three servings of whole grains per day by eating foods such as whole wheat bread, oatmeal, or popcorn, reduce their risk of heart disease by almost 30 percent. By eating a sandwich with two slices of whole wheat bread (instead of just eating a hunk of meat), a woman will get the two servings of whole grains she needs to protect her heart. This, of course, would not be allowed on a high-protein/low- or no-carbohydrate diet.

As I've mentioned earlier, if you're on a high-protein plan that

drastically cuts carbohydrates, you may appear to lose weight more quickly because your body is dumping a lot of water weight. Carbohydrates enter the body in the form of food—either in simple structures that are easily and quickly digested, or in more complex forms that require more time. Complex carbohydrates (starches) must first be broken down to short-chain molecules, and then those molecules and disaccharides (the food sugars) are further broken down to the monosaccharides glucose, fructose, or galactose, all of which are absorbed into the bloodstream as sugar. Fructose and galactose are absorbed a little more slowly and evenly than glucose, which serves as the body's prime fuel to the brain, lungs, and central nervous system. The body needs sufficient carbohydrates to maintain a certain level of glucose in the blood. To ensure an easily accessible supply of glucose, the body stores glucose in the muscles and the liver as glycogen.

If you are eating insufficient carbohydrates, these glycogen stores are broken down and converted to needed glucose. Glycogen molecules are bound with water, which is released as fuel when the glycogen is burned. Once the glycogen

ANOTHER PROTEIN DANGER

Data collected over a fourteen-year period from over 88,000 women enrolled in the Nurses' Health Study indicate that women who eat large quantities of beef, pork, or lamb may be at higher risk for non-Hodgkin's lymphoma (NHL), a cancer of the lymph system. Eating larger quantities of trans-unsaturated fats, as found in margarine, partially hydrogenated vegetable oils, and baked goods, also appears to be associated with a greater risk of that cancer.

After adjusting their analysis for age and other risk factors, the researchers found that women who had a main meal of beef, pork, or lamb daily were more than twice as likely to develop NHL than those who had such meals less than once a week. Women who consumed more trans-unsaturated fats were more likely to develop NHL than those who ate little of this type of fat.

The researchers noted that the major findings from this study are consistent with nutritional guidelines for other chronic diseases, such as colon cancer and heart disease. These findings appear to be "one more reason to eat right," reducing red meat and trans-unsaturated fats, and increasing fruits and vegetables in the daily diet.

reserves are used up, the body will turn to muscle protein to synthesize glucose for vital body functions. It turns first to muscle rather than fat tissue because the body's fat stores cannot be converted to necessary glucose. Fat can be used as an energy source, but not to aid the functions of the brain or central nervous system, and it is also less desirable because only 10 percent of fat can be converted to energy compared to protein's 48 percent. The remaining components have to be excreted as waste products. At this point the metabolism begins to slow down to protect your valuable muscle mass, and the body becomes very efficient at functioning on less fuel. As your metabolism slows, it's a no-brainer to figure out why the weight comes back, surely and steadily, the minute you deviate from the diet.

What about the role of insulin? Eating food (in some cases, even just seeing or thinking about food) will signal the brain to release insulin into the bloodstream. Insulin is a hormone produced by the pancreas that is necessary for carbohydrate metabolism. It is the "key" that unlocks the body's cells to allow sugars to enter the cells and be burned for energy. Insulin influences the way we metabolize foods, determining whether we burn fat, protein, or carbohydrates to meet our energy needs—ultimately determining whether we will store fat. It's true that after eating carbs, insulin levels rise and allow the unused carbs to be stored as fat or glycogen, but that's only part of the equation. Several hours after eating, insulin levels fall and the stored fat or glycogen is released from the cell and used for energy.

Insulin is vital to well-being; but an overproduction of insulin can create an imbalance associated with weight gain, high blood fats, high blood pressure, and even insulin resistance, a precursor to diabetes for those genetically inclined. An overproduction of insulin and insulin surges occur when the system is hit with a calorie over-

SO WHY DOES BREAD MAKE YOU FAT?

Does it? A guy at the office swears he dropped pounds just cutting out bagels. Your neighbor insists that bread makes her bloated. Your sister won't go near any bread at all; she's determined that she's allergic to it—or to wheat.

Bread has a bad rap. But it's not the guilty party; at least, not *all* types are. Bread is a great source of energizing complex carbohydrates and is loaded with heart-healthy fiber and essential vitamins and minerals. A typical slice is low in fat (1 to 2 grams) and can contain 2 to 3 grams of fiber. But the term "bread" is a catch-all word, including calorie-packed high-fat items like muffins, biscuits, and croissants. And any bread can become a fat trap if you slather it with high-fat spreads like butter and cream cheese.

You can see that all bread is not created equal in calories—or nutrition. Any bread made from plain white flour can call itself "wheat" bread, but only those that list "100 percent whole wheat" (having whole-wheat flour as their first ingredient) are high-fiber, healthier breads. Breads that are made from whole-wheat flour naturally contain fiber, vitamins B6 and E, folic acid, copper, magnesium, manganese, zinc—and forty-one other nutrients. Again, these vital nutrients are processed out of white flour, and even though most bread is "enriched," only thiamin, niacin, riboflavin, iron, and folic acid are added back.

Take a look at these numbers:		
BREADS	**Calories**	**Fat**
croissant	300	17
doughnut	280	12
toaster corn muffin	120	12
bagel	250	2
English muffin	140	2
1 slice whole wheat bread	70	.5
TOPPINGS (per tablespoon)		
butter	99	10.5
margarine	90	10.5
regular cream cheese	90	9
fat-free cream cheese	10	0

By the way, although many popular diet books would have you believe the world has a wheat allergy, it is an extremely uncommon allergy. Only 1 to 2 percent of adults suffer from any kind of food allergy, and wheat allergies are rare. The symptoms are not what is often listed on "allergy checklists" (bloating, lethargy, cravings); the symptoms of a wheat allergy are severe: hives, swollen lips, difficulty breathing. Gluten intolerance, also know as celiac disease, causes the body's immune system to attack the small intestine as if it were an invader. This condition is still rare, affecting just one-half of 1 percent of the population.

load—eating too much at one time—and when the body accumulates fat weight. The fat-stuffed cell is resistant to insulin, meaning that as people gain fat weight there are fewer active insulin receptors on the cell—and those don't work as well. Essentially the overstuffed fat cell locks down, preventing fat from being burned. And the more fat you gain, the more insulin the body produces to force those insulin receptors into action. The more insulin, the easier it is to gain weight.

This explains why weight gain can often seem like a runaway train: the more you gain, the easier it is to gain. But this whole cycle of elevated insulin and insulin resistance can be turned around. Healthy weight loss (losing body fat) promotes the creation of new, more efficient insulin receptors. And insulin levels can be lowered through eating small, frequent meals, exercising, and preventing nutrient overload (not eating too much at any one time).

The fad diets that promise weight loss by lowering insulin levels are based on a faulty theory: that high levels of insulin cause a rise in fat weight. In fact, it's the other way around: excess fat causes insulin levels to rise. If we overconsume calories beyond what our body can burn for energy or store as glycogen, the energy will be ushered into the fat cell to be stored as fat rather than into the muscle to be burned as fuel. Overconsuming *any* form of calories will result in fat storage. There is no scientific justification for the claim that healthy people who eat foods high in sugars will automatically gain weight.

It's true that some foods, such as refined carbohydrates, can contribute to weight gain by igniting chemical gymnastics in the body that may increase appetite and spark cravings. And because refined carbs are calorie-dense (few nutrients but lots of calories), they can seem to "turn to fat." When refined carbohydrate intake is combined with a high intake of saturated fats, the ensuing dual mecha-

nism promotes fat storage: by suppressing the lipoprotein lipase enzyme which decreases the muscle cell uptake of energy. In a nutshell, when the calories that come from sugar-laden foods (often fat-laden as well) add up to more than the body can burn at the moment, calorie (or energy) storage occurs. This will be in the form of glycogen (stored glucose) until those stores are filled; the remaining energy will be converted to fat and stored that way.

Diet gurus, and even some scientists, still advise that carbohydrates in the diet are not ideal because any carbohydrate will make blood sugars and insulin levels rise. Much of this research comes from the study of the body's glycemic response to food—the impact that food choices and consumption have on blood sugar levels. Further research continues to reveal that certain foods, particularly refined carbohydrates, do cause a quicker rise in blood sugars than others, and a corresponding rush of insulin. But this can be avoided simply by choosing a different (whole) form of carbohydrate.

Carbohydrates have gotten a bad rap because they're all lumped together. But all carbohydrates are not created equal. The *types* of carbohydrates (and proteins and fats) chosen and the timing and the balance of when they are eaten is the key to healthy weight loss and maintenance. By choosing to eat right foods in the right balance at the right time, the metabolism is activated and blood sugars can be stabilized—and you get the sure reward of appetite control and weight management.

To live well and manage our weight we need a different way of eating—certainly different from that of the typical American. Although most of the world's population eats a high-carbohydrate diet based on whole-food staples such as rice, corn, fish, millet, soy, beans, and bread, not so the developed countries. In developing countries, carbohydrates may still contribute up to 70 to 80 percent

TOP 20 SOURCES OF CARBOHYDRATES IN THE AMERICAN DIET*

1. potatoes (mashed or baked)
2. white bread
3. cold breakfast cereal
4. dark bread
5. orange juice
6. banana
7. white rice
8. pizza
9. white pasta
10. muffins
11. fruit punch
12. Coca-Cola
13. apples
14. skim milk
15. pancakes
16. table sugar
17. jam
18. cranberry juice cocktail
19. french fries
20. candy

SOURCE: Dr. Simin Liu, Harvard University School of Public Health

*These data represent the findings of the Harvard Nurses' Health Study

of a person's calorie intake, but in Canada, the United Kingdom, Australia, and the United States, carbohydrates typically contribute only 40 to 45 percent of the calories consumed—and most of those are refined. Fats make up the rest of the calorie equation.

Let's face it: Our twenty-first century diet is too high in calories, saturated fats, and refined carbohydrates, which are digested and absorbed too quickly (causing a high insulin demand), and are too low in the right kinds of essential fat and whole foods that are absorbed slowly and evenly (allowing a proper insulin release). To make bad worse, our lifestyle is filled with stress, inactivity, and fad dieting, and sparse on exercise, rest, and self-care.

The key to burning excess fat is *not* simply to eliminate or restrict carbohydrates, but to restrict *all* forms of calories while keeping the body mentally and emotionally balanced and physically well nourished. This is best done with a restricted calorie plan that provides the right balance of carbohydrates, protein, and fats. Many weight-loss plans, in attempting to control glucose and insulin levels, will cut all carbohydrate intake drastically. That's because it's easier and quicker than educating people on the healthier approach of choosing carbohydrates and fats wisely throughout life.

A second reason people lose weight on high-protein diets is that excess protein, unlike carbs, must pass through the kidneys, which need to

draw additional water from tissues to flush out the protein and fat waste products produced by abnormal fat metabolism. One of these waste products is ketones, produced from an abnormal breakdown of fat for energy, and they are a very inefficient energy source. They accumulate in the blood and lead to ketosis, a dangerous state of imbalance which causes the body to excrete valuable sodium and potassium. This can result in abnormal heart rhythms and further dehydration, which shows up *quickly* on the scale as lost pounds. During ketosis the body also retains uric acid, which can trigger gouty arthritis, gout, and kidney stones. The circulating ketones can also cause bad breath, frequent urination, interrupted sleep, constipation, nausea, general edginess, and lightheadedness.

Finally, there is that sneaky calorie restriction that explains any true weight loss from a high-protein diet: the high fat intake that accompanies the protein makes you less hungry, so you eat less. If you're cutting out sweets and refined, nutrient-empty, often high-fat foods, if you're eliminating high-calorie desserts, candies, chips, and baked goods, then chances are good you'll drop pounds and feel much better. The tendency to binge-eat is controlled as well because—think about it—are you really as likely to binge on steak or scrambled eggs and bacon as you are on ice cream, pizza, or brownies? It's not the magic of eating protein that's working as much as the elimination of calorie-packed junk foods. These changes are also what spark the dramatic short-term drops in cholesterol and triglycerides that you hear about. Blood fat levels do not miraculously drop because of eating high-fat proteins; they drop because of not eating refined flours and sugars.

Although you could live a lifetime without sweets and white breads, you won't live long or well without the healthy forms of carbohydrate; no one can sustain a diet without them. Eventually, your

cravings win over but rather than steering you toward healthy brown rice, carrots, oats, or broccoli, you fall headfirst into nachos and chocolate chip cookies. This is not because you are weak, bad, or lack willpower; it's the way you were created. Your body is compensating when these diets self-destruct. It's not about your strength or your weakness; it's about survival.

But wait! Most people on these diets will tell you that they don't plan to avoid healthy whole grain carbohydrates and fresh fruits and vegetables for life—just until they lose a few pounds and tame this weight monster. *Then* they'll go back to healthier eating. Unfortunately, research, diet history, and human nature are not on their side. Studies show that after even a short stint with these diets, people rarely go back to healthier eating. And they cling to the erroneous belief that carbohydrates are their enemy. When they regain some of the fluid weight as quickly as they had lost it, it only seems to confirm that the fad diet was right: carbohydrates must be the problem. The crime about such teaching is that a distinction is not adequately made between healthy carbohydrates and unhealthy ones.

The Bottom Line

High-protein–high-fat/low- to no-carbohydrate diets *work* for short-term weight loss through (1) dehydration, (2) muscle breakdown, (3) cutting out calorie-laden sweets and refined starches, and (4) sneakily lowering your calories by keeping you somewhat nauseous and turned off to "all the protein and fat you can eat." These diets are also the *most* effective for weight gaining—go on one, lose a bit, and then regain in spades. What you don't regain is your muscle mass and your health.

WHAT ABOUT *THE ZONE*?

A diet book I am often asked about is *The Zone* by Barry Sears, Ph.D. We'll discuss it here with high-protein/low-carbohydrate diets, because that's what most people think it is. The truth is, it's not. It is *not* one of the dangerous fad diets revived from the seventies; rather, it is a carefully controlled low-calorie diet (the plan allows the average woman only 1,200 calories per day) with an extreme focus on getting an exact "balance" of carbohydrates (40 percent of daily calories), protein (30 percent of daily calories), and fat (30 percent of daily calories). *The Zone* made "40-30-30" a catchphrase among those who subscribe to Sears's claims.

Sears's program was a refreshing breeze for me when it was first released—finally a diet book had hit the best-seller list that actually discussed the need for a balance of protein *and* carbohydrates. It was quite a bit lower in healthy carbohydrates than I was comfortable with (40 percent of calories, compared to the needed 60 to 65 percent), but I was thrilled to get a national spotlight on the need for people, including athletes, to consume the dynamic duo of carbs and proteins. Although higher in fat than I recommend, it's actually a lower-fat plan for most Americans who are taking in 34 percent of their daily calories in the form of fat. If someone were going to go on a "diet," I would prefer they choose *The Zone*.

But the medical and scientific communities have criticized the claims made by Sears for the diet, rather than the diet itself. He puts the total blame for the fattening of America on high-glycemic carbohydrates that stimulate an overproduction of insulin. His remedy goes like this: just eat in the "Zone Blocks" (with the exact balance of 40-30-30 carb, protein, and fat) and you can prevent insulin surges and burn more fat.

Critics say there is no real evidence, just Sears's undocumented claims that excess insulin is the *main* factor in weight gain. The fact is, weight is gained simply because more calories are consumed than burned, regardless of where those calories come from. Sears practically flaunts the lack of traditional scientific proof in support of his run-away best-sellers, *Enter the Zone* and *Mastering the Zone*. Instead, he uses anecdotal accounts as the basis for his theories.

I believe that the body's hormonal response, including insulin surges, does play a part in weight gain, and controlling such surges plays a part in weight loss—but it's certainly not the whole picture.

High-Carbohydrate/Low-Fat Diets

In the early eighties, coming off the high-protein diet atrocities of the seventies, health authorities all over the world began to do research on the value of high-carbohydrate/low-fat diets and to make recommendations. Many people wisely heeded the advice—but they started replacing the fat in their diets with highly refined, high-sugar-and-starch, fat-free products, and lots of them. At the same time that fat-free products were flying off the shelves, the average intake of fat rose by 6 percent. Result: weight gain.

The road to health and weight management is not paved with fat-free brownies and white pasta. This "eat anything as long as it's fat-free" approach was no more healthy or smart than "eat anything as long as it doesn't contain carbohydrates." Once again, a pendulum swing resulted in an ever-fatter America, led by diet programs such as the Pritikin Program and the Duke University Rice and Fruit Diet of the early eighties, followed by Susan Powter's *Stop the Insanity!* in 1993. Even Dr. Dean Ornish's lifestyle plan for heart disease reversal, if used as a casual diet for weight loss and not a carefully planned lifestyle change, can become a high-carb/low-fat nightmare. Often, in the zealous effort to slash all vestiges of fat from the diet, the high-quality protein intake gets slashed as well. Why eat a healthy ounce of low-fat cheese with an apple, when if you ate the apple alone you would get no fat at all? True, no fat—and no body-building protein.

Now, the pendulum is certainly swinging back, with protein-pushing books renewing false hopes that there is an easy, painless way to lose weight and not feel hungry. And carbohydrates are once again becoming public enemy number one.

Reality

If you've been caught on the pendulum swing and are hitting the wall right now, you need to know the truth. *You DO need protein AND fat—and you need carbohydrates, too!* Protein is the main component of the brain, muscles, blood, hair, nails, and connective tissues. Without it, your body cannot be beautiful, nor can you be healthy. Protein is needed to churn out enzymes for digestion and cellular reactions, hormones for living and loving, and the antibodies to ward off illness. You cannot be healthy and lose fat weight without adequate protein and adequate calories.

Even fat is essential to your good health—and weight loss. It is needed for hormone production, lubrication, the absorption of certain vitamins, and much more. It is necessary for healthy weight loss because a moderate intake of fat triggers the production of cholecystokinin, a hormone that helps you feel satisfied. A low intake of fat or a drastic fat loss will produce the galanin hormone that turns up your appetite thermostat for fat. Galanin is released when the body breaks down body fat (as it does in dieting), when the diet is high fat (over 30 percent of calories), or when several hours have passed between meals allowing a fall in blood sugars or insulin levels. Eating more frequently, eating less fat (20 to 25 percent of calories), and eating low-fat protein lowers galanin production. The fact is, you cannot be healthy, nor can you lose weight, without fat.

But carbohydrates are needed as well to protect the protein you eat from being wasted as an energy source. Carbohydrates are also needed to protect the health-giving benefits of its fiber and nutrients and its role in regulating blood sugars. Carbohydrates play a critical role in meeting your body's energy needs and activating your metabolism.

Of course, as mentioned, a high-carbohydrate/low-fat diet also poses problems if the avoidance of fat is taken to such an extreme that the protein baby is thrown out with the fat bath water. This kind of regime so robs your body of essential proteins that it throws off your fluid balance, dehydrates your tissues, tears down your muscle mass, and handicaps the immune system. For a while the scales may look great, but the body begins to looks terrible—inside and out.

The Bottom Line

All nutrients—carbohydrates, proteins, and fats—are vital for living well, and equally vital for healthy weight loss. Losing weight by drastically cutting fat, and sometimes protein, too, is not only difficult, but it also sets up the dieter for malnutrition and a boomerang swing back up the scale. Fat-free does not guarantee that it's good for you!

Food-Combining Diets

Food combining is a concept dating back to the nineteenth century—and one that has been disproved since its first day out of the chute. Food combining is based on the ill-founded notion that the body's digestive tract, as mentioned, is designed like a trash compactor: what goes in first has to be digested before what comes in later. This bogus theory claims that if carbohydrates come in after proteins, which take longer to be digested, they will sit "atop the heap" and putrify, letting off gas and causing metabolic paralysis.

Harvey and Marilyn Diamond's bestseller *Fit for Life* has been hawking the "trash compactor" notion since the eighties, warning us by the millions not to combine proteins with carbohydrates or we will get fat, bloated, and gaseous. It is based on a meal plan of fruit

only in the morning, carbohydrates only at lunch, and proteins only at dinner—never ever eating carbohydrates with proteins.

The Beverly Hills Diet of the seventies, now back in a "new" version for these diet-manic days, was another plan that promoted the idea of eating only one food at a time (like pineapple all day) so various combinations wouldn't "clog" the intestines. It recommends eating fruit by itself and never eating protein with carbohydrates in order for food to be properly digested and not stored as body fat.

During the first ten days on the diet, only fruit is permitted; on day eleven carbohydrates and butter are added; on day nineteen, protein is added. And, of course, fatty treats are permitted.

In the nineties, Suzanne Somers came out with *Suzanne Somers' Get Skinny on Fabulous Food.* So many flaws in this book, so little space to uncover them! Now not just blasting thighs, but blasting balanced, healthy eating as well, the "Somersizing" seven-step program forces you to avoid certain foods (potatoes, corn, bananas, nuts, and olives, to name a few) and to eat other foods in specific combinations (proteins and fats separately from carbohydrates, for example). In the absence of scientific proof to support her theories, Somers says simply, "It works." She also dismisses the U.S. Department of Agriculture's Food Guide Pyramid because "it will make you look like one." Cute, but not true.

Reality

Get Skinny is a rigid and often impractical diet for people whose days are already overloaded. The diet is also very low in calories, which are simply fuel for living, not evil fattening agents. Any diet that contains fewer calories than the number you are consuming now will help you to lose weight, but you don't have to pay $24 for a book or conduct self-experiments with unproved nutrition theories to do that.

As for the theory that the digestive system is like a trash compactor... no way. The biochemical reality is that your body has a very efficient digestive system, and no matter what combination of foods you consume, it will digest them equally in their most efficient site for digestion. Proteins are primarily digested in the stomach, carbohydrates in the small intestine.

What about eating protein only once per day? Although you need to keep your fat intake within safe limits, failing to balance your carbohydrate and protein intake will prevent you from using the protein you do eat in an optimal way. Remember this: You can't store protein; it's a use-it-or-lose-it nutrient. If you don't get enough of it, you will lose your strength and well-being.

The Bottom Line

Any diet that manipulates your intake of carbohydrates and proteins will result in weight loss—but not in a healthy or long-lasting way. Diets based on food combining rely on extremely limited meal guidelines and are not based on any scientific evidence. Besides, such an unbalanced eating plan can be even more hazardous to your health. Basing a life eating plan on erroneous information about the biochemistry of the body is risky business—no matter how effective or lovely the salesperson.

Semistarvation Diets

The Cabbage Soup Diet, the Grapefruit Diet, "power shake" meal replacements, fasting programs... all are seductive to the dieter because they're easy. No need to make choices, no need to have to think. Just eat the starring food of choice—and eat it in abundance. But, because there is a limit to just how much grapefruit or cabbage you can get down before you feel nauseous and bloated, you limit

WHAT ABOUT THE *WEIGH DOWN DIET?*

Gwen Shamblin's popular *Weigh Down Diet* is difficult for me to discuss because I've seen this program help many people come to terms with their overeating—and their true hunger. I have watched people come into new and deep places in their relationship with God through the small group from which this book sprang. Any small group whose members are earnestly and honestly seeking to let go of hurtful habits and self-reliance and embrace the grace of their Creator will produce tremendous spiritual fruit.

The diet plan Shamblin recommends is the problem. It sends shivers down the collective spine of those from the medical and science community because it completely disregards years of research about how to feed the human body for wellness. Although we all need to get in touch with the true needs of our soul and not be controlled by *anything*, feeding our body is about much more than fatness versus thinness. It's caring for our body as something precious. The Bible encourages believers to care for the body as a temple, and not be anxious about anything. It does not teach that we are to ignore the basic principles of how we were created.

Rather than eating just what you "feel" you need or want—and being thrilled to lose weight on a half bag of peanut M&Ms or a plate of biscuits and gravy—learn to eat to bless your body with nutrients that give you energy and fortify your health. You can eat almost any food, if the amounts are small enough, and still lose weight. But "dieting" on candy bars or one meal a day has its price: low energy, fuzzy thinking, and being deprived of the foods that keep you well. Truly, no food should be forbidden or labeled as "bad"—but I will not encourage you to eat foods that are nutritional disasters just because you can. The fact is, you *can* learn to recognize your true need to eat and how to stop when satisfied. But those body signals can only be trusted when you are meeting your body's needs with regular meals, avoiding overeating, and getting plenty of exercise.

Learning how God designed your body for wellness and following these principles is not bondage. A person who is in serious financial difficulty must go to the root issue and examine his or her "love of money" and his or her dependence upon it. But to truly thrive, he or she must go a step further and learn how to budget and manage money. So it is with the person who wants to overcome overeating. It is important to identify the place of power you've given food, dieting, and body image in your life; but then you need to learn how to manage it—for life.

If you have had great success with the *Weigh Down* plan, I rejoice with you. But I encourage you to begin to transition gently to healthy eating, following documented scientific principles that reveal the miracle of our creation.

calories to a dangerous semistarvation level. The vast lack of nutrition has other limits as well—there's a limit to how long you can stay on these diets because they make you sick. Five to seven days is the average limit and enough to take off that promised five pounds. It's water, of course, but it feels as if you'd really been successful.

Each day of a typical seven-day program usually has specific foods that must be eaten, including potatoes, fruit juice, many vegetables, beef, tuna—even ice cream on some. Each day is carefully crafted to be extremely low in calories (less than 1,000 per day), complex carbohydrates, proteins, vitamins, and minerals. You can bet you'll feel lightheaded and weak, and notice a decreased ability to concentrate. Even if you love the particular food at the center of the plan (some people love cabbage!), this diet just isn't worth feeling weak and disoriented—and getting malnourished—for the sake of quick weight loss that won't stay lost once you begin eating normally again.

Reality

When it comes to calories, how much is too little? Less than your body weight times ten—so, less than 1,300 calories for a 130-pound woman. Results of four national surveys show that most people try to lose weight by eating 1,000 to 1,500 calories a day. But, overall, cutting calories to fewer than 1,500 (if you're a woman) or 1,800 (if you're a man) usually doesn't allow enough food for you to be satisfied in the long term. Eating fewer than 1,500 calories also makes it difficult to get enough of certain vital nutrients, such as folic acid, magnesium, and zinc.

Your body, created to survive, interprets long hours without enough food as potential starvation. To prepare for the long haul, the metabolism slows down dramatically so as not to burn much valuable muscle. So what does the desperate-to-lose-weight dieter do in

response? Cuts calories even more. I've seen far too many people cut their calories to below 500 calories per day, and although they are losing their health, they can't lose the weight they want.

Slashing your calorie intake too drastically can slow your metabolism so drastically that it can take up to a year to normalize. That's why you gain back weight so quickly after stopping this type of diet. After starvation, even a return to healthy eating will cause your body to store the calories as fat. What comes off will come back on... and on... and on. Contrary to what you may think, in a starvation state when no carbohydrate is available your body turns first to muscle mass for stored energy and later to your fat stores.

As for fasting, going without all food in order to lose weight can be just as damaging for the overweight person as a binge of eating. Although there is a proper place for fasting and prayer in our spiritual lives, starving in order to lose weight or to even "cleanse the body" has a more mundane motive, and is without the protection of grace! Starving will certainly achieve quick weight loss, but as seen in concentration camps during the war, what you lose is primarily water and muscle weight. This may look great on the scale, but it will look terrible on your body.

The Bottom Line

Fasting, single-food diets, and low-calorie meal replacements aren't the key to long-term weight control and better health—nor is eating whatever you want whenever you want but only half a portion. The only good news about extremely low calorie diets is that people often go off of them quickly—they simply feel too awful to stay on them. Don't rely on dangerous semistarvation diets to lose weight quickly. Instead, learn how to eat.

Blood and Body Type Diets

The newest wave of fad diets base their logic on even stranger theories than insulin resistance or food combining. Take Peter J. D'Adamo's book, *Eat Right 4 Your Type,* for example. This is a particular "favorite" of mine because it is genius-born—it promotes a completely undocumented theory that blood type is a sign of your predestined eating pattern. The diet is therefore tailored to your specific blood type. Here's the theory: If you are type O, like the majority of people, then you were descended from hunters and therefore should eat lots of meat and lots of fat. Gatherers, on the other hand, have type A blood and should be vegetarians and cook a lot. D'Adamo also sells special vitamins for each blood type.

The Body Code, by Jay Cooper, divides dieters into warriors, nurturers, communicators, and visionaries. Nurturers, in addition to eating lots of fruits and vegetables, no doubt do most of the cooking.

Dr. Abravanel's Body Type Diet and Lifetime Nutrition Plan (also known as the Caveman Diet) allows you to eat only what Stone Age people ate. This diet came from the proposition that everyone falls into one of four body types—thyroid, pituitary, adrenal, or gonadal—depending on body shape, food cravings, and other personal traits. Tests within the book with questions about food cravings, personality, cellulite, and sleeping patterns help you identify which is your dominant gland. These glands, the claim goes, are at the root of every weight problem; they trigger cravings for wrong foods and are overstimulated by the foods you crave, thereby slowing down your metabolism and causing you to gain weight.

Once you've identified your body type, you must follow that type's specially tailored diet—eat foods that suppress your "problem" gland while avoiding foods that stimulate it. If you are a thyroid type, you should be eating two eggs for breakfast every morning and

hard-boiled eggs for snacks, but restricting all fruit. If you are a pituitary type, you should *never* eat dairy products, but cooked hamburger would be a great snack. The big drawback of this diet is if you discover that you are a gonad. Gonads can eat only uncooked food.

Reality

The role glands play in regulating body weight is an extremely complex process that could never be remedied by an unbalanced and nutrient-deficient diet. And there is *zero* documentation showing that blood type affects your metabolism one iota. The truth is, cutting out whole food groups not only sets you up for failure, but also for malnutrition by limiting your intake of important vitamins and minerals. Furthermore, suggestions such as "waiting as much as six hours between meals to maximize fat burning" may help to cut calories, but it will also cause blood sugar levels to plummet, leaving you fatigued, irritable, and craving sweets—and your glands or blood type won't have a thing to do with it!

The Bottom Line

The real secret behind any weight-loss success in these diets is the extreme calorie restriction of each diet—too low to meet nutrient needs but low enough and unbalanced enough to allow quick fluid loss and muscle breakdown. Don't fall for a plan just because it sounds new, individualized, scientific, and complicated.

Lose-It-While-You-Sleep Diets

You've probably heard the radio personalities flooding the airwaves—particularly to the teens and twenty-something crowd—promising health and weight loss in a capsule, powder, or herbal brew. It sounds so easy. And these herbal supplements and power

drinks promising weight loss and energy are readily available in health-food stores and even some gyms. They are widely used by bodybuilders and athletes. They are recommended by trainers, friends, and multilevel marketers alike. They seem so natural; they seem so safe. But most people aren't aware they can have serious repercussions.

How to be a savvy user of the myriad of alternative therapies and dietary supplements on store shelves is a vital question, yet a difficult one because it's so hard to check out the science behind the products. They all sound so good, so helpful. There's chromium picolinate, the fat-burner favorite a few years back. Then there's Fat Trapper and Exercise in a Bottle, claiming in infomercials to prevent your body from absorbing dietary fat (eat all the cheeseburgers and fries you want!) and to increase the activity of muscle cells (no exercise required!) so that you can quickly burn the fat that's already been stored. And who hasn't heard of Metabolife, an herbal brew sold in mall kiosks and over the Internet. It has been touted as everything from a safe herbal diet aid to a brain and energy booster (a.k.a., herbal speed). Natural, safe, and quick is the ad's message, but natural, dangerous, and quick may be closer to reality.

Then there's DHEA, or dehydroepiandrosterone—the nineties darling for anti-aging and weight loss. It's a steroid hormone that is produced in abundance by the adrenal glands during youth and early adulthood. Blood levels of DHEA fall considerably as people grow older (production of DHEA starts to decline in the late twenties and dwindles to about 5 to 10 percent of its peak level by age eighty), so the claim is that supplementing with DHEA will remedy the actual cause of middle-age spread. You haven't gained weight because of doing something wrong, but you can lose it by doing something "right"—taking DHEA. The health risk of DHEA

could be great: One danger related to its use in men could be an increase in the risk of prostate cancer. In women, DHEA has been linked with a possible increase in the risk of breast cancer.

It's not just the "natural" supplements that abound with promises to do your weight loss for you. Now a whole new generation of prescription drugs are coming down the pike to help in the weight battle. Heard of Meridia (sibutrammine), the new player on the diet pill scene? There's also Zenical (Orlistat), the medication that works in the intestines by blocking the absorption of approximately 30 percent of the dietary fat consumed. About one-third of users experience unpleasant side effects (such as severe gas, loose stools, and anal leakage). But if it helps with weight loss, the prevailing question seems to be "How do I get a prescription?"

Reality

Do all these products that promise to "do the work for you" *really* do the work for you? Fat chance. Only if you believe in magical thinking. When it comes to herbal and supplement brews, powders, and drinks, the ingredients just haven't been shown effective in significant, healthy weight loss. You lose time and money, but you won't lose weight unless you follow the low-calorie eating plan included with the product.

But what's worse than losing time and money? Losing your health, or your life. Anne Marie Capati didn't tell her family she was taking potentially dangerous herbal supplements to lose weight. Life was a happy whirlwind for the Manhattan fashion designer and mother of two. She was exercising with a personal trainer and working on losing weight, keeping her blood pressure under control. Then, on October 1, 1998, Capati collapsed at her gym while working out with her trainer. She died of a stroke that night.

Anne Marie, it was discovered, had been taking a variety of herbal supplements including Thermadrene, a supplement loaded with ephedra, an ancient herb that stimulates heart rate and the central nervous system. Ephedra is found in many products and under many different names like Ma Huang, Ephedrine, Herbal Fen-Phen, Ultimate Xphoria, and others. Anne Marie was pumping drugs—that she beleived to be safe—as well as iron, and it killed her.

Although the FDA has linked ephedra-containing dietary supplements to more than eight hundred reports of adverse health effects, cases of muscle destruction, and forty-four deaths since

WHERE TO GET HELP

What is good nutrition? Whose answers should you listen to? The average American may have a difficult time telling you, because most of his or her health information comes from the media. A recent study found that 80 percent of women polled relied on the media as their primary source of nutrition information.

You may expect me to tell you that the very best source for accurate nutrition information is, of course, a nutritionist. I won't. Although I am one, the term *nutritionist* is the most meaningless one in medicine. The National Council Against Health Fraud ran a thirty-two–state survey of nutritionists listed in the Yellow Pages. Nearly half had questionable degrees, claiming to be doctors of nutri-medicine (say what?), food counselors, or certified nutritionists—all of which are meaningless titles without qualifications. The institutions from which they "graduated" sounded reputable, but weren't. Diploma mills abound—from which your dog or cat can get a doctorate degree as easily as you can for $1,000 cash or $1,200 with a credit card.

If you want reliable nutritional advice—someone to help you sort out reality from fiction and hope from hype, the person who physicians turn to when they need help with a nutrition issue—turn to a registered dietitian, or R.D. Those are my credentials. R.D.s are nutrition specialists who have bachelor's and master's degrees along with a completed residency/internship. They may even have medical degrees, and they must complete continuing education from accredited programs.

1993, they're still on the market. Reported side effects have included abnormal heart rhythm, seizure, stroke, psychosis, heart attack, and hepatitis. But America is still swallowing these herbal threats by the millions.

Just a few of the other weight loss supplements that are life-threatening are *Stephania*, also called magnolia (this herb has caused kidney disease and resulted in kidney transplants and dialysis in Europe); *Germander* (long-term use can lead to kidney damage and has allegedly been linked to a death); and *Kombucha tea* (an "herbal tea," also called mushroom tea, kvass tea, kwassan, and kargasok, which is really a colony of yeast and bacteria; it can cause liver and other organ damage, gastrointestinal upset, and has been linked to a death).

The ingredients in Fat Burners (chromium picolinate), Metabolife, blue green algae, Fat Trapper, and Exercise in a Bottle have not been scientifically proven to be effective, but numerous health concerns have been raised about the harm they can inflict. Many dietary supplements stress the "natural" quality of their products, which many misconstrue as meaning safer and better. But, as already discussed, this is not always the case.

So how do you sort out fact from fiction from outright fantasy amid the swirl of information about vitamin and nutritional supplements? Quite simply, you need to learn what's known about supplements and what's not. You need to learn who needs a supplement and who doesn't. And you must become familiar with critical safety issues in what has become a largely unregulated industry.

Prescribed weight-loss drugs should be used only if you are likely to have serious health problems caused by your weight. You should not use drugs to improve your appearance. Prescribed weight-loss drugs, when combined with a healthy diet and regular physical

activity, may help some obese adults lose weight. But before these medications can be widely recommended, more research is needed to determine their long-term safety and effectiveness.

The Bottom Line

Anything you put in your body has the potential to harm you, as well as help you. Anything you swallow—whether labeled "natural" or not—can act as a drug in your body, bringing side effects and health risks, including death. When it comes to losing weight, the only natural choice is eating well and exercising. You *don't* lose it while you sleep. You have to do your part.

SPRINGING THE TRAP

With countless diets, programs, and products promising to help you shed pounds, it should be easy. But as any veteran dieter knows, it's hard to lose weight. And it's even harder to keep it off. That's why fad diets continue to entrap us.

The medical evidence for the six diet schemes we've discussed is flimsy or nonexistent, but you can find an "expert" somewhere to support almost every one. Even diets that have been widely criticized by the medical community retain their vocal adherents. It is clear that as long as happy dieters and supportive "professionals" keep appearing on talk shows, people with eating problems are going to be suckers for diets that let them eat pork rinds.

After reading so much about the hidden and overt dangers of dieting, you may be immobilized by a sense of hopelessness about weight loss. Perhaps you're even thinking that it's smarter and safer to stay overweight.

Of course, my vote is for you to choose long-term health. That means choosing to lose weight if you need to, but *not* by dieting.

Instead, learn to live in a way that releases you from the diet trap forever and unleashes your body's natural ability to lose weight and feel great.

Even if you've been on a hundred diets, you can reverse the damage—beginning this very day. The question is not, "What have I done to myself?" by becoming caught in the diet trap. Rather, it is, "What can I do differently for myself now?" The secret lies in cracking the code for weight loss and whole-body healing.

PART TWO ▪ CRACKING THE FAT CELL CODE

CHAPTER 4 ▪ Overweight or Overfat?

The doctor of the future will give no medicine, but will interest his patient in the care of the human frame, in diet, and in the cause and prevention of disease.

—THOMAS A. EDISON

Before you set a goal for weight loss, you have to become objective about your weight, which is *very* difficult. You can't exactly trust the mirror—and you sure can't get a good reading from a scale.

Traditionally, "overweight" has been defined as weighing more than the weight listed for your age and height in a weight table. But that doesn't account for differences in body composition. Athletes, for example, are often "overweight" by weight table standards because of a large frame or muscle development. But they aren't overfat. And body fat, not weight, is what concerns health. The key to successful, healthy weight loss is to lower your percentage of body fat, not to lose pounds of muscle and water as a result of a quick-weight-loss diet.

You lower your percentage of body fat in two ways: by (1) losing fat, and (2) building muscle. The problem with using a scale to measure your progress in these two areas is that, pound for pound, muscle weighs more than fat (each pound of muscle is surrounded by four pounds of water) yet takes up only one-seventh of the space. Heavier, yes, but smaller and tighter. If you gain a pound of muscle,

the scale goes up. That's why only your "body feel," your appearance, and a body fat measurement can tell you the whole story.

Again, the question is not, *Are you overweight?* but, *Are you overfat?* It doesn't really matter if you're losing weight on the scale unless you're also losing fat. The key to body fat analysis is having fat estimated by a trained professional using a reliable method, such as skinfold measurements, infrared interactance, bioelectrical impedance, or underwater weighing. But none of these methods will give you better than a ballpark figure. The older you are or the more fat you're carrying, the less reliable the measurement may be. Nonetheless, if you are serious about wanting to lose only the right kind of weight, it would be a wonderful benchmark. Your area's YMCA, health club, wellness center, or hospital can direct you in getting an accurate body-fat test.

CAN YOU BE FIT AND FAT?

Other than clothes not fitting well, is excess weight really a problem? We assume that all obesity translates into health problems, but this is not necessarily so; not all overweight people are destined to be sick. It has been estimated that 10 to 20 percent of overweight people are not "disease prone." They may not feel tip-top but they are not necessarily more apt to be ill than those who are slim.

A vital observation, however, is this: Those who "eat themselves fat" are less healthy than those who are genetically predisposed to being overweight. And *gaining* weight is even more of a problem than *being* overweight.

Another critical fact: Even if you're slender as a stalk, a sedentary lifestyle can endanger your health. Studies have shown that thin people who aren't physically active are nearly three times more likely to die young than heavy people who exercise regularly. One

BODY MASS INDEX

Another measure of your weight and health status, more accurate than the scale, is your body mass index, or BMI. This is your weight and your height factored together.

TO CALCULATE YOUR BMI:

STEP 1: Multiply your weight in pounds by .45. (For example, if you weigh 150 pounds: 150 x .45 = 68)

STEP 2: Multiply your height in inches by .025. (For example, if you're 5'6" (66 inches): 66 x .025 = 1.65)

STEP 3: Square the answer from Step 2 (1.65 x 1.65 = 2.72)

STEP 4: Divide the answer from Step 1 by the answer from Step 3 (68/2.72 = 25)

If you use the metric system, your BMI equals your weight in kilograms divided by your height in centimeters squared.

YET ANOTHER WAY TO FIGURE YOUR BMI:

Multiply your weight by 703 and divide the result by your height in inches. Then divide that result again by your height.

In June 1998 the U.S. National Center for Health Statistics defined being overweight as having a BMI of 25 or more. For a woman of average height, 5-foot-5, that works out to 150 pounds; for the average man, 5-foot-10, it's 176 pounds. Obesity is defined as a BMI of 30 or more—180 pounds for a woman at 5-foot-5, 209 pounds for a man at 5-foot-10. This isn't a perfect formula because it could appear to be high for a healthy body builder or for adolescents not yet at their mature height.

The problem with BMI as an evaluation of obesity is that the measure doesn't really tell you directly about body composition. It's better than weight alone because it adjusts for height, but it's not as good as knowing how much of that weight is fat versus muscle.

study conducted by the Cooper Institute for Aerobics Research in Dallas tracked 25,000 men and 7,000 women for eight years. Those who were the least fit based on treadmill response were twice as

likely as the others to suffer fatalities from heart disease—no matter how much fat they carried. Thin, unfit men fared far worse in health matters than heavy men who were fit.

This research is compelling enough to put forth the opinion that it may be better to be overweight and active than thin and sedentary.

We can't assume that everyone who's overweight overeats. Being overweight actually stems from the interaction of several factors, genetics being one. Those who are predisposed to obesity may have a problem with leptin, a hormone released by the fat cells to signal the brain to stop storing fat. Either because they produce a defective version of leptin, or because their brain cells don't respond properly to the leptin signal, their fat-controlling mechanism is genetically flawed. Yet, their body may also be better equipped to handle the excess weight. But for the normal person who overeats unhealthy foods and exercises too little, excess body fat often contributes to cardiovascular diseases, several cancers, and numerous other medical disorders, including high blood pressure and diabetes.

A recent four-year study of more than 40,000 nurses, ages forty-six to seventy-one, linked even moderate excess weight to a greater risk of dying early. Losing just 5 to 10 percent of body fat was found to help reduce blood pressure, improve triglyceride and cholesterol levels, reduce sleep apnea symptoms, and cut the risk for joint problems such as osteoarthritis. This large-scale study suggested that the best weight for a woman at middle age was whatever she weighed at eighteen plus ten pounds. For every 2.2 pounds of weight she gained above this, the study showed, the risk of suffering a heart attack rose by 3.1 percent.

TAMING THE WEIGHT MONSTER

Clearly, the best course is to nip weight gain in the bud. Even a ten-pound gain is worth paying attention to. It's easier to tame the weight monster while it's small.

That's what Sherri wanted to do when she came to see me. Sherri just couldn't seem to get control of her seesaw eating—sometimes good and sometimes horrid. She wasn't particularly heavy; but she had battled the same ten pounds for so long that the battle itself seemed to have taken on a life of its own.

Sherri's day starts early, and ends late. She starts the day as a wife and Mom—but with an ailing mother in town, she ends up being daughter as well. She quickly turns into chauffeur for the school car-pool—which she does most mornings so that someone else can pick up the kids while she's at work in the afternoon. She then drives straight to work, which is a tense hour-long commute. At work she starts to spin more plates—creative ones, deadline ones, manage-ment ones, political ones, friendship ones—and then she comes home to yet more. Her life is filled with "gotta dos"—gotta do that report, gotta make that meeting, gotta get the kids here or there, gotta get dinner, gotta get that gift, gotta call Mom, gotta exercise, gotta pay bills, gotta lose weight.

Sherri described herself to me this way: "I feel like one of the kid's juice boxes that has about twenty straws stuck all over the place. I've been sucked dry—the box has caved into a vacuum. I'm operating on nothing—and feel just the same—nothing. I've got too much to think about to feel anything." Sherri's churning, spinning thoughts were wearing her out as much as her schedule was.

Bouncing like a pinball between an obsessive-compulsive drive for a beautiful body and a chronic lack of self-care, Sherri was bat-

tling a cycle of unhealthy eating, high stress levels, and depleted energy supplies. She would come home many nights, sucked dry, and—just for the energy to get dinner for the kids—grab a bag of chips and diet soda. Then a few doughnuts, then some cookies—and then the leftover macaroni and cheese from the kid's plates. Afterward, she'd sit down with her husband for a mindless meal. Most nights, she'd fall asleep on the couch at 10:00 and then wake up to drag herself to bed. If she was lucky, she could sleep till 2:30 or 3:00 AM, only to wake with a start of anxiety and be unable to get back to sleep. She'd finally get up and eat something—cheese, chicken, chips, anything. Then she'd catnap the rest of the night and turn off the 5 AM alarm—exhausted.

Turns out that Sherri didn't really eat that much, and the high-fat, sugar-laden foods she loved weren't the only trouble spots in her eating style. The biggest problem was the lack of routine in her eating. She might go all day with little or no food, other than the occasional doughnut grabbed at a morning meeting (she *loved* doughnuts!) and a continuous intake of coffee and diet soda. She typically ate only one "meal" a day—nonstop grazing from the time she got home till she fell into a coma on the sofa.

Because Sherri didn't seem to have time for anything, even to notice how bad she really felt, she would drown out the "I'm so tired" message with sugar, caffeine, and comfort foods. But that would only last for a while, usually until her weight would soar up seven or eight pounds. Then she couldn't stand the way she looked anymore, and felt others were noticing, she would hit bottom and start on a new diet. She had been on four different diets since January 1, and this was only April.

"I do great on diets," Sherri admitted. "It's the one time I focus just on me." Telling words. Sherri knew that diets—any diet—

worked really well for her. "I lose weight and feel great in just days!" But then the inevitable crisis, and after she had stoically starved for a few weeks, Sherri would blow it in one weary night. Then the whole cycle would begin again. She finally conceded, "I just feel like I'm killing myself with my diets, and my failures are making me crazy."

Sherri was truly caught in a trap, but her weight was not the real problem. It was a *life* trap, and her way of eating and dieting was the glue keeping her stuck.

Sherri exemplifies a classic pattern I see every day in counseling. She is a creative television producer, successful in all she puts her hand and mind to—except in the area of eating and taking care of herself. Like so many others, she has tried diet after diet, only to succeed and then fail. She never resolved her underlying problems or educated herself about how the human body was designed to function optimally. She was drowning in a tidal wave of stress—and was turning to food to keep her afloat. Food was being used to meet needs it was never designed to meet. She was feeding her soul with junk food—and it just didn't fit the bill. Every diet, followed by every failure, had her in the vice grip of the diet trap.

THE STRESS RESPONSE

Sherri is not alone in her fight against the tidal wave of stress—and the erratic eating and weight gain that often accompanies it. Nearly nine out of ten Americans say they experience stress every day and high levels several times a week. One in four complains of high stress levels every day.

Stress is as difficult to treat as it is to understand. That's because stress means different things to different people. Our reactions to life events vary from person to person; what frazzles me may chal-

lenge and inspire you. Most people refer to life's challenges as *stress*, when in fact those are *stressors*.

Stress can result from good things as well as bad; from the joy of a wedding celebration to a major loss like the death of a loved one; from minor irritations like losing car keys or a major one like a traffic jam. Research shows time and time again that it's not the number of stressors in one's life that affects health and well-being, but our response to the situations. The body's response is the actual "stress," and it comes from within.

Your body was designed to cope with the stresses you encounter in life. You were created with a "stress tracking system" that is intricately programmed to seek and find stress signals. This "stress sensor" (the pituitary gland in our brain) is much like radar equipment and is constantly on the lookout for what appears to be danger to your survival. When this master gland picks up stress signals, it sends a hormone messenger to your body's adrenal system (located near the kidneys) to prepare you to fight the present danger, or flee to escape it.

These chemical messages set in motion the symptoms of stress. They cause a shift of the chemical balance deep within your system, triggering reactions that slow down the metabolism and other bodily functions (such as digestion). The stress hormones, adrenaline and cortisol, prime your body for action, causing blood to pool in your muscles and fluid to gather in your extremities. Your heart beats faster, your blood pressure rises, your breathing rate increases, and your muscles tense up. Proteins are converted into sugar, which causes insulin levels to surge and your blood sugar to fluctuate wildly. The roller coaster ride your blood sugar takes in response to stress affects your energy levels, mood, concentration, appetite, and cravings.

This "fight-or-flight" response—this surge of chemical reactions—may have helped our early ancestors to survive when facing grizzly bears, but when our twenty-first century bodies think traffic jams, deadlines, financial pressures, or relationship struggles are modern-day grizzlies, the chronic stress response can wear us down and lock down our metabolism.

The key word with any kind of negative stress is *chronic*. All the adaptive mechanisms wired into us by our Creator were intended as a short-term alert/alarm to prepare us to flee or do battle, and to help us recover once out of danger. But today's bodies are exposed to chronic, unresolved stress, and almost never have a chance to recover and break out of the fight-or-flight reaction. When the body is exposed to the same stress again and again with no stress release, energy stores are depleted and the body begins to show signs of damage—with a metabolic slow-down and fatigue being the cardinal symptoms. Being stuck in stress causes chemical surges which can result in headaches, backaches, sleep disturbances, anxiety, depression, arthritic pain, asthma, gastrointestinal upsets, skin disorders—along with weight and eating problems.

Nothing fuels appetite like chronic stress—and nothing puts the body into the fat storage mode more quickly. Whether or not we eat more when under stress, the stressed body does more damage with what comes in than the nonstressed body. There may be other forces at work as well; for example, when a lack of self-care (sedentary lifestyle, sleep deprivation, poor eating habits) is combined with states of imbalance (illness, hormone dysfunction, depression, or worry), the fat cell stays locked in a "store" rather than "burn" mode. While we are waging war against our body, our fat cells are looking out for our survival. And a chemical imbalance occurs that slows our metabolism. The problem is not only what we are eating, but what

the fat cells are storing away. The fat cells become stockpiled with unused energy, and the cells lock down.

The good news is that we all have more power than we realize to take charge of our body's stress response. But most of us just don't recognize the stress warnings, nor how they keep us caught in the diet trap.

GET YOUR BODY WORKING FOR YOU

In order to achieve a harmonious balance within your body and soul and tap into the reservoir of metabolic power and healing within, you must begin by righting the wrongs of your body and getting it to work for you rather than against you. This doesn't just happen when you go on one more diet or try to "be good." It begins when you change the way you live and eat. It requires an understanding of how your body works and what habits you have acquired that either release the natural flow of energy from the cells or lock it down.

To break out of the diet trap, you have to get beyond the weight issue. Weight problems are but a symptom of an ailing and stressed lifestyle. You must focus on the here and now of life.

Start by assessing your day: How do you feel when you wake up in the morning? How much energy do you have? Do you often experience physical or emotional rises and falls throughout your day? Are there times when hunger or cravings seem to overtake you? How do you satisfy that hunger? What logjams are blocking your total well-being?

The good news is, you don't have to push or drag through each day. You *can* have abundant life; you *can* take charge of your wellness, your energy level, and your weight. And you *can* be set free from the life traps of poor eating, stress, too little rest, and too little exercise. You are free to be well; you need only to choose to eat well of the food that gives life: physically, emotionally, and spiritually.

The bottom line goal: Even if you don't lose weight, adopt health-promoting living habits. Losing weight might not guarantee you a longer life, but being active, eating differently, and heading off more weight gain *will* make you healthier. Whatever your need of the moment—weight loss, controlling overeating, embracing self-care, regaining health and energy—the key is to get started and get strong, one step at a time.

CHAPTER 5 ■ Releasing Your Body's Natural Ability to Lose Weight

Good health has more to do with everyday behavior and habits than with miracles of modern science. Prevention is far superior to cure!

—ANONYMOUS

Weight gain is not inevitable for men or women—nor is it inevitable if you have a genetic proclivity. If you have been gaining weight—or been unable to lose it—it's probably because your fat cells are responding in a survival mode. Fighting them with a fad diet only locks them into metabolic slowdown. That's why the only way to manage weight permanently is to forego dieting and begin to live in a new and natural way that unlocks the exit door to your fat cells so they can start releasing fat again.

Getting your body working for you and shedding excess pounds *is* within your control. The key is learning and practicing the seven secrets of *The Smart Weigh*—strategies for staying fit and fueled and getting your body working for you with optimal fat-burning capability.

THE SECRETS OF *THE SMART WEIGH*

S: Stoke your metabolic fire
E: Equip yourself for stress release
C: Cultivate a positive perspective
R: Regulate your blood sugars
E: Equalize your brain chemistry
T: Take charge of your appetite
S: Strengthen your immune system

These methods will unlock your fat cells and restore the balances of your body and soul. They are not vague or complex, nor are they startling discoveries. They are simply keys to the real issues of weight management—to meeting real needs with real answers. In Chapter 11, I'll help you convert these secrets into specific action steps over a seven-week period. Once you get in the habit of living *The Smart Weigh,* you'll be free from the diet trap once and for all, and your natural ability to lose weight will blossom.

SECRET NO. 1:
STOKE YOUR METABOLIC FIRE

It's not the calories taken in but the calories burned that count—and your metabolism makes all the difference. Remember, your metabolism is the chemical process that converts food to energy and is measured by how many calories you burn per minute for body functions—both voluntary activity and movement, and automatic, involuntary functions like breathing, heart beat, digestion, and blood circulation. The largest amount of calories used (70 percent) are those burned to maintain this basic body function.

At a cellular level, our metabolism is activated by a balance of supply and demand: a supply of optimum fuel and oxygen to the

cells for energy metabolism, and a demand from the body systems for energy. As I explained earlier, a combination of factors—especially our stressful lifestyles and lack of self-care—causes our fat cells to lock down, slowing our metabolic rate to a snail's pace, which results in fats being stored rather than burned for energy. This "cocooning" is the result of constant stress and not nearly enough energy supply to meet the needs.

While a calorie is a calorie, your metabolism can increase or decrease (burn or store those calories) depending on your eating patterns. The body was designed to slow itself down to protect against energy deficits. As a result, erratic eating patterns keep our metabolism locked in low gear, storing away every meal as if it were our last.

Think of your metabolism as a campfire that requires fuel to burn, and air to fan the fire's flame. A campfire dies down during the night and must have wood added in the morning to begin to burn brightly once more. Without being "stoked" with new fuel, the spark turns to ash—there's nothing left to burn.

Similarly, your body awakens in a slowed-down state. If you don't "break the fast" with breakfast and continue to feed it through the day to meet your body's demand for energy and boost your metabolic system, your body turns to its own muscle mass (not fat) for energy and slows down even more, conserving itself for a potentially long, starved state. Then, when the evening eating begins, most of that food will be stored as fat because the body isn't burning energy at a fast rate; the fire has gone out. The food you eat, after long hours without, is like dumping an armload of firewood on a dead fire.

Regardless of the number of calories consumed when we do eat, the body can use only a small amount of energy, protein, and other nutrients quickly. The rest is thrown off as waste or stored as fat. Eating the American way robs the body of vital nutrients for the remaining

twenty-four hours—until the next feeding frenzy. We not only go wrong in how much we eat or what we eat; we also eat entirely too much at the wrong time. The vast majority of us get most of our calories after six o'clock in the evening—too much too late.

Starving for Nutrition

To burn the calories you consume—to metabolize them into energy, rather than store them as fat—requires nutrients. These vital nutrients are the vitamins, minerals, and phytochemicals found in foods. Certain nutrients are considered essential for the metabolism because they act as catalysts for calorie burning. The B-complex vitamins, magnesium, and zinc are important examples. (We'll talk more about them in Chapter 6.) Also important is chromium, found in whole grains, which helps to transport glucose through the cell membranes so that it can be burned for energy. Iron is also vital because it delivers oxygen inside the cells, "fanning the flame" of calorie burning.

Many people may be getting plenty of calories, but not enough of the nutrients to help metabolize those calories and activate fat-burning potential. Or, their metabolisms may be so slow because of chronic stress that they cannot burn the calories effectively. Either way, you've got a fat-storing crisis.

Living life in the fast lane (and often, the fast food lane) means that food choices are often based on convenience instead of nutrition. That not only means a junk food diet, but a *junk diet*: lots of calories, lots of fat, lots of sodium, lots of sugar—all promising energy on the run. But the energy runs out and ends up slowing down, not speeding up, our metabolism.

The classic junk diet is notoriously low in the nutrients that provide for consistent, long-lasting energy. We are more apt to eat fries

than baked potatoes, ketchup than tomatoes, and drink orange soda instead of orange juice. And so most of us are deficient in the vitamins and minerals that would keep our metabolism working in high gear.

But we *can* choose to eat well and eat often. To preserve muscle mass and burn fat while losing weight, your best bet is to eat balanced meals and snacks of whole carbohydrates and low-fat protein, evenly distributed throughout the day. This, in combination with eating an adequate amount of calories, is the most important step you can take to unleash your body's natural ability to lose weight.

To activate your metabolism and get your body working for you, you need to *eat*: (1) eat early, (2) eat often, (3) eat balanced, (4) eat lean, and (5) eat bright. Read more about strategic eating in the next chapter.

Fanning the Fire's Flame

Eating strategically is one of the best ways to increase your metabolism, and exercise is a close second. Yet, research shows that most people with weight problems not only eat too much, too late, but exercise too little. And remember: Controlling your intake of food is not an alternative to exercise, nor is exercise an alternative to healthy eating.

Not only does exercise help you to burn the calories you take in better; it also serves to build muscle mass. And that's another weight-control secret: To rev up your metabolism and burn fat, *use*—don't lose—your muscle. Building new muscle through strength training is one of the best ways to reverse the metabolic slowdown of midlife and stressful living. The more lean muscle mass you can preserve, the bigger "engine" you'll have in which to burn calories.

Now, does what you've always heard about the importance of

exercise make more sense? You can boost your metabolism, lose body fat, and gain muscle mass by doing some type of aerobic activity for thirty to sixty minutes at least four times a week. No time? Break up your workouts into shorter bouts throughout the day. Reports show that squeezing in even ten-minute spurts of activity throughout the day yields results. Add in a workout with free weights, exercise bands, or a Nautilus machine twice a week, or take advantage of the humdrum tasks that have to be done anyway by doing them with vigor. Haul the garbage cans to the curb yourself and rejoice when you carry that laundry basket up and down the stairs! Even though regularly scheduled aerobic exercise is best for losing fat, any extra movement boosts the metabolism and burns calories better. Start parking at the far end of the lot, or make several trips up and down the stairs instead of using the elevator. Even foregoing such automated gadgets as remote controls and garage door openers can make a metabolic difference. (Read more about the benefits of movement in Chapter 7.)

Taking Care of Yourself

You might be wondering, *Where am I going to get the energy to do all this extra moving and working out? I can barely keep my pace as it is!* You're not alone. Not only are many of us living in metabolic lock-down as a result of our lifestyle choices, we're living in an energy crisis as well. The very things that result in a slowed metabolism produce the energy deficit, too. One of these factors is sleep deprivation. You'll read more about the power of restful sleep in Chapter 9.

Sleep is the repair shop of the body; without it we cannot be healthy or even happy. Sleep deprivation actually becomes a profound stress to your body, contributing to fat cell lock-down. Research shows that missing just one night of restful sleep can cause

a surge of stress hormones to circulate through your body, weakening your immune system and causing a metabolic slowdown. Conversely, replenishing sleep and time-outs can equip the body for stress release. Again, it's how we were created.

Breathing is another normal body action that can either release stress—or actually cause it. You can't help breathing, but you can help yourself breathe better. Deep, slow, oxygenating breaths are one of the simplest things you can do to relieve stress, activate your metabolism, and keep control of yourself in any situation.

Yet in times of stress, we tend to breathe in a panicked way—rapid, shallow, or deep, heaving breaths—each breath robbing the bloodstream of the right amount of oxygen to take to the cells to fan the metabolic fire. You can think of this kind of stressbreathing as suffocating your blood cells—which signals the release of even more stress hormones. The more stressed and tense you are, the higher your brain's demand for oxygen, yet the shallow breathing that accompanies stress decreases the oxygen intake and transfer. It's a vicious cycle that takes your breath away! The good news is that learning to breathe in a relaxed way immediately defuses the stress response. (Read more about the healing benefits of focused breathing in Chapter 8.)

Drinking adequate water is another critical element for activating your metabolism and total body health. Because your body is comprised primarily of water, every cell in your body relies on this "one-of-a-kind" beverage to dilute biochemicals, vitamins, and minerals to just the right concentrations so that they can be used in energy metabolism. The body also depends on water to keep the blood at the proper fluid concentration to effectively transport these nutrients and other substances from one part to another. Blood volume actually decreases and "thickens" when you are dehydrated,

meaning that the heart has to work harder to supply your cells with needed oxygen. And remember, oxygenated blood is essential for an activated metabolism—to fan the flame for fat burning. A slow-burning metabolism is a symptom of dehydration.

By now you're getting the picture: activating your metabolism is really just a matter of moving into better self-care. That means treating yourself well by eating right, drinking enough water, exercising and strengthening your body, breathing deeply, and getting rest. The opposite behavior—a lack of self-care—is the recipe for fat storage.

SECRET NO. 2:
EQUIP YOURSELF FOR STRESS RELEASE

I serve as a wellness and nutrition coach for a number of professional athletes, particularly those in the National Basketball Association and Women's National Basketball Association. I also have an opportunity to work with corporate "athletes," high-on-the-ladder executives who are under similar performance demands and pressure. But I work with many more *life* athletes—people like you and me with stresses and demands from all of life's arenas: emotional, relational, financial, physical.

Like the pros, we life athletes have an individual "court of life" in which we are expected to perform day by day with perfection, endurance, and stamina. Like basketball players, we, too, have daily "fouls" committed against us, and we are continually stepping up to the "line"—flanked by team players and opposing forces alike. We are charging full steam ahead in life with too much to do and too few resources to do it with. So we become drained emotionally, spiritually, and physically. It's a stressful way to live, and we need a different level of fueling and fitness to rise up to the continuous levels of stress.

That's where strategic eating and living comes in, with a focus on timing, balance, and variety. Just as your body is designed to work for you nutritionally, it is also designed to survive, even thrive, amidst the stresses of daily life. As important as it is to identify how stress affects us, learning how to defuse life's stressors is even more critical. For once the body picks up a stress signal and interprets "danger," chemical reactions tell the body to go into a conservation mode. This includes three predictable physical responses that clearly affect the whole being.

(1) THE BODY'S METABOLISM SLOWS, storing excess energy in the fat cells for fight or flight. This metabolic slowdown explains part of the quick weight gain that often accompanies stressful times. The slowdown affects energy as well, throwing a person into the fatigue ditch.

Gastrointestinal function is also hit through increased secretions of gastric acids and improper movement of food stuffs through the digestive tract. This means constipation for some; gastritis, ulceration, diarrhea, spastic colon, or Irritable Bowel Syndrome for others. Those prone to increased acidity often have difficulties "facing food" when stressed; they keep a low-grade "queeze" at all times and are prone to a vicious "the less I eat, the worse I feel, and thereby the less I eat" mode.

(2) THE BLOOD SUGAR DIPS, stimulating an appetite for high-calorie foods that will provide needed energy. As the blood sugars fluctuate, energy and moods drop, but appetite soars. Yes, there is a physical reason for getting tired and cranky in stressful times. And, yes, there's a physical reason for craving M&Ms (compounded with strained emotions asking for food to tranquilize the anxiety—after all, *stressed*, spelled backward, is *desserts*).

(3) THE BODY RETAINS EXCESS FLUIDS, keeping the system lubricated

and hydrated for the survival defense. Blood pools in our muscles and extremities, and we store the fluids in the extra poundage in our abdominal area, making us feel bloated and sluggish.

All in all, a stressed body is a rotten place to live—and for some of us it's a 365-day-a-year residence. Some days we face intense, crisis-oriented stress. But some of us live with a level of day-to-day stress that makes us feel chronically out of control to some degree. Chronic stress takes a particular toll on the body because, though it fluctuates in intensity, it never really goes away.

Strategic eating and drinking, exercise, proper breathing, and adequate rest will enable you to stand strong even with a particularly heavy stress load.

The Value of Eating Well

Strategic eating strengthens our barricades against attack and feeds our stress-fighting army. When it comes to righting the fat-storage mechanism of stress and having all the metabolic burn you want and need, eating the right foods at the right time is the bottom line.

Unfortunately, when stress comes in the front door, wise eating often goes out the window. "Quick and easy" takes precedence over nutritious—which leads to fatigue. The more fatigued we get, the less we exercise. The less we exercise, the more fatigued—and stressed—we become.

Although we know that healthy eating and exercise would make a world of difference, they seem like more time-robbers and add to our already long list of "shoulds." If this sounds familiar, try transforming "shoulds" to "coulds." Take charge of what you *can.* As the body's metabolism slows, properly timed and balanced eating can gear it up. When the stress chemicals produce more gastric acids, smart eating can neutralize the acids and stabilize digestive function.

As the blood sugars fluctuate more wildly, the right foods at the right time can keep them even. When the body retains more fluids, adequate protein and fluid intake helps restore proper fluid balance.

Strategic eating keeps your body actively metabolizing the nutrients you eat. In addition, it energizes you for exercise and allows for more restful sleep, both of which further equip the body to alleviate stress.

The Power of Exercise

Exercise is a sword that cuts away at the negative symptoms of stress—a powerful offensive weapon in the war against stress.

Aerobic exercise simulates the physical exertion in the fight-or-flight chemical reactions that occur in the body under stress. It prompts the release of endorphins, powerful stress-busting chemicals. Working somewhat like morphine, endorphins tell the body that it is no longer in danger. You defeated or outran the grizzly bear! You took control of the challenging situation; it no longer controls you.

When you hit a tennis ball, your body thinks you've had your fight. When you walk, your body thinks you are fleeing your present danger; ballroom dancing tells your body that you're waltzing away from the threat. Even laughing is an exercise that contains great stress-busting power—it tells your body that the stress is nothing to fret about. It can't be life-threatening if you can laugh.

Nothing can replace exercise; it is the key to a positive response to stress. This is why exercise is considered nature's best tranquilizer. Exercise just thirty minutes—it can even become your quiet time in the midst of a busy life, a time when you can see the stress through a different lens.

Ironically, when life is most stressful, when we have the least

amount of time to exercise, rest and reflect, eat well, or find anything to laugh about, is when we need those things most. Taking charge of our bodies is one thing within our control, even in the midst of situations that feel very out of control. We can respond as victims or victors.

SECRET NO. 3:
CULTIVATE A POSITIVE PERSPECTIVE

A positive mental attitude is a vital spoke in the wheel of wellness— and critical in successful weight loss. In contrast, a negative attitude saps our well-being and aims us toward just what we expect: the worst.

There is both spiritual and scientific wisdom behind having a positive attitude; it is imperative that we set our eyes and our belief on the good things of life. The wisdom behind this is that our mind is a magnet and we gravitate toward what we think about most. We move straight toward whatever we have our eyes on.

Have you ever noticed how often automobile wrecks involve telephone poles? When a car is running off the road, there is much more open space to go toward than there are poles to hit. Yet they are what the driver sees, and they are what the driver hits.

If I continually grouse that nothing ever works for me, that there is never enough time, that nobody cares for me, that only tough things come my way, then I will attract more of the same. Because my eyes are only on my lack, I will overlook opportunity, refuse offers of help, and continue to propel myself into emotional and spiritual bankruptcy.

I have observed that if a person consistently concentrates on what he doesn't have, he will get less and less of what he wants. If we focus on what's wrong, we never find what's right. Alternately, the people who

are continually rejoicing in what life gives them, and are always looking for and expecting the best, lead active and fulfilling lives. Those who have the most beautiful lives are those who value life highly.

I'm not suggesting that all the answers to life's problems come simply through "the power of positive thinking," but I do believe that a positive perception goes beyond our circumstances. True joy stems from deep within our souls and flows from our spiritual connection.

Attitude Lifters

Pessimists blame every setback on their personal flaws or on how rottenly the world treats them, and they feel that nothing they do can make it better. It's a state of mind with huge metabolic impact—the negative "I'm gonna go eat worms" response weakens the immunes and locks down the metabolism. Happiness and success—even in weight loss—will be elusive.

Cultivating a positive, optimistic attitude—the belief that you can take charge of your choices and influence your circumstances—protects you against sagging spirits and a lagging metabolism by protecting you against the stress hormones that accompany hopelessness. Try these ten tips to bolster your self-image and lift up your attitude:

(1) PAY ATTENTION TO YOUR SELF-TALK. A negative perspective and negative self-talk become a habitual thought pattern, and it's a hard habit to shake—particularly when it's focused on our own body image. We can be our own worst enemy or our own best friend. It's all revealed in how we talk to ourselves. It's amazing how often we put ourselves down throughout the day—and it's time to stop! We need to replace the negative thoughts with positive ones. It's much

like giving our mind and soul a healthy dose of weed and feed—weeding out the negative belief system, and feeding the one that allows us to thrive.

Next time you catch yourself making critical comments, fight back by immediately complimenting yourself and marveling at how specially you were created. Turn a phrase like, "No one could like anyone as fat as I am," into a positive statement like, "I am liked and respected by others because of who I am. Beauty is an inner quality that comes from caring about myself and about others, not from my weight on the scale."

You may choose to eat well and exercise, but it will not make you a more wonderful, likable person. And believing that you already *are* that wonderful, likable person is what begins the process of lasting change.

(2) SEE THE WORLD REALISTICALLY. It's common to compare ourselves to people in magazines or movies, but this is almost guaranteed to make us feel inferior. Realize that envy is a mental state with no payoff. It is human nature to feel sure that others are happier than you are. But the better you know the people you envy—whether the wealthy, the famous, the celebrities with gorgeous partners—the more you will realize their facades hide the same worries, hassles, and sadnesses we all face.

If you must compare yourself to others, look at the real people around you. They come in different shapes and sizes, and none of them is airbrushed or highlighted. Rather than studying pictures in magazines or listening to celebrity talk, read articles or books about uplifting subjects that can raise your spirits.

(3) RECOGNIZE YOUR SPECIAL QUALITIES. Make a list of all your positive qualities, not including your physical traits. Are you kind? Artistic? Honest? Good in business? Do you make people laugh? Post your list near the mirror or some place where you'll see it every day.

(4) PUT YOUR BODY BACK TOGETHER. Most of us with negative body images have dissected our bodies into good and bad parts. "I hate my thighs and bottom." "My backside is okay, but my stomach is fat and my arms are flabby." Reconnect with your body by appreciating how it all works to keep you going. Try a daily routine of stretching; the fluid movements are great for getting in touch with your body that is so wonderfully made.

(5) REMEMBER THE KID INSIDE YOU. Give yourself permission not to be perfect. Inside all of us is the kid we used to be—the kid who didn't have to be perfect and worry about everything (or shouldn't have had to!). Give yourself a break. Place a photo of yourself as a child in your bedroom or at your desk at work so you can see it each day and remember to nurture yourself and laugh a little. Spend time with children as well—they are wonderful reminders of how playful and fun life should be.

(6) PEPPER YOUR DAYS WITH SMALL PLEASURES. Big changes won't make you positive or happy permanently. Negative, unhappy people who win the lottery are no happier a year after they win. But every little thing you enjoy gives you an immediate mood boost. Example: Walk in the park, concentrate on a hobby, or take time off to spend an afternoon with your kids.

One step toward being kind to your body, and inevitably yourself, is to indulge yourself with healthy pleasures. Get a massage, take a long, hot bath, use lotions that smell good, treat yourself to a manicure or a pedicure or go hit some golf balls. It makes a positive statement to your inner self—that you're worth it!

(7) ENJOY YOUR FOOD. Eating is pleasurable. So enjoy it! Food gives us energy and sustains life. Don't deprive yourself or consider eating an evil act. Don't make any food a "forbidden fruit." Focusing on what you shouldn't do and what you shouldn't eat only sets you up for

failure. The negative behavior or food becomes an obsession—and it's only a matter of time before you fall headfirst! If you allow yourself to enjoy food, and eat more often, you'll be less likely to overeat. And your body won't feel bloated and uncomfortable.

(8) THINK YOURSELF HAPPIER. When a bad mood overcomes us, a slip-up becomes a life sentence of being no good; a bad hair day becomes an "I've always been so ugly" week.

The good news is that it's possible to reverse this negative outlook by becoming aware of it and working to change it. The next time something happens that puts you into a funk, make a mental list of what's going right. You didn't get that desperately needed raise? Oh well, you have lots of friends, and your boyfriend and your dog love you. If a friend forgets to call you at an appointed time, don't be bitter or stay mad. Replace the negative thoughts with happier ones like "Maybe he/she had an emergency" or "Everyone forgets."

(9) BE ACTIVE. Movement and exercise can make you and your body feel terrific! Not only does exercise help boost your mood, it stimulates your muscles, making you feel more alive and connected to your body. Exercise also distracts you from negative feelings and forces you to concentrate on your breathing, stamina, and physical power. By the time you've completed your workout, your negative feelings are likely to be less intense or even replaced by a positive sense of accomplishment.

(10) THRIVE! Live well—whatever that means for you. Living well according to a strong value system will help you feel better about who you are and how you look. Whenever a problem seems daunting, take action. Define your goal, then plan specific steps to get there. Every "hopeless" situation you turn around this way will make you a more positive person.

You are a unique, amazing person—don't forget it! A healthy, *happy* life can be yours.

SECRET NO. 4:
REGULATE YOUR BLOOD SUGARS

Our blood sugar level is one of the more powerful influences on our well-being, our ability to lose weight, and our appetite. From a chemical perspective, regulating our blood sugar level is the most effective way to release our fat-burning capacity.

When our blood sugars are up and even, but not too high, we are brimming with energy and vitality and our appetite is in control. When the levels are bouncing widely and wildly, our energy, mood, memory, clarity of thought, and overall performance is apt to rise and fall along with them.

Blood sugar levels normally crest and fall every three to four hours, and even more often and intensely when your body is stuck in the stress response. As sugars fall, so will your sense of well-being, energy level, concentration, and ability to handle stress. Your body will need about half an hour to convert what you eat to energy, so waiting to eat until you're cranky and starving doesn't help immediately. If you've starved all day, the drop in sugars will be a "free fall," leaving you weak, sleepy, dizzy, and *hungry*. There's one thing that doesn't fall with blood sugars, and that's your appetite. As the blood sugars crash, the body sends a chemical signal to the brain's appetite control center, demanding to be fed. And your cells are screaming for a quick energy source—not broccoli or cauliflower, but chocolate chips or Reese's Peanut Butter Cups!

Too much sugar and refined carbohydrates is a drain on anyone's energy metabolism, and a serious one for people with sensitive blood sugar responses. Once a person who is sensitive to the rises and falls

ARE YOUR THOUGHTS AND FEELINGS MAKING YOU SICK?

Intriguing research is affirming that chronic insidious thoughts of doom and feelings of hopelessness or unforgiveness can affect the immune system. For instance, doctors at the University of Ohio have shown that significant anxiety can actually lower several of the immune factors in your bloodstream. Other studies suggest that a negative state of mind can increase the risk of infection from a cold or virus, or even more serious diseases.

Medical researchers in California, Florida, and North Carolina have found that chronic worry, irritability, and unresolved anger may increase production of hormones that are responsible for reducing the body's ability to fight disease and can lead to high blood pressure and heart attack. In another study on people with diabetes, a negative state of mind that develops into depression has also been shown to trigger an adverse physiological response, driving up blood glucose and insulin levels and promoting weight gain. How it does this is not yet properly understood; however, it is theorized that the brain chemistry that accompanies these emotions and thought patterns alters levels of the hormone cortisol, which can worsen insulin resistance and lead to heart disease and other killer diseases from the lowered immune response.

in blood sugar has eaten, his or her blood sugar rises quickly, very quickly if the person has consumed a refined carbohydrate with a high glycemic index (one that is fast-released into the bloodstream as glucose). And that's the problem: what comes up quickly will quickly come down. These quick bursts of energy can ultimately cause fatigue and stimulate appetite by creating a drop in blood sugar due to the insulin surges that result. Remember, insulin levels rise in response to the higher blood glucose level that moves the sugar into the cell to be processed. The insulin does so by opening muscle cell doors wide to usher in the glucose that is to be burned for energy. But if you've consumed more calories than you can use at that time for energy, the insulin ushers the calories into the fat cells to be stored as fat. If you're also overloading on fat, those fat cell doors swing open wider still.

Everyone responds poorly to a high glucose load, but some respond worse than others. To estimate how blood sugar will be affected by eating, the glycemic potential of food has been established to show whether a food will

raise blood sugar levels dramatically and quickly (fast release), moderately (quick release), or just a little (slow release). The glycemic rating of pure sugar is set at 100, and every other food is ranked on a scale from 0 to 100, based on its actual effect on blood sugars. Carbohydrates that break down quickly during digestion have the highest glycemic values—the level of glucose in the blood increases rapidly when these foods are eaten. On the other hand, carbohydrates that break down slowly, releasing glucose gradually into the bloodstream, have low glycemic ratings. The fast-releasing carbohydrates will be ranked with a glycemic index of more than 70, quick release carbs rank between 55 and 70, and slow release carbohydrates are given a rating below 55. The higher the number, the faster the blood sugars rise.

When the blood sugar rise is fast, the insulin released into the bloodstream is abundant. The high insulin level will outlast the sugar burst, taking more and more sugar into the cells and dramatically dropping the blood sugar levels to a less-than-desirable level. The result is that the person soon feels spacey, unable to concentrate, weak, sleepy, anxious, sweaty, or dizzy. The quick drop in blood sugar will also trigger a craving for more carbohydrates, the essence of what is termed sugar or carbohydrate "addiction." (If you suspect you may be strongly reactive to sugar level swings, read more in "Out of the Sugar Trap" on page 310.) In addition, the higher levels of circulating insulin stimulate the storage of fat in the cells and inhibit the burning of fat as energy. This is why eating evenly and wisely will keep blood sugar and insulin levels in check and enable the body to burn fat and release optimal energy.

The need to stabilize blood sugar and insulin levels is one area in which I do agree with the pop diets of today: One of the most important things you can do when it comes to losing weight is to

control your body's hormonal response to food. But there isn't just one hormone to worry about (insulin), nor is the answer as simple as just cutting out or severely limiting all carbohydrates or sugar, or restricting carb choices to those with a low glycemic potential. The

FOODS LOW ON THE GLYCEMIC INDEX

Some foods produce a lower glycemic response than others—meaning that they result in a lower insulin surge—and are considered smart choices for day-by-day eating, especially for those seeking stable blood sugars and lower insulin levels. I consider those foods with a glycemic index ranking under 55 to be the better choices.

BETTER CHOICE GRAINS
Oats
Barley
Buckwheat
Uncle Sam's Cereal
Kellogg's Bran Buds with psyllium
Bulgur
Long Grain Brown or Basmati Rice
Tortilla
Whole wheat or artichoke pasta
100 percent stoneground
    whole wheat bread
Whole grain Pumpernickel bread
Whole wheat Sourdough bread

BETTER CHOICE LEGUMES
Chick Peas
Kidney Beans
Lentils
Navy Beans
Soybeans (the best!)
Peanuts

BETTER CHOICE VEGETABLES
Carrots
Corn
Green Peas
Lima beans
Sweet Potatoes
Yams

BETTER CHOICE FRUITS
Apples
Apricots, dried
Small Banana
Cherries
Grapefruit
Grapes
Kiwis
Mangos
Oranges
Peaches, fresh or canned in own juice
Pears
Plums
Tomatoes

fact is, when you eat *anything*, your blood sugar goes up. How fast and how much depends entirely on the food, the amount, the combination, and your own physiology.

The information regarding the glycemic response of food and the body's resulting chemical response are not just a theory or based on preliminary results of research. It is fact, the documented, confirmed results of many studies that have been published by medical and scientific journals around the world. Most of the popular diet plans and books written in the past decade have addressed the hormonal response to food and attempted to solve it in different ways, but the attempts are almost always knee-jerk reactions causing pendulum swings. Cutting out all carbohydrates is not the answer, because all carbohydrates are not the problem. It's the unbalanced diet that's the problem: refined carbohydrates are being eaten to excess, and the excess calories are being stored as fat.

The key to long-term weight loss and maintenance is to get plenty of carbohydrates—but make them whole and don't overload. Their intake needs to be balanced with low-fat proteins. Eating the right proteins increases your level of glucagon, another hormone that works to lower your insulin level. If you eat lunches that are high in refined carbohydrates but low in protein, you will throw off the glucagon–insulin balance and may find yourself feeling tired and craving sweets in the afternoon. It's a normal physical reaction. So keep your metabolism, fat burning capacity, energy, and concentration *up,* and appetite and cravings *down,* throughout your day by eating small amounts more often.

SECRET NO. 5:
EQUALIZE YOUR BRAIN CHEMISTRY

Our brain is amazing. It weighs slightly more than three pounds

and has about 100 billion nerve cells. It conducts our life with every breath we take and every bit of food we eat.

You may not be aware of how much your appetite and satiety, your thinking, your memory (particularly short-term memory), and your moods depend upon your brain chemistry. During the past twenty years, science has learned that our sense of well-being is delicately controlled by a powerful group of chemicals in the brain called neurotransmitters. These neurotransmitters can be affected, often quite dramatically, by a wide variety of everyday behaviors. Our food choices, eating patterns, exercise, creative expression, sleep, intimacy, television, and interaction with others are all examples of ways that we alter our brain chemistry each day, both positively *and* negatively.

One of the neurotransmitters responsible for enhancing your overall feeling of well-being, goodwill, and zest for life is serotonin. This feel-good chemical increases your ability to concentrate on a particular subject or problem for extended periods of time—and to care about the problem. It also provides you with deeper and more restful sleep. When your serotonin is high, you are more relaxed and content. When serotonin is low, energy will also be low and you are apt to be immobilized with bad moods and depression. Concentration becomes difficult and sleep is fitful. Appetite rages out of control— particularly for carbohydrates, which boost serotonin. Many bouts of binges can be traced to a serotonin deficiency.

Dopamine is another vital neurotransmitter, but with the opposite effects of serotonin. A high level of dopamine also brings high levels of energy but in an alert, aroused, "get-things-done" mode. Abnormally high levels of dopamine result in high anxiety, to the point of aggressiveness and paranoia. The resulting message to the brain stimulates production of hormones that contribute to fat cell lock-down.

The stress response causes the production and even flow of dopamine and serotonin to go awry, causing chemical gymnastics. Plummeting energy and brain fatigue result from falling off the chemical high bar. A poorly nourished brain is not able to protect you against the stress response, fatigue, or overeating.

Your Tool Chest for Equalizing Brain Chemistries

We've talked about many of the things you can do to stabilize your appetite and moods and increase your metabolism, but you may not be aware that many of these secrets work because they work in the brain. In order to avoid using food as your chemical boost, use these ten healthy pleasure tools to keep your brain operating optimally.

(1) **EXERCISE!** Nothing will win the brain chemical battle better than a workout. Just a brisk ten-minute walk can produce serotonin that will last for an hour or more. People begin working out for many different reasons—weight control, muscle toning, back pain relief— but equalizing brain chemistries is the number one reason to stay with it. Just the ritual associated with exercise—putting on your shoes, stretching, seeing familiar faces, taking a warm shower afterward—can start the process of making your brain feel great!

(2) **GET OUTSIDE IN THE SUNLIGHT EVERY DAY.** Our brain's neurotransmitters respond well to sunlight. That's why we feel oppressed and trapped in urban centers or enclosed spaces. The more oxygen we get, the more alert we feel. And the more sunlight we get, the more feel-good chemicals the brain produces.

Sunlight, even on cloudy days, helps to set your biological clock, lifts your moods, strengthens your immune system, and even produces vitamin D to keep you healthy. Sunlight is made up of a full spectrum of wavelengths, or colors, each of which affects your body.

The full-spectrum wavelengths produced by the sun create feelings of emotional well-being and physical energy. A few minutes by a sunny window will brighten your day—and a walk outdoors can give you a tremendous boost! Even in the midst of winter, when you can't see the sun, your body responds.

Though not a replacement for natural sunlight, one type of artificial light helps you maintain proper energy levels and good spirits: warm incandescent light. Cool fluorescents have been shown to depress you and deplete your energy reserves. An increase and improvement in office lighting has been found to result in decreased absenteeism and errors—and increased productivity.

(3) CONNECT SPIRITUALLY. Share your thoughts with a trusted friend, pastor, or counselor, and turn to your Creator in prayer. Studies have shown that as little as twenty minutes in reflective prayer a day can prompt an ongoing sense of calm and well-being. The resulting

---

SEASONAL AFFECTIVE DISORDER (SAD) If you are desperately in need of light, suffering from seasonal affective disorder, you may need full-spectrum bulbs that more closely simulate natural sunlight. This form of depression has been linked to inadequate exposure to light, and may be caused by an improper balance of melatonin in the brain. The symptoms of SAD are:

- noticeable lack of energy
- a fairly constant level of sadness
- a desire to sleep as much as possible, but the sleep is fitful
- feeling listless and being less creative than usual
- having less control of your appetite, resulting in significant weight gain.

SAD needs to be treated appropriately. The best treatment has come from bright natural light. Full-spectrum lights are now readily available for both home and commercial use.

change in brain chemistry is believed to be the scientific physiological factor in the proved strengthening of the immunology system
that comes through this spiritual endeavor.

(4) SPEND TIME WITH UPBEAT PEOPLE. And participate in upbeat activities with them. Good moods are catching! Look for ways to help
someone else: encourage a friend, pray for those in need. Research
has shown an increase in serotonin when you refresh someone else.

(5) TAKE CONTROL OF YOUR SPACE. The chronic chaos in your life could
be affecting your brain chemistry by keeping your body in a chronic
state of stress. Even piles of paperwork can affect your well-being.
Researchers have discovered that clutter (paperwork, newspapers,
etc.) send impulses to your brain that can cause stress hormones to
rise and serotonin levels to drop, affecting your pulse and blood
pressure. Just clearing the clutter—even if you hide it in a closet—
can bring you a sense of calm and well-being. That is, until you lose
something! Like so many other self-care principles, organization
takes time and motivation, but it's a tremendous investment.

(6) COLOR YOUR WORLD. Boost the feel-good chemicals in your brain
by warming up the colors in your surroundings. Colors actually give
off electromagnetic wave bands of energy, which send impulses to
the energy control glands in your brain. Just painting a wall or wearing a certain color shirt can energize your day. Fascinating studies
have shown that the blind respond to wavelengths of color just as
those who see—in both energy levels and moods. That's an amazing
thought: color is *felt,* not just seen.

Yellow shades have the most positive effects on brain chemistry,
followed by the other warm colors of orange and red. Anything that
adds these colors of fire—a flowering plant, a painting or poster,
Mexican pottery—will help keep you more alert. Just be careful not
to overdo; too much color can be just as damaging as too little.

Extroverts who are easily overstimulated and distracted often respond best to the calming colors of blue or green, but with a warm yellow-tinted shade.

(7) GET SHOWERED IN ENERGY. When you have the time or the place, a brisk shower can truly wash away brain fatigue, giving you just the chemical boost you need! The spray of the water from the shower peps up your body through a powerful energizing reaction that comes through exposure to negative ions (molecules with an extra electron). Although not completely proved, the theory holds that showers, waterfalls, and ocean waves multiply the negative ions in the air, which in turn affects brain chemistry, releasing energy and positive feelings.

You can get a quick, cheap stand-in for a shower with a small atomizer. Fill it with mineral water, hold it six inches from your face or pulse points, and spray. It's amazingly refreshing, like a rain or waterfall mist. It humidifies the air, hydrates your skin, cools you, feels good, and wakes you up.

(8) TURN ON THE TUNES. If you're in a slump, music can lift you up. If you're stressed, music can calm you. Music can open the door to your emotions, stimulate you, restore you, and awaken your creativity. The best brain power response comes from listening to music with a gentle rhythm such as that of the piano or flute—without lyrics or loud drums. It should be music that keeps your mind focused rather than distracted. Rhythmic music affects brain waves in a way similar to color, particularly by inducing alpha waves that have been linked to enhanced concentration.

This impact on the alpha waves of the brain is only one of music's power to relax. Studies show that listening to rhythmic music can reduce blood pressure, heart and breathing rates, and even stress hormone levels—all important in unlocking your fat cells.

(9) DRINK WATER—and lots of it! Overcoming dehydration will improve your blood circulation, which in turn will take your brain's feel-good chemicals throughout your body more efficiently.

(10) FOLLOW THE EAT-RIGHT PRESCRIPTION. Eat early, eat often, eat balanced, eat lean, and eat bright! Consider taking a multivitamin that contains at least 150 percent of the RDA for B-complex vitamins, which are fuel carriers, to nourish the brain and trigger the release of upbeat serotonin.

Nourish Your Brain

Vital to your brain chemistry is the last tool in the chest—the eat-right prescription: Are you getting enough of the right fuel to nourish your brain and keep essential chemicals stable?

When you eat, your digestive system breaks the food down into individual nutrients, like glucose and amino acids, to be absorbed into your bloodstream. Once absorbed, specific nutrients cross into the brain to speed the production of mood-enhancing neurotransmitters. What we eat—or don't eat—can have a profound effect on our mood, appetite, and fat-burning capacity.

For example, a raging appetite and slowed metabolic rate are clues to a brain fuel deficit, bringing an almost addictive pull toward certain foods. Your brain may need certain nutrients found in everyday foods to bring peace to the warfare within it. Eating, and eating often, is a big part of the solution.

Remember, your brain has only one fuel source: glucose. If deprived of its energy source, the brain functions at a deficit. Fatigue, mood swings, headaches, depression, and poor short-term memory are the early symptoms of insufficient blood glucose levels. By remembering that blood glucose levels normally crest and fall every three to four hours, you can prevent your personal sinking

BRAIN FOOD

Go for the Bs. In addition to fueling the brain with a constant supply of glucose, there are a number of other brainpower boosts that keep your mind sharp, clear, and effective—and your appetite regulated. For example, fuel-carriers are necessary to get the needed glucose supply to the brain. These vehicles are the B-complex vitamins. When the brain sputters along without adequate amounts of B vitamins, disorders like depression—even overeating—may be the result.

Your basic goal is to aim for these daily values: 2 mg of B6, 400 mcg of folic acid, and 6 micrograms of B12. Make foods rich in these brainpower Bs a part of your daily diet.

POWER B FOODS

VITAMIN B6 (needed: 2 mg daily)		FOLIC ACID (needed: 400 mcg daily)		VITAMIN B12 (needed: 6 mcg daily)	
Potato	.91 mg	Chickpeas, cooked (1/2 cup)	140 mcg	Atlantic Mackerel, 3 oz.	16 mcg
Banana	.73 mg	Lima Beans, cooked (1/2 cup)	140 mcg	Beef, 3 oz.	3 mcg
Whole Grain		Spinach, 1/2 cup cooked	140 mcg	Tuna or Salmon, 3 oz.	2 mcg
Cereal (1/2 cup)	.50 mg	Orange Juice, 1 cup	110 mcg	Milk, 8 oz.	1.5 mcg
Lean Beef (3 oz.)	.48 mg	Strawberries. 1/2 cup	110 mcg		
Halibut (3 oz.)	.34 mg				

Go Fish. Ever heard that fish is "brain food"? That's because it's an excellent source of the amino acid tyrosine. This amino acid increases the production of dopamine and norepinephrine, which help the body to buffer the effects of stress. Known as catecholamines, these chemical compounds work to regulate your blood pressure, heart rate, muscle tone, nervous system function, and metabolism. They are "alertness" chemicals of the brain. Studies have shown that people who get an increase in tyrosine foods perform better at mental tasks and show a significant edge in alertness and quick response time. They also experience less anxiety and have more clarity of thought.

Fish is the single best source of tyrosine, and brings it to you in an almost no-fat form. Cold-water fishes like salmon, swordfish, tuna, and mackerel (along with breast milk!) are also the best source of valuable EPA (eicosapentaneoic acid) oils, known to increase the IQ of developing babies. Whether adequate EPA oil intake helps the aging brain has not been established.

spells by eating smaller amounts of food more evenly throughout the day. Not eating sends you into "brain alert," and the brain sends out the call to eat, eat too much, and eat the wrong things.

You can prevent the alert, by eating the minimeals suggested in *The Smart Weigh* plan. (See specific details in Chapters 6 and 12.) "Power snacking" is also a valuable tool for equalizing brain chemistry because it gives you an immediate supply to meet the demand. (Read about power snacking on page 125.)

SECRET NO. 6:
TAKE CHARGE OF YOUR APPETITE

Many people go wrong not in *what* they eat, but in *how much* they eat. Even if they are eating food that is good for them, they often eat too much of it. Calories *do* count, so learning how to say *enough*— before you've eaten way too much—is vital.

I've got another secret for you: The way to tame your appetite and stop overeating is to *start* eating. You've already gotten a glimpse of this in learning of the power that regulating your blood sugars and equalizing brain chemistries can have over your appetite. It's a fact: wise eating all through the day keeps ravenous appetite away. Enjoying food, not shunning it, is the answer. I know that can strike fear in the heart of any overeater who believes that once he or she begins to eat, there is no stopping. And who has time to eat so often anyway?

American society has become so focused on avoiding and getting rid of fat that we've lost the positive and pleasurable aspects of eating. We've settled for foods that are convenient yet incapable of providing the full sensory experience. And that leads to one thing: overeating. When you've pushed your body through the day on fumes and eat steamed vegetables and plain broiled chicken night

LIQUID SNACKS? Don't make the mistake of slugging down soda to keep from snacking on candy or chips, thinking that *at least it's fat free*. (The average American downs fifty-three gallons of soda a year: 79,146 empty calories!)

In a recent study at Purdue University, subjects were fed extra calories in the form of solid food every day for a month. Their total daily calorie intake—and their weight—remained stable. They made up for the snack calories by cutting back elsewhere in their diets.

During a different month, they were given the same number of extra calories, but this time in a liquid form. Their total calorie intake went up, and they put on pounds. The reason, in theory, is that liquids pass through the digestive tract too quickly to trigger a feeling of satiety, so the "take in more" signal persists.

Other studies have shown that even people who drink diet sodas eat more calories. Of course, diet soda itself has no calories, but the sweet taste can trigger an insulin release that signals you to eat more—which is one of the many reasons that diet sodas have not produced a fit and trim world.

Some solid advice: choose snacks you can chew.

after night, pizza and Haagen-Dazs can sound really good—and a lot of it sounds better! Starvation and sensory deprivation is a sure route to a binge.

Managing Cravings

Sarah has a chocolate fit every month just before she gets her period. After a tough day at the office, Jim covets tortilla chips. Debbie suddenly can't resist pasta with a rich, creamy sauce.

Most of us have experienced a strong, nearly uncontrollable urge for a certain type of food. And while we've struggled to keep away from the refrigerator, we may have wondered why we long so intensely for a particular taste. Why do we have cravings? Are they emotional or physical?

Most people don't sell their soul for a stalk of celery. They are driven toward sugar and salt (inborn preferences for infants to drink breast milk) and fat (inborn preferences for children to sustain growth). The problem is that even though children outgrow their biological needs, their tastes persist because of the foods that are cultural and family favorites. They develop passions for peanut butter and jelly, macaroni and cheese, cheeseburgers, and milkshakes. For the more sophisticated palates of adults, it's

Rocky Road ice cream, fettucine alfredo, creamy chocolate mousse, and nachos.

Diet deficiencies fuel the cravings. As you've read, fluctuating blood sugars—enhanced by unbalanced hormones and stress chemicals—stimulate the driving desire for sweets; fluid imbalances drive the desire for salty foods; a sustained inadequate intake of calories (lack of supply to meet demands) fuels the desire for fats. This is the physical side of the craving, driving us in a general direction.

Our emotions help determine the exact food we arrive at. The body sends out the "I NEED" signal, the emotions send out the "I WANT" signal—and both send us directly the comfort food of choice, particularly when comfort is being called for. Our culture's battlecry is "relief is just a swallow away," and for many of us that spells food. The refrigerator light becomes the light of our life.

Learning Your Hunger Signals

It takes time to recognize the emotional issues behind the "I WANT" signal, but you can take charge of the physical side of your appetite this very day by learning to recognize true hunger. If you've been eating too much, too frequently, or too infrequently, it will take some time and adjustments to learn—and obey—your true hunger signals. Everyone is different; your task is to watch for your own unique hunger and satisfaction clues.

Hunger is not always about stomach sensations; it's more often about energy drops, weakness, fatigue, bad concentration, an empty feeling, crankiness, even cold hands and feet. Satiation has occurred when there is an absence of hunger or a fullness, a level of physical energy, loss of interest in food, and interest in other things. You are more than likely overfull (or as my teenage daughter calls it, "at capacity") when you are feeling bloated, lethargic, and short of

breath. Your healthy goal is to eat to your level of satiation. Eat balanced and choose wisely, but *stop* when you are satisfied.

When you're eating right things at the right time, your meals and snacks will satisfy you much more easily. If you find you are feeling hungry between regularly scheduled meals and snacks, wait ten minutes and see if you still are. After ten minutes, ask yourself if there is something going on emotionally—or if you are just bored or stressed. If you're truly hungry, have your power snack at that time, even if you need to add another to that day.

You don't have to rely on iron-will discipline to control your food intake. By following an eating plan that meets the physical needs of your body, you *will* be in control. Follow these ten tips to stay full—and satisfied:

(1) KEEP A LOG ON THE FIRE ALL DAY. Again, the eat-right prescription of eating early and often, balanced and lean, with lots of brightly colored fruits and vegetables will fill you with satisfying protein, appetite-curbing fiber, and energy-boosting carbohydrates. And minimeals or power snacks every couple of hours will keep your metabolism in high gear and your appetite in control. Don't be a rabbit—salad alone won't satisfy you. Eat a well-balanced diet with plenty of fiber.

(2) EAT FRUIT BEFORE EVERY MEAL. These satisfying tidbits can curb your appetite and slow down your eating—*before* you "eat the whole thing!" Listen to your body and focus on fueling it rather than feeding your emotional needs. Remember, it takes most people about twenty minutes to feel full. We often eat too much in three to five minutes, and are left still looking for more. The simple carbohydrates in your fruit appetizer will have reached your bloodstream by then, helping you to reach satisfaction without looking for something sweet.

(3) PAY ATTENTION TO YOUR FOOD. Inhaling a sandwich at your desk or in your car can set you up for overeating—it fills you up, but doesn't satisfy you. We often turn to richly flavored candy bars or fat-filled chips to satisfy the flavor needs we didn't get during our meal. Instead, take the time to focus on what you're eating and savor every bite. And make it great! Forego bland and tasteless, albeit quick and easy, meals—go for flavor and pizzazz!

(4) HAVE A SEAT. Rushing through a meal can leave you feeling deprived even when your body's signaling that you're full. Savor your food, and avoid distractions like watching TV, which encourages mindless eating. Try to dine at the dinner table only. If you always eat in front of the TV, then every time you nestle in with the remote control, it's a cue to eat. Instead, designate an eating spot for all meals and snacks.

(5) DRINK WATER, DRINK WATER, DRINK WATER. And a lot of it! Don't mistake dehydration for hunger. If you yearn for salty foods, a big craving catalyst is probably your lack of proper fluids, which depletes your body's sodium supply. If you're craving chips, try a tall glass of water first! And, have a tall glass of water before and after each meal.

(6) WAIT OUT CRAVINGS. Think before you bite. Creating rituals—like the old standby of waiting ten minutes before giving in to a craving—can stop you from eating when you aren't really hungry. Ask before you reach: are you bored, tired, angry, stressed, or lonely? If so, you won't find the answer in food. If you find that your emotions are fueling your cravings, choose a healthier alternative than overeating. Sure, you can eat a bag of Oreos when you're angry or frustrated, but a five-minute walk will work, too. And you'll feel better, not bloated.

If the craving seems stronger than you are, try to make the most

of it. If you crave ice cream, choose sorbet and yogurt and top it with fresh fruit. If you crave chips, get the baked version and serve with a fat-free bean dip or top with melted low-fat cheese. Give yourself a treat, not a trick.

(7) TALK TO YOURSELF. At heart, we all crave continuity. So when you try to alter long-standing eating habits, inner voices will pipe up to protest the change. Try to remember specifically why you want to change (e.g., "I'll have more energy when I lose weight").

(8) EXERCISE. Regular exercise keeps you energized and may even suppress your appetite for several hours. Remember, exercise boosts your brain's production of serotonin, which reduces carbohydrate cravings.

(9) PUT A MIRROR ON THE FRIDGE. It may sound strange, but researchers found that people who ate at a table with a large mirror on it were more likely to choose reduced-fat or fat-free products than those higher in fat or calories. That doesn't mean that you need to hang a mirror by the dining room table—a small mirror on your refrigerator or inside the pantry door may get the message across. Keeping a food diary can also serve as a sort of mirror for your eating patterns, helping you to get a grip on reality.

(10) BE PATIENT. Very, very patient! Forget quick diet fixes—it can take three to six months to replace bad habits with healthy ones. Answering the call of an appetite that's run wild is a physical as well as habitual pattern; it takes time to learn how to turn down your personal appetite thermostat, and time to learn how to "just say no" to urges that aren't physical at all. The quickest way to become discouraged is to expect quick success. So give yourself plenty of time to change. This will increase the odds that you'll stay motivated for the long run.

SECRET NO. 7:
STRENGTHEN YOUR IMMUNE SYSTEM

A vital part of the master design plan to keep you living life abundantly is a strong immune system. A good way to picture the immune system is as a disciplined and effective personal "border patrol," with soldiers and scouts on permanent duty throughout your body. These warriors include several different types of white blood cells, each with its own special mission. Together they work to identify a threat to the body, call an alert, and divide into army battalions to attack the enemy and stabilize the body. It all happens so quickly, you often don't even know you were threatened.

Your body's natural ability to lose weight is inherently tied to the energy and healing that is scripted into every cell in your body—and nothing will slow your metabolism and lock down your fat cells into "store" mode like being sick. When battle breaks out in your body, your immune fighting army locks up your fat cells tighter than Fort Knox. This is because your body is on a mission to fight the infection at hand—and signals ring out to produce cortisol from your adrenal glands to steer the immune system's production of white blood cells and steer them to the particular area of your body under attack. As mentioned earlier, heightened cortisol levels slow down the fat-burning capacity—putting your fat cells into a "store" mode to provide an adequate stockpile of fuel for the battle against the offending bug.

Although science has yet to discover a cure for the common cold, there *are* ways to outsmart many bugs. Researchers have begun to unlock some of the secrets of strengthening the immune system. In order to keep your border patrol officers alert and strong, the immune system needs to be kept fit and fueled, mobilized for action. Start eating more of the best and less of the rest. The real world can be a deadly place, so protect yourself with power foods and power

living. Outsmart the invisible invaders that get you sick by using these keys to enforce your own personal protective shield—and receive a boosted metabolism as your reward.

(1) EAT POWER FOODS. This is the number-one strengthener of your immunes. Whole-grain carbohydrates not only give you energy, they supply much-needed B6, selenium, and magnesium, which activate your immune troops within. Power proteins provide vitamin D, iron, and zinc. Essential vitamins and minerals keep your immune system humming, so eat lots of brightly colored fruits and vegetables. They are loaded with nutraceuticals like beta-carotene, flavonoids, vitamin A, folic acid, vitamin C, and B vitamins that help to keep natural energy and healing flowing.

(2) TAKE A HIKE. Moderate regular exercise has been shown to boost the immune system significantly. It increases the activity of white blood cells and natural bug-killer cells.

(3) LIFT UP THE STRESS SHIELD. Studies have shown that people who are under chronic stress are more likely to get sick than those under less pressure. This is because during chronic stress situations, hormones (such as cortisol) are constantly circulating in excessive levels—amounts that can suppress the activity of immune system cells and make people more open to attack. It's a different way of responding to stress than the classic "fight-or-flight" response; instead, it's a "play possum" reaction. Just as a possum rolls over and plays dead when threatened, a person may "roll over" in hopelessness, depression, and feelings of being out of control. Physiological reactions include decreased heart rate and muscle tone. When chronic, this kind of "play dead" reaction may actually invite life-threatening illness by deadening the immune system's response, dulling the mind, and causing the organ systems to function less efficiently.

Unprocessed emotions have the same effect on the body, so don't bury them. Instead, deal with problems or get help. As silly as it sounds, even laughing at problems helps. Laughter even helps us fight infection by releasing hormones that can override the immune, dampening effects of stress. You can outsmart the slowdown with a smile.

(4) GET SWEET SLEEP. Studies show that people who are sleep-deprived experience as much as a 50 percent drop in their natural killer cells that fight invaders. The body can bounce back very quickly, though, with a good night's sleep.

(5) BE A GIVING FRIEND. It has been shown that people with a network of friends who give of themselves have four times the immune fighting potential of those who are more isolated and self-absorbed. Showing love can give an amazing boost to the immune system!

WELCOME TO *THE SMART WEIGH*

All of the secrets we've discussed are really process goals: the process of cracking the fat cell code and unleashing your body's natural ability to lose weight becomes your goal and keeps you well and trim for life. These secrets are the foundation upon which *The Smart Weigh* is built. Cracking the fat cell code and living *The Smart Weigh* begins with choosing a way of eating and living that is so comfortable that you can live with it the rest of your life.

The Smart Weigh plan is not a magic formula. It is a nondieting solution to weight management that works to unleash your body's natural healing and weight-loss mechanism. It is based on timeless truths that show you how the body was designed to work and how you can choose food and water, exercise, air, rest, and self-care to work for you, not against you. It enables you to operate from a point of strength physically—and sets the stage for you to meet the deeper needs of your soul.

I won't give you a specific diet to follow because sooner or later you have to go off it—you know that. But I do ask you to do this: throw out your diet books, and just say no to the next "diet answer" that comes to you via your friends, family, or group. Make the decision, today, to turn from the dieting path, and take a small step on the road to looking and feeling better. Refuse to sacrifice your health and your energy at the altar of improper weight loss.

Embrace these simple truths: live *The Smart Weigh*.

THE SMART WEIGH IN ACTION

S: Strategic Eating
M: Movement
A: Air and Water
R: Rest
T: Treat Yourself Well

Is *The Smart Weigh* easy? Quite honestly, because this lifestyle and eating plan represents the ultimate in health and nutrition, you'll probably find *The Smart Weigh* plan a challenge at first, as you adopt some new, powerfully healthy habits. But the results will be worth it. Studies show that each improvement in lifestyle will not only help your weight loss, but also lower your risk of heart attack, high blood pressure, stroke, cancer, diabetes, osteoporosis, cataracts, asthma, diverticulosis, depression, and even PMS.

Many of the steps in the next section will help you change your attitude or lifestyle which in turn will help crack the code of the fat cell. You have to start somewhere—and *The Smart Weigh* is that place. It is not important to enact the lifestyle upgrades in any certain order, or to master one completely before you learn about the others. However, I have put these principles in logical progression,

beginning with meeting your body's most pressing physical needs. You will find that fueling your body well will regulate your blood sugars and stabilize your body chemistries to energize you for exercise. Eating well and exercising will promote more restful sleep. You'll start to feel good enough to notice when you feel bad, which will in turn remind you to slow down and take a breather. The stress reduction will lead to greater productivity and the free time to pursue the quality relationships and activities you value.

Can the image of the perfect body. Instead of thinking that you have to reach some unattainable goal, focus on losing just ten pounds over these next six to seven weeks. Keep that off for a while and let your body adjust. Then, if you want to lose more, you can. Or, don't focus on losing weight at all; focus on a new way of living—free of the diet trap. In the meantime, you'll be rewarded with new energy and wellness—not just from weight loss, but from your new marvelous way of eating and caring for yourself. And as you meet your physical need for proper nourishment, you will be better able to work on the deeper needs of your soul.

PART THREE ▪ **EMBRACING**
            THE SMART WEIGH

CHAPTER 6 ▪ S: Strategic Eating

It is futile to wish for a long life, and then give such little care to living well.

—THOMAS A KEMPIS

What if we stopped trying not to eat, or not to cheat, and started planning how best to charge up our internal motor? Then we'd be eating *The Smart Weigh*—and feel great all day, relax and play all evening, rise to almost any occasion, with activated metabolisms and bodies that are working for us, and with us.

Remember, eating smart isn't about what you *shouldn't* be eating; it's not about how bad potato chips or ice cream or red meat may be

> **SMART WEIGH TIP**
>
> *Stop starving yourself —eat to lose weight* The Smart Weigh.

for you. Instead, it's about the foods and lifestyle choices that power you with high octane energy fuel. The food you eat shapes the optimal performance and effectiveness of all your body mechanisms and allows your metabolism to burn in high gear. Releasing your body's natural ability to lose weight requires a nutrition plan that goes far beyond traditional or fad dieting.

It was only a decade ago that the world of nutrition began to go beyond dieting for weight loss alone and to focus instead on living life well each day while preventing the diseases of tomorrow.

Most of us underestimate the effect of our eating on how we feel. We don't connect morning sluggishness or afternoon sleepiness to when and what we eat. We know that food is our body's fuel, but most of us resist an even flow. As our schedules get full, it's easy for a consistent eating routine to go awry. Eating falls into an erratic, catch-as-catch-can affair that can't supply our body's needs. It seems as if we can't afford the time to eat well—yet the truth is that we can't afford *not* to. Wisely chosen food is a powerful tool to right the wrong of stress, and remove the logjam to your metabolism that it causes. Paying attention to how you eat is a small-time investment with a tremendous return.

Right now, changing your eating patterns may seem like just another duty, another bondage—maybe even another diet. But you will find that choosing to eat the right foods at the right time is choosing freedom. Rather than binding you, wise choices and self-control frees you to be the real you—free from compulsive dieting, overeating, or self-abusive living. Thousands of people have done it—and you can, too!

EDIBLE ENERGY

When it comes to nutrition, calories take a lot of abuse. Most Americans, particularly women, want to cut them, burn them, and otherwise get rid of them. But a certain number of calories are essential. They provide the fuel our bodies need in order to function. The truth about food is simple: food is just tasty units of energy. It takes food to make energy and to activate the metabolism.

As we've already discussed, the food we eat gets converted to glucose, which is the brain and lungs' only energy source and the most efficient and common form for the rest of the body. A single molecule of glucose can trigger the production of nearly thirty-eight

HOW TO REACH YOUR TARGET WEIGHT

To calculate if you are getting enough fuel, use this formula: multiply your current weight by 16 if you're active, by 12 if you exercise by lifting the remote control. This gives you the approximate number of calories you typically burn in a day—and the amount that will give optimal energy and the amount needed to maintain your current weight. An active 125-pound woman burns roughly 2,000 calories, a sedentary one will need only 1,750. An active 175-pound man needs 2,800 calories, a sedentary one will need only 2,100. To gain one pound per week, 500 calories should be added daily; to lose one pound per week, 500 calories should be cut daily—never to less than 1,500 calories for a female or 1,800 calories for a male.

Eating less than 1,500 calories per day can slow down your metabolic rate by 30 percent and leave you without key energy-releasing nutrients. Your memory, concentration, and judgment can all be impaired. Since weight loss means cutting back on those valuable energy-giving calories, it requires upping the ante of quality and timing of eating. To make up the difference, the goal is to become more active and better burn the calories consumed.

To reach your target weight, first figure out how many calories to cut to hit your goal. One pound of fat equals approximately 3,500 calories. Multiply 3,500 by the number of pounds you want to shed. To lose five pounds you'd need to burn about 17,500 calories. If you cut 500 calories daily below what you need for maintenance, you could lose the weight in about five weeks.

An easier approach is to split the equation. By shaving calories from your food intake and simultaneously becoming more active, you can minimize the struggle and maximize the results—reaching your goal sooner. *The Smart Weigh* plan uses the dynamic duo: reducing calories by 250 to 750 per day and burning an additional 250 calories with added exercise.

To Lose	You Need to Use Up	Time to Goal Weight Exercise Alone	Time to Goal Weight Eating well plus exercise
5 pounds	17,500 calories	6 weeks	4 weeks
10 pounds	35,000 calories	12 weeks	8 weeks
20 pounds	70,000 calories	24 weeks	16 weeks

molecules of ATP, the energy molecule that fuels the body's cells. Without ATP, the cells go on a hunger strike and muscles stiffen, refusing to function efficiently. Our moment-by-moment personal energy is, at the most basic level, all about how much ATP our body is producing. Food—and calories—give us the power to breathe, think, move, crack a joke, make love. Taken in appropriate amounts at the proper times, they are a *very* good thing.

Three components in foods provide calories: carbohydrates, proteins, and fats. Per gram (about the weight of a paper clip), each component provides the following number of calories:

Carbohydrates: 4 calories per gram

Protein: 4 calories per gram

Fat: 9 calories per gram

Alcohol also provides calories—7 calories per gram—but no nutritive value. Generally speaking, all calories—whether from carbohydrates, proteins, or fats—supply the same amount of energy. But each provides unique contributions to bodily function and health. Foods high in carbohydrates (including breads and starches) are mostly used for energy. The fiber that is found in many high-carbohydrate foods also helps regulate bowel function and protects against heart disease and certain types of cancer. Carbohydrates should make up about 55 to 60 percent of your total daily calories.

Protein (including meats, legumes, and soybean products) may also be used for energy. But the body uses protein in more vital ways—to make and maintain body tissue such as muscles and organs. In addition, protein is a key component of enzymes, hormones, and many body fluids. When there are enough calories from other sources, the body uses protein for these essential purposes rather than for fuel. Only about 15 to 20 percent of your daily calories should come from protein.

Fat provides the most concentrated source of energy. Even a little fat can provide a lot of calories. In excess, fat can increase the risk of cardiovascular disease and some cancers. Fat comes in two forms: saturated and unsaturated. No more than 30 percent of your daily calories should come from fat, and—ideally—no more than 20 to 25 percent.

Caloric needs vary considerably from one individual to another. A small, elderly, sedentary woman requires fewer calories than a large, young, physically active man. The number of calories you need depends on your age, height, weight, gender, and activity level. But remember, it's not just the energy consumed that counts; it's the energy *burned*. As we've discussed, our stressful, frenzied, and often sedentary lifestyles have slowed our metabolic rate to a snail's pace, resulting in fats being stored rather than burned for energy.

Regardless of the number of calories consumed when we eat, the body can use only a small amount of energy quickly—the rest

> **THE EAT-RIGHT PRESCRIPTION**
>
> Eat Early and Eat Often
> Eat Balanced and Eat Lean
> Eat Bright and Eat Variety
> Drink Water—and lots of it!

is thrown off as waste or stored as fat. And most of us eat most of our calories overloaded into just a few concentrated hours in the evening. Because of this our bodies are robbed of precious energy fuel and a metabolism that's burning in high gear for the remaining twenty hours, until the next feeding frenzy. We not only go wrong in how much we eat or what we eat; we also eat entirely too much at the wrong time. Energy after six o'clock in the evening is just *too much too late.*

Instead, we need to activate our metabolism with *The Smart Weigh* eat-right prescription: small meals of high-energy, whole-grain carbohydrates and power-building, low-fat proteins complemented by

brightly colored fruits and vegetables, at least every three hours, with LOTS of water.

EAT EARLY

Although it may not seem like news, breakfast is still the most important meal of your day—don't leave home without it! Breakfast begins your day by stabilizing body chemistries and starting your metabolism in high gear. View eating breakfast as a primary metabolic booster.

Breakfast is important to "break the fast" of the body's night rest. Remember the campfire story and your metabolism: think of your body as a campfire that dies down during the night and in the morning needs to be "stoked up" with wood to begin burning vigorously again. Your body is very similar; it awakens in a slowed, resting state, having utilized all the easily available fuel, and it needs breakfast to rev the rate at which you burn calories into high gear. After

CAN'T I JUST EAT A BREAKFAST BAR?

There is a wide variety of bars are available, from grain-and-"fruit" bars to granola or chocolate-covered bars pegged as meal replacements. Although there is certainly nothing "wrong" with these products, we are probably misleading ourselves if we say they are an equal substitute for a balanced breakfast.

Most breakfast bars provide less fiber than you would get from a whole-grain cereal or toast, and most contain substantially more sugar than you might realize. (Check the label for sugar content. Remember that every four grams of sugar equals a teaspoonful.) Even products marketed as containing fruit really contain what is more like sugar-filled jam.

Perhaps heading to bed fifteen minutes earlier would allow you to get up with five minutes to spare for a breakfast that includes a more balanced selection of whole grains, proteins, and fruit without too much of a fat and sugar load. Even if you prefer dinner leftovers to traditional "breakfast foods," the key is the balance—and real foods, not packaged pep.

a night's sleep, it takes 250 to 350 calories to get your metabolism percolating again.

If you choose not to eat breakfast, your body turns to internal sources for energy, burning muscle mass (not fat) for fuel. The metabolism slows down another notch, conserving itself in this disabled, starved state. Continuing to starve your body will leave it dragging through the day, unable to work efficiently and more ready to store whatever food is eaten. When the evening "gorge" begins, much of the nutrients you eat will be wasted and the energy stored as fat. All that food can't possibly be used up because your body isn't burning energy at a fast rate—the fire has already gone out. It's like dumping an armful of firewood on a dead fire.

After a big meal, your body puts out an excess of the fat storage hormone, or insulin. Remember, extra insulin locks down the fat cell, inhibiting it from releasing fatty acids to be burned for energy. Eating smaller meals, more often, is a lot like throwing logs on our slow-burning metabolic fires, getting them to burn better and brighter. It all starts with breakfast.

Don't think for a minute that you are wisely cutting calories or saving time by skipping breakfast. The truth is, those calories would be burned by your body's higher metabolic rate. You are only robbing your body of performance and metabolic fuel. And bypassing this morning metabolic boost doesn't just affect your weight—it can also affect your thinking abilities. Research has shown that missing breakfast can undercut reading skills and the ability to concentrate. A recent breakfast study showed a full letter grade differential in children who had breakfast compared to those who did not. Not only that, the study reported a poorer attitude and behavior problems among the children who missed breakfast. A recent study at the University of Wales found that breakfast-skippers were less able

than breakfast-eaters to recall a word list and a story that was read aloud to them.

Because breakfast stabilizes your blood chemistries, you will have more energy and alertness. It allows you to be more productive and effective, allowing you to do what you do quickly and more enjoyably—with fewer mistakes. How's that for a time investment?

But Breakfast Is a Pain!

Actually, people skip breakfast for lots of reasons. Again, some skip it to save calories; others skip it to save time. Some can't face food in the morning, and others just don't like breakfast foods.

If you are not hungry in the morning, it's more than likely because your body has gone through some chemical gymnastics while you've slept, and you may wake up in a state of "morning sickness." It's not that you aren't in need of breakfast—just the opposite. Breakfast will neutralize your blood sugars and stomach acids and make you feel better.

A quite common reason for skipping breakfast is that in some people it seems to start a vicious appetite machine making them hungry every few hours. If this is you, be assured that breakfast is not the problem; you get hungry soon after you've eaten breakfast because you take yourself out of the starved mode and raise your blood sugars. When you starve your body in the morning, the resulting use of your own tissue for energy releases waste products (ketones) into your system that temporarily depress your appetite and give you a feeling of fullness. You can continue to starve for many hours without feeling hunger.

Sadly, this backfires later in the day. As soon as you begin to eat, the appetite really turns on, and you eat too much, too late. In addition, you've let your body go into a slowed metabolic state, and you're

setting yourself up for a gorge. Not only will you overeat because your blood sugar level has fallen so low, but, like the campfire, your body will not be able to burn those calories well. Remember, your body just cannot handle such a large intake of food at one time; your needs go on twenty-four hours a day.

In matters of nutrition, I talk a lot about investment and returns. Breakfast calories are a good example of this; the return is greater than the initial deposit—remaining calories eaten during the day burn more efficiently rather than being stored as fat. A Vanderbilt University study showed that overweight breakfast-skippers who started to eat breakfast lost an average of seventeen pounds in twelve weeks. Not only did eating breakfast speed up their metabolisms, but it also caused them to be less hungry the rest of the day. Because they were eating the right foods at the right times, they were less apt to eat the wrong things at the wrong times.

The bottom line: eat breakfast soon after you get up (within the first half-hour of arising), and have three different foods for breakfast—a quick, energy-starting simple carbohydrate (fruit), a long-lasting whole grain complex carbohydrate (grains, cereals, bread, or muffins), and a power-building protein (dairy, egg, soy, or meat). This good-for-you balance will allow a slow and steady release of glucose into your bloodstream to feed your brain and muscles with vital energy. Selecting whole foods, rather than a Danish and fruit punch, also gives your body the vitamins and minerals it needs to transform the energy nutrients into usable fuel.

Go light and easy if time is a push; try some eat-and-go meals like fresh fruit and skim-milk shakes, cheese-toast and fruit, or freshly fruited yogurt with a muffin. And don't be concerned if the meals are not made up of traditional breakfast-food choices. Some nonbreakfast food lovers start their day with a turkey or tuna sandwich or even a cheese quesadilla.

You may want to try the breakfast recipes on page 272—quick meals designed to give you the perfect start to an energy-filled day.

EAT OFTEN

Once you get your day started with breakfast, the goal is to keep your metabolic system and blood chemistries working for you. To prevent your blood sugar level from dropping and to keep your metabolic rate high, you need food distributed evenly throughout the day. Going many hours between meals causes the body to slow metabolically so that the next meal is perceived as an overload. Even if the meal is balanced and healthy, the nutrients cannot be used optimally—again, it's too much too late. And the lowered blood sugar will leave you sleepy and craving sweets. Snacking on the right foods is much more fun—and a lot more healthy.

This is what I call "power snacking"—eating the right amounts of the right foods at regular intervals—and it's an important component of *The Smart Weigh*.

But I Thought Snacks Were Bad

You may be thinking, *But I thought I wasn't supposed to eat between meals.* Wrong! When most people think of snacks, they picture potato chips, candy, and sodas. These types of snacks are "empty calories," providing high amounts of fats, sugars, salt, and calories, but little or no vitamins or minerals. A healthy snack, on the other hand, provides you with real nutrition and will keep your blood sugar levels from dropping too low. It will keep your metabolism burning high, your needs satisfied.

Your daily eating should consist of three meals with at least two healthy snacks. Ideally, eat 25 percent of your day's calories at breakfast, 25 percent at lunch, 25 percent at dinner, and the other 25 per-

cent in healthy snacks, eaten about every two-and-one-half to three hours. This is not mindless grazing, which has been shown *not* to raise your metabolism; instead, it is eating strategically to go for the caloric burn. On average, weight loss winners eat five times a day.

Wise snacking will also invigorate your mind. Tests have shown that a snack eaten fifteen minutes before skill tests of memory, alertness, reading, or problem-solving greatly increased performance in

POWER SNACKS

- Whole grain crackers or Raisin Squares cereal and low-fat cheese (like string cheese, part-skim mozzarella, or Laughing Cow Lite Cheese Wedges)
- Fresh fruit or small box of raisins and low-fat cheese
- Half of a lean turkey or chicken sandwich on whole grain bread
- Plain, nonfat yogurt blended with fruit or all-fruit jam, or Stonyfield Farms yogurt
- Whole grain cereal with skim milk
- Wasa bread with light cream cheese and all-fruit jam
- Baked low-fat tortilla chips with fat-free bean dip and salsa
- Health Valley graham crackers or rice cakes with natural peanut butter
- Popcorn sprinkled with Parmesan cheese
- Homemade low-fat bran muffin with low-fat or skim milk
- Crisp bread with sliced turkey and Dijon mustard
- Small pop-top can of water-packed tuna or chicken with whole grain crackers
- Half of a small, whole wheat bagel or English muffin with 2 tablespoons light cream cheese
- Veggie tortilla rolls: whole wheat tortilla spread with mustard or low-fat mayonnaise, and sprinkled with a variety of shredded vegetables, and 2 ounces low-fat grated cheese
- Fruit shake: skim milk blended with frozen fruit and vanilla
- Trail mix: 1 cup unsalted dry roasted peanuts, 1 cup unsalted dry roasted shelled pumpkin or sunflower seeds, and 2 cups raisins (make it in abundance and bag up into 1/4-cup or 1/2-cup portions for a whole snack)

test subjects, while those individuals who had eaten breakfast and lunch, but no snack, scored lower.

Iron-will discipline has never controlled food intake and never will. No checklist or rigid diet plan will give that control. Wisely chosen foods and well-timed eating is much more powerful and energizing. Strategic eating is essentially a balancing act, achieved by giving your body the right foods at the right time, and put together in effective ways. This means having both carbohydrates and proteins at every meal and snack, and keeping your healthy snack handy. When you don't have good choices available, you're likely to reach for an unhealthy snack or not eat at all, with either alternative setting you up for a later disaster.

Consider the healthy power snack ideas chart on the previous page, and start making them a regular part of your daily diet. Many power snacks do not require refrigeration, so keep them available in your car, in your desk drawer, in your briefcase—wherever you may find yourself at critical times. They can be as simple as fresh or dried fruit with low-fat cheese or yogurt, half a sandwich, or a trail mix of dry roasted peanuts, sunflower seeds, and dried fruit.

EAT BALANCED

Eating evenly throughout the day is not the only important factor in keeping your metabolism burning high and your body working well. Balancing your intake of carbohydrates and proteins is also vital to utilizing nutrients optimally. Every meal (and power snack) should include both whole food carbohydrates and lean proteins.

I know that this notion slaps every pop diet in the face; all quick-weight-loss plans manipulate and throw off this balance to force quick weight loss from dehydration. But the only way to lose body fat without losing your health is to embrace balance. It's this balance

POWER PROTEINS

Anything that comes from an animal (poultry, fish, meat, eggs, cheese, milk, and yogurt) gives you complete protein, supplying all the essential amino acids that your body can't make or store. The only plant source of quality protein, a miraculous one, is the legume family (dried beans and peanuts). Their pods absorb nitrogen from the soil and become an excellent high-fiber, low-fat protein source. Yet, because they lack sufficient amounts of one or more of the essential amino acids, they are considered "incomplete" proteins. They are best eaten with a grain (corn, wheat, rice, or oat product) or a seed (sunflower, sesame, pumpkin) to be complete.

Examples of high-quality dynamic duos are: peanut butter on bread, black beans over rice, beans and tortillas or cornbread, or a peanut and sunflower seed trail mix. Generally a 1/2 cup of cooked beans serves as two ounces of protein when mixed with an appropriate grain or seed, and 3/4 cup equals three ounces of protein.

EACH SERVING EQUALS 1 OUNCE OF PROTEIN (7 GRAMS)

- nonfat milk or nonfat plain yogurt — 6 ounces
- low-fat cheeses — 1 ounce or 1/4 cup grated
- 1 percent low-fat or nonfat cottage cheese or part-skim or fat-free ricotta — 1/4 cup
- eggs (particularly egg whites) — 1
- fish — 1 ounce or 1/4 cup flaked fish, i.e., tuna, salmon
- seafood (crab, lobster) — 1/4 cup
- seafood (clams, shrimp, oysters, scallops) — 5 pieces
- poultry — 1 ounce or 1/4 cup chopped
- beef, pork, lamb, veal (lean, trimmed) — 1 ounce
- legumes (black beans, garbanzo beans, Great Northern beans, kidney beans, lentils, navy beans, peanuts, red beans, split peas) — 1/4 cup
- Soybeans and soy products (such as tofu and soy milk) — 8 ounces
- natural peanut butter — 2 tablespoons

ENERGY-BOOSTING CARBOHYDRATES

Carbohydrates are found in plant foods (wheat, corn, oats, rice, barley, fruits, and vegetables), and are nutrition heavyweights themselves. When chosen in their whole food forms, they are packed with fiber, vitamins, and minerals that allow your body to stay operative from a point of strength. Contrary to what you may have heard, carbohydrates are low in calories. It's what we cook them in or top them with (butter, mayonnaise, heavy oils, and dressing) that moves us into weight-gaining territory.

Some carbohydrates are digested and absorbed quite easily, allowing them to be quick-burning forms of energy. These are the simple carbohydrates, found in fruits, unsweetened juices, and crunchy vegetables. The closer the food is to how it is grown, the slower will be the release of its sugars into the bloodstream. Complex carbohydrates, found in root vegetables, legumes, and grains that have been processed and refined, require more time to convert into a usable form of energy; they are digested more slowly and absorbed more evenly into the system as fuel. An eating plan high in whole-food forms of carbohydrates is your best bet for living long and well.

SIMPLE CARBOHYDRATES

FRUITS

All fruits and fruit juices like apples, apricots, bananas, berries, cherries, dates, grapefruit, grapes, kiwis, lemons, limes, melons, nectarines, oranges, peaches, pears, pineapples, plums, raisins (Generally one serving of simple carbohydrates is obtained from 1/2 cup fruit, 1/2 cup fruit juice, or 1/8 cup dried fruit. This gives 10 grams of carbohydrates)

NONSTARCHY VEGETABLES

asparagus, beets, broccoli, brussels sprouts, cabbage, carrots, cauliflower, celery, green beans, green leafy vegetables, kale, mushrooms, okra, onions, snow peas, sugar snaps, summer squash, tomatoes, zucchini (Generally one serving of simple carbohydrates is obtained from 1/2 cup cooked vegetables or 1 cup raw vegetables or juice—this gives 10 grams of simple carbohydrates)

COMPLEX CARBOHYDRATES

GRAINS

The following amounts provide one serving of complex carbohydrates, giving 15 grams:

barley, bulgur, couscous, grits, kasha, millet, or polenta, cooked... 1/2 cup

bread... 1 slice

cereals... 1 ounce (1/4 cup of concentrated cereal such as Grape Nuts or granola, 1/2 to 3/4 cup flaked cereals, 1 cup puffed cereal)

1 cup crackers or mini-rice cakes... 5

crispbread or rice cakes... 2

oats, uncooked... 1/3 cup

pasta or rice, cooked... 1/2 cup

fat-free tortillas... 1

wheat germ... 1/4 cup

STARCHY VEGETABLES

black-eyed peas, corn, green peas, lima beans, rutabagas, turnips, potatoes (white and sweet), winter squash (Generally one serving of complex carbohydrates is obtained from 1/2 cup cooked starchy vegetables, giving 15 grams)

that produces the metabolic burn we are seeking the most. In a study published in 1999, researchers found that healthy young women burned almost 50 percent more of their daily caloric intake when they ate meals that were low in fat and high in carbohydrates (with proper protein balance) than they did when eating meals that were lower in carbs but higher in fat.

Remember, carbohydrates and protein have very different functions in your body. Proteins are the vital building blocks for the body. Carbohydrates are 100 percent pure energy—your body's fuel, designed to burn fast, clean, and pure. When carbohydrates are eaten alone, the body uses them like kindling on a fire. It burns brightly and quickly, but the body-building functions of protein do not take place. While protein can be used as an energy source, it has another much more vital function—which is why carbohydrates should be eaten *with* a protein to protect this building nutrient from being wasted as a less efficient source of energy. This allows protein to be used for building new cells, boosting your metabolism, building body muscle, keeping body fluids in balance, healing and fighting infections, and making skin, hair, and nails beautiful.

Women generally need at least 50 to 55 grams of protein per day; men generally need 65 to 70 grams (these estimates are based on percentage of lean body mass). More protein is needed in times of stress, or when actively working to build muscle or to maintain muscle mass while losing fat weight. Generally, one ounce of meat contains about 7 grams of protein, meaning women need a minimum of 7 to 8 ounces per day and men need a minimum of 9 to 10 ounces per day. Generally, your power snacks should include at least 1 to 2 ounces protein, and your meals should provide 2 to 3 ounces (after cooking). If possible, get a food scale and periodically weigh your protein portion to be sure you are getting enough.

But the *amount* of protein eaten is not the only secret to abundant energy and wellness; equally important is the need to take in protein in smaller, evenly distributed amounts throughout the day. Because protein is not stored, it must be replenished frequently throughout the day, each and every day. And this is where people go wrong. Never, never believe anybody who tells you that you don't need protein, or to eat it only once a day. You will be robbing your body of protein's healing and building power all day long.

The bottom line: be sure to eat proteins and carbs together. At every meal and power snack have a balance of high-quality, whole-food carbohydrate and lean proteins. Always remember: carbohydrates *burn* and proteins *build*. You need them both.

Best-Choice Carbohydrates

When choosing carbohydrates, go for the most whole form possible and thus benefit from all the fiber, nutrients, and natural chemicals they were created with. This means eating fruits and vegetables with well-washed skins on, and choosing fruit rather than fruit juice. Choose whole grains when you can, such as brown rice and stone ground 100 percent whole grain breads, crackers, pastas, and cereals. Look for the word WHOLE as the first ingredient on the label. These foods supply much-needed vitamin B6, chromium, selenium, and magnesium, all nutrients that are critical for activating energy production and release. They also have a lower glycemic response.

Whole-grain carbohydrates are particularly valuable because they have not had the outer layers of grain removed; they contain many more vitamins, minerals, and fiber than the refined, white products. Don't be fooled by manufacturers and advertisements. White, refined carbohydrates, even when enriched, are never as good nutritionally as whole grains. In fact, to your body, refined white flour is the same as

sugar, making a diet high in white-flour foods the same as a high-sugar diet. Start reading the ingredients lists of all your grain products and remember to choose the ones made with 100 percent whole grain. Many manufacturers call products whole grain even if they contain only minimal amounts of bran. Brown dye does wonders in making food look healthy.

Whole grains satisfy and keep you full, so you may eat less in general. The fiber they contain slows the rate of nutrient absorption following a meal, reducing the rise of blood sugar levels and secretion of insulin that causes the fat cells to lock down. Fiber serves as a "time-release capsule," releasing sugars from digested carbohydrates slowly and evenly into the bloodstream. This helps keep your energy levels up and even.

EAT LEAN

One of the drawbacks to eating more protein, more often, is that many popular choices are also high in fat. But does fat make you fat? It's not quite that simple, but fat *is* more than just a disease culprit; excess intake is also a culprit in fat storage and metabolic lock-down. It's theorized that overeating fat sends fat molecules into your bloodstream, increasing the thickness, or viscosity, of the blood, and reducing its oxygen-delivery capacity. And it's the oxygen that's needed for energy to be metabolized rather than stored. In addition, the excess calories we consume as fat are converted and stored as fat more readily than those from other sources. One reason for this is that fat is a more concentrated source of calories (all fats contain twice as many calories as equal amounts of carbohydrate or proteins, about 9 calories per gram, or 120 calories per tablespoon). Also, the body is more efficient in storing fat as fat. This is why the weight control experts of today consider "trimming the fat" from our diets to be much more important in weight loss than just watching our calories.

FIBER: A POWERFUL WEIGHT-LOSS BOOSTER

Dietary fiber (the part of plants not digested by the body) promotes weight loss by helping to block the body's digestion of fat. A recent study of 3,700 men and women ages 18 to 30 showed that those who had the highest intakes of fiber-rich whole grains also tended to have lower body fat. The study showed that at all levels of fat intake, individuals eating the most fiber gained less weight than those eating the least fiber.

In another study, people absorbed fewer calories when the fiber content of their meals was increased. Individuals who upped their daily fiber intake from 18 grams to 36 grams (a bowl of high-fiber cereal can contain 25 grams) absorbed 130 fewer calories per day. Over the course of a year, that reduction in calorie uptake would bring a loss of roughly ten pounds.

There are two types of fiber: the water-soluble fibers found in oats, barley, apples, dried beans, and nuts, which have been found to lower serum cholesterol and triglyceride levels and to help control blood sugar levels; and the water-insoluble fibers found in wheat bran, whole grains, and fresh vegetables, which are excellent means of controlling chronic GI problems.

HIGH-FIBER FOODS

Peanuts and peanut butter
Cooked dried beans
Sunflower and sesame seeds
Apples, apricots, peaches, pears, bananas, pineapple, plums, prunes
Broccoli, carrots, corn, lettuce, peas, potatoes (including skins), spinach
Bran (unprocessed wheat and oat)
Bread (whole wheat)
Brown rice
Cereals: whole grain, bran type, oatmeal, Wheatena
Whole wheat pasta

Think of fiber as a sponge that absorbs excess water in the GI tract to curtail diarrhea but provides a bulky mass which will pass more quickly and easily to relieve constipation and diverticulosis and possibly prevent hemorrhoids. Fiber needs water to make it work the way it should, ideally 8 to 10 glasses a day. The best way to drink water is to have a glass before and after every meal and snack rather than with a meal when it dilutes digestive functions. Try filling a two-quart container with water each morning and make sure you have drunk it all before bedtime.

To increase the amount of fiber you get in your diet easily, choose more raw and lightly cooked vegetables but in as nonprocessed form as possible. As a food becomes processed, ground, mashed, puréed, or juiced, the fiber effectiveness is decreased. Add unprocessed raw bran to your cereals. Raw oat bran (from oatmeal) is particularly useful in stabilizing blood sugar and cholesterol levels; raw wheat bran is useful for a healthy gastrointestinal tract. Be careful to add bran gradually. Begin with 1 teaspoon wheat bran and 1 teaspoon oat bran and increase slowly as your body adjusts to more fiber.

Of course, fatness or thinness is not the only issue involved in our food choices. Even if you have been blessed with a metabolism that burns ever brightly, allowing you to maintain your weight easily, excess fat intake can bring problems. You may not be seeing the problem, on the scale or on your waistline, but it's an energy drain and a disease flag just the same.

Intriguing research on fat's effect on our metabolism has come out of Duke University, showing that Type II diabetic mice put on a radically reduced fat intake (10 percent of total calories consumed) were cured of their diabetes. This reflects the impact that an excess fat intake can have on blood sugar levels—of both mice and men. It also makes a statement about the risk of diets that push fat and radically cut valuable carbohydrates as a diabetes cure. The truth is that excess fat fed to animals with a genetic susceptibility to diabetes made them far more likely to develop the disease.

And there's more. Look at these vital facts about fat:

Daily Calories	Grams of Fat Suggested
1,500 calories	42 grams of fat a day
1,800 calories	50 grams of fat
2,000 calories	55 grams of fat
2,500 calories	67 grams of fat

- Excess fat intake increases your cholesterol level and your risk of heart disease and stroke.
- Excess fat intake increases your risk of cancer.
- Excess fat intake, particularly saturated fat, has been shown to elevate blood pressure, regardless of your weight or sodium intake.

The bottom line: choose your proteins wisely by making them low-fat. You certainly do need fat; it is an essential nutrient needed

ALL ABOUT OIL

We eat five kinds of oil: saturated, hydrogenated, polyunsaturated, monounsaturated, and omega-3 fatty acids. Each has the same fat content and number of calories that contribute to the fat budget: 5 grams of fat and 45 calories per teaspoon.

But these oils vary greatly in the effects they have on our bodies—good and bad. Some are damaging to the arteries and heart.

Artery-clogging fats that increase blood cholesterol include:

SATURATED FAT: Found in dairy and meat products, including milk, cheese, ice cream, beef, and pork. It also can be found in coconut and palm oils, nondairy creamers, and toppings.

HYDROGENATED FAT: Also called trans fat, hydrogenated fat is formed when vegetable oils are hardened into solids, usually to protect against spoiling and to maintain flavor. Examples include stick margarine and shortening, deep-fried foods such as French fries and fried chicken, and pastries, cookies, doughnuts, and crackers. Read the ingredient list of any processed foods you buy. If you see the words "partially hydrogenated," look for a different product—especially if it is one of the first three ingredients. Hydrogenation is a manufacturing process that converts a polyunsaturated or monounsaturated oil into a saturated fat.

Fats that do not clog arteries include:

MONOUNSATURATED FAT: Found in olive, canola, and peanut oils. These fats increase good HDL cholesterol and decrease bad LDL cholesterol, and thus the risk of disease.

OMEGA-3 FATTY ACIDS (EPA AND DHA OILS): Found in all fish and seafood, particularly cold-water fish such as salmon, albacore tuna, swordfish, sardines, mackerel, and hard shellfish. The only plant source is flaxseed. Omega-3 fatty acids decrease triglycerides and total and bad LDL cholesterol. They reduce the tendency of the blood to form clots, stabilize blood sugars, improve brain function, and reduce inflammation.

POLYUNSATURATED FATS decrease both bad LDL *and* good HDL cholesterol, so they aren't the desired choice. These fats are those in corn oil, cottonseed oil, safflower oil, sesame oil, sunflower oil, as well as avocado, sunflower seed kernels, sesame seeds, almonds, walnuts, and pecans.

Try to get most of your fat from monounsaturated olive and canola oil (or salad dressings made from them), nuts, and the Omega-3s found in fish and flaxseed. And spread your fat throughout the day—a little fat helps you absorb fat-soluble nutrients from vegetables and fruit.

in limited amounts to lubricate your body, transport fat-soluble vitamins, produce hormones, and fill you after eating. But it needs to come from the healthiest sources, not from bacon fat and butter.

Cutting calories is easier if you focus on limiting fat to less than 30 percent of daily calories. Cutting back on calories from fat allows you to eat more nutrient-rich foods like whole grains, fruits, and vegetables. You can also eat more food for fewer calories.

Determining Your Personal Fat Budget

As much as we need a balancing act of carbohydrates and proteins at each meal, we don't need fat in the quantities we consume. On the average, too much of our calorie intake is from fat—35 to 40 percent rather than the recommended 25 to 30 percent. The typical adult eats the fat equivalent of one stick of butter a day. Even if *you* don't eat that much fat, chances are you are eating a lot more than you realize.

To really understand your fat limit, you need to know your calorie limit. Remember, to lose weight, a moderately active woman will probably need to keep her daily caloric intake to around 1,500 calories. A moderately active man shouldn't exceed around 1,800 calories. To determine your 25 percent fat allowance, use this formula:

25 percent of 1,500 calories = 375 calories
375 calories divided by 9 calories per gram of fat = 42 grams of total fat suggested each day.

Once you know your fat budget, see whether you are staying within the bounds by adding up the grams of fat for all the food that you eat in a day. This is both the fat hidden in foods you eat—what is in chicken, fish, and cheese—as well as the added fat you cook with or

add to your food, like oils or butter. Almost all food labels will tell you the grams of total fat in a serving.

Like any worthy goal, reducing your personal fat intake requires some effort and commitment—to learn new ways to season foods without fat, to order more healthfully at restaurants, to discover the right snack foods. Be assured that the benefits far exceed the effort. Smart eating does not doom you to nutrition martyrdom—eating flavorless foods that taste like cardboard. Nor do you have to become a chemical analyst to stay within these guidelines while dining out, grocery shopping, or cooking. Use the Practical Strategies For Living in Part 4 to help you trim the fat without cutting flavor.

SMART WEIGH TIP
Get back to basics— limit your portions.

Think of a move toward nutritious, low-fat eating as a permanent change instead of a dieting regime that you go on, and off. Don't keep a calculator at your bedside, and don't get stuck in a deprivation mode. Be easy on yourself, and go slowly, taking practical, feasible steps one at a time. Focus on good foods, well prepared, and your desires will begin to shift. Give your taste buds time to return to how they were created; high-fat foods will have less and less appeal as you begin to eat foods that kick up your metabolism and give you energy, better digestion, and a sense of well-being.

If motivation to cut back on the fat in your diet comes hard, consider this mental picture: imagine hamburger grease after it cools and hardens. Then imagine that grease trying to circulate through your bloodstream.

EAT BRIGHT

Brightly colored fruits and vegetables are loaded with antioxidants like beta-carotene and vitamin A, folic acid, and other B vitamins,

along with vitamin C. These nutrients are vital to wellness since they neutralize chemicals believed to damage body processes and serve to boost metabolism by boosting the immune system.

Generally, the more vivid the color of the fruit or veggie, the higher in nutrients it will be. The bright color signals that these are treasure chests of protection, and triggers for releasing energy and raising immunities. That deep orange-red color of carrots, sweet potatoes, apricots, cantaloupe, and strawberries is a sign of their vitamin A content. Dark green leafy vegetables like greens, spinach, romaine lettuce, broccoli, and brussels sprouts, also have the extra bonus of being *the* source of folic acid (folate), a must-have for health and wellness. The presence of folate in the blood seems to lower the level of homocysteine, an amino acid that may be a cause of stroke and heart disease. A variety of foods contain folate, including breakfast cereals as well as beans and green vegetables. Since January 1998 the federal government has insisted that folate be added to all flour. So it's in your bread, whether you eat it sliced, wrapped, or by the baguette.

Without trying to calculate every milligram of this vitamin and that mineral in the foods you eat, the best way to assure that your vitamin intake is optimal is to go for whole-grain carbohydrates whenever possible, and choose meals full of a variety of brightly colored fruits and vegetables.

The ideal is nine servings of vegetables and fruits every day. Veggies and fruit are the foundation of *The Smart Weigh* plan, as opposed to grains, the foundation of the traditional food pyramid. You should be eating nine 1/2-cup servings (about 4 1/2 cups) of a variety of brightly colored fruits and veggies every day.

Sound like overkill? In reality, it could spell extra life. Study after study links diets highest in fruit and vegetables with less cancer,

TIPS TO RETAIN NUTRIENTS

- Buy vegetables that are as fresh as possible. When not possible, frozen is the next best choice. Avoid those frozen with butter or sauces.
- Use well-washed peelings and outer leaves of vegetables whenever possible because of the high concentration of nutrients found within them.
- Store vegetables in airtight containers in the refrigerator.
- Do not store vegetables in water. Too many vitamins are lost.
- Cook vegetables on the highest heat possible, in the least amount of water possible, and for the shortest time possible. Steaming, microwaving, and stir-frying are the best cooking methods.
- Cook vegetables until tender crisp, not mushy. Overcooked vegetables lose their flavor along with their vitamins.

heart disease, diabetes, even osteoporosis. The landmark DASH (Dietary Approaches to Stop Hypertension) diet study found that nine servings a day lowered high blood pressure as much as some prescription drugs. More and more research suggests that nine a day—five vegetables and four fruits—is the optimum. Yet most Americans get only four servings a day.

Antioxidant Power

For fifty years or so, a leading hypothesis has been that aging and disease are promoted by highly reactive molecules called free radicals. The older we get, the more free radicals are released into our systems, where they destroy tissue. The villain is oxygen. In effect, we rust as we get older! But the body also has a network of defenses against free radicals, called antioxidants. Some are produced internally; others are derived from what we eat.

Vitamin E is one such antioxidant. Many other antioxidants also promise protection against diseases. One is lutein, found in leafy green vegetables, which may help protect against degeneration of the macula in the eye, the leading cause of blindness in those sixty-five or older. Another is lycopene, contained in tomatoes, apricots, guava, pink grapefruit, and watermelon, which may help prevent prostate cancer. And exciting beneficial effects are being shown through the antioxidants contained in red wine, blueberries, and strawberries as well.

As the research continues to pour in, this is the best health insurance policy: five servings a day of brightly colored fruits and vegetables will help to keep the doctor away... and ten servings will allow you to thrive, especially if complemented with other antioxidant-rich foods such as garlic, hot peppers, green tea, and soy.

FOOD HEALS

A discussion about strategic eating wouldn't be complete without some comments on the pharmacological wonders of food. If you have been eating foods just to lose weight, or gain weight, or just because it's dinner time, you are missing an important and exciting truth: food is filled with healing agents, like the antioxidants mentioned above, that energize and power you. Food is *medicine* for your body.

If you desire to get well, stay well, and live a life filled with energy, you must expose your body to food because of what's *in* food: natural healing agents, mood enhancers, and energy boosters. There

---

EAT LIKE THE GREEKS!

A Mediterranean diet may help protect people against rheumatoid arthritis, Greek investigators report. Study findings published in the *American Journal of Clinical Nutrition* from the University of Athens Medical School show that a high intake of cooked vegetables and olive oil may reduce the risk of developing the disease.

The research team compared the diets of 145 rheumatoid arthritis patients with the diets of 188 people who did not have the disease. All of the study participants lived in southern Greece, where the average diet consists of less meat and more cooked and raw vegetables, fish, and olive oil than most diets in Westernized countries. Participants who ate the greatest number of servings of cooked vegetables were about 75 percent less likely to develop rheumatoid arthritis than those who reported eating the fewest servings. People with the lowest intake of cooked vegetables ate 0.85 servings of cooked vegetables a day, on average, and people with the highest intakes ate an average of 2.9 half-cup servings a day.

THE NUTRITIONAL TOP TEN

(1) OATS: The b-glucan in whole oats reduces the risk of coronary heart disease. The soluble fiber is instrumental in lowering cholesterol and stabilizing blood sugars.

(2) SOYBEANS: The bioactive ingredients in soy products suppress formation of blood vessels that feed cancer cells. Soy helps stabilize hormone levels in women, as well as decrease the risk of heart disease, osteoporosis, ovarian, breast, and prostate cancer.

(3) TOMATOES: Lycopene, a potent antioxidant, is a carotenoid that fights the uncontrolled growth of cells into tumors. It fights cancer of the colon, bladder, pancreas, and prostate. Men who eat ten servings of tomatoes per week have been shown to decrease their prostate cancer risk by 66 percent.

(4) COLD-WATER SEAFOOD: Healthy EPA/omega-3 oils are shown to turn on fat oxidation, decrease risk of coronary artery disease, stabilize blood sugars, increase brain power, and reduce the inflammatory response. Seafood reduces LDL cholesterol and triglycerides, while raising levels of HDL cholesterol.

(5) FLAXSEED: A unique source of lignans, powerful antioxidants that are believed to stop cells from turning cancerous. Flaxseed also contains alpha-linolenic acid, the plant version of the omega-3s found in fish oils; it makes a great healthy option for people who won't eat fish.

(6) GARLIC: Rich in allicin, which boosts immune function and reduces cancer risk. Garlic also has strong antiviral effects and has been shown to lower blood pressure and cholesterol levels.

(7) HOT PEPPERS: A source of capsaicin, a vital immune, mood, and metabolic booster with powerful antiviral effects. Capsaicin is linked to decreased risk of stomach cancer due to its ability to neutralize nitrosamines, a cancer-causing compound formed in the body when cured or charred meats are consumed. Capsaicin also kills bacteria believed to cause stomach ulcers, and appears to turn on the fat-burning capacity.

(8) SWEET POTATOES: A rival of carrots as a potent source of beta-carotene and other carotenoids, which help prevent cataracts and protect the body from free radicals and cancer—particularly cancer of the larynx, esophagus, and lungs.

(9) GRAPES: Grape skins contain a high concentration of resveratrol, which appears to block the formation of coronary artery plaque, as well as tumor formation and growth. Red grape juice or red wine is considered a better source of resveratrol than white, which is made without the grape skins.

(10) CRUCIFEROUS VEGETABLES: Broccoli, cabbage, cauliflower, and brussels sprouts contain indoles, sulforaphane, and isothiocyanates which protect cells from damage by carcinogens, block tumor formation, and help the liver to inactivate hormone-like compounds that may promote cancer.

are certain foods that pack a powerful punch when it comes to well-ness. In addition to their wealth of vitamins and minerals, these foods contain nutraceuticals, the food pharmacy for the new millennium.

This may be a new thought for you. Most of us are much more aware of the food/*disease* connection: if a person has diabetes, refined sugar is a bad thing; if he's allergic to shellfish, eating lobster is a bad thing; if she has high cholesterol, saturated fat is a *very* bad thing. Yet most people are just becoming aware of the food/*wellness* connection. And it's the most exciting part of health research today—a focus on the essential building blocks in food that make us well and keep us well.

This new perspective takes us beyond Mom's chiding to "eat your vegetables" because they're good for us. Instead, it's an understanding of what, in broccoli, makes it exciting to eat—indoles and sulforaphanes that protect against cancer and aging, folic acid that protects against heart disease, and vitamin C that boosts immunes.

These truths are why I'm a "food pusher." This perspective builds appreciation and awe for lycopene in tomatoes—the antioxidant mentioned above that strongly protects against prostate and cervical cancer. Or for the b-glucan in whole oats that does medical magic by reducing cholesterol levels, increasing protection from cancer, regulating blood sugars, and serving as a gastrointestinal stabilizer.

These are just a few of the foods in my "Nutritional Top Ten" that can make all the difference. Review this list, and then review your food choices over the past week. How are you measuring up? It may be time to go to the grocery store and to start saying *yes*, not yuck, to power foods for your body.

There are *so* many other foods that could be placed on this Nutritional Top Ten list, some that may surprise you—like blueberries as a potent anti-ager and green tea as a brew for a slimmer you.

That's right, energy expenditure scientists in Switzerland have found that the flavonoid in green tea—epigallocatechin galate (EGCG)—has been found to "turn up the burn" in fat oxidation, helping the body to better burn body fat rather than store it. If you must turn to caffeine for an energy hit, turn to green tea instead of espresso.

WHAT ABOUT VITAMINS AND MINERALS?

Vitamins and essential minerals are required in tiny amounts to promote essential biochemical reactions in your cells. Together, vitamins and minerals are called micronutrients. Lack of a particular

---

YOUR SUPPLEMENT GUIDE

Supplements are not substitutes. They can't replace the hundreds of nutrients in whole foods needed for a balanced diet. But if you do decide to take a vitamin supplement, here are things to consider:

STICK TO THE DAILY VALUE — Choose a vitamin-mineral combination limited to 150 percent DV or less. Take no more than the recommended dose. The higher the dose, the more likely you are to have side effects.

DON'T WASTE DOLLARS — Generic brands and synthetic vitamins are generally less expensive and equally effective. Don't be tempted by added herbs, enzymes, or amino acids — they add nothing but cost. If you are going to use an herbal remedy, do that separately.

READ THE LABEL — Supplements can lose potency over time, so check the expiration date on the label. Also look for the initials USP (for the testing organization U.S. Pharmacopeia) or words such as "release assured" or "proven release," indicating that the supplement is easily dissolved and absorbed by your body.

STORE THEM IN A SAFE PLACE — Iron supplements are the most common cause of poisoning deaths among children. Keep them out of little hand's reach—and in a cool place.

DON'T SELF-PRESCRIBE — See your doctor if you have a health problem. Tell him or her about any supplement you're taking. Some supplements may interfere with medications.

micronutrient for a prolonged period can cause a specific disease or condition, which can usually be reversed when the micronutrient is resupplied.

A vitamin deficiency takes you down over time. It may take months, but it's a slow decline into fatigue and weakness. As your body becomes depleted of certain vitamins, various biochemical changes take place that result in a general lack of well-being. This occurs long before any symptoms of a specific vitamin deficiency can be noted. For example, a thiamine deficiency can ultimately exhibit itself as nerve damage, but appetite loss, weakness, and lethargy will proceed it.

Your body can't make most vitamins and minerals. They must come from food or supplements. Vitamins are organic minerals that the body does not produce on its own but cannot do without. As chemical catalysts for the body, they make things happen. Though vitamins do not themselves give energy, they help the body convert carbohydrates to energy and then help the body to metabolize it.

There are thirteen vitamins. Four—vitamins A, D, E, and K— are stored in your body's fat (they're called fat-soluble vitamins). Nine are water-soluble and are not stored in your body in appreciable amounts. They are vitamin C and the eight B vitamins: thiamine (B1), riboflavin (B2), niacin, vitamin B6, pantothenic acid, vitamin B12, biotin, and folic acid (folate).

In addition to their impact on your metabolism, vitamins in the right amounts are needed for normal growth, digestion, mental alertness, and resistance to infection. They enable your body to use carbohydrates, fats, and proteins. They also act as catalysts in your body, initiating or speeding up a chemical reaction. But you don't "burn" vitamins, so you can't get energy (calories) directly from them.

Your body strives to maintain an optimal level of each vitamin and keep a constant amount circulating in your bloodstream. Surplus water-soluble vitamins are excreted in urine. Surplus fat-soluble vitamins are stored in body tissue. Because they're stored, excess fat-soluble vitamins can accumulate in your body and become toxic. Your body is especially sensitive to too much vitamin A and vitamin D. For example, taking large amounts of vitamin D can indirectly cause kidney damage, while large amounts of vitamin A can cause liver damage. Even modest increases in some minerals can lead to imbalances that limit your body's ability to use other minerals. And supplements of iron, zinc, chromium, and selenium can be toxic at just five times the RDA. Megadose formulas can also cause stomach pains, diarrhea, and kidney stones. Virtually all nutrient toxicities stem from high-dose supplements—more is not necessarily better, and can even be harmful.

Minerals, unlike vitamins, are inorganic compounds. Some minerals are building blocks for the body structures such as bones and teeth. Others work with the fluids in the body, giving them certain characteristics. Some thirty minerals are important in nutrition, though most are needed in small, yet vital amounts.

Like an insufficient intake of vitamins, mineral deficiencies also zap your metabolism, particularly when there is a lack of the high-energy nutrients iron, magnesium, and zinc. Your body also needs fifteen minerals that help regulate cell function and provide structure for cells. Major minerals include calcium, phosphorus, and magnesium. In addition, your body needs smaller amounts of chromium, copper, fluoride, iodine, iron, manganese, molybdenum, selenium, zinc, chloride, potassium, and sodium.

Vitamin hucksters spend millions planting the fear: "Are you getting enough vitamins?" They recommend vitamin, mineral, and

nutritional supplements as "vitamin insurance." But there's no need for most people to bank on vitamin insurance. The American Dietetic Association, the National Academy of Sciences, the National Research Council, and other major medical societies all agree that as your first choice you should get the vitamins and minerals you need through a well-balanced diet. Although certain high-risk groups may benefit from a vitamin-mineral supplement, healthy adults can get all necessary nutrients from food. But most people don't.

And they don't due to a different reason from what you might think—it's not a nutrient deficiency of our food supply, it's that most people don't eat properly. Only one person in ten, for example, regularly consumes the recommended five to nine servings a day of fruits and vegetables. Skipping meals, dieting, and eating meals high in sugar and fat all contribute to poor nutrition. For these people, taking supplemental vitamins would be reasonable and wise, although the best course would be to adopt better eating habits.

Food is better than supplements because food contains hundreds of additional nutrients, including phytochemicals. As already discussed, phytochemicals are compounds that occur naturally in foods containing important health benefits. Scientists have yet to learn all the roles phytochemicals play in nutrition, and there's no RDA yet established for them. But this is known: If you depend on supplements rather than trying to eat a variety of whole foods, you miss out on possible health benefits from these natural protectors. In addition, only long-term, well-designed studies can sort out which nutrients in food are beneficial and whether taking them in pill form provides the same benefit. In the meantime, it's best to concentrate on getting your nutrients from food.

Having said which, it is admittedly difficult to get enough of

some vitamins from the most conscientious diet. Vitamin E, for example, in high dosages may help prevent some cancers and cardiovascular disease. To get that much from your diet, you'd have to consume 1 1/2 quarts of olive oil a day! Overall, however, it is better if your vitamin sources come from natural food rather than supplementation. But a cautionary note: the full benefits of a high dosage of vitamin E are not yet proved. In fact, still troublesome research reports are cropping up showing that antioxidant supplementation can actually trigger cancer cell growth and depress immunities.

The most intelligent course is to get the maximum vitamin and mineral intake you can from food—then use supplements. If you choose to take a multivitamin mineral supplement, look for one that has no more than 150 percent of the RDA. Name-brand multivitamins sold at pharmacies are fine.

And be aware that a multivitamin mineral supplement will not fully meet your needs for certain nutrients like calcium and it will never be a substitute for food. The additional supplements I most commonly recommend are: 100 to 400 international units (IU) of vitamin E and 100 to 500 milligrams (mg) of vitamin C. On days when you may eat only two calcium-rich foods, take 500 mg of calcium if you're under fifty; take 1,000 mg of calcium (divided into

MINERAL TONICS: DO THEY HELP?

So-called tonics of "colloidal" minerals (tiny particles of minerals suspended in liquid), which are touted to increase energy, are brisk sellers in multilevel marketing organizations and health stores alike. But there's no evidence that these drinks do any good, and because they contain potentially toxic heavy metals, they may do a great deal of harm. Many contain arsenic and dolamite, which can build up to toxic levels in the body.

two separate doses of 500 mg each) if you're fifty or older. Calcium citrate has been found to be the most absorbable supplement form.

The bottom line: If you want to improve your nutritional health, look first to a well-balanced diet. In most cases, making changes in your diet has a far greater chance of promoting health than taking supplements. However, even if you don't have a documented deficiency, your doctor or dietitian may recommend a vitamin-mineral supplement if:

YOU'RE OLDER — Lack of appetite, loss of taste and smell, and denture problems can all contribute to a poor diet. If you eat alone or are depressed, you also may not eat enough to get all the nutrients you need from food. Evidence, moveover, shows that, if you're older, a multivitamin may improve your immune function and decrease your risk for some infections.

In addition, if you're age sixty-five or older, you may need to increase your intake of vitamins B6, B12, and D because your body may not be able to absorb these as well. And women, especially those not taking estrogen, may need to increase their intake of calcium and vitamin D to protect against osteoporosis.

YOU'RE ON A RESTRICTIVE DIET — Although certainly not advised, if you are eating fewer than 1,000 calories a day, or your diet has limited variety due to intolerance or allergy, you may benefit from a vitamin-mineral supplement.

YOU HAVE A DISEASE OF YOUR DIGESTIVE TRACT — Diseases of your liver, gallbladder, intestine, or pancreas, or previous surgery on your digestive tract may interfere with your normal digestion and absorption of nutrients. If you have one of these conditions, your doctor may advise you to supplement your diet with vitamins and minerals.

YOU SMOKE — Smoking reduces vitamin C levels and causes production of harmful free radicals. The RDA for vitamin C for smokers is

higher—100 milligrams (mg) compared to 60 mg for nonsmokers. Still, you can easily get this much by eating foods rich in vitamin C. If you smoke, try to stop. And don't depend on high-potency supplements to provide necessary nutrients. Two studies of beta carotene have shown an increased risk of lung cancer in smokers who take these supplements.

YOU DRINK ALCOHOLIC BEVERAGES TO EXCESS — If you regularly consume alcohol to excess, you may not get enough vitamins due to poor nutrition and alcohol's effect on the absorption, metabolism, and excretion of vitamins through the urine.

YOU'RE PREGNANT OR BREAST-FEEDING — If you're pregnant or breast-feeding, you need more of certain nutrients, especially folic acid, iron, and calcium. Your doctor can recommend a supplement.

YOU'RE IN ANOTHER HIGH-RISK GROUP — Vegetarians who eliminate all animal products from their diets may need additional vitamin B12. And if you have limited milk intake and limited exposure to the sun, you may need to supplement your diet with calcium and vitamin D.

The beautiful thing about good, balanced nutrition is this: everything fits together in such a perfect way that just eating a wide variety of different foods in their whole form will more than likely give you an adequate intake of essential nutrients. Eating well is the time-tested answer to the vitamin–mineral question, so don't let a junk diet vandalize your metabolism and energy stores any longer. Determine to make changes for the long haul. Learn how to eat and live with it for the rest of your life.

Eating to boost your metabolism and wellness has another payoff: it energizes you to exercise! Eating smart is only half the battle in your quest for an active metabolism—regular exercise is also a key to keeping your body burning calories at a high rate.

CHAPTER 7 ▪ M: Movement

You cannot get fit in one workout, just as you cannot live your life in one day.

—JOHNNY G., creator of spinning cycling classes

E xercise is critical to weight management success. In fact, it's the single best predictor of whether you'll keep off excess weight once you've lost it. A study done in Boston over a decade ago showed that weight loss people who dieted but did not exercise gained back nearly all their weight, while those who exercised along with dieting, and continued to do so, didn't regain any.

This is primarily because of the impact exercise has on muscle mass. When you start using muscle during exercise rather than losing it to dieting, you release your fat-burning

potential. Strong muscles are a lot like the Energizer Bunny: they just keep going and going, activating your metabolism and boosting your calorie burn even while you sleep. New research shows that by building muscle, you can further boost the calorie burn you get out of any kind of exercise.

You probably know that the amount of calories that you burn during exercise depends on what type of exercise you do, your level of effort, and how much you weigh. Yet when researchers at the

Human Performance and Fitness Department at the University of Massachusetts compared bodybuilders with lots of muscle and little fat to men of the same weight who had less muscle and more fat, they found that the bodybuilders burned about 100 calories more during the same thirty-minute walk. They theorize that the good news will hold true for anyone building muscle, in any amount. Strong muscles rev up the body's calorie-burning ability. That is why exercise, particularly strength training, is the anti-aging solution. Lifting weights curbs muscle loss—along with shaping a sleeker, firmer body.

Aerobic exercise (meaning, "with oxygen") is a powerful metabolic enhancer because it boosts the oxygen-carrying capacity of the bloodstream. During aerobic exercise, your heart pumps more blood, your lungs take in more oxygen, and your blood carries more oxygen and fuel to your muscles. The glucose from your food combines with oxygen in your cells, producing and releasing the energy molecules you need for a fast-burning metabolism. This means exercise gives you more metabolic-boosting oxygen where you need it, faster, and more efficiently. And by making your heart more efficient in its function, aerobic exercise improves brain circulation and function as well.

In addition to increasing your caloric burn while you're running the track or pedaling the stationary bike, exercise is a gift that keeps on giving. The "after-burn" of exercise boosts your metabolism so you use up more calories for hours *after* you finish your workout. This is the real impact of exercise and is especially beneficial if you exercise at higher rather than lower intensities—walking, running, or riding just a little faster, or adding some hills or incline to crank up the calorie burn and keep it up, even after your workout.

Exercise also decreases your appetite and gives you a healthy out-

let for stress—it douses the emotional fires behind overeating. Endorphins—the powerful morphine-like chemicals that promote a sense of well-being—are also released in your brain during exercise. And moderate regular exercise can create a change in biochemistry that launches you into a state of confidence and exhilaration. Studies have proved that just thirty minutes of aerobic activity—all at once or in three, ten-minute spurts throughout the day—will boost your energy, moods, and alertness. The overall effect of consistent exercise is to provide you better fuel to work with and a better engine to put it in.

Yet most people don't exercise at all. Surveys show that only 40 percent of Americans are involved in any kind of focused exercise on even a weekly basis—which adds up to from 40 to 50 million people.

"JUST DO IT!"

Why *don't* people exercise? I believe the answer is simple: too many of us are stuck in a viscious cycle of exhaustion. We know we need to exercise, but we are simply too done in to get it done. That's why I usually develop a phased *Smart Weigh* plan for my clients, first getting them to eat well and to start easy walking. After two to three weeks, a more focused exercise plan will emerge as a result of the overflow of energy. With this dynamic duo, the exercise adds significantly to their energy level and a positive cycle replaces the negative, downward energy cycle.

When you feel too tired to "just do it," keep reminding yourself of this: *the fastest way to feel energized is to exercise.* That "I'm too tired to work out" feeling will get out of your head once you start moving. You just have to override the message of your stressed-out brain and do something—anything—physical when you're in an energy slump. When you get home feeling totally beat, push yourself a bit:

change into sneakers and go out for a brisk walk. You'll feel a burst of energy afterward. Then the next time you're feeling too pooped to exercise, you'll remember that "buzz" and be quicker to get off the couch. You may even be inclined to expand your workout into a more ambitious run or bike ride, or even a visit to the gym. Soon you'll be healthfully hooked on the buzz of working out and won't even hear those "I'm just too tired" messages from your brain.

Not exercising is associated with an increased rate of illness and disease of nearly every type, from the common cold and flu to heart disease and stroke. People who don't exercise are more apt to die from cardiovascular incidents than to survive them. And because of the interconnected nature of the muscular system, brain, and other processes of the body, being sedentary also depresses your mood, your thinking, and your ability to work productively.

Here are fourteen motivators to get you going and keep you going:

(1) YOU'LL LIVE LONGER. An apple a day may keep the doctor away, but a two-mile walk may keep the coroner at bay. Researchers at the Honolulu Heart Program found that adults who walked an average of two miles a day reduced their risk of premature death by half. For the subjects who walked even more, the risk of death fell even further.

(2) YOU'LL BURN CALORIES. Particularly when you walk. Researchers at the Medical College of Wisconsin and Veterans Affairs Medical Center in Milwaukee tested the calorie burn of six indoor exercise machines and found the treadmill burned the most. When study participants exercised "somewhat hard," they burned a full 40 percent more calories walking on the treadmill than when on the stationary bike.

(3) YOU'LL GIVE YOUR BACK A BREAK. The best thing you can do for a painful lower back is to perform moderate, low-impact exercise, like

walking thirty to forty minutes, three to five days a week. Just avoid hills (which stress your back) and use good technique. Stand up straight, and don't let your stomach stick out or your head droop down.

(4) YOU'LL BUILD BONE MASS AND SLIM YOUR MIDDLE. Weight-bearing exercise like walking or weight-lifting promotes bone growth—a big plus in the battle against osteoporosis. And if you walk at a brisk clip (four mph), you may encourage your body to secrete more growth hormone, which strengthens bones and increases lean body mass.

(5) YOU'LL FEEL LESS PAIN. Researchers at the University of Florida in Gainesville corralled sixteen brave volunteers willing to have their index fingers pinched for two minutes before and after thirty minutes of exercise, then again after thirty minutes of quiet time. Once they recovered the power of speech, all the volunteers reported that the pain was most bearable right after exercise.

(6) YOU'LL NEUTRALIZE PMS SYMPTOMS. Regular aerobic exercise like walking can tame even the worst case of premenstrual syndrome (PMS) by raising the level of endorphins in the brain and by increasing your circulation, which helps minimize bloating.

(7) YOU'LL GET A GOOD NIGHT'S SLEEP. A Stanford University study of forty-three men and women with mild insomnia revealed that those who walked briskly for thirty to forty minutes four times a week for four months slept almost an hour longer per night and fell asleep faster.

(8) YOU'LL LOOK BETTER. Regular exercise gets your blood as well as your body moving. This increased circulation transports nutrients to your skin and quickly flushes out waste products. This leaves your skin glowing with enhanced health.

(9) YOU'LL OUTSMART MIDDLE-AGE SPREAD. You know it's true: metabolism slows naturally with age—but not necessarily because of aging. The decline in metabolic rate over time has less to do with advanc-

ing age than with declining activity. A University of Colorado study revealed that middle-aged and older women who exercised regularly didn't experience the age-related decline in their resting metabolic rate as did their sedentary counterparts. As a result, they stayed thinner and healthier—despite their advancing age.

(10) YOU'LL TAKE STRESS IN STRIDE. When you're confronted with a stressful situation, your body prepares to fight or take flight, in part by secreting catecholamines, chemicals that raise your heart rate and blood pressure and pump blood to large muscles in your legs and arms. Your fight-and-flight response then "burns off" those calories. The problem is this: Most often you don't have the option to fight or flee, yet your body is still releasing catecholamines that it doesn't use up. And your heart rate and blood pressure, as well as your stress level, remain elevated. The best way to get rid of those chemicals? Simulate the fight or flight: walk or run.

(11) YOU'LL HAVE A HEALTHIER HEART. Exercise helps to clear the fats that contribute to disease by stimulating fat-clearing enzymes. Fats are either broken down and excreted, or taken up by muscle and fat tissue. Either way, they're out of the bloodstream and less able to increase LDL cholesterol and heart disease risks. This also raises levels of HDL, which protects against heart disease. When a heart is well conditioned, it is like any other muscle: it becomes stronger and more efficient. A normal heart beats at a rate of approximately seventy beats per minute at rest or about 100,000 beats a day. The well-conditioned heart can actually beat as few as forty times a minute at rest or approximately 50,000 beats per day. A well-conditioned heart conserves energy and can supply oxygen-rich blood to the rest of the body with half the effort.

(12) YOU'LL BE A MORE CREATIVE THINKER. According to many recent studies, regular aerobic exercise can improve your memory, enhance

your imagination, and make you more creative. The right side of your brain—the area that specializes in creative thought and solving problems—becomes more active when you exercise. It ignites your ability to solve problems, thrive under pressure, and perform at peak levels of effectiveness. As you dramatically increase your oxygen uptake, as well as the production of the red corpuscles that carry oxygen to your brain, the influx enhances the functioning of every organ in your body. Your thinking power receives a forceful boost because 25 percent of your blood is in your brain at any time during exercise.

(13) YOU'LL PROTECT AGAINST SERIOUS DISEASE. A Harvard University study found that women who run regularly produce a less potent form of estrogen than women who don't, resulting in half the risk of developing breast cancer. Researchers at the Harvard School of Public Health found that a thirty minute brisk walk or jog cut the risk of colon cancer in half. And physicians at Case Western Reserve University and University Hospitals of Cleveland report that regular exercise seems to reduce the risk of developing Alzheimer's. Exercise enhances your immune system, and generally improves the function of almost every organ and system in your body. One study found that people who walked briskly for forty-five minutes a day, five times a week, had half as many colds and flus as nonexercisers.

(14) YOU'LL HANDLE STRESS BETTER. Regular exercise can also help protect against the physical effects of daily stress, according to a report in the November 1999 issue of the *Annals of Behavioral Medicine*. In the study, college students who exercised on a regular basis were more likely to take life's daily stresses in stride, compared with their less physically active counterparts. Previous studies have shown that mental stress takes a toll on physical health, causing such problems as increases in blood sugar levels among diabetics, worsening of

joint pain in people with arthritis, and symptoms of psychological distress such as anxiety and depression. Minor, everyday stress contributes to the development and exacerbation of physical and mental health problems. However, people experiencing minor stress develop different degrees of symptoms, depending on their level of physical activity. During periods of high stress, those who reported exercising less frequently had 37 percent more physical symptoms than their counterparts who exercised more often. In addition, highly stressed students who did less exercise reported 21 percent more anxiety than those who exercised more frequently. Exercise helps people get their mind off stressors. This temporary escape from the pressure of stressors acts as a kind of rejuvenation process.

GET F.I.T.T.

You don't have to take up the latest exercise craze in order to become fit. Instead you can forge your own path, at your own pace, and in your own direction. The frequency, intensity, and duration of your workouts will influence the extent of the health benefits you reap. The type and time of exercise you choose will determine whether you stick with it.

Consider this exercise guide to be F.I.T.T.:

FREQUENCY—Four to six days a week. Exercising *less* will produce some benefit, but not enough. Exercising *more* may be useful for athletic training, but can lead to injury.

INTENSITY—At a level where you feel slightly out of breath, *without gasping*. Exercise should not hurt. If something hurts, stop and rest. If the pain persists, check with your doctor.

TIME—Thirty to sixty minutes, at a time of day when you feel good and your schedule allows you to build a routine.

TYPE—Whatever type of aerobic exercise you enjoy (or could enjoy) and can do regularly.

Choose a time of day that best suits your schedule. Is it early morning? This is a great choice to beat schedule surprises later in the day. Research has shown that those who begin exercising in the morning are more likely to be at it a year later. Another reason to set the alarm for morning exercise: after a night's fast, two-thirds of the calories you burn come from stored fat rather than stored glycogen.

If you do exercise first thing, grab a glass of energy-boosting juice first (4 to 6 ounces of apple, white grape, or unsweetened cranberry juice is great), then eat breakfast right after your workout. If you exercise outside, pay attention to the weather. If you live in a hot climate, be sure you are drinking lots and lots of water to replenish the fluids you are losing to perspiration. And don't forget your water needs even when it's very cold outside. You can still exercise in winter, but be sure to bundle up in layered clothing that can "wick" the perspiration away from your skin. And cover your head and hands.

If you choose midday as your exercise time, don't let it interfere with your lunchtime fueling or let the exercise break turn your lunch break into a frenzied spin. If you don't have at least an hour, exercise will best wait for another time of day.

If you combine lunch and a workout, be sure you have your mid-morning power snack about two hours before your midday workout, then have a piece of fruit (a quick-release carbohydrate) and a twelve-ounce glass of water right before you warm up. Exercise for thirty minutes, freshen up, and then have at least a fifteen-minute lunch.

Is early evening best for you? Although this is a difficult time to stay consistent (easy to "just say no" after a hectic day), it's a tremen-

dous time to take advantage of the stress-busting, energizing power of exercise. By diverting yourself from your day's activities, you can downshift from stress to relaxation. It's a good time also to review the day's events—the good, the bad, and the ugly—and get a pulse on how you feel about them.

If you exercise after dinner, make it a half-hour afterward so you won't be doing battle with your natural digestion process. And don't exercise within half an hour of bedtime; your geared-up metabolism can interfere with restful sleep.

Aerobic workouts are best for morning and midday, serving to maximize energy, reduce tension, and enhance physical and mental performance. Cross training and interval training (more about these later) can energize your performance even more. Anaerobic work, such as conditioning and strength training, may tire you out and is best saved for later in the day.

JUST GET MOVING

No time to get to the gym because of all those household chores? Just get busy and get them done—and you'll get a fitness reward in the process. Studies have shown that you can ward off weight gain, lower blood pressure, and improve your cholesterol levels just by adding even a *little* extra activity to your day, instead of a full-fledged workout. Research done at the Cooper Center for Aerobics Research in Dallas shows that to improve your fitness you have to get your heart rate up, but that can be done if you just *get moving*.

The ways to increase your level of activity without having to adopt a program or invest chunks of time—or money—are endless. And, over time, being more active during the day can have a significant effect on weight loss and maintenance. Each activity below

will burn off about 250 calories. And bear in mind that the harder you work, the more calories you'll burn. By pushing yourself to walk faster, scrub harder, or dance more vigorously, you can burn as much as 40 percent more calories in the same amount of time.

I recognize that these kinds of guidelines can sound like heresy for the avid fitness buff—or simply a nod of the head to our sedentary society. But just look below at the metabolic burn that can come from even moderate daily activities, and what it adds up to for a 130-pound woman by week's end.

The point is that *any* amount of physical activity can improve your level of fitness. Fitness is not thinness or being bulked up—it is being able to perform demanding activities without getting out of breath or becoming unduly fatigued.

Monday total: 525	Tuesday total: 342	Wednesday total: 537	Thursday total: 462
Walk (30 min) 141	Take dancing lesson (1	Walk (30 min) 141	Weed the garden (1 hr)
Cook dinner (1 hr) 162	hr) 180	Mow the lawn (1 hr) 396	228
Do light housecleaning (1 hr) 222	Cook dinner (1 hr) 162		Do laundry (1 hr) 234
Friday total: 342	**Saturday total: 726**	**Sunday total: 618**	**Grand total: 3,552**
Cook dinner (1 hr) 162	Walk the dog (1 hr) 282	Cook dinner (1 hr) 162	
Take dancing lesson (1 hr) 180	Baby-sit nephew (2 hrs) 444	Do laundry (1 hr) 234	
		Do light housecleaning (1 hr) 222	

NO PAIN, NO GAIN?

If you don't like exercising for the sake of exercise, just do fun things to make you active: take the dog out for a walk, chase a football with the neighborhood kids, get your toddler out for a power stroll, jog, swim, bike, dance. Even gardening and mowing the lawn counts. Or find a passion: ballroom dancing, tennis, volleyball, hiking. If you love it, you'll do it.

A NEAT WAY TO TURN UP THE BURN

In one study, researchers correlated the calorie burn from daily activities to why some people can seemingly eat whatever they want and not gain weight. They burn off the extra calories they consume through everyday activities such as walking, climbing stairs, doing household chores, even fidgeting and maintaining posture—a process researchers call NEAT (nonexercise activity therogenesis).

When researchers fed sixteen normal weight people an extra 1,000 calories a day for eight weeks, the amount of weight they gained varied from 3 to 16 pounds. The reason for the difference: some burned fewer calories (just 98) per day through NEAT than they did before the study, while others burned more (up to 692 calories). As reported in the January 8, 1999, issue of *Science*, it appears that when some people overeat, their NEAT switches on to burn this excess energy. Conversely, the failure to switch this on allows the calories to be stored as fat.

Better news: it appears that you can train yourself to increase NEAT. Here are five ways to do it:

1. Every time the phone rings, stand up before you answer it.

2. Whenever a commercial comes on TV, take out the garbage, put in a load of laundry, pick up the newspaper—anything to get moving.

3. Put on music when you're doing dishes or ironing and folding clothes and bop to the beat.

4. A bit obsessive, but helpful: Set your watch timer to beep every thirty minutes or so. When it goes off, tap each foot ten times.

5. Even more obsessive, but effective: Pick a cue word when you're at the movies or in a meeting, and whenever the speaker says the word rotate each ankle five times or shift the way you're sitting. Remember, you're in training!

The goal is simply to stand instead of sit, sit instead of lie, and walk instead of standing still.

The notion of "no pain, no gain" is an exercise lie. If you are in pain, you'll stop exercising or get hurt, and the benefits of activity will come screeching to a halt. The key with exercise is not to let it

become a stress. Too much, too hard—two to three hours of hammering the body—zaps energy. Moderation in all things, even exercise, is the age-old word of wisdom.

Before beginning or increasing physical activity, you should take some precautions to ensure a healthy start. To avoid soreness and injury, start out slowly and gradually build up to the desired amount to give your body time to adjust. Most healthy individuals can do this safely.

But if you have chronic health problems such as heart disease, diabetes, asthma, or obesity, you should consult your doctor before you increase your level of physical activity. Also, the American College of Sports Medicine recommends that healthy women over fifty and men over forty who wish to start a vigorous exercise program should check with their doctor to make sure they do not have

LOSE TWICE AS MANY POUNDS

Researchers at the University of Pittsburgh School of Medicine found that women who exercised for at least 150 minutes a week (that's 30 minutes, five times a week) lost nearly twice as many pounds—25 versus 14—as women who exercised less. Losing weight and keeping it off may require more exercise than previously thought—maybe as much as an hour each day, according to this new research.

In another study from Brown University, researchers found that 2,500 people who lost an average of 60 pounds and kept it off for a year exercised about an hour a day. Most of the people in this study walked about 10 miles a week, then did aerobics, weight lifting, or other activities.

A key to remember is that the more fit you are, the more efficiently you'll burn the calories you eat. If three people of similar weight exercise for 50 minutes at a moderately high intensity, the least fit person would burn about 250 calories, the moderately fit person about 400 calories, and the very fit person about 600 calories.

TWENTY-FIVE WAYS TO BURN 250 CALORIES	
Activity	Minutes to burn 250 calories
Cleaning the House	68
Cooking	93
Dancing	58
Doing Laundry	64
Frisbee Playing	43
Gardening	56
Golfing	50
Hiking	52
Ironing	132
In-Line Skating	36
Jumping Rope	26
Making Love	36
Mowing the Lawn	38
Playing the Piano	104
Playing Racquetball	24
Playing Tag with Kids	29
Playing Tennis	39
Playing Volleyball	83
Scrubbing Floors	39
Shopping	81
Surfing the Net	148
Swimming	27
Vacuuming	66
Walking the Dog	54
Walking Fast	44

risk factors for heart disease or any other health problem. Women under fifty and men under forty should also see a physician if they have two or more risk factors for heart disease, such as elevated blood pressure or cholesterol levels, smoking, diabetes, or obesity. And at any age, you should check with your physician first if you have cardiovascular, lung, or joint-muscular disorders (or symptoms that suggest such disorders).

At the very least, you may want to begin your exercise program with a fitness physical, which can be performed by your doctor or wellness professional. An ideal fitness physical is an "all points check" testing the following: cholesterol, EKG stress test, VO2 max, fat/lean body composition, blood pressure, and resting heart rate. This battery of tests helps you to discover if there are any potential risk factors in your planned exercise program, and to set realistic goals. It's a terrific benchmark, and can be highly motivating.

A WELL-ROUNDED WORKOUT

Fitness is most easily understood by examining its components. Basically, four types of exercise are needed to provide the best workout and to work all the muscles of your body: warm-up/cool down, aerobic exercise, conditioning/strength exercise, and stretching for flexibility.

Warming Up/Cooling Down

Use warm-up exercises, such as light side-to-side movements, to limber up your muscles and prevent injuries from the other types of exercise. Never skip the warm-up—it prepares your muscles for the workout (muscles work best when they're warmer than normal body temperature). A warm-up also allows your oxygen supply to get ready for what is to come, alerting your body to oncoming shock or stress.

You can warm up with stretching, jumping jacks, skipping rope, or jogging in place. You can also warm up with stretching and then beginning a less intense version of your exercise activity—for example, walking before jogging. An adequate warm-up time is three to five minutes.

Then, at the end of your exercise time, spend three to five minutes cooling down. This allows your body's cardiovascular system to return to normal gradually, preferably over a ten- to fifteen-minute

---

EXERCISE BEFORE YOU INDULGE

Take a long, brisk walk before your friend's wedding, and the hors d'oeuvres and cake may not be a heart attack on your plate. In addition to its benefits to your waistline, exercise can help override some of the nasty effects of fat in your blood.

High-fat meals cause spikes in the amount of triglycerides in the bloodstream, which wreak havoc on cholesterol by decreasing good HDL and increasing bad LDL. Over time, these contribute to atherosclerosis and heart disease. But researchers recently found that the timing of exercise can affect these fat levels significantly.

When a group of twenty-one men exercised twelve hours before a high-fat meal, they cut the mount of fat in their blood by half. (Exercising one hour before the meal lowered fat by nearly 40 percent.) Working out *after* a high-fat meal reduced it by only 5 percent.

EXERCISE ON TARGET

When doing aerobic exercise, it's a good idea to keep track of your heart rate. This is especially important when you are building up to a pace and distance that's ideal for you.

Your maximum heart rate is the fastest your heart can beat. The best activity level is 60 to 75 percent of this maximum rate. The 60 to 75 percent range is called your heart rate target zone. In this zone, your muscles are moving, you're breathing deeply, your blood is delivering ample amounts of oxygen to your body systems, and you're burning fat as your major fuel source. At this level, you should be breathing deeply but comfortably enough that you can hold a conversation or sing to yourself.

To find your heart rate target zone, subtract your age from 220. Your exercise zone will be 60 to 75 percent of that number. So, a forty-five-year-old would subtract forty-five from 220, getting an average maximum heart rate (100 percent) of 175. Sixty to 75 percent of this number would be 105 to 131 beats per minute.

When you begin your exercise program, aim for the lower part of your heart rate target zone (60 percent) during the first few months. As you get into better shape, gradually build up to the higher part of your target zone (75 percent).

To see if you are within your exercise heart rate zone, take your pulse periodically throughout your exercise time. Place the first two fingers of your hand at either side of your neck just under your jaw. You should feel your pulse easily at your carotid artery. If not, try the underside of your left wrist. Using your watch or the clock, count for six seconds, then multiply by ten. This is your heart rate per minute.

A fun way to determine whether you are exercising within your ideal zone is to buy a pulse meter, a gadget worn on the wrist or chest that monitors heart rate. It works great for those who have a difficult time mastering the art of checking their heart rate while continuing to exercise.

If you don't exercise hard enough to get your heart rate up into your target zone, you won't produce the changes in your body and brain that boost your metabolism, energy level, and mood. But exercising harder than your target heart rate is self-defeating; it can diminish the effectiveness of your workout. Working to such elevated levels causes you to burn more glucose as an energy source, detracting from fat loss and conditioning of your body. It can also leave you feeling exhausted rather than exhilarated.

period. This can be considered a "warm-up-in-reverse" because it consists of the same types of exercises as your warm-up.

Warm-up and cool down are just as important as the main event. Both can prevent many of the common injuries that take you out of the race.

Aerobic Exercise

Aerobic exercise is any large-muscle activity that gets your heart pumping and that you can sustain for twenty to sixty minutes. Jumping rope, jogging, cycling, stepping, and other cardiovascular activities are aerobic exercises that leave you energized.

Your heart and lungs work together to supply oxygen to tissues in your body. Aerobic exercise forces the lungs and heart to work harder and, in so doing, strengthens and conditions them. It is crucial for overall body wellness and for fanning the flame of the metabolic fire that burns fat. *Continuous* activity most activates the metabolism, not the stop-stand-start type that you do in softball, volleyball, or golf. And the routine of exercise is what builds a conditioned body—one that adapts much more resiliently to stress.

> **SMART WEIGH TIP**
>
> *Up the ante. If you walk, try walking faster or running.*

The minute you start to exercise, your metabolic rate (the amount of energy you expend) immediately increases to somewhere between five and twenty times what you expend sitting down. This change is very healthy when done on a regular basis. The goal is to try for some kind of activity every day. Even if it's not a hard workout at the gym, just a walk after dinner can do miraculous things for your body.

Vary your routine to rev up the calorie burn—different forms of

exercise build and strengthen muscles in more parts of the body. Cross training is a technique you can employ that drives up the effectiveness of your aerobic workouts. Quite simply, it is alternating the aerobic activities you do. Instead of using a treadmill four days a week, alternate it with two days of biking. Instead of running every day, run three times a week, swim for two, and cycle for another. Your body perceives the different forms of exercise as more demanding (even though they may seem less demanding), and will trigger greater internal exertion. As a result, you will burn more fat for fuel and become a more efficient energy producer.

Interval training is a technique in which you vary the intensity at which you exercise. If you normally jog at a slow pace, periodically pick up the pace to a run, maybe for a minute, and then return to a slow jog. Alternate this during your entire exercise time. It can give a significant boost to your fitness gains and energy levels.

If your main concern is shedding some body fat, the key is to do longer, more frequent aerobic sessions at an easier pace. This approach burns more calories. Even though vigorous exercise burns more calories per minute than an easy effort, an extra fifteen or thirty minutes of easy exercise will more than make up the difference.

Longer bouts of exercise also burn proportionally more fat. Harder, but shorter exercise draws more on carbohydrates. If you walk or do some other activity for more than an hour, your body will start to burn significantly more fat for the rest of the workout. Why? Because the carbohydrate stores in your muscles begin running low after an hour.

Once you've settled into a routine of exercise:

■ Do five to seven aerobic workouts a week.
■ Make your effort as easy as possible so that you're able to exer-

cise continuously for forty-five to sixty minutes without strain.

■ Try to do one or more "long" workouts (over sixty minutes) per week.

■ Ignore any pounds lost in the first week (which are mostly water) and concentrate on a steady, consistent weight reduction of about a half-pound to one pound per week.

Conditioning/Strength Exercises

Conditioning or strength exercises are those that tone, shape, and define various muscles through repetitive movements against resistance. Conditioning exercises activate the metabolism by making demands on the muscles that change their chemistry, making them more energy efficient. Conditioning increases muscle strength and mass by putting more than the usual amount of strain on a muscle that stimulates the growth of small force-generating proteins inside each muscle cell. These proteins feed the "fibers" that grow during exercise. When you make muscles work harder, you actually tear these fibers. As they rebuild, they get stronger and bigger, resulting in harder, tighter, and more defined muscles.

Resistance training can also have a beneficial effect on your body composition. As sedentary people age, from about age twenty or so, they lose 1 percent of their muscle mass each year. By age forty, it has amounted to 20 percent. Between the ages of twenty and sixty, inactive people can lose up to 40 percent of their muscle mass. And the

WEIGHT TRAINING INCREASES:
Muscle strength
Muscle mass
The body's average calorie-burning rate
Tendon and ligament strength
Bone density

WEIGHT TRAINING REDUCES:
Body fat
Risk of diabetes
Risk of osteoporosis
Risk of heart disease
Risk of colon cancer
Lower back pain
Arthritis pain
Blood pressure
Cholesterol

WEIGHT TRAINING IMPROVES:
Balance
Digestion
Mood
Sleep

flabbier muscles are, the less muscle fuel (energy) they can store. That means less strength and stamina for you. By the age of forty, up to one-half pound of muscle—and the energy stocked inside—is generally replaced with a half-pound of fat.

By reversing this process, weight training can see you into middle age with the energy, strength, and metabolism you had at twenty. As your muscles grow and become more active, the level of energy within the muscles increases, making you more vital. In addition, stronger muscles offer more support to your joints, pump up your sports performance, improve your balance, and help prevent injuries. And regular weight training exercises can boost your cardiovascular health by improving your levels of good cholesterol (HDL). Resistance training also strengthens your bones and helps increase bone mineral mass to help prevent osteoporosis, a disease that afflicts twenty million women in the United States.

A conditioning or resistance workout usually involves various exercises that focus on different muscle groups. This is the essence of circuit training on machines like Nautilus, which were built for this purpose. Normally the exerciser does one to three "sets" of each exercise (a set can be anywhere from eight to fifteen repetitions, and takes about one minute to complete). A typical session lasts about thirty minutes. But any kind of repetitive resistance training is effective, whether it's circuit training on weight machines; an arm workout with barbells or full soup cans; calisthenics such as chin-ups, push-ups, and sit-ups; or arm and leg extensions with exercise bands.

Just doing a few simple ten- to fifteen-minute strength-training routines at home or at the gym, two times a week, can turn the tide on muscle loss and activate your metabolism. You may notice an increase in the strength and the size of the exercised muscles in just a few weeks.

The good news is that strength and conditioning exercises are easy! You don't even need to change your clothes to get all the benefits with little or no sweat. A few years ago, I made a $20 investment in a pair of three to five pound dumbbells and a rubber exercise band, which is about four inches wide and three feet long and comes in different resistance levels. My best way to build strength has been to lift weight in three sets of eight to twelve repetitions. Lifting a lighter weight for more repetitions is the technique I use to build endurance and tone.

Here are some other tips to keep in mind as you build conditioning into your workout:

- If you have access to a gym or health club that has Nautilus machines or other weight-lifting machines, sign up for an orientation to learn the proper use of each machine. You may consider a session with a certified personal trainer to get an individualized program worked out for you to reach your goals.
- If you plan to work out at home, purchase a pair of three to five pound hand-held weights or adjustable-weight dumbbells (with metal plates that can be added or taken off).
- Before trying any strength exercise, practice it several times with a very light weight, to learn the movement correctly.
- Start with weights that feel comfortable for you and that allow you to do eight to twelve repetitions without pain. If you can't make eight repetitions of a given exercise, switch to a lower weight. Each lifting motion should take two seconds (counting "one-1,000, two-1,000"), while the recovery motion (returning to starting position) should take four seconds. If you're using a weight machine, one set per exercise is enough.

If you're using dumbbells, two sets (with a couple of minutes of rest in between) are recommended.

■ As you work out for several weeks or months, your muscles will get noticeably stronger, to the point where you'll need to increase the amount of weight you're lifting to continue improving. Whenever the twelfth repetition becomes easy on a given exercise, add three to five pounds to each dumbbell, or ten pounds to the load on the weight machine for that exercise.

■ Each strength workout should include a variety of exercises that work both the pushing and pulling muscles of the upper body (arms, shoulders, abdomen, and back) and lower body (legs, hips, and buttocks).

■ Always allow at least forty-eight hours of recovery time between strength workouts, to give your muscle tissue time to rebuild.

■ Choose your equipment wisely. For example, vinyl-coated dumbbells are comfortable to lift, and the bright colors lift your spirits, too. These are great weights for beginners because they come in one-pound increments (up to eight pounds), with a ten-pound option as you progress. (Beyond ten pounds, you'll have to opt for the more traditional chrome or cast-iron types.) Hand weights are also a good option for beginners, especially for people who have arthritis in their hands. Designed with either a strap or handle, you don't have to use a tight grip to hold onto them. Strapping weights to your ankles or wrists instead of carrying them in the hands is another great choice for people with arthritis, high blood pressure, or any other condition in which you should avoid tight grips. And whether you exercise at home or travel a lot, elastic exercise bands are a great way to enhance your workout.

These bands are lightweight, easy to use, and allow you to do exercises that normally require expensive machines.

THE EXERCISES

These are some exercises that can form the core of a regular strength-training program. You may want to begin with the first four exercises below and supplement them with the next four exercises if and when you want to expand your strength training program.

DUMBBELL SQUAT (LOWER BODY) OR LEG EXTENSION MACHINE

Stand holding a dumbbell in each hand with your feet flat on the floor, shoulder-width apart, and your arms down at your sides. Keeping your head up and your back straight, slowly lower your hips until your thighs are parallel with the floor. Then return slowly to starting position, still keeping head up and back straight. Repeat eight to twelve times.

DUMBBELL LUNGE (LOWER BODY) OR LEG CURL MACHINE

Stand holding a dumbbell in each hand, with your arms down at your sides and your feet slightly less than shoulder-width apart. Looking directly ahead and keeping your left leg straight, take a long step forward with your right leg, bending your right knee so that the knee is lined up directly above your right ankle. Distributing your weight equally on both legs, bend your back leg until your knee is almost touching the ground. Then push slowly off your right foot, stepping back into your starting position. Repeat eight to twelve times, then switch legs and repeat.

DUMBBELL CHEST PRESS (UPPER BODY) OR CHEST PRESS MACHINE

Lie face up on a flat bench or on the floor, with your feet flat on the

floor, and hold a dumbbell in each hand. Extend your arms and then lower them to starting position against your chest (your elbows should point out to either side). Slowly push the dumbbells upward together until your arms are fully extended and the dumbbells are directly above your chest. Repeat eight to twelve times.

DUMBBELL ROW (UPPER BODY) OR LATERAL PULL-DOWN MACHINE
Holding a dumbbell in your right hand, rest your left knee on a low bench or step, and place your left (free) hand down flat in front of your knee on the same bench. You should be leaning forward so that your back is horizontal, and your right foot should be flat on the floor, with the right knee slightly bent. Lower the dumbbell so that your right arm is fully extended and slowly pull it to your chest, then return slowly to starting position. Do eight to twelve repetitions, then switch sides and repeat.

DUMBBELL CURL (UPPER BODY) OR BICEPS MACHINE
Holding a dumbbell in each hand, stand comfortably with your arms down at your sides. Slowly bend your arms, curling both dumbbells up to your shoulders, then slowly return to starting position. Keep your head up and your eyes looking straight ahead at all times.

DUMBBELL TRICEPS EXTENSION (UPPER BODY) OR TRICEPS MACHINE
Holding a dumbbell in your right hand, place your left knee on a low bench or chair, and place your left hand in front of it, flat on the bench. Hold the dumbbell with your palm facing inward, and your right elbow slightly bent so the weight is at hip level. Keeping your right shoulder still, slowly straighten your right arm, then slowly return to starting position. Repeat eight to twelve times, then switch arms and repeat.

DUMBBELL SHOULDER PRESS (UPPER BODY) OR OVERHEAD PRESS MACHINE

Holding a dumbbell in each hand, sit on a bench or a chair with your feet flat on the floor. Position both dumbbells at shoulder level, with your elbows pointing downward. Then slowly press both dumbbells upward, until your arms are straight but not locked (think of squeezing your shoulder blades together as you lift). Then return slowly to starting position. Repeat eight to twelve times.

DUMBBELL DELTOID RAISE (UPPER BODY) OR LATERAL RAISE MACHINE

Standing comfortably and with a dumbbell in each hand, hold your arms at your sides so that your elbows are bent at right angles, with your palms facing downward. Slowly raise both dumbbells until your upper arms are parallel to the ground. Then slowly lower your arms to starting position. Repeat eight to twelve times.

Here are three sample exercises you can do with exercise bands:

■ Keeping your arms parallel to the floor, hold the band in front of your chest (at armpit level) with your hands about six inches apart. Slowly bring your elbows toward your back, as if you were squeezing a pencil with your shoulder blades. Hold for two seconds, then bring your elbows forward again. (If this is too difficult for you, use a band with less resistance; if it's too easy, switch to a band with more resistance.)

■ Stand on one end of the band and hold the other in one hand. With your palm facing upward, slowly bring the band up to your shoulder, using only the lower part of your arm. It's important to keep the elbow close to the body and the upper arm straight. Repeat with the other arm.

■ To target the large latissimus dorsi muscle of your back, a

muscle particularly difficult to get at using dumbbells, attach a band to the top of a door using a specially designed door anchor. (If you don't secure the band, it may slide off the door and smack you in the face!) Then sit or kneel on the floor, facing the door and holding the band so that it and your arms are fully extended. Your hands should be about shoulder-width apart. Squeezing your shoulder blades, pull your hands down toward your chest. Elbows should be pointing behind you and down. Hold, and then release.

CALISTHENICS TO REDUCE BELLY BULGE

No matter what the cause of extra abdominal fat—a recent baby, too many brews, or too much time on the sofa—this program will work for you. Do these six exercises three or four times a week to tone and tighten your abs.

Get started today! But go slowly for best results. Forget doing hundreds of crunches. You'll get a flatter tummy quicker if you slow down. Each repetition of an exercise should take about six to eight seconds to complete. For example, slowly count one, two, three, four as you lift during a crunch, and then five, six, seven, eight as you lower. If you experience back pain with any of these exercises, stop the exercise and check with your doctor before continuing. Do each exercise three or four times a week.

CRUNCH

Lying on a mat or carpeted floor, place your hands lightly behind your head, bend your knees, and put your feet flat on the floor. Using your abs, slowly lift your head, shoulders, and upper back off the mat. Keep your abs tight and exhale on the way up. Hold, and then lower. Do ten to fifteen repetitions.

TWISTING CRUNCH

Start in the crunch position. As you lift, twist your torso, bringing your left shoulder toward your right knee at the top of the crunch. Hold, and then lower. Repeat on the other side. Do ten to fifteen repetitions on each side.

ROLLDOWN

Sit on the floor with your knees bent, feet flat. Keeping your arms out in front of you, slowly roll down—one vertebrae at a time—until you're lying on the floor. Then roll to your side and sit up. Do four to six repetitions.

LEG DROP

Lying on your back, bend at your knees and hips so your legs form a right angle. Keeping your back pressed to the mat, slowly lower your right leg until your toe touches the mat. Then slowly return it to the starting position. If your back starts to arch, stop at that point. As your abs get stronger, you'll be able to go farther. Do four to six repetitions with each leg and then do both legs together.

SITTING KNEE LIFT

Sit up straight in a firm, armless chair. Place your hands on the sides of the chair in front of your hips. Tightening your abs and supporting yourself with your hands, slowly pull your knees up toward your chest. Hold and then slowly lower. Keep your lower back against the chair back. This is an advanced exercise, so you may want to start by alternating your legs, lifting one at a time. Do four to six repetitions.

As with any other exercise program, before starting a strength-training regimen, you need to get a medical exam to rule out any possible underlying health problems or any existing conditions that could be aggravated.

EXERCISING FOR FLEXIBILITY

Flexibility is the ability of joints and muscles to achieve a full range of motion. Exercising for flexibility helps prevent injuries, improves your posture, provides for better breathing, and even lowers blood pressure. Despite popular opinion, there's no evidence that you should lose flexibility as you build muscle.

Flexibility exercises use gentle, stretching movements to increase the length of your muscles and the effective range of motion in your joints, allowing you to perform better at daily tasks—from bending over to tie your shoe to lifting a baby out of a car seat to carrying a heavy computer bag. They may consist of a series of specific stretching exercises or be part of a larger exercise program such as aerobics or dance classes.

Since one of the main goals of stretching is to lengthen the connective tissue surrounding your muscle fibers, flexibility exercises should be done after you've already warmed up your muscles with a few minutes of aerobic activity. A typical session involves a minute or two on each stretching exercise. As with aerobics, you can break up your stretching routine into shorter sessions before and after your other workouts.

All stretching movements should be done slowly, to the point where you feel a gentle pleasant tension—not pain—in the muscle being stretched. For an effective stretch, you need to hold the position for fifteen to thirty seconds, then work toward holding all stretches for a full minute. Breathe deeply through your nostrils, concentrating on the muscles you're stretching. Never "bounce" as you hold a stretch, because this will activate your stretch reflex (an automatic, protective contraction). If you feel any pain, stop immediately.

If you regularly stretch your muscles after they're fully warmed up—at the end of an aerobic workout, for example—you can grad-

ually increase their resting length by lengthening the connective tissue that surrounds your muscle fibers. Improving flexibility in this way will make movement easier and more fluid. The more often you stretch, the longer your muscles. For maximum benefits, do a stretching routine several times each week.

THE STRETCHES

Here are some flexibility exercises to add in to your exercise routine. The ideal is to do two thirty-minute flexibility workouts each week, or ten minutes each day incorporated into your aerobic workout.

HAMSTRING STRETCH

Sit with your right leg extended in front of you, your left leg bent with your left sole resting against your right thigh. Place your right hand on the floor slightly behind you as you slowly reach forward with your left hand. Grasp and flex the toes of your right foot, if you can. Repeat four times, then switch legs.

THE BIG V

Lie on your back with legs straight and stretched out to the sides so that they form a V in the air. Your feet should be flexed. Place your hands on the inside of each thigh just above the knee and slowly press until you feel a gentle tension in your inner thighs. Repeat four times.

TOWEL STRETCH

Stand with your feet together, knees soft. With your arms overhead, hold a towel taut (if you feel too much tension, get a longer towel so that your hands are positioned farther apart). Take the towel a few inches behind your head, then slowly lower it. Keep your elbows

soft. When you feel the stretch across your chest, take a few deep breaths and hold it. As your flexibility improves, slide your hands closer together.

CALF STRETCH

Stand comfortably with your hands on your hips, or place both hands on a wall (shoulder's width apart), and step forward with your right foot (about a half-shoulder's width). Bend both knees, keeping your feet flat on the floor, and shift your weight to your forward foot. Slowly lower your hips, until you feel a gentle stretching sensation in the calf muscle and Achilles tendon of your left (rear) leg. Hold for fifteen to thirty seconds, then switch legs and repeat.

TRICEPS STRETCH

Stand tall, with your feet shoulder width apart. Reach down the middle of your back with your right hand, pointing your elbow toward the ceiling. Keeping your shoulders down, use your left hand to pull your right elbow gently toward the center of your body. Imagine that you're trying to align your forearm with your spine to form a continuous straight line. Repeat four times. Switch arms.

CROSS-LEGGED PULL

Lie on your back with your right leg bent, foot planted on the floor. Cross your left ankle over your right thigh. Clasp your hands behind your right thigh and gently coax the leg toward your chest. Feel the deep stretch in your left hip. Repeat four times, then switch sides.

WALK FOR LIFE

Want to drop a size, stabilize hormones, sleep better, and live longer? I can't say it enough: putting one foot in front of the other does your body, mind, and spirit a world of good!

There are many unquestionably good exercises, but all are not everyone's cup of tea. For those that cringe at the thought of jogging, can't easily get to a pool for swimming, and don't have the time, place, or desire for aerobic dancing, fitness walking is a tremendous alternative.

Walking is structured, simple, easy, quick, and cheap—and is guaranteed to make you feel better and look better in just a couple of weeks. It's also a social contribution: researchers have concluded that you help the national economy just by taking a walk. Two doctors at Brown University have calculated the amount spent nationally each year on heart-disease treatment and the added amount wasted as a result of lost employee productivity. They estimated that $5.6 billion in health care costs would be saved if only one out of ten nonexercising adults started a regular walking program.

Even if you haven't exercised in a long time, remember that walking is natural and easy. You need not "gear up" mentally, so walking is easy to build into your life's routine. Even if you don't walk far, just get out and move.

SIX REASONS WHY WALKING RULES

YOU CAN DO IT FOR LIFE. Forty years from now, you may not be rollerblading every morning. But you could still be walking— around your neighborhood, to the park, maybe in the mall. With little risk of injury and great opportunity to see gains in fitness, walking is a sport you can keep for life.

YOU CAN RUN OR WALK NO MATTER WHAT YOUR BODY TYPE. You may not ever have the muscular makeup to do marathons, but as long as you start slowly to prevent injuries, anyone—short, tall, big, or small— can walk or run.

YOU CAN WALK NO MATTER WHAT YOUR CONDITION. Whether you're pregnant, elderly, or obese; with arthritis, diabetes or osteoporosis; even recovering from heart surgery or chronic fatigue—you can walk safely. **YOU CAN LOSE WEIGHT WALKING.** The faster you walk (and the more you weigh), the more calories you use.

YOU CAN GET WELL WALKING. Walking's health benefits include an increase in HDL levels, a reduced risk of bone loss and resulting fractures, a decrease in blood pressure, a stabilization of blood sugar levels in diabetics, and an increase in mobility for people with arthritis.

YOU CAN FEEL WELL BY WALKING. Walking has immense emotional benefits: it counters depression, relieves stress, and refreshes your spirit. You can talk to God, yourself, or a walking companion.

TURNING A WALK INTO A WORKOUT

Find a block of time in the morning (before breakfast) or after work (ideally, before dinner) to go for a brisk walk around your neighborhood. If you are traveling, or don't feel comfortable walking in your own neighborhood, stop off on the way home at an area where you feel safe. Just remember to pack your walking shoes!

Look for a shoe that offers stability, good arch support, and durability, with a half-inch maximum heel height. The heel should be rolled and tapered, and the heel cushion should be about one-half to three-quarters of an inch thick. Combine good shoes with good-quality athletic socks that fit smoothly and evenly on your feet. Don't wear running shoes for walking; walking shoes help your feet roll along in a heel-toe motion and have more flexible soles for faster walking.

Before and after each walk, gently stretch to keep muscle soreness and tightness to a minimum. Do gentle, nonbouncing stretches for your shin muscles, calf muscles and tendons, hamstrings and front

thighs with a slow, steady pull until you feel the muscles ache slightly. Trunk rotations (turning the upper body while feet remain planted) and side bends are helpful as well. Hold each stretch for fifteen seconds. Do these stretches even on days you don't exercise, to keep your muscles from tightening.

Walk fast enough to work up a light sweat (swing your arms, take long, but comfortable strides), but not so fast that you become breathless. This is your ideal "aerobic" pace. You should always be able to talk to a companion (or hum to yourself) during exercise. If you can't do this, slow your pace. When you feel like extending yourself a bit more, research indicates that you will benefit as much from extending time as from increasing pace and stepping more frequently rather than trying to stretch your stride, which can injure your knees.

Proper posture is very important to protect against fatigue and injuries. Stand up straight and walk with your ears, shoulders, hips, knees, and ankles in a vertical line. Keep your head erect, chin pulled in toward your neck, back straight, and buttocks and stomach tucked in. Avoid leaning forward when walking to prevent back strain.

Walking will satisfy all your body's needs for aerobic exercise if you do it in such a way to raise your heart rate to its training zone. If your heart rate is not elevated at the end of a forty-five minute walk, try walking faster, at least part of the time, or look for some long, gradual hills to climb. You may also try walking with weights.

Plan to get some walking in every day, or at least four to five days a week. In a few weeks, your exercise program will be a habit and you'll feel uncomfortable if you have to miss a day. I've done a lot of different forms of exercise at different times in my life, but I always come back to walking. It's simply the best exercise for me to rely on to keep my body operating at its metabolic best.

STICKING WITH IT

Just knowing the benefits of exercise isn't enough; more people *don't* exercise than do. What's the problem? For a lot of us, it's just that exercise is no fun—and it's hard to stick with something every day that's not. To "Just Do It," and keep on doing it, we have to find an exercise that matches our lifestyle, our fitness needs, and our own definition of enjoyment. Follow these guidelines to increase your enjoyment of an exercise routine.

KNOW YOURSELF. The exercises you'll find most enjoyable will probably be those you feel you can best handle. If you have difficulty with eye-hand coordination, you may be frustrated by a sport like tennis but would do well with walking or swimming. If you are not naturally flexible, you may be happier with bicycling than ballet. And you may just want to choose aerobic gardening! Exercise doesn't have to be running a marathon—you just need to get moving, get your heart rate up to your target zone, and keep it there for at least twelve minutes. Playing with your kids or grandchildren may work just fine!

CONSIDER YOUR CURRENT CONDITION. If you are overweight, beginning with an activity that involves pounding on your feet, such as running or aerobic dance, may stress your joints by placing too much weight on them. Try riding a stationary bike or swimming instead. And remember, if you're over thirty-five, see a health professional for an "all-points" check before beginning an exercise program.

USE THE BUDDY SYSTEM. Exercising with a friend will not only give you an opportunity to socialize, but you'll also be more motivated to show up and keep your commitment. Other people's enthusiasm and energy may be just the inspiration you need.

DISTRACT YOURSELF. If your exercise of choice isn't particularly interesting, combine it with something that is. Do the Stairmaster while

listening to books on tape, or sing along to uplifting music while walking on the treadmill.

HAVE FUN. Take up a sport that allows you to get exercise while working on skills and having fun. Volleyball, racquetball, in-line skating, even badminton, are activities that provide terrific fitness benefits but don't feel like exercise. Pick activities that reduce stress, not those that add to it. If risk-taking isn't your idea of fun, leave skydiving to someone else!

REMEMBER THE PAYOFF. Keep your focus on how good you'll feel after you exercise. Keep envisioning exercise as a sword that cuts away at the stress response. Remind yourself of the long-term benefits you're getting: better energy, a better body, and better health. Choosing to exercise daily is giving yourself a precious gift. And your body was created to reward you by strengthening your "armor": building up protective barriers against heart disease, diabetes, bone loss, arthritis, even cancer.

FINE-TUNE YOUR WORKOUT. You're thinking of chucking it all because you're not seeing the payoff? You're still carrying around an extra fifteen pounds? Or maybe you're not getting stronger, faster, or any more energized? Before you give up, use these five steps to fine-tune your workouts for maximum results:

(1) **BE A LITTLE PUSHY.** If you've been doing the same type of exercise for more than three months, you may be stuck. It's easy to amble on walks or coast along on your bike. But for meaningful results, you've got to challenge yourself. Push to go just a little faster, a little longer (even an extra five minutes can do the trick), or to do it more often. (To avoid injury, increase only one aspect of your workout at a time.)

(2) **EXPERIMENT.** The more proficient your muscles become at a

particular activity, the fewer calories you burn. Add a new activity such as biking, swimming, jumproping, even kickboxing or volleyball to your usual exercise routine. You'll burn more calories as you master a new skill—and you'll have fun! Cross training is also a great way to prevent injuries and boredom.

(3) BE ACTIVE ALL DAY. Don't think that you can veg out the rest of the day just because you took a low-impact aerobics class or a brisk hour-long walk. The 300 to 400 calories that you likely burned won't make up for all the calories you're not burning throughout the day thanks to the TV remote, automatic garage-door opener, e-mail, and more. It's estimated that in the past twenty-five years, labor-saving devices have decreased the number of calories we burn daily by 800 or more.

(4) CHECK YOUR FRIDGE. Exercise is key to losing weight and keeping it off, but you can't ignore what you eat. An extra slice of pizza, for example, can put right back the 240 calories you burned jogging for half an hour. And even if you're choosing low-fat, nutritious foods, eating too much of them can have the same effect. Be aware of what and how much you're eating so that you don't negate the calorie-burning benefits of exercise.

(5) TAKE A BREAK. Doing too much, particularly vigorous, high-intensity exercise, can actually hinder your progress. Your body needs time to recover from intense workouts in order to get stronger. Take at least two or three days off between these high-intensity workouts to let your muscles recover, or mix in some lower-intensity walking, swimming, or stretching.

If you are ready to move beyond the reasons why *not* to exercise and join the ranks of those who successfully develop a regular exercise routine and enjoy its benefits, take note: initiating a well-designed

exercise plan will create a wave of positive changes in your life. You'll work with a higher level of energy, think with greater mental clarity and concentration, build confidence, quell negative anxiety, and cut away at the stress response—and all the while lose body fat; build and tone firm, lean muscle; stabilize blood chemistry; and increase your strength. It's an incredible package that shouldn't be hard to sell, even to ourselves!

Exercise is a powerful tool in your stress-fighting and pound-shedding tool chest. Another is healthy, full breaths of air—and lots and lots of water.

CHAPTER 8 ■ A: Air and Water

One reason for doing the right thing today—is tomorrow.

—ANONYMOUS

Ever breathe a sigh of relief? Gasp in shock or pain? Feel the need to vent at someone? These all express the close connection between the way we breathe and how we feel.

The pressure of a deadline can leave us wiped out for the afternoon. Fear makes us tense our muscles, which leads to fatigue, just as if we were working out. Fear can also make us hold our breath, depriving us of oxygen. This not only can lead to fatigue, but it can kick up the stress response and slam shut the fat cell door.

Breathing isn't something we normally have to think about—we inhale and exhale at a fairly steady pace, without much thought or worry over how we're doing. We take on average 28,000 breaths each day. But how we take those breaths contributes to our body's metabolic response—it revs it up or locks it down. While losing weight, we have much to gain from learning how to breathe *correctly*.

In addition, deep and slow oxygenating breaths are one of the simplest things you can do to relieve stress, energize yourself, and

> **SMART WEIGH TIP**
>
> *Just breathe.*

keep control of yourself in any situation. Healthy breathing can help you to overcome the low energy and high stress levels that result from rapid, shallow, or deep, heaving breaths.

Again, because breathing seems so simple, so automatic, it's difficult to think that our metabolism and energy can be boosted just from taking a breath of air. And it certainly is automatic, but so is eating. And how many people do that right?

BACK TO BASICS

Getting the right amount of oxygen into the bloodstream depends on a balance of carbon dioxide and oxygen in the blood. When you breathe in a panicked way, each breath throws that balance off. But you can actually train yourself to breathe in a way that energizes you.

When you're relaxed, you breathe slowly and deeply, inhaling vital, energy-producing oxygen. When you're tense or just not breathing correctly, you tend to breathe lightly and rapidly from your chest, which delivers less oxygen to your body's cells. As professional singers will tell you, only 30 percent of your full oxygen capacity is available when you're not breathing in a deep, diaphragmatic way—it suffocates your blood cells.

To test your breathing, place one hand on your upper chest and one hand on your abdomen. If the hand on your chest rises when you inhale and contracts when you exhale, you're chest breathing. This type of breathing brings in large amounts of air at one time and activates the fight-or-flight alarm reaction. This is good in a life-threatening emergency, but not in daily living.

Chest breathing keeps your body in a state of chronic stress. It also impairs circulation, depletes energy, and slows the metabolism because, without adequate oxygen, the body cells cannot burn fat effectively nor produce a full measure of energy. The brain reads this

as stress, and produces stress hormones. Yet the shallow breathing that accompanies stress decreases the oxygen intake and transfer—and we become even more stressed. Another vicious cycle.

Studies suggest that 80 percent of us don't know how to breathe in a metabolically activating and energizing way; we put our emphasis on inhalation, but the energy and stress release is in exhalation.

Freeze for a moment, holding your body in its exact position. Notice that your shoulders may be shrugged or tense. Correct your posture; imagine being suspended from above with your head erect, light and alert. Next, exhale slowly, draining your lungs—concentrating on the stress being blown out of your body, out through the mouth. Now, slowly fill your chest with air, taking the air in through your nostrils. Expand your diaphragm (the cone-shaped muscle that forms the floor of your chest cavity) by pushing your stomach down and out. Then breathe again... in and out... fully. In and out... in and out.

A RELEASING BREATH WORKOUT

Breathing in this way—from your diaphragm—tells your body: "Everything is okay... you are in control." So, before the pressures of life attack again, take two minutes to practice this type of breath work.

The best way to get started in a focused releasing/relaxing breath pattern is to place one hand on your upper stomach, just below your chest. Inhale while you imagine you're filling a small balloon inside. Fill it in all directions—top, bottom, forward, backward. Breathe in until you feel comfortably full, but not too full. Your stomach should gently rise and then fall as you exhale. Make the exhalation a little bit longer than you think you should. Hold it for a half-second before you inhale again. Your upper chest should stay flat

throughout. Once you're breathing from the right spot, focus on making your breath as even and steady as possible. You'll find that your tension dissipates.

Ready to blow a gasket because your computer just froze *again?* Put your hands flat on your desk and take about fifteen slow, deep breaths. Breathe in, breathe out. You'll feel calmer, and you'll unwind all the energy-depleting tension before it has a chance to overtake you. Practice this energizing and relaxing deep breathing so that you can do it automatically when under stress. Try it whenever the tension builds—in meetings, during a crisis, when you feel tired, unfocused, confused, mad, scared, anxious, or bored.

Repeat breathing "in and out" fully, at least ten times, whenever you feel tired or stressed. Your body and mind will soon feel the release and refreshment.

HYPERVENTILATION

Many people are being robbed of energy and metabolic power because they breathe shallowly and rapidly (more than eighteen times per minute), leading to an excessive loss of carbon dioxide. The loss of carbon dioxide due to chronic hyperventilation syndrome (HVS) affects the blood's hemoglobin, making it less able to carry oxygen throughout the body. So even though you are breathing quickly, you are getting less air. Among the symptoms are fatigue, anxiety, frequent sighing or yawning, and a tingling, coldness, or numbness in the fingers. Many of these symptoms are due to holding your breath to make up for the carbon dioxide lost in hyperventilating. In addition, you have to work harder to breathe, which in and of itself is tiring.

How to overcome hyperventilation problems? First, sit or stand up straight—correct your posture. Keeping your tummy firmly

tucked in when you stand or sit up straight will relax your diaphragm muscles and improve their movement during breathing. Second, if you breathe from your nose, keep your mouth closed. Your nasal passages are too narrow to allow for hyperventilation. Third, practice breathing into a closed paper bag held tightly against your face. With this bag-breathing, carbon dioxide is trapped into the bag where it is recirculated, preventing carbon dioxide levels from falling. Finally, learn the art of breathing to release stress—getting your breath working for you, not against you.

TWO/ONE BREATHING

You can further expand your stress-busting expertise by learning how to manipulate the way you exhale. Since exhaling slows the pulse, a technique called two/one breathing—in which you exhale for twice as long as you inhale makes diaphragmatic breathing even more effective.

To practice the two/one breathing technique, follow these steps:

(1) Sit quietly and do diaphragmatic breathing.

(2) When your breathing becomes balanced and even (it will take a few minutes), gently slow your rate of exhalation until you are breathing out for about twice as long as you breathe in. The easiest technique: count six when you exhale, three when you inhale—or eight and four. You shouldn't end up doing deep breathing; you want to alter the rhythmic motion of your lungs, not fill or empty them completely.

(3) Once you've established your rhythm of breathing, stop the mental counting and focus on the smoothness and evenness of your breath flow.

You receive more than air through proper breathing—you invite regeneration into your body. Breathing for energy gives you a recharge, along with a sense of rest and relaxation. So take a nice, long, slow breath. Now, take another one. Feel better?

SCENT THE AIR

Now, consider the air you are breathing in—is it pure and clear? Toxic air depresses your immune system—and slows your body. Even the scent in the air can lessen your body's ability to lose weight because of the air quality's affect on your brain chemistry.

Pleasant scents stimulate a nerve in the body that triggers wakefulness and alertness. They also can impact the nerve response that triggers appetite—and satiety.

You don't need fancy fragrances or potpourris—they sometimes overwhelm the olfactory sensors, particularly when synthetic. Go the most natural way you can: keep a basket of oranges or lemons on your desk, and slice one when you're feeling fatigued. The sniff will trigger alertness. A mint plant on your desk will provide the same boost when you break off a leaf to breathe in its aroma. Because of intriguing research, many Japanese corporations pipe the scent of peppermint through their air-conditioning systems in midafternoon to perk up energy and boost concentration and productivity.

Another energizing scent is jasmine, which actually alters brain waves and energy levels. It increases the beta waves in the frontal lobe of the brain, stimulating alertness. Jasmine plants or essential oils will supply the refreshment.

A splitting headache, and still more to do on the report? Well, a green apple a day may keep your migraine away—smelling it, that is! Research by Dr. Alan Hirsch of the Smell and Taste Treatment and Research Foundation in Chicago found that for those who like

the smell of green apples, the scent produces a marked reduction in the severity of their headaches. This may also be related to the alteration of brain waves.

Feeling overwhelmed by the stress of the day? The scent of lavender has been found to induce alpha waves in the back of the brain which relax and calm. Certain scents, such as those from strawberries and popcorn, can even distract you from the stress you are feeling.

The easiest way to provide the specific scent you need is to purchase a small vial of an essential oil, a concentrated mixture extracted from a plant. (Be sure to get pure, natural scents only, available from natural foods stores, bath and body shops, and certain drug stores.) An effective way to put the scent where it counts is with a small atomizer (less than a dollar) filled with water and just a few drops of the essential oil. Shake before using, then lightly spray on the pulse points of your wrists, or into the air as a freshener.

Some of the more stimulating scents are lemon, peppermint or spearmint, pine, rosemary, eucalyptus, jasmine, and basil. Among the known relaxing scents are lavender, chamomile, orange blossom, rose, marjoram, sage, and patchouli.

PURIFY THE AIR WITH PLANTS

Plants give off low levels of hundreds of different chemicals that purify the air. Although the chemicals are designed to protect the plant against insects, they also help and energize *us* by protecting against "sick-building syndrome." In addition, plants absorb many toxins like formaldehyde and benzene; the root systems of plants actually feed off pollutants and toxins in the air. After absorbing the contaminants, the plants "breathe back" clean air.

The build-up of air contaminants in many buildings and homes can cause flu-like symptoms and fatigue, even cancer. Plants are a

friendly, "green" way to clear the air. Just seeing the plants may stimulate a sense of well-being. One study of surgery patients showed quicker recovery rates when their hospital rooms gave a view of a garden or an area with trees.

It is suggested that maximum air purification comes when you have a minimum of one plant for every 100 square feet of living space. Don't worry about overestimating—the more the better, especially if you have central heat and air. The plants will help control the humidity of your living space, absorbing the humidity when it's thick in the air, releasing it when it's dry. That adds up to you being more comfortable—and energized.

To get the best humidity control from your plants, keep them well watered but not drowned. Water them the way you need to be watered—when needed. This will keep your plants thriving and more healthy than a massive watering once a week. They also need more water in the winter when the humidity is low, just as you do. A good watering can do you both a world of good.

DRINK PLENTY OF WATER

Too tired for that walk? It may be hard to believe, but the number-one factor in fatigue is dehydration. If you do nothing else in your quest for weight loss but begin to drink water each day—and drink a lot of it—you will experience a phenomenal boost in your energy and sense of well-being. Few of my clients think of water as their most important energy enhancer, yet many of the symptoms of fatigue that we blame on too much stress and too little sleep are simply the result of thirst.

At the end of a long workday, when you feel rotten and headachy and unwilling to exercise—in a strange zone between sore and numb—your body is crying out to be hydrated. Chances are you've

only drunk enough water to wash down a few aspirin and have had little else since that coffee or diet soda this morning. You've been breathing dry, air-conditioned or heated air at the office, and the chronic stress in your routine has caused some moments of intense perspiration. And of course, you've been losing fluids through the day through normal body functions—fluids that haven't been replaced. You're parched!

Water is important for your energy metabolism for several vital reasons. Consider that your body is comprised primarily of water (it's

> **SMART WEIGH TIP**
> *Drink water—and drink a lot of it!*

92 percent of your blood plasma, 80 percent of your muscle mass, 60 percent of your red blood cells, and 50 percent of everything else in your body). Every cell in your body relies on water to dilute biochemicals, vitamins, and minerals to just the right concentrations. Your body also depends on the bloodstream to transport nutrients and other substances from one part to another, and this too depends on optimal fluid concentration. Blood volume actually decreases and "thickens" when you are dehydrated, meaning that the heart has to work harder to supply your body with needed oxygen. And remember, oxygenated blood is the key for effective energy metabolism.

Water is also vital for maintaining proper muscle tone, allowing muscles to contract naturally and increase in mass. When dehydrated, the muscles are more injury-prone and will not work to optimal performance. In fact, dehydrated muscles will only work to 30 or 35 percent of their capacity. This spells mediocre performance for athletes, tiredness, achiness, and headaches for you—and an inability to build body muscle while losing body fat. Without oxygen getting to the cells, fat cannot be burned for energy.

DRINK YOURSELF WELL

Drinking more water is a challenge for most of us. Most Americans have grown up drinking just about anything but water. We list our favorite beverages as soda, coffee, tea, juice—with water only for washing down pills, washing away dirt, and brushing teeth.

Water is an essential nutrient. Without food, a person can survive (although not well) for days, even months. But without water, the human body can survive only three to five days.

Again, water is a metabolic booster because it is a critical component of basic functions to your body's health. First, along with proper protein and salt intake, water works to release excess stores of fluid, much like priming a pump. It is *the* natural diuretic. No other beverage works like water to prevent the body from holding excess fluids. Second, water transports the energy nutrients throughout your body and is essential for maintaining your body temperature. Third, water helps you digest food and maintains proper bowel function and waste elimination. Being a mild laxative, water actually activates the fiber you eat, allowing it to form a bulky mass that passes through the gastrointestinal tract easily and quickly. Without proper water, fiber becomes a difficult-to-pass "glue" in your colon. Big water drinkers get less colon and bladder cancer.

Water is the only liquid we consume that doesn't require the body to work to metabolize or excrete it. Even fresh juices do not provide the solid benefits of pure, wonderful water, since your body must process the substances they contain. With soft drinks, your body has to work overtime to process and excrete the chemicals and colorings. Although based on water, sodas are "polluted" water.

Many other beverages, particularly those with caffeine, actually remove more water than contained in the beverage itself. Coffee, tea, and some sodas contain tannic acid, a product that interferes with

iron and calcium absorption and competes for excretion with other bodily waste products such as uric acid. When not properly excreted, this uric acid can build up in the body and crystallize around the joints. This build-up leads to joint pain in elbows, shoulders, knees, and feet, especially former injury spots, and is a type of gouty arthritis. Men are particularly prone to uric acid excesses. This is one reason why a cup of tea or coffee, although fluid based, just doesn't do the job. Furthermore, water works to lubricate joints.

If you're still not convinced about the wonders of water, consider this: Water also works to keep the skin healthy, resilient, and wrinkle-resistant. It could honestly be labeled an "anti-aging" ingredient!

HOW MUCH DO I NEED?

Eight to ten eight-ounce glasses each day—more when you exercise, travel by plane, or live at high altitudes. Sound overwhelming? Never thirsty? You're not alone. The water prescription brings out cries of anguish from many people.

But you really do need that much because you lose that much every day. Your body continually loses water as it performs necessary functions. Even breathing uses up your fluid stores; every time you exhale you blow off water—a total of about two cups per day. Water evaporates from your skin to cool your body, even when you aren't aware of sweating. These losses, along with what is lost in regular urination and bowel movements, total up to ten cups per day. When perspiring heavily, the amount lost can double or triple.

Take heart! As you begin to meet your body's needs by drinking more water, your natural thirst will increase. You may find water drinking habit-forming; the more you drink, the more you want.

Start increasing your intake any way you can: through a straw, in a sports sipper, from a silver pitcher. Add fresh lemon or lime, drink

sparkling water, buy bottled water—just drink it! Try filling a two-quart container with water each morning, and then make sure it's all gone before you go to bed. I also encourage drinking a twelve- to sixteen-ounce glass of water right after each meal and snack throughout the day. If you are eating as often as you should, every three hours or so, this will provide a large proportion of the fluid you need.

TIPS FOR STAYING HYDRATED

START YOUR DAY WITH EIGHT TO SIXTEEN OUNCES OF WATER. While the coffee or tea is brewing, drink a cup or two of water. You wake up with a water deficit, so drinking water soon after waking will gently restore hydration. Many of my clients swear by a cup of warm water with a squeeze of lemon first thing in the morning to jumpstart their digestive system gently. They declare it's the answer to their "regularity" problems.

GET YOUR EIGHT-A-DAY. This isn't a diet principle; it's just how your body is wired. Take water breaks routinely, at least every thirty-five to forty-five minutes, even more frequently when the air is dry or hot. Try to drink little or nothing with your meals (sip water if you must), because washing food down with water dilutes the digestive function.

GET MORE WHEN YOU NEED IT. You may not automatically know when you need more, but look for the subtle signs of dehydration—dry eyes, nose or mouth, impatience, slight nausea, flushed skin, dizziness, headaches, weakness, and mild fatigue. Also, drink when you're more stressed than normal. Not to make you obsessive, but it's a good idea to glance at your urine occasionally. Other than first thing in the morning, a dark yellow color is a sign your kidneys are having to concentrate the waste in too-small a volume of liquid. Pale-colored urine indicates good hydration.

DON'T WAIT UNTIL YOU'RE THIRSTY TO DRINK. It's already too late. Once

you feel thirsty, you've already lost a significant amount of fluid. So don't rely on your thirst mechanism. It will prompt you to replace only thirty-five to forty percent of your body's hydration needs. And if you don't take in adequate water, your body fluids will be thrown out of balance and you may experience fluid retention, constipation, unexplained weight gain, and a greater malfunction in your natural thirst mechanism.

KEEP WATER WHERE YOU ARE. You're more apt to keep up with water needs if you keep drinking water close at hand. Freeze large bottles of water overnight and pull them out in the morning. The water thaws through the day, but is still chilled. Keep a glass or a pitcher of water at your desk, and refill it often. At home, keep a pitcher or large bottle of water in the refrigerator, with a glass on the counter as a reminder.

AVOID DEHYDRATING FOOD AND DRINKS. Caffeine-containing and alcoholic beverages act as dehydrators, further increasing, and never replacing, your fluid needs. In fact, each cup of coffee or tea adds an extra cup of water to the eight- to ten-a-day basic requirement. Who has the room—or time?

FILL UP BEFORE YOU WORKOUT. Drink sixteen ounces of water fifteen to thirty minutes before your workout. Avoid starting to exercise when you're already thirsty; you're guaranteed a substandard performance.

CONTINUE TO FILL UP WHILE YOU'RE WORKING OUT. Drink six to eight ounces of water every twenty minutes during your workout or training. This may seem like a lot, but even this doesn't begin to keep up with typical sweat losses. When possible, drink cool water—it is absorbed into the system more quickly. No need for a sports drink to replenish electrolytes unless you're exercising longer than ninety minutes.

PRACTICE AIR TRAVEL SMARTS. Drink as if you're going into an exercise workout: sixteen ounces before your flight, then at least eight more every hour aloft. Stick with water or juices.

IF YOU START CRAVING SALT, GO FOR WATER. Once your fluid stores drop below a certain level, your thirst mechanism cuts off altogether. (Possibly to preserve your sanity if you're lost in the desert?) What turns on is a desire for salt—or salty foods. It's one of those magnificent things the body does: because extra sodium holds more fluids in the body, the salt craving is a survival mechanism to slow life-threatening dehydration. Notice a craving for hot dogs and nachos at the beach? Look for a water bottle instead.

IS TAP WATER OKAY?

Be sure not to let the bottled versus tap versus treated water controversy get in the way of your health. Many people do; they don't trust their tap water, so they drink no water at all.

Public water systems today are well monitored for safety, and bottled water companies are now beginning to fall under similar standards. You can assure yourself of the purity and safety of your local drinking water by checking with your local EPA or health department, or by contacting EPA's Safe Drinking Water Hotline at 800-426-4791. If you lack confidence in the answers you receive, you can have your water tested privately. The agencies listed above can give you the names of testing laboratories.

If you drink bottled water, choose brands that bottle their water in glass or clear plastic containers and are able and willing to provide an analysis or certification of purity. And buy only spring or purified water—a bottle labeled "drinking water" may just come from your municipal water system. You would do just as well turning on your faucet.

The biggest concern with tap water is that it is treated with chlorine to remove contaminants. As important as chlorine is for purifying our water, questions have been raised about its contribution to heart disease risk, to miscarriage, and to long-term effects on the immune system. I encourage my clients to avoid, when possible, water that has an obvious taste or smell of chlorine. When you travel, consider ordering bottled water.

You may want to get information on a water purifying system for your home. Steam distillation is the most reliable, and most expensive, form of filtration. The next best is reverse osmosis, which forces the water through a cellophane-like, semipermeable membrane that acts as a barrier to contaminants like asbestos, copper, lead, mercury, and even some microorganisms. Reverse osmosis systems require a good bit of water pressure to function and are often difficult to access for necessary filter changes. And the replacement filters can be quite expensive.

Activated carbon filters use granules, precoat (a fine powder), or a solid block to remove unpleasant odors, colors, and bad tastes from drinking water, and do a very good job in removing chlorine and some contaminants. If all you're after is good taste and less chlorine odor and aren't concerned about microorganisms or other contaminants, a simple table-top pitcher with a carbon filter (such as Brita) will suffice. If you drink tap water, the taste may improve after refrigerating it for twenty-four hours (the chlorine will dissipate). This can be a low-cost way to get the more refreshing taste of bottled water without the cost. Your choice of which water to drink comes down to taste, cost, and availability.

Regardless, the bottom line is this: drink eight to ten glasses of water every day, and more if you exercise heavily. Don't allow anything to become a substitute for the beverage your body likes best: water, the beverage of champions!

CHAPTER 9 ■ R: Rest

The best bridge between hope and despair is often a good night's sleep.

—ANONYMOUS

Rest is something we read about, talk about, and long for, but don't often get. How many of us fall into bed at night, literally "dead to the world" (or is it dead from the world?), seeking a few hours of relief from our lives? Too many days of doing whatever it takes have taken their toll. Too many hours of just getting through have gotten to us. Bedtime comes, but refreshing sleep may not.

For some, it's as difficult to turn off the day as it is to turn off the TV. There is simply too much to do and not enough time to do it, and robbing from sleep seems an easy way to make up the difference. Ask ten people how disciplined they are with a sleep schedule and you'll

> **SMART WEIGH TIP**
>
> *How well you live your day affects how well you rest at night.*

be likely to hear variations on a single theme: "I go to bed when I finish doing what I have to do." Bombarded by increasing demands on their time from work, travel, play, family, and social obligations, most people steal time from sleep. In fact, some are downright proud of under-sleeping. Getting by on four hours has a superhuman sound.

A National Sleep Foundation survey found nearly two out of three people do not get the recommended eight hours of sleep each night. A third of those get less than six hours of sleep. Other surveys have shown that in the past year, one-third of American adults have had trouble falling asleep or staying asleep and two-thirds complained of sleep-related problems such as insomnia, snoring, or restless legs. The late hours designated for rest mirror our days: we fight through them.

LACK OF SLEEP

Sleep is a little known and often missed component in the weight-management game: a bad night's sleep might do more than give you the early-morning blues; it can actually play a central role in locking down your fat cells. Results from studies of the impact of sleep deprivation on the body indicate that a chronic lack of sleep may affect metabolic function as much as living a sedentary lifestyle. Being consistently deprived of sleep can also increase the severity of age-related chronic disorders, including diabetes, obesity, and hypertension.

Sleep is the repair shop of the body and brain, the process that most thoroughly restores our psychological and physiological vitality after the strain and exertion of life. Along with building and repairing our muscle tissue, bones, cells, and immune system, restful sleep allows the release of important hormones such as the human growth hormone, which is critical for vitality and metabolic burn.

Sleep researchers have shown that cheating on sleep for only one night increases evening cortisol to levels that can adversely impact health by lowering immunes and slowing the body's fat-burning potential. Because cortisol helps to regulate blood sugar concentrations, the sleep-deprived body metabolizes glucose less effectively.

Increased levels of cortisol can also damage brain cells, causing shrinkage in the hippocampus, the critical region of the brain that regulates learning.

Small sleep losses can be cumulative. Research has revealed that after even one week's lack of sleep, there are striking alterations in metabolic and endocrine function and a rapid deterioration of the body's functions. The good news is that these studies also show that the negative effects of sleep deprivation can be corrected by normal sleep. Just as a lack of sleep can harm the body, getting sleep can help it.

HOW MUCH IS ENOUGH?

Believe it or not, research still shows that the average adult needs seven-and-a-half to eight hours of deep, restful sleep a night to stay healthy and alert. There are exceptions: one in ten needs ten hours of sleep each night, one in one hundred can be refreshed with five. Again, new studies show that cutting back on sleep to below the seven-and-a-half hours most of us need can be as dangerous to health as a poor diet and no exercise.

> **SMART WEIGH TIP**
>
> *Sleep is the repair shop of the body—aim for 7 1/2 to 8 hours a night.*

There appears to be a biological feedback loop between the body's use of energy, its need to resupply it, and the brain's mechanism for maintaining the proper energy balance. This need of the brain for energy helps to explain why lack of sleep dulls the brain, saps energy, increases irritability and depression, and turns up the appetite thermostat. We think we can lose sleep and be a little tired, but otherwise we'll just be fine. The truth is we won't—we ultimately have to pay the piper. We may be living life in the modern age, but we still have the same bodies, living by the same principles, that we were created with.

If you desire more sleep, but your body simply won't cooperate, check this list for sleep robbers that may be stealing your much-needed rest.

SLEEP ROBBERS

BLOOD SUGAR FLUCTUATIONS. Sleep deprivation and the resulting cortisol production causes impaired blood sugar regulation. In turn, blood sugar fluctuations are a prime culprit in restless sleep. A sudden drop in your blood sugar level, characteristically occurring at 2:30 to 3:00 AM, causes a surge in adrenaline. This can bring on a panic response, which is why you often wake with a start, with your heart and mind racing. Once awakened, it's difficult to get back to restful sleep.

HOT FLASHES AND NIGHT SWEATS. The results of blood sugar crashes, menopause, and panic attacks last only a few minutes but are notorious for disrupting sleep. If they are hormone related and you're a female approaching menopause, please don't ignore the hormone issue. Let troublesome hot flashes and night sweats motivate you to consider hormone replacement therapy or healing soy foods.

GETTING OLDER. It's a myth that you need less sleep as you age. But, your sleep patterns will likely change. You may sleep less in one stretch. You also get less of the deeper, most restorative sleep. Consequently, you awaken more often and are more easily aroused by a snoring spouse or a call to the bathroom.

STRESS. It's the top cause of short-term sleep problems due to the chemical gymnastics it causes in your body. Even worrying about your insomnia can worsen the problem.

MEDICATIONS. Steroids and some drugs can disrupt sleep. The most common troublemakers are some blood pressure medications, diet pills, diuretics, antidepressants, cold and allergy remedies, and asthma medications. Check with your physician and pharmacist.

(6) CAFFEINE. Americans drink 400 million cups of coffee each day, and get extra doses of caffeine in tea or cola-type sodas, cocoa, and chocolate. Caffeine's stimulants are still at work five to seven hours after you've ingested it, preventing your body from falling into deep sleep and often awakening you prematurely by disrupting sleep patterns.

A NIGHTCAP OR NIGHT SMOKE. Alcohol in the bloodstream makes staying asleep more difficult. In addition, it suppresses dreams, depriving your body of its normal, refreshing sleep cycle. Nicotine is also a stimulant that keeps your body from easily falling asleep. One more reason to kick the habit!

ILLNESS. Arthritis, asthma, and sleep apnea (breathing cessation characterized by loud snoring and gasping) can interfere with sleep. **DEPRESSION** can also cause insomnia, just as insomnia can bring on depression.

ABCS OF GOOD ZZZS

If it's a little harder for you to shut off the business of your mind than it is to shut off the light, you may need some tips for sweet sleep. Rather than endure one more sleepless night or another morning dragging out of bed, use these tips to keep your body programmed for restful sleep.

BE CLOCK-DRIVEN. When it comes to catching up on lost sleep, timing is everything. Block in sleep as a priority part of your schedule. By doing this you are making an advance decision that sleep is important because being your very best is important.

Your body's internal time clock is daily reset by getting up at the same time each day. "Sleeping in," even for an hour, can disrupt your biological clock and end up making you feel even more fatigued. This is why getting to bed earlier in the evening is better than sleep-

ing late the next morning—it gives you the extra rest without upsetting your rhythm. Stick with it. People who are just starting to make up lost sleep can take six weeks to recover fully.

I know this is hard, but try to get up at the same time every day, regardless of when you fall asleep. Set your alarm clock—then put it out of sight. You want to be clock-driven, not clock-obsessed.

CHOOSE NIGHTTIME SNACKS WISELY. Overeating, or high-fat, high-sugar snacks after dinner can so overload your body that it will resist getting to sleep or staying asleep. The classic pattern is being awakened around 3:00 AM, eyes open, heart racing, unable to get back to sleep. Eating too much too late has put your body into chemical gymnastics. Going to bed hungry can be a sleep-robbing culprit as well. When you're hungry your brain will try to keep you alert until you eat.

A great bedtime snack is a small bowl of whole grain cereal with low-fat milk or half a turkey sandwich or a banana with skim milk. All keep the body chemistries undergirded through the night, allowing you to waken rested and refreshed.

WORK YOUR BODY DURING THE DAY. Exercise, with its ability to physically process the stressors of our day physically, gives sweeter sleep; it's nature's best tranquilizer! People who work out for thirty to forty minutes, four times a week, fall asleep faster and sleep longer than nonexercisers. Just don't exercise less than an hour before bedtime—the rise in your body temperature can keep you awake.

KEEP IT COOL, DARK, AND QUIET. People sleep best in rooms that are between 60 and 65 degrees, pitch-black, and silent. If that's a far cry from your bedroom, put up heavy drapes or a light-blocking shade. To drown out traffic noises or a snoring spouse, try wearing ear plugs or adding "white noise" like a fan or air-conditioner.

CHECK YOUR NIGHTTIME POSTURE. One of the often overlooked causes

of daytime fatigue is nighttime posture. Sleeping on your stomach can cause a strain on your back that might be just painful enough to keep you from getting a good night's sleep. For the most restful repose night after night, sleep on your side. This promotes easier breathing and reduces snoring, which can wake you up. Consider keeping a pillow under your knees; this comfortably flexes your lower spine, making it say Ahhhh.... To avoid neck and shoulder aches, use a pillow that's low enough to support your head without flexing your neck. Down pillows work best; foam ones are often too springy. Also be sure you're warm enough. If you have to stay curled up all night to keep warm, your back is likely to get sore.

DEVELOP A SLEEP RITUAL. Remember the bedtime story that helped to calm you down as a child? An adult bedtime routine gives your brain strong cues that it's time to slow down and prepare for sleep. It can be as simple or as elaborate as you like—a warm bath, lighting a candle (particularly a calming lavender one), putting a "brow pillow" on your forehead, snuggling up with your loved one, or listening to classical music. (Just ten minutes of Mozart has been shown to rein in the racing mind—both for sleep and performance.)

Some people are avid writers before bed, particularly when their mind is racing. Writing down what you're thinking and feeling helps to "drain the brain" for restful sleep. I have more than a few clients who lie down for five minutes, then get up and make a to-do list, writing down everything that needs to be attended to the next day. Then they set it aside, and set aside time the next day to deal with their list.

LET BED BE BED. Don't let it be an office, a place to pay bills, or a home theater. Make your bed restful by using it only for sleeping and romance.

Don't force the sleep issue. If you're still awake thirty minutes

after going to bed, get up and do something calming, such as reading, until you're groggy enough to fall asleep. Try to stay awake until your eyes close involuntarily. This works best if you don't keep track of time.

OTHER BRIGHT IDEAS—LIGHT

Sunlight is the "spark of life," without which there would be no plant growth, no photosynthesis, no oxygen. On a more personal level, light causes normal physiological fluctuations that can affect the way we feel, think, and sleep. Depending on personal sensitivity and the extent of light changes in your environment, the effects can range from mild fatigue to severe depression.

What keeps us tied to light is a cleverly balanced internal clock, known as circadian rhythm, which synchronizes a wide variety of physiological systems including heart rate, body temperature, and sleep cycles. This internal clock is set by light; it can be reset by changes in the timing or duration of light exposure.

Most of us don't think twice about our circadian rhythms. We take for granted that we become tired and sleepy at night, awake and alert during the day. We notice the effects only if our internal clock is "out of sync." Most people notice the effects of circadian rhythms when they gain or lose time such as in traveling, or during seasonal changes in light. Even small changes can cause dramatic symptoms in some people.

To help smooth out your sleep-wake cycle, try these simple measures to manipulate your exposure to light:

■ If you get up in the middle of the night, avoid turning on bright lights. Light suppresses melatonin production and may

make it more difficult to fall back to sleep. Put dimmer switches or nightlights in bathrooms and hallways.

- If you have trouble rising in the morning, maximize the amount of light in your bedroom as soon as you wake up.
- If you wake up too early in the morning, minimize the amount of dawn light. Wear a sleep mask or put blackout shades on your windows. When you wake, keep lights dim to help gradually shift your usual pattern.

In all of creation, the principle of rest is modeled for us. The soil of the earth needs a rest from time to time, allowing it to become more productive. Bears hibernate, fish sleep with their eyes open, the most beautiful plants have a period of dormancy. Our needs are no different: we need rest in order to heal and rejuvenate. So treat yourself well: give yourself time to recharge and replenish so you can keep your metabolism burning brightly.

CHAPTER 10 ▪ T: Treating Yourself Well

Climb the mountains and get their good tidings.
Nature's peace will flow into you as sunshine flows into trees.
The winds will blow their own freshness into you, and the storms their energy,
while cares will drop away from you like leaves of autumn.

—**JOHN MUIR,** Naturalist who helped establish Yosemite National Park

The lives of so many of us are two-dimensional—work and food. Doing and eating. It's hard to find a place for relaxation and replenishment—sometimes even relationships. You know you should spend more quality time on yourself but just thinking about how to fit it in gives you a migraine. It's easier just to hit the sofa—take in some food and tune out with TV.

Many of us push ourselves into prolonged periods of exertion without adequate periods of rest and relaxation. Some of us push ourselves through long days with barely time for a bathroom break, and definitely no time for lunch.

> **SMART WEIGH TIP**
>
> *Indulge yourself in healthy pleasures that replenish, refresh, and relax you.*

Some go months, even years, without a vacation, or a relaxing weekend. No wonder we get run out and run down, and robbed of the joy and peace we so desire.

This breakneck pace not only inflates your stress level, but takes a hefty toll on your metabolism and your quality of life. It signals the body to eat, and overeat, in order to provide the energy to keep up with the demands of your daily grind, yet slows you down to

conserve what energy you do have. When life borders on depletion, food (and storing that food) takes center stage. Losing weight becomes impossible.

If you are approaching meltdown, the best thing to do, ironically, is nothing at all. You were created with a need to rest, to recreate, to reflect, and to be regenerated. Treating yourself well is really a lifestyle—it makes a statement that "you deserve a break today."

Here are some ways to achieve a wiser, saner, and metabolically boosted you.

CHILL OUT!

Countless studies have documented the benefits of chilling out. Anything that relieves stress also boosts physical, spiritual, and emotional energy and becomes a metabolic booster. Fatigue disappears; backaches vanish; colds and flu are kept at bay; blood pressure drops; and chronic conditions—such as migraine, irritable bowel syndrome, insomnia, even acne—improve.

Sure, it used to be a little easier to get a break. Ten years ago, most stores were not open on Sundays. Now, Sunday is a day for shopping. The notion of the Sabbath being a day of rest has disappeared. You can go to the all-night supermarket and get your entire week's food at 3:00 AM. And holidays—even those like Labor Day and New Year—are a merchant's delight: a time for some of the biggest clearance sales of the year.

To really enjoy life physically, emotionally, relationally, and spiritually, we must have a way, and take the time, to recharge our physical batteries and renew our spirits. Here's how.

TRIM YOUR CALENDAR

Just because you *can* do everything doesn't mean that you *must* do

everything. Ruthlessly cross out unnecessary events in your calendar. Time pressure is a huge metabolism zapper. Research tells us that although we feel more rushed and harried than we did twenty or thirty years ago, we actually have more free time than we used to. We just feel pressured to do more because of our super-speedy culture. E-mail, laptops, and cell phones create the illusion that we can, and should, be busy and productive every minute of the day.

While you can't always stop responsibilities from piling up, you can pick what requires immediate attention and what can be put on the back burner. So go ahead, cancel some social events and not-so-vital work commitments and do *exactly* what you want. It will energize you beyond words and remove a major logjam to your metabolic burn.

MAKE A DATE WITH YOURSELF

At least once a week, carve out one hour (or longer) for your own— an hour in which you have nothing to do. Plan ahead on when the hour will be, but don't plan what you'll do—otherwise it will become one more thing on your "to-do" list.

I actually try to spend one day a week in time-out rest, whether it's Sunday or another day, I need a consistent weekly withdrawal to do replenishing activities. A day of rest for me means a day of activities that personally revitalize me. It may mean reading novels, taking leisurely walks, napping, enjoying friends, window shopping, or just sitting, daydreaming, and writing.

For some people, this kind of activity would *provoke* anxiety. To relax and be replenished, they need to be skydiving, or driving a race car! And that's fine—"relaxing" means different things to different people. But just switching to a *different* activity, even if it's physically strenuous, can revive you. Studies have shown that curiosity increases our performance capability. When devoid of stimulation,

people become disorganized, lose their intellectual ability to concentrate, and decline in coordination. So read a new book, paint your masterpiece, and seek out new situations, work opportunities, and challenges. We are stimulus-hungry beings, and denying our nature can lead to inertia and listlessness.

Does all this sound more like the ideal than reality? It needn't be. This is a great time to carve out our personal hours of renewal, because living in contemporary society has made our need desperate. With determination and a little creativity, anyone can make the time for time-out.

Something happens to me when I choose to relax and be replenished. I return to what I was created to be: a *human being*. With time invested in recharge I can review how I'm normally spending my time and reevaluate according to the purposes that have been placed in my heart. Otherwise, I stay too busy for issues of the soul.

START YOUR DAY WITH A TIME-OUT

Many of us have learned the power of starting the morning with a quiet time of reflection and spiritual connection. This is a daily part of my life because I know that I could be doing nothing more important, and that it is the only way to start my day with strength. It is a time-out in the midst of my busyness to reflect on what my source of strength really is, who I really am, and that nothing, NOTHING, is worth being robbed of the joy of life. Starting my day with quiet reflection is like the warm-up for my exercise—a time to stretch spiritually and get my soul circulating.

I get up and eat breakfast (body fuel) while reading inspirational words (soul fuel). Then, I walk. While walking, I'm also reflecting—not just going through a mental checklist and to-do list, but taking a step beyond to look at the "why" of my life: What's the pas-

sion, what's the purpose, why am I doing all these things, and why am I spinning all these plates? Sometimes I need to focus more on what I need to say no to, more than on what to say yes to. After this time of listening and reflecting, writing is my way to get my thoughts and feelings into a place where I can take action. Writing down what's inside is a ten-minute investment that yields huge dividends for me.

TAKE POWER BREAKS—EVEN POWER NAPS

Research shows that no matter how busy people are, they would work better, faster, and more productively if they took a break. True, withdrawing from your endeavors for a few moments temporarily halts your output, but research shows that doing so can erase tension, enhance optimistic attitudes, focus the mind, jump-start creativity—and give a significant energy and metabolic boost. Why work hours on end at a slightly unfocused 75 percent performance, when a fifteen-minute power break can help you work at an efficient 100 percent for the next few hours?

And that's exactly what happens. Research shows that after every few hours of focused activity, your brain and body take a downturn. Blood sugars begin to drop, energy levels fade, alertness dims, and metabolism slows. You need to get up, get a snack, get water, get moving, and get your mind off the work. If you ignore this need, or try to shake it off, you'll only achieve a lower level of productivity.

You may need to write breaks into your schedule as a priority appointment—as important as any other. It *is* that important. Even the busiest people—a surgeon doing open-heart surgeries, a judge hearing back-to-back cases—can manipulate their difficult schedules to allow for break time. If you realize how important it is, you can make it happen. Remember this: *More breaks, more breakthroughs!*

Using your break for a power nap can also be very refreshing—relaxing your body, clearing your mind, improving your mood, and boosting your energy levels. Studies show that you don't really have to sleep to get the rejuvenation you need—just shut the door, unplug the phone, turn off the lights, and close your eyes. Rest and be replenished. Then get up and have a power snack. Stretch or take a quick walk at the end of your break to rejuvenate yourself for the work at hand.

If you choose to nap, make it short and sweet. Don't tell toddlers this, but a fifteen- to twenty-minute nap seems to be ideal for the maximum energy boost. You can stretch it a few extra minutes, but don't go over an hour. Napping too long can be counterproductive; long naps can allow you to enter into the deeper delta-type sleep, causing a groggy, disoriented state when you wake that takes a long time to snap out of. If you seem to need more than an hour's nap in the afternoon, you're probably not getting enough sleep at night.

END YOUR DAY WITH A TIME-OUT

I have recently begun to end my day with a time-out. This is very difficult for me; I have to tell myself more than once that *there is nothing more I should be doing.* I then enjoy some of my favorite things that don't seem very productive in the scheme of life, yet I know are vital to recharge my energy: reading travel magazines, listening to favorite music, whatever.

Again, it doesn't come naturally for me; I'm a "doer" by nature. The first one up in our household, I go nonstop till the sun goes down and beyond. Even my "breaks" have often been purposeful: planning, researching, meeting with a small group. I have laughed for many years about being a "human doing" rather than a "human being," but only in recent years have I realized it's not something to

laugh about. Ending my day with a time just to "be" reaffirms in my own mind that I am only human—and that's more than enough!

EXTEND TIME-OUTS TWICE A YEAR

I try to begin each year with a personal retreat, a time to write and reflect on where I've been and where I'm going. Is it the direction I want, propelling me toward my dreams?

I try to take another time to pull away midyear to do a midpoint check. What have the past six months done to me and for me? Am I on track with the goals and priorities I established six months earlier? Am I treating myself well—and honoring my body, soul, and beliefs?

At least twice a year, schedule time to pull away and completely change your scenery. Even if it's only for a weekend, physically separating yourself from your daily obligations can do a world of good for your energy level. Leaving your familiar environment is a surefire way to recharge and refresh your batteries. Viewing life in a new context is itself invigorating. When you return, you'll have a new perspective.

> **SMART WEIGH TIP**
>
> *Divert Daily, Withdraw Weekly, Abandon Annually.*

Let your time away build your motivation for making your day-to-day world more beautiful, more relaxing—and definitely more energizing. Treating yourself well is more than just taking action—it is a state of mind, a state of soul. You can enter into rest anytime you choose to let go of all the stuff you don't want, won't use, and don't need. You feel uplifted and drawn to the new because you aren't struggling to carry the old.

SHAKE THINGS UP!

Embracing *The Smart Weigh* will work wonders with your metabo-

lism and well-being—and it will bring something else into life: *change*. We humans are prone to fall into ruts in life—in the way we eat, the way we live, the way we interact with others. These ruts may provide safety, but they also bring boredom and weariness. So shake things up! Taking different actions will give you a different point of view, and that will remind you that you're in control of your choices and can change things for the better.

You probably have a suitcase full of habits and ruts that you aren't even aware of. By becoming conscious of them and then breaking or altering them, you can stir up your old thought patterns and emerge from your slump. Consider moving the furniture; mix up your schedule of doing things in the morning; do your work in a different location; eat a different breakfast; listen to some new music; cross train in exercise; take a new route to the office or school; change the lighting; paint a room; try some unfamiliar fruits and vegetables.

The power of rearranging one's external environment has been well documented in studies since the 1960s when it was first reported. For years, Weight Watchers and other eating modification groups have used this strategy to help countless people to lose weight by modifying their behavior and "stimulus environment." For example, external changes like eating from smaller plates or eating only at the table with a place mat—even just rearranging the refrigerator—can have a huge impact on the inside of you.

You will see how all these truths operate as you learn to implement them through the seven-week plan in the next chapter. Let it become the beginning of a new way of living!

CHAPTER 11 ▪ Your Seven-Week Plan to Lose Weight and Feel Great

The task ahead of you is never as great as the power behind you. You have been created with a genetic heritage for wellness—claim that power.

—ANONYMOUS

T here's a good reason why most people fail at sustaining a new way of living: they don't plan to fail, but fail to plan. The best way to reach long-term goals is with short-term steps. But most people try to make changes without understanding that changing behavior is a process, not a once-a-year New Year's resolution.

The reality is that change is difficult—especially if you haven't figured out the steps. You must know where you are beginning, you need to know where you are going, and you have to figure out how to get there. By implementing certain behavioral steps, you can increase the likelihood of achieving your goal.

> **SMART WEIGH TIP**
>
> *Don't focus on perfection, rather focus on progress. Look at how far you've come!*

For instance, when the goal is weight loss, the first step is to set a realistic weight-loss goal within an appropriate amount of time— about one pound per week. Accept that the healthful weight loss is slow and steady. If you want to keep it off, you have to change your behavior and eating habits permanently. But you don't have to do it all at once. Make small changes, like walking two or three days a

week, cutting out frequent desserts—things you can achieve without much trouble. If you set goals you can achieve, it reinforces a positive feeling that helps you go on. And success breeds success.

PLAN FOR SUCCESS

Many people have had excellent long-lasting results in making change with the SUCCESS plan, a series of steps to help them reach their goals developed by Harold Shinitzky, Psy. D. Consider these elements in your own plan for SUCCESS.

Set Your Goals

Decide what changes you want to make, keeping in mind that you should be specific and realistic. "Lose weight" is a broadly defined goal. A more specific and realistic goal would be, "Lose ten pounds within two months." The key word here is *realistic*—try achieving a comfortable weight you maintained easily as a young adult. If you've always been overweight, reaching a weight at which levels of triglycerides, blood sugar, blood pressure, and energy improve may be a realistic goal for you.

"My first goal was to lose only ten pounds," says Rebecca. "I had very high blood pressure, and my doctor said if I would just lose ten pounds, he believed that I could get off the pills. Every other doctor before said I had to lose 100 pounds, and I thought, 'I can't do that.' But ten pounds—I thought, 'Maybe I can do that.' Doing it one bite at a time made it more achievable for me."

Write down your goals and then let others know about them. That will increase the likelihood that you'll follow through and get support when you need it.

Understand Your Passions

Lose weight because you want to, not to please someone else. You must want to lose weight because it's what *you* want to do. Know what really makes you feel good, what you like to do, and use that to help guide you to your long-term goals. If you want to be fit, or to become a better athlete, focus on what it will take, such as increasing your cardiovascular workouts or weight training. This step requires you to narrow your focus to one or two specific goals. Which goals do you value most? These will become your priorities.

Critically Plan Your Steps

Determine small steps that will lead to the larger one. If your goal is to become more fit, you can join a gym and/or schedule a workout three times a week. If you want to drop ten pounds, follow the guides for weight loss that will bring your calories down and your nutrition up. Exercise appropriately to come up with a 500-calorie-a-day deficit. This will allow you to lose the weight in one- or two-pound increments per week.

Challenge Yourself

That means be willing to work hard, push yourself, and feel a little discomfort (not pain) if it means helping you to reach your goals. Realize that if you want to lose weight, you might feel discontented sometimes, or feel a little out of breath while working out. Acknowledge that change is not easy. If it were, you would have already accomplished your goal.

When things get difficult, we tend to revert to previous comfortable behaviors. But now is the time to develop *new* lifestyle behaviors. To do that, you have to change the behaviors that resulted in weight gain in the first place. Lifestyle changes involve taking a

realistic, sometimes painfully honest look at your eating habits and daily routine. Were you taught as a child to clean your plate? If so, do you still feel compelled to eat everything, even when you're full? Examine your eating style. Do you eat fast? Do you take big bites? When do you eat? While watching TV? All the time? Examine your shopping and cooking techniques.

Evaluate Your Progress

Are you making headway? If not, why not? Adjust your plan to meet your long-term goal. Are you meeting your weekly or monthly weight-loss goals? If not, determine what the problem might be. Do you need more consistency with exercise? Do you need to be eating more often—or become more careful with portion sizes?

Stay Focused

That means not being deterred by obstacles that threaten to obscure your goal. Are you invited to a great party where there's lots of food? Look past the buffet table and envision yourself as the fit and trim person you want to be. That should help you control yourself. Remember, "if it's meant to be, it's up to me."

Savor Your Accomplishments

Reward yourself for reaching small goals along the way. As you lose weight and become more fit, buy yourself some new clothes. Have you developed a pleasant routine of walking? Treat yourself to a walk on the beach or around a lake.

BUILDING A HEALTHY FOUNDATION

I have taken the principles from the previous chapters and arranged them in the form of week-by-week suggestions to help you change

your lifestyle in a way that releases your body's natural ability to lose weight. Each week's suggestions build on what you have done in the previous week; after seven weeks, you will have created the foundation of a healthy lifestyle—one that is free of the diet trap. This exclusive plan combines the best of the best: it combines every top strategy shown by research to increase your chances of reaping the joys of fitness and good health.

There is no need to do this plan in just seven weeks. You may want to slow the pace and incorporate the principles over the next seven months, or even over the next year. Remember, it has taken you a lifetime to accumulate your current habits and attitudes; it will take longer than a few weeks to weed out the negative ones, plant new ones, and allow them to grow into a new you. Of course, I have many clients who are the all-or-nothing type people, and they make a total about-face and dive into the whole seven-week plan the very first day. But, as I've said before, these truths are simple, but they are not easy. Give yourself time to succeed.

Read over the plan below, then try to set a date to begin. You may not be ready now to invest yourself fully in these changes. You may already be on a diet and thrilled with it—for now—and not too thrilled with my opinions about it. If that is the case, I'd love to see you make an appointment with yourself and this book to reexamine your feelings about that diet in two months, or next year. Ask a friend or family member to check in with you at that time, and see if you are then ready to embrace a new way of living—for life.

YOUR SEVEN-WEEK PLAN

WEEK ONE:
STOKE YOUR METABOLIC FIRE

Begin to eat early, often, and balanced; drink water,
get moving, and get some sleep.

ACTION STEPS

■ For the first three days, keep a diary of everything you eat and drink, the time that you eat, how you are feeling, and any exercise you may do (see sample and blank diary pages on page 389). As you keep track of how you are living each day, look for the areas that may be contributing to your metabolism slow-down and fat cell lock-down. What patterns do you see with your eating, your exercise, your moods, and your feelings?

■ Next, begin a new food diary for the remainder of the week using the "Eat Right Prescription" to activate your metabolism (eat early, often, balanced, lean, and bright). This is a time to focus on what to eat rather than what to avoid. Have a balanced breakfast every day, and power snacks or meals every two-and-a-half to three hours (see page 125 for power snack ideas or creatively put together your own). Also keep track of the eight to ten glasses of water you drink each day.

■ Try to walk at least ten minutes a day for five days of this week. If you are already exercising aerobically at least four times a week, keep it up—and do the walk in addition.

■ Look at your sleep patterns and the hours you invest in this vital key to wellness. If you aren't getting at least seven to eight hours of sleep each night, try to get to bed a bit earlier two nights this week.

WEEK TWO:
EQUIP YOUR BODY FOR STRESS RELEASE

Be sure to eat early, often, and balanced—with special attention to eating lean and bright. Choose whole-grain foods, low-fat proteins, and a variety of brightly colored fruits and vegetables. Increase your exercise time, using it as a time to reflect and be refreshed. Breathe *deeply and fully.*

ACTION STEPS

■ Compare your last week's food diary to the guidelines of *The Smart Weigh* eating in the next chapter, and note adjustments you might want to make in timing or balance of eating. After you've evaluated your present-day eating habits and have found your weak spots, you can get on your way toward eating *The Smart Weigh.* Begin to eat in a focused way, using a goal-appropriate meal plan in Chapter 12 as your guide.

■ This week, choose foods and portions for your meals and snacks based on your new plan. Keep in mind that these are guides for minimum portions and proper balance to achieve your desired goals for healthy living, putting you on the road to losing weight and feeling great. Get started with these amounts for the next two weeks to allow your body to stabilize before making adjustments, and keep a diary of what, when, and how much you eat and drink as well as exercise times and types, and how you feel. The sample diary on page 389 provides space for you to list your protein choice, carbohydrates, and added fats.

■ Increase walking to twenty minutes a day, either at one time or in two, ten-minute sessions. If you are already exercising aerobically four times a week, do the twenty-minute walk on the other days.

■ Begin to do the releasing/relaxing breathing described on page 189. Choose a time every day to practice your new focused breathing to release stress and breathe in life. Start with fifteen deep breaths at a time.

WEEK THREE:
CULTIVATE A POSITIVE PERSPECTIVE

Treat yourself well by eating well, exercising, resting, and making time for time-outs to reflect on your attitude and life purpose.

ACTION STEPS

■ Review your day. Is there adequate time for time-outs? Carving out even ten minutes to reflect and be redirected is an excellent beginning. You may focus on writing this week as a way to study your thoughts. What negative thoughts about your progress seem to be recurring? What positive thoughts can you replace them with?

■ Continue the breathing exercises. Practice the relaxing breath exercise whenever you feel anxious or upset, as well as at the beginning of your quiet time and exercise time. Try to have two focused breathing sessions each day.

■ Treat yourself well by doing something nice for yourself: Go to a park or art museum, get a massage or pedicure. Or maybe just take a long, warm bath.

■ Go through your pantry and refrigerator and aggressively remove the foods that no longer fit into your healthy lifestyle. Why keep them? Box up unopened cans and cake mixes and donate to a local shelter for the disadvantaged. After planning your meals and snacks for the coming week, use *The Smart Weigh* grocery list on pages 263-266 to shop smart. Pick up some fresh flowers to enjoy.

■ Increase your walking to thirty minutes, at least five days this week. If you are doing another form of aerobic exercise, continue to walk on the other days.

WEEK FOUR:
REGULATE YOUR BLOOD SUGARS

Use the dynamic duo of healthy eating and exercise to stabilize the rise and fall of your blood sugars and body chemistry.

ACTION STEPS

- Continue to choose foods and portions for your meals and snacks based on the meal plan that is appropriate for you. Review your food diary—are there times of the day when you are hungry, or crave certain foods? How about your moods and energy? Are there times of the day when you are particularly high, or low? Adjust the timing of your eating to best undergird your blood sugars. Also review your diaries for food choices that may contribute to better stabilization. For example, you may need to choose more of the best-choice whole grains and legumes on page 92.

- Check the mileage you are walking in your thirty minutes. If you are walking less than two miles, pick up your pace a bit. Continue exercising at least five days a week, and add in the conditioning exercises on page 171-173 on two of the days.

- Choose four nights this week that you will go to bed early enough to get seven to eight hours of sleep. If you are waking up in the middle of the night, unable to get back to restful sleep, try a bowl of whole-grain cereal as your bedtime snack to stabilize your blood sugars through the night. Also review your day to be sure you are eating in even ways. Remember: how well you live your days affects how well you rest at night.

WEEK FIVE:
EQUALIZE YOUR BRAIN CHEMISTRY

Change your body physically by changing your environment and habits.

ACTION STEPS

- Look around your world. Is there something that may be preventing a positive balance of the chemicals in your brain? Use the tools on pages 95-99 as a guide to look for ways to brighten up your world.

- Do an activity outdoors, weather permitting. Even if it's a cloudy day you will still receive the serotonin boosting effect of light. And warm up the indoor lights by changing the light bulbs, when possible, to a warm incandescent light. Listen to some inspirational music during your quiet time or your walk, and do ten minutes of inspirational reading.

- Experiment with the meal ideas and recipes in Chapters 12 and 13 and break out of your rut! Add pizzazz by selecting at least three recipes you intend to try this week. Boost your B6 and magnesium intake by including some of the foods from the lists on page 100, and try to have cold-water fish or flaxseed at least twice this week.

- Practice releasing/relaxing breathing for five minutes each day using the exercises on page 189 as your guide. Add in rhythmic two/one breathing.

- Continue to exercise, increasing your time to thirty-five minutes. Continue your conditioning work two days a week, and add in the flexibility exercises on pages 177-178 on two other days.

WEEK SIX:
TAKE CHARGE OF YOUR APPETITE

Work toward proper portions of the foods you eat—and letting food be food: nourishment for your body. Slow down your eating and dine; don't inhale your meals.

ACTION STEPS

■ How do you feel after eating? If you still feel hungry, or are craving something sweet, examine your food diary for the timing of the day's meal. Become a student of the setback; longer hours without eating will turn on your appetite and crank up cravings. Also, review "Learning Your Hunger Signals" on page 103, and begin following the ten tips to stay satisfied.

■ If you've not yet begun to write, choose a day this week to write or reflect for ten minutes. Examine how you're "feeling" using the questions on page 363. Are your feelings fueling your appetite? What are some ways to express them that treat yourself well?

■ Try some variety in your power snacks and breakfasts. Look at the "grab and go" suggestions in Chapter 13 for some fresh ideas.

■ Continue to walk, increasing the time to forty minutes, five times a week. Check your heart rate according to the chart on page 164. If you are not reaching your target zone for burning fat, pick up the pace and think about adding in some light (three-pound) hand-held weights, or cross train, adding in some new activities. If you are doing another form of aerobic exercise, monitor your heart rate to stay in the fat-burning zone.

WEEK SEVEN:
STRENGTHEN YOUR IMMUNE SYSTEM

Eat power foods—try to include each food on the Nutritional Top Ten in your daily eating plan. Keep exercising, breathing, and taking care of yourself. Add a time to connect spiritually and to connect with others.

ACTION STEPS

■ Review the Nutritional Top Ten on page 140 and assess last week's eating. Are there immune-boosting power foods that you do not normally choose? Plan to include each of these foods in at least one meal or snack this week. You might begin with broccoli or salmon. If you are not a fish eater, plan to visit a natural foods store to pick up some flaxseed. Grind them, and sprinkle them over your cereal or salad. While shopping, look through the refrigerated and frozen sections to familiarize yourself with the many different products made from soybeans. Pick one to try as your protein source at a meal or snack.

■ Add in calistenics to your aerobic, conditioning, and flexibility exercises. Use the abdominal exercises on pages 174-175 as a guide.

■ Make a list of friends in whose company you feel more alive, happy, and optimistic. Pick one with whom to spend some time with this week. In your quiet time, read about the power of spiritual connection on page 364. Identify some ways that you may begin to receive a new level of peace and power.

ACCEPT PROCRASTINATION, SOMETIMES

When we procrastinate, we are failing to get started on something— or to finish the thing we want to do. By definition, the very word procrastination appears condemning. Yet not all delay comes from poor discipline or lousy work habits. In some circumstances, procrastination may be necessary and may actually serve you well by postponing action to a time when you're more likely to be successful.

> **SMART WEIGH TIP**
>
> *Don't compare yourself to others or adopt their standards—set your own goals for wellness.*

Don't set yourself up for failure by trying to improve your lifestyle if you're distracted by other major problems. It takes a lot of mental and physical energy to change habits. If you're having marital or financial problems or if you're unhappy with other major aspects of your life, you may be less likely to follow through on your good intentions. Timing is critical, and sometimes procrastination can be a good thing.

But if procrastination is not helping you, you can overcome it without beating yourself up. Ask yourself these questions to examine the WHY behind it:

(1) WHAT AM I NOT DOING, AND WHERE HAVE I COME TO A HALT?

- Have you never gotten started?
- Did you stop at the first obstacle?
- Have you run out of steam before the finish?

(2) DO I HAVE A HIDDEN PAYOFF IN PROCRASTINATING?

- Are you being protected from a bigger hurt, like failure or grief?
- Are you fearful of something?

(3) AM I JUST NOT READY TO DO IT?

- Are you still incubating the idea, allowing your mind to work out the solution?
- Is it just not a priority at this time?

(4) CAN I COMBINE IT WITH SOMETHING I LOVE TO DO?

- Make your challenge easier to embrace by inviting your best friend to work it out with you.
- Listen to your favorite CD while planning a meal.

(5) CAN I CHANGE MY ENVIRONMENT?

- Get away, or walk around a lake, for a fresh perspective.
- Rearrange the pantry and fridge to give healthy choices center stage.

(6) CAN I DO IT A DIFFERENT WAY?

- Think about how Jane Fonda would exercise.
- Think about how Julia Child would plan dinner.

(7) DOES MY GOAL NEED TO BE CHANGED?

- Did you try to run too far and too long for your current fitness level?
- Did you plan to lose fifty pounds this winter rather than five pounds over the next month?

THE BIG PICTURE

As you begin to make healthy changes in your lifestyle, be sure to keep your focus on the big picture of looking better and feeling better *for life.* You are not on a diet. You are choosing to take care of yourself and become the best you can be.

Ask yourself more important questions than just what weight you are striving for and how quickly you can get there. Ask yourself where you would like to be in the areas of:

HEALTH _____

ENERGY _____

MOOD _____

APPEARANCE _____

MUSCLE TONE _____

WEIGHT _____

CLOTHING SIZE _____

FITNESS LEVEL _____

EMOTIONAL WELL-BEING _____

SPIRITUALITY _____

This is how one of my female clients answered these questions:

MY HEALTH: I want to stop getting sick every season—and lower my cholesterol and blood pressure.

MY ENERGY: I want to wake up feeling energized and rested, and I want to have energy through my 3:00 PM slump time.

MY MOOD: I want to manage my moods, rather than allowing my moods to manage me. I no longer want to feel like "Ms. Jekel/Ms. Hyde," positive one minute and cranky the next.

MY APPEARANCE: I want to have firmer skin, strong nails, shinier, fuller hair—and less fullness in my midsection.

MY MUSCLE TONE: I want to get a "gravity" lift so that things aren't so saggy!

MY WEIGHT: I think I want and need to weigh about 148. I'm 5'7" and that's been a good weight for me in the past when I'm fit. But I

really don't care about numbers on the scale as much as the size of my clothes.

MY CLOTHING SIZE: I want to be back into size 8s and 10s again—I'm in big 12s and 14s now.

MY FITNESS LEVEL: I want to be able to walk/run around the neighborhood and go up my stairs without getting winded.

MY EMOTIONAL WELL-BEING: I want to feel emotions fully, and express them in healthy ways. I no longer want food to be my substitute for connecting with my own emotions or with others—I want to let food be food, not an emotional or relational gap-filler.

MY SPIRITUALITY: I want to operate with a full spiritual tank—with a reservoir of peace and joy. I want to feel connected spiritually.

Remember, *The Smart Weigh* plan is intended to create a healthier lifestyle—not just shed pounds (though you'll do that, too).

You may be thinking, *But this will take too long! I want to be thin now!* Well, the truth is, it *will* take longer, but the results will last this time. You won't be fighting the same battles day after day, month after month, year after year. This is a strategy *gradually* to change the habits and attitudes that may have sabotaged your past efforts. It's not enough to eat healthful foods and exercise for only a few weeks or even several months. Remember, it's not a diet—it's a new way of living.

Breaking free of the diet trap takes thought, planning, and action. But living *The Smart Weigh* builds a powerful momentum that will support healthy goals for a lifetime. But this momentum will only be maintained through establishing practical strategies for living *The Smart Weigh*—while traveling, eating out, grocery shopping, and preparing foods at home.

PART FOUR ■ **PRACTICAL SRATEGIES FOR LIVING *THE SMART WEIGH***

CHAPTER 12 ■ *Smart Weigh* Meal Plans

We live in a society that sends mixed messages. You are supposed to live on fast food and have a figure like Twiggy. That's not possible.

—PAMELA SMITH

My *Smart Weigh* meal-planning guides give you a detailed strategy for fueling your body with the right foods at the right time. The emphasis is not on just what to eat, but how, when, and how much.

The weight-loss meal plan for women of normal activity provides approximately 1,500 calories a day; the weight-loss meal plan for men and very active women provides approxi-

> **SMART WEIGH TIP**
>
> *We all want to lose it yesterday, but it just doesn't work.*

mately 1,800 calories per day; the weight-loss plan for very active men provides 2,200 calories per day. I have also provided tips for boosting your energy quickly, and even a weight-gain plan for those who want to build up—not fluff up!

Portion sizes in each of these plans may need to be adjusted for individual caloric needs. Remember, the number of calories you need depends on your age, size, weight, level of activity, and even stress levels. So don't get caught up in counting every calorie you eat. Instead, focus on eating great foods, prepared in great ways, that

will work with your metabolism to release your body's natural ability to burn those calories!

You'll be eating plenty of food at meals, plus two or three snacks, properly balanced in whole-food simple and complex carbohydrates, proteins, and fats. But if you get really hungry at other times of the day, have a piece of fruit with 1 ounce low-fat or soy cheese or 1/2 cup skim or soy milk. Drink as much water and seltzer as you like—but definitely get in 64 ounces every day. Attempt to limit your intake of caffeinated beverages such as coffee, tea, or soda.

> **SMART WEIGH TIP**
>
> *Start fresh, ASAP. If you have a slip, don't wait until Monday or even tomorrow to get back on track—start with the very next power snack.*

It will take two to three days for your body to stabilize—and for you to feel an increase in energy and to regulate your appetite. In about ten to twelve days, you will notice when your body reminds you that it's time for a power snack or meal—every two to three hours. This is a very good thing—a sign that your body chemistries are stabilizing.

As you familiarize yourself with the meal plans below, refer to the lists of healthy carbs and proteins on pages 127-128 to refresh your memory about your best choices. The power snack choices on page 125 will give you direction in converting the following snack guidelines into a variety of minimeals. I've also provided a *Smart Weigh* grocery list (page 263) with many specific suggestions of what to bring home from the market so you'll always have handy the makings for healthy meals.

MEAL-PLANNING TIPS

- **Go for color, go for grains.** Go for blueberries, raspberries, mangoes, papayas, watermelon, honeydew, cantaloupe, apples, oranges, or grapefruit. Go for broccoli, spinach, romaine lettuce, sweet potatoes, and carrots. And vary your breads: try whole-grain English muffins, pita pockets, tortillas, or rolls.
- **Eat beans five or more times a week.** Legumes are one of the highest-fiber foods you can find. Beans are especially high in soluble fiber, which lowers cholesterol levels, and folate, which lowers levels of another risk factor for heart disease, homocysteine. (Quick Tip: To reduce sodium in canned beans by about one-third, rinse off the canning liquid before using. Or look for canned beans with no added sodium.)
- **Have a soy food every day.** This could be soy milk, soy protein isolate powder added to a power shake, soy cheese, tofu, soy nuts, a boca burger, or tempeh.
- **Eat fish four times a week.** To get the most omega-3s, choose salmon, canned white albacore tuna in water, rainbow trout, anchovies, herring, sardines, and mackerel. Or get a plant version of omega-3 fat in flaxseed and canola oil.
- **Eat nuts five times a week.** Learn to incorporate these luscious morsels into your diet almost every day. The key to eating nuts healthfully is not to eat too many; they're so high in calories that you could easily *gain* weight. To help avoid temptation, keep nuts in your fridge—where they are safe from oxidizing and turning rancid and where they are out of sight. Sprinkle 2 tablespoons a day on cereal, yogurt, veggies, salads, or wherever the crunch and rich flavor appeal to you.

The Smart Weigh Weight-Loss Meal Plan for Women

BREAKFAST (WITHIN 1/2 HOUR OF RISING)

SIMPLE CARB: 1 serving fresh fruit

COMPLEX CARB: 2 slices whole-wheat toast OR 1 whole-grain English muffin/bagel (may top with 1 teaspoon all fruit jam, the melted cheese or lite cream cheese from protein, or use the optional 1 teaspoon butter) OR 2 homemade whole-grain low-fat muffins OR 1 1/2 cups whole-grain cereal with added bran/flaxseed★

PROTEIN: 2 ounces low-fat cheese or 1/2 cup low-fat cottage/ricotta cheese OR 4 tablespoons lite cream cheese OR 2 eggs (three times/week) or 2 egg whites or egg substitute OR 1 cup skim milk or nonfat yogurt for cereal

OPTIONAL FAT: 1 teaspoon butter for toast or muffin OR 1 teaspoon olive or canola oil for cooking OR 1 tablespoon chopped nuts as topping for cereal or yogurt

MORNING SNACK (2 TO 3 HOURS AFTER BREAKFAST)

As a whole power snack, may have 1/4 cup trail mix (page 125) OR choose a combination of:

SIMPLE CARB: 1 piece of fresh fruit

PROTEIN: 2 ounces part-skim or soy cheese OR 1 cup nonfat yogurt OR 8 ounces skim or soy milk OR 1/2 cup low-fat cottage/ricotta cheese

LUNCH (2 TO 3 HOURS AFTER MORNING SNACK)

SIMPLE CARB: Begin your meal with 1 piece fruit OR 1 cup cooked vegetables OR 1 cup low-fat vegetable soup

COMPLEX CARB: 1 slice whole-grain bread OR 1 baked potato OR 1/2 whole-wheat pita OR 1 whole-wheat tortilla OR 1/2 cup brown rice/whole-grain pasta

PROTEIN: 3 ounces cooked poultry, fish, seafood, lean beef, or low-fat cheese OR 3/4 cup cooked legumes

HEALTHY MUNCHIES: Raw vegetables as desired (up to 2 cups) with lemon juice, vinegar, mustard, salsa, or no oil salad dressing

OPTIONAL FAT: May use 1 tablespoon salad dressing OR 1 teaspoon olive or canola oil to make your own salad dressing or to cook with OR 1 teaspoon butter for bread or potato OR 2 tablespoons sour cream on potato OR 1 tablespoon light mayo on a sandwich OR 1 tablespoon chopped nuts sprinkled on foods

AFTERNOON SNACK (2 TO 3 HOURS AFTER LUNCH)

COMPLEX CARB: 5 whole-grain crackers OR 1/2 whole-wheat pita OR 1 ounce baked tortilla chips (with salsa, if desired) OR 1 slice whole-wheat bread OR 1 whole-wheat tortilla

PROTEIN: 1 ounce part-skim or fat-free cheese (on bread) OR 1 ounce lean meat OR 1/3 cup low-fat bean dip (with chips above or wrapped in tortilla) OR 1/2 cup nonfat yogurt OR 1/4 cup low-fat cottage/ricotta cheese

DINNER (2 TO 3 HOURS AFTER AFTERNOON SNACK)

SIMPLE CARB: Begin with 1 piece of fruit or 1/2 cup mixed fruit OR 1 cup low-fat vegetable soup AND then enjoy another serving of fruit OR 1 cup nonstarchy vegetables with dinner

COMPLEX CARB: 1/2 cup cooked brown rice or whole-grain pasta OR 1/2 cup starchy vegetables OR 1 small baked sweet potato

PROTEIN: 2 to 3 ounces cooked skinless poultry, seafood, fish, lean beef OR 1/2 cup cooked legumes

HEALTHY MUNCHIES: Raw vegetables (up to 2 cups) as desired with lemon juice, vinegar, salsa, or no-oil salad dressing

OPTIONAL FAT: May use 1 tablespoon salad dressing OR 1 teaspoon olive or canola oil to make your own salad dressing or to cook with OR 1 teaspoon butter for bread or potato OR 2 tablespoons sour cream on potato OR 1 tablespoon light mayo on a sandwich OR 1 tablespoon chopped nuts sprinkled on foods

NIGHT SNACK (AT LEAST 1/2 HOUR BEFORE BEDTIME)

COMPLEX CARB: 3/4 cup whole-grain cereal OR 1 slice whole-grain bread

PROTEIN: 1/2 cup skim or soy milk or nonfat yogurt (with cereal) OR 1 ounce lean meat OR 1 ounce low-fat or soy cheese (melted atop bread)

★Begin adding 1 tablespoon oat bran, 1 tablespoon of wheat bran, and 1 tablespoon flaxseed to cereal; gradually increase to 2 tablespoons of each.

The Smart Weigh Weight-Loss Meal Plan for Men and Very Active Women

BREAKFAST (WITHIN 1/2 HOUR OF RISING)

SIMPLE CARB: 1 serving fresh fruit

COMPLEX CARB: 2 slices whole-wheat toast OR 1 whole-grain English muffin (may top with 1 teaspoon all fruit jam, the melted cheese, or lite cream cheese from protein, or use the optional 1 teaspoon butter) OR 2 homemade whole-grain low-fat muffins OR 1 1/2 cups whole-grain cereal with added bran/flaxseed★

PROTEIN: 2 ounces low-fat cheese or 1/2 cup low-fat cottage/ricotta cheese OR 4 tablespoon lite cream cheese OR 2 eggs (three times a week) or 2 egg whites or egg substitute OR 1 cup skim milk or nonfat yogurt for cereal

OPTIONAL FAT: 1 teaspoon butter for toast or muffin OR 1 teaspoon olive or canola oil for cooking OR 1 tablespoon chopped nuts as topping for cereal or yogurt

MORNING SNACK (2 TO 3 HOURS AFTER BREAKFAST)

As a whole power snack, may have 1/2 cup trail mix (page 125) OR choose a combination of:

SIMPLE CARB: 1 piece of fruit

COMPLEX CARB: 5 whole-grain crackers OR 1/2 whole-wheat pita OR 1 ounce baked tortilla chips (with salsa, if desired) OR 1 slice whole-wheat bread OR 1 whole-wheat tortilla OR 2 pieces whole-grain Crispbread

PROTEIN: 2 ounces part-skim or soy cheese OR 1 cup nonfat yogurt OR 1/2 cup low-fat cottage/ricotta cheese

LUNCH (2 TO 3 HOURS AFTER MIDMORNING SNACK)

SIMPLE CARB: Begin your meal with 1 piece fruit or low-fat vegetable soup AND then enjoy another serving fruit OR 1 cup cooked vegetables with your lunch

COMPLEX CARB: 2 slices whole-grain bread OR 1 baked potato OR 1 whole-wheat pita/tortilla OR 1 cup brown rice/whole-grain pasta

PROTEIN: 3 ounces cooked poultry, fish, seafood, lean beef, or low-fat cheese OR 1 cup cooked legumes

HEALTHY MUNCHIES: Raw vegetables as desired (up to 2 cups) with lemon juice, vinegar, mustard, salsa, or no-oil salad dressing

OPTIONAL FAT: May use 1 tablespoon salad dressing OR 1 teaspoon olive or canola oil to make your own salad dressing or to cook with OR 1 teaspoon butter for bread or potato OR 2 tablespoons sour cream for potato OR 1 tablespoon light mayo on a sandwich OR 1 tablespoon chopped nuts sprinkled on foods

AFTERNOON SNACK (2 TO 3 HOURS AFTER LUNCH)

SIMPLE CARB: 1 piece of fruit

COMPLEX CARB: 5 whole-grain crackers OR 1/2 whole-wheat pita OR 1 ounce baked tortilla chips (with salsa, if desired) OR 1 slice whole-wheat bread OR 1 whole-wheat tortilla OR 2 pieces whole-grain Crispbread

PROTEIN: 2 ounces part-skim or soy cheese (on bread) OR 2 ounces lean meat OR 2/3 cup low-fat bean dip (with chips above or wrapped in tortilla) OR 1 cup non-fat yogurt OR 1/2 cup low-fat cottage/ricotta cheese

DINNER (2 TO 3 HOURS AFTER AFTERNOON SNACK)

SIMPLE CARB: Begin with 1 piece of fruit or 1/2 cup mixed fruit OR 1 cup low-fat vegetable soup AND then enjoy another serving of fruit OR 1 cup nonstarchy vegetables with dinner

COMPLEX CARB: 1 cup brown rice or whole-grain pasta OR 1 cup starchy vegetables OR 1 baked sweet potato

PROTEIN: 3 ounces cooked skinless poultry, seafood, fish, lean beef OR 3/4 cup cooked legumes

HEALTHY MUNCHIES: Raw vegetables as desired (up to 2 cups) with lemon juice, vinegar, mustard, salsa, or no-oil salad dressing

OPTIONAL FAT: May use 1 tablespoon salad dressing OR 1 teaspoon olive or canola oil to make your own salad dressing or to cook with OR 1 teaspoon butter for bread or potato OR 2 tablespoons sour cream for potato OR 1 tablespoon light mayo on a sandwich OR 1 tablespoon chopped nuts sprinkled on foods

NIGHT SNACK (AT LEAST 1/2 HOUR BEFORE BEDTIME)

COMPLEX CARB: 3/4 cup whole-grain cereal or 1 slice whole-grain bread

PROTEIN: 1 cup skim or soy milk or nonfat yogurt (with cereal) OR 2 ounces lean meat OR 2 ounces low-fat or soy cheese (melted atop bread)

★ Begin adding 1 tablespoon oat bran, 1 tablespoon of wheat bran, and 1 tablespoon flaxseed to cereal; gradually increase to 2 tablespoons of each.

The Smart Weigh Weight-Loss Meal Plan for Very Active Men

(Weight Maintenance Plan for Men of Normal Activity and Very Active Women)

BREAKFAST (WITHIN 1/2 HOUR OF RISING)

SIMPLE CARB: 2 servings fresh fruit

COMPLEX CARB: 2 slices whole-wheat toast OR 1 whole-grain English muffin (may top with 1 teaspoon all fruit jam, the melted cheese, or lite cream cheese from protein, or use the optional 2 teaspoons butter) OR 2 homemade whole-grain low-fat muffins OR 1 1/2 cups whole-grain cereal with added bran/flaxseed★

PROTEIN: 3 ounces low-fat cheese or 3/4 cup low-fat cottage/ricotta cheese OR 6 tablespoons lite cream cheese OR 3 whole eggs (times a week) or 3 egg whites or 3/4 cup egg substitute OR 1 1/2 cups skim milk or nonfat yogurt for cereal

OPTIONAL FAT: 2 teaspoons butter for toast or muffin OR 2 teaspoons olive or canola oil for cooking OR 2 tablespoons chopped nuts as topping for cereal or yogurt

MORNING SNACK (2 TO 3 HOURS AFTER BREAKFAST)

As a whole power snack, may have 1/2 cup trail mix (page 125) OR choose a combination of:

SIMPLE CARB: 1 piece of fruit

COMPLEX CARB: 5 whole-grain crackers OR 1/2 whole-wheat pita OR 1 ounce baked tortilla chips (with salsa, if desired) OR 1 slice whole-wheat bread OR 1 whole-wheat tortilla OR 2 pieces whole-grain Crispbread

PROTEIN: 2 ounces part-skim or soy cheese (on bread) OR 2 ounces lean meat OR 2/3 cup low-fat bean dip (with chips above or wrapped in tortilla) OR 1 cup non-fat yogurt OR 1/2 cup low-fat cottage/ricotta cheese

LUNCH (2 TO 3 HOURS AFTER MORNING SNACK)

SIMPLE CARB: Begin your meal with 1 piece fruit or low-fat vegetable soup AND then enjoy another serving fruit OR 1 cup cooked vegetables with your lunch

COMPLEX CARB: 2 slices whole-grain bread OR 1 baked potato OR 1 whole-wheat pita/tortilla OR 1 cup brown rice/whole-grain pasta

PROTEIN: 4 ounces cooked poultry, fish, seafood, lean beef, or low-fat cheese OR 1 cup cooked legumes

HEALTHY MUNCHIES: Raw vegetables as desired (up to 2 cups) with lemon juice, vinegar, mustard, or no-oil salad dressing

OPTIONAL FAT: May use 2 tablespoons salad dressing OR 2 teaspoons olive or canola oil to make your own salad dressing or to cook with OR 2 teaspoons butter for bread or potato OR 4 tablespoons sour cream for potato OR 2 tablespoons light mayo on a sandwich OR 2 tablespoons chopped nuts sprinkled on foods

AFTERNOON SNACK (2 TO 3 HOURS AFTER LUNCH)

Repeat earlier snack choices

DINNER (2 TO 3 HOURS AFTER AFTERNOON SNACK)

SIMPLE CARB: Begin with 1 piece of fruit or 1/2 cup mixed fruit OR 1 cup low-fat vegetable soup AND then enjoy another serving of fruit and 1 cup nonstarchy vegetables with dinner

COMPLEX CARB: 1 1/2 cups brown rice or whole-grain pasta OR 1 1/2 cups starchy vegetables OR 1 baked sweet potato

PROTEIN: 4 ounces cooked skinless poultry, seafood, fish, lean beef OR 1 cup cooked legumes

HEALTHY MUNCHIES: Raw vegetables (up to 2 cups) as desired with lemon juice, vinegar, or no-oil salad dressing

OPTIONAL FAT: May use 2 tablespoons salad dressing OR 2 teaspoons olive or canola oil to make your own salad dressing or to cook with OR 2 teaspoons butter for bread or potato OR 4 tablespoons sour cream for potato OR 2 tablespoons light mayo on a sandwich OR 2 tablespoons chopped nuts sprinkled on foods

NIGHT SNACK (AT LEAST 1/2 HOUR BEFORE BEDTIME)

SIMPLE CARB: 1 piece of fruit

COMPLEX CARB: 3/4 cup whole-grain cereal or 1 slice whole-grain bread

PROTEIN: 1 1/2 cups skim or soy milk or non-fat yogurt (with cereal) OR 2 ounces lean meat OR 2 ounces low-fat or soy cheese (melted atop bread)

★ Begin adding 1 tablespoon oat bran, 1 tablespoon of wheat bran, and 1 tablespoon flaxseed to cereal; gradually increase to 2 tablespoons of each.

BUT I NEED TO GAIN WEIGHT

"People absolutely hate me, but my problem has always been that I can't *gain* weight. I've always been naturally thin, but I'm all of a sudden feeling very scrawny—and I'm tired of people looking at me like I'm anorexic."

Nicole is thirty-two, extremely active, but always a bit fatigued. She had come to me after three months of doing "gainer" shakes, and actually losing two pounds rather than gaining. She had been sick three times in the three months, and she was mad about that—"Here I'm taking great steps to get healthier and I'm just getting thinner, sicker, and more tired. How can I gain weight and get healthy at the same time?"

Nicole's plea is not such an unusual one; many of my clients find it as difficult to gain weight as it is for others to lose it. Why? Their metabolisms are on high burn, and they've developed patterns that rev it up even more. When they seek to gain weight, they want the extra pounds to be muscle, not fat. And that's just more difficult to achieve—especially since many people who have bodies that tend to burn fat rather than store it have never paid much attention to nutrition. Nicole said it this way: "I know there's been a lot of information out there about how to eat right, but I just never bothered with it. Now I'm in terrible shape, thin but exhausted, and what I'm doing isn't working for me. I *want* to meet the needs of my body the best way I can. But I clearly don't have a clue how to do that."

Nicole needed a lot more than a weight-gaining meal plan, she needed a crash course in nutrition. She needed some firm directions for a new way of living her daily life. These are some of the tips I gave her for gaining weight *The Smart Weigh*:

- ■ **MAKE EVERY BITE COUNT.** Eat power meals and power snacks *every 2 hours*, and choose foods that are nutrient-dense, low-fat, and healthy. Eat by the clock, not by your appetite.

- **DON'T START OFF MEALS WITH FILLERS LIKE SOUP OR SALAD.** Eat the high-calorie part of the meal first.
- **ADD NUTRIENT-RICH FOODS TO YOUR MEALS.** Increase your intake of dried fruit, peas, carrots, baked potatoes, lean beef, bananas, peanut butter on crackers, and low-fat milkshakes.
- **EXERCISE DIFFERENTLY.** Limit your cardiovascular workouts to thirty minutes, and add strength-training at least twice a week to build muscle. You can also do upper body strength-training two days per week and work on the lower body on two different days. Just provide time for recovery.
- **GET YOUR CALORIES FROM PROTEIN AND CARBOHYDRATES.** Hold fat to 30 percent of your daily calories. Have your fat sources be good-for-you choices such as olive oil, nuts, and fish.

This last point about fat can be a confusing one, especially if your weight-gain attempts have centered on shakes, ice cream, gravies, and fried foods the way Nicole's had. Even if you have a metabolism that allows you to maintain your weight easily, excess fat and sugar intake can nonetheless cause big problems with your immune system and energy levels.

When counseling even the thinnest people, I develop a meal plan that, though high in calories and focused on protein, is nonetheless very low in fat. I've worked with professional athletes who have needed to build up additional muscle mass. Sometimes their *Smart Weigh* meal plans include 9,000 calories! But this very high-calorie plan is still low in fat. High-fat eating doesn't add up to healthy, muscle-mass weight gain for an athlete, and it doesn't work to increase performance and stabilize energy for you. By choosing the low-fat versions of protein foods, you will get all of their goodness without the risk.

The Smart Weigh Weight-Gain Meal Plan

ON RISING

8 ounces unsweetened juice

BREAKFAST (WITHIN 1/2 HOUR OF RISING)

SIMPLE CARB: 2 servings fresh fruit

COMPLEX CARB: 3 slices whole-wheat toast OR 1 1/2 whole-grain English muffins (may top with 1 teaspoon all fruit jam, the melted cheese or lite cream cheese from protein, or use the optional 2 teaspoons butter) OR 3 homemade whole-grain low-fat muffins OR 2 cups whole-grain cereal with added bran/flaxseed★

PROTEIN: 3 ounces low-fat cheese or 3/4 cup low-fat cottage/ricotta cheese OR 6 tablespoons lite cream cheese OR 3 whole eggs (twice a week) or 3 egg whites or 3/4 cup egg substitute OR 1 1/2 cups skim milk or nonfat yogurt for cereal

OPTIONAL FAT: 2 teaspoons butter for toast or muffin OR 2 teaspoons olive or canola oil for cooking OR 2 tablespoons chopped nuts as topping for cereal or yogurt

1ST MORNING SNACK (2 HOURS AFTER BREAKFAST)

SIMPLE CARB: 1 piece of fruit

COMPLEX CARB: 10 whole-grain crackers OR 1 whole-wheat pita OR 2 ounces baked tortilla chips (with salsa, if desired) OR 2 slices whole-wheat bread OR 2 whole-wheat tortillas OR 4 pieces whole-grain Crispbread

PROTEIN: 2 ounces part-skim or soy cheese (on bread) OR 2 ounces lean meat OR 2/3 cup low-fat bean dip (with chips above or wrapped in tortilla) OR 1 cup non-fat yogurt OR 1/2 cup low-fat cottage/ricotta cheese

2ND MORNING SNACK (2 HOURS LATER)

Choose from first morning snack options OR 1 cup trail mix (page 125)

LUNCH (2 TO 3 HOURS AFTER 2ND MORNING SNACK)

SIMPLE CARB: Begin your meal with 2 pieces fruit OR 12 ounces unsweetened juice AND then enjoy another serving fruit OR 1 cup cooked vegetables

COMPLEX CARB: 4 slices whole-grain bread OR 1 large baked potato OR 2 whole-wheat pitas OR 4 whole-wheat tortillas OR 2 cups brown rice/whole-grain pasta

PROTEIN: 4 ounces cooked poultry, fish, seafood, lean beef, or low-fat cheese OR 1 cup cooked legumes

HEALTHY MUNCHIES: Raw vegetables as desired (up to 2 cups) with lemon juice, vinegar, mustard, or no-oil salad dressing

OPTIONAL FAT: May use 2 tablespoons salad dressing OR 2 teaspoons olive or canola oil to make your own salad dressing or to cook with OR 2 teaspoons butter for bread or potato OR 4 tablespoons sour cream for potato OR 2 tablespoons light mayo on a sandwich OR 2 tablespoons chopped nuts sprinkled on foods

1ST AFTERNOON SNACK (2 HOURS AFTER LUNCH)

Repeat earlier snack choices

2ND AFTERNOON SNACK (2 HOURS AFTER FIRST SNACK)

Repeat earlier snack choices OR 1 power shake (page 273)

DINNER (2 HOURS AFTER 2ND AFTERNOON SNACK)

SIMPLE CARB: Begin with 2 pieces of fruit or 1 cup mixed fruit OR 12 ounces unsweetened juice AND then enjoy another serving of fruit AND 1 cup nonstarchy vegetables with dinner

COMPLEX CARB: 2 cups brown rice or whole-grain pasta OR 2 cups starchy vegetables OR 1 large baked sweet potato

PROTEIN: 4 ounces cooked skinless poultry, seafood, fish, lean beef OR 1 cup cooked legumes

HEALTHY MUNCHIES: Raw vegetables (up to 2 cups) as desired with lemon juice, vinegar, or no-oil salad dressing

OPTIONAL FAT: May use 2 tablespoons salad dressing OR 2 teaspoons olive or canola oil to make your own salad dressing or to cook with OR 2 teaspoons butter for bread or potato OR 4 tablespoons sour cream for potato OR 2 tablespoons light mayo on a sandwich OR 2 tablespoons chopped nuts sprinkled on foods

NIGHT SNACK (AT LEAST 1/2 HOUR BEFORE BEDTIME)

COMPLEX CARB: 1 1/2 cups whole-grain cereal or 2 slices whole-grain bread

PROTEIN: 1 1/2 cups skim or soy milk or nonfat yogurt (with cereal) OR 2 ounces lean meat OR 2 ounces low-fat or soy cheese (melted atop bread)

★ Begin adding 1 tablespoon oat bran, 1 tablespoon of wheat bran and 1 tablespoon flaxseed to cereal; gradually increase to 2 tablespoons of each.

BOOST YOUR ENERGY *THE SMART WEIGH*

If you are in need of immediate energy, working to stabilize your blood sugars due to hypoglycemia (or just trying to break the sugar habit), trying to overcome gastric distress (even morning sickness), or dealing with high stress levels, follow your appropriate meal plan with these adjustments:

■ Have 4 to 6 ounces unsweetened juice (if citrus is "hard" on your stomach first thing in the morning, try "soft" juices like unsweetened apple or white grape juice) immediately on rising; follow with breakfast within the next half-hour.

■ Add in an extra power snack (see page 125) both morning and afternoon so that you are eating more often—every two hours. Adjust the timing based on your day's schedule (if you are up earlier or later). Follow this plan for two to three days—up to three weeks is advised. By then, you may be energized enough to maintain the basic *Smart Weigh* meal plan that's right for you.

■ Drink more water, but after meals and snacks rather than on an empty stomach.

■ Always have your meal's simple carbohydrate at the beginning of the meal or snack to get the quicker energy release that it provides.

WHAT ABOUT ALCOHOL?

You may have watched it on *60 Minutes*; you may have read about it in the newspaper. It's called "The French Paradox," and it's all about wine, particularly red wine, being good for you. You read that a moderate amount of alcohol, in any form, actually extends life, and may help to offset the negative health effects of a high-fat diet. Your friend's cardiologist recommended that she drink a glass of Merlot

WHAT ABOUT POWER BARS AND ENERGY SHAKES?

The question is, are nutritional bars and canned shakes the nutrition panacea they are touted to be? Well... they are certainly better choices than downing a cola and fries and calling it lunch, but they are a much worse choice than a grilled chicken salad. Better than no lunch at all—but not better than the real McCoy. A can a day won't keep the doctor away!

The problem with manufactured nutrition in a can—or a bar—is that they simply can't duplicate naturally the collection of nutrients in real food. They lack adequate fiber and valuable phytochemicals such as isoflavones, carotenoids, and other plant-derived compounds that get you well and keep you well. Even fruit and dairy-based shakes don't comprise a whole healthy diet—but they can be great as a snack or part of a meal.

And it's not just about nutrient needs—it's also about pleasure. When people turn to liquid lunches or a bar, they deprive themselves of the pleasure of real food, with all its varied textures and smells. In addition, although an energy bar or shake may provide the calories of a chicken sandwich, a bowl of strawberries, and a glass of milk, you're not getting any of the nutrients naturally found in those foods. And that's the long-term problem when these energy bars become chronic substitutes for meals or when eaten in large quantities.

The average person, even the moderately active one, doesn't need energy to come from an engineered bar—he or she simply needs to eat, and to eat often and well. Yet, the "energy" term is very seductive; people feel they're getting more than they are. What you get from one of these bars is really calories, but the term "calorie bar" wouldn't gross the same sales!

Still, if push comes to shove, and the choice is an energy bar over a candy bar, or no meal at all, then choose those that have about 220 to 250 calories, less than 2 grams of fat per 100 calories, over 10 grams of protein, and about 45 to 50 grams of carbohydrate—a snack for a would be weight-gainer, a meal for a would be weight- loser or maintainer. Just be sure to get real food at the next stop.

every night to raise her HDL cholesterol; it would be good for her. But is it true? And, if so—how does that advice fit into *The Smart Weigh* meal plan?

It is true that a moderate intake of alcohol has been found to have some positive health benefits, and the research is strong and promising enough that many physicians actually recommend a glass of wine to their patients. But also true is that, over time, excessive alcohol can result in a chronic energy drain; its impact on blood sugars increases appetite, interrupts sleep, and interferes with nutrient absorption. The extra calories it adds to your diet can contribute to weight gain, or prevent weight loss. And more than moderate intake can damage your internal organs (such as your liver, intestines, and heart) and increase risk of cancer, particularly that of the liver and breast.

The fact is, the medical benefits of wine or other spirits are just not compelling enough to encourage people who don't drink to begin. The U.S. dietary guidelines say this: "If you drink, do so in moderation." But what is moderation? It's considered to be a 4 to 6 ounce glass of wine, one light beer, or 1 1/2 ounces of hard liquor a day. Because of the impact of alcohol on your blood sugars, it's best to fit it into *The Smart Weigh* meal plan as a simple carbohydrate, substitut-

WHEN BIGGER ISN'T BETTER!

The next time you add that economy-sized box of cornflakes to your shopping cart, think twice. A recent University of Illinois study asked women to take enough spaghetti from a box to make dinner for two—no measuring allowed. When the women were given a standard one-pound box, they grabbed an average of 234 strands of pasta, enough to make two 350-calorie servings. Not bad. Yet, when they were given a two-pound box, they averaged 302 strands—a 29 percent increase, and a whopping 102-calorie difference per serving.

Researchers got the same result with cooking oil. The women poured 192 more calories' worth into a pan when they used a 32-ounce bottle as opposed to a 16-ounce bottle.

The lesson? If you're buying the family pack, be sure to measure!

ing it for one of your pieces of fruit at a meal. But before you go out and buy more booze, how about a refreshing mineral water with lime instead?

WHAT ABOUT SWEETS?

Reserve for special occasions. *The Smart Weigh* meal plan is designed to load every calorie with life-enhancing nutrition. High-sugar foods bring you lots of empty calories and little else. People who avoid all sugar for a month or two often find that they lose their craving for it. It's worth trying!

Use the guidelines in Chapter 15 if you need help to kick the sugar habit. But remember not to make *any* food absolutely forbidden. That could just set you up for a binge on what you "can't" have.

WHAT ABOUT FASTING?

As a nutritionist I am asked as many questions about wise fasting as about wise eating. These are the answers I give:

■ **PURIFY YOUR FAST.** In my opinion, fasting is a physical act of great spiritual significance: It is a commitment and a decision not to look to the world for physical food, but instead to look to God for spiritual food. Don't let the spiritual power that comes through fasting be nibbled away by the wrong motives: to jump-start weight loss, to lose weight quickly, or to rid the body of toxins. Actually, research shows that going without food for prolonged periods of time produces many more toxins than those that come through eating; plus, the metabolism slows drastically, causing fat cell lock-down.

> **SMART WEIGH TIP**
>
> *Go back to basics—are you getting the right portions.*

■ **PREPARE FOR YOUR FAST.** Eat smaller meals and snacks every two-and-a-half to three hours the day before a fast. To increase your body's store of energy, eat extra complex carbohydrates (whole-grain bread, pasta, rice) at each of these meals and snacks, along with low-fat proteins. Include a bedtime snack of cereal with milk or yogurt and fruit.

■ **CONSIDER YOUR TYPE OF FAST.** I recommend a juice fast for busy people desiring to fast for spiritual reasons. Citrus juices should be avoided when fasting because their citric acid is difficult on an empty stomach, but "soft" juices like unsweetened apple juice, apple-cranberry, or white grape juice are fine. Drink 12 ounces of juice at mealtimes and 6 ounces of juice every 2 hours between meals, along with 2 or 3 quarts of water evenly throughout the day. Avoid caffeine beverages and strenuous exercise. I recommend a water fast only if you are going into a retreat, withdrawing totally from the physical demands of daily life. Drink lukewarm or cool water throughout the day and exercise moderately.

■ **CONSIDER YOUR HEALTH STATUS.** Some people should never fast, not even for a day: women who are pregnant or breast-feeding; anyone who is diabetic or hypoglycemic; anyone with liver or kidney problems; anyone who is malnourished. A better choice if you are in one of these groups is, with the same spirit of fasting, to sacrifice a particular favorite food.

■ **BREAK THE FAST WISELY.** Don't break your fast with a huge meal or a feeding frenzy but with a small snack, then your first meal two hours later. Your metabolism has slowed down in response to no food, and it will quickly store away large amounts of food taken in after the fast. This is why any weight lost during fasting is quickly regained. Guard against "fasting" break-

fast, working through lunch, then going out for a huge meal in the evening. By following sound guidelines, your fast can be a wise—and meaningful—one.

GREAT AND GREAT FOR YOU!

For food to be enjoyable, it needs to taste great; if it doesn't taste good, it has limited power to satisfy. But let's face it: time is short. On weeknights, especially, spending less time in the kitchen becomes a clear necessity if we are to spend more time enjoying our food, friends, and family, in addition to some quiet time for personal recharge. But too often, in our catch-as-catch-can way of doing things, something is compromised: taste, health, or the entire satisfaction of making and enjoying

> **SMART WEIGH TIP**
>
> *Don't toss those measuring cups. It's a good idea to measure out portions once a month to be sure those sizes haven't enlarged.*

a home-cooked meal. Yet, many interesting and delicious meals can be made in short order.

Most cooks spend 16 to 45 minutes preparing dinner, according to a recent survey by market research firm The NPD Group. Small wonder that there's a boomlet in convenience foods, recipes that rely on pantry staples, and cookbooks and magazines promising to cut kitchen time. Studies show that people want to make a contribution to the meal they've made their families, but they don't necessarily want to make the whole thing.

That's where convenience products that call for minimal kitchen work, such as chopping fresh herbs for a rice mix or adding chicken strips to a frozen pasta-and-vegetable entrée, come in. Most people don't really hate to cook; what they hate is the stress and spending more time in the kitchen. They hate having to clean up more mess and to feel overwhelmed.

But it needn't be so! The key to great foods that are great for you is being equipped—with a well-stocked kitchen and the knowledge of how to put meals together that are quick and easy. Learning to shop and cook meals *The Smart Weigh*.

WHAT ABOUT SALT?

Although salt is certainly not the number one nutritional evil, it is a concern. The main problem is the amount we use—way, way too much. The average American consumes more than eight times his or her daily requirement—about fifteen pounds per year. This is the equivalent of two to four teaspoons of salt each day. Hypertension, fluid retention, and kidney dysfunction are just a few of the health problems to which those little white granules contribute.

In America today, approximately sixty million people have abnormally high blood pressure, and two million more are adding to the ranks each year. This means that one out of five people are predisposed to high blood pressure—and salt's impact. However, it's not possible to identify who is at risk, so it's wise to practice prevention and cut back on excess salt-even before a doctor tells you that you must.

Salt is made up of 60 percent sodium and 40 percent chloride. In the human body, excess sodium becomes a troublemaker, creating a temporary buildup of fluids, making it harder for the heart to pump blood through the system, and causing a rise in the blood pressure (hypertension). Other factors besides salt intake, such as heredity, a low intake of fruits and vegetables, a high saturated fat intake, and obesity, can also contribute to hypertension.

Unlike heredity, salt consumption is a factor within our control; unfortunately, for the majority of Americans, it is out of control. Shaking the salt habit can be difficult because salt plays a big part in the enjoyment of food. It serves as a catalyst for flavor, enhancing the taste of other ingredients. The key to making this good-for-you cutback is to learn to prepare foods in ways that naturally enhance flavor so less salt is needed for good taste. You'll notice *The Smart Weigh* recipes in the next chapter use herbs and spices which allow you to drastically reduce the amount of salt.

CHAPTER 13 ▪ *Smart Weigh* Shopping Guide and Recipes

Our problem is not in knowing what is right, it is doing it.

—ANONYMOUS

Healthy home cooking is still possible—even in the express lane. Keeping a well-stocked pantry, planning a week's worth of healthy menus, and knowing some shortcuts can simplify weekday meal preparation enough to make it, if not a joy, at least less of a hassle. Healthy home cooking is cheaper, and you can control the calories and fat a lot better.

With that said, here are some suggestions to beat the last-minute dinnertime blues and to put together meals that are destined to satisfy the taste buds and the time-budget:

> **SMART WEIGH TIP**
>
> *Plan ahead. An empty fridge after a stressful day begs for pizza. Don't leave meals to chance.*

▪ **SET ASIDE FIFTEEN MINUTES A WEEK WITH YOUR FAMILY TO PLAN DINNERS.** After a couple of weeks, you'll have menus that you can use over and over.

▪ **STREAMLINE SHOPPING.** With a week's worth of menus in hand, it's easy to cut back on last-minute trips to the store. Choosing recipes with fewer ingredients will speed you through the checkout lane.

■ **USE THE SUPERMARKET SALAD BAR FOR DICED OR CUBED FRESH VEG-GIES—YOU BUY EXACTLY THE AMOUNT YOU NEED.** Also stock up on bags of precut salad greens from the produce section—they are dated for freshness, so go for the latest date possible.

■ **GET PEELED, FRESHLY COOKED SHRIMP AT THE SHRIMP COUNTER, GRILLED CHICKEN BREASTS FROM THE DELI.** Instead of cooking turkey breast, buy 8 ounces of unsliced cooked turkey breast, then dice at home.

■ **KEEP YOUR CUPBOARDS WELL STOCKED AND ORGANIZED.** Besides canned broth, canned tomatoes, and whole grain pastas, have a few nonperishables on hand to add interest to those basics: chutneys, dried mushrooms, flavored vinegars, etc. It's time-savvy to group similar items together and always restock in the same way. Knowing what's on hand saves rummaging through cabinets when cooking and making shopping lists.

THE WELL-STOCKED KITCHEN

Take a long look at what typically is in your grocery cart. If it's a grease and sugar trap loaded with butter, bacon, and Twinkies, chances are you're not going to be producing slim fixings on the home front. A well-stocked kitchen makes the difference between efficiently putting together healthy flavorful foods versus a meal-time-blues headache or a fast-food nightmare. Now is a good time to strengthen and streamline your grocery shopping, your fridge, and, thereby, your body.

Here are some guidelines for adding the health advantage to your shopping cart—and your *Smart Weigh* grocery list to be sure you bring home "the right stuff:"

■ **CHOOSING CEREALS AND BREADS:** Whole grain is a must for fiber and nutrition. The word "whole" should be the first word of the

ingredient list, such as "whole wheat," and "whole oats." Also check labels for hidden fats and sugars; some cereals, like granola, are nutritional nightmares in a bowl. Cereals should have less than 5 grams of added sugar, excluding that from any dried fruit it may contain. Also, remember the now-available variety of whole-grain English muffins, bagels, tortillas, pitas, and crackers—your natural foods store is most apt to have 100 percent whole wheat in these bread varieties.

> **SMART WEIGH TIP**
>
> *Stock frozen veggies. With pasta or stir-fry sauces, they are quick and healthy meals.*

■ **BUYING THE BASICS:** Stock up on whole wheat or artichoke pastas and brown rice. Incorporate barley, oats, cracked wheat, and cornmeal into recipes. Include dried or canned beans, split peas, lentils, and chickpeas.

■ **FENDING AGAINST FATS AND OILS:** Do not use polyunsaturated oils, but instead use olive or canola oil in small amounts. Select reduced fat or light mayonnaise rather than the fat-free (chemical-filled) varieties. Avoid hydrogenated fats whenever possible—label-reading is a must here.

■ **PICKING PRODUCE:** For the best produce, choose what is in season—a good price and an abundant supply will tell you a fruit or vegetable is at it's peak. Ask at your grocery store or farmer's market which are the freshest buying days and where the produce is grown; search for locally grown and in-season fruits and vegetables. Out-of-season produce is more expensive and often imported. If it's imported, it may be only spot-checked for pesticide residues. When fresh is not possible, frozen is the next best choice—but avoid vegetables prepared with butters or sauces, or fruits packed with sugar. Freezing foods doesn't destroy their nutrients and quality as readily as canning does.

SHOPPING *THE SMART WEIGH*

I advocate "real foods" rather than highly processed packaged food. For example, real orange juice or frozen concentrate is far superior to fortified orange-flavored drink. Think "Mother Nature" when you shop. Your grocery store is crammed full of healthful foods, and you don't have to shop at a health food store to get them.

Follow these "trim the fat" tips when you're ready to shop for, plan for, and prepare food that looks great, tastes great, and is great for you:

- Switch from whole milk dairy products to skim or 1 percent milk, buttermilk, and nonfat plain yogurt. Look for fat free or lower fat versions of favorite cheeses such as ricotta, pot, or farmers cheese; skim-milk mozzarella; cottage cheese; and fat free or "light" cream cheese. Check the label to be sure they have less than five grams of fat per ounce. You may also want to try some of the new soy food versions of dairy. You'll get more than you're bargaining for—they are loaded with substances that bless you with disease protection.
- At the deli, go for the leanest cuts. Select sliced turkey or chicken, lean ham, and low-fat cheeses instead of the usual "lunch meats." Limit use of high-fat, high-sodium, processed sausages and meats, hot dogs, bacon, and salami.
- Use this formula for figuring the fat percentage of calories when assessing whether food products are as good as they claim: 9 calories per gram of fat x grams of fat divided by calories per serving. Buy foods that derive less than 25 percent of their calories from fat.
- Buy whole-grain and freshly baked breads and rolls. They have more flavor and do not need butter or margarine to taste good.
- Use the new all fruit jams on breads or toast, rather than fat spreads like butter or margarine.

■ Keep an abundant supply of fresh fruits and cut, munchy vegetables on hand for snacking. Buy light popcorn, breads, and low-fat crackers rather than chips and cookies. Substitute sorbet or frozen juice bars for ice cream.

THE SMART WEIGH GROCERY LIST

GRAINS AND BREADS
❑ Barley

Brown rice:
❑ Instant
❑ Long-grain
❑ Basmati
❑ Wild rice

❑ Buck wheat
❑ Bulgar
❑ Cornmeal
❑ Couscous

Tortillas, flour:
❑ Mission
❑ Buena Vida fat-free

❑ whole-wheat bagels
❑ 100% whole-wheat bread *("whole" is the first word of the ingredients)*
❑ whole-wheat English muffins
❑ whole-wheat hamburger buns

Whole-wheat or artichoke pasta:
❑ Angel hair
❑ Elbows
❑ Flat
❑ Lasagna
❑ Orzo
❑ Penne

❑ Spaghetti
❑ Rotini (spirals)

❑ whole-wheat pastry flour
❑ whole-wheat pita bread

CEREALS *(whole grain and less than 5 grams of added sugar excluding dried fruit):*
❑ All Bran With Extra Fiber
❑ Cheerios
❑ Familia Müesli
❑ Bran Buds with psyllium
❑ Grape-Nuts
❑ Grits
❑ Kashi
❑ Kellogg's Just Right
❑ Kellogg's Low-Fat Granola
❑ Kellogg's Nutri-Grain Almond Raisin
❑ Kellogg's Raisin Squares
❑ Kellogg's Special K
❑ Nabisco Shredded Wheat
❑ Ralston Müesli

❑ Post Bran Flakes
❑ Shredded Wheat 'N Bran
❑ Wheatena

Oats:
❑ Old-fashioned
❑ Quick-cooking

Unprocessed bran:
❑ Oat
❑ Wheat
❑ Rice

CRACKERS
Crispbread:
❑ Kavli
❑ Wasa
❑ Crispy cakes
❑ Health Valley graham crackers
❑ Harvest Crisps 5-Grain *(not all whole grain, but good for variety)*
❑ Ryvita Wholegrain crispbread
❑ Ry Krisp

DAIRY
❑ Butter
❑ Light butter

Cheese: *(low-fat — fewer than 5 grams of fat per ounce)*

Cheddar:
❑ Kraft Fat-Free
❑ Kraft Natural Reduced Fat
❑ Cottage cheese *(1% or nonfat)*

Cream cheese:
❑ Philadelphia Light (tub)
❑ Philadelphia Free

❑ Farmer's
❑ Jarlsberg Lite

Mozzarella:
❑ Nonfat
❑ Part-skim
❑ String cheese

Soy Cheese:
❑ Veggie Slices

Nonrefrigerated:
❑ Laughing Cow Light
❑ Parmesan

Ricotta:
❑ Nonfat
❑ Skim milk

❑ Sun-Ni Armenian String
❑ Egg substitute
❑ Eggs
❑ Egg whites
❑ Milk (skim or 1%)
❑ Reduced fat sour cream
❑ Nonfat plain yogurt
❑ Stonyfield Farm yogurt

CANNED GOODS

Chicken broth:
❑ Swanson's
❑ Natural Goodness

❑ Evaporated skim milk
❑ Hearts of Palm

Soups:
❑ Healthy Choice
❑ Pritikin

❑ Progresso:
❑ Hearty Black Bean
❑ Lentil
❑ 99% Fat-Free Chicken Noodle

Tomatoes:
❑ Paste
❑ Sauce
❑ Stewed
❑ Whole
❑ Fresh Cut

CONDIMENTS

❑ Honey

Hot pepper sauce:
❑ Pickapeppa sauce
❑ Shriracha Chili Sauce
❑ Jamaican Hell Fire
❑ Tabasco

Mayonnaise:
❑ Light
❑ Miracle Whip Light

Mustard:
❑ Dijon
❑ Spicy hot

❑ Pepperoncini peppers

Salad dressing:
❑ Bernstein's Reduced Calorie
❑ Good Seasons
❑ Kraft Free
❑ Jardine's fat-free Garlic
❑ Vinaigrette
❑ Pritikin

❑ Soy sauce (low sodium)
❑ Salsa or picante sauce

Spices and herbs:
❑ Allspice
❑ Basil
❑ Black pepper
❑ Cayenne
❑ Celery seed
❑ Chili powder
❑ Cinnamon
❑ Creole seasoning
❑ Curry
❑ Dill weed
❑ Five spice
❑ Garlic powder
❑ Ginger
❑ Mrs. Dash Original Blend
❑ Mrs. Dash Garlic and Herb Seasoning
❑ Mustard
❑ Nutmeg
❑ Oregano
❑ Onion powder
❑ Paprika
❑ Parsley
❑ Pepper, cracked
❑ Rosemary

❑ Saffron
❑ Salt
❑ Thyme

Fresh herbs:
❑ Basil
❑ Chives
❑ Cilantro
❑ Ginger
❑ Parsley
❑ Rosemary
❑ Thyme

❑ Vanilla extract
❑ White wine
 Worcestershire
 sauce

Vinegars:
❑ Balsamic
❑ Cider
❑ Red wine
❑ Rice wine
❑ Tarragon
❑ White wine

FRUITS
Fresh fruits:
❑ Apples
❑ Apricots
❑ Bananas
❑ Berries
❑ Cherries
❑ Dates (unsweetened, pitted)
❑ Grapefruit
❑ Grapes
❑ Kiwi
❑ Lemons
❑ Limes
❑ Mango
❑ Melon
❑ Nectarines
❑ Oranges

❑ Papaya
❑ Peaches
❑ Pears
❑ Pineapple
❑ Plantains
❑ Plums

Dried fruits:
❑ Apricots
❑ Peaches
❑ Pineapple
❑ Raisins (dark and golden)
❑ Mixed

VEGETABLES
❑ Asparagus
❑ Beets
❑ Bell peppers
❑ Broccoli
❑ Brussels sprouts
❑ Cabbage
❑ Carrots
❑ Cauliflower
❑ Celery
❑ Corn
❑ Cucumbers
❑ Eggplant
❑ Garlic
❑ Green beans
❑ Greens
❑ Hot peppers
❑ Kale
❑ Mushrooms
❑ Okra
❑ Onions
❑ Peas
❑ Red Potatoes
❑ Radicchio
❑ Romaine lettuce
❑ Salad greens
❑ Shallots

❑ Simply Potatoes hash browns
❑ Spinach
❑ Squash (yellow, crookneck)
❑ Sugar snap peas (frozen)
❑ Sun-dried tomatoes
❑ Sweet potatoes
❑ Tomatoes
❑ Whole potatoes
❑ Zucchini

BEANS AND MEATS
Beans and peas:
❑ Black
❑ Chickpeas/ garbanzo beans
❑ Cannelini
❑ Kidney
❑ Lentils
❑ Navy
❑ Pinto
❑ Split peas

❑ Garden Burger

Beef (lean):
❑ Deli-sliced
❑ Ground round
❑ London broil
❑ Round steak

Fish and seafood:
❑ Clams
❑ Cod
❑ Grouper
❑ Mussels
❑ Salmon
❑ Scallops
❑ Shrimp
❑ Snapper
❑ Swordfish
❑ Tuna

Lamb:
- ❑ Leg
- ❑ Loin chops

Pork:
- ❑ Canadian bacon
- ❑ Center cut chops
- ❑ Tenderloin

POULTRY

Chicken:
- ❑ Boneless breasts
- ❑ Legs/thighs
- ❑ Whole fryer

Turkey:
- ❑ Bacon
- ❑ Breast
- ❑ Ground, extra lean
- ❑ Deli-sliced
- ❑ Whole

Veal:
- ❑ Chops
- ❑ Cutlets
- ❑ Ground

Water-packed cans:
- ❑ Chicken
- ❑ Salmon
- ❑ Tuna
- ❑ Charlie's Lunch Kit

Soy:
- ❑ Tofu

- ❑ Silk (milk)
- ❑ Boca Burgers
- ❑ Tempeh

MISCELLANEOUS

All-fruit spreads and pourable fruit:
- ❑ Knudsen
- ❑ Polaner
- ❑ Smucker's Simply Fruit
- ❑ Welch's Totally Fruit

- ❑ Baking powder
- ❑ Baking soda

Bean dips:
- ❑ Jardine's
- ❑ Guiltless Gourmet

- ❑ Bread crumbs

Cooking oils:
- ❑ Canola
- ❑ Olive
- ❑ Cornstarch

Fruit Juices *(unsweetened):*
- ❑ Apple
- ❑ Cranberry-apple
- ❑ White grape
- ❑ Orange

- ❑ Nonstick cooking spray

Nuts/seeds *(dry-roasted, unsalted):*
- ❑ Flaxseed
- ❑ Peanuts
- ❑ Sunflower kernels
- ❑ Pecans
- ❑ Pumpkin seeds
- ❑ Walnuts

Pasta sauce:
- ❑ Pritikin
- ❑ Classico Tomato and Basil
- ❑ Ragú Chunky Gardenstyle

- ❑ Peanut butter *(natural)*

Popcorn:
- ❑ Orville Redenbacher's Natural
- ❑ Light or Smart Pop microwave popcorn
- ❑ Plain kernels

Tortilla chips:
- ❑ Baked Tostitos
- ❑ Guiltless Gourmet

- ❑ Water *(spring or sparkling)*

Wine:
- ❑ Dealcoholized
- ❑ Red
- ❑ White

NOTES: _____

Once your pantry and fridge are stocked with the "right stuff," you're equipped to put together meals in short order. These tips will help to stream-line your time in the kitchen.

- **USE YOUR FREEZER AS A PANTRY AS WELL.** If you're grilling two chicken breasts, why not grill twelve and store ten? Besides storing defrost and serve meals and leftovers, use the freezer for quick-to-thaw meal makers such as frozen veggies, extra cooked brown rice, and freezer-to-oven proteins, such as your advanced grilled chicken or meats.

- **WORK ON MORE THAN ONE RECIPE AT A TIME.** People tend to do one recipe, finish it, and go on to the next. And that just takes too much time. Whatever takes longest, do first. That way, the rest of the meal prep falls into place at the right time.

- **USE SPEEDIER COOKING METHODS.** Forget roasting or braising and go with broiling, sautéeing, or steaming. And try pressure cooking—particularly for preparing whole grains. It can cut cooking time by a third.

- **INVEST IN GOOD SHARP KNIVES.** You may not even need to haul out the food processor or chopper.

- **QUICK-THAW WITH YOUR MICROWAVE.** Stick frozen chicken breasts in the microwave on defrost, cook them at full power for 2 to 3 minutes, then slice the still partially frozen chicken into strips. Throw them into a skillet—they will be thin enough to heat through quickly.

- **CUT DOWN ON CLEANUP.** Try to keep the number of utensils to a minimum and use nonstick pans whenever possible. And my best tip: get someone else to wash the dishes!

- **DESIGNATE A FALL-BACK RECIPE.** Find one recipe you love and tape it into your cupboard door nearest your stove. Keep the

ingredients for the recipe on hand at all times. You'll make it when time is crunched to the max. My favorite quick meal is Baked Spaghetti. (See recipe on page 276.)

When you're planning meals and cooking *The Smart Weigh,* remember to pay attention to added fat in preparation. Follow these tips for trimming the fat from your diet:

SMART WEIGH TIP

Don't give in to peer pressure. If the cookies, chips, or ice cream you buy for the rest of the family is sabotaging your efforts, stop buying it.

- **EAT MORE FISH AND SKINLESS POULTRY, AND FEWER RED MEATS.** If you eat red meats, buy lean and trim well (before and after cooking)—and cook them in a way that diminishes fat, such as grilling, broiling, or roasting on a rack.

- **USE MARINADES, FLAVORED VINEGARS, PLAIN YOGURT, OR JUICES WHEN GRILLING OR BROILING TO TENDERIZE LEANER CUTS OF MEAT AND SEAL IN THEIR MOISTURE AND FLAVOR.** Mix these marinades with fresh or dried herbs such as basil, oregano, and parsley to add flavor.

- **LIMIT PROTEIN PORTIONS TO 5 OUNCES PRECOOKED.** After cooking, the size will resemble that of a deck of cards. This is the typical lunch portion of fish or chicken served in a restaurant. (The typical dinner portion is 9 ounces.) Let brown rice, whole-grain pastas, potatoes, and vegetables become the centerpiece of your meals.

- **USE NONSTICK COOKING SPRAYS AND SKILLETS.** These will enable you to brown meats without grease; and sauté ingredients in stocks and broths rather than in fats and oils. If a recipe calls for basting in butter or "its juices," instead, baste with tomato, lemon juice, or stocks.

■ **SKIM THE FAT FROM SOUPS, STOCKS, AND MEAT DRIPPINGS.** Refrigerate and remove the hardened surface layer of fat before reheating. As you do, think about that fat hardening in your body, and the great favor you are doing for yourself by getting rid of it!

■ **USE LEGUMES (DRIED BEANS AND PEAS) AS A MAIN DISH.** These meat substitutes can be a high nutrition, low-fat meal. Attempt a switch at least twice each week. If beans have been gaseous in the past, try Beano (available from your pharmacy or health food store); it's a natural enzyme that works wonders for digestion of beans and other gas-forming foods while your body is becoming more tolerant on its own.

■ **SUBSTITUTE PLAIN, NONFAT YOGURT OR FAT-FREE RICOTTA CHEESE IN DIPS OR SAUCES CALLING FOR SOUR CREAM OR MAYO.** Also, use these as toppings for baked potatoes and chili. (And don't forget low-fat, flavorful salsa, a great low-cal topping for almost anything.)

■ **USE TWO EGG WHITES IN PLACE OF ONE WHOLE EGG.** Egg whites are pure protein; egg yolks are pure fat and cholesterol.

In the pages ahead are suggested menus that incorporate all of my principles for preparing specific dishes and meals *The Smart Weigh*. Each menu is made up of recipes that have been designed to form a pleasing whole of contrasting flavors, textures, and colors. Each meal is designed with the proper balance of protein, complex carbohydrates, simple carbohydrates, and fat as outlined in *The Smart Weigh* meal plans in Chapter 12.

The nutrient balance and calorie count is roughly the same for each breakfast, lunch, and dinner. If you really like one of the meals, or don't care for another, just mix and match meals from one day to the next. A tuna sandwich is fine for breakfast, and an egg-white

omelet works just fine for dinner. Substitute green beans if you're not craving asparagus; leave out a spice or herb if you don't have it available. You can also use healthy foods you have on hand to create something new and personally yours.

I have analyzed each recipe for its nutritional value. Besides the calories, carbohydrate, protein, and fat grams, I have included information about sodium and cholesterol for those of you watching these numbers as well. The fat grams are also expressed in terms of the percentage of calories derived from fat in each particular dish. My meals are designed to give less than 25 percent of the calories from fat, with the average dish yielding 17 percent.

Individual recipes that are higher in percentage of fat calories are paired with those having low or no fat to balance the whole meal properly. I have used these profiles to plan balanced meals that give appropriate levels of nutrients. Portion sizes may need to be adjusted to fit caloric needs according to your own individualized meal plan. Don't get caught up in counting every calorie or fat gram—just focus on eating great foods, prepared in great ways, that are great for you.

Most of the recipes in the pages ahead have been my favorites, many are those I've developed for restaurants interested in healthier menu offerings. Many have been passed on to me by friends (often chefs) and family. Some have been developed, others "made over" for *The Smart Weigh*. There is an endless array of cooking tricks—part art, part science—to turn unhealthy, full-of-fat dishes into tasty, nutritious ones. I have used them all in these recipes, and you may want to use them on some of your favorites as well.

Basically, I use four methods to reduce the amount of fat, calories and other detrimental substances in a recipe.

- I reduce the amount of high-fat, high-salt ingredients and look for ways to enhance flavor, texture and nutritive value.

- I replace a high-fat, high-salt ingredient with a different one that is lower in fat and sodium and higher in flavor.

- I use smaller amounts of fattier foods that pack a powerful flavor punch: feta cheese, Parmesan, coconut, toasted nuts, sesame oil, and turkey bacon or sausage made from turkey. I cut the quantity to less than fifty percent of what is called for in the typical recipe.

- I use a cooking method that reduces fat yet enhances moisture and flavor. This reduces or eliminates the need for fats, oils, and rich sauces. Some of the techniques I use most in cooking *The Smart Weigh* are grilling and broiling, parchment cooking, poaching, sautéing and stir-frying, steaming or boiling, and microwaving.

GETTING STARTED

You'll find that these meals are fresh, fun, and flavorful—they will fill you with good food and good health. The key is getting started—and remember it's progress, not perfection that counts. You may start with some of the following "grab 'n go" breakfasts. Or you may start packing a more interesting lunch that's healthier and more energizing. It may be one fabulous dinner a week or elements of *The Smart Weigh* cooking sprinkled throughout all your meals. Wherever you choose to begin—get cooking and have fun!

MY QUICKEST BREAKFASTS

Don't resort to the food industry's versions of "instant" breakfasts, like toaster fruit pies, granola bars (just candy with oats), and artificially flavored and colored powdered drink mixes. Instead of going for breakfast in the fast lane—and getting much more fat, calories,

and sodium than you've bargained for—grab and go with your own quick and easy breakfast:

POWER BREAKFAST SHAKE

SERVES 1

You can put all these together in the blender container and place the whole thing in your fridge before bed. In the morning pull it out and place it on the blender apparatus and zap: you've got a drinkable "instant" breakfast that's loaded with whole food nutrients.

1/2 cup frozen fruit
1 cup skim milk
1 coddled egg white, or 1/4 cup egg substitute
2 teaspoons honey
1 teaspoon vanilla
1 tablespoon wheat germ

Blend together until smooth and frothy.

Gives 1 complex carbohydrate (wheat germ), 2 ounces protein (milk and egg whites), and 1 simple carbohydrate (fruit).

NUTRITIONAL PROFILE PER SERVING: 37 GRAMS CARBOHYDRATE; 17 GRAMS PROTEIN; 0 GRAMS FAT; 0 CALORIES FROM FAT, 2 MILLIGRAMS CHOLESTEROL, 88 MILLIGRAMS SODIUM, 216 CALORIES.

SCRAMBLED EGGS BURRITO

SERVES 1

Heat a nonstick pan or griddle over medium-high heat. Add the tortilla to heat and soften, turning it over after 15 seconds. After another 15 seconds, remove the tortilla from the pan and wrap it in foil to keep warm. Spray the pan with nonstick spray, continuing to heat. Beat together the eggs, grated cheese, and creole seasoning.

1 10-inch whole wheat flour tortilla
1 egg, lightly beaten, or 1/4 cup egg substitute
2 tablespoons (1 ounces) 2-percent milk cheddar or soy cheese, grated
1/4 teaspoon creole seasoning (or salt and pepper to taste)
2 tablespoons salsa
1/4 cantaloupe, sliced

Add to the pan and scramble. Place the egg mixture on the tortilla and spoon on the salsa. Wrap it up burrito-style. Serve with the sliced cantaloupe. Gives 1 complex carbohydrate (tortilla), 2 ounces protein (eggs and cheese), and 1 simple carbohydrate (cantaloupe).

NUTRITIONAL PROFILE PER SERVING: 32 GRAMS CARBOHYDRATE; 13 GRAMS PROTEIN; 5 GRAMS FAT; 20 PERCENT CALORIES FROM FAT (WITH EGG SUBSTITUTE), 8 MILLIGRAMS CHOLESTEROL, 613 MILLIGRAMS SODIUM, 223 CALORIES.

4 egg whites
1 cup nonfat ricotta cheese
2 tablespoons canola oil
1 teaspoon vanilla
2/3 cup old-fashioned oats, uncooked
1/4 teaspoons salt
nonstick cooking spray
4 tablespoons all-fruit jam or pourable all-fruit syrup
2 cups mixed berries

HOT OATCAKES WITH BERRIES

MAKES 12 3-INCH PANCAKES

Measure the egg whites, ricotta cheese, oil, vanilla, oats, and salt into a blender or food processor and blend for 5 to 6 minutes. Spoon 2 tablespoons batter into a hot skillet sprayed with nonstick spray. Turn the pancakes when bubbles appear on the surface; cook for 1 more minute.

For one serving, spread 3 pancakes with all fruit jam or fruit syrup. Top with mixed berries. Freeze any leftovers in individual freezer bags. When ready to use, toast the pancakes to thaw and heat. Each serving gives 1 1/2 complex carbohydrate (oats), 2 ounces protein (ricotta and eggwhites), and 1 simple carbohydrate (fruit and fruit jam)

NUTRITIONAL PROFILE PER SERVING: 35 GRAMS CARBOHYDRATE; 12 GRAMS PROTEIN; 7 GRAMS FAT; 26 PERCENT CALORIES FROM FAT, 3 MILLIGRAMS CHOLESTEROL, 97.5 MILLIGRAMS SODIUM, 251 CALORIES.

2 egg whites, lightly beaten
2 tablespoons skim milk
1 teaspoons vanilla
1 10-inch whole wheat flour tortilla
nonstick cooking spray
2 tablespoons Grape-nuts or low-fat granola
1/2 cup mixed berries
1 tablespoon all-fruit pourable syrup

SOUTHWESTERN FRUIT TOAST

SERVES 1

Beat together the egg whites, milk, and vanilla. Dip the tortilla into the mixture, letting it absorb the liquid for a minute or so. Coat a nonstick skillet with nonstick spray and heat. Gently lift the tortilla with a spatula, place it in the skillet and cook until it is golden brown on each side. Sprinkle one half of the tortilla with cereal and berries. Fold the tortilla over omelette style and slide it onto a plate. Drizzle it with all-fruit syrup. Gives 2 complex carbohydrates (tortilla and cereal), 2 ounces protein (milk and egg whites), and 1 simple carbohydrate (fruit and fruit syrup)

NUTRITIONAL PROFILE PER SERVING: 44 GRAMS CARBOHYDRATE; 13.5 GRAMS PROTEIN; 2 GRAMS FAT; 7 PERCENT CALORIES FROM FAT, 8 MILLIGRAMS CHOLESTEROL, 266 MILLIGRAMS SODIUM, 249 CALORIES.

ORANGE VANILLA FRENCH TOAST

SERVES 4

4 egg whites, lightly beaten

1/2 teaspoon ground cinnamon

1/2 cup skim milk

4 slices whole wheat bread

2 tablespoons frozen, unsweetened orange juice concentrate, undiluted

4 tablespoons all-fruit jam or pourable syrup

1 teaspoons vanilla

nonstick cooking spray

Beat together the egg whites, milk, orange juice concentrate, vanilla, and cinnamon. Add the bread slices one at a time, letting the bread absorb the liquid; this may take a few minutes. Coat a skillet with nonstick cooking spray and heat. Gently lift each bread slice with a spatula and place it in the skillet; cook on each side until golden brown. Serve each slice of toast topped with 1 tablespoon all-fruit jam or all-fruit pourable syrup. Freeze the leftovers in individual freezer bags. When ready to use a slice, toast it to thaw and heat. Each serving gives 1 complex carbohydrate (bread), 1 ounce protein (egg whites and milk), and 1 simple carbohydrate (juice and all-fruit jam).

NUTRITIONAL PROFILE PER SERVING: 28 GRAMS CARBOHYDRATE; 8 GRAMS PROTEIN; 1.5 GRAMS FAT; 11 PERCENT CALORIES FROM FAT; 2 MILLIGRAMS CHOLESTEROL; 250 MILLIGRAMS SODIUM; 152 CALORIES

BAKED BREAKFAST APPLE

SERVES 1

1 small Golden Delicious apple, cored

1 tablespoon raisins

2 tablespoons old-fashioned oats

2 tablespoons apple juice

1/4 teaspoon cinnamon

1/2 cup nonfat ricotta cheese

Place the apple in a microwavable bowl. Mix together oats, cinnamon, and raisins. Fill the cavity of the cored apple with the mixture. Pour the apple juice over the apple, and cover it with plastic wrap. Microwave on high for 1 minute. Turn the dish around halfway and microwave for 1 minute more. Spoon the ricotta cheese onto a plate, and top it with the apple and the heated juice mixture. Gives 1 complex carbohydrate (oats), 2 ounces protein (ricotta), and 1 simple carbohydrate (apple, juice, and raisins).

NUTRITIONAL PROFILE PER SERVING: 30 GRAMS CARBOHYDRATE; 14 GRAMS PROTEIN; 1 GRAMS FAT; 6 PERCENT CALORIES FROM FAT; 23 MILLIGRAMS CHOLESTEROL; 100 MILLIGRAMS SODIUM; 183 CALORIES

1/2 banana, quartered lengthwise
1/4 cup crushed unsweetened pineapple
1/2 cup nonfat ricotta cheese
2 tablespoons Grape-Nuts or low-fat granola
1/4 cup strawberries, sliced
1 teaspoon honey or all-fruit pourable syrup

BREAKFAST SUNDAE SUPREME

SERVES 1

Place the banana quarters star-fashion on a small plate. Scoop ricotta cheese onto the center points. Surround with the other fruit; then sprinkle with cereal. Drizzle with honey or all-fruit syrup. Gives 1 complex carbohydrate (cereal), 2 ounces protein (ricotta), and 2 simple carbohydrates (fruit).

NUTRITIONAL PROFILE PER SERVING: 42 GRAMS CARBOHYDRATE; 15 GRAMS PROTEIN; 1 GRAM FAT; 4 PERCENT CALORIES FROM FAT; 5 MILLIGRAMS CHOLESTEROL; 111 MILLIGRAMS SODIUM; 224 CALORIES

2/3 cup old-fashioned oats
1 teaspoon vanilla
1 1/2 cups skim milk
1/2 teaspoon cinnamon
1/2 cup apple or white grape juice, unsweetened
1/2 teaspoon pumpkin pie spice
2 tablespoons raisins, dark or golden

HOT APPLE CINNAMON OATMEAL

SERVES 2

In a small pot, bring the oats, milk, and juice to a boil. Cook for 5 minutes, stirring occasionally. Add raisins, vanilla, cinnamon, and pumpkin pie spice. Remove from heat, cover the pot and let the oats sit for 2 to 3 minutes to thicken. Combine all ingredients and cook for 5 to 6 minutes on high. Gives 1 complex carbohydrate (oats), 1 ounce protein (milk), and 1 simple carbohydrate (juice and raisins).

NUTRITIONAL PROFILE PER SERVING 29 GRAMS CARBOHYDRATE; 11 GRAMS PROTEIN; 1 GRAM FAT; 5 PERCENT CALORIES FROM FAT; 3 MILLIGRAMS CHOLESTEROL; 97 MILLIGRAMS SODIUM; 169 CALORIES

MY QUICKEST LUNCHES

(1) **CHEESE QUESADILLAS:** Fat-free whole wheat tortilla sprinkled with 2 ounces shredded part-skim cheddar cheese and drizzled with salsa—folded and browned in a nonstick skillet until cheese melts. Serve with apple slices.

(2) **BAKED SPAGHETTI:** Cooked whole wheat angel hair pasta in a sheet

pan—topped with one jar of Classico Tomato Basil Sauce, sprinkled with 1 pound shredded mozzarella cheese, and baked for 8 to 10 minutes on 375 degrees. One 3x5 (index card size) is approximately one serving. Serve with "salad in a bag" with low-fat vinaigrette.

(3) VEGETABLE TORTILLA PIZZA: Large whole wheat flour tortilla brushed with Classico Tomato Basil Sauce, topped with chopped veggies of choice, and sprinkled with grated mozzarella. Bake until lightly browned and crisp (about 5 minutes) at 450 degrees. Serve with baby carrots to munch on.

(4) GRILLED CHICKEN SANDWICH: Grilled marinated chicken breast (from your freezer) on whole-grain bun with lettuce, tomato, salsa, or Dijon mustard. Serve with fresh fruit.

(5) TURKEY AND WHITE BEAN SOUP: Smoked turkey breast (precooked) made into soup with chicken stock and cannelini beans. Serve with raw veggies and fruit.

(6) QUICK TACO SALAD: Canned black beans, rinsed, then spiced with creole seasoning and sprinkled with shredded part-skim cheddar cheese. Heat and serve over mixed greens and crumbled baked Tostitos with salsa. Serve with sliced oranges.

(7) EVEN QUICKER GREEK SALAD: Mixed greens (from a bag), topped with crumbled feta cheese and shredded Boar's Head turkey or ham, and drizzled with low-fat vinaigrette. Serve with toasted petite whole wheat pita and a piece of fruit.

(8) CHEESE BAKED POTATOES: Microwave potatoes for 4 minutes each, then cut open and top with cooked broccoli florets and Laughing Cow Lite Wedges (2 per potato) or 2 ounces of another part-skim cheese. Microwave again until cheese melts. Top with nonfat sour cream or salsa. Serve with salad and low-fat vinaigrette.

> **SMART WEIGH TIP**
>
> *Enlist professional help. Registered dietitians, certified personal trainers, and psychologists can help you deal with problems that may be hindering your efforts. If you feel like you can't do it on your own, seek help.*

DELICIOUSLY SIMPLE DINNERS

PASTA SHRIMP POMODORO WITH FRESH BROCCOLI SALAD
SHRIMP (PROTEIN) • PASTA (COMPLEX CARBOHYDRATE)
BROCCOLI (SIMPLE CARBOHYDRATE)

1 1/2 pounds shrimp, peeled and deveined

1/4 cup white wine Worcestershire sauce

8 ounces dry angel hair pasta

2 teaspoons olive oil

2 cloves garlic, minced

1 small red onion, chopped

1 each yellow, orange, and red bell peppers, cut into strips

1 teaspoon Mrs. Dash seasoning

1 teaspoon creole seasoning

1 teaspoon dried oregano

1/2 teaspoon dried basil

1 can (32 ounces) whole tomatoes

2 tablespoons grated Parmesan cheese

PASTA SHRIMP POMODORO
SERVES 4

Marinate shrimp in Worcestershire sauce for at least 15 minutes.

In a large saucepan, cook pasta in salted water until done. Drain.

Spray a nonstick skillet with cooking spray. Lightly sauté half of the garlic and half of the onions. Add shrimp and sear on one side for 1 minute; then turn and sear on other side.

Spray another skillet with cooking spray and add olive oil; heat. Add remaining garlic and onions, sauté. Then add peppers, seasonings and herbs. Allow peppers to soften, then add tomatoes, breaking up tomatoes with spatula while heating. Allow to simmer and reduce for about 4 to 5 minutes. Add shrimp, stirring all together. Sprinkle with Parmesan cheese. Serve over cooked pasta.

2 bunches fresh broccoli, trimmed and cut into small pieces

1 cup chopped fresh parsley

2 to 3 green onions, sliced

1/2 cup nonfat cottage cheese (or ricotta)

1/4 cup light mayonnaise

1/2 cup skim milk

2 cloves garlic, minced

1 teaspoon Mrs. Dash seasoning

1/2 teaspoon creole seasoning

3/4 teaspoon dill weed

FRESH BROCCOLI SALAD
SERVES 8

Blanch broccoli for 5 minutes in boiling water. Immerse quickly in ice water to chill; drain. Toss with parsley and green onions.

Make dressing by blending cottage cheese, mayonnaise, milk, garlic, and seasonings in blender until smooth. Stir in dill. Toss with vegetables and chill well.

HERB CRUSTED ORANGE ROUGHY WITH HERB ROASTED POTATOES

FISH (PROTEIN) • POTATOES, BREAD CRUMBS (COMPLEX CARBOHYDRATE)

BROCCOLI (SIMPLE CARBOHYDRATE)

HERB-CRUSTED ORANGE ROUGHY

SERVES 4

Marinate orange roughy in Worcestershire sauce for at least 15 minutes, or up to 1 hour.

Preheat oven to 375 degrees.

Season fish with seasoning and roll in bread crumbs. Spread mustard on top of fish and roll in bread crumbs once more.

Spray a nonstick skillet with cooking spray; heat. Sear fish in hot skillet on both sides, then transfer to oven and roast until done and browned.

Serve on bed of tomato basil sauce with steamed broccoli. Sprinkle with chopped parsley.

4 orange roughy fillets (5 ounces each)

1/4 cup white wine Worcestershire sauce

1 teaspoon creole seasoning

1/2 cup dried bread crumbs (purchased)

2 tablespoons chopped fresh herbs (cilantro, basil, rosemary, thyme)

1/4 cup Dijon mustard

2 cups broccoli florets, steamed until crisp tender

1/2 cup Tomato Basil Sauce (recipe follows)

1 tablespoon parsley, chopped

TOMATO BASIL SAUCE

MAKES 14 1/2-CUP SERVINGS

Sauté onions, garlic, shallots, and herbs in olive oil until onions are transparent, about 3 to 4 minutes.

Add fresh and canned tomatoes. Cook for 5 minutes at full heat. Lower heat and continue cooking until sauce has reduced by one-third.

Add seasonings. Cook for about 1 1/2 hours, stirring occasionally. Leave chunky; do not grind or blend.

This sauce may be made in large quantities and frozen (after cooling) in zip-top bags for later use. Microwave or place in refrigerator to thaw.

1 tablespoon olive oil

2 white onions, diced medium

2 teaspoons minced garlic

1/2 cup minced shallots

1 tablespoon chopped fresh thyme

1 teaspoon chopped fresh rosemary

1 tablespoon chopped fresh oregano

2 tablespoons chopped fresh basil

5 tomatoes, skinned, seeded, and diced★

1 can (32 ounces) whole tomatoes

1 tablespoon creole seasoning

1 tablespoon Mrs. Dash Garlic and Herb seasoning

★*Tomatoes are easily skinned by immersing them in boiling water for 10 seconds. Remove with slotted spoon. Skins will "slip off."*

2 pounds (about 5 large) red-skinned potatoes, scrubbed and quartered

2 cloves garlic, minced

2 teaspoons olive oil

1/2 teaspoon creole seasoning

1 teaspoon Mrs. Dash seasoning

1 tablespoon chopped fresh rosemary (or 1 teaspoon dried)

HERB-ROASTED POTATOES

SERVES 4

Preheat oven to 450 degrees.

Spray a shallow roasting pan with cooking spray. Add potatoes, garlic, olive oil, seasonings, and rosemary, and spread in an even layer. Bake until the potatoes begin to brown, 20 to 30 minutes, turning them once midway through roasting.

SEARED PORK TENDERLOIN WITH CINNAMON SWEET POTATOES AND FRESH ASPARAGUS

PORK (PROTEIN) • SWEET POTATOES (COMPLEX CARBOHYDRATE)
ASPARAGUS (SIMPLE CARBOHYDRATE)

1 1/2 pounds pork tenderloin, trimmed of all visible fat

1/2 cup white wine Worcestershire sauce

1/2 teaspoon creole seasoning

2 tablespoon chopped fresh herbs (cilantro, basil, rosemary, thyme)

1 teaspoon Mrs. Dash seasoning

2 garlic cloves, minced

1 large red onion, sliced thin

SEARED PORK TENDERLOIN

SERVES 4

Preheat oven to 400 degrees.

Marinate pork tenderloin in Worcestershire sauce, seasonings, herbs, and garlic for at least 1 hour.

Sear pork on both sides in hot ovenproof skillet, then top with sliced onions. Place whole skillet in oven for 15 minutes or until internal temperature reaches 150 to 170 degrees. May pour on additional marinade while roasting.

4 sweet potatoes

cinnamon

CINNAMON SWEET POTATOES

SERVES 4

Preheat oven to 400 degrees.

Wash and scrub sweet potatoes. Place in oven for 35 minutes. (You may add the skillet of pork tenderloins to the oven after 20 minutes.)

Cut open sweet potatoes and push ends together to "mash" toward center and fluff. Sprinkle with cinnamon.

FRESH ASPARAGUS

SERVES 4

Microwave asparagus in chicken stock and seasonings for about 7 to 8 minutes or until crisp tender.

1 pound fresh asparagus, trimmed

1/4 cup chicken stock (fat-free/low salt)

1 teaspoon Mrs. Dash seasoning

1/2 teaspoon creole seasoning

CHICKEN LAURENT WITH BROWN RICE PILAF
CHICKEN (PROTEIN) • RICE (COMPLEX CARBOHYDRATE)
ASPARAGUS, RED ONION (SIMPLE CARBOHYDRATE)

CHICKEN LAURENT

SERVES 4

Preheat oven to 375 degrees.

Marinate chicken breasts in Worcestershire sauce for at least 15 minutes.

Place asparagus spears with 1/4 cup water in a glass baking dish; cover with vented plastic wrap. Microwave on high to blanch for 3 to 4 minutes.

Spray nonstick ovenproof skillet with cooking spray. Add olive oil and heat. Add garlic and shallots to pan; lightly sauté. Add marinated chicken breasts and brown on both sides, sprinkling with seasonings. Lay asparagus and red onion slices on top of chicken.

Stir together wine and chicken stock in a small stock pot; add cornstarch mixed with 1 tablespoon cold water. Stir over moderate heat until thickened. Pour over chicken and vegetables.

Bake in oven for 30 minutes.

4 boneless, skinless chicken breast halves (1 pound)

1/4 cup white wine Worcestershire sauce

2 teaspoons olive oil

2 cloves garlic, minced

2 teaspoons shallots, minced

1 teaspoon Mrs. Dash seasoning

1/2 teaspoon creole seasoning

1 pound asparagus, trimmed

1 red onion, sliced thin

1/3 cup white wine★

2/3 cup chicken stock (fat-free/low salt)

2 teaspoons cornstarch

★ or substitute dealcoholized wine or more chicken stock

1 teaspoon olive oil

1/2 red onion, diced

2 cloves garlic, minced

1 3/4 cups chicken stock (fat-free/low salt)

1/2 teaspoon creole seasoning

1 tablespoon chopped fresh herbs (cilantro, basil, rosemary, thyme)

2 cups instant brown rice

BROWN RICE PILAF

SERVES 6

Spray a medium saucepan with cooking spray; add olive oil and heat. Add diced onion and garlic, and lightly sauté about 1 to 2 minutes; then add chicken stock, seasoning and herbs.

Let mixture come to a boil, then stir in brown rice. Let boil for 1 minute, turn down heat to low and cover. Let simmer for 5 minutes, uncover skillet, and fluff rice with fork. Cover again. Let sit for another 5 minutes.

CHICKEN PAELLA WITH SPICY TOMATO AND CUCUMBER SALAD

CHICKEN (PROTEIN) • RICE, PEAS (COMPLEX CARBOHYDRATE)

TOMATO, CUCUMBERS (SIMPLE CARBOHYDRATE)

1 pound boneless, skinless chicken breast, trimmed of fat and cut into chunks

1/4 cup white wine Worcestershire sauce

2 teaspoons olive oil

2 cloves garlic, minced

1 small onion, diced

1 cup arborio (or medium grain) rice

2 cups chicken stock (fat-free/low salt)

1/4 teaspoon crushed saffron threads (or 1/8 teaspoon powdered)

1/2 teaspoon creole seasoning

1 teaspoon Mrs. Dash seasoning

1 cup frozen peas, thawed

1/3 cup jarred, roasted red peppers, drained and cut into strips

CHICKEN PAELLA

SERVES 4

Marinate chicken breasts in Worcestershire sauce for up to 1 hour.

Spray a large nonstick skillet with cooking spray. Add olive oil and heat over medium-high heat. Add garlic and onions and sauté 30 seconds, then add marinated chicken chunks. Sauté until slightly browned on the outside and opaque inside, 3 to 4 minutes. Remove chicken from skillet and set aside.

To skillet, add rice and stir to coat well. Stir in chicken stock, saffron, and seasonings. Cover and cook over low heat for 20 minutes. Gently stir in cooked chicken, green peas, and roasted red peppers. Cover again and cook, stirring occasionally, until rice is tender, about 5 minutes more. Serve immediately.

SPICY TOMATO AND CUCUMBER SALAD

SERVES 6

In a medium-sized bowl, mix together all ingredients. Cover and refrigerate about 2 hours or until chilled.

2 large tomatoes, cut into wedges
1 cup diced cucumber
1/2 cup finely chopped red onion
1 clove garlic, minced
2 tablespoons chopped fresh cilantro
2 tablespoons red wine vinegar
2 teaspoons chopped fresh hot green chili pepper (or 1/4 teaspoon crushed red pepper)
1 teaspoon honey
1/2 teaspoon creole seasoning

POACHED SALMON OVER BLACK BEANS AND CORN WITH APPLE WALNUT SALAD

SALMON, BLACK BEANS (PROTEIN) • CORN, BLACK BEANS (COMPLEX CARBOHYDRATE) • VEGETABLES, FRUIT (SIMPLE CARBOHYDRATE)

4 SALMON FILLETS (5 OUNCES EACH)

POACHED SALMON

SERVES 4

In a large nonstick skillet, bring poaching stock to boil. Add salmon and asparagus spears; simmer 5 to 7 minutes until done.

Spoon Black Bean and Corn Salsa onto plate. Add fresh spinach leaves and place poached salmon and asparagus spears on top of the leaves.

Sprinkle with chopped chives and garnish with twisted lemon slice.

POACHING STOCK:
1 cup white wine★
2 cups chicken stock (fat free /low salt)
1 whole shallot, quartered
2 cloves garlic, minced
2 sprigs fresh thyme
2 bay leaves
1/4 teaspoon cracked black pepper
1/2 teaspoon creole seasoning

1 pound asparagus, trimmed of tough stalks
2 cups Black Bean and Corn Salsa (recipe follows)
2 cups fresh spinach leaves, washed and stemmed
1 tablespoon chopped chives
1 lemon, sliced
★or substitute dealcoholized wine or more chicken stock

BLACK BEAN AND CORN SALSA

2 cups black beans, drained and rinsed

1 cup frozen corn kernels, thawed

2 plum tomatoes, diced

1/2 red onion, minced

1 serrano pepper, minced

1 tablespoon chopped fresh cilantro

1 tablespoon olive oil

4 cloves garlic, minced

juice of 2 limes

1 tablespoon balsamic vinegar

1 teaspoon cumin

2 teaspoons hot pepper sauce

1 teaspoon creole seasoning

MAKES 10 1/3-CUP SERVINGS

In a large bowl, combine all ingredients and mix well. Allow to marinate at least one hour before serving.

APPLE WALNUT SALAD

2 Granny Smith apples, cored and sliced thin

2 tablespoons chopped walnuts

2 tablespoons chicken stock (fat free/low salt)

1 tablespoon white wine vinegar

2 teaspoons walnut oil (or olive oil)

1 tablespoon finely chopped shallots

1 teaspoon Dijon mustard

1/4 teaspoon salt

1/4 teaspoon cracked black pepper

8 cups washed, dried, and torn mixed greens (red leaf, romaine, frisee, radicchio, arugula, or bibb)

In a small, dry skillet over low heat, stir walnuts until lightly toasted, about 3 minutes. Transfer to a plate to cool.

In a large salad bowl, whisk together chicken stock, vinegar, oil, shallots, mustard, salt, and pepper. Add greens and apples and toss thoroughly. Sprinkle with the toasted walnuts.

RED LENTIL CHILI WITH SOUTHWEST CORNBREAD AND CRUNCHY JICAMA AND MELON SALAD
LENTILS, CHEESE (PROTEIN) • LENTILS, CORNBREAD (COMPLEX CARBOHYDRATE)
VEGETABLES, SALAD (SIMPLE CARBOHYDRATE)

RED LENTIL CHILI
SERVES 10 (1 1/2 CUPS EACH)

In food processor, finely chop carrots, zucchini, squash, eggplant, and onion. Spray nonstick skillet with cooking spray. Add olive oil. Heat over medium high heat. Add chopped vegetables. Sauté for 5 minutes. Add lentils, chicken stock, seasonings, herbs, spices, garlic, jalapeño peppers and tomatoes. Simmer for 2 hours.

1/2 pound carrots
1 small zucchini
1 small yellow squash
1/2 large eggplant
1/2 large red onion
3/4 tablespoon olive oil
12-ounce bag red or brown lentils, rinsed
2 cups chicken stock (fat free /low salt)
1 teaspoon Mrs. Dash seasoning
1 teaspoon creole seasoning
2 bay leaves
1/2 tablespoon oregano
1/2 teaspoon cumin
1 teaspoon chili powder
3/4 teaspoon cayenne
3/4 teaspoon nutmeg
2 cloves garlic, minced
1 jalapeño pepper, chopped
2 cans (32 ounces each) plum tomatoes

2 tablespoons canola oil
1/2 cup finely chopped onion
1 egg, lightly beaten
1 tablespoon honey
1 cup skim milk
1 cup whole wheat pastry flour
1 cup yellow cornmeal
1 tablespoon baking powder
1/2 teaspoon salt
1 cup fresh or frozen corn
1/2 cup shredded part-skim cheddar cheese

SOUTHWEST CORNBREAD

SERVES 16

Preheat oven to 375 degrees.

Heat oil in a small skillet. Add onion and sauté for 5 to 8 minutes or until onion is soft.

Beat together egg, honey, and milk; set aside.

In a separate bowl, combine flour, cornmeal, baking powder, and salt. Add to liquid mixture. Add corn, shredded cheese and onions along with all excess oil. Mix well. Spread into an 8-inch square pan coated with cooking spray.

Bake for 25 to 35 minutes or until brown and firm on top. Cut into 16 pieces.

1 medium jicama, julienned
1 medium cantaloupe, cut into 1/2-inch cubes
3 tablespoons lime juice
3 tablespoons chopped fresh mint (or 1 tablespoon dried)
1 teaspoon grated lime peel
2 teaspoons honey
1/4 teaspoon salt

CRUNCHY JICAMA AND MELON SALAD

SERVES 4

In a medium-sized bowl, mix together all ingredients. Cover and refrigerate 2 hours or until chilled.

RISOTTO WITH SPRING VEGETABLES AND MIXED GREENS WITH CITRUS VINAIGRETTE
CHEESES (PROTEIN) • RICE (COMPLEX CARBOHYDRATE) • SALAD (SIMPLE CARBOHYDRATE)

RISOTTO WITH SPRING VEGETABLES
SERVES 4

In a medium-sized stockpot, bring chicken stock to boil over medium heat. Add carrots and cook 3 to 5 minutes until almost tender. Add asparagus and snap peas, and cook 1 minute longer. Remove vegetables with slotted spoon and place in bowl to cool. Reduce heat and keep stock simmering.

Spray a nonstick skillet with cooking spray. Add olive oil; heat. Add garlic and onions, and sauté until translucent, about 3 minutes. Add rice and stir to coat grains. Add wine and cook until most of liquid has been absorbed, about 2 to 3 minutes. Add 1/2 cup simmering chicken stock and cook another 2 to 3 minutes.

Continue adding stock, 1/2 cup at a time, until rice begins to soften, about 15 minutes.

Stir in the seasoning and basil, adding more stock to keep mixture creamy. Stir in reserved vegetables and cheese. Sprinkle with herbs.

5 1/2 to 6 1/2 cups chicken stock (fat free/low salt)

16 baby carrots, shaved and cut in half

8 medium stalks asparagus, trimmed and cut into 2-inch pieces

1 cup sugar snap peas (thawed if frozen)

1 red bell pepper, cut into strips

2 teaspoons olive oil

2 cloves garlic, minced

1 red onion, diced

1 cup arborio or medium grain rice, uncooked

1/2 cup white wine★

1/2 teaspoon creole seasoning

1 1/2 tablespoons chopped fresh basil

1/2 cup grated Parmesan cheese

2 tablespoons chopped fresh herbs (cilantro, basil, rosemary, thyme)

★or substitute dealcoholized wine or more chicken stock

MIXED GREENS WITH CITRUS VINAIGRETTE
SERVES 4

Just before serving, toss lettuce leaves with Citrus Vinaigrette. Top with curly-leaved onion and sprinkle lightly with herbs and diced tomatoes.

12 cups washed, dried, and torn mixed greens (red leaf, romaine, frisee, radicchio, arugula, or bibb)

1/2 cup Citrus Vinaigrette (recipe follows)

4 green onions, leaves curled

2 tablespoons chopped fresh herbs (cilantro, basil, rosemary, thyme)

2 plum tomatoes, diced

2 tablespoons olive oil

2/3 cup rice wine vinegar

1/3 cup orange juice

1 tablespoon Dijon mustard

1 teaspoon honey

2 teaspoons minced garlic

1 tablespoon minced shallots

1/2 teaspoon creole seasoning

2 tablespoons chopped fresh cilantro

CITRUS VINAIGRETTE

SERVES 12

Mix all ingredients together. Refrigerate.

CHAPTER 14 ▪ *Smart Weigh* Dining Out and Travel Guide

Do what you can, with what you have, where you are.

—THEODORE ROOSEVELT

f it seems as if you hardly eat at home anymore—you're right. The home-cooked meal is not yet an endangered species, but meals prepared and eaten at home are at an all-time low, according to the fourteenth annual NPD Group report on Eating Patterns in America. The newest statistics show that 47 percent of U.S. food dollars are spent eating away from home.

> **SMART WEIGH TIP**
>
> *Be picky when you're eating out—ask for what you want.*

In the last decade of the twentieth century alone, dining in restaurants increased by 14 percent—and fast food restaurants captured more than 80 percent of that growth in the past five years. Every day 160 million people eat out at restaurants and 2 million children eat at one of the three major burger joints. Each day, 100 million M&Ms are downed, along with 30 million hot dogs. No wonder we're in the shape we're in!

But I can't always eat at home, you might be thinking. No, most of us in the twenty-first century are on the run, and having every meal at our own dining room table is unrealistic. But the typical scenario when dining out is to eat too much of the wrong foods prepared in

unhealthy ways. In a small study of 129 women, researchers at the University of Memphis and Vanderbilt University found that those who ate out more than five times a week consumed an average of 2,056 calories per day, compared with an average of 1,768 calories for those who ate out five or fewer times a week. That may not sound like much, but that higher calorie consumption could add up to two to three pounds on your body every month.

The challenge before the person choosing to dine out *The Smart Weigh* is to enjoy fine food without compromising health and weight. The main threats to healthy dining out lie mostly in the "hidden fats" of restaurant preparation. A typical restaurant meal packs in the equivalent of twelve to fourteen pats of butter. To sidestep some of the land mines of eating out, follow these guidelines.

DINING OUT *THE SMART WEIGH*
Plan Ahead
When you're in charge, choose a restaurant that you know and trust for quality food and a willingness to prepare foods in a healthful way upon request. Many progressive and responsible restaurants have begun to offer healthy menu selections—recognizing that healthy eating is not a passing fad.

Order Smart
Never be timid about ordering foods prepared according to your needs. After all, you are paying (and paying well) for the meal and service. You also have a right to know the content of what you are going to eat. Remember, it's your health, your money, and your waistline—so speak up! Don't be intimidated by the waiters or chef; they generally want to please you.

Most foods can be prepared without fat and butter; just order

meats, poultry, or fish grilled without butter or oils, and request sauces on the side. Good choices: marinated, grilled breast of chicken, grilled or broiled fish or seafood, and steamed shellfish. Entrées that are poached in wine or lemon juice are good options as well as those simmered in tomato sauces.

When fresh vegetables are available, order them steamed without added butter or sauces. When ordering salad dressing for salads, mayonnaise for sandwiches, butter or sour cream for a potato, ask for it on the side, and apply them in limited quantities. For example, lightly drizzle 1 tablespoons of dressing on your salad for flavor, and use extra vinegar or lemon juice for moisture.

Restaurant menus give you plenty of clues about what the selections contain. Avoid items with these words attached:

FAT LADEN WORDS

à la mode (with ice cream)	bisque (cream soup)	escalloped (with cream sauce)
au fromage (with cheese)	buttered (with extra fat)	pan-fried (fried with extra fat)
au gratin (in cheese sauce)	casserole (with extra fat)	hash (with extra fat)
au lait (with milk)	creamed (with extra fat)	hollandaise (with cream sauce)
basted (with extra fat)	crispy (means fried)	sautéed (fried with extra fat)

If you see these words, be bold enough to ask for the entrée prepared in a healthful way; that is, if the description says "buttered," ask for it without added butter; if the description says "pan-fried," ask for it grilled or poached instead.

Watch Your Portions

The typical restaurant serves twice as much as you need. And believe me, as an adult there are no rewards for cleaning your plate. You can make better choices: ordering appetizers instead of entrées, lunch portions at dinner, sharing a meal with a willing partner, or taking home leftovers for a great meal tomorrow.

Remember not to give meat the starring role in your meal choices. A healthy serving of meat is the size of a computer mouse or a deck of cards. You'll get the right foods in the right proportions for a healthy meal every time if half of your plate holds veggies, one quarter holds the protein serving, and the other quarter holds the starchy foods (rice, pasta, or potatoes).

Have a carbohydrate and a protein at each meal, never just a salad. You may order a chef's salad with extra turkey rather than ham, or a shrimp cocktail with your salad; but be sure to include a protein. Many salad bars offer protein sources in cottage cheese, grated cheese, or chopped eggs. Your carbohydrate may be a roll, crackers, or baked potato.

Finally, guard against the desire to eat all you can at all-you-can-eat brunches, buffets, or even salad bars. Your overeating ("I want to get my money's worth") is not going to cheat the restaurant out of anything, but it can cheat you out of many healthy years.

EAT-SMART IDEAS

Let's look at the good and bad qualities of various cuisines and restaurants. Use this guide to help you make better choices when eating away from home.

Mexican

EAT-SMART MEXICAN
black bean soup; chili or gazpacho; chicken burrito, tostada, or enchilada; soft chicken tacos; chicken faji-tas (without added fat).

Ask that a salad be served immediately (with dressing on the side) in place of the chips. It will help prevent the "munch a bunch" syndrome. And don't eat the fried tortilla shell your salad may be served in; those shells are grease sponges with upwards of twenty-two grams of fat per shell.

Always order à la carte rather than a combo plate, which is often

laden with high-fat side dishes such as refried beans (refried beans are made with pure lard). You can also request that the sour cream and cheese toppings be omitted from your dish. These carry ten grams of fat per ounce.

And beware of the margaritas—they are loaded with both salt and sugar, to say nothing of alcohol!

Asian

Chinese, Korean, Thai, or Vietnamese food is an excellent choice for dining out, as stir-frying is the main method of cooking. This terrific technique cooks the vegetables quickly, retaining the nutrients, and, if requested, uses very little oil.

> **EAT-SMART ASIAN:** bamboo-steamed vegetables with chicken, seafood, or fish; Moo Goo Gai Pan; shrimp or tofu with vegetables (with no MSG and little oil); wonton, hot and sour, or miso soup; udon noodles with meat and vegetables; Yakitori (meats broiled on skewers).

Order dishes that have been lightly stir-fried (not deep-fried like egg rolls) and are without heavy gravies or sweet and sour sauces. Half a dinner portion is appropriate, with steamed brown or white rice; fried rice is just that—fried!

Many restaurants will prepare food without MSG if you ask, and be careful to watch the soy sauce you add. Both are loaded with sodium.

Sushi is awesome for the enthusiast, but be sure you are eating it at a high-quality restaurant that is serving the freshest fish from the best sources. If in doubt, have grilled teriyaki instead.

Italian

Controlling the size of the portion is especially important here; the typical plate of spaghetti is five times too much. Although pasta with red sauce is a relatively low-fat choice, order it in a side dish or appetizer

portion topped with steamed or grilled seafood, chicken, or fish. Ask for your salad with dressing on the side, and never hesitate to request a red sauce rather than a butter or white sauce.

Seafood

When possible, order fresh fish/seafood—steamed, boiled, grilled, or broiled without butter. A small amount of cocktail sauce is a better choice for dipping than butter (two dips in butter = fifty calories). Remember that small seafood items such as shrimp, oysters, etc., are deadly in terms of fat and calories when fried; the surface area is so high that more breading adheres and absorbs more fat.

Steak Houses

Portion control is also crucial here. A 16-ounce steak or prime rib will give you far more protein and fat than you need. Order the smallest cut available, and plan on taking some home.

Health/Natural Food Restaurants

Do not feel "safe" here by any means! Although you will have an opportunity to get whole grains and nicer fresh vegetable salads, you still need to avoid the fats and sodium. Many foods are prepared in the same way at "health food" restaurants as at the drive-through; they just have healthier sounding names. Beware of sauces and high-fat cheeses smothering the foods, as well as high-fat dressings on salads and sandwiches. If you

have a cheese dish, be sure to use no other added fats in the meal; the cheese will contain enough for the day.

Fast Food Restaurants

If you have to eat in a hurry and can't request special preparation for a sit-down meal, at least become more aware of the hidden fats in the foods you consider while you're on the run.

- Special sauces: it's the mayonnaise, special sauces, sour cream, etc., that triple the fat, sodium, and calories in fast foods. Always order your take-out without them.
- Stuffed potatoes may seem a healthy addition to the fast food menu, but not if they're smothered in cheese sauce (equivalent to nine pats of butter per potato). Ask for grated cheese, and no butter, instead.
- Chicken is a lower-fat alternative than beef, but not when it's batter-fried. One serving of chicken nuggets has the equivalent of five pats of butter—more than twice what you would get in a regular hamburger. And the fat it's soaked in is purely saturated—usually just melted beef fat. A chicken sandwich is no health package either—it usually has enough fat to equal eleven pats of butter, unless the chicken is grilled.
- Croissant sandwiches aren't a whole lot more than a meal on a grease bun. Most take-out croissants have the equivalent of

EAT-SMART STEAK HOUSE: petite cut filet; shish-ka-bob or brochette; slices of London broil (no sauces); Hawaiian chicken or marinated grilled chicken breast; char-broiled shrimp (grilled without butter).

EAT-SMART HEALTH/NATURAL: vegetable soup and 1/2 sandwich (avoid tuna/chicken salad due to mayo); "chef"-type salad (no ham) and whole grain roll; stir-fry dishes, asking for "light" on oil; marinated breast of chicken; fresh fish of the day, grilled when possible; vegetable omelet with whole-grain roll; pita stuffed with vegetables and cheese; fruit plate with plain yogurt/cottage cheese and whole-grain roll.

more than four pats of butter, and the toppings add insult to injury.

■ Salad bars can add fiber and nutrients to a meal, but it's only salad vegetables that do so. The mayonnaise-based salads, the croutons, and the bacon bits should be left on the bar, and dressing used sparingly. Use extra lemon juice or vinegar instead.

■ Frozen yogurt, although lower in fat and cholesterol than ice cream, contains more sugar—so it is not a perfectly healthy substitute. This also applies to frozen tofu desserts. Substitute one of the new sorbet-like frozen desserts that are primarily fruit. They will contain some sugar, but usually not in such high amounts.

While many unhealthy foods await you in the fast food lane, some are also available that can make eating "fast" a part of your *Smart Weigh* plan. Use this guide to help you eat smarter at the take-out counter.

BURGER KING: Although no burger is truly lean, the smaller the portion, the less fat you get. A Whopper Jr. without mayo is filling and tasty and delivers twenty-eight fewer grams of fat than the Big King. Also try the B.K. Broiler Chicken Sandwich (without dressing or mayo; try BBQ sauce for a bit of extra flavor) or Chunky Chicken Salad with reduced-calorie Italian Dressing and your own whole-grain crackers or whole-grain bread.

WENDY'S: Order a plain baked potato (without cheese sauce—get a side of chili instead as a topping). Or try the salad bar, filling up on raw vegetables rather than potato or macaroni salad, etc; use garbanzo beans or chili for protein. Other smart choices include the Jr. Hamburger (without mayonnaise), Grilled Chicken or Spicy

Chicken Filet Sandwich, Chicken Caesar Pita (without the dressing), Garden Veggie Pita (without the dressing), or Caesar Side Salad (without the dressing) topped with Grilled Chicken using reduced-fat and low-calorie Italian dressing instead of the Caesar.

MCDONALD'S: Choose the Grilled Chicken Deluxe Sandwich (try it with barbeque sauce); Grilled Chicken Salad Deluxe (with lite vinaigrette dressing and your own whole-grain crackers or bread for carbohydrate); or a small hamburger.

CHICK-FIL-A: CharGrilled Chicken Garden Salad (with no-oil salad dressing) is a smart choice, as is the CharGrilled Chicken Deluxe Sandwich without mayonnaise and the Hearty Breast of Chicken Soup with a side salad with no-oil dressing.

> **SMART WEIGH TIP**
>
> *Tackle buffets. You don't have to eat "all you can eat" because it says you can.*

TACO BELL: Order a Grilled Chicken or Grilled Steak Taco. You may also order a Bean Burrito, but it has an extra five grams of fat.

BOSTON MARKET: Don't think "safe" here, even though this spot gives a sense of healthier fast food. The best choices are the Quarter Chicken (without skin), the BBQ Chicken (without skin), or the Skinless Rotisserie Turkey Breast served with low-fat new potatoes and green beans, steamed vegetables, or zucchini marinara. The best sandwiches are the Turkey Breast Sandwich or Chicken Sandwich, both with no cheese or sauce, with fruit salad or low-fat steamed vegetables. A great main-dish soup is their Chicken Chili; have it with fruit salad.

KFC: Tender Roast Breast of Chicken without skin, with green beans or Mean Greens. Another choice is the value BBQ chicken sandwich.

ARBY'S OR RAX: Try the Rax Turkey Sandwich (without mayonnaise) or the Rax Roast Beef Sandwich (no sauce). Or try these items from Arby's lite menu: Light Grilled Chicken, Light Grilled Chicken

Salad, Light Roast Chicken Deluxe, Light Roast Chicken Salad, or Light Roast Turkey Deluxe.

SUB SHOPS OR DELIS: Get a small six-inch sub (turkey or roast beef, no oil or mayo). Subway's Roasted Chicken on whole wheat, Tuna with light mayo, Seafood and Crab with light mayo, or the Subway Club on wheat are also good choices.

PIZZA PLACES: Order the personal-size pizza, with vegetable toppings if desired. Eat only half the pizza and save the remaining half for another meal. Or, if you're sharing the pizza with others, try a thin crust cheese pizza (topped with veggies, banana peppers, or chicken, if desired—no sausage or pepperoni). One slice for women, two slices for men.

BALLPARKS AND ARENAS: You may not know about all the positive culinary changes that have taken place at the Big League ball parks and arenas. Don't worry, you can still warble "Take me out to the ball game" and "Buy me some peanuts and Cracker Jacks," but now you can add, "Buy me some veggie wraps and carrot juice." Lower-fat foods are tentatively establishing a toehold in the Majors. Some hardcore fans—guys with protruding bellies and painted faces—may stick with beer and foot-longs, but others can choose to eat from the smart parts of the food pyramid while cheering the home team.

For example, at Edison International Field, home to the Anaheim Angels, health-conscious fans can pick three-bean salad over French fries and sausage sandwiches. At the Cleveland Indians' Jacobs Field, garden burgers and turkey breast on whole-wheat compete against fried fish, chips, and pepperoni pizza.

Of course, not all ballparks are into soy burgers and granola. At the Toronto Blue Jays' SkyDome, McDonald's serves as the main food vendor. And a typical SkyDome dessert is funnel cake—deep-fried dough covered with confectioner's sugar. But for the most part, the new foods are catching on—Subway is there providing their

low-fat-on-multigrain-roll subs, and salads with grilled chicken are standard. Water—even sparkling spring varieties—is sold right next to flowing beer.

Your eat-smart strategy is not to go into the stands starving and parched, but to top off the tank before you go—and go for the best choices you can while you're there.

Appetizers

Many restaurants specialize in appetizers: fried cheese; nachos; fried potato skins loaded with bacon, sour cream, and cheese; fried zucchini and mushrooms; those gigantic onion "blossoms." These are cardiovascular nightmares when you consider that two potato skins or two pieces of fried cheese are basically the fat calories of a whole meal (and should be used as such). Many restaurants are offering raw vegetable platters, but the dip will negate the value of the veggies. If you indulge, do so very carefully.

> **EAT-SMART APPETIZERS:** chicken burritos or fajitas; grilled seafood; marinated chicken breast; non-creamed soup.

Breakfast

Breakfast can be a special meal out because most restaurants offer safe and easy choices. If breakfast is later than normal, energize with a snack when you arise, then the later meal. You also may choose to have your larger lunch portions for breakfast and a smaller lunch three to four hours later. Follow these guidelines in ordering:

> **EAT-SMART BREAKFAST:** Eggs scrambled (without fat), or egg substitute, and whole wheat toast or English muffin; French toast (with whole wheat bread) and berries; fresh vegetable and egg-white omelet and toast; whole-grain cereal with skim milk and fruit; Fresh fruit bowl with cottage cheese and whole wheat toast.

- Order whole wheat toast or grits unbuttered; then add one teaspoon of butter, if desired.

- Ordering à la carte is usually safer so that you are not tempted by the abundance of food in the "breakfast specials" or buffets.
- Be bold and creative in ordering. Rather than accepting French toast with syrup and bacon, ask for it prepared with whole wheat bread, no syrup, and a side of fresh berries or fruit instead. Some restaurants will substitute cottage cheese or one egg for the meat. Many also serve oatmeal and cereal even though it's not always on the menu. It's a nice carbohydrate with milk and fresh fruit, especially strawberries or blueberries.
- Always look for a protein and a carbohydrate source. A Danish doesn't do it!

SMART WEIGH SNACKS

Your best eat-smart snack strategy is to keep wisely prepared power snacks wherever you are. Human nature is such that if the right food isn't available, we're apt to reach for the wrong thing—or push through on fumes with no fuel at all. Instead, keep power snacks in your desk drawer, briefcase, or suitcase (refer to the power snack suggestions on page 125).

If the best-laid plans fail and you find yourself face-to-face with the vending machine, wondering which buttons to push, think of this chart below—and go for the tasty, easy-to-find, low-fat yet high-voltage alternatives to all your favorite "sure-to-burn-out-quick" treats.

TRAVELING THE SMART WEIGH

Traveling is stressful and depleting in the best of times—even if you're on your way to a week in the sunny Caribbean. And for the road warrior—the one who does business "by air"—there seems to be no end to travel. While your friends and neighbors might think

your job is glamorous, we both know traveling is exhausting. It's not unusual to arrive at your destination dehydrated, drained, and disoriented—surely unfit to be productive or even to have fun. This is especially the case when traveling by air.

Flying causes anxiety. So does rushing to the airport at the last minute, unloading those bags, and lugging that briefcase. Try to arrive at the airport with enough time to relax for a few minutes. Give yourself (and the ticket counter staff) adequate time to get you checked in and your luggage safely on board.

EAT-SMART IDEAS:

INSTEAD OF...	CHOOSE...
Snickers bar (280 calories/14 grams fat/6 grams protein)	Crisp apple, mozzarella string cheese (115 calories/ 4 grams fat/ 7 grams protein)
1.74 ounces bag peanut M & M's (250 calories/13 grams fat/5 grams protein)	2 whole-wheat Wasa crisp breads with 8 ounces Stonyfield Farm nonfat yogurt (270 calories/1 gram fat/12 grams protein)
60 Ruffles potato chips (560 calories/35 grams fat/7 grams protein)	24 Baked Lays potato crisps, 1 ounces part-skim cheddar cheese (300 calories/6 grams fat/11 grams protein)
16 ounces Coca-Cola Classic, 6 Ritz crackers (299 calories/5 grams fat/2 grams protein)	Bottle of water; turkey sandwich with 1 slice bread, 1/4-pound turkey, lettuce, tomato, mustard (214 calories, 5 grams fat/24 grams protein)
4 cups microwave popcorn, 1 bottle Snapple Iced Tea (240 calories/7 grams fat/3 grams protein)	4 cups light microwave popcorn, tall Starbucks Frappuccino (248 calories/4 grams fat/6 grams protein)
1 jelly doughnut (220 calories/9 grams fat/4 grams protein)	1/2 whole-grain bagel with 2 tbsp light cream cheese, 1 teaspoons all fruit jam (141 calories, 4 grams fat, 8 grams protein)
Wendy's medium Frosty (440 calories/11 grams fat/11 grams protein)	1/2 cup vanilla yogurt and fresh berries sprinkled with 1/4 cup low-fat granola (205 calories/1 gram fat/6 grams protein)

Use these tips to help keep you in tip-top shape for the rest of the trip: energized, strong, and healthy.

Drink Up

Water, that is. Flying is dehydrating; the pressurized cabin air is ten times more arid than the desert, causing you to lose fluid through your skin. This leads to puffy hands and ankles, fatigue, and a bloated feeling. So drink lots of water—the suggested 8 glasses a day plus an additional 8 to 12 ounces for each hour in the air. And limit your consumption of alcohol on planes; it is a major dehydrator and has more impact in the air than on the ground. Hint: When the flight attendant asks what you want to drink, ask for water.

Jet Fuel for Jet Travel

Whether a business traveler or a vacationer, you want to be bright-eyed when you arrive at your destination. So don't forget to maintain good nutrition while you're traveling. To short-circuit the stress sequence that accompanies you on your trip, eat adequate pre-flight complex carbs (some whole-wheat bread, cereal, or a banana) with low-fat proteins. Moderate your intake of refined carbohydrates and sugars before and during the trip. Eat more protein and low-fat fare (low-fat dairy products, grilled meats, eggs) to boost your alertness.

On travel days, try not to go more than three hours without a healthy meal or snack. Carry a few convenient power snacks (like trail mix or dried fruit with Laughing Cow Lite Wedges) in your briefcase or purse. While everybody else is eating salted peanuts, you'll be stoking your own furnace with protein and good calories.

Pack some power snacks to keep you on track once you arrive at your destination, too. Eating on some kind of an even schedule will necessitate having your own power snacks available—enabling you

to eat the right foods at the right time regardless of where you find yourself during the day. Power snacks will help you accomplish "smart eating on the move" and will keep your stressed and lagging metabolism burning high. Pack foods that don't need refrigeration, such as the trail mix or dried fruits and cheese mentioned above. I take along boxed milk as well.

Airport and airline food can do real damage to your energy and your plan to eat *The Smart Weigh*. Stay away from caffeine in colas and coffee, and don't get trapped by the high-fat, spicy, and sweet foods throughout the airport. Generally it's wise to order a special meal for air travel (give your airline twenty-four hours' notice). Diabetic meals are highest in protein, fiber, and freshness, and you can enjoy them at no extra cost.

Car Travel

When you drive to your destination, don't be seduced into stopping at the first fast food restaurant or stockpiling a bunch of high-fat, high-sugar snacks when you stop for gas. Surprise everyone—maybe even yourself—by bringing along a bag of healthy snacks. Also make brief stops to stretch, exercise, and breath deeply so you arrive relaxed rather than stiff and bloated.

Rub in Relaxation

During the trip, put your fingers to your shoulder muscles or temple, and massage. If it hurts, it probably means your muscles are tight. If you're flying, use some of the flight time to relax your muscles and to breathe deeply. You'll arrive at your destination that much more rested. If you are at an exit row or by the aisle, use the space to stretch your legs and do some ankle rotations.

Stay in Shape

How many times have you packed your workout clothes but never made it to the hotel's spa or gym? What about those times you attended a conference at a beachfront hotel or golf course, but you never set foot outside the doors once the meetings started? At the very least, plan on a brisk walk each day during your stay, and make time to use the pool or exercise room. You'll be surprised how changing into workout clothes, taking a walk, and breathing deeply will recharge you for the next event or meeting.

Even if you're sightseeing, and are beat from all the walking, you'll still receive an energy and metabolic boost from a focused ten-minute walk that doesn't have you stopping for traffic or great buys.

Give Yourself a Break

Resist the temptation to schedule every moment with activities and people. Leave some quiet time in which to be recharged and revitalized without interruptions. Just a ten-minute time-out—even a power nap—in the middle of your day can restore your alertness and enhance performance.

Finally, Sleep

Road warriors probably know the inside of hotels better than their travel agents. Though there is nothing like your own bed, try to get the same number of hours of sleep at the hotel as you usually get at home. If there's room in your luggage, packing your own pillow will give you a better chance of good shut-eye. And don't use that room minibar for a nightcap as you unwind at day's end. Watch out for those chocolate mints and sweet amenities hotels like to give as your good-night kiss, too.

TIME ZONE BLUES

Jet lag is more than just a sense of being tired; it is an actual discrepancy in the body's intrinsic biological sleep cycle, or "circadian rhythm." Your body's sleep cycle is controlled by the daily alternating sunlight and darkness patterns you experience. When you travel to a new time zone, your circadian rhythm remains on its original biological schedule for several days—so your body's internal clock and the external clock are saying two different things. Your body is telling you to sleep in the middle of the afternoon or turn on in the middle of the night.

Symptoms of time zone blues are fatigue, insomnia, headaches, indigestion, disorientation, and metabolic slowdown—adding up to a serious drain on your enjoyment—not to mention your body's natural ability to process the food you eat efficiently.

Here are some anti-jet lag tips to help reduce the strain:

- Get plenty of sleep during the days and weeks before traveling across time zones, or when daylight-saving time begins (the first Sunday in April) and ends (the last Sunday in October). Starting your trip fully rested will ease the transition.

  Change your bedtime three nights before you depart. If you're traveling west, go to bed one hour later for each time zone difference you experience (up to three hours). If you're traveling east, do the opposite: start going to bed one hour earlier for each time zone (again, up to three hours). Limit your intake of stimulants such as caffeine and alcohol, particularly three hours before you plan to go to bed.

- Get into the day/night cycle of the time zone you're going to as quickly as possible after you arrive. Don't hide in dark museums or hotel rooms upon arrival at your destination—

stay out in the daylight. Light acts as a powerful cue to your body, telling your internal clock where you are and what schedule to keep. So does exercise. When you fly east, attempt to exercise at least thirty minutes in the morning sun. When you fly west, attempt to exercise at least thirty minutes in the late afternoon sun.

This is one time to resist napping; instead try to keep moving during the day and go to bed in the evening.

■ Be careful with sleep medications; they don't resolve the biological imbalance caused by jet lag. Melatonin supplements *can* be used to correct circadian disorders, but don't take this hormone without first consulting a doctor, and definitely not for long periods of time. Other than occasional use as an anti-jet lag measure, melatonin taken at the wrong time or in high doses can *cause* sleepiness, sleep disturbance, and impaired work or driving performance—and it may actually shift circadian rhythms in the wrong direction. Moreover, since the Food and Drug Administration doesn't regulate melatonin and other "dietary supplements" for safety and efficacy, there are no standards for purity or dosages.

Don't be discouraged and think you can't ever eat out or travel healthfully. You can have healthy meals away from home; it's just a matter of learning to make good choices. The trick is to learn what you *can* eat, and then follow through. Rather than feeling dismayed or overwhelmed about everything on a menu that doesn't fit into eating *The Smart Weigh*, use your creativity and knowledge to find good things that do.

PART FIVE ■ LIVING FREE FROM THE TRAP

CHAPTER 15 ▪ Kicking the Habit: Sugar and Caffeine

The man who believes he can do something is probably right, and so is the man who believes he can't.

—ANONYMOUS

Mary had been counseling with me for seven months when her birthday rolled around. Although rejoicing in her new healthy life (and a weight loss of over forty pounds), she was now gripped with fear that birthday treats would sabotage all the progress she'd made.

"Honestly, Pam," Mary confided, "I feel like an addict—and my drug of choice has always been sweets. It may start as just a little piece of birthday cake, but it's a bowl of Haagen-Dazs before I go to bed. And, history has shown that once I've started, it doesn't stop. I just *have* to do it differently this year."

> **SMART WEIGH TIP**
>
> *Don't deprive yourself. There is no forbidden food, just some you may choose not to have.*

Mary's experience is a familiar one. Sweets do taste great, but for many the pull is much stronger than a taste bud tickle. The craving for sugar takes on an unnatural drive.

One of the biggest blunders we make in eating isn't about eating at all. It's about depending on food for a chemical brain boost to get us through the rough times when energy is low and we're being

dealt some bad cards. The two prime examples of substances we give too much power to are sugar and caffeine. Let's take a look at breaking their grip.

OUT OF THE SUGAR TRAP

A heavy sugar intake brings a pleasurable rise in feel-good brain chemicals that will be followed by a quick fall a few hours later. That dip often triggers "eating for a lift" to relieve the fatigue, brain fog, and mood drop. Usually the chosen food is again high in sugar, and the seesaw effect continues. Then the guilt tapes begin to play: *You've already blown it, so go ahead and finish the cookies before you get "back" to healthy eating.* And the more you eat, the more you crave, trying to get that same boost.

Equalizing your brain chemistries is a key to living *The Smart Weigh* because too-low levels of serotonin and endorphins trigger the craving for a drug that will provide fuel for these neurotransmitters. Not everyone is as sugar sensitive as Mary—not everyone turns a bite of chocolate into an addictive drug. But there is evidence that some people use sweet foods and refined carbohydrates as powerful mood-altering drugs—and experience the similar roller-coaster of behavior and thoughts of an addict.

People without such an inflammatory chemical response will experience a pleasurable feeling from the rise in brain chemicals that follows eating refined carbohydrates and sweets. But people with a heightened sensitivity will experience a powerful euphoria—not just feeling good, but feeling *great*. These people can be trapped in a vicious cycle of highs and lows controlled by soaring and plummeting body chemistries. Even those who violently oppose drinking or the use of street drugs can get on a different addiction—sugar, ice cream, chocolate, and soda. And the dependency can be just as

strong. In fact, if you have used alcohol or drugs in an addictive way some time in your life, it's very likely that your body's chemistry responds more intensely to these chemicals than other people's. This body chemistry doesn't change in sobriety from, say, alcohol; it often just finds another "drug of choice"—and that is often sweets.

The amount of sugar added to foods eaten by an average American in one day? Nineteen teaspoons, or 304 calories. That includes sugars added by manufacturers to foods like soda, flavored yogurts, and cookies—as well as those added directly by the consumer, such as to iced tea or cereals. The amount of weight you'll lose in one year if you cut that added sugar in half? Sixteen pounds for an average adult.

If sugar is affecting your well-being, make it your goal to cut back on your daily use of sweets and other refined carbs and eat whole carbohydrates and fruits to stabilize your body chemistries and satisfy your natural craving for sugar. Sweets are not worth robbing yourself of your precious energy and stamina.

For help in kicking the sugar habit, use these tips:

KNOW YOUR ENEMY. Sugar is called by many names—honey, brown sugar, corn syrup, fructose, and so on—but it's all sugar. Much of our problem with sugar lies in the fact that it is hidden in nearly every packaged product on the grocer's shelf. American consumption has risen to 146 pounds per person per year, mainly from prepared foods.

Beware if sugar, or another name for sugar (like any word ending in –ose), is in the top three ingredients in a packaged product. If it is, you're getting more than you're bargaining for. Also realize that sugar is hidden in refined carbohydrates that have been stripped of their fibers and nutrients, giving a quick "rush" into your blood-

stream, followed by a rush of feel-good chemicals from your brain. No wonder it can seem to have such power.

KNOW YOURSELF. How much is enough for you—and how much triggers the desire for more? Does nibbling a little bit of sweets lead to a lot? Mary found that even occasionally eating high-sugar foods was difficult for her—she *was* hurt by "just a little bit." It wasn't about the calories or sugar's health risk, it was the effect it had on her body. The seesaw effect resulted in a "more she has, more she wants" syndrome.

If this sounds familiar, it may be necessary for you to "just say no" to sugar-laden foods for long enough (twelve to fourteen days) to allow your blood sugar and brain chemical levels to stabilize, and to allow your energy and appetite for healthy foods to return. Only then can you assess the impact sweets can have on your body—and on your resolve.

KNOW THAT WITHDRAWAL IS REAL. If you are sugar sensitive, you are apt to experience physical symptoms of drug-deprivation. You may feel shaky, nauseous, edgy, or experience headaches or diarrhea.

As you embark on any healthy lifestyle change—especially as chemically impacting as pulling back from a high intake of sugar—your body needs time to adjust physiologically and emotionally. It will take at least five to six days before the change begins to feel comfortable physically. You can expect the following:

DAY 1 AND 2: You may feel slightly sluggish, irritable, and dissatisfied with your eating.

DAY 3: This will be one of your most difficult days as your body begins to feel the chemical change. It may seem that every cell in your body is crying out for food, particularly something sweet. But the urge for sweets is not impossible to overcome.

DAY 4: If you make it through the third day without overeating or homicide, this one won't be so difficult.

DAY 5: This may be a day of a ravenous appetite; you can expect to be hungry for food—not sweets necessarily, just food. You can eat a full meal and still think: *That was a good appetizer—what else is there to eat?*

DAY 6 AND 7: By now it should be getting easier and easier; you have more energy, and you have more control over your appetite. You are now on the road to a lifetime of good eating. The surprise of feeling good makes it all worth the effort.

I know these symptoms may sound more like withdrawal from hard drugs than simply allowing your body to adjust to a wonderfully healthy way of eating. But let's face reality: putting in healthy foods means leaving out the unhealthy, and that means a chemical change—a withdrawal of sorts. If you recognize that the chemical changes are necessary, but temporary, it will be easier for you to break through to a lifetime of good eating.

KNOW WHEN YOU'RE VULNERABLE. Identify—and avoid—resolve-breakers like fatigue, hunger, anger, or loneliness. If you need something when you're tired, to "get through," break for a nap even if it is more difficult rather than reaching for the cookies. If you have spent a lifetime pushing down anger with food you should switch to the more difficult but healthier choice—write away your anger in a journal or discuss its cause with someone.

KNOW THE DRILL. Resist the "I've Already Blown It" Syndrome. Even when you succumb to temptation and consume foods you know interfere with your health, be assured that a lapse in healthy eating doesn't ruin all the health you have attained over weeks of wellness.

A lapse is just that—a lapse. Don't let it become a relapse, another relapse, and finally a collapse. Look at each meal and snack as an event—don't wrap it all into one bad day or one unhealthy weekend. Instead, get right back on track with the next meal or snack. Your body will stabilize quickly, you'll feel great, and you'll be thanking yourself the next day.

KNOW THAT IT WILL GET EASIER. Although we are born with a natural preference toward foods with a sweet taste, these preferences have been overdeveloped and fueled by a lifetime of high sugar intake and erratic eating patterns. As you cut back, over time, your cravings diminish and your taste buds regain their ability to pick up the sweetness in a carrot or piece of fruit.

"POWER SNACK" THROUGHOUT THE DAY. Just in case it hasn't sunk in yet: eating every two to three hours throughout the day keeps your energy okay and a ravenous appetite away. Go for energy-boosting combos like fresh fruit or a box of raisins with low-fat cheese or yogurt, a half sandwich, or a trail mix of dry roasted peanuts and sunflower seeds mixed with dried fruit. Keep power snacks available wherever you are—they will serve as a lift to your body and prevent the drowsiness and sweet cravings that often follow meals.

RELY ON THE NATURAL SWEET TREAT. Fruit naturally fulfills our sweet desires. And remember to go for the fruit, not the fruit juice; the fiber slows the release of the fruit's simple carbohydrate, which prevents blood sugar spikes and insulin surges.

CONSUME ENOUGH FIBER. Remember that water-soluble fibers—found in oats, barley, brown rice, apples, dried beans, and nuts—serve as a "time-release capsule," releasing sugars from digested carbohydrates slowly and evenly into the bloodstream. This helps keep your energy levels up and even and your cravings down.

SAVE THE BEST FOR LAST. If you do have sweets, add a dessert to the

end of the meal rather than having the treat *as* your meal, or your snack. This allows the balanced meal to temper the insulin surge, keeping blood sugars more stable.

WHAT ABOUT ARTIFICIAL SWEETENERS?

As you become aware (and possibly alarmed) about your intake of sugar, you may be tempted to use sugar substitutes. Don't. There are no absolutes in the safety of chemicals—saccharin, aspartame, or any new one to come along. The long-term effects of their use will not be known for years.

For example, in the short time since aspartame has appeared on the market (as Nutrasweet), cautions concerning its use have accelerated. Questions have been posed about its allergic reaction in some; its impact on brain chemistry due to its crossing the blood barrier of the brain; its danger with possible breakdown in hot foods; its effect on children and the unborn; and it's connection to the rise in brain tumor incidence. The verdict is not in.

And the battle will continue, for even though aspartame is made from natural sources, it is still made in a laboratory and is not found in nature. The possibility that problems might occur from frequent use is real, as, for example, hindering the brain's formation of serotonin, causing the let-down that follows an aspartame intake to bring anxiety and depression—and an increased appetite.

Also consider that aspartame is made from phenylalanine, which is an amino acid. High doses of a single amino acid can throw off the balance of amino acids in your brain and body. Because phenylalanine is a precursor to dopamine and norepinephrine, which are stimulating neurotransmitters, high usage of aspartame can create a "speed-like" effect. There is also concern about aspartame's potential to keep insulin levels elevated, thereby heightening the risk of dis-

ease and adding to the obesity problem. Remember, foods alone don't make insulin rise; just the sight, smell, and taste of food can do it. But, in the case of artificially sweetened beverages, there are no calories for the insulin to work with—so the blood sugar level drops, stimulating hunger.

Finally, understand that as long as you continue to use sugar-laden foods or sugar substitutes, you will keep your taste buds trained for sugar. The goal is to cut back on its use so you no longer need everything to taste sweet. Allow your taste buds to change so that the desire for sweetness can be met in a safe way—from fruits and other naturally sweet foods.

TAKING BACK YOUR POWER

As important as it was for Mary to come to understand the chemical power of sweets, it was also crucial that she identify the emotional war going on within her related to food—particularly sweets. Because, for Mary, the trap was two-pronged: physical and emotional.

Her personal war was rooted in her chemical sensitivity and physical reaction to the foods she ate, as well as in the powerful emotional charge she had placed on food. Breaking free of its grip was going to take more than just a diet, more than just an attitude change. It meant shining light on the real issues: the need to stabilize body chemistries for physical stability, along with demystifying the emotional charge food can have. You'll read more about making peace with food in Chapter 18.

Mary made both of these moves toward freedom, and she was ultimately able to take back the power she had given to sweets, looking at a dessert as just what it was—food. And, yes, she did have a piece of birthday cake at her party. She enjoyed it for the moment but was surprised at how sickeningly sweet it was. She was also sur-

prised at how great it made her feel—almost elated. But it didn't set her up to eat the whole cake—nor to finish it off with a pint of ice cream—because she was now alerted to the drop that would inevitably follow. Sugar no longer had power over her.

How about you? Do you have a sweet that seems to call your name? If chocolate is your sugar seductress, you may be hooked on more than the sugar alone. In addition to the chemical impact of chocolate on the brain's neurotransmitters (research shows it to release similar substances as those released in romantic love), chocolate packs a one-two punch with a double hit of sugar *and* caffeine. Not so different from that double mocha-cappucino that may woo you at midafternoon. Or maybe it's that caffeine/aspartame-pumped diet soda—the equivalent of rocket fuel to many.

ARE YOU A JAVA JUNKIE?

Caffeine is among the world's most widely used and addictive drugs. Ironically, caffeine remains a relatively acceptable way of artificially stimulating the brain at a time when society is being exhorted to "Just Say No" to drugs.

> **SMART WEIGH TIP**
>
> *It's not the Last Supper. This is not your last chance in life to have a particular food.*

Caffeine works to keep you alert by blocking one of the brain's natural sedatives, a neurotransmitter called adenosine. It stimulates the central nervous system, increases your pulse rate and heartbeat, and can even give quite a boost to your mood. A single cup of coffee can seem to work energy miracles when needed—even helping athletes to push a little farther. All in all, it's powerful stuff.

But, like other drugs, there is a downside to caffeine: too much causes a surge of adrenaline. But when the spurt is over, power levels plummet and stress hormones are produced. Even small amounts

of caffeine may cause side effects, including restlessness and disturbed sleep, heart palpitations, stomach irritation, fibrocystic breast disease, and diarrhea. It can promote irritability, anxiety, and mood disturbances. Caffeine can also aggravate premenstrual syndrome and mood swings in women. And studies have shown that the stress hormones still circulate, elevating blood pressure, up to eight hours after the last caffeine hit. And those stress hormones play a key role in fat cell lock-down.

The stimulant effect is thought to kick in with consumption of 150 to 250 mg of caffeine—the amount in one mug of brewed coffee or three glasses of iced tea. And because caffeine is also found in soda (regular and diet), chocolate, and even decongestant cold pills, it adds up quickly. The levels soar when you get java from a gourmet coffee shop. New analysis shows that these specialty brews can contain two to three times the caffeine found in a cup made from your typical supermarket brands. These specialty coffees are stronger because more grounds are used to give the brew its rich flavor and the beans are often roasted, making the coffee even more potent. In fact, one large cup of specialty coffee packs a walloping 280 mg of caffeine, and some have been found to contain 550 mg. It's at these higher levels of intake, about 600 mg, that you can get too energized and start to feel the java jitters: frazzled nerves, the shakes, insomnia, and ultimately, fatigue.

Do you need to cut out caffeine altogether? Not necessarily. Despite its drawbacks, it's definitely an energy boost. My concern is when caffeine becomes your very best friend. I do encourage you to cut back slowly to a ceiling of 250 mg. And if, after cutting back to this amount, you still experience any of the above-mentioned effects, I would suggest withdrawing altogether. You'll also get more of an energy boost from the caffeine you do consume if you have cut back on your intake.

Pain is the word that best characterizes cutting back on caffeine consumption, and that is why you must do so gradually. Again, caffeine is a powerfully addictive drug that will bring withdrawal symptoms as you give it up. Many people experience zombie-like fatigue, irritability, lethargy, and headaches from going "cold turkey," and the symptoms may last for up to five days. They expect to feel better by nobly giving up espresso, but end up feeling horrible instead. Then they drag back to caffeine saying this "healthy thing" just didn't work for them.

Let me tell you about Greg. He is an on-site supervisor for a large development company. He is on the job at 5:30 every morning, and his breakfast used to be a Big Gulp of coffee (that's right, 64 ounce of java). He'd get the crews started and check in at the office by 8:00 AM, then stop for a refill of coffee on the way (another 64 ounce)— and then again on the way back to the job site. In the afternoon, he switched to diet Mountain Dew for his jet-fuel.

Then Greg came to the first session of my *Smart Weigh* series, recommended by his physician to get control of his increasing blood pressure and high cholesterol levels. He listened, targeted the caffeine as his problem, and quit. Cold turkey. He went to the ER three days later thinking he had spinal meningitis because he had an immobilizing headache and felt paralyzed with flu-like fatigue.

Even if you don't drink as much caffeine as Greg, don't put your body through what Greg did. Cut back *slowly* over the course of a week to ten days. Start by cutting back to a safer level of two cups of coffee or three cups of tea. Gradually cut back, a quarter of a cup at a time, until you are down to none. Or substitute a decaffeinated product for the real thing in the same reducing amounts. Withdrawal will be less painful if you follow *The Smart Weigh* meal plan. Eating small, balanced meals throughout the day will stabilize your body

chemistries and reduce your reliance on caffeine for energy. And, if you focus on drinking more water than you have in the past, you won't have room for the other beverages. In addition, try to get outdoor exercise every day to get a boost of feel-good endorphins.

Finally, whether it's a mindset you want to break, or the grip of sugar or caffeine, don't set up any food as a forbidden fruit. As Mary learned, there are no good or bad foods; there is no such thing as a legal or a cheat food. Food is simply food. The power it lords over us is the problem. While it's important to assess the physiological power eating may have over our body chemistries and develop a better plan, setting our focus on what we shouldn't do and what we shouldn't eat only sets us up for failure.

A mind filled with worry can fall into the negative—attracting the very thing we are most worried about. Chronic worry can become toxic to us due to the resulting brain chemical surges that ravage the body—hindering the immune system, slowing the metabolism, and affecting our mood. These chemical surges can also take on a life of their own—wreaking havoc with our whole body chemistry and hormonal status. Negative thoughts can spin into a tornado, swallowing us up in an immobilizing state of imbalance called depression. All affect our ability to take charge of our weight.

CHAPTER 16 ▪ Energy Drains: Worry, Depression, and Hormones

My problem is not the problem, my problem is my attitude about the problem.

If you've ever spent hours mentally replaying a conversation or ruined a weekend because you couldn't quite stop fretting about work, you have a glimpse of how much energy chronic worry can drain. Worry is not a passive pursuit; it requires energy and will result in the body slowing down metabolically to conserve—locking into the fat storage mode.

Some worry may actually be good for us, such as concern about our safety and the safety of our family. Some degree of stress and worry can keep us on our toes and boost performance. But when worry takes on a life of its own it can become toxic, obsessive, and chronic.

> **SMART WEIGH TIP**
>
> *Stop worrying. Remind yourself that you only have control over you. If you can't do anything about it, just let it go.*

It's crucial to discern between good worry and draining worry, and to take action—always the positive response to stress. When there is no action to be taken, then continuing to worry is nothing more than spinning wheels. It becomes as self-destructive as nail-biting or smoking, and wears you down, without bringing you any closer to solving the issues that cause it.

To stop your internal wheels from spinning out of control and into obsession, try these quick fixes for your fixations:

CALM YOURSELF. Sit quietly in a comfortable position, eyes closed. Choose an empowering thought, phrase, or word that is rooted in your faith. These are some of my favorites: *I can do all things through God who gives me strength. I am more than a conqueror through Him. Be still, and know that I am God.* Then breathe naturally, and as you do, repeat the affirmation silently as you exhale. When other thoughts come into your mind, push them out by returning to your affirmation. Continue for ten to twenty minutes, as your schedule allows. You may feel better after just one session. Most people get the most benefit from such a calming time if they make room for it at least once a day.

LISTEN TO YOURSELF. Whenever you feel depressed, overtaken by food cravings, or exhausted, you need to stop, take a few slow, deep breaths, and consider what you're thinking or telling yourself. You may find that your internal voice is yakking away about how bad things are going, and how you'll never get this done, and you'll never do it right. You may be feeding yourself irrational drivel that is making you feel worse—or even making you sick. By simply acknowledging that your mind is filled with too much busybody thought, you can start slowing it down and cleaning it out.

SET ASIDE DESIGNATED WORRY TIME. To ward off that free-floating sense of doom, schedule an hour after work—on the ride home, in the tub—to sort out your anxieties. (Bedtime is NOT the time.) For particularly nagging problems, it can be helpful to write in a journal or talk with an understanding friend. If you start worrying during the day, resolve to hold off until your "obsession session." Whatever you do, don't let worries play over and over again in your mind, like a broken record. Instead vent them—get them out.

Inside your head, you constantly work over the content. Outside your head, you can look at it more realistically—and that's vital to both your emotional *and* physical well-being.

GIVE YOURSELF A REALITY CHECK. If you're dreading an upcoming event, consider the absolute worst-case scenario. (*If I do this exactly right, I still won't do it up to the standard of perfection and I'm going to be fired and I'll never be able to get a job again!*) Sometimes when you ask the question, "What's the absolutely worst thing that can happen," you realize that it probably won't. Remind yourself that, even if disaster were to strike, you would and could survive. Then, try to assemble *real* assessments of what is likely to happen. (*My boss may tell me I need to make a few minor changes before sending this report out.*) Tell yourself, "I can handle it." Reining in your runaway thoughts and replacing them with reality will diminish the negative chatter—and you will relax and release it.

IDENTIFY "STINKING THINKING." When you feel overcome by stressful thoughts, recognize that you need to calm down by saying something gentle to yourself like "Oh, there I go again." Just the admission tells you that the stress is from within, from your own thinking, not just the outside world. When you can, write down the thoughts that are bothering you. Then identify the mistakes in your thought patterns. These are the most common:

PERFECTIONISM. Everything must be perfect; everything you do must be right and correct every time.

AWFULIZING OR CATASTROPHIZING.: Assuming the worst, that a certain event or happening will be horrible.

GENERALIZING. The holidays were bad last year, and they'll be bad every year.

Replace your draining, "stinking thinking" with a positive out-look. If you're worrying about a party you have to go to, then replace, say, the fear of overeating with excitement about the people you will be seeing. Write down, "I'll be happy to see so and so, and I'll spend a lot of time talking to them."

TRY CLASSIC THOUGHT-STOPPING TECHNIQUES. To banish an unwanted thought the moment it occurs, speak to it: say, STOP! Or, wear a rubberband on your wrist and snap it to snap you out of the obsessing moment. Practice the breathing you learned in Chapter 8: inhale slowly through your nose, expanding your diaphragm; hold a moment, then focus on exhaling through your mouth as fully as you can. Taking deep breaths from the abdomen will calm you, and help you to ease out of the panic mode.

DON'T TRY TO CONTROL EVERYTHING. If you have a tendency to obsess, chances are good that you're also a perfectionist. Realize that going over something again and again will not magically produce the "right" answer or perfect solution. More important, accept that you don't always have the power—or the responsibility—to make everything flawless or everyone happy. Some things that weigh you down are way beyond your control or power to change; others just aren't worth the worry. Be more selective about the things you allow to rent space in your mind. Remember, *you* pay the rent with your well-being.

Do look for opportunities to seize what control you can. You may not be able to avoid eating on an airplane, but you can call ahead and order a special meal that tastes better and is better for you.

ZAP YOUR NEGATIVE THINKING WITH POSITIVE ACTION. Instead of staring at your credit-card bill in despair, make an appointment with a financial counselor. Instead of dwelling on how much you hate your job, work on your resume. Instead of agonizing that you may have

offended a friend, call her, talk to her about it. Call it "obsession rehab": you replace a virtual addiction to certain fears with productive, restorative activity.

GET MOVING. Because it burns off anxiety-causing adrenaline and allows the blessed release of endorphins, exercise is a sure bet to change your emotional and mental state, right along with the physical. Even a quick walk around the office will help you walk away from your worries.

GET INVOLVED. When you're self-absorbed, you're much more prone to worry. When you strike a good balance of investing in yourself and being involved with others, it brings richness to your life. Trouble in one part doesn't overtake or overcome you because there's much more to life than that one area.

GET HELP. This is critical when you're miserable. If exhaustive and self-abusive worrying persists, seek out a trusted friend, pastor, or a counselor to talk to. Your energy levels and your quality of life are much too precious to be neutralized by worry. Obsessive worry can sometimes spin out of control, and spin you right into a depression of a mountainous sort. You'll need help to find your way down.

OUR EVER-CHANGING MOODS

Mood colors everything we do: what we eat, what we wear, whether we'll make love with our spouse tonight or end up in a disagreement. We all know what it is to be in a great mood: we feel strong and energetic and have a good self-image. We love, we're lovely, our potential is unlimited, and life is bathed in light.

Bad moods are also easy to identify. We're "off," drained of energy, overwhelmed, and irritable. Bad moods hit us all—only 2 percent of us report feeling cheerful every day. Most of us swing in and out of bad moods fairly regularly and predictably. Polls show

that the average person spends about three days out of ten trying to lift up and over a bad mood.

As we discussed while looking at the factors involved in equalizing your brain chemistry, your moods probably have more rhyme and rhythm than you realize. They are most often based on natural biological patterns and chemical changes from lifestyle and food choices you make throughout the day. You may blame your funk on the day's frustrations, but chances are it's more related to your daily rises and falls of stress chemicals. Becoming a keen observer of your moods will help you to track them and influence them for the better.

But there are times when a bad mood is more than the blues—it's depression, and it's tough to shake. When you're depressed, you feel out of control, hate yourself, hate life, hate the people in your life, feel hopeless and overwhelmed. Everything is dark and grim.

Because a positive mental attitude is so crucial to living *The Smart Weigh*, and a bright, hopeful perspective is necessary to make the lifestyle upgrades that can lead to vitality, I address the possibility of depression with every one of my clients—particularly those battling overeating and a dependence upon food, sugar, or caffeine.

BEWARE THE DOWNWARD SPIRAL

Depression is both a physical and mental condition marked by sadness, hopelessness, and fatigue. It's a monster of a disorder that causes the entire body to slow down, pulling you down and back from life.

Depression can have many triggers—both internal and external. Internal triggers include brain chemical imbalances, hormonal changes, nutritional deficiencies, or illness. Depression may be caused by certain high blood pressure medications, birth control pills, and the hormonal changes that come with menstruation, menopause, childbirth, or breastfeeding cessation. Depression can

also be externally triggered by any loss and its resulting grief. The death of a loved one, financial problems, or life changes such as a move, job loss, children leaving home, or divorce can send you into a downward spiral.

Even the healthiest grieving includes a period of depression, but sometimes losses are compounded or intensified in such a way that you can't resolve them—and you get stuck in the depression. You can also get stuck if you don't give yourself permission to grieve—believing that you are somehow showing weakness or ungratefulness if you give in too much to your sadness. The more you stuff your natural, authentic feelings, the more depressed you get. The converse is also true: the more you allow yourself to grieve, the more rapidly you recover from the loss.

It's not just unprocessed grief that can result in depression. For example, anger that is not released in healthy ways can dam up within you and become depression. This is why depression is often described as "frozen emotion" or "anger turned inward."

When a person gets sucked into a downward spiral, the blues can rapidly progress into clinical depression. The body stuck in depression loses the capability to produce the brain chemicals (neurotransmitters) that fight dark perspectives. Clinical depression is accompanied by several telltale symptoms, including profound sadness; a loss of interest in things once enjoyed; feelings of worthlessness and hopelessness; anxiety; changes in appetite (usually resulting in significant weight loss or gain); sleep disturbances; digestive problems; problems concentrating, thinking, remembering, or making decisions; and recurring thoughts of death or suicide.

Depression is known to exacerbate a range of medical conditions because it is associated with poor compliance to recommended treatment. But it does more than get people off balance emotionally and

off track with self-care; it actually affects them *physiologically.* For example, in people with diabetes, depression has also been shown to trigger an adverse physiological response, driving up their blood-glucose levels. How it does this is not yet properly understood; but the theory is that depression alters levels of the hormone cortisol, which can worsen insulin resistance and compromise the immune system, leading to heart disease and other killer diseases. Whether or not this occurs in the normal population without diabetes has not been confirmed through research.

If overeating and poor self-care is rooted in depression, a professional evaluation is critical. Antidepressant medication, often necessary to correct and replenish brain chemistry gone awry, can often avert serious depression—saving lives, families, marriages, and careers. But antidepressant therapy alone is rarely enough to stabilize the body's chemistries for life—it's just a jump start. The long-term answer for depression-related overeating and fatigue comes through getting help to deal effectively with life and hurts, along with embracing a lifestyle of self-care and expressing emotion. A professional evaluation can identify where the real problems are, and help to determine when depression is as much a physical problem as a chemical one. Again, depression can be caused by a variety of physiological imbalances. One of them is fluctuating hormones.

HORMONE HAVOC

As we've discussed, hormone fluctuations can wreak havoc with a woman's metabolism—not just during menopause, but on a monthly basis. And not just a day or two before her menstrual cycle; many women experience lethargy, mood changes, and a raging appetite from ovulation through the end of their period. They barely get a breath of energy before the symptoms begin again.

If a woman is to unlock the fat cell storage mechanism and turn up her fat-burning potential, she must understand and deal with the hormones that play major roles in her energy and well-being. Two of the hormones most familiar to women are estrogen and progesterone. Estrogen not only serves in the regulation of the menstrual cycle, but acts as a mild antidepressant and greatly enhances a woman's sense of well-being. When estrogen is not produced at proper levels, memory, mood, and energy all suffer—which explains the many changes associated with menopause when estrogen production dramatically falls off. Before menopause, estrogen levels peak in the first two weeks of the menstrual cycle and decrease during the two weeks after ovulation.

> **SMART WEIGH TIP**
>
> *Get inspired. Read a lot about other people who have overcome great obstacles.*

Progesterone is also involved in regulating a woman's menstrual cycle, and works to prepare the lining of the uterus for pregnancy. Progesterone begins to increase at ovulation, at the time the estrogen levels decrease, and stays high over the last two weeks of the menstrual cycle. Progesterone is the hormone culprit for PMS-related symptoms: irritability, fatigue, depression, decreased sexual desire, increased appetite, and achiness. Energy and sexual drives are thought to be diminished due to progesterone's suppression of dopamine, the brain neurotransmitter that keeps us alert, motivated, and poised for action.

The hypothalamus, the body's control center, monitors the levels of hormones produced by the ovaries. And this control center is affected by external as well as internal factors. It is the hypothalamus that is battered by the stress chemicals, causing the metabolism, blood sugars, and fluid balance to go awry in times of intense stress. Little wonder that the symptoms of hormone havoc are metabolic slow-down; blood sugar fluctuations resulting in irritability,

fatigue, and food cravings; and fluid retention and bloating. And approaching menopause is another hormone struggle altogether. The hormonal fluctuations that tended to intensify once or twice a month can now take on a life of their own.

Proper nutrition, exercise, and sleep can be tremendous stabilizers, but can fuel havoc if they are deficient. Women who skip meals or go long hours without balanced eating are setting themselves up for fatigue, moodiness, and fat storage.

Here are some stabilizers you can count on to help calm the hormone havoc within:

ADD CALCIUM. Recent research shows that menstruating women who supplemented with 1,200 mg of calcium had significantly less intense symptoms of PMS, and some had no symptoms at all.

GO FOR SOY. These foods have been shown to alleviate many of the symptoms of hormone fluctuations—even the hot flashes of menopause. Substitute soy-based foods (tofu, soy cheese, soy beans or soy protein powders) for meat proteins at least once a day. To be effective, soy products must contain 35 to 45 mg of soy protein isolates. Read the product label.

EAT SMART. Go easy on sweets and alcohol. Although most often the object of hormone-related cravings, these substances trigger a response like throwing gas on a fire. Refined sugars have been shown to aggravate just about every symptom of PMS. So focus on eating whole carbohydrates throughout your day to even out your blood sugar response.

If you eat whole grains, you will also get the blessing of vitamin B6 and magnesium—two nutrients particularly helpful in stabilizing brain chemical production. Beyond whole grains, good food sources of vitamin B6 include fish, chicken, turkey, potatoes, and bananas (see page 100). And a daily supplement of 150 mg can help

alleviate PMS symptoms for many women. If you supplement with B6, limit yourself to less than 300 mg per day; higher levels have been linked to neuromuscular damage and paralysis.

A magnesium supplement may be helpful as well, although a well-balanced diet including green, leafy vegetables, soy products, and lots of whole grains is apt to fill your magnesium need. The recommendation by most PMS researchers is 350 mg of magnesium per day to lessen the intensity of symptoms. Magnesium gluconate and magnesium aspartate are the most absorbable forms.

LIMIT CAFFEINE. Caffeine aggravates fibrocystic breast pain, and complicates the energy and mood seesaw of PMS.

EXERCISE EVERY DAY. Although this may be the last thing you feel like doing when your hormones are fluctuating, regular exercise can change your entire hormone and brain chemistry makeup. The stress-busting endorphins that exercise releases can calm your personal storm.

CONSIDER HORMONE REPLACEMENT THERAPY. To calm the hormonal hurricane induced by menopause, you have the option of replacing dwindling hormones with synthetic forms of progesterone and estrogen. But certain risks and side effects need to be discussed with your health care provider. Still, don't ignore the hormone replacement issue; more is at risk than moods or hot flashes alone. Hormone deficiency increases the risk of osteoporosis, heart disease, and Alzheimer's—risks that are not worth taking. Find the right choice and balance for you.

THYROID DISORDERS

You may not have identified it as such, but your thyroid gland is also a part of your hormonal system. It's a mysterious gland, most often getting the blame for weight gain, a slowed metabolism, and

fatigue. Although less than 2 percent of all cases of obesity can be traced to a metabolic disorder such as low thyroid function, it needs to be considered because a malfunction has such a detrimental impact on energy and weight.

The thyroid gland controls the metabolism of body energy, regulating your metabolic rate and the number of calories you need to keep your body operating. It does so by releasing hormones to regulate your body systems. One of the more important thyroid hormones secreted into your bloodstream is thyroxine, which serves to regulate your heartbeat, metabolic rate, body temperature, and even the rate at which waste moves through your GI tract.

The reason for thyroid dysfunction is unclear. One possibility appears to be a viral infection that triggers the body into an immune response directed against itself. A common target for this autoimmune response is the thyroid gland. If the thyroid gland becomes overactive, it releases too much hormone; if it is underactive, it releases too little. If the hyperactive thyroid gland works too hard, it accelerates the heartbeat and produces an anxious, uncomfortable excess of energy. A sluggish thyroid function, on the other hand, causes low energy, dry skin, hair loss, lowered immunes, poor appetite, intolerance to cold, weight gain, and constipation. Some women may experience an irregularity in their heart rate, and headaches as well.

One out of five women over sixty have hypothyroidism, often unbeknownst to them. What they do know is that they are experiencing overwhelming fatigue, chilliness, and a host of other maladies that may be mislabeled "aging." Because overeating, exhaustion, and depression are often the most pronounced signs of thyroid problems, it's important to get a thorough physical if your body doesn't respond to positive lifestyle changes. Treating an underactive thyroid is not

difficult, once diagnosed; it just requires a daily dose of a synthetic thyroid hormone.

Along with the medication, your metabolism can be boosted by treating the symptoms naturally. Keep your slow metabolism revved up to a higher gear by following *The Smart Weigh* eat-right prescription. Eating balanced mini-meals every 2 1/2 to 3 hours and getting quality proteins throughout the day can also help to arrest hair loss and cure skin maladies. And keep your sluggish GI tract on the move with adequate fiber and lots of water.

Hormone levels gone awry affect every part of the body—and soul. Because of the intricate interplay between hormones and the neurotransmitters of the brain, being caught in hormone havoc can bring destructive forces into our lives and distort the very way we look at life and at our bodies. And because a positive body image is such a vital part of living free from the diet trap, it's important to see all of our entrapments clearly—and take charge of what we can.

A negative body image can be a powerful force that neutralizes our energy, vitality, and self-control. It needn't be. Once you see a lamp of hope shining on the physical you, it may be time to look to the soul and evaluate your emotional relationship with your body, eating, and food.

CHAPTER 17 ▪ Body Image Battles

Your thoughts and companions are like elevator buttons—they will either take you up, or take you down.

—ANONYMOUS

We live in a culture that has an ideal body type that only a tiny percentage of the population can ever hope to achieve. Trying to live up to that kind of standard is enough to make even the most sensible person a little nuts.

But it may surprise you to know that having a poor body image not only messes with your mind, it can also be one of the major hindrances to losing weight. In a study of 177 men and women, researchers from the Stanford University School of Medicine found those with a healthy body image were more than twice as successful at meeting weight-loss goals—55 percent compared to 26 percent. Those with no history of weight fluctuations also fared well (63 percent versus 35 percent).

> **SMART WEIGH TIP**
>
> *Look in the mirror and say, "I am wonderfully made"—and don't give up.*

Some people who want to be thinner have a reasonable body image in mind—they simply don't want to carry around excess weight. But many people, especially women, do *not* have a healthy body image in mind. Rather, they are seeking to rearrange their figure into perfection.

The crazy thing about body image is that it is often the very thing that lures people into the diet trap—and then becomes the very thing that makes them most miserable about being there. It's also the thing that keeps them stuck. Because with a poor body image, it's never good enough—and neither are you.

People who may be genetically destined to carry more weight than the average person have a particular challenge to their self-image. It's a social challenge because of the abuse and prejudice heaped upon them. It's a personal and vital challenge to overcome, however, because studies show that a poor self-image actually fuels poor health habits. Those who feel uncomfortable with their heavier bodies are less apt to exercise—they don't want people thinking, "You sure need to do more of that!" Or, as one of my clients heard from a car speeding by her while she was walking: "Run, Fattie—it might do that fat some good!" Horribly painful words, and definitely not motivating.

> **SMART WEIGH TIP**
>
> *Quit the numbers game. Forget how much you weigh— go for feeling great and how you fit into the clothes you want to wear.*

Because of this kind of social conditioning, many people put so much emphasis on their looks that they ignore their many other good qualities. They also let their negative body image keep them from vital health-care and social activities. One of my clients, Mary, had not had a gynecological appointment for five years, even though she has a history of irregular pap smears. Why? She didn't want her doctor to see her body or have to stand on the examining room scale. Jim, thirty-two, had not gone to a family gathering for two years for fear of what his family would think when they saw him. Cynthia, forty-one, had stopped undressing in front of her husband and would not let him touch her stomach or thighs— which created distance and hurt in their intimate relationship.

MIRROR, MIRROR ON THE WALL

How about you? Do you ever stand in front of the mirror and dream about where you'd get a few nips and tucks if you could? Do you feel as if life would be better *if only* you had smaller thighs, a flatter tummy, or there was simply less of you?

A critical question for your health and happiness is this: Do you have a healthy image of your body? Answer these questions with "never," "sometimes," "often," or "always," and find out how you measure up. It may be time to give your body image a boost.

1. Do you dislike seeing yourself in mirrors?
2. Do you find shopping for clothes somewhat unpleasant because it makes you more aware of your "weight problem?"
3. Do you ever feel ashamed to be seen in public?
4. Do you avoid engaging in certain activities, sports, or public exercises because of being self-conscious about your appearance?
5. Do you ever feel embarrassed about your body in the presence of someone of the opposite sex?
6. Do you ever think your body is ugly?
7. Do you ever feel that other people must think your body is unattractive, even repulsive?
8. Do you view your shape differently from the way others do?
9. Do you ever feel that family or friends may be embarrassed to be seen with you because of your weight?
10. Do you try to lose weight to look good for someone else?
11. Do you ever compare yourself with other people to see if they are heavier or thinner than you are?
12. Does feeling guilty or uncomfortable about your weight preoccupy most of your thinking?
13. Are your thoughts about your body and physical appearance negative and self-critical?

14. Are you driven by a desire to be thin, equating thinness with success and being in control? Do you think about life in terms of "if only" ("if only I were thinner, then I would be married… have more friends… get a better job…").

15. Do you try to lose weight, thinking that when you shed unwanted pounds, you'll become a wonderful person—forgetting that you are already a wonderful person?

Maintaining negative beliefs—as evidenced by any questions to

MEDIA HYPE

This "Did You Know" was sent via e-mail to my seventeen-year-old daughter. I'm hoping it was circulated around the Internet to millions of young girls like her (and those not so young) to put into perspective the truth about our beauty—and the lies that are pervasive in society. Many thanks to the person who put these facts together.

Did you know ...

- If shop mannequins were real women, they'd be too thin to menstruate.
- There are 3 billion women who don't look like supermodels—and only eight who do.
- Marilyn Monroe wore a size 14.
- If Barbie were a real woman, she'd have to walk on all fours due to her unrealistic proportions.
- The average American woman weighs 144 lbs. and wears between a size 12 and 14.
- One out of every four college-aged women has an eating disorder.
- The models in the magazines are airbrushed, i.e., they're not perfect.
- A psychological study in 1995 found that three minutes spent looking at models in a fashion magazine caused 70 percent of women to feel depressed, guilty, and shameful.
- Models twenty years ago weighed 8 percent less than the average woman. Today they weigh 23 percent less.

which you answered "sometimes," "often," or "always"—is a sign of a not-so-hot body image. Answering "often" or "always" to many of these questions can reveal a body image war that can get in the way of your happiness, thwart your success in losing weight and keeping fit, and even lead to depression and eating disorders. But guess what? No matter what "they" tell you—the magazines, Hollywood, your friends and family—looking like Kate Moss or Ally McBeal isn't the cure-all for the woes of life.

In living *The Smart Weigh*, what's most important is that you feel good about who you are. Until you like yourself as is, and understand who you *really* are apart from how you look, trying to change your body shape will be a losing proposition. High self-esteem is crucial for a healthy, balanced lifestyle—and it's a must for successful weight loss. After all, how can you take care of yourself if you don't like yourself? It just doesn't work. Rather than treating yourself well—and improving your health and weight as a result—you end up using "diet" regimes to beat yourself up and literally whip yourself into shape. And when you fail—which you inevitably will—then you've amassed more evidence that you just can't succeed and you'll never be "good enough."

If this vicious cycle sounds familiar, then it's time to smile back at that image in the mirror and value all the wonderful characteristics about the person reflected there.

When each of my daughters turned ten, we went away for a mother-daughter weekend to celebrate the beginning of each girl's "pre-teen" years. We talked about who they were, who they had been created to be—and how difficult it was to "measure up" to the expectations of their peers. We talked about the pain so many teens experience due to never feeling they have enough "brains, bucks, or beauty."

Following the advice of wise family therapists, we spent time listing all of the things we liked about ourselves physically—hair? eyes? height? sense of humor? sensitivity? Then we looked at all the things we didn't like, and wished we could change—nose? hips? teeth? moodiness? too tall? too short? And we looked at all the things that we could reasonably change with better self-care or practical help: braces, better eating, adequate sleep. The rest we wrote on pieces of paper and burned—because all of the wishing and misery in the world would not make one daughter less tall, and the other taller. It was crucial that they appreciate the wonder of who they were and what they looked like—not who they wished they could be or who they thought they should look like.

I took this exercise right back into my counseling. I realized that, as adults, many of us are still struggling with those same issues of bucks, brains, and beauty—and trying desperately to "measure up" in the eyes of others. I realized that no matter what our age—ten, twenty, forty, or sixty—falling in love with our bodies, being thankful for what we do have, recognizing what we cannot change as well as what we can, is a challenge.

You may want to go back and review the ten tips to boost positive perspective on page 84 in Chapter 5, such as practicing positive self-talk, seeing the world realistically, recognizing your special qualities, and putting your body back together. These tips are not a one-time event, but can become daily affirmations in your life as you learn to embrace yourself for exactly who you are.

THE HORROR OF A SWIMSUIT

It's not just healthy habit patterns that get sacrificed to a poor body image; relationships pay the price as well—with yourself and others. That's why one of the strongest aspects of my counseling with over-

weight clients is my focus on freeing them from self-reproach, end-less rumination about their appearance, and their reluctance to appear in public. The horror of "exposing" yourself to the public eye—especially when that exposure involves bare skin—can keep even the thin among us from good-for-you activities like swimming or walking on the beach. In a recent survey conducted by *Prevention* magazine and NBC, nearly half of American women are so self-con-scious about revealing their bodies that they refuse to be pho-tographed in a swimsuit.

Kay was certainly among them—swimsuits were the reason she started dieting, in her early teens, to begin with. She was a Florida girl and, for the most part, *loves* summer: the hot, hot weather, the long sunny days, trips to the beach, splashing in the pool. "So what is my problem?" Kay asked me at our first session together. "It's that all too often, in the back of my mind, there is this constant nagging thought: *I hate my thighs!*" Actually, it was her "thigh"—the left one.

> **SMART WEIGH TIP**
>
> *Find new measures of success. Use a pair of jeans one size too small —try them on once a month to see how they are fitting.*

Kay explained that she underwent some bone-grafting surgery, due to a congenital leg problem, done at age seven. Surgical tech-nique was not so good then and the resulting huge scar and the scar tissue seemed to become its own special saddlebag. "Ever since I was a teenager, the first hint of cellulite seemed to accumulate around that area," Kay explained. "I've had this creeping self-consciousness about revealing my lower half. I've always wanted to carry a sign to the beach saying, 'I had surgery,'" she said half-laughing, and half-teary. "While my teeny friends were wearing shorts or bathing suits without a care, I was devising ways to cover myself. And shopping for a bathing suit was sheer agony. There was one golden year, when

I was fourteen, when the very in-style suit had a little skirt around the bottom, covering just the right spot on my thigh. I loved that suit; it was pink and white checked.

"Well, that was then. I'm a big girl now, right? And a smart one." Kay is a very smart woman—a professional therapist who, strangely enough, counsels other women on body image. Yet, through the years, she's had to work *very* hard on her perception of her own thigh. Kay has had to learn that who she *really* is has nothing to do with her image in the mirror. It has become very important to her to do the right things for the right reasons. She doesn't want the reason for caring for herself by eating well and exercising to be rooted in her "thigh anxiety." She had worked hard on her perception *(it is not that big)* and her interpretation *(my self-worth is not determined by my thigh)*.

As Kay continues to learn to love herself and give herself the gift of health she deserves, she has let her intermittent self-consciousness teach her some valuable lessons. "It still crops up occasionally," she says, "and it makes me mad that I'm bothered by it at all. I mean, who cares, really? Why do I want beautiful thighs? Who am I trying to impress? When those old feelings of self-loathing threaten to undermine my commitment to self-care, I understand that I'm still in need of unconditional love... and I'm thankful for the reminder. Only a spiritual connection will give me that."

Another thing Kay is learning is how to deal effectively with what's really eating her so she won't automatically turn to food to soothe her moods or solve her problems. Like many of us, she has a history of getting caught in a vicious cycle—turning to food as a comfort when she is sad or anxious. So, the more frustrated and panicked she would feel about her thighs, the more she would eat. A clothes-shopping excursion inevitably ended at Baskin-Robbins.

A healthy relationship with food is one of friendship, where food

is regarded as the nourishment it was created to be. But food is not simply food in the world today. We live in a nation of people preoccupied with food—obsessed by it.

I grew up believing that there was no problem in life that couldn't be solved with a banana split. Eating, and overeating, was my response to every emotion. As a family we ate to celebrate when we were happy; to feel better when we were sad; to give us something to do when we were bored; to gain control when we felt anxious or frustrated. I ate to stuff my anger and to soothe my nerves. I ate when I felt out of control. Although my eating itself would have looked out of control to others, it actually gave me a sense of being in charge of something.

In order to live free of the diet trap, food needs to be given its proper place in our lives. Food can be healthy nourishment. It can be a source of pleasure. It certainly does more than satisfy hunger. It's time to make peace with food.

CHAPTER 18 ■ Making Peace with Food

Life can only be understood by looking backward, but it must be lived by looking forward.

—ANONYMOUS

We just talked about accepting our bodies, but in a nation where fashion models average a size two and thin is perpetually in, you don't have to have an eating disorder to spend most of your waking hours—and sometimes, sleeping ones, too—agonizing over food. If you started your day thinking about what you couldn't have for breakfast or kicking yourself for what you ate for dinner last night, then it's time to call it *war*—a food war.

If your mental conversations follow this script—"Have I been good or bad today?" "How many fat grams did I eat today?" "How many calories did I burn off at the gym?" "Is that brownie going to show up on the scale?

> **SMART WEIGH TIP**
>
> *Challenge the power of food. Determine if you're really eating because you're hungry or eating for other reasons.*

Or worse, on my thighs?" "I won't eat tonight to make up for it"—then, in addition to the diet trap, you may be struggling with food obsession or dependency, which can destroy you.

See how you answer these questions:

- Do you make promises to control your eating, but break those promises again and again?
- Do you skip meals, especially breakfast, and hope your stomach won't notice?
- Do you feel a sense of power when you skip meals?
- Do you regularly go the whole day with little or no food, yet wonder why you are sick and tired?
- Have you tried to get through the day on coffee, tea, or soda?
- Do you deny the physical damage or complications caused by your eating choices?
- Are you constantly dieting or discussing food and weight loss?
- Do you eat more, or at a more frenzied pace, when under stress?
- Have you found yourself unable to stop eating?
- Have you ever thought, "I was bad today; I won't eat tomorrow"?
- Do you go on a binge the week before going on a diet?
- Do you consume huge quantities of food rapidly and often secretly?
- Do you dispose of or hide the evidence because you are ashamed of what you've done?
- Have you eaten to the point of nausea or vomiting, or until your stomach hurts?
- Do you feel "good" when you are eating, but when you stop eating, are overcome with guilt, remorse, or self-hatred? Do you eat more to relieve those feelings?
- Do you avoid social engagements that involve eating if you are on a diet?
- Does eating, or planning to eat, seem to be a hassle?
- Do you fast or drastically cut and count calories to lose weight?
- Do you have an on-a-diet, off-a-diet mentality, rather than eating moderately and wisely as the norm?

- Do you think of any food as bad or forbidden rather than simply as food?
- Have you relied on diet pills or shakes or any product that promises to do the weight-loss work for you?

If you answered yes to a number of these questions, than the food fight has taken on a life of its own. Pick the top three issues you struggle with on the list and personalize them, such as, "I regularly think, 'I was bad today, so I'll starve tomorrow.'" Now, open your mind to some new revelations about food and your body that might help you make peace with both.

IS THE REFRIGERATOR LIGHT THE LIGHT OF YOUR LIFE?

Most of us have been taught that food "makes us feel better," and we have certainly discovered that it does. When we feel sad or anxious, a candy bar or bag of chips can be very soothing. When we are stressed or angry, chocolate chip cookies reduce the inner tension. Many people go back to their normal, more balanced way of eating once the uncomfortable feeling has passed. But others do not return to "normal" eating patterns. Their logic goes something like this: "If food made me feel good yesterday, then it should do the same today; and if today, then tomorrow."

Food doesn't let us down, even if everything—and everyone—else does. We can become as dependent on food as on any chemical substance, and it can be as destructive as any other addiction.

Millions of Americans are emotionally dependent on food. Food dependency and obsession has nothing to do with your weight; you may be very overweight or quite thin. Rather, it has to do with an

improper relationship with food in which food and eating–and often dieting—have assumed an unnatural importance in your life.

In this improper love-hate relationship, food has an unnatural control over you. You may love the way it tastes and makes you feel, but hate it for what it does to your body and how it controls your life. Like any unhealthy relationship, food dependency results in a roller coaster of emotions: gratification and satisfaction, guilt and remorse, being "good" only to be "bad," going "on" a diet only to go "off" a diet. The obsession fills your thoughts and drives your actions, robs you of physical well-being and emotional serenity, and affects your self-esteem. Such captivity has life-damaging consequences.

Food or dieting becomes a trap when it is used as a substitute for love, friendship, or success, or when it's used to cover up more serious emotional issues.

FOOD IS NOT AN EVIL

Human beings must have food to survive and thrive; we are created to depend on it and enjoy it. Food itself is not evil, but many of us use food badly. Sometimes we love eating more than we love ourselves, more than we love other people, and more than we love God.

Take an inventory of your own thoughts about food as you read these commonly held beliefs about food and dieting. Observe how these play out in the lives of Steve, Tori, Karen, Deborah, and Jim.

■ *Food (or dieting) helps me cope with stress, frustration, and the insecurities of life. Overeating seems to smooth away the rough edges and relieve the tension, thus allowing me to cope. It provides a quick fix.*

It sure did for Steve—a man who was the envy of all his friends for his rigid dieting and exercise. And it was not only Steve's willpower that amazed his friends; he had an uncanny expertise in the stock market. The most successful stockbroker in his firm, he had many influential clients with large portfolios. His success had its drawbacks, though: the stress was intense and constant, though he "handled it well"—or appeared to, anyway.

Steve couldn't meet the pressures of his job head-on because the main source of his stress was coming from within—his driving need for perfection. He needed everything to go according to plan, but invariably it didn't. So he resorted to a familiar pattern that would relieve the tensions and fuel his workaholic habits: he would go on a binge of massive quantities of sweets. But those sweet binges tarnished the standard of perfection he'd set for himself—so he would maniacally exercise and diet his guilt away.

■ *Food (or dieting) fills the gaps in my life. Food can be the friend and companion that is with me no matter what. When I'm lonely, eating seems to fill the emptiness. It substitutes for love, attention, and pampering. When I'm happy, it's a way to celebrate—even if I'm not with other people. When I'm working hard with seemingly little recognition or appreciation, food becomes a justly earned reward and comfort.*

Tori saw me during the time she was transitioning into being an empty-nester—and it wasn't coming easy. She had loved motherhood, and had accepted it with joy and a sense of challenge. She had dedicated twenty years to raising her daughter, Meghan. And then Meghan took a job in another state and moved—leaving Tori feeling lost and empty.

Tori felt so abandoned that she demanded appreciation from the

very person who could not give it to her—Meghan. Meghan was struggling with her own emotions of breaking away and could not be the support that her mother craved. Since Tori was going to an "empty well" and coming up dry, she turned to food to fill her bucket. And it did, temporarily. But the more Tori ate, the more weight she gained and the more depressed she got—which only ended up isolating and alienating her from the healthy relationships that *were* available.

■ *Food (or dieting) gives me a sense of identity and control. Loving and controlling food is a lot safer than loving people. When life seems most out of control, rigid denial of food or counting every calorie or fat gram—even planning a binge—gives me a sense of being very much in control of at least one area of life.*

At forty-nine, Karen was heavier than she had ever been—yet she had been on a diet for twenty-two years. She was tired of battling food and the scale and wanted to break out of the diet trap.

But Karen was not willing to give up compulsive dieting because she didn't want to give up control. As long as she could control food—her natural enemy—she felt she had control of her world. But the truth was, she wasn't controlling it—it was controlling her. Every time she broke her rigid diet, she saw herself as a failure. When she would reach her "goal weight" and relax a bit, she immediately gained five pounds as the fluid balance restored itself. That led to horror, which led to more restrictions and more failures.

I watched Karen yo-yo like this for three years before she told me that her husband was a practicing alcoholic. Then it all made sense to me. She had been using her compulsive dieting, alternating with compulsive eating, to cover up her pain and shame related to her

husband's disease. She believed she didn't have any hope for change, and felt out of control. Food and dieting temporarily restored her balance.

■ *Food (or dieting) helps me sabotage the "perfect image" people expect me to live up to. I was an obedient, people-pleasing child, and now I'm that kind of adult. In my "good-girl" world, food is something to be "bad" with. Even though becoming overweight is the result, overeating is a socially acceptable vice and a passive form of rebellion.*

Deborah is a minister's wife and a minister's daughter. She grew up with a rigid set of rules for "acceptable behavior" and never dreamed of breaking them. She was "Papa's precious," always wearing a smile.

But Deborah didn't always *feel* like smiling. In fact, she sometimes felt quite resentful of being the preacher's daughter and having to be perfect to meet the expectations of the congregation. She would be immediately overwhelmed with shame for these "bad" feelings, and found that she could act out how bad she felt she was by bingeing on food. She did it in secret, so no one would ever know just how rebellious she was.

SMART WEIGH TIP

Take an emotional inventory. Ask yourself: "What do you feel guilty about? Resent? Fear? Regret? What are you angry about?" Then deal with it— without food.

When she started gaining weight, she began to make herself sick after overeating—to get rid of the evidence. She developed a secret life-style of overeating and purging that followed her into her marriage. Then one day, she exploded with the truth—when she couldn't contain the secret shame any longer. She couldn't stand the reality that no one—not even her husband—knew who she really was.

■ *Food (or dieting) helps me deal with deep-seated emotions and feelings. Keeping my mind on food can keep it off issues of the heart and soul. Overeating seems like a safe way to express my hidden emotions. Stuffing food, or rigidly denying myself food, is a way to stuff feelings, to numb them, to shut them off.*

Eating to stay Mr. Nice Guy is exactly what Jim had done since childhood.

Because he had a high metabolism and weight was never a problem for him, overeating seemed to be the perfect way to deal with the unexplainable rage that would rise up within him. This was such an established pattern that Jim ceased to recognize that he ever even felt angry. He just knew he was tired all the time.

Jim's business was in the midst of great transition when he first came to me for counseling. His commission rate and his sales territory had been changed three times in two months. He had also recently been passed over for a promotion. Jim was vaguely aware he was eating excessive quantities of sweets and vaguely realized that this had increased with the stress at work. But his wife was very aware of Jim's behavior, and was concerned because of his family's proclivity toward diabetes.

Jim had difficulty reporting any set eating patterns; he said his eating was based on availability and the situation he faced at the moment. He was astonished to begin identifying those situations as the ones that made him angry. As long as he could eat a cookie when he began to feel "something" inside, he could avoid dealing with the emotion.

DEALING WITH WHAT'S EATING YOU

The satisfied feeling we get from food *does* fill the gaps—temporar-

ily. But typically, the more we eat, the more depressed we get, and the more we need to eat to feel better. But because food is a quick fix, we never get the chance to fill in the gaps permanently and in healthy ways.

As long as we're eating (or even actively avoiding eating), we don't have to deal with what's eating us. We might appear calm, even happy, on the outside, yet we're crying or raging on the inside.

Remember Sherri, the woman in Chapter 4 who compared herself to a juice box that had its contents sucked dry all day, every day? Sherri's real problem was that she ate to help her deal with what was eating her.

When she was dieting, she would fill her mind with the dieting "rules" and let those become her focus. But, ultimately, she would have a lapse. For all of her hard work, she would reward herself with a doughnut, which would throw her into the "I've-blown-it-now" syndrome. So she would eat six. Her eat-today, diet-tomorrow strategy meant that today she would eat everything she couldn't have when she dieted tomorrow. As is often the case, her momentary lapse became a relapse, which led ultimately to her collapse.

But today Sherri is off that merry-go-round and doing terrifically with *The Smart Weigh*. Two months after her first visit to me, she made many changes. She was eating in a more even and balanced way than ever in her life. She had lost seven pounds, purely as a side benefit of her change in eating—not by starving or "dieting." And because these were seven pounds of fat—not water and muscle—her "thin" clothes were actually too big. And speaking of muscle, Sherri had started walking at lunch time as a powerful stress release, and doing strength and conditioning exercises three mornings a week.

Yet Sherri would occasionally let her eating habits slip out of control. The "binge" was now generally on good foods (although donuts

still sneaked in occasionally), but it ended then and there. It lacked the frenzy and desperation of previous years. But it still happened—and it scared her.

So I asked Sherri to keep a week's diary of what she ate and when. I asked her to note what she was feeling when she overate or wanted to. We were trying to discover the triggers that would send her into a binge. Her food diary became a mirror in which she observed her emotional responses and how eating had been the reaction.

Sherri saw that if she was eating the right things at the right time she could usually not overeat, though the desire was still there—particularly when she was pressured for time and incapable of "producing." It wasn't her actual job of producing that was the problem—she was talented and loved the work. It was the daily need to meet others' expectations, depending on others to come through, which they didn't, and playing the political games that seemed to be required at work. And she did it all with an edge of anger and resentment because it pulled her away from her daughters. By the time she got home *to* them, she had nothing left *for* them. Food seemed to fuel her for her tense meetings during the day and get her through her nights.

Up until this moment of insight, Sherri had always claimed that she simply loved food—particularly chocolate and especially doughnuts. She now saw that, in reality, she had an emotional relationship with food, one that had started years before when, as a child, Sherri discovered that eating certain foods made her feel better, and eating a lot of certain foods made her feel a lot better. She had grown up in a perfectionistic family and had used food to dull her sense of failure and relieve the stress. Since she had developed a life pattern of depriving herself of food for her soul, doughnuts became a sweet substitute. It was time to make peace. She had to learn how to truly feed her soul.

CHAPTER 19 ▪ Feeding Your Soul

The great thing in this life is not so much where we are, but in which direction we are moving.

—ANONYMOUS

There is more to living well than just caring for and feeding your physical being. I believe we humans are three-parted beings: body, soul, and spirit. I also believe that all three parts need to be nourished. You need to care for and feed your soul and spirit with the right kind of soul food.

Many people get caught in unhealthy habits because they don't get their needs met on all three levels—spiritually, emotionally, and physically. And because legitimate needs are not being met in legitimate ways, it's just a matter of time before they are met in illegitimate ways. Like falling headfirst into food.

> **SMART WEIGH TIP**
>
> *If you feel like you can't do it on your own, seek help to deal with what's eating you.*

Before I embraced nutrition as a profession, I was handicapped in all three areas of my life. I was searching for real answers to my questions about the purpose of life—especially my life. I knew I was spiritually empty, but I didn't have a clue about how to get filled. I was carrying a lot of emotional baggage, and food became the easy way to fill up my vacuums and get the fuel I needed to carry the

emotional burden. While overfeeding my physical body, I was starving my soul and spirit.

I could cover my eating dependencies with pendulum swings in my weight. I gained weight—but I always lost it again. And, I could overcome overeating as long as I was trapped in the iron-will discipline of a diet. To cope with my unresolved emotions, I could replace the obsessive use and intense preoccupation with food with an obsessive and intense preoccupation with dieting. But, unfortunately, it always came back up.

As I changed career paths and began to learn more about nutrition and taking care of my physical body, I became strong enough to overcome many of my unhealthy eating patterns. Dieting was no longer an answer for me. It would be some time before I learned about—and responded to—my emotional and spiritual needs, but just meeting my physical needs allowed me to break free enough from food and dieting to see the gaping holes in my life.

Many of my clients experience this also. As they become stronger physically, getting their bodies on an even nutritional keel, they are free to see the deeper emotional and spiritual needs that hinder their health. The goal of *The Smart Weigh* is to live well, free, and whole in all these areas—spirit, soul, and body. The people I see getting free of the diet trap and getting well—and staying that way—acknowledge and care for all three. This is not easy to do, but it is possible.

DEALING WITH ROOT ISSUES

We have been created with an intricate design for our physical growth—no one is born an adult. To grow and thrive, our human body requires certain nutrients; without them, it becomes malnourished and growth is stunted.

A similar design exists for our emotional growth: at birth we are emotionally immature and must be fed love and be nurtured to thrive. Without this food for our souls, our emotional growth is arrested, and we fail to thrive. Even though our bodies may have been clothed and fed, our emotions may have been starved and neglected in our homes. As adults, we may appear to cope well with day-to-day life, until stresses, hurts, and challenges overtake us. Then our childlike emotions reveal themselves, and we respond in an emotionally disabled way.

One woman, who struggled for years with both anorexia nervosa and overeating, described it this way: "I grew up in a single-parent home with a young mother who was understandably overwhelmed by the challenge of caring for me. For many reasons, she was unable to 'be there' for me emotionally, and I learned early that staying 'out of the way' and taking up as little room as possible was the best strategy for survival. Because I was convinced so early that I deserved— and could get—only 'crumbs' emotionally, it seemed natural and desirable literally to starve my body and soul as I grew older.

"Now I'm nearly forty years old, and I'm still 'starving' to some degree. While I no longer starve literally, I still have that mentality: I know I can survive 'just fine' on very little, and so it continues to feel natural to withhold good food, good fun, and good love from myself. And when I can't stand the 'crumbs' anymore, I dive headfirst into a whole loaf of bread (with lots of butter) to fill me up.

"I want so much to discover that what happened to me as a child need no longer dictate how I treat myself. I want to know—and live as though—my Creator longs to give me the bread of life."

Not all families, well intentioned as they may have been, planted healthy seeds of love into the souls of their children. Hurts happened, abandonment occurred, shame resulted. As children from

these families grow into adulthood, these unhealthy emotional seeds grow into invisible weeds of guilt and fear, poor self-image, and lack of healthy boundaries, limits, and trust. To thrive—not just survive—and walk in freedom from the diet trap or any life trap, we must identify and root out these toxic weeds in our soul.

FACING FEELINGS

A good place to start with nourishing your soul is to begin to identify—and face—your feelings. You were created with feelings that you can't ignore. They don't just "go away" because you deny them. Processing your feelings requires that you understand and celebrate how you were made—as an emotional being who *feels*.

If, as a child, you were discouraged from expressing your feelings—particularly negative ones such as anger, guilt, or frustration—you quickly learned which feelings got positive or negative reactions. Perhaps now, as an adult, your life has become a list of emotional shoulds and should nots, leaving you believing that what you feel is bad, wrong, or unacceptable. But if your emotions can't be expressed, they have to be bottled up some way, somehow. Maybe with business, maybe with a smile—or maybe by stuffing them or soothing them with food.

Emotions produce energy (e-motion = energy in motion), and if we don't release that energy, we must spend energy to keep it in. But like a dam springing leaks, feelings stuffed inside can come out "sideways" through physical ailments—joint and muscle pain, insomnia, ulcers, even cancer. Instead of crying, we get headaches. Instead of saying we don't want to go someplace with someone, we get stomach cramps. Instead of saying no to another work project, we push ourselves to exhaustion and develop fatigue or high blood pressure. Or we overeat.

Our bodies react to repressed emotion whether we like it or not. The unreleased energy robs us of our well-being by causing increased tension, anxiety, or depression. New research is revealing that

FAMILY SYSTEMS THAT SET THE TRAP

*Eating dependencies most often come out of three types
of unhealthy family systems:*

THE PERFECT FAMILY. This family places high priority on appearances—the family's reputation, identity, and achievements. Its ruling question is: What will people think? Mistakes are not allowed. This family can appear close, loving, and caring from the outside—a perfect front for a rigid set of rules, many of which govern emotions: don't cry, don't get angry, don't mope, smile when you feel like crying. It takes a lot of eating to hold those emotions in.

THE ENMESHED FAMILY. This family emphasizes the need to be close—very close. There are no boundaries; everyone is community property, with a fence protecting them from the "outside." Secrets stay in. The ruling slogan is: "You can't trust anyone outside of the family." Because of the enmeshment within this family, members have a difficult time developing an independent life or unique personality. As a result, food sometimes becomes the only thing the person feels he or she can control. Overeating becomes the one thing in life that is daring, risky, and rebellious.

THE CHAOTIC FAMILY. There are no rules in this family—or they stay hidden and inconsistent because the parents are emotionally unavailable to their children. It may be alcoholism, workaholism, abuse, or any number of issues that distance the children from their caregivers—but it teaches the children not to talk, trust, or feel. They become well-trained experts at deadening their feelings with food—or any substance of choice.

All of these family systems are the result of unhealthy rules and belief systems that have been passed down from generation to generation; the accompanying pain has been passed down with them. It's important to identify the problems your childhood upbringing may have caused so you can begin to resolve the ways in which old beliefs keep you trapped. But don't get stuck in blaming others. Blame can become just another trap.

repressed emotion can lead to a depressed immune system. And unprocessed feelings like fear, anger, and resentment keep us bound to a spiritual hopelessness—a particularly threatening place to live. The bottom line: the feelings you don't express must be repressed, causing you to be depressed, and opening the door to be oppressed.

To prevent emotions from building up in an unhealthy way, it is vital to allow yourself to feel whatever feelings are inside and to fight the desire to judge them as good or bad. The feelings are simply a readout on where you are in life. Identifying and revealing your feelings enables you to cut a clear path through inner turmoil and get to your real needs. Even socially unacceptable feelings like anger, sadness, fear, or guilt can be celebrated because they can help you discover the needs they're covering up. And that's important when you're trying to overcome a fixation on food or the couch. If food becomes your life raft in a sea of unmet needs, it prevents you from discovering what can really satisfy and nourish your soul. Unless you know what you need, you will rarely get it.

RELEASING FEELINGS

Rather than keeping feelings in, you can identify them and then choose to express them in an active, positive way. Your feelings do not have to control you; they do not have to dictate your behavior. Being angry doesn't mean you have to scream and hurt someone, nor does it mean that you're a bad person. Feeling rejected doesn't mean you have to withdraw.

You can release feelings in a number of positive ways: writing and lifting up your words in prayer, creating something with your hands, singing, talking, exercising. Permit yourself to feel the feelings and process them. Realize it is normal to have many conflicting feelings, and it takes practice to identify them correctly. Being

stressed or upset are not feelings, so continue to dig until you name what you are really feeling. Being "stressed" could be feeling tired, guilty, out of control, afraid. Feeling "bad" could be feeling lonely, sick, or scared. Allow that feeling to come over you—and then watch it fade as you release it. It will, and you can. The next step is to learn to match the feeling with the appropriate need. If you are sad, you may need to cry or talk. Eating is not the answer.

This process may seem like a journey into very unfamiliar—even frightening—territory.

> **SMART WEIGH TIP**
>
> *Look up. Focus on the power that you need to make lasting change.*

But it's a vital part of releasing the healing mechanism within you, including your ability to lose weight and keep it off. Quietly and repeatedly asking yourself "How do I feel?" is a way—your own way and at your own pace—to uncover slowly what needs to be brought out into the light.

JOURNALING FEELINGS

The most effective—and freeing—step I took in this area was to begin to keep a journal. In that privacy, I can frankly say whatever I am feeling.

I had been encouraged to keep a journal for quite a while, but I always protested, "That's not for me!" I didn't feel that I had the time, or patience. And what if someone got hold of it?

A loving friend challenged me to look honestly at my protests, asking if they were really excuses. Out of respect for her, I began to write. I found ten extra minutes in my day, and began a miraculous journey to a new kind of freedom. Instead of my age-old pattern of putting off dealing with things until later, I found that by looking at my life's happenings *as they were happening*, I could discover how I really felt about what was occurring. I found that under my "nice and busy " smile, there was often hurt and anger.

Slowly my self-consciousness began to fade, and I was able to write out more and more of the feelings and thoughts that flooded my heart and soul. Through journaling I came to know the reality of the words penned by wise Solomon: "A heart at peace gives life to the body" (Proverbs 14:30).

I've used an inexpensive spiral-bound notebook to record my feelings, and I've used my portable computer. If your journal is not portable, keep a small notebook with you to jot down notes about your appetite, feelings, and the things that affect you throughout the day. Keeping a food diary is often a good place to begin if you want to change your eating habits. A small notebook will allow you to record what you eat and when you eat it at the time you are doing so—it is much more accurate than relying on memory. Add to this journal notes about how you feel physically before and after eating: are you energetic, alert, full, and strong, or fatigued, foggy, starved, unsatisfied, and shaky? You may be so used to feeling bad that you haven't noticed how serious it really is. Recording this information will help you see the connection between what you eat and how you feel physically and emotionally.

You can examine the feelings you've written about during a time set aside to reflect and be strengthened. If possible, be consistent about the time of day for your journaling, a time that best suits who you are. I write early in the morning, almost every morning, because I'm a morning person. Some people write on their lunch break; others before they go to sleep; some once a week; still others just when they feel the need.

Consider choosing a place in your house that has a particular ambiance for you—somewhere pleasant to "go to" when you write. In this room, desk, table, corner, bed, or sitting area, you should feel safe to write about your feelings. If you wonder, "What in the world

do I write about?" let me give you a jump-start: I begin every journaling time with "Yesterday, I..." I write about what happened in
my yesterday and, more important, I write about how those events
made me feel. Journaling gives me a chance to express my fears,
inadequacies, regrets, joys, hopes, and discoveries. When I feel
happy, I can write about that. When I feel sad or angry or worried,
writing helps me identify those feelings. The act of writing also
helps me to name vague, free-floating feelings. Believe me, there is
enormous power in calling a spade a spade. Once you name how you
feel about something, you begin to receive power over it. It is no
longer an unknown assailant.

If it is difficult for you just to pull your feelings about a particular situation "out of the air," you may find it helpful to make a list
of strong emotion words: ANGRY, AFRAID, SAD, REJECTED,
HUMILIATED, LOVED, GUILTY, DEPRESSED. Chose one, then
write quickly (without censoring yourself) whatever things, events,
people, or thoughts are called up by that word at that moment.

WHEN TO STOP, LOOK, AND LISTEN

WHEN YOU FEEL BAD: angry, sad, afraid, guilty, lonely, hungry, tired, sick, numb, depressed, hostile.

WHEN YOUR THINKING BECOMES A HINDRANCE: thinking about food when you aren't hungry or it's not an appropriate time to eat; thinking about your weight when it's not the real problem; worrying obsessively; thinking about anything too much.

WHEN YOUR CHOICES INVOLVE TOO MUCH: eating, drinking, spending, working, drugs, dangerous overactivity, compulsive sex or pornography, reckless actions.

WHEN YOUR ACTIONS INVOLVE TOO LITTLE: recreation, replenishment, healthy pleasures, sleep, exercise, intimacy, friendship, or social contact.

Don't worry about how strange or bizarre or mean it might sound, and don't worry about your writing skills or grammar. Remember, your journal is just for you.

Feeling an emotion is not a problem—it is what you do with a feeling that takes you toward or away from health and wholeness. As you look at it on paper, you can gain new perspective about the situation that may have caused the feeling in the first place. You can ask, "Why did that person or situation trigger such a feeling?" Did it remind you of something in your childhood? Did it make you feel ashamed or inadequate? Is there tension with another person that needs to be discussed and resolved?

Carve out that soul time for yourself. It may be enough just to feel your emotions and acknowledge them—or you may need to do significant work to resolve deep-seated soul wounds. Letting go of negative feelings opens up space within you for joy, freedom, and health. Your journal can be a powerful vehicle to help you break free of the diet trap.

SPIRITUAL CONNECTION

When I was twenty-four and had all of the trappings of success, I felt empty and without purpose. My relationships weren't working, and even though I was "living well," I wasn't *feeling* well. I was physically tired and emotionally weary. Although I had been raised with religious tradition, that was all I had known—tradition, rules, and rituals. I did not have a personal connection with my Creator.

From this very low point I looked up and came to know a living God who could affect every part of my life. That changed my entire life—and changed how and why I was living it. My new focus on wellness took on a higher significance. I was now interested in the bigger picture: on caring for the magnificently created human being

I knew myself to be so that I could feel well, be well, and do well in gratitude to my Creator. In the years since, I've continued to experience the joy of knowing I am loved by the One who created me, and that has given me the ability to love and care for my body and my soul—and others.

I am convinced that striving for physical wellness and freedom from the diet trap without addressing spiritual and emotional health is a futile exercise—we are a sum of our parts, and spiritual needs cannot be separated from physical ones. The body-soul-spirit connection is an amazing one: the care that we give, or don't give, to our body certainly not only affects our physical energy and well-being, but also our ability to think clearly, to see life through a positive lens, and to connect spiritually and relationally.

Our deepest needs are met through relationships. We fill our souls through connecting with others in positive ways and connecting with ourselves through reflection and recreation. We fill our spirits by connecting and feasting with God. A vital, personal relationship with God and honest relationships with others pave the way to our healing. To thrive, we must be connected physically, emotionally, and spiritually.

Like many people, I have my own definition for what being spiritually "connected" means. My personal religious orientation is the traditional Christian faith, and my use of the term "spiritual" is rooted in the Bible, the Old and New Testament theology. I don't believe that God is a disconnected higher power that I am struggling to reach up to, struggling to perform for and receive acceptance from. I believe that God, in His love, reaches down to humanity—and to me, personally. He empowers me by living within me. By inviting His Spirit to dwell within my spirit, my life has been linked with the unlimited love, power, and wisdom of the Divine. When I view the

world, my relationships, and my struggles through the eyes of my Creator, it makes all the difference in my attitude and my personal power.

At some point in our lives, we all experience feelings and circumstances that challenge us, sometimes beyond what we think we can handle. Your struggle with your weight and eating might be one of these points. Tragic circumstances can also change our lives in a heartbeat, seemingly with no explanation. And it is in these most difficult times that feel so out of control that we can allow our weaknesses to be covered by the great power of God. We can connect with that power.

The scientific and medical fields are beginning to identify an incredible current of healing power that comes through spiritual connection. Studies from around the world are emerging suggesting that humanity has been "wired" for God. There is now medical evidence that prayer and other forms of spiritual connection can help significantly to heal the ravages of stress, fatigue, and illness.

The latest revelations about spirituality and wellness emphasize the power of three components of religious experience: (1) personal faith, (2) religious practice, and (3) prayer. One such study, conducted at Duke University Medical Center, revealed that all these were powerful tools in the fight against illness and stress. Another study showed that regular prayer can positively affect a person's heart and respiratory rates, lowering blood pressure and slowing brain waves—without drugs or surgery. Studies have even shown a powerful impact on health even when the ill do not know they are being prayed for.

Choosing to let go of my own vision of personal strength and live empowered by God is my path to living a life of spiritual connection and significance. Rather than trying in all my human power to

make things work, I now know, deep in my soul, that I will see change through prayer, not by attempting to control the situations or the people in my life. The energy needed to hold onto—and attempt to accomplish in my own strength—the things that I was never meant to control wears on my body, soul, and spirit. This "wear" shows up clearly in physical messages: fatigue, sickness, and excess weight to carry the burden. These physical and emotional "diseases" are but symptoms—telling me and warning me that I have diverted from my spiritual path of peace.

You might wonder how a mere human being can connect with the Divine. I have connected with God through prayer, through listening to powerful music, through reflecting on the beauty of God's creation, through the quietness of a church or garden, through helping another in need. I've learned to pray about my own needs and the things I'm concerned about, asking for divine guidance and strength. Rather than focusing on specific results and demands, I ask for heavenly perspective about specific problems—an ability to see with clear vision the way my Creator does. The result is renewed strength and power.

It is through this power that I have discovered that personal, long-lasting change is possible. Connecting spiritually nourishes the soul the same way that food and water nourish the body. I must nourish my soul with Spirit-inspired "food"— the truth of who I am and why I was created. Knowing the truth about who I am is critical to my emotional well-being. It's critical to yours as well. It determines how you live, what you accomplish, and how you treat—and are treated by—others.

Many of us are so focused on caring for others that we tend to put our own needs on the back burner. Is it because we get more strokes that way? Or, is it that we don't believe we are worth being taken

care of? If you don't feel valuable, taking care of your body seems unimportant and it will be easy to get caught in destructive patterns of eating. If you think you are junk, you will eat junk food.

But once you can see yourself through your Creator's eyes, you will desire new ways to care for yourself.

When you see yourself in a new light, your image of yourself will not depend so much on how others see you—or their response to you. With a correct image of who you are, you will wince at the idea of a binge, cringe at the thought of falling asleep on the couch in a food coma, and wonder "Why would I do that to myself?" You deserve to live free of the diet trap—and you can.

As you move forward on your journey—not just "following a diet" but embracing a new way of living—change begins to occur in every arena of your life. Physically, you are developing new habits, rituals, and routines—and letting go of old ones. Emotionally and relationally, you are choosing new ways of relating to the world and yourself, and processing feelings in differing ways. Spiritually, you are coming more alive and discovering that you are worth loving and caring for in new ways. New beliefs, new thoughts, new feelings, new behavior—all are changes with lasting power.

The results are wonderful—but change never comes easily. Resistance comes clothed in sabotage—often from within, and sometimes from others. To learn to identify and overcome sabotage is to learn a life lesson that will serve you well in all areas of living and loving.

CHAPTER 20 ▪ Overcoming Sabotoge and Setbacks

What lies behind us and what lies before us are tiny matters compared to what lies within us.

—OLIVER WENDELL HOLMES

"I don't know what's wrong with me," Sandy lamented. "I love the new way I'm living. I love the way I'm feeling. I love telling others about my new life. But I started sobbing this morning for no reason I could see. I just don't know what I'm feeling, but I've been depressed all day."

Sandy spoke these words six months after making amazing changes in her lifestyle and perspectives. You may remember reading about Sandy's lifetime struggles with weight in Chapter 1. She was overcoming those struggles, day by day, and she looked and felt marvelous physically. She had lost forty-two

> **SMART WEIGH TIP**
>
> *Know your triggers. You have to know which moods send you to the cookie jar before you can do anything about it.*

pounds and truly knew that she could keep them off for life. Yet clearly, on this day, something was wrong. "Do you know what's going on with me, Pam?" she asked, confusion evident in her eyes.

Yes, I did have a clue about what Sandy was feeling. She was experiencing the challenge of change—and it was threatening to sabotage her new-found freedom. Strange as it may sound, she was

grieving, and thereby experiencing a myriad of emotions from a variety of sources. As thrilled as she was with the positive changes in her life, she was sad and mad, panicked and helpless, all at the same time.

It is very natural for lifestyle changes like Sandy's to trigger a sense of loss. She had hated the way she used to eat, but she'd eaten that way for a long time. She loved the new foods and patterns of eating, but she missed regularly indulging in the comfort foods that had meant so much to her for so many years.

Most important, Sandy was seeing some of the patterns that had caused her to fail in her previous diets. Through counseling and team support, Sandy had learned that being overweight had, on a subconscious level, actually helped her throughout her life. The excess weight was her "voice"—it spoke for her without Sandy ever having to say a word.

To her parents, her inflated size spoke silently but loudly: "You can't control me." To men, her larger size said, "Don't touch me." And to her husband, her extra weight said quietly, "I don't want intimacy."

As difficult as it was, Sandy was now finding the words for those silent messages and admitting them to herself. She was no longer willing to keep weight on just to speak for her. But that didn't mean that letting go of the old patterns was easy. Yet, Sandy had to in order to embrace fully the new. And that meant letting go of grief as well.

Sandy's emotional battle symbolizes the battle we all fight any time we enter the process of change. It's a battle we must identify and win—because defeat means imprisonment in the same old self-defeating ways. Often, in the throes of change, we get stuck—in old patterns, old thinking, and old ways of doing things. Let's face it,

change stirs up old buckets of fear within us and can be terrifying. But if we cave in to the fear, we remain stuck in old patterns simply because of our own resistance to change—a powerful trap in and of itself. The old, no matter the misery it has delivered, is familiar and less frightening.

Even a life filled with constant chaos may be comfortable and "safe" because it's all we've ever known. Battling weight and fighting food may be exhausting, but if you've only lived in a war zone, making peace can bring a deafening calm. So expect internal resistance. Habits and thought patterns that have been learned through a lifetime require supernatural power and patience to unlearn.

The fact is, real change is most apt to happen—really happen— only when the misery of where we are is greater than the fear of where we might be going. In matters of health, I often see crisis as the wake-up call that tells people it's time to change—or else. It may be a doctor telling you to change your eating habits or go on medication for diabetes, hypertension, or elevated cholesterol. It may be an expensive suit that no longer fits, screaming at you to get in shape. It may be that you are picking up every cold, flu, and virus that's around and you're sick and tired of being sick and tired. The desire to change must rise up and face the fear head-on.

OVERCOMING SELF-SABOTAGE

As you feel your fear or resistance swirling within you, you might ask, "What in the world is there to be frightened of? We're just talking about a different—and healthier—way of living! What's so scary about that?" Actually, there are a myriad of fears that arise as saboteurs of lasting change: fears of failure, commitment, disapproval, even of success.

FEAR OF FAILURE is a powerful force in resistance to change. It may be best expressed in the question I'm often asked by my clients: "What if I try this new way of living, and don't stick with it? I've never stuck with any diet before, so why should I believe I'm capable of changing my whole way of eating and living? Won't I just end up a failure and a laughingstock, like always?" They expect themselves to do everything right from the get-go, miraculously changing lifelong patterns overnight, rather than accepting that they'll need to invest time into a *process* of change. The fear of not being able to change—perfectly, quickly, and once and for all—keeps them from even starting. Or, when they experience the inevitable setbacks inherent in the change process, they use the "evidence" of failure to condemn themselves into staying trapped. When the old inner voices chide, "See, you never could do it right and you never will," self-sabotage is often the next step.

FEAR OF COMMITMENT is another common obstacle to setting firm goals or accomplishing them. People manage to keep postponing what they might like to do with their lives for fear that if they accomplish a goal they will have to hold onto it—and that just seems impossible. After all, how good is their track record—especially in the area of health and self-care? Why start anything, why make *any* improvements, if you're not positive you can sustain them perfectly for life? And what if the goal you set is the wrong one? What if it doesn't meet your needs?

This kind of thinking is similar to that of the alcoholic considering whether to choose sobriety over continuing physical and spiritual demise. If a jittery alcoholic, just admitting she is powerless over her disease and considering her next step, were to believe she had to make a rock-solid commitment *today* to stay sober till the day she dies, she may never choose sobriety. That's simply too big a bite to chew.

That's why in programs like Alcoholics Anonymous, newly sober members are urged to take recovery "one day at a time." Thinking ahead is simply overwhelming—and unnecessary. What matters is what they choose *today*. Only in time do they discover the liberating truth that a good choice today usually leads to a good choice tomorrow, and the next day, and the next. But they only have to live them one day at a time. So don't let fear of committing to your well-being become an obstacle or excuse. Choose *The Smart Weigh—just for today*.

FEAR OF DISAPPROVAL OR REJECTION is another saboteur of positive change. This is a valid concern but it needn't be hindering. A major challenge in any personal process of change is dealing with the reactions of your family and friends. Your change may be as scary to them as it is to you.

When we make changes that are in our best interest, friends and family often say, "I liked you better the way your were!" or "Please don't change any more—I like you the way you are!" Psychologists call this subtle or overt pressure to change back to our old ways "changeback pressure." Those pressuring us often feel threatened by our changes because they are losing someone or something familiar. Often they like the old you a bit better, particularly if the old you met their needs—even at the expense of your own. They may want you to change back to being their "binge buddy," or to one who never shows feelings, or to the person who by "being the one with the *real* problem" could help them deny their own struggles.

Sabotage from "inside the camp" is sometimes very real. Many family members and friends want to see weight loss and success for their loved ones as long as they can control it. If they can take the credit, and if their loved ones do it *their* way, they will help. As badly off as you may have been in your "old ways," it may have been more comfortable for them—especially for spouses.

Husbands often try to motivate their wives to lose weight. But, ironically, they are sometimes the least helpful since they are too personally involved. Some typical "motivators" employed by spouses: "You have such a beautiful face; if you could just lose that weight…" or "I'll pay you ten dollars for every pound you lose." Or, "Get into that bikini, and we'll go on that cruise you've been wanting." All fall short of offering positive assistance.

Why? Subconsciously some husbands fear their wives' success. There is so much at stake: loss of eating as a form of entertainment; new foods being served and old ones disappearing; a more physically attractive wife, causing insecurity in some husbands. The sabotage may take the form of subtle complaints about the new way of eating ("Why don't we ever have anything good to eat anymore? You used to be such a good cook!" Or "Honey, you eat anyway you want, but don't mess with my food—I'm not the one with the problem.") Sometimes the sabotage is more direct—he may bring home ice cream or donuts or boxes of candy to reward you for your success.

Similarly, wives often sabotage their husbands' attempts to change their eating patterns. They start out being supportive, often making the appointment to see me, or buying the book. They go "all out" on the new grocery shopping patterns and cooking techniques. But when the husband shows signs of succeeding in his health goals (slimming down, gaining energy, maintaining an exercise regimen), things can change on the home front. Some wives fear their husbands' growing good looks and the new sense of confidence they exude. The husband's success can actually be a double-edged sword to the wife, who may feel that his improved health is a reproach on the way she was previously feeding her family.

How do you hold your own against the sabotage of a spouse or others who may not even be aware of the harm they are inflicting?

First, anticipate and prepare for your loved ones' possible reactions. By expecting negative actions and comments, you can minimize their effect. Write and seek counsel with a friend or a professional to help you identify how you are feeling—and to learn how to communicate lovingly and effectively with your saboteurs.

Most important, make the decision that you are changing your living patterns for yourself—not to please others or to be rewarded with approval, or a vacation. Gaining your personal freedom is reward enough. And remember that the only person capable of gaining the freedom you desire is *you*. Another person cannot force you to change, nor can he or she prevent you from doing so. You decide what you eat, the way you breathe, the water you drink, the exercise you do.

FEAR OF SUCCESS believe it or not, also prevents many people from making positive changes. We may feel that we don't deserve to succeed, feel good, or live free. Some of us won't allow ourselves to trim down to an attractive size because we fear being a sexual target. Or maybe we've been taught as children that we are being selfish when we take care of ourselves.

> **SMART WEIGH TIP**
>
> *Do it for yourself. As long as somebody else is pushing you, no matter what you do or what you try, it'll never work.*

These fears not only serve as obstacles to change, buy are often the vacuum that sucks us back to the old entrapping behaviors. I love the motivational speaker Zig Ziglar's declaration, "Courage is not the absence of fear; it is going on in spite of the fear." And an exciting thing often occurs when we do go on: we may find that by facing the fear, it evaporates.

How often have you avoided doing a task that you thought would be impossible or particularly embarrasing, such as the first time you drove a car, or attempted to water ski? When you finally did it, it

wasn't half as bad as you anticipated, and the joy and freedom—of driving, for example—was surely well worth facing your fear.

One of my clients, Kim, helped begin some of the first aerobic dance classes in our area. At the time she started the franchise, she was carrying fifty extra pounds that she just couldn't drop after a difficult pregnancy. She was attracted to the idea of fun exercise, and out of her own need to start doing *something* to get moving, she organized an aerobics class.

The idea of fun exercise to music stirred lots of excitement and attracted many to come to the first class. But Kim passed on the first class, and the second, and the third. Her fear of others seeing how out of shape she was—and how easily out of breath she became—kept her from fulfilling her dream for quite a while. The day she finally walked into the class, leotard-clad and all, she did so with eyes almost closed and shaky knees. But five minutes later, she was having a great time, dancing alongside others to a new life of wellness. She determined just to look at the class—and not in the mirror.

A few years later, Kim was *teaching* three classes a day—in five locations. Her weight finally fell, but her joy of outfacing fear is what she prizes most. And now she does take a glimpse in the mirror now and then!

THE POWER OF A DREAM

Fear is a natural response to change, but it loses its power when healthy motivation shines brightly. This is why the first best step in overcoming self-sabotage is to identify the *why* of the change you desire. What is your personal dream for wellness? Take a few moments to review pages 234-235, where we explored this issue. Your underlying motivation in living free of the diet trap has to be rooted in a genuine and personal passion for positive change, for the

right reasons. The only way to turn a goal into a living reality is through emotionally connecting to it—with passion.

In this process, refuse to look at what you need to do, what you should or should not do, or what you must or must not do. It is impossible to be emotionally connected to or be passionate about a list of rules for very long. This kind of focus keeps your eyes on the behavior you are trying to avoid rather than on the new way of living life you want to embrace.

As I discussed in Chapter 5, having a positive perspective and positive goal is powerful because we are destined to hit whatever we have our eyes on. Instead of keeping your focus on what *not* to do or aim for, look at what you *want* to obtain and how you desire to live. You may want to make a list that looks something like this:

- I want to live a life overflowing with energy and well-being.
- I want to be fit; I want a body that works for me.
- I want to be well; I want an immune system that protects me from sickness and disease.
- I want to be healthy and vital as I age.
- I want to be at peace with my body and with my food.
- I want to treat myself well—and believe I deserve it.
- I want to provide the framework for a healthy attitude about food for my children.

We need to be honest with ourselves and commit to a few, simple, heartfelt goals that are close to our heart. Even if our initial list turns out to take us just partway down the road, it will at least get us *on* the road—and we will learn a lot in the process.

MAKING YOUR DREAM A REALITY

The next step in the process of change is to identify and become educated in the new habits that will help you to realize your desires. This is the "work stage" of change—and many people actually enjoy it. You may take classes, read books (including this one), and gather more information about how to "just do it." There's a sense of personal power in this stage—of working hard to figure out the solution to your problem.

Letting go is the third step of change: we must make room for the new in our lives. And that means we must let go of destructive thought patterns and leave behind self-defeating behaviors. There is a time for everything, and a season for every activity... a time to tear down and a time to build up. There isn't room within you for both the old patterns and the new.

To unlearn habits and thought patterns that have been developing for a lifetime requires motivation, patience, and courage. Whenever you let go of the old—even self-sabotaging behavior and thinking patterns—you experience loss. In every transition, happy or sad, letting go of what was involves grief.

Grieving the loss is the fourth step of change. Yes, this is painful. This is where Sandy was. She was doing the right things, but getting what felt like wrong results. Instead of getting easier, her process of change was getting harder. She was expecting to feel wonderful, but at the moment she was just feeling awful.

As you make changes, you may, like Sandy, feel depressed, lonely, guilty, helpless, angry, panicked, resentful, hopeless, hostile—and perhaps silly about it all—before you finally feel relief. This stage had been a secret agent of sabotage to Sandy in the past. The grieving and letting go of the familiar had always driven her back to seeking comfort in food.

But not this time. As she saw her lifelong weight problem dissolving, she didn't want to go back to the same old defeat. This time she got support to push through her fears and claim her new life of health and vitality. A setback—whether physical, emotional, or spiritual—became merely an inevitable event along the road of change rather than a step off a cliff.

Sandy finally began to learn from her own experience that the pain of loss would be balanced by the joy of change. For the first time in her memory, she felt physically vital and emotionally fulfilled, and connected—spiritually and relationally. She was learning to look in places other than the refrigerator for strength and support.

> **SMART WEIGH TIP**
>
> *Practice early detection—weigh yourself once a month. If you've crept up two pounds, get back on the weight loss track.*

DO YOU NEED SUPPORT?

Like Sandy, you may want to ask yourself if you need support. Learning to reach out for help is a huge step on the road to freedom and overcoming self-sabotage—yet it's one of the more rewarding aspects of healing. Why? Because asking for help undergirds your desire for lifelong progress. I know from my own experience that reaching out can be scary; it reveals my vulnerability and challenges my "old tapes" of "I don't need anything; I can (and should be able to) do this on my own." But, believe me, your success in changing your life for the better is much more likely if you stop trying to go it alone. Isolation and self-reliance are not only symptoms of our old entrapment, they practically guarantee that we'll stay stuck.

Acknowledging a problem to at least one other human being says that you know you need help and that you are worth helping. We were created with a natural need to be understood and accepted. Nonjudgmental relationships—whether with trusted friends, a coun-

seling support group, a small home-care group, or a ministry team—
show wounded people that they can trust again. Choose your confi-
dante carefully and prayerfully. I encourage my clients who are dealing
with issues such as sexual or alcohol abuse in the family to seek professional counseling. These are deeply painful issues that affect every
part of your being. A professional therapist has the skills to help you
walk through—and out of—painful memories, family systems, and
current traps. Not everyone needs a professional counselor, but a person with whom you can honestly share your soul is vital.

Human support is vital for breaking the back of any dependency
and busting out of any trap. It can meet the need for intimacy and
build our self-esteem in ways that our family and life-up-till-now
may never have been able to do. But realize that while others can
care, they cannot fix. Just as food is not your ultimate comforter,
neither are people your ultimate source of health and well-being.
They will never be able to anticipate your needs quickly enough or
understand you fully enough. No one can be there for you twenty-
four hours a day. Only God can do that. But putting trust in a tangible relationship and opening yourself up for human support will
give you strength for change—especially for the long haul.

The supportive relationships you cultivate can be a beautiful
reflection of your Creator's love and hope for you. So find the right
kind of support. A nag won't do; neither will a partner in crime.
Look for people who can empathize with you, encourage you, and
believe in you.

WHEN YOU WANT TO HELP SOMEONE ELSE

We all feel that we have infinite wisdom and the right perspective
into someone else's situation. We've spent a lifetime learning from
all sorts of mistakes—and it's natural to want to share the wealth.

This is especially true when we have a vested interest in seeing the people we care about change for the better. If we're learning to live *The Smart Weigh* ourselves, we want others to join us. That would make our own journey easier, we think, and may even be *the* difference in our long-term success or failure.

You know what? That's stinking thinking. Remember, *you* are responsible for your own choices; *you* have the power, through your spiritual connection, to stay true to your healthy path without the full support of everyone around you.

But, naturally, we want the people we love to be well and happy, and to benefit, as we have, from positive lifestyle changes. This can be frustrating because we certainly can't control others; but our support, offered in effective ways, can be life-shaping, maybe even life-saving. It requires some innovative strategies and time, but it can make a critical difference in someone's well-being. Supportive spouses seem to be particularly strong motivators. A study by Yale University researchers found that overweight people whose spouses were positively involved in their weight-loss programs lost almost three times as much weight compared with subjects in other studies that focused on the individual alone. Another study from Indiana University found that married couples who joined exercise programs together were more likely to have stuck with it after a year, compared to those who had joined solo.

So what's the right track to take when trying to get a loved one on board the healthful-living bandwagon? Here are some guidelines:

HELP THEM SEE THEIR CURRENT LOCATION. Don't hard sell, but gently nudge them toward the healthy door's threshold. Don't try to nag or push them across it. Next time you get the urge to offer all your wisdom, consider this: Advice, as most people tend to give it, is rarely helpful. Solicited or not, when you make someone's decisions for

them, you enable them to remain dependent on you. And if they don't accept your advice, they're likely to feel as if they've disappointed or offended you.

The bottom line is this: No one makes long-lasting personal change unless *they* want to. But gently helping them to see how they *really* feel in their current health situation—how they sleep, their productivity and stamina, their quality of life, the things that are hindering them from enjoying life—might help them to determine *for themselves* where they want to go, and why.

HELP THEM SEE THEIR DESTINATION. The best support is to give concrete reasons and reminders about *why* they should stay the course to better health. A man might need to be encouraged by how well he will hit the golf ball with less weight on his frame. A teenager may need to see how a clearer mind will yield better concentration and studying. A woman may want more energy—what she can do *with* her body when she's fit and well rather than *to* her body to beat it into submission.

HELP THEM FIND DIRECTIONS. Your loved ones may now have recognized the value of change, but don't have the tools or know-how to get there. Helping them to do some research of their options—a fitness class to join, a community health program that's soon to begin, a highly recommended nutritionist to counsel with, a book like this one—will steer them to the right road. Just remember that what they do with the information you give them is their choice—and it may be to do nothing at all.

USE THE EIO TECHNIQUE. That's Empathy, Information, Options. Here's an example: A friend who has been struggling to overcome a poor body image has been invited to join the office volleyball team but is self-conscious about being seen in sports attire. Rather than saying "Don't worry about that—you *need* the exercise!" give (1)

Empathy ("Wow, that's a tough problem"); (2) Options ("What's the worst thing that could happen? How will you feel if you don't? Would it be less stressful to play on a community volleyball team where you don't know and work with your teammates?") ; and (3) Information ("I think if it were me, I'd figure, 'Hey, what have I got to lose? They know me, they want me, they've asked me'"). When you encourage, you're helping your friends to help themselves.

BE THEIR CHEERLEADER. Downsize your expectations, and expect your loved ones to stall, take occasional wrong turns, maybe even drive off the road. Help them to see that long-term change is best achieved by taking it slowly and getting there alive. Cheer them on and assure them that you believe in them, no matter what rate their progress. Just as you cannot be made to feel guilty about your personal healthy choices, you do not have the power to make others feel guilty about their own unhealthy choices. Keep your eyes on your own road.

A journal is a great gift to give your loved one because they can record even the tiniest steps of progress. When they are reminded of how good an accomplishment, even a small one, feels, they may be encouraged to stay faithful to the whole healing journey.

GROWING UP, GROWING FREE

"Just Say No" has been a powerful campaign slogan warning children and teens against drug use. The irony is that we adults often can't even say no to a chocolate chip cookie! And peer pressure didn't die in high school. No matter what your age, you must learn—and remember—to say one simple word that tends to get stuck in the human throat: *No.*

When you are offered a food that doesn't fit into your wellness plan, there's no need to give a reason. Neither is there a need to feel guilty, especially if the other person knows what efforts you are mak-

ing to change. (If they made the cookie "just for you," then there's another issue going on.) A caring friend or family member will respect your desire for freedom and will understand a simple "No, thank you," or "I don't care for any—thank you." Period. These words communicate strength and decisiveness: the truth is that you *can* eat anything; but some foods you choose not to eat *today*.

When you reach the point where you can make an adult commitment to live and live well, you can break free of the diet trap once and for all. Nonetheless, you may sometimes crave some foods. If so, don't overreact. Good health is not affected by one hot fudge sundae, one piece of birthday cake, or one hot-dog at a ball game. Don't try to fast the next day, punish yourself with restrictive eating, or take a laxative. And don't fall into the trap of, "I've blown it now, so I may as well keep going!" Just get back on track.

> **SMART WEIGH TIP**
>
> *Repeat this to yourself:*
> *"I can lose weight—*
> *and I will."*

This is especially important when you are most stressed and most vulnerable to emotional messages that signal you to eat. When feelings and stressful situations get too hot to handle, it may seem simpler to return to your old way of eating than to change your way of dealing with life. Overcoming each difficult time—and learning from the ones that overcome you—will make the next one easier. You will not just change old habits, you will establish new ways of living that really work.

WILLPOWER DOESN'T WORK

Once understood, the secrets of *The Smart Weigh* are relatively simple. But, embracing these principles and making genuine change will require more than education alone. Information does not change lives; only revelation promotes lasting change.

Information can be received as head knowledge and may give momentary inspiration, but revelation is received in the heart. It is not just a good idea or something we "should" do. We begin to change our way of eating and living only when we see—truly see—the difference it makes in our personal lives.

BECOME A STUDENT OF YOUR SETBACKS

There will be times when your momentum with healthy eating and living will get seriously off track—but that doesn't mean you have failed, or that *The Smart Weigh* "doesn't work." It does mean that you are human and you were not designed to be the Master or Mistress of your Universe.

If you encounter some rough waters, use journaling as a tool to help you study the setback and see what's going on—*really*. Reflect and write on the past hours and days and ask yourself:

1. *Have I gotten off track in taking care of myself?* Am I tired, hungry, or stressed? Did I go long hours without eating? Am I missing the balance in nutrients? Have I been getting too little sleep?
2. *How do I feel—really?* Anxious? Discouraged? Depressed? Afraid? Sick of focusing on weight loss? Mad at my wife, husband, mother, or boss?
3. *What do I need?* A break? To be less of a perfectionist? Someone to say "good job" or notice how well I'm doing?
4. *What am I expecting?* To lose weight more quickly? Not to have cravings? Never, ever to have a setback?
5. *Is that reasonable?* No.
6. *What is reasonable?* To lose one pound a week—and to expect to have hard times. That's how life is sometimes.
7. *What could I say to myself that would be positive?* That I don't have to be perfect; *progress* is great. That I'm doing the best I can with what I have to work with, and that I feel *so* much better.
8. *What can I do to get back on track?* Eat a power snack this afternoon, and go for a walk when I get home. Journal everything I'm feeling this evening. Talk to my spouse about how I've been feeling at work. Call a friend and ask for some encouragement.

Yet, once envisioned, our tendency is to rely on our own strength or willpower. The problem is, it's just not enough—and never has been. It's not natural to "control" eating; it's unrealistic to think that any of us can muster up enough willpower to control it for a lifetime. We need to receive help from a greater power than we can "conjure up" ourselves.

But for many people, willpower and self-reliance are the goals—they are going to do it the right way, in their own way, or not at all. Yet, research shows that people who successfully shed bad habits actually have the same number of slip-ups in the first month as those who ultimately fail to change. The difference is that those who succeed don't let a lapse become a collapse. They don't aim for perfection because they accept that it's impossible. Instead, they accept that they will make "less than best" choices occasionally, and accept "progress" as enough. With this mindset, a slip-up does not seal their fate; instead they study their setbacks and simply move on.

I believe that the final and winning step of change is a life principle: Each day we must decide whom to believe about our habits and hang-ups, our successes and our slip-ups. I believe we have a very real enemy—one who will ceaselessly attempt to cast a pall of hopelessness over us. The voice may say, "You can never change. Just count how many times you've failed. Look at the life you've had, what you've done, what's been done to you. You could never live another way."

This enemy attempts to steal our hope and self-worth and to detach us from the spiritual connection we were created for. When we lose our spiritual connection, we lose our vision and purpose for our life. Hating ourselves, hating our bodies, and living in a self-destructive manner not only prematurely takes our life, but takes the life out of us. The unspoken message we too often follow is: eat, drink, and be merry, for tomorrow you die.

But I believe there is another power in this battle. This is the Voice of truth—my Creator—speaking into my life. His voice tells me that I have been created to be a mighty winner, that I am loved, that I need only to receive and trust. The Voice says that I am to value myself because I am of infinite value to God, and that by choosing to live life well I can continue to receive a power that is greater than I.

Each of us has the deciding vote. You and I break the tie; we decide with whom we will side. I chose many years ago to cast my vote with God—the genuine transformer of my life.

STAYING THE COURSE

Over the course of these past seven weeks you've done what few people do—you've followed through on a vision and a commitment. Research tells us that it takes twenty-one days to break a habit, and thirty days to establish a new one. It takes forty days to start feeling comfortable with your new way of living. So your efforts during these seven weeks have worked to start sealing your new behavior of eating, exercising, resting, and self-care into lifetime patterns. As you continue to live free of the snare, you will need to keep putting into daily practice what you now believe.

May your journey be one that leads you to a fulfilled life—body, soul, and spirit. May you be filled with good food, good health, and great joy!

SAMPLE FOOD DIARY

YOUR NAME: _Lynne_   WEEK BEGINNING _3/2_

	BREAKFAST	LUNCH	DINNER	COMMENTS AND EXERCISE
FRIDAY	PROTEIN: 6:35 am 2 eggs	PROTEIN: 11:30 am 1 chicken breast	PROTEIN: 7:00 pm salmon steak	up at 5:45 am – 6oz apple juice, walked 40 mins.
	COMPLEX CARB: whole wheat toast	COMPLEX CARB: 1 large baked potato	COMPLEX CARB: wild rice	4:45 pm afternoon snack
	SIMPLE CARB: 1 orange	SIMPLE CARB: 1 side veggie, dish of strawberries	SIMPLE CARB: 1 orange	
	ADDED FAT:	ADDED FAT: 1 Tbsp. sour cream	ADDED FAT: salad dressing	
	SNACK★: 6 crackers, 2 string cheeses	SNACK★: 1/2 of a turkey sandwich	SNACK★: cereal and skim milk	☑☑☑☑☑☑☑ CHECK YOUR WATER AS YOU DRINK
SATURDAY	PROTEIN:	PROTEIN:	PROTEIN:	
	COMPLEX CARB:	COMPLEX CARB:	COMPLEX CARB:	
	SIMPLE CARB:	SIMPLE CARB:	SIMPLE CARB:	
	ADDED FAT:	ADDED FAT:	ADDED FAT:	
	SNACK★:	SNACK★:	SNACK★:	☐☐☐☐☐☐☐ CHECK YOUR WATER AS YOU DRINK
SUNDAY	PROTEIN:	PROTEIN:	PROTEIN:	
	COMPLEX CARB:	COMPLEX CARB:	COMPLEX CARB:	
	SIMPLE CARB:	SIMPLE CARB:	SIMPLE CARB:	
	ADDED FAT:	ADDED FAT:	ADDED FAT:	
	SNACK★:	SNACK★:	SNACK★:	☐☐☐☐☐☐☐ CHECK YOUR WATER AS YOU DRINK

★ REMEMBER TO HAVE A CARBOHYDRATE AND A PROTEIN AS A POWER SNACK.

WEEKLY FOOD DIARY

YOUR NAME: _____ WEEK BEGINNING _____

	BREAKFAST	LUNCH	DINNER	COMMENTS AND EXERCISE
MONDAY	PROTEIN: COMPLEX CARB: SIMPLE CARB: ADDED FAT: SNACK★:	PROTEIN: COMPLEX CARB: SIMPLE CARB: ADDED FAT: SNACK★:	PROTEIN: COMPLEX CARB: SIMPLE CARB: ADDED FAT: SNACK★:	❑❑❑❑❑❑❑ CHECK YOUR WATER AS YOU DRINK
TUESDAY	PROTEIN: COMPLEX CARB: SIMPLE CARB: ADDED FAT: SNACK★:	PROTEIN: COMPLEX CARB: SIMPLE CARB: ADDED FAT: SNACK★:	PROTEIN: COMPLEX CARB: SIMPLE CARB: ADDED FAT: SNACK★:	❑❑❑❑❑❑❑ CHECK YOUR WATER AS YOU DRINK
WEDNESDAY	PROTEIN: COMPLEX CARB: SIMPLE CARB: ADDED FAT: SNACK★:	PROTEIN: COMPLEX CARB: SIMPLE CARB: ADDED FAT: SNACK★:	PROTEIN: COMPLEX CARB: SIMPLE CARB: ADDED FAT: SNACK★:	❑❑❑❑❑❑❑ CHECK YOUR WATER AS YOU DRINK
THURSDAY	PROTEIN: COMPLEX CARB: SIMPLE CARB: ADDED FAT: SNACK★:	PROTEIN: COMPLEX CARB: SIMPLE CARB: ADDED FAT: SNACK★:	PROTEIN: COMPLEX CARB: SIMPLE CARB: ADDED FAT: SNACK★:	❑❑❑❑❑❑❑ CHECK YOUR WATER AS YOU DRINK

★ REMEMBER TO HAVE A CARBOHYDRATE AND A PROTEIN AS A POWER SNACK.

	BREAKFAST	LUNCH	DINNER	COMMENTS AND EXERCISE
FRIDAY	PROTEIN: COMPLEX CARB: SIMPLE CARB: ADDED FAT: SNACK★:	PROTEIN: COMPLEX CARB: SIMPLE CARB: ADDED FAT: SNACK★:	PROTEIN: COMPLEX CARB: SIMPLE CARB: ADDED FAT: SNACK★:	❑❑❑❑❑❑❑ CHECK YOUR WATER AS YOU DRINK
SATURDAY	PROTEIN: COMPLEX CARB: SIMPLE CARB: ADDED FAT: SNACK★:	PROTEIN: COMPLEX CARB: SIMPLE CARB: ADDED FAT: SNACK★:	PROTEIN: COMPLEX CARB: SIMPLE CARB: ADDED FAT: SNACK★:	❑❑❑❑❑❑❑ CHECK YOUR WATER AS YOU DRINK
SUNDAY	PROTEIN: COMPLEX CARB: SIMPLE CARB: ADDED FAT: SNACK★:	PROTEIN: COMPLEX CARB: SIMPLE CARB: ADDED FAT: SNACK★:	PROTEIN: COMPLEX CARB: SIMPLE CARB: ADDED FAT: SNACK★:	❑❑❑❑❑❑❑ CHECK YOUR WATER AS YOU DRINK

WEEKLY COMMENTS _____

_____

_____

_____

_____

_____

GLOSSARY

ADENOSINE—a brain chemical that produces a sedative effect. The production of adenosine is blocked by caffeine.

ADRENALINE—a chemical produced in the adrenal system when the brain puts the body on alert for survival. Adrenaline surges during the stress response, heightening the alerting and protective systems in the body that stimulate the fight or flight reaction.

AMINO ACID—the units comprising protein. Some are essential, meaning that the body can neither make them nor store them. A complete protein is one that supplies all eight of the essential amino acids.

ANTIOXIDANTS—substances that trap wayward oxygen and prevent the process of cellular oxidation, the equivalent of cellular "rusting." Antioxidants can target and neutralize damaging free radicals in the body.

BLOOD SUGAR—the level of glucose in the blood. Blood sugar levels have a powerful influence on our health and well-being—affecting our energy, moods, concentration, appetite, and disease risk.

CAROTENOIDS—phytochemicals that serve a strong antioxidant function, protecting against disease. Found primarily in dark green leafy and bright red or orange fruits and vegetables.

CARBOHYDRATE—an essential nutrient that comes mostly from plant sources. The energy carbohydrates provide for vital body functions is critical, as are the essential vitamins, minerals, phytochemicals, and fibers it contains.

> **COMPLEX**—commonly called starches and found primarily in grains and starchy vegetables, these carbohydrates require a longer time to be digested into sugars and taken into the system as energy. In their unrefined form, these foods are a source of much-needed fiber.

> **SIMPLE**—commonly called sugars and found primarily in fruits and nonstarchy vegetables, these carbohydrates contain a wealth of fiber, vitamins, minerals, and phytochemicals and are digested and released into the system as energy much more quickly than the complex type.

> **REFINED**—complex carbohydrate (starch) that has been stripped of its natural fibers and most of its vitamins, minerals, and phytochemicals. These carbohydrates break down quickly during digestion and are rushed into the bloodstream to be metabolized.

> **WHOLE**—carbohydrates that have been prepared without destroying their nutritive value or fiber. These carbohydrates are broken down more slowly in digestion, gradually and steadily releasing glucose into the system to be burned for energy.

CHEMICAL GYMNASTICS—wide fluctuations in body chemistries. These occur when the body is thrown out of balance because of overconsumption of food, increased emotional or physical stress, or inadequate fuel or sleep.

CHOLECYSTOKININ—a hormone with practically the opposite action of galanin—it promotes the feeling of satiety and fullness. This hormone is triggered into production by a moderate intake of fat.

CHOLESTEROL—a fatty, wax-like substance produced by the body and present in all animal products. Cholesterol is necessary for hormone production, for digestion, and to form cell membranes. But, when cholesterol accumulates in excess levels in the blood, it can deposit and harden in blood vessel walls, causing atherosclerosis, which can increase the risk of stroke and heart attacks.

> **HDL CHOLESTEROL**—high-density lipoproteins. Considered the "good guy" form of cholesterol that protects the vessels from building fatty deposits and decreases risk of cardiovascular disease.

> **LDL CHOLESTEROL**—low-density lipoproteins. Considered the primary culprit in increased heart disease risk. It is the substance that builds up as plaque in the arteries.

CORTISOL—a hormone produced by the adrenal system in response to chronic stress. Cortisol exerts great influence on immune function, blood pressure, pulse rate, metabolism, and fat storage. It also inhibits the production of testosterone and increases the production of insulin.

DOPAMINE—a vital chemical neurotransmitter that brings high levels of energy, alertness, and arousal. Abnormally high levels of dopamine result in high anxiety—to the point of aggressiveness and paranoia. Excessive "brain alert" stimulates production of hormones that contribute to fat cell lock-down.

ENDORPHIN—a morphine-like brain chemical that kills pain and contributes to feelings of self-esteem, euphoria, and emotional well-

being. Endorphins are natural calming agents that release you from the stress response and are responsible for what is termed "runner's high."

ESTROGEN—a hormone that serves to regulate the menstrual cycle. It also acts as a mild antidepressant and gives protection against diseases such as osteoporosis and cardiovascular disease.

FAT—an essential nutrient found in animal products and plant oils. Fat is vital for growth, lubrication, hormone production, and the absorption of certain vitamins. It is also a concentrated source of calories that is easily stored as fat on the body.

> **SATURATED FAT**—found in dairy and meat products, including milk, cheese, ice cream, beef, and pork. It can also be found in coconut and palm oils, nondairy creamers, and toppings.

> **TRANS FAT**—formed when vegetable oils are hardened into solids, usually to protect against spoiling and to maintain flavor. Examples include stick margarine and shortening, deep-fried foods such as French fries and fried chicken, and pastries, cookies, doughnuts, and crackers. Read the ingredient list of any processed foods you buy. If you see the words "partially hydrogenated," look for a different product—especially if it is one of the first three ingredients. Hydrogenation is a manufacturing process that converts a polyunsaturated or monounsaturated oil into a saturated fat.

> **MONOUNSATURATED FAT**—found in olive, canola, and peanut oils. These fats increase good HDL cholesterol and decrease bad LDL cholesterol, and thus the risk of disease.

> **OMEGA-3 FATTY ACIDS (EPA AND DHA OILS)**—found in all fish and seafood, particularly cold-water fish such as salmon, albacore tuna, swordfish, sardines, mackerel, and hard shellfish. The only

plant source is flaxseed. Omega-3 fatty acids decrease triglycerides and total and bad LDL cholesterol. They reduce the tendency of the blood to form clots, stabilize blood sugars, improve brain function, and reduce inflammation.

POLYUNSATURATED FATS—found in corn oil, cottonseed oil, safflower oil, sesame oil, and sunflower oil, as well as avocado, sunflower seed kernels, sesame seeds, almonds, walnuts, and pecans. These fats decrease both bad LDL and good HDL cholesterol, so aren't the best choice.

FAT CELL CODE—an intricate communication system in which the body's production of hormones and chemical neurotransmitters determine how the body processes fat. Fat will either be burned, or stockpiled into the fat cell for storage.

FAT CELL LOCK-DOWN—a state in which the fat cells are stockpiled with fat, which causes the cell doors to slam shut and prevent the body from naturally releasing fat. The fat cell becomes resistant to insulin's ability to unlock it and allow the natural fat-burning capacity to be released.

FAT STORAGE FORMULA—when stress, a lack of self-care (sedentary lifestyle, sleep deprivation, erratic or over eating), and states of imbalance (illness, hormone dysfunction, depression, or worry) put the body into a survival mode of energy storage through the slowing down of the metabolism.

FREE RADICALS—unstable compounds produced in the body that can damage vital cell structure. Many chronic diseases and premature aging are linked to the damage caused by free radicals circulating in the body.

GALANIN—a brain hormone that regulates the fat that you store as well as your body's desire for fat. The higher your galanin level, the

higher your propensity to seek and find high-fat foods, and the more fat you store. Galanin is released when the body breaks down body fat (as it does in dieting), when the diet is high-fat (over 30 percent of calories), or when several hours have passed between meals, allowing a fall in blood sugars or insulin levels. Eating more frequently, eating less fat (20 to 25 percent of calories), and eating adequate low-fat protein lowers galanin production.

GLUCAGON—a hormone that serves to balance insulin levels. The higher your glucagon level, the lower your levels of insulin. Glucagon levels are increased with an adequate and frequent protein intake.

GLUCOSE—a simple sugar that is the building block of starch. In the small intestine, digestive enzymes break down large molecules of complex carbohydrates (starch) into smaller molecules. These and simple carbohydrates (sugars) are then broken into simpler monosaccharides (glucose, fructose, and galactose) to be absorbed into the bloodstream where they are available as a source of energy to the cells. Glucose is the most critical of these monosaccharides, because it is the source of fuel used by the brain, central nervous system, and lungs. It is so important to your body that if your diet doesn't provide enough carbohydrates to supply glucose, the brain will signal a shortage, and muscle tissue will be broken down to supply the shortfall. That means you lose body muscle (not fat) to feed your brain.

GLYCEMIC INDEX—A measure of the glucose-loading power of a food. The index ranks foods from 0 to 100, estimating whether the food will raise blood sugar levels dramatically and quickly (fast release), moderately (quick release), or just a little (slow release). Carbohydrate foods that break down quickly during digestion have the highest

glycemic values—the blood sugar increases rapidly and the rise is fast and high. Carbohydrates that break down slowly, releasing glucose gradually into the bloodstream, have low glycemic ratings.

GLYCOGEN—the body's readily available storage supply of glucose—stored in the liver and muscle. The body maintains a certain level of glucose in the blood to serve the brain, lungs, and central nervous system. To ensure an easily accessible supply of glucose, the body stores it in the muscles and the liver. This stored glucose is called glycogen.

INSULIN—a hormone produced by the pancreas that is necessary for carbohydrate metabolism. It serves as the "key" to unlock the body's cells to allow carbohydrates to enter the cell to be burned for energy. Insulin influences the way you metabolize foods, determining whether you burn fat, protein, or carbohydrates to meet your energy needs—and ultimately determining whether you will store fat.

KETONES—a waste product of abnormal fat metabolism. Ketones are produced when carbohydrate intake is inadequate and the body is insulin-deprived. Fats instead of carbs are broken down to be used as an inefficient energy source.

KETOSIS—a dangerous state of inbalance wherein the body is circulating high levels of acidic ketone waste products. Symptoms of ketosis can include bad breath, frequent urination, interrupted sleep, constipation, nausea, general edginess, and lightheadedness. In clearing ketones, the body excretes sodium and potassium, which can result in dehydration and abnormal heart rhythms. The body also retains uric acid, which can trigger gouty arthritis, gout, and kidney stones.

LEPTIN—a hormone produced in the body to give a sense of satiation and hinder the amount of insulin released. Leptin targets and blocks

neuropeptide Y, a brain chemical that increases appetite for carbohydrates and increases insulin production.

LIPOPROTEIN LIPASE (LPL)—an enzyme that enables fat to enter muscle cells to be burned for energy and enter fat cells for storage. Saturated fats, a too low fat intake, and high insulin levels suppress LPL at the muscle cell and activate it at the fat cell-directing fat to the fat cell to be stored.

MUSCLE—a complex body system that uses energy to propel the body and body functions. Muscle stores glycogen and essential fatty acids to be used as energy.

MELATONIN—a hormone produced by the pineal gland in the body that contributes to the regulation of circadian rhythms—the wake and sleep cycles.

METABOLISM—a measure of how many calories we burn per minute for body functions. This includes automatic, involuntary functions like breathing, heart beat, digestion and blood circulation, as well as voluntary activity and movement. The largest amount of calories used (70 percent) are those burned to maintain our basic body functioning.

MICRONUTRIENTS—essential vitamins and minerals that are needed by the body in minute quantities, yet have critical functions. These nutrients are often found in foods in trace amounts, requiring a variety of foods to be eaten to meet the body's needs.

MINERALS—inorganic compounds that serve as building blocks for structures such as bones and teeth, and work with fluids and electrical transmissions. Over thirty minerals are crucial to good nutrition and fat release.

NEUROTRANSMITTERS—brain chemicals responsible for sending specialized messages from one brain cell to another. Examples are sero-

tonin, endorphins, dopamine, and adenosine.

NUTRACEUTICALS—compounds in foods that go beyond the nutrients alone. They carry preventative and healing properties against disease.

PHYTOCHEMICALS—powerful plant compounds filled with detoxifying enzymes and antioxidants. Phytochemicals help to protect the body from diseases and aging—along with powering the immune system for wellness. Only a few hundred have been identified, and it is estimated that plants contain hundreds more. They can be received only by eating plant foods.

PROGESTERONE—a hormone that, like estrogen, is involved in regulating the menstrual cycle and works to prepare the lining of the uterus for pregnancy. Progesterone is thought to be the hormone culprit for PMS-related symptoms due to its suppression of the brain chemical dopamine.

PROTEIN—an essential nutrient that comes primarily from animal products and legumes. Protein serves as a vital building block for the body's growth, healing, and repair. It can be used as a more efficient energy source than fat when carbohydrate intake is deficient.

SEROTONIN—a chemical neurotransmitter that brings calm, increased well-being, a bright perspective, a sense of satiety, and appetite control. Serotonin is called the natural feel-good chemical and master weight control drug. It suppresses the tendency to binge and controls increased appetite triggers.

TRIGLYCERIDES—a body fat that serves to transport nutrients throughout the body. Triglycerides often rise to a high level in the blood when there is a nutrient overload (too much food at one time), a high intake of refined carbohydrates, or excessive intake of alcohol.

VITAMINS—organic molecules that the body does not produce on its own, but cannot do without. Vitamins do not give energy, but as chemical catalysts for the body they contribute to its production and allow the body to use it correctly. They make things happen! Vitamins A, D, E, and K are fat-soluble; B and C vitamins are water-soluble.

RESOURCES

BOOKS AND TAPES
BY PAMELA M. SMITH, R.D.

THE ENERGY EDGE

If you are like millions of Americans who allow fatigue to control their lives. Pam's best-selling book, *The Energy Edge,* is for you! The 300 pages of this, deluxe hardcover book are filled with Pam's blueprint for life—giving you the energized tools you need to outsmart the energy "vandalizers" that drain your energy supply. The simple strategies and high octane meal and snack ideas laid out for you will allow a river of energy and stamina to be released from within. (Also available in soft-cover.)

THE GOOD LIFE—A HEALTHY COOKBOOK

A wonderful feast of Pam's most savory recipes. This cookbook offers complete meals for breakfast, lunch, and dinner, plus scrumptious desserts and power snack ideas. Cooking techniques and plate design are presented easily and practically. Food that is good for you tastes great! For the novice or gourmet cook, this book is designed for every-one to enjoy—and it's beautiful! It's a deluxe hardback edition with full-color photography.

EAT WELL—LIVE WELL

A bestseller, this is Pam's nutrition guidebook for healthy, produc-tive living. This large, hardback edition presents "The Ten

Commandments of Good Nutrition" in detail, along with directions for menu planning, grocery shopping, and dining out—from fast food to gourmet. The large cookbook section contains innovative, time-saving recipes. Meal plans for weight loss and weight management are included.

THE SEVEN SECRETS TO LIVING THE GOOD LIFE
A video and audio tape series
In this dynamic four-tape series (audio or video), you will learn how to fit healthy living into your busy schedule, turbo-charge your metabolism and your immune system, seal all the "energy leaks" in your body, and recharge and refuel while you lean down. Pam demonstrates her healthy and delicious cooking techniques and gives easy tips for traveling and dining out healthfully. Available in: 4–tape video series or 4–tape audio series.

FOOD FOR LIFE
More than a nutrition guide and cookbook, *Food for Life* shows how to eat smart and walk in abundant life. It presents Pam's secrets for staying fit, fueled, and free—helping you to explore your relationship with food and yourself. You will discover how to choose the best food, manage weight, and develop a proper perspective for feeding yourself emotionally and spiritually. Meal plans, recipes, and specific action steps are included. Available in: deluxe hardback edition or softcover edition.

FOOD FOR LIFE: A-DAY-AT-A-TIME
This thirty-day devotional guide will equip and empower you to break free from the food trap—forever!

COME COOK WITH ME

This is the kid's cookbook! A wonderful way to teach children nutrition through the basics of healthy cooking. Great for picky eaters! Includes kid-proven recipes, how to set a table, and some great lessons on manners. Handwritten and fun.

ALIVE AND WELL IN THE FAST LANE

A lighthearted and informative nutritional guidebook for the whole family—in a fun, handwritten, and illustrated format. Includes tips for healthy eating on the run.

HEALTHY EXPECTATIONS

This is the expectant mother's handbook with the latest information for nourishing mom and baby. It includes an extensive question and answer section with a proven, natural technique for overcoming morning sickness. This book is filled with love and wisdom. Meal plans and tips for direction before, during and after delivery are included. (An optional mom's journal is available to complement this beautiful book.)

FOR ORDERING INFORMATION ON PAM'S BOOKS AND MATERIALS,
SPEAKING AND WORKSHOPS, PLEASE CONTACT:

LIFE COMMUNICATIONS
PO BOX 541115 • ORLANDO, FL 32854
800–896–4010

LifeLine
Press
202–216–0600
VISIT PAM'S WEBSITE AT WWW.PAMSMITH.COM

INDEX